ANGEL'S FATE

THE COMPLETE SERIES

TESSA COLE

Angel's Fate: The Complete Series

Copyright © 2020 Tessa Cole

All rights reserved. No part of this book may be reproduced in any form or by any means without written consent, excepting brief quotes used in reviews.

This is a work of fiction. Names, places, characters, and events are entirely the product of the author's imagination or are used fictitiously, and any resemblance to persons, living or dead, actual locals, events, or organizations is coincidental.

Gryphon's Gate Publishing

550 King St. N.

PO Box 42088 Conestoga

Waterloo, ON

N2L 6K5

Print ISBN 978-1-990587-27-6

FATED BONDS

ANGEL'S FATE, BOOK 1

AMIAH

I'd thought he was *the one*.

The moment I'd locked eyes with him, the ghostly swirling white lines of my not-yet-awakened angelic mating brand had started to ache, which meant he was my destiny.

Except the magic in the mark hadn't risen to the surface of my skin alight with the golden glow of our soul bond. It had remained buried, a constant throb, reminding me that he hadn't been ready. It hadn't been the right time. I'd needed to be patient.

And I had been. I'd been blessed with the sacred angelic mark and promised from the moment I was born that I'd have a love so rare and great and beautiful other angels would talk about it for centuries. The brand was eternal, destined, and could never be broken. I would wait centuries for him — if by a twist of magic his mortality let him live that long before our bond extended his life. I'd already waited one and a half centuries, keeping my secret because I didn't want all the curious looks and questions a formed but not awakened brand would get. What was a little more time?

I'd do whatever it took.

At least I thought I'd been willing to do whatever it took.

Until I met *her*.

Essie Shaw. His actual mate.

She'd shown me how horrifying the brand was, how it stole her independence and all her choices. She'd been crazy with fear and on-her-knees shattered when her mates had been injured and in trouble, and I had no reason to believe her situation was unusual. The angelic mating brand created a soul bond deeper than any other bond in all the realms. The death of one mate caused the death of the other — or drove her insane, which wasn't the better option.

I shuddered and wrapped my arms tighter around me even though the summer's night was still warm and muggy with almost no breeze sweeping across the Joined Parliament Operations Building's rooftop.

No, the cold was soul deep and had sunk into my core the moment I'd seen Essie on the floor, screaming in agony and fear.

I didn't want that. I couldn't live with that. I'd lost my freedom once before, and I swore I'd never lose it again. Just the thought of being trapped made my pulse race. And yet I was already branded, the ache growing stronger every day.

Another shudder slipped down my spine. My soul mate was drawing closer. It was the only explanation for the growing pain — although I had no idea why it had started four and a half years ago when I hadn't really met my true mate.

I swept my gaze over the skyline of Union City's Supernatural Quarter. This part of the city had been restored after Michael's war of extermination as a place to live for those supernatural beings who'd come out of hiding to defend humanity, and where I'd called home for the last twenty years.

Except I wasn't sure I could call it home anymore. I hadn't really lived since I'd met *him*.

I'd been waiting.

Like a good angel.

And I'd escaped that nightmare by the skin of my teeth... for now.

Before me, in an apartment building a few blocks away, a light turned off, while a streetlight on the next street over flickered off then back on. A car with blue neon glowing from underneath it sped by most likely headed to the vampire section of the Quarter, the heavy *thump thump* from its stereo so powerful I could feel it in my chest even five stories up.

If I looked to my right and slightly behind me, I'd be able to see the UV-blocking purple-glass canopy over the vampires' section catching hints of the light of the half moon along with the strobe lights from the half dozen nightclubs occupying the vampires' main strip.

There were some vampires and shifters who'd indulge in a flashy, obnoxious vehicle like that, but given that the car had come from the direction of the park separating the Quarter from the human part of the city, the occupants were more likely young human males out to party with the creatures of the night.

Which surprised me a little. But then the path to humans accepting supers hadn't been as rocky as I'd expected. The monsters who'd hidden in the dark had become saviors and for the most part, humanity was welcoming, or at least tolerant, of supernatural beings. Yes, there were a handful of humans who still feared supers, and many who still didn't want to live next door to them, but the terror of extinction from a common monstrous enemy had certainly eased a lot of fear between species.

It also didn't hurt that supers had representation in government in the Joined Parliament — and therefore weren't fighting to be recognized as citizens — as well, they had laws to abide by and an enforcement agency — the Joined Parliament Bureau of Supernatural Law Enforcement — with JP teams to uphold those laws.

And for the last three years, I'd been the chief physician for Union City's JP Operations' Building because *he* had joined Union City's JP team.

I'd thought if I was near him, my mating brand would be awakened and our bond would fully form and we become more than just friends. I yearned for our bond, for him. He was passionate and strong and fiercely protective. His shifter nature gave him a wild edge that I knew I'd never find in another angel, and I'd thought our bonding meant I needed a counterbalance to my reserved angelic nature and my need to always be in control.

I just hadn't realized how much our bond— *any* bond would rip away all control. I liked my life, liked who I was, liked how I had freedom and a job that released the constantly building pressure of my healing magic. A bond would take all that away.

And yet my heart ached for the loss of something I no longer wanted.

Which didn't make any sense.

How could I mourn something that terrified me?

Except it wasn't the angelic mating brand and everything it entailed that I was mourning. It was the loss of what could have been, the promise of joy, passion, unconditional love and acceptance, and the dream of a soul-deep connection with someone.

Well, no more! So the brand wasn't what I thought it was and its terrible fate was headed my way. I wasn't going to just accept its inevitability. Yes, a soul bond, once formed, was impossible to break, but my brand hadn't awakened yet. Maybe there was a way to remove it, or block it, or something before my soul bonded with a complete stranger's and made me fall in love with him.

And maybe I only *believed* a soul bond was impossible to break.

I'd been wrong about how beautiful the mating brand was. I could be wrong about the finality of its soul bond. The only way to know for sure was to stop feeling sorry for myself and do something, gather information, find someone powerful enough who might be able to break or suppress my mating brand—

I bit back a groan. There was only one person who could possibly be strong enough, and I really didn't want to see the arrogant, lascivious faekin again.

Except Sebastian Bane wasn't a faekin — half human half fae — glyph witch. He was a full fae sorcerer in hiding... probably because he'd slept with someone's mate or sold stolen magical artifacts to the wrong super, or done something stupid and had a hit out on him.

He'd proposition every woman I'd seen him come in contact with, and while that hadn't been many, he was still at a hundred percent propositions to encountered women — myself included.

I'd promptly turned him down of course. There wasn't any way I'd have sexual intercourse with a man like him. I was saving myself for my soul mate—

Except I didn't want a soul mate any more.

And if I wasn't going to have a soul mate, why wouldn't I take a lover?

Because that lover could end up being my soul mate... although Sebastian and I were such opposites, there was no way he could be my mate.

Another shudder swept through me. I couldn't believe I was actually thinking of saying yes if he propositioned me again... which he wouldn't because I'd already clearly and firmly turned him down.

The door to the stairwell opened, and my heart skipped a beat. Essie liked to come up to the patio, her angelic nature drawing her to rooftops and open sky as much as it did me. And while I knew I needed to work on creating a truce between us — since I'd been less than kind to her when I thought she was going to emotionally shatter my mate — I wasn't ready. Every time I saw her, I saw my wasted years — thank goodness only four! — and my lifetime of naiveté.

Thankfully, Cassius stood in the doorway and not Essie, although he appeared harder and more imposing than I'd ever seen him before, even in those darkest days during Michael's war. He looked like a statue who'd been sculpted by a master with his broad muscular shoulders straining his simple black T-shirt, strong chiseled jaw, and piercing blue eyes. He wore his blond hair buzzed short — something he'd started doing during the war — and it made him look like the dangerous warrior I knew he'd made himself into. Gone was the thoughtful warm angel I'd become friends with almost a hundred years ago, replaced with a solemn soldier.

And now that soldier was even more solemn, acting cold and angry toward everyone, including me. But then Essie Shaw's life hadn't been the only one to be turned upside down in the last couple of months, and while things had turned out all right in the end, it wasn't just Essie who'd gotten scars.

Except Cassius's scars weren't anything I could heal. My magic only worked on physical injuries, and the one person who could help him emotionally — Essie Shaw with her empathic healing magic — was the one person he was angry at.

"They're about to leave," he said. "Did you want to say goodbye?"

"They're only going to be in Rome for a few weeks. Why would I?" I asked, my anger at Cassius's anger making my tone sharper than I intended.

I wanted to heal him, heal all of them, everyone. It was a compulsion deep within my soul, one that had pulled me into the mortal realm when Michael had started his war, one stronger than my need for order, control, or open sky. I'd felt all those wounded souls crying, their physical agony making my magic burn through my whole body even while I was in the Realm of Celestial Light, and even if Cassius hadn't asked me to join the Angelic Defense with him, I would have joined.

"Right." The muscles in Cassius's jaw flexed and he turned his gaze to the Quarter's skyline.

The weight of his judgment sat heavy between us. I wasn't being a team player. I'd been purposefully mean to Essie to get her to leave in order to protect Marcus and the rest of the team... and, if I was being honest, to protect myself. I knew I should have chosen a different way to protect everyone, but I'd been shocked seeing her there in my office. Four and a half years ago, she'd been the cause of enormous physical and emotional pain to Marcus, pain my magic hadn't been able to ease, and I didn't want that for him again or anyone else.

Except I'd been fighting destiny, and it didn't care who it hurt to reach its outcome.

At least everyone had survived the terrible battles that had happened about a month ago — although I had no idea how — and life had returned to a new normal with Essie as part of the team.

But that meant I needed to admit I was wrong and make nice with the new girl. And I would. I wanted to. Just as soon as looking at her didn't remind me of the nightmare coming my way, and the heartache of an illogical loss.

And really, Cassius should talk. Really. He should. As far as I could tell, he'd barely said more than a dozen words to Essie or anyone of her guys with the exception of his brother. He needed to make nice as much as I did.

"The sooner you work it out with Marcus—"

"There's nothing to work out." Jeez. Did everyone know that I'd been an idiot over him? Cassius had been on assignment out of town for the last two and a half years and had only returned for a visit once. Someone must have told him about Marcus... probably Cassius's brother, Gideon. Gideon had seen and heard enough to have known how I'd felt about Marcus.

And while yes, I'd admit, I'd had an emotional attachment to Marcus, everything I'd done had also been practical. Essie hadn't branded him at the time, and her bonds with her other men would have made her love them more. Marcus hadn't deserved to be slowly abandoned, his love unrequited. No one did.

And no one deserved the nightmare of the angelic mating brand. Not even Essie Shaw.

Another shudder swept over me and I pushed my fear of my fate as deep down inside me as possible. "I was looking out for the health of Union City's JP team. That's my job. She didn't understand the nature of the mating brand." And neither had I. "If they hadn't had a soul bond, it would have eventually shattered him no matter how strong his will."

"But they do have a bond." Cassius kept his gaze locked on the skyline, his posture rigid, and for a second it felt like he was talking about his brother, one of Essie's other mates, and not Marcus.

"And now we have the strongest JP team in the mortal realm," I said. This wasn't the conversation I wanted to have. As much as Cassius and I had been good friends, we'd never really talked about our romantic relationships— or rather, he never talked about his, since I'd spent my life secretly and stupidly waiting for my soul mate and hadn't had any. "Have you talked with Nathaniel and Chris?"

They worked as operational support but the head office had decided that with Cassius as team leader, the three of them could handle the day-to-day activities of the JP in Union City, first for the two and a half weeks while the primary team was out of commission recovering from their terrible ordeal, and now when they went to Rome for advanced training.

"They've been briefed. They—" He cocked his head to the side and squinted as my magic swelled under my skin. It rushed into my palms not yet manifested and visible, but ready to burst free at my command.

Someone was in desperate need of immediate medical attention, and my magic had latched onto them. I gritted my teeth. I hated when my power did this, hated the lack of control and choice. But there wasn't anything I could do once my healing magic had connected with a soul in need, so I yanked my gaze to follow Cassius's and caught a hint of shadow rushing past a pale gray cloud. The shape hurtled across the front of the Quarter's tallest building and a bank of windows with the lights still on.

My pulse stalled. "Is that a person?"

The big, bulky shape took out the top of the spire of the next building, careened off the wall of the six-story high rise beside it, and crashed into the park ring forest with a resounding *boom*.

My thoughts lurched as my power surged, burning up my forearms to my elbows. That *was* a person. A man. A big one by his size and build. Even if I hadn't clearly seen him, my magic knew it.

I reached for my phone but realized I'd left it in my office and there wasn't time to go and get it. There also wasn't time to change out of my pastel blue silk camisole and tan linen pantsuit. But this wasn't the first time I'd ruined my clothes to save a life, and I doubted it would be the last.

"Tell Cassey to prep triage." I pushed a trickle of power into my back and, with a white flash of angelic light, released my wings, the magic allowing them to manifest through my clothing without damaging what I was wearing — something I highly appreciated. I didn't release my wings often, but when I did, it was usually an emergency and while my clothes might end up bloody, they could sometimes be saved. Very little would save them if my wings had ripped massive holes in the back.

"Amiah, wait." Cassius grabbed for me, but I leaped off the roof before he could stop me. Light flashed at the corner of my eye as he released his wings and flew after me. "Just wait."

"Some supers can survive a fall like that, and my magic says he's still alive." But he wouldn't be if I didn't get to him right away.

I pushed myself to fly faster headlong into the breeze that hadn't been there moments ago. It whipped my long blond hair out of its tight chignon and away from my face and cut through my thin clothes, chilling my skin everywhere except for my hands and forearms where my magic pulsed.

Everything within me narrowed to a pinpoint focus on the man. I could get to him in time. I could save him. I had to save him—

My thoughts lurched at that. I'd never *had* to save anyone before. The possibility of death had always been an option. My magic knew that. As long as I did everything in my power to save someone, I didn't experience any backlash. If I didn't do everything possible, my magic turned inward, sweeping through me and painfully incapacitating me.

"Stop. I'm the agent in charge. We know nothing about this situation." Cassius flew close and tried to grab me again.

I jerked away and held up my now-glowing palms. "We know someone down there needs medical attention." I dove into the alley between two four-story buildings. There was no way I could shake him or even out fly him. He was the stronger flyer, the stronger angel in every way, but maybe I could dodge him long enough to get to whoever had fallen out of the sky.

I took a quick turn out of the alley onto the next major street. Cassius drew close and reached for my ankle again, but I darted back into another alley and jerked to the side narrowly avoiding the metal fire escape clinging to the building's red-brick wall.

"I don't want to write you up," Cassius said. "Amiah, please. We have to follow protocol. We're already on probation with head office."

"You know I *have* to go to him." He knew how my magic worked, knew that if I fought it when it locked on to someone like this, I'd be useless for hours, sometimes even days.

"I promise. You'll go to him. But we have to follow protocol."

"I can't wait for protocol. If I don't want to be useless tomorrow, I can't." No matter how much it made my heart race to disobey the rules, the call of my magic was the stronger compulsion. It always was.

I shot out of the alley, across the empty two-lane street at the edge of the Quarter, flying so low I skimmed the roof of a small silver sports car parked at the curb, and barreled into the dark shadows between the thick tree trunks into the park ring.

My magic urged me on. *Fly faster. Save him. Go go go.*

I twisted avoiding branches and kept low to the ground, half trusting my night vision that allowed me to see reasonably well in low light and half trusting my instincts as I followed a dirt path heading deeper into the forest.

Cassius was right on my heels. If he put in a push, he'd be able to grab me. I didn't know why he didn't, but I was grateful he let me keep going. Probably the practicality of not wanting Operations' chief physician incapacitated by something that could be avoided. And with the amount of magic building in my hands, if I didn't try to save whoever had fallen out of the sky, I'd be out of commission for days.

My magic jerked me to the left toward thick underbrush and dense evergreens. With a pulse of power to my back, I yanked my wings into my body, hit the ground running, and shoved through the foliage.

I broke through into a clearing illuminated by the pale light of the half moon. A wide deep groove had been cut into the forest floor, the dirt pushed to the sides and heaped at the back, and broken branches littered the area.

At the far end, Sebastian Bane, his skin so pale it seemed translucent and radiating a pale icy blue light, knelt beside the broken, bleeding body of a massive, completely naked man.

AMIAH

"Amiah?" Sebastian's eyes widened at our arrival. "Cassius?"

My thoughts stuttered over his presence... and, if I was being honest with myself, his breathtaking appearance. If the man had been a demon, he'd have been an incubus. And a part of me wondered — since no one knew much about fae or their realm — if he wasn't the fae equivalent of one given his lascivious nature.

His stunning good looks, unusual pale eyes, and spiky white and silver hair gave him an exotic appearance, and with a body that I knew from treating him was all sculpted lean muscles covered in mesmerizing black tattoos, he probably had just as much success satisfying his needs as an incubus. He'd certainly know what he was doing—

"What the hell—?" Sebastian said, leaning forward, pressing his hands harder against a laceration in the naked man's abdomen and doing little to slow the blood oozing between his pale fingers. "What are you doing here?"

I ignored him and heaved my thoughts back to the immediate problem. Assess the situation and save the man. From his essence and his lack of clothing, I guessed he was some kind of shifter — since a shifter's magic destroyed his clothing when he shifted — but I wasn't sure what type. His essence seemed wilder, more primal than Marcus's, so I didn't think the man was a werewolf, but he also didn't have the sleek predatory feel of a feline.

Whatever he was, he was something that could survive that terrible fall, although just from looking at him, I was certain he'd broken every bone in his body, and his left fibula and ulna protruded through his skin. He probably had ruptured organs as well. This was going to take everything I had and then some. If we could get him to Operations, I'd be able to supplement my magic with human surgery, but first I'd need to stabilize him so we could move him.

"Why aren't you calling triage?" I snapped at Cassius. I didn't wait to see if he pulled out his phone or not, and dropped to my knees in the dry crunchy summer weeds on the other side of the man from Sebastian.

Even broken and bloody, the naked man was a stunning specimen, his massive body a study in powerful musculature. He wasn't as gorgeous as Sebastian or handsome as Cassius, but with his mussed dark red hair — longer than that of both Cassius and Sebastian — and a few days' worth of scruff along his jaw, he had a hard, rugged appearance that spoke tantalizingly of power and passion which was just as attractive.

The pressure of my magic grew stronger, the glow from my palms bright in the dark forest. If I didn't connect with him soon, I'd pay the price.

I placed my hands over his heart and let my senses slide into his body. It didn't matter if Sebastian still kept pressure on the man's wound. Until my magic released me, it would heal the most grievous injuries first, not letting me go until this man was stable or someone else was in greater need. Given the state of the naked man, I doubted any of my magic would go into Sebastian at all before I ran out.

My power connected and I instantly knew that yes, almost every bone in his body had been broken, some, like his right femur had been shattered. Both of his lungs had been pierced by broken ribs, his spleen had ruptured, and he was bleeding out from numerous deep lacerations.

It was a miracle he was still alive, and I could feel his life rushing out of him. There wasn't time to be gentle and slowly seep my power into him. But in his condition, I doubted he'd feel the painful burn of being healed too quickly, so I drew in a steadying breath and released my magic without restraint. It crashed into him, a massive, hot wave, that always felt like blood pouring down my arms and over my hands and into my patient even though it wasn't actually blood.

He screamed and jerked upright.

Oh, my goodness!

With his eyes still closed, he rammed his palm into my chest. The air burst from my lungs, and I flew back, slamming into a large rock at the edge of the clearing. Hot agony blazed through my chest and the forest lurched around me as my power surged inward, threatening to drown me.

Sebastian grabbed the naked man's arm — too little too late — and the man collapsed back to the ground as if he hadn't just sat up and hit me with his broken arm.

Cassius scrambled to my side and cupped my cheeks between his palms, trying to lock gazes with me. But I couldn't get my vision to steady. It had been a long time since I'd been hit so hard that the world spun, my breath had been knocked out of me, and my ribs had been cracked — which I knew with certainty two of them were. And never before had I been hit by a patient like that. Yes, I'd been hit and clawed and bitten, but that—

"Amiah." The angelic light radiating from Cassius's eyes flared as his concern intensified.

"I'm okay," I gasped, trying to push his hands aside. The naked man was still dying and my pain was nothing compared to that. I could deal with it later, and even if I hadn't been okay, my magic still wouldn't have allowed me to leave him.

Cassius didn't let go and his eyes narrowed. "You're not okay."

"And he's dying." I matched his glare. "Call triage."

"No, don't," Sebastian said, his hands back on the gushing gut wound, seemingly unaware that his white button-down was getting bloody. "It's too dangerous. Just get him stable. I'll take it from there."

"Stable doesn't mean he's out of the woods." I shoved at Cassius, shooting agony through my chest. He glared at me but sat back, letting me pass, and I scrambled back to the naked man.

Sebastian's lips quirked and he rolled his pale eyes at me. "You did not just say that."

"Say what?" I placed my hands back over the naked man's heart but held my power back. I didn't want a repeat of the first time I'd flooded him. "Both of you hold him down. I don't want to get hit again."

The hint of Sebastian's smile turned wicked, heating my insides with a yearning I'd spent my entire adult life ignoring and one I was going to continue ignoring because I was certain Sebastian was about to make fun of me.

"If you stabilize him," he said, "I'm pretty sure he *will* get out of the woods."

...because Sebastian would drag whoever this man was out of the park ring... which was more of a woods than a park.

"That wasn't in the least bit amusing," I huffed.

"You just don't want to admit you like a little word play," he said, making *word play* sound like it was supposed to be something else, something hot and dirty, that increased the aching heat inside me.

Cassius grabbed the naked man's shoulders, and Sebastian pressed down hard on the man's gut wound.

I drew in another steadying breath and, even though I didn't really have the time for it, strained to release my magic slowly, praying I could increase the flow without making him lash out again. All the while my magic screamed to work faster. *Hurry up. Save him.*

My power flowed back into him, thick and viscous and clinging to his damaged cells while the excess leaked down my forearms, making them burn. *Slow and steady. Build it up gently.* I'd resisted the compulsion before — not often, but I had — and I could do it again.

"Okay, Bane," Cassius said. "Start talking. Why is it dangerous to take this guy to Operations?"

"Titus is—" Light flashed from a small tattoo almost completely covered in blood on the inside of Sebastian's wrist. "Fuck."

He jerked around as a man materialized out of the shadows behind him. One moment there was nothing, the next, a man — or rather fae from his delicately pointed ears — had appeared, the shadows partially bleeding out of his face and hands, leaving a few billowing clouds of darkness undulating under his skin. He wore all black and had a scarf pulled up covering his mouth and nose like a bandit... or an assassin.

He stabbed at Sebastian's heart with a knife the length of my forearm, and only Sebastian's sudden turn to face the other fae saved him. The blade sliced into Sebastian's side, his white button-down soaking up his blood in a dark, growing stain. With a grunt of pain, Sebastian seized the man's wrist, but the man jerked back, breaking free of Sebastian's hold, and lunged in again.

My power flared, the sudden shock of being attacked breaking my control of my magic. The power leaking down my forearms slammed into the naked man— what had Sebastian called him? Titus? It burned through his body, making him scream and his muscles seize.

"Because of this," Sebastian gasped, as he twisted just enough so the blade cut his shirt but not skin, allowing him to get close to his assailant.

He seized the man's wrist again and punched him in the gut, drawing a surprised *oomph*.

Cassius leaped to his feet, his fire magic bursting around his right hand, and he snapped a fire whip around the assailant's neck, but another man— no— demon from the hellfire in his eyes— no— vampire from his still lifeless essence rushed out of the shadows, his long black hair tied back in a ponytail sweeping behind him with the movement.

He sliced Cassius's whip with a black katana, the blade only visible from the momentary glint of moonlight and firelight off the metal, and sparks showered the ground, catching in the dry weeds and turning into small fires that were sure to get out of hand quickly.

They did, however, offer better illumination, and it was clear I'd been right about Cassius's assailant on both accounts. The man had both the hellfire of a demon in his eyes and the fangs of a vampire, which meant he had to have been half demon half human in order to be turned by a master vampire since the ritual didn't work on pure demons.

He, too, wore all black: black leather pants and a black wrap tunic with an East Asian feel to the cut and fabric. It hung past his knees, was bound tight across his chest, and secured by a wide sash and a leather belt.

He barreled toward Cassius and slashed at him with his katana. Cassius drew the flames in the weeds back into his palms putting out the mini fires as he jerked out of the way of the blade, but the demon-vampire didn't press his attack, instead shifting to lunge at me.

My pulse froze. I had to move, get out of the way, but my magic held me captive, refusing to release me until Titus was healed enough to move or I was physically pulled away.

This was why I never did field work. It was too dangerous. No matter how hard I concentrated or mentally fought my power, if it had locked onto someone, it wouldn't let go, even if I was in danger.

"Amiah, move," Sebastian shouted, but the glow of my power burned brighter and the hot sticky flow seized my muscles, keeping me locked in place.

Cassius snapped his fire whip around the demon-vampire's neck as a force-wave rushed from Sebastian's palms and slammed into me, ripping my hands away from Titus and knocking me onto my back. Pain sliced through my chest from my cracked ribs, stealing my breath, and my magic surged inward with the promise of a crushing backlash.

The demon-vampire staggered but didn't go down, and Cassius yanked him a few steps away from me with his fire whip before the demon-vampire twisted and severed the whip with his katana.

I heaved myself back to Titus, my power reconnecting with his injuries and taking control of my body as the weeds beside me caught fire.

"Cassius." I gritted my teeth and forced my hands to slide down Titus's body to get away from the flames. But I only managed to get to his abs before my power jerked me to a stop, not allowing me to move farther from his heart, the place where my magic had the easiest access into his body since he didn't have just one grave injury to concentrate on.

My heart pounded with a mix of fear and frustration. If I hadn't been locked onto him, I'd have been able to move my hands anywhere. It had been years since I'd let myself end up in a situation like this. Working in a medical center, first for the war, then the emergency department at the supers' hospital in the Quarter, and then in Operations had been enough to keep this nasty part of my magic at bay.

"Cassius. Your fire," I said, determined to keep my voice stern but calm. No one liked it when their physician panicked.

Except everything within me screamed. *Fire!* But also *save him!*

The heat seared my skin, the flames singeing my pantleg. Even if Titus's condition wasn't dire, I didn't want to have to waste magic healing myself since it took a lot more magic to heal myself than someone else.

I scrambled over Titus to his other side to get away from the flames and, grabbing his shoulder while my other hand was still stuck on his heart, tried to roll him out of danger. But the man was heavy — he must have been solid muscle — and I couldn't get him to roll, at least not while my healing magic was still rushing out of me into him, taking my strength with it.

"Cassius!" I wrenched my attention from my patient and the flames in search of help.

Sebastian still fought hand-to-hand with the shadowy fae, with two more growing blood patches staining his sliced shirt and a black tattooed glyph near his neck glowing with icy-blue light.

Cassius was a few feet away, his flames dancing around him and the demon-vampire, who lunged in with a quick jab. Cassius started to sidestep, then froze, the angelic light glowing in his eyes flaring. The blade plunged toward his chest and my pulse tripped. If I was still locked on Titus, I might not be able to save Cassius if he took a serious injury. But at the last minute, with a burst of fire around his hands and a scream, he heaved to the side.

For a second it looked like he'd managed to avoid getting cut, then the firelight shimmered in the blood soaking into his black T-shirt and the fabric parted revealing a laceration slicing across his upper chest from shoulder to shoulder.

"Don't make eye contact with the nightmare," Cassius gasped. He shot a ball of fire into the trees directly across from him as he scrambled out of the way of another sweep of the demon-vampire's katana.

A demon with hellfire hair licking around tall thick horns that protruded from his forehead burst from the shadows. He was, without a doubt, a nightmare, a demon who, in both his human and horse form, could paralyze you with fear.

"Amiah, can you run?" Cassius asked.

"Not even to get away from your fire," I snapped back. The flames now burned my patient's shoulder and the pressure of my magic surged.

"How long until he's stable?" Sebastian asked, slapping his ribs and activating another tattoo, although it didn't seem as if anything magical had happened.

"I—" I scrambled to hold back my rushing power, but with a scream, Titus jerked awake again, and his eyes flew open revealing striking golden irises that stole whatever I was going to say. For a second there was just him, his predatory gaze boring into me, seeing straight into my soul.

Then pain twisted his expression. His breath turned into ragged gasps, and he grabbed the front of my suit jacket and shoved me to the ground, impossibly rolling on top of me and pinning me with his still mostly broken body, his weight crushing me. The movement, with the strength and power rushing out of me, made my head spin.

Blood from his wounds splattered on my face and clothes, and he snarled, revealing pointed elongated canines, suggesting that maybe he was a werewolf.

"You can't have it," he growled, his eyes wild as he clamped a huge hand around my neck and squeezed.

AMIAH

I gasped, clawing at Titus's hand with my weak still-glowing fingers, my other hand still pressed against his chest. I tried to tell him I didn't want whatever it was he was protecting, but couldn't draw enough breath to speak. Without a doubt, all he needed to do was tighten his grip and he'd crush my windpipe.

"I won't let you have it," he growled, but for some reason, his grip didn't tighten, and his body trembled, his strange golden eyes wide with fear and pain.

"Amiah, is he stable?" Sebastian asked, either not noticing I was in trouble or not caring.

Help me!

I whimpered, the most noise I could make, but knew the moment the pathetic sound came out it wasn't loud enough to draw anyone's attention.

Please, look at me.

The forest grew darker. I was going to pass out soon.

I heaved against Titus's massive weight but couldn't move him.

"Doesn't matter, we have to get out of here," Cassius said, also not looking my way or he definitely would have come to my rescue. "Teleport us."

I dug my short nails into Titus's wrist. His gaze never left mine, his expression more dangerous beast than logical man.

Help.

The trembling in his body increased. "You can't have it. I won't let you." Now it sounded like he was begging.

"A teleport is not happening," Sebastian said. "We have to run for it. I can put them down long enough to get to my car if you can carry Titus— Oh, fuck. Titus. Let her go." Out of the corner of my eye, I saw Sebastian leap toward me, and Titus's attention jerked to the fae.

"Seireadan?" Titus gasped, and his eyes rolled back. He collapsed on top of me, stealing what little breath I had left and sending agony screaming through my chest.

My magical compulsion to heal him until he was stable finally released me — thank goodness for that! — leaving me weak with miniature convulsions racing through my muscles. I struggled to push him off, even just enough to squirm free, but I'd used too much magic too quickly and barely had the strength to breathe against his weight.

Cassius shot another fireball at the demon-vampire, tossing him into the nightmare although not dropping either of them, and heaved Titus off me as Sebastian slapped two more tattoos and hissed a sibilant — probably fae — word.

Another force-wave shot from his hand, this one stronger than before, picking up rocks, fallen branches, and flaming weeds. It put out all the fire and slammed into the fae, the demon-vampire, and the nightmare, tossing them deeper into the forest.

Sebastian jerked to face us. "I wove a bit of sleep in with that blast but that won't keep them down for long." He held his hand out to me and I batted it away and scrambled to my feet.

The forest darkened and lurched, and my legs shook, but I gritted my teeth. There was no way I was going to let Sebastian see how dizzy I was. It would just give him more to make fun of and the dizziness would pass... eventually.

"I'm parked down the path," Sebastian said, and Cassius hefted Titus over his shoulders.

We crashed through the underbrush and back down the path. Sebastian ran straight to the small, sleek silver two-door sports car parked at the side of the road and opened the passenger side door.

"Are you kidding me?" Cassius asked. "You came here in that?"

"If I'd known you were coming, I would have driven a bigger vehicle," Sebastian said, his tone dripping with sarcasm. "You're welcome to run with him all the way back to my place."

Cassius's eyes narrowed and the muscles in his jaw flexed. "We're not going back to your place."

Oh, my goodness.

The street darkened and whirled and I fought to keep standing. *Were they really having this conversation right now?* "You're all bleeding. Those men could catch up with us any minute. Get in the car!"

Cassius stiffened and Sebastian's eyes widened and I realized my tone had been a lot sharper than I intended. But I wasn't going to take it back. I didn't need them to like me. I just needed them to not get hurt any worse than they already were, because I was already running low.

"You heard the lady," Sebastian said, gesturing to the open passenger door.

Titus was too big to fit in the back with someone else even if Sebastian pulled the front seats all the way forward, so Cassius set the big man in the front passenger seat and squeezed his not-nearly-as-big but still pretty-big frame into the barely there back seat.

I squished in beside him onto the soft black leather, grateful that I was about average size and build, and grabbed Titus's shoulder, easing more healing magic into him, and assessing his condition. Yes, he'd been well enough to be moved, but that didn't really mean much. Most of his organs and some of his bones had barely been stitched back together while other bones were still broken, and he still bled profusely. At least most of the internal bleeding had stopped.

Sebastian hopped into the driver's seat, drew in a shuddering breath, and activated another glyph along his right ribs. Icy blue-white light flared from the tattoo, turning his white shirt see-through, revealing the dark swirling lines covering his torso but also accentuating the large patches of blood soaking the fabric. He was going to need medical attention, if not my healing magic — which I could give him now that I'd been released from the need to heal Titus even though I didn't have much left — then certainly stitches, and Cassius would as well.

With another shuddering breath and a grip on the steering wheel that made the tendons in his forearms flex, Sebastian sped away from the curb, the wheels squealing against the asphalt.

"Okay," Cassius said, his voice low. "What was that?"

Sebastian swerved around a corner, putting a three-story building between us and the entrance to the park then took a hard left and raced down the road.

Cassius bit back a strangled grunt. "And that was a red light."

Titus moaned, my healing magic starting to pull him out of unconsciousness even though it would be better if he didn't wake. The agony of his broken body would still be overwhelming, and given his strength and violent reactions, it would be best if he didn't lash out while we were all crammed into Sebastian's tiny car. Except there wasn't anything I could do. My magic knitted broken bodies back together. It didn't sedate or dull pain.

"He needs a sedative and more medical attention. All of you need medical attention," I said, forcing my words to be firm and professional, and not letting my increasing dizziness and weakness affect my tone. I didn't want an argument. And I didn't want either of them to see how surging that much magic into someone affected me. Knowing Cassius, he'd get all worried and treat me as if I was fragile. He hadn't looked at me as if I was fragile in a long time and I intended to keep it that way. Because no one took a fragile woman seriously and I wasn't going to let anyone take my control away like that. "You're taking us to Operations."

"No." Sebastian's gaze jumped to the rear-view mirror and caught mine, his expression deadly serious. "You saw what happened. I'm taking Titus to my apartment."

"You don't think we can protect him?" Cassius's eyes narrowed. "Or will I find out the truth and have to arrest him?"

"Neither," Sebastian said. "I can only keep the protection spell I cast on Titus going for so long, and Operations doesn't have the kind of protections my apartment has. Those men will still be coming after him."

"What kind of protection?" Cassius demanded.

Sebastian snorted. "A glyph witch never casts and tells."

"So an illegal spell," Cassius huffed.

"Go ahead and prove it." Sebastian sped around a corner, going through another red light and making the muscles in Cassius's jaw flex.

With a scream, Titus jerked in his seat and slammed his knee into the dashboard, cracking it.

I pushed more magic into him, repeating my mantra in my head over and over again.

Just keep looking strong and calm. Just a little longer. Strong and calm.

But the speeding car did little to ease the growing whirl in my head, and my hunched forward position to maintain contact with Titus made it painful to draw each breath. That and my neck where he'd grabbed me was starting to hurt, which meant he'd squeezed hard enough to bruise. "He needs to be properly sedated. He's dangerous in this condition."

"He's dangerous in any condition." Sebastian pulled into a short driveway leading into the underground parking for a four-story office building. The heavy metal door rolled open, and he drove down the steep ramp, past row upon row of mostly empty parking spots, to the back of the garage that I was pretty sure was now in the basement of the next building over.

"This is none of your business, angel." Sebastian parked between an expensive looking SUV and another sleek sports car, this one black. He shoved open his door and got out, revealing that the whole left side of his button-down was soaked with blood.

Cassius climbed out after him. "A fight between supers makes it my business. I could bring you in for running those red lights."

"No you can't. You can only write me a ticket. Call a cab and go home." Sebastian shoved past Cassius, limped around the front of the car, and opened the passenger door. His breath was too fast and his expression tight. Even without my magic telling me, I knew he was in pain.

Titus moaned again, and Sebastian turned his attention to me. "Can you revive him? It'll be easier if I don't have to carry him."

"His broken legs are barely knitted back together, and even if I could revive him, given his injuries and his violent outbursts, that's a bad idea."

"Right. Of course. Dangerous in any condition," Sebastian said, his tone clear he thought he was stupid for having forgotten what he'd just said. He pressed his forehead against the doorframe and squeezed his eyes shut. "You God damn fucking idiot."

"Bane—" Cassius growled, but I cut him off before he could utter whatever he was going to threaten Sebastian with.

"Pick him up, Cassius, and let's get him cleaned up and in a bed." I glared at Cassius. There was no point in Titus bleeding out in Sebastian's fancy sports car when it would be more comfortable for him and me to finish what I could in Sebastian's apartment. "You can arrest Sebastian, or both of them after *all* of you have stopped bleeding."

Cassius huffed but pulled Titus out of the car and hefted him over his shoulders again as Sebastian led the way to a plain, cinderblock wall. The fae pressed his palm to one of the bricks, and the illusion shimmered then vanished revealing an elevator door.

The door slid open and the guys marched in as I clenched my hands and squared my shoulders, struggling to not show how weak I was, then I joined them. Sebastian hit the top of two buttons and the door slid shut. Guess the elevator only went to two floors. The garage and up to wherever we were going now.

Tense silence broken by sharp breathing from all the men and punctuated by moaning gasps from Titus filled the elevator. Darkness danced at the edge of my vision, and I tightened my fists, determined not to grab the side of the wall to keep my balance.

I will not look weak. I will be strong and calm. I wouldn't ever be weak again.

A moment later, the door opened to a long opulent hall. I'd only been to Sebastian's apartment once before, but I didn't think I'd ever forget the white marble floor or the complicated gilded frescoes on the walls and ceiling of the hall outside his door. All that money wasted on decorations when it could have been spent on medical attention for those less fortunate.

The elevator had opened at the end of the hall. A quarter of the way down stood a heavy door with a large frosted blue and white stained-glass window, and at the far end were the stairs leading up to the roof and directly down to the ground level without any doors to the three other floors in the building. The soft *thump thump* of music from the nightclub below filled the silence but wasn't nearly as loud as I'd have expected this close to midnight, which suggested Sebastian had enspelled his floor to mute the sounds below.

Sebastian unlocked his front door, flicked a switch turning on a shimmering crystal chandelier hanging from the vaulted ceiling, and limped across his stunning white-on-white with hints of blue and silver living room toward his kitchen, leaving a trail of blood droplets on the white marble floor.

"Put him in a bed," Sebastian said, "then go. I can take it from there. He's a pretty fast healer so he'll probably be fine soon."

I huffed. No one healed that fast.

"Are you going to tell us who he is?" Cassius asked, adjusting his grip on Titus, and I realized Cassius didn't know where the bedrooms were. "And who were those men who tried to kill you?"

The last time we'd been here— or rather *the only* time was when Cassius had been magically poisoned and we, along with the main JP team, had been running for our lives. He probably didn't even remember arriving, and he certainly hadn't been conscious when we'd left. At the time, I'd been terrified I was going to lose him. Without Marcus, all I had were Cassius and my fellow healer, Priam. I didn't make friends easily and I'd thought I'd found my soul mate and hadn't needed anyone else. Even if Cassius did always take assignments out of town, he'd been my one constant for almost a century.

The room started to tilt and I dug my nails into my palms. I'd been conscious the last time I'd left, I'd be conscious this time, too.

"I've already told you," Sebastian called from the kitchen. "His name is Titus and that's all you need to know."

"Not good enough, Bane. There are three dangerous men in my city."

"It's not *your* city," Sebastian said. "It's your brother's. And there are lots of dangerous men and women here. Three more you're never going to see again are not your concern."

"They didn't look like the kind of men to give up. If they know anything about angels, they'll know Am—" The light in Cassius's eyes blazed. "They'll know all angels live in the JP Operations building. We left with their target. You or Titus. They're going to show up at Operations looking for you whether we like it or not."

Sebastian limped out of the kitchen with a small red first aid kit that I doubted had much of anything helpful in it. "They know Operations doesn't have an area concealment spell. They'll know Titus isn't there."

"You don't know that," Cassius said.

Titus moaned and jerked, forcing Cassius to shift to keep hold of the big man, the movement sliding his foot into the growing blood pool at his feet.

"The protection of everyone in that building and in this city are my responsibility right now."

"Then put Titus in a bed and go fucking protect them." Sebastian limped around his conversation area of two couches and a coffee table, past his grand piano to the hall with the apartment's other rooms, and threw open the first door on the right.

Cassius glared after him.

"Just follow him." I wasn't going to be able to remain standing, not with the whirling lightheadedness threatening to steal my consciousness, and I certainly wasn't going to be able to hide my trembling for much longer. I didn't want either Cassius or Sebastian to see me give in and sit. Or worse, pass out. "You can argue while I heal you two then finish with Titus."

With a grunt, Cassius marched to the door and pushed past Sebastian. Inside was a clean, elegant bedroom done in the same white, blues, and silver as the rest of Sebastian's apartment. The room was lit by another, smaller, crystal chandelier, had a king-sized bed with a pristine white duvet, and an en suite bathroom with marble countertops and a standup shower.

I yanked the duvet off the bed, tossed it on the floor out of the way, pulled off the white sheet underneath, and laid it on the bathroom floor. It wasn't ideal and there wasn't a whole lot of room in the bathroom for all four of us, but it was the best solution to clean Titus up.

"Oh, for the love of— Just put him in the bed," Sebastian said.

"Once I've stopped the bleeding and he's cleaned up, then yes, we'll put him in a bed." I pointed to the big, heavy man on Cassius's shoulder. "I doubt you want to have to remake the bed around him."

Cassius set Titus on the sheet then perched on the closed toilet lid, his knee bouncing with what I knew was pent-up frustration, his expression hard. A wisp of smoke curled around his fingers, the precursor to his fire magic escaping his control and wrapping around his hands with dangerous flames.

The muscles in his jaw clenched and the smoke broke apart as he got his emotions back under control.

I'd seen his control slip more times in the last few weeks than I ever had during our friendship, but I had hoped that with things finally settling down, he'd no longer be struggling to keep his flames at bay.

Of course, it probably didn't help that we were just attacked and he was in pain. Something I could take care of. But first—

I sank to the floor beside Titus and pressed my hands over his heart to assess if moving him had damaged any of the work I'd already done. Somehow, he'd gotten through being hauled out of the park ring and up to Sebastian's apartment without redamaging any of his still-fragile organs, leaving me a few bones and most of the lacerations to heal, many of which could wait until tomorrow when I'd recovered some of my power. And, much to my surprise, he didn't have a single burn on his body from Cassius's accidental flames.

"I'm assuming you don't have a suture kit," I said to Sebastian, "and that first aid kit isn't big enough for all the gauze and bandages I'll need so—"

"So come up with something. Fine." Sebastian dropped the first aid kit on the counter and ran a hand over his spiky white hair, streaking blood over the tips. "You're not going until he's stopped bleeding, are you?"

I met his crystalline gaze. "Until *everyone* has stopped bleeding."

His lips quirked and desire heated his eyes. "Does that mean we all have to get naked?"

A foolish shiver of need swept through me, but I was pretty sure he was flirting to change the topic, not because he was actually interested in me, so I squashed the emotion and forced my focus to the job at hand: healing my patients.

"Get her bandages, Bane," Cassius growled.

Sebastian snapped his attention to Cassius. "Only if you promise to get the hell out of my apartment."

"Tell me who's after your friend and we'll go."

Jeez, neither man was going to budge figuratively on the topic and likely literally with their physical positions. Which wasn't going to help me hurry through healing everyone. I hadn't thought Sebastian was as stubborn as Cassius, but then I guess I didn't really know him.

Either way, I couldn't let this go on.

I jerked to my feet, slicing pain through my chest, and pointed to the door behind Sebastian. The room spun and darkened, and I grabbed the counter to steady myself. "Bandages. And you—" I tightened my grip on the counter to keep my balance and forced my expression into a hard, professional mask, praying neither man noticed how weak I really was. "Take off your shirt so I can assess your injuries without using my magic."

Sebastian snickered. "So we *do* get to get naked." He limped out of the bedroom, leaving me with Cassius and his hardened emotions.

"He's as bad as an incubus," Cassius growled. "Couldn't get Gideon's mate so he's going after you."

"Which implies I'm second best. Gee, thank you."

Cassius's eyes widened as he realized what he'd said. "That's not what I meant."

But it wasn't wrong. I'd made a point of making it clear to everyone that I wasn't interested in a romantic relationship... well, everyone except Marcus, because I'd been waiting for *the one*. I doubted anyone at Operations ever saw me in a romantic way — including Marcus — and I had no one to blame but myself. Except that hadn't bothered me until I'd realized what a fool I'd been and how even just waiting for my inevitable soul mate took away my choice for who and how I wanted to first be intimate with someone.

And I *had* to stop thinking about that. There was no point wallowing when I had a job to do. There wasn't even any point in planning. Once I'd healed Cassius, Sebastian, and Titus and had recovered, *then* I'd take action.

Hunh. I could use the excuse of checking up on Titus to come back to Sebastian's. If I was lucky, Cassius would be busy and I'd be able to discreetly hire Sebastian to remove my mating brand.

The man would make a big deal about it, me coming to him, but I could live with a little humiliation if it meant I'd be free.

"You know that's not what I meant," Cassius said, a whisper of smoke curling from his hands.

"I know." I heaved my attention back to business. Why was it so hard to focus these days? "How badly are you hurt?" I asked as I shrugged out of my ruined suit jacket, turned on the tap, and pumped soap from the dispenser into my palm.

"I'll be okay." He shrugged and winced.

I cocked an eyebrow at him, dried my hands, and checked the first aid kit for gloves more out of habit from using a combination of human and angelic healing than anything else because my healing magic wouldn't let me transmit diseases or infections. The kit didn't have any gloves, so I turned my attention back to Cassius.

"I can manage," he said, his tone returning to hard and commanding as if I were an agent under his command... which I wasn't. Trauma trumped agent-in-charge every time. Just silly agents liked to forget that.

"I'm not letting you go after those men while injured," I replied, matching his tone because I knew once he'd pulled enough information out of Sebastian he was going after them. "Take off your shirt and let's see."

I didn't really need for him to disrobe for my magic to work, but given I was low and still had Sebastian to heal and Titus to top up and the fact that I was in a bathroom with limited resources and not an OR, I needed to be smart about how I used what I had left.

"Amiah, I'm—"

"You already know it's useless to lie about your physical condition. Why do you insist on it every time?" He always did this, always pretended he wasn't hurt, or it wasn't as bad as it was, and always told me to take care of someone else first, as if I couldn't assess how best to use my magic. "Take your shirt off, agent. Don't make me work any harder than I have to."

I shuffled past Titus to stand in front of Cassius. His eyes narrowed. The icy hard edge that had been his almost constant expression since he'd returned to Union City just under a month ago grew into a silent challenge to my command.

Well, he could challenge it all he liked. I wasn't giving in. I could be just as hard and icy as he could. I'd spent a lifetime hiding my emotions for the sake of my patients, and right now I was exhausted and dizzy and trying not to tremble. I had every reason to be angry, more reasons than he did. I just wanted to go home, crawl into bed, and pretend I could stop thinking about Marcus and my brand, but I couldn't ignore the compulsion to heal Cassius, Sebastian, and Titus. Even if my magic hadn't locked onto them, I was still compelled to help. It would drive me crazy if I had an opportunity to help and I didn't take it. At least now I could choose how much I healed them.

"You're the agent on duty, you're going to put yourself in a dangerous situation. I *can't* let you walk out of here still bleeding. Please."

The look in Cassius's eyes softened, and his piercing blue gaze locked with mine.

My breath caught and my pulse stuttered at the intensity in his eyes. It sent a shiver racing down my spine, bringing back with a vengeance the yearning Sebastian had awoken in the park ring, defying my iron grip on my emotions, and making my body throb with need.

Cassius dragged his sliced and bloody shirt up over his head, revealing his gorgeous sculpted body and making my pulse stall completely.

AMIAH

I WAS CERTAIN CASSIUS DIDN'T MEAN FOR HIS GAZE CAPTURING MINE TO BE sexual. We didn't have that kind of a relationship and never would. But I couldn't stop my thoughts from jumping straight to desire... for him?

That wasn't possible. We were friends. Nothing more.

No, I just yearned for anyone at this point. How long could an angel go without intimacy before she lost her mind? Especially knowing that my not-soul-mate was being intimate with his actual mate, quite possibly at this very moment.

Which I didn't want!

Why was that so hard to remember?

Because it wasn't intimacy I didn't want. I didn't want the control-stealing soul bond. And now my reason for celibacy was gone.

That, and I missed physical contact. We might have just been friends, but Marcus had needed physical contact. I doubted he'd even been aware of his need since he wasn't a naturally born shifter and probably didn't know shifters had a much smaller personal space than most people, especially angels. I'd selfishly not told him and allowed him to stand too close and to embrace me when he'd thought I needed comfort... when I *did* need comfort, and now that I'd gotten used to that kind of closeness, that touch, it was gone.

Except Cassius was the last person I'd get physical comfort from, even platonic comfort. That need for closeness just wasn't in his nature.

He'd fight all my battles if I let him, but he'd never sit just a little too close. And now I'd gone weeks without something I'd had for the last four years. I hadn't thought I'd need physical contact on the same level as a shifter, but maybe I'd been wrong.

And again! I wasn't supposed to be thinking about that right now.

I refocused my attention on Cassius, his gaze still boring into me, his chiseled muscular torso on display. Blood smeared his skin and the parts not bloody were red and swelling with the beginning of heavy contusions. The laceration across his chest still wept, along with another gash at his ribs.

I contemplated telling him to take his pants off since his left pantleg was pasted to his thigh with blood, but we weren't in triage, and I doubted he'd appreciate me asking him to strip to his underwear in Sebastian's apartment... especially since Sebastian had already teased us about getting naked.

"Just slow the bleeding," Cassius said, dropping his gaze from mine, his voice strangely gruff.

"I know how to do my job." I sagged to the floor, using the counter to help lower myself, mindful of my cracked ribs, and laid my trembling hands against the laceration across his chest. If I didn't think he'd go headlong after those men, I *would* just heal him enough to slow the bleeding. Angels didn't have the fastest innate healing among supernatural beings, but they did have some, and with a partial healing, the wounds would be fully shut within twenty-four hours. They'd scar unless I gave him another session, but he'd survive.

Except I knew Cassius. He wouldn't allow those men to endanger anyone else, and he'd been more dogged about protecting everyone since the mess a few weeks ago where he'd helped his brother take down Lilith, the Hellfire Queen.

My magic swelled into my palms, the oozing heat weak compared to the flood I'd poured into Titus. I closed my eyes to concentrate and gently pushed my power into the wound. He didn't need to be healed quickly so there was no point in hurting him while I healed him.

My power billowed but instead of staying in the chest wound, it slipped down to the laceration in his side, heading to the worst injury first. Except the added distance thinned my magic, stretching it taut, and that required more magical strength to heal him, so I moved my left hand to his side to ease the pressure growing inside me.

A shiver trembled through his body and his muscles tensed. "You can go faster."

"This won't take long. You can wait." Through my connection to his body, I felt the flesh in his side start to knit together. And now that the laceration in his side was no longer the worst injury, a stream of my magic split off and sank into his thigh, thinning my power even more.

Another split and my magic swelled back through the laceration across his chest. My muscles contracted, my body drawing into my deepest reserves to keep going, and even with my eyes closed, I could feel the bathroom spinning.

"Amiah."

The voice was far away and yet close at the same time. Tender yet stern.

Just a little more, just to ensure he was at full strength when he put his life on the line again.

"Amiah."

Fingers clasped around my wrists — Cassius's fingers — and he jerked my hands from his body.

The connection between us snapped, jolting through me with a ghost of a backlash and another sharp slice of pain from my ribs, and I wrenched my attention up to him. Or at least I tried to. The light in the bathroom had dimmed and he was slightly out of focus.

"That's enough," Cassius said, and for a moment he had the same look of pity and concern that he'd had when he'd found me chained in that tent all those years ago. A look I swore I'd never see again on his face or anyone's. A look I desperately wanted to forget, but couldn't.

I wasn't helpless. I wasn't. And I'd never be helpless again.

I tightened my mask of cool professionalism and dropped my gaze, unable to hold his. The lacerations on his chest and side were sealed shut, but because he'd pulled me away and my magic hadn't withdrawn from him, I knew they weren't completely healed. They, along with the laceration in his thigh, were probably still tender to the touch under all that blood.

His eyes narrowed. "You need to rest."

As much as I wanted to argue with him, I couldn't. I was exhausted, except I wasn't done. Sebastian and Titus were still bleeding, and my compulsion to heal them, the compulsion that had left me weak and helpless all those years ago, made my pulse pick up.

I loved and hated my magic. I saved lives, gave people second chances, but I often did it whether I wanted to or not. Sometimes I could ignore the compulsion, but right now I was too tired to fight it. It was easier to just give in, finish what I could, and be done with it.

Which made me want to scream in frustration. It didn't matter how hard I tried to be in control, I never truly was.

I searched inside my palms, the place where I always felt my magic, to see how much I had left. A spark still warmed my hands. If I was careful, I could partially close the worst of Sebastian's and Titus's wounds, but that was the best I was going to get.

"I've a little left for Sebastian and Titus," I said, standing. The bathroom lurched and darkened, and I clutched the counter. "Then I'm done."

"You might be able to convince everyone else you're still fine, but I know you're more tired than you look," Cassius said, his expression softening even more, worry dimming the angel glow in his eyes. "Bane is a big boy. He can take care of himself."

"He sure is and he sure can," Sebastian said as he limped into the doorway, holding a pair of scissors and a folded white sheet. He'd thought to wash the blood from his hands and forearms, but hadn't changed his clothes yet. "Especially if that means you get out of my apartment."

Except he looked pale— or rather paler, which I hadn't thought was possible with his complexion, and his skin had a grayish hue and wasn't as luminescent as usual.

"Just sit and take off your shirt." I pointed to the toilet where Cassius sat then turned on the tap again out of habit and scrubbed Cassius's blood from my hands.

"No, Amiah," Cassius insisted, "you're going home."

"Don't tell me what I can and cannot do." And really, if I didn't want a bigger fight about it, I shouldn't waste time arguing. I should just heal Sebastian and Titus and end the conversation.

I split the magic I had left in half, lurched to Sebastian, and grabbed his forearm with my clean but still wet hand. With a forceful burst, I shoved one half of my power into him and partially knitted the worst of his injuries together. He screamed at the sudden painful blast of magic into his body and dropped the sheet and scissors to clutch the doorframe, his breath ragged his eyes wide.

"Jesus," he gasped.

The muscles in my legs gave out and I dropped to the floor at Titus's feet, painfully jarring my ribs. Cassius leaped from the toilet seat to grab me, but I shoved the rest of my power into Titus before he could reach me.

Titus howled and his eyes flew open. His hand snapped up to hit me, and Cassius seized it and yanked it back, as Sebastian pressed one hand to his shoulder activating a glyph, dropped to Titus's side, and placed his other hand over Titus's heart. The big man's eyes rolled back with Sebastian's spell and he collapsed, unconscious again, onto the bloody sheet on the floor.

"Jeez, Amiah," Cassius groaned as he leaned against the side of the counter. "Of all the stupid—"

"You don't want to finish that sentence." We'd argued before about me overexerting myself — a lot, actually, during the war — but I'd thought he understood how I had to help. I'd had power left and both Sebastian and Titus had needed it and I just couldn't fight the compulsion. It was really that simple.

I jerked a trembling hand over Titus, falling back on my cool professional persona to stay in control. "Now he still has a few broken bones and his condition is fragile. Clean him up, pack and bind the wounds that are still bleeding and get him into bed."

"You know that in your condition, I now have to escort you back to Operations," Cassius said, standing and washing his hands. At least he was going to do as I'd asked and finish with Titus first.

"You weren't going to before?" Sebastian rolled his eyes. "She just used who-knows-how-much magic. Chivalry really is dead."

"I was going to call her a cab and then ensure her safety by going after those men."

Which was such a Cassius thing to do. He didn't do friendly, warm gestures. He abandoned you to go out and bring you justice.

"And I've already told you she's not in danger." Sebastian grabbed the scissors and cut into the sheet.

"Someone threw your friend out of a plane or helicopter and sent men after him to make sure he was dead," Cassius said, soaking a hand towel and ringing out the water. "They tried to kill him. Don't you want justice?"

"Capture him." Sebastian ripped a strip from the sheet.

"What?" The light in Cassius's eyes flared.

"They tried to kill *us* so they could *capture* him. I'm not bringing anyone else into this. Believe me when I say, if you're not near Titus, you're not in danger."

"You'll pardon me if I just don't take your word for it," Cassius said, kneeling beside Titus and getting to work on cleaning him up.

Oh, for goodness sake. Again? They were going to be stuck in a standoff all night and there wasn't any way now that Cassius would agree to let me leave by myself, no matter how much I argued with him. If I had more energy, I'd smack both of them. "Stop talking in circles. Sebastian, what's your evidence? How do you know for certain the Quarter and Operations are safe? Cassius isn't going to leave without more information."

A hint of a victorious smile curled Cassius's lips.

Yeah, no. You're not going to think you've won this. "And Cassius, believe him. He's helped the JP enough to get the benefit of the doubt."

"Yeah, but not out of the goodness of his heart. He sent us a bill," Cassius said.

Sebastian shrugged, and a whisper of wicked sexual playfulness gleamed in his eyes. "I had to see if the JP would pay."

"Your evidence," I repeated before Cassius could argue about that as well.

"Fine." Sebastian sighed. "Titus is from the fae realm and those men were bounty hunters of the Shadow Court. He's their only target." A ghost of something passed across his expression but vanished before I could figure out what it meant. "They won't make trouble in the mortal realm unless they have to, such as finding us with Titus, and they won't do a full assault of any place. That would draw too much attention. The only people in Union City in danger will be me and Titus as soon as you two get the hell out of my apartment." Sebastian tore another strip from the sheet with a sharp *riiiiip*. "Oh, and no, I don't want the JP's help."

"I'm going to hold you responsible if you're wrong." Which was as much of an acknowledgment as Sebastian was going to get from Cassius that he was backing down.

"You go right on ahead and do that," Sebastian shot back.

I was sure Cassius was going to go home, sleep on it, and return at the crack of dawn demanding answers, but that was a problem for tomorrow.

Cassius harrumphed, but he and Sebastian did get to work cleaning and dressing Titus's wounds. In strained silence, but they did it. At least they were no longer arguing.

By the time they were finished and had hauled Titus into the bed, I'd regained enough strength to stand and walk without assistance. I could almost pretend I hadn't been weak and had just been sitting and supervising the guys' work. Except if I'd said that out loud, I was sure neither man would have believed me. And if I thought too long about it, my cheeks would flush with embarrassment. I was supposed to be a professional. Calm, in control, a rock in the painful chaos of a patient's injuries. I wasn't the one who was supposed to need help, not ever again.

"I'll come back in the morning and check on you and Titus." I grabbed my bloody suit jacket from the bathroom floor, mindful of hiding my sore ribs from Cassius because he'd make a fuss over that if he knew about them.

"It's better if you don't," Sebastian said, escorting us to his front door. "Unless you want to stay the night?" His tone turned sultry, and that damned desire heated low within me again.

Except I was pretty sure his offer was to tease me and Cassius. It wasn't real. Not even in the sense of a one-night stand… which I wasn't interested in. Really. That, and I needed to get back home and have my friend Priam discreetly heal my cracked ribs and what I was sure was going to be a spectacular bruise around my throat.

Not to mention, I had no clothes here and mine were covered in blood. Oh, and I really wanted a shower. If I stayed, that meant getting naked… in Sebastian's apartment… with him close by.

A shudder swept through me, but with excitement at the prospect, not the nerves or fear I'd have expected.

I tightened my expression to hide my surprise. There was something very wrong with me.

What I needed Sebastian for was to see if he could remove my mating brand before it fully formed. Nothing more. *Then* I could find someone to ease my need for physical contact. Someone who wasn't flirting just to get a rise out of me. Someone more appropriate.

"I'll be by midmorning," I said, heading out the door before Sebastian could argue and making my head spin with the sudden movement.

Cassius fell into step beside me and Sebastian's door closed, the deadbolt sliding shut with a heavy *click*.

"I might not be able to escort you back here in the morning," Cassius said, his voice low. "And yes, I know you don't need someone to walk you around, but those guys are still out there."

The spinning didn't ease up as I reached the stairs, so I slowed my pace — hopefully not enough for Cassius to notice — and grabbed the railing to steady myself. As much as I wanted to remind him that I wasn't helpless, I couldn't argue with his assessment of the situation.

"There's no way I'm going to be able to convince Sebastian to bring Titus to Operations." I reached the landing of the third floor, my slower pace doing nothing to ease the spinning and my breath painful and shallow. "I don't believe for a minute his friend heals so fast that he'll be fine in the morning. He's going to need another session or a lot of bedrest."

"And given the situation, I doubt Sebastian will think bedrest is a good idea," Cassius said.

"Would you?" Even I knew enough that the longer they stayed in one place, the greater the chance of being caught. Just because Sebastian said those men weren't going to cause trouble, didn't mean they wouldn't start asking around about a faekin. There were so few of them in the world and only one in Union City. Sooner or later someone would point them to Sebastian.

"I'm just afraid of what he's going to do." Cassius blew out a heavy breath. "I shouldn't have let it go."

"You should have figured out how to get him onto your side." I let go of the railing to go around the corner on the second-floor landing, and stumbled, just a little bit, but managed to catch my balance by leaning against the wall as I walked. "You've worked with him before."

"Not sure the fight against Lilith counts. He was working with Gideon's team. I was setting my career on fire."

"You did what you thought was right." I struggled to draw in a deeper breath. The shallow pants weren't enough and my dizziness was growing, and now it felt as if Titus was lying on top of me again, crushing my chest.

Cassius glanced at me and frowned. "You don't look good."

"Just tired." He was one of a very few who knew firsthand what overtaxing myself did to me. Although it was starting to worry me that maybe I wasn't recovering as quickly as usual because I'd completely drained myself too soon after the last time I'd drained myself — that being the fight against Lilith a few weeks ago.

"You know finishing Titus's healing isn't your responsibility," he said. "Bane has more than enough money to afford medical attention."

"But it wouldn't be magical," I gasped, struggling to breathe. Only angels had the ability to magically heal, and the three other angels in

Union with healing worked at Mercy Memorial. They didn't keep private practices.

"Still not your problem."

It wasn't, but I had every intention of returning to Sebastian's, might as well heal Titus when I did.

We reached the bottom of the stairs and stepped out onto a small patio lit by a single light hanging above the door. The *thump thump thump* of the music from the dance club throbbed in my chest the moment we'd passed through the doorway, adding more evidence to the theory that Sebastian had a sound-muting spell on his residence.

The patio was just big enough to comfortably hold a wrought-iron bistro table with two chairs, its boundaries marked by four planter boxes with evergreen shrubs. Beyond, cloaked in darkness, lay a narrow alley and our way out to the street to catch a cab.

I took three steps away from the door and the air around me vanished. One minute I could breathe, sort of, the next, nothing. The weight crushing my chest swelled, making the pressure from before seem like nothing, with a pain that went beyond just my cracked ribs, and my lungs burned, desperate for oxygen.

I staggered and grabbed the edge of the bistro table, but didn't have the strength to hold myself up. My knees smacked against the concrete ground and I crumpled onto my side. The patio spun around me, getting darker and darker, the light above the door growing smaller and smaller.

My pulse stuttered, fighting to keep going, and I desperately dug inside myself for magic, even just a spark, to save myself. But I was empty. I'd given everything to save Titus and heal Cassius and Sebastian.

And on top of that, I had no idea what was wrong with me! How could I not know? I could connect with the life force inside someone and know what was wrong with them in an instant, and that included me.

But I couldn't get my thoughts to focus past the encroaching darkness and the burning in my lungs. All I knew was that I was suffocating, but I had no idea why.

Cassius's face leaped into my line of vision. His expression was filled with fear and he cupped my cheeks between his strong hands, his skin hot against mine, his fire magic on the verge of releasing. His mouth moved, but I couldn't hear him past the rushing in my ears. The darkness swelled, blotting out everything except a weak glimmer from the angel glow in his eyes, and my fingers and toes went numb as a chill settled inside me.

AMIAH

Time lurched, and I gasped in a ragged breath that sent screaming agony through my chest. One minute I was on the ground dying, the next I was in Cassius's arms, my ear pressed against his chest hearing the rapid thud of his heart. It was like that day all over again when he'd found me. I'd been weak, barely alive not just because I'd been physically abused but because my own magic had compelled me to heal so many people without rest.

The worst part was that I'd had no one to blame but myself for my condition. If I'd resisted the urge, held my power back, I might have been strong enough to escape. But there'd been so many suffering people, many of them children. How could I have refused them? How could I have not helped them just to free myself?

Except by the time I'd realized saving my strength was my only way to escape, that the human who'd enslaved me was going to profit off my healing magic until I'd withered and died, I was too weak to resist my healing compulsion.

"Put her on the couch," Sebastian said from somewhere ahead of me.

"How did you not know this would happen?" Cassius demanded as he set me down on something soft. "You should have warned us there was a spell on her."

"Right, because I always know when there's a spell around."

I pried my eyes open and struggled to focus on my surroundings. We were back in Sebastian's apartment, and my gaze caught and stalled on a rainbow of refracted light from the crystal chandelier shining on the marble floor near my foot. My thoughts spun around and around, crushing pain still seized my chest, and I couldn't catch my breath.

"Don't you?" Cassius demanded. "Those men were dangerous. You should have checked or something. That should be standard practice."

"Not an agent," Sebastian shot back. "There is no standard practice."

"Not good enough." Cassius cupped my cheeks again with his too-warm hands, smoke curling from his skin. He was starting to lose control of his fire. He raised my head, pulling my attention away from the rainbow to meet his gaze, his eyes filled with worry.

I still couldn't figure out what was wrong with me, why I'd suffocated. It was like my mind had completely turned off and I couldn't get it started again. Draining myself might have made me blackout, but it shouldn't have suffocated me, and even if I had blacked out, it should have happened right after healing Titus.

"What happened?" I asked, my lips numb, my words embarrassingly slurred. I needed to pull myself together so he'd stop looking at me like that.

"Just a minor complication," Sebastian said, drawing close and pressing a hand over my heart.

Cassius stiffened, his gaze dipping to Sebastian's hand just above my breast before leaping back to mine. "He says you're linked with Titus. That's why you passed out."

Everything within me froze. "I'm what?"

No.

No no no. This wasn't happening, it couldn't be happening, please don't let it be happening.

"No. I can't be. I won't be. I—" I lurched forward, but Sebastian pressed me back onto the couch, my body so weak I doubted he had to use much force.

"Just take it easy," he said.

Take it easy! As if this wasn't my worst fear come to life?

My pulse leaped into a rapid tattoo and panic stole what little breath I'd managed to recover. I couldn't be bonded. Not so soon. Not when there was a hope, albeit a slim hope, but a hope nonetheless, that I could escape that fate. I hadn't even had a moment to talk with Sebastian. But without a doubt, now that the brand had formed, it'd be impossible to break. The one shot I had at freedom was gone, all because my stupid magic had locked onto a stranger and compelled me to save him.

"It'll be okay," Sebastian said, and an icy tingle of his magic seeped into my skin, doing little to ease my panic. It tugged at something inside me then melted into nothing. "Damn. I was right. Well, no matter. I'll break it and then you can be on your merry way."

"You're just going to break it? Just like that?" A harsh laugh escaped my lips. If it was that easy to break a mating brand, surely angels would have known about it.

My thoughts stuttered over that. Unless maybe no one knew because no one wanted to know? Maybe he was right and I could be free before the brand compelled me to fall in love with Titus. I didn't even know Titus. How was that fair? I didn't want to lose my life to a stranger. I didn't—

Sebastian frowned. "Okay, maybe not *just* like that."

"Of course not." My heart sank and my eyes burned with tears that I was *not* going to cry. I needed to keep it together and regain control. If I looked strong and acted strong, eventually I'd be strong. I wouldn't let this define me. Not like it had for my whole life. I'd find a way out. I would. Please.

"Hey," Cassius said, shifting to sit beside me on the couch — with an appropriately modest amount of space between us — and drawing my attention back to him. "You're not trapped."

"Don't," I said, my throat tight. If he tried to convince me this was a good thing, I'd start crying. And I was *not* going to cry! "Don't tell me it's magical and beautiful and sacred."

Sebastian huffed. "A leash spell? Yeah. It's anything but. It's not even close to a soul bond and certainly not that kind of permanent. I can break it. I just need a resonance charm."

His words tripped in my mind. "So you're saying...?"

I pressed my hand against my hip where my aching mating brand was. It didn't hurt more than before and it wasn't warm like the stories said a newly formed brand felt like. The need to pull up my camisole and shove down the waistband of my pants to check made my pulse race even faster. But I couldn't do it in front of Sebastian or Cassius. Cassius would probably be awed and amazed that I was destined to have a soul mate, and Sebastian would make some remark about taking my clothes off.

Sebastian chuckled. "You thought you were branded?"

"What other option was there?" I glared at him, fighting tears that were a mix of panic and relief. I still had time. I could still be free.

"I suppose leash spells are rare here." He sat on the edge of his coffee table. He still wore his bloody clothes and blood still streaked the tips of his white and silver hair, and while I was sure he wasn't bleeding as badly as before I'd healed him, his complexion was still a little gray. "The good news is it won't fuck with your emotions like a soul bond and it's not permanent."

"And the bad news?" Cassius asked, his voice dark and dangerous.

"You can't go far. A leash spell links a prisoner to their master, so if the prisoner goes beyond the designated distance, they'll suffocate. Well, technically it removes the air around the prisoner and that suffocates them. And by the looks of it, you can't go more than a hundred feet from Titus."

My breath hitched, and the panic that had eased when I'd learned I wasn't mated to Titus surged, squeezing my chest and turning my breath into shallow quick gasps again. "So I'm Titus's prisoner?"

"No. Titus started suffocating as well. That's why I ran down to get you," Sebastian said. "I thought he was the prisoner half of the spell. But I think what happened is that he somehow managed to break a leash spell originally on him, but didn't completely dispel it. When you healed him, the spell must have reignited. But it's as if you're both the prisoner."

I couldn't be anyone's prisoner. Not again. Even if it hadn't been intended, I couldn't be trapped like this.

The urge to go, get as far away from Titus as possible, made my stomach roil because that was the very thing I couldn't do.

"And those men were the ones holding him captive?" Cassius asked.

"No." Sebastian rolled his eyes at Cassius. "Those were the men hired by the man holding him captive. Someone who casts a leash spell doesn't do his own dirty work."

Please. I can't be trapped.

And I couldn't let this fear control me. *You're stronger than this, remember?* There was a way out. Sebastian said he could break the spell.

I clung to that thought and sucked in a steadying breath that shot agony through my cracked ribs and drew a whimper that I couldn't keep back.

More smoke curled from Cassius's hands, and Sebastian sat forward, pressing his palms against my knees, the gesture honest and pure without any hint of sexual intent.

"Just take it slow," the fae said. "Depending on the spell, it could take a while for the effects to wear off."

Except everything within me screamed at the idea of being trapped a second longer.

"You said you need a resonance charm to break the spell," I forced out, fighting to keep my tone even and calm.

"Yeah, I need it to find your magical resonance, Titus's, and the spell's so I can get in and pull it apart." Sebastian squeezed my knees in reassurance, then stiffened as if he'd just realized what he was doing, and leaned back, drawing his hands away. "It's not simple, but I'm more than capable of handling it," he added, his tone deepening, turning his words into a sexual innuendo.

Cassius's eyes narrowed. "Then get the charm and break this spell."

"Would love to, because that would get you the hell out of my house, but I need sleep." He shoved up to his feet and stared down at me. "And since you can't get more than a hundred feet from Titus, it looks like you're staying the night."

"You're not going to do it now?" I squeaked. Now. I had to be free now. I couldn't be trapped. *Let-me-go-let-me-go-let-me-go.*

"You don't want me fucking this up," Sebastian said. "The spell won't do anything to you if you don't get too far from Titus. You'll be fine until the morning."

But I was trapped!

"All right then," Cassius said as he pulled out his phone. "I'll call Chris and get him to bring over a change of clothes for us."

"Of course, you're staying, too." Bane threw his hands up. "Well, I hope you like sleeping together because I only have one other guestroom."

Cassius's eyes widened. "We're not— I mean—" He cleared his throat. "That wouldn't be appropriate."

"I'll take the couch in the study." I stood, the movement making the room tilt. My body trembled with the effort to hold my panic at bay and not let them see it. I wasn't going to last much longer. I needed to get alone before either of them realized the truth: that I couldn't handle what they thought was so simple, that I was weak.

Cassius jerked up and grabbed my elbow, helping me steady myself. "I'll take the couch. You should have the bed."

"Great. Now that you've got that all sorted, I'm going to bed." Sebastian shook his head and headed down the hall, not bothering to turn the light on.

"Do you know if the other guestroom has an en suite?" Cassius asked as Sebastian went into the room at the very end of the hall.

"It does." I dragged my attention back to Cassius. Surely he could feel my pulse racing, but he didn't react as if he knew I was falling apart. He wasn't even giving me *the look* any more. I just needed to hold out a little longer.

"Then have a shower. I'll leave your clothes outside the door," he said.

My gaze dipped over his still bare and bloody torso. "You should probably have a shower, too."

Which meant I'd have to hold out even longer while I waited for him to use my bathroom. My trembling increased, my mind screaming, *trapped, trapped, trapped*. I couldn't do it. I—

No. I wouldn't let him see me weak again. Ever. I squared my shoulders. "We're already unwanted houseguests. We shouldn't get blood on his furniture." I glanced at the blue-gray couch we'd been sitting on and the blood smeared on its cushions. "On any *more* furniture than we've already ruined."

"Yes," he said, his voice gruff. "Right. I'll wait out here until you're decent." The muscles in his jaw clenched, but I didn't know if it was because of his frustration at the situation or something else. "Unless... ah... you think you're too dizzy to shower by yourself."

My pulse leaped and my body heated with embarrassment and desire, which I quickly squashed, desperate to keep my expression from revealing my surprise and my unreasonable yearning.

This was all Sebastian's fault. Flirting with me and making me think of having sex — with apparently anyone if I was considering Cassius. Cassius's offer had been purely practical. I'd been perfectly fine all these years without sexual intercourse, educating and exploring myself so I wouldn't be a complete disappointment for my soul mate, and waiting. I would be perfectly fine now.

Except I wasn't fine. I was trapped and tired and heartbroken.

"I'll manage."

Cassius frowned.

"I'm already breathing better," I said, which was true. The massive weight of the leash spell had finally eased and now all I needed were shallow breaths to avoid aggravating my ribs. "And the dizziness has subsided." Subsided but wasn't completely gone. But I was *not* going to get naked with Cassius. I needed a friend now more than ever, and, given my desires, showering together would ruin that.

I squared my shoulders and took a few steps past the coffee table, determined to look like the living room wasn't slowly spinning. "See. I'll be okay. Now call Chris and get us some clean clothes."

His frown deepened.

"The guestroom is the second door on the left." I turned and made it into the hall without staggering.

Behind me, I heard the front door open and close as Cassius went to get our clothes.

"Didn't take Cassius up on his offer to share a shower I see," Sebastian said from the far end of the hall, still wearing his bloody and ruined clothes while holding a pile of folded clean ones.

A shiver of anticipation trembled down my spine. I didn't understand how I kept responding to him like that. I *knew* he wasn't interested in me, that his flirting was just a game he played with every woman, and yet no one had ever really flirted with me before, and it made me feel... desired.

"It wasn't necessary," I forced out.

"It usually isn't." His clear gaze captured mine, and another shiver swept over me.

I clamped down on my yearning. "He only made that offer because he thinks I'm still dizzy." *And weak. So pathetically weak.*

"Sure he did," Sebastian said, crossing the distance between us.

"You know he did. Don't make it into something it isn't."

"You mean you and he haven't...?"

"Of course not!" How was I even having this conversation? Because I was trapped, bound to Sebastian's friend unable to leave his apartment. My pounding heart sped up and my trembling grew stronger. I gritted my teeth, forcing my expression icy. "Do you need something, Sebastian?"

His lips quirked.

Crap. That just opened me up for more teasing. *Please don't. Please just end this conversation.*

The sensual gleam in his eyes softened. "I thought you might want something to sleep in." He held out the clothes, a T-shirt and a pair of cotton knit shorts.

I didn't know what was more surprising. That the man who always wore a dress shirt and slacks had clothes like that or that he was thoughtful enough to offer them to me. Especially since I was sure he'd love to tease me in the morning about having no choice but to sleep in my underwear or worse, naked.

"Thank you," I said, taking the clothes, trying and failing to hide my shaking hands.

"Yeah, well, leash spells are nasty."

The look in his eyes softened even more, making my gut churn. He could see right through me. He knew I was weak and couldn't handle being trapped even for just a night, and yet I still squared my shoulders and hardened my expression to hide my emotions, the habit so ingrained that I couldn't stop myself even when I knew it was pointless.

"But *you* don't need anyone or anything, do you?" He rolled his eyes at me. "Accepting a little help won't kill you, you know."

"You should talk. Cassius has all but formally offered the JP's help for you and your friend."

"Not the same thing."

"Of course it is," I said. "He has the skills and assets you need to deal with those men, and you have the skills and assets I need to break this leash spell."

Sebastian's wicked smile tugged at his lips again and more need heated low within me. "So you admit it. I have something you need."

I opened my mouth to say I could easily call in another witch to break the spell. There were some powerful ones in the JP — although none of them as powerful as Sebastian — and I was sure they could handle this leash spell just as easily as Sebastian could — it would just be a matter of keeping it together long enough for them to get into town. But Sebastian *did* have something I needed... or at least I hoped he did: the power and knowledge to remove my not-yet-formed mating brand. And if I wanted his help, I was going to have to swallow my pride.

"You do," I said quietly.

His eyes widened. "You must really be exhausted. I expected more of a fight."

"I want—" I glanced behind me, checking for Cassius. He'd be furious to learn I was trying to remove the most sacred mark an angel could have.

He still hadn't returned with our clothes but that could change at any time, and if I was going to broach the subject with Sebastian tonight, I had to do it now.

"What do you want, Amiah?" Sebastian asked, his voice sliding into a low sensual drawl.

"I want to hire you to break a mating brand." The words came out in a rush and my pulse pounded with the fear that he'd laugh at me.

But his eyes narrowed instead. "I'm not breaking any of Esther's bonds," he said, jumping to the most natural conclusion. Angelic mating brands were rare and Essie's bonds were the only ones anyone in the realms knew about. But that he'd think I was so jealous of Essie that I'd want to break her soul bonds—?

Was that what everyone thought of me? I knew I wouldn't win any popularity contests, but I didn't think they thought I was heartless. I'd dedicated my life to saving people. People who, if they just thought things through and weren't so reckless, wouldn't need me.

Well, fine then. If that's what they thought, that's what they thought. I didn't need to be liked. Things were just fine the way they were.

Except they weren't. A part of my soul was missing. The aching brand was proof of that. It was also proof that I'd be trapped again.

"I have a partially formed mating brand that hasn't awakened," I said, fighting to keep my fear from my voice. "I want it gone before it turns into a soul bond."

"Holy fuck," Sebastian gasped. "An angel wants her brand gone."

"I won't be trapped like Essie. I won't lose my independence to a stranger." My breath picked up. I was going to lose control and have a panic attack in front of Sebastian. I clamped down hard on my fear. "I want it gone. Are you powerful enough to do that or do I need to look for someone else?"

"Oh sweetheart, there isn't anyone else." His wicked smile grew but didn't reach his eyes as if this was more of an act than anything else. "If I can't do it, no one can."

"But you'll try?" *Please say yes. Please.* He was my only hope.

"It'll cost you."

"I wouldn't have expected anything else." *Whatever the cost.* My fear melted into relief. I was going to be free. I'd be able to keep my life. "But I expect you to start as soon as possible."

"I have a leash spell and a group of kidnappers to deal with first," he said. "That could take some time."

"Not if you accept the JP's help." It was a win-win for everyone. Sebastian would be able to protect Titus, Cassius would know those men were in custody, and I'd deal with my brand before it was too late.

"Not happening," Sebastian said with a shudder. "Not until Esther gets better control of her magic."

"You don't have to worry about that. The primary team is in Rome. You'd be working with Cassius."

Sebastian's eyes narrowed. "That doesn't make it better."

"Sebastian, please." I couldn't risk the brand fully forming while I waited for him to deal with whatever was going on with Titus. "I know it'll be impossible to break if it forms and then…"

"Then you'll be stuck with someone forever."

I didn't want to beg, but I would if I had to. The mating brand could awaken at any time. "I know whatever is going on with Titus is complicated, but I'll pay—" God, I was going to regret this. "I'll pay whatever the price."

"Whatever?" This time his wicked smile did reach his eyes, filling them with heated sexual desire and making my body ache again with that frustrating need I desperately wanted to ignore.

I opened my mouth to tell him I wouldn't pay with sex, but the moment I thought that, I realized I would. Many supers used sex as a currency, and given Sebastian's constant flirtations, I should have expected it.

"Whatever the price." I held his gaze to show I was serious.

He stared back as if he was searching my soul for the truth in my words, and my skin heated with a mix of desire and embarrassment.

"Well, then," he purred. "Let's have a look at this unformed brand."

"You'll need more light," I said, my voice breathy.

"I meant look with my magical senses. I don't have to see it, just touch it to figure out what it is."

"Right." I knew that. His magic probably worked in similar ways to mine, sensing spells like I could sense injuries.

I set his clothes on the floor, not wanting to get them dirty before I'd even worn them, and tugged up the hem of my camisole and pushed down the waistband of my pants.

His gaze locked on my bared skin and my pulse pounded faster.

"The brand runs from just above my waist, over my hip, and down my thigh." The ghostly white lines curling under my skin were hard to see in good light unless you knew what you were looking for, but in the dim light in the hall, they were invisible.

Sebastian stepped close and brushed his fingers along the top of my hipbone with a whisper of a touch that made my not-yet-formed brand throb and my breath hitch.

"Ah, I see." His eyes fluttered shut and he traced the line that trailed up to my waist and curved around to my back with his index finger, the movement slow, sensual. My trembling increased, no longer with fear, but with that pesky yearning I'd been trying to ignore.

I fought to stay where I was and not lean into his touch. Maybe my willingness to pay with sex wasn't just because I'd do anything to not be trapped by a soul bond, but because I wanted it, wanted to be caressed and kissed and filled. There'd be no strings attached with Sebastian. I wouldn't have to continue aching like this while I waited for the right man to come along. I could satisfy a need and move on.

His icy magic prickled under my skin and raced along the brand's lines swirling over my abdomen. The sensation made my inner muscles clench and drew a surprised gasp of pleasure.

"I can't make any guarantees," he said as his magic slid down my thigh, drawing another breathy gasp. "And I still expect payment if I can't break it."

"I understand."

"But I'm sure we can work out a payment that'll suit both of us." He opened his eyes and raised a gaze without a hint of sexual invitation to mine. His expression was serious, all business, and it was clear, he'd just been toying with me, like all the other times before.

The heat of my desire swelled into embarrassment, burning my cheeks and twisting in my chest. He didn't want me. Of course, he didn't want me. How could I have been so foolish to think he'd actually be interested in me when he could have any number of strong, confident, easy-going, experienced women?

"I'll start tomorrow after I break the leash spell and—" He shuddered. "—after Cassius and I come up with a plan to help Titus. There should be some downtime while things are getting sorted for me to check my library."

"Thank you," I said, trying to keep my disappointment from my tone. I didn't know why his rejection stung so much. It was supposed to have been a transaction, nothing more.

CASSIUS

I called Agent Karsten for a change of clothes for Amiah and me, and, after checking to make sure I wouldn't be locked out, waited at the edge of Bane's patio. Fire dripped from my hands, sizzling on the concrete at my feet, small sharp flashes against the night as my emotions roiled in a furious, fearful sea. Amiah was enspelled and exhausted and there wasn't a damned thing I could do about it.

God, she was so willful. If she'd just listened to me, followed protocol, we wouldn't have been in this mess.

Except I knew that wasn't fair. Amiah had no control over who her magic locked onto. The best she could do was avoid situations where she was likely to come across someone gravely injured. If she hadn't been standing on Operations' roof or if I hadn't seen Titus and said something, she might have been fine.

But draining herself to exhaustion... that was her fault. She knew better. And yet she kept doing it over and over again.

I bit back a growl of frustration. Neither I nor Bane would have died from our injuries. She hadn't needed to heal either of us, and she certainly hadn't needed to completely seal shut all my wounds. It had been like she was in a trance, lost in her magic, and unaware of how much power she was pushing into me.

And I'd been an idiot, distracted by her kneeling close, her warm hands pressed against me, and her breath feathering over my aching flesh. I hadn't realized until it was too late that she was going to heal everything completely and drain herself dry.

My power flared and curled up my forearms, and molten fire poured onto the ground.

Shit.

I clenched my jaw and heaved my fire back under my skin. It writhed and snapped against my will, searing my insides as I fought to get my emotions back under control.

I needed to take another assignment out of town. It was the only way to regain what little hold I had on my emotions.

My brother was safe. He didn't need my protection — not that I'd been able to protect him or anyone in the last few weeks. Hell, he was mated to a powerful super who I had no doubt would destroy the world if something happened to him, and he was happy.

Amiah wasn't.

But I couldn't give her what she desired. Not without risking burning everything around me.

My emotions churned stronger, my fire threatening to break free. I hadn't realized I'd fallen in love with my best friend until the war had pulled us apart. When it was done, things between us were different. Because I was different.

She hadn't gotten through the war without psychological scars, I don't think anyone had, but my psychological scars were bigger and deeper. My magic was best suited for the front lines and special ops, and I'd turned myself into a force of destruction, my rage at the injustice of a senseless war turning my magic into a firestorm that burned everything to ash.

And a part of me had enjoyed it. I'd embraced the monster inside me, finally released my hold on my emotions, and wreaked vengeance on Michael's army for the murder of millions... for the murder of my youngest brother. I hadn't cared about rules or order, only justice.

I couldn't lose control like that again.

Except my fire magic had gained strength during the war and had become harder to control. Moderate levels of emotions that hadn't affected it before affected it now, and it wasn't just rage that made it burn hotter. It was every emotion.

And at the moment, I was barely holding on with the memory of that demon-vampire hybrid stabbing at Amiah playing over and over again in my mind. I'd almost failed her, just like I'd failed to protect my brother, Dominic, against Michael, and Gideon in the fight against Lilith.

I'd thought once I'd figured out how to control my fire, I could tell Amiah the truth, tell her that I'd really fallen in love with her the moment I found her chained in that faith healer's tent, drained, and clinging to life. But then she joined the JP to follow Marcus, and I realized I'd never be able to be the man she wanted.

Marcus was fierce, his emotions powerful and untamed like many shifters, and he was free to show them. Most shifters loved hard whether they were mated or not, and with Amiah setting her sights on Marcus, it was clear. She'd finally figured out what she wanted. Passion.

Which I had. But like all my emotions, rage, fear, joy, it too was connected to my fire, and I could never let go enough to fully show it.

A hot spark snapped against the concrete, the sound sharp and loud even against the noise from the nightclub under Bane's apartment.

I was barely holding it together as it was. Letting go to embrace and show my desires was too dangerous. People would get hurt. Amiah would get hurt.

She'd always been careful with her heart. I wasn't even sure I'd ever seen her show interest in anyone until Marcus, and even then, unless you knew her well, you probably wouldn't have noticed... not until Essie Shaw had shown up.

I didn't know what Amiah had been waiting for with him, but I was glad she'd never made a move on her feelings. It made me ache and my fire burn hotter knowing how hurt she must have been — must still be — when he formed a soul bond with Essie. I couldn't imagine how much more she'd be hurting if she'd actively pursued him or if they'd had an intimate relationship before everyone realized he was fated to love someone else.

But just because Marcus wasn't the one for her, didn't mean she didn't still deserve the intense passion of a shifter. She deserved everything she wanted. And I was God damned going to protect her to make sure she got it.

An average-height, muscular figure dressed in typical black JP fatigues strode into sight from down the alley. He had a backpack slung over one shoulder and his gait was sure, strong, radiating the power of a werewolf. Chris Karsten. He and Nathaniel usually secured crime scenes after the main team had dealt with the dangerous situations, and from what I could tell from his JP files, he was easy-going, orderly, and highly competent. Competent enough that he could probably put in a transfer and request to join a primary team. Except his family and his pack were in Union and, in the time we'd spent working together over the last couple of weeks, I'd learned he was happy being a secondary agent in order to stay where he was.

I clamped down even harder on my emotions, turning my fire into curling smoke, before Chris realized how close I was to losing it. It wasn't good that I couldn't get my flames fully under control, but it was the best I was going to get, what with Amiah's condition and whatever this mess was with Bane and Titus.

"Jesus," Chris said, as he approached, his gaze sliding over my bruised, bloody, and shirtless body, his expression tight with concern. "What the hell happened? Is Amiah okay?"

"She is." No thanks to me. "She's fine." But that was all I was going to say. She wouldn't appreciate me saying she'd foolishly drained herself to exhaustion, and she certainly wouldn't want me mentioning the leash spell. Especially since she'd be free in the morning.

"Good. I figured something had happened if you both needed a change of clothes, but I didn't expect—" He blew out a heavy breath, and handed over the backpack.

"Thank you for this. Get Nathaniel, Jasmine, and Summer and go to the park ring. We were attacked by a male nightmare, a male demon-vampire hybrid, and a male shadow fae."

Chris's eyebrows shot up. "A shadow fae?"

"Yeah. He can blend into the shadows like a wraith." I pulled out my phone to send him the location of our fight. "I want everything you can find, forensics, tracks, if you pick up scents that don't match me, Amiah, or Bane. See if you can figure out where they came from or where they went. But," I said as I leveled a hard glare at him to ensure he understood I was serious, "if you see them, don't approach, not until we have a better idea who they are. These guys are dangerous."

"Copy that." Chris's attention shifted to the door behind me and I could see the question in his eyes. Why weren't we back at Operations? There was no reason for Amiah to treat someone outside of her medical facility. "Anything else I need to know?" he asked.

"I'm sure lots, but I don't know it either." The smoke curling from my hands thickened and I sucked it back before it turned into flames. "I hope I'll have more in the morning."

"Yes, sir," Chris said with a tight nod. "I'll text you if I find anything that can't wait."

"Thanks." I watched him stride back down the alley as I took deep breaths that twinged the still tender cuts across my chest and side in an attempt to lock down my emotions before I went back inside. I still had to talk to Amiah again before this night was done, and I needed to lock everything down to do it. The moment Bane had told her she was magically linked to Titus that same look in her eyes that she'd had when I'd found her all those years ago had flashed across her expression. Desperate, terrified, hopeless.

A spark snapped from my hands.

She'd recovered her composure quickly, but it was all an act and I had no idea how to help her and that was making it nearly impossible to keep my emotions in check.

AMIAH

I SLEPT FITFULLY, THE AGONY IN MY CHEST AND THE ACHE AROUND MY throat, making it impossible to get comfortable. That, and my mind kept whirling, spinning between being trapped by the leash spell and having told Sebastian about my brand, something I'd never told anyone else about... not to mention how I'd actually considered paying Sebastian with sex or how much it had stung when he'd offered different payment terms.

I couldn't believe I'd done or thought that, and I prayed he wouldn't say anything about it in front of Cassius. I wouldn't be able to keep a strong appearance if Cassius's concern grew — I was barely holding it together as it was — and without a doubt, he'd be concerned that I'd want to get rid of my brand.

It also hadn't helped that I'd slept in Sebastian's borrowed clothes, too tired to change into the scrubs Chris had brought over after I'd dragged my exhausted, aching body out of the shower and let Cassius have his turn. I'd thought I'd be fine sleeping in Sebastian's T-shirt and shorts, but all night long, all I could smell was a fresh evergreen scent that without a doubt was Sebastian's. I hadn't been able to stop thinking about him, about the heated look in his eyes and that whisper of a touch that made my body throb and how he'd just turned it all off, clearly not interested.

I gave up on sleep just before dawn and went into the bathroom to splash water on my face in the hope that I wouldn't look as run down as I felt and Cassius wouldn't be as worried as he'd been last night.

Except a quick glance in the mirror revealed that splashing a little water wasn't going to do much to mitigate any of Cassius's concerns. Sure, he wasn't going to notice my dimmer than usual angel glow, or my tired expression, because he was going to be staring at the massive dark red bruise around my neck in the shape of Titus's large hand.

Just wonderful. If I didn't want him fussing, I was going to have to heal myself. Except my magic wasn't even halfway back to full and I'd need at least a full night's sleep more to recover all of it. Which meant I needed to see how much more healing Titus needed before turning my magic on myself. Because without a doubt, Sebastian would want to go on the run with Titus or start a fight or something dangerous to deal with those men, and I couldn't risk Titus still being injured when they did that.

My injuries could wait. It took a lot more magic to heal myself than everyone else and just like when I healed everyone else, I couldn't pick and choose what to heal. My magic always mended the worst injury first. Which meant it would heal my cracked ribs before my bruise, and that meant healing to the point of getting rid of the bruise would drain what little power I'd managed to recover. I wasn't so vain as to let Titus continue suffering especially when his life was in danger just to avoid an argument with Cassius.

With a sigh, I ran my fingers through my long blond locks, combing out the tangles and braiding it back so it was out of my way — which was only a temporary solution because I didn't have anything to tie off the braid. I considered changing into the scrubs, but some of Titus's deepest lacerations could still be bleeding, and it was better to get Sebastian's clothes bloody than the only change of clothes I could reasonably wear to walk out of Sebastian's apartment. No way was I showing up at Operations wearing his clothes and giving everyone something to gossip about.

Besides, after this morning everything would be fine—

Well, maybe not *fine*, but at least on track. I'd no longer be trapped by the leash spell, I could get away from Sebastian and his flirtation and regain my composure, and I wouldn't have to worry about Cassius seeing me as that weak, pathetic angel he'd rescued all those years ago. I'd be back in control and soon free of my mating brand.

So long as I didn't think about the fear currently squeezing my heart

— and the cause was going to be gone before the morning was out — I was okay. There was hope and I could hold out a few hours longer.

As quietly as possible, I tiptoed across the hall to Sebastian's other guestroom and eased open the door, hoping Titus was still sleeping and I wouldn't wake him. Given his violent reaction last night, it was foolish of me to check on him without Sebastian or Cassius, but I'd snuck in and checked on hundreds of patients before, many with highly acute senses, without waking them. I could check on Titus, top him up, and be gone before he stirred without needing to bother anyone, and more importantly without Cassius realizing I'd slept in Sebastian's clothes.

And yes, that was an irrational thought. What did I care if Cassius saw me wearing Sebastian's clothes? What did I care if Sebastian saw me? But I did care. It would open me up to questions from Cassius and teasing from Sebastian, and after last night's concern and rejection, I didn't want to deal with either.

Inside the bedroom, Titus lay on his side facing me, his shaggy dark red hair veiling one eye, the other eye closed and his chest rising and falling with the steady breath of sleep. The comforter had slipped down to his waist, and in daylight, without the chaos of the fight, he looked even bigger and bulkier — and more intimidating — than he had last night.

A thick ragged scar encircled his one visible wrist, and I could see a hint of another scar on his neck, injuries I knew too well from healing Michael's captives.

The sight sent a shudder racing through me. My captivity at the hands of that human almost a hundred years before Michael's war hadn't resulted in physical scars, but I knew many held in captivity weren't so lucky.

Titus's skin, what I could see around the many bandages, was mottled with dark purple bruises, some with hints of green as if they were almost a week old, not less than twelve hours old, and the lacerations that had been too small to worry about bandaging had sealed shut and were faint pink lines.

All of which spoke to an exceptional level of healing, and a deplorable degree of imprisonment.

If his healing was that good, it would have taken a lot for a long time to make scars like the ones he had on his wrist and neck.

At least his exceptional healing meant I wouldn't need to give him much more to finish knitting his broken bones back together and strengthen his newly healed organs. Then a quick shift into his beast would finish the job. That might even leave me enough magic to heal my ribs and my neck and avoid comments from Cassius.

I crept to Titus's bedside, placed a gentle hand on his massive biceps, and let my magic connect with his body.

All of his bones, even the ones I hadn't had enough power to heal, were healed, his organs were strong as if they hadn't been damaged at all, and every laceration had sealed shut, although the deepest ones looked like they were still tender.

Sebastian hadn't lied. Titus was a fast healer. I didn't think I'd ever come across someone — incubi and succubi excepted — who healed so quickly, not even a greater demon.

For a second, I contemplated leaving him as he was and letting his natural healing finish the job. If he shifted in and out of his beast form then stayed out of trouble, he'd be fine by the evening, even his bruises would be gone.

But those were the key words: if he stayed out of trouble.

I had no idea what Sebastian was planning, and while Titus was big and Sebastian magically powerful, that didn't mean they'd be able to get through the next fight without serious injury.

The thought of Sebastian gravely injured made my stomach churn. I might not like the way he did things or how he teased me, but he'd come through for the JP recently when we were desperate. That, and I'd already saved his life once before. I didn't want all that hard work to go to waste. I wouldn't be able to live with myself if I didn't finish healing Titus and something happened to Sebastian. And unlike Sebastian and Titus, I wasn't about to jump headlong into trouble.

I drew in a steadying breath, sliced agony through my chest, and pushed past the pain to reach the still-weak spark of magic in my palms. It flared at my mental touch, pushing against my mental grip, but I easily kept it contained. There was no need for this healing to be painful, and besides, painful would wake him up, defeating the purpose of healing him without him noticing.

I focused my magic into the hand I had pressed against his arm and released a small stream, but before the stream could flow into him, he seized my wrist and wrenched me forward.

With a yelp, I tumbled on top of him, and in one swift movement, he rolled, pinning me under his massive body, shooting agony through my chest.

His hand clamped around my throat again and our gazes locked, his expression stunned.

For a second there was only him. No fear, no pain, nothing, as if my mind and soul had stalled unable to register on anything else but him, not even the danger he presented.

He radiated a wild, unbridled intensity that stole all breath and thought. My body heated at his quick exhales washing over my cheeks, the press of his thighs on either side of mine boxing me in, and his pelvis pinning me to the mattress.

The vein in his neck pulsed under the ragged scar, the beats growing faster, and with a blink, the shock vanished from his golden eyes. He jerked closer, lurching my thoughts back into action, and snarled, revealing sharp extended canines.

"Don't scream and answer my questions and I won't snap your neck." His grip around my throat tightened.

The fear I should have had the moment he'd grabbed me slammed into me and my lungs screamed for air. I clawed at his hands and jerked against his weight, but that only sliced more pain through me, stealing what little breath I had left and sending flecks of darkness across my vision.

"Nod if you understand," he said, his expression hard, his intention clear: if I even squeaked too loudly, he'd kill me. Rage and fear and determination now filled his eyes, I wasn't even sure if I'd seen his wide-eyed stunned look or just imagined it. What I did know was that someone had cast that horrible leash spell on him and imprisoned him. He'd do anything, kill anyone, to be free, and I was about to become a casualty.

I gasped against his grip, instinct making me continue to heave against him, desperate to be free. Pain burned my chest and the darkness in my vision swelled.

"Fucking hell," Sebastian said, his voice cutting through the darkness. "Don't kill her."

Titus stiffened, and his attention jerked to Sebastian standing in the doorway. He wore a pair of dark blue pajama pants that hung low on his hips and nothing else, giving me a spectacular view of his sculpted arms and torso and the swirl of black glyphs tattooed on his pale skin. Behind him stood Cassius with his angel glow blazing, his smoke curling around him, and fully dressed in a black T-shirt and fatigues as if he'd slept in his clean clothes.

"Get off her," Cassius commanded.

"Seireadan?" Titus's grip relaxed a bit, but he didn't let go or get off me. "Is she yours?"

"No," Sebastian said.

"But she smells like you."

"Because she borrowed my clothes." Sebastian took a slow step closer to the bed. "You bled all over hers."

"I said, get off." Cassius's smoke thickened.

Titus bared his canines and growled low in his throat. "No, not until I know I'm free."

"You honestly think I'd enslave you?" Sebastian asked, taking another step closer.

"Deaglan did," Titus growled.

"I said. Off." Cassius shoved Sebastian out of the way, snapped a fire whip around Titus's throat, and yanked him off the bed with a vicious jerk.

Titus hit the floor with a heavy thump, the comforter tangling around his legs and tugging me half off the bed toward him. He grabbed the whip with his hands as if it wasn't made of flames, tore it apart, and lunged at Cassius, who snapped up another whip. But Titus tackled him, using his massive body to slam Cassius against the marble floor, throwing off Cassius's strike.

"Jeez, stop," Sebastian said, jerking out of the way of the two men and activating a glyph on his left forearm that curled from his wrist past his elbow, snaking in between other glyphs. "Deaglan betrayed me too."

Cassius shot a blinding spark into Titus's face. The big man flinched and Cassius managed to shove him off him with the help of a fire blast into Titus's chest. The bandage-made-of-sheet around his gut burst into flames and turned to ash, and my pulse stuttered. Cassius was going to ruin all the hard work I'd done last night, and there was no need for them to be fighting. Titus just needed to know he was safe.

More flames roared around Cassius's hand and I scrambled from the bed, agony blazing through my chest.

Titus's fingertips extended into thick claws with razor-sharp tips unlike any claws I'd ever seen on a shifter. He jerked his hand back to slash at Cassius, and I grabbed Titus's wrist.

"You're free," I said, praying my words would be enough to stop him since there was no way I was strong enough to hold him back.

He jerked to me, snarling, and I pressed my palms around the ragged scar on his wrist. "I promise. No one here will hurt you."

My throat tightened. Those were the words Cassius had said to me when he'd rescued me. *He won't hurt you ever again. You're free.* Behind him, the burning tent and cart had lit up the twilight sky, brighter than the blazing sunset, a fiery announcement that Cassius's justice had been served.

And now I was trapped again.

Titus's eyes narrowed and he growled low in his throat, making Cassius tense and flick his wrist, reforming his whip.

"No," I said to Cassius then locked gazes with Titus. "You're free. I swear." *And I know how afraid you are to hope, and of the thousands of times you've dreamt of this moment. You'll be completely free just as soon as Sebastian breaks the leash spell.* But I couldn't mention that, not until he'd calmed down, because with his current fury, I doubted he realized being bound to me had been an accident.

"You are, Titus," Sebastian said, also not mentioning the still-active leash spell, his hand still on his glowing glyph. "Deaglan betrayed me too."

"Try to take me back and I'll kill you," Titus snarled, his voice low and dangerous, his gaze locked with mine.

"That would mean I'd have to go back." Out of the corner of my eye, I saw Sebastian drop his hand from his arm and release the power in the glyph, its light going out. "Not happening."

With a growl, Titus jerked his wrist out of my grasp and sat back, conceding the fight, but the tension didn't leave his body. He remained a predator, ready to pounce the moment he sensed danger... or weakness.

"If I'd known Deaglan had you, I would have come for you." Sebastian crouched beside me, his bare shoulder brushing mine, sending an inappropriate shiver of attraction through me. "If I'd known you'd ended your hibernation..."

"I'm not sure I would have trusted you," Titus said, his body language saying he still didn't trust him.

I inched away from Sebastian, but Cassius sat up on my other side and I couldn't put as much distance between me and Sebastian as I wanted. Cassius's gaze jumped to my neck and the muscles in his jaw flexed at what he saw.

Thankfully he didn't say anything — although it was clear he wanted to — and I fought to keep my shallow breaths even for fear Cassius would notice that I was in pain, too. That would only make it harder for me to look in control... which I wasn't. I was trapped—

Focus on Titus. Not the spell.

"You were seriously injured. Do you remember what happened?" I asked. Maybe a change of topic would help him relax. Especially since it was clear that right now there was no way he was going to let me put my hands on him to finish healing him.

I swept my gaze over him. Thankfully he didn't have a single burn from Cassius's fire, not even on his hands, which meant the plan for a little healing top up and a quick shift was still possible... if I could convince him it was safe.

"No." Titus snagged the comforter beside Sebastian and covered himself with a surprising amount of modesty for a shifter. "Deaglan's leash spell weakened and I broke it. Then I ran. I thought I'd found a portal out of Faerie, but if you found me..." He glanced at Sebastian.

"No, you're out," Sebastian reassured him, his voice quiet and calm as if he, too, saw that Titus could snap again at any second. "We're in the mortal realm."

"You left Faerie?" Titus asked, surprised. "With Enowen?"

"No." Sebastian's expression grew grim. "And it's a long story, which—"

"Which you can talk about later. We need to deal with what's going on right now," Cassius said, smoke curling from his hands. "You said Deaglan is the leash spell guy and he's the one in charge of the men who attacked us? What do we know about them?"

Sebastian opened his mouth to say something, but Cassius cut him off.

"And I don't want an argument." The light in Cassius's eyes flared. "The JP *is* helping you deal with them. The sooner those guys are off the streets, the sooner your friend is safe."

I glanced at Sebastian, afraid of his response. Last night he'd said he'd work with Cassius, and now Cassius had actually offered assistance instead of taking over — which was a huge concession for Cassius — but there was still a chance Sebastian would go back on his word... or mention our deal.

"I was going to say before we *all* deal with Deaglan, we need to address the most immediate problems. Breaking the leash spell between Titus and Amiah and getting proper protection spells on Titus."

"What?" Every muscle in Titus's big body tensed and the pulse in his neck picked up again. "You said I was free. I broke that spell."

"Technically you only disconnected it and when Amiah here—" Sebastian jerked his chin at me and Titus's gaze returned to mine, making my heart stutter at the intensity in his eyes along with the fear that I was magically bound to him. "When Amiah saved your ass with her healing magic, it latched onto her."

"So you lied," Titus said, his voice low. "I'm not free."

The panic I really needed to ignore surged, making my breath pick up. "Neither am I."

And I needed to be free. I had to be free. *Now. Please now. Never again.*

Something dark and sad flashed across his expression as if he could see the fear threatening to overwhelm me.

"You've both got the prisoner end of the spell, so it's sucky for both of you." Sebastian stood and headed to his office across the hall. "Let me get my resonance charm and fix that."

Titus's glare softened a bit, but he didn't look away and I couldn't tell if it was because he thought I was a fellow predator or prey... probably prey.

That, at least, was Cassius's assumption since he tugged on my elbow, urging me to put some distance between me and Titus. "Why don't you get off the floor?"

"How about I finish healing you first?" I said to Titus. "Why don't you shift then shift back and we'll see what's left."

"No."

I waited for him to say more, but he didn't.

"I'm not comfortable with you dealing with those men while you're injured."

"I don't care what makes you comfortable," Titus said, which made Cassius tense and more smoke curl from his hands.

"Titus, please. It'll only take a few minutes." *And it'll distract me from our situation.*

"What will?" Sebastian asked as he strode back into the bedroom carrying a small wooden box.

"Titus's healing. If he just shifts and shifts back, I'm sure there won't be much left." Why were people, particularly the men around me, so difficult? It wasn't as if I didn't know what I was doing.

"Yeah, no." Sebastian nudged Cassius with his foot. "You should move."

Cassius glared at him. "I'm not moving."

"You don't want to be too close to this and I really don't want to argue with Amiah about you being hurt. Especially when it'll be your own damned fault," Sebastian said as he cocked an eyebrow. "Do you?"

Cassius's fire flared, dancing over his forearms before sinking back under his skin, but he moved a few feet back.

"Don't change the topic," I said as Sebastian took Cassius's spot, sitting cross-legged on the floor beside me. "What do you mean, no? It's Titus's decision."

"And Titus is just as capable of doing the math as I am. He shifts into a thirty-foot dragon. He'd barely fit in this room and he'd break all the furniture." Sebastian opened the box and pulled out a thin coin with a complicated glyph etched on its surface. "I like my furniture."

He said it so nonchalantly that his words almost didn't register in my brain.

"You're a dragon?" I asked.

Titus couldn't possibly be a dragon. Dragons were one of a few types of shifters natural only to the fae realm and they'd been rare to begin with. And while I hadn't spent any time researching dragons, all reports I'd heard said they were extinct.

"I didn't think there were any dragons left," I said. Which was the stupidest, most insensitive thing I could say if he really was a dragon.

Titus harrumphed, but I couldn't tell if it was in agreement or not. I supposed I could see it, his unusual gold eyes unlike any shifter I'd ever seen, his wild intense energy similar to a wolf's or a wild cat's and yet more ferocious. If I really looked at him, there was a sense of barely contained power radiating around him, as if his human form was too small to hold in all his energy.

"The last dragon died half a millennium ago," Cassius said.

"No, the last dragon went into hibernation half a millennium ago," Sebastian corrected.

"The last dragon was *leashed* half a millennium ago." The rage and darkness I'd seen in Titus's eyes when he thought he needed to take a hostage returned.

Sebastian's expression turned somber. "Never again. I promise."

"Don't make promises you can't keep," Titus said. "The Heart has awakened and the other courts will eventually learn I'm still alive. They're going to come for me."

"Which is why I need to separate you and Amiah." Sebastian held out his hand with the coin resting in his palm. "Both of you take my hand, palm over mine."

I set my hand on Sebastian's, our fingers brushing as my palm settled over his, sending another unwanted shiver of attraction sliding through me. I wished he'd never teased me by asking for his payment with sex. Or that he'd put a shirt on before running into the room. Now I couldn't keep my eyes off the mesmerizing swirls on his body, or the lines that disappeared past the waistband of his pants. All I could think about, when I managed to not think about being trapped, was having sex, as if that one teasing suggestion had shattered over a hundred years of restraint.

But it hadn't just been the suggestion that he wanted sex, it was the other times he'd propositioned me on top of learning that my hopes and dreams and the whole reason I'd been waiting had been a lie.

Titus laid his massive hand on top of mine, fully encompassing it and making my wrist look small and fragile in comparison to his. I was captured between his warm rough hand, and Sebastian's cool smooth one, a strange mix of hot and cold. Another shiver taunted me at the thought of being embraced between them. Essie had more than one mate. Why couldn't I have more than one lover?

Which — oh my goodness! — wasn't something I should be thinking about. Especially about Sebastian, who didn't really want me, and Titus, who was a complete stranger.

Sebastian's eyes narrowed. "It's just a little magic," he said, thankfully thinking my shiver was because I was afraid. "It'll be over before you know it."

"It didn't sound like just a little magic last night or just now when you told me to move," Cassius said. "Which is it?"

"Maybe I just wanted Amiah to stay the night." Sebastian flashed me a wicked grin, and I bit down on the desire swelling inside me. "Maybe I just wanted to get close to her."

All a game. Just a game. He isn't interested.

"So she *is* yours?" Titus growled.

"I'm not anyone's," I said before Sebastian could continue teasing me or reject me again — and I wasn't sure which response would upset me more. "Can we get on with this? I have things to attend to at Operations."

"Please," Cassius added. "The sooner Amiah is safe, the sooner we can go after those men."

Sebastian rolled his eyes. "One of these days I'm going to find an angel with a sense of humor."

"We have a sense of humor," Cassius said. "You're just not funny."

Sebastian snorted. "You keep thinking that."

Before Cassius could respond, Sebastian closed his eyes and set his other hand on top of Titus's.

Icy blue-white light rippled over the back of his hand and cold nipped just under my skin. He didn't activate any of the magical glyphs tattooed on his body which meant what he was doing was pure, fae sorcery, channeling raw magic from his core realm, Faerie, and weaving it into his spell by only the force of his willpower. Which was a lot more dangerous than using his essence to power the spell — in glyph form — already on his body. Too much magic too quickly and he could burn up. And given that Titus and I were connected to the spell, he could burn us up as well. I suspected the charm helped mitigate some of the dangers by focusing his power, but I had no idea by how much.

Cassius shifted and sparks danced over his forearms. He'd noticed that Sebastian wasn't using a glyph either, but he sucked in a quick breath and managed to quench his flames before something in the bedroom caught on fire. His angel glow, however, continued to blaze bright, revealing his worry.

The cold nipping under my skin turned to sharp, painful bites and crawled up my forearm to my elbow.

Across from me, Titus tensed, his hand on top of mine trembling and his gaze focused solely on me. The rage and fear had returned to his eyes, and for a second, a blink of an eye, it felt as if I was his lifeline, the only thing holding him in place. As much as he was participating in Sebastian's attempt to break the leash spell, he still didn't trust the fae. I didn't know if he trusted anyone.

I tried to reassure him with my eyes that it was going to be okay — afraid that if I said anything I'd break Sebastian's concentration. Sebastian was many things, but I'd yet to see him be malicious. Of course, I had very little experience with him. We'd only really met a few weeks ago, and before then, I'd only heard comments from the main team about buying hard-to-find magical items from him and his questionable morals.

The tendons in Sebastian's neck flexed and he rolled his shoulders, the soft glow emanating from his skin rolling down his body in a gentle wave. But instead of looking more relaxed, he looked worse, the light dimming, giving his complexion a grayish hue before flaring back to life.

"There you are," Sebastian whispered, and his cold magic swept into my chest and contracted around my heart.

I gasped, the sudden breath slicing pain through me, and fought the following whimper, afraid that if it looked like Sebastian was hurting me, Cassius would interfere. And I couldn't let Cassius interfere. I had to be free.

The cold burned, no longer just stinging bites, but a full-body burning, bringing with it a pressure that made every breath with my cracked ribs agonizing. The darkness of unconsciousness swelled at the edge of my vision, and I fought to hold on until Sebastian was done. Surely it wouldn't be much more. Surely I was strong enough to hold out—

No. I *was* strong enough. I wasn't weak. I'd never be weak again.

I ground my teeth. Across from me, Titus's whole body was also tense, his breath quick gasps. He growled low in his throat, and his pupils slitted as his dragon strained to rise to the surface.

"Seireadan," he hissed, his voice thick with warning.

"Just... a little... more," Sebastian gasped. "There."

The pressure snapped into a pull, ripping at my insides with a pain unlike anything I'd ever experienced before, tearing a scream from my clenched jaw. The darkness in my vision swelled and tears streamed down my cheeks. Far off in the distance, Titus roared, the sound filled with agony, and someone else cried out.

Then the ripping pressure and cold vanished, leaving only pain and darkness, and I sagged forward, unable to stop my sobbing no matter how hard I tried to hold it back. God, I was so pathetic.

Strong hands drew me into a warm embrace, pulling me tight to a chest shuddering with ragged breaths, and I didn't bother fighting it. It was clear I was weak. I couldn't hide it if I wanted to.

"Is it done?" Cassius demanded... his voice across from me?

I dragged my eyes open, my throat tight as I fought to stop my tears. Cassius knelt in front of me, his hands on fire, glaring at Sebastian who sat with his forehead pressed against the floor, his back heaving with desperate breaths, while I lay in Titus's arms.

A spark caught in the comforter, igniting it, and Cassius's eyes flashed wide with fear. With a growl, he wrenched it and the rest of his flames back under his skin.

"Bane." He jerked to his feet and stormed into the en suite bathroom where there wasn't as much that could catch on fire, his body shaking with his bottled-up emotions. "Is she free?"

"No." Sebastian shuddered and his glow dimmed again, revealing that worrying ashen complexion.

No?

My pulse froze.

I wasn't free?

No, please. I can't stay like this. I can't. And I didn't want to go through that kind of agony again.

A tear trailed down my cheek and I leaned into Titus's embrace, not caring that he was a stranger, just needing the comfort of being held, something I hadn't had in over a month and desperately missed. I was still trapped and my heart ached. I was sure he would be back to keeping everyone at arm's length, including me, when this moment was done. It was just his shifter need for physical contact during stressful situations that made him hold me.

I could handle that. In fact, it was better than Cassius or Sebastian comforting me. I had no connection to Titus and he'd be gone once the leash spell was broken. It didn't matter if he judged me for leaning on him, and I could just tell Cassius that I didn't want to fight his shifter nature because he was so much stronger than me.

"I thought the charm was supposed to free her," Cassius said, as a spark snapped from his hand and hissed as it hit the marble floor.

"It was." Sebastian shuddered.

"You should have been able to break it," Titus said. "You're just as powerful as Deaglan."

"No shit." Sebastian turned his head just enough to glare at Titus with one eye, but surprise flashed across his expression when he saw me in Titus's arms.

Embarrassment heated my cheeks, but I was still sore and shaking too much to focus on rebuilding my in-control demeanor. And I missed this. Missed the heat and security and reassuring pulse of life from another being.

"So now what?" I asked, hoping to cut off any teasing before it started. "There has to be something else you can do." As soon as I voiced that out loud, my pulse beat faster with the fear that there wasn't anything else to do and I was stuck never able to leave Titus's side.

Titus's grip tightened, putting pressure on my cracked ribs and making me gasp. His eyes widened and his arms relaxed a bit, but he didn't let me go, as if he, too, still needed physical contact with someone, anyone.

"There is." Sebastian grabbed Titus's shoulder and sat up, using the big man to steady himself. "But it involves going to Left of Lincoln."

"Left of Lincoln?" That was the underground market that originally had been set up in an abandoned storefront just off the last left on Lincoln Street. Hence the name.

It wasn't there anymore and supposedly had grown from just a few illegal vendors to hundreds, but the name had stuck. After Michael's war, many people had decided to live off the grid, unwilling or unable to return to normal life, creating a whole underground society, and Left of Lincoln was the main place in Union City for those people to buy the supplies they needed or desired — be they legal or illegal — using a variety of currencies, including standard cash, magical essence, magical abilities, blood, and services that were more often than not sexual in nature... or at least so I'd heard. I'd never been to the market.

I hadn't needed to learn much about the off-grid world, since all I did was heal people regardless of how they chose to live their lives. I only knew what Left of Lincoln was, and that the JP, for the most part, turned a blind eye to it in favor of going after more dangerous criminals.

"If the charm is specifically attuned to our resonance, it'll be easier to unravel the spell from your essences. But I don't want to risk waiting around on a specialist to come to us. It's better if we go to him. Which means all three of us have to go to Lincoln."

"You mean all four of us," Cassius said, stepping to the edge of the bathroom door, his fire gone but heavy smoke still curling from his hands and forearms. I was kind of surprised he hadn't set off the smoke detector yet.

"Of course you're coming," Sebastian groaned. "Fine. All four of us. I need a shower and Amiah and Titus need clothes."

"Amiah has clothes," Cassius said.

"I saw, but she can't go to Lincoln in scrubs. It's bad enough both of you are angels. You, in your military chic, I can pass off as hired muscle, there are a few angels that do that sort of thing, but Amiah can't go looking like a physician. Everyone will know she's with the JP and no one will do business with me."

"I'm not leaving to go to Operations to get a different change of clothes for Amiah," Cassius said.

"It's okay. I'll be fine," I assured him.

"Don't worry about it." Sebastian climbed to his feet. "My assistant has to bring clothes for Titus since nothing I own will fit him. I'll just get her to bring something for Amiah too." He staggered out of the bedroom, the soft glow emanating from his skin dimming and flaring back to life. "And Amiah, I suggest you do something about your neck. That bruise will attract all the wrong kind of attention."

Titus's golden gaze dipped to mine filled with a heart-stopping intensity. It made me ache, the look reminding me so much of Marcus and all his ferocious emotions. I hadn't experienced his all-in love, not the love he gave to his mate, but I'd desired it, thought if I was patient it would be mine.

I pushed out of Titus's arms and stood on shaky legs. It was a mistake to have let him hold me, to give in to my desire for physical contact. Now his embrace just reminded me of what I'd never have—

No, of what I didn't want. Really.

SEBASTIAN

I made it into my bedroom and closed the door before my knees gave out, dropping me to the hard marble floor, pain wracking my body.

Fuuuuck.

Fuck fuck fuck.

The resonance charm was supposed to have made it easier to break the leash spell. My old self would have been able to do it without the charm. A hard pull on my connection to the primal magic of Faerie combined with the charm should have been enough to do the trick.

But I wasn't my old self. I was the new fucked up version thanks to my inability to mind my own fucking business.

God. I shouldn't have agreed to help stop Lilith. What would it have mattered if she'd taken over this realm? There were other realms I could go to. I didn't have to go back to Faerie. But damned if I didn't like the mortal realm. No one gave a shit who I was, no one played sick games with me or anyone I cared about, and I'd been doing just fine until I'd stuck my nose where it didn't belong.

I pressed my forehead to the cool marble floor and dragged in a ragged breath, trying to ease the pain. It burned through my magical channels in my head, heart, and hell, to the tip of every nerve ending with the caustic poison of demonic magic, something that wasn't supposed to be in my body. Ever.

I couldn't connect with the Realm of Celestial Darkness to use its magic. I couldn't even make a connection to that realm. Which was why I couldn't get the damned magic out of my system and push out the poison.

Now, because the demonic magic kept getting in the way, I could barely reach the magic in Faerie, able to only channel a trickle of power when it used to be a flood. And yet I still risked all the side effects of channeling too much magic, because every time I tried to weave a spell, with or without a glyph to focus my power, the demonic magic exploded into an inferno, like a spark suddenly given oxygen.

As if just thinking about it gave it power, the demonic magic flared again, setting my skin on fire, forcing me to bite back a groan.

I doubted anyone was standing outside my door, but I didn't want to risk them hearing me, just in case. They needed to think I was powerful enough to break the leash spell. Hell, I *needed* to be powerful enough to break the leash spell, because Titus and Amiah needed to be free of each other. Not to mention if I couldn't break the leash spell, there was no way I'd be able to remove Amiah's not-yet-awakened mating brand... if there was even a way—

No. There had to be a way. There was always a way. A soul bond was similar to any bonding spell, just on a more powerful level. If I figured out how to break or block her soul's potential to make a bond, she should be able to live her life bond free.

And — I was a damned idiot — I really wanted her to have that. The idea of being permanently bound to someone for life was terrifying. I didn't care how happy Esther Shaw was with her mates, the idea scared the shit out of me, and I knew Amiah had the same fear.

I'd seen a hint of that fear in her eyes when she'd swallowed her pride to ask for my help, and I'd seen all of that fear, clear and raw, when she thought the leash spell had been her soul bond. It had been a look of absolute panic, just for a second, before she'd regained her composure, but it had been clear as day.

Except if I couldn't break a simple leash spell, how the hell was I going to deal with her soul bond?

I drew in another breath and, gripping the doorknob for balance, stood. I was going to have to get power from an outside source even though that still risked burning me up, and that was going to cost a lot... if I could even figure out how to break or block the mating brand.

Which wasn't the thing I should be worrying about.

Why the hell did I keep thinking of Amiah? And why had it scared the shit out of me to see Titus's hand around her throat, or pissed me off to see him mauling her like she was his security blanket while she'd been fighting her tears?

She was a pain in my ass with her ice queen attitude, and her sharp tongue, and her God damned insistence on spending every ounce of her magic healing people when she should just leave well enough alone.

Except fuck if I didn't just love seeing that little flash of surprise every time I hit on her and then her following angry frustration as she tried to hide the fact that I'd caught her off guard.

Although her reaction last night had been different. Yes to the surprise, but consideration instead of anger.

Which shocked the hell out of me. I couldn't believe she'd seriously thought about sleeping with me as payment to get rid of her mating brand.

But that only told me how desperate she was to have it gone.

Except that also pissed me off.

She thought I'd have sex with someone to make them pay off a debt. Yeah, there were a lot of supers who worked that way, but that was disgusting. A little no strings attached fucking was great. It was the way I preferred it. But everyone involved had to agree.

I staggered to my bathroom and turned on the shower, hoping the warm water would help me relax — since being tense made the demonic magic blaze hotter inside me even when I wasn't trying to use my magic.

What Amiah thought of me didn't matter. So what if we shared the same fear of being permanently bound to someone for the rest of our lives? I shouldn't let that influence how I did business, and I needed to come to terms now with the fact that I wouldn't be able to do anything for her and move on.

Which, God damn it, I didn't want to accept.

Jeez.

What I really should be thinking about was helping Titus and the fact that he hadn't been in hibernation all this time, but leashed like an animal in Deaglan's court.

After Deaglan's failed assassination attempt on me, I should have sent spies into his court. I shouldn't have said fuck it and abandoned everyone, and I sure as shit shouldn't have gone realm hopping without at least checking on Titus.

Except he hadn't told me where he'd been hibernating. No one was supposed to have known. He'd just said he'd wake and find me when

Faerie's Heart started calling to him so I could remove or block that bond and he'd be free of his species' curse.

Which was yet another bond I was supposed to be able to break.

I pulled off my pajama pants, stepped into the shower, and pressed my palms against the cool tiles, trying to focus on the spray hitting me.

I couldn't believe the Heart had awakened already. Faerie was going to be a battleground with each court desperate to get their hands on it or stop someone else from getting it. That was how Titus ended up the last of his species. There hadn't been many dragons to begin with, but the last time the Heart had awakened, the Summer Court had decided no one should have it, and the only way to ensure that was to exterminate the only species with a direct connection to it: dragonkind.

I didn't know if the king of the Summer Court had changed his mind since then, but I had no doubt even if he had, some other monarch would decide Titus was too dangerous to live.

I couldn't allow Amiah to get caught up in this mess. She might be a pain in my ass, but she didn't deserve what was coming Titus's, and now my, way. I had to separate them as soon as possible, which meant I had to get my shit together.

And that started with telling Titus to stop calling me by my birth name. Seireadan had died the night Deaglan and Enowen, my betrothed, had tried to kill me, and I sure as shit didn't want to keep being reminded that I'd been a lovesick fool. I didn't need Titus bringing up details about a time I'd worked damned hard to forget, and I certainly didn't need Amiah asking questions about it.

TITUS

Seireadan — who didn't look or smell like Seireadan — left. The only reason I recognized him was because of the spell he'd wrapped in my soul so I could find him once I'd come out of hibernation and he could sever or block my connection to Faerie's Heart.

I didn't know why he had a glamour spell on him hiding his identity, and I had a terrible feeling a lot had happened in the five hundred years I'd been Deaglan's prisoner.

Amiah and the other angel left as well, closing the door behind them, and I headed into what had to be the bathing room to clean off the blood crusted to my now mostly healed body. My reflection in the large mirror over the white marble sink would have been laughable with all the bandages wrapped around me if it hadn't been proof of how injured I'd been — since Seireadan, who knew how fast I healed, had still let Amiah bind my wounds.

My pulse raced at the thought of her and I rubbed my face as if that would help me think straight... which it didn't.

I sliced off the bandages with a claw then turned my attention to what I hoped was a waterfall or rain-shower stall. Even taking the time to figure out that the silver handle with the dial made water spray from a disk near the ceiling and that turning the handle adjusted the temperature — not like Faerie where magic adjusted the temperature with a thought — couldn't get her off my mind.

I had no idea why I'd grabbed her and held her close.

She'd been crying from what I knew was agonizing pain — a pain that had seized me as well — and my instincts had kicked in and all I'd wanted was to hold and reassure her.

Which was crazy. I didn't know her, and I sure as hell didn't know if anything was going to be okay.

But we were in the same boat, and I'd seen the fear and hurt in her eyes when she'd tried to tell me I was safe. She knew what it was like to be imprisoned. I didn't know how or why an angel like her would end up in such a terrible situation, but without a doubt, she'd felt that fear before.

With that look and her crying, I'd been unable to resist my nature, the nature that made dragons entwine their bodies with their mates. I had to touch her, steady her soul against mine, show her she wasn't alone — as well as use her to steady my own shaking soul.

I stepped into the washing stall that was barely wide enough for me and let the warm water rush over my skin.

It would have been even better if she'd been naked. Full flesh to flesh contact to properly ground us... or rather me since she wasn't a dragon and didn't have the same need. Except that would have created a whole new problem.

My beast wanted her, and her being naked would have made it close to impossible to rein in that even more powerful primal emotion. An emotion that had roared to life the moment I'd pinned her to the bed and met her gaze — probably because I'd been without sex or even a compassionate touch for half a millennium and was starved for contact.

Yeah. That was it. My beast had latched onto the first female I'd encountered since escaping.

Except, as much as I wanted to deny it, there was more to my desire for Amiah than her just being female. While there'd been surprise and fear in her eyes when I'd grabbed her, there'd also been a fierce determination that had excited my beast.

That excitement had only grown when she'd risked her life to stop me from ripping out the other angel's throat even though she knew it'd take nothing for me to hurt her. And it had grown again with the look she'd given me when Seireadan had been trying to break the leash spell, as if she, by herself, would keep me safe from whatever was coming.

Which was the stupidest thing ever. She was small and fragile, and given that she had healing magic, I doubted she had another power that could hurt me or anyone else if she was threatened. She couldn't protect herself let alone me.

But that only made my beast more excited, and I was glad I'd covered up before Seireadan had noticed my raging hard on. Because if she wasn't Seireadan's female like her scent implied — along with the fact that I couldn't smell the woman he'd been betrothed to on him or anywhere in the room — Amiah was surely the other angel's given how enraged he'd been to see me on top of her.

And my beast didn't give a fuck about that. Its desire for Amiah— No *any* female, Amiah was just an easy target, made my cock so hard it hurt.

This was going to be a problem. The best I could hope for was that getting myself off along with the promise of finding an appropriate female soon, would satisfy my beast.

I gripped my cock, and brought to mind the last female I'd had sex with. My female. She hadn't been my true mate, but not every dragon found their soul's mate. I'd won her affection and she would have been mine to the end of our days or until either of us found our soul's mate or another dragon challenged me for her and I lost the fight. She'd been a fire dragon like me, with red hair slightly paler than mine, gold-green eyes, and a powerful body — both in human and dragon form.

I pumped my hand up and down my length, remembering the intimate times we'd spent together, her hot flesh against mine, her lips teasing my body, and my cock sheathed in her tight heat. Except the moment I thought about driving into her, the image in my mind's eye shifted. The woman wrapped around my cock turned into delicate Amiah, with her blue glowing eyes partially hidden by lids lowered with pleasure, her long blond locks splayed on the pillow behind her giving her a shimmering halo, and her lips parted on a sensual moan.

My balls tightened and I tried to turn her back to my long-dead mate, hell, to anyone else, but couldn't. My beast wanted to be wrapped in *her* tight sheath, wanted to feel *her* come around my cock. Wanted to hear *her* moans and screams of pleasure.

My fantasy Amiah locked gazes with me as I drove into her, the look in her eyes said she understood me, understood the fear and hurt of being enslaved, and still wanted me, craved me as much as I craved her. Then her body tensed, her head tipped back exposing her delicate neck to my canines in invitation to mark her as mine, and she screamed her release which set off mine.

I came hard, biting back a roar, and digging my claws into the shower tiles to keep steady... and not to go storming out of the bathroom to find Amiah and make the fantasy real.

Fuck. This was really going to be a problem.

AMIAH

I lay on the bed in Sebastian's guestroom, staring at the ceiling, exhausted and dizzy. Healing my cracked ribs and the bruise around my neck had taken everything I'd managed to regain with last night's meager sleep. All I wanted was to crawl into bed and sleep, but that would put off breaking the leash spell, and the panic of being trapped that had eased when I'd thought I'd be free in a few hours had returned with a vengeance.

I had to be free. *Now.*

Now now now.

Cassius was already back to looking at me like I was fragile, and I didn't know if I'd ever be able to get him to see me as an equal again, able to stand on my own just as much as he could. I shouldn't have let Titus hold me. But I was weak.

And now they all knew it.

The sooner Titus and I were separated the better. Cassius's honor wouldn't let him leave my side until he knew I was safe, which meant he wouldn't go after the men, and that would delay Sebastian in finding a solution to my problem.

A problem which I was now acutely aware of. With the pain from my ribs and throat gone, there was nothing distracting me from the warm ache running from the bottom of my ribcage, over my hip, and down my thigh. The pain in my not-yet-awakened mating brand felt stronger than before, but I had to be imagining that. It hadn't gotten worse. I was just more aware of it because I was trapped — *trapped trapped trapped!* — by the leash spell.

I drew in a slow pain-free breath, fighting to steady my nerves and to get the room to stop spinning.

I could handle this. Just a few more hours and I'd no longer have to act like I was strong and calm. I would be.

With another deep breath, I turned my attention to the scrubs sitting at the foot of the bed. I'd feel more like myself if I was dressed like myself, but that just seemed like too much work, especially since I was going to have to change again to go to Left of Lincoln. Better to have breakfast, regain some strength, and then change into whatever Sebastian's assistant was bringing over. Cassius had already seen me in Sebastian's clothes and hadn't said anything, so my irrational worry that he'd be upset had been unfounded and our friendship, the friendship I desperately needed right now, wasn't on rocky ground because of that.

No. It was because I'd never experienced such pain before and had given in to my weak, base need for physical comfort.

I pushed that thought aside. Regardless if Cassius thought I was weak or not, he'd be there for me. Just like he always was.

I drew in another breath. *All right, Amiah. Time to get up and be a professional. Just a few more hours and you'll get your life back*

At least until my mating brand awakened.

My panic surged and I pushed that thought back.

Strong and calm. No one is supposed to worry about their physician. You can do this.

Another breath and I slowly sat up.

The room stayed at its ever-so-slight spinning but didn't get worse. That was the best I was going to get, so I squared my shoulders and made sure my mask of cool professionalism was in place and didn't reveal how exhausted I really was.

With my guard fully up, I carefully stepped into the hall and was met with the rich aromas of freshly brewed coffee and frying eggs.

Oh, thank goodness. Someone was making breakfast. I could only hope I could convince them to share since I wasn't sure I'd be able to stand at a stove long enough to make something at the moment.

I followed the smell to Sebastian's sleek high-end white and stainless-steel kitchen, where I found all of the guys.

Titus, sitting at the small kitchen table tucked into a corner by a tall window with the purplish hue of UV-blocking glass, was the first to notice me. He sat with his back to the wall with a towel, barely big enough to cover all of him, wrapped around his hips. His attention jumped to me the moment I stepped through the wide opening, his gaze filled with a confusing mix of emotions.

At first glance, he looked... hungry and not in the way a beast looked at dinner but in the way a man looked at a woman he desired. But that quickly shifted to a banked anger, which I couldn't blame him for. I'd been angry at everyone for a long time after my rescue even though I knew I had no reason to be angry with them.

Sebastian sat beside him, dressed in beige summer slacks and a light-blue button-down. His lips were quirked in their perpetual mischievous smile as if he knew a dirty joke, most likely about me, and was dying to share it in front of everyone to embarrass me. The grayish hue to his complexion was gone, and he looked like he always did, with a blue-white glow emanating from his skin at the soft, almost imperceptible levels of a faekin, not the more powerful glow of the full fae that he really was.

Cassius, much to my surprise, stood at the stove frying up a big pan of scrambled eggs. He had his back to me and didn't notice my arrival, and I took the moment to appreciate his broad shoulders, narrow waist, and firm glutes. A part of me was surprised he hadn't settled down in a serious relationship by now. He was a good, handsome man who cared deeply, or at least he'd cared before the war. Now I was sure he still cared, but the signs were harder to notice and he hid it behind an overbearing protectiveness.

"How can I help?" I asked, the idea of Cassius making me breakfast without me at least helping suddenly making me uncomfortable despite my exhaustion. I could probably lean on the counter and make toast or something. Really.

Cassius glanced at me and his eyes narrowed. "I'd rather you sit and eat before you pass out."

"I'm not going to pass out," I said, old habits making me square my shoulders as I headed to the sleek, single-serve coffee machine. But Sebastian stood, blocking my way, and held out his chair for me.

"I need a refill," he said, his cup still half full. "I'll make yours while I'm up."

"I—" I bit back my sharp response. I couldn't afford to alienate him and risk him refusing to remove my brand, but I also didn't like him doing something for me that I could just as easily do myself, especially when it was clear he was just getting up for me.

He cocked an eyebrow as if daring me to finish what I was going to say.

This wasn't the conversation I wanted to have so I pressed my lips together and sagged into the offered chair.

"Atta girl," he chuckled as if he'd just scored a point, making me bristle because he had. I'd just given in and sat like he'd asked.

"She takes a little sugar and a lot of cream," Cassius said, dividing the finished eggs onto four plates. "What's the ETA on the clothes?"

"Anytime now." Sebastian grabbed a mug from the cupboard above the coffee maker and set it in the machine. "I'd like to get to Lincoln as soon as possible. Titus is going to stick out like a sore thumb so the fewer people who see him, the better."

My stomach tightened. That meant I'd be free soon. Likely within an hour or two.

"You honestly think less of a crowd will be better?" Cassius asked going to the fridge and pouring a glass of orange juice. "There'll be fewer people to blend in with."

He set the juice, a plate of eggs, and a fork in front of me as the tightness in my stomach turned into a cold stone. Waiting until there were more people in Lincoln was the better plan no matter how much I wanted to be free. *Right now.*

Sebastian rolled his eyes and jerked his thumb at Titus. "Don't tell me you think he's going to blend in with anyone. He's as big as a greater demon or an ogre but with the wrong essence and the wrong coloring. It doesn't matter how big the crowd is, everyone is going to notice him."

I took a bite of the eggs not really tasting them. "We should get a glamour and a concealment spell on him first." If Titus was going to draw attention, magically changing his appearance was the most logical first step. It was illegal for anyone except the military or the JP to cast those spells but we were trying to hide from dangerous men. We were going to have to break the rules.

That thought made my stomach churn, adding to the worry that getting concealment and glamour spells on Titus meant putting off breaking the leash spell for even longer.

I glanced at Titus, fighting to keep my expression calm. "Can you handle being leashed a little longer to get a proper glamour put in place?"

Could I?

My heart raced at the thought. But disguising Titus first was the safest plan.

"Sure," he said, his voice gruff, his gaze dropping to his breakfast.

"A glamour first would be logical if you two weren't bound with a leash spell." Sebastian set my coffee on the table and slid into the chair beside me. "The glamour, along with a concealment spell, needs to be strong and long lasting. The leash spell will suck power during the casting, making it harder to cast and set the spells. I'm not sure whoever we get to set the spells will be able to do it while you two are connected. At least not someone I completely trust."

"You can't set them?" Cassius took the last chair between Sebastian and Titus and shot me a worried glance. He was still looking at me like I was fragile and a part of me feared he'd never stop. At least he wasn't freaking out over the conversation about casting illegal spells... which only spoke to how serious the situation was.

"I can do a lot of things," Sebastian said, "but I can't set a spell in someone."

Cassius sighed. "And there isn't anyone at Operations right now who's strong enough to set one."

Which left us with the risk of Titus being seen or waiting until a strong enough witch flew in to Union City to meet us.

Cassius pinched the bridge of his nose and a wisp of smoke curled from his hand. "This is a terrible idea. We're just going to walk around Left of Lincoln without a glamour or a concealment spell. That's almost as bad as putting up a billboard saying where we are."

"Jeez, I'm not that stupid." Sebastian took a sip of his coffee. "Yes, we're going to be walking around Lincoln without a glamour, but I have a group concealment glyph. I can keep it active long enough to get the charm attuned to our resonance and get back here, so they at least won't be able to track us with magic."

The muscles in Cassius's jaw twitched, likely at Sebastian's confession that he had an illegal spell tattooed on his body. "That's another issue. Those men saw you. They're going to start asking about you and someone is going to point them here." He frowned and shoved his fork into his eggs with an angry thrust. "I'm surprised they haven't shown up by now."

"They haven't because I have a look-away spell on the apartment. Yeah, people know I do business in the office I keep downstairs, but only a select few know I actually live here." Sebastian drained his coffee mug. "Anyone who shows up looking for me will find my office closed and leave."

"What about your landlord?" Cassius asked. The master vampire who owned the building wasn't the most trustworthy and wasn't on the best of terms with the JP.

Sebastian's expression hardened. "She won't be a problem," he said, and I didn't want to ask what that meant. It was probably something illegal, and while I might be able to look the other way, Cassius would have a harder time doing so.

More smoke curled around Cassius and he shifted, clearly coming to the same conclusion, but his phone chirped, saving him from having to decide if he should push for more details or not.

He answered and had a quick conversation, most likely with Chris, then hung up. "Chris lost the trail of those men in the middle of the Quarter near Winfield, and Summer is still working on the forensics they found in the park ring—"

"Tell her not to bother. She won't find anything useful," Sebastian said. "Those were professionals. They probably cast a spell to remove all trace of themselves and Titus. The only DNA she's going to find is yours, mine, and Amiah's, which means the JP won't be able to cast a tracking spell. This can't be handled in your traditional ways. The only way to get these men are for them to come to us."

"Which we're not going to let happen until Amiah is free of this situation," Cassius said.

Yes, free. Now. I had to be free. I took a large sip of my orange juice, grasping the glass in both hands to hide the fact that I was shaking.

Come on. It's just a few more hours.

And while I logically knew that, I couldn't convince the rest of me of it.

"You say that as if we have a choice in when they find us." Sebastian met Cassius's glare, all mirth gone from his expression. "Like I've been saying from the beginning of this clusterfuck, the first priority is separating Amiah and Titus."

"So long as we understand each other—" Cassius stiffened and held up his hand for silence. "Someone's here."

"Sebastian," a sultry alto called, the word punctuated with the sharp click of heels on the marble floor.

"It's my assistant." Sebastian stood, and took his empty plate and mug to the dishwasher. "In the kitchen, Nova," he called as a stunningly beautiful demon with the onyx skin of a babaus stepped into the archway between the living room and the kitchen.

She wore a vibrant green pantsuit, but only in the pretext of appearing professional since the skirt was obscenely short, showing off her long, shapely legs, and the form-fitting top under her jacket showed an equally obscene amount of cleavage.

But despite that, she didn't come across as cheap. It was more like she oozed sex as if she was a succubus, even though babaus didn't possess sexual magic. And with her lingering gaze on Cassius and Titus, she knew how alluring she was.

Cassius drew in a sharp breath and gave her a tight nod, before turning his back on me to go to the sink, so I had no idea what he thought of Nova. She wasn't like any of the women he'd dated in the past, but then as far as I knew he'd only ever dated angels, and angels, no matter how beautiful, just didn't have that kind of sexual magnetism. And really, Cassius could be attracted to her. He had needs, just like everyone else.

Which made me think of Titus and the hungry look he'd given me when I'd first entered the kitchen.

My gaze jumped to him of its own volition. As irrational and ridiculous as it was, I didn't want to see his desire for this woman, and yet I couldn't help looking. The man had spent a long time in captivity where I doubted his needs had been met. He was going to look at every woman that way. Except instead of the hunger I'd seen when I'd first entered the kitchen, his expression was pained. Then he shifted and grunted and his banked anger returned.

"You've *come* right on time," Sebastian said with a hint of his wicked smile, his inflection turning his words dirty.

"Don't I always," she purred, and his smile deepened, making embarrassment heat my cheeks.

To think I'd actually considered accepting his proposition for sex... if he ever propositioned me again. But of course he wouldn't. He wasn't interested in me. Why would he? Not when he had someone like Nova in his life. He probably had dozens of Novas at his beck and call, and I was a naive, inexperienced angel. All I had was research and self-exploration. No firsthand experience and that was probably clear as day to someone like Sebastian, which was why he teased me in the first place.

And jeez, why did that even bother me?

Because I'd been a fool to even entertain the possibility of releasing my own pent-up needs with him.

Nothing more.

Nova prowled to the table and set a full cloth bag in front of Titus. "I take it you're the big and tall—" Her gaze dipped to the towel around his hips. "—and extra large."

Titus sat forward, a strange desperate hope flashing across his expression for a second before returning to anger. With a huff, he grabbed the bag — and the ends of his towel to keep it secure — and marched out of the kitchen

"And you're the sundress." Nova set a second bag in front of me and sank into the chair across from me, but her attention was back on Sebastian and Cassius, barely giving me a cursory glance. "I changed today's meeting to tomorrow like you asked."

"You really think this will be solved by tomorrow?" Cassius handed Sebastian his dirty plate to put into the dishwasher.

I prayed it would be. Then he could get to work removing my brand.

"Maybe we'll get lucky." Except Sebastian didn't sound as if he believed that, making my hope wither. "But I'm meeting someone I don't want to piss off."

"That would be a first," Cassius said.

"There are lots of people I don't want to piss off." Sebastian's smile turned wicked. "But you're just too much fun."

"Oh? You think it's fun to piss me off?" Cassius demanded.

"Guys—" I bit the inside of my cheek. What was the point? At least they weren't arguing about anything serious.

Sebastian chuckled and glanced at me, but I grabbed the bag with the sundress and left the kitchen. The sooner I changed, the sooner we could get to Left of Lincoln and separate me and Titus.

I reached the bedroom and for a second I wasn't sure I wanted to look inside the bag. Whatever the dress was, it wasn't going to be appropriate for the chief physician of Operations.

But then not looking like myself was the whole point, and I wouldn't have to wear it for long.

Much to my surprise, the dress was tasteful. It was white with large blue flowers the color of my eyes and skimmed my curves perfectly. The skirt flared a bit and hung a modest one inch above my knees, and the sexiest things about it were the sweetheart neckline revealing a little more cleavage than I usually liked and its behind-the-neck strap that exposed most of my back, forcing me to go without a bra. Thankfully, I wasn't as well-endowed as Nova and there was enough support in the dress for me to feel comfortable going without.

To top it off, a pair of white sandals in my size with a practical heel had been included.

I was dressed and about to put on the sandals when someone knocked on the door.

"Are you decent?" Cassius asked.

"Just putting on my sandals."

"Not what I asked," he said as he opened the door.

His gaze swept over me, his eyes wide with surprise, and a hot curl of desire unfurled low within me even though I was sure his surprise wasn't at my appearance. He'd seen me in a dress... although not recently. But still—

"It surprised me too." I gave a slow twirl — still mindful of how tired I was — making the skirt gently swish around my legs. "I can't believe Sebastian had his assistant pick up something reasonable."

"Ah... yeah," Cassius said, his voice gruff. "I expect Nova has a different taste in clothes than you."

"That much is obvious." I sat on the edge of the bed to put on the sandals. "Is everyone waiting on me?" I hadn't spent a lot of time changing, but I had moved slower than usual. Breakfast had helped a little and now the room wasn't spinning, but I was still exhausted and my magic was still low and I was struggling to keep my fear at bay.

"Yeah." He crossed his arms and his expression hardened. "I called Priam to cover your shift at Operations."

"Good." My fingers shook as I tried to secure the catch on the sandal, but the more I fought to still my hands and not let Cassius see me tremble, the stronger my shaking became. "Tell him I should be able to take the afternoon portion of the shift," I said with as even a tone as possible.

"No." He knelt and nudged my hands away to buckle my sandal. "You look almost as exhausted as you did last night. If the situation wasn't so urgent, I'd make Bane wait a day."

"And by urgent you mean those men coming after Titus." Not the fact that I was trapped. Again. Which, if the idea of being controlled by someone didn't terrify me so much it wouldn't have been the most urgent issue to me. Without the men coming after Titus, being leashed to him didn't endanger me.

"I mean this whole mess," he said as he buckled my other sandal.

"You're magically bound to a man we know nothing about, who has dangerous men coming after him for reasons we also know nothing about. For all we know, Titus broke out of jail where he was sent for committing a crime."

"You don't really believe that?" I didn't. Although I didn't know why. Titus's hurt and anger didn't seem like it came from a criminal who'd been caught. Except I had no proof. All I had to go on was my instinct. Cassius, however, was right. We didn't know anything about Titus or Sebastian for that matter... and if I couldn't get rid of my mating brand, I could find myself trapped in the same situation, bound to a man who I knew nothing about. "If those men had been fae law enforcement officers they would have identified themselves, not tried to stab Sebastian in the back."

"I'm not willing to risk your life by letting you stay around Bane and his friend to find out." He finished with the buckle on my sandal and stood.

He did *not* just say that! "Not *letting*?"

"The situation is dangerous," he insisted, missing the point.

"And I don't need your permission." I pushed past him and strode out of the bedroom. "I'm as capable of assessing this situation as you."

"No. You're not," he said, falling into step beside me, smoke curling from his hands. "You don't have any tactical training."

"I don't need to have tactical training. I healed your injuries. I know how dangerous they are."

Cassius huffed. "You have no idea how dangerous these men are."

"I do know." I glared at him even though I knew I'd never win this fight.

The light in Cassius's eyes flared. "No, you don't."

"You know, you two should just fuck and get it over with," Sebastian said from his spot by the door.

Titus, standing beside him dressed in a black T-shirt, black fatigues, and combat boots like Cassius, stiffened.

"Don't be crude," Cassius snapped.

"Don't be a prude," Sebastian shot back. "Man with all that *restrained decorum,* angel sex must be boring... or fucking wild as hell." His pale gaze met mine, making me instantly throb with need. "Which is it? Are you an animal in bed?"

I bit back my frustration. How was this the same man who'd offered me something to sleep in and bought me a tasteful dress? And why did I still react to him like this? It was just a game. *Just. A. Game*

"My sexual predilections are none of your business," I said, painfully aware that just saying *predilections* made me sound like a prude as well. "Are we getting this leash spell broken or not?"

Sebastian snorted and opened his front door, gesturing for all of us to leave. Titus marched out first and Cassius followed.

"Sweetheart, you need to work on your comebacks," Sebastian said as I passed.

"Well then," I replied, pitching my voice so only Sebastian could hear me, "given that we're going to work out a type of payment suitable for both of us, I guess you'll never know what I'm like in bed."

Heat flooded my face and I quickly turned away from him.

Why did I just say that? Words had just come out of my mouth and—

And now he was going to tease me more. There'd be no end to it, and with it just being a game to him, all it would do would rub in the fact that I irrationally ached for him and he didn't want me.

AMIAH

THE RIDE IN THE ELEVATOR DOWN TO THE PARKING GARAGE WAS TENSE. Cassius stood stiffly at the back with Titus, who didn't even look at me as I entered, while Sebastian stood beside me with that look in his eyes that said he knew a secret dirty joke about me. I prayed he wouldn't carry on our conversation where Cassius and Titus could hear—

Actually, I prayed he wouldn't continue our conversation at all.

Why had I said that! If anything proved that I was losing my self-control, that was it, and without a doubt, given the heat in my face, my cheeks were bright red, giving it all away.

The door slid open to the cool damp underground garage, and I hurried out needing space. I couldn't think with the guys standing so close and having just been reminded of what I'd been avoiding for years and painfully ached for.

Sebastian walked past the SUV and sports cars to an old maroon sedan with a dented front fender, parked in a dark corner of the garage, and opened the driver's side door without unlocking it.

"I see we're traveling in style," Cassius said, his tone dry.

"You wanted bigger," Sebastian replied with a shrug. "Flashing too much money around Lincoln is dangerous. It's bad enough it looks like I have two bodyguards and angel arm candy."

Cassius got into the front passenger seat. "Amiah is *not* arm candy."

"She looks pretty hot to me." Sebastian flashed me his wicked smile, making my insides warm with desire and frustration, and slid into the driver's seat.

Titus grunted, but I didn't know if it was in agreement or not and, eyeing the car with suspicion, got in the seat behind him.

"Flattery wouldn't get you into my bed," I said, shoving my feelings down and getting in as well.

"Oh?" Sebastian asked as he started the engine, his gaze meeting mine through the rear-view mirror. "Does that mean something else will?"

No, because you don't really mean it.

A hint of smoke wrapped around Cassius and he rolled down his window. "Can we focus on the job at hand?"

"There isn't much more to it," Sebastian said, pressing a hand to his side and activating a glyph. Light flared from the glyph, bright in the garage's low illumination, before dimming to an almost imperceptible level against his natural glow. "We go to Lincoln and get the resonance charm attuned to our resonances. And you—"

He pulled out of the garage into early morning sunlight. The street was empty since we were in the vampire section of the Quarter and even with the UV-blocking canopy vampires were still mostly creatures of the night, but he still promptly stopped at a red light even though there wasn't a single car on the road. "You keep yourself under control and don't arrest anyone."

"I've already promised I wouldn't," Cassius said, surprising me. Upholding the law was one of the main things that drove him, and he clung to it as if it kept him steady in a world of chaos. He hadn't been so strict with rules and regulations before the war. He could let things slide if it meant justice prevailed. But after the war, it was as if the rules were the only thing holding him together, and while that had eased a bit in the last twenty years, it hadn't gone away... and had gotten worse again in the last month. "Breaking the leash spell is the priority. Anything else would jeopardize that."

Sebastian turned onto the main street leading out of the Quarter and headed to the park ring that separated the supers' part of town from the humans' part. "You just remember that once we get there."

Dappled early morning sunlight flickered through the thick branches overhead as we drove into the park then filled the car in full as we crossed its threshold into the human part of Union City.

I didn't often leave the Quarter, and I was always a little amazed at how different and modern the rest of Union felt compared to the Quarter.

The Quarter had originally been an older part of town, expropriated by the city to create an area for supers so they could live with humans but not necessarily right beside them. No one had known how the supernatural beings who'd come out of hiding to help save humanity from Michael would be received, but almost everyone had agreed they had as much right to live out in the open as humans. And while yes, there were modern buildings in the Quarter, most of the original structures had survived Michael's assaults giving the Quarter an older feel with its nineteenth century brick buildings.

The buildings directly on the other side of the ring, however, were towering residential high rises that had been built in the mid to late twentieth century. Most were plain utilitarian concrete without any charm, and I had no idea why anyone would want to live there, although I suspected people did because they couldn't afford some place better.

Which spoke volumes for those living there since a number of nice neighborhoods in Union had survived the assault while a significant number of the population hadn't, making good places to live cheap and plentiful in the beginning. But that left out those from the smaller towns in the area who'd been forced to abandon their communities and move to Union. Those who took too long to realize the Joined Parliament wasn't going to send revitalization money to their small town and instead focus on the larger cities lost out.

Sebastian headed south and I rolled down my window to alleviate the growing heat. Titus, after watching me, did the same. The day's humidity was already building and without a cloud in the sky, it was going to be another beautiful, hot summer's day. The breeze ruffled his shaggy red hair, and he leaned into it with his eyes closed and drew in a deep breath that expanded his massive chest.

"They didn't let you fly, did they?" I said, the sudden realization breaking my heart. Not letting a dragon fly had to be as horrible as not letting a wolf run.

"No."

"Did they even let you shift?" He'd been imprisoned for five hundred years. Not flying was terrible. Not shifting and releasing his beast would be soul crushing.

While shifters were still one being, they had two very distinct aspects to their soul that often made them feel like they were two separate entities in one body. And not being allowed to embrace both halves, be it beast or man, was psychologically and physically damaging. It was why shifters who weren't naturally born shifters, those rare few infected with lycanthropy, had difficult transitions. Not only did the lycanthropy painfully rewrite their DNA, but they often saw their beast as a separate being and fought it instead of accepted it.

"No," Titus said, his voice low, making my throat tighten.

"Have you shifted since you escaped?" I asked, trying to focus on his situation clinically and not emotionally. If he hadn't, he was going to need to do so soon and appease his primal nature.

"Yes."

Oh, thank goodness.

"You flew out of Faerie, didn't you?" Sebastian said, driving into a deserted part of town, the buildings mostly rubble. "That's why you fell out of the sky. You found a sky portal but didn't account for the fact that if you have a shape more acceptable to the mortal realm a Faerie portal will shift you into that."

"And I was struck just before I went through and couldn't shift back in time," Titus said, his face still turned to the wind and sun.

Sebastian swerved around a pothole. "That must have been some blow. You used to be one of the fastest shifters I knew."

And it had been. My magic had locked onto Titus the moment he'd materialized in the mortal realm, which meant he'd already been seriously injured before he'd even hit the ground.

Titus grunted.

I reached out and firmly pressed my palm against his biceps, hoping that my small skin to skin touch would help calm his shifter's soul. There wasn't much I could do for the psychological trauma, but I could at least help steady him.

He stiffened, and for a moment I feared I'd gone too far by invading his personal space. Then, without turning away from the sun and wind, he rumbled low in his throat and captured my hand under his.

We stayed that way until Sebastian parked the sedan at the still-standing support for an overpass that ended fifty feet away in a nasty drop.

As if stopping was his cue, Titus climbed out of the car before Sebastian had even shut off the engine, and pulled on a black ball cap that shaded his eyes so I couldn't easily read his expression.

A mix of disappointment and sadness churned in my gut, fueled by my compulsion to heal. I understood, in part, the wounds in his soul, and I yearned, not for the first time, that my power was stronger and more complex. There was more to healing someone than just fixing his or her body and at times it felt like I was working with one hand tied behind my back.

Cassius pulled on a ball cap as well and added sunglasses that hid the glow from his eyes, although that wasn't a perfect disguise. Yes, no one would be able to see his eyes, but anyone with the ability to sense essences — which was most of the super population — would know he was an angel. It was, however, better than nothing. Especially if the whole point was to avoid as much attention as possible given our unusual party.

I got out as well, forcing my gaze over the area to distract myself from my need to help Titus and my inability to do so. The area looked like it had been a mix of residential and small commercial buildings. Those behind us in the direction we'd come from were mostly leveled with only a few concrete shells of three- and four-story apartment buildings standing ghostly sentinel.

The destruction lessened as I turned my attention to what lay in front of the car as if we were standing at the edge of the radius of a tremendous blast. And given the powerful magic Michael had commanded during the war, it could have been just one blast.

Ahead stood a modest, two-door mechanic's garage. The roof had been ripped off — probably from the blast — and so had half of the sign, leaving only "& Son" creaking in the breeze. On its left sat another business, the sign gone so I had no idea what it had been. The big front window was broken, and the insides had been torn apart, likely from people scavenging everything that could be reused or recycled.

Sebastian led us down an alley between the two businesses that was so narrow Titus's shoulders brushed either side and along an uneven dirt path heading down into a wooded ravine.

"I would have thought Left of Lincoln would be easier to get to," Cassius said.

Sebastian skidded down a sharp incline in the path with the ease of someone who'd done that before. "We're coming in the back way. There's parking and easier access if you arrive by the main roads, but also a lot of people just hanging around. I'd rather avoid that kind of notice."

Cassius huffed. "So you actually can come up with a plan." He followed Sebastian down the slope then held out his hand to help me.

I contemplated not accepting his help. The way he looked at me was still verging on that same look of worry and pity he'd had all those years ago, and every part of me screamed that I needed to look stronger, *be* stronger.

But his look would only get worse if I slipped and landed on my rear end. And with my luck as of late, my skirt would fly up and I'd end up flashing all of them.

And then Sebastian would have something else to tease me about.

I took Cassius's hand and half skidded like Sebastian and Cassius. But the skid quickly turned into a slip, toppling me forward, and I crashed into Cassius's firm body.

His arm wrapped around me — it had to have been instinct, nothing else — and he held me close.

Unable to help myself, I melted into his embrace. I always felt safe in those rare instances when he held me, and I wanted to savor this moment, wanted it to last longer than I knew it would. It wouldn't come again anytime soon, even though I needed it.

"You okay?" he murmured, making my pulse pick up... because Sebastian had teased me and now I craved a connection with anyone, even Cassius. Except...

Was his faster too?

It couldn't be.

But before I could figure that out, he gripped my shoulders and took a step back, putting an appropriate amount of distance between us.

Sebastian rolled his eyes and for a second it looked like he was going to comment — probably say something snide — but he snapped his mouth shut and continued down the path. Maybe he, too, realized we all needed to play nice with each other to get through this.

I bit back a huff of frustration. It was more likely he was just waiting for a better opportunity to make a stinging remark.

A few minutes later, we stepped out of the woods into an alley of sorts running between the forest and behind a row of tents, trucks, and trailers.

Even at this early hour, standing in the shadow of a large red nylon tent, my senses were assaulted with the rumble of many voices and the smell of cooking food and pungent spices, reminding me of the Middle Eastern bazaar I'd visited — modern tents and vehicles aside — a few years before my abduction.

My impression didn't change when we made our way between the tent and a blue van and stepped onto a narrow street half full with people. It was almost hard to see that the area originally had been a small parking lot — most likely for access to the forested ravine — across the street from an unusual V-intersection where one street ran parallel to the ravine and two other streets met it in a V.

At the center of the market, standing in the point of the V, was an intact narrow three-story building with a sign advertising blood bunnies — for any vampire who'd managed to purchase a rare and expensive charm against the sun or were visiting after sunset — and prostitutes for everyone else. A few other buildings — a couple of small houses and three small storefronts — also remained standing, while the rest of Left of Lincoln were tents and vehicles crowded down the streets and around rubble creating a maze of passageways.

Sebastian held out his elbow and flashed me his wicked smile, making my pulse frustratingly stutter. "Remember who we're supposed to be, Angel Arm Candy."

I took his arm and he tugged me close, reigniting my desire, while Cassius glowered, and Titus focused on the area around us, his gaze darting over everything, his body tense.

"Hawk keeps a tent on the edge of the market. It's usually this way," Sebastian said, heading toward the three-story building.

"Usually?" Cassius asked. "I don't particularly want to be wandering around. It's bad enough that we're already drawing attention."

And we were. People were looking at us with a mix of curiosity, suspicion, and jealousy. I felt like I was on display, and in a way I was. I didn't know how many people here knew or knew of Sebastian Bane, but he was still a rare faekin, and at the moment, he had two angels and a massive shifter with him. And while there were a few men with bodyguards and pretty young women hanging on their arms, there weren't a lot and none in as an unusual combination as us.

"Lincoln never stays the same," Sebastian said as if he didn't notice the stares. "Hell, two months ago it was on the other side of town near the old arena and last year it was about ten miles out of town."

Cassius harrumphed. "We should ask for directions."

"I agree," Titus rumbled.

"I'm not asking for directions." Sebastian tugged me even closer to avoid running into a monstrously large ogre with thick, grayish-green skin who was even bigger than Titus.

"The sooner we find Hawk, the sooner we get out of here," Cassius pressed.

"Asking for directions will just make us more memorable," Sebastian replied, leading us past a food truck with whole plucked chickens and skinned rabbits hanging from the metal awning. "Surely you're smart enough to know memorable is bad."

"So is spending more time than necessary," Cassius said.

For the love of—!

"This is Sebastian's turf. He knows the area and the people best."

Sebastian flashed me a satisfied smile, and Cassius's glower deepened.

Yeah, I don't think so.

"If you can't find this Hawk person in ten minutes," I added, "*I'm going to ask for directions.*"

Sebastian rolled his eyes at me. "That's not—"

"Nine minutes and fifty seconds," I said. "Or do I start asking now?"

I started to step away from him to talk to a heavyset woman selling...? I had no idea.

But Sebastian tightened his grip on my arm and tugged me back to his side. "Fine. Ten minutes."

"Nine minutes and thirty seconds, now," Titus rumbled.

Sebastian glared at him. "You, too?"

We hurried past the unofficial blood house/brothel down the narrower of the two streets that made up the V-intersection and made our way past a pickup truck with — probably stolen — electronics, a tent with colorful lady's clothing, and a cube van with a complicated glyph painted on the side. The van's back door was open, revealing stacks of old-looking books, and wooden and metal boxes of various shapes and sizes.

If I was magically sensitive, I was sure that van would have been glowing like a sun or pulsing like a pressure wave with all the magic inside... *if* the woman standing at the open door selling the magical items wasn't trying to cheat her customers. But by the sudden tightness in Sebastian's body and the way he picked up his pace to move past the van, I was certain the woman was selling the real, magical deal.

We left the road two trucks and a small still-standing house later, moving into a tent city with even narrower passageways. Here the smells of cooked food, smoke, sweat, and urine clashed with each other in a strange mix of appealing and disgusting. People talked in hushed voices, stared at us as we passed, or hurried inside their tents.

The tension in Sebastian's body didn't ease and neither did his pace.

"You okay?" I asked softly, although I was pretty sure Cassius and Titus were still able to hear me.

"Yeah," he said, "just a lot of magic in this area. Not really a fan of letting it all hang out like this."

"You never were," an incubus said, stepping out of a large white canvas tent, far too similar to the tent I'd been kept in all those years ago.

I shuddered and the gorgeous demon slid his attention to me, hellfire simmering in shockingly gray-blue eyes — a rare color for a demon.

He radiated raw, unbridled sex that stole my breath, and he made no attempt to hide it like the other incubus I knew. It made me ache to run my hands through his jaw-length sandy blond hair, tease the base of his small horns fully knowing they were an erogenous zone, and let him do whatever he wanted to me. Like all incubi, he'd be perfection under his T-shirt and shorts, all sleek, sculpted muscle, and I instantly needed to see him naked, run my hands over him, have him pressed against me, inside me—

"Hawk," Sebastian said, making my pulse pick up.

This was who we were meeting? An incubus? I was already having trouble closing the floodgate on my desire. How was I going to hold myself together sitting near sex incarnate and not look like I was affected while Sebastian conducted his business?

AMIAH

Desire throbbed between my thighs as if proving the point that I no longer had any restraint, and the hellfire in the incubus's eyes swelled.

"You moved your tent," Sebastian said.

"I got pushed out by a blood witch." Hawk gave a sensual shrug, his gaze never leaving mine. "You here on business?"

"Yeah." Sebastian drew closer — and as a result, drew me closer.

My pulse beat even faster and I struggled to get myself back under control. I'd been around incubi before. This shouldn't be that difficult.

"Well, then." Hawk raised the flap on his tent and gestured for us to enter.

A whisper of fear fluttered through my chest, chilling my desire. I didn't want to go inside even though I *knew* it wasn't *that* tent. Cassius had burned it almost a hundred years ago, and if he hadn't killed the human who'd enslaved me, that human would still be long dead, not here in Left of Lincoln.

The thought made me furious.

All these years later and that human was still controlling me. How many times was I going to have to tell myself I was strong, I was in control, I was free before my soul believed it?

And maybe yesterday I would have believed it.

But today, I wasn't free.

I was magically bound to Titus and soon I'd be magically bound to someone else if Sebastian couldn't remove my mating brand.

Well, the first problem I could take care of. It was just a matter of going inside that tent. And the sooner I dealt with the leash spell, the sooner Sebastian could get to work on my brand.

Sebastian frowned and tugged gently on my arm, urging me forward and making embarrassment heat my cheeks. I'd hesitated for too long and now he knew something was wrong.

Fighting the urge to straighten my back — that would give me away even more — I made myself enter with him.

Inside was completely different to the traveling faith healer's tent from my past. That man had tried to portray a pious nature — even though he was nothing of the sort. He'd kept a clean tent with a simple cot for my patients during the day and him at night, a table with his bible, a wash basin, clean rags, and a locked chest filled with stones that was too heavy to move, which he chained my ankle to during the night.

Hawk's tent was stuffed with multi-colored pillows, Persian rugs, and gauzy curtains. The morning sun shone fully on the tent top, providing more than enough light to see clearly, and yet the space still had a soft, intimate feel. The temperature was also comfortable — most likely cooled by magic. A large chest with an intricate design carved into its wooden surface sat at the back, and a low table sat in the center. At the edge of the table, on a metal tray, was a pitcher of pale yellow liquid with condensation beading on its glass surface along with two delicate wine glasses beside it.

Hawk gestured to the pillows in front of the table, but walked to the chest at the back and pulled out a third wine glass.

Sebastian sat on one of the cushions, drawing me down to sit beside him, and glanced at Cassius who gave a tight nod, his expression icy. He stayed at the entrance, just inside the flap, while Titus took up position kneeling at the side of the tent halfway between Cassius and the table — since he was too tall to fully stand.

"You don't usually come with muscle," Hawk said, oozing sexual grace as he eased into a cushion across from us and poured the yellow liquid into one of the wine glasses. "You also never come with a companion. Have you decided on an alternative payment this time?"

He flashed me a heart-stopping smile and Sebastian huffed.

"No," the fae said.

"Too bad." Hawk handed me the glass, brushing his index finger along my baby finger as I took it and sending his sensual magic rushing straight to my core. "I find angels intriguing."

I fought to keep my expression the same and not shift to ease the heat and pressure building low within me before remembering that it didn't matter what my outward appearance was, the incubus could sense my desire.

My cheeks heated and Hawk's smile deepened.

"Very intriguing," he purred, the hellfire in his eyes flaring.

"Are you planning on doing business today?" Sebastian demanded. "There are half a dozen Sensitives in Lincoln who can do what I need done."

"We both know you'd never go to those hacks." Hawk turned his attention to Sebastian, releasing me from his captivating gaze, and his smile shifted from sensual to friendly. "What do you need?"

Sebastian pulled the resonance charm from his pocket and set it on the table. "I need a three-way alignment."

Hawk cocked an eyebrow. "You can do a three-way alignment."

"I wouldn't be here if that had worked. The spell I'm breaking is warped and I need the charm aligned with more precision than I'm capable of."

"How much more?" Hawk asked, his expression becoming serious, all sense of sensuality or even warm friendship gone.

"As much as you can manage," Sebastian replied, just as seriously.

Hawk poured another glass of the pale yellow liquid and took a long sip. I watched the muscles in his neck flex as he swallowed, unable to help myself, fully knowing that was the effect of his magic.

"That'll cost you," Hawk said.

"I expected it would."

Hawk's eyes widened. "You're a better haggler than that."

Sebastian leaned forward, his expression hard. "Which should tell you how serious I am about you doing your best work."

"It tells me you're rattled." Hawk took another sip and closed his eyes. "Let's just see what you're up against—" He sucked in a sharp breath. "Shit. A leash spell?"

"You're familiar with it?" Sebastian asked, his voice grim.

"Yeah." Hawk opened his eyes now fully consumed by hellfire and turned his attention to me, his expression fierce. "Whoever cast that should be shot. Keep your money, Bane, and let's free the angel and the

—" He glanced at Titus then turned back to Sebastian, his eyes wide. "Are you shitting me?"

"Nope," Sebastian said. "What's your usual order for the alignment?"

"You first. You're the one breaking the spell. Then the—" Hawk shook his head as if he still didn't believe what he was going to say. "Then the dragon, the origin of the spell, and finally Miss Angel here."

He finished his drink, picked up the charm, and stood.

Sebastian jerked his chin at the wine glass still in my hand as Hawk knelt behind him. "You're going to want to drink that."

I brought the glass to my lips and took a quick sniff then a sip. It was wine. One with a nice light slightly sweet flavor, but wine nonetheless. "It's the middle of the morning."

"Trust me." Sebastian turned to face Hawk. "You're going to want it."

"If it's that bad, why aren't you or Titus drinking?"

Sebastian quirked an eyebrow at me as if I should have already figured out the answer. "This isn't going to affect me or Titus as much as it will you. Guys aren't our thing."

My thoughts tripped over that.

Right. Hawk was an incubus.

Heat seared my cheeks again and my pulse picked up. I was about to get firsthand experience with an incubus's sex magic, and Sebastian wanted me to drink first. Of course he wanted me intoxicated. That would offer the best opportunity for me to embarrass myself and give him more fodder to tease me with.

"One drink isn't going to release my inhibitions," I said, putting the glass on the table.

Sebastian drew in a deep breath and rolled his shoulders making his glow undulate down his body. "No, but it might relax you."

"And it's always better if you don't fight me," Hawk added, using his palm to press the charm against Sebastian's chest over his heart. "You ready?"

"To get blue balls? Oh, yeah," Sebastian said, his tone dripping with sarcasm. "Always."

Hawk chuckled and closed his eyes. "Pretty sure you'll be able to remedy that soon enough like you always do."

Sebastian shuddered and bit back a sensual groan that made my pulse pick up.

"Jeez, man," Hawk hissed. "You're spun so tight, it's painful. Take your own advice." He slid his free hand to the back of Sebastian's head and urged him forward to lean his forehead against his shoulder. "Just take a—"

Both of them stiffened and Sebastian's soft glow flickered, revealing that sickly gray pallor for a second. Then Sebastian groaned again, but this one sounded more like pain than pleasure.

"Shit, Bane." The muscles in Hawk's jaw flexed, and a surge of sensual desire brushed against my senses. "What the hell did you do?"

A husky moan escaped Sebastian's clenched jaw the sound back to pleasure and starting a slow throb between my thighs. "It'll be dealt with tomorrow," he said through gritted teeth.

"Then use the charm before then. That shit has messed with your resonance." Hawk drew in a deep, slow breath, and the heated desire that had been caressing my skin without me really knowing it, vanished, leaving me cold and aching. He must have released his power.

That thought made my pulse race even faster. If that was what his magic felt like without him touching me, what would it feel like to have his hands on me?

Hawk nudged Sebastian to sit back and withdrew his hand from Sebastian's heart, his expression tight with worry. He opened his mouth to say something but Sebastian's eyes darted to me and Hawk gave a tight nod.

Gasping, Sebastian leaned back against the table, his breath still too fast, and poured himself a glass of wine. He emptied it in one gulp and turned his gaze, heavy with desire, toward me, making me think of how much I ached for him—

No. Anyone. I ached for *anyone*, not Sebastian specifically.

"You really should drink yours," he said, his voice husky, sending a thrill racing through me.

I yanked my attention away as Hawk turned to Titus, who watched the incubus with the eyes of a predator ready to attack.

"May I?" Hawk asked.

Titus grunted and nodded his assent, his body stiff and his expression hard.

"You might want to relax." Hawk pressed the charm over Titus's heart like he had with Sebastian, and closed his eyes.

Now that I was aware of it, I could feel Hawk's sensual magic whispering against my skin as he released his power. It made my insides heat but seemed to make every muscle in Titus's body tense.

"Take a breath," Hawk said. "Don't fight me."

Titus drew in a huge breath, expanding his massive chest, and released it on a shuddering growl.

Hawk's magic swelled and Titus's growl turned into a strangled groan. With another groan, he tipped forward, his breath suddenly fast, and Hawk caught Titus's forehead on his shoulder like he had with Sebastian, cupping the back of Titus's head. The tendon in Titus's neck flexed, and his face scrunched in pain as another groan, a strange mix of pain and pleasure, tore from his throat, sending more heated desire sweeping through me.

"How much longer?" Titus gasped, his back heaving with ragged breaths.

My breath picked up, matching his, and I fought to regain control over myself, but that only increased my fear. Hawk hadn't even touched me yet, and his power already made me ache for him.

"Just.... a little... more." Hawk's power swelled, stealing my breath, and Titus slammed his fist into the tent floor, his whole body shaking.

"And we're done." Hawk's power snapped off leaving me cold.

He withdrew his hand from Titus's heart and urged him to sit back like he had with Sebastian. With a snarl, Titus jerked away from Hawk, his eyes still closed, his body even more tense than before they'd started.

Then Hawk turned to me and my pulse stalled.

I didn't want his magic to affect me like Titus or even Sebastian... Except Sebastian had said Hawk's magic was going to affect me more.

Oh, God.

I downed the wine.

Hawk's lips quirked and he held up the charm. "May I?"

A part of me wanted to say no and run out of the tent. I didn't want to risk losing control, and without a doubt, Hawk's magic was going to make me want sex even more than I already did. But saying no wasn't an option. I had to be free. Now. I couldn't hold back my fear for much longer, which meant I had to suck it up and let Hawk touch me.

Please, touch me.

No! Don't.

I nodded, afraid I wouldn't be able to get any words out. Hawk lifted the charm to place it over my heart and I realized with horror that I didn't have the protection of clothing that Sebastian and Titus had. The neckline of my dress was too low. His flesh would be touching mine and that only enhanced an incubus's connection with his lover.

Hawk shifted closer. Heat from his demonic body temperature radiated from his hands as he raised them to set the charm over my heart and press his hot palm over top of that.

My mouth went dry and I wished I'd had another glass of wine. I wasn't relaxed enough for this. I didn't think I'd ever be.

"Just take a breath," Hawk murmured, his tone like silk against my senses.

I forced myself to inhale, and as I released it, he released his magic. It unfurled hot and slick and sensual, and I instantly ached for his touch. I needed to be caressed and kissed. I needed to know what it felt like for a man to move inside me and I was tired of waiting.

I can't be patient anymore. Please release this ache. Please, please touch me.

But that wasn't why I was in Hawk's tent. He was using his magic sensitivity to reach deep into my soul to attune the resonance charm to my resonance. That was it. Not to mention I would hate myself if I begged Hawk — like all but a small part of me wanted to do — to take me with Sebastian, Cassius, and Titus watching. Cassius would never look at me the same and it would just become more fodder for Sebastian's teasing.

My heart pounded faster and my body throbbed with need. I had to hold on until Hawk was done. My yearning would ease up once he withdrew his magic. Surely I could last for the few minutes it took for Hawk to get my resonance.

But his power swelled, and I released an embarrassingly sensual moan then another one as he slid his fingers into my hair and urged me to rest my forehead on his shoulder.

Except I didn't want to just lean on his shoulder, I wanted to rip off our clothes and take him deep inside me.

Now. God. Please now.

"So much desire," he whispered, his breath feathering across my neck and his magic swelling in my core. "Wound so tight. I can help you release it."

Yes. God, yes!

My breath grew ragged, each inhalation reminding me that Hawk's hand was on my breast and I desperately wanted it to move lower, to tease my nipple, taunt me in the best way before satisfying me.

I slipped my hands inside his shirt, trailing my fingers over his six-pack, making him hum with pleasure. The sound twisted my desire tighter, and I reached for the button on his fly when my brain finally caught up to my need.

Cassius, Sebastian, and Titus were in the tent! Watching. Had they noticed I was about to undress Hawk?

I glanced at Sebastian through a veil of lashes afraid of seeing that wicked smile that said he was never going to let me live down that I wanted to have sex with an incubus I'd just met. Surely he saw where my hands were. He was the closest.

But instead of mischief, his gaze was heavy with raw desire, his pupils dilated. He was turned on and I got the sense he wanted to watch Hawk pleasure me.

And that idea excited me even more. My muscles clenched and my body trembled on the verge of an orgasm.

"Sweet Jesus," Hawk groaned, his voice so low I could barely hear him. "When you're free of the leash spell come find me."

He shot a hot spike of magic straight to my core and ignited my orgasm. My breath caught as the pleasure swept through me and I clutched the waistband of his shorts — only because that's where my hands had been when he made me come.

"That's just a taste," he murmured in my ear and his sensual magic melted away, leaving me panting and trembling and craving more.

I clung to him, fighting to catch my breath and regain my composure before I lifted my head and faced the guys. Embarrassment heated my cheeks that I'd orgasmed with everyone watching, but so, too, did excited desire for the same reason. And while it could have been Hawk's magic influencing me, I had a suspicion it wasn't.

"We need to go," Cassius said, his tone sharp, jerking my attention from my still trembling body. Something was wrong.

Hawk chuckled, the sound thick with male satisfaction. "Pretty sure Miss Angel can't walk yet."

"Then Bane, carry her," Cassius commanded. "It's gotten too quiet outside."

I drew in a ragged breath and forced myself to sit up.

"What do you mean too quiet?" Hawk asked.

"You might want to close up shop for a month or so," Sebastian said to Hawk as he stood and held out his hand to me.

"I can't afford to close up shop for a—"

A sharp *rip* came from the back of the tent, and with a yell, a wiry man with a knife leaped inside through the large slit he'd just made.

AMIAH

SEBASTIAN GRABBED HIS LEFT FOREARM AND HISSED A SOFT SIBILANT WORD as two more men leaped through the slit at the back of the tent. The glyph on his arm lit up and a moderately powerful force-wave shot from his left hand and knocked the men over, tumbling them into the tent's canvas back.

"Grab Amiah and let's go," he said to Hawk and staggered toward the flap at the front.

Hawk threw me over his shoulder before I could tell him I could manage.

The three assailants, all human males with similar builds to Sebastian and all with foot-long knives, scrambled to their feet and raced after us.

We ran out of the tent, and Hawk dropped me to my feet and shoved me into Sebastian's arms. "You should take her."

He then turned to face the men, and I pushed away from Sebastian before he could get a good grip on me.

"I can stand," I said, even if I was still a little unsteady.

Behind him Cassius and Titus fought with at least a dozen more assailants, a mix of men and women, humans and shifters, while people screamed and ran away, tripping over each other, tent lines, and knocked-over merchandise.

Cassius side-stepped a jab from one of the men, snapped a small fire whip around his neck — mindful of all the flammable tents and people around us — and wrenched him into a shifter behind him. Another shifter leaped at him, her claws aimed for his back, and he jerked around to face her, blocking her attack with his forearm and pushing her claws away from his body.

Titus snarled and slashed at a man with a sword, tossing him into a small red tent, as another man, a shifter, took the man's place. Inside the damaged tent, someone screamed and a woman scrambled out the front flap as the man Titus hit staggered to his feet then dropped to his hands and knees, gasping.

My magic surged to my palms and locked onto him, even though I'd only recovered a little magic from this morning.

Oh, no. My pulse stuttered. I didn't want to go running into a fight to heal someone let alone someone trying to hurt us. But my magic didn't care if that man was trying to hurt us or not. He was gravely injured and I *had* to try to save him.

I strained to stay where I was. I wasn't a reckless fool. The worse thing I could do was run into danger. That could distract Cassius and he could be killed. But the burning pressure to go to the injured assailant jerked me forward despite my desires.

Sebastian grabbed my arm. "What are you doing?"

"Keep me here," I gasped.

"Keep yourself here."

Behind me, someone yelled, and Sebastian yanked me out of the way to the other side of the narrow path by a pair of tall metal trailers. Hawk and the man who'd first entered the tent tumbled onto the ground where I'd just been standing, and Hawk rammed his elbow into the guy's face while Sebastian shot another small force-wave at a man about to stab Hawk in the back.

"What the hell have you gotten me into?" Hawk demanded, as more men hurried out of the tent.

"You really want an explanation right now?" Sebastian shot another force-wave, but my body jerked me away before I could see the results.

Weak light radiated from my palms, visible only to me, a testament to how little power I had, but the pressure to use it on the dying man was just as ferocious as if I was at full.

I stumbled, fighting the pull, but I had no idea if I'd be able to resist long enough for the fight to end and Cassius to drag me away.

Someone yelled and a woman tumbled to the ground beside me

unconscious. Not dead. All around me, people yelled and screamed. Cassius had released more of his fire, his whip almost full size now, hissing and crackling as it struck flesh. Titus snarled and slashed someone else. Both Cassius and Titus were bleeding, their T-shirts cut, and blood splattered the hard-packed dirt at their feet.

Ahead, the injured man, still on his hands and knees, panted short shallow gasps, each breath coming farther and farther apart. Blood gushed from the wound Titus had inflicted with his claws, and from the amount on the ground, he was losing it quickly.

Pressure screamed through me with the promise of an excruciating backlash if I resisted much longer.

The man sagged to his side and I lurched forward another step. I was now at the edge of the chaos. There was no point in fighting the compulsion now. I was already in danger.

I scrambled to the fallen man's side just as the pressure inside me vanished, releasing me, replaced with anger and frustration. He was dead and I'd been forced to run into danger for no good reason.

A woman landed beside me with a *thud* and a heavy *oomph*. Her attention jerked to me and I froze. But a tall muscular man with a stern expression yelled at her and she scrambled back into the fight, only to be replaced by another man with a compound fracture, the bone protruding through the flesh of his right arm.

My magic flickered and I lunged for Titus. He was the closest, and if I wanted to get out of danger, I needed to use up my magic so it wouldn't lock onto someone else.

Titus jerked around to swipe at me but froze, and I slapped my palms against his side and released my magic. The sudden surge drew a wild howl filled with pain and Cassius wrenched around to face us.

"What are you doing?" He grabbed my arm and yanked me away before I'd given Titus all my power.

A slice of backlash cut through me, stealing my breath, and I grabbed Cassius's wrist and gave him the rest, all but the little bit that was always in the core of my being deep in my palms, a flame of magic that never went out.

He grunted against the pain of suddenly being healed and his gaze met mine, hard and icy with understanding.

Exhaustion flooded me and the world lurched and darkened, but at least I wasn't going to heal the enemy.

"Bane," Cassius yelled, seizing the assailant between him and Sebastian with his fire whip and slamming him into the side of a pickup truck. "Get her out of the way."

Bane's attention jerked toward us and Cassius shoved me toward him.

I staggered, fighting to stay upright and conscious. The weariness would pass. I just needed time to recover.

Sebastian yanked me to his side. "What the fuck is wrong with you?"

I opened my mouth to respond but he jerked his gaze away from me.

"Fucking crazy angels," he hissed and sent another force-wave into two shifters barreling down the path toward Hawk.

I swept my gaze around the chaos. There were dozens of assailants, and they were making no attempt to go unnoticed. The stern man yelled something else and two more men scrambled back into the fight. "I thought you said they wouldn't make a public attack."

"That was the Shadow Court. My glyph would light up if they were shadow fae." Sebastian pointed to a small glyph on the inside of his wrist, which flared to life with a brilliant white glow. "Oh, come on!"

With a curse, he shoved me back, hard. I lost my balance and fell onto my rear end, the impact jarring up my spine and sending darkness shuddering across my vision, but it saved my life as the fae with the shadows writhing under his skin darted out from between the two trailers his blade slicing the air where I'd just been.

He swiped his knife again, this time at Sebastian, who jerked out of the way. The blade cut through Sebastian's shirt, but thankfully didn't draw blood, and Sebastian grabbed the shadow fae's wrist and twisted it in an attempt to disarm him. But the shadow fae rammed his heel into Sebastian's knee, knocking him off balance, and wrenched his wrist free.

I staggered to my feet and scanned the area for somewhere to hide. The best place for me was out of the way. Even if I had combat skills, I was in no condition to fight, but a shifter, who'd been knocked to the ground by Hawk, noticed me and bolted toward me.

I glanced at Sebastian. He was busy with the shadow fae. And while Hawk had managed to get one of his assailants' knives, he was still fighting with four of them.

No one was going to help me, so I squeezed a trickle of magic out of the core of my being and released my wings. Up was the best place to go. Everyone would be able to see me — and up my skirt — but at least they wouldn't be able to get to me.

I leaped, caught the wind, reached the top of the trailers, and the nightmare from the park ring lunged out from behind one of the trailers and grabbed my ankle. He wrenched me down, slamming my back against the hard-packed dirt and knocking the wind from me.

For a second I was drifting in quiet darkness, then my vision partially cleared and the sounds of the fight roared back to life around me.

"No flying away and going for help," the nightmare sneered, capturing me with his hellfire gaze.

Icy fear seized me. The faith healer's tent materialized around me and he smashed his Bible against the side of my head, making the world spin. I'd displeased him. I'd been unable to heal as many people as he'd wanted before I'd run out of magic, and he hadn't made the profits that he'd wanted.

With a snarl, he seized my throat and pushed me onto the table. Would this be the time he raped me? I'd told him I'd lose my magic if I wasn't pure, but I had no idea how long he'd believe that lie.

Tears streamed down my cheeks and his grip tightened, cutting off my air. *Please, don't. Please—*

Except the faith healer had never raped me and I wasn't in his tent. Cassius had freed me. This wasn't real. It was the nightmare's magic.

I gritted my teeth and felt for his magic in my mind. There. A sour, nauseating darkness.

The faith healer squeezed tighter and reached for his belt buckle.

No. Please no.

My thoughts stuttered, my fear swelling, and I heaved my focus back to the nightmare's magic. With a scream, I mentally shoved him out of my mind and the faith healer's tent vanished.

The nightmare snarled and lunged at me, but the demon-vampire, now beside him, grabbed his arm, stopping him.

"Not our target," he said to the nightmare, his voice so soft I could barely hear him above the roar of the fight.

The nightmare glared at him, the hellfire in his eyes blazing, then he jerked his arm free. He slammed his fist into the face of one of the other assailants, knocking him to the ground, and charged down the path toward Titus and Cassius.

"This doesn't involve you, angel," the demon-vampire said. "You should run."

In one swift motion, he drew his katana, turned, decapitated an assailant rushing up behind him, and strode after the nightmare.

I stared at the headless body, its blood rushing into a thick pool and soaking into the ground. It had happened so fast I almost couldn't make myself believe what I'd just seen. Sure, I'd just seen Titus kill someone, and I'd watched people kill and die during the war, but that man's death had been so quick and emotionless. As if the demon-vampire had felt nothing when he'd taken that life.

Sebastian dropped to the ground beside me as I sat up and pulled in my wings. Behind him, Hawk now fought with the shadow fae, his attacks with his knife not as sleek or efficient as the fae's but still confident as if he'd fought with a knife before.

"Are you hurt?" Sebastian asked.

"No. I'm—" I tried to catch my breath, still stunned from my fall and the horror of the nightmare's magic. The world was still spinning and I was so exhausted it was hard to keep my head up. "I'm—"

I dragged in another breath, this one harder than the last.

Hawk grunted and Sebastian's attention jumped back to him. The shadow fae yanked his dagger from Hawk's shoulder and rammed his fist into Hawk's gut.

"I'm—" I fought to draw my next breath against a rising pressure squeezing my insides. It was as if I'd cracked my ribs again. Each inhalation was agonizing, and darkness started to creep around the edges of my vision. "I'm—"

An invisible weight slammed into my chest, stealing what little air I had left and making my pulse race. I gasped, but there was no air to breathe in. Every muscle in my body tensed and I collapsed onto my side, my lungs burning.

"Amiah!" Sebastian's eyes flashed wide. His attention jerked up, and he yelled for Titus.

The world spun faster as the darkness in my vision swelled. I desperately reached for any glimmer of magic I had to save myself. But just like the last time, I had nothing left. And even if I did have magic, it wouldn't save me. There was no air to breathe. That wasn't something I could fix.

AMIAH

"Where the fuck is Titus?" Sebastian yelled and he rolled me to my back, captured my face with his cool palms, and pressed his lips against mine.

I froze. Shocked. Sebastian was kissing me. I was dying, and he was kissing me. I'd wondered what it would be like to kiss him, how it would make me feel. Would he surprise me and tease me with something gentle or be strong and brash like he always was? Except I couldn't tell if I felt anything. Everything within me was howling, desperate to breathe.

Then he released his breath into my mouth and I gasped it in against the pressure in my chest.

He turned his attention back to the fight around us. "Find Titus!"

"Little busy," Hawk said, his voice barely audible against the rushing in my ears.

Sebastian gave me another breath. "You're going to need to hold the next one." He pressed his lips against mine and gave me a bigger breath.

I tried to gasp in as much as I could, forcing my burning lungs to expand against the invisible weight crushing me.

"Find Titus. The big guy. Now." Sebastian pressed his hands to his chest, and both the sleep glyph on his shoulder and the force-wave glyph on his forearm burst to life, along with a third glyph that curled across his ribs.

With a scream, he released a massive blast of power that swept dust into my eyes and made the world darken and spin. Hawk staggered into the trailer, leaning against it to keep standing, while the shadow fae fell to his hands and knees. Beyond them, everyone along the path collapsed, some completely unconscious. All except the tall stern guy. He staggered, dropped to one knee, and his attention jerked to us.

"Fucking hell," Hawk hissed and he jabbed his blade toward the shadow fae's back, but the fae dropped and rolled under the trailer.

Gasping and trembling, Sebastian gave me another shallow breath, and Hawk dropped to his knees to chase after the shadow fae.

"No. Titus," Sebastian barked. "They're too far apart and everyone won't be down for long."

Hawk's attention jumped to me. "Shit." He bolted down the path.

Sebastian gave me another weak breath, his expression tight with pain and his eyes filled with fear. The glow in his skin was gone and his complexion was gray. Whatever he'd cast, it had taken a lot out of him.

The darkness in my vision swelled. His breaths weren't going to sustain me for much longer.

Another warm breath filled my mouth and, too late, I tried to breathe it in, but it vanished before I could inhale it. Sebastian's hands, back on my cheeks holding me steady, trembled and he gave me another shallow breath.

Someone yelled. Sebastian's cool presence disappeared and strong hands picked me up.

Whoever held me clutched me tight and started running, and I gasped in a painful breath, the crushing pressure still present, but at least the air was back.

Titus had to be near. I dragged my eyes open to find him and looked up into his ferocious golden gaze. He didn't look nearly as affected as I was, and I didn't know if I should be furious or grateful for that.

He barreled around the only remaining brick wall of what used to be a house into another tent alley. Ahead, Hawk and Sebastian — Hawk with his arm slung around Sebastian's waist helping him — slipped between a wooden stall with a red awning and a blue pickup truck, and Titus followed.

"We can't keep running," Cassius said from behind Titus.

"There's a storm drain overflow up ahead. Do you have enough juice to eliminate our trail?" Hawk asked Sebastian, who nodded.

We cut between two more tents, across ten feet of waist-high grass and weeds, and skidded down the concrete incline into the currently dry, man-made runoff creek. Ahead lay the dark mouth of the storm drain, its metal grate twisted back providing an opening big enough for us to enter.

The guys didn't slow once inside. They kept running deeper into the cool, damp darkness, Hawk leading us down one pipe then another and another until we reached a hole where part of the wall had collapsed.

"We can catch our breath in here," Hawk said, helping Sebastian climb over the rubble and up a short, steep incline.

Titus set me on the ground at the top of the incline — which was actually a blue-tiled floor littered with debris, rubble, broken glass, and dirt. I lifted my gaze to a high, domed ceiling covered with a blue and white mosaic. The intricate design flowed around tall windows close to the ceiling, letting in just enough light to soften the darkness — the glass long broken — and ran down the walls and the half dozen pillars supporting the dome. A few feet away sat a curved bench, one of many ringing a large recessed area in the center. It looked like we'd entered what had once been a fancy European bathhouse.

With a grunt of pain, Titus climbed up beside me then moved past me so Cassius could climb in as well. He stopped beside me on his knees, his expression icy and his angel glow blazing.

"You okay?" A spark snapped from his hand and he shifted away from me.

"Are you?" I asked back.

Blood oozed down his cheek from a gash above his left eye and his T-shirt had been cut in numerous places.

"Nothing you can do about it," he said.

"I've more than just my magic." I could still treat them with non-magical methods. Even dizzy and exhausted, I was sure I could manage something. "We still need to take stock. What's everyone's condition?"

And I wasn't going to think about how I'd almost died because Titus had moved too far away from me.

I struggled to push away my fear and turned to face the rest of the guys to assess their conditions.

Except Hawk knelt in front of me, blocking my view. He ducked in close, grabbed the back of my head, and before I could say anything or pull away, captured my lips with his.

I gasped in surprise and he pushed his tongue into my mouth, raking it against mine.

Holy smokes. *This* was a real kiss.

Desire ignited within me. All the desperate need I'd been fighting for far too long, need that had been behind a wall of restraint that Sebastian and now Hawk had shattered, surged inside me.

I tangled my fingers in his hair, purposefully brushing the base of his horns, and kissed him back. He groaned, the sound low and dark, and his kiss turned ferocious. His grip in my hair tightened and he pulled my head back, arching my back and pushing my breasts forward. His other hand plunged down the front of my dress and he roughly palmed my breast, the sensation rushing through me, drawing a moan.

My core throbbed and I strained to move against his grip and straddle him, but he held me firm, fully controlling my body. Then a whisper of his sensual magic caressed inside of me and a soft climax rolled through me.

I shuddered with my release and whimpered into his mouth, satisfied and yet disappointed it had happened so fast and softly.

"Let her go." Cassius wrenched me out of Hawk's embrace and slammed his fist into the incubus's face with a resounding *crunch*.

"Fucking hell," Hawk gasped, blood running from his nose. "I just needed a top up."

And boy had I given him a top up. Succubi and Incubi survived on sexual energy. Anything that was lustful: thoughts, kissing, touching, and of course intercourse. And while they didn't need to participate in any of the activities, flesh-to-flesh contact provided more powerful energy than just standing nearby, and being the focus of the lust and participating was the most powerful of all.

He pushed his broken nose back into place, his enhanced healing stopping the bleeding and starting to set it already, proving just how much of a top up I'd given him.

"Pretty sure she didn't mind," he said, giving me a smug smile and making my cheeks heat with embarrassment. "And I didn't just take. I'm generous like that."

Oh, my God! If it hadn't been obvious to the others that I'd orgasmed — again — it was now.

"Just because you seduced her with magic doesn't mean she consented." Smoke billowed around me and Cassius's hands grew searing hot, stinging my skin.

"Cassius." His lack of control was really starting to concern me. I tried to push out of his embrace before his fire manifested and burned me. "Cassius, please."

His attention dropped to me and his smoke.

"Shit." With a growl, he set me on the floor and wrenched away. His smoke vanished but now he was so tense, trying to hold it back, he shook. "You don't get to use your magic on anyone you like."

"Oh, there was no magic involved." Hawk's smile turned wicked, renewing my aching desire. "Well, not until—"

"That's enough," I said before Hawk could go on. "I'm exhausted—" And embarrassed and frustrated on so many levels. "And my chest still hurts from the leash spell."

And I'm still trapped.

I fought to shove down everything I was feeling and focus on the situation. "Hawk is now healed. Who else is bleeding and how badly?"

"I'll manage," Cassius said, even though his clothes were ripped and bloody and the right side of his face was starting to swell, making it hard for him to fully open his eye. "If everyone else can manage as well, we should get back to Bane's and regroup."

"Not until we stop leaving a blood trail," Sebastian said, leaning back against the pillar beside us, his appearance the opposite of Cassius's. His shirt wasn't overly bloody, but he must have had a serious injury somewhere because his complexion was still gray and there was a small pool of blood beside him. "Both the Shadow and Spring Courts will be able to track us by our blood, and I don't have enough juice to hold up the group concealment spell *and* remove all traces of us as we make our way back home. The minute we move on and our blood is no longer within the concealment spell, they'll be able to hone in on it."

"Which means none of us can bleed until the samples they've no doubt taken from our fight degrade." Cassius shifted, sucked in a sharp breath, and pressed his arm to his side. He probably had broken ribs as well. "In fifteen or sixteen hours?"

"I'd go with at least twenty-four to be safe," Sebastian said. "And I can't keep up the concealment that long without a break. Amiah, have you got enough magic to stop our bleeding?"

"No." I had nothing. "If I rest, I can recover some. How long can you hold the concealment?"

"If I'm just holding the concealment spell, I can keep it up for a while. How long do you need?" Sebastian asked.

"Honest inventory everyone," Cassius said, saving me from confessing I didn't even have enough magic to assess anyone's injuries. "I took some really nasty cuts from some of those shifters, but I've seared the worst of them shut so I'm not even close to bleeding out." Which had to have been excruciating.

Sure, his fire magic gave him the ability to cauterize wounds that regularly couldn't be cauterized and he now wasn't bleeding, but he'd replaced those lacerations with nasty burns. Burns he normally wouldn't have because unless he purposely set his mind to it, his fire didn't burn him. "I'm also pretty sure I have at least one broken rib."

I started to stand to move to him, but the room twisted and darkened before I'd even gotten off my knees, and I sagged back down to the floor. "Come here and take off your shirt so I can see just how many ribs you've broken."

The muscles in his jaw flexed and his expression grew icier. But he got up, knelt before me, and pulled off his ruined T-shirt, revealing an angry patchwork of second degree burns and lacerations, many of which were oozing blood, along with bruises and swelling skin.

Hawk drew in a sharp breath. "Jeez. I'd hate to see how bad it gets that you can't manage."

"I fought on the front line in the war. I've been hurt worse," Cassius said, his voice gruff.

My throat tightened. He *had* been hurt worse. A number of times. And every time he'd come back to me a little harder and colder.

I ran my hands over his ribs trying not to think about his pain or how stunning he normally looked or how much I still ached with desire.

Because I had no magic, I had to put pressure on each rib and judge by feel and his reaction to determine how many were actually cracked or broken. "You've got three broken ribs on your left side, and I'm worried about two more on your right."

This was going to take a lot more magic than just healing lacerations. If Sebastian wanted me to stop all of the bleeding, I was going to have to heal Cassius's ribs first — and no way was I going to let him use his fire magic to burn the rest of his wounds shut.

"Titus?" I asked, turning to the dragon. He looked the best out of everyone, but then the people who'd attacked us weren't trying to kill him, just hurt him enough to abduct him. Yes, his shirt was also ripped and bloody, but I suspected the lacerations weren't serious, and even if they were, Titus was a fast healer.

"If we sit here for a few hours, I'll be fine," Titus said.

Hawk huffed. "The angel said honest inventory. I saw you get run through with a sword. A shifter can't heal that fast in a few hours."

"It wasn't that bad." Titus shrugged, and I didn't know if he was telling the truth or lying to hide how fast he healed. As it was, there was no blood gathering around him and his complexion was good, so he'd probably be in decent shape by the time I had enough magic to heal Cassius's ribs.

I shifted my attention back to Sebastian and fought to keep my expression even. It wasn't good if your physician looked worried, but he looked terrible. The blood pool by his leg had grown in the few minutes we'd been talking, his breath was shallow, and the light in his skin still hadn't recovered.

"I was cut a few times and I think the one on my thigh is pretty deep," he said.

"Let me see." I prayed it wouldn't need a tourniquet. I'd already need at least five hours of rest to recover enough magic to heal Cassius's ribs and cuts. That would leave the tourniquet on for too long, which could cause nerve damage and would require even more magic to fix.

He shifted so I could get a better look at the nasty laceration on the side of his upper right thigh without any comment about needing to take his pants off.

Jeez, he really was in bad shape.

I tore the hole in his pantleg wider and tried to get a good look without having anything to wipe the blood away.

The wound was deep and long, and blood flowed slowly and steadily. It cut through muscle, but, given the pace of his blood loss and the laceration's location, he'd gotten lucky and no major vessels had been severed. Yes, it would take at least a few more hours of rest for me to recover enough magic to heal it and any other injuries he had, but he wasn't in immediate danger.

"I'd like to just bind this and avoid a tourniquet. Take off your shirt."

"Pretty sure that's the wrong article of clothing. Or do you finally want to see me naked?" Sebastian's lips quirked and a glimmer of the annoying man I knew flickered in his pale eyes. Thank goodness.

"You have the cleanest shirt," I said, too exhausted and worried and relieved to give him the reaction he was probably looking for.

He unbuttoned his shirt and shrugged out of it as I fought to keep my expression even. He was even more breathtaking than Cassius, with his sculpted muscles and the dark tattoos swirling over him, and I'd clearly lost my mind because I couldn't stop thinking about sex.

I handed the dress shirt to Titus, who was the most capable of the group to make me a bandage with his strength and claws. "Please tear off the longest piece you can."

"Sure." Titus took the shirt and, with a sharp claw, cut a piece off the bottom, keeping the seams intact to make one long strip.

"So, given everyone's injuries and the fact that we can't lose a drop of blood, we're going to be here for a while." I took the rest of the shirt from Titus and folded it into a makeshift dressing and pressed it against Sebastian's wound. "Hold this here. I'll need at least eight hours of rest."

Which meant eight more hours magically bound to Titus.

No. I can handle this. I'm strong. Just a little longer.

Sebastian held the dressing in place and I secured it with the bandage Titus had cut.

"I'll need less if I can fall asleep, but given that we've just run for our lives and have people hunting us, I doubt I'd be able to relax enough to get a deep enough sleep. Unless…" Sebastian had a sleep glyph. But was I comfortable enough around these men to be magically put to sleep?

And did it really matter? We couldn't hide there forever. We needed to get back to Sebastian's apartment, and the sooner the better. Having to wait six hours was bad enough. What I was and wasn't comfortable with was nothing compared to the danger we were in.

"If you use your sleep glyph," I said to Sebastian, "we can take two hours off the time I need. Do you have enough power for that?" Technically, because he was a sorcerer he had all the power in Faerie, but the more exhausted he was, the harder it would be to control the flow into his body and avoid burning up.

"Six is better than eight," Sebastian said. "Get comfortable."

"Is it even safe to be here for that long?" Hawk asked.

Cassius wiped away the blood from the gash over his eye. "It'll have to be."

I settled against the pillar beside Sebastian so he wouldn't have to move to put me to sleep. It wasn't the most comfortable way to sleep, and I didn't know how I felt about passing out beside him, but I didn't really have much of an option since I didn't want to make him move and make the laceration in his thigh worse.

With a soft word, Sebastian activated his sleep glyph, pressed his hand over my heart, and a cool thread of his magic slipped into me, bringing with it a frustrating shiver of desire.

I bit back a groan. I shouldn't be thinking about sex. Even if I was pretty sure Sebastian wasn't my soul mate, we were running for our lives. That, and he'd already made it clear he wasn't interested.

Why did my desire keep going back to him? If I really wanted my first time to be with someone experienced, Hawk was the one to go to. He at least was interested. Of course, he was an incubus, he was always interested. But that also meant he wouldn't fall in love — well, it was rare if an incubus did — which meant the odds of Hawk being my soul mate were even less than Sebastian's.

Hmm. Maybe when all of this was done I *would* seek out Hawk.

SEBASTIAN

Amiah's eyes closed as my sleep spell took her, and she sagged against me, her head on my shoulder. Just that little touch made my already hard cock harder.

I was going to fucking kill Hawk. It was bad enough his magic made me hard as hell, but then to make Amiah come twice right in front of me—

I bit back a groan. She'd come in front of *all* of us. The show hadn't just been for me... which wasn't really a problem for me, either.

And man, when her guard was down and that bitchy ice queen act was gone, she was so fucking sexy. The sounds she'd made and the look on her face when she came... and that had just been a taste. It was obvious she'd tried to hide her reaction to Hawk's magic, and that he'd only given her a small amount of it — full power, and she would have come screaming then passed out. What would she be like if she truly let go?

And why the fuck did I want to make that happen? I wasn't interested in her. I didn't even like her.

Except the image of her lying on the ground suffocating flashed through my mind's eye and a whisper of the panic I'd felt trembled through me... because she was a valuable healer and leashed to Titus. That was all.

She sighed, turned into me, and wrapped her arm across my waist.

Her warm breath feathered across my bare chest which brought back the memory of Hawk kissing her, his hand shoved down the front of her dress, and the mewling gasp she'd made.

Fuck. I couldn't do this.

I raised my gaze to Cassius sitting across from me. Wisps of smoke curled from his hands, a precursor to his fire reigniting, which would be bad for Amiah. Titus, to my left, was tense. Holding Amiah would be good for him, but he, too, probably had a raging hard on from Hawk's magic and the man had been imprisoned for half a millennium. Letting him be her pillow right now would be cruel.

Which left Hawk, who I wasn't handing her to, and me.

Swell.

"So," Hawk said with a smirk that said he knew exactly what his magic and Amiah had done to me. Asshole. "I'm not going to be able to return to my business even after our blood samples degrade, am I?"

"Not until things with Titus are cleared up," I replied, struggling to keep my tone even and not show how much I needed my own release not to mention the agony of the demonic magic screaming through my body from the fight. He already knew I was infected with power from the Realm of Celestial Darkness. I couldn't let him see how badly it affected me.

Except every inch of me burned like I'd been dipped in acid, and the pain wasn't letting up because I had to keep pushing power into my group concealment glyph. I couldn't even feel my injuries. The only reason I'd known the cut in my leg had been bad was because of the growing pool of blood on the floor beside me.

I shouldn't have cast that last force-wave. I shouldn't have woven in sleep, which meant I'd needed to weave in an exclusion for Titus, Cassius, and Hawk. I'd needed to channel too much raw magic to do all that and I was paying for it now.

But Amiah had been dying, and as much as I hated to admit it, I'd panicked.

Cassius sat forward. "What exactly are *things*?" He frowned. "And why did Amiah nearly die but Titus could keep fighting?"

"His leash has to be longer. I must have stretched it when I first tried to break the spell." And I really didn't want to think about that because that meant the spell was completely warped and was going to be challenging to rip apart even with a perfectly attuned resonance charm.

"I don't think my end is as strong, either," Titus said. "I felt a pressure and there were moments when it was hard to breathe, but it didn't come close to suffocating me. I thought she was okay." He clenched his hands and stared at Amiah, his gaze so intense it hurt to watch. "Things are only going to get worse. You have to separate us."

"One problem at a time." The demonic magic swelled. I bit back a groan and Hawk's eyes narrowed. "We can't risk another mess like that. We need to get a proper concealment spell and glamour on you first."

If I could get a concealment spell on Titus along with a glamour that changed his appearance as well as his essence, we could run and hide until this mess blew over.

But the Spring Court was now involved and unlike the Shadow Court, they'd go after everyone who'd had contact with Titus. Amiah, Cassius, and Hawk were now in the middle of it, and it was going to be hard to convince the angels to abandon their lives until Faerie's Heart went back to sleep.

Except they were going to have to if they wanted to live... or until one of us could come up with a better plan to defend ourselves against all of the courts in Faerie.

"I thought you said breaking the leash spell was our first priority." Fire sparked from Cassius's hands even though his expression remained hard. "Amiah almost died. We've set the resonance charm, what more do you need?"

"To recover all the magic I spent saving her ass. Just like she needs sleep, so do I." The demonic magic swelled again, stealing my breath. Fuck. "Breaking the leash spell will use a lot of magic which will leave me vulnerable."

"And you think the original caster will be able to sense the spell when you pull it apart and use that to track you?" Hawk asked.

"Isn't that what you wanted?" Cassius asked. "To lure those men to us so I can arrest them."

"That was before the Spring Court showed up a hell of a lot sooner than I anticipated." Plus, despite my confidence earlier, a part of me feared that shadow fae had somehow seen through my glamour and recognized me, which was why he'd come after me again and let his friends go after Titus.

I'd hoped after all these years Deaglan had given up on trying to kill me. And maybe he had. No one had come looking for me for over a century. Running into me was probably just a bonus to his hunt for Titus.

"So that's why those men from the park ring were killing the other guys coming after us," Cassius said.

"Is that also why half of those guys who looked like humans were glamoured?" Hawk asked. "They weren't really human, were they?"

"No. They were spring fae. Their seneschal, Balwyrdan, is a sorcerer with a particular talent for glamour." Only those with a high magic sensitivity were able to sense his glamour, and even then, you had to be on guard to catch it. Just one of the many reasons I'd gotten out of Faerie.

Balwyrdan also had a vicious streak. I'd been surprised to see him commanding the spring fae assault team, and even more surprised he hadn't joined the fight.

"The fae might not be members of the Joined Parliament, but they do recognize the mortal realm as a sovereign realm," Cassius said. "They can't just come here and kill people, just like we can't go there and kill people."

Hawk snorted. "I'm pretty sure they don't care."

"Because Faerie's Heart has awakened," Titus said, shifting. The movement inched him closer to Amiah and I didn't know if he'd done that on purpose or not. "You have the Heart, you control Faerie."

"And by control Faerie, he means the very essence of the realm. You can remake it as you see fit, eliminate whole courts, kill thousands with a thought, and lock away the magic of the realm from others until they wither and die." It was a fucking nightmare and all the courts should have banded together to destroy it the first time it had manifested over two millennia ago.

But the court monarchs had been greedy. They still were. And only the dragons had had the wherewithal to lock it away.

Except that was all they'd been able to do. It would have taken the combined effort of half a dozen full sorcerers to destroy it, and even locking it away had backfired, linking all of dragonkind to the Heart, making them compasses to the keys that could release it.

"So how are you involved in this?" Cassius asked, turning his hard glare on Titus, who didn't notice because he was still staring at Amiah.

"Dragons have an innate connection to the Heart," I said. "They—"

Titus's gaze jumped to me and for a second he had the same look he'd had when he'd realized he was the last dragon.

God. I was the worst friend ever. I'd let him suffer in captivity and now I'd reminded him he was alone.

"Titus can find the keys to unlock the Heart. No one else can." The demonic magic inside me surged, making me gasp, and Amiah's hand slid from my waist up to my heart, her palm warm against my skin, as if even in sleep she was trying to heal me. Except all she'd done was remind me of how much I needed to fuck someone. "The courts won't stop coming after Titus until the Heart goes back to sleep."

"And when will that be?" Cassius asked.

"I don't know," Titus replied. "No one does."

"That's not the worst of it." I set Amiah's hands back in her lap and turned her slightly away from me. With luck, she'd keep her hands to herself until Hawk's magic had left my system — hopefully by finding someone to sleep with and not having to wait it out for the long fucking hours it would take to work its way out of my system. "The Shadow Court will only come after me and Titus. I'm not familiar with this team, but so far, they've behaved like the other Shadow Court teams I've seen. They stay in the shadows and strike quickly and efficiently."

"There was nothing about staying in the shadows in Lincoln," Hawk said.

"Because those other guys forced their hand," Cassius said, showing his combat experience by seeing through the chaos of that fight. "They couldn't afford for the spring fae's greater numbers to overwhelm Titus. In fact, it looked like they were willing to let Titus get away to ensure the spring fae didn't get him."

"The spring fae's team isn't as powerful as the Shadow Court's, but they have greater numbers and they don't care who sees them," I continued. "They'll also go after everyone involved with Titus even if Titus is no longer around."

Hawk rubbed his face, his expression growing more concerned. "Why the hell would they do that?"

"Information. Leverage," Cassius said, his voice low. "Possibly to cover Titus's tracks. If the others going after him don't know or can't find who he's been in contact with that could give the Spring Court an advantage."

"Two more points for the angel," I said.

"Jeez. Fuck this." Hawk sat forward. "I'm not just up and leaving my life. There has to be something we can do that's better than waiting for who-knows-how-long for this to blow over."

"I agree." Cassius glanced at Amiah and his angel glow flared.

I had no idea how she hadn't figured out he was in love with her. It was painfully obvious. Honest-to-goodness in love, not just wanting to sleep with her. Of course, there were times it seemed that she wasn't even aware of — or perhaps didn't want to acknowledge — her own sexuality, so the fact that she was oblivious to Cassius's desires shouldn't have surprised me. And while almost every angel I'd come across was uptight, Amiah took that to a whole other level... which was why it was so much fun to keep pushing that particular button.

"We can't take on all the courts," Cassius continued. "What are our other options?"

"You should kill me," Titus said. "That will solve everything. That will keep everyone safe."

"Really? Have you forgotten what Balwyrdan is like?" No one was sacrificing themselves to this ridiculous cause. "Even if you're dead, he'll come after us out of spite so your death would be a waste, and that doesn't account for the other monarchs and their seneschals or warlords. We hide until the Heart goes back to sleep."

"And what about in five hundred years or a thousand or whenever it reawakens and I go through this again?" Titus asked, his voice low, *still* not looking away from Amiah. Jeez.

Maybe I should have told him to be her pillow. And maybe he was just as horny as I was and was staring at her because she was the only woman in the room.

"The last time I lost my kin and then I lost my freedom," he said. "What will I lose this time or the next?"

"No one is killing you." The light in Cassius's eyes flared. "Amiah would kill herself trying to save you and I won't let that happen. If it's a race to get the Heart then we have to win."

"You want to go after it?" I couldn't have heard that correctly. That was crazy and everything I knew about Cassius said he didn't do crazy. "Going after the Heart would make us bigger targets. The minute the courts figure out what we're doing it won't just be the Spring Court coming after all of us, it'll be all of the courts, and Amiah will be in the middle of it."

"Amiah is in danger regardless," he said his voice hard and icy. "There's no guarantee that we'll be able to hide until the Heart goes back to sleep. It needs to be destroyed or lock away for good or we need it for leverage. Whatever we do, it means we have to get it. What other option do we have?"

"I vote for the option that doesn't get me killed," Hawk said.

Cassius's eyes narrowed. "And which one would that be?"

Hawk glared back at Cassius, his hands clenched as if he wanted to punch the angel. "Not the one where we join a treasure hunt where the competitors are trying to kill each other."

"You're welcome to sit around and hope someone doesn't come after you." Cassius turned his attention to me. "If we can get the Heart, we can redirect the courts' attentions away from Amiah and Titus. What are the possibilities that you can destroy or permanently locked away this thing? No one should ever have absolute control over anyone let alone a whole realm."

I had to agree with that… and fuck, I also had to agree with his assessment of the situation. "I don't have the power to destroy it or permanently lock it away." Even if I wasn't infected with demonic magic, I doubted I'd be able to channel enough raw magic to destroy it or lock it away without burning up. "But you're right. The only play we have is to get the Heart."

And then pray it would actually be enough to protect us.

AMIAH

I woke to someone brushing my hair out of my face, the caress cool and gentle, and a hot throbbing ache in my hip from my mating brand. I knew I had to get up and heal the guys, but I didn't want to move. I didn't want to face the reality of my situation, leashed to Titus and with a worse fate coming my way. I wanted to just savor this touch, this closeness. I missed it so much, felt so unsteady without it, and I had no idea if I'd ever get anything like what I had with Marcus with someone else.

"Time to get up," Sebastian said, and I looked up into his pale, almost colorless gaze. There wasn't a hint of mischief or flirtation in his eyes. This was the man who'd tried to reassure me when I'd first been panicking about the leash spell and offered me something to sleep in. His complexion was still gray, but not nearly as bad as before which meant he must have recovered a little magic as well even though he was still powering the concealment glyph.

"If you stay there much longer," Hawk drawled, "he's going to expect you to do more than just lie there."

Sebastian's lips quirked.

"He's what—" My brain kicked in, clearing my sleepy thoughts. My head was in Sebastian's lap, right beside—

Heat rushed across my face — not just with embarrassment — and I quickly sat up. Hawk might have inside knowledge of my desires, but no one else needed to know them. I could only pray that once the spring fae could no longer track him, he'd go on his merry way.

It was bad enough Sebastian kept teasing me. I didn't want to have to deal with two of them. And I doubted propositioning Hawk and arranging for something later would get him to stop.

"How are you feeling?" Cassius asked, now sitting at the edge of the cave-in where we'd entered, his breath shallow, likely to ease the pain of his broken ribs and possibly the nasty burns on his torso.

I closed my eyes and focused on my magic. It welled in my palms, hot and warm and thick. Almost at three-quarters of what it should be, which was a little more than I anticipated I'd recover with six hours of sleep.

"I'm good. Unless any of you've lied to me, I should be able to heal everyone and have a little to spare." If, of course, I was smart about how I used it. And I was going to be smart because I had no idea when I'd need to heal them again.

I dropped my gaze to Sebastian's thigh. He was the closest. Might as well heal him first. He'd bled through the makeshift dressing and bandage, but the blood that had pooled on the floor beside him had dried, which meant he hadn't lost much more while I was asleep.

Blood oozed from the wound when I untied the bandage and I quickly pressed my hands against it. Even though I had enough magic to push my power through clothing, directly connecting with the injury was always the best.

My magic swelled into my palms, warm and strong, and, while concentrating on controlling its flow, I pushed it into the wound. It slid between his cells, thick and viscous, tugging them together and mending muscle and flesh before a thread split off toward the next most serious wound, a cut in the back of his shoulder. My magic split again and again and soon every injury was sealed shut and I pulled my power out of him.

"The wounds will still be pink and a little sore," I said, sitting back on my heels, "but I'd rather hold back as much magic as possible just in case."

"Just means you'll have to come back to finish the job." Sebastian flashed me his wicked smile, making my body heat, and I rolled my eyes at him, trying to hide the fact that his proposition excited me more than bothered me.

I really had reached my breaking point, and it was getting harder to care about the fact that I wanted to throw years of restraint out the window. I wanted more of the sensations I'd gotten from Hawk, but I also wanted to be touched and kissed and held more. So much more it was getting harder to remember that I needed to be careful and not get too close to anyone who could be a potential soul mate.

I got up and sat beside Cassius, who tensed when I placed my hands on his bare skin, probably anticipating the pain of a quick healing.

"I'll go slow. There's no need to do this quickly," I said. "We've already spent six hours here, what's a few more minutes?"

"Yeah," he said, his voice gruff, and he drew in a shallow, shuddering breath that did little to relax him.

Without waiting for another breath — I didn't need him to relax and I doubted he would — I pushed a gentle thread of magic into him. It flowed straight to his broken ribs, enveloping the bones and knitting them back together.

Again, I concentrated on slowing the flow of magic and withdrew it once all of his ribs were mended but before completely healing his burns. Now they looked like they'd been painful a month ago instead of only a few minutes, and if I didn't finish healing him, he'd have thick ugly scars marring his stunning body, but he wasn't going to be leaving a blood trail, which was the point of the exercise.

I moved to Titus next, who kept his gaze locked on the ground by his feet, refusing to look at me. He also tensed when I touched him to confirm he wasn't bleeding, but I didn't press either issue. As much as he'd held me after the pain of the failed attempt to break the leash spell, we didn't know each other. He didn't owe me or anyone eye contact let alone anything else. And while I didn't know exactly what he was feeling, I suspected he was still dealing with a mess of confusing emotions from his captivity and recent escape.

With everyone healed, we found concrete stairs at the back of the room that led up to what once was an opulent foyer of a fancy hotel, and walked out onto an abandoned street.

Less than half of the buildings still stood and there wasn't a soul in sight. And thank goodness for that because two of the guys were shirtless and everyone was covered in blood making us stand out.

The sun was well past noon, the day hot and humid, and it continued to sink as we made our way back through the ruined and deserted streets to Sebastian's car. No one wanted to call a taxi — if one would even drive into the neighborhood — and no one wanted to call a friend.

I was filled in about our situation, about how more fae were after us and would be after anyone we had contact with. Cassius had sent a text to Chris telling him not to dig too deeply into the mess at Left of Lincoln and that he and I had to go dark for an undetermined amount of time.

I couldn't imagine how hard that had to have been since that meant Cassius was abandoning his job again. We were clearly breaking the rules, and we'd surely get written up again or fired this time, especially since he hadn't given Chris an explanation.

The idea of disobeying protocol made my insides churn, but not nearly as much as endangering someone just because I talked with them.

Hawk and Sebastian had both cleared their schedules, and Sebastian had told Nova to leave town, which was why we were walking back to the sedan. They, like Cassius, had destroyed their phones and scattered the pieces as we went, leaving us without a way to communicate but also safe from being tracked that way.

I tried not to think about how I was even more trapped than I was before or about the reckless plan to go after Faerie's Heart. Except that meant thinking about my aching need, which wasn't any better, or my throbbing brand, which was even worse.

It took us an hour to get back to the car, and we piled into the oven-on-wheels with me in the back with Hawk and Cassius — thankfully with Cassius in the middle and me cramped against the door so I wouldn't have to sit beside Hawk.

It didn't take us long to drive back to the Quarter. But instead of returning to Sebastian's underground garage, we parked at the end of an alley in the middle of Squatter's Row.

The Row was a neighborhood on the far side of the Quarter that, because the supers' population was still relatively small, had yet to be redeveloped. Most of the buildings were in good shape, having survived the war like the rest of the Quarter, but had no electricity, gas, or running water and weren't supposed to have tenants. However, those who didn't care about the lack of utilities, or had no other choice, had taken up residence in many of the buildings.

For the most part, the JP ignored the area, letting the individual species police their own and saving their resources for more powerful and dangerous criminals. But that meant most *businesses* in the Row offered less than legal services, and I was pretty sure we'd arrived at one such business since we needed illegal concealment charms.

Sebastian shut off the engine and turned to Cassius. "Don't be a dick and arrest Mavis once this mess has blown over."

"I managed to get in and out of the market without arresting anyone," Cassius huffed.

Sebastian quirked an eyebrow. "How much of that was because we ended up running for our lives?"

"I gave my word. I give it now." Cassius nudged me, and I opened the door and got out.

"And an angel's word is everything," Hawk said with mock innocence.

"It is." The light in Cassius's eyes flared. "So trust me when I say if you use your magic on Amiah again without her consent I will lock you up for assault."

Hawk snorted and slid out of the car with a grace that made me shiver with need. Only an incubus could make something so mundane look so sexy. "That would require you having access to a jail."

"Would you rather I just burn you?" Cassius got out and slammed the door, smoke curling around his hands.

Oh yeah, agreeing to all work together to get Faerie's Heart was a great plan.

"So now you're judge, jury, and executioner," Hawk said. "Didn't know *that* was the law."

"Extenuating circumstance," Cassius growled back.

"So we're all agreed," Sebastian said, heading down the alley. "You want to get it on with Amiah, you need Cassius's permission."

He did *not* just say that!

"There will be no *getting it on* with Amiah," Cassius insisted.

Oh, my God. And neither did he!

"There'll be whatever I want," I snapped. Jeez. Even with Hawk's seductive magic tempting me, I was perfectly capable of taking care of myself... or rather in my current situation asking someone to take care of me. "You don't get a say in who I do and do not have intercourse with. None of you do."

I jerked my head indicating they should follow Sebastian. Cassius stared at me, shocked, clearly thinking — and rightly so — that I was keeping open the possibility of having sex with Hawk, while Hawk's gaze turned hungry, clearly coming to the same conclusion. Titus still wouldn't look at me, and with a growl, he strode after Sebastian.

Heat seeped across my cheeks and I squared my shoulders. If I wanted to sleep with someone, I would. If I wanted to take a page out of Essie's book and take multiple lovers, I would... just as soon as I was free of my mating brand and the risk of being permanently bound to someone was gone. Oh, and we were no longer being hunted by all of Faerie.

AMIAH

I hurried to catch up with Sebastian and Titus as they reached a plain metal security door that opened into a long hall. A low light coming from everywhere and yet nowhere filled the hall along with a purple haze with a cloyingly sweet smell. Cool air that could only have been chilled by magic swept over my skin, drawing goose bumps, and a heavy sense of dread settled in my chest.

"Cut the theatrics, Mavis," Sebastian said. "You know it's me."

"And you're not welcome," a raspy alto replied as a woman with dark skin and wild dark hair barely contained by a gold multi-strand chain headpiece stepped into the hall.

She wore a billowy yellow blouse cinched at the waist by a black corset that drew the eye immediately to her ample cleavage, and a full gauzy skirt, also yellow, that, when she shifted, turned partially see-through, giving a teasing glimpse of her legs.

"No more referrals. No more angels and pretty boys and whatever the hell you are." She jabbed her finger at Titus, making the numerous gold and silver chains around her neck and bracelets around her wrists tinkle and catch the dim light.

"I can pay," Sebastian said.

"You don't have enough money to pay me, after sending the JP here to make me cast illegal concealment charms."

The sense of dread grew, twisting in my chest, and I took an involuntary step back, bumping into Cassius.

Hawk shifted past me and a whisper of his seductive magic caressed my skin. "We'd be grateful on top of paying," he said, his tone clear that *grateful* meant he'd sleep with her. "We really need your services."

"Of course you do. You all look like you've lost a fight. Let me guess." She propped her hands on her hips. "You all need concealment charms."

"And a glamour for the big guy," Sebastian said.

Her gaze flickered back to Hawk as if she was seriously considering his offer. "No."

"It's a matter of life and death," Cassius said.

"With an angel it always is," she huffed.

"Mavis." Sebastian drew closer to her and her gaze slowly slid down his body as if she couldn't help herself from appreciating his fine physique and the tattoos swirling over it. "Do I need to remind you who holds the cards here? The wrong word to the wrong person..." He shrugged and the pale light emanating from his body rippled over him. "Take my money."

Her eyes narrowed. "I want the incubus, too."

"You've already turned him down," Sebastian replied before Hawk could. "Take fair payment for the job and be done with it."

She glared at him and Sebastian cocked an eyebrow.

"Fine. Whatever." The sense of dread vanished, and she jerked around and stormed into a large room lit by dozens of thick candles.

Dark wood bookcases crammed with boxes and books and other magical paraphernalia lined the walls, and to the right sat a short length of stainless-steel counter, sink, and stove that looked like they belonged in a commercial kitchen. The counter was cluttered with jars, pots, and bowls, the sink full with dirty dishes, and a large pot sat on the stove. The element on the stove was off, but I had no doubt even though the building didn't have power, the element worked, powered by magic like her air conditioning.

In the middle of the room were an intricately carved wooden table and a matching high-backed chair. Mavis took a metal box with a complicated glyph carved on the lid from one of the shelves and sat. With a resigned sigh, she flipped open the box. Inside, on a bed of red silk, lay a thin knife, a small jar with dark ink, a thin paintbrush, and a handful of coins with another complicated glyph etched on them. Everything she needed to cast an illegal concealment spell.

"Who's first?" She pointed to a stool across the table from her.

"Titus, with a concealment and a glamour, then Amiah. Just concealment," Sebastian said. "They're leashed, so you're going to need extra juice."

Mavis's eyebrows shot up. "I'll need to use external magic to set the spells." She flicked her finger and another metal box floated from the shelf behind her and landed on the table. "You're lucky I have a full orb. It's double for the two of them and I expect you to refill the orb."

"Agreed, but I can't refill it today."

"Of course you can't." She rolled her eyes at him and turned her attention to Titus. "You're up, big man."

"The glamour doesn't have to be significant," Sebastian said. "Just a shift in his facial structure, eye color, hair color, and a change of his essence. A wolf or bear would probably be easiest."

"Want to lean over my shoulder and watch me do it, too?" she asked as Titus settled on the stool across from her. "Give me your wrist."

Titus, his whole body so tense it broke my heart, set his hand on the table. Mavis flipped it over so the inside of his wrist faced up, dipped the paintbrush in the ink, and drew a simple glyph on his skin. Then she picked up the knife.

"Cassius should probably sterilize that," I said before she cut Titus. Given the pile of dirty dishes in the sink, I wasn't going to assume the blade was clean.

Mavis rolled her eyes. "Angels are a pain in the ass."

Yeah well, better a pain than have to deal with gangrene. I bit the inside of my cheek. She was going to cast a spell on me next. It was best not to upset her.

She handed the knife to Cassius who wrapped the blade with fire for a moment then handed it back to her. With another eye roll, Mavis made an incision through the glyph the diameter of the coin, hissed a sharp word, and set the coin in the blood oozing out of Titus's wrist.

"You might want to sit," Sebastian said, drawing up beside me and grabbing my elbow.

"Sit?" I didn't like the sound of that. I looked around for a chair or another stool but didn't see any.

Mavis opened the other box and pulled out a glowing marble filled with magical power. She clenched it in her fist, the light bleeding out between her fingers, hissed a long string of words, and the weight of the leash spell slammed into my chest.

Oh, my goodness!

My knees gave out and Sebastian caught me. He swept me into his arms, cradling me against his chest, and I fought against the spell's weight to regain my breath.

"You could have mentioned this earlier," I gasped. At least the air was still around me... although it felt thin. Or perhaps that was just because each shallow breath was a painful struggle.

"I should have," he said. He squeezed his eyes shut and the muscles in his jaw flexed. "Just concentrating on a lot of things right now."

"Are you all right?" Cassius asked, drawing close, the light in his eyes blazing.

I didn't know how to answer that. I was being crushed from the inside by a spell that every fiber of my being screamed I had to be free of.

Mavis hissed a few more words. The magic in her fist flared, blindingly bright making my eyes water, and the coin sunk into Titus's skin. The pressure increased, shooting agony through me, and I clenched my teeth against a groan.

Titus also tensed, and his breath grew ragged.

"Amiah?" Cassius asked.

"I'll be okay," I forced out. "It'll be over soon." *Please let it be over soon.*

Sweat beaded on the back of Titus's neck, his fingers extended into claws, and he dug the ones on his free hand into Mavis's table. The air around him wavered, like heat radiating off hot asphalt on a summer's day, and the pressure grew.

Dark specks crept at the edge of my vision, and my breath grew shallower.

Mavis hissed another word, and Titus's hair darkened to a warm brown and his essence shifted, now clearly saying he was a wolf.

Please be over. Please. I wasn't going to be able to take much more.

Another hissed word, and the pressure, along with most of the blazing glow from the marble, vanished. One minute I was being crushed to death, the next nothing. It made the world jerk, the sudden change jarring.

Mavis sat back with a gasp as I drew in desperate quick breaths, trying to clear my vision and steady myself.

"Next," she said, sweat glistening on her forehead despite the cool temperature. "And I don't want to hear any complaints about the glamour."

Titus stood and turned to face us. Except it wasn't Titus facing us, it was a still-big, but average looking guy. He now had brown hair and eyes and a slightly crooked nose. His once rugged appearance had softened and, if I really thought about it, he didn't seem quite as imposing as before.

"It's boring and perfect," Sebastian said, setting me on my feet by the stool.

I sat, my nerves thrumming and my chest still sore. I really didn't want to experience that pressure again, but I didn't have any other choice. Even if the plan was to hide until Faerie's Heart went back to sleep, I'd still need the charm.

Mavis cracked her neck and rolled her shoulders, and I placed my arm on the table while Cassius sterilized the knife again, my attention stalling on my bloody hands, the blood a mix of Cassius's and Sebastian's.

Mavis noticed the blood too and, with a hint of a smile, tsked.

"Let me take care of that for you." She closed her eyes, and the blood pebbled into droplets on my skin even though it was mostly dried. It rolled off my skin, onto the table, and gathered in the groove at the edge.

"Gee, Mavis," Sebastian said, "what do you take me for?"

"What do you mean?" she asked, batting her eyelashes at him.

Did that work with any man?

"Really?" Sebastian asked incredulously. With a sigh, he pressed a small glyph on his chest, lighting it up, and the blood evaporated. "You honestly think I'd let you get away with collecting my blood?"

"Oh, well, you know." Mavis shrugged. "I had to try."

"Sure you did, and I'll just accidentally say the wrong thing to the wrong person." He cocked an eyebrow and her eyes narrowed all pretense of innocence gone. "Cast the spell, Mavis."

With a huff, she jerked her attention back to my wrist, painted on the simple glyph, and made her incision. She hissed the same sharp word from before, set a coin on the now-bloody glyph, and picked up the marble, which now glowed a third as brightly as before. Three more hissed words started her spell, and the crushing weight of the leash spell returned.

This time I did groan, unable to hold it back, and out of the corner of my eye I saw Cassius jerk forward and Sebastian put a hand on his chest to remind him to stay back.

Another hissed word and agony sliced through me with each panting breath. Specks of light and darkness flashed across my vision, and the room lurched.

I clenched my teeth and fought to hold on. It wouldn't take long. *Please, don't let it take long.* I'd never had a concealment spell on me before. I knew from talking with active agents that it was a pretty quick and simple spell. Surely my spell would be quicker than Titus's because he'd also needed a glamour.

The pressure swelled and I leaned onto the table, unable to keep myself upright. Then the coin sank under my skin, taking the blood and ink with it, along with the enormous weight from the leash spell and leaving no evidence that Mavis had cast the spell.

Gasping, I sagged against the table, tears I was *not* going to cry burning my eyes. At least I'd been right and it hadn't taken as long as Titus's spell.

Cassius tugged on my arm, urging me to stand, and helped me stagger to the stainless-steel counter, where I leaned against it, trying not to look like I was shaking. It was bad enough I'd looked weak since Hawk's tent. Much more and Cassius wouldn't want to let me out of his sight or go anywhere or do anything... which was just as bad as being trapped by a spell or a soul bond.

"You okay?" he asked, his angel glow bright with worry.

"Yeah. Sebastian will break the leash spell tomorrow and things will get—" Well, they wouldn't go back to normal, not with the Spring Court coming after us, but they would get better. I'd no longer be trapped. I could leave if I wanted to. It wouldn't be safe or wise, but I could. *Please, I had to.*

Except I wanted to leave *now*. My soul screamed. I had to be free. I'd sworn I'd never be someone's prisoner again, never be foolish or reckless enough for someone to take me and hurt me again. Never be so helpless.

I dropped my gaze, afraid he'd be able to see the fear squeezing my chest.

"Things will get... less restrictive," I said, awkwardly finishing what I was going to say.

He brushed a finger across my cheek, drawing my gaze back up to him, and tucked a strand of hair behind my ear.

The gentle action surprised me. He'd never touched me like that before. He barely ever touched me because touching wasn't appropriate for angelic friends, and the sudden soft contact ignited my desire... because everything right now seemed to make me yearn for sex, which then made me angry with myself. I had more control than this. I'd had over a hundred years of proof of my control.

"I'll make this right," he said.

"You're up, Cassius," Sebastian said as Hawk got up from the stool.

"I promise." A whisper of smoke curled around him and he took Hawk's place in front of Mavis.

Hawk sidled up to me, rubbing his wrist where Mavis had implanted the charm, his hellfire banked and his gaze appraising. "You are one complicated woman. When was the last time you got any?"

"Excuse me?" I don't know why it surprised me that he was so blunt.

"Sex," he said, lowering his voice. "You're awfully tense. When was the last time you had sex? And I don't mean the little treats I gave you today."

"You've already made your offer. Do you honestly think now is an appropriate time?"

"Baby, I'm an incubus," he said and a curl of his seductive magic caressed my cheek, mimicking Cassius's touch and making me throb with need. "There's nothing appropriate about me." He leaned in close, his demonic heat radiating from his body and his breath feathering across my neck making my pulse pick up. "And there's nothing appropriate about you, either."

"My situation is complicated." Why had I just said that? I should have just rejected him. Even if I wanted to take him up on his offer, now certainly wasn't the time.

"More complicated than being leashed to a man wanted by all of Faerie?" he asked and his magic seeped across my chest and started to sink.

"Yes," I breathed. Oh, my goodness! I had to get ahold of myself.

"Which is why you need to do more to relieve your stress."

I squared my shoulders determined to resist his magic. "What I need is food and sleep." *And to get free.*

My panic surged, overwhelming my desire.

Hawk's hellfire snapped to tiny red pinpricks and he shifted away from me, his hands raised. "Hey, I'm not going to *make* you do anything," he said thankfully mistaking my fear for fear that he'd manipulate me into doing something I didn't want to do. "It's no fun if you don't really want it."

"So you think I wanted you to kiss me in the abandoned bathhouse?" I asked, realizing as I said the words how stupid they were. I hadn't expected his kiss, but I'd certainly wanted it, and Hawk with his ability to sense sexual desire knew it.

He cocked an eyebrow. "Pretty sure you wanted more than just a kiss. Pretty sure you still do."

Thankfully, Sebastian stepped close, rubbing his wrist like Hawk had, saving me from coming up with a response and drawing Hawk's intense gaze away from me.

"We're all done," Sebastian said. "Can you walk?"

"Yes," I replied, my voice still embarrassingly breathy.

I clamped down on my emotions and pushed past Hawk, hurrying down the hall, out the metal door, and into the stifling summer heat.

This was getting out of hand. I had to regain my control. Somehow. I just had no idea how.

Shadows filled the alley and dusk was starting to darken the sky. My stomach rumbled and exhaustion dragged at my senses. It had been a long day and I'd only eaten once and spent all of my magic twice. I was exhausted... which was probably why I had no self-control.

We returned to Sebastian's apartment in silence, the drive thankfully short, and the ride in the elevator grim and awkward. Everyone was worried. Yes, now we didn't have to worry about being magically tracked, but the spells, no matter how expertly they'd been cast, would only last for so long.

"Everyone should eat something before going to bed," I said as Sebastian unlocked his door and let us in.

"Speaking of bed..." Hawk purred with a sensual smile.

"You've got the couch in the living room, and you and I are using Titus's bathroom," Cassius said, striding past him toward the kitchen. "You're also going to be useful and help make dinner."

"Oh, I am, am I?" Hawk asked as he crossed his arms and narrowed his eyes. "I'm not even going to get anything out of it. Food isn't what I eat."

"It's okay," I said. I was too tired to deal with a fight between them and I was pretty sure Hawk, like Sebastian, would escalate the situation just to amuse himself. "I'll help you."

"No. You're going to sit and drink a glass of orange juice." Cassius jabbed a finger at me. "You've expended your magic twice today and you look terrible."

Hawk snorted. "You should probably take that back."

"I'm perfectly capable of assessing my condition." Jeez, and now all I wanted was to prove him wrong even if the smartest move was to let him take care of dinner. But I wasn't helpless. I'd never be helpless again, and it made my insides squirm knowing he was doing something I was perfectly capable of doing myself.

"No, you're not," Cassius said. "You always push yourself too far."

"You did not just tell me I don't know my own body."

Hawk snickered and I glared at him which only made him flash me a heart-stopping smile.

"I'll help," Titus said. "Seirea— sorry, Sebastian, any suggestions?"

"Make whatever you want. I had Nova stock up the fridge and pick up more clothes for everyone before she left. It should all be in the kitchen." Sebastian rubbed his face and for a second his complexion was gray again... which it shouldn't have been because I'd healed everything that was wrong with him.

Or at least everything I could heal. There wasn't anything I could do for magic depletion.

He turned and headed to the hall leading to the bedrooms. "I'm going to get cleaned up."

"You should eat first," Cassius said. "We haven't eaten anything since breakfast. You can survive if you're filthy. You can't if you're starving."

"Whatever." He didn't turn around and gave Cassius the finger.

"Bane—" Cassius growled.

I set a hand on Cassius's arm. "Let him go. He used a lot of magic today, too."

No one, except for maybe Hawk who'd gotten more than enough sexual energy in the last little while, had much energy to cook anything, so we settled on sandwiches. All three guys — even Hawk — helped assemble sandwiches, and while Sebastian's kitchen was big, so were all three of the guys. So to stay out of the way, I ended up sitting at the kitchen table cutting vegetables for a salad.

Sebastian didn't come out to join us, and a worry that there was something wrong with him, something I'd missed started gnawing away at me. Maybe it was something deep, an infection that was slowly affecting him.

I'd been so concerned about the laceration in his leg and sealing shut all his other cuts that I might not have noticed it, and I'd pulled my magic out before I was finished fully healing him, trying to conserve it. If there had been the beginnings of an infection in any of his wounds, I could have withdrawn my magic before removing it and it could have been growing inside him since... well, since last night's fight.

Which was ridiculous. Surely my magic would have noticed it.

But the need to heal him twisted in my gut along with the selfish fear that if he was sick, I'd have to wait even longer to be free. And I had to be free.

I wasn't going to be able to get any rest until I eased the compulsion from my healing magic and the fear of being trapped, and I was too tired to fight either, so I grabbed a sandwich from the pile on the platter in the center of the table and stood. "I'm going to check on Sebastian."

"He's probably just fallen asleep," Cassius said.

I hoped so.

"Something you—"

I glared at him and he cleared his throat, making Hawk snort, not even trying to hide his amusement.

"Something *all of us* should do," Cassius finished.

"That's the plan," I said. "I'm taking him this sandwich then going to bed. Good night."

His expression softened, verging on that look I hated so much. Why did he always see me as the weak, pathetic angel he'd saved? Why could I never put that nightmare behind me?

Because it had been my own fault. I'd made a bad decision, first to go to the human realm by myself, then to keep healing those humans when I knew it would keep me weak. I never wanted to make a bad decision like that again, and yet I knew, if put in the same position, I would. I'd drain myself dry to save lives. I'd never been able to stop myself.

Which meant I couldn't allow myself to be put in that kind of position again. Ever.

I marched to the door at the end of the hall and firmly knocked. I doubted Sebastian was modest, but it was always polite to give fair warning. "I brought you something to eat."

No answer.

I strained to hear anything inside.

Nothing.

He probably *had* fallen asleep, and while it would be best if I returned the sandwich to the kitchen and went to bed as well, I couldn't ignore the compulsion to ensure he was okay.

I cracked open the door and peeked in. The lights were off and only a thin band of light from the barely open en suite door cutting into the room offered weak illumination. His bed was empty, the sheets still pulled up, and I could hear the soft rush of running water.

"Sebastian?" I called. "Are you okay?"

He still didn't answer and my need to heal twisted tighter. I had to confirm he was okay and that there wasn't anything else I could do to help him. He had, after all, saved my life. And I had no doubt we wouldn't be able to get out of this mess without him.

I certainly wouldn't be able to be free of the leash spell... or my mating brand.

The thought made my pulse race. It didn't matter if he was angry at me, so long as he wasn't hurt and could break the leash spell in the morning.

I stepped inside and closed the door behind me. His bedroom wasn't much bigger than his guestrooms and was done in the same white and blues as the rest of the apartment. Unlike the simple plain guestrooms, he had a large painting hanging on the far wall of a winter forest scape, a wide, masculine dresser with a stack of books and two small wooden boxes on top, and a large bookshelf also crammed with books. More books sat on a bedside table and in a pile on the floor in front of it.

I'd known he liked books — the man had a whole office with floor-to-ceiling bookshelves crammed with books — but it was always so easy to forget his scholarly nature with his brash flirtations.

"Sebastian," I called again, as I headed to his bathroom. "I brought you dinner."

Still no answer. Now I was really starting to worry.

"Are you okay in there?" I knocked on the door and it creaked open a little wider.

The air inside was humid. Mist had gathered on the large mirror above the sink and the glass wall of the large shower stall, but not enough to obscure my view of Sebastian's incredible body.

He stood with his back to me, his forehead pressed against the white tiles, the water rushing over his sleek muscles and the mesmerizing swirls of ink covering him. All of him. The ink encircled his neck, snaked down his spine, curled around one shoulder blade, and twisted on top of the other. A lattice of thin lines accentuated the firm muscle of one butt cheek and trailed down the back of his thigh, while a thick line cut along the curve of his other hip and wrapped around his other thigh.

My mouth went dry and my pulse picked up again for a completely different reason. He was breathtaking. I'd known he was. I hadn't seen him fully naked, but I'd seen enough to know he was in as good a shape or better than any JP agent I'd worked with, but this... This was so much more than I expected. I ached just looking at him.

AMIAH

My desire throbbed low within me, and I wanted to scream with the day's frustrations. I needed to regain control of my emotions, but I didn't know if I'd be able to do that, not while being trapped in this situation with Sebastian and now Hawk always around.

No. The best plan was to get it out of my system. Surely if I released this pressure, I'd be able to think straight again. Hawk would be my best choice. He'd already offered. Except there was no guarantee he'd be discreet, and I wasn't ready for everyone to know I'd invited him to my bed.

I bit back a groan. There was no good way to deal with this.

"Fucking hell," Sebastian gasped, and I yanked my attention back to him. I hadn't even realized my gaze had dropped to the floor. "What are you doing in my bathroom?"

Heat rushed across my cheeks and I turned my back to him. I'd seen many naked men before and I had no doubt many women had seen Sebastian naked, but given what I desired, looking at him was inappropriate. As much as I wanted to, I couldn't pretend I was just an impartial physician. "I came to check on you."

"So you just decided to walk into my bathroom?"

"You didn't answer when I called." I squared my shoulders, trying to draw on my cool professional persona and ignore my desires. "And you didn't get anything to eat."

"For fuck's sake," he hissed. "I'm fine. I'll get something to eat when I'm out."

"You're not fine. You're too pale."

"I'm supposed to be pale," he shot back. "I'm winter fae."

"You know what I mean," I said, shifting closer to the shower but managing to keep my back turned to him despite the urge to look... because I wanted to assess him, not ogle his gorgeous body. Really. "Just let me check you."

"I'm not a patient and we're not in your hospital. Go away."

"If you have an infection, it'll be easier to treat now than in the morning." I couldn't let it go. The compulsion to heal and my fears were too strong.

I set the plate with the sandwich beside the sink and walked backward until my back bumped against the shower wall.

"Let me check you." I reached my hand around the edge of the glass shower stall, even knowing I should comply with his wishes, that I shouldn't force my magic on him. But just thinking that made my compulsion twist tighter. "Please, Sebastian. A quick check, and I'll be gone."

"Amiah," he said, his voice low, filled with warning, and sounding like he stood right beside me.

Unable to help myself, I slid my gaze to the opening into the shower and my breath caught.

He did stand right behind me, his face inches from mine, and the desire burning in his eyes seared my insides. "You won't like my reaction if you touch me right now."

But I knew he didn't really mean it. He was just trying to get me to go away. He'd already made it clear that he could turn that look on and off with a thought, that he only pretended to want me because it shocked me.

This was just another tease and if I fell for it, he'd just make fun of me later. "We both know you're not going to do anything." I huffed trying to sound like the look in his eyes didn't affect me. "All you do is tease. At least Hawk has follow through."

I reached up to press my palm against his cheek and check him, but he seized my wrist and yanked me into the shower, pinning me against the tiles with his body.

Water soaked into my dress, plastering it to my body, and his erection pressed hard against my pelvis. My thoughts tripped. He did desire me...

or at least he was sexually excited. I wasn't sure if it was because I was a woman or because I was me.

"You think I have no follow through?" He captured my head between his palms and smashed his lips against mine with a hungry, angry kiss. It stole all breath and thought. There was only my aching desperate need and my certainty that Sebastian couldn't possibly be my soul mate.

Somehow, I managed to regain enough conscious thought to slide a thread of magic into him. Absolutely no infection. He was tired and the lacerations weren't completely healed, but beyond that, there was nothing for my magic to fix.

He thrust his tongue into my mouth, and my thoughts scattered again. His fingers tangled in my hair and he ground his erection against me as if he needed to get closer. But the only way he could get closer would be to be inside me.

With a moan, I hooked my leg around his hip. The action tilted my hips and rubbed him against my clit, sending a shock of sensation zinging through me.

"Fuck," he groaned as he pulled his lips away and pressed his forehead against mine. His breath was ragged and his grip tightened in my hair. "Tell me to stop."

"No." I burned with a need that had only been growing since last night. I missed being touched and held, and I ached for more, so much more.

"You've been influenced by Hawk's magic." He shifted, the movement grinding him against me and making me gasp in pleasure. "*I've* been influenced by Hawk's magic. If we wait, it'll pass," he said, trailing his lips down my neck.

"Is that what you want?" I asked. Of course, that was what he wanted. He'd already made his feelings clear.

"Fuck no," he murmured against my throat. "But if *you* can't wait, you should go to Cassius. Not me."

"I've told you we've never slept together." I tipped my head back and he reached behind my neck and unhooked the strap of my dress. "We're just friends and even if we weren't, he'd want a commitment I can't give him. I can't commit to anyone until my brand is gone. It'll make me love someone else."

"Maybe he's your soul mate." Sebastian slid his hands over my shoulders, slowly pushing the top of my dress down until just a fraction of material maintained my modesty.

"That would make it worse." My breath picked up with a mix of anticipation and fear. "I can't be trapped like that."

"Maybe I'm your soul mate. Having sex with me might seal the deal," he said with a ghost of his wicked smile.

"Do you honestly think we're soul mates?"

He raised his gaze to mine, his eyes filled with barely contained need, his body trembling. "Last chance to say no."

I captured his lips and gave him my answer with my body. He kissed me back with the same ferocity as before and pushed down the front of my dress. Sensation rushed through me, overwhelming everything else. There were just his lips on mine, his hand tangling in my hair, and his fingers tweaking my nipple. I was on fire everywhere our bodies touched and it was amazing, so much more than what I'd imagined.

My breath picked up and I dug my fingers into his scalp, not wanting to let his lips go. I couldn't get enough of the heat and hunger he inspired. I'd thought the kiss with Hawk had been incredible, and it had been, but it had only been a taste of what a kiss could be like.

"So wild it is," he gasped as he grabbed my rear and pulled me into his arms. "Let's get out of the cold."

"The what—?" I wrapped my other leg around his waist, realizing, through the heated haze rushing through me, that the water had grown cold.

He carried me to the bed, both of us still dripping wet, and laid me on the comforter. His lips found mine again, stealing my breath with a quick passionate kiss, before pulling away.

I reached to draw him back to me as he flicked his tongue over my nipple, sending a shock of sensation zinging through me, stopping my reach and drawing a surprised gasp. With a groan, he sucked my nipple into his mouth, building the throbbing need within me as he worked my other nipple with his hand, teasing it into a tight peak.

This was just as good as kissing. More so. God, I'd been such a fool. I could have been feeling like this for years. This was so much better than just pleasuring myself, and right in that moment, there was only him. No fear about being trapped by the leash spell or my brand, no thought about how I appeared or if he thought I was strong and in control. I wasn't in control. He was and it felt amazing.

He unzipped my dress and pulled it and my underwear off, tossing them to the floor, but didn't return to lie on top of me. Instead, he looked down at me with a heated hungry look that made my pulse stall. I'd never been naked in front of a man before, and I'd certainly never had one look at me the way Sebastian was looking at me now. I didn't care if he just wanted to have sex with me because I was a woman and not because of who I was. In that moment I felt beautiful and sexy and desired.

I slid my gaze down his body, drinking him in like he was drinking me in, and stopped at his impressive erection. I bit my lip. This was really going to happen. I was really going to have intercourse.

His lips quirked. "I have plenty of follow through."

"I can see that," I said, my voice breathy.

He tapped a finger against a glyph on his hip and activated it.

"I wouldn't have thought you'd need help," I said. It couldn't have been a birth control spell because angels could only be impregnated by other angels, so it had to be something else.

"This is for you." He pressed his palms against the insides of my knees and urged me to open for him. "A sound block." He leaned in, traced the vein on the inside of my thigh with his tongue, and settled his head between my legs.

Oh, my.

He flicked his tongue over my clit, making me gasp.

"The sounds you make tonight are mine, no one else's, and I have every intention of making you scream." His tongue swept over my clit again, and if I had a response, it vanished with the rush of sensation.

His mouth was even more amazing down there. He drove me crazy with his tongue, and with the spell blocking any sounds from leaving his room, I fully gave in, moaning and gasping my pleasure.

My breath grew ragged and my muscles began to tremble. "Oh, Sebastian."

He groaned and slid a finger inside me. Withdrew it and returned with two, pumping them into me, hitting a spot that made my trembling muscles start to tighten. With a hard suck on my clit, he made my muscles contract. Sensation crashed through me, radiating into every cell in my being and I cried out, not even bothering to try to hold it back.

But he didn't give me time to recover. My muscles were still clenching and my mind still spinning with my rushing breath and pulse as he moved up my body and pushed partway into my opening.

Oh, yes. I never imagined it could be like this.

"Shit, you're so tight." He squeezed his eyes shut and drew in long breaths to steady himself then slowly withdrew and pushed back in a little farther, his erection stretching me, urging my body to accommodate him.

The aching heat of need swelled within me again as if I hadn't just had an orgasm, and with another withdrawal and push, he fully sheathed himself inside me.

My breath hitched, my muscles already trembling again around him, and something in my essence clicked — not my mating brand, thank God. My skin grew luminescent similar to Sebastian's, making me moan, part in pleasure and part in embarrassment. It wasn't unheard of for an angel to glow his or her first time, but it didn't always happen, and I'd really hoped I wasn't one of the lucky few.

"Ah, fuck." Sebastian froze, his expression horrified. "You're a virgin?"

My pulse froze with him and my fears started to rush back in. *No. Please.* I didn't want this to end.

"It doesn't matter," I forced out. It shouldn't matter. *Please don't let it matter. Please don't stop.*

"Sweetheart, it always matters," he said. "An angel like you is a virgin for a reason, and I'm not that reason. You haven't been waiting for me. That's for sure."

"I'm not waiting for anyone." Not anymore. I rocked my hips, trying to urge him to continue. I didn't want to lose the trembling promise of another climax. *Make me forget I was a fool. Make me forget I'm going to be trapped forever. Please.* "Sebastian, make me scream."

I grabbed his head and urged him down to capture his lips in a desperate kiss. I needed my mind to stop whirling, to forget everything. I could taste myself on his lips and a shudder of pleasure whispered through me at the memory of his mouth on me.

He hesitated, just for a second, then groaned and kissed me back, plunging his tongue inside my mouth, ratcheting up my desire.

He kissed me until I was breathless and squirming and my mind blissfully empty. My core throbbed, my body teetering again on the edge of another release. With a groan, he sat back, still fully sheathed inside me. His hungry expression turned wicked, and he brushed his thumb over my clit, the sensation stealing my breath.

God, he was going to ruin me for other men. He knew just how to touch me, how to bring me close without letting me crash over, and he teased me again and again until I was gasping, the room spinning with my quick breaths, and my body was on fire, wound so tight I was sure I'd explode. Then he finally — thank God, finally! — seized my hips and started to move inside me.

"Oh, yes." This was what I wanted. This was amazing. The slide of his erection in and out of my body and the glorious friction. He fully possessed me, claiming me as only a man could claim a woman, just as I hungrily welcomed him in.

His pace grew faster and his thrusts harder. The promise of my climax spun tighter and tighter until every muscle in my body contracted and shattering bliss roared through me, tearing a scream from my throat.

Sebastian gave another few hard thrusts and tensed, his own release drawing a cry, sending another wave crashing through me.

"Fuck me," Sebastian groaned and he shuddered, which sent another, small wave rushing through me.

Yes, I had.

He gave me a fierce kiss and rolled off me, his chest heaving with his rapid breaths, and wrapped me in his arms, my back against his chest. I snuggled in, savoring the feel of his body pressed against me and the pulse of his life force thrumming against my senses.

This was the way it was supposed to be. This was right.

And oh my goodness, I'd just had sex.

With Sebastian Bane.

It had been amazing. So much more than I'd fantasized about. I was still spinning and glowing and floating, my body so lax I wasn't sure I'd be able to move. But oh my, goodness—

I'd had sex with Sebastian Bane!

How was I to know he'd actually cast a sound blocking spell? And even if he had, he was surely going to use this against me in the morning.

God, what had I been thinking?

I hadn't been, and for the first time in my life, I'd been free of my fear, my self-restraint, of everything. I hadn't thought of looking strong or of the nightmare branded in my skin. There'd only been his mouth and hands and body bringing me immense pleasure.

He pressed his lips against the back of my neck, his breath teasing my skin making my pulse pick up again and need throb between my thighs.

What was wrong with me? How could I crave more when I was still — literally — glowing from round one?

He hummed low in his throat, a sound of pure masculine satisfaction, and slid his hand down my belly and dipped his fingers into my curls.

I pulled away from him, need and panic a sudden whirling mix of hot and cold in my chest. "I should..."

I didn't know what to say. I wanted to let go again, stop thinking, and just feel, but my spinning thoughts were taking over and I couldn't push them aside.

I'd just made a horrible mistake.

No, I hadn't.

Sebastian had been everything I wanted for my first time and more, so much more. But at what cost?

"I should clean up." And take a moment to think. I had no idea how I felt about what had just happened. I just needed some time by myself to regain my mental equilibrium... as much as I— God! I loved being held in his arms like that.

He raised his gaze to me, his pupils dilated with desire, but his lips quirked in that wicked smile that said I amused him.

I scrambled off the bed and grabbed my dress. I didn't know where my underwear had gone but if I stayed to search for it, I'd have sex with Sebastian again.

And while a part of me was certain that wasn't a bad thing, the part that needed to be in control was having a meltdown. My pulse was already racing and my breath getting faster, and it had nothing to do with desire. I'd done something without considering the consequences. Again.

"You don't need to get dressed to clean up," he said. "I have an en suite."

"I know. I just— I need to think."

"That's a bad idea." His smile deepened, his eyes filled with mirth... and was that a hint of softness?

No. I was imagining it. I only *wanted* him to understand my fear, but logically I knew he didn't care. Which had been the whole point of sleeping with him.

I pulled on my dress. The zipper got caught in the wet fabric halfway up, and I didn't bother fighting with it, hoping I'd be able to slip into my room without anyone seeing me.

It shouldn't have mattered. I should be able to have sex with whoever I wanted whenever I wanted, and yet I was torn with so many conflicting emotions and thoughts.

I was supposed to be waiting... for someone I didn't want anymore.

I should never have given up control like that.

I should have picked someone more appropriate, someone who actually cared for me.

Except the fact that Sebastian and I didn't have an emotional attachment was the very reason I'd considered him. There were no strings attached with him. Now that he'd conquered me, this would likely be the one and only time we'd have sex.

And I had no idea how I felt about that, either.

I hurried out of his bedroom, pulled the door closed, and pressed my back against it, desperate to slow my racing heart.

That had been amazing.

And so foolish.

The lights in the hall and living room were off. Sebastian's apartment was dark and everyone had gone to bed. Which meant — thank goodness — no one would see me slinking back into my bedroom, and I had until morning to figure out how I was going to react to what I'd just done.

I squared my shoulders and headed to my room as Hawk stepped around the corner in the living room into the hall.

Oh, no.

My stomach bottomed out as realization hit me. I might have been able to hide what I'd done from Cassius, and if I showered I'd be able to hide it from Titus as well, but Hawk, with his incubus ability to sense sexual energy, knew exactly what I'd just done.

AMIAH

Hawk drew closer and the hellfire in his eyes flared, casting his beautiful face in flickering illumination and making him look dangerous.

"Why did you leave?" he asked, his voice low. "You weren't done."

"I was," I insisted, embarrassment heating my cheeks, even though I logically knew I had nothing to be embarrassed about.

"Oh, baby," he purred, leaning in. He brushed the back of his warm finger along my jaw and sent a shiver of aching need sweeping through me without even using his magic. "You weren't done."

"Yes. I was." I needed to get my thoughts under control, but I couldn't make myself push past him to go to my room. He was mesmerizing.

Like he was supposed to be. Because he was an incubus.

And as much as I'd said I was done, I wasn't. My body wanted to go back to Sebastian for round two and feel that all-consuming bliss again. But my mind wouldn't let me. I'd made a mistake. I'd lost control. I'd—

I shifted to put some space between us and my back hit the hall wall.

Hawk pressed close and, with a smirk, slid his hand under my skirt and up the inside of my thigh, stopping at the crux between my leg and pelvis.

My breath hitched, anticipation of what would happen if he just moved his fingers an inch reigniting my desire. I wanted him to touch me, wanted more, and that terrified me.

"Oh, no." He teased his fingers against my wet and swollen folds. Just a whisper of a touch, and my thoughts scattered. All the reasons I'd run from Sebastian's bed vanished, and, with just that touch, I was instantly trembling on the verge of an orgasm again. "You weren't done at all."

He slid two fingers inside me, and I moaned, my body melting into the sensation. *Oh, yes.*

"He wants you again." Hawk slowly slid his fingers out then pushed back in. "Even after you ran, he still wants you. But I think it's his turn to know someone else is fucking you. He can't sense it like I can, so let's give him something to listen to."

He brushed his thumb against my clit, sending another teasing tremor through me, and I fought to swallow a moan of pleasure.

It came out as a desperate mewl that deepened Hawk's smile. "Or would you rather he watched?"

The memory of Sebastian's hungry look when we'd been in Hawk's tent and the thought of him watching while Hawk pushed inside me rippled pleasure through me, torturously close to an orgasm but not quite.

"Fuck, yeah," Hawk murmured, increasing the pressure on my clit and sliding his fingers in and out at a torturously slow pace. "How about instead of watching, we invite him to join us."

Oh, God yes. I wanted that. I wanted all of it. Everything I'd learned about while I'd waited and prepared for my soul mate, and what better way to do that than with men as experienced as Sebastian and Hawk who were without a doubt *not* my soul mates.

My muscles clenched around Hawk's fingers and another orgasm swept through me. He captured my lips, swallowing my moan, and slipped a curl of his hot sensual magic into me that made the sensation swell. Stars flashed behind my eyelids, my release stealing all breath and thought.

"You're going to be so much fun," he murmured before sauntering away through the living room into the kitchen leaving me panting and trembling and clinging to the wall to stay standing.

Oh, God.

God.

That was—

And I was—

What was wrong with me? I wanted to call him back, wanted him and Sebastian so much it hurt, wanted the escape of not thinking and just feeling. No—

I sucked in a ragged breath. What I needed to do was think. My reasons for leaving Sebastian's bed hadn't changed, and I needed to figure out how to pull myself back together. Something, I wasn't going to be able to figure out in the guestroom any more. It was too small. I needed more space and sky to steady myself. I had to have sky.

I raced out the front door before common sense kicked in but managed to force myself to slow down so I could notice the moment the leash spell activated. It always started with a pressure before the air vanished. If I felt that, I'd turn around, but not before.

Please, don't activate. Please let the stairs to the roof be within the limits of the spell. I needed the sky too much. I needed to find my balance.

Thankfully, there was only a hint of weight in my chest, and I crashed out the metal security door onto the roof, the coarse surface rough against my bare feet and the summer's evening heat wrapping thick and humid around me. A mix of relief and desperation brought me to my knees.

There had to be something wrong with me. I wanted to go back to Hawk and Sebastian. I craved it. But the things I desired surprised me.

And yet just thinking about Hawk's proposition for a *ménage à trois* sent an aftershock rushing through me.

I wanted both of them. Together. But did I want *them* or just two men? I wasn't sure I'd feel comfortable agreeing to anything with men I didn't know. Except I barely knew Sebastian and I didn't know Hawk at all.

Which meant it wasn't them I craved, but sex... really? No, there was something about them that I trusted... or was that just because my control had finally shattered and my psyche needed to justify my desire for them by making me think I trusted them.

I swept my gaze over the Quarter's skyline. The lights across from me were tinged purple by the UV-blocking canopy which was attached to the side of the roof — marking this building as being at the edge of the vampire's section of the Quarter. The canopy rose up seven feet, stretched over to the roof across the street as well as the buildings up the street, protecting a whole, long block.

My insides squirmed, my worry and confusion growing. I'd thought seeing the sky would help, but with the glass canopy, I still felt trapped. Trapped by my fear and now trapped by my desires.

I couldn't take back what I'd done with Sebastian and I didn't want to. I'd hoped my aching need would go away if I satisfied it, but now I knew what I'd been missing, and I wanted more.

A part of me feared I wouldn't be able to get enough and another part feared if I propositioned Sebastian he'd refuse me.

As it was, Sebastian or Hawk would let it slip, and Cassius would know what had happened by the morning and would no doubt be concerned, since sleeping with Sebastian was out of character for me... because I wasn't a sexual woman.

Well, if I didn't want to go crazy and make even worse decisions, I was going to have to become one. I needed to own my desires. I was sure I could still practice some restraint, but I didn't want the celibacy of before. Surely I could convince the part of me that was still screaming at my lack of control that taking charge of what I wanted *was* an act of control.

The thought made my cheeks heat.

Taking charge meant being forthright and asking for what I wanted.

Funny how I could say what needed to be said in a medical situation no matter how blunt, but the idea of asking for what I desired embarrassed me.

I drew in a deep breath, trying to calm my fear. I was still in control. My destiny was still my own. Sebastian would break the leash spell and remove my mating brand and I'd be free. I had a lifetime to find my courage to ask for selfish things, sexual things, anything I wanted.

A footstep crunched on the roof behind me and I turned around, my heart pounding with the hope that Sebastian or Hawk had followed me.

But instead, it was the stern man from the market who'd been commanding the spring fae and their hired thugs. Behind him stood half a dozen shifters, their fingers extended into razor-sharp claws.

"Just the bait I was looking for," he said

Bait? My pulse leaped into a rapid tattoo. Bait meant he was going to capture me, use me. The thought shot icy fear through my limbs. I couldn't be someone's prisoner again. I swore. Never again.

My mind raced through my options. I didn't know how to fight and even if I did, there were too many of them. I had to flee. And flying was my best defense. I couldn't jump off the roof behind me — the way was blocked by the glass canopy — but I was still close to the side of the building. I hadn't gone too far from the staircase.

I bolted for the edge and release my wings. The leash spell wouldn't let me get far, but chances were none of these men could fly so hovering just out of reach would keep me safe until I could figure out how to get to Cassius.

The man laughed, the dark sound making the hair on the back of my neck stand up, and a sharp, sudden weight — too similar to the weight of the leash spell — slammed into my chest. I crashed to the rooftop before reaching the edge and the weight disappeared as quickly as it had appeared.

"How far do you think you'll be able to go?" he called.

I scrambled back to my feet. I just needed to get off the roof. It was only ten feet away.

The man's laughter grew and I put on a burst of speed as the weight slammed into me again. I hit the rooftop hard, spiking sharp pain up my right wrist in a failed attempt to protect my face. My cheek smashed against the ground and a fiery burn spiked through my knees.

The weight didn't go away and I heaved back to my feet, flapping my wings to help me rise. The edge was now only five feet away. If I could get there, I could fight the pressure in my chest and hold myself aloft.

But the weight swelled, stealing my breath, and yanked me around to face the man. He sneered at me, his eyes bright with pleasure, and he curled his finger at me in a come-hither gesture.

The weight jerked me forward a step. I heaved against it, flapping my wings, desperate to keep back. But it was as if a chain was embedded in my chest and fighting it felt like it was tearing out my soul with the same excruciating agony I'd felt when Sebastian had first tried to break the leash spell.

I stumbled forward another few steps, panting against the pain, fighting with everything I had. But I wasn't strong enough. I was weak. I was always weak. And this man was going to take me.

No, please. I couldn't go through that again. Even if it was just being trapped here on the roof while this man made his demands. My life for Titus's. And I had no idea what Cassius would choose. It wasn't right to give Titus over to this man, and the JP didn't negotiate with hostage takers, but Cassius's need to protect people was also strong. Would it be stronger than his need to follow the rules? He'd already turned a blind eye to the illegal activities in Lincoln and at Mavis's. Would he sacrifice Titus to protect me? And could I live with that?

I took another staggering step and another, my mind screaming —

fight. Resist. Be stronger. Stop. Please stop — until I stood before him, straining to breathe.

I glared at him. It was the only act of defiance I could manage, and the man's sneer deepened.

"Grab her and let's go," he said.

"Go?" I gasped. I couldn't go. If he took me out of the radius of the leash spell, I'd suffocate. Titus would suffocate. "No, please. I'm caught in a leash spell—"

"I'm aware." The man flicked his finger and the air around me vanished.

I futilely gasped, instinct making me draw breath even though I knew there was nothing to breathe, and sagged to my knees. Dark specks crowded my vision and my lungs burned as the world began to spin.

The man grabbed my hair and yanked my head up to meet his gaze. Dark pleasure filled his eyes, making cold fear churn in my stomach.

"I've hijacked the leash spell." Then he flicked his finger again and the air returned — although the crushing weight of the spell remained. My fear grew, making me tremble no matter how hard I tried to hide it. This man wasn't just going to kidnap me. He was going to hurt me.

"I can't kill the beast, but I'll make him suffer through you until he comes to me and admits I'm his master." He jerked my head back, shooting agony through my neck and making me whimper. "We're going to have so much fun together."

CASSIUS

I LAY IN THE DARK ON THE COUCH IN BANE'S OFFICE SURROUNDED BY FLOOR-to-ceiling bookshelves unable to get to sleep and my fire burning under my skin as I fought to contain it. With the exception of the window at the back — its UV-blocking glass tinting the Quarter's streetlights purple — and the fireplace across from me, there wasn't an inch of wall that didn't have a shelf filled with flammable material.

If I was smart, I'd go down to Bane's patio and relieve some of the pressure by releasing my flames on the concrete.

Except I didn't want to go that far from Amiah. It was already driving me crazy that she was out of sight.

Which was also driving me crazy.

I shouldn't have to literally watch her to watch out for her. She could be perfectly fine in another room.

But my need to protect her squeezed my chest and made my fire threaten to roar out of control.

She shouldn't be in this mess. She should be safe at Operations, back to life as normal — or as back to normal as it was possible for her given she'd just had her heart broken.

But I'd failed her. Once again I'd been unable to protect the people I cared about. It didn't matter that it was Amiah's magic that had gotten her into this trouble by locking onto Titus. Somehow I should have been able to stop that, or gotten her out of the situation once I knew what a mess it was, or something.

I should have been able to do God damned something.

My fire flared, billowing smoke from my hands, and I clenched down on it, the heat searing my skin.

I couldn't believe I'd said we had to go after Faerie's Heart. Except no matter how I looked at the situation — and I'd spent all day trying to come up with any other solution that ensured Amiah's safety — there wasn't any option... if, of course, Bane was telling the truth.

I really wanted to doubt him, wanted him to be the lying bastard I'd thought he was before he'd helped my brother fight Lilith, but given how much he'd wanted us out of his apartment last night, he'd never come up with a story that forced us to stay together.

Which meant until we could get Faerie's Heart, Amiah was in danger, and even then, unless we could make an iron-clad arrangement with someone who I seriously doubted would keep their word, she was still in danger.

It also meant we were stuck with Bane. The man who made sexual advances on everyone.

God, he drove me crazy. He'd propositioned my brother's mate and now he kept propositioning Amiah. Not that she'd ever say yes. He wasn't her type. He was a one-night stand guy. Have some fun and be done, and I doubted he even bothered to learn his lovers' names. He made no attempt to hide that, and if I knew one thing about Amiah, she was a full commitment kind of woman. She was careful with her heart, so damned careful, and she'd never say yes to his advances.

And really, he was the least of my worries. Now we were stuck with an incubus who didn't care who his magic affected.

I'd thought Essie's incubus mate had been a sexual harassment complaint waiting to happen, but he was restrained compared to Hawk. I couldn't feel the incubus's magic, but I had no doubt Hawk did little to hold it back. It was the only thing that explained why Amiah hadn't resisted his kiss in the abandoned bathhouse, why it looked like she'd *wanted* him to touch and kiss her like that.

The thought made my heart clench and my fire flared again.

I jerked off the couch, strode to the fireplace, and shoved my hands inside.

I wanted to touch her and kiss her like that... well, not like *that*—

Actually. Yes. Exactly like that.

I wanted to kiss her, comfort her, and convince her that while I'd never be as passionate as a shifter, I could fulfill her desires and be a good mate.

Fire sparked from my hands, proving just how wrong I was. I couldn't be passionate. I'd burn her if I ever let go enough to show her how I felt. Hell, just thinking about her like that made it impossible to control my magic. How could I be a good mate if I couldn't even touch her?

I sagged to the floor, keeping my hands in the fireplace and letting my flames drip onto the cleaned concrete hearth and metal grate. I had to focus on my priorities: keeping her safe.

That was the only thing that mattered.

It had barely bothered me to see the stolen goods as well as the health and magic code violations at Left of Lincoln or at Mavis's. My need to protect overwhelmed everything else. I'd failed my youngest brother, Dominic, and I'd been useless protecting my other brother, Gideon. I couldn't fail Amiah.

Something banged against the floor out in the hall and I jerked up to my feet.

"Seireadan!" Titus roared. "Seireadan. She's gone."

My pulse skipped a beat. There was only one *she* Titus would be yelling about.

I threw open the office door. The bedroom door across from me — Titus's door — had been ripped off its hinges and lay half on the bed, while Titus, dressed in the sweatpants Bane's assistant had provided him, was already at the end of the hall. He shoved open Bane's bedroom door, revealing the naked fae scrambling out of bed. Of course the fae slept naked. Had Amiah walked in on *that* when she'd gone to check on him after dinner?

"She's gone," Titus said, his grip crushing the doorknob, his massive muscular chest heaving with rapid breaths. God, he was strong and dangerous. And another one I needed to protect Amiah from.

"She can't be gone," Hawk said rushing from the living room into the hall. "She knows the dangers of the leash spell."

Titus wrenched around to face Hawk and snarled. "She's gone. I can feel it."

I hurried into her bedroom and turned on the light. The bed was still made, and the scrubs Chris had brought over yesterday were still neatly folded at its foot. My stomach bottomed out and fire snapped from my hands.

"She's not in her room." I sucked my flames back before I burned anything and returned to the hall. "Would she be in the other room?" I asked, pointing to the only other door in the hall.

"That's my clean room for complicated spell casting. No furniture or windows," Bane said, pulling on a pair of slacks. "Would she be in there? Last I saw her, she said she needed to think." Bane's gaze flickered to Hawk before jumping to me.

"She'd want open sky," I said as Titus threw open the clean room door. "She'd go to the roof if she could."

"Would she risk the roof access being outside of the leash spell?" Bane asked.

"If she was upset enough." And God, she had so much to be upset about.

I shoved past Hawk and stormed out the door.

If I really thought about it, it should have surprised me that she hadn't gone to the roof sooner. Amiah's need for open sky was stronger than most angels'. I didn't know if it was the way she'd always been or if her captivity at the hands of that human had exacerbated the compulsion, but for as long as I'd known her, she'd sought out rooftops and large open spaces.

The others caught up to me and I fought to keep my pace even. There was no point in panicking. She was on the roof thinking. She probably just wanted some peace and time to think and was going to be upset we'd all come up to find her.

I pushed open the metal door and strode outside into humid evening air. Ahead stretched the wide, empty roof.

My pulse picked up.

Maybe she was on the other side of the stairwell.

"Amiah?" I called, heading around the other side.

She wasn't there, either.

I wrenched around, scanning the rooftop as if I'd somehow missed her. She had to be here. She couldn't be gone. Gone meant she was suffocating to death somewhere.

Titus groaned, clutched his chest, and sagged to his knees.

Panic seized my heart. If she was far enough away for Titus to feel the effects of the leash spell, she was in dire need. I had to save her. I couldn't fail her too.

I grabbed Bane's arm, not caring that fire raced over my hand and up my forearm. "Find her."

"Shit." He wrenched free of my grip, his fae glow undulating around him. "It'd be easier to concentrate if you weren't burning—" His attention locked on the rooftop a few feet away and his eyes widened. "Oh, fuck."

"What is that?" Hawk asked as he crouched in front of a shiny pebble. "It just lit up like the sun."

Titus's attention jumped to the pebble. All the blood drained from his face and a wild fury filled his eyes. "He has her."

"Who has her?" I demanded.

"Balwyrdan," Titus snarled. "We have to find her."

"We have to be smart about this," Bane said, crouching in front of the pebble.

"If Titus is feeling the effects of the leash spell, she's suffocating," I snapped. Suffering. Dying. How long had she been gone? How long would she last without air?

We had to find her. Now.

Fire dripped from my hands, snapping and hissing around my feet. "There's no time to think this through."

"Balwyrdan is enough of a sorcerer to hijack the leash spell to force Titus to come to him. If she dies, he loses his connection to Titus." The muscles in Bane's jaw flexed. "No, he'll keep her alive until he gets what he wants."

"That's not better," Titus said, his tone dark.

I didn't like the sound of that. "He can compel Titus to come to him?"

"It's not like a compulsion spell," Bane said.

Titus groaned again, his expression tight with pain.

Bane jerked his chin at the pebble. "Touch the charm, Hawk."

Hawk tapped it with his finger. A burst of white light flared from the pebble and a life-sized flickering image of Amiah appeared on the roof.

She lay on her side, curled in a ball. Her hair veiled her face and she gasped deep ragged breaths. Dirt stained her dress, and from the angle of her arms, it looked like they were tied behind her back.

Relief whispered in my chest. She was alive. She had to be terrified — this was too similar to the nightmare I'd rescued her from all those years ago — but she was still alive. I could still save her.

I strained to see anything in the background that might tell me where she was, but everything except for her was out of focus and dark.

Someone chuckled, the sound dark and masculine, and a hand reached into the line of sight of the spell. He seized a fistful of her hair and yanked her head up and back, lifting her to her knees and straining her neck. She bit back a cry of pain and her hair fell away, revealing blood oozing from a broken nose and a right eye that was starting to swell shut.

My stomach bottomed out, and I jerked forward a step even though I knew I couldn't reach her through the spell. This was so much worse than before. That human had hit her, but that had been nothing compared to this, and whoever had kidnapped her now had only had her at most for a couple of hours.

The man from Left of Lincoln who looked to have been in charge of the spring fae stepped fully into sight.

"Balwyrdan," Titus snarled.

"Do you think the beast has found my little note?" Balwyrdan asked, his eyes bright with sadistic pleasure. "We should probably give him more incentive to find it, just in case he hasn't."

He flicked his finger and Amiah's body went rigid. Her mouth opened and closed like a fish out of water, gasping for air that no longer existed, her good eye widened with pain and fear, and her face turned red.

Titus collapsed forward onto his hands. His claws extended and dug into the roof, and his eyes squeezed tight with pain.

Balwyrdan flicked his finger again and Amiah gasped in a desperate breath, but he didn't give her time to recover and smashed her across the face with the back of his hand.

"Jesus," Hawk hissed, as she toppled over with a strangled cry.

"You can do better than that," the man said. He grabbed the front of her dress and wrenched her up, his other hand cocked back to strike her again, but the catch on her neck strap broke. She collapsed back to the floor, leaving the man holding the front of her dress and exposing her breasts. Her head hit the ground and lolled to the side, her face fully in the sight of the spell. Blood now oozed from a cut in her lip as well as from her nose and her eyes were unfocused.

With a huff, the man flicked his finger again and she went rigid.

Titus groaned, and I turned my back on the nightmare projected on the rooftop. My fire seared my insides and raced up my arms past my elbows, snapping and hissing and threatening to pull free of what little control I had and ignite my clothing. "Turn it off."

The sound of Amiah's gasps and sobs vanished, but continued to echo in my head, and I couldn't get the image of her beaten face or her ripped dress out of my mind's eye.

I *had* to go to her right now. Protect her. Except if I was going to save her, I needed to get my emotions and my fire under control. I knew next to nothing about this man or where he was or how many men he had. Rushing in without a plan would get her killed.

"Where is she?" Titus growled as he lunged forward to grab the pebble, but Bane snatched it up before he could get it.

"Don't tell him, Hawk." Bane jerked away from Titus, but the dragon seized his throat and yanked him forward.

"Give me the charm," he snarled. "I'm getting her away from that monster."

"Not until you've calmed down," Bane gasped, clutching Titus's wrist but not fighting back.

"He won't stop." Titus's pupils slitted and his body shook. "Seireadan, you know him. Suffocating her is for me, but the beating is for him. He's going to beat her to an inch of her life until he gets bored and then he's going to give her to his men."

Bane's expression turned icy. "But he won't kill her."

"Fuck man, that's cold," Hawk said.

"But right." I heaved my fire back under my skin, clenching it so tightly it felt like my blood was boiling. "What do we know about this guy?"

"He's a nasty piece of work," Titus snarled.

"No shit," Hawk replied. "We've already figured that one out."

"Bane?" I asked, giving Titus a hard look until he let the fae go. "Tell me everything you know." I was going to get Amiah back. Whatever it took. Even if that meant breaking every rule or burning down the world to do it. I would not fail her like I'd failed my brother.

TITUS

It took everything I had not to gut Seireadan with my claws and take the charm. Every instinct I had screamed at me to protect Amiah, comfort her, avenge her. I needed to hold her small fragile body and steady her soul, and once I had her, I wasn't ever letting go. She should never have had to experience the terror of captivity again let alone be beaten like that, and just knowing that even when Balwyrdan got bored with her, she was going to face the same torture and worse at the hands of his men, made me furious. I was going to tear that bastard to pieces and let her eat his heart—

Except she wasn't a dragon. She probably wouldn't want to eat his heart.

And she wasn't mine to hold on to.

She was Seireadan's. I don't know why he'd denied it this morning. Her scent was all over him along with the taunting smell of sex — recent sex — which made my beast furious and my cock hard. Of course, Hawk smelled of her arousal, too, although not nearly as much as Seireadan, and that made my beast even more angry. She was Seireadan's and the incubus needed to keep his hands to himself.

I bit back a roar. They both needed to keep their hands to themselves. She was going to be mine and I would fight Seireadan and Hawk and Cassius and anyone else to keep and protect her.

Mine.

The roar escaped, a low, dangerous rumble in my chest that drew everyone's attention.

Fuck.

Not mine.

Not fucking mine. Why the hell couldn't I convince my beast of that? I didn't want *her*. I. Did. Not. Want. Her. I just wanted a female. Any female.

"Balwyrdan had at least two dozen men at Lincoln. He'll already have replaced the ones we injured or killed and added more," Seireadan said. "It looks like he still prefers hired thugs in an attempt to hide his court affiliation, so I suspect his new men are the same."

The weight of the leash spell slammed into my chest, stealing my breath and making the world tilt. I released a half groan half roar and dug my claws into the roof again to stay put. As much as I wanted to give in to my beast and stop Amiah's suffering, Seireadan was right. We had to be smart about this. I might not care if I died trying to save her, but rushing in could get her killed and that was unacceptable.

"Okay," Cassius said, smoke whirling around him, his eyes filled with the same burning rage I felt. "Tell me her location and a safe place to break the leash spell. Your apartment is compromised and we're not returning here once I get her back."

"Once *we* get her back," Seireadan corrected with an icy fury I'd never seen from him before, proving she really was his... and not mine.

"And *is* there a safe place to hole up?" Hawk asked, his expression grim. "We've all got concealment charms and there's another concealment spell on your apartment. The spells are good too. I can barely sense them or the glamour on Titus and only because I know to look for it. How did they find us?"

"Are any of us tagged?" Seireadan asked Hawk, who closed his eyes and drew in a slow breath.

"Not that I can tell," the incubus said after a moment.

"You're the most sensitive Sensitive I'd ever come across. Which means we aren't tagged. Someone has betrayed me, and that's a very short list." Seireadan ran a hand through his hair, the muscles in his arm bunching with the movement drawing my attention to the black glyphs swirling over his body. I wondered if they were a part of the glamour hiding his identity or real. Had he had all those spells inked onto his body? And why?

"If that's the case, then we find an abandoned building and regroup there." A flame flickered around Cassius's hands then vanished with a gust of smoke. "Hawk. I know you're still stuck in this mess, but I don't expect you to risk your life for Amiah. How about you meet us at the corner of Tyndal and Maingate. That whole neighborhood is abandoned but not completely rubble. Titus, you should go with him."

"Not happening," I growled, as the weight crushed my chest again, stealing my breath and making me groan in pain.

"You're compromised. The moment Balwyrdan sees you, he'll suffocate Amiah and you'll go down. At best, you'll be useless in this fight. At worst a liability." Cassius turned to Seireadan. "Bane—"

"I'm going," I said cutting him off, "and I'm tearing that bastard to pieces."

I stood, fighting the pressure of the leash spell, and let my canines and claws extend in full to show Cassius how serious I was. I didn't want to, but I'd go through him to protect what was mine. And while a part of me knew he was right, that I endangered Amiah's rescue, my beast didn't care. Just like it didn't care that she was Seireadan's.

Cassius squared his shoulders and met my gaze without flinching. From the look in his eyes, he was well aware he was challenging me for dominance, and that only made my beast's fury stronger. "You'll get her killed."

"Seireadan already said Balwyrdan won't kill her until he has me," I said. "I'm glamoured. He can't recognize me."

"He'll know it's you the moment he activates the leash spell and you drop to your knees," Cassius shot back. "You're going with Hawk."

"Except Hawk is going with you, sparky," Hawk said. "You're going to need all the help you can get."

"I can manage just fine." Cassius's flames reignited around his hands. "Someone needs to show Titus where we're meeting since we can't come back here and he doesn't know the city."

"I'm going," I insisted, releasing just enough of my beast to gain more height on him and widen my chest and shoulders. If I hadn't been glamoured, my red-gold scales would have covered my neck and hands as well.

Cassius stood his ground and molten flames dripped from his hands, setting the roof on fire around his feet. "You're not."

"I am." I grew another foot up and across, grateful for the elastic waistband on the jogging pants. A partial shift wouldn't disintegrate my clothes like a full shift would, but I could still rip them.

"For fuck's sake." Seireadan touched a tattoo on his chest. It flared to life and ice swept through the flames around Cassius extinguishing them. "I'll free Titus from his half of the spell so he's not a liability and I'll break Amiah's half when we get her back."

"It'll be harder to free them one at a time." Hawk frowned. "And won't Balwyrdan and the original spellcaster feel it and be able to find our location when you free Titus?"

"Not if I move the spell from Titus to the resonance charm instead of breaking it." Seireadan stood and headed to the stairs.

Hawk grabbed his arm, stopping him. "Except you're the foundation of the charm. That'll just move Titus's half of the spell to you."

"But at least it won't blow his glamour. We can't risk any survivors knowing what Titus looks like," Seireadan said. "The Spring Court isn't the only court after him."

"There won't be survivors," I growled.

"We still shouldn't risk your glamour being blown," Cassius replied, pulling the rest of his fire back under his skin, "and we'll give them a chance to run first. If they're just hired thugs they're not responsible for Balwyrdan's actions."

"Speak for yourself," I shot back. They were involved, they clearly hadn't done anything to stop Balwyrdan. They were just as guilty.

The muscles in Cassius's jaw flexed, but he turned to Hawk and didn't argue with me. "Hawk, you know where she is?"

Hawk gave a tight nod.

"Okay. Bane, move the spell, everyone finish getting dressed, and pack a small bag." Cassius headed to the stairs and the other guys followed as the leash spell slammed into my chest again. "We don't have time to waste and I want to scout the area first before we make our move."

Which was the smartest choice. But neither I nor my beast wanted to wait and it was getting difficult to rein him in. It wanted blood and I was going to let him have it.

AMIAH

The dimly lit abandoned reception hall spun around me, and tears I'd desperately tried to hold back rolled down my cheeks. Terror squeezed around my heart, and even when there was air to breathe, I still couldn't catch my breath.

I'd been taken.

Again.

And this man — his men had called him Balwyrdan — was a hundred times worse than the human who'd taken me all those years ago. He didn't care what I looked like. He wasn't trying to sell my services to an unsuspecting public.

Balwyrdan's fist smashed into my cheek with a sickening crunch, fracturing the bone. Agony exploded in my face and stars shot through my vision. My other cheek hit the dusty floor, and I prayed for unconsciousness. But I already knew Balwyrdan had experience beating someone like this. It had been clear after his first few blows that he knew just how much force to use to take me to the edge of oblivion but never over.

I tried to shut my mind away from my body, curl my consciousness into a tiny trembling ball deep in the core of my soul and ride it out until Cassius came for me — *please, God, come for me*. But my concentration broke every time Balwyrdan activated the leash spell and my desperate need for air wrenched me back to the agony again and again.

Oh, God. Stop. Please stop.

I'd wanted to be strong and had glared at him defiantly at the beginning, but that had only excited him more.

Except I couldn't bring myself to be meek and obedient in the hopes it would stop the torture. Not again. Never again. That hadn't worked for the human, and even if it would work for Balwyrdan, I couldn't make myself do it. Not even to survive. I didn't want to be weak any more. I swore I never would be... except I was. I always would be—

No. I would survive this. I might not be able to fight, but I could still run... so long as he didn't break my legs. I wasn't going to sit around being helpless, waiting for Cassius to show up. One wrong hit and my broken ribs could puncture my heart or lungs. And given that I still had low reserves from healing the guys this afternoon, I didn't know if I had enough power to save myself from an injury like that because it took so much more to turn my power inward.

I couldn't wait. I needed to search for an opportunity, any opportunity, to make my escape. I just needed to hold out until then.

He seized my hair and wrenched me up. The fear of another blow made my ragged breaths stall and all thoughts of biding my time, waiting for a chance to escape, evaporated.

"Sir," one of the shifters on the other side of the room called out.

"What!" Balwyrdan's attention jerked to the man who'd spoken.

The man nodded at the open doorway, and Balwyrdan tossed me to the floor, my head hitting the legs of the large stacked tables behind me.

With a snarl, he strode to the far side of the large room to the reception hall's wide main doors.

The pale glow from the half dozen magical fae orbs hovering at the ceiling flashed off of something metal, and Mavis with her gold and silver necklaces, bracelets, and chain headpiece sauntered through the entrance.

"You've been paid, witch," Balwyrdan said.

"But I didn't tell you everything, and now you know my information is good." Mavis flashed him a cocky smile and walked her fingers down the front of his chest. "For double, I can give you the dragon."

She could what—?

Realization cut through my whirling thoughts and the fear churning in my gut hardened and heated into anger. Mavis had betrayed us. She'd told Balwyrdan where we were— or rather from the sounds of it, where *I* would be. She was responsible for my fear and pain and now she was back to give Titus up and get more money. Had she even bothered to ask what Balwyrdan wanted with Titus? Which was a stupid question. She clearly didn't care.

"For double, hunh?" Balwyrdan asked, his voice lowering and turning sensual.

Now I really had to escape. I had to warn Cassius. Without a doubt, Balwyrdan would take Mavis up on her offer, and she'd tell him what Titus now looked like.

I yanked my gaze away from them and glanced around the room. I wasn't sure how many men Balwyrdan had, but of the dozen in the room, the only one closest to me — fifteen feet away — was staring out the large bank of windows along the back wall that surprisingly still had glass in them. Beyond, lay a sloping field of grass and weeds with clusters of trees and bushes shrouded in darkness.

No one was watching me.

This was my chance.

I slowly rolled to my knees, trying to be as quiet as possible. My body screamed in pain and my pulse raced. *Please don't look my way. Oh God, please.*

"I should be charging you triple," Mavis purred. "But that faekin thinks he can keep sending angels and JP agents to my shop. I want you to teach him a lesson."

I shifted to bring one knee up but Mavis's gaze flickered to me, and I froze, my gaze locking with hers. There wasn't a hint of remorse in her eyes.

My heart thudded and each rapid breath sliced agony through my chest. Did she know I was trying to escape? Would she alert Balwyrdan?

Her smile deepened and she turned her attention back to Balwyrdan. "I want you to make the faekin suffer. Something it seems you're quite good at."

I brought my knee up, ready to stand, and searched the room for my quickest escape route.

There. A door. A few feet past the guard at the windows. I didn't know if it was unlocked, but if I could get outside, I could release my wings and fly away.

No. Bad idea. Balwyrdan would see me and suffocate me—

My thoughts stuttered. He didn't even need to see me. The moment he realized I was gone, he'd use the leash spell to kill me or bring me back.

Why hadn't I thought of that?

Because I was in shock and pain and still reeling from the beating I'd taken.

All I wanted was to be strong and in control, but I wasn't.

For a second, I contemplated what my chances were that I'd be able to find Cassius and warn him before Balwyrdan suffocated me. He was still walking into a trap. Even if I died, perhaps I could save them.

Except would Balwyrdan be able to sense if I moved farther away from him, just like I knew when I'd moved too far away from Titus? How far would I be able to go?

"I usually don't hire my services out," Balwyrdan said, "but I may make an exception for you. How do you know the faekin will show up with the beast?"

Mavis gave a sensual shrug. "There's a chance he won't."

"Then you'd be losing out on one-third of your payment."

My throat tightened. There wasn't anything I could do to survive this or even help the guys except uselessly pray Balwyrdan didn't kill me before Cassius came for me.

"Oh, I can think of a few ways to get that one-third." She pushed her pelvis against Balwyrdan's and stroked her palms across his pecks.

More tears rolled down my cheeks.

It didn't matter what I wanted. I had no control. I never did.

"And what makes you think I'd take you up on your offer?" He slid his hand to her back. "What makes you think I'd even pay double for something I already have?"

"But you don't have the dragon." Mavis tried to pull away, but Balwyrdan tightened his grip, crushing her against him. "He still has my concealment charm and glamour on him."

"And when I first came to you, I asked you for the dragon," Balwyrdan hissed.

He grabbed the long knife from the hip sheath of the man beside him and plunged the blade into Mavis's heart.

Oh, my God!

Mavis screamed and tried to shove out of Balwyrdan's grip, but he held tight, capturing her against his body, and twisted the blade, driving it in all the way to the hilt.

My magic rushed into my hands and locked onto the woman responsible for my suffering, turning my fear and rage to frustration.

"You said you couldn't give me the dragon," Balwyrdan said.

Mavis gasped, her eyes wide.

I gritted my teeth and fought the building pressure to move my battered body across the room.

I was *not* going to save her. Saving her would take all my strength, and I wasn't going to make that mistake again. Just because I couldn't run, didn't mean I couldn't try to hold out until help arrived. It was the only thing I had left in my control.

God, I couldn't even control my own magic.

Balwyrdan yanked out the knife and slammed it back into her chest, drawing another scream. "And now you say you can give me the dragon."

A part of me hated how selfish I was. I had the power to save her and I'd picked me over her. But picking me also picked Cassius, Sebastian, Titus, and Hawk. Wasting my power on someone who'd betrayed us, whose greed was the reason she'd been mortally wounded meant not having the power to save one of the guys, and that was unacceptable.

My power burned up my forearms and heaved at my soul.

Save her.

No. Not at the expense of the guys.

Mavis weakly struggled to break free and clawed at Balwyrdan's hand, her mouth opening and closing on gasped words too quiet for me to hear on the other side of the room.

"You think I'll just accept your lie and pay you again?" he demanded, yanking out the blade and plunging it back in. "What made you think I was the kind of man who would play that game?"

Save her.

The pressure burned past my elbows and squeezed my chest. It heaved me up and I threw myself forward, curling into a ball and pressing my forehead to the floor to keep from moving.

She's dying. Try. I had to at least try.

No. I won't save her. Please. I can't.

My power surged and impossibly, a thin thread, just enough to assess injuries, connected with Mavis even though I wasn't touching her. I could feel her life force draining from her, pooling in her blood at Balwyrdan's feet. The pressure to go to her, heal her, screamed through me and my body struggled against my will to sit up.

Go. Save her.

Mavis screamed again, and the sharp burst of being stabbed shot through my connection to her. I wasn't touching her. I wasn't even looking at her. I shouldn't have been able to feel her pain or her life force. But it was there, inside me, overwhelming me, snapping, and writhing, desperate to stay alight, begging me to use the power I'd been born with to save her.

Another scream and slice of pain and Mavis's life force stuttered, flared, and went out.

The fiery pressure inside me vanished, replaced with the trembling ache of backlash. I tried to bite back a sob, but it escaped anyway. Frustrating useless tears leaked from my eyes. I was never going to be in control. If I wasn't someone's prisoner or trapped by my mating brand, I'd still be a slave to my power.

"I told you to run," a quiet, emotionless voice said.

My heart leaped into my throat and I jerked my head up to face the demon-vampire, the sudden movement sending agony screaming through me.

He crouched beside me, his handsome sculpted features just as emotionless as his voice, but his fangs were fully extended and his hellfire angry red pinpricks in his black eyes, revealing a wild hunger — the kind a predator had for its prey. His attention dipped to a cut on my cheek and he swallowed, the muscles in his throat flexing with the movement.

My breath picked up, making my pulse pound faster, which I was sure only made me look like a more appealing meal. It was against the law for a vampire to feed on someone without his or her consent, and with the plethora of humans more than willing to experience the euphoria of a vampire's bite and legalized blood houses, very few broke that law. But I doubted this vampire, given how emotionless he'd been when he'd decapitated that man in Lincoln, cared about laws.

Balwyrdan kicked Mavis's lifeless body, now lying on the floor with the knife still in her chest, and glared at the man beside him. "Get rid of this."

The hellfire in the demon-vampire's eyes flared and he shifted closer to me.

I shivered, half in fear and half at his lifeless essence. I didn't mind vampires, they were who they were, but they always felt wrong to me. Empty and cold. I couldn't *feel* them like how I felt others, like they didn't have a proper life force even though they still had a soul.

"Where is that beast?" Balwyrdan flicked his finger without even looking at me and the air around me vanished.

My body seized, my lung screaming for air, and darkness swirled through my vision. I collapsed forward, tears rolling down my cheeks, and my fear swelled. After this, Balwyrdan would yank me up by the hair and hit me again and again. *No more. Please.*

"I want a report from the men outside," he said and my air returned.

I sucked in a ragged breath, shooting more agony through my chest, and squeezed my eyes shut. I had to shut myself away, had to endure this until help arrived.

But a cold hand grabbed my wrist and fear shattered my concentration.

"Please," I begged, ashamed that the word had slipped out.

Something yanked against the rope binding my hands and the pressure keeping them back vanished.

My eyes flew open and I met the demon-vampire's gaze. His hunger was gone, replaced with a hard, emotionless expression. He pressed something into my hand as someone outside the main door yelled, then he darted into the shadows behind me with his enhanced vampiric speed and disappeared.

My thoughts stuttered. He'd freed me... sort of.

But why even free my hands?

Orange-red light flashed somewhere beyond the bank of windows, and my heart skipped a beat. Had Cassius finally come? *Please, let this be Cassius.*

The men in the room all started running for the door.

"Hold your position," Balwyrdan snapped still standing at the doorway.

The orange-red light flashed outside again and someone screamed.

I glanced at what the demon-vampire had given me. It was a small switchblade, the blade only a few inches long. It didn't make any sense that he'd give me a weapon now when he'd tried to kill me in the ring park, and I wasn't sure I'd be able to use it. With my surgical knowledge, I might know the most effective places to cut, but I didn't know how to fight. And since resisting my magic and refusing to save Mavis hadn't resulted in a serious backlash, I still risked my magic locking onto whoever I cut.

"Let them walk into the traps."

My pulse stuttered. *Them? Traps?* It wasn't just Cassius who was coming to my rescue?

"Then I'll kill everyone except the beast," Balwyrdan said, striding toward me.

I shoved my hands behind my back, praying my skirt hid the knife. With my lack of experience, I'd only be able to get one strike. But if Balwyrdan was close enough that strike could kill him.

It would have to kill him. Fast.

It was the only way to prevent my power from wanting to save him.

And I was *not* going to save him. Taking his life would stain my soul — the act went against the very essence of my being — but if it meant saving Cassius and the other guys, I would pay the price, the consequences be damned.

AMIAH

BALWYRDAN STRODE BACK TO ME AND SEIZED ME BY MY HAIR. WITH A snarl, he yanked me to my feet, wrapped his arm across my chest, his hand capturing my throat, and jerked me tight against his body. "Looks like Mavis was right. You are valuable."

My pulse pounded with fear and hope. Outside people yelled and screamed, but everyone was out of sight. All I could see were the bursts of orange-red light from Cassius's fire. It cast long flickering shadows across the lawn in front of the windows of human-like shapes jerking and running in the throes of battle.

Someone roared, the sound filled with fury and pain, and for a second, I thought it was Titus. But it didn't sound right. Not as deep as the roar I'd heard before. Which meant it had to have come from one of Balwyrdan's shifters.

Please let it be one of Balwyrdan's shifters and not Titus.

"Sounds like they even brought backup," Balwyrdan chuckled. "Or was there always a bear or wolf in your little group?"

A ball of fire tossed a large gray wolf across the lawn into the thick trunk of a lone maple tree near the door where I'd originally hoped to escape. Flames caught in the dry grass and weeds and swept around the wolf, burning fur and flesh, before Cassius — still out of sight — sucked the fire back into his body, leaving a charred corpse without a hint of life force.

Bile burned my throat. It had happened so fast my magic hadn't even had time to lock onto the man. At least the shifter's death had been swift. But for Cassius to kill so quickly and violently...

Was this what it had been like for him during the war? No wonder he'd come back hard and icy.

Another scream tore me away from the horror of Cassius's power.

Was that one of the guys? Please don't let it be one of them. I couldn't let any of them die. Not to save me. *God, why had I wished for them to come for me?* Surely they'd already figured out they were walking into a trap. Cassius had experience with these kinds of things, and Sebastian, while full of himself, was smart. They had to know. *Please, let them know.* I had to find a way to tell them. I couldn't just stand there, helpless. There had to be something I could do.

Anything.

Please.

Blinding white light lit up the lawn outside and someone screamed in agony.

My heart leaped into my throat and Balwyrdan chuckled.

"I wonder which one of them walked into the trap." He wrenched my head back to look me in the eyes, his gaze filled with the same dark pleasure he'd had when he hit me. "The new shifter? The faekin Mavis wanted tortured?"

A blast of fire raced over the lawn in front of the windows, and a nauseating mix of relief, guilt, and dread churned in my gut.

Cassius was fine. Was Sebastian? Titus? Hawk?

"Well, the angel is still conscious."

The strange roar that could have been Titus sounded.

"And so is the new shifter."

Which left Sebastian and Hawk.

One of Balwyrdan's men ran into sight at the far edge of the windows. Cassius's fire whip snapped at him and he jerked out of reach, falling onto his butt. Two more men appeared, one wrenching out of the way as Hawk lunged at him, while the other swiped at Hawk. Hawk leaped to the side and the man's claws narrowly missed his shoulder.

More fire flared just out of sight and someone screamed, then Titus lurched into view and tossed a charred body, the clothes still on fire, through the window on the far side of the room.

The glass shattered, sending shards skittering across the floor, and the corpse tumbled all the way to the main door.

Titus's gaze locked on me and with a snarl, he stormed through the opening. Hawk, Cassius, and — thank God! — Sebastian rushed in behind him.

They were alive. *They're all alive.* And they were terrifying.

Sebastian, the least terrifying of them, without any blood on his clothes and a gray complexion, had a hard and calculating expression. Without a doubt, he wouldn't hesitate to kill any of Balwyrdan's men, and he probably already had.

Beside him, stood Titus, his hands and arms covered in blood up to his elbows and his T-shirt soaked with it.

Next was Hawk. Blood splattered his shirt as well, although not as much as Titus's, and coated his hand holding a wickedly curved blade. He, too, looked ready to kill anyone who stood in his way.

But most terrifying of them all was Cassius. Molten fire dripped from arms and hands fully engulfed in flames, and the inferno raced along the top of his wings all the way to the tips. His body shook, and from the searing ferocious look in his eyes, he shook from a rage that was on the verge of slipping his control.

I'd never seen him so angry before. I hadn't even known he was possible of such rage. Rescuing me this time wasn't compelled by justice but by vengeance, and God help anyone who stood in his way.

Cassius took a step forward and blinding white light flashed around them. Dark thick strands burst from the ground, capturing them in a magical spider web. Hawk and Titus slashed at the strands, but more strands swept around their arms, immobilizing them.

Balwyrdan huffed. "That was too eas—"

Cassius yelled and his fire exploded into a massive fireball that ignited the web. Flames rushed through the strands sending ash to the floor and thick black smoke to the ceiling, freeing the guys without burning them, which was an extraordinary demonstration of Cassius's control.

"Let her go," Cassius said. He didn't even offer to let Balwyrdan live like I'd expected.

Balwyrdan's men who'd been told to hold their position tensed, shooting nervous glances at each other and waiting for Balwyrdan's command to attack.

"Hmm. Which one do you think is the beast?" Balwyrdan asked, his voice filled with dark mirth as if his spell hadn't just been burned to a crisp. "I know he isn't the angel or the faekin. It would be too obvious to make him a wolf, so my guess is the incubus."

Cassius's fire billowed from his wings. "Let. Her. Go."

"Give me the beast," Balwyrdan said in a mocking singsong, "and you can have her back."

"This isn't a negotiation," Cassius growled.

"You're right, it isn't." Balwyrdan released my throat and flicked his finger.

I gasped in a quick breath just before the leash spell slammed into my chest and the air around me vanished.

Sebastian groaned and pressed a hand to his chest.

"Come now. Which one of you is the beast?" Balwyrdan released the spell and slammed it back into place with so much force my knees gave out. His grip in my hair tore at my scalp, and I fought to regain my balance without grabbing his hand and giving away the fact my hands were no longer bound.

Sebastian screamed and dropped to his hands and knees, his chest heaving with desperate gasps.

"You took the leash spell?" Balwyrdan asked, his tone sharp with surprise, and air flooded back around me as if he needed to concentrate to keep the spell active. "You. You little faekin," he said incredulously. "*You* manage to take the spell and warp it enough so you wouldn't suffocate. You must have had help. That witch must have double-crossed me and helped you take on the spell."

"No help." Sebastian climbed back to his feet, his fae glow so weak it was barely visible, and shrugged. "The last dragon isn't coming, either. He's already left town and you'll never be able to find him."

"So I'm what?" Balwyrdan asked with a dark chuckle. "Just supposed to hand her over?"

"Yes," Cassius replied.

"You really didn't think this through." Balwyrdan jerked my head back, spiking agony through my neck and chest. "If I can't get the beast with the leash spell then I have no use for her."

I gasped in a quick breath, knowing what was coming, but the leash spell pounded into me, stealing what little breath I'd managed to get. Cassius bellowed and rushed toward me, but Balwyrdan's remaining men ran to meet him.

My body strained to breathe, gasping against nothing, and my lungs started to burn.

Titus and Hawk dove into the fray, Titus slashing the neck of a big, bulky man with his claws, sending blood spraying everywhere, while Hawk ducked under a similar swipe to his neck and sliced his blade through his assailant's gut.

My magic exploded under my skin, locking on Titus's man, then jerking to Hawk's for a second when Titus's man died.

Cassius seized the man closest to him with his fire whip and tossed him through another one of the large windows. He turned to head to me, but another man jumped in his way, slicing his right biceps before Cassius tossed him aside with his fire whip.

Flames danced along the floor on the verge of getting out of control, and Balwyrdan's men still blocked the way of all the guys. They were getting closer and there were only about six assailants left. But dark specks crowded my vision, and my body shook with the effort to stay standing. I was running out of time, and even if the guys could take out all the men right now, none of them were close enough to get to me before I passed out.

Titus roared and ripped out another man's throat. Hawk slashed at his assailant, but the man jerked out of the way and rammed his fist into Hawk's side. Cassius sucked in his fire before he burned the abandoned reception hall down around us as another man lunged at him, managing to slice through his fire whip with his claws. With a yell, Cassius sent a blast into the man's chest, tossing him into the stacked tables behind me.

Balwyrdan stiffened and Cassius's gaze locked with mine. His eyes were filled with rage and soul-crushing terror. He knew he wasn't going to be able to get to me in time, knew Balwyrdan was going to kill me.

He raised his hand, his whip hissing and crackling. Balwyrdan would still be able to kill me before his whip connected, but it was the only option.

I knew it. He knew it. And Balwyrdan could see that too.

He jerked me closer, wrapping his arm across my chest and using my body as a shield. The room darkened and spun around me, and I had no idea if Cassius was going to use his whip or not. All I knew was that I had to get away from Balwyrdan or break his concentration or something. I *had* to do something. Now.

I yanked my hand out from between our bodies and without a deadly place to strike, sliced the blade through his arm.

He howled and seized my hand before I could cut him again. Air rushed back around me and I gasped in a ragged breath. But he wrenched my hand back and broke my wrist, exploding agony through my hand and arm.

"You need to do more than that to get free," he sneered, and the leash spell pounded into me again, just as his blood splattered on my bare foot and my power instinctually connected with him.

The wound was deep, but not deadly.

And that didn't matter. It was all I needed.

I shoved my magic into him with a forceful blast, making him scream. The leash spell sputtered out and his grip loosened. I wrenched free of his hold and tried to scramble out of the way but only managed a few staggering steps before my battered body lost its balance.

Sebastian caught me and yanked me back. We fell to the floor, me half in his arms, as sudden ferocious heat seared my back.

Someone screamed, and I turned to see Balwyrdan fully engulfed in a massive pillar of fire. The inferno burned so hot he barely had a chance to move before he dropped to the floor and burst into a pile of ash and glowing embers.

Cassius sagged to his knees and all of his fire, the fire that had consumed Balwyrdan and the flames dancing over his skin, went out. He'd used a lot of his magic and it was amazing he was still conscious. Hawk stared at him, wide-eyed and pale, as Titus killed the last of Balwyrdan's men.

I couldn't tell how badly everyone was hurt, but my magic hadn't locked on to any of them so none of them were in mortal danger.

Thank God. Oh, thank God.

With a groan, Cassius sucked the remaining fire in the building back into his body. He shuddered, heaved his wings back in as well, and pulled off his T-shirt. Somehow he'd managed to get through that fight with just that cut on his biceps, only the ugly red burn scars from his fight in Left of Lincoln marred his torso. Of course, he hadn't held back, hadn't cared if he ran out of magic or who or what he'd set on fire. I doubted anyone had managed to get close to him.

"Here," he said, tossing the shirt to Hawk who caught it in his free hand. "Give that to Amiah."

Hawk knelt beside me, his gaze filled with concern without a hint of sexual invitation even though I was half naked.

The look made my throat tighten with frustration. It was the same look Cassius had given me all those years ago when he'd first rescued me.

"Can you sit up?" he asked.

"Yes," I insisted, even though I had no idea if I could. I didn't want to move. I wanted to pass out until my body stopped hurting. Except the only way I'd stop hurting was if I healed myself and that was going to take time. A lot of time... that I didn't want to spend topless.

I struggled to rise, shooting blazing agony through me that made the room darken and lurch, and left me panting.

"Jeez," Sebastian said. "You just had the shit beaten out of you. Stop trying to do everything yourself."

He helped me sit, and I held up my arms, my muscles trembling even with something as simple as that, and Hawk dressed me. Biting back a moan, I sagged against Sebastian, gasping shallow breaths and fighting my tears.

I wasn't strong. I'd never be strong.

I'd never be free.

Titus crouched beside Hawk with the same pitying expression. "Can you break the leash spell?"

"We should move someplace safer first," Cassius said, his head bowed, his body language saying he wasn't going to move anytime soon. "We don't know who betrayed us. We could still be in danger."

"It was Mavis," I gasped. "Balwyrdan killed her."

"Good," Titus growled.

"Does that mean your apartment is safe again?" Hawk asked. "Wait." Hope flashed in his eyes. "Does that mean I can go back to my life? Sparky barbecued that monster and we killed all his men. The bitch who betrayed us is dead and the spring fae don't know about us anymore."

Cassius groaned, pushed up to his feet, and staggered to the rest of us. "Are you willing to risk that?"

"Hell, yeah." Hawk's gaze jumped to mine for a heartbeat but he yanked it away and stood before I could figure out what the look meant. "This situation is fucked up, and you're all insane."

"There were more than just spring fae at Lincoln," Sebastian said, gingerly stroking a lock of my hair out of my face and drawing my attention to his pale eyes. His expression was still tight with pain and his complexion gray. "Let's break this leash spell."

"I can wait." As much as I wanted to be free — *now now now* — he was in no condition to cast anything... and if it was going to be as painful as the last attempt, I wouldn't be able to handle it. "You're too pale."

"Winter fae, remember?" His lips quirked. "And while I love the fact you can't go more than a hundred feet from me, I'm pretty sure Sparky here hates it."

Cassius bristled at his words. "Call me Sparky again. I dare you."

"So you don't care that Amiah is stuck with me?" A hint of Sebastian's usual wicked gleam lit his eyes. "Just the nickname."

"I didn't say that," Cassius shot back.

"Sure sounded like it to me," Hawk said.

"It's not an either or." Cassius crouched and held out his hands. "Give me Amiah and let's get out of here."

But before Sebastian could hand me over, the air a few feet away burst into a shimmering liquid mirror. A pale tiny woman in a dark flowing gown with gossamer wings and the same bluish-white and silver coloring as Sebastian stepped through. Two enormous identical men taller and broader than Titus who looked like they'd been carved from ice followed her and took up position behind her. They carried long spears and wore a strange shimmering breastplate that could have been made of ice, and loose white pants.

Cassius jerked to his feet and clenched his hands as if to summon his fire, but not even a hint of smoke curled from his skin. Titus extended his claws and snarled, and Hawk widened his stance, ready to fight.

"Fuck," Sebastian groaned.

"Faekin," the woman said. "You've been summoned to the Winter Queen's court to swear your allegiance."

Something shifted in the shadows on the far side of the room behind the woman, drawing my attention, and I met the demon-vampire's solemn gaze.

"I've already sworn my allegiance," Sebastian said.

The woman's eyes narrowed. "You have not."

"Yeah, well." Sebastian shrugged, the movement making me gasp in pain. "Tell her majesty, thanks but no thanks."

"This wasn't a request." The tiny woman clapped her hands and the air turned to liquid magic. It crashed around us before any of the guys could attack, sweeping us into a ferocious whirlpool and sucking us in.

We were going to Faerie whether we wanted to or not. Right into the realm where everyone wanted to capture or kill us, and the Shadow Court's assassin knew exactly where we were going.

FATED WINTER

ANGEL'S FATE, BOOK 2

AMIAH

THE SHIMMERING LIQUID PORTAL SPAT US OUT INTO FAERIE AND JERKED Sebastian forward who was still kneeling and holding me. The sudden jolt made him tighten his grip and shoot agony through my bruised and broken body, drawing a whimper that I struggled to hide. I didn't know why. There wasn't any point. They'd just seen me at my worst — and a lot more of me than I'd wanted — and I had every reason to be in pain.

A few feet away, Hawk stumbled and fell to his knees, and Cassius and Titus staggered but managed to keep standing.

We'd arrived at the back of a massive hall that looked like it had been carved entirely of ice even though I couldn't feel the cold. Pale glowing balls of light hovered above us, not even close to the vaulted ceiling, illuminating the space and reflecting in the semi-translucent pillars and walls.

But the sense of ice, gleaming walls, and vastness was all I could really register. Agony from the beating I'd taken at the hands of Balwyrdan, the Spring Court's seneschal, wracked my body along with the horror of what I'd gone through. I'd been taken. Again.

God, again!

And while I had a glimmer of healing power inside me, it wasn't enough to heal any of my broken bones, since healing myself took a lot more power than healing someone else. Even if I'd been at full, it still wouldn't have been enough because my thoughts spun, ripped apart in a whirlwind of fear and pain and I couldn't focus long enough to pull my power from my palms and direct it to my injuries.

All of my ribs were broken, my wrist was broken, my nose was broken, and a hairline fracture sliced through my cheek. I also had a concussion, which explained, in part, why I couldn't focus my magic. Most of my face and torso was one big swelling bruise, and I could only see out of one eye — the other had swollen shut — and my vision was blurry and dark while the room spun and lurched around me.

I wasn't sure if there was anyone else in the room other than us, the tiny woman with the gossamer wings who'd pulled us into the portal, and her massive ice guards with their ice spears.

I could only pray she wouldn't force me to stand. I wouldn't have been able to, no matter what I wanted.

"God damned fucking shit," Sebastian hissed, his body shaking and his heart pounding. But I couldn't tell if it was from the fight we'd just won or our abduction into Faerie to the Winter Queen's court. As it was, his complexion was gray from all the magic he'd been forced to expend to save me, and I doubted he had anything left to use if we needed to fight our way free.

"We can't stay here," Titus growled softly, his claws fully extended — the glamour making his dragon claws look like wolf claws — and his hands and forearms covered in blood. Blood also dampened his ripped T-shirt and pasted his right pantleg to his thigh where he'd been injured. I couldn't tell what other injuries he might have had, but my magic didn't lock onto him so he couldn't have been in immediate danger, and with his amazing natural healing, whatever injuries he did have would be healed sooner rather than later.

The woman with the wings flew to the center of the room, leaving the guards who stood a few feet away to glare at us, and a murmur of voices on the far side of the room greeted her.

"Your majesty. The winter faekin to swear his allegiance," she said, her voice echoing off the icy walls.

Cassius shifted closer to us, his hands clenched but not a hint of smoke curling from his skin. He'd also used every last drop of his fire magic to save me in a terrifying display, burning Balwyrdan to ash in a matter of seconds, and there was no way he'd be able to fight us free, either. "Just swear your allegiance so we can go."

"It doesn't work that way," Sebastian said.

"Of course it doesn't." Hawk stood and tightened his grip on his wickedly curved knife. His T-shirt was also bloody and torn, and he had a nasty set of lacerations along his ribs, likely from a shifter's claws. He was going to need an influx of sexual energy to heal and I wasn't in any kind of condition to help him.

"Step forward, faekin," the woman called from her spot in the center of the room, "and bow to your queen."

Sebastian staggered to his feet, jostling me. I whimpered again and a tear I didn't want to cry rolled down my cheek. I hated that I was in pain and weak even though I had good reason to be at the moment.

Because I'd been taken.

I fought to shove that thought aside and think about anything else, the guys' injuries, concentrating past the whirling room, trying to breathe without slicing pain through my chest. Anything but what had happened.

Taken. Again.

And this time I'd been seriously beaten. I swore I'd never be anyone's prisoner ever again, done everything in my power for the last hundred years to keep that vow, but I'd been helpless to save myself. So damned helpless. I was tired of being helpless, but in a world of supernatural beings, an angel with a healing magic that could compel her to heal her enemy was weak and useless in a fight.

"Give her to me," Cassius said, holding out his arms, the muscles of his bare chest flexing with the movement. He'd given me his shirt because Balwyrdan had ripped my dress's neck strap.

I didn't want to think about that, either. All of the guys had now seen me topless. And if I didn't hurt so much, I would have been embarrassed.

"No," Sebastian said. "If I'm holding her, they're less likely to separate us."

"Right." The muscles in Cassius's jaw flexed at the reminder that Sebastian and I shouldn't be separated.

Sebastian had taken on Titus's half of the leash spell that had bound us together and now I couldn't be more than a hundred feet from Sebastian or I'd suffocate.

I wasn't sure how I felt about that, either. The last time Sebastian and I had talked was just after having sex and I'd fled his bedroom, too stunned at what I'd just done. It had been amazing and surprising and completely out of character for me. Over a hundred years of celibacy broken in one amazing, confusing moment, and yet at the time, I'd desperately wanted him, wanted to be kissed and touched and filled in a way that I'd been holding back from because I'd been foolishly waiting for my soul mate.

"In fact, everyone stay close." Sebastian took a careful step forward, but even that sent blazing pain rushing through me and drew a whimper.

"They must know about T," Cassius whispered, falling into step beside Sebastian and keeping his gaze locked on the front of the room. "Why else would they come after you?"

I tried to make my breath as shallow as possible. But it didn't matter how slightly I breathed, every miniscule movement hurt.

"I'm hoping because someone from the Spring or Shadow Courts told Her Majesty there was a winter faekin in the mortal realm who most likely needs to vow his allegiance to the queen in an attempt to get us out of the way so they could have T to themselves." Sebastian's trembling increased. "I really hoped I'd never have to come back."

"Faekin," the woman snapped. "Disobedience is death."

Sebastian barked a quiet bitter laugh. "Maybe we'll get lucky and this won't take long."

"There's only one way to manage that," Titus said under his breath.

"I know." Sebastian glanced at Hawk, whose expression was pinched. "Can you give Amiah a bit of a distraction to ease her pain?"

"Ah… sure." Hawk brushed a finger down my bare calf and a warm sensual curl of his incubus magic unfurled within me. For a second, I was drifting in a heated ocean of desire, my pain a whisper at the edge of my senses, my fears and worries muted, my focus entirely on the bone-melting sensation coursing through me. There was no hall, no guys, just blissful nothingness.

Then light flared around me and Hawk's magic stuttered, jerking me out of my haze. Sebastian had released his hold on his glamour that kept the glow emanating from his skin at a low faekin level, letting it blaze at its full fae radiance. His ears, already with a small delicate point, grew pointier. But unlike the last time I'd seen him in his full fae form, his face also changed. His eyes became bigger, his nose narrower, his cheekbones and chin sharper.

I hadn't thought it was possible for him to be more stunning. He'd already had the looks to compete with an incubus. Now he wasn't just breathtaking, he was mesmerizing. Everything within me tripped, stunned, unable to think past his appearance.

"Kneel, fae—" The woman with the wings turned to us and gasped, which drew a big gasp from the people gathered at the front of the room.

A murmur rushed through the crowd and I strained to focus on them and see just who we were facing. There were maybe a hundred people in the room, a mix of men and women some with the full-body glow of fae, but others were small with wings, or tall and bulky... actually, they were all manner of shapes and sizes, although most looked humanish. The women all wore diaphanous dresses in white, silver, and blues and they all dropped into low curtsies. The men wore knee-length tunics and loose pants in the same colors, and they knelt on one knee, their heads bowed.

Behind them on a raised dais sat a tall, beautiful fae woman on a massive throne that looked like it was made entirely of ice. She had the same white and silver hair as Sebastian, although she wore hers half up with braids and half hanging past her waist instead of Sebastian's short and spikey.

A small, delicately spun ice crown rested on her head, the thin strands woven into a complex filigree, and she wore a shimmering midnight blue gown made of diaphanous layers of fabric tailored to perfectly accentuate her slim figure and tease with glimpses of pale glowing flesh beneath.

To her right stood another beautiful fae woman with striking black hair, the color unlike any other fae in the room. An intricate ice circlet held back her hair, and she wore a similar dress to the queen's in white as if she were the queen's opposite.

At their feet, were a dozen men, half of them fae like Sebastian, the rest a mix of shifters and demons. They lounged on thick blue rugs and cushions, dressed only in loose pants made of the same light fabric as everyone else's clothes, but in varying shades of red, each one of them with an exquisite physique.

All of them, the men in red and both of the fae women on the dais, stared at Sebastian with guarded expressions.

"Oh, shit," Hawk hissed.

"The day has finally arrived," the Winter Queen said, her voice breathy as a single, shimmering tear rolled down her cheek. "You've come home."

Sebastian slowly dipped into a shallow bow. I could tell he was trying not to jostle me, but the movement still made me whimper and the room darken and lurch. "Your majesty."

"Formalities? Really Seireadan? I haven't seen you in over three hundred years." The queen clapped her hands and a dozen people, a mix of men and women who looked like they'd been carved from ice like the two guards — although not nearly as tall or muscular — scurried from a small door behind and to the right of the dais. "Seireadan, prince of the realm, heir to the throne of the Winter Court has returned home. This calls for a celebration."

The men on the dais all bowed their heads, but the woman standing beside the throne continued to glare.

"Prince?" Hawk asked under his breath. "If I'd known you were royalty, I would have charged you more."

"Not any more. I abdicated and got the fuck out of Faerie," Sebastian murmured back, giving him then me a pointed look. "Your magic for Amiah."

"Shit. Right. Sorry." Hawk brushed his finger over my calf again, stealing my breath with another sensual curl of power and sending me spinning, half in pain and half with desire.

"Yes," the queen cooed, her eyes bright. "This will be the biggest celebration in court since your betrothal. Bigger."

"Your Maj—" Sebastian started but the queen's eyes narrowed, and for a second it looked like something dark and ugly flashed behind her bright joy. But it happened so fast I wasn't sure I'd actually seen it.

"Mother," Sebastian corrected. "We're in no condition for a celebration."

"Of course you are." The queen leaned back on her throne and raised a hand. Most of the crowd scurried out of the room followed by half of the ice people, while the other half of the ice people knelt to the right of the dais and five women gathered demurely to the left — although all of them kept glancing at Hawk, unable to keep their eyes off him even though it seemed they were supposed to keep their heads bowed.

I couldn't blame them. Hawk was as handsome as Sebastian and with his magic oozing through me it was difficult to think of anything other than begging him to satisfy me. And while the other women didn't have his magic inside them, he, like all incubi, naturally radiated sexual desire, and I doubted he did much to hold it back.

"Oh, you look tired but I'm sure you're more than perfectly capable of handling a celebration in your honor and selecting a bride." She gave Cassius, Titus, and Hawk a dismissive wave. "Give your bodyguards and

—" Her lips pursed and she studied me with a cold calculating look that made my insides churn. I hadn't imagined that ugly darkness.

The man closest to her, a werepanther with a sleek, lean-muscled body, leaned toward her and mumbled something, and her grip on the arms of her throne tightened.

"I see," she said, the darkness shifting to something else, something more... calculating? "Give your men and your concubine time to relax."

Cassius stiffened at her words, as Titus growled low in his throat and Hawk snorted.

Concubine? I wasn't his concubine... although I had slept with Sebastian — and with Hawk's magic heating me, I was starting to think sleeping with Sebastian again was a good idea despite my injuries. But that didn't make me his concubine. We weren't in a relationship.

"I'm not going to a party," Sebastian insisted, "and I'm not choosing a bride. I'm going home. Allow us to pass through the portal."

"But you are home, dear, and you must choose a bride." Actual darkness bled over the queen's eyes, and crackling frost rushed down the dais's three shallow stairs and across the floor toward us. "You'll be king. You must produce an heir."

"I don't need to produce an heir," Sebastian said. "Padraigin already has an heir."

The woman beside the throne stiffened and more ice crackled across the floor around Sebastian's feet. The temperature in the room dropped, making me shiver, and the agonizing blaze in my body devoured Hawk's magic.

"Padraigin isn't *my* heir," the queen said. "You are."

"Mother—"

"You just needed time to think after that silly business with Enowen." The queen sat forward and all the men around her straightened, ready for her command. "And now you're back."

I strained to breathe as darkness crept around the edges of my vision, and Hawk's magic fought to overwhelm my pain.

"Pick a wife." The queen gestured to the ladies who now openly stared at Hawk. I didn't know if he was purposefully letting his incubus magic affect them or not. He seemed oblivious to them, all of his attention on me, his expression tight with concern... or was that concentration? How hard was it to use his magic to distract me from my pain without making me ignore my injuries to satisfy myself?

"I'm not picking a wife."

"You are." The temperature dropped again and snowflakes lazily drifted from the ceiling. "And tell your incubus to pull his power back or I'll neuter him. The maids are for you. I'll not have him manipulating your future wife." The queen's smile turned wicked. "Not until you've made your vows. Then you can do whatever you like with her."

Sebastian shot Hawk a quick glance, who frowned and squinted at Sebastian before his magic evaporated.

The agony in my body surged — I hadn't realized how much he was actually muting my pain — and I tried to bite back a sob but it escaped, a pathetic, mangled whimper.

"You've had your fun, Seireadan." The queen stood and all of her men stood with her. "Now pick a wife. Your whore can always remain in your harem. They all can."

"I can't do that," Sebastian said, his voice low.

"Of course you can." More ice crackled across the floor and the snow falling from the ceiling thickened. "If none of them appeal to you, I'll send for more."

"I can't. I..." Sebastian's almost-colorless blue gaze met mine filled with apology and resignation. "I've already made the vow to Amiah. You know it can't be broken."

"You vowed your fertility to a being you can't have children with?" The snowfall burst into a blinding freezing flurry. The flakes turned to ice pellets, stinging my already burning skin and sending tears streaming down my cheeks.

"I have," Sebastian yelled into the storm, hugging me tighter and hunching forward in an attempt to protect me from the storm. "Amiah is my wife."

The light in Cassius's eyes flared and he jerked close. "You better be lying."

"I'm not," Sebastian replied.

My heart skipped a beat and my thoughts whirled, caught between pain and confusion. "We're married?"

"Hey, man," Hawk said. "Just because you licked her, doesn't mean she's yours."

When did we get married? It couldn't have been because we had sex. I was sure in his very long life that Sebastian had slept with hundreds of women. He had to be lying. It couldn't be the truth. I couldn't be trapped like that. I couldn't be trapped, period. Never again.

Please, no.

Sebastian was supposed to be helping me remove my not-yet-awakened angelic mating brand and avoid the horrible fate of having a soul bond with a complete stranger, not trapping me to him. And if he couldn't remove my angelic mating brand, married to him or not, the brand was going to make me fall in love with someone else... and I wasn't in love with Sebastian. I didn't even know if I liked him.

AMIAH

The Winter Queen's storm picked up, the wind howling around us, the temperature so cold my nose, cheeks, fingers, and bare toes grew numb even with the pain wracking my body. I huddled against Sebastian's chest, fighting to breathe.

I can't be trapped. I can't be. I can't—

"How are we married?" I gasped. How was this even possible? I didn't vow anything to him. We'd just had sex.

"I used the binding ritual and everything," Sebastian yelled into the storm, ignoring me.

"You what?" I yelled back as the storm vanished, my cry suddenly loud in the silence.

A flicker of sadness flashed across Sebastian's face before he jerked his attention away from me. "Check for yourself, Mother."

Icy magic swept into my chest, stealing my breath completely before I could deny that I was married to Sebastian, that I hadn't agreed to anything. My shivering increased turning my pain into an inferno. For a second, darkness filled my vision and the promise of unconsciousness taunted me, then the pain surged, making me cry out.

"I see." The queen's power tore out of me and she glanced at a stunningly handsome fae who stood at her right and slightly behind her. He gave a tight nod and she huffed. "Well then."

Tears streamed down my cheeks, and Sebastian hugged me closer, his pulse racing even faster than when we'd first arrived.

"Prepare a room for the heir apparent, his bodyguards, and his... wife." The queen spat out the word and the remaining ice people rushed from the room. "Out!" she snapped at Sebastian's prospective brides, who scrambled to leave.

"We're not staying." Sebastian glanced at Cassius who, from his expression, if he had fire magic left, would have been dripping flames onto the floor. "My wife needs medical attention."

"Take her to the pools," the queen said, and the ice guards who had been hanging twenty feet back stepped up behind us. They looked identical both big, muscular, bald, and wearing strange shimmering breastplates and loose white pants, and they towered over all of us except for Titus who was only a foot or so shorter than they were. "We'll postpone your return celebration until she's recovered. Can't have the princess consort of the Winter Court missing her own celebration."

The queen flashed a disturbingly sweet smile and stormed off the dais. Her men followed, and the other woman jerked forward a step but stopped as Sebastian gave her a tight nod.

"Padraigin," he said.

"You shouldn't have come back." Her expression was as hard and icy as the queen's.

"I wasn't given much of a choice."

Her attention jumped to the ice guards then back to Sebastian. "Congratulations on your nuptials, your highness."

"Not any more," Sebastian said. "I left a note. I abdicated."

"Her majesty didn't accept your abdication." The woman, Padraigin, gave a shallow bow and marched out of the room.

"What the fuck?" Hawk demanded.

"You'll address his highness with respect." The guard on the left jabbed the butt of his ice spear at Hawk's chest.

Hawk jerked out of the way, and tensed, ready to slash the ice man with his knife, but Cassius grabbed his arm and jerked his chin at me. I wasn't sure what he was trying to tell Hawk, but after a moment with a pinched frown, Hawk seemed to understand and relaxed his fighting stance.

The other guard gestured to the back of the room. "Attendants are waiting for you in the pools, your highness."

"Dismiss them," Sebastian said, heading to the back with a confident stride, his back stiff, each step setting my body on fire. "My bodyguards are adequate protection and I wish to attend to my queen alone."

"Sebastian," I gasped. "I'm not—"

"Ready to discuss us staying here. I know, my love," he interrupted, a strange desperation flashing in his eyes. "We'll *talk* when we get to the pools."

My mind tripped over his emphasis of the word talk. Whatever he wanted to say, he didn't want these guards to overhear.

"Your highness, we can't leave you." The first guard stepped ahead of Sebastian and led the way down a wide, white hall while the other guard took up position behind us. "But I'll dismiss the attendants when we get there."

"And you'll wait in the hall," Sebastian said.

"Your highness—"

"Have I not made myself clear?" Sebastian asked, his voice suddenly low and dark, promising danger if the guard disobeyed. "I'll not have her majesty's constructs ogling my wife while she bathes in the healing pools. She's not fae. Her sensibilities are different and you'll learn to respect that."

The guard dipped his head with the sound of heavy ice creaking, but I didn't know if that meant he was embarrassed that he'd insulted his prince or upset at Sebastian's command. "Of course, your highness."

The guard led us down long icy hall after long icy hall that all looked identical. The floor was smooth but didn't seem slippery since none of the guys had problems keeping their balance, and the walls looked like they were carved with an intricate pattern. Except with the glow of the faerie lights in the semi-translucent white-on-white walls, it was difficult to make out the design.

No one said anything, and my pain continued to grow with every body-jarring step. Soon the world was dark and spinning and my breath shallow ragged pants. I wasn't going to last much longer. If we didn't stop, I was going to pass out and then I wouldn't be able to even try to focus what little magic I had to start healing myself. Which meant I'd be in even more pain when I woke, and that would keep the cycle of not being able to focus my power going.

"Sebastian, I have to stop," I gasped, fighting my tears. I didn't know why I fought them. It wasn't as if he and everyone hadn't seen me crying in the queen's hall.

"Almost there," he murmured. "We just need to get inside."

We rounded a corner and reached a large intricately carved ice door. Six petite ice women, all identical to each other, and if I thought about it, identical to the ice women who'd been in the hall, dressed in white flowing dresses, waited outside the door holding bundles of fabric. All of them bowed low as Sebastian approached.

"Set the towels and change of clothes on the bench inside and leave," the guard commanded as he pushed open the heavy door.

Sebastian didn't wait to see if the women obeyed or not. He strode inside, into a grotto nestled in a dimly lit cave filled with the gentle sound of flowing water. The floor was polished granite, but uncut rock also jutted out from the walls and floor, creating four different levels, each with at least one pool sunk into them. Holly bushes and evergreen shrubs added hints of privacy among the pools — and maybe more than hints since there might have been other pools I couldn't see because of them. Their scent filled the warm, humid air, and soft light from glowing orbs reflected off the floor and water, while starlight shone through a skylight.

"We'll be just outside the door if you need us, your highness," one of the guards said and the door closed with a resounding boom. Trapping us in.

Trapped. Again. God, again!

I dragged my attention to the skylight. Even on the verge of passing out, I needed sky and open spaces. I couldn't be trapped. I was now trapped to Sebastian. I couldn't—

Sebastian sagged to the floor and his glow stuttered, revealing an ashen complexion.

"What in the ever-loving fuck?" Hawk hissed.

"She's your wife?" Cassius demanded. "When did she become your wife?"

With a groan, Sebastian set me on the floor and activated a glyph on his hip, the one he'd claimed while we were having sex was a sound blocking spell.

"You shouldn't be using magic," I said. "You don't look well."

"No choice. We need to have a conversation and my mother's ice constructs will be listening." Sebastian squeezed his eyes shut. "Someone get Amiah in a pool. Any pool will do. The water isn't as effective at healing as angelic healing, and the body can't stand submersion for more than an hour at a time, but it'll still help."

Cassius grabbed the front of Sebastian's shirt and hauled him to his feet, but Sebastian's legs didn't brace to hold him. "How the hell is she your wife?"

"Cassius, please," I gasped as I sat up with a sharp slice of agony that made the room darken. "Look at him."

Cassius turned his glare on me. "You married him?"

"What if I did?" I blurted out. I didn't know why I said that. I was just so sore and angry. He didn't have a say who I married, just like he didn't have a say who I had sexual intercourse with. And Sebastian had no right to do a ritual marrying us without my consent, trapping me.

My pulse stuttered, the memory of Balwyrdan beating me threatening to overwhelm me.

Don't think about it. Just don't think about it.

A wisp of smoke burst from Cassius's hands. "Amiah—"

"For fuck's sake," Sebastian groaned, managing to get his balance. "My mother wasn't going to stop until I picked a wife and she wasn't going to let us go. I needed to say something that kept us together until I can break the leash spell on Amiah."

"So we're not—?" A strange mix of emotions crashed through me, fear, regret, anger, relief.

"No. We're not. Jeez, you really think I'd marry you?" he asked.

My throat irrationally tightened at that. No, of course he wouldn't. It was surprising enough that he'd had sex with me given how he clearly hadn't been interested before, just teasing me. Now that he knew I'd been a virgin and was inexperienced, I doubted he'd ever have sex with me again.

Which sent another confusing mix of emotions rushing through me. It shouldn't have mattered that he didn't want to have sex again, but it did. He already knew the truth about me, knew about my partially formed mating brand, and without a doubt wasn't my soul mate. In this particular instance, he was the safest person to satisfy my desires, desires I was tired of resisting.

And the fact that this upset me just proved how sore and exhausted I was.

"You still shouldn't have told her you gave Amiah your fertility," Titus said, his pupils slitted, his beast close to the surface. "You've put Amiah in danger. The only way now that you'll be able to have offspring with anyone else is if Amiah dies and you perform the ritual again." He yanked off his shirt and pulled off his boots.

"Without the binding ritual, my mother would never have accepted

Amiah as my wife." Sebastian tugged at Cassius's grip but wasn't strong enough to break free. "It had to be irreversible."

"Yeah, but it's *not* irreversible," Hawk said, also taking off his shirt and shoes and reaching to unbutton his fly. "Amiah's death fixes your mother's problem." He flicked open his fly and stepped out of his shorts. No underwear. I wasn't in the least bit surprised.

My breath and thoughts stuttered at the sight of Hawk's stunning physique and impressive... equipment. I barely even noticed the lacerations along his ribs and right biceps and the large bruise on his left side.

"Hey," Cassius snapped. "Put your shorts back on."

"I'm not going into a bath with clothes on."

Oh, wow. For a moment there was no pain, no fear, nothing, only heart-pounding bliss.

"—hoping we'll be out of Faerie before it comes to that," Sebastian said, now sitting on the floor and unbuttoning his dress shirt, time having stuttered while I was mesmerized by Hawk.

The shirt fell open revealing the complicated black tattoos still covering Sebastian's torso. They really had been real and not a part of the glamour he'd apparently had up hiding his true identity.

"At least the leash spell is good for something," he said. "My mother is powerful, but she's not a sorcerer, so she could feel Amiah and I were bound together, just not how."

"Shorts." Cassius grabbed Hawk's shorts from the floor and tossed them at the incubus.

"Don't be an asshole," Hawk shot back.

I heaved my attention away from them to focus on the closest pool. It lay about twenty feet away and was big enough for all five of us. Steam curled from its gently undulating surface, the movement coming from a small waterfall at the back where water from the previous level up fed into the pool.

I couldn't afford to stay in my current condition. Especially if we needed to flee the Winter Court at a moment's notice, so I gritted my teeth and started crawling the twenty feet to the pool.

But I'd barely crawled a few feet before my body was on fire and the world so dark I couldn't see my hands on the floor in front of me. The adrenaline I'd had during the fight with Balwyrdan was finally well and truly gone and all I wanted to do was curl into a ball and cry.

I will not think about it.

"You shouldn't be moving," Titus said as he gently drew me into his muscular arms. He looked at me with sadness and pity and a small hot ember of rage, and I closed my eyes, my throat tight with tears I was tired of crying.

I would get through this. I'd heal myself and the pain would end. I just needed to be strong. Just for a little longer. But it was so hard to concentrate, let alone be strong, especially with all the proof that I wasn't.

Titus carried me into the warm soothing water still fully dressed — or at least as dressed as I had been when Balwyrdan had kidnapped me in only a dress without shoes or underwear. Soft tingling magic sank into my skin and oozed into my veins and between my cells. It curled around my heart, seeped into my essence, and, for a heart-stopping second, heated the delicate lines of my not-yet-formed mating brand.

Panic stole my breath. *Is he the one? Please, not him. Not now. Don't trap me now.*

Then Titus shifted, sinking us lower until the water lapped against my jaw, and the tingling magic swept out of my brand and muddled my thoughts, leaving me still in pain and yet drifting.

I tried to concentrate on my power and pull it from my palms into my body, but my thoughts floated farther and farther away from me. Which wasn't good. If I had a concussion, I needed to stay awake for the next three to six hours before it was safe for me to sleep.

"Don't let me pass out," I said, my lips numb. "Not for a few hours."

But Titus didn't respond. He just kept looking at me with that frustrating mix of grief and pity and anger. I mustn't have said that out loud, and with the tingling magic of the pool dragging at my senses, I didn't have the strength to try again.

AMIAH

Every nerve in my body was on fire and my fingers trembled as I fought to undo the last button on my shirt. I'd spent too much magic just moving Titus's half of the leash spell to the resonance charm — and as a result to me — and had been in pain before we'd even begun our fight with Balwyrdan.

The demonic magic trapped inside me had coursed through my veins like acid, like it did now, and it had taken everything I'd had to stay conscious while that Spring Court asshole had been using the leash spell to suffocate Amiah and figure out which one of us was Titus. And while Titus's half of the spell hadn't had the same deadly effects as Amiah's half, it had still been excruciating.

And now we were trapped in Faerie, a realm I'd sworn I'd never return to.

"Jeez," Hawk said, tossing his shorts back to Cassius for the second time and hopping into the pool beside Titus. "You should have undressed her."

"She's fine as she is." Cassius yanked off his army boots and stepped out of his fatigues, which left him in black boxer briefs. He grabbed a small towel off the bench by the door and slid into the pool on Titus's other side as if he was unwilling to have the incubus between him and Amiah. And given how I was sure Cassius was in love with Amiah, that didn't surprise me. "I'm sure she wouldn't appreciate us seeing her naked. It's bad enough we've all seen her without a top."

"Well one of us is going to have to see her naked," Hawk said. "If she's going to heal herself, she'll need sleep to recover her magic and we can't put her to bed in wet clothes."

"And let me guess." Cassius shot Hawk a dirty look as he dipped the towel in the water and started gingerly washing the dried blood from her face. "You volunteer."

"I was thinking her *husband* should do the job. Surely being married to her means he's already seen her naked." Hawk flashed me a dirty grin then shrugged. "But if you insist."

"Stop trying to push my buttons. We need to get serious," Cassius said, carefully wiping at the blood crusted on her upper lip from her broken nose. "You know as well as I do that I didn't insist on you undressing Amiah, and Bane has already said he isn't her husband."

"She is Seireadan's though," Titus said, hugging her closer to his massive chest.

I bit back a groan and prayed Titus's possessiveness had everything to do with the fact that he was a shifter and took comfort from physical touch and closeness, and not because he, too, had feelings for her.

But then, he couldn't have real feelings for her. He didn't know her.

Except the fury in Titus's eyes when he'd seen Balwyrdan beating Amiah...

It had been the same fury in Cassius's eyes.

Which had been the same fury I'd felt. So no. Titus couldn't be in love with Amiah like Cassius. Seeing anyone beaten like that was enough to get my blood boiling, Titus's too, not to mention Hawk's. He hadn't even thought twice about joining us and killing Balwyrdan's thugs.

That had to be it. Titus's reaction to Amiah was sympathy for her injuries and a need to be touching someone because he was a shifter. There was also probably a big helping of sexual frustration because he'd been imprisoned for half a millennium and likely hadn't had any sexual contact in that time, either. Amiah was the first woman he'd come across, and he too had been fighting Hawk's magic from aligning our resonance with the resonance charm — and maybe still was since it took hours, sometimes days, for it to work its way out of a person's system if he didn't have sex to release it.

"She doesn't belong to Bane," Cassius said. "She doesn't *belong* to anyone."

Titus flashed his canines at Cassius. "She's his female. She bears his scent."

Oh, crap. He knew we'd had sex.

God, I was a moron. But of course he knew.

I'd still been lying in bed thinking about the amazing surprising sounds she'd made and how, even after she'd run from my bed, I wanted to make her let it all go again and scream my name. Titus had ripped open my bedroom door and would have smelled her and sex all over me.

"Because she slept in his clothes," Cassius replied. "She—"

"She's not mine," I interrupted before Titus could tell Cassius Amiah and I had slept together. That was something she definitely wouldn't want to get out even though, out of all of us, Cassius was the only one who didn't know — since Hawk would have felt us having sex with his ability to absorb sexual energy.

But in no way was Amiah mine. For fuck's sake, she'd freaked out and ran the minute she'd realized what we'd done.

And I had no idea why that bothered me so much. Even if she hadn't been a virgin — and holy shit I'd popped her cherry — she would have run. Having sex with me would have worked all of Hawk's magic out of her system and reality would have sunk in.

Except she'd considered paying for my help to remove her angelic mating brand with her body before she'd met Hawk. Had she actually been interested in me before then?

And that didn't matter. Clearly she'd realized sleeping with me had been a mistake, which, at the time, had been amusing — because oh, the things I could tease her about! One knowing look or the right innocent word and her cheeks would go red and she'd get flustered then angry.

But now the thought made me furious. If she hadn't run— if *I* hadn't given in to my need to release Hawk's magic from my system and slept with her, she wouldn't have been on the roof. Her beautiful face and body wouldn't be swollen and bruised and bleeding, and she wouldn't be in pain that even now, while unconscious, tightened her expression.

And now I'd told my mother I'd completed the fae marriage ritual with Amiah, making me fertile for Amiah and Amiah alone when angels could only have children with other angels.

We had to get out of the Winter Court before the assassination attempts started. Except there was no way we could fight our way to the

Winter Court's portal to escape back to the mortal realm in our condition, and no matter how much I wanted to, I couldn't summon my own portal like my mother's seneschal could. Even if I wasn't in pain and infected with demonic magic, I still wouldn't have been able to make a portal. That just wasn't one of the things I could do despite my sorcerer's ability to weave the raw magic of Faerie to my will however I wanted it.

Biting back a groan of pain, I eased into the pool. At least the magical waters, unlike Amiah's healing magic, would help restore some of my magic.

But the warm water didn't relax me and the pool's magic, its soft tingling sensation seeping into my essence, set my nerves on edge.

I was back in Faerie and I'd brought Amiah with me.

"We just need to hold out until Amiah has recovered," I said to myself.

"You're going to need time to recover too," Hawk replied.

Crap. I'd said that out loud.

The incubus turned a pained gaze to me. Which was confusing as hell. His injuries hadn't been that bad and, unlike angelic healing that wasn't effective on incubi, the pool would heal him just like everyone else.

He squeezed his eyes shut and took in a shuddering breath and realization hit me.

He was a Sensitive, able to sense magic, and he was one of the most sensitive Sensitives I'd ever met. Faerie had to be overwhelming.

And while I was also on the sensitive end of the Sensitive scale, the magic that made Faerie *Faerie*, that seeped from the ground and drifted in the air, was a part of me. I accepted it and it me, at least in the courts, and I couldn't sense its full power. Hawk, a being from the Realm of Celestial Darkness, was a foreign body without the acceptance of Faerie's magic. He had to be sensing *all* of its power.

Jeez, I was missing everything right now.

"We need to get a shield on you first," I said. The demonic magic swelled and I bit back a groan.

"I can manage until you've recovered." Hawk jerked his thumb at Cassius. "That and it'll make Sparky feel better."

Cassius's eyes narrowed. "What will?"

"The fact I can't see shit. Faerie is so fucking magical it's like I'm staring at the sun. I'm surprised I haven't walked into a wall yet. At least people have different colored auras to differentiate them and I can sort of make out faces."

"So great. You're in rough shape," Cassius said to me, missing the fact that Hawk couldn't get a good look at Amiah even if she was naked, "and you can't see. Anything up with you?" he asked Titus.

"Aside from the fact that we need to figure out what to call you since we can't use your real name?" I asked.

"I can't shift." Titus carefully brushed a strand of wet hair away from Amiah's bruised cheek, his pupils still slitted, his dragon still threatening to take over even though we weren't in immediate danger. "No glamour is going to make me look like a wolf if I do a full shift."

"And right now I'm out of fire." The muscles in Cassius's jaw flexed. "We need to recover. All of us. If we keep T's identity under wraps, how safe are we?"

"We're not," Titus said. "The Winter Queen wants Sebastian to produce an heir, which means she wants Amiah dead."

"Except we're in no condition to fight our way free," I forced out as the demonic magic flared again. "If we're careful and Amiah is never left alone, we should be okay for a while. My mother won't make her move right away and when she does, it won't be overt. If I have proof she attacked or killed my wife, I'll be able to demand a blood price."

"But only if you have proof," Titus growled, shifting to curl a little more around Amiah as if he was already trying to protect her with his body. "We can't count on the royal blood price to keep her safe."

"And it takes her longer to heal herself than others," Cassius said. "Her nose is broken, her wrist is broken, and I'd bet at least half of her ribs are as well. We're not talking a good rest and a few hours of healing. She's probably going to have to drain herself a few times and that's if she can concentrate past the pain."

"We'll supplement with the pools." I sank deeper into the pool so I could rest my head back against the ledge and fought to focus on the soft tingling magic flowing into my body and not the demonic magic burning through my veins. If I could just hold out, the pain would ease up.

Except it wouldn't fully ease up until I stopped channeling magic and released my sound blocking spell. God, how the hell was I going to break the leash spell between me and Amiah let alone remove her mating brand if just keeping something as simple as a sound block spell active hurt?

I wasn't.

If I could get back to full, I could probably manage the leash spell, but even with an external source, I wasn't going to be able to remove her brand. Not unless a miracle happened and someone pulled the demonic magic out of me — which was supposed to happen tomorrow... in the human realm.

Yeah, it looked like I was going to miss that meeting and piss off one powerful demon.

Someone else was going to have to remove Amiah's brand... although now that we were in Faerie, I might know someone who could... if he was still trustworthy.

"I'm not saying we stay here forever," I said. "Just long enough for Amiah to fully recover, and she's going to recover faster than my mother expects. As long as we can keep Amiah's magic a secret—"

"And we *are* going to keep it a secret," Cassius said. "Only angels have the magical ability to heal others and if her power is revealed, she's in danger of being abducted again."

Something I prayed would never happen again.

"So what? Pretend Amiah is worse off than she actually is?" Hawk asked. "I'm not sure how that's much of an advantage."

"But it is an advantage." Cassius rubbed his face. "I'm just too tired to figure out how."

"My mother knows the pools will heal Amiah's cuts and bruises faster than her broken bones so we can convince her to put off my welcome home celebration until we've had time to get the lay of the land before we make our escape," I said.

"You don't trust that your knowledge of the Winter Court is still accurate, and you don't think we can just make a break for it." Cassius pursed his lips, his gaze growing unfocused with thought. "And you can't make a portal?"

"No," I said. "I have to use a preexisting one."

"Well, if we're going with that," Hawk said, "then the best plan is to use your party as a distraction for our escape."

Titus leveled a hard gaze at me, his golden eyes blandly brown, changed by the glamour hiding his identity. "We should avoid the court portal and go into the Wilds, find a portal there or sneak into one of the other courts and use theirs."

I bit back a groan. Going into the Wilds was a terrible, dangerous idea, and where Deaglan and Enowen had left me to die. But no one went into the Wilds because of how dangerous it was, especially to high fae like me. Which made it the perfect place to hide. "Agreed."

"And the Heart?" Cassius asked. "We can't forget that after Amiah's well-being, it's our top priority." Hawk opened his mouth and Cassius glared at him before he could speak. "No matter what you think of Amiah, she can keep us alive. That makes her more valuable than any of us."

And she'd do it at her own expense, no matter what anyone else wanted, or how it pissed off anyone else.

"I wasn't going to argue Amiah's usefulness," Hawk huffed. "I was going to say fuck the Heart."

"So you'd rather hide for who knows how long until the Heart goes back to sleep?" Cassius asked.

"This treasure hunt is going to kill at least one of us." Hawk's gaze jumped to Amiah then back to Cassius, his worry clear that the treasure hunt was going to kill Amiah. She was the least able to defend herself in a fight... and I had no idea what to make of his concern. "But hey, you want to go after it? That's fine by me. I'm good with keeping the pretty doctor company until this blows over. I'm sure I can keep her entertained," he said, his tone clear he was going to *entertain* her with his body.

The light in Cassius's eyes flared, smoke curled from his shoulders, and the water around him started to bubble.

Hawk flashed him a wicked grin. "You're welcome to join us if you'd like."

"I'm not having sex with Amiah," Cassius said, "and neither are you."

"Pretty sure that's her choice," Hawk drawled.

Cassius glared at him. "Only if you don't use your power to coerce her."

The demonic magic inside me flared and I bit back a groan. "We can't sit back and wait. We have to go after the Heart."

A part of me hated that I agreed with the uptight angel, but Cassius's original assumption was still right. Our best hope for survival was to get Faerie's Heart, the one magical thing that could destroy all of Faerie, and use our possession of it as leverage to protect ourselves.

"T—" Another agonizing flare stole my breath. Jeez. I'd hoped the pool's magic would have been more helpful easing the pain. "Can you sense any of the keys? Have any of them been empowered yet?"

Titus closed his eyes and slowly rubbed his hand up and down

Amiah's arm, his palm never leaving her flesh. She looked small and fragile leaning against his massive body, the whole right side of her face an enormous swollen bruise.

I wanted to kill Balwyrdan again. Slower this time. Cassius had turned him to ash, but it had happened too quickly and the fae hadn't had enough time to suffer. He'd deserved to suffer.

The thought shocked me. Oh sure, if you wronged me, I got even. But I never set out to make anyone suffer.

Clearly I'd spent too much time around angels. There was a fine line between vengeance and justice... and I usually didn't give a shit about either. I certainly didn't give a shit about getting it for someone else. After my betrothed, Enowen, and one of my best friends, Deaglan, had tried to kill me, I swore I'd never be blinded by love or friendship again. No one and nothing took precedence over me, especially a woman. They were a good time and that was all. Including Amiah. If I was smart, I'd keep my distance from her before Cassius burned me for looking at her the wrong way.

Hell, if I was really smart, I'd find a way for Cassius to admit his love to Amiah so those two could finally get married, fuck, and make little angel babies like I'm sure Amiah wanted.

Except even if Amiah was in love with Cassius — which I also suspected — she'd never sleep with him until her mating brand was removed because she didn't want to get trapped in a soul bond.

And I couldn't blame her for that. I'd almost permanently bonded myself to a woman who'd only been marrying me to take the throne of the Winter Court. I still had no idea why she and Deaglan had jumped the gun and tried to kill me before Enowen and I had completed the marriage ceremony, making her the princess consort. Guess, Queen of the Shadow Court as Deaglan's wife was the better position. Although I didn't have any proof that she and Deaglan had actually married, that was just the most logical step for that power-hungry bitch.

Titus opened his eyes and for a second — because I knew what lay under his glamour and I was a Sensitive — his glamour wavered and they were strikingly gold, reminding me that he was the last dragon. The Heart had taken the lives of his entire species, and God help me, I didn't want it to take Amiah's life too.

"I can't sense any of the keys," Titus said.

"Which means what?" Hawk asked.

"It means we focus on using Bane's party to hide our escape," Cassius said. "If that changes, the plan changes. Until then, we protect Amiah until she's recovered."

Amiah, still unconscious, shuddered and whimpered, and Cassius's attention snapped to Titus, who froze as if he was afraid moving would hurt her.

"What did you do?" Cassius demanded.

"Nothing," Titus replied.

She whimpered again and threads of glowing faerie magic snaked through her cheek.

"It's the pool. We need to get her out." I didn't know why she was already showing the signs of being in the pool for too long. We'd barely been in the water for fifteen minutes. Perhaps it had something to do with her healing magic conflicting or augmenting the pool's magic.

Titus got out of the pool careful not to jostle her and headed to the towels and robes sitting on the bench by the door.

"Okay, so who's changing her?" Hawk asked, hopping out of the pool and striding to the towels.

The light in Cassius's eyes flared and a wisp of smoke curled from his shoulders as he got out. "Not you."

"You should do it, Cassius," I said. No way was I volunteering since he wasn't going to be happy with anyone else. And hey, maybe a little intimacy would start to break the ice between them.

Cassius stared at me as if I'd suggested he'd run naked through the halls or something. Then his expression grew pinched and he gave a tight nod.

Jeez. That man had so many issues. I staggered out of the pool, agony still burning through me. The pool's magic had done little to ease the acidic burn of the demonic magic, and I pushed aside the niggling worry that the demonic magic was a bigger problem than I feared. At the moment, there wasn't anything I could do about it, so I was just going to have to push through.

Titus sat Amiah on the bench but didn't let go of her shoulders when Cassius approached.

"T," I said, grabbing a towel from the pile on the bench and offering it to him.

Amiah groaned and her eyelids fluttered open, but her breath picked up with short sharp painful gasps and her gaze was unfocused.

"Hawk, a little distraction," I said as I eased onto the bench beside her, leaning close to Titus's arm since he refused to move.

Hawk brushed a finger across her neck then stepped back, allowing Cassius to draw closer.

Her eyes rolled back and her expression softened with the seductive slide of Hawk's magic, reminding me of the look she'd had when I'd first pushed into her tight hot sheath and making me grateful I'd kept my pants on so no one could see my reaction. And I made a point of not looking away to see Hawk's expression, too. He knew I wanted to sleep with her again. There was just no getting around that. But given how she'd reacted, I doubted she'd let her defenses down long enough to return to my bed.

"Guys?" she asked, her voice too soft for the stern, desperate-to-be-in-control angel that she was. At least her eyes were clearer as her gaze slid from Hawk to Cassius to Titus to me.

"Cassius is going to help you change out of your wet clothes," I said.

She bobbed her head for a second in agreement then her eyes flashed wide. "I— ah... I can manage myself," she gasped.

"You can't," Cassius said, his expression hard and icy. He gave Titus a nudge, who snatched the towel from me and strode to the far side of the grotto to get out of his wet pants and dry off.

"No. I'm good with Hawk's magic," she insisted. "See." She sat forward and managed not to make a sound but it was clear she was in agony.

"Stop being stubborn." Cassius crossed his arms and glared at her, the light in his eyes blazing. "You're in worse shape than the last time and I can't just take you home."

Last time? Good Lord, had she been beaten before?

"You're not changing by yourself," Cassius said, "and I'm pretty sure you'd rather I saw you in your underwear than T, Hawk, or Bane."

Her eyes widened even more. "I'd rather Sebastian."

"You what?" Cassius looked at her stunned as if he couldn't believe what she'd just said.

And hell, I couldn't believe it either. I probably hadn't heard her correctly, what with the demonic magic burning through me.

"Sebastian can help me change," she said.

Smoke burst from Cassius's hands and with a growl, he yanked it back under his skin. "I see." His stunned expression vanished behind a hard, icy mask, and he gave me a tight nod before grabbing a towel and joining Titus and Hawk on the other side of the grotto.

"Are you that afraid of your brand awakening you'll refuse his help?"

I asked, keeping my voice low so the others couldn't hear. "The mark is so pale he won't be able to see it. Hell, Hawk wouldn't be able to see it unless he actively looked for it. Pretty sure just seeing you in your panties won't do anything." I rolled my eyes at her, trying to ease the fear still in her expression by making light of the situation. "Those panties weren't even much to look at."

"And those panties are still somewhere in your bedroom," she said, refusing to make eye contact with me. "I don't want Cassius thinking Balwyrdan raped me. It's bad enough I was— Again—" She grabbed the hem of Cassius's T-shirt with her one good hand to pull it over her head but clutched the fabric instead, her hand trembling. "I swore I'd be strong, swore—"

Her breath hitched and a tear rolled down her cheek.

"But I'm not strong," she whispered. "I never was."

Frustration and anger squeezed my heart even as relief flooded me at the fact that Balwyrdan hadn't raped her. His usual M.O. was beating to achieve maximum pain, but there'd always been a chance he'd try something different or already given her to his men for their entertainment.

"And no one else... you know?" The words slipped out before I could stop them. *Please, no... Because Cassius will lose his shit if she's been raped, and I don't want to deal with a rampaging angel. Really.*

"No." She raised her gaze to meet mine, her angel glow dim in her shockingly bright blue eyes revealing just how exhausted she was. Then, with an effort that made my chest hurt to watch, she slid her icy mask of professionalism into place. "And feel free to tell Cassius that so I don't have to have this conversation again. Now. All of my ribs are broken so I might pass out. Be ready for that," she said, her tone brusque. "And don't let me stay unconscious. I need to deal with my concussion first. *Then* I can pass out."

Jeez. And she didn't think she was strong.

AMIAH

I WOKE WITH FIERY AGONY FLOODING MY BODY AND IT TOOK ME A terrifying moment to focus my whirling thoughts to remember where I was and what had happened. We'd been dragged to the Winter Court in Faerie, Sebastian had told his mother — the Queen! — that we were married, then after a momentary dip in a magical pool that made my own healing magic stutter and flare uncontrollably, Sebastian helped me dry off and change.

And I wasn't going to think about him seeing me naked again, or the fact that I'd refused Cassius's help because I didn't want him to know I'd lost my underwear. As it was, Cassius had barely said more than a few words to me, which might have had something to do with me barely hanging onto consciousness... but probably not, and I was sure I was going to have to give him an explanation as to why I'd chosen Sebastian to help me and not him.

After that, Hawk had sent another bone-melting swell of his seductive magic into me, somehow making it easier to focus past the pain, and I concentrated on healing my concussion. Thankfully my magic recognized it as the worst injury since it hindered my ability to heal anything else.

Then Titus carried me to the suite the Winter Queen had assigned us. The big shifter had tucked me into a massive plush bed big enough to hold all of us, and the guys argued about who would stay with me.

Sebastian had suggested Hawk so when I woke he could ease my pain enough for me to use my magic again. Cassius had said absolutely not.

In the end, they'd all stayed, Hawk in a chair pulled up to the side of the bed, Sebastian in another chair on the other side of the large bedroom, Titus on the floor by the door, and Cassius perched on the far side of the bed as far away as he could get from me.

Shortly after that, I expended the last drop of my magic and passed out.

With a groan, I cracked open my good eye — my right one was still partially swollen shut — and a gentle wave of seductive magic unfurled low within me as a warm body lying beside me shifted closer.

My heart picked up. Someone was in bed with me. For a second I ached for whoever it was to wrap his arms around me and just hold me. I missed the comfort of being in a warm strong embrace and feeling the soft pulse of life force from someone. But as much as I craved that, my body wasn't ready for that kind of contact. It was a miracle I hadn't punctured a lung or my heart or any number of organs while being carried around the Winter Court.

I turned my head, my muscles screaming at the movement, and came nose to nose with Hawk. He was under the covers with me and I had no idea if he still wore the clothes he'd changed into after bathing in the pool or not.

Heat flooded my cheeks.

He could be naked.

I could be naked.

Just because Sebastian had helped me put on a robe, didn't mean someone hadn't undressed me while I was unconscious. And even if I was still in the robe, only a soft silky tie held it together.

"Why are you in bed with me?" I squeaked, my reaction embarrassing me more than realizing I was in bed with the sexy incubus.

"Why not?" He traced a finger along my jaw, sending another swell of magic heating my insides.

"Didn't Cassius tell you no?" I was pretty sure that had been part of their argument, which was why Hawk had ended up in the chair.

"He's not here. It's just you and me and what Cassius doesn't know won't hurt him." He flashed me a wicked grin, but it didn't reach his eyes. In fact, the hellfire in his unusual blue irises was banked and his expression was pinched. He was still breathtakingly handsome, but he also looked exhausted and in pain.

Had he been hurt worse than I thought? I'd been in too much pain and hadn't checked him or anyone else for serious injuries.

I eased my good hand out from under the thick white comforter and rested it on the side of his neck, pushing a small thread of magic into him to assess his injuries. Nothing more serious than what I'd seen before. The lacerations on his ribs and right biceps were scabbed over but still painful and the bruise on the left side of his torso — that curled around his back to his left kidney — was still tender.

My compulsion to heal kicked in and, before I realized what I was doing, I pushed a stronger thread of power into him, even though logically I knew it took more power to heal an incubus than it did to heal myself. The best way to heal him would be to kiss him — which I wasn't going to do because my face throbbed.

"Whoa," he said, gingerly grabbing my wrist and pulling my hand from his neck. "What are you doing?"

A small snap of backlash from being disconnected from him jolted through me and my thoughts stuttered. What *was* I doing? I was in worse shape than he was and it was a waste to use my magic on him.

His hellfire swelled and so, too, did his sensual magic seeping through my veins. "There are more effective ways to heal me."

"I'm not up for *that*." As much as a part of me was starting to think it was a great idea.

"Oh, I know. But I'm not that hurt. A few naughty thoughts will do the trick." He gave me his wicked smile again and this time it did reach his eyes. The look sent a small shiver of desire racing through me that reignited the agony in my chest, which he melted away with another surge of magic.

This was a bad idea.

And yet when I'd been with Sebastian, just for a moment, I'd been free of worry, of my need to be in control, of everything.

And I'd been taken again.

I shoved that thought back. I wasn't going to think about it. Ever. And Hawk pleasuring me would be the perfect distraction.

"What if I want more than just thoughts?" It wasn't fair if Hawk was just going to tease me. I was done with being celibate and he'd already proven more than capable of satisfying me with his magic. Hadn't I decided before Balwyrdan kidnapped me that I'd take control of my desires?

My pulse stuttered, and the part of me that screamed for control demanded I take it back and never be a victim again. Asking someone to pleasure me meant they controlled my pleasure. I couldn't allow that and even if there were sexual situations where I had control, I was in no condition for that and I still needed to ask someone to do that with me.

"Hey." Hawk hooked a finger under my chin and drew my attention back to him. "Whatever you're thinking, it's not a naughty thought." His hellfire dimmed. "Bane said Balwyrdan didn't force himself on you."

"He didn't and I don't want to talk about it." I didn't ever want to think about it. I'd tried to escape and been helpless against Balwyrdan's control of the leash spell. And even if he hadn't controlled the leash spell, I'd still have been helpless. I was just so damned helpless and pathetic. After being kidnapped by that human all those years ago I'd vowed never to be foolish and helpless again, and yet I'd spent my life letting my mating brand control me, waiting for a soul mate who'd then control my life.

And with the brand, there'd be no escape and no one to save me. Especially if Sebastian couldn't remove it before it fully formed. Once formed there wasn't even the hope of being free.

How could I keep control of my life when my loss of control was inevitable?

I struggled to shove those thoughts deep down inside me as well. There wasn't anything I could do about it and if I wanted to be useful — not the pathetic helpless angel that I was — I needed to heal myself. I was only useful as a healer and I wouldn't be able to heal anyone in my condition.

Focus on Hawk. Let him distract you. After this mess was done, I'd never see him again. He, like Sebastian, couldn't possibly be my soul mate so there was no fear of my mating brand awakening. That, and I didn't know if Sebastian would welcome me to his bed again after running out on him last night. He'd had a strange look in his eyes when he'd helped me change, but I could have imagined that since I'd barely been conscious. Hawk, however, survived on sex, and if he was going to be stuck with us, we were going to have to figure out a way for him to feed.

"Let's get you healed," I said.

His lips quirked and a flicker of his hellfire danced in his eyes. "Because you get nothing out of it."

"Only if you just tease me. But you wouldn't do that," I replied, my heart pounded with the fear that he'd reject me. *Please. I need this.* I needed it more than he needed healing. "You said you're generous. Was that a lie?"

"Oh, I am." His magic swelled, rushing heated desire through me. It wasn't the powerful bone-melting hunger when he'd kissed me in the abandoned bathhouse, but a softer, languid need. "I just need to be careful about this. And you need to lie there and enjoy it."

"What makes you think I wouldn't?"

"I barely know you and I already know you're terrible at letting others do things for you." He slid a hand between my knees and shifted closer. The demonic heat radiating from his body seeped into my skin and swirled with the warmth of his magic. My body grew heavy, my senses drifting on a gentle sensual ache. "You gave it up for Bane and then freaked out."

"I didn't freak out."

"Baby, from the sexual energy radiating off him, he would have fucked you all night long." Hawk's fingers teased up the inside of my thigh, and the languid need intensified in my core and my aching grew into insistent throbbing. "And from the energy radiating off of you, you would have let him, but your mind got in the way."

"I didn't expect to sleep with him. I needed to figure out what that meant?"

"Amiah." He leaned close, his breath feathering against my tender, bruised neck, swirling with his sensual heat. "It didn't have to *mean* anything. All you had to do was let go and enjoy it."

The thought sent a frozen snap of fear cutting through Hawk's sensual heat. Letting go meant risking I'd do something foolish, that someone could hurt me again.

And yet that was all I wanted. To let go of my fear and my desperate need to be in control. I wanted my mind to turn off, just for a little while, and to just feel.

"You know you want it." He brushed a finger through my folds and sent another rush of heat into me, melting my fear. "You want his cock inside you again. You want mine."

He flicked my clit and sensation shot through me. I gasped, spiking pain through my chest, but his power billowed, softening the agony, turning it into a shocking, exquisite pleasure.

"You want both of us at the same time."

I shuddered at the memory of Sebastian's heated gaze while Hawk had used his magic to make me orgasm in his tent yesterday, and my breath picked up. Watching Hawk seduce me had turned Sebastian on, and the idea of him watching Hawk slide into me turned me on. God, the idea of both of them filling me, moving inside me, sent the whispering ripples of an orgasm through me.

I wanted their hands and lips on me, their bodies pressed tight against mine. I wanted to give up my desperate, exhausting need for control. I wanted them to— God, I wanted them to pleasure me until I couldn't think straight.

"Now that's a naughty thought." Hawk hummed low in his throat, dipped a finger inside me, and rubbed the slickened tip over my clit, drawing a soft moan from me. "When you're all healed up, we're going to have so much fun."

Another whispering ripple of an orgasm swept through me.

"And we'll make Bane watch."

He pushed two fingers inside me and ground his thumb against my clit. His magic sharpened to a pinpoint inside me at the perfect spot where his fingers rubbed again and again, faster and faster. My breath picked up and he melted the pain of each inhalation into a desire that built inside me until I couldn't contain it any longer.

Hot, sensual pleasure rushed through me, infused in my cells, teasing my essence, and my muscles clenched around his fingers. The orgasm wasn't shattering like the ones with Sebastian. My body wouldn't have been able to handle that. But it still filled me with overwhelming, breathtaking bliss, and I rode the sensation, letting it steal my thoughts. There'd be time to worry about everything later. Right now, I felt amazing. I felt free. And I never wanted the feeling to end.

AMIAH

Hawk cleaned up in the en suite bathroom and left, and I, still warm and drifting on my orgasm and his magic, pulled my power from my palms and focused on knitting my broken bones back together.

I didn't know how long I lay there with my eyes closed concentrating on the slow agonizing process of healing myself, but it was long enough to drain every last ounce of my magic, which was only enough to partially heal my ribs.

Now I lay, still under the covers, the bliss of Hawk's magic a memory, staring at the softly glowing, translucent ceiling. Because of its plain surface, it was the only place I could look where the room's spinning didn't nauseate me even though the walls with their hint of swirling glyphs were pretty plain as well. They, too were translucent and softly glowing, giving the suggestion that I could see through them without actually being able to see through them. Which I appreciated since I didn't want people watching me. But there also weren't any windows, and that made my heart pound. I didn't like being unable to see the sky. I needed—

I squeezed my eyes shut and struggled to slow my breathing against the pain of my partially healed ribs. Even with my eyes closed, I could feel the room whirling and the walls pressing close.

I had to find space and sky. I couldn't just lie there in the closed off room. I needed to think, focus, figure out... everything.

Except exhaustion dragged at my limbs from having drained all my magic — and I wasn't even moving. And while my mind screamed to run, the rest of me dreaded the thought of getting up.

But no matter what my body wanted, at some point, I was going to have to rise. I wouldn't be able to restore my magic without eating and then sleeping again, and before I did that, I wanted to clean up — *and see sky. Please.*

The dip in the healing pool had helped my cuts, bruises, and achy muscles a bit, but it hadn't been completely cleansing, and my insides squirmed with the need for a more open space as much with the need to scrub the grime of last night's events from my body — some physical but most of it emotional grime.

Biting back a moan of pain in the hopes that the guys, wherever they were, wouldn't hear me, I sat up and slid my legs over the side of the bed.

The room lurched and darkened and I sucked in more, painful breaths. I really didn't want to vomit with broken ribs, but I also needed to prove to myself that I could do this, that I wasn't completely helpless.

After being rescued from that human faith healer, it had taken years to get Cassius to stop looking at me and treating me like I was fragile, and that time I'd just been a little beaten up and drained of all my magic. He was going to be impossible now.

I stood on shaky legs and shuffled over to the wall to keep my balance. At least my legs hadn't been injured. And while draining my power had left me dizzy and exhausted, I was still able to move without help... although I was sure that was something Cassius would also disagree with.

I was halfway to the bathroom — really only a handful of feet away from the bed — when the bedroom door opened.

"For the love of—" Cassius growled. "What are you doing?"

I didn't even try to look at him. Moving my head that much would make the room whirl and my stomach was already threatening a revolt. "I'm going to the bathroom."

"You should have called for help." He strode to my side and reached for me, but I waved him off as best I could with my elbow since my good hand held me steady against the wall and my broken one was drawn protectively close to my chest.

"My legs aren't broken. I'm just a little dizzy."

"And if you fall and injure yourself worse?" he asked. He wore a loose white tunic that hung to mid-thigh and loose white pants, a match to what the fae men had been wearing in the Winter Queen's throne room.

"Then you'll be able to say I told you so."

"What's gotten into you?" The angel glow in his eyes flared, revealing his concern. Not that I needed it to tell me he was concerned. "You know this isn't practical."

I bit back a sigh and shuffled a few steps closer to the bathroom. He was right. Me trying to do this on my own wasn't practical... and yet I had to do it, had to prove I could do *something*.

God, when had I become that person? The one who willfully did something that went against common sense?

And if I was being practical, it wasn't safe for me to take a shower by myself, not until I was steadier on my feet. Which meant no matter how much I wanted to scrub off the memory of the pleasure in Balwyrdan's eyes every time he'd hit or suffocated me, I needed to eat first and get the room to stop spinning. Because I really didn't want to shower with Cassius or anyone else watching me.

Jeez, I really just want a shower.

Cassius stiffened and a wisp of smoke curled from his hand. "I'll get Bane then."

"You'll what?"

He turned on his heel and rushed from the room, leaving the door partially open and letting me see into what looked like a sitting area. The walls were the same as the bedroom, translucent and glowing — although the glow was much brighter out there than in the bedroom — and I still couldn't see a window. A dark blue couch sat with its back to me, and I could see the front edge of an armchair.

"Bane," he barked. "Help Amiah."

"What?" Bane asked as he sat up on the couch and rubbed his face — had he been sleeping there? For a second his complexion was gray, then his full-body fae glow flickered back to life.

"Amiah wants to shower," Cassius said, "and she's not doing it by herself."

Guess I'd said that thought out loud.

"You didn't need to announce it." Sebastian rolled his eyes at him. "Have fun."

"She's already made it clear which of us can see her naked," Cassius ground out.

"She *is* his female," Titus said from somewhere out of sight.

"She's not my female," Sebastian insisted.

"If none of you want to help her—" Hawk said, sauntering into sight, oozing sex and sin and flashing me a wicked grin. He too wore the loose white pants, sitting dangerously low on his hips, and no tunic, showing off his amazing physique. "I wouldn't mind more alone time with the pretty doctor."

"Absolutely not." More wisps of smoke curled from Cassius's hands.

"We're going to have to figure out how he's going to feed," Sebastian said. "Especially if we don't trust anyone in court."

"He's not doing it while Amiah is naked," Cassius said.

"Well if you want to be naked, I roll that way, too," Hawk purred, walking his fingers down Cassius's chest.

Fire sparked up Cassius's forearms and he slapped Hawk's hand away. "Why don't you seduce information out of the fae? That should keep you going for a while."

"We agreed, no one leaves this suite alone," Sebastian said, "so unless you want to join Hawk with his seduction, that option is off the table."

Cassius stiffened.

"And it still doesn't address who's helping Amiah," Hawk said, his grin deepening.

"Her mate," Titus replied.

"For fuck's sake." Sebastian threw his hands up in exasperation. "I'm not her mate."

"She chose you to help her change," Titus said.

This was ridiculous.

"I can handle it just fine on my own." I didn't want any of them to help me shower, and I certainly didn't want them arguing over who I belonged to or who could sleep with me or who my mate was.

"No, you can't," Cassius shot back, his eyes filled with that worried, pitying look I hated.

I wasn't going to win this argument with him. No one was. He'd dug his heels in, determined to *protect* me whether I wanted his protection or not, commanding me like I was one of his agents.

"Fine. Sebastian, if you would." I shuffled the last few steps to the bathroom and clutched the smooth stone counter to wait for him.

The door to the bedroom clicked closed, and Sebastian, in a dark blue version of the tunic and pants with silver embroidery sewn around the neck and cuffs, walked toward me.

"You're going to get me burned alive," he said, stopping in the doorway.

"Cassius wouldn't do that."

I purposefully avoided looking in the mirror in front of me and turned my attention to the rest of the bathroom. It looked a lot like a smaller version of the healing grotto with natural rock and winter greenery. The sink was a bowl carved in a wide stone pillar jutting from the floor and the toilet was also stone. Beyond that lay a pool sunk into the floor large enough for all of us — like the bed — and a waterfall, its flow gently tumbling into a shower-like area. A second, thinner waterfall diverted from the first and trickled down the wall to fill the pool.

"You didn't see him trying to get to you last night and he's been pissed since we got you in bed."

"He's been upset since he thought his brother's soul mate was a human who endangered his life." If I thought about it, he'd been upset for the last twenty-three years. Ever since his youngest brother had been killed in the war.

I reached for the tie on my robe, my thoughts stalling on the shower. No curtain to hide behind. Sebastian couldn't just wait in the bathroom to ensure I was okay. He was going to see me naked. Again.

I'd been in too much shock in the healing grotto for that to really register... him seeing me naked... again. Now my pulse picked up with uncertainty and embarrassment heated my cheeks.

"That doesn't make me feel better," Sebastian said. "The next time you need someone to see you naked, don't pick me. Pick him."

"I don't *need* for anyone to see me naked now." My throat tightened. It was an irrational reaction, but his words still stung. He didn't want to see me naked again. Of course, I didn't want him to see me naked either. Not to mention I'd run from his bed. That had probably stung as well. And really, we weren't even friends. Just two people forced together by horrible circumstances who'd had a momentary lapse in judgment. "And why would I pick Cassius? I'm not adding anyone else to the list of men who've seen me naked."

He snorted. "You might want to tell Hawk that in front of Cassius. I'm sure he's convinced Cassius that he wants to see you naked, and Cassius doesn't know him well enough to know he's not going to risk his life and do something."

My cheeks grew hotter at the memory of Hawk's magic and fingers inside me.

Okay, so maybe I *did* want to add to the list of men who've seen me naked, and I would beg to differ on the incubus not doing anything. But that was none of Sebastian's business... unless we invited him to participate.

The thought sent a shiver rushing through me and I gasped, which shot agony through my chest and forced me to clutch the counter to keep standing.

"Fucking hell." Sebastian rushed up behind me, grabbed my hips, and gingerly drew my back against his chest to help steady me.

His breath feathered against my neck and my pulse picked up even as a part of my essence sighed at his closeness. I didn't know what I craved more. Just being held or being satisfied.

"He's determined to protect your virtue," Sebastian said.

"I never asked him to, and it's not the Dark Ages. I can do whatever I want with my virtue."

"Not if it's going to turn me into a pile of ash. It's obvious he's barely in control, but fuck— I had no idea he was that powerful. Did you?"

"No." I knew Cassius's magic was stronger than most angels and I'd seen him create a wall of fire to keep people away from us, but I'd never seen him make anything that burned as hot as the pillar he'd encased Balwyrdan in.

"If I'd known he was that powerful, I'd have never slept with you."

Fantastic! So now Cassius was controlling me just by being Cassius. I couldn't get away from it. God, I wanted to scream. I was free. I was strong. I was in control. And maybe if I told that to myself enough times it'd be true.

"Well, then," I said through gritted teeth as I pulled out of Sebastian's embrace and staggered the rest of the way to the shower then turned to glare at him. "I suppose it's a good thing I left your bed when I did. Wouldn't want Cassius to know two consenting adults had sexual intercourse. I didn't think you were a coward."

The muscles in his jaw flexed and something dark flashed across his expression. "It's called self-preservation and I wouldn't talk about being a coward."

"What's that supposed to mean?"

"That you're in love with Cassius, but you're too scared of your mating brand to admit it."

"I'm not in love with Cassius. We're friends." And I'd never allowed myself to think of him in any other way because my mating brand hadn't woken when we met, and at the time, I'd been waiting for my soul mate.

Was I in love with Cassius?

I'd ached to be closer to him when I'd healed him in Sebastian's bathroom. But that had just been my yearning for sexual release and my lack of willpower because Sebastian had kept teasing me and reminding me about sex. I hadn't really wanted Cassius, just sex.

And could I love someone who didn't see me as an equal? In Cassius's eyes, I was a pathetic, weak angel he had to keep protecting. He'd never be able to stop seeing me as the angel he'd rescued all those years ago.

"You don't look at him like he's a friend," Sebastian said. "You look at him like you want to fuck him."

"I'm sure I look at all of you like that, no thanks to you and Hawk." I dipped my hand into the waterfall, unable to hold his piercing gaze. The water was cool. It wasn't going to be the warm relaxing shower I wanted, but it was better than nothing. "I'm over a hundred and twenty. That in itself is a strain on a vow of celibacy, and then I met you, and…"

"So it's my fault you broke your ridiculous vow? I gave you more than enough opportunity to say no. I warned you. Told you to get the fuck out of my shower," he snapped.

"You did. But that's—"

"You angels are unfucking believable. You have a glimmer of humanity, freak out, and blame it on someone else. You and Cassius deserve each other. You're so God damned uptight."

"I'm not in love with—" There was no point in denying it, and it didn't really matter if my love for Cassius was deeper than just a friendship or not. Sebastian and I weren't friends.

Why was that so hard to remember?

Because I'd liked the way he'd looked at me last night, like I was the most beautiful woman in the world, like I was, in that moment, even with all my flaws, perfect. And I'd loved the way he'd made me feel.

I wanted him to look at me that way again, to feel that way again.

Except was it him I wanted or just *someone*?

Well, it was clear, it was never going to be him again.

"I realize we were just getting something out of our system. I know it will never happen again." The water sluicing over my hand started to warm up. Guess the magic of Faerie warmed the water when someone wanted to use it. Thank goodness, because with my broken ribs and throbbing face, I didn't want to be shivering through my shower.

"Once you've removed the leash spell and this situation with the Heart is resolved, I expect you to keep your word and attempt to remove my brand. Now please," I said, not giving him a chance to respond, "wait for me in the bedroom. I didn't ask for your help and it's not needed."

"Of course you didn't. You don't need anyone," Sebastian said, his voice low, his words stinging yet again.

I didn't understand why the idea of never sleeping with him again hurt so much, why not needing him made me feel lonely, or why I couldn't close my emotions off like I used to be able to.

But then Sebastian was the first and only man I'd ever slept with. Even if I didn't want a romantic relationship with anyone, the surprising, amazing moment with Sebastian last night would be forever branded on my soul.

CASSIUS

THIS WAS A NIGHTMARE. *PLEASE LET IT BE A NIGHTMARE. PLEASE LET ME WAKE up and everything be fine. Let Amiah be fine, not bruised and broken. God, she has to be fine.*

But she wasn't, and I didn't know, even after she'd healed her injuries, if she ever would be again. Abducted twice. Hurt twice— this time worse.

I didn't know how I could have protected her from Balwyrdan, but I should have. I should have paid more attention to her, not assumed she'd be okay when she'd left the kitchen last night to check on Bane. So much had happened in just one day. Hell, I was still reeling from it all and I'd seen heavy combat during the war. Amiah had only ever seen the results of combat, she'd never had to deal with anything like—

My throat tightened and fire snapped up my forearms before I could control my magic and suck it back under my skin.

Hawk, who'd taken Bane's place stretched out on the couch, raised his eyebrows. "You know staring at the bedroom door isn't going to make their shower any faster."

Their shower.

She'd wanted Bane's help.

Not mine.

And I had no idea why.

Sure, our relationship had never been more than friends, but out of all of us, I would have thought she'd have trusted me the most. The friend who'd been by her side for a hundred years, not some sex-craving fae she'd met only a few weeks ago.

What did that say about us? About my hopes to be more than friends?

Another spark burst from my hands and hissed on the floor that felt like marble but looked like ice, reminding me why I couldn't be anything other than a friend to her. I'd hurt her if we got intimate and I couldn't live with that.

God, I could hurt her just standing too close.

My magic burned under my skin, scorching through my veins, and I couldn't get it to calm down. Seeing Amiah beaten by that monster had been the final straw. I'd been struggling all day and that horrible moment on the roof where Balwyrdan had been hitting her and I'd been helpless to stop it had been more than I could take. Whatever had been inside me holding back my inferno, the fire that I had let roar to life during the war and hadn't been able to extinguish, had shattered, and now all I had was a tenuous strength of will keeping me from constantly dripping a stream of molten flames on the floor.

And I hadn't even gotten a full night's rest. I wasn't at full power yet. How the hell was I going to keep it in once I was?

I'd have to find the time to release it. Except letting go last night and letting my power rage hadn't burned it out. Probably because my rage and fear still squeezed my heart.

She could have died.

And my failure to protect her was clear as day, red and swollen on her body.

Bane had said the pool would heal her from the outside in — unlike her magic which worked inside out — but she hadn't looked any better clinging to the bedroom wall in a stupid, headstrong act to take a shower without help.

Now she was in the shower with Bane — Bane! — who without a doubt, even in her broken condition, was going to hit on her. He'd hit on her every chance he got, seeing her naked — and this time while she was more coherent — would be an opportunity he wouldn't be able to pass up.

Another spark leaped from my hand and hit Hawk's bare shoulder.

"For fuck's sake." He jerked up, his hellfire blazing and his unique healing making the minor burn vanish between one blink and the next.

God, was he getting sexual energy as we waited?

I tried to shove that thought aside. As Amiah had pointed out, she was her own woman, she could do as she pleased with whomever she pleased. But there was no way she was thinking straight after last night, and someone had to watch out for her until she was.

I jerked away from the bedroom door and dragged my attention across the sitting room. It looked like a sitting room from the mortal realm with a couch and three chairs and a table, and I didn't know if that was normal for the fae realm or if the Winter Queen had provided us with furnishings we were more familiar with.

Probably not. All she cared about was Bane— or rather Seireadan. I doubted she'd put us in a suite where her son's bodyguards would be comfortable, and given what Titus and Bane had said in the grotto about her wanting Amiah dead, I doubted she'd put us in a room to make Amiah comfortable.

Aside from the sitting room and the main bedroom, there was one other bedroom with a dozen cots, presumably for a few guards and servants, and another simple, adjoined bathroom.

And no windows.

In fact, I hadn't seen a window since we'd gotten here.

My insides squirmed at that, even though my need for sky and open spaces wasn't as strong as other angels... as Amiah's.

"Would you just take a breath," Hawk said.

I glared at him and realized I was smoking with little flecks of fire dancing up my forearms. Jeez.

"I know angels are high-strung," Hawk said, "but man, you're going to burn yourself up if you don't relax."

"My fire doesn't burn me. Not unless I want it to." Most of the time. I took a deep breath and heaved my smoke and fire back under my skin.

I could handle this and my out-of-control emotions. I had to handle this. I just needed to wrap my heart and mind in ice and freeze the blaze inside me into submission. It was the only way I was going to be able to think straight.

"You mentioned the Wilds in the pool last night," I forced out, turning my attention to Titus who'd squeezed his massive frame into one of the armchairs. "Tell me about them."

"The Wilds is the space between the Faerie Courts where the magic of every court has no control. At times it's a wasteland, at others a wild untamed jungle." Titus shrugged. "It all depends on what it feels like at the time."

"So even the Wilds are semi-sentient?" Everything I'd been told about Faerie — which hadn't been much — implied that the realm itself was alive... sort of. That sentience was muted in each court, the Monarch's will taking over their bubble of existence in the realm, but everything else was wild and free, and—

And that was everything I knew about Faerie. Less than two dozen fae sorcerers had come to the mortal realm to help the Angelic Defense fight Michael and save humanity and earth's supernatural beings, and they'd pretty much stuck to themselves with the exception of a few dalliances that produced about a dozen faekin worldwide.

"The Wilds are the soul of Faerie where it's the most free and unrestrained from the courts and it doesn't like most high fae, that's what Seireadan is, so they avoid it."

"So there's less of a chance the Winter Queen will send her men after us." I could see why the Wilds was our best option. "How dangerous will it be for us and Bane?"

"I don't know how it will react to beings from other realms, but it will try to take back the magic inside Seireadan," Titus said. "My ancestral nest is in the Wilds. If we can get to it, we'll be safe within its magical walls for a while."

"How long is a while?" Hawk asked.

Titus shrugged. "I don't know. Depends on how much Faerie wants Seireadan."

The door to the outside hall flew open and I jerked to face it, my fire flaring, searing my insides and blazing around my hands. Titus and Hawk also jumped to their feet, ready to fight, as a pair of identical looking ice women in white flowing dresses carried in two large platters of food and set them on the table.

Outside, the two guards who'd been watching us since we'd left the throne room, stood statue-still on the other side of the hall, not watching out for trouble but watching in at us.

"Her majesty is concerned. His highness hasn't requested food yet," one of the women said, her gaze searching the room, clearly looking for Bane.

"His highness is with his wife," Hawk said, the words screeching against my soul. His wife. As if she'd ever marry a man like Bane. As if she'd ever be interested in a man like him—

Except right now she was naked in the shower with him.

"Tell her majesty, he'll eat when he eats," Hawk flashed a wicked grin at the woman, who didn't respond to his seductive nature. In fact she didn't even seem to notice he was half naked as he ushered her and the other woman out the door.

"Hmm," he said, pressing his back to the door his expression tight. "I can't affect the servants with my magic."

"Because they're constructs," Titus said, examining the trays of food. "They're beings made of ice and controlled by the queen's will. They live only to serve. They have no other desires."

"Well, shit," Hawk said, "I can't even flirt out a snack with the servants. I *am* going to have to get my meals from Amiah."

My fire flared and I gritted my teeth, managing to keep even my smoke inside. *Frozen blizzards. Encased in ice. Hard and cold.*

Hard and God damned cold.

"You can go a few days without a meal. We'll be out of Faerie by then." We were *going* to be out of Faerie by then. I would not have Amiah offering herself up to feed Hawk. And she'd do it, too, because she always gave everything she had to help someone.

And I wasn't going to let Hawk or anyone take advantage of that.

"Or," Hawk said, drawing out the word and leveling his gaze on me as his hellfire flared, accentuating the wicked gleam in his eyes. "You could relieve some of that stress and sleep with her. A little secondhand sex will also keep me going. You and she have a thing going, don't you?"

"A thing?"

Hawk shrugged. "Yeah, you want to sleep with her and she's waiting for you to make your move, and neither of you are doing anything about it." He rolled his eyes. "Because angel courtship is so fucking complicated and awkward and uptight."

"You think I want to—? No, I—" My gaze jumped back to the bedroom door and my inferno seared around my heart. "After what happened she can't be thinking straight. I'm not going to— That would be—"

Terrifying.

Amazing.

Wrong.

So very wrong. She wanted someone with a ferocious passion. Not someone who couldn't fully show her how he felt. She'd never want someone like me. We'd known each other for almost a century. If she wanted someone like me, I would have known by now. It didn't matter that I hadn't even known my true feelings for her until only twenty-five years ago. Surely she would have said something. Which meant we weren't meant to be. The best I could hope for was friendship.

"She's like a sister," I forced out, praying my hard tone ended this conversation.

I wasn't going to discuss my love life or lack thereof with an incubus, and I sure as hell wasn't going to let him take advantage of Amiah.

"You keep telling yourself that," Hawk drawled.

I jerked my attention away and reached for the first thing on the platters of food that my gaze landed on, an apple nestled among a pile of grapes. Even if I wasn't going to allow Hawk to eat, the rest of us should, and whenever we could since I had no idea when we'd get our next meal.

But Titus grabbed my wrist, stopping me before I could take it.

"It could be enspelled," he said. "We wait for Seireadan to check it out. He can sense spells."

I opened my mouth to ask if the Winter Queen would actually enspell food and give it to her son, but given that she'd demanded he take a wife the moment he'd returned to her court with barely a welcome home, it wouldn't have surprised me if she did.

"I'll check." Hawk dropped back onto the couch, leaned close to the food, and closed his eyes. The muscles in his jaw flexed and his eyelids squeezed tighter with pain. "You're good."

"Are you sure?" Titus asked. "Seireadan would be able to tell."

"I'd be able to tell what?" Bane asked, standing in the bedroom's doorway with Amiah leaning against him.

My heart clenched at the sight of her. She still wore the robe Bane had helped her put on in the grotto, the fabric closed all the way up to the base of her neck and the belt tied tight, and she looked exhausted and in pain — both of which were natural since it was going to take more than one session to heal her broken bones, and it'd been clear when I'd walked in on her that she'd already expended all of her magic healing what she could.

And God I *did* want to make my move and tell her how I felt. Except she'd never accept me and that would ruin our friendship.

"If the food is enspelled," Titus said.

"Hawk is more sensitive than I am," Bane said, helping Amiah to the couch. "If he says the food is safe, it's safe."

Amiah sagged onto the couch beside Hawk and he grabbed a hank of grapes and offered them to her.

The grapes were a good choice, bite-sized and didn't require a lot of chewing, but she still struggled to pull one free with just her one good hand.

I shifted forward to help, but Hawk noticed the problem right away and plucked a grape from its stem and fed it to her.

Damn. Biting back a growl, I grabbed the apple I'd originally wanted to take, viciously bit in, and paced to the front of the room and back again. This really was a nightmare. Now the incubus was hand feeding her!

"How many more sessions do you think you'll need?" I asked her, fighting to keep my emotions cold.

Hard and cold. Hold it together.

"It depends on how much the healing pool helps," she said, her words half-mumbled because of her swollen face. "At least one session, more likely two to be sure my bones are properly healed."

"And how many are broken?" I asked, determined to keep my tone steady and professional. I didn't want to know, but I needed to if I was going to properly assess the situation and come up with a plan.

The light in her eyes flared.

I could see her pride warring with her practicality in her gaze. She'd never wanted to be the one being cared for, always determined to be strong and put others first. It was one of the things I loved about her *and* that drove me crazy at the same time. *I* wanted to help her, wanted to do things for her, even silly little things that she could do herself. But she never let me and she never asked for help unless it was absolutely necessary.

"If things go sideways and we need to run, I need to know what your condition is," I said.

Her gaze dropped to her lap. "He broke all of my ribs. Half are mostly healed. My wrist and nose are also broken, and there's a hairline fracture in my cheek," she said matter-of-factly as if she wasn't talking about herself but a regular patient... except she didn't raise her gaze, didn't look at any of us, and that made my inferno flare. "But that's as serious as it gets. It could have been worse."

Titus, back in the chair, stiffened, and release a low, barely audible growl.

I wanted to growl with him. It could have been worse? God, it shouldn't have happened at all.

"We should get back in the healing pool," Bane said, grabbing a roll and sitting in the chair farthest from Amiah. "My magic is still low and I want another dip before I remove your half of the leash spell."

"You sure you want to do that?" Hawk asked. "It's what's making your mom think you and Amiah are married. You break it, she notices, and she's going to make you marry someone else."

"And punish Amiah for your lie," Titus added.

"Fuck," Bane hissed, raking a hand down his face, looking gray and almost as exhausted as Amiah.

I'd known he'd expended a lot of magic yesterday, but I hadn't known a sorcerer, someone able to tap into the primal magic of Faerie, could be drained like me or Amiah, whose power came from an internal source.

"Fine. We wait until we're out of the Winter Court. I'll warp the spell so it looks like a marriage bond just in case," he said. "There aren't a lot of sorcerers in the Winter Court, but I don't want to risk one of them getting curious and taking a serious look at it."

"No." My fire flared and I fought to keep it under my skin. "It's too dangerous. You need to break the spell. If you're separated, she could die."

"If the Winter Queen learns Seireadan lied, she'll die," Titus said, his voice low.

"I can stretch the leash and adjust its side effects, but I can't disguise it *and* change it at the same time. I don't have the power at the moment." Bane stood, dropped the roll back onto the tray, and knelt in front of Amiah.

Without asking for permission, he pressed his hand over her heart, drawing a small gasp that could have either been pain or surprise.

I gritted my teeth. *Icy cold. Hard. Frozen. God damned frozen.*

He closed his eyes, and Amiah's breath picked up. Her angel glow — terrifyingly weak, exposing how little magic she had left — fluttered brighter and this time her gasp was one of pain.

"Bane?" I asked. I didn't want Amiah in danger, but I also didn't want her in pain.

"Let him concentrate," Hawk said.

Amiah squeezed her eyes shut and her body trembled. A tear leaked from beneath her lashes and rolled down her cheek, and she released a strangled whimper, one she'd been trying to hold back.

My fire churned, boiling my blood. I clenched my hands, fighting to stay put, fighting to hold my magic back, fighting every instinct I had to yank Bane away and beat the shit out of him for hurting her.

Bane began to shake as well, his fingers over her heart digging into her robe and the soft flesh of her breast, his other hand clutching the couch cushion beside her.

"Almost there, man," Hawk murmured, squinting as if he was looking into a bright light.

Amiah's breath turned ragged and another tear rolled down her cheek, but she clenched her jaw tight, keeping in any sound.

Her strength tore at my heart. She didn't deserve any of this and I should have been able to stop it.

The apple in my hand burst apart, my grip crushing it, covering my hand in juice while little fiery pieces fell on the floor.

"Fuck," Bane groaned. His glow flickered, dimmer for a second, and he sagged forward.

Hawk caught him before he fell against Amiah and helped him sit on the floor then pressed a hand against Amiah's neck. She groaned and sagged back, her body going limp with the flood of Hawk's power, her ragged breath evening out as her pain melted into pleasure.

I tossed the crushed apple back onto the tray and paced back to the front door.

Ice. Hard. Frozen. Frozen. Frozen.

"Amiah and I need to make a trip to the pools," Bane groaned. "Cassius, you come with us while T and Hawk do some recon."

"Agreed." I paced back to the couch.

Frozen. Just be frozen. Don't burn Amiah.

AMIAH

Pain wracked my body even with Hawk's magic flooding me, making me feel boneless and achy. Whatever Sebastian had done to the leash spell it had hurt and I just wanted to breakdown and sob. But Cassius already looked like he wanted to punch Sebastian, and the other guys stared at me with concern and pity, and crying would just make the situation worse.

So instead, I tried to eat another grape. But my face hurt too much and after chewing one, I gave up. Here was hoping the pools would ease some of the pain and I'd be able to get down more food before I passed out because being hungry made it harder to replenish my magic even if I slept.

Hawk put on a tunic, and he and Titus left — although for a minute Titus's expression grew dark and angry and it looked like he was going to argue with Sebastian about staying — then Sebastian insisted Cassius carry me to the pools.

"It's not far, but at the pace you walk, it'll take us forever to get there," he said, and I couldn't tell if he wanted Cassius to carry me because he was too weak to hold me or if he wanted nothing more to do with me so Cassius wouldn't hurt him.

Which made me want to scream. At both of them.

As I'd requested, Sebastian had waited in the bedroom while I'd showered and changed, and he'd only made a move to help me when I shuffled out of the bathroom and admitted I needed help. Just showering and trying to dry off with one hand had sucked away what little energy I'd had and had left me exhausted and dizzy, forcing me to cling to the front of my robe with my good hand and lean against the wall to stay upright.

But he hadn't seemed happy about helping me and now he was out the door without waiting to see if Cassius was going to pick me up or not.

With a huff, his expression hard and imposing, Cassius carefully picked me up.

He was back to the cut-from-stone angel who'd stood on Operations' rooftop with me two nights ago. If I hadn't known his power was fire, I might have guessed it was ice from all the emotional warmth he was giving off. I wasn't even getting comfort out of my magic sensing his life force.

The two guards from the throne room fell in step behind us as we walked down a long wide hall to the very end and down another hall back to the large, intricately carved ice door of the healing grotto.

"Stay here," Sebastian commanded to them, "and no, we don't require assistance."

"Your highness—" the guard on the left started.

"Have the towels and robes been replaced?" Sebastian asked, although I suspected he already knew the answer.

"Yes, your highness," the guard on the right replied with the same voice as the one on the left.

"Then obey me." Sebastian pushed the heavy door open and strode inside.

Cassius followed and one of the guards pulled the door closed behind us, trapping us in the humid, steamy grotto.

"There's a pool at the back that's better for restoring magic," Sebastian said, grabbing a towel from the bench by the door. "The first pool is better for Amiah. It seems you can't stay in it for long, so when glowing threads start snaking through your skin or it gets painful, get out."

He strode up three wide steps cut into the rock wall and disappeared around a rough rock pillar and a narrow blue spruce that reached all the way to the ceiling.

Cassius stared at the wide pool ahead of us, its water gently rippling and lapping against the sides. "I'll call him back to help you undress and..." For a second his hands grew warm then his angel glow flared and he was back to cold and stern. "And I'll keep my eyes closed while you're in the pool."

Heat swept across my cheeks, and Hawk's power swelled low within me. How *was* I going to bathe? Even if Sebastian had stayed and Cassius didn't look, I wasn't going into the pool naked, no matter how impractical that was. Sebastian had made it clear he didn't want to see me naked again, and Hawk's magic still surged through me. The irrational desire that I'd thought — had prayed — I'd squashed when I'd slept with Sebastian, that I shouldn't have had because of the pain I was in, taunted me. And Hawk, bringing me to a gentle climax with his magic, fingers, and words less than an hour ago hadn't helped.

I ached to go back to bed. Although I wasn't sure if it was for sex I was too tired to have or to be held and feel the warmth of someone's body, their life force humming against my senses. None of which I was getting from Cassius at the moment.

"I'm sure we can manage without him. There are extra robes," I said, trying to ignore my aching desire. "I'll just go into the pool wearing this one so you can keep an eye on me. I can change into a dry robe when Sebastian returns." If he'd even be willing to help me again since he'd made it clear he wasn't even interested in that. Maybe I could manage untying the knot and drying myself off one-handed again.

"Right." Cassius's gaze slid over the pile of towels on the bench and the robes hanging on hooks on the wall behind it.

There wasn't a change of clothes for him unless he wanted to wear a robe. He wasn't going to be able to go into the pool still clothed like I was.

Would he strip to his briefs like he had last night? He certainly wouldn't strip all the way down like Hawk had.

My pulse picked up, need throbbing between my thighs. I ached to feel Sebastian filling me again, or Hawk teasing me with his fingers. What would Cassius be like as a lover? Cool? Reserved? Or would he finally release his hold on his emotions and join me in the consuming sensations, letting it burn away all the fear and heartache until there was only bliss?

He strode the few feet to the closest pool, knelt while still holding me, and eased me into the pool's warm soothing waters. My robe billowed up, exposing my thighs and the large bruises and scrapes on my knees, and I clutched at the front of it, holding it down between my legs so I didn't flash him.

His gaze locked on my hand between my thighs and a hint of embarrassment, but not enough to quell my desire, heated my cheeks. Then my rear end reached the submerged bench ringing the pool and he pulled away, both his body and his gaze, looking anywhere but at me.

The glimmer of magic I had left, that flickering core of power that I could never consume but wasn't powerful enough to even sense someone else's injuries, stuttered like a small flame in a strong wind, and the pool's tingling magic sank into my skin, rushing straight to my heart.

I gasped as it curled around the organ, no longer the lulling power from last night, flooded my veins, and gathered, cool and sharp along the lines of my mating brand, making its ache stronger than the rest of my injuries for a terrifying moment. My pulse pounded faster, fear consuming my desire, and I yanked my gaze to the skylight, seeking comfort from that small square of clear blue sky.

I won't be trapped. I can't be trapped. Not even by love. Especially the uncontrolled love of a soul bond. I didn't want my brand's cruel magic making me fall in love with someone I didn't know, making me lose myself in their soul. I didn't want the terror of knowing they were hurt or the inability to control myself when they were.

It was bad enough my magic compelled me to heal people. What happened if my soul was locked on my mate while my magic was locked on someone else? Who would I pick? Would I even be given a chance to pick or would my soul bond and my magical backlash tear me apart?

I fought to shove those thoughts aside, adding them to the list of things I didn't want to think about. I didn't know how long I'd be able to ignore them and prayed it would be long enough to get through this situation... even though I had no idea how long this situation was going to last.

"How are your burns?" I asked, jumping on the first thing that popped into my mind and gritting my teeth against a painful flare of magic in my palms. Yesterday, after the fight in Left of Lincoln, the illegal off-the-books market, Cassius had cauterized his wounds with his fire, leaving ugly, painful burns all over his torso. I'd managed to heal them enough that they were no longer painful, but I hadn't had enough power to eliminate the thick scars, and if I didn't get to them soon, they'd be permanent.

"I'm fine," he said. "Save your magic for yourself."

"I'm aware that your scars are less severe than my bones," I replied, my tone sharper than I intended. How many times were we going to have this conversation? "Stop assuming I don't know how to best use my magic."

"That's not what I was saying." His gaze jumped to me and slid down my body. Heat simmered in his eyes for a second, making my pulse thrum faster, before they widened and he jerked his attention away again.

Jeez. Did I look that terrible?

Except he'd already seen my battered face.

I dipped my attention to my body and my heart froze as a hot flash of embarrassment flooded my entire face and scorched down my neck. The white robe clung to my curves, leaving nothing to the imagination, and had turned see-through, exposing the ugly red bruises covering my torso... as well as my nipples. Thank goodness I was holding the robe down and my hand was in the way, or he'd be able to see a whole lot more.

"I'm saying stop worrying about us for a minute and worry about yourself," he said, his voice gruff.

Except if I worried about myself all the thoughts I didn't want to think would come crashing in. I couldn't just sit there and wallow. I had to keep busy, not think, do something.

"Cassius, please. Let me do my job." *Let me do something I know how to do. Let me be useful, not helpless and pathetic. Let me be an equal. Don't let this nightmare change our friendship, because I need you. You're all I have.*

A wisp of smoke curled from his hands then vanished.

"The pool last night helped them along," he said.

"Then let me see. I think my injuries are too severe to get a good sense of how this pool heals," I said, hoping that if I turned his examination into an educational experience for me I'd get him to take off his tunic and show me his scars. "How far along are they? Would another dip finish the job?" I asked, clinging to the questions of how effective the healing pool actually was. "You could change into a towel and join me and we could find out."

"No," he said, appalled. "I'm not— Not while you're—" He gestured at me, his gaze starting to slide back to me then jerking away as his back stiffened. "Out of all of us, why him? Why Bane?"

Because there's no chance he's my soul mate and he doesn't feel obligated to start a relationship. The memory of Sebastian's mouth on me made Hawk's power surge again. I just wished it had been more than a one-night stand.

Except I knew what Cassius was really asking. Why not him? Didn't I trust him? Weren't we friends?

But it was because we were friends, because there was a chance he could be my soul mate, that I couldn't let him get close. Not until my partially formed mating brand was gone.

"After this, I'll never see him again," I said, saying the first thing that came to mind. "Don't you think seeing me naked would make things awkward between us?"

The pool's tingling magic flickered with my power, sending tiny painful bites through my skin, and I sucked in a shallow breath, focusing on Hawk's magic still seeping through me instead of the pain.

Hot and sensual. Achy thrumming need.

God, his fingers pumping into me, bringing me to climax.

"You're a physician," Cassius said. "I'm sure you see naked people all the time. How would me seeing you naked be different?"

Because it was different. My robe had turned see-through and I was blushing and so was he. Except I couldn't say I didn't want to show him my body because I was attracted to him — because I ached for sex with anyone, not just him. Really — that would open the door to a conversation I wasn't ready to have. Not until my brand was gone. And I wasn't telling him about my brand either. He'd think it was wonderful and magical like every other angel, not the nightmare I knew it to be.

"You're right." I bit the inside of my cheek, my heart pounding, my core throbbing. If I didn't feel anything for him, hiding my body was illogical, and eventually he'd come to the same conclusion. If I didn't want him to think I felt something more for him and have a relationship conversation forced on me sooner than I wanted, I needed to be coolly professional about the whole situation. Right now, he was able to help me and I needed help. Nakedness shouldn't matter.

Fine.

"You might as well strip and get in the pool then," I said. "A body is just a body, be it mine or yours."

AMIAH

HEAT FLOODED MY FACE. *WHAT IS WRONG WITH ME? WHY DID I JUST SAY that?* I'd just told him to strip and get in the pool with me.

"Amiah—"

"There's no point in you having scars or me wasting power removing them when you can just join me in the pool," I insisted, doubling down on my argument unable to stop myself.

"I'm not joining you in the pool," he snapped back.

"Agent. If you're shy, wrap yourself in a towel. But it's not like I haven't seen a man's genitalia before." And recently. I shuddered at the memory of Sebastian's hard and thick erection pushing into me. "You've briefly mentioned your romantic relations in the past, I'm sure you've a seen a woman's before as well. Don't be foolish. Take this opportunity for free healing."

He glared at me, his angel glow blazing.

"Fine." He marched back to the bench and pulled off his tunic.

Oh. My. God! Something was really wrong with me. I was supposed to be keeping our friendship a friendship, not invite him to strip and sit mostly naked—

He pushed his pants and briefs off his hips, giving me an amazing view of his glutes and muscular thighs.

Fully naked!

My mouth went dry and Hawk's power made the muscles between

my thighs clench. Cassius was stunning with his sculpted arms and shoulders, his broad back tapering into a narrow waist, and the ripple of flexing muscles in his back and shoulders as he bent, grabbed a towel from the bench, and wrapped it around his hips.

Then he turned back to me and my heart dropped into my stomach. His expression was icier than before, almost pained, as if he hated the idea of joining me in the pool, but didn't want to argue with me.

I forced my gaze to his chest and studied his scars as he slipped into the pool on the far side, far enough away that our feet wouldn't accidentally brush. The scars were in better shape than I'd left them, and a few were no longer bright pink just rough shiny discolorations in his skin as if I'd already spent extra time working on him.

"How long were you in the pool last night?" I asked as the tingling snaps from the pool's magic grew sharper.

Focus on learning about the pool and the pain. Nothing else. Not what happened to me and not how much I want him.

My gaze dipped lower to his hands, one holding the towel closed, the other holding the front of it down, aching for just a peek.

Jeez. Focus.

Embarrassment heated my cheeks again and I wrenched my attention back up to his eyes. Except he wasn't looking at me. He'd locked his gaze on the skylight above us, the muscles in his jaw tight. His whole body tight, actually.

"We couldn't have been in the pool more than fifteen minutes," he said.

"So not as powerful as me, but still impressive." It would have taken me only a few minutes — faster if I didn't care about hurting him — to do that amount of healing, but fifteen minutes in the water was still good. Maybe I should have looked at myself in the mirror. Perhaps I didn't look so bad. Except I felt horrible. Broken bones aside, my face didn't feel like I'd spent any time healing my bruises. "What rate would you say my bruises have healed?"

"They're maybe a day or two old." His gaze remained locked on the skylight.

"So the pool isn't as effective on me." I let my gaze wander back to his hands, the throbbing between my thighs increasing and my insides hot... or was that the water?

This was a mistake. A huge mistake.

"Bane thinks it has something to do with your healing magic."

Cassius's breath picked up and he shifted his hips, trying to get comfortable.

I jerked my attention up and found him staring at me. His bright blue gaze, a match to my own, captured mine, and for a second I could see wild, seething emotions in his eyes. Fire and fear and an aching—? Was that desire?

No. It had to be my desire reflected back at me.

Still, my breath caught and a heavy tension filled the air between us. Maybe Sebastian was right. Maybe I was in love with Cassius.

And maybe I'd just spent over a hundred years without sex and my libido wanted to make up for lost time.

That had to be it. I'd commanded Cassius to get in the pool because my subconscious wanted this moment, wanted to feel this burning need of being near a naked man, wanted more. I yearned for Cassius to cross the distance between us, yearned for the courage to cross to him.

Would it really hurt if I just kissed him?

My thoughts stuttered.

What was I thinking?

Of course it would hurt if I kissed him. That would ruin everything. If he didn't reject me, he'd want a commitment I couldn't give him. I was destined for someone else, and even if he was my soul mate, I didn't want to be trapped in a permanent magical bond.

Fear sliced through my desire, and the memory of last night flooded my mind. Terror. Pain. Helplessness.

I swore.

I started to tremble and fought to clamp down on my emotions. Not now. Not when Cassius was looking at me. Not ever. I wanted to pretend it had never happened, pretend I hadn't broken my vow to never be a victim again, pretend—

My throat tightened.

I swore.

The pool's magic snapped with a sudden biting sting, and grew into a painful electric shock, searing through my body.

I swore. I swore. I wasn't going to think about it.

Cassius frowned. "Amiah?"

"I'm fine." *Fine fine fine.* It hadn't happened. I wasn't weak. I was strong. So strong. *Please, I have to be strong.*

"You don't look fine."

Another agonizing bite from the pool and my magic flared. The pressure built inside me, a mix of magics fighting for control, each surging to gain dominance even while I was drained, and there wasn't anything I could do about it.

So don't think about it. Think of something else. Anything else.

Except it was getting harder and harder to think past the pain and fear. Not even Hawk's magic and Cassius's nudity were helping.

I heaved my gaze up to the skylight, but the square in the ceiling was too small. Even the sky felt crowded and the walls of the grotto were closing in on me.

"I can do this." I had to do it.

"It's not a matter of whether you can or not," he said, his voice suddenly close, the water around me getting hotter.

I turned to look at him as the edge of his towel brushed my arm. So close. Would he kiss me? *Please kiss me and take it all away.*

"Bane said you couldn't spend a lot of time in the pool." The muscles in his jaw flexed and consideration flashed across his expression, then he released his towel, picked me up, and set me on the edge of the pool.

I tried not to look at him. I really did. But my gaze leaped to his sculpted chest and sank lower.

He grabbed his towel before I could see anything, the now-bubbling and steaming water billowing the fabric forward, unfortunately hiding everything.

"If you can hold on, I'll dry off first then help you."

The pool's magic snapped again, thankfully not as strong as before now that I was just wet, not immersed in its waters. "If you help me stand, I think I'll be okay."

In fact, while I was still tired and in pain, I felt a little stronger. But Cassius had already hopped out of the pool, steam rising from his skin, and rushed to the bench, his back to me and his wet towel in a heap on the floor, giving me an amazing view of his glutes again.

"You're just going to let her sit here?" Sebastian asked as he came down the stairs, fully dressed, his wet hair, the towel in his hand, and the healthy glow radiating from his skin the only indications he'd been in a pool.

I shifted to face him, not ready to stand just yet. His gaze dipped to my chest and his eyebrows raised.

"Ah," he said, drawing close and holding out his hand to help me. Desire dilated his pupils and his eyes raked over my body again, making me ache with need. "Decided to be cruel to him."

"Hardly. I doubt the bruises are attractive." I took his hand and he helped me rise with a tug that toppled me into him, although thankfully not forcefully enough to spike pain through my ribs or broken wrist. My good hand slid out across his muscular chest to his shoulder and my breasts pressed against him.

His pale blue, almost colorless gaze captured mine, just like Cassius's had a moment ago, stealing my breath and making my pulse pound.

He'd kissed me like he'd desired me. He'd looked at me like I was beautiful. He'd taken the time to satisfy me with a passion I hadn't expected from a one-night stand kind of guy like Sebastian, as if I'd been important to him.

He was the only one who knew my secret, knew how terrified I was of my mating brand, and knew I'd never been with a man before.

And now he wanted nothing to do with me.

"Now who's being cruel?" I breathed.

"So fuck him," he whispered, his breath heating my skin and sending a shiver racing through me. "I bet he left you sitting here to hide a raging hard on."

"Remove my mating brand and maybe I will," I murmured back, making his eyes widen in surprise.

"Can you untie the belt?" Cassius asked, his voice gruff as he approached, now fully dressed.

I fought the urge to see if Sebastian was right about Cassius desiring me. *Not until my brand is gone.*

"Sure." Sebastian stepped back, slung the towel over his shoulder so he had the use of both hands, and reached for the belt's wet knot, his gaze on my breasts.

He licked his lips and my nipples hardened. I wanted his mouth on them again, teasing me, building the heat within me. I didn't care that most of my ribs were still broken and I looked horrible. I needed him, needed to forget about being trapped, being taken, being—

Oh God, please. I needed to have sex again to forget it all. I was going to lose my mind, break down, and start sobbing, and I couldn't do that. That would be admitting it was all true, that it had happened, that I'd been helpless.

But I certainly wasn't going to ask either man for intercourse, and I doubted my body could handle that. I was just going to have to wait until Hawk and I were alone again and beg him to use his magic to satisfy me.

Sebastian jerked his attention back to my eyes, untied the belt around my waist, and slipped the robe off my shoulders then hurried back to the bench to get another robe, as Cassius gently helped me dry off while keeping his gaze averted.

The whole moment was tense and awkward, and if I was being honest with myself, a little thrilling. I had two gorgeous men helping me change my clothes. If I hadn't been hurt and they hadn't been... well, if they hadn't been *them*, I might have found the courage to embrace the throbbing desire inside me. I might have been bold enough to ask for what I wanted.

And I wasn't going to acknowledge what a mess I was, being worried about Cassius and Sebastian seeing me naked while at the same time fantasizing about being intimate with both of them... at the same time.

"You should carry her," Cassius said stepping back and leaving Sebastian to tie my robe closed.

"I'd rather you did," Sebastian replied, tying the belt and also stepping back.

Jeez. Really?

I headed for the door. I didn't know if I'd be able to swing it open — it looked pretty heavy — but I wasn't going to stand around and wait for one of them to give in and pick me up. Yes, I was exhausted, and yes, I was still moving slowly, but the pool had helped and I no longer felt like I was going to fall over or pass out.

Thank goodness most of today's awkward problems would be solved by tonight — and I wasn't going to think about my fears or my desires. A little food and eight to ten hours of sleep, and I'd have restored enough magic to knit the rest of my ribs and my broken wrist back together. Then I could breathe easier and I'd be able to dress and undress without help.

Cassius hurried past me and opened the door, making Sebastian roll his eyes and sigh.

"Fine." Sebastian scooped me into his arms, jarring my broken ribs and making me gasp, which made Cassius glare.

"Hey, I told you," Sebastian said, "you should carry her."

Cassius's gaze jumped to the ice guards as they fell into step behind us and his body stiffened. "If your highness would prefer it."

"I would," Sebastian replied, a wicked haughty gleam lighting his eyes.

"Just don't," I insisted before Sebastian handed me over which would jar my ribs again. "I'm not a sack of potatoes. Every time you move me, it hurts."

Cassius's expression grew harder as if for a second he'd forgotten about my injuries and the gleam in Sebastian's eyes vanished.

"I just want to eat something and go back to bed," I said... with Hawk.

No!

Not with Hawk.

To sleep. Alone. And restore my magic.

"We can do that," Cassius replied, pity sliding into his expression and making my stomach churn.

I wished he'd stop looking at me like that.

I wished I hadn't given him another reason to look at me like that again.

Don't. Think.

Sebastian turned the corner to the hall leading to our suite and stopped. The door was open, two more ice guards stood on guard in the hall, and ice servants scurried in and out carrying empty dishes, silverware, crystal glasses, and table decorations.

"What's happening?" Cassius asked, his voice low.

"My mother, that's what." Sebastian stiffened and glanced at the glyph on the inside of his wrist that alerted him to the presence of shadow fae. It flashed a soft white glow then dimmed. "And trouble."

He squared his shoulders and strode confidently to our suite's door, stopping in the doorway.

Inside, the living room furniture was gone, replaced with a large wooden dining room table that was being set with fancy china, crystal, and silver place settings, along with lit candelabras, decorative floral arrangements of winter greenery, and bottles of wine. Half a dozen wide high-backed matching wood chairs, generously spaced out, surrounded the table, and at the far end, on a wide couch, tall enough for her to sit properly at the table sat the Winter Queen.

She wore another diaphanous gown, this one in blood red, cut low to draw the eye to her cleavage. As if the cut of the dress wasn't enough, a large diamond pendant surrounded by gold filigree hung on a delicate gold chain between her breasts. Two of the gorgeous men who'd been on the floor around her throne — one fae, like Sebastian with red and silver hair, the other the werepanther — sat on either side of her, still not wearing shirts, their pants still red now matching the queen's dress.

The woman who'd been standing beside the throne, Padraigin, sat stiffly in a chair to the queen's left. She wore the same simple white tunic Cassius did, and while I couldn't see her legs, I suspected she also wore the same loose pants. The delicate ice circlet that had been holding back her long black hair was gone and her locks were now only held back with two simple braids at her temples.

On the queen's right sat a breathtakingly handsome shadow fae, the shadows under his pale skin undulating, slowly, seductively. He wasn't the same shadow fae who'd attacked us in the park ring or in Left of Lincoln, even though he had the same shoulder-length black hair pulled back at the nape of his neck. The lines of the fae's face were sharper, more refined, and more beautiful, but that didn't make me feel safe because he wore a similar black leather outfit as the other fae, and behind him stood the demon-vampire, his cold lifeless essence making me shiver.

The demon-vampire still wore black leather pants and a long black wrap tunic. It was similar but not the same as the clothes the seated shadow fae wore, hinting at an East Asian style where the seated fae's clothes seemed more modern-day North American. His black hair hung halfway down his back and was half pulled back in a ponytail and half loose, and while his katana was sheathed at his hip along with a matching wakizashi, I knew how fast he could draw his weapon and slice someone down.

This was the man who'd tried to kill me in the park ring, decapitated someone in Lincoln without a second thought, and then given me a knife when I'd been Balwyrdan's captive. I had no idea why he'd given me a weapon when he'd tried to kill me earlier, and there was no hint of emotion on his face or in his black eyes — his hellfire banked to small red embers — indicating he thought anything about me or even recognized me.

"Seireadan," the Winter Queen purred. "Look who came to visit. His Majesty of the Shadow Court, your friend, Deaglan."

The shadow fae flashed a warm friendly smile that sent a chill racing through me. I didn't care how friendly he smiled. This was the fae who'd cast the horrible leash spell on Titus and had held him prisoner, trapped in his human form unable to shift and fly and satisfy his beast's needs, for five hundred years. This was a monster.

AMIAH

SEBASTIAN'S GRIP ON ME TIGHTENED, AND HE FLASHED HIS OWN WARM smile with no indication to Deaglan that he knew what he'd done to Titus or any fear that Deaglan would recognize that our marriage bond was actually a warped version of his leash spell.

"What an unexpected surprise," Sebastian said, striding the few remaining steps to the chair at the end of the table opposite his mother but not sitting.

"I heard you were back in court and married, your highness," Deaglan said, his voice warm and enticing, nothing about it implying darkness like the undulating shadows under his skin or the fact that he was the King of the Shadow Court and an all-around monster.

"Come, Deaglan," the Winter Queen cooed, "no need to be overly formal. You and Seireadan grew up together."

"And I'm no longer a prince of the Winter Court." Sebastian jerked his chin and one of the ice maids pulled out the chair in front of him. He sat, still holding me, and settled me in his lap.

Cassius took up position behind us, mirroring the demon-vampire's stance with his hands behind his back and his feet slightly apart like a soldier at rest.

"You still are a prince of the Winter Court," the queen said. A delicate mist curled around the table legs and a whisper of cold swept across my skin. For a second that something dark and dangerous that I'd seen in the Winter Queen's expression in the throne room returned to her eyes.

"Although you have made it challenging to produce an heir," Deaglan said, "what with marrying an angel and all."

"Because I don't need an heir." Sebastian pressed a kiss to the top of my head, sending a shiver of desire slipping down my spine even though the kiss was about as chaste as a kiss could get. "Once my bride has recovered, I'm returning to the mortal realm."

Deaglan cocked an eyebrow and pursed his lips, and the hellfire in the demon-vampire's eyes sparked, drawing my attention to his hard, emotionless expression.

Why did he help me? Why give me a weapon? It didn't make any sense—

Except it did. The demon-vampire had seen me with Titus and if he hadn't seen Titus come to my rescue, he'd probably been hoping I'd lead him back to Titus...

But he could have just as easily let me die and kept watching Sebastian or Cassius or even Titus-in-disguise in the hopes of finding Titus.

Another shiver of desire breathed down my spine, reminding me of the ache between my thighs that I'd been trying to ignore since seeing Cassius strip in the grotto— No, since seeing Sebastian standing over Titus's broken body in the park ring two nights ago.

"Now Seireadan, don't be foolish. You're not returning to the mortal realm. The future king of the Winter Court must *stay* in the Winter Court." The queen waved at no one in particular and maids scurried to pour wine and bring in plates with food, setting them on top of the plates already in front of us. "I'm sure the Winter Court will grant you fertility with your angel like the other courts do with all the other species."

She turned and captured the mouth of the werepanther in a deep passionate kiss, moaning when he teased his palms over the top of her breasts and cupped them, kneading them through her dress's gauzy fabric.

Padraigin picked up her fork and stared at her plate, while Deaglan's smile darkened, openly appreciating the sexual display.

"Angels are certain they can only have children with other angels," Sebastian said, smoothing a wrinkle in my robe along my thigh and resting his hand on my bare knee, not reacting to his mother making out in front of us. "I'm in love with Amiah. I didn't marry her for children."

My chest irrationally ached at his words. Oh, how the lie just slid off his tongue and how he touched me as if there really was something between us.

A part of me yearned for that, his— No, *someone's, anyone's* affectionate touch, his warmth, his thrumming life force near mine, his desire. I yearned with a need almost as strong as my need before I'd slept with Sebastian even though we were in a dangerous situation and surrounded by strangers and most of my body still hurt.

The Winter Queen broke off her kiss, but her hand dropped below the table, reaching out — for her lover's lap? — and the werepanther pressed sensual kisses against her neck as the other man joined in, kissing the other side of her neck. "Angels only *believe* that they're only fertile with other angels. The Winter Court tells me no angel has tried to become pregnant with a high fae in Faerie."

Sebastian tensed. "You asked it?"

"You are a royal and a full sorcerer," Padraigin said, her gaze jumping to the red-haired fae then to Deaglan then back to her untouched plate. "Her majesty says the Winter Court will grant you an heir."

"And there's already a precedent for a half-breed becoming heir." Deaglan caught Padraigin's gaze when it jumped back to him, and the heat in his eyes grew.

She stiffened, a hint of pink coloring her cheeks, and she dropped her attention back to her plate, stabbing a small white square that could have been a piece of potato or apple or something-only-found-in-Faerie with her fork.

"The heir to the Autumn Court is a half-breed," Deaglan said, "and his court has already claimed him and granted him royal privileges."

The werepanther's breath picked up and he slid a hand inside the front of the Winter Queen's bodice, roughly palming her breast.

The sight of their rising desire made my pulse quicken and my own aching need throb hotter between my thighs.

Deaglan took a long slow sip of wine, turning his heated smile to me. "Still, you're usually more affectionate with your lovers. I'm not sure I believe you love her."

"I made the vow." Sebastian's hand on my knee inched higher and shifted to the inside of my thigh.

Heat pooled low in my core and I leaned in to him, savoring the feel of my body pressed against his, broken bones and everything.

"I can see the bond." Deaglan shrugged. "Maybe all isn't right in your wedding bed? I could always work her in for you like I worked in Enowen." His gaze dipped to my chest, and I realized the robe had slipped open and was no longer pulled up to my neck, revealing a generous amount of cleavage.

My pulse beat faster, but I couldn't tell if it was with fear or desire at the thought... which was crazy. Deaglan was a monster. I wasn't attracted to him, and yet it felt as if my body didn't care what the rest of me wanted.

Another whisper of cold tickled under my skin and the mist curling around the table legs billowed. The demon-vampire's attention slid to mine and his hellfire sparked again, a sharp flash of red in his black eyes.

For a second, he looked hungry, in the way a predator *and* a man looked at a woman, sending another shiver of desire and fear sweeping through me. Then he blinked and his cold, emotionless expression returned. Except his gaze remained locked on me.

"You used to share all the time," Deaglan said, his voice dark, dangerous, terrifying, and sensual.

"I didn't share Enowen."

"You would have, eventually." The heat in Deaglan's eyes grew. "Just cut to the chase, Seireadan. Her majesty doesn't care what you do in bed."

"Only that I get a grandchild, and the Winter Court will only give the heir to you. It doesn't matter who else fucks her," the queen said, making Cassius stiffen and the light in his eyes flare. "Whatever fixes your problems in bed."

"I have no problems." Sebastian's hand slipped higher up my thigh, the tip of his fingers a breath from my slick heat.

The ache inside me grew and I squirmed my hips, shifting just enough in his lap to slide his fingers against my folds, showing him just how much I wanted him.

Sebastian pressed his lips against my neck and softly groaned into my skin as two of his fingers dipped inside me.

My desire spiraled tight, making my pulse race and my breath pick up.

The demon-vampire's hellfire swelled, now actual miniature flames in each eye instead of just red embers, and the heat in Deaglan's eyes grew, as Padraigin's hands trembled, her attention still on her food. The queen leaned back, her smile smug, and Sebastian groaned again and tensed.

"Fuck," he murmured against my neck as he withdrew his fingers, clutching the inside of my thigh. "Amiah is injured and an angel. She doesn't have the same sensibilities as a high fae."

"If she's going to be queen, she'll have to get used to it," Deaglan replied.

"Yes," the queen purred. She jerked her chin at the fae man who slid off the couch and went under the table, while her hand was still in the werepanther's lap, his jaw clenched as he fought to control his breath — and presumably his release for some reason. "You should start now."

"Is that why you've made the Winter Court fill the air with an aphrodisiac?" Sebastian's fingers dug painfully into my flesh and I reached under my robe and grabbed his hand, urging him to slide his fingers back to my core.

God, surely I had more control than this. Surely I could wait until we were alone. But just that thought made my yearning twist tighter. I needed him. Needed him inside me. *Oh, please.*

Then my thoughts tripped over what he'd just said. The Winter Court had released an aphrodisiac. That was why I couldn't seem to control myself.

"You clearly needed some encouragement," the Winter Queen said.

"I don't need help sleeping with my wife."

"The guards said you were distant toward her on the walk to the pools. I can't have that," the queen said, her voice thick with need. "I want a grandchild."

"You have one. Padraigin's son," Sebastian replied through gritted teeth.

"That child is a half-breed," the queen moaned, "and the court hasn't claimed her."

"Mine will be a half-breed as well." Sebastian's hand inched closer to my core again and I bit back my own moan, fighting to keep my expression as neutral as his.

"But yours will be the rightful heir and the Winter Court agrees." The queen's eyes fluttered shut and the werepanther groaned.

Her eyes snapped open and she glared at him, her expression filled with icy danger. "Did I say you could come?" she asked, her voice suddenly dark.

The man's eyes rolled back and he trembled. "No, your majesty."

"Good." The queen leveled her glare at Sebastian. "But you,

Seireadan, should. Now and often until your wife—" she spat out the word "—has made me a grandchild."

My heart skipped a beat. I desperately wanted to sleep with Sebastian again, let go of everything and feel that amazing bliss. I wanted it so much I feared I'd shatter.

"Fuck your wife." The queen tipped her head back, her breath coming fast with whatever the man under the table was doing.

The heat building inside me surged with the memory of Sebastian's mouth bringing me to climax. Without a doubt, that was what the man under the table was doing.

And that was what I wanted. Now.

No.

"No," I forced out, "I'm in no condition to have sex."

"I don't care what condition you're in. You're the princess consort. Your duty is to my son and my court. You just have to lie there and get pregnant."

She waved at the bedroom door and it magically opened by itself with a rush of cool wind. The bed had been made, the white comforter replaced with a dark blue one to show off the shimmering, diamond-like snowflakes scattered over its surface like rose petals, and a soft white light pulsed around it. Four women in see-through gowns knelt in a row at the foot of the bed facing us. I didn't recognize them from the throne room, but I'd barely been conscious so they could have been in the group the Winter Queen had presented for Sebastian to choose his bride. Their heads were bowed, their breaths too fast, and their bodies trembling as if they, too, were affected by the Winter Court's aphrodisiac.

In fact, it looked like everyone in the room except the ice maids, Cassius, and the demon-vampire were being affected. Unless the queen always had sex at her dining room table, and Deaglan always looked at women like that. Padraigin certainly looked like she was trying to hold herself together.

I glanced at Cassius. He trembled and smoke curled from his hands. No, he fought some great internal battle. The court was influencing him too.

My gaze slid to the demon-vampire whose hungry look had returned, sending another confusing shiver of fear and desire rushing through me. A vampire's bite caused sexual euphoria. Some people threw themselves at vampires in the hopes of being bitten.

And now all I could think about was being bitten while having Sebastian push inside me.

"We don't need help," Sebastian said, his voice gruff, "and I'm not going to have sex with her right now."

The Winter Queen stood, drawing the werepanther up with her, her hand still in his pants, the fae man still on his knees under her skirt. "You can't resist the will of the Winter Court. My will."

Two ice maids picked up the couch and took it into the bedroom.

"Oh, no," Sebastian said, his fingers digging painfully into my thigh. "You're not watching."

"You're going to watch?" I squeaked before I could stop myself.

"Queen's prerogative." The Winter Queen gave me a wicked smile. "If it bothers you, Deaglan and his bodyguard can watch... or help." She pumped her hand inside the werepanther's pants, drawing a strangled groan. "But I want proof of your heir's conception."

My gaze jumped to Deaglan, who had the same dark hunger in his eyes that I'd seen in Balwyrdan's, except instead of getting off on just hurting me, I had the sickening sense that he wanted me screaming, crying, bleeding, *and* be inside me.

Fear sliced through my desire, but didn't completely diminish it, which only made Deaglan's smile deepen. Behind him, the demon-vampire shifted, anger bleeding into his hungry expression.

"No," I gasped. I wasn't even sure if I said the word out loud. I wouldn't let anyone hurt me like that again. I couldn't—

"No," I said more forcefully, and Sebastian's grip on me tightened.

A sharp flash of pain cut through my hip where my sleeping mating brand lay and the aching need inside me vanished, fully consumed by fear.

Oh my God! Was Sebastian—?

No, he couldn't be my soul mate or my brand would have formed already... when we'd had sex... wouldn't it have? Except the bond from a mating brand could form at any time. Surely sex was enough of an intimate act to make a bond form between us... if one was going to form.

And God, I wanted to have sex with him again, feel him fill me, sink into the bliss of sensation without thought or worry—

"No. I'm not having sex with Seb— Seireadan for your entertainment."

A gust of freezing wind blasted through the room and everyone's eyes widened, the queen's, the werepanther's, Padraigin's, Deaglan, the demon-vampire's, *and* Sebastian's.

I gritted my teeth against the Winter Queen's power.

She wasn't going to trick, coerce, or force me to have sex with Sebastian. "And I'm not asking the Winter Court to give me a child so your heir can have an heir."

The wind gusted again, sweeping around me and Sebastian as if we were in the eye of its storm.

"Well, that's interesting," Deaglan said, as the demon-vampire inched closer to Deaglan and the muscles in Padraigin's jaw flexed.

The Winter Queen's glare turned dark and frozen. She flicked a finger and the wind died. "The Winter Court responds to you. It's made its choice. Seireadan is heir apparent and you're his queen." Her eyes narrowed. "You will fuck my son. Now."

"Pretty sure I get a say in this, too," Sebastian drawled, his trembling belying his confident tone. "She's in no condition for sex. I won't risk hurting her."

"Fine then." The queen's glare turned wicked. "I'll make the appropriate arrangements for you to consummate your marriage at your party when she's healed up. All of court will witness the impossible conception and know you, my dear, belong to the Winter Court." She strode from the room, her men, and the four maids in the bedroom following her.

Padraigin stormed after her as Deaglan leaned back in his chair.

"You should have just let me watch," Deaglan said with a shrug. "Now everyone gets to see your milky white angel ass."

No no no no.

I wasn't having sex with Sebastian and no one was seeing anything. We were leaving before it came to that. *Oh, God. Please.*

"The Winter Court's wind gusted for her, Seireadan. Just like it gusts for her majesty and like it used to gust for you. It hasn't gusted for your sister in centuries." Deaglan's gaze raked over my body, making a mix of desire and nausea churn in my stomach. "Guess you really did marry her."

He flashed me a wicked smile and strode out of the suite. The demon-vampire shot me one last hungry look, the hellfire in his eyes licking across his cheeks, before he schooled his features back to coldly emotionless and followed Deaglan.

"What. Was. That?" Cassius growled as soon as the door closed.

"My God damned fucking mother," Sebastian groaned, yanking his hand out from under my robe.

"We're leaving before the party." My pulse was racing too fast and I couldn't catch my breath, each quick gasp shooting agony through my chest. "I'm *not* having intercourse with you with the whole Winter Court watching."

And we're not married. We couldn't be married. Please, don't let us be married.

I pushed out of his arms and stood, trying to put some space between us, but my hip bumped the table, making me stumble, and Sebastian grabbed my waist, steadying me, his touch searing through the thin robe.

His pale blue gaze captured mine, and time stuttered for a second, caught on my stalled breath.

"I'm not having intercourse with you, period," Sebastian said, jerking away from me.

Cassius moved toward me, but stopped and crossed his arms instead as if he didn't want to touch me. "Can the Winter Court really make you conceive with him?"

"How am I supposed to know?" I squeaked. "As far as I know no angel has ever tried to get pregnant with a fae." Yes, at some point I thought I'd want a family... if my soul mate had been an angel since I wouldn't be able to conceive with any other species, but not now and not with Sebastian. It was clear he didn't do commitments. Without a doubt, he'd run the minute I got pregnant and I'd never see him again.

"It can't," Sebastian said, "no matter how much magic my mother uses. I haven't vowed my fertility to Amiah so I'm still shooting blanks."

The door to the suite banged open and we all jerked to face it. Fire rushed over Cassius's arms then vanished as Hawk staggered inside with Titus close behind him.

"Holy fuck," Hawk said, his words slurred and his hellfire blazing.

His gaze locked on me with a hunger that made my pulse trip, and he stormed toward me. Before I could stop him, he cupped my face with his hot hands, shooting agony through my fractured cheek, and dipped in to kiss me. But Cassius grabbed his shoulder and yanked him back before our lips could meet.

With a groan, Hawk turned on Cassius, grabbed his head, and captured his lips in a searing kiss instead.

AMIAH

Cassius froze, his eyes wide with shock at Hawk's lips locked with his. The incubus hummed low in his throat, a sound of pure masculine desire, and leaned into Cassius, not caring that Cassius wasn't kissing him back. A curl of his seductive magic somehow swelled in my chest even though he wasn't touching me, and I fought to keep back a surprised gasp.

Then horror flashed across Cassius's expression and he jerked back, holding Hawk at arm's length. "Back off."

"Oh come on, hot stuff," Hawk moaned. He leaned into Cassius's grip, and grabbed for the hem of Cassius's tunic at his thighs but couldn't quite reach. "I want to see you let it go and light the bed on fire."

Another swell of Hawk's magic rushed through me, this one even stronger than the last, teasing me with the promise of an amazing climax. I tightened my grip on the table, my legs wobbly.

"Fuck," Sebastian hissed, his body trembling.

Cassius's eyes rolled back and smoke swelled from his hands. "Would you pull it back? You're bleeding magic."

And excessive amounts as if he had so much power, he wasn't able to contain it.

"Because— Fuck—" Hawk squeezed his eyes shut and clenched his jaw. His expression fluctuated between playful and pained as if he couldn't figure out what he was feeling and his breath grew ragged. "I need to— Fuck. Someone. Anyone. Hell, if you don't want to fuck me, Sparky, let me give you and Amiah a boost. Trust me. You'll thank me in the morning."

Titus stiffened, his gaze jumping to me, the same sexual hunger in his eyes that I'd seen in Sebastian's kitchen the other day.

"I'm not having sex with Amiah," Cassius snapped.

Another rush of Hawk's magic tightened hot and needy between my thighs. Where had all this extra power come from? I doubted Titus had helped Hawk get it or waited around from the incubus to seduce I-don't-know-how-many-women to gather that much power. It was like he had too much, was overflowing with it—

Oh, no.

Whatever the Winter Queen had done to try and get me and Sebastian to have sex, had to have affected Hawk. That sexual energy had to have broken through Hawk's shields and flooded his system.

"Come on," Hawk cajoled. "You know you want to."

"No one is having sex with anyone," Cassius said, his voice gruff, his attention on my cleavage, his gaze adding to the heat building inside me.

In fact, all of the guys were looking at me with a hunger that made my pulse pound.

Jeez. The Winter Queen hadn't had to come here to try and force me to sleep with Sebastian, she just had to flood Hawk with too much sexual energy and let nature take its course.

"What did he get into?" Cassius asked. "How can he be this... high?"

"My mother mustn't have specified our suite when she made the Winter Court release the aphrodisiac," Sebastian said.

"You mean *everyone* in court was feeling that?" I asked. "Why didn't you dispel it?"

"Because it wasn't a spell." Sebastian took an unsteady step away from me and crossed his arms. "It was her will on the Winter Court making it turn us on, and her will over the court is stronger than mine. She's the queen and the court hasn't claimed another, not even me."

All that sexual energy must have overwhelmed Hawk. And how many in court had actually given into their feelings and had sex? His natural shields that regulated how much power he took in wouldn't have been able to withstand that, not if he hadn't known it was coming and hadn't consciously bolstered them ahead of time. That surge had probably torn right through them and drowned him in power. Which meant he could be ODing and I had to do something. *Hawk* had to do something.

"He has to release his excess power," I said as his magic churned hotter inside me. "Hawk, look at me."

I needed to know how bad his condition was. If he was just high, he could carefully bleed off some of the excess and sleep off the rest. If he was ODing, I'd need to do the equivalent of pumping his stomach, forcing as much of the excess magic out of his system as fast as possible before it killed him.

I reached for him but managed to stop myself before making contact. It was bad enough that I was about to orgasm, touching him could flood me with too much power.

Hawk turned to move toward me, but Cassius held him tight, his fingers digging into Hawk's shoulders making him shudder and groan.

His eyes rolled back and his breath grew ragged. "Jesus fucking Christ, someone fuck me."

I gritted my teeth and shifted closer to Hawk. "Open your eyes, Hawk."

He did. His hellfire flared erratically, indicating an OD. But before I could figure out what to do, another blast of magic shot into me, this time making me come with a powerful wave that stole my breath and made my legs give out. I tried to cling to the table but couldn't support myself and managed to sag forward instead of dropping to the floor, knocking over a crystal wine glass and spilling a pale yellow liquid over the white tablecloth.

Oh my God, oh my God, oh my God.

Sebastian jerked forward to catch me and ended up pressed against my rear, his erection grinding into me. I pushed back against him before I could stop myself even though I'd just climaxed, desperately seeking another one, and his fingers dug into my hips, his body trembling.

"Take it," Hawk murmured and his power exploded inside me again, twisting me to the edge but not crashing me over again. "Please."

"No." Sebastian heaved away from me.

This had to stop. Even if the guys wanted to sleep with me, I was still injured. It was just so hard to remember that with bliss blazing through my veins. With this much out-of-control power, Hawk had to focus it away from them or they wouldn't be able to control themselves and end up hurting me — not to mention that would make everything more complicated.

My desire swelled at the thought of all of them pleasuring me, worshiping me.

I gritted my teeth and fought to think beyond their powerful gorgeous naked bodies pressed against mine.

Jeez.

I wasn't going to have sex with them.

Which meant Hawk needed another way to release his excess power.

He could just release his power into me, but even if I wasn't hurt, I didn't know if I was strong enough to take the full force of it all without it killing me. And it wouldn't be pleasant. It'd be painful.

Come on, think. Do something,

Hawk groaned and heaved against Cassius's grip. His hellfire snapped and flared and his breath turned to short sharp gasps. He was running out of time. He needed to release the excess. Now.

Another wave of pleasure crashed through me, ripping a moan from my throat.

Smoke curled from Cassius's hands and he stared at me, hungry and desperate. Titus snarled, dropped to his knees, and dug his claws into the floor, his massive chest heaving.

Think.

Maybe Hawk could find someone else in the Winter Court.

No. If I sent him into the hall, he might not find a good target fast enough before his power burst his heart.

Crap. The best solution was to take his power into myself and just deal with the pain. But he'd still need to bleed some off first to be safe—

"Cassius, burn him," I gasped.

Cassius's eyes widened. "What?"

"Burn him, make his power redirect itself to healing him until its low enough that I can take the rest."

"You're not taking any of his power," Cassius growled. "I'm burning it all off."

Hawk heaved in Cassius's grip, his eyes too wide. "I'd rather have sex."

"With who?" I asked, using the table to hold me up as I inched toward him. "I'm in no condition to take the full force of your power, and if none of the other guys are bisexual, you'll just make them unable to stop themselves from coming after me."

"Come on, Bane," Hawk begged, closing his eyes and panting. Sweat slicked his brow and hellfire snapped from beneath his lashes. "Surely you swing both ways."

Sebastian wrenched another step back from me. "I'm always up for a *ménage a* whatever, but you've used your power on me enough times to know if you flood me with your magic, I'll want Amiah over you or any of the other guys."

"Your body won't be able to take this for much longer," I gasped. "Look at me, Hawk."

Hawk's eyes snapped open, and his power surged inside me with the promise of an excruciating climax, drawing another throaty moan.

I fought to keep standing and hold his gaze. "I've got you. You just need to lose enough so you don't kill me. Cassius will make it quick."

A fiery tear rolled down Hawk's cheek and he shuddered.

"Take a deep breath and let it out," I ordered.

Hawk drew in a ragged breath and I gave Cassius a tight nod. He switched his grip from Hawk's shoulder to his bare forearm and, as Hawk released his breath, molten flames exploded around Cassius's hand with a sudden flash.

All of Hawk's muscles jerked taut and his head snapped back. He screamed with gut-wrenching agony, the sound tearing at my heart. Every instinct inside of me howled that I had to stop this, had to heal him. My compulsive need to heal twisted tight as his power stuttered inside me, freezing and burning with painful sharp flashes.

His knees gave out, and Cassius eased him to the floor. I sank with them, cupped Hawk's cheeks with my palms — now that the redirection of his power made it safe — and forced his gaze back to mine.

"I've got you."

Heal him. Stop his suffering.

His hellfire tears stung my hands and his body shook, but I wasn't going to let go. Even if my compulsion would let me, I still wouldn't — and thank God for being completely drained of magic or, without a doubt, I would have locked onto him making this whole mess more complicated.

Heal him, heal him.

"Take another breath," I said, trying to sound calm and soothing despite the urgency to heal him and his seductive magic still building inside me. "You're almost done."

I flicked my gaze to Cassius and — thank goodness — he sucked his fire back inside his body.

The sickening smell of charred flesh filled my nose and bile burned the back of my throat.

My fault. His suffering is all my fault.

Hawk's right forearm and hand had been burned down into his muscle and bone, his flesh charred and waxy. The assault had happened so fast, he hadn't even bled.

"Just breathe," I murmured, reconnecting our gazes, trying to keep him lucid through the pain so he'd heal faster.

"It doesn't help," Hawk snarled, agony and anger and betrayal in his eyes. "I fucking hate you all."

"You're almost done."

His hellfire still blazed bright, snapping and flaring erratically, and I hoped he'd used up enough power because there was no way I'd be able to tell Cassius to burn him again. Just thinking of the words tightened my throat and sent panic surging through me.

Blood oozed from Hawk's burn, splattering onto his pants, the red stark against the white fabric, ironically a sign he was healing. His magic turned his fourth degree burn into third then second, mending muscle and flesh.

With a groan, he clenched his jaw and his hellfire stuttered, flared, snapped, and flared again. He hadn't lost enough. He was still in danger of ODing. But then I knew that would be the case. I strained to keep my breath even, but my pulse was racing.

His bleeding, blistered skin, turned pink, his magic healing him fully, his flesh now just smeared with blood, the only indication he'd been injured.

I didn't want to do this, didn't want to experience the need and pain of his power. But better me suffering than him again.

"Now release the rest," I said, letting the words rush out before my fear choked me.

Cassius tensed and smoke rushed around his hands as if he was going to burn Hawk again.

My heart lurched. I couldn't let Cassius stop me and take control. This was my call to make. I was the only woman in the group and the only healer, and I needed to be in control of this. I had to be in control. I wasn't in control of anything else and I was barely holding it together.

I pulled Hawk's mouth to mine before Cassius could reignite his fire.

A shot of pain from my fractured cheek made me gasp and a flood of Hawk's power poured into me, rushing down my throat.

Need wrenched into a sharp painful ball around my heart. It shot agonizing threads of power through my veins, along the lines of my mating brand, then swept into my cells and sliced into my essence.

I couldn't think, couldn't breathe. Hawk's magic had sucked all the oxygen out of my lungs and replaced it with desire, burning, searing, screaming desire. It consumed me, like Cassius's fire had consumed Hawk's flesh. Fast, ferocious, and without mercy. My soul wailed. I was pretty sure I wailed. But I couldn't hear anything past the roaring in my ears... my head... my whole body.

All my muscles contracted in the mockery of a full-body orgasm as my body and essence burned. Hawk's power consumed it all until all that was left inside me was an agonizing bundle of twitching raw nerve endings.

I collapsed onto Hawk, sobbing, each breath slicing into my body and soul.

It hurt. Oh God, it hurt. I didn't know where the pain ended and I began, and I couldn't stop crying, not even in an attempt to ease the agony, let alone appear strong.

Hawk pulled me into his arms and held me tight. Too tight.

"I could have killed you," he gasped, pressing his forehead against mine and rocking back and forth. "I could have killed you."

He kept repeating the words over and over again, his grip getting tighter and tighter. But I didn't care. It didn't matter that he was squeezing broken and tender ribs. My soul was on fire.

"She can't stay on the floor," Sebastian said, his voice close and soft.

"I could have killed you."

"It was her choice," Sebastian replied.

"Next time it won't be," Cassius snarled. "Now let her go."

"I could have killed you. Why the fuck would you do that?" A fiery tear plopped onto my cheek. "You don't even know me."

"Let her go, Hawk," Sebastian pressed.

Strong hands pulled me out of Hawk's arms and smoke curled around me. Cassius. His heart pounded and he shook, clinging to me almost as tightly as Hawk had as he stood.

"Come on, man," Sebastian said, his voice getting farther away... except it was really me and Cassius who were getting farther away, heading to the bedroom. "You should sleep the rest of it off."

"Don't you ever do that again," Cassius growled as he laid my burning body on the bed.

I curled into a ball as if that would somehow protect me from the pain. But of course, it didn't. Not unless I could separate myself from my flesh, and that wasn't my angel power.

"I swear to God—!"

Something snapped and hissed. Cassius's fire hitting the floor?

"I hate— I— God damn—!"

Blazing hot air rolled over me and Cassius screamed, a gut-wrenching cry of rage and frustration and pain.

HAWK

Why? God, why? Why?

I was stuck on that word, my thoughts whirling and my stomach churning. My whole body was raw from that sudden, uncontrolled blast of magic, and I couldn't stop shaking.

Why had she taken all that power? Why risk her life when Cassius could have burned me again?

I could have killed her.

"Why?"

"Because she's a fucking angel," Bane said as he helped me stagger into the servants' bedroom.

"You still should have stopped her, Seireadan," Titus growled.

Someone should have stopped her.

I should have stopped her.

Except I hadn't stood a chance. I'd been wasted on that massive surge of sexual power that had blasted through my magical shields as if they hadn't been there. My heart had pounded so hard I thought it'd explode and my body had been on fire from Cassius burning me, and then Amiah had kissed me.

Any hope of control erupted the moment our lips touched. My power had found its release and there hadn't been a damned thing I could have done to control it.

My knees hit a cot that I could barely see through the blazing glow of

Faerie, and I collapsed onto it, my power still rushing through me setting my nerves on fire. "I could have killed her."

Out in the living room, Cassius howled a wordless scream of rage and frustration and pain. A door crashed shut and the angel stormed into the room bringing with him a ferocious heat. Fire roared around him, somehow not catching on his clothes, and dripped on the floor, crackling and hissing.

He barreled toward the back of the room, snapping fire whips around the frames of two of the cots at the back as he moved. He tossed the cots into the row beside me, crashing them against two other cots then seized two more and flung them into the pile.

"I'm going to kill her," he snarled, sending a blast of fire into the space he cleared, scorching the wall and floor. "I'm going to God damn kill her."

He reached his clearing and jerked around — the angel glow in his eyes cutting through Faerie's glow making it clear he'd turned to face us. Fire poured from his hands, pooling around his feet, and his aura blazed angry and red, only partially visible through his flames. "I should have burned you again."

I shuddered and I couldn't tell if he was going to burn me now just to release the rage consuming him or not.

I didn't have a lot of experience with angels — they didn't run in the same kind of circles I did — but I'd never seen one so angry before. I wasn't sure I'd ever seen *anyone* this angry before. He was literally on fire, his power raging out of control.

Bane pressed the ice glyph tattooed on his chest and hissed a quick word. His brilliant white aura flared, blinding me for a second, before the demonic magic infecting him shot ragged black and red spikes through him. A frozen wind gusted into the room and ice swept around Cassius, extinguishing his fire and encasing him up to his thighs.

"Just take a breath." Bane sagged onto the end of the cot across from me and rubbed his face, the demonic magic's light still slicing through him even though he'd finished casting his spell and didn't need to keep pushing power into it to maintain it.

Cassius released another blast at the floor, melting the ice, and dropped to his knees into the puddle, his chest heaving and his fire dancing over his skin, still powerful and yet a fraction of what it had been before. The angry red light in his aura grew clearer now that his fire had weakened, writhing against whatever hold he'd managed to regain of his power and straining to burst free and turn him into a fireball again.

This was more than just frustration, and while Amiah's recklessness had triggered it, it spoke to something deeper, something broken within him. And maybe if I could see more than just his aura, I'd be able to say what was wrong with his power. If he'd let me touch him and use my magic, I wouldn't need to use my eyes to *see*. But even if he let me touch him, I still wouldn't be able to fix it, and I didn't want to touch anyone right now.

Everyone was struggling to keep their urges controlled, and their only ideal outlet was Amiah. Their willpower was already strained. Without a doubt they were all going to find their release, adding to it would only make it harder for them to stay away from her and just jack off in private.

"It's like she wants to hurt herself," Cassius said, sucking in a heavy breath and pulling back more of his fire, which only made the light in his aura blaze stronger.

"You saw her face when you burned Hawk," Bane replied. "It's not that she wants to hurt herself, but I doubt she'd have been able to stand it to see Hawk in that kind of pain again."

I hadn't seen her full expression, but then I hadn't been able to look away from her eyes. Her angel glow had been so weak, proving how little magic she'd had left and how exhausted she was, and her eyes had ensnared me in their vast blue depths, holding me captive with her strength and determination and pain.

No one had ever looked at me the way she had.

Even with my power raging through her, heightening her desire for me — for all of us — she looked at me as if she could see me, my truth, my soul, not just my body or my power, like I was important, precious, and she'd do whatever it took to carry me through the pain... through anything.

I knew it was just her physician's need to get me through the agony, that if it had been anyone else, she'd have given them the same look, but it had still stolen my breath.

I'd never been more than a body, an obsession, a craving to women and a few men. Which had suited me just fine before. Incubi didn't fall in love, didn't have that soul to soul connection that other species had because we couldn't sustain ourselves on one person. It was like a genetic failsafe. Having a single lover ended in the lover's death — by being drained of too much life force — or the incubus's — by starving himself.

But now—

God, it went against everything I was and I still ached for that look again, that acceptance, that being seen.

"How am I supposed to protect her through all this when I also have to protect her from herself?" Fire sparked from Cassius's arms then vanished back into his writhing aura. "She's my responsibility. She's not a field agent. She never wanted to be in the field because of her magic."

"You're not the only one trying to protect her," Titus said, his red-gold aura blazing almost as brightly as Cassius's and a ghostly wolf's head superimposed on top of his. He was losing it too, his beast barely contained. Thankfully the glamour still held, but I wasn't sure how long that would last.

"Hey." Bane barked a bitter laugh. "At least my mother isn't trying to kill her."

"Not sure using the Winter Court's magic to make you sleep together so you can impregnate her is better." The water around Cassius's knees started to steam. "And if we can't figure out how to escape, regardless of whether you can get her pregnant or not, your mother is going to make you have sex in front of the entire Winter Court."

My pulse stuttered in shock.

"You're what?" Titus jerked forward from his spot by the wall, his aura flaring around his hands, his claws extending from his fingers.

I didn't know Amiah well, but I knew having something like that forced on her would break her. I'd known from the moment I'd met her she'd been repressing her sexuality and now desperately wanted to embrace it but didn't know how and was afraid to. Being forced to perform in public would push her into a shell she'd never come out of.

No, she needed to be encouraged without judgment, worshiped until she recognized how beautiful and strong she was, and I wanted to be the one to show her.

Anything long term between us was out of the question. Amiah might fancy a *ménage à trois* but eventually, she'd want something permanent with someone.

That someone wouldn't be me, and I was okay with that.

"I'm not sleeping with Amiah for my mother's entertainment," Bane said, his need for her swelling, radiating against my senses. "I'm not sleeping with her, period."

Well, if he wouldn't. I would. I'd give her whatever she wanted, and not because of the power in her desire — which had been the original reason I'd begged her to return to my tent — but because I selfishly wanted to have that connection with her again, of being seen for who I truly was, however brief, and I wanted her to feel it, too. With my incubus nature, I didn't know if I was capable of giving it to her, but I was damned well going to try. And even if I failed, I'd still be giving her the gift of pleasure, something she deserved.

"Why would your mother think you could get Amiah pregnant?" Titus asked. "You're fae and she's an angel."

"She seems to think the magic of the Winter Court can make it happen," Cassius replied, more fire sparking from his hands and arms.

I would, however, need to be careful of Cassius. He was overprotective of her for good reason, but that was getting in the way of something my magic assured me she desired, all because he wasn't willing to admit he wanted to have sex with her.

"You also didn't need to reinforce the lie that you're married to her by making it look like the Winter Court responds to her," Cassius said, "or whatever it was you did to make the queen and Deaglan think Amiah can control the court's wind."

"Deaglan is here?" Titus's aura exploded, his beast's power blinding me. My instincts screamed to move, to run, his beast was breaking free with a fury that would blindly kill everything in its way.

I heaved onto my side to get off the cot and run — although I had no idea how the hell I was going to run, I wasn't even sure I could stand.

"T," Bane snapped and Titus growled and thankfully stayed where he was. "Hold it together. Everyone just God damn hold it together. Yes, the bastard is here, but now isn't the time for revenge."

"Every time is time for revenge," Titus snarled.

If I was smart, I'd also be mindful of Titus.

Given that he and Amiah had just met, his powerful desire for her had to come from his captivity, not because he was in love with her. But I'd seen him release part of his beast to rescue her from Balwyrdan, and I didn't want to be on the wrong end of that ferocious rage.

"Sure. And you'll just release your beast in the middle of the Winter Court. That'll go well," Bane snapped. "He has that demon-vampire hybrid with him. The rest of his assassination team is probably here as well. If they don't capture you, my mother will use the Winter Court's magic to imprison you, and then you'll be her bitch."

"*And* you'll endanger Amiah," Cassius said.

Titus's beast surged again, forcing me to squint to even catch a glimpse of him, and he jerked toward the door. I didn't know if he was going to go after Deaglan right now or to Amiah to protect her, but he slammed his fist into the wall instead. "I *will* kill him."

"And I'll help," Bane said, "but our priority is keeping you out of the hands of anyone in any of the courts."

"And protecting Amiah," Cassius insisted, the steam around him thickening and the water starting to boil. "You have power over the Winter Court. Can you use that to help us?"

At least Bane, who was already sleeping with her, would understand what I was doing. But even he'd been acting strange since we got here. Yes, Amiah wasn't in any condition for sex and her appearance was shocking and heartbreaking and enraging, but for someone who wanted to sleep with her again, he sure was giving her the cold shoulder. He'd looked like he'd been walking to his death when he'd gone into the bedroom to help her shower.

"I barely have power," Bane said, the demonic magic snapping through his aura, making him gasp. He was going to have to do something about that soon. It hadn't been good when I'd used my magic to get his resonance yesterday and it had gotten worse since then. The demonic magic that wasn't supposed to be in him grew every time he used his magic, be it a spell in one of the glyphs tattooed on his body or a spell woven with raw power with his sorcerer's ability.

"You made the wind gust when Amiah refused your mother," Cassius said.

"I didn't." Bane rubbed his face. "That was all Amiah."

"So you are mates," Titus said, his aura writhing as his beast strained to get free. "It's the only way she'd be able to control the wind."

"For the last fucking time, we're not mates, she's not mine, and she's not a dragon. She doesn't adhere to five-hundred-year-old dragon social norms. She can have whoever's scent she wants on her, whenever she wants it. Hell, if it so strikes her fancy, she could fuck all of us all at the same time or the whole fucking court and still not *belong* to anyone."

Fire rushed over Cassius's arms as his need for release pounded through him. "Amiah wouldn't *fuck* all of us."

"Fine." Bane rolled his eyes at him. "*Make love*. She's her own woman. If you want a sexual relationship with her grow a pair and tell her."

"But the court recognizes her," Titus said.

"We're not mates and we'll never be mates. I will never make the marriage vow. Ever." The demonic magic flared again, sending painful angry spikes through Bane's aura, and he tried to bite back a groan — he was probably successful at hiding it from the others since they couldn't see the magic inside him. "I have no fucking clue why the Winter Court responded to her. Maybe it's the leash spell, maybe it's my mother's desperate desire to get her pregnant, maybe it just God damned likes her."

Like they all did.

Like I did.

Any of them would be a better long-term relationship than me, but none of them at the moment were going to give her what she craved... what she needed.

Well, until they figured themselves out, I'd give it to her. Discretely of course. There was no point in making the situation more complicated since we were all stuck together until we could get out of Faerie. But I wasn't going to let Amiah go without when it took nothing from me to give it to her.

AMIAH

CASSIUS HAD SLAMMED THE DOOR BEHIND HIM AND I'D CRIED INTO MY pillow until I'd finally passed out. I must have slept for only a few hours because when I woke, still curled in a ball, my body was still burning like a painful smoldering ember and my power was still low.

For a second, I had no idea where I was, only that I wasn't in my apartment at Operations. I couldn't hear the familiar soft rumble of traffic on the street outside... although maybe it was very early in the morning. The Quarter was often quiet those few hours before dawn...

Then my thoughts tripped and the horror of the last few days flooded me. My pulse pounded and I fought to catch my breath. I'd been taken. Again. Helpless. Again.

I swore—

I clenched my jaw, fighting the storm of emotions threatening to drown me. If I didn't think about it, I'd be fine. Fine. That was the way it had worked the last time. *Stay in control. Don't be foolish and put yourself in dangerous situations again—*

Except I hadn't *put* myself in that situation. I hadn't chosen to get caught up in all of this, and yet, even if my magic hadn't locked onto Titus, I would have still rushed to save him the moment I saw him fall from the sky.

My stomach rumbled and clenched, reminding me that I'd drained my magic and hadn't eaten anything in over twenty-four hours — the few grapes I had when I'd woken not counting — which meant I might have been asleep for more than just a few hours. Without proper sustenance, it was harder to restore my power.

If I was going to heal properly, I needed to get up and find something to eat.

But I didn't want to move. I was afraid if I moved, I'd find out just how much I still hurt. I'd never experienced that kind of pain before. Not even the pain when Sebastian had tried to remove or change the leash spell had compared to the blaze of Hawk's power erupting in my cells.

My nerves were still raw, even after getting a little sleep. Just the miniscule slide of my skin against the soft comforter hurt, and I didn't know if this was something I could heal with my magic or not. I'd never had a patient who'd been flooded with an excess of sexual magic.

Except, if I was going to pull myself together and regain control — *please, any control* — I needed to restore my magic. There was nothing I could do for my soul or my fear, but in the very least, I needed to finish mending my broken bones.

With a groan — I didn't care if anyone including Cassius heard me, I wasn't going to fight to keep it in — I uncurled and sat up. My nerves lit up with agony and I panted, praying if I just kept breathing the sensation would pass.

I could do this. I was strong.

My throat tightened.

I didn't need Cassius to help me. Even if the smart thing would be to call out for help and have someone bring me food.

When had I become that person? The one who ignored practical logic and did something foolish just—

Tears burned my eyes.

Just to stay in control.

Because my control had been taken from me. Again.

Not going to think about it.

I stood on shaky legs and staggered to the door before realizing there might not be any food in the suite. Which meant I was going to have to at least ask Sebastian for help if I wanted to eat.

Jeez. I was going to have to call out and alert everyone to my condition and then deal with Cassius again.

Couldn't I just do one thing on my own? I needed to be able to do something by myself for myself. I couldn't stand being helpless and pathetic and weak, the angel who'd been foolishly captured by that human and now brutally beaten by that fae. I didn't want to accept that that was who I was.

With a trembling hand, I opened the door. The living room turned dining room was still a dining room, the table still set with plates of uneaten food and glasses of undrunk wine. The light emanating from the walls and ceiling was low — guess the guys were in the other room sleeping — but I could see well enough with my night vision. I shuffled to the closest place setting where Deaglan had sat and reached for the fork. He hadn't touched his food, and while it would be cold, at least it would still be food.

"Don't," Titus said, his gruff voice coming from the back of the room, making me jump a little and setting my nerves on fire. "The food could be enspelled."

He sat in the corner with his knees pulled up to his bare chest, his claws dug into the floor, his breath too fast, and his body tense. His gaze, a muddy brown because of the glamour that changed his appearance and not the striking gold that had first stolen my breath, locked on me, filled with a ferocious desperate intensity. His beast was straining to rise to the surface.

"You should shift," I said, holding the edge of the table to keep my balance and shuffling toward him. He hadn't fully shifted and released his beast since I'd met him, and before that, he'd only shifted once in the last five hundred years. And what with the influx of Hawk's magic that had to have been influencing all of us not just me, his beast was probably going crazy.

"I don't want to risk it." He squeezed his eyes shut. "Shifting could break the glamour and with Deaglan in court—"

My throat tightened, my heart aching for him. My captivity had been nothing compared to his, a blink of an eye. I didn't know if Deaglan had hurt Titus as much as Balwyrdan had hurt me — and I wasn't going to think about that, not now, not ever — but not being able to release his beast for five hundred years was bad enough. And I doubted Titus had gotten the physical contact that as a shifter he needed to help calm his soul.

"Let me help you."

"Your magic can't heal this," he said.

"No. But maybe I can help steady your soul. May I?"

"My beast is raging. I could hurt you."

"You won't." I didn't know if that was true or not, but it didn't matter.

He needed help and I could give it to him. That was at least something I could do, something I could control. *Please, I need to be in control.* "Why fight this alone when you don't have to?"

I sagged to the floor beside him and he stiffened. I hadn't thought it possible that he could get tenser.

Then he rumbled, a rough, desperate sound and wrapped an arm around me, carefully drawing me against him. "Thank you."

I pressed my hands and cheek against his massive bare chest, giving him as much flesh-to-flesh contact as I could manage. His pulse raced and he trembled, the movement making my skin burn, but I gritted my teeth and took slow steady breaths, trying to will him to relax.

There was a chance he wouldn't be able to, that his beast was too enraged at being held back that physical contact, especially with someone who wasn't his mate — or the same species — wouldn't be able to steady him.

I didn't know what I'd do if that was the case. We were stuck in the Winter Court, hiding him from all of Faerie, and he was the last dragon. The only thing I could do was give him physical contact.

But then he took in a slow, shuddering breath, and his pulse began to slow and his trembling eased.

Thank goodness.

I'd done something. I wasn't helpless, not like when—

I leaned into him, my own soul aching for this contact. I needed it as much as he did, needed to feel his life force warm and thrumming against my senses, needed the distraction. I'd gone almost two months without this kind of contact, contact I hadn't thought I'd needed until I'd mistakenly believed I'd met my soul mate. His shifter nature had made him more physically affectionate than an angel even though we'd only ever been friends and I hadn't realized how much I wanted to be held until it was gone.

I bit back a bitter huff. I hadn't realized a lot of things. Like what a nightmare a soul bond would be, how my mating brand would trap my soul to someone's, possibly a complete stranger's. I'd be helpless to resist, I'd be desperate if something happened to him, and, whether I wanted to or not, I'd fall in love with him.

My pulse picked up and Titus took my hand, rubbing gentle circles in my palm with his thumb calming me — I wasn't even sure he was aware he was doing it.

"I missed this," he said.

"Me, too."

He tensed again. "You have someone?"

"Had. A shifter friend." And I'd been such a fool over him. "I hadn't realized how much I needed his touch until it was gone."

"*His* touch?" Titus asked.

"His. Someone's. He found his mate and that connection, that contact I'd become used to was suddenly gone and I..." I didn't know how to explain the loss of something so small and simple. Couldn't I have just asked someone for a hug? Even if other angels were naturally standoffish, I could have asked a non-angel. But I didn't know how to explain why I, an angel, wanted it. I wasn't supposed to need it, not as deeply as I did.

"You felt lost," he said, "empty, even though you weren't mates."

"Yes." Empty and alone and heartbroken. Although my heartache had more to do with the death of a dream, the childish fantasy that my soul bond was an amazing, beautiful gift.

"I lost my mate the last time the Heart awakened." He tipped his head back against the wall and closed his eyes. "She wasn't my soul's mate, but we'd been happy."

For a second I saw his true rugged appearance and not the glamour, his wide cheeks, slightly crooked nose, and hard square jaw dusted with pale golden-red stubble. He wasn't as breathtaking as Sebastian or Hawk or as classically handsome as Cassius, but there was something stunning and beautifully primal about him. A ferociousness. The promise of a powerful passion that tugged at my heart... and reminded me of Marcus, the man who wasn't my destiny.

The lonely ache I'd been trying to ignore since Essie Shaw had walked into my life squeezed around my heart. "I'm so sorry."

"I lost everyone. I think I would have killed myself if it hadn't been for Seireadan and—" His thumb stopped moving and his grip on my hand tightened. "And Deaglan. I think they would have gotten me through the worst of it if Faerie hadn't called me to hibernate."

"You and Deaglan were friends?" No wonder he hadn't trusted Sebastian when we'd first found him.

"We'd grown up together. Been friends for almost eighty years before —" His hand holding mine started to tremble. "I was such an idiot. Seireadan gifted me with a spell to find him wherever he was, saying that when I woke, he'd be strong enough to sever or block my connection to the Heart. Deaglan gave me chains."

Both magically with the leash spell and physically. I pressed my free hand over the scar on his wrist, a match to the one on his other wrist and around his neck. The glamour hid them, but I knew they were there and that he'd forever bear the horrible proof of his captivity, a constant reminder of Deaglan's betrayal.

"I got those trying to free myself from his shackles." He set his hand over mine, holding it against his wrist, his heartbreaking tremor growing stronger. "I fought every day."

Of course he did. Because he was strong. Not just physically but mentally. I'd barely fought, either time. I hadn't even realized that first time that I'd needed to fight until it was too late.

"I wish I had." Tears stung my eyes. God, I'd been so naive and weak.

I still was. I always would be.

"I didn't even fight the first time when it was just a human holding me. I could have released my wings and flown away." I should have released my wings. "He never had me chained when I was healing the sick for his profit. But I couldn't leave them."

I blinked, fighting back my tears. I'd been young and curious about the mortal realm and had found that human in the middle of nowhere, dying from a particularly aggressive strain of influenza. He'd left his village to find someone to help fight the illness killing his people and I'd willingly drained my magic and saved them.

Then he'd asked me to help the next village down the road and by the time I realized he was demanding money, choosing who lived and who died, it was too late. He was already chaining me up at night to a trunk filled with rocks too heavy for me to move and I was too weak to resist my compulsion to heal the never-ending line of sick and injured people to escape.

"So many of them were children with parents desperate to try anything, *pay* anything to save them." And my power had trapped me.

I slid my hand out from under Titus's and stared at my palms. Pale light — that only I could see because it was still weak — radiated from them, proof that I had some power available to heal someone, that if someone was in dire need, I'd have no choice, I'd have to try to save them.

"It's who you are," he said, cupping my hands between his and reestablishing that point of flesh-to-flesh contact. "You risked Hawk killing you to save him from more pain."

"Because I'm weak. I can't bear to see someone in pain if I can prevent it and I can barely control my magic. I'd have never been held captive if it hadn't been for my power, if I had an ounce of self-control. I knew that human was going to drain me to death, knew the only way to survive was to hold back my healing magic." From those desperate, sick children.

"If Cassius hadn't found me—" I fought to push the memories back, but I couldn't force them out of my mind and couldn't make myself stop talking. Perhaps it was because I'd kept it bottled up for so long that the minute a crack had formed it was breaking free, or perhaps it was because Titus knew the fear of being held prisoner. No one else could relate, certainly not Cassius.

"I knew eventually he was going to hit me more than just a few times, he was going to stop being careful about leaving bruises that others could see, he was going to—" My breath picked up. "He was going to rape me."

I squeezed my eyes shut. I wouldn't cry.

I. Would. Not. Cry.

My months with that human had been nothing compared to my few hours with Balwyrdan. I'd thought I'd known fear, but I hadn't had a clue what true fear was.

A tremor swept through me and Titus's arm around my shoulders tightened.

Don't think about it. Just don't think about it.

But I couldn't get my body to stop shaking and the memory of Balwyrdan's fist slamming into my face rushed into my mind. His first punch had completely stunned me with shock and pain, my brain unable to fully register what had happened. The next strike had frozen me with fear.

Don't think about it.

He would have killed me if Cassius and the others hadn't rescued me. He would have drawn out my pain until I wished I was dead, then given me to his men for their entertainment, then—

Stop thinking!

Terror clenched my heart and tightened my throat. "If I'd stayed in Sebastian's apartment, if I hadn't gone up to the roof— If I—"

"You couldn't have known Balwyrdan would be there," Titus replied, releasing my hands to draw me tighter against his body, my trembling growing so strong my teeth chattered.

"But I swore." A tear broke free. "I swore to be smarter, to be more careful, to stay in control." Another tear raced after the first. "I swore never again."

Stop thinking.

Please. Stop thinking.

But the panic and desperation that I'd been determined to ignore had broken free. I couldn't think of anything else. He would have killed me. He would have hurt me until I begged him to kill me and then kept going.

I shouldn't have just lain there. I should have fought back, fought through the pain and shock, should have stopped him from kidnapping me in the first place, or avoided it, or something. I should have done something! Anything. Again. Always.

I swore. "I swore."

And my vows were useless.

It didn't matter what I wanted. I hadn't been strong enough to escape Balwyrdan or even that human. There was no way I'd be strong enough to avoid the fate of my mating brand. I'd never be strong.

Why couldn't I be strong? All I wanted was to be strong. Titus had survived five hundred years in captivity. Five hundred! He'd fought to free himself every day. Probably every hour.

I didn't even have a sliver of his strength because I'd done nothing.

Not a damned thing.

"I didn't even try." I didn't want to be weak. I was so tired of being weak. "Why didn't I do something?"

"But you did do something."

I barked a bitter laugh. "Yeah, I cried and cowered."

Titus hooked his finger under my chin and lifted my gaze. A glimmer of gold shone in his glamoured eyes, his expression filled with sorrow and rage and heartbreak. "You survived. You held out until we came for you."

"Is that all I'm capable of?" *God. Please.* "I just wanted to be strong."

"You are." Titus pulled me into his lap and hugged me to his chest, wrapping his body around me. "There are more kinds of strength than just physical and you're one of the strongest people I've ever met. You faced Hawk's magic without blinking an eye even though you had to have known it would hurt. You didn't cower when I threatened to kill you when we first met and then offered to keep healing me, and you sure as hell didn't cower when Balwyrdan had you. I saw the look in your eyes. If there'd been an opportunity to fight him you would have taken it."

I pressed my face against Titus's broad chest and clung to him, sobbing. "Then why couldn't I stop him?"

Why couldn't I?

Why?

"Because he controlled the leash spell," Titus said, pressing his lips to the top of my head. "You knew that. You knew your best move was to hold on, and you did."

And that was the horrible truth. The truth I didn't want to admit because it meant it didn't matter how strong I was or how prepared, or in control. Balwyrdan could have taken Titus or Cassius or any of the guys — with the possible exception of Sebastian — and none of us would have stood a chance against him and his control of the leash spell. None of us would have been able to run away, not from the rooftop or in the abandoned reception hall. None of us would have been able to do anything.

I wanted to scream at the injustice of it, to tear into my pain and terror and helplessness, defy it, defeat it, rip it to God damned pieces.

But all I could do was cry, hacking angry sobs of frustration and grief. Balwyrdan had stolen all those years of determination, of trying to prove to myself that I was no longer the angel Cassius had rescued. He'd shattered my illusion that if I was just strong enough and smart enough and in control enough everything would be fine. I could *do* something, take action, control my fate. But I could have been as strong as Titus, and Balwyrdan still would have taken and hurt me.

It wasn't fair. It wasn't God damned fair.

But then life wasn't fair. And I cried for the loss of another dream, the dream that if I'd just prepared, I could keep myself safe against everything. I cried because I hadn't cried after Cassius had first rescued me or when I realized the horror of the mating brand. I cried because it felt so good to be wrapped in Titus's arms and because that terrified me and because I'd been keeping so many people at arm's length, afraid they'd see how out-of-control I was.

And I cried because fate was a wild raging storm I couldn't control. No matter what I wanted or how hard I tried.

TITUS

I HELD AMIAH AS SHE CLUNG TO ME AND CRIED HEARTRENDING SOBS, HER face pressed against my chest, her small hands clutching my shoulders. It made both me and my beast furious that she thought her inability to do something when there had been nothing anyone could have done against Balwyrdan meant she was weak. Physically, sure. She was delicate and fragile. She didn't stand a chance in a fight, but her willpower and her soul—

Her soul was so damned fierce, her determination powerful, as powerful as any dragon I'd met. More so because she was so fragile. She gave life, pulled it from her very essence and handed it away at her own expense despite her fear. She hadn't cared that my beast could have hurt her. She'd sat beside me and offered everything she had to help ease its turmoil, and it yearned to go back in time and rip Balwyrdan to pieces before Cassius had set him on fire. How dare Balwyrdan make her afraid, make her doubt herself and her worth. How dare that human! My beast wanted to find that human who was probably already dead — probably at Cassius's hands — and give Amiah the justice she deserved.

And it was furious that Cassius was the one to have given her that. It should have been me. Always me.

It didn't matter that I hadn't known her back then. My beast didn't care that its desire wasn't logical. It wanted to protect her. *I* wanted to protect her.

Because she's mine.
I bit back a snarl.
Not. Mine.
Not yet.

Seireadan was right. She didn't belong to anyone. Except I couldn't convince my beast of that, and with her crying in my arms, taking comfort in my body, it was more certain now than ever that she was mine. Even the raging need that had consumed me when Hawk's power had been out of control had eased because she didn't need to have sex, she needed soul to soul comfort, needed to be steadied and reassured.

Yes, I still wanted her. I'd gotten off in the shower — Seireadan and Cassius thankfully letting me go first — and couldn't think of anyone else but her. I'd tried to focus on her injuries, how she was in no condition for sex. I imagined her in bed with Seireadan and then Hawk, but nothing worked. My thoughts kept turning her into the stunning woman I'd first met, determined, and filled with life and kindness. My beast didn't just want a woman because I'd been locked away for half a millennium, my beast wanted *her* and her alone, and it would kill anyone who hurt her. And right now, with her delicate body shaking in my arms, her tears trailing down my chest, I agreed.

Mine.

I would fight for her, and I would go through anyone who stood between us.

Which wasn't healthy. I didn't really know her. We'd only just met. I couldn't possibly be feeling the things I was feeling for her, not to mention she already had complicated relationships with all the other guys, especially Seireadan. He might have said he didn't want her, but my beast found that hard to believe. Who would willingly give her up? Once I'd proven myself to her and she was mine, the only way I'd leave her would be if someone killed me. No, Seireadan would go back to her once he realized what a fool he was, and I needed to figure out how to control my beast and not kill him until I could convince Seireadan she was mine.

For a long time, I just held her as she cried, my soul thrumming at her nearness, and my beast coiled tight within me ready to protect her, possessively satisfied that she felt safe enough in my arms to release her hold on her emotions in front of me.

I didn't know how long she cried, but eventually, her tears subsided, and with a heavy sigh, she sat back and wiped her eyes, sending panic clenching around my heart.

She was done. She didn't need me anymore. I had to accept that. But I didn't want to. I wanted more. I wanted it all with her.

Mine.

"I'm sorry," she said, looking up at me, her eyes rimmed with red and her shockingly blue gaze capturing me as if she didn't already possess me.

My pulse stalled and my beast strained against my control not to break free and shift, but to kiss her, show her how much I desired her.

But the part of me that was man and not beast knew her emotions were still a confused mess. Making a move could scare her and make her push me away, and then my beast would really lose its shit.

"I was supposed to be steadying your soul," she said, "and here you are letting me cry on you."

"It doesn't have to be one or the other." I fought the urge to tighten my grip around her and instead freed a strand of blond hair stuck to her damp cheek and tucked it behind her ear. "You needed my touch and I needed yours."

I still do.

"I should—" She glanced back at the bedroom and another tear trickled down her cheek. "I don't want to leave."

"Then don't."

"Sitting on the floor like this can't be comfortable."

"It doesn't bother me." *I have you.*

"I—" She pressed her hand over my heart — I wasn't sure she was aware she was doing it — and returned her gaze to mine.

My whole essence stalled trapped in the gravity of her soul. *Stay. Please.*

"I wish the Winter Court had windows," she said, sagging back against my chest.

Oh, yes.

"I really need to see the sky. Please tell me there's more to the court than just that square of sky in the healing pools."

"So much more," I said, tightening my embrace. "The Winter Court has a lot of storms, but when the queen is happy, the sky is stunning." *Like your eyes.* "Clear and crisp, the sun reflecting off the ice and snow making it brighter than the brightest day in the Court of Light."

And I wanted to show her all of it.

I'd lost my mind. I swore that if I ever escaped from Deaglan, I'd never return to Faerie, but now I wanted to soar through the Winter Court's ice canyons, ride the thermals at the edge of the Lusaline Desert in the Summer Court, and lie in a meadow of sweet-smelling primrose with her, watching the clouds drift by in the Spring Court. I wanted to show her all the things I'd loved about Faerie before the Heart had awakened and my kin were slaughtered and I was imprisoned.

My beast tensed. The Heart was awake again. Just my very presence put Amiah in danger.

She shifted, snuggling closer, and instantly eased my beast. It would protect her, no matter what, whatever it took. Always. Mine.

"Are all the courts affected by their rulers' moods?" she asked, closing her eyes, relaxing even more into me, the tension in her body starting to melt away.

"Yes, their will shapes their court by harnessing the wild magic of Faerie. Without a monarch, there is no court, and without a strong monarch, the court is in chaos." Of course, a weak monarch usually didn't survive long. If the monarch was weak, Faerie would attack the court's high fae, trying to pull its magic out of them, killing them until it found a fae strong enough to withstand it. That fae became the court's new ruler.

Except being strong only protected a high fae in a court and the moment Seireadan stepped into the Wilds, Faerie would try to claim its magic back until we reached the safety of my ancestral home.

"Is that why the queen is so determined to make Sebastian her heir?" she asked, her word slurring with sleep. "She thinks Padraigin isn't strong enough because the court's wind doesn't blow for her."

"If the Winter Court doesn't respond to her, then she won't be able to control its magic when she ascends to the throne." I shuddered. The Autumn Court had nearly been decimated when its ancient queen had lost her will to live and was consumed by Faerie's magic. Her son hadn't been strong enough and the screams of the court's high fae had filled the Wilds all day and night for days. "But I'm surprised that it doesn't. She's not a sorcerer like Seireadan, but her water magic has always been strong."

"I don't think Sebastian wants to be king," she murmured. "He shouldn't be trapped by that. No one should."

"No. No one should. Ever." Not my best friend, and not my angel. Never again.

It didn't matter how irrational it was, my beast had decided. It would give everything to protect her, be it against a monster like Balwyrdan or the full power of the Winter Court and its queen.

Mine. Always and forever.

And the sooner she figured that out and accepted that, the safer Seireadan and the others would be from me.

AMIAH

I woke completely alone in the enormous bed and feeling better, lighter, like a massive weight had been lifted from my chest. Last night hadn't healed all my emotional wounds, but it had helped release a pressure that I hadn't realized had been building inside me.

A part of me, however, was sad Titus hadn't stayed when he'd tucked me in. It had felt so good being held by him, his life force soothing, the warmth of his body relaxing. I'd felt safe, if still raw and shaky from my breakdown. I wasn't even embarrassed that I'd cried in his arms. I'd needed to cry in someone's and he, out of all of the guys, could at least relate to what I'd gone through. That, and he'd needed a physical connection as much as I had, his soul had been in as much turmoil as mine.

But if he'd joined me in bed, I might have given in to my desire for a deeper physical connection — not to mention my craving to lose myself and my worries in the sensations of sexual intercourse. That would have made things complicated between us, between me and Cassius, heck, between me and all of the guys... well, maybe not between me and Hawk. As an incubus, he didn't have the same emotional connections other species had.

Besides, even if my not-yet-fully-formed mating brand hadn't awakened, there was still a chance Titus was my soul mate and having sex could awaken our bond, and I wasn't going to risk it. Maybe when Sebastian removed my brand...

Except what about Cassius? Did I love Cassius? There was something between us, but I could also feel something between me and Titus... and between me and Sebastian... and me and Hawk.

It had to be lust.

Yep, that was it. I was confusing honest, long-term emotions with lust because I'd finally broken my vow of celibacy, now knew what I'd been missing, and wanted to make up for lost time.

I couldn't possibly be in love with four men, three of whom I barely knew.

Except Essie was.

Because fate had forced that upon her with her mating brands.

A whisper of pain raced along the ghostly lines of my brand, shooting from the middle of my thigh up over my hip and around my back to my ribcage.

It was a fate I was going to avoid.

I wanted to be with someone because I wanted to be with them. Not because my brand made me.

The pain subsided into an ache that was a little too warm for comfort, making me keenly aware that it was there, that my destiny was coming, and coming soon. It hadn't been this warm the last time I'd felt it... which had been the last time I hadn't been in pain.

My thoughts stuttered at that.

I wasn't in pain.

Somehow all of my broken bones had healed while I'd slept and I couldn't have unconsciously used my magic. My power didn't work that way. I needed to concentrate to heal anyone including myself, and I was at full, my magic warm and overflowing around my hands.

How was I healed?

Just crying in Titus's arms wouldn't have healed my body like it had helped to mend a part of my soul, and surely Sebastian would have said something if the Winter Court could heal someone like this.

Someone knocked briskly on the bedroom door and cracked it open.

"You need to get up," Cassius said. "You've been asleep for almost twelve hours and you need to eat something."

My stomach grumbled, reminding me that I hadn't eaten in far too long. "I'm awake."

"Are you decent? Would you like to freshen up first?" Meaning, he was going to help me to the bathroom whether I wanted him to or not.

"I'm fine." I sat up as he opened the door wider — not waiting for me to confirm my state of decency — and I scrambled to make sure my robe was pulled closed after falling open while I'd slept.

Behind him, the living room was back to being a living room. Titus sat squished in an armchair still only wearing the loose pants and showing off the broad expanse of a chest still beautifully muscular even with the glamour disguising him. Our gazes locked for a second and relief flooded me. He looked more relaxed than I'd ever seen him, more in harmony with both aspects of his nature, and a part of me was thrilled that I'd helped steady his soul even though I wasn't his mate or a dragon.

"You're hardly fine," Cassius said, his expression completely frozen and shutdown. "You still have some broken ribs and a broken nose—" He frowned. "Why does your nose look fine?"

Because somehow I was fine.

Hawk groaned. He sat in the other armchair — strangely enough wearing a shirt — with his head tipped back and his complexion gray. He looked like he had a hangover. Of course, given the amount of magic that had flooded him, I wasn't surprised. I might have taken on a huge amount of his power but he'd still had too much in his system. Not enough to kill him, but certainly enough to make him feel terrible for a good while even with his enhanced healing—

Wait a minute.

I'd taken a huge amount of his magic.

"Oh, my goodness! You did an energy transfer because I forced you to release your power through a kiss." That explained why I was completely healed.

Incubi and succubi consumed life force from the people they seduced, but they could also give it back. That influx of magic helped heal a person. I just hadn't realized so much of it could help someone rapidly heal like an incubus.

"Nope," Hawk moaned. "That's just a myth. We can't transfer energy into someone to heal them."

"Except I know you can." One of Essie's mates had done it to save her life and then swore me to secrecy—

Oh, no.

I shouldn't have said anything in front of the other guys. I was just so surprised Hawk had done it. I'd been told incubi and succubi didn't want it getting out that they could do energy transfers. It was dangerous for them. It wasn't like how I healed someone. I had magic and when it ran out, I was just drained and exhausted. An incubus gave someone their life force. If they ran out of power, they died.

"No point in lying about it," Sebastian said from his spot on the couch, a flash of pain tightening his expression for a second. Something was still wrong with him, but I had no idea what. "It's the only way to explain how her nose is no longer broken and her power is still at full."

"And now Sparky and T know about it." Hawk glowered at him. "Thanks for that."

"If you'd known you could do that—" Cassius started.

"I hadn't realized I was doing *that*." Hawk turned his glower on me. "And don't you dare think about telling any of your healing angel friends or writing a paper about me. I'm not going to become anyone's lab rat."

"Never," I said. I couldn't believe I'd slipped up so badly. I'd just been caught completely off guard by it. "And don't you dare do it again. I was told doing a transfer like that is dangerous for you."

"At least the idiot who let it out of the bag told you everything." Hawk rubbed his face. "It's potentially deadly to us, especially if we can't get a recharge in time. I think the only reason I wasn't immediately incapacitated was because I was already ODing on too much energy."

Titus sat forward, his attention still locked on me. He hadn't looked away from me since the door had opened. "So Amiah is healed. That means we can leave."

"No," Cassius replied, surprising me. "I don't want the Winter Queen knowing what Amiah's magic is. Your unusual energy transfer aside, angels are the only species with healing magic and only a few have it. Our original reasons for drawing this out still stands. I don't want Amiah becoming any more of a target than she already is."

"Are you crazy?" Hawk asked. "The longer we stay here the longer we're *all* in danger. I'm sure none of you want a repeat of last night... this morning...? God, I don't even know what time it is in here."

"It's the middle of the afternoon and man, I hate that I'm agreeing with him again, but Cassius is right." Sebastian gave me an apologetic look. "Best not to give my mother another reason to search for you after we leave."

Except that meant they were all unnecessarily putting themselves in danger to protect me.

"If that's the only reason we're putting off leaving, then we should leave." I pushed back the comforter, stood, and headed to the door. Not a hint of pain — with the exception of my aching brand. That energy transfer had been a lot more powerful than the one Essie's mate had done. Of course, I'd paid for it with excruciating pain, and even if it wasn't potentially deadly for Hawk, I didn't want to repeat that. "There are four of you and one of me. It doesn't make sense for us to stay."

"It makes perfect sense," Titus said.

"Yeah, if something happens to you and I get hurt, I'm not kissing that asshole," Sebastian said, jerking his thumb at Hawk.

"You know I like it when you play hard to get." Hawk half-heartedly waggled his eyebrows at Sebastian before his expression returned to I-feel-terrible. "If we stay, we still need to figure out a way for me to eat. That should be reason enough for us to get the hell out of here."

"After last night, you should be good for a few days." Cassius stepped aside, giving me way too much room to pass, making my heart squeeze.

I hadn't expected him to just get over me risking my life by taking Hawk's power, but a part of me had hoped he'd understood why I'd done it. He, out of all of the guys, knew how my magic worked, knew how I had a compulsion that was hard to ignore — and impossible to ignore when my magic locked onto someone. It had been hard enough to tell him to burn Hawk the first time. I couldn't have watched him do it again.

Someone knocked on the door and Sebastian, Titus, and even Hawk stood, joining Cassius, instantly ready for a fight.

"Amiah, look weak," Cassius said, stepping between me and the door.

I crossed my arms and tried to make myself look as small as possible. I didn't know if that made me look weak or not, but I didn't have a lot of experience pretending to be weak. All of my pretending had been to try to look stronger than I felt.

"Enter," Sebastian called and two ice maids each carrying an enormous silver platter covered with a large lid, and a third with a tray holding a silver pitcher and glasses hurried inside. They were followed by two more maids with a table made entirely of ice. "Set the table and food by the door and don't bother with the chairs."

"Yes, your highness," they said in unison. They quickly obeyed while the five other maids holding chairs waited in the hall with the two ice guards then curtsied and left.

"Told you we wouldn't need to wait long for something to arrive." Sebastian strode to the table and lifted one of the lids.

Inside were three plates with large servings of... I wasn't sure what. It looked like a roasted small bird of some kind, on a pile of something purple and grain-like, with green, blue, and red chunks of something else.

I headed around the couch to get a plate, but Titus grabbed my wrist, stopping me. "Wait until Seireadan checks it for spells."

"It looks okay," Sebastian said. "Just sit and I'll bring you a plate."

"Gee, thanks," Hawk replied.

Sebastian snorted. "I was talking to Amiah. You don't need a plate."

"But—" Hawk batted his eyelashes. "I can still enjoy the taste and I healed all her broken bones."

"And I'm perfectly capable of getting my own plate," I said.

"He just about killed you and I'm already standing here," Sebastian insisted.

"That's not fair," Hawk groaned as he stood. "She *made* me almost kill her."

"You should still be getting her a plate," Titus said, tugging on my wrist and urging me to sit on the couch.

"Come on, guys. Can't you see I'm dying here?" But Hawk was already at the table, pouring himself a drink. "And jeez, you should have let them bring in chairs so you could sit at the table."

"Sure, and that would be five more of my mother's constructs getting a look at Amiah and wondering if she looks healthy or not," Sebastian said, picking up two plates and two sets of cutlery and returning to the couch.

He set a plate on the coffee table in front of me then sat on the couch as far away from me as possible.

Him too?

But of course, he'd made it clear that he wasn't going to risk Cassius's wrath by having any more contact with me.

"So we're going to be fucking idiots and stay," Hawk said, sitting back in his chair with his drink. His gaze lifted, met mine for a second, and the hellfire in his eyes flickered. My pulse fluttered, surprisingly not in fear at the memory of his power roaring through me, but in anticipation of it sliding sensually into my body and heating my desire again.

A whisper of a smile tugged at his lips and he gave me a slight nod. I wasn't sure what that meant, and Titus sat on the floor at my feet, drawing my attention away from Hawk, before I could figure it out.

The big dragon leaned close, pressing his bare biceps and shoulder against my leg and giving me flesh-to-flesh contact. I wasn't sure if it was for him or me, and I didn't care. Just this simple touch felt good, steadying. With him, I could handle this... whatever *this* was going to be.

"We're also going to keep making trips to the healing pools to keep up the ruse," Sebastian said.

"The plan is still good." Cassius took Titus's chair and dug into his food. "I want a little more time to get a sense of the Winter Court's security and then we'll use the party as a cover for our escape. We just need to time it right."

The party where everyone was supposed to watch Sebastian and me conceive an heir to the Winter Court's throne. I set my plate in my lap and with a trembling hand poked a blue chunk with my fork. "I don't care what the timing is, so long as we leave before I have to have sex in public."

"That's a given," Sebastian said as Titus wrapped his large hand around my ankle, adding another point of contact and easing my shaking.

"Okay, so the first order of business is to lengthen the leash spell and adjust its effects on Amiah, then you and Sebastian should go to the pools," Cassius said, not even glancing my way. "T, you and I will wander back to the ballroom and its receiving rooms."

"You should take Hawk." Sebastian turned his attention to Titus. "You should stay here. I don't think you should be wandering around with Deaglan in court."

Titus tensed and his grip around my ankle tightened. "I'll go with you and Amiah to the pools."

"That's not—" Sebastian started but Hawk interrupted him.

"It's going to take a lot of magic to change the leash spell. If something happens, you might not be able to protect her." Hawk's gaze slid to mine again and this time his expression was clear. He was worried for me.

Sebastian narrowed his eyes and something subtle passed between him and Hawk. Hawk knew something that Sebastian didn't want the rest of us to know, and while I wanted to respect his privacy, if it endangered any of the guys—

"Sebastian—"

"It's fine," he said. "You don't need to worry. We've got you covered." He shot me a 'don't you dare' glance and shoveled a forkful of the purple stuff into his mouth.

I opened mine to protest then snapped it shut. I had secrets I didn't want the others to know too, and without a doubt if I forced Sebastian to reveal his, he'd reveal mine.

"So we're decided." Cassius cleaned his plate and set it on the coffee table. "Hawk, when you're ready?"

"I'm always ready," Hawk replied, flashing me a wicked smile even though he still looked hungover.

Cassius pinched the bridge of his nose and headed to the door. "I really hate working with demons."

"That's not fair," Hawk said, joining him at the door and slinging an arm over his shoulders. "You don't really know me."

"You're an incubus." Cassius shoved Hawk's arm off him and opened the door. "That's more than I need to know."

"Oh, come on, hot stuff. Don't tell me you're not even curious." Hawk shot me another smile and followed Cassius into the hall, closing the door behind him.

"He's going to get himself killed," Sebastian said, and I took a tentative bite of the purple stuff. It was pretty good with the consistency of rice and an earthy, fresh basil kind of taste.

"Says the man who used to give him just as much grief," I replied. Had it only been a few days since Sebastian had been teasing us—teasing me? It had made me so frustrated and now I wanted that Sebastian back... because now I wanted to take him up on his flirtations and have sex with him again.

"And then I saw how powerful he is," Sebastian said. "I'm never poking that bear again."

"He wouldn't do anything to you." I tried the roasted bird. It tasted like chicken, thank goodness. "That's not who he is."

"Yeah, you keep on thinking that, princess," Sebastian said, taking another mouthful of the purple stuff.

Princess? Was he implying I didn't do anything for myself? "I'm hardly a princess. None of you are letting me do anything for myself. Besides—" I said with a chuckle, trying to keep the mood light, "I'm not a princess. I'm a future queen."

I took a bit of the purple stuff and Sebastian stiffened. "Not even if you fuck me in public. You're not my wife and you never will be."

The purple stuff turned to a lumpy, tasteless paste in my mouth, his words irrationally stinging... just like he'd intended them to. Except I didn't know why they'd hurt.

It had to be because he'd rejected me. That was all. Not because I wanted any kind of a relationship with him. He wasn't my type. He clearly wasn't my soul mate. Why was that so hard to remember?

And yet I couldn't push aside my hurt feelings. He'd put me in my place and he'd been mean about it.

Well, fine.

A whisper of a cool wind caressed my cheeks.

"That wasn't what I meant and you know it." I met his pale, almost colorless blue gaze, daring him to say something else mean.

Something sad and angry slid across his expression. "You're right. I'm sorry." He ran a hand over his spiky white and silver hair. "I'm angry at my mother and Enowen, not you."

"Enowen?" There was that name again. Both his mother and Deaglan had mentioned her.

"No one important." He let out a heavy sigh and set his half-finished plate on the coffee table. "Let's get this leash spell stretched and adjust its side effects."

Except I was pretty sure she was very important. I'd never seen him react that way to anything.

AMIAH

LENGTHENING THE LEASH SPELL AND ADJUSTING IT SO I DIDN'T SUFFOCATE if Sebastian got too far away from me was as painful as before. I would have thought after experiencing the agony of Hawk's power burning through me, changing the leash spell would have seemed like a skinned knee in comparison. But no, it was still like major surgery without an analgesic or sedative, and I didn't even bother trying to fight my tears.

Titus wrapped me in a firm embrace the moment Sebastian withdrew his hand from over my heart, and I trembled in his arms trying to get my breath back, while Sebastian sagged forward, his head between his knees.

"Fucking hell," he gasped. "I'll be really glad when I can get rid of this spell."

Which I knew was going to hurt as well. But at least it would be the last time.

I shuddered.

Would removing my mating brand hurt like that? Working with the leash spell always felt like Sebastian was tearing into my essence, and the leash spell wasn't a deep connection, it didn't feel rooted in my soul like my mating brand did.

I pushed that fear aside. I would deal with that when I had to. We had to get out of Faerie first and possibly deal with Faerie's awakening Heart.

But that thought only made my pulse race faster. I was running out of time and too much was happening for Sebastian to be bothered with my brand.

"Let's get to the pools so I can get my magic back," Sebastian said.

"I'll go get changed." Titus pressed his lips to the top of my head, released me, and headed to the servants' room.

Sebastian glanced up at me and his eyes widened at what he saw. "You can get through this one more time."

"That's not what I'm worried about." I brushed my hand over my hip before I realized what I was doing then tried to hide the movement by standing. The sudden action so soon after Sebastian had adjusted the leash spell made the room spin.

"Hey." Sebastian stood as well and grabbed my shoulders, steadying me, his expression soft with concern. "I haven't forgotten."

My pulse stalled and time froze. For a second I thought I glimpsed the real Sebastian, the man who hid behind sharp words and bravado, who'd fled his home, hid his identity, and swore never to return, and who'd been a generous lover and a fierce protector.

Then he rolled his eyes at me and his expression turned mocking, reminding me that he flirted — and probably slept with — every woman he could, and that now that he'd had me, he wasn't having me again. "Trust me. You're on the list right after escaping my mother. Cassius seriously needs to get laid."

"Gee, thanks." But I wasn't going to argue with him that I still didn't know how I felt about Cassius. If that's what motivated Sebastian to get rid of my brand, I'd take it.

"Now." He stepped back, his full-body glow dimming for a second revealing that gray complexion that concerned me so much, and held out his arms. "Let me carry you so you look weak and my mother doesn't pay us another visit."

"Are you sure? You look pale."

He quirked a hint of a smile. "I told you. I'm winter fae. I'm supposed to look pale."

"And I told you that's not what I meant." Not when I'd first said it to him in his bathroom two days ago and not now.

"Yeah, well. I'm good enough to carry you to the pools and I really don't want my mother to get more concerned about our marriage. That could make her add something magical to our public display and make it harder for us to avoid it."

"Good point." I shuddered at the thought, and let Sebastian pick me up.

Titus returned wearing a plain white thigh-length tunic that matched his pants. His gaze landed on me in Sebastian's arms and his eyes narrowed. For a second it looked like his pupils had slitted, his beast straining to get free, but he turned his back on us and marched out the door before I could get a good look at him.

Sebastian followed him and we headed down the hall with the ice guards a few steps behind, but when we turned the corner, an ice maid holding a small silver tray stood in front of the large intricately carved door blocking our way.

"You have a message, your highness." She curtsied as we approached and held out the tray with a small black coin on it that at one second looked like it glowed and the next didn't.

"Who's it from?" Sebastian asked, setting me on my feet but not reaching for the coin.

"I wasn't told," the maid replied, still holding her curtsey.

"Deag—" Titus glanced back at the guards then cleared his throat. "His Majesty of the Shadow Court?"

"It's not his magical signature," Sebastian said.

"He could be hiding it." Titus inched protectively close behind me but didn't touch me.

"He could, but there's only one way to find out." Sebastian tapped the coin with his finger. Light burst from it and his full-body fae glow flared bright for a second. His eyelids fluttered shut, his head tipped back, and he tensed. Then the light vanished and he opened his eyes. "I have to meet someone."

"Who?" Titus asked.

Sebastian turned to face us with a strange — was that happy? — expression, but his gaze jumped past my shoulder and his expression returned to grim. "Help *my wife* in the pool. I won't be gone long."

Titus tensed and also glanced back again at the ice guards looming half a dozen feet behind us. "It's not safe for you to be alone."

"I'll be fine. I have my mother's constructs to protect me." He stepped closer, capturing me between him and Titus and making my thoughts jump to being caught between them while wearing a lot less clothing.

I tried to push the inappropriate thought aside, but Sebastian hooked a finger under my chin and brushed his lips against mine.

I knew it was just an act for his mother's guards and maid, but that whisper of a caress from his lips stole my breath and heat rushed between my thighs. Just a touch and I was lost, as if the desire I'd had when all this had started had never been extinguished, just muted by my pain. I ached for him, ached for his mouth to return to mine, ached for it to go lower like it had the other night.

"You should stay," I murmured. *Stop worrying about Cassius's wrath and make me feel amazing again.* "T's right. It's too dangerous for you to be by yourself." My thoughts stuttered. "And what about the spell... connecting... you know." He could have made a mistake and not lengthened the leash spell or weakened its deadly effects. We hadn't had time to test it.

"It'll be okay. Trust me," he whispered back, "you don't need to worry about that and you want me to make this meeting. I'm hoping it'll be good news for you."

"Good news?"

He slid his hand over my left hip and met my gaze, his message clear. He was meeting someone about my brand. I could be free.

Oh, my goodness, I could be free!

"Can we trust this person?"

"That's what I'm going to find out." Sebastian stepped back and raised his gaze to Titus's. "I'll meet you back here."

"Stay safe," Titus said, his voice gruff.

Sebastian commanded the guards and the maid to not enter the healing grotto then hurried back down the hall with one of the ice guards following him.

With a growl, Titus pushed open the heavy door and ushered me inside, as the remaining guard closed it behind us.

The grotto's warm humid air wrapped around me and I sagged onto the bench by the door and stared up at the small square of bright blue sky in the skylight.

I was going to be free.

My mating brand was going to be removed and I'd be able to pursue a relationship with anyone I wanted. I wouldn't have to look to Sebastian or Hawk to relieve my desire... although Hawk would certainly be a good choice to help explore everything I'd learned about in anticipation of meeting my mate.

Free.

If whoever Sebastian was meeting could be trusted.

Fear and anticipation twisted in my gut.

Please let them be trustworthy. Please.

I didn't know why Sebastian wasn't removing my brand himself. He'd said he was the only one who could. Except when he'd said that we'd been in the mortal realm where he was likely one of the most powerful beings around. Here in Faerie there could be someone else better able to remove it. *Oh, please.*

My mixed emotions twisted tighter and swelled into my chest—

No, not my emotions, the leash spell. Sebastian had reached the end of its range, gone beyond, and now the weight of the spell squeezed around my lungs, tight and a little painful, but not agonizing like it had been before.

"Are you okay?" Titus asked, crouching in front of me.

I pressed my hand over my heart and strained to draw in a full breath. I could, but it was still hard. "Well, the spell hasn't removed all the air around me, so that's an improvement."

"Not sure by how much," he said, holding out his hands to me.

I took them and he closed his fingers completely covering mine.

"I'm not suffocating," I said. "I'll have to consider that a win."

"Can you walk or would you like me to carry you?"

"I'm fine here. I don't need to go into a pool." So there was no point going any farther from the door.

"Carry it is." He tugged me to my feet and picked me up. "I want to show you something before Seireadan returns."

"What?" I asked as I leaned into his embrace and savored the feel of his body and his essence brushing against my senses.

"You'll see." He strode to the back of the grotto to a hidden set of stairs carved into the side of the wall and took them up to a small landing mostly hidden by winter greenery. At the back stood a simple narrow ice door.

With ease, Titus held me with one arm and opened the door, and — turning sideways to get his broad shoulders through — stepped out onto an ice and rock balcony set into the side of a mountain. Cold crisp winter air swept across my face and teased down the neck of my robe and vast blue sky stretched out before me, stealing my breath at its vast openness.

I didn't care that it was too cold for just the thin robe I was wearing. I barely noticed the goose bumps rushing over my skin. There was just so much space. It was so open, so free, so beautiful and steadying. I'd known not being able to look out a window had been crushing my soul as much as everything else that had happened, but I hadn't realized just how much I needed to see open sky.

The balcony was about twenty feet by twenty feet with an intricate ice railing at its edge. About thirty feet to the left was an identical balcony with an identical plain ice door, and ahead, lay a sprawling mountain range of snow topped peaks. Far off in the distance a flock of white birds, the sunlight catching in their feathers, soared and dipped, riding the thermals.

"This is amazing." The spot between my shoulder blades where my wings appeared ached and I yearned to release them and join the birds — something I'd never desired before. But then, I'd never been so unsteady and stuck underground before. Even when that human had held me, I'd been able to see the sky.

"I wanted you to see this," Titus said, his voice gruff.

"It's beautiful. Will you let me down?"

"It's a little cold."

"I don't care." I needed to stretch out my arms, feel the air rushing around me and breathe it in.

He set me down. The balcony floor was smooth and cool under my bare feet, but not stinging cold like ice, and I crossed to the edge and leaned against the railing. The wind picked up and I stretched out my arms and turned my face into it, letting it sweep my loose hair back from my face and tug at my robe as I drew in a deep breath. Even with the leash spell squeezing around my lungs, it was easier to breathe.

Space. Sky. Free. So free.

"There are ice canyons over there." Titus drew close behind me, this time close enough that his chest brushed against my back, and pointed to a deep V in the mountain range. "It's so deep sunlight never reaches the bottom."

I leaned into him and he wrapped his arms around my waist, holding me tight. The warmth from his body radiated into my skin and seeped into my muscles. God, this felt so good.

"It has tiny blue flowers that pulse with the power of the Winter Court and tinkle like little bells when the wind blows just right or if you gust them with your wings. And at the very end is an enormous frozen waterfall, hundreds of feet high, with ice passages riddled throughout."

"It sounds amazing."

This was amazing, having the open sky I'd desperately needed and the physical contact I wasn't supposed to need. I could feel Titus's life, his energy, pulsing with power against my magical senses. He was healthy, well, even mostly content with his beast. For the moment, they were almost properly aligned, almost completely merged into one whole ferocious soul, filled with strength and power and certainty.

"It is." His voice softened and he pressed his lips to the top of my head.

That was the second time in a few minutes that he'd done that small, soft intimate act.

It sent a shiver of need whispering through me, and he curled more of his body around me probably thinking I was cold. I didn't correct him. I felt so safe and strong with him embracing me like this. And while I knew this kind of contact didn't necessarily mean anything coming from a shifter, that it could just be his nature making him more intimate than an angel, I also knew it *could* mean something, something I could explore once my brand was gone.

"You should see it all," he said. "You should make the flowers chime and play tag flying through the waterfall."

The wind changed directions and showered us with a flurry of ice crystals that caught the sunlight and sparkled like diamonds. I held out my hand to catch some on my palm, but instead of landing and melting, they sparkled and danced less than an inch from my skin held aloft by a miniature whirlwind.

"You should watch the sunrise from the top of the Silver Mountain on a clear day, and lie on the Calmarine Ice Plains at midnight looking at the opalescent glimmer of the Winter Court's protective boundary."

He cupped my cheek with his large hand and gently urged me to face him. His pupils were fully slitted with a hint of gold shimmering behind the plain brown of the glamour. His beast had fully risen to the surface with his emotions. But it wasn't rage fueling the ferocious aspect of his nature, it was desire.

Its intensity stole my breath. Marcus had never looked at me like that. I'd only glimpsed a fraction of his powerful emotions because I hadn't been his soul mate. I'd known the look he'd give his true mate would have been intense, consuming, and the longer I'd waited for him to look at me like that and for my brand to awaken, the more I yearned for it. Would it have looked like this?

I wasn't sure anyone could match Titus's ferocity. He was more powerful, wilder, and more primal than a wolf. Perhaps this was how he'd looked at his mate before she'd been killed, the one who hadn't been his soul mate. He'd been without sex for a long time, and Hawk's loss of control had to be straining Titus's willpower.

That was it. And yet, I still yearned to kiss him, give him that connection that he hadn't had in such a long time.

Except if I kissed him would my brand light up? Would we be bound together for the rest of our lives?

With him looking at me like that, his yearning inflaming my own, it was so hard to remember that I didn't want a connection forced on me, that I wanted to fall in love like everyone else. I wanted to *choose* my happiness.

His gaze dipped to my lips and my pulse stuttered.

I ached for him to kiss me.

And that terrified me.

Something skittered down the mountain behind us, and Titus jerked around as an ice man in the same kind of ice armor as the queen's guards — although only as big as Titus and not bigger like her guards — half-slid half-jumped from the cliff face above the door. He landed on the balcony between us and the door with a dark light emanating from inside his semi-translucent body. Above him, still clinging to the jagged rock and ice were dozens more identical ice men.

"You're supposed to still be in the grotto," the man said, drawing an ice sword that without a doubt was as hard and sharp as steel.

AMIAH

I BACKED UP AND HIT THE RAILING, MY HEART POUNDING IN A CHEST STILL tight with the pressure of the adjusted leash spell. Another gust of wind showered us with ice crystals, and three more ice men landed in front of the door.

They now blocked us from our only means of escape, and while I could release my wings and fly, I wasn't strong enough to take Titus with me. Sure, he could also shift and fly, but that might break the glamour hiding him and leave Sebastian, Cassius, and Hawk still in the Winter Court. And the queen would be furious to know Sebastian had been hiding the last dragon and the only connection to the most powerful magic in all of Faerie right under her nose.

"Tell me where the dragon is and I'll let you run away from court instead of killing you," the ice man said.

Titus stepped in front of me and flexed his hands, extending his fingers into wolf-like claws. "Step away from the door and I won't kill *you*."

"This is just a construct, wolf," the ice man said. "Destroying it won't hurt me."

"Sure it will," Titus snarled back. "The harder I have to work to protect Amiah, the more I'm going to rip into you when I find you."

"And how do you plan to do that?" another ice man asked in the same voice as the first as he dropped from the mountain face and joined the line in front of the door.

"Prince Seireadan will be able to find you."

"Prince Seireadan will be dead just as soon as I finish with you," the first man replied.

My pulse stalled. Sebastian was low on magic and he hadn't had a chance to go into a pool to restore it. Had the message about removing my mating brand been a trick, a way to separate us? And how soon would the ice men attack him? How many could he fight off by himself in his condition?

"You can either join him or just become a widow," the man said. "Tell me where to find the dragon."

"I don't know what you're talking about," I said.

Another gust of wind, suddenly frigid and making me shiver, showered us with more ice crystals.

"You and your bodyguard aren't from this realm. There's no point in sacrificing yourself by lying." The man took a step forward and Titus tensed. "Tell me and you can run off with him."

"Now who's lying," Titus growled. "You can't let her live. The court responds to her. You kill his highness and she becomes heir."

The dark light inside the ice man flared. "You're awfully knowledgeable of court ways for an outsider."

"His highness warned me of the dangers of court politics," Titus said.

"You *will* tell me where the dragon is."

The ice man swung at Titus's head with a powerful two-handed strike, but Titus lunged in, blocked the man's attack, and tore his claws through the man's arm. The man didn't even utter a sound as his arm shattered and Titus tossed him into one of the other ice men who was blocking the door, knocking them both back.

The rest of the ice men in the line leaped at Titus who batted one into another and twisted to avoid getting impaled by a third. Two ice men dropped from the rockface above and grabbed Titus's right arm before he could get in a good swipe at either of them, and two more grabbed his left.

"Fly." Titus wrenched the men on his right arm off balance and jerked his hand free. "Get to the door at the next balcony and warn Seireadan." He grabbed one of the men on his left arm and tossed him over the railing, but another ice man lunged in, plunging his sword into Titus's gut.

Blood seeped into his white tunic and splattered on his pants, but the wound wasn't serious enough for my magic to lock onto him. With a roar, he swung the man still on his left arm into the man who'd stabbed him, sending them tumbling into two more men.

Another ice man slashed at Titus's arm, but he yanked a third man into his way and the sword dug deep into that man's shoulder. Except the man didn't react to getting cut, just stumbled because the sword was caught in his body.

"Fly," Titus snarled. "I can handle them."

My pulse beat faster, and the wind sweeping around the balcony grew stronger. I didn't want to leave him, but if I stayed, I'd just get in the way, and I needed to leave before my compulsion to heal forced me to stay. Someone needed to warn Sebastian.

Another man sliced at Titus. He twisted just enough so the blade slipped past his side, and raked his claws through the man's face. The man's nose and cheek shattered and with a loud crack, a fissure sliced through his head and chest. He collapsed, bursting apart as he hit the floor, his pieces skittering across its smooth surface in all directions.

I pushed a trickle of power into my back and released my wings with a flash of white angelic magic, but an ice man leaped from the cliff onto me, pinning me against the railing.

"Tell me where the dragon is," he demanded.

"No." I pushed him off, but another man fell onto me before I could launch myself into the sky.

"Tell me."

I shoved at the new guy and the wind snapped, knocking him over the railing. But the first man grabbed my wing before I could fly away, and painfully twisted it.

Tears sprung to my eyes and I heaved against his grip, but he wrenched hard, shooting agony into my back.

"Don't make this harder on yourself."

The wind — it had to be the Winter Court's wind — gusted around me, tugged at my hair and robe, and jostled the man holding my wings. His grip loosened and I pulled my wings back into my body, but more men grabbed me. Something sharp bit into my thigh and I was yanked to my knees before I could figure out what had happened.

Somewhere, beyond the crush of ice bodies, Titus roared.

My breath caught with the fear that he was mortally wounded, but my magic still didn't lock onto him, and two of the ice men holding me down were yanked away.

Ice shards showered me, and Titus seized another ice man, threw him over the railing then shattered two more.

"Come on." Titus threw me over his shoulder, bolted the three steps to the left side of the balcony, hopped onto the railing without losing momentum, and jumped to the other balcony in one great leap.

We landed with a heavy thump and Titus set me on my feet but didn't let go. His gaze, strangely brown and gold at the same time and filled with rage and fear, captured me. Then he grabbed the back of my head and smashed his lips against mine in a ferocious kiss that stole all breath and thought. Time froze and there was only Titus, his strong arms holding me close against his hard body, his warmth, his life, and his mouth igniting a sudden desperate desire.

Oh, wow.

His kiss was filled with a wild, passionate need as if he didn't have the words and could only show me how he felt, how much he wanted me. It sent heat swelling through my body, radiating from his lips and rushing to my toes in a giant, breathtaking wave.

Oh, no.

He jerked away, gasping, and shoved me toward the door. "Run. I'm right behind you."

The kiss had only lasted a second and yet my senses were reeling from it. I was warm... was I too warm? It didn't feel as if the heat radiated from my brand. Did that mean he wasn't my soul mate?

The ice men scurried up and across the sheer cliff face from the grotto's balcony and dove toward us.

Titus shoved me again. "Run. Find the others. Warn Seireadan."

I scrambled to the door and wrenched it open as Titus roared and an ice man shattered on the floor behind me, its shards stinging the backs of my bare calves.

Another ice man dropped from the cliff face above me, trying to cut me off, but the Winter Court's wind surged, frozen and sharp, and blew him over the side of the balcony.

I ran inside before someone else could reach me and Titus slammed the door shut between us.

"What are you doing?" He was supposed to be behind me.

"Find Seireadan," he said through the door.

"T—"

"Seireadan," he roared and something heavy crunched on the other side of the door. "We can't trust the queen's constructs. He's by himself."

And magically weakened.

Right.

Titus was hurt but he was a fast healer. He could handle the ice men. *Please let him be able to handle the ice men.*

I raced across the wide empty room to the only other door. I had no idea what the room was supposed to be, there wasn't any furniture or decorations, only a pale light emanating from the walls and ceiling and none of that mattered. I had to find Sebastian.

I just had no idea how.

I was pretty sure I wasn't even on the same floor as the grotto so I couldn't just go down two halls back to our suite and hope Cassius and Hawk were there. I'd have to find some stairs and preferably someone to show me the way.

Except could I trust anyone? I didn't know who controlled those ice men, and while they hadn't looked like the ice people I'd already encountered who belonged to the Winter Queen — who I doubted would try to kill me after going to so much trouble to make Sebastian sleep with me — that didn't mean they would help me or that all the other ice people I met were safe.

I threw open the door and stared into a wide, white hall that stretched left and right. It looked like all the other halls I'd been in and I had no idea which direction to go.

Left or right.

Left.

Right.

Behind me, the door to the balcony jerked open then slammed shut. My heart leaped into my throat.

Titus is fine. He's a fighter. Sebastian isn't, not without his magic.

I bolted right, praying I would find...

I had no idea what. I needed to find someone I could trust. But who?

The hall ended in an L intersection and I careened around the corner and slammed into a hard body.

The sense of cold lifelessness shivered across my senses and I looked up into black eyes with smoldering red hellfire.

Deaglan's demon-vampire.

My stomach bottomed out and fear rushed frozen through my chest.

I jerked back, the court's wind sweeping around me, as Deaglan strode out an open door between me and the demon-vampire.

They both still wore black leather, the demon-vampire's clothing the same as before, but this time Deaglan wore a leather jerkin with a dozen silver buckles and no shirt underneath, leaving his sculpted, muscular arms bare.

"Ah, the future queen of the Winter Court." His lips curled back in a wicked sneer and a dangerous gleam lit in his eyes. Shadows billowed under his skin, gathering like a storm, and his gaze slowly trailed down my body, hesitating on my cleavage and making fear churn in my gut.

I stumbled back a few more steps, getting out of arm's reach, my thoughts whirling. I needed to get away from him, needed to get to Sebastian before the ice men did—

Was Deaglan controlling the ice men?

I didn't know what kind of magic he possessed, and even if he didn't control the ice men that didn't mean he hadn't told someone else to.

The demon-vampire rested a hand on the scabbard of his katana sheathed at his hip, his emotionless gaze locked on me, and Deaglan took a step toward me.

I stumbled back another step. My foot slipped on something wet on the floor and I staggered into the wall to keep my balance, my gaze dipping down to the thin red streak in the floor.

Blood. I'd stepped in blood.

My thoughts stuttered and I realized warmth trickled down the side of my right thigh and the back of both of my calves. Somehow I'd been hurt and with all the adrenaline pumping through me hadn't realized it.

"You seem to have gotten hurt and misplaced your husband," Deaglan said, his voice dark, sounding too much like Balwyrdan's when he'd taken and beaten me. "Not even a bodyguard to keep an eye on you."

My pulse roared in my ears and I started to tremble. I was going to get taken again, hurt again. Worse. I could see it in his eyes.

"My hybrid says you don't know where the dragon is, that Seireadan took his half of my broken leash spell."

"That's true." There was no point in denying that I knew about Titus. The demon-vampire had already seen me with him, I could only pray that Deaglan wouldn't figure out that Titus was Titus.

"He also says the Spring Court's seneschal couldn't break you."

I glanced at the demon-vampire. His hellfire still smoldered, small red pinpricks, but a hunger now also burned in his eyes and his mouth had parted slightly, his fangs partially extended.

"Is Rin right?" Deaglan took another step forward, forcing me back again. "How much can you take?"

None. No more.

The Winter Court's wind gusted around me, ruffling Deaglan's hair, and making Rin's sash and long ponytail sweep out behind him.

"So Seireadan really didn't control the wind back in your room," he said.

Never again.

"I thought Seireadan had disguised my leash spell and that's what was binding you together, but it really does look like he married you." Deaglan's sneer deepened. "I'm going to enjoy the look on his face when he realizes I broke you."

No. Never. I wouldn't be taken again. I had to run back to Titus. It didn't matter if he was still fighting the ice men or if Deaglan saw him. I didn't know how to fight and I didn't have magic I could use to defend myself, not against Deaglan let alone both him and his demon-vampire.

"I broke in his other betrothed," Deaglan purred.

Except vampires, even ones a few hundred years old, had enhanced speed, and I doubted someone like Deaglan would put a baby vampire on a three-man assassination team and send him after the most valuable being in all the realms.

Which meant running wasn't an option.

And I didn't want to run. I was furious that running was my only choice, furious that I was so scared, furious at that human for making me doubt myself for over a hundred years, and furious at Balwyrdan for terrifying and hurting me.

"Rin says you never lost that look in your eyes," Deaglan sneered.

God, I wished I knew how to fight, was strong, had some kind of power. If I couldn't run away, the best I could hope for was to stall him until Titus found me and then pray he was strong enough to get Deaglan to back down — and that Deaglan wouldn't recognize him.

"Yeah, that look." Deaglan glanced at the demon-vampire. "Do you think I can wipe it from her face? Want to bet her blood?"

The demon-vampire's expression didn't change, and Deaglan huffed.

"Stop trying to hide your hunger," Deaglan said. "You can have her once I break her."

"As my lord wishes," the demon-vampire said, his voice so soft I could barely hear it and without a hint of emotion.

No.

Not going to happen.

Never again.

The court's wind grew colder and more bitter, reminding me I wasn't entirely helpless. It had thrown ice men off the balcony to protect me. Could I create a storm like the Winter Queen had in her throne room? Could I actually stand my ground?

Deaglan took another step forward, his horrible gaze raking up my body again. "Now where should I begin? Here?"

He reached for my neck and the wind snapped around me, knocking his hand away. My power surged into my back with a sudden spike of fear and adrenaline, and my wings released. "No."

Never again. Deaglan didn't control the leash spell like Balwyrdan. I might not be able to get him to leave me alone, but I *could* hold my own until Titus came. I wouldn't cower any longer. I would fight with whatever I had, even if that was with a magic I didn't know how to control and a bluff that I wasn't afraid of him.

I pushed my power into my hands, forcing them to light up even though I was the only one injured. Deaglan didn't know what magic I possessed, and I prayed he'd assume I had offensive magic. "You don't want to threaten the future queen of the Winter court."

"Oh, I don't?" Deaglan asked with a chuckle and the shadows under his skin swelled, bleeding across the floor and over the walls. "But I'm more powerful than you. I'm the *king* of the Shadow Court."

I clenched my hands, fighting to hide my trembling, and glared at him. I just had to buy time until Titus arrived. That was all.

Except the shadows devoured the light from the walls, and thick, sticky tendrils twisted around my ankles and dug into my flesh.

I wrenched against the shadows, jerking my legs and flapping my wings, but they twisted up my calves and past my knees, creeping painfully higher, drawing closer to the crux between my thighs.

"You really thought you could challenge a king?" Deaglan asked, drawing close and reaching for my robe's belt.

I slapped his hand away but more shadows captured my wrists and yanked them up.

No, please.

Panic seized my lungs and the court's wind exploded into a whirling frigid storm, shoving Deaglan back and sweeping shards of ice through his shadows and tearing them apart. The icy gale pounded into him, slicing his cheeks and bare arms, and toppled him into the demon-vampire then knocked both of them over and shoved them thirty feet down the hall.

He jerked to his feet with murder in his eyes and the court wind knocked him down again. "I'm the king of the Shadow Court," he snarled at me.

"But you're not *in* the Shadow court." I stretched my wings, brushing the tips against the walls on either side of me, knowing the glow in my eyes blazed with my fear and determination and rage, while praying I looked as angry as I felt.

I knew it was foolish to embarrass him like that, knew the next time he came after me — and from the look in his eyes there'd be a next time — I might not have the power of the Winter Court protecting me, but God, no more!

I was done feeling like a victim. I needed to fight back, even just this once, and the Winter Court was giving me that chance. Right now, against this monster who'd held Titus in captivity for five hundred years, I was going to vent my years of fear and anger. I was taking my power back.

SEBASTIAN

I raced down the hall, desperate to get to Amiah and Titus. It had been a long time since the Winter Court had spoken to me — it hadn't even spoken to me when I'd first entered it again — but its rage had exploded with fiery agony in my chest while I'd been in the middle of my meeting with Karthick.

Someone was threatening Amiah and the court was pissed. Except the court didn't even have to compel me to go to her. Amiah hadn't deserved anything that had happened to her and she didn't deserve any more. Sure, technically it had been her fault for getting caught up in this mess, but if she hadn't rushed to heal Titus, he would have died and I'd never have gotten my friend back. In the short time I'd known her, she'd only really asked for two things for herself: for me to get rid of her mating brand and for me to show her the pleasures of sex. And a part of me feared I'd failed her on both accounts.

I'd yet to remove her brand and at the first sign of danger from Cassius, I'd pushed her away, and as a result had put a stop to her sexual awakening — something she'd already waited far too long to explore.

I'd bolted from the Winter Forest, not bothering to go out the way I'd come in and pick up my mother's ice guard. I didn't want to have to explain to it what was going on and there was a chance it would stop me if it thought I was running into danger.

The court led me to the level above the healing grotto, its fury and fear building, gusting frozen around me so strongly I almost missed the spike of heat and flash of light in my wrist from my shadow fae alert glyph.

Shit.

I really hoped it wasn't Deaglan who was nearby, but given that he'd made a point of visiting me, I had a bad feeling it was.

God. He'd looked at Amiah with the same predatory hunger with which he'd looked at Enowen—

No, more. His look in our suite yesterday hadn't just been a desire for sex but pain as well. In the three hundred years since he'd tried to assassinate me, it seemed he'd developed a taste for sadism, and not the kind that would stop with a safe word.

I raced around a corner, afraid of what I'd find as a massive blast of frigid wind parted around me, tugging at my tunic and pants. At the far end of the hall Deaglan fell onto his demon-vampire hybrid already on the floor, and thirty feet beyond them stood a furious, spectacular angel.

"I'm the king of the Shadow Court," Deaglan snarled.

"But you're not *in* the Shadow court." Amiah stretched out her wings. Her angel glow blazed from her eyes and her power filled her palms with a bluff I hadn't thought she was capable of. The Winter Court's wind gusted around her. It rippled through her robe — which was on the verge of falling open and exposing everything — and swept her long blond locks around her head.

She was breathtaking. An enraged goddess, worshiped by the Winter Court. Its wind defended her and its essence called to me to protect her. Even Deaglan, with his eyes ever-so-slightly too wide, saw it.

He'd assumed— Hell, *I'd* assumed because she wasn't fae, the court wouldn't race to fulfill her will like it used to do for me. But it had never behaved this ferociously for me even when I'd fully accepted that I was one day going to be the king. It only behaved like that for my mother and she had to force it to her will. I doubted Amiah even knew she could force the court to do anything.

Fucking hell. Had I actually married Amiah and not realized it? I hadn't thought that was possible. We hadn't done the ceremony and bonded our souls together.

And if I hadn't married her, was I going to remain a fool and continue to push away this determined, amazing, powerful woman?

She'd said while we were having sex that she was certain I wasn't her soul mate, but seeing the Winter Court fully embrace her made me seriously doubt her words. Maybe we *were* meant to be together. Just because her brand hadn't awoken when we'd had sex didn't mean it wouldn't. An angelic mating brand could form at any time, before sex, during sex, after lots and lots of sex. Maybe the Winter Court's connection had just awakened before her brand had.

Jeez, what the hell was wrong with me?

I didn't want a wife. And I certainly didn't want that wife to be Amiah. She drove me crazy. Besides, she was meant for Cassius — that much was obvious, even if both of them were too blind to figure it out — and I was pretty sure Cassius wasn't the sharing type. He was far too uptight for that... although his brother who was also pretty uptight was soul bound to a woman with three other mates and he hadn't had problems sharing...

The Winter Court's wind snapped around me and shoved me forward a few steps, reminding me why it had summoned me.

It would continue to protect Amiah, but if Deaglan really wanted to put up a fight, he could, and that could get nasty even without his hybrid to back him up.

"I see you've found my wife." I plastered on my over-confident asshole expression and strode closer, catching a glimpse of the fear and relief barely hidden behind the rage in Amiah's eyes. "Spectacular, isn't she?"

Deaglan glared at me and stood as the hybrid rose behind him, an expressionless deadly shadow among the Shadow King's other deadly shadows.

"And here I'd thought she was a kitten," Deaglan said, wiping his thumb through a trickle of blood that was slowly oozing down his cheek, "with little kitten claws trying to stand up against the Winter Queen by refusing to fuck you."

"You honestly think I'd marry a kitten?"

"You were going to," Deaglan replied, "and I never would have thought you had it in you to take a wild cat to bed, especially one certain to draw blood." Dark desire lit up his eyes at that and I clenched my jaw, fighting the urge to punch him in the face.

No way in hell was he getting anywhere near Amiah's bed. Ever.

"But you surprised me," he said. "You're not that same starry-eyed fae I grew up with. You've changed."

"Being poisoned by your best friend and your betrothed and left in the Wilds for Faerie to rip its magic out of you will do that to a fae." I'd barely survived and only because Karthick had found me. Another hour and the only thing left for Faerie to have ripped out would have been my essence and soul.

"I couldn't let you live. You were going to figure out I had Titus chained up in my court if that fool Enowen didn't tell you first." Deaglan's eyes narrowed. "And of course the first thing the beast did when he broke free was go running to you."

"Because I promised to sever his connection to the Heart."

"And he was stupid enough to believe that?" Deaglan huffed a dark laugh. "Don't pretend you don't want the power too. You crave it just as much as I do, as every high fae does."

"I don't want it. I don't even want the Winter Court." Yes, I missed Faerie, missed the feel of the court's magic always at the edge of my senses, missed breathing air always crackling with a power that fed my soul, but that was it. In the mortal realm, I wasn't chained to a role I was born into and didn't choose, and I had all the same power and wealth but none of the duties and a hell of a lot less of the danger. I could do as I pleased, love how I pleased, and leave as I pleased. No one to answer to and no responsibilities.

"Well that's good," he said, "because the Winter Court won't be yours. When your mother finally decides to fade, the court will pick your wife to rule, not you, and then you'll have no way of breaking her."

"A king shouldn't break his queen." The thought of breaking Amiah's will made my stomach churn. She didn't deserve to be broken, no woman did, she deserved to be built up, cherished, worshiped.

God, how amazing would she be if she released her fears and embraced all of who she was.

"I doubt you could, even if you wanted to. Word from the Spring Court is that Balwyrdan couldn't break her." Deaglan chuckled the sound dark and grating. "Such a difference from Enowen. She broke without me even trying. I had her crawling through shadow thorns to suck my cock on the first day. Just dangled a throne in front of that kitten and she jumped at it."

Just one punch. Right in that smug smile.

Except I wouldn't be able to stop at one punch and I didn't have enough power right now to stand up against him and his hybrid, especially since the Winter Court didn't respond to me like it did Amiah.

"Poor Seireadan," Deaglan mocked, "I bet your angel is too high and mighty to suck cock."

My cock tightened at the thought, even as my brain decided she probably wouldn't. Miss Prim-and-Proper probably thought it beneath her to wrap her soft lips around a cock. And if she wasn't interested, I wasn't going to make her. Sex was only good if it was good for everyone.

Deaglan turned to Amiah. "You'd never kneel for Seireadan, would you?"

"You think having him in my mouth and knowing that with my lips I bring him pleasure and with my teeth I bring him pain isn't a position of power?" she asked with a dangerous glint in her eyes that made me even harder. "Then please, by all means, bring your cock closer."

Fuck me. Did she just say that?

"No?" she asked.

Deaglan glared at her, and that dangerous glint tugged at her lips, making her look downright wicked. God, I'd had that in my bed and I'd pushed her away.

What the hell was wrong with me?

"Then excuse us, your majesty of the Shadow Court," she said, her tone brusque, a clear dismissal. "I'd like a word with my husband."

Deaglan raised his chin and she matched him, everything about her screaming strength and defiance. The Winter Court gusted, shoving him back a step and bumping him into his hybrid as if telling him where to go, and Amiah raised a delicate blond eyebrow, not backing down from his challenge. She had the full force of the Winter Court protecting her. Did he really want to turn this into a fight?

"You're going to wish you'd just let me fuck you in private," he spat at Amiah before storming past me with his hybrid close at his heels.

He marched around the corner and Amiah pulled in her wings and rushed to me, cupping my face with her palms and sending a warm thread of magic into me, checking my condition, and making my pulse pound with a fucked-up mix of fear for her wellbeing and desire for her body.

"Are you okay?" She gazed into my eyes, searching for an answer her magic was already giving her.

I was fine. Or at least I was as fine as I was going to get given that I'd just had the shit scared out of me seeing her facing off against Deaglan, and was infected with demonic magic that I couldn't get out of my system.

"The court told me you were in danger. Are you all right?" I asked.

Her robe at her right thigh was ripped and stained with blood, and she looked like she was running on fear and adrenaline. "You're bleeding."

"And Titus could be worse." She turned to rush down the hall in the opposite direction Deaglan had gone when Titus barreled around the corner at the far end.

His eyes were wild, his pupils slitted, and he radiated dangerous ferocious power, his beast's fury barely contained. Blood stained his white tunic and pants. A lot of blood. Dozens of cuts, some deep, crisscrossed his arms, and blood oozed from a nasty gash above his right eye. His gaze landed on Amiah and his expression grew darker.

With a growl, he pounced on her, yanking her to his chest and baring his teeth at me.

Oh shit. His beast wasn't straining to get free, it was free. It just had enough sense not to shift and break the glamour.

"T, I'm okay," she said, somehow not panicking at Titus's sudden attack or trying to pull free. She pressed her palms to his cheeks just like she'd done to me a moment ago, and her eyelids fluttered shut. "We need to get you back to our rooms so I can stop your bleeding."

"I'm fine," he said. "I'll heal. I'm taking you back to our rooms then killing whoever threatened you." He shoved past me and headed in the same direction Deaglan had.

"Let's go the other way." I reached for his arm to stop him, but he jumped on me, seizing the front of my tunic, wrenching me off my feet, and shoving me against the wall.

"I'm glad your safe," he snarled. "Don't get in my way."

Fuck. What the hell was wrong with him? I'd never seen him like this before, never seen him with this little control over his beast. But he'd spent five hundred years unable to calm his beast with physical contact or shifting. I should be more surprised that he'd managed to control his beast for as long as he had already.

"Deaglan went that way," I said, straining to resist the urge to struggle. If it looked like I was fighting, his beast would strike and I didn't want to have to hurt him to defend myself — that could get Amiah hurt. "I don't want to run into him again."

"Is he responsible?" Titus asked.

"I don't even know what happened," I replied.

"This isn't a conversation we should be having in the hall." Amiah tried to push out of Titus's hold but he released me and added his other arm to his embrace, making it impossible for her to escape.

"You're right." He marched — thankfully — back the way he'd come, and I hurried to catch up with his stride.

Amiah met my gaze over his shoulder and a whisper of court wind fluttered through her hair. She was worried and upset and still too wide-eyed from her encounter with Deaglan and whatever else had happened.

Jeez. Whatever it had been, it had scared the hell out of her and sent Titus into beast mode.

We needed to get the hell out of court and fast... just as soon as I took Amiah to Karthick and got her brand removed.

Titus took a set of servants' stairs down to the next floor, and I followed, trailing my fingers along the hall wall, asking the court to summon Cassius and Hawk back to our rooms.

I prayed my summons would go through the court itself and not my mother, but given how bad the situation looked, I didn't care if my mother knew I was calling Cassius and Hawk back or not. We needed to regroup, and someone needed to tell me what the hell was going on.

We reached the door to our suite as Cassius and Hawk came barreling down the hall.

"What's wrong?" Cassius asked, fire snapping over his hands. "We just got the urgent sense that we had to return here." His gaze landed on Amiah in Titus's arms, both of them now covered in Titus's blood, and his eyes narrowed.

"Jesus," Hawk hissed.

Titus wrenched open the door — I was surprised he didn't yank it off its hinges — and stormed inside.

"Watch Amiah," he snarled to no one in particular as he set her on her feet. "I'm hunting the bastard who tried to kill her."

"Who?" Cassius grabbed Titus's wrist and the dragon tossed Cassius to the far end of the room.

Cassius landed with an *oomph*, tumbled across the floor, and hit the wall.

"T, stop. You need healing. You're still losing blood," Amiah said.

"And you need a plan," Hawk added.

"Kill him," Titus's beast growled.

Cassius rose, fire blazing up his forearms, and stalked back toward him. "That's not a plan."

"I know!" Titus roared back. "My beast doesn't care."

"So take a breath." Amiah rose on her toes, leaned into him, and tangled her hands in his hair. She pressed her forehead against his — as best as she could with their height difference — and gave him the firm physical contact that should have helped calm his beast, but his breath picked up instead of slowing and his canines extended.

"He tried to kill you. They piled on top of you and I thought—" His fingers shifted into claws and hints of red and gold scales swept over the back of his arms.

Ah, shit. He was losing it.

"I won't let him threaten you again." He shoved her, knocking her into Cassius's flaming arms and making the angel yank his fire back under his skin, and jerked to the door.

Fucking hell. I couldn't let him storm around court, not with him barely holding onto his human form.

God damn it. This was going to hurt.

I pressed my hand to my shoulder, awakening the power I had stored in my sleep glyph, and slapped my other hand over his heart. The spell activated and the demonic magic surged, screaming through my veins, a black acid consuming me from the inside out.

Titus growled and swatted me across the room — thank God he didn't use his claws — and I slammed into the wall. Pain snapped through my chest and the back of my head, and I sagged to the floor as my sleep spell took hold and Titus dropped to his knees.

"Seireadan, please. I have to protect—" His eyes rolled back and he collapsed.

"What the fuck just happened?" Hawk asked, hurrying to close the suite's door.

"We were attacked." Amiah rushed to my side and captured my head between her hands again. She forced me to look at her, staring into my eyes looking for... I had no idea what. With the demonic magic consuming me, I could barely think straight.

Then the gentle warmth of her power swelled into me, stronger than the fire of the demonic magic, soothing the pain in my head and chest. For a second it felt as if she was calming the demonic magic as well, but it was really just easing off because I was no longer using my magic.

"Someone sent ice men after me. They wanted to know where the last dragon was and they wanted both me and Sebastian dead." The light in her eyes flared and her hands on my cheeks started to tremble.

I pressed my hands over hers, trying to reassure her with my touch. Which was stupid because she was an angel, not a shifter, and didn't respond to touch like they did.

And yet her trembling eased and a primal need heated inside me. I'd give her more than my hands if it wiped away that look in her eyes.

Fucking hell.

Wasn't I supposed to be helping her and Cassius realize they were in love with each other?

If I didn't get my shit together, I was going to do something stupid. And I'd sworn I'd never do something stupid for a woman again.

Except Amiah wasn't just any woman. If the Winter Court's response to her meant anything, she was supposed to be my queen. Something she'd never want, and I'd do whatever it took to ensure she'd never be permanently bound to me.

AMIAH

A strange look passed over Sebastian's face. His gaze dipped to my lips as if he wanted to kiss me, making me ache for more than just his hands on mine, then he gently shifted his grip to my wrists and nudged me away, reminding me that Titus was still hurt. I was hurt. Someone had tried to kill me. Deaglan had almost—

If Sebastian hadn't shown up, Deaglan could have seriously hurt me.

My pulse picked up and a whisper of wind fluttered around me, reminding me of how much power I currently had at my command.

God, I'd wanted to hurt Deaglan, wanted to take out my frustration over everything on him. I finally had the power to defend myself. I'd knocked him and his demon-vampire off their feet and I'd seen fear in their eyes.

A shuddering mix of desire and revulsion swept through me. I was supposed to heal people, not hurt them.

"We were afraid you were in danger," I said as matter-of-a-factly as I could.

Maybe if I embraced my cool professionalism I'd stop thinking about how afraid and angry I was. Really. Whoever attacked me and Titus was still out there, still wanted me and Sebastian dead.

Except I couldn't do it, couldn't rein in my emotions and my hands were trembling again.

I turned to Titus and placed my palms on his back over his heart and released a small trickle of magic to assess his condition. Most of his lacerations were already on their way to sealing shut, and it wouldn't take a lot to heal everything.

"I was trying to find you when I ran into Deaglan."

"Deaglan?" Cassius jerked a step toward me, glanced at the smoke curling from his hands, and stopped, shoving them into his armpits as if he needed the reminder not to touch me. "Did he hurt you? Is any of that blood yours? Where the hell were you, Bane?"

My heart skipped a beat and I glanced at him. *Please don't tell him. Please.*

"I was making contact with someone who might be able to get me some protection against the Wilds," he lied. "And she looked a lot less bloody before Titus picked her up."

"Most of it's Titus's," I confirmed. Because he'd protected me, risked his life so I could get away... and kissed me.

God, that kiss! It had been amazing and shocking and added to the whirling mix of emotions that I had no right indulging in because he was hurt and we were in danger. And while I was pretty sure my mating brand hadn't awakened, I couldn't check with everyone watching me.

I pushed a little more power into him, letting it ooze through his veins to the worst of his injuries, warm and gentle. It would take a little longer to heal him this way, but doing it too quickly would hurt him and that could wake him from Sebastian's sleep spell, something I was sure Sebastian didn't want to cast again. Two of his ribs had been cracked and he'd gotten a minor concussion from Titus's strike. The next time could be worse. Titus could use his claws.

"Tell me about the ice men," Sebastian said.

I finished with Titus and sat back on my heels. My fear and anger and God, all my emotions surged, and I forced my gaze to slide over Cassius and Hawk, trying to visually assess them as a way of distracting myself.

"They all looked and sounded the same," I said. *Focus on the guys. Just them, their health, nothing else.* "And they had this strange black glow inside them."

My power flared, warming my palms, and somehow my magic connected with them even though I wasn't touching them. Which was supposed to be impossible. Yes, my magic locked onto someone when they were dying, but it didn't connect with them and tell me their injuries, just compelled me to go to them. I always needed physical contact to properly assess and heal someone. Except I'd connected with Mavis when Balwyrdan had murdered her, and now I was connecting with the guys.

"Did you recognize them?" Cassius asked.

"No. But I've barely been outside of this room." And I was trapped again in this windowless suite with people outside wanting to kill me. I was sure others would have felt safe with only one way in and out, but it felt like the walls were drawing closer and closer together, now more than ever, and I had nowhere to run.

Focus on how weird it is that you connected with Cassius and Hawk without touching them.

My trembling increased.

Focus.

"Titus took me up to the balcony so I could see the sky," I forced out. "The ice men knew we were in the grotto and knew you'd been called away," I said to Sebastian.

God, I wanted to go back to that balcony and stare at that vast open expanse of blue. Maybe then I'd be able to figure out what I was feeling, why my magic could connect with them and tell me they were fine, how I'd so badly wanted to hurt Deaglan, and why I couldn't stop being afraid. I was so tired of being afraid.

"How many people could have known you weren't in the grotto?" Hawk asked.

"Depending on who it is and how powerful they are they could have placed a scrying spell outside the grotto doors." Sebastian ran a hand over his spikey white and silver hair. "But that would mean they've got some serious power. It would take a lot to hide something like that from me."

Hawk's eyes narrowed.

"Even in my weakened condition," Sebastian said, meeting his gaze. "I need to check out the grotto and the balcony and then maybe poke around court. If at all possible, I'd like to avoid being caught off guard when we leave." The muscles in his jaw flexed. "Especially with Deaglan around."

My chest tightened at his words, partly in fear but mostly in anger for myself, Titus, and Sebastian. Sebastian's mother had said he'd just needed time to get over that silly business with Enowen, but from the sound of it, the situation had been anything but silly. I already knew Deaglan had confessed to seducing her, but I hadn't realized Sebastian was going to marry her and then they'd tried to kill him. It made me angry to think of how horrible that must have been.

The court wind gusted around me, blowing my hair back from my face.

"I won't let him touch you," Sebastian promised, mistaking the wind's reaction for just fear.

"None of us will," Hawk added.

"Cassius," Sebastian said as he stood, "will you have my back? Your power is more deadly than Hawk's and from the look of Titus, those ice men weren't an easy fight."

Cassius glanced at me and the smoke billowing around him thickened. Was he actually considering staying instead of going out and hunting down whoever had attacked me? I wasn't sure if I should be surprised that he wanted to stay or be worried that he thought I was in so much danger he felt he needed to.

"The Winter Court won't let anyone past that door who wants to hurt her," Sebastian said.

The light in Cassius's eyes flared. "Because your mother is so desperate for you to have an heir?"

"No, because it likes her. It knocked Deaglan on his ass to protect her."

Cassius opened his mouth and Sebastian raised a hand, silencing him.

"And I have no idea why, so don't bother asking." But something flickered across Sebastian's expression. He might not know for sure, but he was definitely working on a theory.

I started to rise and Sebastian held out his hand, offering to steady me. Without thought, I accepted his offer, savoring the feel of his cool skin against mine and remembering his fingers roaming my body, bringing me pleasure.

Funny how just a few days ago I'd adamantly refused his help even though I'd nearly drained myself saving Titus's life. Now I embraced the simple gesture, craved it, and didn't care if it made me look weak. He'd already seen me at my worst. They all had. I couldn't look weaker if I tried, and I selfishly wanted to feel his touch again.

A hint of a wicked smile tugged at Sebastian's lips, his victory at getting me to accept his help lighting his eyes, then his gaze jumped past me to Cassius, and he slid his hand out from mine. "Let's get Titus in a bed first," he said.

Cassius and Hawk carried Titus and laid him on a cot in the servant's room. Then Cassius and Sebastian left to try to find whoever had attacked me, while Hawk left to quickly check the hall for any extra spells.

I went to the bathroom to heal and clean my wounds, grabbed a small cloth from a shelf between the tub and the shower, and held it under the sink's tap — having managed to figure out earlier that holding something under the tap made the water run.

A stunned, pale, wide-eyed version of myself stared back at me in the mirror above the sink. My hair was a wild, wind-blown mess, and my robe was on the verge of falling open, revealing a shocking amount of cleavage and an indecent display of inner thighs.

And I didn't want to think about the kind of show I could have given the guys when I'd rushed to help Sebastian and Titus. Had they seen it all? How had I not noticed that the guys might have gotten a view of everything?

Because I was in shock and desperate not to think about the attack, not about Deaglan, Titus, or the ice men.

I hadn't even been able to fly away. Those ice men had grabbed me and would have killed me if Titus hadn't pulled them off me.

My pulse pounded.

Deaglan would have hurt me worse than Balwyrdan and then given me to his demon-vampire to feed.

Don't think about it. Just don't think about it.

I pushed my magic away from my hands and into my body, something I should have done long before now. The cut in my thigh was deep and so was one of the cuts on my calves, and I concentrated on flooding those injuries with power and sealing the wounds shut.

But I couldn't stop thinking about Deaglan, about how scared I was, how much I'd wanted to hurt him, wanted to fight back, and how satisfied I'd been when the Winter Court had cut him with ice shards and knocked him and his demon-vampire to the floor.

My magic might force me to heal anyone and everyone regardless of who they were, but that didn't mean I'd lost my angelic desire for justice. Yes, my desire for order and goodness and justice wasn't nearly as strong as most angels. Compared to Cassius it was almost non-existent. But it was still there, and Deaglan deserved more than just being knocked down for imprisoning Titus and trying to kill Sebastian.

A shiver swept down my spine and I hugged myself.

Except when I left the Winter Court, I didn't know if I'd be able to keep its magic, and I wouldn't be able to use it fully, not to hurt Deaglan the way I wanted. My healing magic would kick in and force me to heal him.

I bit back a scream. It wasn't fair.

And I was sick and tired of thinking that.

But I had no idea how to come to terms with that. I'd never be able to defend myself, let alone those I cared about. I'd always be dependent on someone else. All I could do was be around to pick up the pieces afterward, and even then, I could only heal the physical injuries.

"Hey," Hawk said, his seductive tenor sliding across my senses and drawing a very different kind of shudder.

My pulse stuttered and my gaze jumped to him.

He leaned in the doorway, his posture casual, confident, and radiating raw sexual energy. He was breathtaking. The hellfire in his unusual blue-gray eyes flickered, little more than embers but enough to show he wasn't holding back his power, and his complexion was back to normal — his magic finally having dealt with his hangover. I ached for him to step closer, to touch me, kiss me, and direct all his heated sensual magic toward me again.

"You okay?" he asked.

Please touch me, make me forget. Make me forget who I am.

Except I couldn't force out the words.

God, I was such a coward.

"I only got a few lacerations and I've already healed them." I tugged my robe closed, set my foot on the closed toilet lid, and wiped at the blood on my calf, but I couldn't get my hands to stop shaking.

"Not what I was talking about."

It wasn't. I knew that. He wanted to know how I was feeling. But I didn't want to talk about it, and for some reason, I couldn't say what I really wanted to say.

"There isn't anything I can do about it," I said, moving back to the sink, putting the cloth under the tap, and activating the stream of water.

"So you're just going to ignore it?" Hawk stepped up behind me, close but not touching, not even his hands on my arms.

Heat radiated from his body — his body temperature, like all demons, naturally higher than humans or other supers — and it seeped through my thin robe, bringing with it a seductive whisper of sensual magic, promising me everything I desired if I'd just speak up.

"Yes," I breathed, but I didn't know if I was answering his question or asking him to have sex with me.

With his magic and his body, he could make me forget everything: the look in Deaglan's eyes, the look in Balwyrdan's eyes, and the fury building inside me that I needed someone's help to find justice. His caress and kiss, his body against mine, and the thrum of his life force against my senses could take me away, free me, even if it was for just a moment.

What was I so afraid of? I'd already asked him to satisfy me before. He'd already seen me at my absolute worst and still wanted to sleep with me.

So what if he sees you like Cassius does, weak and helpless? So what if you're just using him?

I met his gaze in the mirror, my pulse pounding with the irrational fear that he'd reject me. He was an incubus. He survived on sex and he'd already made it clear he wasn't afraid of Cassius.

"Make love to me." *Please. Make me forget.* I said the words in a rush, knowing if I didn't blurt it out, I never would.

AMIAH

The hellfire in Hawk's eyes flared and I held my breath, anticipating his rejection, but he didn't even hesitate, didn't have to think about my request. He drew closer, brushed my hair aside, and pressed a tender kiss to the divot behind my ear. A soft tendril of seductive magic unfurled from his lips and curled down my neck, sending a shiver of need racing to my core.

"Anytime. Anywhere," he murmured against my suddenly sensitive skin.

Thank goodness.

I released a shuddering breath and leaned into him, savoring the feel of his strong body supporting me and the hard proof of his desire pressed against the small of my back.

Just focus on the sensations, not the loss of control.

"Tell me what you like," he murmured against my skin.

"I don't know." My eyes fluttered closed and I tipped my head back, offering him better access to my neck. I certainly liked it when he kissed my neck and when he let his power slide into me.

"You don't know?" He hooked his index fingers into the neck of my robe and slowly followed the fabric over my collarbone, his knuckles grazing my skin, inching closer and closer to my nipples.

I liked that too.

"Or you don't want to admit it?" he asked.

Which was also the truth.

"I—" My breath picked up with a mix of desire and fear. I didn't want to think, not about what I did or didn't like or anything else. I didn't *know* what I liked. I knew from all the things I'd researched what intrigued me but I'd barely experienced any of them. I couldn't say for certain if it felt good or not until I tried it. And now my mind was spinning, worrying about wanting him and about being inexperienced.

"I won't laugh at you or judge you."

"I—" Embarrassment heated my cheeks.

Stop thinking. Just answer his question and get back to not thinking.

"Hey." He hooked a finger under my chin and urged me to look at him. "Whatever it is, I'm into it."

"It's—" *Jeez, just tell him. He'll figure it out soon enough anyway.* I squeezed my eyes shut, unable to meet his gaze while I made my confession. "Sebastian was my first."

"That's okay," he said. "I just didn't realize you were that young."

"I'm not. I'm over a hundred. I was—" My throat tightened. I was a naive fool thinking my mating brand was wonderful and beautiful and not realizing it was a life sentence. "I'd made a vow. I'd thought I was waiting for someone."

"For Sebastian?" he asked, surprised.

"No."

"Fuck." He tensed, my one word chilling his seductive magic leaving me aching and cold. "I pushed you over the edge to do something you didn't want to do, didn't I? That's why you freaked out after you two had sex."

He started to step back, but I grabbed his hand, still tauntingly close to my nipple, and captured it against my chest, not allowing him to step away. "It's okay."

Please, don't reject me.

"No, it's not."

I caught his gaze in the mirror again and tried to will him to understand how desperately I needed to forget, to not think, to just *feel*. "I didn't have intercourse with Sebastian because of your power. You just gave me the push I needed."

"But then I—"

"Made me orgasm again with your hand and promised me more later?" The muscles in my core trembled at the memory of his fingers sliding into me. I wanted to go back to that moment and chase after him instead of running up to the roof. Everything would have been different if I'd just taken him up on his offer for the both of us to go into Sebastian's bedroom and finish what had been started.

"I didn't realize— You wanted it so badly your desire hurt."

It hurt now. Couldn't he feel it?

Make me forget. Make me feel good.

"I thought you'd just gone without for too long," he said.

"I had." My whole life. "Hawk, I'm done waiting and holding back. I was done before I'd decided to sleep with Sebastian. I want to have sex with you. I want to feel good with someone, connect with someone."

The hellfire in his eyes flared and he offered me a soft, sad smile. "You know I can't do a relationship."

"Which is why you're perfect," I said. A bitter huff escaped my lips before I could stop it. "It was why Sebastian was perfect until he decided it was too dangerous to risk upsetting Cassius." Although it probably hadn't helped that I'd run from his bed right after having intercourse.

"So that's his problem." Hawk wrapped his free hand around my waist and drew me tight against his chest. "The idiot."

His sensual magic unfurled again between my thighs, and I throbbed with the need that hadn't even gotten close to being satisfied with that one moment with Sebastian. Hawk had merely teased me with that gentle orgasm when I'd woken in bed with him, and since then I'd had his power and the Winter Court's aphrodisiac swelling inside me. I needed a release, from my desire and worry and fear, from everything.

And Hawk was the perfect man to give it to me.

"Just to be clear," I said, my voice breathy, "I'm using you."

He drew his hand free from my grip and teased his thumb over my nipple. It was a barely-there brush over the thin fabric of my robe but it shot hot, sultry desire straight to my core and made his hellfire blaze stronger. "Yeah, because I get absolutely nothing out of this."

His hand traveled down my body to the belt holding my robe together, his touch light and slow, building the ache inside me, so different from the sex I'd had with Sebastian.

That had been wild, unrestrained, both of us desperate and aching for release. This was just as intense and made my pulse race just as quickly, but Hawk was taking his time to build a throbbing tension inside me. He was in complete control, his hands and mouth and magic in command of my desire, and that should have made me panic. If he was in control, I wasn't. But for some reason, knowing I didn't have to be in control relaxed me. I could just let go, just feel and not worry. I didn't know why I trusted Hawk, but I did, and I knew he was going to make me forget everything and feel good. He already was.

He undid the knot on my belt. My robe slid open, exposing the curls at the crux between my thighs, my still almost invisible sleeping mating brand curling over my left hip, and even more cleavage — the robe catching on my taut nipples instead of falling completely open.

With a low hum of pleasure, his gaze stroked down my body's reflection in the mirror, filled with a heated need that made the muscles in my core clench.

God, he could make me come with just a look. I wanted him to make me come with a look. In his eyes, just for this moment, I wasn't the weak angel who couldn't defend herself. I was beautiful, perfect, and desired. It was the same look Sebastian had given me when he'd first undressed me and I wondered if this was how all men looked at a woman before they made love to her. It had to be, because I wasn't special and neither man loved me.

I pushed that thought aside. I didn't care if Hawk looked at every woman like this. Every woman *deserved* to be looked at like this. And right now I was going to wrap the feeling around my heart and pretend the look was for me and me alone.

The hellfire in Hawk's eyes sparked and his expression grew hotter. His gaze, along with his hand, stroked slowly, sensually back up my body, inflaming my sensitive skin and making my breath pick up. He brushed aside the edge of my robe and kneaded my breast while his other slid over my brand, his fingers tracing the seam between my thigh and torso, heading toward my inner thigh.

My breath caught, but I had no idea if it was at the intensity of his look, his teasing touch, or the chance that he'd noticed my brand.

"So beautiful," he murmured, releasing my breast to slide the robe off my shoulders and let the silky fabric pool at our feet,

His lips pressed back against my neck as his fingers dipped into my curls and brushed my already slick folds with a whisper of a touch that made my desire twist tighter.

Oh, yes. This was what I wanted.

"Lace your fingers behind my neck, give me your lips, and let me make you feel good."

I obeyed, sliding my fingers through his soft sandy blond hair at the nape of his neck and turning my head just enough to kiss him.

The kiss was slow, sensual, and released a bone-melting curl of power inside me, stronger than before. It swelled around my heart, making my breath pick up again, which pushed my breast against his palm. Then it sank lower, filling me with sultry, breathtaking need.

I moaned, aching for more, for his finger to find my clit, for his hand on my breast to tighten. I knew he wanted me. His erection pressed hard against me, and his breath had gotten faster too. But he continued to tease me, his touch light, his slick fingers close but never hitting the right spot, building my need until I was squirming against him, every nerve throbbing in anticipation.

Oh, yes. My fear had vanished. All thoughts had vanished. There was only his touch, the heat and strength of his body, and the thrum of his life force pulsing against my senses. Each caress twisted my desire tighter, drawing me closer and closer to climax.

Then he brushed my clit. I gasped and my muscles clamped tight, the wave of an orgasm starting to form, but his power swelled. It yanked me back to teeter once again on the edge, trembling and ready — God more than ready — my need tight, promising a shattering release that I'd only just caught a glimmer of.

"Not yet," he said against my lips, brushing my clit again, making me shudder, still at the edge, desperate for release and yet loving the pressure continuing to build inside me.

"I didn't know you could stop an orgasm like that," I breathed. Of course, I hadn't thought I'd ever have sex with an incubus, so I hadn't spent a lot of time researching their sexual powers.

"I usually don't. I think it's cruel, but that was too fast. You deserve more than just a little flick." He pushed two fingers inside me and pressed his thumb against my clit.

"Oh, wow," I moaned, my eyelids fluttering shut at the feel of him slowly invading me. "Pretty sure you've already given me more than just a flick."

"Yeah, but this is better." His grip on my breast tightened and he rubbed his thumb over that sensitive bundle of nerves, picking up speed as his fingers, pumping in and out of me, picked up speed as well.

My breath grew ragged and my need twisted tighter and tighter until I couldn't stand it any longer.

I crashed over the edge again, crying out, my muscles clamping around his fingers. My orgasm hit me hard. I didn't even need more of his magic for stars to flash behind my lids. It roared through me, a giant wave of sensation that scattered my thoughts and made my knees weak.

Hawk held me tight, his fingers buried inside me as I rode the wave, staying put until I was completely satiated, then he picked me up, took me into the bedroom, and laid me on the bed.

I squirmed, savoring the bliss radiating through me and the feel of the soft covers against my hyper-sensitive skin. This was exactly what I needed. I felt so good, so sexy. God, I wanted more. I wanted to feel like this all the time.

He smiled at me, a breathtaking grin of pure joy, and shrugged out of his tunic, showing me the gorgeous expanse of his muscular chest.

My pulse stuttered. "*Now* you're getting undressed? I can barely move."

His smile turned wicked, sending an aftershock of my climax trembling through me and making my eyes roll back in pleasure.

"I'd be a piss poor incubus if you only got one orgasm." He pushed his pants off his narrow hips, freeing his erection, and my pulse stalled completely. I hadn't imagined his size when I'd seen him in the healing grotto... and it was much more impressive fully engorged.

With a groan, he settled on the bed beside me. He captured my lips in a deep kiss, stealing all breath and thought and worry that I wouldn't be up for more, and added fuel to a desire that hadn't even been close to going out from my first orgasm. I kissed him back, tangled my fingers in his hair, and rubbed my thumbs against the base of his horns.

His breath quickened and his erection pressed against my hip, hot against my mating brand. He kneaded and pinched my nipples back into aching peaks before nudging my legs apart with his knee, settling one leg between my thighs, and teasing his fingers through my folds.

Oh, wow. I arched into his hand, moaning into his mouth, aching for him to fill me, bring me to the edge of pleasure and send me soaring again.

His sensual magic trickled from his lips into my cells, and he moved his other knee between my thighs, his erection pressed against my mound.

My pulse pounded, anticipation making my muscle clench.

But instead of entering me, he grabbed my hips and rolled, pulling me up to straddle him.

"I *gave* you pleasure in the bathroom," he said. "Now I want you to *take* it, be in control."

I stared at him stunned for a second. I didn't know how. I mean academically I *knew* how, but there was a difference between reading and doing. And yet the only way to know was to try.

I dropped my gaze to his erection nestled against my curls, thick and hard with a drop of pre-ejaculate glistening on his tip, and my pulse picked up. He was larger than Sebastian and Sebastian had been a tight fit.

"You're good and wet, and I promise I won't let it hurt." He set his hands on my hips, urging me to rise up. "Just take it slow."

I can do this. God, I want to do this, need to do it.

I rose and he wrapped his fingers around his shaft, running his hand down its length and leaving a glistening slick substance.

"Did you just—?"

"Add a little extra lube just in case," he said, aligning himself with my opening. "You really don't know much about incubi, do you?" He raised his hips just enough to press his tip against me and brushed his thumb over my clit.

I shuddered, and he released a soft heat inside me and gently urged me down to slowly impale myself on his shaft, his magic turning the pain of stretching to accommodate him into a heart-racing pleasure. Each fraction of an inch slid against already heightened nerve endings, rebuilding my desire along with a growing awareness of his life force, something I hadn't noticed with Sebastian, although at the time I'd likely been too distracted. It was as if having him inside me heightened my senses, making my pulse throb in time with his.

I was panting with need by the time I'd reached his base, every nerve in my core thrumming— No every cell in my whole body thrumming. God, this felt so good.

Hawk's grip on my hips tightened and his breath hitched. "Holy hell."

I tensed. "Good hell?"

"Oh, yeah, gorgeous," he purred, as his hellfire blazed and his seductive magic swelled inside me. "Fuck yeah. Now let's figure out what feels good for you, what angle, what pace, what motion."

He urged me into a slow rocking motion, his hands resting lightly on my hips just to steady me and giving me full control. For a moment it was hard to concentrate on anything but the feel of him inside me, his sultry magic sliding through me, and his life force heightening all of it. It felt amazing just as it was, then I accidentally shifted and caught a sliver of what it *could* feel like, what it was *supposed* to feel like.

"Oh," I breathed, the sudden brush of amazing sensation making me tremble.

"Exactly." Hawk's face lit up with masculine satisfaction, and he shifted my angle bringing me back to the position that flooded me with sensation.

The feelings swelled from my core and entwined with Hawk's power, filling me with pulsing, aching bliss. He raised his hips in time with my rocking, and I tipped my head back and closed my eyes, giving in to all of it, letting my body's natural instinct take over. It was overwhelming and amazing and so much more than I'd ever expected.

My desire surged into an urgency, making my heart pound and my breath ragged. I clung to Hawk's wrists to keep my balance, moaning and panting, holding on for dear life as the promise of an amazing climax surged inside me.

"Oh, Amiah," he groaned, and I glanced down at him.

His gaze captured mine and for a second there was a softness to the desire burning in his eyes, an awe… that I couldn't possibly have seen because I wasn't anything he hadn't already experienced before.

Then he rubbed his thumb over my clit with strong fast circles, ratcheting up the sensations beyond what I thought possible until every muscle in my body contracted with a full-body orgasm. Hawk sat up and captured my mouth, muffling my scream of pleasure and groaning his own, as bliss tore through every cell in my body. I was on fire again from Hawk's magic, but this time it felt amazing, crashing through me over and over again, sending me spinning, my essence thrumming.

Oh.

Oh my.

There weren't words to explain how I felt.

I was totally and utterly ruined for other men.

Sebastian had been amazing and now so had Hawk, and I doubted every man could make me feel like this.

AMIAH

"Hey, Amiah," Hawk murmured, brushing hair out of my face, his fingers sending rippling aftershocks rushing through me.

I cracked open my eyes and realized I lay on Hawk's chest with his arms wrapped around me. He was still inside me and I could feel the throb of his rapid pulse against my cheek and between my thighs.

"When did we lie back?"

"When you passed out," he said.

"I passed out?"

"Also common with my magic," he said with a chuckle. "Way back when, it used to be a defense mechanism so we could escape after feeding."

"And the magical formation of lubricant?"

"So we can get the best possible meal with anyone." He slid a hand down to cup my rear, his implication clear he meant anal sex which sent more shivering aftershocks rushing through me as well as a whisper of renewed desire.

Oh my! I guess that interested me as well, especially if it went with the suggested *ménage à trois*.

But right now it didn't interest me enough to move and leave Hawk's embrace.

No, right here and now is perfect. My naked body was pressed against his with his life force strong and sure, steadying my soul.

Hawk moaned and drew his hand away from my rear. "I really want to stay here, make you come again, but Sebastian and Cassius are coming closer. Or at least two people with the same frustrated sexual energy, and I suspect you're not ready to tell them about this."

My throat tightened. He was right. I shouldn't feel bad about having consensual sex with Hawk, and yet I wasn't ready to deal with everything that came with everyone knowing that I'd slept with him—

No, that wasn't true. It wasn't everyone, it was just Cassius. I wasn't ready to deal with his overbearing protectiveness when he learned what I'd done.

"Hawk, I—"

He shifted me to his side, sliding out of me but still holding me tight, and met my gaze. The hellfire in his eyes flickered in a mesmerizing dance, making my heart race. "It doesn't bother me if you don't want them to know about this—" He flashed me a wicked smile. "About us."

"Us?" That one word filled me with such hope. It implied there was more to our... arrangement than just this one time. With him, I could explore my desires without fear of my soul bond awakening or him wanting a committed relationship.

"Of course." He captured my lips with a breathtaking kiss. "For as long as you want me. Even after this mess is over."

"Pretty sure you have more experienced lovers you can turn to once we get back to the mortal realm."

"Silly angel." He rolled his eyes at me. "That doesn't mean I still can't give you what you desire until you meet someone you want to settle down with."

"But I'm—"

"Gorgeous, amazing, determined, strong?"

"Inexperienced."

"We can fix that." The hellfire in his eyes flared and a curl of sensual magic swelled inside me. "We've already started. Get over your worry. I said I'd make love to you anytime and anywhere and I meant it." He kissed me again just as passionately as before, his embrace tightening and his erection pressing hard against my thigh.

Oh, yes. No—

Wait a minute...

He pulled back with a groan. "If you don't want Sebastian and Cassius to see me coming out of your bedroom, I have to go."

"Yes... of course..." I said, trying to focus my scattered thoughts.

He pulled his pants back on — the loose fabric doing nothing to hide his erection — and grabbed his tunic. With another strange, soft look, very much like the look he'd had when he'd said my name during sex, he left.

I stared at the ceiling, my lips tingling from his kiss, my body aching to have him fill me again, and only a slight heat radiating from my mating brand. Hawk wasn't my soul mate, and sex with him had been amazing. God, what would it be like to have both Hawk and Sebastian? I wasn't sure I'd be able to handle that.

And given how Sebastian was keeping his distance, that wasn't going to happen at all.

I got out of bed and — on wobbly legs that brought a smile to my face... because I'd had sex with Hawk! — took a quick shower.

I was putting on a new robe, frustrated that the only thing for me to wear were robes when the guys got pants and tunics, when I heard them talking in the living room.

"I don't like that we don't have a clue who was behind the attack," Cassius said as I opened the bedroom door.

His gaze jumped to me and the light in his eyes flared, the intensity in his look stealing my breath. He was tense, the tendons in his neck standing up, but there wasn't a hint of smoke curling around him which meant he was trying to hold it all in.

Sebastian's attention also jumped to me, and for a second the look in his eyes was just as intense as Cassius's with an expression I couldn't read, then he yanked his gaze away and dropped onto the couch, stretching out to take up all the seats like a spoiled house cat. "I don't like it either, but it is what it is."

"Not acceptable," Cassius growled.

"What's not acceptable?" Hawk asked, coming out of the guy's bedroom with wet hair and wearing just his pants.

Water dripped from his jaw-length locks and trailed over a sculpted pec.

My pulse stalled— goodness, everything stalled and the memory of what we'd just done flooded me, heating my face.

"Pull it back, incubus," Cassius snapped. "She deserves to be a part of figuring out what we're doing, not enthralled by your magic."

Hawk winked at me and shot Cassius a wicked smile. "Don't be jealous, Sparky, there's more than enough of me to go around."

"I don't want to sleep with you." Cassius pinched the bridge of his nose and the muscles in his jaw twitched. "Can you be serious for just a moment? Someone tried to kill Amiah and they're still out there."

"Someone is trying to kill both me *and* Sebastian," I corrected, taking the other chair and wishing Sebastian had ordered more food. Even though it had only been a few hours since I last eaten, I hadn't gotten nearly enough. A snack would be lovely. Ideally something that wasn't purple or bright blue.

Hawk's expression flashed from playful to serious. "You've got no clue who made the attempt?"

"No," Sebastian replied, "so we need to come up with a plan that involves leaving soon. I still need to conclude my business and get magical protection from the Wilds so I'm not incapacitated, but once that's done, even if my mother hasn't announced her party, we have to go."

"Will the Wilds kill you?" Cassius asked.

"No, but—"

"Then getting protection isn't worth risking Amiah's life by sticking around," Cassius said.

"Yes, it is. But I want to be ready to run the moment I've got it." Sebastian shot me a quick look and his gaze dipped to my left hip, making me suddenly hyperaware of the heat radiating from my brand. This wasn't about getting protection. This was about freeing me from my fate, a fate that I might have been able to ignore in all the pain and chaos, but one that was still coming my way.

I could be free before the day was done.

Free.

My pulse pounded and I tried to keep my expression calm.

"Why don't I wake Titus and we'll figure out a plan first," Hawk said.

"Don't." Sebastian jerked up. "Not until we know what we're doing. We need to give him something he can focus his rage on or he won't be able to control his beast."

"We need a contingency plan for if he loses control." Cassius paced to the front door and turned to come back.

"If he fully loses it, he'll shift and we'll be fucked," Sebastian said. "My mother will lock the court up so tightly no one will be able to get out."

"Hawk, are you strong enough to carry him by yourself?" Cassius asked.

"Yeah, but he'll seriously slow me down." Hawk slid into one of the chairs, oozing heart-stopping sensuality and I fought to not stare at him.

Moments ago I'd had all that sensuality, all that desire, focused on me and it had felt amazing... and not what I was supposed to be thinking about.

Jeez.

Except if I wasn't thinking about sex with Hawk, I was thinking about the heat in my brand.

I wrenched my attention to Cassius who had paced to the back wall and was making another pass to the front door.

"I'll try to keep his beast calm, but I don't know if I can keep it at bay." I turned my attention to Sebastian. "I couldn't do it before and you had to cast your sleep spell on him."

"The sleep spell and carrying him is the best option," Cassius said. "I don't want you endangering yourself by getting close if his beast takes over and he loses it."

"Hey, maybe we'll get lucky and we won't have to worry about it," Hawk said, but from his expression, he didn't believe that we would.

"Yeah," Sebastian huffed, "because we've had the best luck so far."

"It is what it is, we'll deal with it," Cassius said. "Okay—"

Someone knocked on the door to the hall.

Cassius stiffened and glared at it.

"If they mean Amiah danger, they won't be able to get in," Sebastian said as he stood, his body tense.

"How sure are you?" Hawk asked, also standing.

The door opened, revealing an ice maid carrying a large silver platter with a jug of something pale yellow, and a plate with fruit, cheese, rolls, and cold cuts. All of it looked very mundane and mortal, just like what I'd been wishing for. Behind her followed another maid with a platter of glasses, plates, and cutlery.

"More food?" Cassius demanded. "Really? Didn't we just eat a few hours ago?"

"Hey." Sebastian raised his hands in defense. "I didn't request it."

The ice maids set the platters on the coffee table, curtsied, and scurried out.

Hawk's eyes narrowed. "So your mother sent it?"

"Guess so," Sebastian said, giving me a strange look then turning his attention to the food. "It's safe."

I filled up a plate with food and dug in, unable to stop thinking about being free and the achy heat building in my hip... because it wasn't building, that was just my imagination because my attention was focused on it.

As I ate, the guys talked about what they'd learned while Sebastian and I had been visiting the healing grotto, what the security was like, and what our first and second choice exits out of the Winter Court were. The biggest problem was the ice guards. Sebastian didn't know if we'd be able to lose them — something that would have been easier to do during the party — so we were going to have to make a run for it and pray we could get out before the Winter Queen noticed her guards were damaged and backup arrived.

"It'll be tight, but if we make our move by the silver sitting room, they shouldn't be expecting anything and we'll have time to get out," Sebastian said.

"That's still four long halls from our closest way out," Cassius replied. "We should do it closer to the exit."

"Any closer and they'll get suspicious and then it won't be a matter of catching them off guard, we'll have to actually fight them," Sebastian said. "We might have a reason to go to the silver sitting room, but not farther."

"Fine." Cassius rubbed his face. "Go deal with whatever it is you have to deal with and let's go."

Sebastian glanced at me, making my pulse pick up, as I bit into a sweet roll with white frosting on top.

Soon. Soon. But—

Was he going to tell Cassius the truth? How was he going to get us out of the suite without anyone else knowing?

A heavy knot formed in my stomach. He wasn't. I was going to have to accept that. It'd be safer if all the guys came with us. They'd know the truth, but at least I'd be free. Free to choose my destiny, be in control of my life, and to fall in love like everyone else.

Soon.

"Yeah, about that..." Sebastian said.

The light in Cassius's eyes flared. "Bane?" he said, his voice dark with warning.

"Remember when we went searching for evidence of whoever attacked Amiah and Titus and no one attacked us?"

"No," Cassius said. "Whatever you want. No."

"It'll be fine. I promise," Sebastian insisted.

"Hey man," Hawk said, "even I think this is a bad idea and you haven't even said anything yet."

"How about we hear him out." I set the rest of my roll on my plate and licked frosting from my index finger, trying to look calm and not reveal the panic racing inside me. This was it. Sebastian needed to tell Cassius I had to go with him and he was going to have to explain why.

I could do this. I could handle it if it meant I was free.

I could. Really.

Hawk's hellfire flared and his lips quirked, sending a shiver of desire racing through me, while the muscles in Cassius's jaw flexed.

Hunh?

Then realization hit me. They, along with Sebastian, were watching me suck the frosting from my finger.

Really? All of them? Hawk's power must still have been influencing them.

I jerked my finger away from my mouth and clutched my hands in my lap, determined to hide my trembling.

Sebastian raised an eyebrow at me, a hint of his wicked smile tugging at the corner of his lips. "The deal to get protection from the Wilds is that I introduce Amiah to Karthick, and we come alone."

My thoughts stuttered. He'd lied.

Smoke erupted from Cassius's hands. "No."

"I'll protect her," Sebastian huffed. "And so will the court."

Was it really safe for us to leave the suite alone? Someone was trying to kill both of us.

And yet I couldn't deny the desperate hope twisting inside me that I could be free and no one would ever know.

"Absolutely not." Fire snapped up Cassius's forearms and with a growl, he yanked both it and his smoke back under his skin.

I sat forward, my pulse racing, praying this lie would actually work — which was completely out of character for me. It didn't even bother me that Sebastian was lying even if it wasn't logical to go knowingly into danger. But the voice inside me screamed that I had to be free, above everything else, that I couldn't wait any longer, and it was stronger than my need to be honest and any common sense I still had left.

If my brand was gone, I could allow myself to look at Cassius as more than just a friend. I could look at anyone I wanted. I could have a committed relationship if that was what I desired.

I glanced at Hawk.

Or I could wait. But it would finally be my choice.

"How important is it for you to be protected from the Wilds?" I asked.

"He said it wouldn't kill him," Cassius growled.

But Sebastian had also said when we'd been facing off against Deaglan and his demon-vampire that when he'd been left to die in the Wilds Faerie had ripped its magic out of him. There were a lot of painful degrees between healthy and dead, and this sounded like something I couldn't heal.

"If my mother chases after us, you don't want to be carrying both Titus and me," Sebastian replied, never looking away from Cassius even though he was answering my question. "I swear, I'll keep her safe."

Cassius's eyes narrowed.

I had to put a stop to this. Yes, I should be smart and not go, or I should confess to Cassius the truth. But that would become another fight and there might not be another chance anytime soon to have my brand removed.

"It's not your decision to make," I said, setting my plate on the coffee table and standing. "Sebastian needs this protection. All I have to do is go, protected by the court, Sebastian, and his mother's constructs."

"There are people trying to kill you." Cassius grabbed my wrist and I glared at him, my heart pounding.

"And unless they're listening in on us right now, they don't know exactly what we're doing." I dropped my gaze to his hand then back up to his eyes and raised my chin, daring him to keep holding me. "We can't afford to have both Titus and Sebastian out of commission. That would mean you and Hawk would be carrying them and I'd be the only one with free hands. Do you expect me to fight the Winter Queen's men by myself?"

The light in Cassius's eyes flared. "Amiah—"

"Let me go." I tried not to sound like I was begging even though everything within me was. I had to do this, had to be free, and I was this close to doing it without Cassius's judgment.

And really! This was my life, my choice. He had a right to express his feelings, but not to tell me what to do, even if I was always going to be the weak pathetic angel he'd rescued all those years ago.

"Fine." Cassius jerked away and fire crackled over his hands.

"Great. Now that we have your permission," Sebastian said, his tone dripping with sarcasm as he stood and strode to the door. "If we're in trouble, the Winter Court will tell you, just like it told you to meet us back here after the first attack."

"That doesn't make me feel better," Cassius said.

Hawk sat forward and brushed his index finger against mine, just a whisper of flesh against flesh that sent a shiver of desire racing through me. His hellfire flared and a hint of that soft strange smile swept across his expression again then vanished, the moment so quick I wasn't sure I'd actually seen it.

"We won't be long." Sebastian opened the door, revealing the two large ice guards standing at attention in the hall.

I hurried out, Sebastian right beside me, and we headed down the hall — the ice guards falling into step a dozen feet behind us.

"Thank you," I said, keeping my voice low.

"Doing it for myself, remember? Sparky needs to get laid."

AMIAH

Sebastian led me down long, white, shimmering hall after long, white, shimmering hall without a window in sight until we reached an enormous arch with two towering statues of the Winter Queen standing guard on either side. Each statue held a massive sword, its point on the ground and its pommel reaching her waist, and each wore an intricate crown larger and more detailed than what I'd seen her wearing in the throne room when we'd first arrived.

Beyond lay a thirty-foot stretch of perfect untouched snow, glittering in the late afternoon sunshine, along with a vast expanse of cloudless sky framed by snowy mountain peaks and a forest made of both deciduous and evergreen trees as well as shimmering ice trees mimicking their live counterparts.

I hesitated at the threshold as a frozen wind ruffled through my robe, reminding me that was all I wore and that I didn't have shoes. This was the first time I'd actually felt the cold in the Winter Court, and walking in the snow was going to be painful. I'd have to monitor my feet carefully to watch for frostbite. But I could heal that and it was worth the use of my magic to be free.

Soon. Soon.

Except before I could grit my teeth and step into the snow, Sebastian swept me into his arms.

I tensed, habit making me ready to argue that I could make it without his help, but shoved aside the urge to say anything. It was safer for my feet if he carried me. He knew that, I knew that, and him holding me didn't mean anything... no matter how much I loved the feel of his arms around me.

It was just touch I wanted, and not specifically his. That was all.

Still, I relaxed into his embrace, savoring the feel of being pressed against his muscular chest, his arms wrapped around me, and the heat radiating from his body — which was odd since he was usually on the cool end of the body-temperature spectrum.

"We really need to get you some real clothes," he said, striding toward the forest, his footsteps crunching in the snow.

"Ideally before we leave," I replied.

"Yeah," he said, his voice gruff. "Although no clothes might speed things up between you and Cassius."

Given how Cassius had reacted to me in the healing grotto I wasn't so sure about that. He'd tried his hardest not to look at me or touch me, and I, unlike Sebastian, wasn't going to assume that was because he wanted me.

Behind us, the ice guards took up position at the archway and stared at us as Sebastian drew farther away.

"They aren't following us." And I hadn't heard Sebastian order them to stay behind like he had every time we'd gone into the healing grotto.

"They can't. The Winter Forest is sacred. The court only allows a select few to enter." Sebastian's grip tightened and his pulse under my ear beat a little faster. "But the Winter Court likes you, so it was safe to assume you'd be on the approved entry list."

"Except you didn't know the court liked me until after you had your first meeting with Karthick. What would have happened if I wasn't?" I asked, shivering as the cold seeped into my skin and making me even more aware of the warmth in my not-yet-awakened brand.

"You would have hit a magical barrier. Which would have been awkward with me holding you. But you are and this is the most discreet place for this meeting."

He stepped into the shade of the trees, making my heart sink a little bit as branches partially obscured most of the sky, and headed down a path, its edges marked with little snowbanks. Sunlight streamed through the trees' naked limbs and shimmered in ice branches and the air grew heavier and colder. It chilled the inside of my nose and throat as I inhaled and released as a glittering mist when I exhaled.

Sebastian's pulse slowed back to normal and he drew in a deep breath. The light radiating from his skin swelled and beat in time with his heart, and the rhythm of his life force thrummed against my senses. "God, I missed this."

"The forest?" This was the first time I'd seen him at ease in the Winter Court and it broke my heart to think he'd been forced away from his home for centuries.

I might have left the Realm of Celestial Light, but I could return whenever I wanted. There wasn't much for me in my native realm, my parents had passed away just before the war and my sister worked in Tokyo with her earth magic, calming earthquakes, but Sebastian had said he'd never wanted to return. He clearly didn't want the life that waited for him in Faerie and it was obvious that if he returned, he wouldn't be able to avoid it. Case in point, everything that had happened since we'd arrived.

"I miss the magic," Sebastian replied, his voice wistful, then he chuckled. "Poor Hawk needed a shield against all of it and I'm pretty sure I wasn't able to completely block it out for him."

"Because he's magically sensitive?"

"And not from Faerie. I'm sensitive too but my essence is a part of Faerie. More so because I'm a sorcerer and can directly connect with it. The mortal realm is like walking around at high altitude for me. I can survive, but the air is thin." He drew in another deep breath and released it with a heavy sigh, his breath misting, filled with glittering flecks of... well, I guessed magic even though I wasn't magically sensitive and shouldn't have been able to see it. "But the power is the only thing I miss about this place."

He rounded a corner and the trees opened up, revealing a large clearing with a shimmering ice gazebo in the center. The structure looked like it had been spun from delicate threads of ice, the pillars and roof woven in an intricate design, offering some shade, but also allowing in light — and more importantly letting me see more of the sky again. A dark blue rug and dozens of pillows in various shades of blue surrounded a small metal brazier radiating a glorious warmth, and the moment Sebastian set me on my feet, I dropped onto a pillow close to the brazier and held out my cold hands.

Sebastian sat beside me, within arm's reach but still a proper Cassius-amount of distance away as if he hadn't just carried me here.

I bit back a sigh. He'd made his choice and I had Hawk. I shouldn't be feeling upset that he'd suddenly decided to respect my boundaries... and yet I missed the Sebastian who used to tease me.

"Karthick should be here soon." Sebastian's full-body glow dimmed for a second and his expression hardened. "Then we can get the hell out of here and away from my mother and Deaglan."

Guilt twisted in my stomach. If it hadn't been for me, we would have left already and Sebastian wouldn't be risking his life. "You didn't have to insist on this."

Except if we'd left, I'd still be trapped with no guarantee that Sebastian would be able to find the time to free me before my brand fully formed.

"I don't know if I can remove your brand, but I know Karthick can. This is your best chance." He shrugged and turned his gaze skyward. "And maybe I wanted to return to the forest one last time before I left for good. I hadn't gotten a chance the last time."

I opened my mouth to tell him... I wasn't sure what. That I was sorry he'd been forced to abandon his home, that I was furious on his behalf that his friend and his fiancé had tried to kill him. But heavy footsteps crunched in the snow on the far side of the forest, drawing his attention away from me and I let the moment go.

A squat, bulky man marched out of the trees across from us on the other side of the clearing from where we'd entered. He wore heavy brown pants with the legs tucked into black boots that laced up to his knees, and a dark green shirt, the sleeves rolled up to his elbows revealing thick, muscular forearms. A bandolier with dozens of small pouches was slung across his broad chest and he wore a pale green knitted scarf, the only indication he noticed the cold.

"It's been a long time since the Winter Forest has had heat," he said, his voice low and gravelly. "Winter fae don't usually notice the cold even in the forest."

"The Forest doesn't usually allow a being from the Realm of Celestial Light to enter," Sebastian replied as the man sat a few feet away from me, putting me in the center between him and Sebastian. "And you knew it would, Karthick."

Karthick shrugged and held out his hands to the brazier like I did. "The Winter Forest was always going to welcome your wife, Seireadan."

Sebastian rolled his eyes at Karthick. "You know very well she's not and never will be."

Karthick turned a bright green gaze on me. "Because you belong to another."

"No." *Not yet. Never.*

Flecks of gold danced in his eyes, mesmerizing me, drawing me in, as if he could hold me captive, see into my soul, and pull out my secrets... like how I was still attracted to Sebastian and yet desired Hawk... and maybe Cassius... not to mention how I wanted a repeat of my kiss with Titus—

I jerked my attention away from him. It was just my pent-up sexual frustration making me desire all the guys around me. It wasn't that I desired them specifically. Just men.

And maybe if I told that to myself enough times, I'd believe it.

But even if I did like them, even if they were my soul mates, I didn't want a soul bond, not with any of them. Ever.

"I don't *belong* to anyone." I didn't want something that killed me or made me insane when my other half died, and I didn't want my death to mean someone else died or went insane. Neither option was acceptable. I couldn't believe I'd been foolish enough to think it had been, to have thought it was beautiful.

My pulse picked up, fear chilling me so deeply I barely felt the brazier's warmth, only the heat from my brand. The moment my soul bond awakened I'd be trapped. They'd be trapped. *Please. This might be my only chance.*

"Seireadan says you can remove it," I forced out, my voice frustratingly small, exposing my fears.

"If I do, you'll never be able to form a soul bond with anyone," he said. "You'll always feel as if a piece of your soul is missing."

A small part of me felt like a piece of my soul was already missing, but it wasn't enough for me to wish for a bond that made me fall in love with a stranger.

"An angelic mating brand is rare even among angels and no other species can form a bond like that," he pressed. "Are you absolutely sure? This can't be undone."

I raised my gaze to his and held it. "Everyone says the bond is beautiful, but I've seen the truth. I've seen it crawling on the floor desperate and I've seen it turn caution into recklessness."

My thoughts stuttered at that. I'd already become reckless. I'd done things that defied common sense, tried to do things on my own when it was more practical to ask for help, and had risked my life to save Hawk. I was already becoming the thing I feared, the thing I'd admonished others for.

I had to put a stop to it, regain some self-control — and I owed a certain someone a huge apology. It had been all too easy to make the choices I had to not burden those around me and to protect them even if it meant endangering myself.

"I want to choose who I fall in love with."

"You'll love your soul mate." Karthick's eyes narrowed.

"Because the bond will make me. Please." I'd beg if I had to. I'd do anything to be free of this fate. "I've had my choices taken away from me before. I can't do that again." My throat tightened. "I'll never let anyone have that kind of power over me again. Ever." I didn't know what I'd do if Karthick refused to remove my brand. I'd already lived through someone controlling me, using my natural compulsions against me. I couldn't do it again.

Never again. Never.

Sebastian pressed his hand against my back, the soft touch instantly steadying me, and I glanced at him. He had the same look I'd seen on Cassius's face when he'd rescued me from the faith healer. Concern— No, pity. Because I was weak. And in this case, I was. I couldn't fight or deny that truth. I wasn't strong enough to deal with an unwanted soul bond, and my heart raced at the thought of it forming.

"I've already told you I'll pay her debt," Sebastian said.

I stiffened. "Sebastian, no. It's my price to pay." I squared my shoulders and a gust of frozen wind swept through the gazebo making the fire in the brazier snap and flicker. "What do I owe?"

Karthick's eyes widened and he glanced over my shoulder at Sebastian. "So she does control the wind."

"You're a little late to the party," Sebastian groaned. "She used it to knock Deaglan on his ass, probably would have pummeled him into tomorrow too if I hadn't shown up and put it at ease."

"Yeah, and then he'd have just run a shadow blade through her heart. But boy I would have loved to have seen the look on that bastard's face." Karthick's gaze returned to mine and he held out his hand. "The price hasn't been decided. You'll owe me a favor."

My mouth went dry. What kind of a favor would a fae ask for? Would it be something I'd be able to do or would my natural compulsions prevent me?

I stared at his hand and instinctually my magic connected with him, again without me needing to touch him. It rushed through his body, a whisper of power, connecting with each cell and making my compulsive need to heal surge.

Every joint in his body was painfully inflamed, the cartilage and bone damaged from advanced osteoarthritis... and the cause was extreme old age. It was astounding he could walk. In fact, it was a miracle he was walking normally. And I wasn't even going to try to wrap my head around the thousands of years he'd been alive. I hadn't even met angels who'd been alive that long.

"You must be in such pain." I raised my hand above his heart but didn't touch him. "May I?"

"I'm not in pain," Karthick said as Sebastian grabbed my arm and pulled it back.

"Remove her brand and she'll heal you."

"It doesn't work that way," I said. The urge to heal Karthick twisted inside me. If he said no it would ease off. His condition wasn't serious so my magic hadn't locked onto him, but I had the power to help him, ease what had to be constant agony. If he'd let me, I'd help. No strings attached.

"It does in Faerie," Sebastian said. "Having a debt with Karthick isn't bad. There are worse fae to be indebted to, but you have something valuable to trade. It's a good deal."

"If I charged for my services you'd be up to your eyeballs in debt," I shot back. I'd already healed Sebastian a number of times, at one point draining myself to save him. "Would you like me to send you a bill?"

He glared back at me. "Go ahead. I'd be able to pay, no problem. Then I'll send you a bill for removing your brand."

"But you're not going to remove my brand, Karthick is." This was not the conversation I wanted to have, and we could argue about it after my brand was removed and we'd escaped the Winter Court. I jerked my attention back to Karthick, who wore an amused smile. "This won't take long."

"Those are her terms," Sebastian insisted. "I can vouch for her power."

"You'll still owe me for pulling you out of the Wilds," Karthick said. "And for protection against it now."

"I'd expect nothing less." Sebastian released my arm and I held my hand back up to Karthick's heart.

He nodded and I pressed my hand to his chest. My power rushed into my palm, glowing around my fingers, eager to take action, but I held it back, only allowing a thick thread to ooze into him, and not the sudden painful rush that it wanted. There was no need for this to be fast. While Sebastian and I didn't have all the time in the world, I could still take a little time so healing Karthick wouldn't be painful. He'd already suffered with pain for too long.

My magic slid through his body, seeping into each cell and clinging to his joints. I closed my eyes and let my power take over, maintaining just enough control to restrict its flow. It wove his swollen, damaged cartilage back together, starting at his feet and moving up.

I savored the feel of my power, thick and sticky like blood around my hands and teasing up my forearms, and yet always flowing out of me into someone else. I felt his body and life force strengthen and my soul sang with joy. I'd done that. I'd stopped his suffering. This was who I was. Always and forever.

With all the recent pain and fear and heartbreak, it felt as if I'd forgotten that, forgotten who I truly was, *what* I truly was. Life.

My magic surged, a great final swell healing the last of Karthick's arthritis, and dissipated from his body, releasing me.

With a sigh, I sat back and drew in a deep relaxed breath, my pulse steady and sure, my hands still glowing. The compulsion to heal him had vanished, less than half of my power had been used, and my soul felt steadier than it had been in days.

Karthick stared at his hand, his expression shocked, and he slowly curled his fingers into a fist. "I never thought I'd feel this way again."

"If you take care of yourself, you should be pain free for a long time." Perhaps another thousand years.

"Thank you." He cupped my hands between his and met my gaze, a soft warm smile making the gold in his eye sparkle.

"No, thank you. It was nice to just let go." *Accept who I'm supposed to be and not care about anything else.*

He barked a wry laugh. "That wasn't you letting go. I could sense you holding your power back, slowing it down."

"If I'd let go completely, you'd have been healed in a heartbeat and it would have been painful."

His smile melted away, replaced with a grim determination. "I won't be able to do the same for you. This will hurt and there's no way around it."

My throat tightened and my fear returned, his words chilling my joy. "I understand. I figured as much."

I'd already realized this was going to hurt. He was tearing out a piece of my soul. There wasn't any way it could be painless. But I could do this. I'd be free after this. Free.

"Take a breath and release it," Karthick said as he closed his eyes.

I obeyed, and warm, gentle power swelled over the back of my hand and up my arm. For a moment it was comforting. It billowed into my chest, gathering around my heart, and sank to my hip. But the moment it reached my brand it burst into sharp, stinging bites. First rushing along the complicated lines of the brand that trailed from the middle of my left thigh, over my hip and waist, and curled around my back to my bottom ribs, before surging back to my heart.

I gasped and Karthick's magic snapped, crushing around my heart and searing down my leg. It burned me from the inside out, liquid fire rushing through my veins, consuming me. Then Karthick's eyes opened, his green gaze captured mine, and blazing agony sliced into me.

My muscles seized and I screamed. Darkness swarmed my vision and I strained to stay conscious, strained to draw in each breath. But the pain kept growing, the fire tearing into me, ripping at the long, powerful threads of my bond woven into my soul.

The world lurched and dimmed. Karthick's power shredded my insides. Each breath grew into a battle, a fight against the pressure and pain, and I fought to stay conscious.

I could do this. I had to do this.

Please. God. I had to be free.

I clung to that hope, repeated it over and over again — *free, free* — desperate to shut my mind away from the pain. But I couldn't shut it out, couldn't do anything but sob as Karthick ripped a ragged tear in my soul... because that was what I wanted.

Then the fire vanished and Sebastian gathered me into his arms before I collapsed onto Karthick. I pressed my face into his tunic and cried, my body shaking with painful tremors.

"Is it done?" he asked.

"Check for yourself," Karthick replied.

Sebastian pressed a cool hand against my knee and his chilly magic whispered through my enflamed skin for a second as he searched for my brand with his magical senses.

"It's gone," he murmured against the top of my head.

"Let me see." I grabbed the hem of my robe with a shaky hand and drew the fabric up high enough to see my upper thigh.

The barely-there shimmering lines that had been on my body for as long as I could remember were gone, and, if I concentrated, so too was the heat and ache.

I was free to love who I wanted, how I wanted, and when I wanted. The terrible destiny that awaited me was gone.

Finally. I was free.

CASSIUS

I paced the living room unable to stand still *and* keep my fire under control. It was one or the other and my fire was the priority. And no matter how hard I tried to focus on being hard and icy, my internal flames blazed through those thoughts, yanking me back to Amiah and my worry, urging me to go, take action, protect her.

She wasn't safe. I couldn't lose her like I'd lost my brother. She and Bane had been gone for too long — which probably wasn't true. It was hard to tell time in the suite, but I didn't think they'd been gone for more than half an hour.

"He'll keep her safe," Hawk said, thankfully not telling me to calm down.

"I still should have gone with them." I should have forced Bane to let me go. Except Amiah had been right. If both Titus and Bane were incapacitated that left her to defend us or her trying to carry Bane, and neither option was acceptable. We couldn't afford for the Wilds to incapacitate him which meant going ahead with his deal for protection.

"He's just as concerned about her safety as you are." The hellfire in Hawk's eyes flared and the muscles in his jaw flexed. Was he worried too? "He'll protect her."

"She's not his responsibility." And I knew if Bane got a better offer, he wouldn't think twice about betraying her—

Except that was the person I'd thought Bane was. It wasn't the man

I'd seen the last couple of days — and if I was being honest, it wasn't the man who'd put his life on the line to help save my brother, Gideon.

Flames sparked over my hands and I heaved them back under my searing skin.

Just because he wasn't the mercenary I'd thought he was, didn't mean he'd be able to keep her safe. The only way I could be sure she wasn't in danger, was if I was protecting her.

"She'll be fine," Hawk insisted, but again it sounded like he was worried and trying to convince himself.

Which was strange. He didn't know Amiah. They'd only met three days ago.

"What's your story, incubus?" I growled.

Jeez. Not the most diplomatic way to ask the question, but I was sure everything I said right now was going to come out angry. And I wasn't even sure what I was asking. I didn't know him, I didn't know why he seemed concerned about Amiah, and I didn't know what Bane and Amiah were walking into.

God damn it. I didn't know anything.

My power surged and I strained to keep it controlled, wishing that the floor and walls were actually ice and they'd be able to help cool me down.

"What do you mean what's my story?"

"Who are you?" *Should I be worried about any outstanding arrest warrants? Can I trust you and why the hell have I been trusting you?* Because I had been. Which wasn't like me at all. Not without at least doing a basic background check.

But my raging power was making it difficult to stay calm and concentrate. I couldn't lose her. Even if we were only ever friends, I had to keep her safe.

"I'm nobody," Hawk said, his gaze sliding to the hallway door.

"Only somebody who's somebody says they're nobody." My gaze followed his, my fire churning stronger. Was she about to arrive? Could he sense her energy — and did I want him able to sense her energy? Because that would mean Bane was flirting with her and she was enjoying it. "How do you know Bane?"

"We met during the war." He ran a hand through his jaw-length sandy blond hair. "And no, I'm not talking about it."

"That's not an option." I didn't want to talk about the things I'd done in the war either, but demons had no problems lying. Just because he said he was a vet didn't mean he actually was and requiring him to provide details might help me see through his lies. "What was your rank and deployment?"

Hawk gripped the arms of his chair. "You don't get to interrogate me."

"I don't know you and we're stuck in this together. If I want to ensure Amiah's safety, I have to know what kind of experience you bring to the table." It was a logical argument. Just like when I'd needed to know Amiah's physical condition. It was important to understand the strengths and weaknesses of each one of us.

Hawk was decent in a fight. I didn't know how he handled a sidearm or rifle since — much to my surprise — Bane hadn't had any firearms in his apartment, but Hawk had been deadly with the karambit and its wickedly curved blade, and taken out his fair share of Balwyrdan's mercenaries. I still, however, didn't know how he'd manage if faced with more powerful supers.

The hellfire in Hawk's eyes flared. "And I've just got to take your word that you've the experience to keep her safe."

"I've been keeping her safe for a hundred years," I said before realizing how possessive that made me sound, especially since I'd announced that we weren't in a relationship.

"As a sister," Hawk said, his tone clear he didn't believe me.

"Yes," I forced out. If I corrected him, he'd keep on taunting me, trying to get me to confess I wanted something more with her when that would put her in more danger.

"That doesn't mean you have the experience to protect her."

"You're just trying to get me to tell you what I did during the war." Which, even if I didn't like it, was fair. He didn't know me either. Except he didn't have a responsibility to keep Amiah safe. I glared at him. This wasn't a conversation I wanted to have. She wasn't his concern... and I didn't want her to become his concern.

Hawk glared back, his expression serious with no hint of sexual playfulness. "You tell me yours and I'll tell you mine."

No.

Except I needed to know who he was.

But would he even tell me the truth?

I jerked away from him and paced to the back of the living room. God damn it. I was just going to have to hope he would.

"Fine. I was a lieutenant in special operations before I was moved to the second division on the front line." I'd assassinated a dozen of my own kind who'd sided with Michael in his quest to exterminate humans and supernatural beings before my rage had become a liability to the team. Then they'd put me up front and I'd let my fire burn through everything and everyone. All the misguided humans and supers who hadn't realized Michael's end goal, all the angels who'd agreed with him, and all the mindless nephilim he'd created.

My fire surged, racing up my arms, snapping and crackling, and I strained to pull it back. It had felt so good just to let go, to let my fire rage.

And it had been terrifying to realize I was a monster too.

"You're the Salamander," Hawk said, his voice tight, edged with awe and fear.

"Not anymore." I yanked my fire back under my skin. Except not being the Salamander was only a fantasy, a desperate wish that I could regain control of my fire and become just plain Cassius again.

"I was the canary for the forty-third infantry."

Hawk said it so softly, so matter-of-factly that his words almost didn't register. Canary was slang for a magically sensitive soldier in a squad. Because of their sensitivity, they were the first to notice magical traps and attack spells, hence the term. They were the magical canary in the coal mine of the battlefield. But that wasn't what had made my thoughts stutter.

"The forty-third?"

"Yeah."

No wonder he didn't want to talk about his experiences.

The forty-third had been assigned to check out a warehouse with some unusual activity and had come across one of Michael's labs. Except instead of creating unnatural monstrous nephilim for his army, he'd been conducting horrific experiments on human children.

The forty-third had lost two-thirds of its men trying to take the lab and Michael's soldiers had slaughtered half of the children, attempting to destroy the evidence. The remaining children had been so horribly mutilated, physically and mentally, that none of them could have been saved, not even with the help of angelic healing.

"In short Bane, who I'd thought was a faekin glyph witch at the time, and I were assigned the magical cleanup."

"And by cleanup you mean...?"

"Killing children. Michael made us kill children because it was that or let them suffer in agony for days, maybe months, before they died." Hawk's grip on the chair's arms tightened, turning his knuckles white.

"He fucked with their DNA and the healing angel who'd been assigned to the mess couldn't save any of them. His magic couldn't reverse whatever Michael had done and we couldn't even pump them up with drugs to ease their suffering. Ever been in a room with over a hundred wailing dying children that you can't sedate?"

So not only had he fought a bloody battle, he'd had to suffer through the aftermath, too.

"Don't doubt my resolve, Salamander. I'll do what I have to. And don't doubt Bane's," Hawk said. "We're not besties — I'm pretty sure Bane doesn't let anyone get that close to him — but I know what kind of man he is."

"Tell me both of you visited a lethe demon at least once since then." If they hadn't had a *lethe* devour the emotions of those memories and soften the edges, the two of them could break down the moment Amiah needed them the most.

"It's none of your business, but we have," he said. "That and a little more than years later it just feels like a bad dream or a horror movie, not something I actually did... unless some asshole makes me think about it."

Hawk's attention jerked to the door before I could reply and it opened, revealing Bane and Amiah. They entered and my heart skipped a beat at the sight of her.

She was pale, her eyes rimmed with red as if she'd been crying, but she had a soft smile that made my breath hitch.

I took a step toward her, drawn to the gentle warmth in her expression before I realized what I was doing and my fire burst over my hands, my affection and desire for her making it blaze stronger.

Hawk sat forward, clearly drawn to her as well, the hellfire in his eyes flaring.

"Are you okay?" I asked, the urge to move closer twisting in my chest.

Instead, I forced myself back a step and heaved at my power.

Icy cold. Frozen. Hard. Just be frozen.

My priority was and always would be to keep her safe, and that included being safe from me.

"We're okay," she said, her smile disappearing behind her usual mask of cool, determined professionalism. "Has Titus woken?"

"Nope," Hawk replied, standing. "It hasn't even been an hour since the sleep spell was cast. Are we finally good to get the fuck out of here?"

"Oh yeah." Bane grabbed a roll from the tray of food on the coffee table with a trembling hand, and I realized he was shaken. He was trying to hide it, but whatever had happened during their meeting, it had set him on edge. "An appropriate change of clothes for Amiah should arrive in a minute or two and then we're good."

"Who wants to help me wake Titus?" Amiah asked, heading to the door of the bedroom with the cots. "I think if I do it, he's less likely to attack, but I'm not going to wake him by myself."

My chest tightened at the thought of her getting close to Titus. He'd tossed me across the room as if I'd weighed nothing, and there was no guarantee that his beast's fury would be gone when he woke. But she'd also gone forehead to forehead with him in an attempt to calm him down and the worst he'd done was shove her into my arms. Out of all of us, she was the one most likely to get the best response from him.

And even as I came to that conclusion, my fire burned hotter with my need to protect her. I couldn't fail her like I'd failed Dominic. Except I also couldn't lock her away to keep her safe, as much as a part of me really wanted to do. Someone had already locked her up and it had killed me to see her like that and to watch her struggle to regain her strength and confidence.

No, the best I could do was watch her back like a good friend.

Except I wanted so much more than that.

Flames snapped around my hands.

But more was too dangerous. I was an uncontrolled inferno, and I put her in more danger than anyone else.

TITUS

My angel's soft voice shivered across my senses and my beast roared inside me, straining to break free and take control. She was in danger, someone had tried to kill her, and everything within me screamed to protect her with my very life if I had to.

Except somehow, I'd given her the first key to unlocking Faerie's Heart, something I hadn't thought was possible without killing the original keyholder, and she was in even more danger. Deaglan would eventually figure out she had it and come after her.

He'd been overjoyed when the first key had become empowered, ready to unlock the spell containing the Heart, and the compulsion to go to it had seized me. And he'd been completely pissed when I grabbed it before he could and it had somehow helped me break his leash spell, allowing me to escape.

I'd hoped to never tell anyone about the first key, not even Seireadan — it was safer for everyone that way — and then I'd somehow gone and given it to Amiah by kissing her.

It was as if some strange instinct had taken over, some knowledge that the key would be safer with her, or perhaps the key had possessed me. I'd smashed my lips against her, my need for her overwhelming, and the key had rushed out of me into her.

My beast heaved and clawed inside me. Protect her. Kiss her. Again.

It had felt so good, so right, and had been too quick. I'd wanted to explore her mouth, her body, show her how much I wanted her, how she was mine and always would be. But I'd only had a few seconds and the need to give her the key to keep it out of Deaglan's hands had been overwhelming. If I'd died, the key would have fallen from my body and anyone could have picked it up, and I had no idea if having one of the keys would allow someone who wasn't a dragon to find the others. It didn't matter that it put her in more danger. I'd had to do it.

"Titus."

Yes.

Call on me. Need me. Let me protect you. Always.

"Titus." Her essence warmed my cheeks and entwined with my beast's raging power.

My pulse picked up and my beast's claws dug into my soul. Whoever had tried to kill her was still out there and still a threat.

Kill. Protect. Mine. I would go through anyone who stood in my way to keep her safe. Not just my beast, but all of me.

Mine.

And the other guys had tried to stop me—

No, they'd tried to make my beast see reason. But it had no reason. It was pure, primal instinct, and seeing those ice men pile on top of her and thinking it had lost her had sent it into a desperate, ferocious rage. Hell, *all* of me, both man and beast, had panicked.

If she'd died—

If I'd lost her—

I couldn't. Please. *Mine. Always.*

I had to go. Now. Kill. Protect.

I jerked awake and stared into her shockingly blue gaze, captured, mesmerized, drowning. For a second, there was only her, leaning over me, her hands against my cheeks, and the warmth of her soul steadying mine. My beast reveled in the closeness, ached for more contact, ached for more flesh.

Then panic seized me, my fear taking over. I grabbed her around the waist as I sat up, and pulled her protectively tight to my body. The other guys standing a few feet away near the doorway to the living room all jerked forward.

I snarled, flashing my canines to show how serious I was even though I logically knew they didn't endanger her. If Seireadan hadn't stopped me, I would have raged through the Winter Court, revealing my true nature, and put Amiah at greater risk.

And my beast didn't give a shit about that.

"You put me to sleep," I growled.

"Because you weren't thinking straight," Amiah said, shifting to get more comfortable against my side but not trying to pull away, which made my beast extremely happy. But that also made Cassius's glower deepen, the hellfire in Hawk's eyes flare, and Seireadan frown.

Mine.

I resisted the urge to hold her tighter, but couldn't keep back my snarl.

Jeez. Not mine. Not yet.

And really, I *knew* I hadn't been thinking straight, my beast's desire for blood had been too strong. Seireadan had probably saved my life, and I'd thanked him by bashing him into a wall.

Something my beast didn't give a shit about. He'd gotten in the way.

I gritted my teeth. Losing control wouldn't help Amiah, and neither would alienating the other guys. My beast might want to be the only one protecting her, but it was better if I had help.

"Are you all right?" I asked Seireadan.

He shrugged. "Nothing Amiah couldn't fix," he said, which made my beast heave against my control.

She'd touched him, comforted him, given life from her body to heal him.

Because that was her magic. It didn't mean anything.

I bit back another growl. I had to get ahold of myself. I hadn't proven myself to her yet and I couldn't just claim her. Seireadan had been right. She didn't adhere to five-hundred-year-old dragon social norms. I had to figure out how angels claimed their soul's mate—

No...

Those weren't the words I'd meant. It couldn't have been. She wasn't my soul's mate. She wasn't even a dragon. Sure, my beast had decided she was mine, but that didn't mean she was *mine* mine. My beast was confused. *I* was confused. That was it. My soul was in turmoil from my captivity, my beast enraged because I'd been unable to release it.

"I have to get out of here." I needed to think, needed to tell my beast to shut the fuck up. Yes, I wanted her as my mate, because she was amazing and strong and her soul sang to mine, but—

Fuck.

Amiah cupped my cheeks again and pressed her forehead to mine, instantly sending soft warmth into my soul and steadying me.

If she was my soul's mate it was going to be even harder to keep my beast controlled while she worked out her relationships with the other guys.

And what if she didn't choose me? What if she picked Seireadan? They'd already had sex and the Winter Court responded to her. No matter what Seireadan said, they were practically mated already.

"I have to leave." I met her gaze. *Please pick me. I want you and I don't want to hurt them.*

"We're going to. We have a new plan and we're leaving soon," she said.

Thank goodness. If we could get to the Wilds, I could release my beast and the emotions threatening to crush me.

"Can you stay in control?" she asked.

No. "Yes."

"You better," Cassius snapped. "I won't let you endanger Amiah by pulling that shit you did earlier. For better or worse, we're a team right now. If we're going to survive this, we need each other."

Someone knocked — presumably on the door to the hall — and everyone jerked to face the door out of the bedroom.

"Must be Amiah's change of clothes." Seireadan stepped into the doorway to the living room and froze then dipped into a deep bow. "Your maj— Mother."

My beast dug into my soul and I tightened my grip on Amiah. The queen might not want Amiah dead, but that didn't mean she wasn't going to hurt her.

"Shit," Hawk hissed, stepping up behind Seireadan.

Cassius joined him, the three of them creating a wall with their bodies in the doorway.

"A little snowflake told me your wife is in better health," the queen said, her tone sickeningly sweet. "I've come to see the miraculous recovery for myself."

"Your little snowflake is mistaken," Seireadan replied. "The pools couldn't possibly have healed her injuries this soon."

"Unless you've been lying about how hurt she was." A gust of wind swept through the door. "Tell me, Seireadan. Have you been lying to me?"

"No, Mother." Seireadan dipped into another bow.

"No?" The wind picked up, then snapped, forming a barely visible rope. It wrapped around Seireadan's neck and yanked him stumbling into the living room and out of sight.

Cassius and Hawk stepped forward to fill in the doorway and Amiah tugged against my hold.

"Let me go," she whispered.

"It's not safe," I hissed back. I didn't know what she was going to do, but there was no way in hell I was letting the Winter Queen see her. "She won't hurt him too badly, but she might hurt you."

"Except she's still going to hurt him," Amiah said, but she stopped trying to break free of my grasp as if coming to the same conclusion I had: there wasn't anything she could do.

"Do you honestly think you can protect her?" the Winter Queen asked. "That if you waited long enough, I'd forget that she *chose* to fuck you in public?"

The room's temperature dropped and ice crackled over the floor in a thick uneven coating, sweeping past Hawk and Cassius's feet and inching toward my cot.

Something thumped and Seireadan groaned. Hawk jerked forward a step, but Cassius grabbed his arm, stopping him.

"You will conceive an heir and everyone in court will bear witness."

"I'm still concerned for her condition," Seireadan gasped.

"Then fuck her gently," his mother snarled.

"Mother—"

"I'm tired of waiting. The King of the Shadow Court assures me she can take it. So she either puts on a dress and acts like a queen, or I tie her naked to the bed in the ballroom until she does her duty."

"There's no need for th—" Seireadan gagged as if he was being choked and Amiah tensed, her fingers digging into my forearms.

"If any other words except 'yes, Mother' come out of your mouth, I'll let the entire Winter Court fuck her first to remind you that you've been self-indulgent enough. A monarch never marries for love."

Amiah froze, her eyes flashing wide with fear, and my beast snarled. It strained to be free even knowing it would put Amiah in more danger if it attacked the Winter Queen like it wanted.

Seireadan was smart. He wouldn't disobey his mother like that, wouldn't risk Amiah's body like that. Please.

"Yes, Mother," Seireadan said. "I'll show her the delights of the Winter Court and we'll conceive an heir."

The room's temperature flashed back to normal, suddenly too warm in contrast to the queen's cold, and yet Amiah's skin under my hands remained cold and her body trembled.

"That's a good boy," the queen purred. "I'll even supply the good winter wine so you can melt her frigid angelic inhibitions. I expect to see you in the ballroom in ten minutes."

A door slammed shut and fire erupted over Cassius's body. He jerked away from Hawk and stormed to the back of the room where he'd had his other meltdown — the cots still piled out of the way.

"We're leaving. Now." He sucked in desperate deep breaths clearly trying to regain control of his power and failing.

"It's okay," Seireadan gasped as he staggered into the doorway, a large, bleeding welt encircling his neck.

"How is this okay?" Hawk asked, helping Seireadan to the closest cot.

"Let me go." Amiah pushed against my grip and this time I forced my beast to let her go. She hurried to Seireadan's side and sat on the cot beside him.

"I thought you said the court wouldn't let in anyone who would hurt Amiah," Cassius growled, his fire dripping from his hands and sending black smoke billowing to the ceiling.

"The court still bows to my mother's will and clearly it doesn't think conceiving an heir in public will hurt her," Seireadan replied as Amiah reached to place her hands on his neck. But he grabbed her wrists and pulled her hands back before she made contact. "Don't. If you heal me, my mother will know for certain that you have healing magic. Right now she might suspect, but it's more likely that I'd lied about your condition."

Amiah huffed. "Fine. Hawk give—" Her gaze swept over his bare torso then turned to me. "Titus, give me your tunic."

I yanked my top off and tossed it at her then dug my claws into the mattress so I wouldn't pull her back into my arms. If I did, I'd hold on tight and make a break for it. To hell with the other guys or the fact that I probably couldn't get out of the Winter Court alone. "You said we had a plan."

"The new plan isn't going to work," Seireadan said as Amiah wrapped my tunic's sleeve around his neck. "The guards will only take us to the throne room and all of my mother's other constructs will be on the lookout for us. We'd never be able to make it out of court."

"Hold that and apply pressure," Amiah instructed.

Seireadan wrapped his hands around his neck and offered Amiah a small smile. "No, we're back to the original plan," he said, "slipping away during the party when my mother's concentration isn't focused entirely on her constructs."

"I'm not having sex with you in public." Amiah's breath picked up.

"I won't let it come to that," Seireadan said.

"We'll fight our way out before it comes to that," Cassius added, his fire back under his skin, but his body was so tense the tendons in his neck stood out and he shook with the effort to hold his flames in.

Amiah's gaze jumped to him then slid to me. My beast snarled his agreement. I would kill everyone to protect her. I would sacrifice myself to prevent her suffering.

The light in her beautiful eyes flared and her fear deepened with a horrible realization. "Against all of the queen's constructs? Against the Winter Court itself? It's too dangerous."

That didn't matter so long as she was safe. And I was certain that at least Cassius believed that as well.

"Promise you won't fight. Please." She jerked her attention to Hawk. "Promise you'll enthrall me so it won't hurt, so I'm not thinking."

Hawk dropped to his knees before her and grabbed her hands. "It won't come to that. I swear."

"Promise me anyway," she begged. "If you fight, she could kill you, and Sebastian and I will still have to do it. I can't get through it without you." Her terrified gaze jumped to Seireadan then Cassius then me. "Being humiliated isn't worth your lives. It won't break me if you're all alive, if I know we can still escape."

But my beast wasn't going to listen to her. If it looked like she and Seireadan were going to be forced to have sex, there was no way I'd be able to control it. It wouldn't be able to just stand there and watch, no matter how practical her request. I didn't think any of us could.

HAWK

WE ALL PROMISED AMIAH WE WOULDN'T RISK OUR LIVES BY FIGHTING OUR way to freedom if she was going to be forced to have sex in public, and without a doubt, we all lied, even the angel.

What shocked me was that Cassius and Titus agreed to go along with Bane's plan instead of grabbing her and running since Cassius was barely holding onto his fire and Titus his beast. But everyone had to admit Bane's plan was the best— or rather the one we were all most likely to survive.

Bane assured us there wouldn't be a lot of guards in the ballroom, and the plan was to split into two groups, mingle with the crowd, and make our way to a narrow hall at the back of the room. The hall led directly to the Winter Forest, where only a select few could enter and hence wouldn't be watched, but just before the way was magically blocked there was a door leading into the catacombs and a hopefully forgotten way out.

All we had to do was survive a little time at the party.

"My mother will want to build up the suspense," Bane said, still holding Titus's tunic to his neck, his pale gaze never leaving Amiah. "She won't make us have sex right away."

"But she will punish us if we're late." Titus stood. His pupils were still slitted and his canines extended even though he'd managed to calm down a bit while we went over the plan. "Did she leave us clothes?"

"They rolled in a rack," Cassius replied. His expression was back to stern and icy, but his aura writhed around him, angry and red as if his expression was just a mask and he still seethed inside.

"Okay." Amiah drew in a steadying breath and squared her shoulders, her fear hardening into determination. "Let's do this."

I gave her fingers a reassuring squeeze and stood, keeping hold of one of her hands as we followed Titus and Bane into the living room.

The servants had left the rack by the door, having scurried in with it after Bane had agreed to his mother's terms and then scurried out. It had three pairs of heavy leather dark blue pants that had laces instead of a zipper for a fly and three red sashes, along with a pair of white leather pants with the same lace-up fly and a white sleeveless leather jerkin with blue and silver embroidery and intricate silver clasps down the front. At the end hung a white gown made of soft gauzy material.

Cassius went through the hangers of the men's clothes, the muscles in his jaw twitching. "We just get pants."

"And a sash," I said brightly, unable to help myself.

Cassius scowled at me. "Not all of us enjoy walking around half naked."

"Well that's a pity." I slid my gaze down his body, letting it show in my eyes that I appreciated his physique even though he was fully dressed. I'd seen him in his briefs in the healing grotto. He had nothing to be ashamed of. His chiseled musculature, honed from his years as a soldier and then as a JP agent and his classic handsome features could attract women just as easily as my good looks. I doubted the man had trouble finding companionship... if he hadn't completely closed himself off from everyone.

"Back off," he said, yanking a pair of pants from a hanger and holding them to his waist to check their size. "I'm not having sex with you."

"Aw, come on." I knew I shouldn't. Cassius had no sexual desire for me. The closest I might get to having sex with Cassius was if he let me join him with a woman and the jury was still out on whether he was open to that. But it was just too easy to push his buttons and it actually relaxed him a little, surprising him into forgetting that he had to keep a tight hold on himself.

"Flirt with Bane," he said, tossing me the pants that were too small for him.

I caught the pants one-handed and batted my eyelashes at Bane who rolled his eyes at me.

"I think we've already established you don't do it for me, pretty boy." Bane headed back to the bedroom with the cots. "I need to clean up before I put on all that white."

"You probably shouldn't be calling Hawk pretty, pretty boy," Amiah said, sliding her hand from mine, making me ache at her absence.

I'd only had her once, but now I craved her. She'd felt amazing, both physically and magically, and she'd truly been a goddess when she'd thrown her head back and ridden me until she'd orgasmed.

But there'd been something else, something more than just sex. It had whispered within me the moment I was sheathed inside her and had swelled into an amazing, stunning sensation just before she'd climaxed. It was a connection that was deeper than our physical bodies, except she hadn't used any magic. Even if by some twist of fate Amiah was one of the rare angels able to create a soul bond with someone, I still would have sensed and seen the power of a bond forming — Bane's shield on me blocked out a lot, but not everything. But that moment with Amiah... I had no idea what it had been, only that it had felt amazing and absolutely right.

Bane's desire for her flared and he flashed her a wicked smile. "Gee, you think I'm pretty?" Then his eyes widened for a second and his gaze jumped to Cassius before he strode into the bedroom.

Jeez. Both of them were completely fucked up.

Titus huffed, his beast still straining to get free, his desire for Amiah ferocious.

Correction, all of them were fucked up.

Amiah took the dress and went into her bedroom to change, and I reached to yank off my pants where I stood, but my cock was hard and I hesitated.

Crap. I was supposed to have more control than that. Just thinking about a lover shouldn't have been enough to make me hard, not unless I'd wanted it to, and I hadn't been purposely desiring her... except I had been. I'd been thinking about her from the moment I'd left her bedroom, and I wasn't sure I'd ever be able to stop. I wasn't sure if I'd ever get enough of her.

And while I usually didn't care who saw me naked and hard, Cassius was barely holding his shit together. He'd either rightly assume I was hard for Amiah or wrongly assume I was hard for him and both would make him react badly. Thank God the leather pants were heavier than whatever our other pants were made out of and would keep me in.

Titus grabbed the remaining pants and sash, and followed Cassius into our bedroom, while I quickly stepped out of my loose pants and pulled on the leather ones before Cassius realized I wasn't following him.

"Hey. You should change in here," Cassius said, leaning out of the bedroom's doorway as I jerked the heavy leather pants over my ass and started to lace myself in.

"Nah, I'm just about done," I called over my shoulder.

"Don't make things more uncomfortable for Amiah than they already are. She— ah... She..." he stuttered, his desire suddenly spiking, hot and desperate.

I looked up to see what the problem was and my gaze locked on Amiah.

She was breathtaking in the gauzy dress with her long blond hair hanging loose in soft curls and blushing so hard it colored her cheeks and ran all the way down her neck into her cleavage — which with the dress's plunging neckline was a whole lot of cleavage.

I'd thought all the gauzy layers of fabric would have made the dress hard to see through, but it was shockingly sheer and, with its sleeveless faux Grecian cut covered very little. And while it didn't show *all* the goods, it was awfully close and would if she didn't watch how she sat. Especially with the slit up the left side that went all the way to her waist. There were also cut-outs over her abs and at her sides and when she turned to Cassius, I could see that the dress was backless and cut so low it showed a teasing glimpse of the top swell of her amazing ass.

She crossed her bare arms, drawing my attention back to her breasts and the silver and blue embroidery embellishing the bodice. Embroidery also accentuated the hem along the slit and I had no doubt she and Bane would match when they stood side by side.

"You look amazing," I said, drawing her attention back to me.

Her striking blue gaze captured me, stealing my breath, and I was grateful I was more or less tied in or Cassius would know for certain how much I wanted Amiah — and if I were to guess, he would be more upset if I was hard for her than if I was hard for him.

"I'm practically naked, and I still don't have any shoes." She huffed even as her gaze slid over my body just like mine had slid over Cassius's and her desire billowed, teasing through my veins with glorious seductive power. "Not that any shoes that would go with this impractical dress would be practical for fleeing."

"Well, fuck," Bane said, stepping up beside Cassius, adding his desire to the mix. He'd discarded Titus's tunic and washed the blood from his hands and neck. The welt had stopped bleeding, but it was still obvious, a stark contrast to his pale skin. "At least my mother has good taste."

"This is not good taste," she insisted.

"Yeah, you're right. The white virginal bride thing is a little on the nose," he said, making her stiffen and her blush burn brighter, "and inaccurate." He gave her a dismissive shrug and a hint of a sneer, reminding her that he'd been her first and silently telling her he was done with her, even as his desire for her grew.

Her desire vanished and, because I knew to look, I could see the hurt in her eyes before she quickly hid it behind a stern mask of professionalism.

I bit back a nasty retort to defend her. Saying anything would just make Cassius aware that something had gone on between them and she wasn't ready for that. Which Bane clearly knew and had used against her.

When we finally got out of here, I was beating some sense into the asshole. She could have gone to any of us for her first time. She could have gone to Cassius, someone she already knew and trusted. But she'd chosen Bane, trusted him to give her what she needed.

He didn't have the right to use that against her, especially to protect himself. No one should ever be made to feel bad or guilty about sex.

"But it does effectively show off your body." He grabbed his clothes from the rack and headed back to our bedroom. "And for my mother, the point of this is to publicly humiliate us... well, you, which is supposed to upset me."

"It should upset you," Cassius said, following him into the bedroom to change.

"Don't think it doesn't just not for the reason my mother thinks," he replied. "I don't want to fuck Amiah, let alone in public."

Liar.

All of us wanted to have sex with her. Something about her drew us to her and it wasn't just her good looks. There were women out there more beautiful than her, more confident, and not nearly as uptight. Perhaps it was her sexual awakening, her desire to explore all the things she'd been denying herself that called to us on a subconscious level. Or perhaps it was her fierce determination, her strength to carry on when the four of us knew, in part, the horrors she'd been through. Perhaps it was her scarred soul resonating with ours... maybe that was what I'd felt when we'd had sex. The connection with a kindred spirit just as wounded as me.

"Hurry up and get dressed," Titus said as he opened the bedroom door, striking an imposing figure. Wearing just the pants and sash made his massive, muscular chest appear bigger and broader even with the glamour changing his appearance. Where Cassius was honed, and Bane and I with our leaner frames were sculpted, Titus was bulky heavy muscle. Rugged and raw.

His attention instantly jumped to Amiah and his gold-red aura flared as his desire surged.

With a snarl, he stormed toward her, the ghostly image of a wolf's head superimposed over his own, indicating his beast was trying to gain control of his body.

Oh, shit.

I jerked forward, instinct moving me to protect her, but she stepped up to meet him and rested her palms against his massive chest. The wolf's head sank back under his skin, his beast instantly calmed, and he pressed his hands over hers.

"The Winter Queen is going to regret giving you that dress," he said, his voice gruff. "No one will be able to keep their eyes off you."

"I hope that isn't the case. The whole point is to blend in with the crowd and slip away." She leaned into him, making his desire burn hotter but his aura soften, his beast relaxing even more. "You need to shift the moment we're out of the Winter Court and it's safe. I don't care if it destroys the glamour changing your looks, you're not going to be able to keep your beast at bay for much longer."

"I'll manage."

She leveled an unimpressed glare at him. "You've shifted once in the last five hundred years. If you don't let your beast out, you'll permanently damage the connection between you two and then you won't be able to control him. That's not something I can heal."

"I agree," Bane said, striding out of the bedroom looking regal. The white strangely suited him even with his pale skin. It made him more luminescent, to the point where I had to concentrate to see the demonic magic writhing inside him. It also accentuated the black glyphs tattooed on his bare arms and curling up his neck out of the collar of his jerkin.

Not only did he look regal, but with that many spells on his body, he also looked dangerous, and I wasn't sure if his mother had realized that or not when she'd selected our clothing. "Now let's get this shit show on the road."

He stepped into the center of the room and offered his arm to Amiah. She strode to him, her expression icy as the dress fluttered behind her. Titus followed her, and I quickly tied my sash around my waist. Cassius hurried out of our bedroom, looking uncomfortable in just his pants, and as a team, we stepped out of the suite.

Two ice guards waited for us and walked a dozen feet behind us as Bane led us down long, white, softly glowing halls.

We heard the ballroom before we reached it. The rumble of many voices mixed with lilting music carried down the hall, growing in volume as we approached the grand entrance. The woman with the gossamer fairy wings who'd yanked us into Faerie waited in the doorway and two more ice guards stood at attention on either side of two, fully open, massive doors. Beyond, was a wide balcony that ringed the room and a two-sided grand staircase.

Bane strode through the door, a slight arrogant smirk pulling at his lips, and led Amiah to the wide ice railing at the balcony's edge. His gaze swept over the large room below, filled with hundreds of people all wearing fancy gowns and suits — as well as a few just in pants like us who carried themselves like fighters and were most likely personal guards.

The room was strangely lit with dancing fae light orbs the brightest biggest ones hovering around the edges of the room and dimming the closer they got to the center, but that only accentuated the beam of shimmering moonlight pouring through the massive skylight high above. It landed like a spotlight on a large bed swathed in red shiny sheets, dusted with glimmering flecks of white reminiscent of scattered rose petals.

The muscles in Amiah's back tightened and her breath picked up.

I gritted my teeth against the urge to pull her into my arms and tell her she wouldn't have to perform in public. I was pretending to be Bane's bodyguard. I couldn't just hold his queen. So I forced my attention to the crowd, looking for potential dangers instead. I might not have been much of a soldier compared to Cassius, but I knew enough to get a good idea of who was a possible threat.

At the back on a large raised throne, in a red gown to match the sheets, sat the Winter Queen with her men on cushions on the floor around her, also in red — pants only as well. Her crown was tall and more imposing than before and a gentle breeze danced around her, ruffling her long loose hair, adding to the sense of power. She was queen and the Winter Court's wind was hers to command. She gazed across the room to the balcony and her lips curled back in a wicked smile.

Between us was the packed ballroom. People danced in the center around the bed while others mingled, talking and eating and drinking. I suspected they'd gotten more than the ten minutes to get party-ready than we did. Their bodyguards — the female guards in leather pants and halters with red sashes — mostly kept to the edges of the room.

A hint of hellfire caught my attention and I focused under the balcony, halfway between the grand entrance and the throne. The demon-vampire stood by a pillar, shirtless and wearing black pants and a black sash, the hellfire in his eyes blazing, his attention locked on us... no, locked on Amiah.

A shiver rushed down my spine. His expression was flat, more closed off than Cassius's when he tried to contain his power, and the hybrid's aura was a strange, barely visible black, unlike any aura I'd ever seen even on a demon or a vampire. I'd only ever seen a hybrid once before and that had been during the fight at Left of Lincoln, which meant this was the King of the Shadow Court's hybrid and that the king and possibly the rest of his assassination team were close by.

"Demon-vampire hybrid, three o'clock," I murmured.

Bane rolled his shoulders, the only indication he heard me. Cassius gave a slight nod and Titus grunted as a hush descended on the crowd.

The woman with the fairy wings fluttered into the air and everyone below stopped what they were doing and looked at the balcony.

"His Royal Highness, Prince of the Realm and Heir to the Throne of the Winter Court, Seireadan and wife," the woman proclaimed.

Murmurs rushed through the crowd and everyone dropped into a low bow or curtsey.

The queen stood and the breeze swept around her, making her dress billow dramatically. "Tonight I celebrate my son's return, his marriage, and the conception of a new heir."

She raised her hands and the crowd released a heartfelt cheer on cue.

"Welcome home, Seireadan."

Another heartfelt cheer. When I'd met Bane, I would have never in a million years have guessed he was a Faerie prince. The only reason I'd known he was full fae was because we'd combined our magic in a desperate attempt to save those children.

The queen gave a dismissive wave, telling the crowd to return to their merrymaking, and glided down the three steps to the ballroom floor. Two of her men followed her as she made her way toward us — parting the dancers instead of weaving through them — while the rest of her men dispersed among the crowd.

Bane led us down one side of the wide stairs. He'd told us we were going to have to meet his mother as a group, but after that, he and I would distract her for a bit, while the others slowly made their way to the narrow archway three-quarters of the way down the left-hand side of the ballroom.

The queen stopped at the bed, of course. It was the grand finale of her night and given that she wanted to remind Amiah of her place, the location to meet us didn't surprise me.

The queen's eyes narrowed as we reached her. "I can't believe you covered your arms in those disgusting spells."

"Mother." Bane dipped into a bow, wisely not responding to the queen's comment and telling her those *disgusting* spells covered more than just his arms.

Amiah curtsied and the rest of us bowed.

Bane gestured to the ballroom. "You've outdone yourself."

"My heir has returned and I'll soon have a grandchild." The queen flicked her finger and the wind gusted through Amiah's skirt, parting the fabric at the slit and making her flash the entire room.

Amiah grabbed the front of her dress, holding it down, but the back still billowed out, giving me, Cassius, and Titus a front row seat to most of her ass and making it clear she wasn't wearing any underwear.

Cassius and Titus both tensed — I did as well — but we all managed to at least look calm. We only had to play this game for twenty minutes. Doing anything else might jeopardize our escape.

"I'm so looking forward to your performance," the queen purred.

"Amiah and I are looking forward to our first child." Bane swept a lock of hair out of Amiah's face, his knuckle caressing her cheek. The touch was surprisingly affectionate but it didn't awaken any desire in Amiah.

"I am too." The queen raked her gaze down Amiah's body and gave her a wicked sneer. Then the wind suddenly vanished and her attention snapped to Bane. "Come, Seireadan, I've heard the Heart has awakened. We need to discuss how you're going to get it."

"Of course, Mother." Bane brushed his lips across Amiah's cheek, another tender motion, and if I hadn't known better, I would have sworn he was in love with her. "Enjoy the party, my love."

"Yes," Amiah murmured. She turned to leave, and Cassius and Titus moved to follow her.

"No, you're with us," the Winter Queen said, her gaze turning heated as she studied Cassius and Titus. "The incubus is more than enough to watch your queen. Do you want him to loosen her up first? He can't use this bed, but I can have another one brought out."

"That won't be necessary," Bane said. "Cas and T, you're with me."

The queen led them away, leaving me with Amiah.

"How long do you think they're going to be discussing the Heart?" Amiah asked.

"I don't know."

"It's probably a good thing," she mused. "Now we'll have inside knowledge of her plans, even if Sebastian isn't going to be the one fulfilling them."

"At least there's that."

They exited through a side door near the throne, and Amiah and I wandered in the opposite direction — and across the room from our escape hall — to a long buffet table set against the wall. I didn't recognize much of the food, but none of it was enspelled, so I made a small plate of what looked like finger food for Amiah in the hopes that holding something would help distract her from her revealing dress, not to mention everything else.

I wasn't sure if it did, but it at least gave her something to do with her hands.

A few minutes later, a man with the icy coloring and stunning looks of a winter high fae approached, bowed, and offered his congratulations. A rotund woman with a shockingly cold body temperature that I could feel standing four feet away from her joined him, along with a few other men and women, all congratulating Amiah and engaging her with small talk.

I divided my attention between watching for Bane and the others to return and looking for potential danger. The hybrid had disappeared into the crowd while we were talking with the queen, and I'd yet to see any other members of his team.

One of the younger women asked Amiah about how she and Bane had met, and Amiah spun a romantic tale about him coming to her rescue during the war while she was attempting to evacuate children from one of the many war zones that had sprung up all around the world.

It was a complete lie... well, Amiah probably had been part of a team rescuing children. Cassius had said she didn't want to do field work, but that didn't mean she hadn't. I didn't know all of the shit Bane had done during the war, but I doubted their relationship was twenty-five years old. No, they reacted to each other as if they were still pretty much strangers.

By the end of the tale — which thankfully Bane wasn't going to have to repeat because we were leaving — the women were sighing over their romantic prince and the men were puffing out their chests at their heroic prince. Without a doubt, the tale was going to go through the crowd like wildfire and everyone was going to end up in love with Bane. Jeez, if he wanted, he'd probably be able to usurp the throne before the night was done... depending, of course, on how afraid everyone was of the Winter Queen.

Bane and the others emerged from the doorway soon after Amiah's tale, and Cassius caught my attention and pressed his palm to his shoulder two times. We were leaving in ten minutes.

Thank God.

I reached to touch Amiah's arm and get her attention when a wave of desire swept through me that wasn't from any of the guys or Amiah.

Crap. If it was someone desiring Amiah, we couldn't afford to be caught up in anything that slowed us down or drew attention.

I glanced around, searching for the source. We were at the end of the buffet table, near a narrow dimly lit hall... where the desire came from.

There. A couple about fifteen feet down the hall.

They were mostly hidden in the shadows of a statue, but they stood close, their foreheads touching and her hands cupping his cheeks. Desperate desire, the kind that came with heartbreaking longing, not hot wild need, radiated from both of them.

They were in love and they couldn't be together.

And they weren't a threat.

I started to turn back to Amiah when the couple broke apart and stepped out of the shadows. It was Bane's sister and someone's personal guard, wearing only a pair of dark pants and a sash. He was a pale and gorgeous winter high fae with his long red and silver hair pulled back into a ponytail that reached his waist and he looked really familiar.

Bane's sister turned sharply, making the skirt of her dark dress swish around her and she hurried away deeper down the hall. For a second it looked like something dark oozed through her aura, but then it vanished and my attention slid to the man now heading toward the ballroom.

I brushed Amiah's arm. "My lady." I didn't know if that was what I was supposed to say to a future queen but it sounded appropriately formal.

She excused herself from the group and drew close to me.

"Ten minutes," I said, keeping my voice low.

"Thank goodness," she breathed. "It's starting to get hard to keep track of my lies about Sebastian."

I chuckled and we turned to head toward the stairs — there was no way we were going to get closer to the throne to cross the room — but Amiah bumped into a werepanther in the queen's red pants as he was turning to head in our direction.

Amiah yelped and lost her balance.

I grabbed her shoulders and caught her as something flashed at the edge of my vision.

A spell?

Close?

Time stuttered and I glanced toward the glimmer. The fae man who Bane's sister was in love with — who, holy shit was one of the queen's men but not wearing red pants! — stepped close and jabbed a knife at Amiah. He kept the blade low, partially hidden by his body, and with everyone's attention on the werepanther almost knocking Amiah over, no one had noticed him.

Thankfully, the blade wasn't enspelled. The glimmer had just been a flash of the fae lights on the metal, but I didn't have time to let Amiah go and stop the man's attack.

On instinct, I drew close and turned her, blocking the blade with my body. I could heal just about anything quickly. Getting stabbed would still hurt but it wasn't a problem.

The blade pierced my side with a slice of pain, sliding through my sash as if the fabric hadn't even been there, and plunged into my flesh all the way to the hilt.

The fae man's eyes flashed wide with surprise and he yanked the blade free and jerked away.

"Hey." I reached to stop him and blinding agony, as painful as Cassius's fire, tore through me.

Oh, God.

I'd been poisoned. That man had tried to kill Amiah with a poison so potent even my rapid healing wasn't going to be enough to save me.

AMIAH

Hawk painfully clenched my shoulders as the crowd that had been drawn to my stumble dispersed, and my magic flooded my hands and locked onto him, demanding I save him.

Oh, no.

My pulse stuttered and the court's wind fluttered around me. Everything within me started screaming. *Save him. Save him. Now. Fast.*

He was dying.

Poison.

I knew the source before I'd even realized I'd connected with him. The poison was attacking his cell membranes and was so strong his natural healing wasn't able to eliminate it, let alone hold it back. All it could do was draw out his suffering which would entail massive bleeding from his eyes and nose and organ failure.

Save him. Save him.

I grabbed his wrist, and my power ignited, wild and urgent, ready to blast into him, but he dug his fingers into my skin and the hellfire in his eyes blazed.

"Don't you dare let the queen know your power," he gasped. "She'll imprison you and the others will kill themselves trying to free you."

I opened my mouth to argue with him, but he was right... well, maybe not about Sebastian trying to save me, but Cassius definitely would do whatever it took for me to escape.

Except I couldn't let Hawk die. My power wouldn't let me and neither would the rest of me.

I strained to hold my magic back enough that my hands didn't glow and raked my gaze over the crowd. But I couldn't see any of the other guys and there wasn't time for a more thorough search.

Save him. Save him.

The wind ruffled my hair, gaining strength but not nearly as strong as it had been when I'd been facing Deaglan, and my power swelled. It had barely awakened and already it roared through my body, straining for release, promising an excruciating backlash if I didn't save him. Now now now.

God, I had to save him.

But I couldn't endanger the others.

And really the best way to heal Hawk was to give him sexual energy. Using my magic on him was worse than using my magic on myself.

Except my power didn't care. I had to use it, had to save him, no matter that it was better to do something else. Even if I did manage to shove it aside and give him sexual energy, I couldn't do it in the ballroom with everyone watching... well I could, but I really didn't want to.

Behind us was an unguarded dimly lit hall. Statues in shadowy alcoves lined the walls on either side blocking my view of any possible doors, but surely we wouldn't have to go far to find a room.

I wrapped an arm behind his waist to help support him and we hurried to the hall.

"Amiah—"

"Don't you dare tell me to stop," I hissed as my power burned up my forearms, hot and sticky, and the pressure in my chest continued to grow. "There has to be a room somewhere."

Please, let it be close. Please. I have to save him.

He stumbled, his weight yanking me forward, and the wind gusted, helping me catch my balance. His breath was ragged and sweat slicked his skin. He hadn't been poisoned more than a minute ago and already it was overwhelming his natural healing. I didn't have a lot of time left. I had to do something. Now.

There. A recess in the wall that didn't have a statue. Was that a door?

I hauled him toward it. His legs barely held him up and his head lolled forward. Pressure screamed in my chest and my power burned not just around my hands but around my heart as well. I had to use it. If I waited any longer the backlash would tear through me and possibly knock me out and then I'd definitely lose Hawk.

But the recess wasn't a door, just a deeper alcove.

Hawk tensed and he released a strangled cry. The poison had flooded his heart. We were out of time. There wasn't anywhere else we could go.

I shoved him into the alcove. It was wider than the opening, and with the court wind's help, I heaved him into the front corner so the only way we'd be seen was if someone caught a glimpse of us while heading to the ballroom or if they purposefully looked in the alcove — but we'd only remain hidden if we were standing.

He groaned and his eyelids fluttered open. His hellfire was barely visible, tiny red pinpricks that sparked with sudden erratic flashes of light, desperate to stay lit and keep him alive.

God, I had to save him.

My power burned stronger, heaving against my control and lighting up my palms. It wrenched my hands over his racing heart, the place where it had the easiest access into his body, and I leaned in, using my body to help brace him against the wall.

"Don't... waste... your magic."

"I don't have a choice." All I could do was pray it would be enough to save him. "This will hurt."

His eyes rolled back and his lids shut again. "Already... does."

I released my magic, straining to control it, so it wouldn't hurt him as much as it could, but it blasted out of me, drawing a sharp scream.

Shit. Hold it back. I had to hold it back. Except I couldn't. My magic howled to save him — *now now now* — fast before the poison killed him, and I couldn't resist it.

I tried to move one of my hands to his head to draw his lips down to mine and stifle his cry, or even just cover his mouth, but my power held tight, locking both of my palms over his heart.

Fear churned with my power's desperate need and the wind picked up strength tugging at my dress and hair. Someone was going to hear us. We were going to get caught. The queen would learn the truth and everything would get worse.

No, nothing could be worse than Hawk dying.

My throat tightened. It didn't make sense. I barely knew him and I'd lost patients before, even lost a few I was close to. The idea of losing Hawk shouldn't crush me. And yet it did. I felt safe with him, wanted to spend more time with him, learn who he was—

No, it was my natural angelic sense of duty and justice. He didn't deserve this. He'd been in the wrong place at the wrong time and had gotten caught up in this mess. He hadn't volunteered like I had by rushing to save Titus's life.

My power swelled into a massive weight crushing my chest and stealing my breath.

Save him. Save him.

Another scream escaped his clenched jaw.

Hold. It. Back.

Just enough so it wasn't agonizing.

I gritted my teeth against the rising pressure of trying to control it so it wasn't blindingly painful, yet having to shove my magic into him because his natural healing fought me as well as the poison. I should be kissing him or giving him a handjob or a blowjob. That would have been more effective, but I couldn't move my hands from his heart, couldn't resist my magic's compulsion.

Save him. Now. Now.

I wouldn't be able to give him any kind of sexual energy until I'd used up all of my power or I'd healed him. Except for every molecule of poison I burned away, two more appeared, and for every damaged cell I healed, the poison destroyed three.

His body shook and his breath had become shallow, desperate gasps.

I was going to lose him. I couldn't lose him. The wind turned frigid with my fear and my soul screamed, panicked, desperate.

I had to work faster. I couldn't afford to hold back.

Save him.

I wrenched my power into a ball in my palms, holding it against the burning, howling need to push it into his body. If I could do a powerful enough blast, I could burn out the poison and then his natural healing could save him — *please let it be enough to save him* — but I had to blast all of my remaining power all at once. Fast. Explosive. Painful.

The pressure in my chest grew, threatening to rip me apart if I didn't push my power into him, but I held on, spinning it tighter and tighter until my hands and forearms felt as if they were on fire with Cassius's magic.

With a strangled sob — my attempt at holding back my own cry of pain — I slammed all but a glimmer of power into Hawk.

He wailed. My compulsion released me — because I had nothing left to give him — and I grabbed his head and smashed his lips against mine, stifling his scream, even as the court's wind whipped it away.

I could only pray no one had heard that and that it had worked.

Hawk wrapped his arms around me, clutching me to his trembling body, his forehead against mine, and exhaustion flooded me, weighing down my limbs. The world darkened, turning the alcove almost pitch black for me and what little I could see slowly spun.

Only a glimmer of power flickered in my palms and I couldn't catch my breath.

But neither could Hawk. And his pulse didn't slow.

"You shouldn't have done that." His grip on me tightened and the remaining wisp of my power connected with him... and the poison.

No.

My throat tightened. It hadn't been enough. Except I knew it wouldn't be. It would have taken almost everything I had just a heal a few broken ribs in an incubus. I had no hope of eradicating such a powerful poison. All I'd done was bought him a little time... and released myself from my compulsion so I could heal him properly.

"My power had locked onto you. It wouldn't have let me go until you were no longer dying or I was out of power," I said in my clipped doctor voice and leaned back to look him in the eyes, but my vision wavered and I couldn't get it to focus. "Let's finish this. Kiss me."

"Amiah—"

"I'm not letting you die." I reached between us and with trembling, numb fingers worked to unlace him from his pants.

He cupped the back of my head and captured my lips in a searing kiss that made me forget I was trying to unlace him. It stole all breath and thought, and I melted into his embrace. Even dying his kiss could inflame my desire and make me forget about the exhaustion threatening to overwhelm me.

But his hold on me tightened and his fingers dug into my scalp and waist. He tipped his head back against the ice wall, gasping, and groaned in pain. The kiss wasn't enough, not even if we kept going. He needed stronger energy.

I fumbled with the rest of his laces and slid my hand inside his pants. I didn't know if a hand job with kissing would be enough, either, but I didn't think he was in any condition to have intercourse, he could still barely stand.

"Hey," he gasped, his gaze sliding to the alcove's opening. "We're in here."

My heart leaped into my throat and the Winter Court's wind gusted with my fear of getting caught and then Sebastian stepped into the alcove. Oh, thank God. Someone else who could help.

"What the hell?" he hissed. "Why did you leave the party?" Then his gaze landed on me and his eyes flashed wide. "Your eyes. Where's your power?"

"He's been poisoned. Help me." I knew Sebastian didn't want to have sex with me, but maybe a little foreplay with Hawk drawing energy from both of us would be enough to save him.

"Fuck." Sebastian jerked close and pressed one hand over his hip where he had his sound blocking glyph and the other on his shoulder. "I've blocked sound and put up a veil behind me. We don't have a lot of space, but no one will see or hear us."

Hawk moaned in agony, his body trembling, and turned my head back to him to capture my lips again. The poison was growing again, painfully destroying his cells as if I hadn't just pushed all of my power into him. I wrapped my fingers around his penis, but he was only partially erect. That wasn't good. An incubus had control of his erection, and Hawk knew he needed sex to survive.

Sebastian drew up behind me, the clasps on his jerkin cool against my bare back. He slipped one around my waist and over my belly and drew my hair aside with the other.

Except I didn't react to his touch. Not even a glimmer of desire.

God, what was wrong with me? I'd been fantasizing about being with Sebastian and Hawk since I'd first met Hawk.

But I couldn't get my thoughts to focus on anything other than the fact that Hawk was dying and I had no magic left. I was also still selfishly hurt over Sebastian's words in our suite. He didn't want me again. He'd made that perfectly clear.

"This isn't going to work," I said. "If neither of us can muster up any desire, we won't be able to save you."

"Bane isn't the problem," Hawk gasped. "He's been wanting to make love to you again since you ran out of his bed." Hawk tensed and moaned. "And that dress is driving him crazy."

"But I'm not the one you're supposed to be with," Sebastian murmured against my neck his voice soft and strange. "I'm not in love with you. Cassius is."

For the love of—!

"I don't want you to be in love with me," I snapped, making the wind gust. "I just want someone to have sex with."

"But now your reasons are different," he replied.

"Yes. Hawk is dying." *Dying! Save him.* I had to save him. But what Sebastian had really meant was that my brand was gone and I could be with Cassius without fear of being permanently bound to him.

"And you need to relax for this to work," Sebastian said. "Hawk, can you give her a jump start?"

"I'll try," Hawk groaned against my lips.

A whisper of sensual heat slid down my throat, a teasing promise of what Hawk's power could be. It made my heart ache, churning with the growing fear in my gut and filling my chest with pressure again.

I couldn't lose him.

Except I had no idea why I couldn't lose him. Why?

Sebastian's hand on my belly slipped beneath my dress, gliding to the edge of my curls, while his other hand cupped my breast. Hawk pushed his tongue into my mouth, deepening our kiss, and I tried to forget he was in agony, or that I desperately needed to save him, or that my limbs were heavy with exhaustion.

I needed to relax, feel good, forget about everything.

Sebastian dipped his fingers into my curls.

This was the fantasy. Caught between both of them, having both of their hands and mouths on me.

Sebastian brushed tauntingly close to my folds, trying to work up the sexual tension and make me ache for him. And I did. I hadn't stopped aching for him even after having sex. But I was also still too afraid, my mind and body out of habit clinging to stern professionalism and shoving my feelings deep down so I could appear calm.

Just forget about the poison.

I sucked in a ragged breath, released it, and tried to relax in Sebastian's embrace. Hawk had held me like that only a few hours ago. He'd slowly built up my desire and let his magic swell inside me.

I focused my whirling thoughts on the memory of that, of how he looked at me with such heated need, or how he'd caressed me, teased me, brought me pleasure. He'd built up the tension inside me until I was aching with want then twisted it tighter and tighter until I'd exploded.

Sebastian moaned against my neck and brushed his cool fingers through my folds, drawing a shiver of desire.

Yes. Focus on that. Focus on how Sebastian's body is cool and Hawk's is hot.

Except the moment I thought about Hawk's body, my mind jumped to his condition. Sebastian and I had given him more power and slowed the poison's spread, but it still burned through him, his sweat-slicked body still trembled, and his erection was still only half hard. He was barely holding on.

I pulled away from him to look him in the eyes again. His hellfire was barely lit. Even the sparks had died down. "We have to give you more." A lot more.

"Come for me," he gasped, and Sebastian slowly slid a finger inside me, giving me a teasing reminder of what it had felt like to have him there filling me.

I groaned, my need surging with the memory of him pushing inside me, but I wasn't even close to coming, I was barely wet. It was going to take a lot more than that to make me come.

Then a strong thread of sensual magic slid down my throat, ratcheting up my desire. My breath hitched half in need and half in fear.

"Stop using your magic," I said, my voice low and breathy. "You need it."

"You need a strong orgasm for this to work," he said, his grip tightening and his face scrunched in pain.

Except I wasn't sure if just me orgasming would be enough.

But if Sebastian also came—

"You need two," I said. "I've never seen a poison this potent before. One isn't going to be enough."

"I don't have time for you to have two," he gasped.

"Not from me." I couldn't believe I was going to say this, but we were out of options. If Sebastian still desired me, I could make this work. I had to make this work. I couldn't lose Hawk.

"Sebastian, we have to have intercourse." The words came out sharper and colder than I intended, but we didn't have time to be polite. Hawk was dying.

"I—" Sebastian withdrew his fingers from me and shifted away.

"I know you don't want to. I know you think I should have sex with Cassius instead, but he's not here and Hawk is barely holding on. It has to be you." I turned to face him, to kiss him and get things started, but Hawk whimpered, grabbed my head, and turned me back to him, making the world lurch with the sudden movement.

"Don't stop kissing me," he begged.

Crap.

Fine. Sebastian and I still needed to have sex, so I reached behind my back and drew my dress aside, offering Sebastian my naked rear end. "Not anal. I'm not ready for that yet."

Hawk's trembling grew. His breath had become shallow and I had no idea how he was still standing. If we waited any longer, Hawk would start bleeding out.

The court wind turned cold and gusted with my fear, stinging my bare skin. I sucked in a breath that did little to calm me.

Come on, Amiah. Relax. You can do this. Think about when you had sex with Hawk, when you had sex with Sebastian.

Sebastian didn't draw closer or say anything.

What was he waiting for? Had Hawk lied and Sebastian didn't really desire me?

"Sebastian, we're running out of time. Are we clear?" I glanced at him from the corner of my eye. He stared at me with a strange look on his face, but his image was out of focus so I had no idea what his expression meant. "Please. He's dying. Have intercourse with me."

He ran a hand over his spiky white and silver hair. "Fuck me."

"No, Sebastian," I begged. "You're supposed to fuck me."

AMIAH

SEBASTIAN GROANED. "FUCKING HELL. I'M GOING TO REGRET THIS."

"I won't make you do it again," I promised.

"That would be the problem." He unlaced himself, and used his body to sandwich me against Hawk. "I didn't want to stop the first time, but I also don't want to be burned to a crisp."

"Cassius wouldn't burn you," I said, as he pushed aside the fabric over my breasts and roughly worked my nipples into taut peaks.

My breath picked up and his erection hardened against the swell of my rear, but I trusted he'd respect my wishes. While I didn't know Sebastian well, I'd never seen him do something to purposely hurt someone, and forcing me into a sexual act I didn't want would hurt me and Hawk, because if I wasn't into it, Hawk wouldn't get the sexual energy he needed.

I fought to stay focused on the sensation of Sebastian's hands on me and his hard body pressed behind me along with the memory of having sex with him. His desire had barely been contained, just like mine because of Hawk's magic. I had ached for him, ached for his hands and mouth, ached for him to fill me. And he had. God, the things he'd done with his mouth had been amazing, the way he'd brought me to climax then worked me back up to crash over the edge again... it had been everything I'd hoped sex would be and so much more.

I moaned into Hawk's mouth, remembering the throbbing desire that had swelled through me just before Sebastian had filled me and imagined that need pulsing in my core now, growing stronger than my fear and exhaustion.

Hawk deepened his kiss, and Sebastian's breath picked up. He dipped a finger back inside me then slid the slickened tip over my clit. My focus jerked to the sensitive nub and the real throb building there.

Oh, yes.

Another moan slipped out, and Sebastian's hold around me tightened.

"That's it, sweetheart," he murmured. His thumb replaced his finger on my clit with a delicious firm pressure that made my desire twist tighter, and two of his fingers pushed inside me. "Show him how fucking hot you are."

He worked his fingers, sliding them in and out, and rubbed his thumb against my clit as Hawk devoured every gasp and moan. His tongue pushed inside me like Sebastian's fingers, claiming my mouth and fueling my desire. It overwhelmed the memories of them making love to me, pushing me into the here and now, and stole all conscious thought. There was no past, only present, only the feel of their sculpted bodies boxing me in, their hands and mouths bringing me pleasure, and the growing need building inside me.

Hawk's erection grew firmer in my grip, but with my whirling thoughts and the flood of sensation, all I could do was hold on.

Oh wow. This was the fantasy, the feeling I'd been craving. And oh my goodness! It was so much hotter than I imagined.

My desire twisted tighter and my breath grew ragged. If Sebastian kept doing what he was doing I'd orgasm soon, and even though it was possible for me to come and then Sebastian, I really wanted to come with him inside me. I wanted to feel that connection again, the thrum of his life force caressing my senses that was enhanced when we joined.

"Sebastian, I'm close," I gasped. "I want you in me."

Sebastian groaned, pulled out his fingers, and tugged my hips back to offer him better access then pushed part way into my opening, making me tense in anticipation.

"Oh, fuck," he panted and inched farther in, his girth stretching me, making me whimper. "Sorry. I know you need slow. But—"

"It's okay. Hawk needs this."

"Right," he said with a sudden sharpness. "You're just doing this to save Hawk." He fully sheathed himself with a quick push and my essence sang, despite the whisper of pain. Sebastian filled me, body and soul, his life force thrumming, drawing me to vibrate in harmony with him.

God this felt so good. His essence, his life, and him inside me.

I pulled away from Hawk's lips so I could look at Sebastian. The world was still out of focus and spinning, but I met his pale almost colorless gaze as best as I could, determined to show him how serious I was. "I'll never get tired of how you make me feel. I was momentarily confused last time, but I know what I want now. I don't want this to be the last time we have sex."

"Fucking hell," Sebastian growled, his voice dark and husky, and he slowly started to pump inside me, reconnecting me with my desire.

"But you have to be willing to share." Hawk drew my lips back to his.

"You have to ask her first," Sebastian said.

"Hey, Amiah..." Hawk said into my mouth.

"Yes," I moaned, saying it to the feeling of Sebastian moving inside me and Hawk's request.

"It's not fair to ask her while she's distracted."

Sebastian's thrusts picked up speed, twisting my need closer to the edge, and my desire and essence roared with his life force. I didn't even need Hawk's magic to feel that glorious pressure building in my core, promising to crash through me.

"Oh, God, Sebastian."

His thrusts grew harder and my orgasm rolled through me. I threw my head back with a gasp and a throaty moan, and Sebastian grunted low in his throat and tensed with his own release.

My connection to his life force swelled, adding to the bliss rushing through me, stronger than the last time we'd made love.

I never wanted this feeling to stop, but no matter how good it felt, we were still doing it to save Hawk.

I dragged my whirling thoughts to focus on him and concentrated on my weak thread of power still connected to him. There wasn't a hint of poison left, and his hellfire blazed, strong and healthy, licking his cheeks. He looked at me with the same awe that I'd seen the last time we'd made love, as well as with a heated desire that made my breath hitch and my body ache.

God, I needed him in me, needed to feel his life force like I'd felt Sebastian even though my magic told me he was fine.

I captured his head and pulled his lips to mine with a hungry kiss.

He lifted me off Sebastian, and I hooked my legs around his waist and aligned him with my entrance. He plunged into me, a curl of his seductive power turning the pain of the sudden invasion into breathtaking pleasure.

I clung to him as he clutched my hips and drove into me with hard wild thrusts. The ferocity of his passion filled me, igniting already hypersensitive nerves and ratcheting up my need to new panting heights.

His life force sang inside me, so powerful, so sure, and I gave into the feeling of him moving inside me, giving him full control of my body.

God, yes.

This. This was the way it was supposed to be, what I'd been denying myself for far too long.

"Open your eyes and look at me, gorgeous," he gasped. "I want to watch you come."

I open my eyes and was drowning in hellfire and need and that soft awe that I'd seen before. I still had no idea what it meant, but it sang to something deep in my heart and my power made my essence stutter and matched my pulse with his, entwining our life forces with a breathtaking swell.

Then he pushed a whisper of magic into me. It wasn't much, but it sparked an explosion inside me, crashing me over the edge.

I tried to keep my eyes open. I really did. But every muscle gloriously contracted and I wasn't sure what I did after that. All I knew was that I cried out his name as his release took him and he moaned mine and the court's wind whipped around us. The most amazing sensation rushed over me, stealing my breath, and the world went black.

Once again, I was whirling, floating, swept away on bliss, stunned at the force of Hawk's power and the overwhelming sense of life from both him and Sebastian. It was as if a new sense had awakened within me, one that could only be felt when I joined with someone.

Panting, Hawk held me in a firm embrace as if he never wanted to let me go. His breath was heavy and his pulse raced, but he was healthy. All of the poison was gone. He was going to be okay.

Thank God, he was going to be okay.

As if thinking those words gave me permission to relax, the adrenaline rushed out of my body. It left me with an exhaustion that dragged at my limbs and even with my eyes closed, I could feel the world spinning.

"Thank you," Hawk murmured, his lips brushing my neck sending glorious aftershocks rushing through me. "God, you're amazing. Thank you."

"Jesus, Amiah," Sebastian groaned, and he drew close and pressed a tender kiss to the back of my neck. "I wish I could let you pass out and enjoy that, but we have to get going."

"Come on, give her a minute," Hawk replied. "She just gave all of her magic and her body to save me."

"I can't. Deaglan and my mother started talking. That's why I came looking for you. We need to leave before he convinces her to jump straight to the night's grand finale." Sebastian kissed my neck again. "As much as I really want a repeat of what we just did, I don't want us to have to do it in front of an audience."

My heart skipped a beat and the fear about the night's plans that I'd managed to momentarily forget flooded back with a vengeance.

"Okay," I said, my voice still shaky and soft. "We should go."

"I'm not sure you can walk, gorgeous," Hawk murmured. "And you didn't just drain your magic. I took a lot of life force from you, too."

I knew that. I was just too exhausted to remember. That was why incubi couldn't be monogamous. One lover wasn't enough to sustain them because they needed to feed faster than a single person could restore their life force, and that lover slowly emaciated until they withered to a husk and their organs failed.

"And neither of us should carry you through the ballroom," Hawk said. "That would definitely draw attention."

"I can walk. Put me down." God, I hoped I could walk.

I unwrapped my legs from Hawk's waist. He lowered me to the floor and I sucked in a few deep breaths to try to get the alcove to stop spinning.

"See. I'm fine."

Hawk's eyes narrowed. "I haven't let go yet."

"If she needs help, I'll help her. That will be believable. I can say you're still too weak and spending time at the party has exhausted you." Sebastian closed his eyes and his full body glow undulated around him.

Something whispered across the inside of my thighs, drawing a shiver of desire, and the ejaculate slowly oozing down my legs vanished.

Sebastian groaned — and not in the good way — and he grabbed the wall to keep standing, his breath suddenly ragged. His glow dimmed, and even in the weak light, I could see that his complexion had turned gray. Then his glow flared again, back to its normal luminescence.

"Whatever you cast, you shouldn't have," Hawk said. "Especially after casting the sound block and veil spells. I took life force from you, too."

"Amiah can't walk into the ballroom dripping our cum. She needed a clean-up and we don't have time for her to go to a bathroom." With another groan, Sebastian straightened, then reached for my breasts and slid them back into my dress.

Jeez. I was so dizzy I hadn't even thought to fix myself... and so dizzy I'd just stood there and watched while Sebastian had tucked me back in instead of insisting I could do it myself like I usually did.

I drew in another breath then another as Sebastian laced himself back into his pants. The dizziness of having used all of my magic and being drained by Hawk would pass... eventually. I just had to power through until then.

"Okay." I ran my fingers through my wind-blown hair. "I'm good." Or as good as I was going to get in the next minute or so.

Sebastian offered me his arm and I took it, drawing close and using him to help me keep my balance, and Hawk released me.

The hall's spinning picked up and I gritted my teeth.

I won't pass out.

My body trembled and the hall's dim light darkened.

I. Will. Not. Pass. Out.

Hawk laced himself back in and we stepped out of the alcove and headed back to the ballroom — which was farther away than I expected. I hadn't thought Hawk and I had gotten very far, but I'd been so desperate to save him, I hadn't been paying attention. And now a part of me regretted that. I was already exhausted and we hadn't even gotten to the end of the hall, let alone crossed the ballroom to the hall leading to the Winter Forest.

But passing out would draw attention and the queen would either revive me and jump to her grand finale or send me back to the suite where it would be harder to escape.

I forced myself to keep moving, determined to keep my back straight and my expression calm, but my body and mind were heavy and numb as if I was walking and thinking through water.

Around me, the hall heaved in and out of focus, and the bright light from the ballroom ahead of us got dimmer and dimmer.

Come on. Don't pass out.

We were halfway to the ballroom when my feet tangled and I lost my balance. I tried to tighten my grip on Sebastian's arm but my hands and fingers were weak.

"Amiah—" Sebastian gasped as he caught me and pulled me into a firm embrace.

"I'm okay. I just need a minute," I said, clinging to him and squeezing my eyes shut, desperate to get the hall to stop spinning.

"You're not." Hawk placed a warm hand on my back and my senses instantly connected with his life force, strong and sure. "You need at least ten minutes, ideally more and something to eat."

Except the longer we stayed the greater the chance I'd have to have sex with Sebastian with everyone watching.

That thought made my stomach churn. Yes, I wanted to have sex with Sebastian again, but I wanted the next time to be because we wanted to not because we had to, and I certainly didn't want to do it with a bunch of strangers watching.

"I can do this." I tried to push out of Sebastian's arms and stand on my own, but he wouldn't let go. "I can't do sex in public for your mother's entertainment."

"It's better to wait and risk it," Sebastian said. "You're not going to make it to the ballroom let alone to the other side."

"Well," a dark masculine voice purred from the direction of the ballroom, sending a shiver of fear racing down my spine.

Sebastian stiffened and I dragged my attention up to see Deaglan and his demon-vampire hybrid between us and the ballroom.

AMIAH

DEAGLAN AND HIS HYBRID STOOD IN THE DARKNESS A FEW FEET AWAY FROM the edge of the bright light spilling into the hall from the ballroom, blocking our way and threatening our escape. Their faces were cast in shadow and only my night vision and the simmering hellfire in the hybrid's eyes allowed me to make out their features.

"Trying to sneak away?" Deaglan asked.

"Letting my wife have a quiet moment," Sebastian replied. "She's not accustomed to court functions and she's not fully healed."

"Of course." Deaglan flashed a wicked grin. "I'm sure there are a lot of things she'll have to get accustomed to." His dark gaze slid over my body his meaning clear. I'd have to get used to having sex in public and soon. "You should really have your incubus warm her up."

"That's my business," Sebastian said.

"Just giving you a warning," Deaglan said with a shrug. "Your mother will be unimpressed if she just lies there, especially since we know she's a wild cat."

My pulse beat faster and a hint of the court's wind fluttered around me. Except it was a soft breath compared to the gale it had been the last time I'd faced Deaglan. But then I'd been filled with fear and adrenaline before, and now I could barely keep from passing out...

And Deaglan didn't know that. I'd scared him last time. Maybe if I showed a little backbone, I could get the wind to gust stronger and make him go away.

Please, just go away so we can get out of here.

I straightened my back as best I could in Sebastian's embrace and leveled my sternest, iciest glare on Deaglan, but the court's wind didn't gain strength. In fact it vanished, taking with it some of the air around me.

I forced my expression hard, praying I could carry through with my bluff and not let the fear of suffocation brought on by having been caught by the leash spell make me gasp. "Do I need to remind your majesty who's court we're in?"

"Not yours," Deaglan said and his shadows exploded from the darkness around us as a blast of shadow slammed into me and Sebastian.

Sebastian stumbled and the hybrid leaped forward so fast that with my spinning, wavering sight I could barely see him. He grabbed my arm and wrenched me from Sebastian's grasp while he was off balance.

Deaglan's shadows shoved between us, knocking Sebastian back seconds before he burned it away with a blast of light, but it was enough for the hybrid to wrap a strong arm around my waist, yanking me farther from Sebastian and Hawk and pinning my back against his cool bare chest.

The sense of cold lifelessness shuddered across my senses and the hall whirled and darkened around me.

Don't pass out. Please. Don't pass out.

Hawk jerked forward to help me, but a shadow wrapped around his neck and wrenched him off his feet. Gasping, Hawk clutched at the shadows choking him but couldn't rip the darkness apart and free himself.

"Get your hands off her." That sounded like Cassius.

I dragged my gaze to the mouth of the hall. Cassius and Titus stood in the bright light pouring in from the ballroom. Smoke curled from Cassius's hands and Titus snarled, his lips curled back showing his extended canines.

"This isn't a fight you want to have," Sebastian said, and a glyph on his left arm and one curling around his neck lit up with power. "Let go of my wife and my guard."

"I think you've forgotten who holds the queen's favor," Deaglan sneered, his shadows writhing around Sebastian but not attacking.

"You've been gone, Seireadan, and someone needed to reassure your mother that you'd eventually be found."

"What a load of shit," Sebastian shot back. "You tried to ki—"

"Her majesty won't stand for you abandoning your duties again," Deaglan interrupted as if he thought someone else was listening instead of gloating like he had before. "You can't run out on this like you ran out on the Winter Court three hundred years ago."

"I said let her go," Cassius repeated and flames swept over his hands.

"Enough," the Winter Queen commanded as she strode into the hallway, her blood red dress billowing around her. The werepanther who'd pleasured her when she'd first tried to get Sebastian to sleep with me was one step behind her along with two other fae men — neither man the fae who'd joined the werepanther pleasuring her. They all wore the red leather pants of her harem.

Ice enveloped Cassius's hands and a frigid wind blasted down the hall, stinging my skin and pasting my gauzy dress to my legs — and thankfully not flashing my privates to Deaglan.

Titus jerked forward and wind slammed him into the hall wall and pinned him there, as Cassius's fire melted the ice containing his power and he tensed, about to stand and fight.

"Stand down, Cas and T," Sebastian said, the light in his glyphs fading. "Mother—"

"Don't 'Mother' me," she snapped. "Deaglan said you'd try to slip away and if he's holding your man and your wife then he was right."

"We weren't. Amiah just needed a moment to rest," Sebastian insisted, as Cassius sucked his fire back under his skin but didn't relax and Titus continued to heave against the queen's wind.

"Then what is this?" Deaglan clenched his fist.

Sebastian stiffened and his full-body glow flared, his eyes narrowing in concentration for a second before squeezing tight in pain, and he released a strangled scream. The small shimmering orb of magic that Karthick had pushed into Sebastian to protect him from the Wilds after he'd removed my mating brand, emerged from his chest with a sickening tearing sound and floated into Deaglan's outstretched hand. "You've protected yourself from the Wilds. It sure looks like you're trying to sneak away."

"I won't let you run away from your duty again," the queen said and the wind gusted around us laced with pieces of ice that sliced shallow stinging cuts across my skin. "If you hate this court so much, you can leave once your heir makes a connection to the Winter Court. All I want is the child."

"Amiah just needed a moment," Sebastian gasped, his hands pressed to his chest where the orb had been.

"If she's so exhausted, your majesty," Deaglan said, turning to the queen, "it would be best to conceive the next Winter Court heir now."

My pulse stuttered and I weakly pushed at the demon-vampire's grip but he held tight.

No.

No no no.

Sebastian had to buy us time, find a way for us to slip away. I had to. Someone did. Please.

"There's no need to rush and ruin your party," Sebastian said.

"No, the King of the Shadow Court is right," the queen said. "It's time for you to sleep with your wife."

I had to think of something, anything for us to get away, but I couldn't get my thoughts to focus beyond the exhaustion threatening my consciousness and the fear of being naked and exposed in front of everyone.

"Perhaps he needs more incentive," Deaglan said.

The queen's eyes narrowed. "My constructs say you're friendly with your bodyguards. How friendly?"

The court's frozen wind whipped around Cassius's neck and jerked him to his hands and knees. His fire roared up his arms but was extinguished by more ice.

Titus snarled and the wind capturing him against the wall pounded into him with crushing force, drawing a guttural scream of pain.

"Fuck your wife or I'll kill your men," the queen said.

No, please.

My pulse tripped and the court's wind gusted for me, frozen and flecked with ice. But the Winter Queen flicked a finger and it vanished.

"This is my court," she said, stalking toward me, frost crackling over the floor with each step and inching closer to my bare feet. "My power. You can't use it against me. My will is stronger than yours, little angel."

Sebastian stepped between me and his mother. "There's no need for this."

"Fuck your wife." Darkness swept over the Winter Queen's eyes turning them black. "I'll even help you along. Deaglan, have your hybrid bite her to get her going."

Deaglan's eyes lit up with dark pleasure. "Rin."

"Let her go," Titus growled. He heaved against the wind and it snapped his head back into the wall with enough force his eyes rolled back and his eyelids fluttered shut for a second.

A few feet beside him Hawk gurgled and gasped for breath, his feet skimming the floor, while Cassius tried to stand, but the wind whip yanked him back to the floor and another wave of ice swept over his hands and up his forearms.

"She's weak," the hybrid said, his voice barely more than a whisper. "Blood loss won't help her."

I dragged my attention over my shoulder and met black eyes with a smoldering pinprick of hellfire and an emotionless expression that told me nothing about why he hadn't immediately obeyed.

"I didn't ask for your opinion," Deaglan snapped and he clenched his fist.

The hybrid tensed and what little magic I had left connected with him.

Pain. Agonizing breathtaking pain burned through his veins for a blazing second then vanished, leaving me gasping.

"Yes, my lord," the hybrid said his voice still that emotionless, barely audible whisper with no indication of the agony that had just burst through him.

He tangled his fingers in my hair, jerked my head to the side, and sank his fangs into my neck without further hesitation.

More pain, a fraction of what I'd felt from him moments before, sliced into my neck.

"No, please." I weakly pushed against his grip, my heart pounding. I didn't want this, didn't want a stranger holding me in an intimate embrace, consuming my blood. And I didn't know how much I could take before I collapsed. I was already weak, my magic and life force drained, and what little magic I had left snapped, a dying flame in a ferocious wind, desperate but unable to save me.

Titus howled and bucked against the wind, while Hawk strained to break free of Deaglan's shadows, and Cassius clutched at the wind whip choking him, his face turning red with effort and lack of oxygen.

Then the hybrid took a long, hard pull on my vein and bone-melting bliss swept through me, rushing straight to my core, filling me with sudden aching need, and dragging at my already weakened limbs.

The hall darkened, my pulse stuttered and slowed, and for a terrifying moment there was nothing, not even the bliss of the hybrid's magic.

Then panic seized me and wrenched me back to the hall. My muscles had given out and only the hybrid's grip in my hair and around my waist kept me upright.

"Fucking hell," Sebastian hissed. His cool hands cupped my cheeks and he urged my head up the fraction of an inch needed to meet his pale gaze, suspending me in a cold, clear nothingness, the heart of the Winter Court captured in Sebastian's almost colorless eyes. For a second, sparks of magic flashed in his irises and I could see a vast, breathtaking expanse of power there.

Then he blinked and the endless expanse vanished and the hybrid's power surged drawing a throaty moan that I tried but couldn't keep back.

My body throbbed, aching for a release I didn't want, and I shivered at every sweep of wind against my suddenly too-sensitive skin. I was hyperaware of the feel of Sebastian's cool hands on my cheeks and the thrum of his life force, as well as the hybrid's hard body pressed against mine, his breath a little too fast, his arms trembling, and the cold absence of his life force. His fangs slid from my neck and he replaced them with his lips in a barely-there kiss. The warm flicker of heat of his miniscule healing magic — a magic all vampires possessed — sealed the puncture wounds shut and sent an aching shudder racing through me.

"Your highness," he said and he eased me into Sebastian's arms.

"Now fuck your wife," the Winter Queen said.

"Jesus." Sebastian hooked an arm under my knees and lifted me, cradling me against his chest. "You're not going to get much of a show now."

The queen's eyes narrowed. "My original offer to have the court fuck her first still stands."

"Your majesty, Rin and I will be happy to show him how it's done," Deaglan said.

Sebastian's grip on me tightened and Hawk made desperate choking sounds, his rapid healing the only thing saving him from suffocation.

Titus growled low in his throat. He extended his claws and the massive muscles in his arms and neck bulged with the effort to break free of the Winter Queen's wind.

"Amiah," Cassius gasped, his breath short and ragged, every muscle straining to break free and his fire racing over his arms as more ice encased him over and over again. His angel glow blazed and his eyes were filled with ferocious determination.

He was going to fight and so was Titus and there was a chance, a good chance, they wouldn't survive, because even if they could break free of the Winter Queen's power there was still Deaglan and all of the queen's guards.

I met Cassius's gaze, begging him with my eyes. *Don't. Please don't. Remember your promise.*

He tensed and I dragged my gaze away from him before he could respond and leaned into Sebastian, the hall still spinning and dim and the hybrid's magic throbbing low within me, making my stomach churn with frustration and fear that my body craved something the rest of me didn't.

"I'm waiting." The queen wrenched her hand down and Titus smashed face-first onto the floor.

Blood rushed from his now-shattered nose and from a gash above his right eye. My power stuttered, still too weak to do anything but twist my compulsion to heal tight in my chest.

"What's more compelling?" the queen asked, her voice dark and dangerous. "Avoiding the pleasures of the King of the Shadow Court and the rest of my court, or saving your soldiers?"

Cassius released a strangled cry and blood oozed down his neck as the wind whip tightened and cut into his skin. His eyes bulged and his mouth opened for a breath he couldn't draw.

No, please.

My power stuttered stronger, desperate to help them, but it was still a weak useless glimmer in my palms.

The Winter Queen sent another wind whip around Hawk and wrenched him free of Deaglan's shadows and slammed him onto the floor beside Titus with crushing force, drawing a sharp scream.

Please stop. Just stop.

"This isn't necessary," Sebastian said, his body tense and his grip on me tightening.

The wind gusted stronger around us, filled with thick snowflakes and sweeping through the queen's hair and dress making her look ferocious and dangerous. "Make your choice."

Cassius's eyes rolled back and Hawk released another sharp scream. *Stop. Please, God, stop.*

My throat tightened. I couldn't lose them. I couldn't be responsible for their deaths.

I had to do it. I had no choice.

"Just do it, Sebastian," I begged, "before the hybrid's magic wears off." *Before she kills them.*

Because the hybrid's magic would wear off. I wasn't bite-locked which meant I didn't need an orgasm to release his magic, it would just naturally fade away and then I wouldn't even have that to distract me from what was going to happen.

"Amiah—" Sebastian whispered.

"Please. You promised. You all promised." I couldn't let them die. It was just my body. It wasn't my soul and it was with Sebastian. I could do this. I had to do this.

The court's wind stuttered then snapped colder than before. My fingers and toes grew numb, my teeth started to chatter, and the hall grew darker.

"Please," I gasped. "Don't let her kill them."

Sebastian's expression turned sad and soft, and my throat tightened. This wasn't the way we were supposed to have sex again. It was supposed to be beautiful, purposeful, not because we needed to save Hawk and certainly not desperate and on display to save Cassius, Hawk, and Titus.

"Okay," Sebastian murmured against my forehead.

Titus howled and all three of them wrenched against the queen's control, but the wind picked up, slamming their heads into the floor, stunning them, and Deaglan's shadows wrapped around their necks, choking them.

"After you," the queen said, her wind slamming the guys against the floor again.

Sebastian jerked away from them and marched down the hall to the ballroom. The Winter Queen and Deaglan, arm in arm, strode behind us with the hybrid a few steps behind them, while Cassius, Titus, and Hawk, barely conscious, were behind the hybrid, dragged along by the court's wind, and guarded by the queen's three men.

Sebastian stepped into the ballroom and headed straight to the bed, while the queen and Deaglan led everyone else to the raised throne at the back of the room.

Cassius, Titus, and Hawk were wrenched to the floor in front of the dais's steps with the rest of the queen's men standing guard on either side of them, and if any of the queen's guests noticed, they didn't react to the bleeding, stunned men being held captive at her feet.

The light in Cassius's eyes blazed so brightly I could barely make out his facial features and smoke billowed around him. Beside him, Hawk gasped for air, clutching the wind whip around his neck, while Titus heaved and snarled, his eyes wild, blood on his face from the cut above his eye and his shattered nose.

Stop. Please stop. They had to stop fighting. They couldn't win and I couldn't lose them. I could get through this if I knew they were safe.

The queen sat on her throne, raised her hands, and the room went silent. "The time has come to welcome a new heir to the Winter Court."

The room burst into wild cheers and all eyes turned to me and Sebastian as we drew closer to the center of the room.

Oh God oh God oh God.

My pulse pounded so fast my chest hurt and I couldn't catch my breath.

The room grew dimmer, and the beam of moonlight shimmering from the skylight onto the bed grew brighter.

I couldn't do this. I couldn't.

But I had to.

Please. I couldn't be responsible for their deaths. I couldn't lose them.

Sebastian paused at the edge of a thin, barely visible sparkling line encircling the bed. "Amiah—"

"Just make it quick."

He pressed his lips to my forehead and murmured, "If we don't loosen you up more it'll hurt and Hawk won't be able to help you."

"I don't care. I just want this over with. This doesn't count. It's not real. We'll get real again when this is over and we're safe."

The muscles in his jaw flexed and the grief in his eyes deepened. "She'll want a show."

"Then pick an interesting position."

"You're too weak for that." But he still squared his shoulders and stepped across the sparkling circle.

A whisper of ice shivered through my veins and the hybrid's magic billowed. I tried to hold back my moan, but it still escaped, low and breathy.

Sebastian sat me on the bed, knelt in front of me, and captured my cheeks between his palms.

I tried to stare into his almost colorless eyes, tried to find that vast expanse of power and lose myself in his gaze again, but I couldn't focus and couldn't concentrate past the exhaustion and fear and throbbing desire of the hybrid's bite.

I can't do this. They're all looking at me. They're all going to see me. I can't, I can't.

I have to. Please.

"I won't make it if you draw it out." I wasn't sure I could make it now. "Just rip off the bandage. Hard and fast. Make me cry, that'll make your mother and Deaglan happy."

"I'm not making you cry." He captured my lips in a tender kiss filled with such concern and gentleness that it broke my heart and my wavering vision grew glassy with tears I didn't want to cry.

The court's wind gusted around us, ruffling my hair and another shiver of ice swept through my veins.

I tried to find my strength, my resolve to do what had to be done, and appear brave, but a tear frustratingly rolled down my cheek.

"I'm going to cry anyway," I said. "I'm crying now. I don't want this. I don't want your mother to kill the others. I can't—" My throat tightened and I couldn't catch my breath. If he treated this like we were actually making love I'd shatter. I wouldn't be able to get through it.

I captured his face with my palms and pressed my forehead against his. "Please, Sebastian. Just make it quick. Get me through this as fast as possible."

He stared into my eyes as if he could see into my soul for a long, terrifying moment. He had to do it fast. I wasn't going to make it if he didn't. I didn't know how to convince him. All I could pray was that he could sense my desperation and just do it.

Then he gave a tight, barely-there nod.

"Okay," he murmured back, his voice heartbreakingly soft. "I don't mean any of this."

"I know."

He seized a handful of my hair, painfully jerked my head back, and smashed his lips against mine in a bruising kiss. It happened so fast, the room darkened for a second, then another shiver of ice swept through me and the skylight lurched back into sight.

He shoved his tongue into my mouth and his hand between my

thighs. One finger slid inside me, testing how far the hybrid's bite had gotten me, making the magic inside me twist tighter in my core. But the hybrid's magic had only gotten me started. Sure, I was mostly lubricated, but even with that I wasn't relaxed enough to accommodate Sebastian's size without still taking it slow.

And still I shuddered at the invasion, my body aching for more even as my pulse raced with shame and embarrassment.

They were all watching me, all waiting for Sebastian to shove himself inside me, all thrilled that they got to see us like that.

My stomach churned at the thought. Didn't I like the idea of being watched? Wasn't that what I'd wanted in Hawk's tent when I'd seen Sebastian's desire at my reaction to Hawk's magic? But this wasn't like that at all. Intimacy didn't just have to be between two people, it could be between three or four — or, oh my goodness! five people — that I cared about and desired. There was nothing intimate about what was happening right now. Even if I remained clothed, I was still being exposed and violated. Both of us were.

I dragged my wavering gaze to the throne. The queen smirked with satisfaction while Deaglan watched with dark desire. At least the aggressive kiss seemed to be satisfying her.

Then my gaze dipped to the guys and my throat tightened and another tear escaped. Titus wrenched against the wind again and again, his eyes were wild with rage, and fire sparked from Cassius's arms even though they were encased in ice. His breath was hard and fast and his angel glow had sharpened into a cold fury.

The court's wind gusted stronger, whipping my hair to the side and stinging my skin.

They were still fighting. They had to stop. They were going to make this sacrifice pointless and get themselves killed.

Sebastian had to hurry this up, not just for me, but for them. If we finished there'd be no reason for them to fight. But he roughly rubbed his slick finger against my clit, trying to build on the hybrid's magic.

Except it wasn't going to be enough. Nothing would be enough, not to get me to relax or forget everyone was watching or that the Winter Queen was going to kill the others.

I grabbed the front of Sebastian's jerkin and weakly struggled against his grip, trying to tell him to just get it over with. But he wouldn't let me go and wouldn't ease up enough on his kiss for me to speak. All I could do was gasp shallow shuddering breaths.

He kissed me as if he was furious, as if he could vent all of his frustrations out through his lips, and I couldn't tell if it was an act or not. He twisted my neck to a painful angle, dug his nails into my scalp, and bit my lip, drawing blood.

I whimpered against his mouth, not needing to pretend it hurt, and he snarled back at me.

The Winter Queen's smirk deepened and Deaglan's breath picked up.

Then Sebastian yanked his hand out from my thighs, quickly unlaced himself one-handed, and shoved me back onto the bed, the sudden movement making my head spin. My gaze caught his and my heart broke at the pain in his eyes. This wasn't him. It wasn't us.

"It's okay," I murmured, trying to hide my terror and give him the strength to get through this. Because if he couldn't, I couldn't. I didn't have the willpower to shut myself away from what was happening. I needed him strong, steadying me, needed to cling to the strength of his soul and his compassion to survive. "Make it good so we never have to do this again."

Titus's struggling grew frantic, desperately bucking and heaving against the wind, the Winter Queen sat forward, and Deaglan's hand slid inside his pants.

My stomach churned with a nauseating mix of fear and unwanted desire. More ice crackled through my veins, stronger than before, and the court wind gusted, picking up speed.

I dragged my attention back to Sebastian.

It's okay. We can do this.

Sebastian aligned himself with my opening, his gaze locked with mine.

We can do this. We can save the others. Because this isn't really us. Not our souls, just our bodies.

He seized my hips.

Not us. Not us. This doesn't count.

Then he plunged into me with a forceful thrust.

I cried out, my body tensing, and tears spilled down my cheeks at the pain of his savage invasion and the horror of what was happening, as the people in the room cheered.

The court wind whipped into a gale that tore through the room and swept inside me, following the ice in my veins to explode around my heart in a wild, ferocious torrent that threatened to tear me apart.

Titus howled, a great bellowing roar, that carried through the gale.

He wrenched against the wind holding him and his body swelled, his muscles and chest growing enormous and his hips and thighs tearing through his leather pants. Red and gold scales swept over his neck and hands and raced over the rest of him. With another great howl, he tore through the Winter Court's wind and shifted...

Into a massive, furious dragon.

FATED FEAR

ANGEL'S FATE, BOOK 3

AMIAH

ICE AND WIND AND SOMETHING ELSE, SOMETHING POWERFUL AND FOREIGN tore through my chest, overwhelming the fear of having sex in public as well as the exhaustion of having spent all my magic and some of my life force to save Hawk from a vicious poison.

Time stuttered and for a second my senses narrowed to the pain, the power, the bed's red silk sheet against my back, Sebastian's fingers digging into my hips with his furious grip, and his erection buried deep inside me.

He stared at me, his eyes wide with shock. Something in my soul clicked and my skin lit up again like it had the first time we'd had sex even though I was no longer a virgin.

His expression turned to horror. "Oh, fuck."

Then time lurched, yanking me back to the chaos erupting in the Winter Court's ballroom. People screamed and bolted for the exits, and Titus, now a massive red dragon, roared and snapped his tail at the Winter Queen sitting on her throne.

The queen stretched out her hand and a wall, half ice and half wind, stopped the strike, but exploded on the impact.

Cassius yelled, flames erupted over his body and poured from his hands onto the floor. He released his wings with a fiery burst and heaved free of the court's icy wind, while Hawk continued to wrench against the wind's control.

Titus jerked his attention to me and even with his face transformed, I could see the ferocious desperation in his golden eyes. He leaped toward me, his wings catching air, but Deaglan, the King of the Shadow Court and the man who'd held Titus captive for five hundred years and who'd tried to murder Sebastian, shot shadows from his hands and seized Titus's neck and legs and jerked him back to the floor.

"Fuck fuck fuck." Sebastian yanked himself from me and hurriedly secured himself back into his leather pants. "Amiah, are you okay?"

The court's wind blasted around us, filled with stinging ice that sliced my skin and Sebastian's and shattered against Titus's scales. It whipped open the front of my dress — a dress with a slit that went all the way up to my waist and barely covered my breasts — exposing my privates to anyone who might have been looking my way, but I couldn't get my thoughts to focus even to grab it and cover up. I should grab it. I should run. I should—

Cassius snapped a fire whip around the wind capturing Hawk in front of the queen's throne and freed him, and they both scrambled out of the way of Titus's tail as he smashed it against another wind wall while trying to break free of Deaglan's shadows.

"Amiah." Sebastian leaned over me and cupped my cheeks in his hands, dragging my whirling attention back to him.

I tried to focus on him, but the room kept spinning, and exhaustion weighed me down determined to drag me into unconsciousness.

If I passed out everything would go away, the fear, the pain, the shame, and the ice.

Everything was happening so fast. My worst fear had come true. Sebastian's mother had threatened to kill Hawk, Cassius, and Titus, and Sebastian and I had been forced to have sex in the middle of the Winter Court's ballroom with everyone watching.

"Amiah. Are you all right?" Worry tightened Sebastian's expression.

He'd hurt me, pulled my hair, bit my lip, and thrust himself into me before I was ready. Because I'd asked him to. Because I wouldn't have gotten through it if we'd actually made love and I'd connected with his life force. And because I was too weak to give his mother and Deaglan any other kind of show to please them and save the guys.

And then Titus had gone crazy and shifted, shattering the glamor hiding his identity and protecting him from everyone in Faerie... where we were... right now...

"Fuck. Amiah. Stay with me."

I dragged my eyes open.

"Atta girl." He glanced over his shoulder then captured me again with his pale blue, almost colorless gaze. "I can fight Deaglan long enough to get away, but you have to take control of the Winter Court from my mother."

His words tripped in my mind.

"But she's the queen." She'd already proven she could take away what little control I had of the court's wind with a flick of her finger.

"The Winter Court just claimed you as a rightful heir. I can feel its power rushing through you."

"I—"

Titus roared, drawing my attention to him as a pillar of ice shattered against his side, making him stumble, and sending massive shards shooting into the windstorm whirling around us.

Both the Winter Queen and Deaglan wanted him. Everyone wanted him.

Sebastian ducked close, protecting me from the shards with his body.

"I know you can feel it. It's like ice and power in your veins," he said, his breath strangely warm against my cheek when it was usually cool. "Amiah, take it, use your will to overpower my mother's and get us the hell out of here."

"But this is her court." *And yours.* Whether he wanted it or not, he was the next King of the Winter Court in Faerie, he would have a more powerful connection to the court than me.

Another pillar of ice shot toward Titus. He opened his mouth and blasted it with a stream of fire, melting half of it before the rest shattered on his scales.

I wanted to scream at him. We'd already decided there was no way we could fight our way free, but he'd shifted anyway, giving us no other choice. Now we had to escape or die trying... and the odds weren't good for escaping.

Faerie's Heart and its powerful magic had awakened and Titus, the last dragon and the only one able to find the keys to release it, had revealed himself to the entire Winter Court and the King of the Shadow Court. They would do whatever it took to keep him in their grasps.

"Bring me my son and his wife," the Winter Queen yelled, her voice carrying through the wind. "The queen's favor to whoever brings them to me."

Most of the men in her harem bolted toward us along with a few personal guards that were dressed only in leather pants like my guys — and likely worked for other winter court nobles or the few visiting nobles from other courts who'd come to the queen's party.

Hawk grabbed the long white hair of one of the queen's men, a stunningly beautiful high fae, and yanked him off his feet. Cassius blasted another in the back with a ball of fire, shoving him onto the floor and drawing a scream of agony before two more of the queen's men encased Cassius in ice. But liquid fire roared from his hand's melting it before my sluggish thoughts could fully register the danger.

Towering and bulky guards, beings constructed of ice and Winter Court magic, stormed in from the halls. They headed straight for my guys, and Deaglan threw more shadows around Titus's neck and his snout.

Titus heaved and jerked against the shadows and his gaze, still locked on me as if not even fighting for his freedom mattered, turned desperate.

With a triumphant yell, the queen raised her hands. The frozen magic in my chest thudded like a powerful second heartbeat, and a barrier swept around all of us, trapping us in a magical icy dome.

"Amiah. I can't fight Deaglan *and* my mother. Take control of the court."

One of the queen's men, a bulky muscular werewolf, dove for me, and Sebastian rolled me out of the way, pulling me on top of him. But another man grabbed my hair and wrenched me off Sebastian with a painful jerk.

The sudden movement made the room darken and lurch and the ice inside me swelled. A blast of wind snapped out of the queen's storm and broke the man's arm.

With a scream, he released me and jerked back, and the wind, *my* wind, slammed him into another of the queen's men, knocking both of them over.

I staggered but managed to keep standing in my weakened condition, and my compulsive need to heal twisted in my chest. *Heal him. His arm is broken.* It didn't matter that he wanted to hurt me or the guys. God, I'd never been so grateful to be out of power.

Sebastian scrambled out of the way of a naga wearing the red leather pants of the queen's harem, his red scales — covering his chest and arms — protecting him from the flying ice. His thin prehensile tail flicked behind him, helping him keep his balance, but Sebastian activated a glyph on his left forearm and shot a force-wave at the man, and his tail wasn't enough to keep him upright. He staggered back and the windstorm threw him to his knees as three more of the queen's men barreled toward us.

Cassius snapped a fire whip around the neck of one of them and yanked him to the floor, but Deaglan shot a shadow spear at Cassius before he could stop the two others. The spear slammed into Cassius's shoulder, shoving him back and pinning him to the ice barrier.

"No." My pulse stuttered. How could they have been so stupid? They'd promised they wouldn't fight. They knew some or all of them wouldn't survive battling the queen, her men, her guards, and the Shadow King. Why had Titus shifted? He'd just had to control his beast a little longer and we'd have been free.

I'd been willing to sacrifice my body to save them? It had been the only option. It had almost been done. With the Winter Queen satisfied, we could have just slipped away. Why couldn't they have just let me save them.

Fire roared around Cassius, but the ice barrier behind him, keeping all of us captured, didn't melt, and the queen's men encased him in wave after wave of thick ice, rebuilding it as fast as he could melt it.

Hawk screamed, jerking my attention to him, and my pulse stalled altogether. One of the queen's guards had shoved his enormous ice spear through the center of his chest, and while the incubus could rapidly heal and take a lot of damage, there was still a limit to his powers. And if we didn't get out of the Winter Court soon, we'd find it.

"Amiah," Sebastian snapped. He held up his hands and shot light through the shadow pinning Cassius to the dome, freeing him. None of Sebastian's glyphs that I could see glowed which meant he could have been using his sorcerer's power — not the power of the many spells tattooed in his skin — and dangerously channeling the primal, raw power of Faerie itself, risking burning up if he couldn't control it. "Break the dome."

The werepanther who'd been by the Winter Queen's side since we'd arrived in court ran toward me. He shifted between one step and the next, his body melting into a sleek black cat with liquid effortlessness, and leaped at me.

I lurched out of the way, but the movement made the room whirl, and I tumbled back onto the bed. The werepanther's canines gazed my legs, slicing into my skin but not getting ahold of me, and the ice in my chest thudded again.

A blast of my wind shoved him a few feet away, forcing him to dig his claws into the floor to keep from tumbling even farther.

"Amiah, get us out of here," Sebastian yelled. His full-body glow had dimmed, his complexion was gray, and his breath was too fast. His light magic twisted and writhed with Deaglan's shadows while also tethering Deaglan's demon-vampire hybrid to the back of the dome to keep him out of the fight. Sebastian was stretching himself too thin and if he kept going, he was going to burn up.

The hybrid sliced at the light tethering him with his claws and jerked forward a step, but the tether quickly reformed and shoved him back again.

"How long can you hold both of us?" Deaglan called in a singsong. "You're not as strong as you were three hundred years ago."

"I can hold just fine." Sebastian's light surged, but Deaglan formed more shadows, catching the blast then shooting a flurry of spikes in my direction.

I tried to jerk out of the way but I wasn't going to be fast enough.

At the last second, Sebastian tackled me onto the bed and rolled us off the other side and my wind tore the shadows apart.

"Get us the fuck out of here," Sebastian snarled at me, before jerking up and throwing another blast of light in Deaglan's direction.

Titus howled and I glanced over the edge of the bed. Only a few strands of shadow still captured him. With a powerful flap of his wings, he broke free of the rest, but the Winter Queen seized his neck with a lasso of wind and wrenched him to the floor with a bone-rattling boom.

Icy fear roared through me and my wind tore the lasso apart without me trying to control it.

The Winter Queen's gaze, her eyes fully black with her terrifying power, jumped to me.

"This is my court." Her wind exploded into a hurricane that tore at my hair and dress and slammed me into the far side of the dome. My breath exploded from my lungs at the impact and the wind whipped it away as the room darkened.

"Amiah." That sounded like Hawk.

I forced my eyes open to see him barreling toward me. He'd broken free of the spear, leaving a large pool of blood on the floor, and had managed to draw closer.

But the queen's wind gusted and tossed him sideways toward Cassius, who fought three more ice guards, as well as the queen's fae men. The wind tore at Cassius's fire, yanking it from his body and extinguishing it, and thick ice threatened to immobilize him.

With a guttural yell, he erupted in a ferocious blaze, radiating so much heat I could feel it halfway across the room. The ice encasing him shattered, and he snapped a massive fire whip around a guard's neck and tossed him at the Winter Queen. She wrenched her hand up, sending a blast of wind knocking the guard to the side, and the storm pummeling me stuttered.

The icy power inside me thudded again, and I mentally clutched at its cold slicing through my veins. I willed it, begged it, promised it everything if it would just give me control, just long enough to save them.

The hail and wind vanished and the room fell deathly quiet. Only Titus's snarls as he fought the wind pinning him to the floor and the crackle of Cassius's fire broke the silence.

I'd done it. I'd stopped the storm. Somehow I'd taken control of the queen's wind.

All eyes jumped to Sebastian who panted a few feet away, his complexion gray, his body trembling, then their gazes slid to me, their expressions filled with a mix of fear and horror and rage.

"I said," the queen hissed, her voice low, barely carrying across the room, and filled with a dark, deadly rage, "this is my court."

She wrenched both hands up and wind pounded into me. It stole my breath and crushed me against her barrier, cracking my ribs and sending a pain I was far too familiar with screaming through my chest.

Cassius yelled and shot a fire whip at the queen, but both of her fae men encased it in ice and the two remaining ice guards stabbed at him with their spears.

The wind's pressure grew. I heaved against it, strained to regain control, but couldn't breathe and could barely think.

Deaglan sent a flurry of shadows at Sebastian, wrenching him off the ground and slamming him into the floor before he could defend himself.

One of my ribs snapped, exploding agony through my chest, and then another.

Hawk leaped toward me, but the werepanther dug his claws into his side and yanked him around with a wild spray of blood that was whipped up into the queen's reawakened storm.

Another *snap*.

I screamed and the wind tore the cry from my mouth and devoured it.

Titus wrenched and spat fire. His wings wildly flapped and his claws dug rents into the floor as he fought to break free of the queen's hold.

All of the guys fought, desperate, panting, and bleeding. Cassius's fire stuttered, and Hawk staggered as the werepanther raked his claws against his back. Light snapped from Sebastian's hands burning through some of Deaglan's darkness but the demon-vampire seized him by the throat and pinned him to the floor.

Another *snap* and darkness swept over me, promising blissful nothingness. I struggled to stay conscious, to regain control of the wind, do something, anything. I had to do something.

It didn't matter that I didn't have any power of my own. Everything within me screamed that I had to save them. Somehow. Whatever it took. I would pay it. Whatever the cost. *Please. Someone, anyone, save them.*

AMIAH

My soul screamed, *save them, save them,* but it was more than just my compulsive need to heal. It was deeper, more consuming, and it twisted with the ice in my chest.

I have to save them. I have to find the power.

I couldn't let the Winter Queen kill them and I couldn't let her or Deaglan imprison Titus. He'd suffered too much already for too long. He'd already lost everything, his whole species, what he'd thought was a friendship with Deaglan, and five hundred years of his life.

He didn't deserve that. No one did.

Sebastian screamed and blasted light into the demon-vampire, breaking free of the hybrid's grasp and tossing him to the dais at the back of the room. Cassius barely held his own, his inferno ripped from his body by the queen's ferocious wind, and Hawk tumbled out of the way of the werepanther's teeth, blood gushing from his wounds.

The Winter Court's magic thudded in my chest, my veins, my soul, an overwhelming second heartbeat, and I gasped in an agonizing breath.

Whatever the cost? it asked.

"Yes." *Yes yes yes.*

The ice thudded again and locked in. The court's cold swept through my cells and wove into my essence, and frost crackled over my skin. There was no going back. The Winter Court had claimed me and I'd let its wild magic in without restraint.

A small part of me screamed, desperate to take back my consent. I was trapped. I'd let myself be trapped in a permanent bond, the very thing I'd been trying to avoid, the very thing I'd begged Sebastian to help me avoid when he'd helped remove my mating brand. Worse, I'd enslaved myself to a magic I didn't understand.

And the rest of me didn't care.

It was the only way out, the only way to save everyone. And I *was* going to save everyone.

I seized the ice inside me, willing it, begging it to obey my command and only my command. I was stronger than the Winter Queen. I had to be stronger than her. The guys weren't going to survive if I wasn't.

I. Will. Save. Them.

I forced everything I had into one powerful command to the Winter Court. Mine. Right now, it was mine. The wind would stop. The dome would break. And the court would help us escape.

The ice inside me shuddered, not because it wanted to resist me, but because the Winter Queen still possessed its power.

"Mine!" I screamed, releasing all of my fear and determination into that word and seizing control of the court.

Ice tore at me from the inside out and the queen's storm vanished, taking all the air in the room with it for a gasping, heart-stopping moment and making my world whirl.

The Winter Queen howled and the dome shattered with a sharp *crack*, showering us with massive chunks of ice.

A piece slammed into Sebastian, knocking him to the floor and drawing a cry of pain. Hawk twisted out of the way of another piece, barely managing to dodge it, while Cassius shoved one of the ice guards into the path of another chunk.

The queen raised her hands, blocking the ice falling on her with a wind shield then tossed the pieces at me.

I jerked my hands up and threw myself to the side as my wind battered her ice out of the way, but another piece from above crashed against the side of my head and sent me reeling.

Titus wrenched free of the Winter Queen's wind, leaped across the room for me, and snatched me up in his large front claw.

Without waiting for the others, he shot straight up and smashed through the skylight.

"Stop that dragon," the queen screamed.

Cassius extinguished his flames, grabbed a barely conscious Sebastian, and slung him over his shoulder, while Hawk scrambled to join him. With the incubus clutched against his other side, Cassius took off as well, but with the extra weight he couldn't fly as fast as Titus and we were leaving them behind.

"Titus, the others," I gasped, my teeth chattering with the cold inside me.

Titus snarled and rose higher into the freezing night sky, strangely lit not with stars but with a shimmering, opalescent barrier.

If his beast had fully taken over there was no way I'd be able to reason with him. He'd be working purely on primal instinct, and I could only pray that after having been forced to deny his beast for five hundred years Titus the man hadn't been locked away in the deepest recesses of his beast's mind for good.

"Titus, please."

He jerked around, pulled his wings back, and divebombed Cassius, whose eyes flashed wide. The wind of our fall whipped my hair and dress around me, stung my bare skin, and made the world whirl. Fire snapped over Cassius's hands, drawing a yelp from Hawk and a moan from Sebastian, and Titus seized Cassius and Sebastian in a large claw — Hawk managing to jerk out of the way at the last minute and cling to Titus's leg.

With a roar, Titus shot fire in ferocious defiance into the ballroom. Then he flapped his wings with powerful strokes, gusting the air around us, and soared away from the heart of the Winter Court.

Below, ragged snowcapped mountains stretched as far as I could see in every direction, and above, thick storm clouds started to rush in around us. They brought a vicious, freezing wind, filled with ice shards, and I knew in my heart this was the Winter Queen's fury.

The wind tossed us, adding nausea to my spinning vision and I fought to control the icy magic freezing my soul and regain my hold of the Winter Court.

But the queen's fury was too strong and I'd been exhausted and weak to begin with and getting weaker and it didn't seem to matter that I now belonged to the Winter Court.

Titus roared, fighting the wind, his grip around me — and most likely Cassius and Sebastian as well — tightening, while Hawk, with his fingers locked together, clung to his leg.

You thought you could keep the dragon for yourself, the wind howled. *Too impatient to wait for me to fade to inherit my court.*

A blast of wind slammed against Titus's back, dropping us toward the jagged mountain spikes. He twisted, narrowly missing crashing into the stone and shot through a crevasse barely wide enough for his body.

"Mother, please," Sebastian gasped pinned against Cassius's body. His full-body glow flickered and disappeared for a terrifying second then stuttered back to life, but it was barely visible.

I won't let you leave my court. I won't let you take my dragon. I will kill him before I let you or anyone else possess my Heart.

An enormous vortex roared to life in front of us. Titus jerked, trying to avoid it, but it seized him and wrenched him in.

The air was sucked from my lungs and the world went frigid and dark. Wind stung my skin and we spun around and around and around making my stomach heave.

Titus roared and fire sparked from Cassius but the flames were whipped away the second they appeared. Hawk wrapped his legs around Titus's and locked his ankles, desperately trying to hold on.

Winter court, please, I begged.

Not. Your. Court, the Winter Queen's wind howled.

Command me, the court said inside me, its ice snapping and cracking as if it tried to keep hold inside me but the queen's control kept breaking it. *Command me.*

Let us go.

A massive blast of wind slammed into us and we were tossed out of the vortex and through the opalescent barrier protecting the Winter Court from the Wilds, the magic of the barrier painfully tearing at my essence as we tumbled through.

For a second we were suspended in a cold, clear sky filled with glittering stars above a barren, mostly flat landscape stretching as far as I could see, then Titus faltered and plummeted to the ground.

He tossed me and the guys and started to shift — using the magic that changed his shape to partially cushion the impact. But I hit the cold, hard-packed cracked earth, agony screaming through my chest, and tumbled over and over again before I could see if he succeeded.

My shoulder hit something hard, bringing me to a jarring halt lying face down, and my stomach immediately heaved. It threatened to expel the little bit of food I'd managed to eat during the party, and my uncontrollable shivering with the Winter Court's ice inside me and the agony of my broken ribs didn't help.

"Amiah," Cassius groaned.

I struggled to not throw up and raised my head, but that only made my stomach clench tighter and my world darken.

"Amiah, answer me," Cassius said, his tone sharp. Footsteps pounded toward me, smoke enveloped me, and burning hot hands rolled me over, making me cry out in pain and straining my mental hold on my stomach's contents.

Cassius's striking blue gaze met mine and for a second I was floating in brilliant blue, embraced by angelic light, home and safe. I'd felt that way when he'd rescued me from that faith healer. I hadn't thought I'd ever see the familiar glow of a fellow angel's eyes again, had believed that I'd be alone until the faith healer had drained me of all my power and I'd died.

Then Cassius had found me and looked into my eyes like he was doing now, his gaze filled with fear and rage and... something else, something I couldn't quite place, something stunned... or was that awe... desperation? Need?

My stomach clenched tight and his eyes widened.

"Crap." He jerked back, fire erupting over his body as I threw up, barely managing to avoid his boots.

"Jeez, Amiah," Hawk gasped.

Cassius staggered farther away, his fire pouring onto the ground around his feet, hissing and snapping as if he couldn't control it. Smoke billowed around him, and every muscle in his body tensed.

Hawk scrambled to my side and brushed my long blond locks, tangled and windblown, out of my face, keeping the ends out of my vomit.

Heat radiated from his body in massive, suffocating waves, burning down my nose and throat with every breath. Sweat burst from my skin even though my insides remained frozen, and I inched away from him making him frown.

"Are you okay?" he asked, his voice tender, his usual blue-gray gaze filled with concern and a barely smoldering prick of hellfire.

"Are you?" I asked back through chattering teeth despite the heat coming off of him and fighting to keep my breath shallow. I wasn't okay. I didn't know if I'd ever be okay again. I was exhausted, in pain, out of power, freezing cold on the inside, and possessed by the Winter Court.

"You," Titus snarled, dragging my attention past Cassius and Hawk to the enormous naked shifter — the magic that transformed him having consumed his clothing. He stormed toward Sebastian who had barely managed to get to his hands and knees. "You hurt her."

"Titus—" Sebastian started to raise his head, but Titus grabbed the back of Sebastian's white leather jerkin and slammed him back into the ground.

Everything within me froze, unable to fully comprehend what I'd just seen.

"You made her cry." Titus jerked Sebastian back up again and smashed his fist into Sebastian's face with a sharp crack that resounded through the quiet darkness. "You rammed your cock into her and made her cry, you fucking bastard."

Blood gushed from Sebastian's nose and he opened his mouth but Titus punched him again. Another sharp crack that snapped Sebastian's head to the side.

My mind jerked into motion and my heart leaped into my throat. After all that, Titus was attacking him?

"Titus, stop." I staggered to my feet. Pain sliced through me, and the barren landscape lurched along with my stomach. Cassius reached for me but jerked back at the last moment and Hawk grabbed me instead, pulling me into a blazing hot embrace, searing my skin and making me whimper in pain.

"You weren't supposed to have sex with her," Titus roared, his voice booming in the stillness.

"Titus, stop." I pushed against Hawk's grip, but I was too weak to fight him, and he wouldn't let me go. "It's not his fault."

"How could you do that, Seireadan? She cried. In pain." Titus smashed his fist into Sebastian's face again. *Crack*. Sebastian's full-body glow flickered, his eyes rolled back, and my compulsion to heal twisted in my chest, adding to my nausea, even though I barely had any healing magic left.

Fear quickened my pulse and I weakly heaved against Hawk's grip. I had to stop this. Didn't he know it hadn't been Sebastian's fault? I would have cried if it had been any of them.

"Stop. Just stop," I begged, the ice in my chest swelling, numbing the agony of my broken ribs, and making me shiver despite Hawk's burning body temperature.

But Titus smashed his fist into Sebastian's face again. "She cried." Another crack even though Sebastian's head lolled to the side, his eyes barely open. "Because of you."

My need to heal twisted tighter. God, Titus was going to kill him. He might have shifted back into a human, but his beast still had control and he was furious that Sebastian hadn't been gentle when he'd been forced to have sex with me... because I'd asked him to.

Titus snarled, wrenched Sebastian close, nose to nose, and bared his large, wickedly sharp canines. "You even think about touching her again and I'll rip your heart out and eat it."

"I said stop!" I commanded, letting my fear and frustration and pain harden my voice, but Titus wrenched his hand back to hit Sebastian again.

AMIAH

"Just stop!" I screamed again. *Please, God, stop.* Sebastian wasn't going to be able to take much more. I could feel his life force stuttering even though I wasn't touching him and I was supposed to need contact to sense someone's life force. And while I also wasn't fully connected and had no idea how serious his injuries were, I knew a few more blows would kill him.

"Please, Titus."

Titus jerked to face me, a wild fury blazing in his golden eyes, making his body shake.

Blood filled with sparkling flecks of white light gushed from Sebastian's nose and a cut along his cheek. It splattered onto the hard earth and was instantly absorbed. His breath was ragged and he hung limp in Titus's grip.

"Please." I pushed against Hawk's embrace but he still wouldn't let go, and to be honest, I wasn't sure I could stand without his help, but I had to go to Sebastian. Even if I couldn't heal his injuries, I had to check on him, prove to my magic there wasn't anything I could do. *But please, God, let there be something I can do.*

"Let me go," I said.

"You're not going anywhere near him," Titus snarled. "Not after what he did to you."

"I said let me go. You don't get to tell me what to do. None of you do,"

I snapped. *Not after what I'd just been through.* "I *need* to check him," I added, putting emphasis on need hoping Cassius would understand that I was too tired to ignore my compulsion to heal even if I barely had any power. "And you certainly don't have the right to hit him for something I told him to do."

"You what?" Cassius asked, smoke billowing from him, his fire a molten pool around his feet, bright in the darkness. "You told him to assault you?"

"He didn't assault me." How could they possibly think Sebastian had assaulted me?

"Yes. He did," Cassius spat out. And now *he* looked like he wanted to pummel Sebastian into the ground, too.

The light in Cassius's eyes flared, revealing a hard, furious expression in bright angelic light. I wasn't sure if I'd ever seen him that angry before. The last time I'd seen him let his fire pour around him like that had been when I'd been kidnapped by Balwyrdan, and that fae had seriously beaten me.

Oh, God. Did he think Sebastian was as bad as Balwyrdan? Had it really looked that horrible? It couldn't have. Yes, Sebastian had been rough, but Balwyrdan had been brutal.

"That was hard to watch," Hawk said, his grip tightening, burning against my skin, "especially knowing you weren't enjoying it." Which was something I couldn't deny. Not that I wanted to. With his ability to sense sexual energy, he knew exactly how I'd felt about what had happened and could probably guess that the reality of it hadn't fully hit home because I was still too exhausted and stunned.

"It had to be done," I said.

"Not like that," Cassius growled.

"She was going to kill you. If we didn't put on some kind of a show, she'd make us do it again, and I was too weak for anything else."

My throat tightened with the fear that I'd felt — still felt, because now all of Faerie knew we were with the last dragon and was coming after him — along with a rapidly growing rage. The Winter Queen had threatened whatever had been building between me and Sebastian by forcing that on us. And now it looked like she'd threatened his relationship with the other guys as well.

"I wasn't going to do it again. I just wanted it over with. Hurting me, making me cry, getting it over with fast was the best way to satisfy her so we could get out of there."

Wild sparks snapped from Cassius's body and the smoke billowing around him thickened. "He could have built up the hybrid's magic."

"Do you honestly think Sebastian could have done anything to make me enjoy that?" I shot back, my eyes burning with tears I didn't want to cry. Yes, I'd had the seductive magic of the demon-vampire's bite coursing through my veins, but it would never have been enough. I would never have relaxed enough to even partially enjoy it, not with everyone watching, not knowing the guys' lives hung in the balance.

"Amiah—" Cassius took a step toward me then jerked back as if he remembered he was still on fire.

"The only way I could have gotten through anything else was if you'd enthralled me," I said to Hawk. "And you weren't in a position to help."

He, Cassius, and Titus had all been trapped at the foot of the queen's dais and while an incubus's magic could affect someone from a distance, he needed to touch a person to fully enthrall her.

I shot a glare at Hawk and Titus. What was wrong with them? Didn't they know Sebastian would never do something like that to me? I'd had to beg him to do it. "You know him. Do you honestly think he'd have done that without my consent?"

The muscles in Hawk's jaw flexed. "Just because you agreed to it, doesn't make it right."

"Don't you think that hurt him as well? Didn't you see our first kiss?" I pressed. I hadn't known Sebastian very long, and even if I'd only met him that night, that first kiss had been so gentle, so caring it had broken my heart. He might wear a cocky overconfident demeanor the rest of the time, but in that moment, he'd revealed his true heart, someone who cared deeply for others, who didn't want to hurt others because he'd been horribly hurt himself.

It all made perfect sense now why he flirted with everyone and had a reputation for sleeping around — which he probably did. If he kept the same lover for too long, he'd become emotionally involved, and I was willing to bet the last time he'd been emotionally involved with someone was with his fiancé who'd slept with his best friend and then tried to kill him.

Sebastian groaned and his glow flickered and went out again. His muscles clenched tight and his breath picked up, making my pulse trip.

I *had* to check on him, had to use what little magic I'd managed to recover in the short time since I'd pushed everything I had into Hawk to help Sebastian.

"Now let me go." I heaved again against Hawk's grip, shooting agony through my chest and gritting my teeth, refusing to cry out in pain. "Don't make me fight my healing compulsion on top of everything else."

"Fine," Cassius growled. He gave a tight nod and Hawk released me — which made me furious because Hawk had done what Cassius had said and not what I'd wanted. "Titus, back away from Sebastian."

Titus snarled at Cassius and didn't release Sebastian.

"Titus," Cassius snapped.

"He won't hurt me," I said, staggering to them.

"Amiah—" Cassius started, but I jerked my head back to glare at him, making my stomach heave and the world lurch.

"He's beaten Sebastian to a pulp because of me." I sucked in a steadying breath, shot agony through my chest, and ended up panting. "He's not going to hurt me."

A flurry of sparks exploded from Cassius's blaze and flew into the night sky,

I turned my attention to Titus. "You're not going to hurt me," I said, keeping my voice soft and trying to look confident and in control while hiding my shivering body and chattering teeth.

"No," he growled as I reached him and placed my hands on his massive muscular arm, praying that the flesh to flesh contact would help calm his beast. As much as I really wanted to tend to Sebastian — now now now — I needed to deal with Titus and his beast first. If I didn't calm him down more and steady his soul, he could break down and attack Sebastian again.

"For fuck's sake, Amiah," Hawk hissed.

"Back away from the dragon," Cassius demanded.

Titus tensed at my touch and turned his golden gaze on me, his pupils fully slitted and a hint of red-gold scales curling over his neck and jaw.

"If there'd been any other way, you know he wouldn't have hurt me like that," I said, pressing my forehead against his biceps, adding another point of contact, and letting a whisper of my magic connect with him, just enough to gage through his vitals when he'd gotten his beast under control.

A shudder swept through him and he growled low in his throat.

"Amiah, please," Cassius begged.

"He could have fought," Titus said, but his pulse and breath were already starting to slow, my contact helping to steady his soul and let his human side regain control.

Oh, thank God. Because I had no idea what we were going to do if he remained furious with his beast in control. We needed him. *I* needed him. I needed all of them right now... and I wasn't going to think too hard about what that might mean.

"We barely escaped," I murmured back. And we'd only escaped because I'd given myself to the Winter Court. Something else I didn't want to think about.

Sebastian moaned and I strained to stay with Titus, my need to heal twisting, its pressure mixing with the pain and cold in my chest.

"Titus, I'm okay."

"You're not," he said, his voice a low rumble. "I smell your blood. I smell sex from him and the incubus."

My pulse stuttered and I prayed Cassius was too far away to hear that. I wasn't ready to tell him I was having sexual intercourse with both Sebastian and Hawk... which was silly given everything that had happened. What he thought of me, how he saw me, was nothing compared to what I'd just gone through.

"The light in your eyes is gone. You've spent all your power and I wasn't there to protect you." Titus dropped Sebastian, drawing a grunt of pain. He embraced me, curling his massive body around me — thankfully without putting pressure on my ribs — and a part of my soul sang at the physical contact, the closeness. And not completely because I was being held by a ruggedly handsome naked man. No, part of my satisfaction was because of the strong, ferocious pulse of his life force caressing my senses and the knowledge that all of his injuries, all the lacerations and contusions he suffered during the fight, were melting away with his unusually fast healing.

But instead of the embrace calming him, his breath picked up and he started to tremble, his beast suddenly struggling to take over again. "I should have protected you. You're fragile. You're hurt—"

"I'll be okay," I insisted. Just as soon as we got someplace safe and I could recover some of my magic and heal Sebastian and myself... and Cassius. Jeez, I hadn't even thought to check on Cassius, and with his fire blazing, any injuries he might have gotten during the fight weren't easily noticed.

"You. Were. Hurt," he growled, his muscles bunching around me.

"Titus, please." He was losing control again, the contact wasn't enough to calm him, and I had to get him calm. If Sebastian was out of commission, Titus was the only one who knew Faerie well enough to get us to safety.

I reached up and cupped Titus's cheeks, urging him to look down at me, hoping eye contact would help him regain control, but it wasn't Titus the man who looked down at me. It was Titus the beast, his eyes filled with a wild, ferocious intensity that stole my breath, half in awe and half in fear.

"You were hurt. I should have protected you. *He* should have protected you, not hurt you," he snarled. "He doesn't deserve you."

"Titus, please. Control your beast. Just for a little longer." I knew what I was asking might be impossible. He'd spent five hundred years in captivity and had only shifted one other time since. His connection with his beast had to be strained, and I could only hope it wasn't completely broken because that wasn't something I could heal.

"He hurt you." Titus heaved in a ragged breath, his nostrils flaring, and bared his teeth at me.

I met his glare without flinching, not in a fight for dominance — there was no way I'd ever be dominant to Titus — but in earnestness. There'd been no other way and his beast knew that, had to accept that. "I told him to."

His battle with his beast raged in his eyes. He wanted to protect me, wanted to support me, wanted to believe me. His primal instincts had to be tearing him apart because he'd denied half of his soul for far too long. And all I could do was press my body against his and pray that even though I wasn't a dragon or his mate my essence was enough to calm his and help him regain control. It was the only thing I could do.

"We thought it was our only way to keep all of us alive." *Please believe me. Please calm your beast. Please don't hurt Sebastian anymore.*

His eyes narrowed and his gaze dropped to Sebastian, who moaned in agony, more flecks of light sparking from his body, now not just from his blood but his skin as well, all of it sucked into the hard, barren earth.

"He was your best friend. You know him."

"I do," he spat out, pain tightening his expression, his whole body trembling.

"You know he wouldn't hurt me on purpose." Well not physically. He'd tried to hurt me emotionally to get me to turn my desires to Cassius when I wasn't at all certain I was in love with Cassius. But then he'd confessed that he wanted to continue having sex with me when we'd saved Hawk... and if I thought too hard about that right now with my whirling unsteady thoughts, I'd make myself crazy trying to figure out what that had meant. All I really wanted was to have sex with him, to explore what I'd denied myself for too long. And he'd been perfect because he didn't want a relationship.

More sparks exploded from Sebastian's skin and his full-body glow stuttered and went out again for a second.

My need to heal clenched around my heart. "You know we did what we had to in order to get out of there," I said, forcing my voice calm.

"I do." He yanked away from me. For a heart-stopping second, I thought he was going to attack Sebastian. His hands curled into tight fists and he bared his teeth. Then he jerked away. "I need a minute. Faerie is already ripping out his magic. We can't stay here."

He stormed a few feet past Cassius, his whole body tense with his beast's fury, stunning me at his sudden change of mind. He released a wild, ferocious howl, dropped to his knees, and punched the earth again and again as if he could scream and beat out his rage and regain control.

I sagged to the ground beside Sebastian, my magic connecting with him before I'd even touched him. His nose was broken, his cheek fractured, and his right orbital bone shattered. But more than that, a different kind of pain tore through him, turning his breath into shallow, desperate gasps. Except I couldn't find the source. It was everywhere and nowhere. In his veins, igniting his nerves, and consuming his fae light from the inside out. This had to be Faerie taking back its magic.

"Holy fucking hell." Hawk scrambled to my side and drew me back into his too-hot arms, sending agony screaming through my chest and making me gasp in pain, while Cassius stayed where he was, fire pouring off his body as if he'd given up on trying to control his magic.

"Don't you do that again," Cassius snarled. "God, please." He sank to his knees, his fire undulating around him in a ferocious burning pool.

The eyelid of Sebastian's one good eye fluttered open, and his gaze instantly met mine, making my pulse stall. There wasn't even a glimmer of the power in his eye that I'd seen before, only writhing painful darkness.

"Fuck man, you need to get that dealt with," Hawk whispered.

"Sure, find me a demon in Faerie that can pull it out." Light sparked from Sebastian's body and sank into the earth. He bit back a strangled moan and raised a trembling hand to my cheek, his skin strangely warm. "I'll fix this. I promise."

"We did what we had to. Titus will understand that. Cassius will too." A whisper of my healing magic sank into him, but it wasn't enough to knit any of his broken bones back together let alone mend all the lacerations he'd gotten from the ice in the queen's storm. "I don't have enough power to heal you. You're going to have to hang on for a while."

"I wasn't talking about that." Another spark snapped from his body and he panted in quick shallow breaths. "I'm talking about the court, about this." He drew my hand up. My skin still glowed like it had the first time we'd had sex as if I'd still been a virgin, except now I could see threads of white shimmering magic trailing through my skin like veins. "I'll get the court to release its claim on you and take back its magic. I promise."

"What? The Winter Court claimed her?" Hawk's grip around me tightened, making me whimper and he quickly eased up on his embrace. "That's why she's lit up like the sun and is freezing?"

"Yeah," Sebastian huffed then groaned as more light sparked from his body. "Guess what Amiah, you're now high fae. Soon you too will get the pleasure of having Faerie's magic ripped out of you if we stay here much longer."

"I'm what?" I must have been too exhausted and sore and cold to have heard that right. "How can I be fae. I'm an angel."

"You've Faerie's magic running through your veins now," he gasped.

"Because you two had sex on your mother's magic bed?" Hawk demanded.

"Best guess," Sebastian said as Cassius, his fire pulled under his skin with what had to be an extraordinary force of will — his frigid hard expression proof of his effort — drew closer. "Titus somehow gave her the first key to unlocking Faerie's Heart without killing himself and the Winter Court latched onto its magic inside her soul."

AMIAH

My thoughts stuttered. "I have a key to unlocking the Heart? When did I get the key?" Wouldn't I have known I had the key? In my soul? "How did I get the first key?"

Then my memory jumped to the kiss with Titus on the balcony when we were being attacked by the ice men.

Heat had filled me and I'd thought, since it hadn't been my mating brand awakening — the brand I no longer had, thank goodness! — it had just been a rush of adrenaline and desire. Because I did desire Titus. I'd been drawn to him from the moment I'd met him, and I wasn't sure anymore if that was just because he was a shifter and could give me the physical contact I craved or not.

"I don't know how I gave it to her. It just happened," Titus said, stepping up beside Cassius. His pupils were still slitted, but he was no longer heaving in giant breaths in a desperate attempt to calm down.

Another spark snapped out of Sebastian's skin, drawing a moan and making his good eye roll back for a second. "You didn't think that was something we should have known? The power of the key mixed with the court's power and my mother's will to make us conceive a supposedly impossible child. It connected Amiah to Faerie. If I'd known, I could have stopped it, woven a spell to lock Faerie out, something. Then Amiah wouldn't have a permanent glow."

"So you're not glowing because that was your first time?" Smoke billowed from Cassius's hands and he blew out a heavy breath. "Oh, thank God."

"Why?" I snapped suddenly irrationally angry. "Because fragile little me wouldn't have been able to handle it if I had?"

Jeez, I had no idea why I was so angry. But my sex life was none of Cassius's business... unless I wanted it to be—

Not the point.

I was sick and tired of him trying to protect my virtue when it wasn't his to protect and looking at me as if I was still that weak, pathetic angel he'd rescued all those years ago — even if right now I was weak and pathetic.

"I'm allowed to have a sex life. Just because I've never told you about it doesn't mean it doesn't exist. You've been keeping your distance from me ever since the war ended. For all you know I've been having wild, crazy sex for years and I can't wait to get back home and pick things up where I'd left them with my lover."

"Oh, really?" Cassius glowered at me, fire rolling up his arms, his control starting to slip again. "So you didn't just spend the last four years pining over a man who didn't love you and never would. You've been fucking every Tom, Dick, and Harry that came along."

"You really want to take that back," Hawk said, tightening his grip around me.

"All you really know is that I haven't been fucking you," I said to Cassius, the curse word flying out of my mouth like it had his.

His angel glow flared, but I didn't know if his reaction was at me swearing or if I'd hit my unintended mark. Sebastian had said Cassius was in love with me and if I'd stopped to think about it, I'd just said the most hateful thing I possibly could.

"Not sure this is the best place for this conversation," Hawk said.

Sebastian moaned, jerking my attention back to him and the sparks snapping from his body.

I turned my glare back to the guys. "Just to make things perfectly clear, my sex life is no one's business but mine and whoever I choose to sleep with. Sebastian did what he did because I asked him to, and he barely had a chance to do anything so no one has to worry about a half angel half fae nephilim abomination baby making their life complicated." If conceiving had even been possible... which it shouldn't have been.

He hadn't ejaculated and even if he had, he'd said he was shooting blanks because we hadn't completed the fae marriage ritual where he became fertile for his wife and only his wife.

Cassius heaved his smoke back under his skin. "Amiah—"

"We're *not* having this conversation again. We're *not* breaking anyone's bones about it. And we're not discussing how all of you made my sacrifice pointless," I said, my voice turning shrill, my breath short, desperate pants that sliced agony through my frozen chest.

Oh, God. It hadn't meant anything. Letting myself be exposed and hurt like that hadn't meant anything.

No. Stop thinking about it. Just stop.

But I couldn't focus my thoughts. Everything was whirling, the world around me, all my thoughts, even my soul. I spun, encased in ice and pain, and I was never going to be free.

God, I'd been beaten by a monster, I'd been forced to have sex in public, I'd begged a kind man to do something horrible to me because I hadn't been strong enough to handle it, and I'd lied to Cassius.

I was weak. So horribly weak. I couldn't handle any of it.

No. Not true.

I'd given myself to the Winter Court to save the guys and I'd do it again in a heartbeat.

Okay, so I was trapped. Again.

I bit back a sob.

Fine. I could handle this. I *would* handle this.

I'd pull myself together and get through this. We weren't safe. The Winter Queen could still send men after us into the Wilds not caring that it risked their lives, and I had no idea how far we'd been flung away from the Winter Court. I couldn't see its barrier, but for all I knew that didn't mean it wasn't close, since I knew next to nothing about the fae realm.

I clamped down on everything, all the desperate panic screaming through me, and heaved my professional doctor's persona in place. It would get me through this. It had gotten me through the war, and through watching the man I thought was my destiny fall in love with someone else. I clung to the persona, praying, begging, that it would hold me together until there was a more convenient — and private — time to have a breakdown.

"I've got you," Hawk murmured, his lips pressed against the back of my head. "Whatever you need."

And with just those few words some of the tension eased from my body. Hawk had my back. He didn't want anything from me and didn't need me to be anything to him. I could be who I was with him and not have to worry.

"Okay." I drew in a shallow, steadying breath that still sliced agony through my chest. "We have to get someplace safe. Sebastian? Titus? Where should we go."

"My ancestral nest," Titus said, his voice gruff, and he marched a good twenty feet away and shifted into his massive dragon.

I loved watching a shifter change, loved the magic that was woven into their very cells that allowed them to melt apart, multiply or merge their cells and transform into something beautiful. And this close, Titus in his dragon form, was stunning — and I suspected he'd be more beautiful when I saw him in daylight when I could see the different shades of red and gold in his scales that I'd only really caught a glimpse of in the ballroom.

"Before we go," Sebastian gasped, drawing my attention back to him. "Knock me out. You're fae now, you've Faerie in your veins, so you should be able to power my glyphs." He took my hand and placed it over the sleep glyph on his right shoulder. "Put your other hand over my heart, imagine pushing power into the glyph, and say ignite. The glyph will do the rest of the work."

My throat tightened. God, I wanted to be able to knock him out. Anything to help him get through the pain while he waited for me to regain my magic. But— "Even if I could power your glyph, I'm out of magic."

Fire popped inside me, shockingly hot against the ice, and a brilliant white spark exploded from my body with a sharp pinch and was sucked into the ground.

"Faerie disagrees." He quirked a ghost of his wicked smile, making my throat tighten even more because of what we'd just gone through. Then he groaned, his expression shifting back to pain, and more sparks exploded from him and were sucked away. "You've more Faerie magic than me right now. The less you have, the more painful losing it will get."

"Which means we need to get going," Cassius said, not meeting my gaze. His expression was harder and icier than I'd ever seen it and I knew my words had cut him. Well fine. He'd hurt me too. His overbearing protectiveness constantly implied I didn't know what I wanted and couldn't handle my own life. "If you're going to power his glyph, do it now, since we have no idea what other effects Faerie will have on you."

And as much as I wanted to argue that there wasn't anything else Faerie could possibly do to me that was worse than claiming me and filling me with frozen magic, he was right. There were probably hundreds of things this realm could do that I couldn't even imagine. I was a being from the Realm of Celestial Light. I wasn't supposed to have Faerie's magic in my veins ever.

I wasn't supposed to be trapped here.

I shoved that back.

"Okay." *Focus on what needs to be done. Focus on staying in control.* I had no idea if I would be able to activate Sebastian's glyph — very few angels had the ability to use glyph magic and they were rarer than angels with healing magic — but if Sebastian said I could do it, I had to try.

I pressed my free hand over his heart and imagined pushing power into the glyph on his shoulder. Ice thudded in my chest, misting my breath as if we were outside at wintertime and sending thick frost rushing over my hands. Power flooded me, frozen, biting, overwhelming. It was just me and the ice... no me and the Winter Court.

Then its power exploded out of my hand, ignited Sebastian's glyph before I could even think the word to activate it, and kept going, pouring into his body, blazing through the thick, painful darkness, and flooding his heart.

He sat up with a strangled scream, his full-body fae glow suddenly bright. "What the fuck—?"

Then his non-swollen eye rolled back and he collapsed, unconscious, his body radiating more light than I'd ever seen before as if I'd just imbued him with Faerie magic.

I jerked my hands back, terrified that I'd hurt him even as that whisper of healing magic inside me connected with him, assuring me he was fine... still injured with lacerations and broken bones and still filled with that strange consuming darkness, but I hadn't made things worse.

"Is he still alive?" Cassius asked, but his tone was so cold I couldn't tell how he felt about his question.

As if in response, a spark snapped from Sebastian's body and he groaned in his sleep.

"I just hope he's asleep long enough for me to regain some power."

"And to heal yourself," Cassius said, squatting to pick up Sebastian. "You're the priority. We lose you and we lose our healing."

He heaved Sebastian over his shoulder and marched to Titus before I could respond.

"Because that's all I'm good for I guess," I said to Hawk as he gathered me against his too-hot body.

"You hurt him. He's gone into soldier mode and shut his emotions down. I saw it all the time during the war."

"You were in the war?" I didn't know why that surprised me. After Michael's first few vicious attacks that had decimated some of the largest cities in the world, millions of people had volunteered to join the newly formed Angelic Defense. Humanity's survival as well as the survival of all supernatural beings depended on winning the war and very few souls were willing to sit back and hope for the best.

"Yeah." His voice turned soft and I sensed a great sadness in that one word, one that spoke of a grief deeper than the usual grief I'd seen in other vets. Whatever he'd gone through, it had really affected him. "Maybe someday I'll tell you about it."

"You don't have to." I leaned into him despite the heat radiating from his body. "I'll listen if you want to tell me, but I don't need to know."

He pressed a kiss against the top of my head and carried me to Titus. We climbed onto his back, and with the guys clinging to his spine ridges, Titus leaped into the air, flapped his wings with a powerful stroke, and took off into the cold night sky.

If Faerie is kind, Titus said, using the telepathy all shifters had in their shifted form, *it'll reveal the aerie sooner rather than later.*

"God, I hope so," Hawk said. Guess Titus had said that in everyone's head, not just mine.

No one else said anything and I, finally getting used to Hawk's hotter-than-normal-even-for-a-demon body temperature, gave in to the pain and exhaustion and let myself drift.

I dreamed of ice. Unending frozen, consuming ice. Wherever I looked, wherever I went, there was only ice. It groaned, massive pieces grinding against each other, and squeaked when I walked on it like a heavy snowfall or snow that was bitterly cold. It froze my blood and replaced my heart with a ball of ice. I belonged to it. I was it.

There was no escape.

I was trapped. The one thing I desperately didn't want. I'd voluntarily accepted agonizing pain and had a part of my soul ripped out to eliminate my mating brand in an attempt to remain free, and now I was trapped.

Trapped trapped trapped.
Because I made a choice.
Mine.
And if it kept the guys safe, I could live with that.

I jerked awake, shooting agony through my chest and crying out in pain, despite the determination that had filled me in my dream. I'd made the right choice. I had. I'd chosen my destiny and while I didn't like it, everyone was alive and free... except for me. What was one soul compared to four others or even all of Faerie?

"Hey." A seductive curl of magic unfurled inside me, Hawk's magic, muting but not completely getting rid of my pain.

Hawk still held me, his bare chest against my mostly bare back still uncomfortably hot. We were still on Titus's back, the wind rushing past us, and I was still out of magic... or rather out of my *healing* magic — I was still frozen inside so I guessed I was still brimming with Winter Court Faerie magic. Regardless, low healing magic meant I mustn't have been out for very long.

Ahead on the horizon loomed a flat-topped mountain that got bigger and bigger the closer we approached, a giant, jutting protrusion reaching out of the barren wasteland below as if an enormous rock had been dropped and left there.

Titus flapped his wings, picking up speed, and hurtled toward it. His pulse picked up and a new energy sang through his life force. This was home. This was a place he hadn't been to in over five hundred years.

He banked, soaring around a solid, sheer cliff face, climbing almost to the top and into a wide cave. For a second we were flying in absolute darkness then magical red flames burst to life along the ceiling, revealing a wide passage that quickly opened up into an enormous cavern as if the inside of the mountain had been hollowed out.

Only part of the cavern was closed off from the sky, and on the cavern floor, a dozen stories below us, was a small lake — its water lapping against the far side of the cavern — as well as a small forest and a meadow in the middle. Outcroppings jutted from the cavern's sides, big enough to hold one, two, or three dragons — if all dragons were Titus's size — and the walls were riddled with passages, some of which were dragon size while others were closer to human size.

Titus landed on an outcropping halfway down with a human-size passage, and, with Hawk's help, I slid to the ground where he promptly picked me up again and cradled me against his chest.

I leaned into him. Yes, he was still too hot, and yes, his life force was weak from all the injuries he'd taken during the fight, but he had me. I was safe with him. I could give in and trust him to take care of me... something I used to feel about Cassius.

The human quarters "are this way," Titus said, half in our heads as he shifted and half out loud once he was done.

Cassius adjusted Sebastian's unconscious body on his shoulder and we followed Titus down the passage. More flames burst to life as we walked, but the light couldn't ease the growing sense of dread squeezing my chest. We were heading deeper into the mountain, farther away from any open space and sky. I was going to be trapped inside a mountain again, just like when I was trapped in the Winter Court.

We passed dozens of doorways, none of which had doors, until we reach the doorway at the end of the hall. Without hesitation, Titus led us into a large sitting area filled with pillows of all different shapes, sizes, and colors, along with low, intricately carved wood and stone tables, all in perfect condition and arranged into a number of conversation areas. Flecks of white light shimmered in the air, mixing with the dancing magical flames near the ceiling, and with a soft *pop* the musty smell of age and decay vanished and the room felt fresh and clean as if it hadn't been abandoned for half a millennium.

And directly ahead of us, stood a window — or rather opening since there was no glass — that stretched from one side of the far wall to the other and from the floor to ceiling with only a waist-high spindly stone railing to stop someone from a terrible fall.

The weight in my chest vanished at the vast open expanse stretched before me.

Oh, thank goodness.

"I won't trap you underground," Titus said, his voice gruff.

I guess I'd said that out loud.

"I'd never do that to you." He shot a dark glare at Sebastian then hopped over the railing, shifted, his body turning to liquid flesh and changing from one second to the next, and took off.

"Shit," Cassius hissed. "He shouldn't be out there alone."

"Then go after him," I said, "Hawk and I can take care of Sebastian."

"Fine." Cassius set Sebastian on the floor and leaped over the railing like Titus had. With a burst of fire and white angelic light, he released his wings and glanced back at us, his expression still hard and frozen, before he soared away.

It broke my heart and made me furious at the same time. He didn't have a right to tell me what to do, and yet he was— *had been* my best friend for over a hundred years. I missed him. I'd been missing him since the war ended. I wanted the thoughtful, warm angel who'd been by my side, supporting and encouraging me, back. Even if he'd driven me crazy by being overprotective, I wanted that Cassius back.

CASSIUS

SHE'D TOLD BANE TO DO IT. OF COURSE SHE'D TOLD HIM TO DO IT. I WAS an idiot to think she hadn't thought of the horrible plan for Bane to attack her because she'd do anything, sacrifice anything to save people. So she'd done the biggest, stupidest thing she could think of to save us.

The God damned idiot. The God damned fucking idiot.

I screamed, shooting fire into the sky, doing little to ease the inferno burning through my veins, an inferno that shouldn't have been there because of all the magic I'd used during the fight.

How the hell could I protect her if she kept doing things like that? How could I keep her safe? God, I had to keep her safe. She'd already been horribly beaten because I hadn't been paying enough attention. For her to think having Bane assault her like that had been her only option—

I screamed again and fire poured off my wings and showered onto the wasteland below.

He'd shoved inside her and she'd lit up and I'd thought I was going to die. I'd thought she was a virgin and that this had been her first, horrific time having sex.

And now I didn't know if I was furious because I'd been horrified or furious that she'd been angry at me for having feared that. And for her to have pointed out we weren't having sex! To have shoved it in my face—

She had no idea how much it hurt to know I couldn't be with her, couldn't show her how I felt because I'd burn her, and yet she'd cut straight into my heart. She'd zeroed in on the one thing that could truly hurt me and struck her blow.

But worse was the fact that she'd been right, that I didn't know her anymore, not really. I'd withdrawn from her after the war because I knew I was going to hurt her, and while I hadn't burned her, she'd still been hurt. She'd fallen in love with Marcus and I hadn't been there for her when his soul mate had come along and broken her heart. What kind of protector was I? What kind of friend? How could I tell her I didn't think she was weak when my actions, my need to keep her safe, belied those word.

Except the thought of letting go, of trying to prove that I thought she was strong by holding back my protective instincts made my heart pound. I couldn't lose her like I'd lost Dominic. I couldn't fail her. I'd told Dominic to take that mission to infiltrate Michael's army, told him he was perfect for the job with his dual magic. Angels rarely had two powers and with his light magic, Michael would never know Dominic could also read minds. But somehow Michael had known and had killed him.

Because of me.

I'd sent my youngest brother to his death.

My fault.

And now Amiah was in danger.

All of Faerie was hunting us and I had to keep her safe. I couldn't fail her. Not like I'd failed Dominic. And now wasn't the time to hold back my protective instincts just to make her feel better.

I released another scream and blast of fire, lighting up the night sky.

If I wanted to keep her safe in all of this, I couldn't be her friend. I'd rather she hated me for being overbearing than her being dead. Like Dominic. The only thing that mattered was that she got through this mess alive and unharmed, and I'd already failed on the unharmed part of my mission.

Once again she was hurt and out of power, and the moment I managed to calm down and Bane was awake I was finding out why the hell her power had been spent when Titus and I had found her, Bane, and Hawk being accosted by Deaglan and his hybrid in that hall.

Something serious had happened and I needed to know what. Not because I needed to know everything that might have happened between her and Bane — although a part of me feared I did want to know — but because I needed to know if whatever had happened was going to continue to be a problem. It took a major injury for Amiah to fully drain herself by healing someone... unless, of course, she was the one who'd been hurt.

My pulse picked up again at the thought of someone hurting her and me not being there to protect her. I couldn't lose her. God damn it. I just couldn't.

Except I'd already lost her. I couldn't touch her, not even to carry her now. It took everything I had to hold back my fire and it was getting harder and harder to do so. From the moment she'd risked her life by taking in that massive blast of Hawk's power when he'd been ODing on sexual energy and saving him, I'd been burning up, my heart and soul on fire. I couldn't release enough fire to ease the inferno inside me, and I couldn't turn it back into the small waiting flame that it used to be in my heart.

And now every time I opened my mouth, I upset her, and I had no idea why. She no longer trusted me and that hurt more than not being able to carry her out of danger.

Now she turned to Hawk. She let Hawk hold her like she used to let Marcus as if she needed physical touch for comfort like a shifter did. She leaned into him, was comforted by his words, and I had no idea why she was demonstrating such unangel-like behavior because I knew she was smart enough to know Hawk would never fall in love with her.

Except she'd already broken her heart over a man who hadn't loved her.

God, she was doing it again, and there was nothing I could do about it.

Not a God damned thing.

And right now it didn't matter. Hawk might eventually break her heart, but at least he was comforting her, something she desperately needed right now and apparently on a more physical level than a typical angel. Her world had been turned upside down, she'd thought she'd needed to make Bane hurt her to save our lives, and now she had a foreign magic inside her.

And I was *not* going to think about her having sex with Hawk, because eventually his nature would get the better of him and he'd use his magic to seduce her or she'd sacrifice her body again to feed him and they'd be intimate.

And she'd made it clear that was her business and absolutely none of mine.

Except I desperately wanted it to be mine... which it could never be...

Fuck!

More fire exploded from my body.

Fuck fuck fuck. God damn fucking shit.

And fuck Bane, because it had to be his influence turning me into a foul-mouthed angel. I didn't think I'd ever sworn this much in my life, not even during the war.

Stop following me, Titus growled in my head, his massive form a dark shadow on the edge of a horizon just starting to lighten with a golden dawn.

None of us should be outside alone, I growled back.

I can take care of myself.

Right, I said, filling my mental voice with as much sarcasm as I could, *that's why you risked Amiah's life by shifting in the middle of the Winter Court.*

He was hurting her, Titus snarled, turning and flying toward me.

Yeah. The asshole had been hurting her, and I should have known he wouldn't have done that because he'd wanted to. He'd propositioned her and every woman I'd ever seen him come in contact with every chance he'd gotten and had business dealings with a lot of unsavory people, but he'd proven time and again that he'd never have purposely hurt her. Push her buttons — definitely push mine — and make her blush, but never hurt her. Hell, he'd willingly suffered by taking on Titus's half of the leash spell so we could rescue her from Balwyrdan.

You nearly got her killed by revealing yourself to the Winter Queen and Deaglan, I said. *She asked Bane to hurt her to save us. What do you think she would have done to save you from another five hundred years of captivity?*

Which was the truth I despised. I'd been relieved when she'd stopped doing fieldwork during the war because her compulsive need to heal, to do whatever it took to save someone, made her take terrifying risks. She had realized that too, thankfully early on, and had been smart, getting herself stationed in the Angelic Defense's main hospital, far away from the front line.

She used to have so much common sense. So much control. When had she lost it? When had she decided risking herself was better than protecting herself so she could continue to heal people?

The blaze inside me surged. She'd lost it when she'd had her control taken away, when Balwyrdan had proven it hadn't mattered what she did, or how hard she tried, she'd never be completely safe. She could be taken like she'd been taken by that faith healer all those years ago.

More fire burst from my body. *We only got out of the Winter Court because of a miracle.*

Because the Winter Court claimed Amiah, Titus said, his mental voice filled with regret. *She broke the Winter Queen's hold on the court and now everything is worse for her.*

He swooped past me, soaring back to the flat-topped mountain towering over the wasteland.

I trailed after him, releasing one last burst of fire, hoping I'd used up enough magic that I could pull the rest of my flames inside my body and regain some semblance of control.

She can't stay in Faerie, he said, lightly landing on a narrow ledge jutting from the top of the mountain as if he weren't a thirty-foot dragon who likely weighed thousands of pounds. *The minute Seireadan can find a portal, you all have to leave.*

I heaved my flames back under my skin, revealing all the bruises I'd gotten during the fight and the angry burns I'd seared into my body to cauterize my wounds. At least with my fire blazing through me, I couldn't feel much of anything else, even the pain of my injuries. *She's not going to let you stay here by yourself,* I said, landing on the ledge beside him.

Make her. Titus snorted fire and curled his front claws over the edge of the ledge. *She's not safe here and the rest of you are not safe with me.*

What does that mean? Except I had a feeling I already knew. He was barely keeping hold of his beast. One flight across the Wilds to his ancestral nest wasn't going to be enough to erase five hundred years of not shifting.

My beast would have killed Seireadan if Amiah hadn't stopped me. It still wants to kill him. You have to take her back to the mortal realm and leave me.

One, she wouldn't leave you, not knowing there are people still after you and that you're struggling to heal the connection between you and your beast. No matter how practical it was to leave, it was clear she was committed to helping Titus, and even though her magic couldn't help his connection, she was still going to use the rest of her extensive medical knowledge to help. *And two, can she even leave with the Winter Court's claim on her?*

I had no idea what being claimed by a Faerie court really meant. Bane, heir to the Winter Court's throne, had left and lived in the mortal realm for who knew how long, but had the court claimed him?

She has to. She has one of the keys. If she leaves, the Heart can never be freed.

But that only complicated the matter, because if anyone figured out she had a key, all of Faerie would be hunting her as well.

That thought made my fire boil my blood and filled me with a desperate need to see her.

Are you going to fly off again? I asked. God, I hoped not, because I had to see with my own eyes that she was still okay. The compulsion was overwhelming and shocking and infuriating, and I was too tired to fight it.

No. I think I'm okay if I'm not near Seireadan.

When they wake, we'll need to come up with a plan, I said, stretching out my wings and straining to hold back my flames. *And as much as I'd love for her to return to the mortal realm, I'm not sure we'll be able to convince her of that.*

Then don't convince her, Titus said, his mental voice gruff. *Just take her.*

Which would make her furious. But it would keep her safe... or rather safer... until someone in Faerie figured out she had a key and then we were back where we started.

I stepped off the ledge and caught the wind with my wings. She'd never forgive me if I forced her to return home. If she even could return home. But she would be safer there for a little while longer at least.

I glided around the side of the mountain, looking into dark caves and crevasses, and other sitting rooms magically frozen in time waiting for someone to enter until I found our sitting room.

Bane had been shifted to a thick rug and pile of fluffy pillows a few feet from where I'd left him, and Amiah and Hawk lay on another pile of pillows beside him, Amiah curled half on top of Hawk with his arms wrapped around her.

Seeing her didn't comfort me, and my compulsion to protect her grew stronger.

Her whole body glowed a soft white light, a reminder that I'd failed her again and she had a foreign magic inside her that could be hurting her in unimaginable ways, and she was splattered with blood, some of it ours from when it had been swept around in the Winter Queen's storm and some hers from all the little cuts all over her body from the ice in that storm.

I should have kept her safe. I didn't know how, but I should have.

And here was Hawk, holding her like a lover, like how I wanted to hold her as if it were nothing to just wrap his arms around her and let her use his body as a pillow.

Ice and snow and God damned frozen things. Thinking of the cold had barely worked when we'd been in the Winter Court, but it was all I had. *Just keep it frozen. Keep her safe even if she hates you.*

I quietly landed on the far side of the window, determined to not disturb them, and was about to turn my attention to the half dozen doorways at the back of the room when Hawk's eyelids cracked open.

"Hey," he said, his voice soft, his hellfire small flickering flames in his eyes, not fully banked but not fully released either. "Find the big guy?"

"Yeah. That's more or less under control." And was the best it was going to get for now.

"Good. He's angry now, but I have a feeling he'd never forgive himself if he killed Bane."

There was that, too.

Amiah whimpered and snuggled closer to Hawk, and my fire surged. *Ice. Frozen ice.* I could hold my fire in. I would hold my fire in.

"You should hold her," Hawk said. "I could use a stretch and she seems to need body heat."

"Seems to? I doubt you tried to avoid holding her," I snapped, my tone a hell of a lot sharper than I intended.

"Actually I did after she fell asleep. I wanted to explore a little, but she wouldn't let me go." His gaze dipped, sliding down the length of her body.

She'd been stunning in that dress. Showing so much skin it had embarrassed her — and I'd never make her wear it again if she didn't want to — but God, I was grateful I had the memory of seeing her in it. Just thinking about it— hell, seeing her now with it bloody and torn, made me yearn to touch her, kiss her, give her pleasure. Would she let it all go? Would I finally get to see her without worry or struggling to stay in control? I wanted to give her that moment, those sensations, fill her with bliss. I wanted—

My fire surged and smoke billowed around me.

I wanted things I'd never have. I'd never be her mate and she'd never want me to be her mate. The most I could do for her was keep her safe.

I would not fail her like I'd failed Dominic. I'd die first.

"Take my place," Hawk said, tugging the slit in her dress closed and covering her up a bit more. "I want to look around, find her a bathroom so when she wakes, she can clean up a little."

More smoke curled from my hands.

There was no way I'd be able to hold her and keep my fire inside. I'd probably set the whole room on fire.

"No."

"Come on, man. I'm pretty sure with your fire magic you can run your body temperature as hot as a demon's."

God, I wanted to. Wanted the incubus to stop giving her what I wanted to give her, but— "How do you think she'll react when she wakes and finds me holding her instead of you? She's made her position clear."

"That you two aren't sleeping together?" Hawk asked. "Doesn't mean that's the way it's going to stay." He huffed a soft laugh. "Of course, if you keep yelling at her and telling her what to do, she'll never invite you into her bed."

"Like she's invited you?" *Shit. I shouldn't have said that.* Because it was none of my God damned business.

"Just take my place. When she wakes, apologize for being an asshole," Hawk replied, not answering my question. "That'll go a long way toward getting into her bed."

"I can't."

Hawk's hellfire flared and his eyes narrowed. "Apologize or hold her?"

"Both." I clenched my hands, fighting my fire, but smoke still curled from my skin. "I'd rather she hate me and be safe than like me and be hurt again. I won't lose focus and let her be hurt again." I glared at Hawk. "That includes her heart."

Whatever it took. I wouldn't fail her.

AMIAH

I woke completely confused on a soft bed in a dimly lit room, snuggled against a blazing hot body, and my chest screaming in pain. Cassius had left Sebastian on the floor and flown after Titus, and Hawk had moved all of us to a thick rug and a pile of pillows and I'd passed out in his arms. I had a vague memory of Cassius returning, but that could have been a dream, and then sometime after that Hawk had picked me up. I guess he'd carried me to this bed and I'd fallen back asleep.

Beneath me, Hawk's chest slowly rose and fell, his breath deep with sleep, and his life force thrumming against my senses. He was alive but his magic was low and he hadn't been able to fully heal all the lacerations, fractured bones, and bruises marring his beautiful body. If he was going to finish healing, or worse survive another fight, he was going to need to feed.

The thought made my pulse quicken. I really liked the idea of that, of having sex with him again without the fear of losing him. Except we weren't going to be able to do much until I'd healed my broken ribs. Which I wasn't going to do until I'd healed Sebastian's broken face. And as much as Cassius had said I should heal myself first there was no point in Sebastian suffering. Yes, only five of my ribs had been broken this time, but I was still going to need to drain myself twice to mend them.

At least my power was mostly at full again, which meant I had to have been out for at least eight hours.

My heart pounded faster, and the ice in my chest sank and churned into a stone in my stomach. I'd drained myself because someone had poisoned Hawk and my power had locked onto him. The queen had threatened the guys. Titus had shifted. I'd yelled at Cassius that we weren't having sex. And, oh God, I'd been claimed by the Winter Court.

I shoved those thoughts deep down, straining to ignore the ice and fear, and concentrated on Hawk. He was too hot... because of the ice now permanently frozen in my soul.

No. Well yes, but don't focus on that. Focus on his life force, on its thrum.

I drew in a steadying breath, shot agony through my chest, and gritted my teeth, determined to keep my focus. The sense of simmering hellfire crackled through the energy of his life force. Fiery and dark, because he was a being from the Realm of Celestial Darkness. Surprisingly, it slid against the light inside me, caressing my essence instead of grating against it and easing the freeze of the Winter Court.

As if thinking about it made it stronger, the Winter Court's power swelled. But it wasn't painful and wasn't consuming. It just was. Neither good nor bad. Merely a miniscule flicker of power now embedded in every cell in my body and woven into my essence. In my mind's eye, it sparkled, like snow in brilliant sunlight after an icy storm, and it connected with another life force behind me. A life force surging and straining against an oozing, consuming darkness.

I turned my head, trying not to aggravate my ribs or wake Hawk.

Sebastian lay beside us on the bed, his swollen bruised face tight with pain, his breath fast and shallow. Yes, his injuries were hurting him, but there was something more, something dark sliding through his veins, fighting the thread of ice from the Winter Court and the shimmering radiance of Faerie's raw magic. I'd felt the pain when I'd connected with him last night and now, somehow, I could also feel the power staining his life force.

My healing magic swelled in my palms, thick and sticky, determined to burst free, compelling me to heal him — although thankfully not locking onto him — and I eased my hand out from under my body.

Just moving made my power surge stronger, and it fully connected with him before I'd even gingerly pressed my fingers against his temple, forcing me to strain to hold it back and turn its flow into a soft trickle. I didn't have to heal him quickly, there was no reason for the healing to hurt or to even wake him.

He groaned and my power oozed into his face, immediately splitting three ways and sinking into his shattered orbital bone, fractured cheek, and broken nose. It flooded his cells, knitting bone back together with an effortlessness that it wouldn't have when I healed my ribs, and struggled to blast into the rest of him, sealing every laceration, even the smallest cuts, shut.

I kept the flow down to a steady, warm stream even as my power burned hotter up my forearms and past my elbows, and I reveled in the feel of his body mending until there was no evidence that he'd ever been in a fight. Not even a scar. He was still in some pain, his life force still struggling against the darkness my magic couldn't even recognize, but the agony of his shattered face was gone.

He murmured in his sleep but didn't wake and I turned to lie back on Hawk's chest, still at half power but ready to go back to sleep.

"He could have lasted a little longer," Hawk murmured, stroking my hair back from my face. "You could have gotten started on yourself."

"I'm going to take longer than just one healing session," I said, carefully easing my weight back onto him and waiting the few seconds it took for my cheek and chest to get reaccustomed to his body heat. "The Winter Queen broke a few of my ribs."

"You've got to stop doing that."

"Oh," I said with an eye roll he couldn't see, "because I planned on having my bones broken again."

He tensed beneath me and for a second I thought he was going to bring up Sebastian hurting me, then he pressed his lips to the top of my head and a whisper of seductive heat unfurled inside me. It mingled with the ice, also not grating against it like it hadn't grated against my celestial light essence. It eased some of my pain and a slow, gentle throb pulsed in my core.

"Is that better?" he asked.

"Yes," I breathed. God, I could get used to having an incubus lover. "A little more and we could get some of your magic restored as well."

"But not just a tease." His tone turned wicked, reminding me of the last time I'd woken in bed with him, my body burning with pain and I'd begged him to not just tease me. "I know how much you hate being teased."

My insides squirmed, my desire building at just the thought of Hawk's magic bringing me to a climax again. "If you do more than just tease, you'll get more power back."

"True, that." He eased me into my back and captured my lips in a soft tender kiss that made my heart flutter. It made me feel safe and cherished... and loved. And I wasn't going to think too hard about that because Hawk couldn't love me, it wasn't in his nature. I was just going to enjoy the feeling and pretend it was real for the meantime.

"But you've got to remember to lie there and enjoy it like last time," he said.

"And we've got to keep it subtle and quiet." I glanced at the open doorway. There wasn't even a door we could close.

"Titus is far below us, probably at the bottom of the cavern," he said, trailing kisses along my jaw and down my neck. "And Cassius..." he murmured against my collarbone, his hot breath feathering over my skin, sending a shiver of desire racing through me. "He's a good hundred feet at least to our left, so not outside our bedroom door."

"I didn't know incubi could sense where people were."

He brushed his lips along my dress's plunging neckline, teasing the inner swells of my breasts, and another seductive curl of magic unfurled in my chest, easing away more of the pain of my ribs.

"We usually can't get so specific," he said, inching lower and lower down my body, his heat sliding away letting the Winter Court's cold grow stronger. "But I'm a Sensitive too and we're literally the only people here so there are no other sources of desire to muddy the waters. That and both of them could use a release. Their desire is particularly strong at the moment."

"Have they not gotten over being influenced by your magic?" I asked, my pulse picking up with the memory of Hawk's power raging out of control when we'd been in the Winter Court and how it had affected all of us.

He pushed a hot hand under the hem of my indecent dress and slowly slid his fingers up the inside of my thigh, urging me to open for him. Oh, yes.

"They're probably still thinking about you in this dress."

I huffed a bitter laugh. "I believe that was the Winter Queen's plan with the dress. To embarrass me and make all the men in the room want to sleep with me." I didn't know if the latter had worked, but I'd certainly been embarrassed. I'd never worn anything so revealing before and I'd never wear anything like it again.

"Well it certainly made four of us want to sleep with you." He pressed a kiss to the inside of my knee. "And I really enjoyed it. You know, after you and Sebastian saved my life and all."

He trailed his lips up my thigh, his breath caressing my skin drawing closer and closer to where I really wanted him.

Oh, that felt good.

Okay, so I might consider wearing something like that again. It certainly gave Hawk easy access and if I didn't think about the panic of trying to save him, having Sebastian push into me from behind and pinning me between him and Hawk had been incredibly... stimulating.

"Yeah, like that," Hawk purred, nudging my other thigh with his elbow and settling his gorgeous, muscular, shirtless body between my legs. "Are you thinking about Sebastian satisfying you or me?"

"Does it have to be one or the other?" I asked, my voice deliciously breathy.

"Nope. I'll never make you choose, gorgeous." He brushed his tongue against the inside of my thigh at the crux where my leg met my torso.

I gasped at the feel of him against my skin and the sudden breath shot agony through my chest, but Hawk's seductive heat swept through me before I could even whimper.

"You're going to spoil me." I ran my fingers into his sandy-blond locks, curled them around his horns, and rubbed my thumbs against their base. It was one of the most sensitive spots on an incubus and a major erogenous zone, like the base of an angel's wings, and if he was going to stay down there, I was going to explore just how erogenous they were.

He groaned at my touch.

"I like spoiling you," he said. "And I like the sounds you make."

He brushed his tongue through my folds, making me softly moan.

"I love how you taste."

Another slow, drawn out brush that spiraled heated desire in my core. *Oh, yes.*

"I love the feel of your body."

He slid his hands up the outside of my thighs and captured my hips, stopping me from squirming against his mouth and hurting myself.

"And I love the feel of you letting go, that you'd even want to share something like this with me."

He pushed his tongue inside me, my nerves suddenly hyperaware of his slick heat against my cool insides, and my eyes rolled back with the sensation.

Oh yeah, I could definitely get used to having an incubus lover.

I rubbed my thumbs harder against the base of his horns. His breath grew faster, his sculpted muscles rippling with every shift of his body, mesmerizing me like he was supposed to. And I fully gave into his allure as he carefully built up my desire, licking and sucking and adding whispers of heated magic to soothe my pain.

The pressure inside me grew, and I fought to keep my moans quiet so I didn't wake Sebastian, but with my desire spiraling tighter and tighter, it got harder and harder to remember to hold it all in.

Then Hawk sucked on my clit and pushed a soft swell of power into me. My orgasm swept through me, a glorious, gentle wave, and I released a breathy, satisfied moan.

"Well, that's one way to wake up," Sebastian said, his voice gruff.

I let my head roll to the side to look at him and met a stunning, pale blue, almost colorless gaze, his eyes filled with heated desire. The look sent another soft ripple of orgasm through me and Hawk's fingers dug into my hips and he moaned against my folds.

"Guess having me present wasn't just a dirty little necessity to save his life." Sebastian slid his gaze down my body as if he didn't know where he wanted to start first, and the still-swirling heat of Hawk's magic swelled.

"You're just going to frustrate yourself," Hawk groaned, rising up on his forearms and giving me a look just as heated as Sebastian's. "She's got broken ribs. She can't do much for you. But if you want to get her off again, I won't stop you."

Concern bled into Sebastian's eyes and he reached to caress my face but hesitated. "Would you want me to? After I hurt you like that?"

I slid my hand up to his and interlaced our fingers, his self-doubt scaring me. While I didn't know him that well, I'd never seen him be tentative about propositioning anyone.

"That didn't count. I told you I like the way you make me feel," I said. "I thought I'd made myself clear. I don't want a relationship right now, I just want sex. With you."

"But you're free now. Your reason not to commit is gone." His gaze dipped to my left hip where my partially formed mating brand used to be but thankfully didn't say anything in front of Hawk who, like everyone else, didn't know I'd been cursed with an angel's most sacred mark.

"And when I'm ready to commit to someone I'll commit." It was the first time in my life that I had the freedom to love how I wanted to, and I didn't want to just jump into a committed relationship. I wanted to explore my sexuality, who I was, and what I desired. Hawk and Sebastian — if he was interested — were perfect. "My reasons for having sex with you haven't changed. You don't want me to fall in love with you and you're not going to fall in love with me, and you've plenty of experience."

"So I'm just a good fuck then?" he asked, but he didn't sound upset about that.

"Hmm, I don't know." I gave him my wickedest smile, which was probably terrible since I had no experience with that kind of thing. "I've had sex with an incubus now. Do you think you can rise to the occasion and match his prowess?"

"That's quite the challenge," Sebastian said, his tone turning seductive and thoughtful. "You've had a quick fuck against a wall. You haven't had the full incubus experience yet. And while I'm good, Hawk *is* a professional. He's going to blow your mind when you finally get down to it."

I pursed my lips and Hawk, with a Cheshire cat grin, crawled back up beside me and gingerly tugged me into his embrace, using his magic to ease the spike of pain caused from moving me.

Sebastian's eyes widened. "Holy fuck. You've already slept with him. That's why you didn't bat an eye when you had sex in the alcove."

"And yeah, it was mind blowing." My pulse picked up with fear. God, I was actually going to say it. I was going to proposition Sebastian for a *ménage à trois*. "But there are things I'm curious about that I can't do with Hawk alone."

His eyes widened even more. "Oh, fuck me," he groaned.

"Not yet, her ribs are still broken," Hawk replied with a chuckle.

"Who the hell are you and what have you done with the annoying as hell, uptight angel I first met?" Sebastian asked me.

Jeez. I was not going to beg for this. "Are we going to keep having sex or not?" I asked, my fear of rejection making my tone sharp.

Sebastian's face lit up with a glorious, heart stopping grin, reminding me of the Sebastian I'd first met, the one who'd relentlessly teased me about sex.

"There she is," he said, and he captured my lips in a breathtaking kiss that made the remnants of Hawk's magic surge inside me.

God, I wanted to get started now, and yet I was going to have to wait until my ribs had healed. How had this become my life? How had I suddenly become free of the nightmare of a forced, permanent soul bond? And how had I ever ended up in bed with both Sebastian and Hawk?

Of course, we were also on the run from all of the Faerie courts, the Winter Court had claimed me, and my relationship with my best friend had somehow been torn to pieces.

I leaned into Sebastian's kiss, determined to let the feel of his mouth against mine, his desire for me, and the residual heat of Hawk's magic make me forget.

"Hey," Hawk murmured, gently tugging me away from Sebastian's lips. "Your ribs are still broken and Cassius is coming our way... Unless you've changed your mind about him knowing about this."

I bit back a heavy sigh, managing not to shoot agony through my chest. "I should rub this in his face given how he'd reacted to the idea of me having a sex life."

"Please don't," Sebastian said, rolling onto his back and staring at the ceiling, but he interlaced his fingers with mine again and I wasn't sure if he was conscious of the act or not. "I was barely conscious last night and even I know he's barely holding his shit together. I swear to God he's in love with you."

"So that makes trying to slut shame me okay?" I snapped back. "I should be able to have sex with whoever I want and however I want it."

"Which is why I didn't turn you down," Sebastian said.

"Gee thanks. You make it sound like having sex with me is a chore." Except while I hadn't wanted him to feel like it was a job, I also hadn't wanted his emotions to get involved. Which was the whole point of having sex with him and Hawk. They weren't going to fall in love with me.

"That wasn't what he meant." Hawk hooked a stray lock of my hair behind my ear, the motion softly stroking his hot fingers across my cheek and sending a shiver of desire racing through me that shot agony across my chest.

"It's okay," I said, trying not to show my pain. I squeezed Sebastian's fingers and he glanced over at me. "This isn't an emotional arrangement. I understand that. When it stops being good for any of us, we stop."

A strange expression flashed across Sebastian's face and disappeared before I could figure out what it meant. "Deal. But you have to promise to mend things with Cassius. If we're going to survive what's coming, we're going to need him thinking clearly, and he's eventually going to figure out we're having sex."

"I'm sure both you and Hawk have experience being discreet."

Sebastian gave me a look so heated it made my heart skip a beat and my insides throb with need. "It's not us I'm worried about giving it away."

"You don't think I can be discrete?"

"What he's saying, gorgeous," Hawk whispered in my ear, his hot breath teasing me, "is that a man, even an uptight angel like Cassius, can recognize a thoroughly satisfied woman, and you, my dear, are going to be thoroughly satisfied."

AMIAH

Oh, my God! I wanted to get started on being thoroughly satisfied. Right now. To hell with my broken ribs... although a part of me was terrified I'd taken on more than I could handle with the two of them.

Sebastian, however, was right. Not about me letting Cassius know we were having sex, but about mending things with Cassius. Even if we hadn't been hiding from all of Faerie, I still should at least talk to him.

But he just made me so angry. It didn't matter that his belief that I was weak and unable to defend myself was right. He needed to stop barking orders at me like I was an agent under his command and he certainly had to stop protecting my virtue as if we were in the Dark Ages.

"He's just about here," Hawk said and Sebastian slid his fingers from mine and moved to the far side of the bed.

I felt Cassius's fiery life force blazing across my senses before I heard his soft steps to the doorway. His life force was so strong, so determined, stronger than Hawk's or Sebastian's, but it was as if a part of him was struggling to break free and he was desperately trying to hold it back, as if he weren't in harmony with himself, which heightened my sense of him.

"You healed Bane first, didn't you?" he said, his tone icier than the ice inside me.

Of course that would be the first thing he said to me.

"I have broken ribs again. There's no point in Sebastian suffering for days while he waits for me to heal myself," I said as Hawk helped me sit up.

Cassius's eyes narrowed and smoke curled from his hands. He'd cleaned up and found a change of clothes, and while he still wore leather pants, they were now brown instead of dark blue and looser fitting. He'd also found a loose cotton shirt, the soft beige fabric covering up most of his honed muscular chest, but he'd rolled up the sleeves to his elbows as if he were too hot even in the thin material. Dozens of scabbed-over lacerations covered his forearms, and more marred his neck as well as the hint of chest I could see through the V of his shirt. His angel glow was bright, indicating he was brimming with power, but his eyes and expression were that of a man running on too much stress and too little sleep.

"Did you get any sleep?" I eased myself over Hawk's legs and got off the bed, the Winter Court's chill swelling and growing stronger the farther I got from Hawk. My teeth were chattering and my whole body shivering, shooting agony through me by the time I was within arm's reach of Cassius, and while his body heat was a fraction of Hawk's, it still drew me inappropriately close. "How bad are your injuries?"

"I'm fine." The muscles in his jaw flexed.

"Let me check." I leaned toward him, even knowing he wouldn't want me to snuggle up to him, and reached to press my palm against his chest.

"Heal yourself first." He grabbed my wrist, but my magic connected with him anyway, and I instantly knew he had three cracked ribs and half a dozen nasty burns where he'd used his fire to cauterize his wounds.

"You're not fine." I released a thread of magic into him, using his hold on my wrist to gain entry into his body, and it rushed straight to his ribs.

"I said, heal yourself first." He jerked away from me, but my magic stayed connected and surged. It roared through him, using up almost everything I had left, even though mending that amount of damage normally wouldn't have. With one sudden, agonizing blast, it healed his ribs and burns and drew a strangled, pain-filled scream.

Gasping, he dropped to his knees, his chest heaving and his body trembling. Smoke billowed from his hands and his life force snapped as if I could somehow feel his fire through his life force. "God damn it. I said heal yourself first."

"Don't tell me what to do with my magic," I snapped back, even though I shouldn't have healed him like that. I certainly shouldn't have spent all my magic, and I had no idea how I'd done it without touching him.

The room darkened and lurched, and the exhaustion at using all my power swept through me. I sagged against the doorframe, my shivering growing stronger, and didn't even bother trying to look strong. What was the point? They'd all seen me at my worst. No point in hiding the truth. Besides, just being myself wasn't nearly as exhausting as putting on an in-control strong demeanor. Especially since none of them would have believed me anyway right now.

Hawk picked me up in his too-hot arms before I collapsed on the floor, and his heat seeped into my skin. "We need to do something about your body temperature."

"If you can hold out a little longer for me to get some power back, I'll see what I can do." Sebastian rubbed his face and sighed. "And I need to finally deal with the leash spell as well."

"Well, first we all need to eat," Cassius gasped. He staggered back to his feet and glared at Hawk, the light in his eyes flaring. "Do you? You took some serious damage during the fight."

"My options are somewhat limited," Hawk said, not giving away that I'd just given him an influx of sexual energy.

"I'm aware of that," Cassius forced out refusing to make eye contact with me. "I found a stocked kitchen and some food for the rest of us," he said, jerking away and heading toward a low table in the middle of the room. "Let's eat and figure out how the hell we're going to get out of this mess."

A platter with strange looking fruit, a small wheel of cheese, a knife, and a pile of dried meat sat on the table. Cassius took a seat on one of the cushions in front of it and grabbed a piece of meat.

"Hunh," Hawk said as he approached and sat cross-legged. He set me in his lap but kept me close, letting me press my barely covered torso against his bare chest. "Where did the fresh fruit come from? And do we honestly think that cheese and meat is safe? How old is it? I'd hate for Amiah to have to use her magic to deal with food poisoning on top of everything else."

It's safe, Titus said in our heads, and his massive dragon form hurtled toward the window, his life force wild and ferocious, mixing with Cassius's burn, Hawk's darkness, and Sebastian's ice and pain inside me.

Titus shifted as he reached the threshold, his body shrinking and melting in the blink of an eye, and he transformed into a ruggedly handsome, completely naked man.

He'd broken the glamor changing his appearance when he'd shifted in the Winter Court's ballroom, and now he was back to the man I'd first met with his stunning powerful musculature, dark red shaggy hair, square jaw dusted with red-gold stubble, and mesmerizing golden eyes.

Those eyes met mine for a second and the world stood still. The intensity of his gaze was breathtaking, powerful, predatory, and I was his prey. Except that didn't terrify me like it probably should have and reminded me of the sudden ferocious kiss we'd had when we'd been attacked. I shivered at the thought of all that passion and power directed at me, embracing me, filling me, thrumming against my senses.

He jerked his gaze from me to glare at Sebastian as he dropped onto a cushion on the far side of the table.

Sebastian met Titus's glare for a second then lowered his gaze, wisely giving Titus dominance. I had no doubt if Sebastian was at full power Titus wouldn't stand a chance, but Sebastian was also smart enough to know Titus's hold on his humanity was still tenuous, and challenging him right now would only cause problems.

"Faerie always magically preserves the aerie while it waits for occupants," Sebastian said. "That's why none of these pillows, the clothes Cassius found, or the bedding has rotted into nothing even though there hasn't been anyone here in over five hundred years."

"And the fruit comes from the trees in the cavern." Titus grabbed a piece of meat and tore a chunk off with his teeth. "This morning the Wilds were a jungle instead of a wasteland so I stayed close to the mountain and did a bit of hunting. There's fresh meat in the cold room so we won't have to just eat this."

"How long do you think we can be here?" I asked, reaching for a dark blue, apple-like fruit, sending agony screaming through me, and making me gasp.

Sebastian grabbed it for me and Titus's glare deepened.

"It all depends on how much Faerie wants Seireadan," Titus growled. "The aerie can only protect you for so long."

"Painfully aware of that," Sebastian replied, grabbing his own apple-like fruit. "I'll eventually need to get into a court or get out of Faerie."

"So we find a portal and get the hell out of here," Hawk said. "Your realm won't eat you alive and I'll be able to properly feed."

"We'd either need to use a portal in one of the courts or try to find one hidden in the Wilds," Sebastian said. "So neither option is easy. I've got at least a few days before Faerie breaks through the aerie's defenses and comes after me. We've got time to catch our breath. Not to mention, only a dragon can find the aerie so we're safer here for now than anywhere else, including my apartment in the mortal realm."

"Great, so we're staying at least until Amiah heals herself," Cassius said, cutting off a piece of cheese and not sounding happy about staying. But it was the most logical plan, especially if it was going to be dangerous getting to a portal to return home. He turned his gaze to Hawk. "Can you manage?"

"If everyone has a few really sexy thoughts, I'll be able to get by." Hawk slid his hand up my thigh, nudging the slit of my dress open a few more inches, not even enough to be considered indecent by my — old — standards. Every eye dropped to my leg, and Hawk hummed low in his throat, the sound only audible to me. "God, I love this dress."

Cassius stiffened and his attention jerked up to my eyes, dipped again to my cleavage then back up to my eyes. He cleared his throat and a layer of emotional ice settled over his expression.

"We also need to discuss what happened last night," he said, his voice gruff.

Titus stiffened and the memory of the fear and pain of everything that had happened heaved against my mental barrier.

"No." I shoved those emotions further down. I was doing just fine as I was. I didn't need to have a breakdown, I could pretend none of it had happened... except for some amazing sex. *That* I was going to remember. "I said we weren't going to bring it up again and you're not."

"Not that." Cassius raked a hand over his blond buzz cut, his angel glow flaring. "You were out of power. What happened between the Winter Queen pulling us away to discuss her plans for the Heart and us finding you in that hall?"

Heat seeped across my cheeks. One of those amazing sex moments.

"Someone poisoned Hawk," I said. "My magic locked onto him and it took everything I had to save him."

"Actually one of the queen's men who I saw making out with your sister by the way," Hawk said to Sebastian, "tried to stab Amiah with a poisoned knife."

My thoughts stuttered at that, then realization hit me and panic squeezed my chest. That poison had nearly killed Hawk with his extraordinary healing. There was no way I would have survived, even if I'd flooded myself with my magic.

"That was Padraigin?" Sebastian asked. "Well, shit. I'd thought if there was anyone at court we could trust it would be her."

"Amiah stands between her and the throne," Titus said.

"No, I don't." But as soon as the words came out, I knew I was lying. The Winter Court had claimed me and I'd taken control of its power from its current queen. I might have more claim to the throne now than even Sebastian.

Sebastian pursed his lips, confirming what I feared.

My pulse picked up.

I was trapped.

And I would handle it.

I. Would. Handle. It.

"Come on," Hawk said, drawing me tighter against his chest as if he could sense my fear. "It's been obvious since the beginning that your return pissed Padraigin off."

"Yeah. I know. I'd just hoped—" Sebastian rubbed his face, his glow flickering and his complexion sliding back into that unsettling gray for a second. "It doesn't matter. I don't care who's sitting on the throne of the Winter Court so long as it isn't me."

"Or Amiah," Titus growled, his canines extending and his beast straining to break free.

Sebastian's gaze jerked to him. "I said I'd fix the court's claim on her and I will. Just give me a minute to catch my fucking breath. It takes longer to restore magic ripped away by Faerie."

"Hey." I reached out for Sebastian's hand before realizing what that might look like then decided I didn't care and interlaced my fingers with his. "I know you will."

Surprise flashed across his expression and his gaze, filled with concern and something else, something softer, captured mine. For a second I was drowning in a vast universe of power and yet writhing in a painful darkness.

"I promise," he said, his voice soft, and he slid his fingers free, taking with him the power and pain and dimming my connection with his life force.

"Okay." The Winter Court's ice swelled, as if filling in the emptiness left when Sebastian pulled away. "Sebastian and I need to regain our power with more rest, and the three of us still need to clean up and change clothes."

"Right." Cassius's gaze jumped from me to Hawk then Sebastian. "Who's helping you?"

"I can clean up on my own." Sure, I wouldn't have minded a shower with Sebastian and Hawk, but later, when my ribs weren't broken and I wasn't freezing and I could do all the things I wanted to do.

"You're still dizzy and you still need body heat," Cassius said, his posture getting more rigid by the second.

"I can manage by myself long enough to clean up and get back into a bed."

He opened his mouth, and I glared at him. "This isn't a discussion." I turned to Hawk. "You go first, then I'll meet you back in bed."

"There are other bathing rooms in all the other suites," Titus said. "Just go back into the hall and pick a doorway."

"I'll go change the sheets on your bed." The muscles in Cassius's jaw flexed. "The last door on the end is a bathroom and I put a variety of clothes for everyone on a rack with the towels just inside the door." He jerked to his feet and strode from the room, a wisp of smoke curling behind him.

Hawk carried me to the last doorway, down a short hall with a sharp ninety-degree turn so no one could just look in and see into the bathroom. It was almost identical to the one in my room at the Winter Court with a stone sink and toilet, a waterfall shower, and a tub carved into the stone floor.

He set me on my feet at the edge of the tub while Sebastian grabbed a towel, a washcloth, and a change of clothes from the rack and brought them over.

"I'll meet you back in bed," Hawk said, his hot breath washing across my cheeks and down my neck. Oh man, I couldn't wait to be healed.

"But *I* won't be waiting in bed for you," Sebastian added, "not until you talk to Cassius."

The two of them left, and I sank to the floor shivering uncontrollably with the Winter Court's cold, agony screaming through my chest. But I wasn't going to call them back. I wasn't sure I could resist either man's allure at the moment if I was naked and I'd just end up frustrating all of us and hurting myself.

And I was going to think about that and only that. How they made me feel. How I ached just thinking about having sex with them again. How I could just let go of everything.

I untied the hidden laces at the side of my dress, pulled off the bloody and ripped fabric, and dipped my foot into the tub's cool water.

God, if you'd asked me about having sex with them a week ago, I would have said it was the most terrifying idea ever.

The water in the tub started to warm up, and I eased into its soothing heat.

I'd never have given someone else control over me like that, let alone them, and I'd never have let someone see me without my rigid hold on my body and my emotions. Now I couldn't wait to let go with Sebastian Bane of all people and an incubus.

And I really wasn't going to think about how everything would change the moment we returned to the mortal realm. I'd have to go back to my real life and both Hawk and Sebastian would remember who I really was.

TITUS

I stared at the bathroom doorway, my beast straining to regain control. Seireadan and Hawk had left with their changes of clothes and towels and now it was just me and my angel in the suite.

Except she wasn't mine, no matter what my beast wanted. The Winter Court had claimed her so Seireadan had to have lied and married her and Hawk had her scent and arousal all over him. And I'd have believed just her scent being on him because he'd been holding her since we'd crashed into the Wilds, but the scent of her arousal could only mean one thing.

In fact, both he and Seireadan had smelled of sex when Cassius and I had found them in the hall off the ballroom facing off against Deaglan. The scent had been so strong and her angel glow so weak it had taken everything I had just to hold my beast in.

Then seeing Seireadan kiss her like he hated her and then ramming himself into her making her cry on top of all of that had been too much. My beast had torn free of my mental hold and the only thing I could think of was getting to her, protecting her, and making Seireadan pay.

I sucked in a heavy breath that did nothing to calm my beast. Fuck, I should have stayed in my dragon form and not joined her and the others for that meal. She'd spent the entire time cuddling with the incubus, which only pissed my beast off more. And while logically I knew she needed his heat — she'd been freezing when she'd leaned into me in the

Wilds and stopped my beast from killing Seireadan — my beast didn't give a fuck. She needed to be cuddling with me. Using me for comfort. Using me to satisfy her sexual desires and not them.

Not fucking them.

My beast snarled, heaving inside me.

She was only a few feet away and naked. *I* was still naked. It was perfect.

My fantasy of sliding into her hot tight sheath, of her stunning radiant gaze capturing mine, and the look of pure pleasure when she came could come true.

Except she was hurt and exhausted. Now wasn't the time to have sex with her... even if the incubus had... although I hadn't smelled *his* arousal on her, not this time, which meant he'd just pleasured her.

Which I was just as capable of doing.

Really.

I jerked forward but managed to stop myself just before I reached the ninety-degree turn and saw into the bathroom.

My beast was wrong. I hadn't had a sexual touch from a female in over five hundred years. There was no way I'd be able to control myself let alone my beast if she was naked and in my arms. Hell, that barely-there dress the Winter Queen had made her wear had strained my control even with the fear that she was going to get hurt by the night's events.

If I was smart, I'd fly around the nest again and try to mend the connection between me and my beast. Except my beast didn't want to shift. That would mean it wouldn't be able to hold Amiah, and it *had* to hold her, be comforted by her soul, bring her pleasure.

I dug my claws into the wall and sucked in another breath.

Leave. Just turn around and jump out the window.

Go into the bathroom and comfort her. Neither Seireadan or Hawk can comfort her like I can. They aren't her soul's mate.

And yet the Winter Court had claimed her with a connection strong enough to take away the queen's control. That spoke of a deeper connection between her and Seireadan...

Except Seireadan had said the connection had happened because I'd given Amiah the key.

So he wasn't her mate.

She was still mine.

I bit back a roar and clawed chunks from the wall. Damn it. She wasn't mine, not until she'd chosen me... or whatever it was that angels did to recognize their soul's mate.

"Hey," she said, jerking my attention to her as she eased to my side and pressed her freezing hands against my forearm.

She was fully dressed now in a pair of loose, soft cotton pants and a cotton shirt that was too big for her, the open V-neck exposing a glorious amount of cleavage. My beast shuddered with pleasure at the sight as well as her touch, and my soul rang with the truth.

Mine.

With a growl, my beast captured the back of her head with my free hand and smashed my mouth to hers before I could stop it. And the moment our lips touched I was lost.

My cock went rock hard and all of my senses locked on her. The rightness of connecting with her, the thrum of her soul against mine reassuring my beast, the feel of her lips, her soft sweet scent, her too-cold body, and her shivering even though she was fully dressed.

She gasped in surprise at our sudden connection, and I seized the opening created by her breath, raking my tongue into her mouth and deepening the kiss. This kiss was going to be so much more than the desperate locking of lips when I'd somehow given her the key. I was going to show her with my mouth — and my mouth alone — how she was mine, how it didn't make sense to choose anyone else but me, how I could satisfy her.

I slid my arm free of her hands, shifted closer, and gently captured her delicate body against the wall with mine. She was so small, so unlike any female dragon, and yet absolutely perfect. My erection pushed against her belly, letting her know in no uncertain terms how I felt, and I slid my hand under her shirt and softly — oh so softly so I didn't hurt her — brushed my fingers up to her breast.

She moaned into my mouth, the scent of her arousal thickening and her breath coming faster, but also sharper.

Somewhere in the back of my mind, I knew I was hurting her. I needed to stop, to pull away.

Except this might be my only chance to show her how I was her mate, how we were meant to be together.

Shit.

I heaved against my beast, but it snarled back at me and rubbed the pad of my thumb against a nipple pebbled and begging for my mouth.

She moaned again and arched her fragile perfect body into my hand, making my beast growl with pleasure.

"Titus, please," she gasped, cupping my cheeks in her small freezing hands, her voice tight with pain. "I can't."

Because she was Seireadan's—

No, because she was hurt, her ribs broken, and each breath had to be agonizing.

Shit.

Her hands on my face trembled, her breath sharp and shallow. "Titus."

Shit shit shit.

I wrenched myself away from her and pressed my back against the other side of the hall, fighting my beast and holding myself there. The loss of our connection, even just that few feet of distance, made my soul cry. I needed her, needed her soul to steady mine.

Her gaze dipped to my cock, painfully hard and standing at full attention. Heated desire dilated her pupils and her arousal taunted me.

My beast clawed at my insides. She wanted me. Why the hell was I holding back? It could be steadying her soul — and it wasn't going to recognize that she wasn't a dragon and didn't need her soul steadied — and it could be making her feel good. It would protect her for as long as I had breath. It would do anything to see her smile, to feel her soul, to be with her. It would die to protect her.

"Be my mate," I blurted out. I wasn't going to be able to hold it back much longer. She had to know how I felt, had to know what I wanted. If I didn't say anything, she'd keep sleeping with Seireadan and Hawk, and I didn't know how much longer I'd be able to hold my beast back before it challenged them for her.

Shock swept through the desire in her eyes. "Titus."

"Be my mate."

"Titus, you don't know me."

"I do. You're powerful and kind and you calm my beast." Just being near her settled me. She felt right, more right than my mate before the Heart had awakened.

Because she's mine, my beast growled, heaving against my control.

"Can't you feel it?" I asked. "When you touch me, we connect."

The light in her eyes weakly flared, barely a glimmer of what it should have been because she was low on power. "You've just gone without for too long. You haven't been able to completely calm your beast and he rules your primal needs. You're mistaking lust for love."

"I'm not," I snarled back. How could she not see we belong together?

"Titus." She raised her hands, palms up toward me. "Take my hands, let me help you calm your beast. You're not in love with me. You just need to have sex, that's all."

"Is that what you're doing with Seireadan then?" I glared at her hands and dug my claws into the wall behind me. If I took hold of her, my beast would take over and I'd hurt her. "Just having sex? He's not your mate?"

"I'm having sex with Hawk too. Also not my mate." She took a step toward me, her hands still extended as if she weren't afraid of my beast like she should have been, proving all the more that she was mine.

"If they're not your mates, then be mine." If they truly weren't her mates then I didn't have to win her, my beast wouldn't have to hurt them.

"I don't want a mate."

My beast heaved inside me. Of course she wanted a mate. She wanted me. She just hadn't realized it yet. She was my soul's mate. We were destined to be together... unless my beast was wrong and she was right. What if it was just my damaged connection with my beast making me think there was more between us than there really was. Surely if we were soul mates she'd feel it, she wouldn't reject me.

"You really don't want a mate? You don't feel anything between us?"

My beast howled and wrenched against my mental grasp. It had to break free, had to claim what was his—

It was going to hurt her.

How can she so easily calm me if she isn't my soul's mate? How? How?

"Titus." She inched closer and the cold radiating from her body swept over my skin. She was trembling, shaking from the cold and yet still trying to calm me.

Damn it. "If there's nothing between us, why aren't you afraid of me?"

I jerked toward her and snarled, trying to get her to back off before my beast grabbed her and hurt her.

But she pressed her hands against my chest instead of stepping away. "Because you *need* someone. You need another soul to stabilize yours. I'm not going to let you suffer with a damaged connection. You don't deserve that."

My beast shuddered again at her touch, its tension melting away, and it leaned in. It couldn't do anything else.

Mine. She's mine. She has to be.

And yet another part of me was so certain she was Seireadan's because the Winter Court had claimed her. But both her and Seireadan had said I was wrong about that. She was claimed because I'd given her the key. Maybe I was wrong about us.

"You don't love me?"

"I don't really know you. I don't love Sebastian or Hawk either." Her weak angel glow flared again and her gaze dipped to her hands. "All I know is that I need this too. With you. With them. I don't know how to explain it. I'm not a shifter. I shouldn't *need* this. And yet it's like a part of me that I didn't know was asleep comes awake when I connect with all of you."

She raised her brilliant blue eyes to meet mine and my pulse stalled. This time instead of holding me captive like she'd done before, it was like she'd pulled back a veil and I could see into her soul. There was a rawness there, a soul-deep need that she didn't understand and feared. It was as damaged as my connection with my beast, and was so much bigger than a connection with a single person. And I wasn't even sure she realized all of that, only that there was something wrong with her.

Mine.

But my beast was mistaken. It was confused. If she felt a connection with all of us then she couldn't be my soul's mate.

And even knowing that, I still wanted her. My cock was still hard.

Because I hadn't gotten laid in over five hundred years, and because I understood the desperate need in her soul for a connection.

Even if she wasn't my mate, I could still give that to her like Seireadan and Hawk... if I could keep my beast at bay... and if she'd still accept me... which she did. Her arousal still filled my nostrils and her pupils were still dilated. Her desire for me hadn't diminished because I'd begged her to be my mate, and that desperate need to heal a connection within her that she didn't understand still filled her eyes.

She was already giving so much to help me calm my soul, the least I could do was give her my body to help calm hers. I just had to figure out how to get my beast to shut the fuck up and not hurt anyone.

AMIAH

"I CAN GIVE YOU WHAT YOU NEED," TITUS SAID, HIS VOICE GRUFF, surprising me.

That wasn't what I'd expected him to say at all.

"I just need time to get my beast to settle." He jerked back a step and stroked a heated gaze down my body. "And you need to heal."

Desire shuddered through me even as my thoughts stuttered over his words.

"I don't want you to be with me if you have to fight your beast. I don't want it to make you hurt the others." How had this suddenly turned into us discussing a sexual arrangement?

"I won't. It understands your situation." He turned before I could respond, strode to the window, and jumped out.

In the blink of an eye, he shifted into his magnificent dragon, caught a wind current, and lifted out of sight.

I sagged against the hall wall, exhausted from having used all my magic again and shivering not just from the Winter Court's cold. There was something broken inside me, something as an angel I wasn't supposed to have and didn't understand. And it hadn't just been years of ignoring my desires that made me crave sex, it was the years of denying something deeper inside me.

My life force *needed* to connect with someone else's life force. It was the foundation of my magic, why, if I didn't use it often enough, a pressure would build inside me, and why, if I was pulled away before it was done or resisted its compulsion, I'd suffer a debilitating backlash.

Denying that needed connection for so long had damaged it just like Titus being unable to shift had damaged his connection with his beast. Now we both had to figure out how to heal ourselves.

And much to my surprise, I believed Titus when he said his beast understood what I needed. Which was good, because I ached to connect with Titus physically, but I also knew, especially now that I was aware of my broken connection, that I needed more than just his touch. It was why I still wanted to have sex with both Hawk and Sebastian, why my soul thrilled at the idea of connecting with both of them at the same time. Just like someone else I knew, I was *supposed* to have multiple lovers. Not because I was destined to have multiple mates like her but because my soul needed the strength of multiple connections.

"Amiah?" Hawk asked, hurrying across the living room toward me, his fiery dark life force sliding against my senses and sending a thrill through my soul. "You okay?"

No. I needed to connect with him, to have him inside me.

He'd changed into clean leather pants like Cassius but hadn't put on a shirt and I had a perfect view of his stunning sculpted body. A body made for sex... which I was in no condition to have, and was going to have to wait for.

I just needed to hold out until I'd healed my ribs.

I could do that. Really.

"Just cold and tired," I said.

His eyes narrowed.

Yeah, I wouldn't believe me either.

"Titus just jumped out the window again." He picked me up, cradling me against his too-hot body, and I leaned into him, not waiting to grow accustomed to his body temperature before trying to get as much flesh to flesh contact as possible. "He looked upset and you're both horny as hell."

"Can't hide anything from you." I slid my hand over his pec and savored the feel of his hard, honed muscle as well as the gentle snaps under my skin of his life force responding to mine.

"Is he going to be a problem?" he asked, carrying me back to the bedroom and laying me on the bed. "You keep putting your hands on him and I get the impression dragons are like wolves and they have trouble sharing."

"We've worked it out."

"You sure?" Hawk settled in behind me and pulled a heavy blanket over top of us.

Mindful of my ribs, I carefully snuggled against him, letting his heat melt the cold inside me and the physical contact strengthened my connection with his life force. All of it relaxed me, dragging me closer and closer to sleep. "He understands what I need."

"Doesn't mean he won't be a problem," Hawk said, his hot breath feathering across the back of my neck.

"He won't." Because once again Titus was the one most likely to understand my situation. Just like being held against our will, we were the only ones in the group with souls that needed a connection with another soul.

"Okay then," Hawk replied without further argument.

Which struck me as funny. If it had been Cassius, we'd still be arguing. We'd argue about it all night long because he didn't trust my judgment—

Not true.

He couldn't let even the slim chance of danger threaten me... because I was weak and he saw me as his responsibility.

That thought twisted around my heart. I didn't want to be his responsibility. I wanted my friend back, wanted the easy relationship we used to have before the war, wanted more. If my stupid brand hadn't gotten in the way, I'd probably be married to him now.

And then I'd never have had sex with Sebastian or Hawk or realized the truth about my soul. Angels, compared to other species, were distant with each other, even with their lovers. Unless they were soul bonded, they never opened their souls to anyone, and without a doubt, Cassius would never open his to mine. He certainly wouldn't open his now.

Which twisted my grief tighter. The war had torn a hole in his soul, and it wasn't just because of his youngest brother's death. All I wanted was to heal him. Except I couldn't heal souls. His other brother's mate could with her empathic healing magic, but it was going to take a lot of convincing to get him to even consider seeing Essie. And first, we'd have to get out of this mess and find our way back to the mortal realm... if I could even leave Faerie now with the Winter Court's claim on me.

My eyelids slid shut and my exhaustion pulled me into a strange sleep. I dreamed of ice again and also fire, twirling around and around inside me, trapping me, freeing me, filling me with power and life and something else I couldn't find the words for. It crushed and pulled and threatened to consume my soul and there wasn't anything I could do about it.

Because I was trapped.

Trapped.

I woke with a start, gasping for breath, my power full and burning in my palms. My body ached, but it wasn't screaming in pain, and a whisper of Hawk's sensual magic pulsed in my chest and throbbed between my thighs. I still lay under the blanket in his arms with my back against his chest, but now his hand had slipped under my shirt and was cupping my breast and his erection was hard against my rear.

My thoughts instantly jumped to him pushing inside me, and his magic swelled. He murmured, still asleep, and started kneading my breast, making my nipple harden in anticipation.

A soft moan escaped my lips and he shifted his hips forward adding a delicious pressure to the press of his erection. His life force crackled against my senses with the promise of so much more if I just took him inside me, and my whole body throbbed with need at the thought.

Which was a terrible idea since I really needed to heal my broken ribs first.

I shifted so I could touch his face, wake him, and look him in the eyes. The movement slipped his hand from my breast, and with a throaty, masculine groan, he slid his hand inside my pants, his fingers going straight for my clit.

His touch shot sensation through me, stealing my breath, and his power curled tight in my core.

Oh, wow.

"Hawk," I said, my voice breathy.

"Just let it go," he murmured still asleep and he slid two fingers inside me. "I've got you."

My eyes rolled back and my breath picked up, spiking only a glimmer of the pain that I should have felt. Which didn't mean my ribs were healed, just that Hawk's power was growing inside me and I couldn't feel them.

"Hawk, wake up." I caressed his cheek with what I knew was a freezing cold hand to his naturally hot demonic body temperature and his eyelids fluttered open, capturing me with his unusual blue-gray eyes, his hellfire blazing.

"We should probably wait," I said.

He frowned. "We should wait?" he asked his words slurred with sleep.

Then his eyes widened and I guess he realized where his hand was.

"Oh, well," he said his expression turning wicked. "You want to finish?"

The thought sent a sudden rush of desire racing through me. "You have to ask?"

He shrugged. "Not really."

With a swell of magic, he quickly worked me up and over the edge. It wasn't the deep, connection that I craved. His fingers inside me didn't fill me with his life force to the same degree as his erection did, but it still felt amazing, and I wasn't an idiot. I'd never say no to him making me feel like that.

"God, I love how that feels," he said, pulling me back into his arms and wrapping me in his heat.

"That makes two of us, and you'll be able to get a lot more power once I heal my ribs."

"With all the sexual desire in this group, I'm already at full." He kissed the divot behind my ear. "That was purely for the pleasure of it. But yes, heal those ribs. There should only be pain during sex if you're into that."

The memory of Balwyrdan with sexual pleasure gleaming in his eyes as he slammed his fist into my face rushed into my mind's eye chilling my desire.

"Yeah. Didn't think that was your thing," Hawk said. "So what do you need me to do to work your magic and heal yourself?"

"Just keep holding me. You're not injured so there's no chance my magic will slip into you, and it takes a lot of concentration to heal myself. I'd rather not have to try to do that while I'm also freezing." I gathered my power, hot and sticky, in my palms and gave him an apologetic smile. "It's going to look like I'm asleep and it's going to take a while, so it might get boring."

"Gee, holding a sexy woman in my arms." He flashed me a wicked grin. "I think I can manage."

"Just holding. As much as I'd love something else, I can't."

He pressed his lips to my cheek and said, "I've got you." Just like he'd said in his dream.

I closed my eyes and dragged my power from my hands and into my chest, pushing it into my broken bones and agonizingly slowly knitting them back together.

God, it was such a waste. This was why I needed to be more careful. All this magic could have saved someone's life, could have healed all the guys — except Hawk — of serious injuries. If I was supposed to be using it on myself, healing me would have been as easy as healing everyone else.

And as much as staying out of trouble was the ideal, it wasn't the reality. Especially now. I was in the middle of all of it just like the guys and I knew, even if I had a chance to get some place safe, I wouldn't leave them. Getting hurt was a risk I was more than willing to take if it meant I was nearby when one of them needed me.

I pushed power into my ribs until only the small spark in my palms that I could never use up remained. Three of the five ribs had been healed, good as new, and much to my surprise, the fourth's break had been healed into a hairline fracture.

Exhaustion weighed down my body and once again the room was slowly spinning, even with my eyes closed. I drew in a breath not nearly as painful as before in an attempt to ease my dizziness and opened my eyes.

Hawk's gaze locked with mine and worry clouded his expression. "Jeez. I hate seeing your glow that dim."

"I hate feeling it," I replied.

"I'll get you something to eat." He pushed back the covers and eased away from me. "Be back in a minute."

I grabbed his wrist. "Help me into the living room so I can see the sky before I pass out again." There weren't any windows in the bedroom and while Hawk was an amazing distraction, seeing the sky would also help me steady myself and make it easier to regain my power.

"Deal." He picked me up and we stepped into the living room.

Sebastian was the only one around, lounging on a pile of cushions staring out the massive window at a clear blue sky. His icy life force surged against my senses, connecting me with him even though he was halfway across the room and filling me with his pain, the source still invisible to my magic.

"Set her right here," Sebastian said, opening his legs and shifting so he was sitting instead of lying. "I've got enough power to ease the Winter Court's cold. I think that, and not the leash spell, is our first priority."

"Agreed." Funny how the leash spell was no longer the top priority. Sure, Sebastian had lengthened and eased its deadly side effects, but we were still bound together. I was still trapped. And yet that no longer terrified me. Maybe because I knew eventually we'd deal with it, there was a way to be free.

The Winter Court, however, was a different matter.

My gaze dipped to my still-glowing hands. The light had dimmed a bit, or perhaps I was just getting used to it, but I still glowed. I still had Faerie's magic woven in my cells, impossibly making me a high fae and it wasn't just going to go away.

"Can you get rid of all of it?" I asked, even though I suspected I knew the answer. He'd said he'd fix it when we been in the Wilds but he hadn't mentioned that when we'd all discussed our situation.

"No." Sebastian's expression darkened, confirming my fears. "That's going to take a lot of power and I'm not up for that right now. Best to deal with the cold and make things manageable for you until I'm strong enough."

"Are you up for even blocking the cold?" Hawk asked.

Sebastian patted the cushion between his thighs again. "I'm fine. Let's just do this."

I rolled my eyes at him. "You're not fine. You're in pain and it's getting worse."

"Because every time he casts a spell the demonic magic trapped inside him gets stronger," Hawk said, still not putting me down. "You channeled a lot of magic when we escaped the Winter Court."

"No shit. And our other options were...?" Sebastian patted the cushion again. "There's nothing I can do about it and Amiah shouldn't have to spend who knows how long freezing."

So that was what their strange conversation in the Wilds had been about. Sebastian, a being from Faerie shouldn't have been able to connect with the Realm of Celestial Darkness let alone take its magic into his body. If he somehow had demonic magic in him, he might not be able to get it out, which would explain why he'd mentioned needing to find a demon.

Except if he wasn't able to connect with demonic magic— "How do you even have demonic magic in you?"

"Long story." He sighed and patted the cushion again. "It involves teleporting too many people at once, a crazy hellfire queen, and an archnephilim newly awakened to her powers."

And he'd dumped everyone into the middle of the cafeteria in the

Joined Parliament Operations building. He'd saved everyone's lives with that spell, and it had torn up his insides, nearly killing him. Thankfully my fellow healer, Priam, had gotten to him first and stabilized him, stopping my magic from locking onto him, but once we'd all gotten to a safe location, I'd still had to drain myself to heal him.

"Why didn't you say anything?"

"Because it was none of your business." Sebastian glared at Hawk.

Hawk glared back. "Given our situation, I think she has a right to know."

"I don't see how me being infected with demonic magic influences us being fuck buddies," Sebastian snapped. "It's not like it's contagious."

"Because she's counting on your magic to keep her safe and it's going to fail and soon." Hawk's grip on me tightened. "I've been watching it eat you from the inside out since you walked into my tent."

"And again I say, find me a fucking demon in Faerie who can pull it out." He slapped the cushion between his legs. "The sooner I ease up Amiah's chill the sooner Cassius will feel it's safe to move and we'll get back to the mortal realm. Problem solved."

"Fine," Hawk said, setting me on the cushion between Sebastian's thighs. "I'll go find you something to eat."

He stormed out of the living room and with a groan Sebastian tugged me back against his chest. His life force pulsed against my senses, cold and uneven, and his pain slid through my veins.

"How bad is it?" I asked.

He wrapped his arms around me and the heat from his body — the temperature not as hot as Hawk's but still warmer than mine when it shouldn't have been — slowly seeped into my skin. "It used to just hurt when I cast something. Now I hurt all the time."

"Then don't ease the Winter Court's cold. I can manage."

He snorted and lifted one of my softly glowing hands. "Your fingernails have already turned blue again. You've been snuggled up to a natural furnace for hours and you've only been away from him for a minute. Your body isn't made to handle the Winter Court's magic."

"Then why would it claim me?"

"I have no idea." He tensed and his icy magic prickled over my skin then sank under it, rushing in a freezing wave to my heart.

I tensed, anticipating a pain similar to the agony of changing the leash spell, but instead, it filled me with bliss. An icy version of Hawk's seductive magic. It flooded around my heart, making my pulse pick up, then sank lower into my core.

"But fuck if it doesn't like you," he said, his voice husky. "I've never felt my magic do that before."

"If it likes me, will it even let me leave Faerie?" The seductive chill swelled and I breathed out a soft moan.

"Let's just deal with one problem at a time," he groaned back.

Which meant he didn't know... or he did and the answer was no. Meaning even if we got to a portal, the Winter Court wasn't going to let me leave. Ever.

HAWK

FUCKING HELL.

I wrenched open a cupboard looking for a bowl. Just plates. Great. So now I'd found serving platters and plates. Where were the damned bowls?

I'd stormed down the hall to the last doorway where Cassius had said there was a kitchen, finding it attached to a massive dining room.

The kitchen part was constructed from a mix of stone carved — likely magically carved — from the mountain itself and wood. Stone counters ran from the doorway and along the walls in a long L, broken only by a large old-fashioned metal stove and a sink, and jutted out from the wall marking the boundary between the kitchen and the dining room.

Someone had left a pot of stew simmering on what I could only assume was a magically heated element because there was no electricity in Faerie that I'd seen and no fire heating the stove, and I'd decided that something warm would be good for Amiah even if Bane did manage to ease the Winter Court's chill.

God, I hoped he had enough power for that. As much as I loved holding her in my arms, it was clear the constant cold was taking its toll, and she was either putting on a good face or was too worried about everything else to notice.

And now I'd given her something else to worry about.

What the hell was wrong with me?

I shouldn't have said anything about the demonic magic consuming the magical channels in Bane's body in front of Amiah. I should have kept my damned mouth shut.

But it was clear from the way she looked at him that she cared for him more than just for the sexual pleasure he could give her. Sure, she'd made a point of saying love wasn't going to be involved in our arrangement but that didn't mean we couldn't care for each other, and she was going to be shattered if Bane killed himself trying to free her from the Winter Court.

Every time he used his magic the demonic magic got stronger and his connection to Faerie got weaker. Eventually, he was going to be completely cut off and he'd die since a high fae couldn't survive without a connection to their realm.

She had a right to know the danger he was putting himself in for her. Hell, the others did, too, but they wouldn't blame themselves like Amiah would, and I couldn't live with her blaming herself.

Fuck. I couldn't live with her being cold or in pain, and I wasn't sure I wanted to live without her when she finally decided to fall in love with someone and have a committed relationship.

I didn't want to give up the feeling of her desire rushing through my veins, or her body moving against mine, or the sounds she made, and certainly not the look of absolute pleasure when she came. I'd even been dreaming about making love to her and had woken with my fingers buried inside her and my hard-as-hell cock pressed against her butt.

I'd never woken like that before.

I was supposed to have more control than that.

But there was something about her, about the way she looked at me, connected with me. It wasn't love. It couldn't be love. But there was something there, something so deep I'd dreamed about it and had felt so fucking good when I'd woken with her desire rushing through me and her body aching for a pleasure I was more than happy to give her.

Fuck.

We'd only known each other a short time. I'd only slept with her twice and while the hard fuck in the alcove to save my life shouldn't have counted, the look in her eyes, that sense that she was seeing into my soul and embracing all of me not just my body, had been even stronger than before. She'd closed her eyes when her orgasm had swept through her, but just before that there was that perfect moment again where she saw me. All of me. It had stolen my breath and left me stunned. Again.

Fuck.

I wrenched open another cupboard.

Bowls.

Finally!

"Is she awake?" Cassius asked from behind me, making me jump and drop a bowl.

The pottery shattered on the stone floor, sending chunks flying in all directions.

"Jeez." I knelt and started picking up the pieces. "Yes, she's awake."

"And her ribs?" Cassius picked up a piece halfway between us. His aura snapped and heaved, an angry red nimbus around his body, and his expression was hard. If I hadn't known from the turmoil in his aura how much he was struggling to keep his fire inside him, I'd have mistaken his expression for bottled up rage.

"I don't know. She spent a couple of hours healing herself, but when I moved her to the living room, she still looked like she was in pain."

"She's in the living room? Good," he said, surprising me since I was sure he'd want her to stay in bed until she'd fixed all her broken bones. "Seeing the sky will help her recover her magic faster."

"An angel's need for open spaces is that strong?" I'd known angels liked open spaces and claustrophobia was more common in angels than any other species, but I hadn't known the need was so strong it affected their magic.

Cassius's aura flared and a wisp of smoke curled from his right hand. "Amiah's is. She needs to know she's free, that she can escape. I suspect the need wasn't as strong before she was taken." Another *snap* in his aura and the wisp of smoke thickened. "Before the *first* time she was taken."

Right. Which had been the first time they'd met. A part of me wondered if that had been when he'd fallen in love with her, while a selfish part of me was glad she hadn't fallen in love with him then too. I'd never have met her if she had.

Except now that she was allowing herself to feel, I suspected she'd eventually fall in love with him too.

She and Cassius had been friends for a long time and he was completely dedicated to her. Even if he hadn't told me, it would have been clear in how they interacted. They behaved like two people who'd known each other for years, comfortable — for the most part — in each other's company. They had a lot in common, had shared a lot of experiences, and I suspected when he got his head out of his ass, they had fun together... a stuffy angel kind of fun, but still fun. They were perfect for each other.

And yet the part of me that didn't want to lose her to a committed relationship was getting louder and louder. If she committed to Cassius, I'd lose her. She needed to commit to someone who'd accept me as well — since if she committed to me and me alone, I'd end up killing her or starving, because if she committed herself to me, I wouldn't want to sleep with other people outside of our relationship.

Hell, I wasn't sure I wanted to sleep with other people right now.

My pulse stuttered at that.

Fuck me.

It wasn't supposed to be possible, but in that instant, I knew Amiah was going to break my heart.

The realization stunned me.

"Hawk?"

I wasn't sure if I was in love with her yet, but I would be. Even if I'd never been in love before and wasn't supposed to be able to fall in love, I just knew I was going to fall in love with her. With how she made me feel, what I wanted to give her and show her, how I wanted to take care of her... it was inevitable.

"Hawk."

If I was smart, I'd pull away from her and protect myself. I had no idea how a broken heart was going to affect me. Incubi weren't supposed to be able to fall in love, and there were only a few recorded cases of it happening... and ending very badly. Falling in love was akin to a mental illness in any other species.

But the thought of ending what I'd started with her made my heart race.

It wasn't even a matter of want. I *couldn't* do it. Not even to protect my sanity.

I'd always known my time with her would come to an end, no way was I going to be an idiot and end it sooner than absolutely necessary. I'd rather have more time, a bigger broken heart, and end up locked up in a psych ward, than less time and centuries of regret.

"Hawk!"

I jerked my attention to Cassius.

"What is wrong with you? You've cut yourself three times on the same shard."

My gaze dropped to the half dozen blood drops on the floor by my knee and the bloody shard — my finger perfectly fine because of my rapid healing, although the blood drops on the floor indicated at least one of the cuts had been deep.

"We need to get Amiah out of Faerie." The words rushed out of me. She wasn't safe in Faerie. What little time I had with her was going to be cut short because someone was going to kill her.

"We need a plan first," Cassius said, tossing his pottery pieces into the sink, not sounding happy about that at all. "The aerie will protect Bane, and I guess Amiah now too, from Faerie ripping its magic out of them for a few days, but we can't just return to the mortal realm. We're seriously vulnerable there."

"Bane's place has spells hiding it. Balwyrdan only found us because Mavis told him."

"And how much do you want to bet one of Deaglan's assassins didn't get that information too?"

Fuck. "What about the JP Operations building? It has protections and agents." I dropped my pieces in the sink with his. "And an arsenal. God, what I wouldn't give for a rifle right about now."

"You honestly think I haven't already thought of that?" He gripped the edge of the counter, his aura writhing and smoke billowing from his hands. "That's the last resort. I don't want to get any more people involved in this mess than necessary. Amiah has one of the keys. That means Titus got a key while he was Deaglan's prisoner. Once Deaglan figures out Amiah has it, he'll be coming after her whether we like it or not, wherever she might be. We need a better plan than just holing up at Operations."

"Well we're going to need to think of something."

"I said I was going to keep her safe and I will." Cassius's eyes narrowed and his angel glow flickered, shockingly bright for a second. "Back in the Winter Court you said I shouldn't doubt your resolve."

"And I'd meant it." I'd been pissed when I'd said it. Cassius had pressed me for details to prove I was actually a vet and I'd told him about the horrible thing I'd had to do in the war. I should have lied, just said I was a canary for a reconnaissance unit or something, but that would have meant getting my story straight with Bane who'd been with me during that nightmare, and there were more important things to worry about.

"What are you willing to do to keep her safe?"

Anything.

Everything.

I was already going to happily lose my mind and heart to her. I'd give up my soul too if it meant protecting her.

I was so completely fucked.

"What are you asking?"

The light in Cassius's eyes flared again and for a second his expression was filled with heartbreak and resignation before his icy mask slid back into place. "Are you willing to have her hate you if it means protecting her?"

He was. He'd told me so. And yet it was clearly tearing him apart.

Was I? Could I withstand losing her because of something I did and not because it was time for her to move on to someone else?

God, I didn't even want her to move on to someone else.

Except I wasn't supposed to care. Not like that. And if I didn't want Amiah worried about my sanity, I couldn't let her or anyone else know the truth that I was impossibly falling in love with her.

AMIAH

Much to my disappointment, I woke alone, my magic at full indicating I had to have slept for about eight hours, and once again I pushed my power from my palms into my chest to finish healing my broken ribs.

Back in the living room, Sebastian's magic had caressed my insides, turning me on but also making me drowsy, and I'd floated, propped up against him, watching puffy clouds drift across the sky.

Hawk had brought me a bowl of stew, his body not nearly as hot as before — which a far-off part of my brain knew that meant Sebastian had managed to ease the Winter Court's chill inside me — then they'd put me back to bed, each man stealing a breathtaking kiss before I passed out.

Now I lay in the bed, a little too warm under the heavy blanket and fully dressed, trying to figure out what I wanted to do first: eat or take a pain-free shower.

Cassius would have said eat, "you can survive if you're dirty," but the more I thought about it, the more I liked the idea of having a long hot soak. Just lounge in the tub and let my thoughts wander—

To all the things I was trying not to think about...

Best to have a shower.

Unless I could find Hawk or Sebastian and invite them to join me in the bath. That was something I definitely wanted to try. Of course, we'd have to do it in a different suite. It would be best to avoid an embarrassing situation with Cassius walking in on us.

Just the thought heated my cheeks with embarrassment... but also desire.

Jeez. What was wrong with me—

No. There was nothing wrong with me. I had to stop thinking like that. I wanted to connect with all of them because that was who I was, what my soul needed.

Except, did I want to connect with them because I needed to feel their life force and anyone would do, or because they were them?

And the minute I thought that, I knew it was because of who they were. I'd never craved Marcus like I did Hawk, Sebastian, Titus, or even Cassius. Now that the part of my soul that had been asleep had awakened, I knew there was something about them, about their life forces, that resonated with me.

They weren't my soul mates. Or at least Sebastian and Hawk weren't. As much as they weren't the men I thought they were, it was still crazy to think either man was my perfect match. So it couldn't have been my partially formed brand drawing me to them. That, and the draw was stronger now that my brand was gone and the part of my soul that could create a bond had been permanently removed. No, it had everything to do with the power in their souls.

Connection and desire aside, however, I still wasn't prepared for Cassius to walk in on me having sex with Hawk or Sebastian or both of them together. In fact, right now, I didn't want to have anything to do with Cassius. I was still furious about him thinking he had any kind of say in my sex life.

Except Hawk and Sebastian had said I needed to have a conversation with Cassius, and they were right. But it wasn't to clarify who I could and couldn't have sex with. That was none of his business. What I really needed was to figure out how to get my friend back and not the icy soldier who seemed to think he could tell me what to do.

I pushed the blanket back and got out of bed, praying I wouldn't run into Cassius. I wasn't even close to being ready for our much needed conversation and he'd probably make me eat something which meant the shower — or sexy bath — would end up waiting. And, God, I was just so tired of waiting. I was tired of being patient and denying myself something I hadn't even realized was a fundamental part of myself.

For too long I'd forced myself into a tight little box: Amiah the healer who was waiting for her soul mate. I'd tried to ignore everything else, because everything else couldn't be controlled. Everything else increased the risk of making a mistake, of being hurt and held captive again, of feeling things for someone I wasn't supposed to have feelings for because he wasn't my soul mate.

But squeezing into that box hadn't kept me safe or protected my heart. The man I'd thought was my soul mate had been destined for someone else and the brand that I'd thought was beautiful was a nightmare. And the man who I'd thought was infuriating and selfish was a generous lover who was hurting himself to help me.

I hadn't really known anything.

I stepped into the living room and my attention instantly jumped to Cassius. He was the only one in the room and stood at the railing staring out the open window at the clear afternoon sky. He'd released his wings from his body and extended them, letting the gentle breeze caress his feathers, and was absolutely breathtaking. The perfect image of the perfect angel.

For a second he looked like the man I used to know. The thoughtful warm angel who'd saved me, made me laugh, and kept me company without even knowing I was foolishly waiting for a love I now no longer wanted.

Then he turned, his gaze locking on me, and ice swept across his expression, turning him back into the hardened soldier.

My throat tightened and tears pricked my eyes. God, I wanted the old Cassius back. But just like me, he'd learned things that had fundamentally changed him, which broke my heart because it wasn't anything I could heal.

"Hey," I said, unable to think of anything else to say and yet unable to turn away from him.

"Are your ribs healed?" he asked, his voice so cold it made me shiver.

"Yes." Was even a glimmer of the man I used to know in there anymore? I desperately wanted him to be. I needed *him,* not the soldier determined to keep me safe whether I liked it or not.

"I'll get the other guys so we can discuss our next plan of action." He pulled his wings back into his body and started to storm off.

My heart clenched and everything within me screamed that I couldn't let him leave, not with this anger between us. He'd made me so mad and if I thought about it, I'd said something hateful back. If he really was in love with me like Sebastian said, rubbing it in his face that we weren't having sex would have really hurt.

"Cassius, wait."

But he didn't stop, didn't even look at me.

Jeez. I scrambled to the door leading to the hall and put my body between him and the exit, pressing my palms against his chest. The sense of his life force flared, snapping with a burning heat just under my skin, even as he froze, his body going rigid.

"Amiah—" he said, his voice gruff, smoke curling around his hands. "Let me get the guys."

"Let them rest or whatever it is they're doing for a minute." We needed to have this conversation. I needed to get back what was left of *my* Cassius.

I drew in a steadying breath, determined to gather my thoughts and say the right thing but I couldn't pull my attention away from the feel of his firm pecs beneath my hands, only a thin cotton shirt separating our flesh. He didn't have the sleek sculpted physique that Hawk and Sebastian had, but his musculature was just as stunning, just as developed only a little bulkier. What would it be like to have him moving on top of me, those powerful arms holding himself up, his broad chest—

My thoughts stuttered and I realized I'd just stroked his chest.

I lifted my eyes and our gazes locked. For a breathtaking moment, I saw a desperate desire that ignited a matching desire within me.

He wrenched his gaze away, grabbed my wrists, and put more than an angel-appropriate amount of distance between us.

"Amiah, please. If you're still cold, grope someone who'll like it, like Hawk," he said, his tone implying that grope meant sex because of course now that he knew I was having sex I had to be incapable of touching someone without having sex with them.

How dare he!

"Oh, so I do get to have a sex life," I snapped. "Or am I only allowed to *grope*?"

"Don't be ridiculous." More smoke billowed around him and his palms grew painfully hot around my wrists. "I didn't say you couldn't have sex."

"No, you just think it's disgusting that I am."

"Of course I don't." Fire snapped from his hands, stinging my skin, and he wrenched away from me.

"Right, because you weren't appalled at the idea of me having sex with anyone and everyone?"

"No," he growled back, "I was shocked because I didn't think you'd sleep around while trying to win Marcus. I thought you were in love with him."

"I was in love with him." The words leaped out before I could stop them. Crap. I shouldn't have said that, because I hadn't really been in love with Marcus. I knew that now. I'd been in love with the idea of being in love, of his shifter's passion, of how wonderful having a completed mating brand would be. "I *thought* I was. I was wrong."

God, I'd been such a fool. How could I have ever thought what I felt for Marcus had been love? I wasn't in love with Hawk, Sebastian, or Titus, and what I felt for them was so much stronger than what I'd ever felt for Marcus even after four and a half years of being near him.

Because I needed something in their life forces, something that Marcus didn't have.

Something that Cassius also had.

"You know you're not in love with Hawk, either," Cassius said. "He can't love you back."

Jeez. I wasn't stupid. I was well aware Hawk couldn't love me back.

"It's just his magic," he added. "It's influencing you because he can't be bothered to pull back all of it."

Oh, for the love of—

"What does it matter?" I asked. "So what if his magic is influencing me."

Cassius rolled his eyes at me. "So if you have sex with him, you're going to regret it and I'll have to help you mend another broken heart."

I stared at him, stunned. I hadn't just heard that. I couldn't have. "You'll *have* to?"

"That's not what I meant," he huffed, not looking at all like he regretted his choice of words.

"No, that's exactly what you meant." God, I had to stop. I had to shut my mouth and walk away. But I couldn't. I was so angry at everything, and I was furious at Cassius for looking at me like he wanted me, like maybe there could be something between us, then pushing me away and acting like he had the right to tell me who I could and couldn't have sex with. "So I'm some kind of chore? A duty you're stuck with because you pulled me out of that faith healer's tent? Protect poor weak little Amiah from everyone, from life, from herself? She doesn't know what she wants. She's too fragile. She can't possibly make the right decisions, especially about sex."

"That's not what I said at all." Fire rolled over his arms and he glared at me. "Things have happened to you and you're not thinking straight right now."

"I'm thinking perfectly fine."

"Right, that's why you risked your life by taking on all of Hawk's power, why you keep getting close to Titus when he's about to lose control of his beast, and why you had Sebastian practically rape you in front of the entire Winter Court ballroom." Sparks exploded from his hands, catching in one of the cushions and it burst into flames. "Fuck!"

He heaved his fire back under his skin, taking the flames consuming the cushion as well, and stormed back to the window.

"You are *not* fine," he growled at me. "You can't possibly be fine."

"Well neither are you."

"I'm not going to do something I'll regret, like sleeping with Hawk."

"I'm not regretting it," I yelled back.

Shock flashed across his expression.

"I see." He released his wings with a fiery explosion and dove out the window.

Crap.

I'd just yelled at him that I was having sex with Hawk, the complete opposite of the conversation I was supposed to have had with him. Just great.

AMIAH

I didn't even know how the conversation had gone so wrong. The argument hadn't even made any sense. He'd told me to go grope Hawk and then turned around and told me he needed to protect me against having sex with Hawk and falling in love with him.

I released my wings and screamed out the window even though he was out of sight and I didn't really want to fly after him. I wasn't the one who wasn't thinking straight.

Where was *my* Cassius, the man I could lean on, who I'd thought trusted me to make good logical decisions? I hadn't even been arguing with the hard as ice soldier who'd come back from the war.

I had no idea who that had been.

Except I had no idea who I was. I hadn't been thoughtful or logical in that argument. I wasn't sure I'd been logical since this whole mess started.

Now Cassius was flying around somewhere so angry he hadn't wanted to stay in the same room as me and I'd pushed him further away.

And there wasn't a thing I could do about it.

Swell.

Well, since the cat has been yelled out of the bag, I might as well go find Hawk and grope him.

I yanked my wings back inside my body and checked all the bedrooms and the bathroom.

No Hawk or Sebastian.

Just great. The aerie was huge and I didn't want to aimlessly wander around with the hope that I'd find one of them. I could run into Cassius again and as much as a part of me wanted to continue yelling at him, the smart thing to do was just avoid him until both of us had calmed down.

Which brought me back to my original plan: have a shower and then get something to eat.

I grabbed a towel from the rack in the bathroom and stared at the ninety-degree turn. One of the guys could still walk in on me, and I wasn't in the mood for an awkward anything or not being able to move on my desires because I was worried someone in the living room might hear us or walk in on us.

That was a frustration I just didn't want, so I decided to use the bathroom in the suite at the very end of the main hall. But when I left our suite, I ran into Sebastian.

He leaned against the wall in the doorway of the second suite down, watching me approach with his arms crossed and his lips pursed, and not at all looking like he wanted to have a sexy bath.

"Well," he drawled, "that was one way to tell him you and Hawk are having sex."

"I'm aware of that." I didn't want to have an argument about my argument, and that's what it looked like Sebastian wanted. "And I'm not talking about it," I said, marching past him.

He grabbed my wrist, tugged me into the shadows of the suite's long hallway, and captured me against the wall, his palms on either side of my arms, boxing me in, making my pulse pick up in anticipation. Except his expression remained concerned, not even a hint of sexual desire.

"There are a lot of things you don't want to talk about," he said.

"Because there's no point in talking about them." My throat tightened and all the things I didn't want to think about threatened to break free. I leaned in and brushed my lips along his jaw so he wouldn't see I was about to have a breakdown. "There are so many better things we could be doing instead of talking."

"Sex will only be able to distract you for so long," he replied, nipping at my ear.

"It just needs to get me through this mess."

"And then what?" He slid his hands into my hair, capturing my head, and pressed his forehead to mine. "What will you do when this is done?"

His life force tingled against my senses, his icy brightness writhing against the demonic darkness. I didn't want to give up whatever it was that I needed from him, but he'd made it clear he'd never make a commitment to anyone. Ever. And given that the last person he'd been committed to had tried to murder him, I couldn't blame him. Which meant at some point I'd have no choice. I'd have to give him up.

And I'd deal with that when we got there.

"I don't know." I slid my hands under his shirt and ran them up his washboard abs. "Is this really what you want to be doing? Talking about the things I don't want to talk about? I'd rather you were doing me."

He snorted. "Jeez. You have sex a couple of times and all your angelic propriety gets thrown out the window."

"Would you rather I ask you primly for sexual intercourse?" I asked. "Or how about..." I dropped my towel, reached for the laces of his fly, and slowly sank to my knees.

I'd been curious about this, about what it would be like to hold a man's erection in my hands and feel it slide between my lips. It had felt amazing when Sebastian and Hawk had put their mouths on me, I bet it would feel just as amazing for them.

"Amiah," he huffed. "You've made your point. You don't have to do this."

I freed him from his pants, wrapped my hand around his full thick erection, and gave him my answer by slowly running my tongue over his tip.

"Fuck, Amiah," he groaned

His skin was softer than I imagined, a velvety layer over a steel shaft that I knew could bring me immense pleasure, and I slowly licked his tip again, drawing another groan.

"If you're teasing, just stop." He tangled his fingers back into my hair and started to tug me up, but I slid him into my mouth and he froze, his fingers digging into my scalp.

"Fucking hell."

My heart skipped a beat. I was pretty sure taking him in my mouth was how it was done, but he'd gotten tense, his body trembling.

Well, maybe I could convince him to give me some instruction so it felt good for him.

I glanced up at him through my lashes, ready to pull him out and ask for his help, but my words stalled at the look in his eyes.

Desire. Smoldering, dark, hot-as-hell, barely contained desire, that made the muscles in my core clench in anticipation at the possibility of wild, passionate sex. While I hadn't enjoyed what we'd had to do in the Winter Court ballroom, that didn't mean I wasn't excited at the idea of less restraint. It made me wet just thinking about the first time we'd had sex. I'd thought he'd been barely controlled before, but this, from the look in his eyes and the tension in his body, was what it really looked like.

Keeping our gazes locked, I drew him out until just his tip was in my mouth and slid him back in.

"Oh, fuck." He pressed a palm against the wall.

I did another slow withdrawal with my hand sliding up his length following my lips, my eyes still on his, and his breath picked up.

There was something so incredibly erotic about watching him struggle to hold himself together, not because of my oral sex prowess — I was sure it was just adequate at best — but because it was clear he thought he'd never see this. Me, on my knees, with my lips around him, and now I knew he'd been fantasizing about it.

His grip in my hair tightened and his hips rocked forward, pushing him back in, and I freely took him, my own pleasure an insistent throb, growing hot and wet between my thighs.

He rocked his hips back and I let him take over, showing me the pace he liked, never looking away because I couldn't get enough. God, the look in his eyes, the sound of his breath getting faster, the noises he made when he pushed into my mouth, and softly, on the edge of all that, the pulse of his life force teasing my magical senses.

Feeling him slide between my lips and against my tongue was just as stimulating as feeling him pushing in between my legs. It was amazing the things the body could do, the pleasure it could take or give, and my guess that me giving someone this kind of pleasure would turn me on as much as receiving it hadn't been wrong.

What I hadn't expected was the added thrill of maintaining eye contact, watching his need build, his hand in my hair, his pace getting faster as his restraint started to crumble. His sounds got louder too and with a groan, he pressed the sound blocking tattoo on his hip.

A flicker of pain swept through his expression, and his life force snapped against my senses, but he pushed back into my mouth and his burning need returned, inflaming my own.

God, like everything about sex so far, this was so much more than I imagined, the sensations more intense, the surprising desire building inside me even though I was the one stimulating him.

His breath grew ragged, his thrusts almost more than I could handle, but I could see he was getting close and I wanted to feel his release in my mouth, feel his erection pulse between my lips and against my tongue, and taste him.

"I'm going to come," he warned.

I moaned my pleasure in response.

"Jesus. Fuck." He jerked out of my mouth and tugged me up to my feet by my hair.

"Why did you stop?"

"Because— Fuck." He yanked me into the bedroom across the hall from us and smashed his lips against mine in a searing kiss that made me dizzy.

My back hit a wall and, with his hand still in my hair, he angled my neck to deepen the kiss and shoved his other hand up my shirt. The kiss was a lot like the kiss in the ballroom. Hard and wild, but there wasn't anything angry about this one. It was passionate, an overwhelming need that I'd inflamed by taking him in my mouth, and it made my pulse race and my body ache to be filled.

His fingers went straight to my nipple, making me moan, and he pushed his tongue deeper into my mouth. All breath and thought vanished, there were just the sensations of his hard body pressed against mine, his mouth taking what he wanted, his fingers rubbing and pinching my sensitive nipple, and God, I loved it. I was pretty sure I would have loved what we'd done in the ballroom too if we hadn't had an audience and he hadn't forced himself in me before I was ready.

"Take your pants off," he breathed against my lips.

Absolutely!

I fumbled with my lace-up fly, loosening it enough so I could push the soft fabric over my hips and rear. They hadn't been very tight and they easily slid down my legs to pool around my ankles.

"Step out of them and turn around." Sebastian stepped on the pants' crotch so I could step out, but I only managed to get one foot free before he spun me around and pressed me into the wall again.

My pulse stuttered, and for a second I was afraid being pinned like this, my face against the cold stone and his erection hard against my rear, would make me panic. I had no control in this position and I wasn't strong enough to break free. But I pushed my worry aside. I'd had to beg Sebastian to hurt me in the ballroom. He'd never hurt me during sex unless I asked for it, and even then, he might not.

He pulled off my shirt and ran his hands over my back.

"Is it true?" he asked. "Are the bases of an angel's wings sensitive?"

He teased his tongue along the invisible seam beside my left shoulder blade where my wing would emerge. It was just a whisper of a touch but it made my breath stall, the sensation rushing hot and heavy straight to my core. I'd never had anyone touch me there before, not like that, and while I knew academically that the base of my wings were an erogenous zone, I hadn't expected it to feel so good.

"Yes," I moaned.

"Show me."

He stepped back and I pushed a glimmer of power into my back and released my wings. They unfurled out of me with a flash of light, and before I could even stretch them out, Sebastian was close again, his hands roughly caressing the outer curve of my rear and slowly sliding up my back, ratcheting up the anticipation of his touch.

God, he had to be driving himself crazy as well. His breath was still wild, his erection hard as steel against my rear, and his body trembling.

Then his fingers skimmed the base of my wings and the hot, heavy need inside me thickened and all thoughts of Sebastian's amazing control disappeared. It was like his touch on my wings was a direct connection to my core, and every brush of his fingers and—

He leaned in and traced the path of his right hand with his tongue. *Oh God!*

Every tease with his mouth made my desire throb stronger.

He swept his tongue over the base of my other wing and reached around to cup my breasts.

I moaned low in my throat, leaned back, and pushed out my chest, not knowing which way to go, my body begging for more, for all of it. I'd already been turned on by having him in my mouth, feeling him tremble and tighten with something I was doing to him, now I was on fire and quivering.

His licks grew more insistent, his tongue rasping against the base of my wings and his fingers roughly kneading my breasts, and he quickly worked me up until my breath was as ragged as his.

"God, you react to this like I'm sucking your clit." He tugged me away from the wall, pushed me forward onto the bed, grabbed my hips, and pulled my rear tight against his pelvis, sliding his erection through my folds. "And you're as wet as if I was too."

He rubbed his thumbs against the base of my wings and the tremor of a climax clenched my muscles. Gasping, I ground myself against him, seeking the final connection between us, and with a shuddering groan, he pushed inside me.

Oh, yes.

The sense of his life force surged inside me, aligning with that thing in my soul that needed to feel his energy, and my desire surged with it.

SEBASTIAN

I pushed into her slick tight sheath in one smooth slow move and nearly came at the sexy as hell moan that fell from her lips. Fuck. She was going to make me come before I could make her. I'd barely held it together when she'd been sucking me off, and had no idea how I hadn't with her brilliant blue, glowing eyes staring up at me through her lashes. Her gaze had never left mine even after I started to lose control and began fucking her mouth as if this wasn't her first time sucking cock.

It had taken everything I had to pull out, but I'd been fantasizing about pushing back into her and being exactly where I was now since she'd asked me to join her and Hawk in our new sexual arrangement—hell, since she'd told me she loved the way I made her feel back in that alcove when we'd fucked to save Hawk.

A part of me was seriously disappointed that I hadn't been able to see her face and watch her desire build as I rubbed her wings, but I'd needed to get her wet fast because the rest of me had been screaming to get inside her, and had been screaming since I'd almost come in the hallway. And she would have gone the distance too. I'd given her fair warning, thought she wouldn't go so far against her angelic sensibilities to finish the job, and instead she'd doubled down in response. She probably would have swallowed too.

Holy fuck, how the hell did I get this lucky?

I could only pray she wouldn't change her mind about this or at least change it anytime soon, and not because she'd swallow — I could have cared less about that — but because I liked the way she made me feel, too, the way she trusted me and the connection we always seemed to make when I entered her. I'd felt it that first night, but I'd thought it was because she was a virgin and it was her angelic magic affecting me. But then I'd felt it again in the alcove, and again when I'd hurt her in the ballroom, and now here, even stronger.

The connection couldn't be because we were married. It wasn't possible for me to have accidentally married her that first night. But the Winter Court hadn't seemed to care if we were or not. It had treated her like my wife, claimed her body and soul—

And that was a problem I wasn't going to think about right now. I was balls deep in an amazing woman, barely holding myself together, and I needed to focus and make her come first, ideally screaming, because I loved the way she cried my name when she came.

I pulled out to the tip and slowly pushed back in, fighting to stay in control, but she moaned again and my balls tightened at the sound, making me rush the thrust and sheath myself with more force than I intended.

Except that only made her gasp and an amazing shiver rushed over her, a tremor in her physical body and a ripple in her unnatural full-body fae glow. A glow that emanated from every inch of her skin and feathers.

God, she was beautiful. Inside and out. There was something mesmerizing about her glowing wings, the swell of her butt, and the way her hair veiled her face as she tried to watch me fuck her. But what made her really beautiful right now was that she was being herself with no persona, no need to be in control of this, and no worry about what I thought of her or the incredible sounds she was making or the fact that I had her ass in the air and her face on the mattress.

Fucking hell.

I rubbed the base of her wings again and started to pump into her slow and steady purposefully straining my control to build her up as tight as possible. I might not have the magic, or hell, the experience Hawk did, but I still had the skill to make her feel really good.

She arched her back, her wings stretching and contracting with our movement, and her fae glow undulated under her skin like gently disturbed water.

I'd seen the fae glow undulate during sex a few times a long time ago

— not all high fae glowed like that during the act — but I'd never had sex with an angel before and her wings were astounding. It didn't matter if I brush them, rub them, or held on for dear life, she reacted. A gasp, a groan, a rippling of her muscles around my cock promising her release.

It drove me crazy and it was getting hard to hold back when I sensed Hawk's essence drawing close. A hot pressure that filled the air, vibrating with the struggle to hold his power in as much as possible. Which was surprising, since he never used to care whose head he'd turned and he knew he was going to walk in on me and Amiah mid-act.

He stepped into the doorway, casually holding a pair of boots — not his because he was wearing his and they were too small — his shirt off, and his pants hanging low on his hips. Everything about him oozed sex. The hellfire in his eyes was blazing, licking his cheeks, and his lips were quirked back in a wicked, hungry smile.

He leaned against the doorframe and I slowed my pace down just a little so he could watch me pump into her. The wickedness melted from his expression and turned into pure hunger.

Fuck. He desired her as much as I did. He had to, because he didn't need to feed. If that little wakeup call they'd given me hadn't brought him up to full, the frustrating hours of waiting for her to heal herself so I could be buried inside her would have finished the job. There was no reason to want her so strongly other than pure, hot desire.

"Pull your wings in, sweetheart," I said to Amiah, my voice thick with my fight to not go out too soon. "I want you to see this."

Her wings melted back into her body with a flash of white light, and while still inside her, I urged her to sit up and straddle me, her back to my chest. Now she could watch Hawk watching me fuck her.

I ran my hands over her belly and up to her breasts, cupping them, and with a sigh, she leaned back, wrapped her arms behind my neck, and gave me her body. No questions asked, no struggling to maintain any kind of control. She just gave herself over to me, trusting I'd make her feel good, and locked gazes with Hawk.

His breath picked up and I dropped my hands on her hips to steady her and slowly pushed myself in deep.

She moaned, maintaining eye contact with the incubus, and his hellfire sparked, tiny flecks snapping free and drifting to the floor.

Yeah, I know exactly what her eye contact does.

I pulled out, slowly pumped back in, and drew another moan, and my balls grew tighter. Fuck if I wasn't going to lose it. If Hawk wanted in on this, he was going to have to join now or it would be too late.

"Are you going to join us or what?" I asked.

Another spark of hellfire and Amiah moaned.

"Kiss me, Hawk," she said, her voice breathy, her body trembling against me. "Make love to me with Sebastian."

"Anytime anywhere," he murmured. He dropped the boots, took off his pants and boots, his cock standing at full attention, and pressed his lips against hers in a slow passionate kiss that left her gasping.

He started to draw away but she tangled her fingers in his hair and pulled him back to her, deepening the kiss, showing him with her lips how she felt, how much she wanted us. His hands trailed to her breasts and I struggled to keep a slow pace, to build her desire as tight as possible before crashing her over the edge.

But Hawk urged her to grip the back of my neck again then moved his mouth to her breasts, and her breath grew ragged, which turned my breath ragged. Fuck, that was hot. Seeing him turn her on like that, making her arch into his mouth, gasping and moaning with every brush and caress and thrust between us.

Then Hawk dipped lower, flicking his tongue on her clit. The shudder of a climax inside her clenched my cock. Oh, fuck. I lost all sense of control, unable to hold myself back any longer. I thrust into her, faster and harder, striving to bring her crashing over the edge before I came as Hawk suck and licked and teased her clit with his mouth and tongue.

Her nails dug into the back of my neck, her breasts heaving with her wild breaths, and with a scream, she came hard. Her whole body tensed, clenching me tight, making me explode inside her.

For a glorious moment we were locked together, our muscles contracted, and that connection that I'd felt before pulsed again through my veins. If we'd been married and she fae and not an angel, I would have gotten her pregnant right there. Hell, even if I'd worn a condom it would have been torn to shreds.

I collapsed back on the bed and Hawk captured her lips again in another slow kiss, making love to her mouth while I was still buried inside her. But I didn't care. The two of them were so damned hot together. I'd been wanting to watch him have sex with her since he made her come in his tent while we'd all watched, and now I had a front row seat.

He worked her desire back up with a kiss that was starting to get me hard again then pulled her off me, rolled onto his back on the bed, and slowly slid her onto his cock. She released a satisfied moan, captured his gaze again, her desire simmering in her brilliant blue eyes, and started to move with the confidence of someone who'd enjoyed that position before.

The hellfire in Hawk's eyes snapped again sending more sparks drifting around him, going out before they hit the blanket, and he helped her find her rhythm, letting her take her pleasure from him.

Her breath quickly picked up again and her eyelids slid shut as she fully gave in to the sensation of him moving inside her. It was mesmerizing to watch, her body moving with his in perfect rhythm, getting faster and faster as her desire grew, her breasts heaving with each gasp and moan, and her long blond hair swaying around her.

Hawk never looked away, more sparks bursting from his hellfire, and a strange, soft awe filled his expression. No, not just awe, adoration, raw, honest, dangerous adoration.

Then her breath caught and I watched her orgasm sweep through her, starting at her hips where she and Hawk were joined and rushing up her body physically with her muscle contractions and magically with her fae glow.

It tipped her head back and drew a long throaty sigh of pleasure. It wasn't the hard, screaming orgasm I'd given her, but it was somehow more powerful, deeper. It lit up her skin like the first time we'd had sex and turned her into a radiant goddess.

Hawk released a satisfied groan and came seconds after her, his gaze never leaving her, the raw adoration still in his eyes.

"Oh, Hawk," she murmured and her body went completely limp, his magic making her pass out.

He caught her, lying her on his chest with his arms around her and his lips pressed against her forehead, that soft awe in his expression growing stronger.

Oh, shit.

He was in love with her.

It was blatantly obvious. I didn't know how I hadn't seen it before. Maybe because he'd been hiding it really well or I hadn't been looking for it, or he wasn't even aware of it—

And if he didn't realize what he was feeling, then he needed to know before things went too far. He probably didn't even know he was falling in love, didn't recognize the emotion for what it was. He wasn't supposed to be able to do that. But I'd recently seen the same expression on four guys who were madly in love, one of them an incubus, and without a doubt, love was what I was looking at now.

"Hawk," I said, keeping my voice low, hoping not to wake Amiah. If she knew the truth, she'd do everything to save him, which meant sacrificing her sexual awakening to protect him, and deep down a part of me knew that would be very bad for her.

There was something about the way we connected that a part of her needed on a fundamental level because she hadn't just connected with me but with Hawk as well. Except I couldn't recall what and needed to search my library for the answer. And again, a problem for another day.

Hawk shifted his gaze to me and offered me a sad soft smile.

Fuck. He knew exactly what he was feeling and exactly what it meant.

"It's already done. Just let me have it while it lasts."

"Maybe it'll work out." Maybe she would pick us. Hawk wouldn't go crazy if she never left him, and he wouldn't starve or kill her if I stuck around. I'd happily share her with Hawk. The things the three of us could do together...

But my soul knew she belonged with Cassius. She always had. She just hadn't realized it. If she'd still had her partially formed mating brand it would only have been a matter of time before their souls were bound together. She'd needed to accept something in her soul, something about who she was, likely about the way she connected with us through sex, and then her brand would have awakened.

Of course, she hadn't wanted her brand, had suffered agonizing pain and permanently damaged her soul to get rid of it.

Maybe she would pick us. Maybe she'd ask us to make this arrangement permanent. God, I *wanted* her to make this permanent.

Fuck. Had I fallen in love too?

AMIAH

I woke in Hawk's arms, fully satiated, my body wonderfully limp, but with a strange cold pressure in my chest as if Sebastian had gotten too far away and had activated the leash spell. Except I could feel his life force, icy, bright, and writhing against demonic darkness close by, as well as his body pressed tight against my back, and when I cracked open an eye, one of the arms on top of me was pale, glowing, and covered in thick black tattoos.

"Hey, gorgeous," Hawk murmured.

Sebastian hummed low in his throat, snuggled closer, and pressed his lips against the back of my neck. "Go back to sleep. I don't want to get up just yet."

"How long was I out?"

Hawk flashed me a wicked smile, but I got the sense he was hiding something deeper and softer with that look. The awe that I thought I'd imagined the first time we'd had sex had definitely been there this time and my connection with his life force had been stronger, turning my orgasm into something that swept through both my body and my soul.

"You were out for about half an hour," he said.

"Half an hour. Is your magic supposed to do that?"

"No," Sebastian said, his warm breath washing over my still-sensitive skin making me shiver with a hint of renewed desire. "But you were well and thoroughly fucked." He snorted. "It's a good thing you screamed at Cassius that you and Hawk were doing it because you're glowing again."

"Again?" I dragged my still sleepy attention to my hand pressed against Hawk's chest. Radiant light pulsed from my skin in time to my heart, brighter than it had ever been before — even after the first time I'd had sex. "But I'm not a virgin anymore." Jeez, there wasn't going to be any way to hide my sexual activities if I lit up like the sun every time I orgasmed.

"Some high fae get glowy when they're deeply satisfied," Sebastian chuckled.

"Swell."

"Did you really scream at him that we were having sex?" Hawk asked.

I bit back a sigh. "I still don't want to talk about it."

"Oh yeah?" Sebastian's tone turned dark and seductive, making my thoughts jump to the last time I'd said that.

"And yes, I'll happily put your erection back in my mouth to avoid talking about it."

He huffed. "Just to avoid a conversation? No other reason?" He sounded upset and I wasn't sure if he was teasing me or not.

"Sebastian," I said, shifting so I could meet his pale gaze. His eyes sparkled with mischief as if he were daring me to take him in my mouth right now. "If I could fully move, I'd finish the job you wouldn't let me finish. But maybe I should give Hawk a turn. Maybe he'd be more interested in completing the act."

"Maybe I *want* to watch you suck Hawk's cock." His mischief shifted into that hot desire I'd seen when I was on my knees and the idea made my insides throb. Oh, yeah. That was definitely on the list of things to try.

The cold pressure in my chest swelled and I frowned, struggling to get my next breath. Had Sebastian's spell easing the Winter Court's cold stopped working? And why could I barely breathe?

"Hey, if you're not into it," Sebastian said, mistaking my change of expression, thinking his suggestion didn't turn me on.

"It's not that. It's just—" Another swell and now the pressure was almost as crushing as the original leash spell and the cold suddenly bone-deep. And just like the last time, it wasn't anything physical so my magic couldn't tell me what was wrong or fix it.

"God, Amiah. Just look at me and breathe." Hawk pulled his arm out from under me and cupped my cheeks with his burning-hot palms. "You're freezing again. How are you suddenly freezing?"

"Do you know what's wrong?" I gasped, my teeth chattering.

"That's what I'm about to find out." His hellfire flared and slick sensual heat unfurled inside me, drawing a throaty moan.

I fought to keep my gaze locked on his like he'd asked and strained to draw a breath that was picking up with desire.

"Speed it up," Sebastian said, his voice somehow far away even though he was right beside me. "She's having trouble breathing with your magic in her."

"Working on it." Hawk's magic swelled, rushing around my heart, filling me with aching desperate need.

Oh, God. Now that I knew what it felt like, I wanted him back inside me. Now.

The world darkened and spun and my focus narrowed down to Hawk's unusual blue-gray eyes and the hellfire flickering inside them. There was only him, his seductive magic, and the now soul-freezing pressure.

His eyes narrowed and he pressed a hand against Sebastian's shoulder. "Do you know what this is?"

Sebastian tensed and jerked away from him. "Shit. You can let her go. That's the key inside her responding to another key."

Hawk pushed his power through me instead of pulling it away, giving me a soft, satisfying orgasm — *thank God* — and drew me back into his arms as if he didn't want to let me go. Except his body heat against the frozen pressure was too much to bear.

"Too hot," I gasped, pushing out of his grip. "I'm sorry, but you're too hot."

"Amiah—" His eyes widened with surprise then he jerked farther away, the absence of his heat making my teeth chatter. "You need to get dressed."

"And we can't stay here," Sebastian added, rushing off the bed and grabbing our clothes from the floor. "Another key has become empowered. Titus will be compelled to go to it whether he wants to or not and we can't let him go alone."

"Agreed," I said, struggling to sit up.

"How strong is the compulsion?" Hawk took our clothes, looked at me, then handed mine back to Sebastian so he could help me get dressed.

"I have no idea," Sebastian said, helping me stand. "Any idea where the others might be?"

His full-body glow dimmed for a second and a whisper of his magic caressed the inside of my thighs, cleaning me up.

"Stop unnecessarily using your magic." I clung to him, his normally cool body temperature hot against my skin, my legs shaky, and each breath getting harder than the next one. Sure, I still had air to breathe unlike the first version of the leash spell, but this wasn't much better.

Hawk closed his eyes. "Cassius is in the kitchen and Titus is coming our way."

"He probably smells the sex," Sebastian groaned as he set me back on the bed, laced himself back in, having not lost any clothing during our lovemaking, and helped me put on the pair of soft, calf-high boots that Hawk had brought me. "I really hope he doesn't punch me in the face again."

"That shouldn't be a problem," I said, hugging myself in a useless attempt to warm up. At least I hoped it wouldn't be. Titus had said he could give me the connection I craved with him but that he needed to get his beast to settle first... except I had no idea how long that would take.

Titus stormed into the doorway, his life force snapping across my senses powerful and wild. His breath was fast and shallow, although it looked like he was breathing a little better than me, and his golden gaze jumped to me even as he dug his claws into the stone on either side of the entrance as if he needed to hold himself back.

"You can feel it too, can't you?" he growled, his expression desperate.

"Yes." I pulled the blanket on the bed around me but it didn't ease the chill.

"Guess that answers that," Sebastian said. "The compulsion is strong."

"We need to join Sparky in the kitchen. Now." Hawk reached to pick me up but hesitated. "Bane, your body temperature is colder than mine."

"Right." Sebastian picked me up, blanket and all, and we hurried to the end of the hall to the kitchen.

The kitchen was bigger than I expected, although I wasn't sure exactly what I'd expected. The kitchen area proper had lots of counter space and cupboards, and beyond was a dining room area with long tables and benches.

Cassius sat backwards on the end of a bench closest to the kitchen, staring out another long wide-open window. But his attention jumped to us the moment we entered and he stood, his fire snapping over his skin, a sudden flash of light before it turned into billowing smoke and drifted off.

"What's wrong?" he asked, thankfully not commenting on my glow or restarting our argument about my sex life.

"Another key has become empowered," Titus said, his body tense and his pupils slitted.

The muscles in Cassius's jaw twitched and he met my gaze. "And of course you can feel it too."

"Really wish I couldn't," I gasped, leaning into Sebastian's heat and clinging to the blanket. "This is like the first leash spell only with a bit more air and a lot more cold."

"I can fix that. Well, the cold at least," Sebastian said, and he, with Hawk and Titus right behind him, carried me to Cassius and sat me on the edge of the table. "I'll just add more power to the spell diminishing the Winter Court's chill."

"Just wait a second," Hawk said. "Will this go away when someone gets the key?"

"Most likely." Sebastian placed a hand over my heart. "The magic of the key is strengthening the Winter Court's hold inside you. But then I'll just pull the power back out of the spell when you get too warm."

Hawk's hellfire flared and his expression darkened. Every time Sebastian used his magic, he hurt himself and his demonic infection got worse.

I pressed my hands above his, savoring a warmth he shouldn't have had, and met his gaze. "I can manage."

"I can't fix the breathing problem, but you don't have to be freezing," he insisted.

"Just do it," Titus growled, jerking to face the window then jerking back to us, his body tense with a compulsion I could relate to. When my magic locked onto someone, it was almost impossible to ignore it, and from Titus's expression, his compulsion was just as strong.

"No. It isn't worth it."

"Amiah—"

"We don't have time to argue about this. Titus, where's the key?" I wasn't sure if I'd be able to zero in on it, but even if I did, I might not know where it was since I knew nothing about Faerie, and the best way to stop the cold and not let Sebastian hurt himself was to get the key.

Titus closed his eyes and frowned.

His life force snapped, stinging under my skin as if it was trying to get out... or in... or I don't know what.

He sucked in a breath with an effort I more than understood and clenched his hands.

"I can't find it."

"What do you mean you can't find it?" Sebastian asked. "Amiah, can you?"

Another snap, this time around my heart and the cold and pressure swelled. "I don't know anything about Faerie."

"Just try," Hawk said, his expression filled with worry.

"And hurry," Titus growled.

"Okay." I closed my eyes but couldn't manage much of a breath, let alone a calming one.

The cold and pressure heaved, angry and blue slicing through the darkness behind my lids as if I could see its magic when I wasn't capable of seeing magic otherwise, and the sense of Titus's ferocious life force grew stronger. It pulled at the cold in my heart, drawing it out like an elastic band before it *snapped* out of Titus's reach and slammed back into my chest. His life force was trying to connect to the key inside me.

"Titus, take my hand," I said, reaching out to him as his life force stretched out the key again, tighter and tighter.

His big warm hand engulfed mine just before it snapped again and a wave of pressure crushed inside me. Titus tensed and then all sense of him, the others, and the room around me vanished. I was trapped in darkness, squeezed so tight I couldn't move, couldn't breathe, couldn't think.

My pulse roared through my body and soul. Trapped. I was trapped. I couldn't be trapped, please—

Except it wasn't me. At least I was pretty sure it wasn't me... No, that was wrong. It was me. The key was crushing me so *I* had to be trapped. *God, no.*

"Fuck," Sebastian hissed. "Get them apart she's turning blue."

The darkness squeezed tighter and the cold seeped deeper into my soul. Please. I couldn't do it again. I couldn't be trapped again—

Burning hot hands grabbed my shoulders and yanked me back, and both Titus and I cried out.

"Shit," Cassius hissed by my ear and the burning hands vanished.

My vision cleared, but the cold and pressure didn't go away. Titus knelt on the floor in front of me, his chest heaving with desperate gasps. Hawk and Sebastian each held a muscular arm, while Cassius stood a good ten feet behind me, black smoke billowing around him, waves of heat radiating from him and washing over me.

Titus's gaze met mine, his expression fierce and sad. "I'm sorry."

"Sorry about what?" Hawk shifted toward me. I could see in his eyes that he wanted to hold me, reassure me, but knew he couldn't because of his body temperature.

"I can't find the keys now without connecting with Amiah," Titus replied.

"But you know where the next one is," Cassius pressed.

"Only that it's in the Autumn Court. I won't know exactly where until we try again inside the court barrier."

"Shit," Sebastian hissed. "That means Amiah has to come with us."

Fire snapped over Cassius's arms, sending a painful wave of heat sweeping over me, and he sucked in a deep breath and turned the flames to smoke again. "Absolutely not."

"I don't think we have a choice," I said. The pressure swelled again and Titus's life force painfully *snapped* inside me. I really didn't want to go into the field, not while in agony and my power at full. If my magic locked onto the wrong person, I wouldn't stand a chance against it. There'd be no way I'd be able to fight its compulsion to heal.

"And we don't have the time to argue about it," Sebastian said.

His glow flickered for a second, revealing the gray complexion that I now knew was a result of being infected with demonic magic. "Not to mention I still need to deal with the leash spell. I'm not sure how comfortable it would be for Amiah to stay here while I'm in the Autumn Court."

"So deal with it," Cassius growled.

"No," Hawk said before Sebastian could respond. "Breaking the leash spell will take a lot of magic and we might need it to get the key."

Sebastian ran a hand over his spiky white and silver hair. "I really hope we don't."

"Fine." The light in Cassius's eyes flared and an icy mask swept over his expression. "What do we need to know about the Autumn Court?"

"That it's going to be a problem," Titus said. "Let's go."

Sebastian rolled his eyes at him. "All the courts are a problem."

Titus snarled back, his canines extended. "You know what I mean. The court is unstable and shattered. Come on."

Fire flared from Cassius. "Not until I know exactly what that means and how it endangers Amiah."

"Amiah is coming regardless." Red-gold scales rippled over Titus's neck and he strode toward the open window and pulled off his shirt, revealing his massive muscular chest and arms.

"He's right," Hawk said not sounding at all happy about the situation.

"We can discuss it on the move." Titus yanked off his boots and pants and my pulse stuttered at the memory of him kissing me, his erection pressed against my belly, his desire for me ferocious as he begged me to be his mate. "Someone grab these for me."

He didn't wait for a response and jumped out the window and shifted, his body turning to liquid and rapidly expanding into his stunning dragon form.

I hadn't gotten a good look at him the last time he'd shifted because he'd flown away too quickly, but now I had a spectacular view. The late afternoon sunlight shimmered on his red-gold scales, the color shifting from dark red along the top of his head, back, and tail and melting into a pale gold on his underside. Horns swept up and back from his temples and spiky ridges trailed all the way down his spine to his tail. The spine ridges along his neck flexed up then settled back down and he flapped his massive leathery wings, sending air rushing into the dining room. With a hot huff of air from nostrils almost the size of my head, he gently set his back feet on the railing and his front feet on the closest stone table.

Everyone up, he said in my head — and presumably everyone else's as well.

"Okay, problem," Hawk said, gathering Titus's clothes. "How are we going to get Amiah on you without her seizing again?"

"Maybe the connection is only made when it's flesh to flesh," Cassius said.

"Maybe," Sebastian replied. "But you should carry her anyway. Just in case."

"Not a good idea." His angel glow flared and he jerked his attention away from me, his quick refusal stinging. He was still so mad at me that he hadn't even thought about it. "Let's get Amiah and Titus together with that blanket in between them first. Maybe it's nothing to worry about."

"How about I just fly," I said through clenched teeth, trying to get them to stop chattering. "I have wings.

Four dark glares snapped to me and Titus huffed smoke to punctuate his anger. Wow, that was one way to get them to all agree on something.

"You're shivering so hard you can't stand and you can barely hold the blanket shut," Sebastian said, lifting me off the table and back into his arms. "You can't fly."

"And you might be able to ride on Titus," Cassius added, his expression frigid.

Sebastian leaned in and pressed my blanketed side against Titus and before we'd even touched, his life force painfully snapped and a wave of pressure crushed me back into that darkness, trapped, unable to even move.

No. Get me out. Get me out get me out get me out.

Sebastian jerked me away and I sucked in a painful desperate gasp.

"You're up, Sparky," Sebastian said.

Cassius heaved in a deep breath, his expression turning colder than the chill inside me, his body shaking with pent-up rage. With a low growl and a burst of fire, he released his wings and held out his arms. "Okay. Hand her over."

Jeez. Was he really that angry that I was having sex with Hawk? Or was it that I didn't want to take his advice? Maybe he was sick and tired of me being a burden. He didn't want to protect me or carry me around but his angelic honor wouldn't let him say no, just like he felt he *had* to help me heal my broken heart.

And really, what did it matter? He'd made himself clear. The man I'd known was gone, taken away by the war, it'd just taken me twenty years to realize that. Just like it had taken me over a hundred to realize the truth about my angelic mating brand.

"Let's just get through this," I said to Cassius as Sebastian handed me over. "When this is done, you'll never have to deal with me again."

The light in his eyes flared but his gaze remained locked on Titus as Sebastian and Hawk climbed onto the dragon's back.

This way, Titus said and he turned, diving out the window and catching the air currents sweeping around the mountain with his massive leathery wings.

Cassius followed, his grip on me so tight it hurt, and we soared away from the mountain, the Wilds a vast green jungle radiating a thick moist heat instead of the dry desolate wasteland it had been when we'd arrived.

"How long until we reach the Autumn Court?" Cassius asked as he glided into a position beside Titus's neck, close enough to have a yelled conversation with the others but not too close for the key to affect me or Titus.

Faerie wants me to get there, so not long. I can see it on the horizon, Titus replied.

A spark of white Faerie magic burst from Sebastian's cheek, making him wince in pain. "Thank fucking God."

"Then start talking. What are we flying into?" The light in Cassius's eyes blazed brighter and for a second his hands were too warm. "You said the court was unstable and shattered. What exactly does that mean?"

"It means be ready to catch me or Hawk if we fall off a land mass." Another spark burst from Sebastian's skin and whooshed down into the jungle. "The land is literally shattered, its pieces floating around the court barrier with magical pockets that slow time, speed up time, move you to the other side of the court, tear you to pieces, that kind of thing. Think, not just side to side and front to back but also up and down."

Titus's life force snapped in my chest, the cold sinking deeper into my bones, and now something heavy tugged at me, pulling me in the direction we were flying.

When the Autumn Court's ancient queen let herself be consumed by Faerie's magic, her heir wasn't strong enough to hold the court together. Titus heaved in a breath, still struggling to breathe in his dragon form. *Faerie ripped through most of the Autumn Court's high fae as well as the court itself until it found its new king.*

I shuddered at the thought. Back in the Winter Court Titus had said a court monarch needed to be strong or the court would be in chaos. He didn't say it killed high fae and broke the land until it found someone strong enough, but he also hadn't gone into details.

The new king isn't strong enough to put the court back together. All he can do is hold it as is.

"Which is probably why my mother is crazy for another heir," Sebastian said. "If the Winter Court doesn't respond to Padraigin then all the high fae in court could be killed if someone from another court manages to assassinate her."

"So she's crazy with a good reason," Hawk drawled.

"Still doesn't make what she did to Amiah right," Sebastian replied.

"Or you," I said, even though I was sure none of them could hear me, my teeth still chattering despite the blanket, Cassius's body heat, and the heat rising from the jungle.

Fire popped inside me, painfully hot against the ice, and a flash of white Faerie magic exploded from my body, a reminder that the Winter Court had claimed me and turned me into a high fae.

The muscles in Cassius's jaw flexed, but there was nothing he could do about it, he couldn't even try to fly faster because we were already racing toward the horizon as fast as we could.

"So watch where you step," Cassius said. "Got it. Are the dangerous magical pockets identifiable?"

"For the most part, yes. Even if you're not a Sensitive, you should be able to see them," Sebastian replied, which was good since only he and Hawk were Sensitives which would have left the rest of us walking blindly into potential danger.

"Anything else I need to know?" Cassius asked, as another fiery pop seared through me.

Amiah stays safe. You abandon me and the key if you have to.

Oh, hell no.

"We're not abandoning you," I yelled back making sure they could all hear me this time.

I glanced at Sebastian to get his agreement, but he wasn't looking at me. Neither would Hawk.

"Are you kidding? You agree with him?" God, they'd leave Titus behind just to protect one person. "That's not acceptable. I don't care what kind of macho agreement you all have. We're not abandoning anyone. Certainly not for me. Besides, I can take care of myself. I have the Winter Court's magic." Except I'd yet to feel a single gust since we'd gotten out of there.

"Sorry, sweetheart," Sebastian called back as another burst of light flew out of his body. "If you're not the queen or king, the Winter Court's magic only works for you in the Winter Court."

So I was powerless again.

Just great.

"You're the healer," Hawk added. "You're more useful than any one of us."

"But we can only get the keys with Titus," I insisted.

If I'm dead, no one can get the keys.

His life force snapped hard again and the pull in my chest grew stronger. I bit back a moan of pain, fighting to draw more than just a shallow breath. There was no way I was going to leave him behind. I didn't know how I'd stop the guys from dragging me away, but God damn it, Titus wasn't dying. No one was.

AMIAH

Thankfully it didn't take long to get to the Autumn Court's protective barrier, but by the time we'd reached it, the pressure and cold and pull inside me was agonizing. It took everything I had just to stay focused on what was around me and not succumb to the dark prison threatening my consciousness even with the fiery pops of Faerie reclaiming its magic from my body.

On top of that, the reek of rotting flesh started to fill my nose, and I couldn't figure out if it was my imagination, my brain overloading on everything else, or real.

Then we reached the Autumn Court's barrier, and I knew the reek wasn't in my head. The Autumn Court was sick and dying with a gangrenous disease that oozed through its magical essence.

I didn't understand how the court could smell like a corpse, it didn't have a physical body to decay, but my magical senses, the sense that connected with the guys' life forces knew the moment I saw the court's dull gray-brown barrier, that the smell came from the court itself. And the reek was overwhelming, making my stomach heave and my eyes water as we passed through.

"Holy fuck," Hawk gasped. "Look at that."

I quickly blinked away my tears to see what had made Hawk gasp, and my mind stuttered at what I saw, unable for a second to fully comprehend what I was looking at.

It was like we'd flown into a surrealist painting with broken chunks of land consisting of dead and dying meadows, thick, dead leafless forests, hills, low mountains, and putrid lakes and rivers floating all over the place. Below us, above us, right side up, upside down, on their side, at strange angles. Water poured down from one chunk to another, but also up and sideways. Birds flew in strange patterns as if pulled by gravity coming from one direction and then another, dipping and swirling and gliding upside down then back to right side up.

My stomach heaved again as my brain tried to figure out where the horizon was and what was right side up.

But the horizon was everywhere and nowhere.

I couldn't see a sun, but it shone "down" on the ground with the beginnings of a dark ominous sunset regardless of the ground's orientation.

Titus landed on the closest land mass, a floating meadow directly below us about the size of a football field with ragged dead grass. Above us, a flock of birds darted toward us, hit a patch of shimmering air — like air over hot asphalt on a summer's day — vanished, and reappeared sixty feet to the left.

Beyond them stood a city, its walls a deep earth tone like it was made from bricks or adobe with towers spiking out at every angle as if the city was as shattered as the land.

Hawk scrambled off of Titus, leaving Titus's clothes behind, dropped to his knees, and pressed his forehead against the ground. "I think I'm going to throw up."

"Well do it fast," Cassius said, his voice hard and cold and in command, "then pull your shit together." He landed beside Hawk. "The less time we spend here the better."

"Agreed," Sebastian said, not getting off of Titus. "Bring Amiah close and let's find this key."

At the mention of the key, my attention jumped past Cassius's shoulder. It was that way. That was where the agonizing pull was coming from.

You ready for this? Titus asked in my head.

No, but I'd rather not put it off. And Cassius didn't even give me a chance to say anything. He just stepped close and pressed me against Titus's side.

The weight and cold slammed into me and I was gone again, trapped in darkness, squeezed tight, unable to move or breathe. My soul screamed. I had to be free. Get me out. Someone. Anyone. Please. But no one could see me, no one was looking for me, and no one could hear me.

"Did you get it?" Cassius asked, jerking me away.

Yes, Titus replied, as I fought to get my breath back. But I was shaking so hard from the cold, my muscles clenched so tight, that all I could manage were desperate shallow gasps.

"Good. Then let's go." Cassius set me on my feet, the dead grass crunching with my weight, and held me at arm's length. "Hawk, stay with her. We'll be back when we get the key."

I opened my mouth to argue then snapped it shut. I wasn't sure I had the breath for an argument and even if I did, I was still a serious liability if we ended up in a fight. It was safer for all of us for me to stay where I was.

A screeching flock of crows popped into existence above us, dipped low, and skimmed the ground, then soared up into the patch of shimmering air the other birds had flown through.

But instead of appearing sixty feet to our left like the previous birds, they appeared way above us and upside down, skimming the three dead trees crowded on a small island drifting overhead like a cloud.

Sebastian jerked his thumb at them. "You honestly think we'll be able to find our way back here? You can't even count on the fractures to go to the same place every time."

Cassius frowned. "She can't come with us. Look at her."

"I'll be fine here," I gasped. "Take Hawk, he's too heavy for me. When you get the key, I won't be cold and I'll be able to breathe. I'll fly back into the Wilds and wait for you."

"And if we get caught in a time bubble?" Sebastian asked. "You could be waiting for us for years, and without Titus, his ancestral nest will remain hidden to you."

Fire sparked from Cassius's wings and his hands grew painfully hot for a second then vanished as his expression grew even harder.

"Fine." He yanked me back into his arms and leaped into the air. "Let's get this damned key."

"Everyone keep an eye out for any shimmering air," Sebastian said as Hawk scrambled onto Titus's back. "We can't afford to be separated by a fracture or get caught in a magical bubble."

"Just great," Cassius huffed and he glided back into position by Titus's neck, close but not too close, while I fought to relax my clenched muscles and draw deeper breaths.

But the gravity of another dead meadow yanked us off course, tipping us upside down, and my heart leaped into my throat at the sudden loss of right side up.

Cassius's grip on me tightened and he jerked us "down" which was the new "up" narrowly missing a shimmer with three emaciated deer caught in it, frozen in mid-leap.

I shuddered at the thought. "Are they in forced hibernation?"

Or was it something worse given their physical condition? Forced magical hibernation didn't slowly starve someone, it just froze them, stopping time. Even if they'd been starving or on the brink of death before they were frozen, they wouldn't have been dying now, not until someone outside of the hibernation spell dispelled it.

"Time bubble," Sebastian said, clinging, like Hawk, to Titus's spine ridges while the dragon quickly turned to the new right side up. "They're not frozen or dead, they're just moving very slowly."

"For how long?" Hawk asked. He had Titus's clothes captured between his arms, while he clung to the dragon's spine ridge with his head down and his eyes squeezed shut. His complexion was getting paler and paler, and while he'd managed to not throw up when we were on the meadow island, it was clear his hold on his stomach was slipping.

"It's different for each bubble. If you look at it, Mr. Sensitive, you'll be able to see just how much it's slowing time."

"Ha ha. Your shield muting my magical sensitivity only blocks out so much. Not only is the landscape fucking with my stomach, but everything is still just a little too bright," Hawk said. "You really want to risk me throwing up all over you and Titus to take a peek at the bubble?"

Just give me a heads up, Titus said. *I'll turn to the side so none of it hits me. Oh, and don't get anything on my clothes.*

"Gee, thanks," Hawk groaned. "You're too kind." But he didn't ask to stop and I didn't think Titus would even if Hawk begged because the key's pull was overwhelming.

I could barely breathe or think and from Titus's rapid, labored breaths, he was struggling as well. The pressure and cold grew so strong it overwhelmed the painful snaps of Titus's life force in my chest, and I was shivering uncontrollably when we reached a cluster of small islands butted up against each other and the source of the pull.

The terrain was mountainous with cliffs and jutting rocks mostly covered in dead trees, their twisted blackened branches reaching into the sky like skeletal fingers. A fast-moving river, too wide to jump over, sliced around the jutting rocks and tumbled over the cliffs. It started at the far island from an unknown source in the ground, swept off a cliff and twisted midair to run along an island standing sideways, and finally ended at a large roaring waterfall that crashed down onto large jagged rocks and disappeared through a shimmering patch of air.

And there at the edge of the waterfall was a sharp blue pinprick of light as bright as the sun. The key. It wrenched on my soul, begging me to become one with it and twisting with the other key inside me with a crushing, agonizing force.

"It's down there," I gasped, "by the waterfall."

I see it, Titus said and he dipped forward to dive closer.

But a mass of writhing darkness exploded to life above us and slammed into us, knocking the air from my lungs.

The world went black, the air tearing at my hair as we careened down? Up? I had no idea. Even if I hadn't been desperate for breath, I wasn't sure I'd be able to tell which way was up. Cassius squeezed me against his chest. Far off, past the howl of the wind, Hawk yelled, and Titus roared.

Fire sparked through the darkness for a second and I caught a glimpse of blue sky and ominous red sunset, then we smashed into the trees, ricocheting off thick branches and smashing through rotted ones. They sliced my face, yanked my hair, and tore at the blanket.

Cassius curled his body around me, his temperature skyrocketing.

We crashed onto the hard, rocky ground, and I was thrown out of his grip, across jagged rocks, into a solid tree trunk, and showered with dead, rotting branches.

Something hot and sticky oozed down the side of my face.

Blood—

I was bleeding—

I struggled to catch my breath against the pressure and the cold, praying the world would stop whirling... except it wasn't just whirling. What lay ahead of me, across the turbulent water of the river, was the ground side of another island, its "down" perpendicular to the "down" of the island I was on.

And even as I tried to wrap my mind around it, the key's pull tugged my attention to my right, to the blazing pinprick of blue light through the thick dead trees and underbrush and past the jagged rocky landscape.

We were close. We just had to climb that five-foot ridge jutting up from the ground, watch out for those two shimmers, and go through those trees... which also meant the roaring in my head wasn't just because I was still reeling, but from the nearby waterfall.

Cassius was on his hands and knees between me and the glimmer, his breath heaving and his wings trembling. Some of his feathers were damaged, but not badly enough to require my healing magic if he pulled them back into his body. With a groan, his fire burst from his hands and along his wings, and he heaved himself to his feet. Blood rushed from a cut above his right eye, down his cheek, and dripped off his chin onto his thin cotton shirt that had been ripped in numerous places and was now plastered to his body with more blood.

My whirling thoughts lurched, zeroing in on his blood, and my power roared into my palms, painfully hot. Once again a thread of my magic connected with him even though I wasn't touching him and told me nothing was broken. He just had dozens of lacerations, some of them deep.

I breathed a sigh of relief as his piercing blue gaze landed on me, making my pulse pound, and his flames ignited the dead wood around him.

"Shit." He jerked away from me, sucking his flames — and the accidental fire — back under his skin.

Behind me, someone moaned and my magic jerked my attention toward the sound. Hawk sat propped up against a trunk with Titus's clothes scattered around him and a shimmer only a few feet beside him. He held his left arm tight against his chest, blood gushing from a compound fracture of his forearm, his expression tight with pain.

Beside him, Sebastian lay face down in the dirt... and wasn't moving.

My magic snapped to him and my compulsion to heal added to the cold and pressure and pull. I hadn't locked onto him, he wasn't dying, but he was in rough shape with four broken ribs and three broken vertebrae paralyzing him from the waist down.

He groaned, waking up, and his breath turned sharp and fast with the pain from his injuries.

"Just hang on, Sebastian," I gasped, using the tree beside me to help me stand, the cold making me tremble.

"What's his condition?" Cassius barked, the soldier fully taking over.

"Manageable." I clung to my ripped blanket and staggered to his side.

"Hawk?" Cassius's gaze swept through the dead trees searching for danger instead of looking at us. "Titus?"

"I'll be okay in a minute," Hawk groaned, his broken bone already sinking back under his skin.

"Are you sure about that?" an all-too-familiar dark masculine voice asked.

My pulse stalled with fear. Thick shadows rushed in surrounding us in complete darkness and a cold lifeless essence surged close. Deaglan's demon-vampire hybrid.

I tried to jerk away, but I wasn't fast enough.

A warm hand that shouldn't have been warm, grabbed the back of my neck, and a strange barely-there life force shivered across my senses. It was a writhing mix of life and death, frozen and burning, wild and too still, and in pain. So much pain.

Except I had no idea what to make of it, and it didn't eliminate the fact that if Deaglan told the hybrid to kill me he would. He might have hesitated before biting me back in the Winter Court, but he'd still ended up obeying Deaglan, and I'd seen the hybrid decapitate a man with his katana in the blink of an eye without any emotion in his black eyes.

"Don't fight him," the hybrid said in his soft low voice, so quietly I was sure I was the only one who'd heard him. "You don't have to become collateral damage."

AMIAH

Someone screamed, the sound sharp with agony. My senses jerked back to Sebastian, my compulsion to heal him growing stronger, and the shadows melted away, revealing Deaglan with his foot on Sebastian's broken back.

The King of the Shadow Court sneered, the expression turning his beautiful face ugly. He wore the same black leather as before with his black shoulder-length hair pulled back at the nape of his neck, and thick shadows undulating under his skin.

Someone crashed through the dead underbrush coming toward us and the nightmare, his hellfire hair writhing around his tall thick horns, and the other shadow fae on Deaglan's assassination team who was still high-fae-beautiful but nothing compared to Deaglan or Sebastian, dragged Titus into sight.

Titus was in his human form, barely conscious, and completely naked, giving me a perfect look at his mostly unharmed body — thank goodness. He'd probably tried to shift just before he hit the ground, his scales protecting him from the tree branches. But, from his barely conscious state, it was clear he hadn't been as successful with the sudden shift before landing as he'd been the last time when we'd tumbled into the Wilds.

"Well, Seireadan," Deaglan purred, pressing down on Sebastian's back and drawing a scream of pain that made my healing magic burn hotter in my hands and squeeze tighter in my chest. "I didn't think you'd bring the whole gang. Who'd have thought I'd get to kill you and the dragon, and then get to fuck your wife."

Deaglan raked his eyes down my body, his gaze growing heated despite me being covered up in a blanket, and I knew he was imagining me in the revealing dress the Winter Queen had made me wear. Then something dark flashed across his expression, drawing a frown, but a blast of heat billowed from behind me, and his attention jumped past my shoulder before I could figure out what it meant.

"Release your fire, angel. I dare you."

The demon-hybrid tensed. His pain flared and he extended his short, sharp vampire claws in my neck, making me whimper. Now blood oozed down my neck as well as from the cut in my temple, a strange hot contrast to the cold consuming me.

"If you kill Titus, you'll never get the Heart," Sebastian gasped, his pain growing inside me making my magic heave, desperate for me to go to him.

I couldn't stay connected to him like this, knowing I could help him but unable to touch him. I had to heal him, had to ease his suffering.

"You really think I'd kill the last dragon without a way to find the keys myself?" Deaglan snapped a shadow whip around Titus's neck and yanked him out of his men's grip down to his hands and knees. "I just needed him to find the first key so I could confirm that my tracking spell worked."

"So you didn't track us here? You tracked the key," Hawk said, his left arm covered in blood but now no longer bleeding.

"Which means I no longer have a use for Titus." Deaglan rammed his foot against Sebastian's back.

Sebastian screamed and my power surged, painfully hot in my hands, up my arms, and around my heart. It exploded through the thin thread connecting us, and roared into his body in a sudden, vicious blast, using up almost everything I had.

He screamed again and Deaglan's eyes flashed wide with surprise. Sebastian grabbed his left forearm, yelled a sibilant word, and a massive force-wave slammed into Deaglan and his men but not us — a testament to Sebastian's incredible ability that he was able to select who the wave hit.

The hybrid's claws scraped through my neck as he was ripped away, thankfully before he could tighten his grip and rip out my spine. Blood spurted from my neck and I shoved the remainder of my power into me before I passed out and bled to death. I barely had any power left, but it was just enough to heal my nicked arteries — and thankfully they'd just been nicked — leaving me with still bleeding gashes, but no longer on the verge of dying.

Deaglan went flying, crashing through rotted branches and careening off still-solid tree trunks, and the nightmare and the other fae tumbled toward the edge of the island, were sucked up by the sideways island's gravity, and crashed onto the banks of a swamp.

A cloud of greenish-gray air wafted around them, hit the gravity of our island, and was sucked toward us. It billowed around Cassius and his fire ignited the bog gasses with a sudden flash and *pop*.

"We need to get the key," Titus said, grabbing his pants and boots before standing.

I sagged to the ground, exhausted at having spent my power, shivering, and barely able to breathe. I yanked the blanket up and held it tight against my neck to slow the bleeding, but I couldn't do anything about the cold or pressure inside me.

"We need to get out of here," Hawk said, rushing to my side.

He pressed his hands over mine to help add pressure, but his flesh was so hot it felt as if the back of my skin was being burned.

I yelped and he jerked his hands away, his expression filled with worry.

"We can't let Deaglan get the key." Cassius raked his gaze over the thick brush where Deaglan had disappeared.

"What about Amiah's safety? Didn't we agree?" Hawk shot back.

"That was before Deaglan could find the keys on his own. Now we don't have a choice. Hawk, protect her. Sebastian, we need to stall Deaglan long enough for Titus to get the key." Cassius snapped out a fire whip, jerked around, and seized the hybrid by the throat mid-lunge somehow knowing he was about to be attacked.

The hybrid drew his katana and sliced through the whip in one quick move and continued barreling toward Cassius with his faster-than-most-supers vampiric speed. Cassius twisted out of the way at the last second and wrenched up his fire whip, knocking the hybrid's slice off target.

Titus — with pants and boots on but not bothering with his shirt — turned toward the brilliant blue pinprick of light, and grabbed the edge of the ragged five-foot ledge to climb up and head toward the waterfall, but a tendril of shadow shot out of the underbrush and smashed him face first into the rock.

"Ah fuck." Sebastian scrambled to his feet and sent a blast of light into the brush, his fae glow shuddering and his complexion turning gray before it flared back to life.

Hawk reached for me, hesitated a second, then grabbed my arm over top of the blanket — his hand still painfully hot through the thick material — and yanked me to my feet. He bent to pick me up when the other shadow fae swept out of the shadow of the rock beside us and slashed his long knife at us.

"Shit." Hawk shoved me out of the way and grabbed the fae's arm, yanking him away from me.

I stumbled, hit a tree trunk — showering myself with more rotting debris — but thankfully didn't fall to the ground.

"The shadow fae can jump from shadow to shadow between islands," Hawk yelled, heaving forward to keep his grip on the fae's arm and preventing him from being able to fully attack.

And we were surrounded by shadows. The invisible sun sat low on a blood-red horizon that was everywhere and nowhere, slicing thin beams through the trees. But even if it had been midday we'd still be surrounded by the forest's shadows and there wasn't a large clearing in sight. The widest open space was the rushing river and the hole in the canopy — if you could call the lattice of dead branches a canopy — where we'd crashed through.

More of Deaglan's shadows pinned Titus to the ledge while also lashing out at Sebastian who looked like he was barely holding his own, his fae glow weak and his chest heaving with strained breaths. Cassius had split his whip in two, forcing the vampire to draw his second shorter sword, but it didn't look like he was winning either.

An inferno raged around them with billowing waves of heat, making sweat instantly slick my body despite still being frozen on the inside, and I staggered to the next tree, trying to get farther away from the fire and Hawk's fight with the shadow fae.

A part of me was furious that I no longer had the Winter Court's wind. I'd be able to help all of them and Sebastian wouldn't have had to risk his life by channeling magic while infected with demonic magic. But the only thing I could do right now was get out of the way. At least I was out of magic and there wasn't a chance that I'd be forced to heal one of Deaglan's men or worse, Deaglan.

Deaglan's writhing shadows shoved through the trees, breaking the trunks with sharp cracks, and sending them tumbling into the fight toward everyone with resounding *booms*. Everyone scrambled to get out of the way, and Titus wrenched down, the edge of the ledge breaking the fall of the trunk crashing toward him. A reeking cloud of debris and fine particles filled the air and swirled with the black smoke billowing from the fire started by Cassius's inferno. Some of it gusted into a shimmer and froze, a mix of fire, smoke, and particles, caught like smoke in volcanic glass.

Deaglan stormed through the passage he'd made and sent another flurry of shadows at Sebastian and Titus, as well as snapping a shadow whip to the sideways island and yanking the nightmare back onto our island.

My pulse stuttered. The guys were barely holding their own. Adding the nightmare could tip the battle in Deaglan's favor.

And there still wasn't anything I could do.

I couldn't help them. I couldn't heal them anymore. I—

I *could* try to get the key. No one was paying attention to me and with my exhaustion and the key's pressure and cold I couldn't move very fast... which wouldn't help if getting the key turned into a mad dash, but it would help if I didn't want to make any fast movements that could draw someone's attention.

I staggered to the next tree trunk over. Titus was trying to climb an outcropping protruding from the forest floor and there was no way I'd be able to haul myself up, especially while still trying to maintain pressure on my neck wounds, but the outcropping turned into a steep hill the closer it got to the river. If I could ignore the pull of the key screaming at me to go directly to it, and slip between those two large shimmers at the top of the hill, I should be able to climb that slope.

The shadow fae heaved free of Hawk's grip and yanked his blade across Hawk's gut. Hawk jerked back far enough to not be completely gutted, but the blade still sliced flesh. It made him scream and stumble and the shadow fae lunged in, his blade aimed for Hawk's heart.

I cried out, unable to do anything, and a blast of fire slammed the shadow fae into a nearby rock and knocked his knife from his hand.

Hawk dove for the blade, his rapid healing having already sealed the laceration in his gut shut, and grabbed it before the stunned shadow fae could regain his senses. My incubus slashed at the shadow fae who scrambled out of the way, closer to me, and Cassius snapped a fire whip at the man, yanking him away from me. But that opened Cassius up to the hybrid who sliced down at his head.

Cassius wrenched out of the way and for a second it looked like the hybrid had missed. Then blood rushed down the front of Cassius's shredded shirt, the katana's tip having sliced a deep line from Cassius's collarbone to his hip.

With a howl of pain, he turned his fire inward and cauterized the wound, and shot a massive blast of flame at the hybrid, sending him tumbling into the inferno behind him that was growing by the second and starting to threaten Deaglan, Sebastian, and Titus.

Everything within me screamed to help them, heal them even though I had no power left. But the only way I could help was to get the key.

I yanked my attention away from them.

Get the key. The fight wouldn't end if I got it, but Titus and I would no longer be in pain and we could all escape.

Shivering and stumbling, I staggered from one tree to the next, then to a large rock, and another tree trunk, the ground's slope getting steeper and harder to climb. My breath sawed in my chest and my hands were getting tired from holding the edge of the blanket against my neck. The guys yelled and grunted, trees crashed to the ground sending up more clouds of debris, and Cassius's inferno sent waves of heat washing over me.

I just needed to get up this hill. I just needed for them to keep ignoring me.

Someone screamed, the sound sharp, filled with pain, jerking my attention back to the fight.

Hawk yanked the knife from the shadow fae's shoulder and kicked him into the side of the hill where the ledge just started to form, while Deaglan with ragged shadow wings tore through gnarled tree branches overtop of Titus and Sebastian and flew toward the key. But Cassius seized his ankle with his fire whip and slammed him back to the ground.

The hybrid sliced at Cassius's side with his katana and Sebastian sent a force-wave crashing into him, knocking him off his feet toward the sideways island. The gravity yanked on him and he dug his sword into the ground and clung to it with both hands, letting his shorter sword fly into the bog.

Cassius sent a blast of fire at the hybrid, breaking his grip and sending him hurtling toward the bog, but Deaglan grabbed the hybrid with a shadow whip as Titus jerked himself onto the top of the ledge and seized the front of Deaglan's leather jerkin.

With a roar, Titus smashed his fist into Deaglan's face and the Shadow King lost control of his whip, tossing the hybrid into a tree at the top of the ridge, twenty feet away.

Sebastian scrambled up to join Titus, wrapping bands of light around Deaglan, but the nightmare lunged up beside him, slashing a knife the length of his forearm at him and forcing Sebastian to release his light and dive out of the way.

Cassius half flew half dove to the top of the ledge and, yanking his wings inside his body at the last second, tackled the nightmare. They tumbled over the ragged ground and slammed into a tree which burst into flames.

It didn't look as if anyone had noticed me, or at least realized I was heading to the key, but they were still getting closer. If I wanted to get there first, I was going to have to hurry up.

I released one hand on my blanket and heaved myself over a stony outcropping overhanging the river and avoided a shimmer. Below, the water churned and frothed, crashing against rocks and spraying me with a putrid mist before plummeting over the edge of the island.

The pressure and cold pounded inside me, the key's pull tearing at my insides and blood oozed down my neck from the side I'd let go. Just a little farther. That was all.

I staggered the remaining few feet up the hill, each breath a shallow agonizing gasp.

The trees gave way to uneven barren rock, and the key, a miniature blue sun, blazed at the edge of the waterfall about fifty feet away. And between me and it, two shimmers, one with the ground blackened beneath it, and the other small unlike any of the other shimmers I'd seen so far. This one was more like liquid, the air undulating instead of shimmering and quickly growing.

My thoughts stuttered.

I'd seen that before.

That wasn't one of the Autumn Court's dangerous shimmers, it was a portal. The same kind of portal that had yanked us all into Faerie in the first place.

The portal swelled to double a man's size and the Winter Court high fae with the red and silver hair who'd pleasured the queen, along with her werepanther, and a group of ice guards stormed out.

"Get the dragon, Prince Seireadan, and his wife," the winter fae commanded, his gaze jumping to me the second he was through.

I staggered back, hitting a tree trunk before falling on my rear or worse tumbling down the hill or into the river.

"You can sense the key too?" I gasped.

"What key?" the man asked. "I'm tracking your connection to the Winter Court."

"Stop looking at the angel, Noaldar," the werepanther yelled. "Freeze that fire."

The winter fae, Noaldar, jerked his attention up and his eyes flashed wide as if he hadn't noticed there was an inferno blazing around us.

"Hold her," he snapped to an ice guard, then he bolted a few feet across the hill, heading toward the ledge. His full-body glow flared and he raised his hands, sending a frozen blast of wind roaring through the trees and putting out the fire.

All eyes turned to Noaldar, the fight momentarily forgotten for a heartbeat.

"They've got a tracking spell on Amiah," Hawk yelled.

"I can see that," Sebastian snapped back as a blast of cold magic swept through me making my teeth chatter. "Track her now, assholes."

"I don't need to. I'm dragging you back to the Winter Court," Noaldar replied as Deaglan shot a shadow spear through Sebastian's shoulder, drawing a scream of pain.

"Protect the prince," the werepanther commanded, running toward the fight, his fingers extending into claws.

All the ice guards turned toward Sebastian.

"No, one of you secure the prince's wife." Noaldar turned back to face me but didn't make it all the way around, his gaze landing on the key instead.

The ice guard Noaldar had originally commanded to hold me, grabbed my arm, and Noaldar took a hesitant step toward the key.

I heaved against the ice guard's grip, but even if I hadn't been weakened by the key or the loss of my magic, I wouldn't have been able to break free.

A ball of fire shattered the guard's arm into ice chunks, releasing me, and it stumbled back, tumbled into the river, slammed into a large rock, and shattered, its pieces tumbling over the waterfall.

"Amiah," Hawk yelled, running toward me.

"No, protect the key." I pointed at Noaldar bolting toward the key.

But the shadow fae popped up from a shadow in front of Noaldar and attacked, slashing his knife at the winter fae's gut and making him stumble dangerously close to the shimmer with the blackened earth.

Deaglan tossed two of the ice guards onto the sideways island, sending up another cloud of bog gasses that hit the fire pouring from Cassius's arms. It exploded with a violent *whoosh,* stunning three more guards still in the middle of the fight as well as the nightmare.

Hawk changed directions, stabbed the nightmare in the back, and wrapped an arm around his neck, seizing the opportunity to attack the man while he was stunned, while Titus rammed his fist into the chest of one of the ice guards, shattering it. I wasn't sure why he hadn't shifted, although he was still trapped in the trees and even if he made it to the clearing where the key and the waterfall were there still wouldn't have been a lot of room for him and anyone else. He was just as likely to knock a friend off the island as he was an enemy.

I wrenched my attention back to my goal. Noaldar and the shadow fae fought directly in front of me beside the shimmer and I wasn't stupid enough to head closer to the fight with everyone else, which left me the narrow ledge running alongside the river.

I staggered toward it, clinging to the rocks to keep my balance, and inched my way to the other side. If I could make it, I'd be right there. I could get the key and we could escape.

"Secure the prince's wife," Noaldar yelled, sending the shadow fae tumbling back with a blast of frozen air. But the fae hit a patch of shadow, vanished, and popped up beside Noaldar, and sliced at his ribs.

The closest ice guard jerked toward me and grabbed for my arm. I heaved back, but I wasn't going to be fast enough, not without losing my balance so I shoved the last desperate glimmer of my power into my back and release my wings.

They manifested through the blanket as if the blanket was a part of my clothing and I didn't have time to fix the problem.

I leaped in the air to escape and the ice guard lunged at me. He missed my foot but seized the edge of the blanket and yanked me down, using his enormous strength, to bring me crashing back to the river's edge.

"Amiah." Cassius scrambled toward us, blasting the ice guard into the river.

Behind him, Sebastian sent a force-wave at Deaglan, sweeping up debris and ripping more branches from the trees, but Deaglan sliced through the wave with his shadows and flew closer toward the key.

"I don't think so." Cassius seized Deaglan with his fire whip and wrenched him to the ground.

The King of the Shadow Court snarled and his shadows swept around Cassius's fire, rushing down the whip and crashing into Cassius.

With a scream, Cassius dropped to his knees, and the shadows surged under his skin then ripped out of his body, taking his inferno with them in a brilliant, fiery blast. Now not even a hint of smoke curled from his hands.

My pulse stuttered. He was out of fire. Deaglan had taken Cassius's fire.

On instinct, I jerked toward him as Noaldar shoved the shadow fae into the shimmer with the blackened ground, drawing a heart-stopping howl. The shimmer's magic tore through the shadow fae at the cellular level, disintegrating him in the blink of an eye, making Noaldar's eyes flash wide in fear for a second. Then the winter fae bolted toward the key and slammed his shoulder into me to get past, knocking me back. My foot hit uneven stone and debris and I tumbled into the river.

The blanket was instantly soaked, weighing me down. A small part of me knew I had to pull my wings in to get rid of the blanket, but the rest of me was screaming for air, and then I crashed into a rock and my thoughts scattered.

Strong hot hands grabbed me and jerked my head out of the water long enough for me to catch a breath before we crashed into another rock and another.

Cassius's brilliant blue gaze met mine for a second. He'd jumped in and saved me without thought to his own safety. Like he always did.

And then we plummeted over the waterfall, crashing against the jagged rocks and through the shimmer.

SEBASTIAN

Noaldar, a trusted member of my mother's harem, body checked Amiah into the river and my heart froze. Everything froze. My thoughts, fears, even the agony of the demonic magic consuming me from the inside out. There was only that horrific moment where Noaldar collided with her, the blanket tangled around her wings, and she went under the water.

Cassius, without a hint of fire, dove in after her with no hesitation, while Hawk screamed and started running toward her.

My thoughts lurched back into action and I started running too. But just like Hawk, I was too far away to save her. Titus howled and his beast took over, shifting him into his dragon form despite the trees caging him in, his wings crashing through the rotting wood, his tail thrashing trying to break free as he strained to get to her.

Noaldar didn't even glance over his shoulder. He just grabbed the key, created a portal, and disappeared, leaving behind the guards and the werepanther — someone my mother must have acquired after I'd left court because I didn't recognize him or know his name.

I scrambled to the river's edge and caught a glimpse of blond hair and green blanket crash against the rocks then tumble over the waterfall.

Oh, God, no.

"Titus, catch them." I raced to the waterfall's edge and the pressure of the warped leash spell filled my chest, heavy but not painful. It was already too late. They'd already tumbled through the shimmer and gone to wherever the waterfall emptied out, which could have been one spot or many spots.

Titus spat fire at Deaglan, clawing through the shadows holding him down, broke through the trees, and careened to the front of the waterfall as Hawk scrambled up beside me, his chest heaving, his clothes covered in blood.

She's gone. She can't be gone. Titus pulled his wings in to dive into the shimmer after them.

"Titus, wait. It might not take us to her," I gasped. We couldn't afford to be separated anymore than we already were, and frankly Titus was my and Hawk's only way off the island.

Titus snarled at me but didn't go after them, and Deaglan snapped a shadow whip around my neck and yanked me away from the edge.

The werepanther lunged at him, severing the shadows with his claws before I fell over, but I barely managed to keep my balance.

"Secure Prince Seireadan," the werepanther yelled, and one of my mother's ice guards barreled toward me.

The demon-vampire hybrid rammed his shoulder into the guard, sending the construct flying into a shimmer that disintegrated it like it had disintegrated Deaglan's shadow fae assassin.

But I didn't have time to catch my breath. More ice guards raced toward me along with the hybrid and the nightmare.

I turned to face them as the demonic magic surged, searing through my whole body, and my knees gave out.

God damn it. I couldn't afford to go down, not with Deaglan determined to kill us, or in the very least determined to kill Titus. And while my mother's werepanther and constructs would protect me and Titus, they didn't stand a chance against Deaglan. Hell, the three of us with their help didn't stand a chance right now.

God. I couldn't believe Deaglan had figured out how to cast a spell that would track the keys. The kind of power he'd have needed to cast something like that would have been a hell of a lot more than he'd had the last time he'd tried to kill me.

But then, I'd grown in power in the last three hundred years. Deaglan probably had too.

And right now, he wasn't being consumed by a foreign magic.

Hawk grabbed me, slung my arm around his neck, and hauled me back to the waterfall's edge.

"Titus, get us out of here," he said, throwing us over the edge and just trusting that Titus would catch us.

Titus swooped in, snatching us in his claws. He dove around a cluster of nearby islands, hit the gravity of an upside-down island, jerked to the new right side up, hung a quick left, and darted around another large island, all the while keeping something between us and Deaglan.

I tried to keep an eye out for Deaglan's shadows, praying he was also exhausted and wouldn't bother chasing us, but with Titus's erratic flying and the sudden jolts to new right-side ups, it became harder and harder not to squeeze my eyes shut and pray I wouldn't throw up.

After a few minutes, with the key's island long out of sight, Titus landed on the edge of an island with a meadow large enough for him to land and a copse of dead trees big enough for us in our human forms to hide.

He gently set us down, and Hawk, on his hands and knees, promptly threw up. I dragged myself a little farther away to avoid any splatter in case he wasn't done, and Titus did one of his amazing almost about to land shift into human forms just before touching the ground.

"We have to go after her," Titus said, grabbing Hawk by the arm, hauling him to his feet, and helping him stumble into the trees. "She's weak. Even with the key's pressure gone, her angel glow was weak. She used all her power healing you." He glared at me as if her using her power on me was my fault. "She'll be exhausted."

At least he hadn't just left us.

I staggered after them, clinging to the trees to keep my balance.

"Cast a spell like the one your mother's man did to track her," Titus said, "or highjack it or something before he casts it again."

"I destroyed it and Amiah's concealment charm is still working. Noaldar is a decent enough sorcerer but the only way he'd managed to track her was because my mother crafted a complicated spell using Amiah's connection to the Winter Court. Noaldar can't cast it at all, and my mother won't be able to repeat it quickly."

"And you can't cast it?" Titus growled.

"Even if he could, he shouldn't," Hawk said, clinging to a tree trunk looking like he was going to throw up again. "And don't you dare try."

Titus jerked toward Hawk, seized his tattered shirt, and yanked him nose to nose. "So what, you have sex with her but you don't care what happens to her?"

Hawk's hellfire flared and while I doubted Titus could see it, it was clear Hawk was barely holding himself together. He was just as crazy to save her as Titus was, maybe more so, and the only reason he hadn't just run off to find her was because he couldn't fly.

"She's not alone. She's with Cassius. She'll be okay long enough for us to figure out something that doesn't kill Bane," he replied as if he were trying to convince him of that.

"I can try casting something," I said as the demonic magic burned hotter.

I had to.

Yes, she was with Cassius, but she was also without magic and injured. That hybrid had sliced up her neck and she'd still been bleeding when she'd fallen into the river. Not to mention Cassius had been seriously injured. For all I knew they were lying helpless and unconscious and Deaglan was using the key finding spell to find her.

Except if he could have done that, he would have come after her in the aerie. Even if the aerie remained hidden from outsiders, it didn't mean outsiders who had a way to find it couldn't. It just usually took an extreme magical effort that very few fae possessed.

"Don't you dare cast anything," Hawk said, clinging to Titus's hand, his toes skimming the ground. "If the demonic magic doesn't kill you, the effort to channel any more magic right now will burn you up. Your aura is already on fire."

"What's he talking about, Seireadan?" Titus growled, dropping Hawk back to the ground and glaring at me, his beast barely under control.

"I'm infected with demonic magic," I gasped. "Long story."

"And your shoulder is bleeding," Hawk added.

I dragged my attention to my shoulder and the blood gushing out of it. I couldn't even feel that pain, and I had no idea if I had any other injuries.

"You should put pressure on that." Hawk yanked off his shirt and staggered toward me. "Just sit."

His shirt was filthy, but I was more likely to die from blood loss at the moment than I was of an infection, so I sagged to the ground, using the tree to prop myself up. Hawk bunched the tattered fabric on both sides of my shoulder and applied pressure behind me on the exit wound while I tried to press against the entrance wound.

Titus heaved in a big breath, blew it out, and crouched in front of me. "You need Amiah."

We all did. We barely knew her and I was pretty sure we were all in love with her.

Even Titus.

Except if Titus was in love with her, why hadn't he ripped out mine or Hawk's throats? He'd seen us in that bedroom getting dressed, the room smelling like sex. He knew we were still sleeping with her and dragons were like wolves. They didn't share well with others.

And that was a question for another time.

"Fuck." I tried to focus my thoughts, but the demonic magic surged again, stealing my breath.

Fuck fuck fuck.

"How are we going to find her if we can't use magic?" Titus asked. "Can you track her through the leash spell?"

"No. It's too warped." And for a second a part of me wished I hadn't had to change it. If I hadn't, I could have found her... and she'd have suffocated to death by now.

"You shared a connection when the key called you," Hawk said to Titus. "Can I touch you, see if that connection is still there? I might be able to make it stronger so you can find her, but you're not going to enjoy the side effects."

Meaning Hawk was going to make Titus hard and frustrated with few options for release. Which was beyond cruel. The man hadn't gotten laid in over five hundred years. And while he could jack off, that wasn't going to be completely satisfying, just like the last two times we'd had Hawk's magic burning through our systems.

Titus dug his claws into the hard-packed earth. "Whatever it takes. Just do it."

Hawk helped me shift so the tree trunk kept his ruined shirt in place at the back of my shoulder and turned to face Titus. "Take a breath and try to relax."

Titus glared at him and his canines extended into fangs.

"Okay. Don't relax. Just don't punch me in the face, then."

"I can't make any promises," Titus growled back.

"Swell." Hawk pressed his hand on Titus's bare chest over his heart and closed his eyes.

Titus tensed, his breath suddenly fast, and he released a shuddering growl. "Make it quick."

A hint of sensual magic teased my senses, thankfully not overly strong, since Hawk wasn't my type. Sure, I'd happily share Amiah with him and not care about the closeness that came with that, but without Amiah, he didn't turn me on. Amiah, on the other hand, would have been instantly flushed with desire, her pupils dilated, her breath picking up, and her breasts pushed out silently begging for them to be sucked on.

The demonic magic inside me flared, stealing my breath and all thoughts of Amiah. For a second there was only the acidic burn coursing through my veins.

Fucking hell.

I needed to get back to the mortal realm and deal with this infection. And pray to God Sargos, the demon I'd hired to pull the magic out of me wasn't completely pissed that I'd stood him up for our first meeting. I wasn't sure what I was going to do if he refused to help me instead of just raising his price. There wasn't anyone else in the area that I knew of who could do it.

"Got it," Hawk said, his eyes still closed.

Titus groaned, every muscle in his body contracted and trembling. Then he gasped and his eyes flew open, wide with shock. "I can feel her. She's far away, but I can feel her."

Hawk sagged back, his breath too fast as well. With the burn of the demonic magic, I couldn't tell how low Hawk's magic was, but it was a safe bet that manipulating Titus's connection to Amiah had drained him.

"Fuck," Titus groaned. "Just feeling her isn't enough."

I couldn't have agreed more, and from the look on Hawk's face, neither could he. But we had a way to find her. We'd get her back. Safe and sound.

Please, God. Safe and Sound.

AMIAH

THE SHIMMER DUMPED US ALONG WITH A HEAVY BLAST OF WATER INTO A deep, surprisingly clean pool, and the blanket dragged me down. My lungs screamed for air and I tried to kick up and reach the surface but after having spent all my magic, I was too weak to swim against the blanket's weight. I needed to pull my wings in and get rid of it, but I didn't even have enough power to do that and wouldn't for at least ten or fifteen minutes.

Above, the water grew still like glass, and a small, far off part of my mind knew that meant the shimmer on the other end of the waterfall had switched locations and was sending all of its water someplace else. It was peaceful, and heavy, getting darker, and still cold. God, it felt like I was always going to be cold.

At least the agonizing pressure crushing inside my chest and the key's painful pull were gone, replaced by the weight of the leash spell — which was nothing in comparison. Someone had gotten the key.

I could only pray it had been one of my guys.

And that they weren't too badly hurt.

Because I wasn't going to be able to save them.

I couldn't even save myself.

Then Cassius's face swept close, his weak angel glow barely visible in the darkness, and he grabbed my wrist. He yanked me back up to the surface and hauled me to the pool's rocky edge, dragging me half out of the water before collapsing to his hands and knees, coughing and gasping for breath.

I lay face down against the cold rocks, drawing in desperate breaths and coughing up water as well, choking between the two. Exhaustion pulled at my limbs and the world whirled and lurched around me. Warmth oozed from my neck and across my temple.

I was still bleeding.

And I was too tired to do anything about it, let alone move... or think. My thoughts were spinning as quickly as my vision, and getting just as dim and far away.

"What were you thinking?" Cassius gasped, heaving himself up to sit back on his heels and scanning the area around us. "You ran straight into the middle of the fight. Again."

Really? Those were the first words he wanted to say to me after falling over a waterfall?

I tried to glare at him— *wanted* to glare at him. But I couldn't turn the thought into action and couldn't focus on his wavering form for a good glare. Even if I could, he wasn't looking at me so the effort would have been wasted.

A stinging wind gusted around us, rolling dead leaves across the rocks in front of me and rustling through the trees seconds before a sudden, violent rush of water exploded behind us, sweeping waves up from my waist to my cheek.

Cassius jerked his attention to the pond behind me. "We can't stay out in the open like this."

Right.

We needed to move.

I had to get up. But I still couldn't force myself to turn the thought into action. All I could do was lie there and shiver, and pray the world would stop spinning.

"If any of Deaglan's men or the ice guards come through the shimmer we're in trouble." His gaze finally landed on me and his eyes flashed wide. "Shit, Amiah. We have to get you someplace dry and figure out how to stop your bleeding."

Before I could say anything, he picked me up, holding me with one arm under my knees while bracing my chest against his, making it easier to wrap an arm across my back with my wings still out. He didn't even bother asking me to pull them in, which spoke to how bad I must have looked.

The sudden movement sent the world lurching, turning the living autumn forest behind him into a barely visible kaleidoscope of reds, oranges, and yellows, as if we were in the mortal realm and not in the dying Autumn Court.

I caught a glimpse of what could be a path and more large jagged rocks protruding from the ground like the dead island where we'd been, then Cassius turned, making the world lurch again, and headed in the direction of the path.

Now I could see the pond where we'd been dumped, its water trickling down a thin rocky riverbed and disappearing into the forest's darkness. Overhead, was a hint of opalescent glow from the court's barrier as if the gangrenous disease consuming the court hadn't yet reached wherever we were. And I was sure if I could focus past the cold and exhaustion, my magical senses would confirm that.

As I watched, water exploded from a shimmer thirty feet above the center of the pond and poured down, sending waves washing against the shore and a swell of water rushing down the riverbed, before vanishing a few seconds later.

"About thirty seconds," Cassius said, but I was pretty sure he was talking to himself and even if I wasn't sure, I couldn't form coherent words to respond to him.

We crashed through the forest — so maybe that hadn't been a path — Cassius not seeming to care if we left a trail or not, choosing speed over caution.

The forest grew darker, but I couldn't tell if it was because the sun had finally set or if it was because I was on the verge of passing out.

All I wanted was to close my eyes and go to sleep, but my shivering was so violent it kept jerking me awake, and a small part of me screamed that passing out was a bad idea.

Except I couldn't figure out why.

I'd get my power back faster if I slept.

And I wouldn't feel the cold if I was unconscious.

The world lurched and somehow we'd gone from the forest to a cave and Cassius was crouching and setting me on the cold ground.

He leaned me sideways against a rough stone wall and cupped my face between palms that were barely warm. "Just hold on. I need to get wood for a fire. I won't be long. See if you have enough power now to pull in your wings."

He hurried into the darkness and I dragged my thoughts to my wings. I couldn't tell if I had enough power to pull them in or not. The magic flame in my palms that never went out no matter how much magic I used was barely there... or I was barely there. Perhaps my mind was the problem and I needed to concentrate harder.

I struggled to focus. I just needed to push a little bit of power into my back and flex my shoulder blades to pull them in. That was all I needed to do.

Just push a spark of magic.

Just move a fraction of an inch.

My thoughts narrowed down to that. Just an inch. Just a spark.

I strained against the cold and exhaustion and the emptiness in my palms.

Just. Pull. Them. In.

With a desperate ragged cry, I pushed every last scrap of power from my palms into my back and heaved my wings back into my body. The effort left me gasping, my shivers growing stronger, my body weak, and the weight of the soaked blanket slipped from my shoulders.

God, I just want to pass out. Everything will be fine when I wake.

My eyelids slid closed and I leaned my cheek against the stone wall.

It would all just go away, the pain and the cold and the numbness seeping through my muscles, if I just passed out. Just for a few minutes.

Then strong hands jerked me forward. "Come on, Amiah. You've got to stay awake. You *know* this. Open your eyes."

I dragged my eyes open and met Cassius's brilliant blue gaze. Just like I had that night he'd rescued me from the faith healer...

Except there was something wrong with his eyes.

I frowned and raised a trembling hand to his cheek. "Your angel glow is barely there."

"And yours is practically gone." He pulled off my boots, drew me forward, balancing my body against his, and yanked off my shirt.

I slid my hands over his bare shoulders, savoring the feel of his well-developed muscles as he worked to hold me—

Wait a minute.

"You're not wearing a shirt?" I said, my words slurred.

My gaze dropped, as he rose into a crouch, lifting me up with him, and I realized he'd stripped down to his boxer briefs.

He reached for the laces on my pants and my heart lurched.

I wasn't wearing any underwear—

I hadn't had underwear since I'd last been in Sebastian's apartment in the mortal realm—

And I wasn't wearing a top anymore—

I was going to be naked, and as much as I desired Cassius, our relationship wasn't anywhere near being naked together. I wasn't even sure if we were still friends.

"Cassius, wait—"

"You'll die of hypothermia in your wet clothes. If you were thinking straight, you'd know that." He pulled my pants down to my ankles and froze.

"Cassius—" I gasped again.

God, was that the only thing I could get out?

"It'll be okay," he said through gritted teeth, although I couldn't tell if that was to himself or me.

He carried me the few feet to a small fire and laid me on my side facing it, but the flames weren't nearly strong enough to thaw the cold inside me, and no matter how hard I hugged myself I couldn't stop shivering.

"Tell me what else I'm supposed to do," he asked, wrapping his body behind me and holding me tight.

My lids started to slide shut again. Not even the flesh to flesh contact could draw my thoughts beyond the cold and exhaustion.

Cassius gave me a squeeze and my lids flew open. "Amiah. What else am I supposed to do?"

"You don't know?" I frowned, my eyes closing again. "I was sure you knew."

"So tell me." He gave me another squeeze and pressed his palms against my chest discretely high enough that they wouldn't hit my nipples.

My thoughts stuttered at that and I realized his hands were getting warmer, his arms too.

"Amiah. What do I do?"

"What do you—? What were we talking about?" God, I couldn't get my thoughts to focus, and I was sure I should be thinking something or blushing or aching with desire, or being mortified that I was naked in Cassius's arms, but I couldn't keep a thought in my mind long enough to fully register on it.

"Jeez," he huffed, his breath warm against the back of my neck. "Fine. What the hell were you thinking running into that fight like that?"

Really? He was going to reprimand me now when I could barely think?

"Of course you'd want to bring that up," I mumbled back, angry one second, then drifting again as a little flame in the fire, fluttering at the edge of a piece of wood, caught my attention. "Right when I'm exhausted and can't think straight."

"Yeah, I'm a real asshole right now, but—"

The flame sparked, jolting me closer to consciousness. "Did you really just say asshole?" I think I'd heard him swear more times in the last few days than I had in the hundred years I'd known him.

"Bane and Hawk have been a bad influence," he said. "And right now I'm happy being an asshole to find out why you're a complete idiot. You could barely walk and barely breathe, and you thought what? Hey, I'll just saunter into the middle of a fight and risk everyone's lives by distracting them?"

"That wasn't at all what I was thinking." The little flame shrank and grew darker, my lids starting to slide shut again.

Cassius jerked me awake. "Then what were you thinking? You're smarter than that."

God, just let me sleep.

"I was thinking if everyone was busy fighting, I could get the key and we could get out of there." I would have gotten it too if that high fae from the Winter Court hadn't shown up.

"How could you even think that was a good idea? The key had practically incapacitated you, the fall left you bleeding, your neck had been sliced up and somehow you used up all your magic." Cassius jerked me again, and my eyes flew open. "And it wasn't to heal yourself. Your neck is still bleeding."

"Sebastian's back was broken." The little flame flared and joined a bigger flame and the tip of the piece of wood broke off, falling into the heart of the fire. Falling, falling. It was only a few inches, but it sent me spiraling down toward blissful darkness.

"But you didn't touch him," Cassius said.

"I know," I mumbled. *Everything will be better if I just give in.* "It's like when you stepped away from me and I still healed you back in the aerie. It uses up a lot of power and I don't really have control over it."

"Well that's just great," Cassius snapped, his tone cutting through the exhaustion, and jerking me out of my downward spiral. "Something else to worry about."

"I never asked you to worry about me." Of course he'd think that. He wasn't amazed my power had grown, that I could now heal someone without touching them — which if I really thought about it should have been terrifying since at my age, I should have been at my full magical ability already. Angels my age didn't just suddenly become stronger. Only if they branded a mate and formed a soul bond.

No, all he could think about was how it made things difficult for him, how he couldn't be overprotective of me if my magic locked onto someone and drained me without touching that person. I would have thought me not needing to run into danger to save someone was a good thing.

"If you hadn't turned into an idiot I wouldn't have to worry," he said, his tone sharp. "It's like you lost all common sense when you started sleeping with Hawk."

Oh, no. I wasn't going to justify my sex life to him again. I was too tired and, God damn it, it was none of his business.

"We're not having this conversation again." The fire snapped and the wood shifted, sending up sparks into the darkness above us. Up up up. Now I was spiraling up with the smoke, drifting, hazy, swaying. I didn't want to argue with Cassius. I just wanted to pass out—

And yet I couldn't seem to help myself. Words just kept pouring out of my mouth even though I wasn't really sure what I was saying. "Just because I'm not behaving the way I used to doesn't mean I've lost common sense or become a fool. It just means I'm different. People are allowed to change, aren't they?"

"People don't suddenly become different overnight."

They did if their beliefs had suddenly been shattered or their hearts broken like mine had. I hadn't known who I was or what I believed in. I'd never really known. I wasn't sure I knew now. But at least I was making an effort to finally find out instead of waiting for my destiny.

And I'd go back to that after I'd slept.

"It's like you've lost your mind."

God, just let me sleep.

"I realized I'd been a fool over my br— over my Marcus—" *No. Not mine.* My thoughts stuttered. "Over Marcus." That was right. "Not my Marcus. Just Marcus. Because I'd—"

Jeez, just stop talking.

I pressed my lips together. There was no point in telling Cassius about my partially formed mating brand. He wouldn't understand how horrible it was, even after he'd thought his brother had been branded to a weak human who endangered his life. Cassius still believed the angelic mating brand was beautiful and sacred, and he'd be horrified to learn I'd gotten rid of mine.

"So you decided to sleep with Hawk?" Cassius pressed.

"Yes, I did." And I was thoroughly enjoying it. My lids started sliding shut again.

He barked a bitter laugh. "Jeez, I'm an idiot." He gave me a jerk but my eyes didn't open this time. "You're sleeping with Bane too, aren't you? That's why you wanted him to help you change in the healing pool."

"I wanted him to help me because Balwyrdan kidnapped me without any underwear and you were guaranteed to freak out over that." Which was the truth, although I had no idea why I hadn't just come out and told Cassius I was also sleeping with Sebastian

"I wouldn't have freaked out." His embrace tightened, belying his words.

"Yeah, right," I replied, my words slurred, sleep tugging me deeper toward unconsciousness.

Just let me pass out.

"I wouldn't have," he insisted, his back growing gloriously warm and his body heat starting to soothe my shivers.

Oh yes.

The peaceful nothingness of unconsciousness swelled, dragging at my limbs and drawing me in.

"—underwear?"

Cassius jerked me again and my thoughts snapped back to him and the cave, but it was like he was a dream, a frustrating, bad dream, and the soothing darkness was reality.

"Amiah, why didn't you have underwear?"

"Because I'd just slept with Sebastian." There, now he knew the truth. *Now let me pass out. Please.*

"For the love of God! What's wrong with you?"

"What's wrong with me?" I tried to turn my head so I could glare at him but didn't have the strength to move. "What's wrong with you? Why are we arguing about this again? I thought I made myself clear. My sex life is my sex life. And please, I just need to go to sleep."

Cassius gave me another jerk and my lids fluttered open again. I hadn't even realized they'd closed.

"Not until your body temperature is higher."

"Not until what?"

"Your temperature. If you were thinking clearly, you'd know we need to get your temperature up before you can pass out. You were probably suffering from hypothermia before you were even dumped in the river and from the blood and growing bruise on your temple you have a concussion. That and it would be best if you pushed a little more power into your neck and maybe stopped that bleeding a bit more before you passed out."

My thoughts stuttered at that. "So you're arguing with me to keep me awake?"

That didn't make any sense.

"Asking you for detailed medical instructions didn't work," he said, pressing his lips to the top of my head. "But I knew restarting our fight would get you going."

"I'm that predictable?"

"You're that adamant. Especially when you're right."

The fire snapped, sharp and bright, jolting me back to the cave, and I struggled to focus on it and my surroundings and fight the seductive lull of exhaustion. Cassius was right. If I concentrated, my magical senses told me my body temperature was still dangerously low, I did have a mild concussion, and my neck was still bleeding. All of which could get worse if I let myself pass out.

Except focusing on my surroundings made me hyperaware of Cassius's hot flesh against mine, his muscular arms wrapped around me, pulling me tight against his sculpted chest, and his hands so close to my nipples he'd brush them if he just shifted them the right way.

Not to mention his erection pressing against my rear.

I didn't know if Sebastian was right, that Cassius loved me, but he certainly desired me. And while yes, we were both naked — or in his case mostly naked — I was a battered wreck. I doubted I looked attractive so it had to be something deeper than just a physical attraction.

And I had no idea what I wanted to do about that.

My thoughts jerked back to the last thing he'd said.

"I'm right?"

"Who you sleep with is none of my business," he said, his tone soft and suddenly sad.

"But it bothers you that I'm having sex with Hawk and Sebastian."

"It just surprises me. Hawk can't love you back and Bane is looking for a good time with anyone and everyone. He's been adamant about never wanting a commitment."

"Probably because his ex-fiancé tried to murder him. I wouldn't want to commit to someone after that either," I replied. "Hawk and Sebastian are generous lovers, with lots of experience. They're exactly what I want right now. I'm not looking for love."

Except as soon as the words came out my heart squeezed, not necessarily because I wanted Hawk and Sebastian to love me or make a commitment, but because that statement meant what we had would come to an end and I wasn't ready for that.

"And that's what you're looking for. Just experience and no commitment?" Cassius asked. "Just because Marcus wasn't the one, doesn't mean he isn't out there."

"I'm sure." Horribly sure. There *was* someone out there fated to be my mate, and if I met that someone now I might fall in love or I might not. But now, at least, it was my choice. "Someday, yes, I'd like to settle down and have a committed relationship."

Cassius might even be that guy. Right now, in this moment, this was the Cassius who'd rescued me... except this was more than just the Cassius who'd rescued me. This was the Cassius I'd started fantasizing about when my sexual restraint had started to slip. Strong, sexy, and naked.

He could very well have been my soul mate. Or at least this version of him, not the hardened icy soldier he'd become after the war, and if he didn't go back to bossing me around, I could fall in love with him.

He'd always been my rock, my safe place to land. I knew him, knew he loved cricket — of all sports! — hated onions and pineapple on his pizza, liked to go stargazing, and protected those he considered family with a passion verging on obsession.

Maybe I would fall in love with him.

Maybe Sebastian was right and I already had.

At least now I could allow myself to feel whatever I really felt for him without the fear that my brand would force me to fall in love with someone else.

"But I'm not ready. Not yet. I need to figure out who I am first. I wasted too much time waiting." My pulse picked up with a mix of fear at the thought of losing Hawk and Sebastian, and desire for the naked man behind me. My senses, still weak, connected with Cassius's life force and filled me with a hint of what I knew was a raging inferno on the verge of breaking free.

Except it wasn't breaking free at the moment. It was weak, his flame barely lit.

"Waiting for what? For Marcus?"

"No, not Marcus."

"Then passion," Cassius said, sounding certain in his conclusion. "The only man I've ever seen you set your sights on in the hundred years I've known you was Marcus. You want the unrestrained passion of a shifter."

I opened my mouth to argue with him that I didn't want Marcus because of his passionate shifter's nature, but a part of me had been thrilled at the idea, thought it made perfect sense. I needed him to loosen up my reserved angelic nature.

Except if I didn't deny that desire, I might not be able to move my friendship with Cassius to anything else.

And God, even weak and dizzy, the idea of moving our friendship to the next level was starting to seem like a great idea. I wasn't nearly as cold as I was before. Cassius's now gloriously warm body was melting the ice inside me, and his deliciously hard muscles were changing that ice into a soft, aching heat.

But if I didn't tell him the truth, he'd never understand why now, after so many years, I was interested in him.

A hint of the ice returned, this time as a sour churning fear in my stomach at the thought of what his reaction was going to be.

Except my soul yearned to connect with his life force in the same way I connected with Hawk and Sebastian, and in the way it yearned to connect with Titus. I needed that closeness with them.

But did that mean I needed a committed relationship with them?

When we got back to the mortal realm, Hawk was going to return to his other lovers. He said he'd still have sex with me, but he couldn't survive on just me alone, and Cassius wouldn't be able to see the difference between sex and a committed relationship. That was just the kind of guy he was and he'd want me to give up the others. Sebastian, given how he flirted with every woman he came across, would move on and not give me a second thought.

And yet I still wanted to have what I could with them. With all of them. Even Cassius.

Which meant if I ever wanted the hope of having more with him, I had to be honest about why I'd never looked at him that way in a hundred years. I had to tell him about my brand.

AMIAH

I sucked in a sharp breath, trying to steady my racing heart. "I was waiting for my soul mate. I had a partially form mating brand, so I was waiting," I said in a rush.

Cassius stiffened, his muscles flexing around me. "You what? You *had*? Amiah—"

"It's my life. My body," I said before he could reprimand me or try to tell me how amazing a brand could be. "I got rid of it recently and even if it could come back, I'd never want it."

"Why would you do that?" Cassius shifted, sliding me to my back, his body pressed tight against my side still keeping me warm, but allowing him to stare down at me, his expression strange. He wasn't furious like I expected, but I couldn't figure out what he was thinking. "A mating brand is an amazing destiny. For there to be two angels with branded mates in this century is incredible."

"It's not incredible. It's a nightmare," I insisted. "You weren't conscious for it, but I saw what it did to Essie. When her guys were seriously wounded and she couldn't get to them, she was literally on the floor begging for someone to help them."

"But Amiah—"

"And Gideon was a wreck when Essie had been shot and nearly died," I pressed on. Cassius had to understand the truth about the brand. I wasn't crazy. I hadn't made a horrible mistake. "The brand nearly tore him apart when he tried to ignore it because he knew Essie was in love with Marcus." My throat tightened at the memory of their fear and pain. The image of Essie on her knees, screaming for help, of Gideon clinging to the wall outside Essie's hospital room trying desperately not to give into the brand's compulsion and go to her because she wasn't in love with him. "It's just another prison. I can't do that again."

"But to get rid of it you'd have to have damaged your soul."

"I can't be trapped by someone, my life ruled by them again. I just can't." Tears burned my eyes and my breath turned into short sharp gasps, the fear of being trapped, held prisoner, and hurt by someone again overwhelming me. "Cassius, I can't."

Cassius cupped my face with an ever-so-slightly too-warm hand, his eyes filled with a strange mix of grief and something else.

Probably judgment. I was a horrible angel. I'd ripped out a piece of my soul just to avoid the possibility that I'd fall in love with a stranger. For all I knew, Cassius could have been my soul mate.

Except if he was and I'd kept the brand, I wouldn't ever know if I was really in love with him or if it was the brand making me love him.

"I want to fall in love like everyone else. I don't want some brand to force that on me. I put my life on hold for a lie." A tear broke free and trailed down my temple. "I don't even know who I really am. I had no idea that I need sex."

His eyes widened.

"You, ah— You need—" He cleared his throat. "You need sex? You sure that's not the euphoria of Hawk's magic?"

"No, there's something that clicks inside me, like a circuit being completed. It happens with both Hawk and Sebastian, and now that I know it's there, I feel... strange when I've gone without for too long... empty..." I didn't know how to explain it. "It's like I need physical contact like a shifter, my soul settles like a shifter and is stronger afterward, but it's deeper than that, something about needing to connect with their life forces."

Cassius swallowed hard. "You sure they're not your mates?"

"You really think those two are a match to my soul? I know the brand could bond me with a stranger, but it wouldn't be with someone so completely different from me. Essie might have been a being created in a laboratory intended for evil purposes, but her values, her sense of right and wrong, her goodness, perfectly aligns with all her guys."

"And you don't think Hawk and Sebastian share your values?"

I opened my mouth to deny that then closed it. Hawk and Sebastian weren't the men I'd thought they were. They were generous and kind and compassionate, and they were willing to risk their lives for what was right. Just like I was. "I had sex with both of them before my brand was removed. It would have fully woken if either of them was my mate."

Unless I hadn't been ready. No one really knew why a brand formed. Sometimes it formed after years of knowing someone and being intimate with them, and sometimes right away, at first sight.

And none of that mattered anymore. The brand no longer controlled me.

"So you thought your brand would awaken if you and I— if we—?" Cassius's breath picked up and that ache between my thighs, the desire to be with him, swelled again.

"My brand didn't do anything when we first met, so I didn't think you were the one. But Cassius, you're my rock, my best friend. A part of me would be broken without you." Had been broken since he'd returned from the war and had been withdrawing from me. "When I decided to stop waiting, decided I wanted to fall in love like a normal person, I didn't want to risk my brand waking if we ever..." I stared into his eyes, able to clearly see just how brilliantly blue they were with his angel glow so weak.

"If we ever," he prompted.

"If we ever had sex," I said, my voice breathy.

His gaze dipped to my lips as if he wanted to kiss me.

God, please kiss me.

"And you've thought about that?" he asked, his pupils dilating, his voice husky. "About us having sex?"

"Recently. A lot."

I caressed his cheek with a trembling hand — although not nearly as shaky as before — and his expression turned pained.

"Amiah, this isn't right."

"Because I'm having sex with Hawk and Sebastian?"

Because I didn't want to make a commitment and he did.

Or was it because he thought I was a fool? He might have agreed that who I slept with was none of his business, but that didn't mean he had to join my growing list of sexual partners.

Which was actually kind of ridiculous since the total number of guys I'd slept with was two.

"Because I know you're not thinking straight. Your body has warmed up a bit, but you're still losing blood, it's a trickle now, but you're still losing it, and you still have a concussion."

"And if I was thinking straight?" God, I didn't know why I was pushing this. Even if I could see desire in his eyes and feel it from his body, that didn't mean he wanted to act on it. I needed to respect that.

"I wouldn't be able to give you what you want." The strange look in his eyes solidified into sadness, soft, heartbreaking grief. "And I certainly can't give you what *I* want."

"Because you want a commitment?" Which I couldn't give him. Not yet.

"No— well, yes. But I'd wait for you. I've been waiting for you since before the war." He huffed a bitter laugh. "I think I've been waiting for you from the moment I saw you in that tent. I was just too dense to realize it."

He captured my hand against his cheek with his and leaned into my touch.

"God, you don't know how much I've wanted this, wanted to be able to show you that I was in love with you—" His gaze met mine again, the depths of his desire making my pulse stutter, and something in his eyes changed, a realization, a decision. "I've always been in love with you."

He leaned in and brushed his lips against mine, sending a swirl of emotions rushing through me.

Finally.

Yes.

Were we really going to make love?

How would that affect our friendship?

"Cassius—" God I wanted this. It was like his life force called to me, and just like my compulsion to heal, my soul was compelled to connect with him, complete the circuit. "Are you sure? I'm not going to stop having sex with Hawk or Sebastian right away."

"Do they make you happy? Give you what you need?"

"Yes."

"Then when we meet up with them, go back to them. Figure out who you are. I'll wait."

A shadow of sadness flashed across his expression so quickly I wasn't sure I'd actually seen it, then he pressed his lips against mine again.

His kiss was slow and sensual as if he wanted to put the desire of his hundred years of waiting into that one kiss. It reached all the way to my toes, seeped into my cells, and sank into my soul.

There was something so right about it, about finally taking the next step in our relationship. It reminded me of all the warm comfortable times we'd had together, laughing over bad jokes, watching the stars, just being comfortable in each other's company.

And yet there was a new sensation, a thread of heat, of fire, of need growing in my heart. His life force thrummed against my magical senses, and I thrilled at the feel of him, of his magic, his power, his naked body pressed close to mine.

It made the soft ache of desire within me warm and grow, and I kissed him back, sighing with pleasure, letting him know I wanted this as much as he did.

He brushed his warm fingers across my collarbone to the divot at the base of my neck then trailed them to the inner swell of my left breast.

My heart pounded at his touch and I slid my hands over his buzz cut, capturing his head and deepening our kiss.

A part of me couldn't believe this was really happening, that Cassius and I were kissing, while the rest of me thrilled at it.

I slowly teased my tongue against his lips and tongue, something Hawk had done the last time we'd kissed and it had driven me crazy.

Cassius moaned, rewarding my forwardness, but my thoughts scattered as his fingers traced the inside of my breast and his thumb brushed my nipple. Just a whisper of a touch, but it shot a spark of sensation straight to my core and made me gasp.

He did it again, drawing the same spark and another sharper gasp, and I pushed my breasts up, urging him for more than just a teasing touch.

"I wondered what that would sound like," he murmured against my lips.

"What?"

"You letting go." His fingers skimmed across my ribs. "Enjoying yourself."

"If you want me to enjoy myself, go back to my breast," I said.

He chuckled. "But you're still bossing me around."

"Pretty sure you're the one who keeps trying to boss me around."

"Pretty sure I've been failing."

He trailed kisses along the same path his fingers had taken, collarbone, divot, inner swell of my breasts, slowly, oh so agonizingly slowly, as if he wanted to memorize my body not just with his eyes, but his hands and lips too.

I was squirming by the time he flicked his tongue across my nipple, snapping more sensation through me, a mix of my desire and his fiery life force. He worked my nipple into a tight aching bud, then the other one, his pace slow, the building anticipation a glorious torture that made my breath fast and my heart race.

Then his hand shifted from my ribs to my hip where my partially formed mating brand had been and heat swelled in my skin.

My pulse stuttered and a flash of icy fear returned to my stomach.

Oh, crap.

But the moment I thought that, I realized the heat wasn't my brand reforming. The brand was gone. I could feel the hole left in my soul from ripping it out. The heat came from Cassius's palm. His whole body actually. His temperature had skyrocketed, hotter than the most powerful demon I'd ever encountered and his life force blazed against my senses.

This was just me and Cassius. No destiny, no soul bond, no fear. I could let everything go with him like I did with Hawk and Sebastian, and fully embrace my connection with him, a connection that was growing stronger by the second.

He trailed his lips over my belly, his hand skimming down my thigh beyond where the brand had ended, the heat from his skin continuing to grow, along with the heat of desire within me. He raised a gaze filled with need and awe, the look strangely similar to the look Hawk had given me, and captured me body, breath, and soul.

This was the way it was supposed to be between us, where we'd have been headed before the war if my brand had started to wake, and what had been missing in our relationship. I hadn't even realized just how deeply it had hurt me when he'd returned from the war cold and icy.

I knew now, with absolute certainty that I'd been in love with him for a long time too, and had used angelic propriety to keep him at arm's length to protect myself for when I'd met my soul mate.

But maybe that's what he was.

My soul mate.

There were still things I needed to figure out, desires I wasn't sure I could explore with Cassius or not. I wasn't sure how he felt about having sex with more than just me.

But now that we'd realized the truth, that we were in love, we had a lifetime to figure it out. There was no need to rush. We could take it as slowly and explore our relationship as deeply as Cassius was exploring my body now... and I wouldn't have to give up Hawk and Sebastian right away.

Cassius nudged my legs open, shifting his stunning body between my thighs, the honed muscles in his shoulders and arms bunching with the movement. He teased kisses and licks across my skin, his breath hot against my folds before finally — God, finally! — he flicked his tongue over my clit.

More amazing sensation snapped through me. I bucked against his mouth as a throaty moan escaped my lips.

"God, that's the most amazing sound." He captured my hips, holding me steady, and slowly, reverently, as if he was worshiping my body with his mouth, worked me into a gasping, writhing frenzy, until my muscles contracted and a shuddering orgasm swept over me, sending my senses spinning, reminding me that I was still weak.

I clutched his head, riding the wave, and he raised his gaze back to me. His angel glow was brighter, his emotions heightened, and he held me safe and secure in his brilliant blue eyes. I'd always be safe with him, always be protected, he would move heaven and earth to ensure my safety, and I'd move it to keep this Cassius, the one I'd fallen in love with.

"I love you, Amiah. I've always loved you." He pulled off his boxer briefs and captured my lips in a searing kiss, his lips hot, his passion overwhelming, making my desire that hadn't been satiated with that first orgasm surge stronger.

His erection teased my folds, his hands roughly kneaded my breasts, and his warm flesh pressed deliciously against mine.

I curled my hips up, taking his tip inside me, letting him know how much I wanted him, needed him inside me.

"I'll always love you," he said, his voice thick, low.

Slowly — God he was going to drive me crazy with this pace! — so damned slowly, he pushed inside me. The heat of his life force flared and that piece of my soul that needed whatever it was from him, shifted and clicked into alignment, making my muscles tremble around him.

Our gazes locked, completing the circuit, and for a second he froze, his eyes ever-so-slightly too wide, as if he, too, felt the connection.

Then, with a masculine groan, he started a slow sensual rhythm, withdrawing and pushing back in, building my desire.

God, it felt so good, and I held nothing back. I freely gave myself to him, letting the feel of him moving inside me twist my need tighter until my whole body was throbbing, desperate for a release. My breath had become ragged. So had Cassius's.

His pace grew frantic, his body was blazingly hot, smoke curling from his shoulders. Light and love blazed from his eyes, filling my heart, and my muscles contracted tight, my orgasm starting to sweep through me.

"Oh, Cassius," I cried.

Cassius gave another few hard fast thrusts then tensed and gasped my name.

I crashed over the edge. The sensation was glorious, breathtaking. It sent me whirling, tipping my head back and filling me with light and fire. My body lit up again, and his life force roared across my senses, filling me as completely as his erection did.

Fire flooded into every cell inside me and swept into my soul. I was strong like Cassius, a living inferno. My fae glow blazed brighter than ever before, and the connection with him was the strongest I'd ever felt.

I was complete. Whatever it was I needed from him, filled me.

God, I wish I knew what that was, what I needed from all of the guys.

But Cassius said he'd wait. I had time to figure it out before he'd want a commitment, and before Hawk and Sebastian went their own way.

And right now, in this moment, everything was perfect. I was in love with my best friend and I'd finally gotten him back.

CASSIUS

Amiah healed her neck with the little bit of power she'd managed to recover in the time it had taken us to make love — or maybe *because* we'd made love, I wasn't sure. She shrunk the cuts into something that would quickly scab over then passed out.

I pulled her back into my embrace, not bothering to put my briefs back on, savoring the feel of her slightly cool flesh against mine.

I didn't want to let her go.

Ever.

But I wasn't going to have much of a choice in the matter. I could already feel my fire building inside me and had maybe a few hours before I'd have to actively lock it and my emotions back down. And even after I'd locked it away, I didn't think I'd be able to keep holding her. It didn't matter if I put everything into keeping my fire controlled, my feelings for her were too strong and I wouldn't be able to hold it under my skin while touching her.

This was it. All I was ever going to get. I wouldn't ever be able to hold her again.

A satisfied sigh slipped from her lips and my heart twisted tight.

I wanted this forever, wanted to listen to the sounds she made and see the look on her face when she finally let it all go and she let me see the real her.

She was mesmerizing. Her angel's soul radiant.

I'd felt that connection she'd talked about and seen it in her eyes. Those brilliant blue orbs, so like my own in coloring, had blazed bright even though she hadn't recovered most of her magic, and her gaze had reached deep into my soul, capturing me.

I'd never felt anything like it before.

And she was right. It wasn't a soul bond.

After she'd come, her unnatural fae glow had lit up her whole body and the connection had vanished. If we'd been destined for each other—or rather if she'd still had her brand, the connection would have stayed and a matching brand would have formed on my body.

My heart clenched tighter, making it hard to breathe.

I never would have gotten this moment if Deaglan hadn't ripped out my fire.

God, I'd been terrified, helpless against him, afraid my fire was gone for good and without my magic, I'd be unable to protect her.

But my fire wasn't gone, and he'd unintentionally given me the greatest gift I could have asked for: a moment with the woman I loved, had always loved, and would continue to love until I died.

And while yes, she needed to move on, stay with Bane and Hawk or commit to someone else, whatever she desired because she deserved to have the life she wanted, I never would.

I knew I should.

It'd be healthy to.

But she was my one.

Not because our souls were destined to be together, but because I'd completely fallen in love with her, with her determination and kindness and brilliant spirit. I'd fallen in love in the normal way, the way she wanted to fall in love. I'd even share her with Bane and Hawk if that was what her soul needed — what she seemed to think she needed because of the connection she made during sex — and I'd comfort her when they moved on. Because they would. That was their nature.

Except with my inability to hold back my fire, I wouldn't be able to comfort her very well, not the way I really wanted to.

I pressed my lips to the back of her head, trying to get closer, to touch more of her while I could. I needed to memorize how this felt, seal it in my mind so I'd never forget this one amazing moment.

God. There had to be a way to keep this, to fix me.

But the only being I'd ever heard of who had the power to heal an angel's magic had been the archangel Michael, and that bastard was thankfully long dead.

Maybe Bane would be able to help. He'd been able to put my fire out before.

Except that had been by encasing me in ice and my fire had quickly reignited and melted it. Although he hadn't been trying to fix my control over my magic or even remove it—

If Deaglan could pull out my fire, maybe Bane could too. They were both sorcerers able to channel raw Faerie magic and weave it into almost any kind of spell or power they wanted. They just needed the willpower to keep it controlled or they'd burn up and die.

That could give me a few hours with Amiah—

Hell, maybe Bane could take my fire altogether.

Then I could always be with Amiah and I wouldn't have to worry about burning her or anyone else. The war was over and I no longer had to be the Salamander. I didn't need to have magic to live my life.

Sure, I'd have to leave my job as a JP agent, but I'd do that in a heartbeat if it meant I could be with Amiah.

But first I needed to protect her until the mess with Faerie's Heart had been dealt with. Being with her now was a taste of what I might be able to have in the future, but none of it would matter if Deaglan or someone else killed her.

My pulse picked up, pounding in my chest as fear twisted in my gut. Whatever I did, I had to keep her safe. Even if that meant never being able to hold her again.

She murmured in her sleep, soft nonsensical sounds, her skin still radiating a gentle white light. It added to the flickering illumination from the fire, brightening the cave, pushing the shadows into the crevasses between the rocks and deeper into the back of our shelter, and clearly lighting the cave's entrance.

We'd be easy to spot if anyone was looking for us and I could only pray it would be Bane and the others who arrived first because while I didn't want to admit it to Amiah, I was exhausted and injured too. I had a huge burn down my chest and was still weeping blood from numerous cuts.

It actually spoke to how exhausted and out of it Amiah had been for her to allow me to make love to her while in my injured condition. And without a doubt, she was going to be furious with herself when she woke for not noticing that right away.

Which was something I'd deal with when she woke.

I closed my eyes, listening to her slow, soft breathing and savoring the feel of her body against mine, while I drifted on the edge of sleep, trying to stay awake and listen for danger. Her skin wasn't as warm as it should have been, but it was a lot better than it was before and some of her chill could be attributed to my raised body temperature.

At least her lips were no longer blue and she could breathe normally.

Someone had gotten the key and I had a bad feeling about who.

Bane had barely been standing when I'd jumped into the river and I doubted Hawk could have taken a lot more damage. The only one who'd been capable of fighting had been Titus and Deaglan had tied him up with shadows seconds after he'd shifted.

The best outcome was that Deaglan had the key, and everyone else had managed to escape.

Something crunched outside the cave and I cracked open an eye just wide enough to see who was coming. With very little power, my best move was to let whoever it was think I was unconscious and use the element of surprise to defend us.

Another crunch and another that quickly turned into heavy rapid footfalls.

"She's this way," Titus said, and the footfalls — a mix of Titus's heavy tread and lighter ones from the others — pounded close, crashing through the forest then came to a sudden stop.

"Well, fuck," Bane said.

I raised my head so I could look at them clearly. The forest behind them was dark, it was still night, but now they stood within the radius of Amiah's radiance.

Both Bane and Hawk looked like shit, their clothes torn and bloody. Hawk had lost his shirt, and while he wasn't bleeding, he did have bruises, which meant his magic was low. If he took another serious injury, he wouldn't be able to heal it. While Bane held a wadded-up piece of blood-soaked fabric — probably Hawk's shirt — to his shoulder which was probably only slowing his blood loss not stopping it.

Titus on the other hand looked perfectly fine — and I could tell every bit of him was fine because he was completely naked and sporting some massive wood.

"So Sparky finally got laid," Bane said. "It's about fucking time."

But his words felt forced as if he weren't really happy that Amiah and I had finally made love. Although perhaps that was due to his horrible condition. It was actually a miracle Amiah hadn't immediately woken and healed him.

And even before any of us could do anything, Titus growled and stormed toward me and Amiah.

Ah, shit.

"Titus." Hawk grabbed Titus's arm, but he jerked free without missing a step as Amiah's eyes fluttered open.

Her gaze jumped straight to Bane then jerked to Titus and she sat up, sliding my arms to her waist, not seeming to care that she was naked or my hands were now in her lap, and reached out to the furious dragon.

He dropped to his knees in front of her, cupped her face in his massive hands, and pressed his forehead against hers.

My thoughts stuttered at that. I wasn't sure if I was expecting him to beat the crap out of me like he'd beaten Bane, but I certainly hadn't expected for him to kneel before her. Although if I really thought about it, he'd been using her to calm his shifter's soul almost from the moment we'd dragged him back to Bane's apartment.

Titus huffed, a very dragon-like sound, and closed his eyes, the muscles in his powerful thick arms flexing. "You mated with Cassius."

"We had sex," she said. "We're not mates."

The hellfire in Hawk's eyes flared and he frowned. Guess he thought if Amiah and I ever figured ourselves out, we'd end up in a committed, monogamous relationship. And if I hadn't felt that strange connection when we'd had sex, I would have expected the same thing too. That was the way it was supposed to be, wasn't it? Sure my brother was mated to a woman with other mates and there were a handful of other angels who didn't practice monogamy, but I always expected it'd just be me and Amiah.

Except right now it couldn't just be me and Amiah. I couldn't give her what she needed. In a way it was good she needed whatever it was she got from the others during sex and didn't want a committed relationship, because I had no idea how I was going to explain to her that we couldn't have sex again. Hell, I wouldn't even be able to hold her again anytime soon.

Amiah shifted in my embrace, jerking my attention to her, and I realized my hands were smoking and the heat of my fire was building again inside me.

Shit. Too soon.

It was God damned too soon.

I jerked away from her and grabbed my damp briefs and Titus captured her lips in a hard, ferocious kiss, not seeming to care that Amiah had just been in my arms.

There was a frenzy to his kiss, as if he'd been trying to hold back and couldn't any longer. His fingers tangled in her hair, he tilted her head back to deepen it, and she moaned softly into his mouth, her breath picking up.

He growled back in response, wrapped an arm around her waist, and jerked her into his lap, her legs straddling his, her mound pressed against his cock.

God damn it. That's what I wanted again. I'd barely gotten to hold her and my fire was back.

"This isn't the place," I snapped, my voice icier than I intended. "We should get back to the aerie."

"Just because you licked her doesn't make her yours?" Bane said, clinging to the mouth of the cave to keep standing.

Hey!" Hawk said. "That's my line. I think he's just feeling left out. Don't worry, Sparky. I'll kiss you." Hawk batted his eyelashes at me.

For the love of—

"Fuck off," I growled at Hawk and grabbed Titus's shoulder.

He jerked his head away from Amiah, bared his fangs, and snarled at me.

"If you two want to have sex, at least wait until you're somewhere more comfortable," I forced out.

"Says the man who fucked her in this very cave," Bane drawled.

"No, Cassius is right," Amiah said, her cheeks turning bright red with embarrassment as if she'd just realized she'd been about to have sex with Titus in front of all of us. "We should go back to your aerie," she said to the big man. "But first—" Her gaze jumped to Bane and she eased herself out of Titus's embrace. "Sit before you fall over."

"I can last until you've recovered more magic," he gasped.

"I've enough to deal with your shoulder and ease up some of Cassius's pain." She pointed to the ground. "Sit."

Bane glared at her.

She glared back. Her angel glow was brighter than I would have expected for only being asleep for such a short period, but maybe that connection she made when we had sex had helped... or maybe I'd actually dozed and we'd been asleep longer than I thought.

With a groan, Bane gave in and slid down the wall, and Amiah knelt beside him. She peeled away the bloody fabric he had bunched against his shoulder and gave the hole in Bane's shirt a fierce tug, ripping it open more so she could get a better look at his wound. Then she tipped him forward to check out his back.

At least she was being smart about it and checking him out without using her magic. I could only hope she'd do just enough to close the wound and no more, since I didn't want her exhausted and dizzy again anytime soon. I wouldn't be able to handle that. My emotions were already running wild and it only got worse when she was in bad shape.

She placed her hands over Bane's wound, not caring that she was getting bloody, and closed her eyes. Watching her work always amazed me. There was something incredible about her power, the way she knitted muscle, bone, and flesh back together. Before Amiah, I'd never met an angel who had healing magic, and while I'd met a lot more during and after the war, there was something about the way she worked that always made my breath catch with awe.

White light flickered around her palms and Bane tensed, anticipating pain. But she wasn't in a hurry, which meant she could control how fast her magic healed him so it wouldn't hurt and after a second, he realized that as well and breathed out a heavy sigh, tipped his head back, and closed his eyes.

Hawk and Titus watched and I pulled on my damp pants and shoved my feet into my wet boots. I wanted to get moving the moment she was done. She could heal my burns after we'd gotten to the aerie and she'd had a chance to clean up, eat, and sleep.

I was going to insist on that.

Bane needed to be healed, but I didn't. Yeah, I hurt and the burn down my chest was painful, but, like I had in the past, I'd get by.

"Okay," she murmured, pulling away from Bane and turning her gaze on me, her glow not as low as it could have been which meant she'd remained smart and hadn't fully healed him. "Your turn."

"I'm fine."

"You're in pain. I've enough left to ease that up and it'd be easier if I touch you," she replied, reminding me that she could now heal me without making contact.

"Amiah—" I pulled on my damp shirt. "If you're barely conscious and we end up in another fight we've got a problem."

"And you're injured. I'd say that's a bigger problem." She raised an eyebrow, daring me to keep arguing, and held out her hand. "Just take my hand, Cassius. Don't make me work harder than I have to."

Meaning she was going to heal me whether I wanted her to or not and was probably going to end up hurting herself.

"Fine."

I sucked in a sharp breath and clenched at the inferno starting to build again within me.

I would not burn her. God, please don't let me burn her.

It had barely been a minute since I let her go and already my fire seared under my skin.

"You don't have to look so sour about it." Disappointment swept through her expression before she pulled up her cold mask of professionalism.

The look and emotional withdrawal made my heart clench, knowing she thought I was back to my old ways, that the moment we'd had in the cave hadn't really changed anything between us.

"Jeez man, that's cold," Bane said. "She lets you in and now you're back to being an asshole?"

Of course I was. Because I couldn't God damned touch her again. Not the way I really wanted.

Smoke billowed from my palms and fire snapped over my hands and up my forearms. A few sparks flew dangerously close to Amiah, and I jerked back, my inferno surging with the sudden fear that I was going to hurt her, which only made the fire on my hands bigger.

Shit shit shit.

Ice. Frozen ice. Cold. Hard. Frozen.

But the mantra didn't help anymore. It had barely been helping in the first place. My flames raged through me, burning away any kind of control I might have had, suddenly powerful as if Deaglan hadn't ripped all of it out of me a few hours ago.

"Cassius—" Amiah's eyes grew wide with concern and she stood.

God, she was going to come to me and I was going to hurt her.

"Stay where you are." I jerked my gaze to the others. Titus glared at me as if I was the enemy, Bane's expression had turned thoughtful — yeah, he was close to figuring out the truth — and Hawk looked grim and knowing — he'd already figured it out.

God. I hadn't told anyone the truth, hadn't wanted to admit it publicly, but the only way to get her to back away was to confess my problem.

"I don't have full control of my fire," I said.

I wasn't sure if I had *any* control anymore.

I couldn't hold her. I'd never be able to be with her again.

Flames dripped from my hands and hissed against the damp stone beneath my feet.

"It's connected to your emotions, isn't it?" Hawk squinted as if he were trying to get a better look at something. And maybe he could. The man was a Sensitive. Between him and Bane, they were the ones most likely to figure out what exactly was wrong with me. Then he shook his head and frowned. "Sorry, man. I have to touch you to find its source."

"We can deal with this when we get back to the aerie." I sucked in a deep breath. The fire still raged, snapping over my arms, past my elbows, and curling over my shoulders.

Another breath. I had to pull it all back. But the inferno roared through my veins, boiling my blood, stronger than before.

Ice. Frozen. Control. Please, God, just give me some control.

At least I'd had a chance to show her how I felt.

"This is why I lost my best friend, isn't it?" Amiah asked, her voice soft, barely audible over the fiery roar in my head. "And I only got you back because Deaglan took your fire."

"You'll get me back again," I promised her, even though it was a promise I couldn't make.

There was no guarantee I'd ever be able to regain control. In fact what little control I had was getting harder and harder to maintain, and there was no guarantee Bane or anyone else would be able to permanently take it away.

"Right now we need my fire," I forced out. "Eventually Deaglan is going to figure out you have one of the keys and come after you. I'm not going to lose another person I love."

I wouldn't let what happened to Dominic happen to Amiah. I'd protect her. I'd give up everything to keep her safe. And that included having a future with her.

"When this is done, if I have to, I'll get rid of my fire to be with you." In a heartbeat without a second thought. "I love you."

HAWK

My heart clenched at Cassius's words. I knew he loved her, knew she loved him, knew they'd eventually have a committed relationship. They were both angels. It made sense.

But just for a moment, when Amiah had told Titus that she and Cassius weren't mates, that they'd just had sex, I'd had hope.

I could keep what I had with her—

Only if Bane or one of the other guys joined us so I wouldn't kill her or starve, but I could keep her.

Then Cassius had said the words I was too afraid to say and her expression turned soft and sad and her desire for him swelled.

She loved him back. She'd wait for him.

Of course she would.

He was willing to give up his magic for her.

When this mess with the Heart was over, it would be over between me and Amiah as well. Cassius didn't strike me as the sharing kind. Most angels weren't. They weren't as possessive as wolves — and by the looks of it dragons — but they tended toward devout monogamy. It was actually a little shocking that Amiah desired multiple partners... although maybe that had something to do with that connection that she formed between us when we had sex.

Regardless, the end had always been inevitable for us.

I knew that.

I'd just hoped I'd have more time with her.

And while I sort of did, time while we were running for our lives wasn't the kind of time I wanted. I wanted normal time, date time, living together time, just being together time without the fear of death. I wanted to have the time to help her explore her desires, to figure out who she was and what she liked.

And above all, I wanted to connect with her again and again. The very thing I told her I'd never be able to do.

I wasn't sure I'd be able to go back to just being a body. Now that I'd had a lover who saw me, desired me and not just my magic, and connected with my soul, the idea of sex for survival wasn't enough. The idea of sex with anyone else made my pulse race.

Which was crazy.

I was crazy.

Because I was an incubus in love.

Fuck.

"Can you hold your fire back long enough for me to heal you?" she asked, her eyes filled with worry for Cassius.

And rightly so. His aura was a complete mess now. Last time it had looked this way, he'd been furious and terrified because Amiah had risked her life. The situation now wasn't nearly as emotionally heightened but his aura raged like it had before, angry and red and barely under control. Whatever was broken inside him had gotten worse, and I didn't know if it was because Deaglan had pulled out his fire during the fight, or because Cassius had let his emotions go to make love to Amiah and couldn't rebuild the wall that maintained what little control he'd had before.

Except I wouldn't be able to tell the exact cause without using my magic to find what was wrong, and giving him even a hint of my magic right now was a terrible idea.

"Let's fly back to the aerie," he said through gritted teeth. "Maybe by then I'll have enough control to let you touch me."

Amiah's eyes narrowed. She didn't like that suggestion. I wonder if she felt guilty for having sex with him while he was injured or if it was just her nature compelling her to heal him before she'd fully recovered.

"If you haven't gotten it under control by then, I'm still healing you."

"You'll burn yourself," Titus growled, grabbing her clothes by the cave wall, frowning at them, but handing them over to her anyway.

"I can do it without touching him now." She pulled on pants that still looked wet and slid her gaze to Bane then to Titus. "I can do it to any of you. I think I might be able to do it to anyone. I just haven't had an opportunity to figure that out."

Her gaze landed on me and my heart did a crazy little jump in my chest.

"You need more than what Titus and I generated with our kissing."

Yes. I get to be with her again—

Unless she picks one of the others.

Which made me irrationally angry and sad.

I was so completely fucked.

Incubi didn't get jealous.

I forced a wicked smile and let my gaze slide to her still naked breasts. "Are you making an offer?"

"Back at the aerie," Cassius snapped, his body rigid with trying to keep his fire inside him — along with a huge dose of sexual frustration.

Of course, if I couldn't even touch Amiah, I think I'd lose my mind too.

Titus marched out of the cave, shifted, and violently swiped his tail, sending trees crashing to the ground and making an area big enough for him to take off.

Amiah shoved her feet into her boots and pulled on her still-wet shirt. The material clung to her breasts, the light cotton almost see-through, showing her pert nipples, and a wave of desire washed off of Bane and Cassius, giving a small boost to my magic.

"Swell," Cassius grumbled, the muscles in his jaw flexing, and he released his wings with a burst of angelic light and fire.

"Come here, gorgeous." I held out my hand to her and she took it without hesitation, making my heart sing. "Cuddle with me while we fly. That'll help."

Bane climbed onto Titus's back, held out a hand, and together we helped her up.

The dragon's desire surged as I climbed up behind her, wrapped my arms around her waist, and pulled her tight against my chest. I was going to hate myself for suggesting it, but the smart move would be to push Titus and Amiah together to restore my magic. It wouldn't be as powerful a boost as having sex with her myself, but it would be more helpful given our current situation.

Her desire when they'd kissed said she wanted him as much as he wanted her, and he desperately needed to release my magic from his system. His desire was getting painful. The catch would be convincing him to control his possessive nature, because I didn't want to give her up, and neither, I was sure, did Bane — at least for the moment. Although in the end, it would just be her and Cassius.

Titus's body bunched beneath us. He swept his wings down in a powerful stroke and leaped into the air, then flapped his wings to gain altitude, flying away from the large, almost healthy island where we'd found Amiah and Cassius and back into the stomach-churning shattered limbo of the Autumn Court.

I was going to be so glad when we finally got out of this nightmare world. And while it was night and everyone else with their night vision only saw dark shadowy islands suspended in the Autumn Court's nothingness, I saw writhing magic, sharp and angry, and ominous and sickly. It wrapped around islands, drawn in and pushed away by unnatural gravities, and surged like visible wind currents all around us.

"So," Cassius said as he flew in close to Titus, closer than before, now that he was no longer restricted to keeping Amiah and Titus apart. His aura seethed and smoke billowed behind him, but he was managing to keep his flames inside him. "Deaglan has a key."

"Actually Noaldar, my mother's man, has it," Bane corrected.

"I'm not so sure he's your mother's man," I said. Yes, that high fae, Noaldar, had sat beside the Winter Queen in the throne room, but the last time I'd seen him he hadn't been wearing the same clothes as the Winter Queen's other men and had tried to kill Amiah. "He was the man I saw with your sister, the one who'd tried to stab Amiah with that poisoned knife. From the flavor of their desire, I'm pretty sure they're in love."

Although the queen's werepanther had also been involved in the attack. He'd still been wearing the queen's colors, but I didn't want to assume bumping into Amiah had just been an accident.

I shuddered at the thought of them actually succeeding. That poison had been so powerful it would have killed her in seconds. And from the acid that had burned through my veins, that death would have been agonizing. The only reason I was still alive was because Amiah had sacrificed all of her magic and her body to save me.

I slipped a hand under her shirt, needing to be closer, to feel her aura and her desire sliding through me. I could have lost her.

As if sensing my need for her, she turned and captured my lips in a tender kiss filled with gentle yearning, and my hand instinctually slid up to her breast, deepening that yearning and turning it sultry.

She sighed softly and let me take control of the kiss for a moment before pulling away.

"Don't stop on my account," Bane said, his desire pouring off of him in a thick wave and sinking into me. "I don't think I'll ever get tired of watching you two."

"Can we not talk about sex?" Cassius asked, fire rolling down his wings and falling toward a small sideways island and igniting the two dead trees on it. His desire was almost as strong as Bane's but for different reasons. He wanted Amiah. And while Bane wanted Amiah too, he also got off on watching someone else be with her.

"Fine." Bane dragged his attention away from me and Amiah, and I gently, subtly kneaded her breast, carefully building her desire so it wasn't overwhelming and she wasn't going to want to have sex while on Titus's back, but still enough to help restore some of what I'd lost in the fight.

"So Noaldar is banging my sister," Bane said.

"Really, Bane?" Cassius growled. "It's hard enough already."

"Shit. Sorry." Bane gave him an apologetic smile. "So if Noaldar isn't really my mother's man, then he may not tell her about getting the key. He might want to get the Heart for Padraigin."

Can Noaldar make ice constructs? Titus asked in my head.

"He is a sorcerer." The demonic magic in Bane flared, now almost fully consuming his fae essence, and he drew in a sharp breath and tensed, trying to hide his pain from the others. "But it depends on how much he's grown in strength."

"If he can, then maybe he was the one behind the attack at the healing pool," Amiah said, her voice breathy, the only indication that I was turning her on — likely out of respect for Cassius and Titus. "Whoever that was had been after the Heart as well. But why give it to Padraigin? Why wouldn't he keep it for himself?"

"He might end up doing that when he realizes just how powerful it is," Bane said. "But if he's in love with Padraigin and the Winter Court doesn't respond to her, then having the Heart will give her enough power to control the court by force and take the throne. And whoever is queen, has the queen's harem."

"So you're saying if I ended up as Queen of the Winter Court, I'd end up with all those guys?" Amiah asked. "Even if I was your wife?"

"Yep," Bane said.

And then I'd eat them, Titus said.

"Jeez man," Bane said with a chuckle, not in the least bit worried, or making the connection that Titus wanting to eat the queen's harem meant he might also want to eat Amiah's current harem — currently consisting of me and Bane right now.

That would make Amiah cry, Titus said in my head. *And she needs you. I've seen it in her soul.*

You what—? I wasn't sure what to make of his words. A part of me was thrilled that Titus recognized my connection with Amiah, while the rest was confused. And I wasn't going to think too hard about the fact that Titus had responded to a personal thought. It was usually considered rude in the shifter world to eavesdrop on other people's thoughts.

You thought it very loudly. And please, stop seducing her. Wait until we get back to the aerie. All I can smell right now is her arousal and it isn't fun flying with a hard on that you're making harder by the second.

So you won't challenge me for her? I asked, almost afraid to hope, because he wanted her as much as the rest of us, and I had a feeling it wasn't just because he hadn't gotten any in the last five hundred years or because of my magic. *Would you share?*

That's what she asked for. That's what she needs. Titus tilted sideways, making me tighten my grip on Amiah — one hand around her waist the other still on her breast — and soared around an upside-down island.

Her breath grew faster even as she clung to Titus's spine ridge to stay straddling him, and her desire surged, liquid power rushing into my veins, easing the sudden jolt of nausea of no longer being right side up.

"She could just let them go," Bane continued, clearly not hearing the conversation between me and Titus. "Just because they're in her harem doesn't mean they have to stay."

I don't know how to explain it and I don't think she does either, Titus said, *but I've seen it in her soul. It's like she's a dragon, but she isn't, and it isn't just me her soul needs.*

His words whirled through my head.

Her soul needs.

She was an angel and angels, out of all the supers in all the realms, had the ability to create permanent, powerful soul bonds with one or more mates. It was rare. Rumor had it that it only happened every few centuries, but maybe Amiah was one of those rare angels.

"Come on, Titus, tell me you wouldn't eat them," Bane said.

Do you think we're her mates? I asked.

I thought she was mine. Titus huffed, sending smoke pouring out of his nostrils, and dipped below another island, riding a putrid green wave of magic that I knew he couldn't see. *But I'm not the only one in her soul. So I must be wrong.*

Maybe you're not. Maybe we're all hers. God, wouldn't that be perfect? Except that had to be pure fantasy, my desire to keep her. If any of us were her mates, surely she would have branded us by now. She'd known Cassius for a century and they were in love. Surely she would have branded him.

"Your silence is terrifying," Bane said, the muscles in his back bunching with another angry surge of demonic magic.

No I wouldn't eat them, Titus huffed. *Your hand, incubus.*

Right. I was just so stunned that Titus, after clinging to her in the Winter Court and beating the crap out of Bane, would so easily share.

There's nothing easy about it, he growled back.

I slid my hand out from under Amiah's shirt and her desire softened, although her breathing was still a little too fast and shallow.

"So the Winter Queen may or may not have a key," Cassius said, his gaze locked straight ahead, his body almost as tense as Bane's. "And Deaglan has the ability to sense the keys."

"But only when they first become empowered," Bane said. "If he could sense them after they'd been claimed, he would have gone after Amiah in the aerie or in that cave in the Autumn Court."

"So it's even more of a race to get to the keys than it ever was." Amiah let go of Titus to wrap her arms around me and pressed her cheek and chest against my naked chest, the wind rushing around us cooling her already slightly-cool skin even more.

"A race you shouldn't be a part of," Cassius said. "We need to figure out a way for Titus to find the rest of the keys without you."

"And if you did that—" She drew in a heavy breath. "Sebastian would still have a broken back—" Another heavy breath. "And Deaglan would have killed all of you."

Titus hit a seething red stream of magic, lost the air under his wings for a second, dropping us a heart-stopping few feet, and caught his balance.

Cassius's eyes flashed wide and fire poured from his wings as he dipped to rejoin Titus. "What happens in our next fight when we seriously injure Deaglan or one of his men and your magic locks onto them?

You can heal without touching now. Do you honestly think your magic won't just drain you? That'll make you weak and dizzy and a dangerous distraction for all of us."

"I'm with Sparky," Bane said. "When we get back to the aerie, I'll see if I can cast something that will give Titus back the key without killing you."

"Don't you dare," she gasped, shivering.

Titus grunted, but I didn't know if it was in agreement with Cassius or Amiah. He soared around a massive waterfall pouring from one island to the next, and there, ahead of us, was the writhing putrid barrier and our way out of this not-so-fun funhouse.

"I have to agree with Amiah," I said. "You don't know how much power pulling the key out of Amiah will take."

Bane shrugged. "Maybe it'll be easy. Titus just gave it to Amiah, maybe she can just give it back."

Titus grunted again and put on a burst of speed, heading straight to the barrier and then bursting through into the Wilds, but he didn't let up when we were through and kept up the pace, shooting through the night sky over the Wilds' steamy jungle.

"You honestly think taking the key is going to be easy?" I asked, as Amiah's shivering increased and her body temperature grew colder despite the humidity rising from the trees below us. Jeez. We needed to get her out of the wind and her wet clothes. "How far to the aerie?"

"Depends on how Faerie is feeling." Bane tensed and a small ball of magic exploded from his body and was sucked down into the trees below. "And I fucking hope it's feeling generous. I don't have a lot for it to take right now."

"Go quickly," Amiah said as a white ball of magic exploded from her back, drawing a whimper.

Titus beat his wings again, gaining more speed. Except instead of the dragon's mountain on the horizon, it was the opalescent shimmer of another court barrier, and he was headed straight for it.

"Why the hell is Faerie showing us the Summer Court?" Bane asked.

"Go," Amiah gasped, straining to draw a breath, her body frighteningly cold just like when the last key had become empowered.

Oh, shit.

Another key? Already? We hadn't had time to recover from the last one, and Amiah was still with us, still in danger.

"Find a place to land," I said, my voice sharp with panic. "We can't take Amiah with us. Titus land."

But the dragon kept barreling toward the barrier, making my pulse roar through me and my breath quicken. We were weak. We couldn't protect her. We'd barely been able to protect her at full power. If Deaglan realized she had a key and got his hands on her, he wouldn't think twice about killing her to get it.

I could only pray because we'd already been on the move, we'd get there first and would be able to escape before anyone else showed up.

TITUS

I SPED TO THE SUMMER COURT BEFORE AMIAH FROZE OR SUFFOCATED OR whatever it was that happened to her when a key became empowered and we were in physical contact. The key's call clawed at my insides, urging, begging, screaming at me to take it into my dragon body where it belonged.

The guys yelled at me, ordering me to stop, but I couldn't. Not with the compulsion tearing through me. Not for a second. That, and if I let Amiah get off, I'd have to stop and make contact with her again once we were inside the Summer Court.

She was strong. She could handle the pressure and the cold for a little longer. Her breath was labored, but if I concentrated, I could still hear it, and she hadn't pushed Hawk away for being too warm, not yet. We still had time. I could fly fast enough to get to the key before its call overwhelmed her, even if her thoughts were starting to scare me.

I can't be trapped. Not again. Let me out. Please, God. Let me out.

Her desperate mental cries tore at my heart. Whatever the key did to her, it dragged her back into the horror of being a prisoner. She'd been taken. Twice. And by saving me, I'd trapped her with a leash spell, one that still connected her to Seireadan, and now the Winter Court wanted her. She was trapped over and over again and right now her soul saw no way to escape, no hope.

Just hang on, I said in her head and only her head.

I will. Get us... to that... key. Don't... listen to them. Even her mental voice was gasping, fighting for air.

"Titus, slow down," Seireadan yelled. "Her lips are turning blue. Let Cassius take her."

You think he can carry her? He couldn't even look at her without fire pouring from his wings, and taking the time to figure out if he could hold her was time that Deaglan could be getting the key, and I couldn't let him get even one.

Not to mention if I managed to fight the key's compulsion and stopped, I might end up pounding the shit out of Cassius instead of handing Amiah over.

My beast was still raging that he'd stopped us from mating. It didn't matter that he'd been right and it was best to wait until we were back at the aerie and Amiah could clean up and get something to eat. We weren't going back to the aerie and my beast had finally agreed to not kill any of the others if she slept with me and then them again.

She needed them, not just me, and my beast wanted what was best for my mate.

And it didn't matter how many times I tried to tell it she wasn't mine. It wouldn't listen.

I'd been relieved when she'd made the point of saying she and Cassius had just had sex because it had taken everything I had to go to her instead of attacking Cassius and stay with her even with her soul calming mine. If they were mates, my beast would challenge him. My beast still wanted to challenge him.

She was my mate, who just so happened to need sex from the others.

Unless, of course, Hawk's theory was correct and she was all of our mates.

I crashed through the Summer Court's barrier, its magic clinging to my scales as I passed through, and beat my wings, flying as fast as I could over the vast, lush — manicured within an inch of its life — summer garden that surrounded the court's royal villa. The key's compulsion urged me on — *go go, claim me, bring me home* — even though I had a chance to land and let Amiah off. It was so close. I knew exactly where it was.

Except Amiah's thoughts were getting desperate and her shivering violent, and Seireadan had turned around and taken her from Hawk.

Please, let me go. Please, she sobbed, and I couldn't tell if her sobbing was just in her thoughts or not.

Hang in there.

Please. I want out. I have to get out. I can't stay this way.

"For fuck's sake, Titus. Stop," Seireadan yelled, his thoughts flooding me. *She's dying. She can't breathe. I have to save her, sever her connection with the key.*

Almost there, I snarled in his head and plunged down a steep slope of mixed grasses and shrubs, groomed to look like swirling clouds, and landed at the mouth of the Summer Court's luminous cave garden, its entrance too small for me to enter in my dragon form.

It took everything I had to hold myself steady as Seireadan pulled Amiah from my back and Hawk hopped down.

The key's call grew stronger by the second and the moment they were off, I leaped toward the fae-sized opening, shifting between one stride to the next into my human form before my dragon form slammed into the intricately carved pillars on either side of the entrance. It didn't matter that I was naked. I barely felt the flagstone path leading into the cavern under my bare feet. I had to get the key.

Now now now.

"Titus, wait," Cassius called. "Be smart about this. We don't know if Deaglan or Noaldar is already here."

"All the more reason to hurry." Even if I wanted, I couldn't resist the compulsion. It didn't matter that Cassius was right, that it was foolish to run headlong into the cavern. I couldn't stop. Not with the key screaming for me to get it and not with Amiah's desperate begging to be free still gasping in my mind even though I didn't have telepathy in human form.

"Titus." Cassius snapped a fire whip around my biceps and jerked me off balance.

"What the hell," Hawk said. "You'll burn him."

"My fire doesn't burn him, he's a fire dragon," Cassius replied and stormed toward me. "Take a breath. Running headlong puts Amiah in danger."

At the mention of her name, my gaze instantly jumped to her. She huddled against Seireadan, drawing in strained, shallow breaths, shivering so hard she couldn't keep her balance.

I'd done that. I'd hurt her.

She met my gaze, the glow in her eyes barely brighter than the glow from her body, and captured my soul, like she always did.

Mine.

Not. Just. Mine.

Still makes her mine.

"We go in cautiously," she said.

Cassius glared at her. "You're not going anywhere."

"And you'd leave me out here to be found by Deaglan or Noaldar?" His fire snapped and black smoke billowed around him.

"Even if one of you stays, neither of you are well enough to face either man alone. It'd just end up with the two of us captured or dead." Her angel glow flared and her shivering increased. "And neither is an acceptable option."

Her words made my beast heave inside me, not just because it hated either option, but because both of us knew she'd pick death over capture again.

"God damn it." Cassius shot a blast of fire into the ground. "You hide the moment there's trouble."

He jerked his attention to the garden's entrance and heaved his wings back inside his body. "Anyone know what this place is?"

"The Summer Court's luminous cave garden," Seireadan said, lifting her into his arms and cradling her against his chest.

Something I needed to do.

Except I also had to get the key. Now.

"Sounds pretentious." Hawk rolled his eyes then closed them.

"Everything about the Summer Court is," I snapped.

Go now. Claim me. Bring me home.

I ground my teeth against the compulsion. "Unless you can fly, and you're smaller than a dragon, this is the only way in or out."

Now. Go now. Come on.

Cassius stepped past the pillars and peered down the long tunnel leading to the garden. "Can you smell anyone's scent?"

"I don't smell anyone who's been here since the key became empowered," I replied, "and nothing that smells like Deaglan, shadow fae, or Noaldar."

"I can't sense anyone inside, either," Hawk said. "Although that could mean they're shielded or having little to no sexual desire at the moment."

"It's a single passage in, and while there might be a few places to hide, it's mostly one big cavern with glowing rocks and moss," Seireadan added.

"Okay. Eyes open everyone." Cassius squared his shoulders. "Titus, you've got the lead. Stay cautious."

I jerked forward before I fully realized what I was doing, then forced myself to pay attention to my surroundings. Cassius was right. Running headlong put Amiah in danger.

The walls and ceiling of the passage into the luminous cave garden were carved with intricate swirls that looked like flowers and clouds. It was similar to the carving in the Winter Court, although softer, swirlier. Hints of luminescent moss and moonstones glowed throughout the decoration, providing just enough light for me with my night vision to see where I was going.

Ahead, the glow grew brighter, and it took everything I had not to race to the end.

Claim me. Bring me home. Now. Now.

I reached the threshold between passage and cavern and dug my claws into the wall beside me to stop and look for danger. Except my attention jerked to the blazing blue pinprick of light at the back of the cavern on the wide top shelf of three shallow rocky shelves, hovering a few feet off the uneven ground.

Seireadan drew up behind me and Amiah gasped, making my heart clench. I wished I could have taken her here just to show it to her.

The place was stunning, with its numerous stalagmites and stalactites softly glowing in yellows, blues, and pinks, and the patches of green and blue mosses that curled over the stones near the two fae-sized shafts that let light into the top half of the cavern during the daytime. In the center, surrounded by a mesmerizing pattern of softly glowing moonstones, was the cavern's luminescent pool, a deep pool with shimmering specks of glowing algae suspended in its clear water.

"Hawk? Bane?" Cassius asked.

Just get me. Bring me home.

I clenched my teeth. I could wait a few more seconds.

"I think we got here first," Hawk said. "I also don't sense any magical traps, just the power of the key."

"Good." Cassius stepped into the cavern proper and released his wings with a fiery burst. "Titus, get that key and let's get out of here."

Finally. I lunged forward, shifting with the movement and dove for the key. It wasn't practical to be in my dragon form, there were too many rocky protrusions barring the way, but there was enough space to get over the pond.

I jerked sideways to fly between two stalactites too close together for my wingspan, straightened and caught the air over the pond, and shifted, midflight, to land on the other side.

The key wrenched on my soul.

Bring me home. Bring me home.

I ran to it, easily leaped up the rocky shelves — they weren't even as tall as me — and lunged, my hand outstretched to grab the key.

AMIAH

TITUS REACHED FOR THE KEY, HIS HAND INCHES FROM ITS BLAZING LIGHT, and a thick strand of shadow shot out from the cluster of stalagmites behind him. It seized his wrist and slammed him against the ground.

I gasped, barely able to draw that surprised breath against the frozen crushing pressure in my chest.

"I don't think so," Deaglan said, oozing out of the same shadow his strand had come from.

"Are you fucking kidding me?" Hawk groaned, and he bolted out of the cave entrance toward Titus.

Cassius shot a ball of fire across the cavern and burned through the shadow holding Titus, but Deaglan quickly reformed it, recaptured Titus, and tossed him off the rocky shelves, sending him tumbling over the rough ground to the edge of the pool.

"How could you possibly have gotten your fire back so soon?" He demanded as Cassius shot another fireball at him, making him jerk away from the key.

Except Cassius hadn't gotten all of his fire back. If he had, he would have dropped a pillar of fire on Deaglan. The fact that he used a fireball, said he wasn't at full strength and was trying to be smart about how he used his magic.

"Kill them," Deaglan commanded and the shadows around Cassius and Hawk surged. Dozens of shadow fae jumped out of the darkness, their skin a mix of white fae glow and undulating shadows, their life forces dark and thick and suddenly there, thrumming against my senses.

Then my senses jerked my attention up. There were three more life forces in a large shadow descending from a hole in the ceiling. A fiery, sour force, a wild primal force, and a barely-there strange life and death, cold and hot, and filled with pain force. Deaglan's nightmare, a new shifter, and the vampire-demon hybrid.

The shadow deposited them in front of Titus and they immediately lunged into action along with their fellow assassins.

"Fuck," Sebastian hissed, leaning me against the cave wall. "Just stay out of sight."

He stepped into the cavern, the absence of his body heat making me shiver so hard I could barely keep standing, dropped to his knees, and pressed both hands to his chest. Brilliant white light flooded the space, blinding me, and from the grunts, gasps, and cries, everyone else as well.

"Take that, asshole," Sebastian yelled.

"Only makes you easier to kill, Seireadan," Deaglan spat back.

"Hawk, protect Bane and Amiah," Cassius called out and the sound of another fireball exploded against the rocks.

I cracked open one eye, making it water, but forced myself to keep it open. Yes, I didn't need to see to fight, but I still needed to avoid being attacked and distracting the guys, which meant I needed to be able to see the danger coming.

Light filled the entire cavern, reaching into every crack and stretching all the way behind me to the garden's entrance not giving the shadow fae any shadows to hop between.

Sebastian still knelt, his eyes squeezed tight, his complexion gray, and his breath short and shallow. He needed to keep channeling magic to maintain the light spell and he wasn't going to last very long.

Hawk fought with three shadow fae, somehow already getting a knife from one of them, and three more fae rushed toward Sebastian. Titus also fought with a swarm of shadow fae, the nightmare, and the new shifter — although I couldn't tell what animal the woman shifted into — and was unable to get closer to the key, while Cassius flew across the pond flecked with light, and snagged Deaglan's wrist with a fire whip.

Deaglan sliced Cassius's whip with a shadow blade and lunged for the key.

But the air beside him burst into a shimmering liquid mirror and Noaldar leaped through and grabbed the key.

The brilliant blue light flared and sank into his skin and the frozen pressure in my chest vanished.

I gasped in a desperate deep breath even as my chill shifted into a cold dread in my gut.

Noaldar now had two keys.

I didn't know if he knew I had one or not, but I didn't want to bet he wouldn't be able to find out.

Noaldar flashed Deaglan a victorious sneer and jumped back into the shimmer, slamming into something and tumbling onto his rear instead of going through the portal.

Deaglan's shadows seized him and wrenched him into the air, his arms and legs stretched taut. "You really thought I wouldn't cast a one-way portal lock?"

My magic flared in my chest, jerking my attention to Titus and locking on a shadow fae gravely injured among other dead shadow fae lay in a growing pool of blood around Titus.

The fae gasped and died before my power forced me forward, but it continued to snap and heave inside me as my guys battled Deaglan's men.

I clenched my teeth and clung to the wall.

I will not let my magic run free or enter the fight. I'll keep my magic. I'll stay safe. Even if it means suffering backlash. I won't endanger my guys.

"You really think I'll let you have his keys?" Cassius said, and I wrenched my attention back to him.

He landed on the far end of the shelf, pulled his wings in, and sliced through the shadows holding Noaldar.

The winter court fae hit the ground and scrambled to the edge of the shelf behind him, but Deaglan's shadows exploded from his body, capturing Noaldar while also slamming into Cassius, just like they had when Deaglan had taken his fire.

My heart skipped a beat. We hadn't had time to protect Cassius from this attack. It hadn't even come up, and Cassius had to have known if he confronted Deaglan straight on, the Shadow King would take his fire again. He was smarter than that. He had to have a plan. Something that would stop Deaglan.

"Stop interrupting me," Deaglan screamed, and his shadows surged under Cassius's skin, extinguishing the flames roaring over his body.

Then fire and shadows erupted from his chest, drawing a heart-wrenching cry of pain and he dropped to his knees, his chest heaving, once again not a hint of fire or even smoke curling from his skin.

I jerked forward, my heart pounding, not because my magic had locked onto Cassius, but because he was suffering.

Except I couldn't help him. The best I could do was stay put and remain unnoticed.

Just stay put.

Deaglan sneered, turned his back on Cassius, and wrenched Noaldar within arm's reach.

"Those don't belong to you," Deaglan said and he grabbed Noaldar's jaw and forced the man's mouth open.

Noaldar heaved against Deaglan's grip and more shadows wrapped around the winter fae's neck, choking him. His eyes bulged and his fae glow flared bright even in the brightly lit cavern. The glow rolled up his body and focused into a blazing blue stream that poured out of his mouth along with a desperate scream.

Deaglan's sneer deepened and Noaldar wrenched and thrashed against the shadows, his breath wild gasps, his eyes filled with terror. His life force snapped against my senses with a terrifying frenzy, and Deaglan sucked it in.

My magic surged and locked onto Noaldar, my power bursting into my palms and racing up my forearms. I could feel Deaglan not just sucking out the magic of the keys, but the Faerie magic inside Noaldar that made him high fae *and* his life force. All of it. And without a doubt, Deaglan wasn't going to stop until he had every last drop of magic in Noaldar, killing him.

My magic wrenched me forward and I fought to stay where I was. More light than there should have been, given how low my power was, blazed from my hands. Everything within me screamed to save him, heal his rapidly draining life force. And if I didn't go to him, my power would connect with him anyway. There wasn't even a risk of suffering a terrible backlash for refusing. I couldn't refuse. I had no choice. I *had* to save him.

Except I didn't know how to heal his life force. I healed bodies. My magic knitted bone and muscle and flesh together. It didn't heal magic and it certainly couldn't restore someone's life force.

Noaldar gasped, a final desperate, weak breath, and the last drop of his life force swept out of him, leaving a gray shell without any hint of fae glow hanging in Deaglan's shadows.

It had only taken a few rapid pounds of my heart. One second

Noaldar was alive and my power was howling through me, the next he was dead and I was released.

Then Cassius, without making a sound, leaped at Deaglan, a rock clenched in his hands aimed at the Shadow King's head. So that was the plan. Get close and attack when the Shadow King least expected it. But Deaglan wrenched around to face him as if he was able to sense Cassius was attacking, and a massive shadow spear formed beside him.

Cassius hit first, the rock smashing against Deaglan's temple, but the shadow spear still lurched forward even as Deaglan dropped to his hands and knees. The spear missed Cassius's heart but still sliced a deep laceration into his side.

"Cassius." I could heal that.

I had to heal that.

It was deep and would kill him without medical attention, but I had enough magic within me to stop the bleeding. *If* I could get my hands on him in time.

I bolted out of hiding and raced toward him.

"Amiah, get back," Hawk yelled at me.

"He doesn't have fire. He can't cauterize the wound."

An assassin grabbed for me and Hawk tackled him to the ground.

"Amiah. Stop," Hawk screamed, his voice sharp with panic.

More assassins broke off their fight with Hawk and Titus and rushed toward me, but I wasn't going to lose Cassius. Not when I could save him. "Clear the way for me."

Cassius pressed his hands against the wound doing nothing to slow the bleeding and sagged to his knees.

I could reach him. I had to reach him.

I loved him and he loved me. We'd finally admitted the truth to ourselves and each other, and even if my feelings were still complicated, my desire for the other still strong, I knew in the depth of my soul that I was in love with Cassius.

And, God damn it, we were going to figure that out. We were getting that lifetime of being together that I'd dreamed of when we'd had sex.

Someone screamed, but I kept my focus on Cassius.

Deaglan groaned. Blood dripped from his temple where Cassius had struck him, splattering the rocky ground between his hands, and he swayed as if he were on the verge of passing out.

"Just hold on," I yelled to Cassius and his attention jerked up to me, his bright blue eyes, now fully visible because his power was gone, capturing my soul.

"What are you doing?" he yelled at me. "Get back."

"I'm saving your life, you idiot."

"Get back!" He staggered to his feet and one of Deaglan's assassins leaped onto the shelf behind him and yanked his knife across Cassius's throat.

Everything within me froze.

My body, mind, and soul froze then lurched into a desperate, soul-rending scream.

I couldn't stop screaming.

My soul was screaming.

Cassius's eyes flashed wide and he grabbed his neck, but arterial blood sprayed between his fingers, hitting Deaglan in the face.

"About fucking time," the Shadow King snarled.

My power exploded within me, making me stumble and fall to my knees at the edge of the pool. It locked onto Cassius and slammed into him without me even thinking about it. He collapsed on the ground and I scrambled to my feet, heaved my magic back inside my body, and started running again. But I was only halfway around the pool.

"Cassius!" I couldn't let him die. I'd just realized I loved him. We were supposed to have a lifetime together.

God, I wasn't going to get to him in time. I had to release my magic and heal him from afar. It was the only way.

Except I didn't have a lot of power to begin with. I wasn't sure I had enough to heal him while touching him. I certainly didn't have enough power to heal him from a distance. I had to hold it in, fight the compulsion raging through me long enough to get to him. It was his best chance.

I tried to push power into my back to release my wings, but my magic wouldn't move out of my hands and forearms. I was supposed to send it out, use it on others, use it on Cassius, and I couldn't even draw the miniscule amount needed to fly.

God damn it. Why did it have to do that? If I could fly, I could get to him faster. Save him.

Yes, save him.

My soul screamed at me to save him.

I pumped my arms, trying to run faster, my lungs and muscles burning with the effort.

Hawk screamed my name and out of the corner of my eye, I saw a shadow fae diving for me.

I jerked out of the way. I couldn't get caught. Cassius would die if I even slowed down for a second, and maybe, just maybe if I could get to him, I'd have enough magic to stabilize him.

Please let it be enough. It had to be enough. I had to save him.

My power burned so hot it felt as if my hands were on fire and the promise of an excruciating backlash squeezed in my chest making it harder to breathe.

I couldn't lose him.

Please. Please. I can't.

His fiery life force heaved and snapped against my senses, desperate to stay lit, but was growing weaker by the second.

"Amiah, stop, please," Titus roared.

But I couldn't stop. I had to save Cassius. I didn't know what I'd do without him. He was my best friend, my rock. I'd just gotten him back.

Save him.

My toe hit a ridge in the uneven floor and I fell, tumbling face first onto the stone. I was still fifty feet away from Cassius, and he lay in a massive pool of blood, his eyes glassy with death.

I could barely feel his life force.

I was going to lose him, and I couldn't lose him. I just couldn't.

A horrible frozen stone formed in my gut. I wasn't going to have enough power even if I reached him in time.

There had to be a way to get more power. I needed more power, more life.

My senses snapped to the shadow assassin who'd slit Cassius's throat, now rushing toward me. His life writhed with a similar darkness as Deaglan's, strong and sure. It slid across my senses, taunting me. Everyone's life force did.

I could feel all of them, the sense stronger than it had ever been before. Every one of Deaglan's assassins, his nightmare, his new shifter — a bear — his hybrid, and Deaglan himself. He had the most life force out of everyone because he had a life that didn't belong to him, and while I could feel the keys inside him as well, I didn't immediately connect with them and didn't have the time to figure out if I could.

My magic latched onto Noaldar's life force inside Deaglan, and the Shadow King gasped. He dragged his head up and searched the cavern to figure out who was attacking him. Then his dark gaze zeroed in on me and he sent a flurry of shadows at me, but I didn't care. I just needed more power to save Cassius.

I heaved on Noaldar's life force and Deaglan's shadows burst apart, his magic stuttering at the sudden withdrawal of power, and Noaldar's life poured into me and flew back out into Cassius.

Cassius's life force sparked, a dying flame given a speck of fuel to stay alive.

It was working. I could save him. I just needed more.

I grabbed Deaglan's life force. His expression filled with terror and a blast of fae magic ripped through my connection to him and created a wall blocking me from reconnecting with him. The wall was weak, riddled with fissures that I might be able to get through, but no—

No time.

There were other life forces that were easier to connect with. I could feel them, feel every living thing in the cavern, my guys, Deaglan's men, the mice and rats and bugs hiding in small tunnels away from the light, even the moss growing on the glowing stalactites and stalagmites and the algae in the pond.

All of it thrummed against my senses, mine to take and use.

Except the moss, algae, bugs, and rodents didn't have a strong enough life force, and the cost for using the men's was the likelihood that I draw too much and kill them.

And the moment I realized that, I knew I'd pay any price to save Cassius.

Even if it meant staining my soul by killing someone.

And while these men were trying to kill us, and obeyed a man who'd held Titus, his friend, captive for five hundred years, and who wanted Faerie's Heart for his own gain, that didn't lessen the fact that I was going to kill them.

To save Cassius.

God, please.

I pushed my magic into all of Deaglan's men and seized their life forces. The power heaved in my grip and my magic clenched tighter.

I would save Cassius. I would sacrifice my soul for him.

I just needed more power.

I wrenched at the life forces, and every man that I could see collapsed and started screaming.

I didn't care.

I had to save Cassius.

Their life poured into me, burning through my veins and making my skin blaze with power, and streamed into Cassius, making his life force flicker stronger.

"I don't think so, little angel," Deaglan screamed, his eyes wild with anger and fear.

A wall slammed around the hybrid, cutting me off from him.

Fine. I didn't need him. His life force was strange and weak anyway. I still had the others.

But then another wall and another burst around the men and my power weakened and so did Cassius's life force.

Deaglan created shadow wings and flew up to the ledge near the hole in the ceiling where his nightmare and hybrid had come from.

"Kill the angel and get me her key," he yelled and those assassins who were no longer on the ground screaming picked up their weapons, and rushed toward me.

Titus and Hawk jumped into action to protect me, and I fought to keep a connection with the few men I was still connected to. But another wall went up and another.

I was losing all my power, and I hadn't saved Cassius. Healing from afar took an enormous amount of magic, especially something as serious as a slit throat and massive blood loss. I had to focus, and I couldn't do that and run at the same time.

I staggered to a stop about twenty feet from the shelves where Cassius lay, strengthened my hold on the life forces I was still connected to, and rammed my magic through the barriers of the half dozen of Deaglan's men who were closest to me.

Please let this work. Please let this save him.

With a scream, I wrenched on their life forces, drawing a horrific wail that echoed through the cavern before going suddenly deathly silent. Their life roared into my body and swept to my hands as another life force jerked close behind me.

A strange cold, burning, pain-filled life force, life and death at the same time. Deaglan's hybrid.

I wrenched around to see how close he was, and he slid his katana into my heart.

My mind stuttered unable to comprehend what had just happened.

Then agonizing pain exploded in my chest and he wrenched his blade free.

My connection with Cassius shattered and the life forces I'd gathered slammed into my chest, but it was too much, I couldn't control it, couldn't focus it to save myself. Agony roared around my heart, a ferocious fire, consuming me from the inside out. It swelled through my whole body before gathering, a searing inferno in my left hip, and erupted into a brilliant burning golden blaze.

My soul locked onto the hybrid's soul and horror stole my breath.

No, please, God, no.

His eyes widened and his hellfire burst into wild flames.

"What did you do?" he asked in that soft, terrifying, barely audible voice of his.

I'd branded him.

Oh, God.

He'd forced me to lose control of the power I needed to save Cassius and the angelic mating brand that I thought was gone, that I'd damaged my soul to get rid of, had awakened.

I was soul bonded to Deaglan's demon-vampire hybrid.

And I could no longer feel Cassius's life force.

FATED DESPAIR

ANGEL'S FATE, BOOK 4

SEBASTIAN

DEAGLAN'S DEMON-VAMPIRE HYBRID SLID HIS KATANA INTO AMIAH'S CHEST and my world froze, the horrific moment burned into my mind.

It happened so quickly. One moment she was desperately trying to save Cassius by channeling an enormous amount of power stolen from the men around us — since her own reservoir had been mostly depleted — and the next, the hybrid had stabbed her.

I stumbled, caught my balance, and pushed myself to run faster and reach her. I couldn't stop. I had to get to her. I'd been running since Cassius's throat had been slit and she'd started screaming, a soul-deep desperate wail.

Her eyes widened with surprise at the blade in her chest, her mouth open on a gasp, then the hybrid yanked his blade out and her impossible power exploded into a blazing golden light. It overwhelmed her unnatural full-body fae glow and blazed from her eyes with the unmistakable magic of an angelic mating brand.

For a second, I hoped that somehow, even though the brand was newly formed and she wasn't supposed to be able to, she'd be able to draw some of the life force from her mate and it would save her.

I didn't care which one of us she bonded with, so long as she survived. I didn't even care if it was me.

But then she cried out and the golden light blazed in the hybrid's eyes.

Oh, fuck.

He was her mate?

How the fuck was he her mate?

"What did you do?" the hybrid gasped, his expression as stunned as hers.

The brand's magic swelled. The leash spell binding me and Amiah shattered in my chest making me stumble, and another, more powerful spell exploded between the hybrid and Deaglan.

Just like the last time I'd seen a vampire get branded, the power of the forming angelic mating brand severed any other bonds that weren't soul bonds between the two recipients.

Guess the hybrid wasn't a part of Deaglan's team of his own free will. Which was good, because if he was well and truly Deaglan's man, we were fucked.

Deaglan snarled, his expression a mix of rage and shock, and flew out of the hole in the roof. His men, those who were still alive, ran screaming from the cavern.

I dropped my light spell, throwing the Summer Court's luminous cave garden into deep shadows. The glow from the luminescent rocks and moss and algae was weak in comparison to the light I'd summoned to prevent Deaglan's shadow fae assassins from jumping between shadows, but I kept running, trusting my vision to quickly grow accustomed to the darkness.

I knew agony burned through me. It had for the entire fight with Deaglan and his men because I'd had to maintain the light spell, but I couldn't feel anything. All of me — all of my senses, my thoughts, my soul — was focused on Amiah, her hands pressed to her chest, her blood rushing between her fingers and soaking into her beige cotton shirt, and her eyes wide with horror.

It didn't matter that her soul was now bonded to the hybrid. I had to get to her.

Hawk screamed and bolted toward her, and Titus was close at his heels.

She crumpled to the ground, and the hybrid continued to stare at her, his expression still shocked, her blood dripping from his katana.

"What did you do?" he asked again, as if he couldn't get his mind to move past their sudden, horrifying soul bond.

Titus snarled and swiped at him with his claws and my heart leaped into my throat.

"Don't kill him," I yelled. "She's branded him. They're soul bonded. You kill him, you kill her."

Titus's golden gaze jerked to me, then he closed his hand at the last second and slammed his fist into the hybrid's face instead of ripping out his throat.

The hybrid didn't even defend himself. I wasn't even sure if he was aware Titus was there. He never looked away from Amiah until Titus's punch knocked him down, and, even clearly dazed from the blow, he strained to keep his eyes on her as the big dragon pinned him to the ground, the hybrid's body under Titus's knees and the hybrid's head captured under a big hand.

Amiah gasped, the pool of blood shockingly large for the few seconds she'd been down. She needed to heal herself. Why wasn't she healing herself?

Right. Fuck. Cassius. She'd been channeling all her magic and the magic she'd torn from Deaglan's men into Cassius.

Hawk dropped to his knees beside her and cupped her face in his hands, forcing her to look at him, although I was too far away to actually tell if she was able to focus on him.

"Come on, Amiah. Heal yourself. You've got a bit of power left. Use it. Please use it," he begged. "Please heal yourself."

I barreled past them and scrambled up the three shallow jagged shelves at the back of the cavern where the key to unlocking Faerie's Heart had become empowered, and where Cassius was bleeding out—

Please let him still be alive. God, please. Don't do that to her.

I dropped to my knees beside Cassius, not caring that I was in a pool of his blood or that the agony in my body was making me shake, and pressed my hands over his heart. I just needed to sense a glimmer of magic inside him. That's all I needed to keep him alive.

I couldn't heal him. But I could cast a hibernation spell and freeze him in time until Amiah could save his life.

But only if he was still alive.

And only if I could survive channeling that kind of magic.

There. A small, barely lit glimmer of power in his heart. It would take Amiah a massive amount of magic just to bring him back. She'd need to be fully recovered to save him, but she could save him.

I'd make sure of that.

So long as I didn't kill myself.

"Amiah, please!" Hawk cried, his voice breaking with desperation, making my heart clench.

I didn't know how he'd managed to fall in love with her so quickly. They barely knew each other. But the impossible had happened and Hawk's heart belonged to Amiah. And no one knew if an incubus who'd lost his lover could remain sane. Being in love was thought to be genetically impossible and on those extremely rare occasions when it did happen, it was considered a mental disorder.

What I did know from his heartbreaking pleas was that if she didn't save herself, he'd let himself starve to death. Yes, he'd known she and Cassius were going to end up in a traditional angelic monogamous relationship, but she'd still be alive. She'd be happy and have what she desired. That might have been enough for him to keep on living.

But her death was going to break him and he was one of the strongest people I knew.

"Come on, Amiah. Please."

Convince her. Please, God, convince her to live.

Because I could save Cassius. I had to save him. I just needed to focus.

I shut Hawk out. I shut everything out, all the pain, the fear, and the anger, and reached for my connection with Faerie's primal magic.

The demonic magic that wasn't supposed to be inside me, that I couldn't get out, blazed the strongest it ever had, and scorched through my magical channels and veins, setting every nerve on fire.

Everything within me begged me to stop, and yet my soul begged me to keep going.

I was in love with Amiah, too.

It was crazy. I swore I'd never fall in love again, thought she was frustrating and annoying and uptight—

Until she hadn't been anymore. Until she'd let down her walls and let me in, and God, I wanted to keep what we had. Her, me, and Hawk. Hell, if Titus and Cassius wanted to join in, that would be great too, but all of it would be gone if Cassius died.

His death would shatter her and I didn't know if the rest of us would be enough to get her through that, especially with her unwanted angelic mating brand permanently bonding her with someone who'd tried to kill her at least once and who she knew nothing about.

God, she'd done everything, had a chunk ripped out of her soul to get rid of it, and it had still formed.

Maybe it wasn't a real bond. Maybe all the power she'd been impossibly channeling had bonded her to the hybrid when he'd stabbed her and, once I'd regained my full power — *if* I ever regain my power — I'd be able to break it for her.

I captured the small thread of fae magic that should have been a torrent coming through my connection and spun it into the hibernation spell, twisting my intention over and over again, creating the spell from scratch because I didn't have it tattooed on my body.

It needed to be strong. It needed to hold without me having to keep pushing power into it, because after this, I was summoning the man who'd failed Amiah and owed her for a job he apparently hadn't done, and casting that would likely be one spell too many.

Already the fire of uncontrolled magic burned in my chest, my will weakened from constantly fighting the demonic magic and having to keep casting spells day after day.

I strained to stay in control.

Just a little more. I could do this. I could survive this. I could have my Amiah, the Amiah who wasn't heartbroken over the death of a man she loved, the one who wanted to explore her desires, and who somehow magically connected with me during sex.

My willpower stuttered and the weak thread of fae magic stuttered with it, losing shape and burning into my body.

I gritted my teeth and yanked the thread back into the ball that only I, and maybe Hawk because he was a Sensitive, could see. I was almost done.

The spell and my focus.

I just needed a little more.

Another stutter and another flash of fire that threatened to consume me from the inside out.

Almost.

There.

I pushed the last bit of power into the hibernation spell, making it flare to life, and released it in Cassius's chest before my power burned me up. The spell activated and I let go of my magic.

Smoke billowed from my hands and forearms like Cassius with his fire, except I wasn't fireproof like the angel. I sagged forward, gasping, the demonic magic screaming through me. But it hadn't killed me. Thank God.

Just one more spell. That was all I needed to do and she'd be safe... or rather safer.

God, Deaglan knew she had one of the keys to freeing the powerful magic of Faerie's Heart. He'd be coming after her, and I could only pray the others would be able to hide her long enough for her to recover. Because after this, there was no way I'd be able to protect her.

"Hawk, is she stable?" I asked, dragging my attention back to the horrific scene, her laying in a pool of blood, Hawk staring into eyes only partially open, and Titus pinning her newly bonded mate to the ground, his teeth bared.

"She will be," he said, and he pressed his lips to hers.

The pressure of his power, the weight I felt because of my magical sensitivity, swelled and he shoved his magic in Amiah.

Oh, fuck.

He was giving her his life force, something she told him never to do again. Incubi and succubi consumed life force through a person's sexual energy and, unbeknownst to most people, could also give it back.

He could give her enough magic to maybe heal her, in the very least stabilize her, but if he gave too much, he'd kill himself.

And I needed him to help get all of us out of there. Titus had a hold on the hybrid for now, but if he decided to fight back it would be a struggle to contain him and move both Amiah and Cassius. Especially since my next spell could incapacitate me.

Amiah gasped and her fae glow flared, but she didn't open her eyes, and Hawk trembled, the pressure of his power rushing out of him, weakening his essence.

He was going to give her everything.

Of course he was. He was in love with her.

"Hawk, stop." I staggered off the shelves and, with a strength I didn't realize I had left, yanked him away from her.

We both fell back, landing on our butts, and the demonic magic snapped and sliced into me.

"Did I save her?" he gasped before his eyes rolled back, and he collapsed.

My sense of his power flickered and vanished.

Fuck fuck fuck.

He'd given her too much. He needed an infusion of sexual energy or he'd die, and I was God damned not going to let him or anyone die. I crawled to him, pressed my lips to his, and imagined I was kissing

Amiah, since while I found Hawk attractive — everyone in all the realms would find him attractive — he didn't turn me on like a woman did. Like Amiah did.

Except thinking about kissing her made me glance at her and her too-pale skin and her barely-there breaths, and chilled any desire I might have had.

Think of something else. Anything else.

The demonic magic sliced deeper, making my breath short sharp pants.

I struggled to focus. I needed to forget everything and get turned on. Just for the duration of the kiss.

Hell, this would probably turn Amiah on. She'd just love to see this. Me lip-locked with Hawk when I'd been adamant he wasn't my type. Everything else with her and sex had been surprising, I'd bet she'd be into this too. She'd loved it when Hawk watched me make love to her. Hell, she'd loved it when I'd watched her give me a blow job.

Her pupils had dilated, turning into dark bottomless pools surrounded by brilliant blue, glowing sky. I bet they'd go big and dark again, eager to watch us kiss, eager to explore this new dynamic. I had no idea how she'd managed to keep her vow of celibacy for over a hundred years. I think I would have lost my mind. But now that her self-imposed drought was over, it was clear she wanted it all, and I wanted to give it to her.

The memory of her face when I'd first pushed inside her tight slick sheath filled my mind. Her eyes had rolled back, her lashes had fluttered shut for a second, and her expression had been pure bliss. Her cold angelic mask and her desperate need to control everything had been forgotten and she'd let me glimpse the real her. The Amiah I'd fallen in love with.

Hawk groaned into my mouth and captured the back of my head, deepening our kiss and sending a sliver of magic into me to strengthen my desire and give him a bigger hit of sexual energy.

I clung to the memory of Amiah, determined not to pay attention to who I was kissing or the acidic burn of the demonic magic consuming me for fear I'd lose some of my desire.

I focused on all of the delicious sounds she'd made, her cry of release, my name on her lips, and her gasps and moans as she drew closer to the edge. From the first time I'd had her, I'd fantasized about having her again. I hadn't had a lover release her hold on everything like that in a long time, and coming from Amiah, it had been shocking and amazing. And then when we'd had sex to save Hawk's life, I'd started fantasizing about the three of us, but hadn't really thought she'd be into that. I hadn't thought she'd be into blow jobs either.

She just kept surprising me. I wanted more surprises. I wanted to get through this mess with the Heart and have her naked in my bed. With or without Hawk. I didn't care. Hell, I didn't even care if she was naked. I just wanted her, wanted her around, wanted her determination and caring.

Except that would never happen. It wouldn't even happen with Hawk or Titus or Cassius added to the mix.

Her soul had bound her to the hybrid, giving me serious doubts about the belief that an angel's soul mate wouldn't be fundamentally different from her.

What if that was just a myth, like how beautiful the bond was? Amiah had been terrified of it, saw it as a prison that she had to escape from where all other angels thought it was beautiful and sacred. What if being bound to her perfect match was also a lie?

Hawk pulled away from me, his chest heaving with rapid breaths, his hellfire blazing in his eyes. "I didn't think I was your type."

"If it'll get Amiah out of here, everyone is my type," I groaned, the pain of the demonic magic flaring. "Did you save her?"

Hawk ripped open the cut in the front of her blood-soaked shirt to get a better look at her stab wound. She didn't react, her eyelashes didn't even flutter, but she was breathing. Barely, but she was.

"She's still bleeding, but it's no longer gushing. Hopefully my magic has healed the worst of it." He turned a furious gaze on the hybrid, jerked to his feet, staggered then caught his balance.

I grabbed Hawk's wrist, stopping him, sending agony screaming through me. "We'll deal with him later. Get Cassius."

Hawk's expression turned grim.

"Did she save him?" Titus asked, his pupils slitted and his canines extended. He trembled, and from his expression, it was from barely contained panic and rage.

"He's barely alive and I've put him in hibernation. She'll need all her power to heal him." I gasped in a painful breath and met Titus's gaze then Hawk's. "We don't tell her about him until she's fully healed herself."

"But thinking he's dead will crush her," Hawk replied, heaving to his feet and heading to the shelves where Cassius lay.

"And we all know she'll kill herself trying to save him. She ran into the middle of a fight for fuck's sake." The demonic magic flared and the cavern got even darker.

Fuck. Just stay conscious. Just a little longer.

"Cassius is safe," I said through gritted teeth. "Even if I die, the hibernation spell will hold."

"You're not fucking dying," Hawk said. "No one is dying."

"We still need to get out of here." I turned to the hybrid, the little bit of movement shooting agony through me. He still wasn't fighting Titus's grip and he still looked stunned. "Hey, hybrid. Does Deaglan know about my apartment in the mortal realm?"

"No," he replied, his voice barely more than a whisper, his attention never leaving Amiah.

The always-on intention glyph tattooed on the inside of my right thigh didn't respond. Shit. The spell needed an emotional lock on him to work and he was either really good at hiding his emotions, or I was in too much pain to know if he was lying or not.

God damn it.

"If you're lying, I'll put you in hibernation and forget about you," I said, trying to get enough of an emotional reaction for my glyph to work.

"Yes, your highness," the hybrid replied.

Nothing.

Titus snarled and put more pressure on the guy's head.

Still nothing.

Just fucking great, and we really didn't have the time to keep pressing him. I wanted out of Faerie before things got worse, and in Faerie things could always get worse. Even if Deaglan didn't know about my apartment, it still wasn't guaranteed to be safe, but it was the only place where I knew for certain there was a circle with a barrier strong enough to keep the hybrid captive until we could figure out what to do with him.

"If I pass out, demand Karthick portal you back to my apartment and put Talkative here in my clean room and activate the barrier glyph on the circle," I said as Hawk climbed the shallow shelves to Cassius, his movements not nearly as nimble as usual, meaning he wasn't even close to having gotten his power back from our kiss.

I dragged in a painful breath and turned away from Titus and the hybrid.

This was going to hurt. A lot. I pressed my hands to the ground and grabbed the barely-there thread of fae magic inside me.

The connection was even weaker than it had been a few minutes ago. Every time I used my magic the demonic magic got stronger and pushed out more of Faerie's magic, and I had a horrible feeling this final spell was going to push all of Faerie out of me. If I didn't burn up right away, I'd die the drawn-out, painful death of a fae cut off from his realm.

And it didn't matter. Amiah had to get out of Faerie.

I tugged on my connection and the demonic magic surged, tearing through my body and threatening my hold on my power and my consciousness. Fire burned under my skin and I started to smoke.

Come on. Just one last spell.

Just one more.

I heaved everything I had into my hands and with a scream, shoved the power into the ground and demanded Faerie, not just one of its courts, but the entire realm, summon Karthick. He would come and he would come now. I was a royal and a sorcerer. My connection to Faerie was stronger than most fae and so was my ability to command it.

Please work. Please, God, work.

The burning darkness of the demonic magic roared into my cells and flames burst over my forearms. My blood rushed over the ground around my hands as my skin blistered, burst, and blackened.

One of the guys yelled, but with the roaring in my head and the agony in my body, I couldn't tell which one.

I tipped forward, gasping, and the inferno inside me burned up my biceps and across my chest, drawing closer to my heart even though I was no longer pushing power into the spell.

It was cast. I could only hope Karthick wouldn't resist and would answer. He'd be pissed. No one, not even the monarchs of any of the courts, dared summon him like that, but I was out of options.

It hurt to breathe or move or hell, even think. Somehow — I had no idea how — I was still alive. Barely, but I was alive. Every inch of me blazed with agony, and while not all of my outside had second- and third-degree burns, most of my magical insides did.

Please come. Please help us.

"What the fuck is wrong with you?" Hawk demanded, his voice close and yet far away at the same time.

The power of a portal popped against my senses, and a pressure that had been squeezing around my heart released.

Oh, thank God.

I forced myself to sit up and face what was sure to be an angry sorcerer. The room darkened and each breath, each miniscule movement of my muscles, sliced agony through me. I fought to stay conscious. I just had to make Karthick help us. That was all that was left to do.

"You actually summoned me?" Karthick asked his voice thick with disgust at receiving a royal summons. "Oh, high and mighty prince of the Winter—"

His gaze landed on me, and the short, squat summer fae's eyes widened, and his attention jerked to the cavern around him and the shadow fae bodies littering the ground.

The cavern's weak illumination grew even darker and I clutched at my consciousness.

Just stay awake. Just long enough to save her.

"You owe her," I forced out before Karthick could ask for an explanation. I didn't have enough in me to answer questions. I just needed to get her safe. "She paid you to take her brand and she's still soul bonded. With Deaglan's hybrid."

She was God damned bonded with a stranger. The very thing she was terrified of.

Karthick frowned. "Well I can't remove an angelic bond once it's formed."

"Which was why you were supposed to have gotten rid of her fucking brand." And now it was going to make her fall in love with the hybrid and not me. Fuck. "Pay your debt, Karthick. Portal us to my apartment in the mortal realm."

Karthick's attention turned to Amiah and the pressure of his magic crushed inside my chest, adding to my agony.

I clenched my jaw, but a whimper escaped, jerking Karthick's gaze back to me.

"I don't know if Faerie will let her go through a portal to another realm," Karthick said. He almost sounded apologetic.

Well, he should. And while I recognized it wasn't completely fair to be angry at him, that angelic mating brands were a magical force all their own that no one really understood, I couldn't help myself. Everything had gotten worse because he hadn't gotten rid of her brand. She wasn't even going to fall in love with Cassius. I might have been able to get over that. But the hybrid? How the hell could she be soul bonded to the hybrid?

I heaved my thoughts back to the real issue. "She can't stay in Faerie. It's not safe."

The demonic magic sliced deeper, cutting into the core of my being and my connection to Faerie shrunk to a miniscule pinprick. I was running out of time.

"You owe her." I gasped. "I'm calling in your debt. Break her connection... and get us... all of us... the fuck out of here."

"She's too weak. Breaking her connection will kill her."

God damn it.

"Then block it."

"Blocking it will only buy you so much time. Faerie will summon her back and she won't be able to resist."

I knew that, but it was all we had. "Just fucking do it."

I couldn't force Karthick to do anything. On a good day, if I got lucky, I might have been a match for him, but this wasn't a good day. It hadn't been a good day for a long fucking time.

And if we stayed in Faerie, we were dead.

TITUS

THE METALLIC SCENT OF BLOOD AND THE CHARRED REEK OF BURNED FLESH filled my nose, making my beast rage inside me. Amiah barely breathed and I knew she was only clinging to life because Hawk had given her his. She was so pale, her small, fragile body in a terrifyingly large pool of blood, and Seireadan looked like he was about to pass out — and from the horrific burns on his hands and arms, I was shocked he wasn't howling in agony.

It took everything I had to fight my clawing, howling beast and stay where I was. I *had* to go to her. She needed me. Even if I couldn't heal her, she needed my soul, needed flesh to flesh contact.

Except I couldn't. I was the only one in any kind of condition to hold the hybrid — my rapid healing having already healed most of the injuries I'd gotten during the fight. And while he lay perfectly still beneath me, I didn't know if it was because he was still stunned from my punch or waiting for a moment to attack, or if he knew that if he moved even an inch my beast would tear into him.

And I would. The bastard had tried to kill Amiah. Both my beast and I were in agreement on that.

Except Seireadan had said hurting him hurt Amiah.
Because they were soul bonded.
My pulse picked up, and my beast snarled at that.
She couldn't be soul bonded with the hybrid. She was mine.

Mine!

I didn't know how the hybrid had soul bonded with *my* mate, but if Seireadan said he had, then it was true. Seireadan had been just as horrified, and if he was married to her — which was still a possibility that neither him nor my beast wanted to admit — then a soul bond with the hybrid destroyed everything for both of us.

And if we didn't get Amiah to safety and healed, none of it would matter.

The strange Summer Court sorcerer, Karthick, pursed his lips — and it better have been in concentration to form a portal to get us out of Faerie and not trying to decide if he should actually do it. Seireadan had risked burning himself up to summon this guy, he had to have believed the man would help us even if his words to him had been angry and demanding.

Amiah's fae glow fluttered brighter for a second, but she didn't react, making my pulse pound faster, and my beast dig deep rents in my soul.

Go to her. Hold her.

No. She'll take a deeper breath any second now. She'll wake up. Something. Anything. Please.

"Her connection to Faerie is blocked, but I don't know how long it will last," Karthick said as Hawk, staggering with Cassius slung over his shoulder, carried the unconscious angel back to us, leaving a trail of blood on the uneven rocky ground. "Deaglan can't be allowed to get the Heart, and I know that bastard will figure out she has a key."

"He already... has," Seireadan groaned and his head lolled forward as if it was too heavy to hold up. "Why do you think... I'm trying to get her... out of Faerie."

"Call me when she needs to come back." Karthick knelt in front of him and raised a finger to Seireadan's forehead.

"Don't," Seireadan said before Karthick could touch him. "Give the summoning spell to Hawk or Titus."

Karthick's expression grew grim. "Fine." He turned to Hawk and pointed at the ground. "Kneel so I can reach you."

Hawk knelt, still holding Cassius, and Karthick pressed his finger to the middle of Hawk's forehead.

"Decide you want to summon me. That will activate the spell, and I'll pull you back into Faerie."

Hawk shivered and his hellfire flared. "Why don't you just come with us?"

Smart thinking. I should have thought of that. Inviting another sorcerer who wasn't seriously injured to join us would help ensure Amiah's safety.

"Faerie won't let me leave and it isn't anything I can solve with my magic," Karthick replied, making me wonder just what he'd done to make Faerie trap him like that. You had to really piss off the realm or be a monarch without an heir for Faerie to stop you from going through a portal to a different realm. "Now think about where you want my portal to take you. Imagine it in your mind."

Hawk closed his eyes and Karthick clapped his hands.

The air around us shimmered and thickened. It clogged my nose and ears, filling me with the unnerving pressure of a portal, then *popped*, releasing us in the middle of Seireadan's dark living room, the portal shoving his couch and the low table in front of it aside to make room for us.

We'd arrived positioned exactly as we'd been in the cavern with Hawk and Seireadan kneeling, Amiah behind them, and me a few feet away holding down the hybrid. A glimmer of strange purplish-orange light shone through one of the windows at the back of the room, but other than that, it was dark outside.

"Get the hybrid in my clean room and in the circle and touch the lock glyph at the circle's edge," Seireadan said and he collapsed face first onto his floor, drawing my gaze to the growing dark stain of Amiah's blood oozing across the white marble floor toward him. She was still bleeding.

"Crap." Hawk set Cassius on the floor and stood. "Let's get the hybrid in the room."

My beast snarled at Hawk. It wanted to go to Amiah. Now. She needed help. Now. But I wrenched one of the hybrid's arms behind his back instead, moved my hand from his head to his neck, and hauled him to his feet. As much as I needed to go to Amiah, the hybrid was still a potential danger.

And I wasn't stupid enough to tell Hawk I could handle the hybrid on my own so Hawk could take care of Amiah. For all I knew, the hybrid was just biding his time, waiting for us to take him with us wherever we retreated to before trying to finish murdering Amiah.

I shoved him toward the hall where the bedrooms and the clean room were. All the doors stood ajar, with the exception of the guestroom door that I'd ripped off its hinges.

Everything was as we'd left it when we'd raced to save Amiah from

Balwyrdan. The sheets on Seireadan's bed in the room at the end of the hall were bunched to one side. He'd been naked when I'd wrenched the door open and drenched in the scent of Amiah's arousal. My bed also had crumpled sheets, the door half on the floor and half leaning against the bed, while Amiah's room was untouched, the bed perfectly made with a pile of olive green clothes neatly folded at the foot... because she hadn't had a chance to sleep in it that night... because she'd slept with Seireadan... and then been abducted by Balwyrdan.

Had that only been a few days ago? If I thought about it, I'd known even then that she was my mate. I just hadn't wanted to admit it because I'd thought she was Seireadan's or Cassius's.

And she still might be. She might be mated to all of us.

Or none of us—

Or rather, just the hybrid.

I shoved him into the center of the clean room, a white, windowless space with nothing in it except a large circle of glyphs carved into the white floor where Seireadan could protect those around him when he cast dangerous spells.

Hawk waited until I was outside the circle then pressed his hand against the lock glyph. A blue-white light flashed from all the glyphs and a pale bubble, only visible from the corner of my eye, burst around the hybrid. Anyone on the outside could touch the lock glyph and remove the barrier, but only Seireadan would be able to go in or out of the barrier.

The hybrid sank to his knees, rested his hands on his thighs, and closed his eyes, all sense that he was stunned gone. All sense of any kind of emotion gone.

My beast snarled at him. Neither of us could believe this cold lifeless man was Amiah's mate. She was life itself. Passion and compassion and love. Even Cassius who was cold and hard at times was really trying to contain his powerful emotions.

"Come on," Hawk said, stepping into the hall. "Bane built that barrier before the demonic magic fucked him up. No one's getting through that."

My beast huffed and I stormed after Hawk, yanking the door closed, remembering at the last second how weak the hinges were, and managing not to break it.

With a groan, Hawk headed back to the living room, his bare shoulder bumping against the hall wall and leaving a blood smear before he regained his balance. "Cassius is in hibernation. He'll be fine on the floor until we can find time to get to him. I'll get Bane to bed and see what I can do about his burns. You take Amiah, clean her up, and pack that wound. I doubt she has much power, so we'll have to wait a few hours for her to get some back before she'll be able to stop her bleeding."

"Will a few hours be enough?" I asked. It took more power for her to heal herself than it did us, and I had no idea how much magic Hawk had given her and how well it would help heal her.

"I hope so." Hawk knelt in front of Seireadan, who was out cold. "I'm not going to be able to watch her bleed for more than that."

Neither would I.

The muscles in Hawk's jaw clenched, then he hefted Seireadan onto his shoulder, staggered to his feet, and headed back toward the hall.

"Hawk," I said, carefully gathering Amiah in my arms, my beast howling at her pale limp form. *Mine mine mine.* Her breath was so shallow. I had to strain to hear it. Her lashes didn't even flutter when I picked her up. *Mine.* "Thank you."

"You were only going to be able to hold your beast back for so long. You need her."

"And she needs us." I'd seen it in her soul. "All of us."

Yes, my beast believed she was my mate, but it also recognized what it had seen in her eyes back in the aerie. There was something in her soul that needed to connect not just with me but with the others. She thought that meant we weren't mates. Hawk thought it might mean we all were. That would certainly explain why my beast *knew* she was mine while at the same time the Winter Court behaved like she was Seireadan's.

I carried her into the guestroom I'd first woken in, kicked the door off the bed, and went straight into the bathing room. The other guestroom still had its door, but I didn't want to dirty up the bathing room or the bed just in case she wanted some privacy when she was better.

My beast hated the idea. That would mean she wouldn't want to be near me, and right now my beast never wanted to let her go. But she wasn't just mine, and she'd been held against her will before — twice now — and I wanted her to feel like there was a space that was all hers, where she could be with the others or just be alone if that was what she needed.

But that's not what she needs. She needs me.

Right now. Yes.
Because she's mine.
And possibly theirs as well—

Except the horrible truth was that she wasn't mine or even theirs. She was soul bonded with the hybrid. He was her soul's mate. Which didn't make any sense. He was the one who'd stabbed her.

I set her on the floor, propped up between the wall and non-magical rain-shower stall, which was a tight fit for just me, let alone both of us. Not to mention, if I couldn't get her to wake up — and I wasn't sure I wanted to wake her given everything she'd just been through — it would be challenging to shower her while she was completely limp.

I carefully cut off her bloody shirt and pants with a sharp claw, dampened one of Seireadan's small white cloths in the sink, and gingerly wiped the blood from her body.

The hybrid's sword strike had gone all the way through her and both the front and back wounds still wept blood. The only positive was that at least they were no longer gushing. I didn't know if that meant that Hawk had given her enough energy to fully heal her and she'd be fine in a few hours or not.

When she was clean, I wadded up more small clean clothes against her wounds and tightly wrapped a large towel around her chest to hold them in place. The next step was to put her in bed, but both my beast and I had to hold her and I was also covered in blood — hers, mine, and the blood of the shadow fae I'd killed. I needed to clean up, but I couldn't bring myself to let her out of sight for the few minutes it would take to shower.

I moved her out of the mess left from cleaning her up to the other corner in the bathing room by the door, stepped into the rain-shower stall and quickly scrubbed away the blood on my already naked body — because the last time I'd shifted, I'd destroyed my clothing and I hadn't had a chance to replace them.

Once clean, I took her to bed, curling my body around hers, holding her tight, and giving her as much flesh to flesh contact as possible.

A few minutes later Hawk staggered into the doorway, his gaze instantly jumping to Amiah. His hellfire was barely-there smoldering red pinpricks in his eyes and his expression was filled with longing and exhaustion and fear. It was clear he wanted— no, *needed* to be close to her too, but was afraid of my beast.

And my beast was snarling at him for just standing in the doorway looking at her. But it also recognized that Hawk had been willing to sacrifice himself to save her. She'd told him to never do an energy transfer again because it could kill him and he hadn't hesitated. That and he'd been desperate and hopeful at the thought that we were all her mates. I hadn't thought incubi took mates, but his need for her was clear, possibly as strong as mine... which couldn't be, because she was *my* mate—

Except she wasn't, damn it.

"Get cleaned up," I growled. My voice was darker, my beast closer to taking over than I liked, but there wasn't anything I could do about it. My mate was hurt. And I couldn't even give her vengeance and kill the hybrid for hurting her.

Hawk frowned at me as if he didn't understand what I was saying.

"You're not getting in this bed looking like that."

His gaze slid down his body as if he hadn't realized he was covered in grime and blood.

"She needs you, too," I said. And Seireadan and Cassius.

My beast heaved and snarled inside me. It didn't matter that she was soul bonded with the hybrid. I'd seen her soul. She needed all of us.

She has to need me.

And I wasn't going to think about the new horrible possibility that finding her soul's mate changed that. She wasn't a dragon. Her soul wasn't like ours even though she seemed to need the same physical contact to soothe her soul.

She would still need me when she woke.

She would. Please.

AMIAH

I DRIFTED TOWARD CONSCIOUSNESS, FIRST BECOMING AWARE OF A SEARING agony slicing through my chest and then the wild ferocity of Titus's life force along with the fiery darkness of Hawk's life force thrumming against my senses.

From that, I knew Titus was in good health — if exhausted — and lay behind me in bed, both of us under the comforter. His massive body was curled protectively around me, my back to his chest, his muscular arms holding me tight, while Hawk lay close in front of me, also under the comforter, his forehead pressed against mine. He was also physically fine, his magic having rapidly healed any injuries he'd taken during the fight with Deaglan, but he was still exhausted and his magic was dangerously low.

Despite that, it felt good to be in bed with them, even if it was odd to be with Hawk and Titus instead of Hawk and Sebastian. My soul sang with their nearness. This was right. The way it was supposed to be. I was steady with them near. It didn't matter that I wasn't a shifter, that I wasn't supposed to need flesh to flesh contact like this. I needed them. Needed all of them to ground my soul within me.

And then I remembered.

Cassius was dead.

My throat and chest tightened, and my heart rushed into a rapid, desperate pulse.

Oh God oh God oh God.
Dead.

I'd just gotten my best friend back, just realized that I was in love with him. We were just starting to figure ourselves out and now... now...

My breath turned sharp, slicing agony through me.

Please, God. Please.

It had to be a bad dream. A horrible dream. I'd wake up and he'd be angry with me for running into the middle of the fight... to save him...

But I hadn't saved him.

And my soul knew this wasn't a dream. His life force was missing. I hadn't even been aware that I'd been sensing it all this time. But now it was gone and his absence in my soul was as painful as the literal hole in my heart.

Except the physical hole was mending. Given time and power, I could heal my body. I couldn't heal my soul. Not even time would heal the hole left by Cassius's death. It was like I was missing a limb that I hadn't known was there in the first place, and now that it was gone, I realized I needed it, depended on it, couldn't live without it.

My soul started to tremble and it didn't matter that Titus and Hawk were close.

Cassius was gone because of me. Because I hadn't tried harder, hadn't pulled magic faster from those men—

The pressure in my chest clenched tighter, and I couldn't breathe.

I'd killed those men. I'd purposefully taken their lives to save Cassius, and I'd do it again in a heartbeat. I should have killed more of them, gotten more power, gathered it faster, pushed it into Cassius sooner. I should have held on and finished saving him even with the hybrid's sword in my chest and saved Cassius.

All those years trying to convince Cassius and myself that I wasn't weak and when it really counted, I'd failed.

I hadn't even told him I loved him.

God, why? Why? Why hadn't I told him?

But I'd been afraid he'd demand I give up Sebastian and Hawk, and I wasn't ready to make that kind of a commitment. Which was stupid. He'd said he'd wait for me. I could have told him how I felt. It was just three simple words. And it was the truth. He would have given me the time to figure out why I connected with the others during sex. He'd said he would. And now it was too late.

Now the damage to my soul was deeper than anything Karthick had done when he'd ripped out my ability to create a soul bond.

I bit back a bitter huff.

And more permanent.

I'd suffered excruciating agony for him to tear away my partially formed mating brand, but fate was cruel. It took away the man I loved and bound my soul to a monster.

Except I'd used my healing magic to take life. I'd done the one thing I vowed I'd never do. Maybe I deserved to be bound to a monster. An angelic mating brand didn't bind incompatible souls together, which meant I deserved to have my life permanently connected to that lifeless, emotionless man...

Unless of course, that was also a lie. The soul bond wasn't beautiful or sacred. Perhaps it didn't care what souls were bound together, it just happened when it happened. Which had to be the case because how could a man who was the antithesis of life be my soul mate? He wasn't even alive. He was half vampire. He didn't have a heartbeat.

And maybe the bond wasn't a real bond. I couldn't feel it.

Except that didn't mean anything.

The connection formed with an angelic mating brand could develop slowly. An angel might not even know who she was bonded with for days, sometimes even weeks. That, and I couldn't feel much beyond the pain in my chest and Hawk's and Titus's life forces. And even then, all of that was a barely-there sensation compared to the pain in my soul.

But maybe all that power I'd been channeling when the hybrid had stabbed me had accidentally connected us like the leash spell had connected me and Titus. Maybe Sebastian would be able to remove it.

My pulse pounded faster.

Sebastian had been in rough shape before we'd even started the fight. The demonic magic infecting him that he couldn't get out of his system had been consuming him from the inside out, and every time he used his magic it burned deeper into his magical channels.

At the thought, my senses jumped beyond Hawk and Titus and connected with Sebastian. A breathtaking agony swept through me and not just the agony of the demonic magic consuming him. It seared my hands and arms and chest with a nauseating mix of fiery pain and numb nerve damage from a combination of second- and third-degree burns.

My need to heal overwhelmed me and I jerked up, making the room darken and lurch. I was exhausted and low on magic, but it didn't matter.

I had to go to him. I had almost enough to heal the burns to ugly, tender scars. He'd still have some nerve damage, but I had enough to ease most of his pain until I could regain more magic. I couldn't let him suffer. I couldn't lose him too.

Which didn't make sense. He wasn't dying. But I needed him now more than ever. I needed all of them, needed them near, needed to feel their life forces. I wouldn't survive another amputation like I'd suffered with Cassius. I didn't know why I needed them or even how they fit into my soul. I wasn't soul bonded with them. I knew that for certain. All I knew was that my soul was weaker without them.

God, I needed to tell them I loved them before it was too late, even though I wasn't supposed to have fallen in love with Sebastian and Hawk. Even though neither man would love me back. It didn't matter. They had to know.

Titus's arm around me tightened, keeping me from scrambling off the bed, and Hawk's eyes flew open.

"I have to go to him," I gasped. Sebastian needed me. Now.

Tears rolled down my cheeks. I'd been silently sobbing this whole time and hadn't realized it. The pain in my soul had been overwhelming with my grief for Cassius and for Sebastian's agony and because I couldn't lose anyone else. And because Hawk and Sebastian were going to eventually leave me.

"Heal yourself first. He can wait." Hawk said.

"Hawk, please. He needs me. I have to."

His hellfire flared and his eyes filled with sadness.

Did he think I was talking about Cassius?

Who was dead.

No. God, no.

Focus. Sebastian was in pain. He wasn't dead and he needed me. This was something I could do. I could help him like I hadn't been able to help Cassius.

My compulsion to heal squeezed around my heart even as my thoughts jumped back to Cassius.

Dead.

I never got to tell him I loved him.

More tears streamed down my cheeks. They had to know. All of them. Even if it didn't make sense, even if I'd only known them for a few days. I didn't want to let them go. I didn't want to be without them. Somehow falling in love with them was the only explanation for how I felt. And something could happen to them too. I could lose any one of them. I could lose all of them.

I cupped Hawk's face in my trembling hands and met his gaze. "I love you, and I know you can't love me back, and that's okay. I don't expect you to. But I never got to tell Cassius, and—" My throat tightened. "I never got to tell my best friend that I—" The pressure in my chest squeezed, making it hard to breathe. "I didn't get to tell him and I can't lose you too. I love you."

Titus pressed his lips against the back of my head and curled his body tighter around me. I tried to turn in his embrace, but he wouldn't let me move.

"I've fallen in love with you too."

"You don't really know me," he said, throwing back the words I said to him when he'd begged me to be his mate. "You don't really know any of us except Cassius. You're upset and mourning. That's all. Your soul needs something from ours, but that's not love. It can't be. We're not your soul's mate."

His words sent cold rushing through me and more tears welled in my eyes. It didn't matter if I loved any of them. If my bond with the hybrid was real, then eventually I'd love him and only him.

No. I wouldn't let that happen. I'd fallen in love with Hawk and Sebastian and Titus, and I was going to stay in love with them. I'd already lost one man I loved, I wasn't going to lose anyone else. I'd fight my bond, find a way to get rid of it. There was always a way. Everything else about the angelic mating brand had been a lie. Its permanence had to be a lie as well.

My need to heal Sebastian squeezed tighter.

"Please, Titus," I begged. "Let me go."

"You have to heal yourself first, gorgeous," Hawk said, wiping a tear from my cheek, the sadness in his expression darkening into a heartbreaking grief. "My magic healed you more than I thought it would, but you're still bleeding. We've had to replace the washcloths twice now and it's only been a few hours."

His magic?

Horrific realization flashed through me. He'd done an energy transfer to save me and given me enough to mend the hole in my heart. It was barely mended, leaving me with deep puncture wounds on either side, but I wasn't rapidly bleeding out. I could have lost him too.

"Hawk—"

"Heal yourself," he said, fear sharpening the grief in his expression. "Please."

Except I couldn't. My compulsion to heal Sebastian was growing stronger. I'd survive a few more hours without medical attention. I'd be weak from blood loss and having spent my magic, but I'd survive.

"I'll be okay for a few more hours. I have to ease Sebastian's pain." And the moment the words came out, I realized I also needed to be closer to his life force, too.

More tears rolled down my cheeks. I wasn't strong enough to withstand the pain of Cassius's missing life force without their help.

"I'm too weak to fight the compulsion, and I'd rather not waste power healing him from a distance. I'd barely make a dent in his burns that way."

Hawk's gaze jumped past me to Titus.

"I'm not even sure my magic will let me heal myself," I added. Which was the truth. If I was at full power, if I didn't have a gaping hole in my soul, if my heart wasn't shattered, I might have had the willpower to turn my magic inward. "Don't make me fight myself, too."

"Okay," Titus said, his voice heartbreakingly soft.

He tugged the towel wrapped around my chest tighter and pushed back the comforter. With the exception of the towel, we were both naked and so was Hawk, and neither man seemed to care. Even with us being in bed with an incubus there hadn't been anything sexual about it. We'd been more like a small shifter pack, piled together needing the soul-steadying comfort of flesh to flesh contact in our time of grief.

Titus picked me up, the movement shooting agony through me and making the room whirl. I pressed my face against his broad chest and squeezed my eyes shut, praying the sensation would stop, praying I'd wake up from this nightmare, praying for everything to be different. Why couldn't it have been different? Why couldn't I have saved Cassius?

We headed to the door at the end of the hall, Sebastian's bedroom, and Hawk opened it for us. Inside was a room about the same size as the room we'd just left decorated in the same white, silver, and blues. A huge painting of a winter forest hung on the far wall, reminding me of the Winter Forest in the Winter Court that Sebastian loved so much, and books were stacked on every piece of furniture as well as on the floor.

Sebastian lay asleep in his bed with only a thin sheet pulled up to his waist, his full-body fae glow barely alight, his complexion gray, and his expression tight with pain even though he was unconscious. Blood stained the strips of white sheet someone had wrapped around his hands, arms, and chest, and the rest of his torso was covered in the scratches and bruises I hadn't healed when I'd healed his shoulder after the fight at the waterfall.

His life force snapped cold and bright against my senses, fighting the overwhelming darkness of the demonic magic inside him, and for a second all of my pain and exhaustion and grief was gone. There was just Sebastian and his injuries and the fact that I could do something to help him.

"Set me down beside him," I whispered, not wanting to wake him.

Titus set me down and stepped back, taking his ferocious life force with him.

"No, stay." I reached out my hand to him. "Both of you." My throat tightened and my grief for Cassius swelled. "Steady my soul."

Titus didn't hesitate. He eased onto the bed propped up against the headboard and pulled me into the V between his legs letting me lie on his chest while still able to touch Sebastian, and didn't seem to care when Hawk pressed the length of his gorgeous sculpted naked body against his leg and draped his arm across my chest, resting his palm against my cheek.

"What the hell... are you doing?" Sebastian gasped and his eyelids cracked open.

Then his gaze met mine and my pulse stuttered. His pale, almost colorless blue eyes were filled with a pain and darkness that I couldn't do anything about, no matter what I wanted. I could heal his burns, but I couldn't do anything about the demonic magic infection.

"Let me... guess. You're healing me... first."

I released a thread of power into him, straining to hold what little magic I had back so I didn't cause him more pain. My power heaved against my control. It wanted to heal him, needed to. Now now now. It didn't understand how painful it was to have your cells yanked back together to the way they were before. It just healed. That's what it did. And in that moment, I felt more like a vessel, a means for the power to release itself than someone in control of it.

I wasn't in control. I never really had been. If I had, I would have saved Cassius.

"I'm sorry," I said as the last drop of power slipped out of me into him and the peaceful darkness of unconscious dragged me under. "I promised I wouldn't fall in love with you."

But the darkness wasn't peaceful. It was filled with ice and pain and fear.

I was trapped. Again.

God again and again. I was never going to be free. I would always be someone's prisoner.

The Winter Court had claimed me and I could feel it calling to me, its frozen power muffled and far away, but still there, still straining to possess me, and my angelic mating brand had awoken and bound me to a monster.

Why couldn't it have been any of my guys?

My guys.

But they weren't my guys... and yet they were. Except if they weren't my soul mates what were they to me? Why did I need to connect with their life forces?

My life force could have saved Cassius if our souls had been bound together with an angelic mating brand. Why had I waited until I'd had the brand removed to have sex with him? I could have saved him. He could have taken life and strength from me even when my magic failed me.

But now I would save Deaglan's demon-vampire hybrid. The man who'd tried to kill me the first time we'd met and who'd decapitated one of Balwyrdan's men with one emotionless swing of his black katana.

And yet he'd told me to run when we'd met in the illegal market and had given me a knife when Balwyrdan had held me captive.

He'd also been filled with an excruciating pain when he'd hesitated to obey Deaglan's command to bite me.

Except if he hadn't stabbed me, Cassius wouldn't be dead.

I jerked awake, sending fiery pain slicing through me, and found myself alone in Sebastian's bed.

Cold, heart-stopping panic added to my pain, and the profound absence of Cassius's life force filled me, making my throat tighten and my eyes burn.

He was dead.

And I was alone.

A sob broke free and I staggered out of bed. It was foolish. I was still bleeding and should heal myself first, but I couldn't focus on anything past finding my guys and easing the pain in my soul.

Clutching the towel around me, I stumbled out the door. The dim hall whirled around and around and I leaned against the wall to keep standing, heading toward the living room, the direction from where I could sense their life forces. Surely they were there or in the kitchen. They wouldn't have just left me.

I reached the first door, Sebastian's clean room, and my senses leaped to the strange cold and fiery, alive and dead life force inside.

The hybrid.

My mate.

The man who'd killed Cassius.

And while he hadn't slit Cassius's throat, he'd shattered my concentration by stabbing me. If I'd just had a few more seconds, I could have saved him. I wouldn't have a hole in my soul. But I'd still be trapped.

RIN

THE DOOR FLEW OPEN AND THE ANGEL WHO'D IMPOSSIBLY FREED ME FROM the King of the Shadow Court staggered in. She was wrapped in a towel that barely covered her, her hair was a tangled mess, her eyes were red from crying, and she was absolutely stunning.

She stunned me every time I saw her with her sensual body — which I'd gotten an amazing view of in that dress she'd worn to the party where she and Prince Seireadan were to formally consummate their marriage — her powerful determination, and her unusual, heady magic. A magic that was unlike any other magic I'd sensed before. It called to a primal part of my demonic nature, urging me to feed on her, while the rest of her called to the man whose desires had only been satisfied when his king allowed it, and infrequently at that.

But all those desires were overwhelmed as the metallic scent of her blood slammed into me and shattered my tenuous hold on my hunger. My fangs fully extended and I couldn't stop them, and I instantly knew, not even needing to see the bloodstain on the towel at her heart, that she was still bleeding from the wound I'd given her.

"You killed him."

She trembled — I was surprised she was able to stand — and her breathtaking blue eyes were unfocused and barely lit with her angelic glow indicating she was low on power. Even her impossible high fae full-body glow which King Deaglan had said meant she really was Prince Seireadan's wife was weak.

She should have recovered more power in the time I'd been locked in the circle... unless she'd used what she'd regained to heal her husband, a man who obviously cared for her. He'd been willing to burn himself up by channeling too much magic to summon that Summer Court sorcerer to portal us to the mortal realm. The horrific burns on his hands and his collapse the minute we were through the portal was proof of that.

Recklessly using her magic when she was injured and weak would go with what I knew about angels with powerful healing magic. They often died young, a good couple hundred years before other angels, even angels with weaker healing magic. They drained themselves to death because they were unable to fully control the compulsion that came with their powerful innate magic. And I'd known what she was the moment I'd seen her in that forest in the mortal realm where we'd found the dragon. I hadn't even had to sense the flavor of her power to know.

I had no idea how the others hadn't figured it out. It had been obvious by how she knelt over the dragon. But if they weren't going to say anything to the Shadow King, neither was I.

If King Deaglan knew what she was, he'd want her, and I couldn't let him have her. She wouldn't last fifty years as his prisoner. He'd use her in all the horrible ways he used his women until she'd drained herself or killed herself to end the torture, and then he'd toss away her corpse without a second thought.

Except maybe not. Maybe she would last. Maybe she'd be able to escape. Somehow she was more powerful than just an angel with healing magic. Healing angels, no matter how powerful, couldn't break spells, and King Deaglan's spell holding me captive had exploded the moment I'd run her through.

Maybe it had something to do with her marriage to the heir of the Winter Court. He felt powerful, but he also had demonic magic inside him that was blocking his power. Maybe she could channel what he couldn't through their marriage bond.

And none of that really mattered.

I was free. Sort of.

But so was my hunger. Completely.

That had been the only good thing to come out of being taken by King Deaglan. His spell keeping me a prisoner and in constant pain had also held back some of the gnawing, desperate hunger inside me. A hunger that was more powerful than the vampire's who'd made me because my demon half also hungered for magic. Dying and becoming a vampire hadn't changed one hunger to another. It had doubled it. And the little bit of magic inside her, both angelic and fae, called to me as powerfully as the blood leaking from her body.

"You killed him," she said again, one hand clutching the towel around her and the other clenched in a fist. "You killed him."

Power sparked in her eyes, a taunting glimmer of what I craved, and a tear rolled down her cheek.

"I could have saved him. I could have—"

Her breath grew sharp and fast and her heart pounded faster, making her blood rush and my mouth water.

My stomach growled and her eyes widened with horror as if she were finally really seeing me for the monster that I was. I had no control right now and I could feel my hellfire burning across my cheeks. I was starving. King Deaglan had seen to that. And now that his spell was gone, there was nothing holding me in check.

I don't think I'd ever been so grateful to be locked up behind a magical barrier before. I had no idea how I was going to convince Prince Seireadan to let me go, especially after attempting to kill his wife. Hell, I had no idea how I was going to convince him to let me live.

Except he hadn't let the dragon kill me, which meant he had plans for me.

A shudder swept through me. Once he recovered from the fight with King Deaglan, he could still draw enough power to bind and starve me just like King Deaglan. Even with the demonic magic consuming him.

"Oh, God." The angel took a staggering step forward, the look in her unfocused eyes horrified and heartbreaking. "What did he do to you?"

Then her eyes rolled back and she crumpled to the floor. The towel fell open, giving me an indecent view of her beautiful body, and my gaze jumped to the delicate gold lines swirling over her left hip and sparkling with a strange magic I didn't recognize.

The urge to leap to my feet and go to her surged inside me and I forced myself to stay kneeling. I couldn't help her and I needed to keep what little hold I had on myself. I wouldn't let myself become a raging wild hybrid when there was a chance Prince Seireadan would keep me alive. And if I was alive, there was always a chance — be it a slim one — of being free. This angel was proof. I was no longer King Deaglan's assassin.

Besides, with my heightened hearing, I knew the others had heard her talking to me and were on the way.

Footsteps pounded down the hall and Prince Seireadan, the dragon, and the incubus rushed into the room. The prince and the incubus both wore loose pants while the dragon had a sheet tied around his wide hips. All were shirtless, all well-built, all were dangerous in their own way, and all three gazes instantly jumped to the angel as if they were all drawn to her. Like I was.

"Fucking hell." Prince Seireadan ran a hand over his spikey white and silver hair. The burns on his hands, arms, and chest, now partially covering the glyphs tattooed on his body, were still an angry red, but they were no longer weeping blood. She *had* healed him.

He jerked forward a step, glanced at his hands, then moved out of the way so the others could get to her.

But she hadn't had enough to give him full use of his hands which meant her healing magic was either weaker than I thought or the prince's burns were more serious.

"I told you we shouldn't have left her alone," the incubus said, kneeling to grab her, but the dragon got to her first, tugging the towel closed and lifting her into his arms.

She looked broken and fragile nestled against his broad chest, and he looked even more muscular and imposing than before.

He glared at me, his gaze more ferocious than it had ever been even when he'd gone crazy and shifted into his dragon form in the Winter Court's ballroom or at the waterfall in the Autumn Court.

"The woman is impossible," Prince Seireadan snapped. "She couldn't just stay unconscious for ten fucking minutes while we dealt with Cassius? And why the hell didn't she heal herself first before dealing with *him*?" He jerked his thumb toward me.

The dragon's glare deepened and he bared his teeth and snarled.

"Come on." The incubus placed a hand on the dragon's biceps, drawing his attention away from me. "Let's get her back in bed."

The dragon headed out the door and the incubus followed, pausing on the threshold to look back at the prince.

"You need sleep too."

Prince Seireadan looked longingly at his wife then ran his hand over his hair again and drew in a ragged breath. "I need to have a conversation with buddy here first."

The incubus's eyes narrowed. "He doesn't have a tracking spell on him, and the binding spell Deaglan had on him shattered when Amiah branded him."

Branded?

So that's what they thought happened? That was how she freed me from King Deaglan? The prince's wife had branded me with an angelic mating brand? But that didn't make sense. She'd taken the fae marriage vow and bound her soul to Prince Seireadan's. The Winter Court responded to her as if she were already its queen. She wouldn't have been able to create a mating brand... would she?

My thoughts jumped to the delicate gold lines in her pale skin. If that was an angelic mating brand, then she'd definitely branded someone, but it couldn't have been me. She didn't know me. She must have branded her husband as part of taking her vows and for some reason they thought I'd been added to the bond.

Except I didn't feel like my soul was bound to either her or the prince. It felt free. Finally. The pain of King Deaglan's spell that I'd lived with for hundreds of years was gone. Mostly.

Of course, the fight hadn't been that long ago and my hunger was ferocious. Maybe the bond wasn't strong enough, maybe my hunger was too overwhelming for me to feel it.

My hellfire snapped with a sharp *crack*. Had she freed me from Deaglan to keep me for herself as a second subservient mate? An angelic mating brand couldn't be broken and when one mate died the other died or went insane, so her death and the death of Prince Seireadan wouldn't free me.

God, I was still a slave, trapped to the whims of a royal from Faerie.

Panic twisted in my chest and my hellfire snapped again.

I narrowed my focus to the still nothingness in my heart, determined to rise above the turmoil inside me. *I* wasn't the hunger. *I* wasn't the fear. They were just sensations in my body. I might not even be branded. They had no proof. *I* had no proof.

Of course, if I was branded, the mark would be on my hip, a match to the one on hers.

The need to check surged inside me.

No, I didn't need to check right now. And I certainly wasn't going to check while they were in the room with me.

"We still need to have a conversation," the prince said to the incubus. "I won't let Amiah be blindsided again. She's barely holding on as it is, and she's headstrong as hell. She's going to come back to him, probably the second we all fall asleep."

"Fine." The incubus turned to the dragon. "We'll join you in a few minutes."

Prince Seireadan rolled his eyes at him. "I'm perfectly capable of having a conversation with a barrier between us. You need her as much as Titus does. Go."

"And I haven't been able to figure out what kind of demon he is," the incubus replied. "If you weren't so exhausted you'd know no one should talk to him alone even with a barrier between you."

He talked back to his master as if he were an equal, and I didn't know if that spoke to the kind of man Prince Seireadan was or the nature of their relationship — since the prince had passionately kissed the incubus after the incubus had saved his wife.

Prince Seireadan turned his attention to the dragon. "If she wakes, don't let her leave the bed until she's stopped bleeding."

The dragon huffed, a strangely dragon like snort in a human body, and took the angel, Amiah— No. I corrected myself. She was *Princess* Amiah, Prince Seireadan's wife. The dragon took her away while the prince and the incubus sagged to the floor in front of the barrier.

"How about we start with your name?" the prince said.

I glanced from him to the incubus whose gaze was ever-so-slightly out of focus. He'd said he knew I didn't have a tracking spell on me and that Deaglan's hold on me was broken. He had to be a Sensitive and was looking for any other spells on me. Or maybe he was using his sensitivity to figure out what type of demon I was. Which he wouldn't be able to. Some half demons, like me, gave off muddy essences, making it impossible to figure out what exactly we were. And now that I was a vampire, the only things that gave me away as a demon were my eyes.

Prince Seireadan sighed. "I'm Sebastian. This is Hawk. We both think Deaglan is an asshole."

"Way to just lay all our cards on the table," Hawk said, but he didn't sound particularly upset just exhausted.

"Yeah, because he hasn't already figured out who we are or what we think of Deaglan." The prince rubbed his face. "Who are you?"

"Rin." It was just my name. There was no point in holding back that information, especially since I had no idea if this prince would torture me for refusing to say my name like my last master would.

The only positive in this situation was that Prince Seireadan — and I wasn't foolish enough to call him something so personal as Sebastian — was too weak to properly bind me this very minute. He could leave me in this barrier and let me continue starving, but at least there wouldn't be sudden moments of blinding agony in the near future. I'd finally gotten a reprieve.

Of course, that might only be for so long. I'd nearly killed his wife. He'd want justice for that.

"How did you end up in Deaglan's employ?" the prince asked.

"He bought me." He'd paid to have me murdered and turned into a vampire on the off chance that I'd inherited my mother's short human lifespan, because he'd thought I was more valuable and powerful than I actually was.

My father had been a sin eater, able to eat magical energy and, more importantly, the energy that powered spells. Unfortunately, after Deaglan had taken over my connection with my vampire sire and bound me with a carefully crafted spell that was next to impossible for a sin eater to consume, he realized I'd only inherited half of my father's abilities. I could only consume raw magical energy before it had been manipulated into a spell.

I think the only thing that had saved me was my skill as a warrior... either that or it amused him to keep me. He certainly got pleasure out of my hunger, both denying it and, when it was too much to bear, watching it force me into a frenzy.

The prince raised a white eyebrow. He clearly wanted more information, but I wasn't going to offer up anything extra. He might look like King Deaglan's opposite, pale and cold, but that didn't mean they were different. Prince Seireadan was a prince of Faerie, and I had yet to meet any royal who didn't have a hidden agenda.

"How long ago?" the incubus, Hawk, asked.

"The end of the Sengoku period."

Hawk frowned.

"That would be Japan," the prince said to him, "about five hundred years ago."

"Didn't he have Titus for about five hundred years?" Hawk asked. "That seems awfully coincidental."

"Too coincidental. Which means your demon half is something really interesting." Prince Seireadan turned his pale, almost colorless winter fae gaze back to me. "What would Deaglan actually spend money on instead of just taking?"

"What would be easier to buy instead of take?" Hawk shifted right to the edge of the barrier without touching it and stared at me. His hellfire sparked, a sign of frustration... or great concentration... and then his eyes flashed wide. "Holy shit, you're a sin eater."

I clamped down on my own surprise. No one had ever been able to tell what I was. I didn't think anyone was sensitive enough to tell. Deaglan only knew about me because he'd seduced my mother — something else he liked to tell me about — and had learned about my father.

"Well that's just great," Prince Seireadan said. "So you've just been sitting here behind a barrier you could easily take down, waiting for what? You could have escaped at any time. With your magic, you know the only one capable of putting up any kind of a fight right now is Titus. Your odds of getting out of here are good."

I glanced from him back to Hawk, who still looked at me with a slightly out of focus gaze. Would he be able to see the whole truth about me? Was he that sensitive? And if he couldn't, what did I tell Prince Seireadan?

I'd have to tell him the truth. If he bound me, he'd expect me to be able to break spells for him. Of course, if he knew the truth, he might not bind me, he might just kill me—

Except he thought I was soul bound to his wife. If he killed me, he'd kill her.

"He isn't biding his time. He didn't get the full power. I don't think he can break the spell," Hawk said, his expression turning grim. "Your demon parent just gave you the hunger with none of the benefits of being a sin eater."

I gave a tight nod. There was more to this incubus than met the eye. There was more to all of them. The other angel had a fire magic that was so out of control I couldn't grasp onto it long enough to take a sip, and Prince Seireadan radiated the promise of extraordinary power. The most normal person in the group was the dragon and he was a dragon!

"So Deaglan must have taken over your bond with your sire thinking that was the only way to control you, since a sin eater wouldn't have been able to break a sire bond without killing himself." Prince Seireadan's expression turned grim. "He must have been seriously disappointed to find out you couldn't break spells for him."

That was an understatement.

I suppressed my shudder and kept my expression blank as the nightmare of those early days flashed through my mind. I hadn't thought I'd survive the pain and hunger and humiliation. But I'd been a newly made vampire. I hadn't realized just how much damage I could take or how psychological damage could be worse.

My hellfire snapped again, giving me away, and Prince Seireadan's eyes narrowed.

"So what were his favorite games? You're a vampire, you can heal a lot of serious injuries and pretty quickly." The prince pursed his lips. "I bet he got bored with that and started getting more creative. Sengoku period, hunh? With your skill, a ronin? Samurai? Pain *and* humiliation. How did he play you?"

My stomach roiled in anticipation, nausea churning into my hunger. That musing look always preceded pain. Pain through the hold he had on me, pain through my hunger, and the pain of my shame with his sadistic games and, when I was finally allowed to feed, the pain that I couldn't control myself.

"Did you lie when I asked you if Deaglan knows about my apartment?"

"No." That was the truth. Telling the truth hadn't worked for King Deaglan, he hadn't cared either way, but maybe it would work for Prince Seireadan. I had thought it would be better to be Prince Seireadan's prisoner than King Deaglan's. Except with that look in his eyes, the implication that he was going to enjoy the same sick games, I wasn't so sure.

But the prince released a heavy breath and his expression returned to exhaustion, the musing wicked gleam in his eyes vanishing.

"Not a lie. We've bought ourselves some time until my mother finds us or the Winter Court calls Amiah back to Faerie." His eyes narrowed. "When was the last time Deaglan let you eat?"

Just asking about it made my hunger surge, but I kept my expression even.

I'd told the truth and he hadn't hurt me... which he could have done even thinking I was soul bonded with his wife. Hurting me wouldn't hurt her. Only killing me would.

"When?" the prince pressed.

"When His Majesty commanded me to bite your wife," I replied.

She'd barely had any magic left so all I could have safely taken was blood, and given her condition, I hadn't been able to take much. I hadn't wanted to take anything from her. I knew if I'd fed too deeply and she wasn't able to... *perform*, I'd have been punished.

Prince Seireadan's eyes narrowed again, probably because I'd just reminded him that I'd bitten his wife. "And before then?"

I'd been given a dribble of blood and magic before chasing after the dragon. But we'd failed to kill him and we'd all been punished. Before then... I couldn't remember.

"He's taking an awfully long time to answer you," Hawk said.

"Which either means he wants us to think he's weaker than he is or he doesn't want to confess how weak he actually is." The prince stood, looked down at me, and sighed. "Either way, I can't let you out until I know you won't hurt Amiah."

"Again," Hawk reminded, his hellfire flaring, revealing his anger. "Won't hurt Amiah *again*."

Except if I was branded, I wouldn't be able to hurt her without hurting myself.

Of course, if I was faced with an eternity of still being a slave with a bond that couldn't be broken no matter how powerful the magic, then the only way to end it would be to kill myself.

They left and my hellfire exploded, sending sparks spraying around me and hissing against the floor.

I couldn't remain a slave. I couldn't face more years of torture or shame for a royal's amusement.

They were wrong. They had to be wrong. She hadn't branded me. The only time she could have branded me was during the fight and the bond wouldn't have been strong enough to save her from my katana. And she hadn't branded me to take me away from Deaglan. It'd be safer for her to have not bound our souls and just have her bodyguards kill me. She had no reason to brand me.

I yanked up my tunic and shoved my pants off my left hip.

Delicate gold lines swirled over my hip, reaching up to my waist and around my back and down my thigh.

I was still a slave.

HAWK

"We're putting him in hibernation," I said the second we were in Bane's study and the door was closed. "He's not getting anywhere near Amiah."

I didn't care that her profession of love to me hadn't been real and had been brought on by the shock of thinking Cassius was dead. She'd said she loved me and my soul had lit up with joy. Even when she was thinking straight and she realized she wasn't in love with me and took it back, I was going to hold onto that moment. She'd looked into my eyes and connected with me and said those three amazing words and I thought my heart was going to explode. Just three words.

Something the hybrid, Rin, had been short on. He'd barely said two dozen in our brief conversation, which didn't tell us anything about him other than he hadn't been with Deaglan of his own free will. We'd had to figure out for ourselves that he was half sin eater and we still didn't know if Deaglan had let him feed or not. And if he hadn't, his hunger could be deadly... which, from the way his strange black aura seethed around him, was what I'd bet on.

My gaze dropped to Cassius lying on the large carpet in the middle of the floor with no aura, not even a whisper of a spark, looking dead to my magical sight even though I knew he wasn't.

He looked even worse to my non-magical sight. We'd cleaned him up, taken off his bloody clothes, and wrapped a towel around his hips, but his complexion was gray, bloodless, from all the blood he'd lost, and he wasn't breathing. Blood welled in the ragged gash in his side and the horrific slice across his neck, frozen on the brink of pouring out of him, and would start gushing the moment Bane released his hibernation spell.

I didn't know if Cassius would even start breathing again when the spell was released, which terrified me. Amiah would need to work quickly to save him, and if she couldn't, she'd go through the horror of losing him all over again.

As it was, keeping his condition from her was cruel. It tore at my heart to see her grief when she shouldn't be grieving.

But Bane was right. She'd healed him before she'd healed herself. If she knew Cassius was alive, she'd give him everything she had. All her magic and probably everything in her soul if she could force it out of herself just to save him.

She loved him too. Loved him for real.

And he loved her. He certainly wouldn't want the hybrid getting anywhere near her even if they were soul bonded. He'd set the room on fire with his determination to protect her. And with bookcases crammed with books covering every inch of available wall space except the window and the fireplace, the room would ignite in the blink of an eye.

"Even if we're going to put him in hibernation," Bane said, "he and Amiah will still need to seal their bond. If they don't, she'll go crazy. Just as if he died."

Except sealing their bond meant sex.

God, could she even have sex with someone she didn't know? Could she have sex with someone who'd nearly killed her? She was opening up and accepting her desires, but her confidence was still fragile. She'd probably spent a lifetime being told how angels did and didn't have sex, and doing it with a demon, let alone a demon and someone else who weren't her soul mates, was probably frowned upon in the angelic world.

Being forced to have sex with Rin would be like the sex she and Bane had been forced to have in the Winter Court ballroom, except without any of the trust between them. There'd be nothing for her to hold on to that would quell her fears.

"You can't be okay with this," I said.

Sure, Bane had been emotionally closed off since Amiah had professed her love to him just before she'd passed out, but that didn't mean he no longer cared for her. Just that she'd shaken him. It had only been a few hours since her profession. Something that big took a man like Bane time to process, especially if he actually cared for her. And given that he'd sworn he'd never commit to anyone, closing himself off emotionally proved he had strong feelings for her.

"I'm not okay with any of this." He ran his hands through his hair and sagged onto the dark blue leather couch and stared at Cassius. He looked exhausted and the demonic magic trapped inside him, writhing and slicing into his magical channels, had now almost completely devoured his white high fae aura. "But we don't have a lot of options. He's her soul mate. There's got to be a reason for that."

"Yeah, because the universe is fucked up." Because if it hadn't been fucked up, I'd have been her soul mate.

I was impossibly in love with her. If she'd branded me, my love would have made sense. It wouldn't have been a mental disorder.

Of course, if she'd branded me and didn't brand any of the others, we'd still be faced with the original reason why incubi didn't fall in love. I'd starve or I'd drain her to death. And neither option was acceptable.

Except every time we made love she reached into my soul and connected with me. There'd even been a glimpse of that when she'd told me she loved me. I hadn't imagined it. Titus had said she needed us, but her soul bond with Rin was going to make her fall in love with him and only him.

And I had no idea what the hell that meant.

I knew I was going to eventually lose her, knew she was going to commit to someone and that would be the end of us. But I'd thought it would be Cassius, not a complete stranger.

"She branded him and Deaglan had enslaved him. The hybrid—Rin. God, I should start using his name. Rin can't be a monster. Amiah's soul wouldn't pick a monster," Bane said, but it sounded like he was trying to convince himself of that. "From his reaction, Deaglan was torturing him. Making him think I'd do the same was the only way I managed to get enough of an emotional jolt for my intention glyph to register his intent."

"Just because he didn't lie about Deaglan knowing about your apartment, doesn't mean he's safe for Amiah. We saw more than enough of Michael's victims to know some people just don't come back from being tortured, and Deaglan had Rin for almost five hundred years."

Bane raised his gaze to meet mine and for a second I saw a ghost of the same horror that haunted me. Thankfully it wasn't strong in either of us anymore. A lot of time had passed and we'd had the emotions of those memories taken away. But there were still times when I woke up hearing all those children screaming and crying and then the slow, terrible silence as they died.

Neither of us had come back from that the same and we'd only witnessed the torture. I couldn't imagine what hundreds of years of surviving it did to a person.

"She'd said the brand wasn't beautiful and sacred." The demonic magic inside Bane's aura flared, drawing a gasp, and his expression tightened with pain. "I hadn't really believed her, hadn't thought an angel would feel that way about the connection formed by a brand, especially after the brand had formed. I'd thought her determination to stay in control was what had driven her to have it removed—"

"She already had a brand?" How hadn't I noticed? I was a fucking Sensitive. Magic practically assaulted me everywhere I went, and I'd had sex with her. Numerous times. Surely I would have noticed a magical brand on her body being that intimate with her.

"It was only partially formed and you had to go looking for it to notice it," Bane said. "She asked me to remove it, but with this demonic shit inside me I wasn't strong enough, so we paid Karthick to do it."

Which explained the conversation they'd had in the cavern.

"I should have believed her. She'd said it was a nightmare." The muscles in Bane's jaw flexed and his grief turned to rage as the demonic magic spiked again. "*This* is a fucking nightmare. I don't ever want to see her on the ground bleeding to death, and I sure as hell don't want him touching her. If anyone should be branded it should be you and even that makes me angry. Fuck!" he yelled. "I want her brand." His eyes widened with shock as if he hadn't realized that was what he really wanted.

"Bane—"

"Fuck. No." He jerked to his feet and rushed to the bookcase behind his couch, gasping with another flare of demonic magic. "That isn't right. I don't really want her brand. It's got something to do with how we connect during sex. Something about what she is..."

"So you're just going to deny that you've fallen in love with her too?" Was he so afraid of a commitment that he wasn't going to acknowledge his feelings? I thought he already had.

"Of course I'm in love with her. We're all in love with her. I have no idea how, but we are." He yanked out a book and flipped through the pages. "Don't think I haven't thought about the three of us, hell, all five of us in something long term. But I can be in love with her without wanting my soul permanently and irrevocably bound to hers. I don't want her brand. And yet I do. There's something else going on. Something she needs from us."

Which was what Titus had said. There was something in her soul that needed the four of us. Could it be different from what her soul needed from Rin? Would she still want to be with us? And would I be happy sleeping with her to give her whatever she got out of our connection but not being the one she loved?

Bane shoved the book back onto the shelf and yanked out another, bigger one, but the demonic magic burst through his aura with sharp red spikes, stronger than before. He gasped and the book landed on the floor with a heavy thud.

"Shit." He bent down to pick it up, but just kept going, sagging forward on his knees, unable to stay upright against the fiery darkness consuming him.

"Just stop for a second," I said, hurrying to his side. Amiah had barely healed his burns and she wasn't able to do anything about his demonic infection.

"God damn fucking shit," he hissed, pressing his forehead against the floor. "And figuring out what she is isn't the priority. My mother will find us. She'll recast the spell that tracks Amiah's connection to the Winter Court and come after us. Hell, for all I know, Deaglan could figure out how to track her too. He knows how to find the newly empowered keys without Titus." The demonic magic sliced and writhed. "I'm losing my fucking mind. I should be focusing on how to keep her safe, not why she makes a connection during sex."

"You need to sleep." We all needed sleep, even Titus, who was the only one who'd managed to get out of the fight unscathed.

"I need to get this demonic magic out of me. My connection to Faerie is almost completely blocked. I've got maybe a couple of days at most."

"At most?" I knew the infection was bad, but I hadn't thought it was that bad. I thought he had more time. If he couldn't connect with Faerie, he'd eventually die a very painful death. Being shut out for fae was worse than any other super being disconnected from their realm. Faerie's magic was woven into their very cells. They didn't just go insane. They couldn't live without its magic.

"There's a burner phone in my desk. Top drawer," he gasped. "I need to hope I haven't pissed off a really powerful demon and he only raises the price, not demands something else."

"Sargos?" I asked. There was only one demon in Union City who could pull the demonic magic out of Bane and he was a nasty piece of work.

"Yeah."

We were going to need more than hope if Bane had already pissed off that greater demon. The odds weren't good he'd just ask for more money and we had next to nothing to give him at the moment. Except Bane was almost out of time.

AMIAH

I WOKE WITH MY CHEST STILL ON FIRE AND MY HEART AND SOUL NUMB. I didn't know if the numbness was better than the stabbing grief or not. Titus held me against his body, and his breath, heavy with sleep, washed over the back of my neck, while his wild life force taunted me, a constant reminder that Cassius no longer had a life force and there wasn't anything I could do about that.

Hawk lay in front of me again, higher than the last time, letting me use his chest as a pillow — also asleep and alive — and Sebastian lay behind him, his feet tangled with mine. His face was scrunched tight with a pain my magic couldn't touch even though he was unconscious and his breath was too fast and sharp. But he, too, was alive, his cold bright life force struggling to stay lit against the writhing darkness inside him.

They were all alive and Cassius's wasn't.

The puzzle in my soul was incomplete and now always would be. Forever.

My throat tightened, my heartache burning through the numbness and my fear twisting in my gut. All the courts in Faerie still wanted to control Titus or wanted him dead, Sebastian was barely hanging on against the demonic magic infecting him, and Hawk was so low on power he wouldn't be able to heal a papercut. People were coming for us. The Winter Queen and Deaglan were coming for us. I couldn't wallow. I had to heal myself, heal them, come up with a plan to ensure I didn't lose any of my other guys—

Which now also included the hybrid. The mate I didn't want.

That thought left a bitter taste in my mouth. I'd wanted to fall in love like everyone else, not be forced to love someone because of my mating brand. And I had. Somehow I'd fallen in love with four amazing guys, guys I'd never have thought I'd pick.

Well, if I really thought about it, Sebastian had been right all along. I'd always been in love with Cassius, I was just too naive and scare to admit it, even to myself. But I certainly wouldn't have thought I'd fall for Sebastian Bane or an incubus and now the idea of being without them made my soul ache.

Why did my brand have to pick someone else? Why not one of them? All of them. I didn't want to give up any of them.

And yet when my magic connected with the hybrid's strange life force and when I'd looked at him, truly looked at him, I hadn't seen a monster. I'd seen a man suffering. The agony I'd originally felt when I'd connected with him was gone, but he'd suffered for so long, the pain had been imprinted in his cells. I wasn't sure if he'd ever be able to be pain free, and I didn't know if I had the kind of power to heal that.

There was something more to the hybrid than just an assassin who killed for the King of the Shadow Court. But that didn't give my soul the right to take away my choices and permanently bind me to him. He wasn't the one I wanted.

Maybe there was still hope and the brand wasn't real, and Sebastian, once we'd figured out how to remove the infection, would be able to free me.

But that would only happen once all of Faerie wasn't trying to kidnap or kill us.

I drew in a shuddering breath, trying to draw on my professional persona to get through this.

Except the moment I thought that, I thought about Cassius and all the times he'd been at my side and watched me work. He'd been around a bit during the war and then at the hospital in the supers' quarter in Union City. And then he'd been around a lot — at first — in Operations when I took over as chief physician.

I'd healed him and his soldiers, and then him and his agents. I'd been in charge and in control and I'd known what I was doing and where I was going and what fate had in store for me.

And I'd been fooling myself.

I was only grateful I'd realized the truth before my soul permanently bound me to a stranger and I'd had a chance to be free, to be who I was supposed to be. It had only been for a few days, and they'd been far from ideal, but they'd been mine with no fate and no naive daydreams.

Tears burned my eyes. I didn't want to give that up, and damn it, I wasn't going to. Sebastian would figure out a way to break the bond between me and the hybrid, and if he couldn't—

If he couldn't—

My breath picked up. I wasn't going to give up what I had with them. I needed them. I knew that in the core of my being.

If he couldn't break the soul bond between me and the hybrid maybe there was a way to create a soul bond with them as well. I had no idea if any of them would want to permanently join the kind of messed up relationship that would be, but it was an option... it had to be.

And the only way for that to happen was for everyone—

A tear leaked from my eye, traced a path over the bridge of my nose, and plopped onto Hawk's bare chest.

Everyone *left* to get through this mess with Faerie's Heart.

Meaning I couldn't afford to wallow. I had to shove my grief deep down, heal myself, then finish healing Sebastian and Hawk.

Another tear broke free and followed the path of the first one.

I wasn't going to be able to push my grief aside, no matter what I wanted. Everything I thought about reminded me of Cassius, or how I loved him and hadn't told him because I'd been afraid. He'd say I didn't have time to mourn and he'd be right. He'd say I had to carry on, be safe, survive.

I had to honor that wish. It was the only thing left that I could do for him.

I forced myself to focus on the power in my palms. I'd recovered about three-quarters of my magic, but it was still dark outside — and I was pretty sure I hadn't slept through a whole day. I shouldn't have had this much power for the amount of time I'd been asleep.

And Cassius would say don't question it, just use it.

I pushed the power from my hands to the hole in my chest and slowly, agonizingly slowly, started to knit my flesh back together until the wound was partially healed and all the power left inside me was my constant small spark.

Exhausted and dizzy, even just lying there with my eyes closed, I trembled between my guys, my thoughts rushing back to Cassius, my will too weak to ignore them. I thought about his smile, his stern glare, his laugh that I hadn't heard in a long time, and all the time we'd spent together. How had I not known I was in love with my best friend?

More tears leaked from my lashes onto Hawk's chest, and I softly cried, not wanting to wake him or the others, until sleep tugged me back into blissful nothingness.

This time it was nothingness. I didn't dream of pain or cold or my horrible reality.

Except when I woke again, all my worries and fear and heartache rushed back in.

I bit back a sob but couldn't stop my tears. I was still sandwiched between Titus and Hawk, but Sebastian's life force wasn't nearby.

He was gone. Panic seized me before logic kicked in and my senses reached out and connected with him. He was in the bathroom and still in pain. The demonic magic was so strong I could barely sense the cold radiance of his winter fae life force and his burns were still sensitive.

A trickle of power reached out to him and I yanked it, along with my magical senses, back into my body. He'd be furious if I healed him again while I was still bleeding. They all would—

Cassius most of all.

And I was still bleeding. My chest, however, wasn't nearly as painful as it had been before and my power was also back to half.

I cracked open an eye to check the light in the room and try to figure out how long I'd been asleep this time.

The room was dimly lit, but because I was facing away from the window, I couldn't tell if that was because it was early morning or because the heavy curtain on Sebastian's bedroom window was blocking out the sun. And really, it didn't matter. Both Titus and Hawk were asleep and I had the power to finish healing myself. I might even have some left over to help Sebastian.

I forced my power back into my wound, fighting to keep it turned inward when it wanted to go in any other direction but that.

It heaved against my control, jerked this way and that, straining to return to Sebastian, and I clenched down with everything I had and managed to seal my wounds shut. Barely. It was still tender and if I didn't push more power into it in the next few days I'd have a scar, but I was no longer bleeding.

Except the second I let go, the little bit of my remaining power jumped into Sebastian, determined to ease his pain.

Crap.

I wrenched it back under control. It was a waste to heal him from afar. It could just stay where it was until I could touch him.

The catch was getting out of bed without disturbing Hawk and Titus.

Except the moment I thought that, I knew it was going to be impossible. Hawk might be tired enough to sleep through me moving, but Titus's rapid healing had already healed the injuries he'd gotten during the fight. He was just sleeping with me to be with me, using his body to help steady my soul as if I was a shifter.

I tugged at his arm around my waist so I could turn in his grip and look at him.

His stunning golden eyes opened and met mine. They were filled with a deep, pure love that made my pulse stutter. He'd begged me to be his mate and I'd told him I wasn't in love with him.

Then I went and told all of them that I loved them.

And I'd meant it.

I wasn't sure how he was going to take that even though he'd said he would give me the connection I needed with him despite me still having sex with the others. But sex and love were two very different things.

"You're not allowed to get out of bed until you've stopped bleeding," he whispered.

I inched down the towel still wrapped around me and showed him the healed, but still sensitive wound.

His expression turned grim and my thoughts jumped to how I'd gotten it. My mate had stabbed me and Cassius had died.

My throat tightened and I fought my tears even though I knew I hadn't cried nearly enough. I doubt it had even been a full day. All I wanted was to cling to my guys and sob, but my magic wanted to heal Sebastian and that was something I could do. That was useful. That could distract me. That—

I pressed my lips to Titus's, cutting off my whirling thoughts, and letting him know with my mouth how much I cared for him and needed him. Life was too short, and I hadn't kissed Cassius nearly enough before I'd lost him.

I didn't care if they thought I was crazy or that it had happen too fast or that I'd fallen in love with all four of them. Essie had four mates. She was madly in love with all of them and without a doubt, her soul bond with them was only a part of why she loved them. I could love four men. It was that simple.

Titus froze as if he hadn't expected me to kiss him, then huffed softly, a dragon-like sound of satisfaction, and kissed me back. It wasn't a deep kiss or a wild one like the ones we'd had before. It was gentle, just a touch of lips and tongue to steady our souls.

Except I needed more, needed a deeper connection, and I had no idea why. I needed to join with one of them and feel their life force inside me. Kissing Titus was good, but not enough to keep me steady and face my new reality.

The soft *shush* of the shower started, and my magic warmed my palms.

What I really needed was to heal Sebastian.

I eased back. "I've got a little extra left and Sebastian is still in pain."

Titus's gaze jumped to the bathroom door beyond the foot of the bed then back to me, and he gave me a soft sad smile as if he knew what I really needed from Sebastian. "I want you to stay and connect with me, but you're still weak and I..."

His pupils slitted, his beast starting to rise to the surface, and his erection dug into my thigh.

"You won't be able to fully control your beast our first time, will you?" He hadn't had sex in so long and his connection with his beast was still fragile. If his connection was too far gone, it would be best if I didn't have sex with Titus, the man, our first time. His beast would need to fully take over for his soul to mend, and I could only hope it would realize I wasn't as sturdy as a dragon. And yet... if I was at full power, I might be able to satisfy his beast's needs with no problem.

A shiver of anticipation rushed through me at the thought of the ferocious passion that awaited me, along with a hint of fear at his size. He'd given me a glimpse of what sex with him would be like with our first few kisses, and I didn't want him to be afraid to have it with me, but he was also a big man and properly proportioned and I was still very new to sex.

"Make him do all the work," Titus said, pulling me from my thoughts. "It's the least he can do for you."

His words didn't make sense. Sebastian had risked dying to keep us safe during the fight with Deaglan. He'd channeled magic when he shouldn't have to keep the cavern lit so the shadow fae couldn't jump between shadows, and he'd given himself horrible burns for no doubt getting us back to the mortal realm.

I owed him for my life and the lives of my remaining guys.

My eyes burned at that thought and I blinked back my tears.

"Go," Titus whispered. He brushed his lips against my forehead then eased away and pulled down the comforter so I could get off the bed.

Careful not to wake Hawk, whose breath was still slow and deep with sleep — attesting to how low on power he still was — I climbed off the bed and tiptoed to the bathroom.

The door wasn't fully shut, and just like the last time I'd entered Sebastian's bathroom, it opened with a gentle push, letting a soft wash of moist warm air caress my skin.

Inside wasn't as steamy as before since he hadn't been in the shower for as long this time, and the mirror over the sink hadn't completely fogged up. It showed a too-pale woman, clinging to a bloody towel wrapped around her chest, with a wild mess of blond locks, red eyes from crying, and a weak angel glow.

"So Titus let you out of bed," Sebastian said, his smooth tenor drawing my attention from the mirror to the glassed-in shower stall at the end of the room.

And just like the last time, my pulse tripped at the sight of him. I hadn't seen him fully naked since our first time having sex and he was breathtaking. Black tattoos swirled over his sleek sculpted body, the ones on his arms and some across his chest marred by the ugly burn scars, but the rest were perfect, a twisting, mesmerizing black pattern in his pale, luminescent skin. The ink encircled his neck, swept over his chest and washboard abs, wrapped around both thighs, and trailed down to his ankles.

I slid my gaze appreciatively down his body, a part of me stunned that I'd had sex with this man, that he'd want to have sex with a stuffy, uptight angel like me. He wasn't an incubus, but he was still sexy as hell and could have chosen to sleep with anyone — well, almost anyone since Essie had kept turning him down. When we'd first met, he'd proposition every woman he came across and, like an incubus, I doubted he'd ever gone without sex when he wanted it.

When this was done, he'd go back to that lifestyle.

Because he swore he'd never commit to anyone and as much as I'd fallen in love with him, I understood he couldn't love me back. Just like Hawk.

And given our circumstances, that would be the best outcome. As it was, either one or both of them could be killed the next time we faced Deaglan.

Like Cassius.

I needed to make the most of the time I had with him, and right now, my soul desperately needed to connect with his.

My gaze stopped at Sebastian's erection, full and thick and ready for me. I focused on my desire for him and how he always made me feel good and adored and perfect.

"So you just decided to walk into my bathroom?" he asked, repeating what he'd said the last time I'd walked in on him, except this time his voice was thick with desire and not shock at my intrusion.

"I've stopped bleeding." I dragged my attention back to his pale eyes and dropped my towel, giving him a full view of my naked body, something I'd never have done the first time.

His gaze grew heated and he trailed it down to the towel at my feet then back up, pausing at my left hip... where my brand used to be— *was*. Where my brand now *was*.

Was he going to reject me because fate said I belonged to someone else? Like I was fate's property or something to be given away on its cruel whim?

A part of me wanted to follow his gaze and look. I'd only ever seen my brand as a barely-there ghostly swirl under my skin. Had it turned golden? And if it had, did that mean it was a real brand?

He jerked his attention up to my breasts, lingering on where I'd been stabbed then slowly lifted his eyes to capture my gaze, letting me see that he still desired me. I didn't know if he cared about my brand or not, or the fact I'd told him I'd fallen in love with him when I'd promised I wouldn't. Right now, in this moment, he desired me, and a small part of my soul relaxed with relief, while the rest of me tightened in anticipation.

AMIAH

"I've stopped bleeding," I repeated, my voice breathy.

"I can see that."

"I have a little extra left. Let me ease some more of your pain."

"Just my pain?" His lips quirked and for a second he was the Sebastian I'd first met, the one who'd relentlessly teased me and Cassius about sex.

My grief edged into my desire, but instead of diminishing it, my need for Sebastian, for our connection — and to just feel and not think for a little while — grew. God, it was so selfish. But I didn't want to fight it. I'd spent a lifetime fighting myself, denying who I was, and I was just too emotionally exhausted. I needed Sebastian right now. That was just the way it was.

"And my pain," I confessed, letting him look into my eyes and see me. All of me. The woman who was angry and frustrated and heartbroken and throbbing with need.

The desire in his eyes softened and he held out his hand. "Come here."

"Are you going to give me what I want?" I asked, afraid his softening desire meant we weren't going to have sex — even though the rest of him still clearly said he wanted me.

A hint of wickedness sparked back into the softness. "And what do you want, Miss Angel?"

"To connect with you."

"Really? Because I thought you wanted to fuck." He leaned back against the white tiles and put his hands behind his head. The shower spray sluiced down his body, drawing my attention to his stunning physique and his standing-proud erection — as he'd intended — making my breath pick up.

"You know that's what I meant."

"Then say it," he said with a sneer as if daring me to confess something dirty.

Well, fine then. Does he really think I'm still that embarrassed prim angel?

With my heart pounding — because I'd never done something like this before and I was still, just a little bit, that prim angel from a few days ago — I stepped to the shower's entrance and cupped my breasts, making his gaze dip to them. Then I slowly slid my hands down my belly, watching his gaze slide with me, and pushed my fingers into my curls, pointing him to where I wanted him.

"Sebastian," I breathed.

His eyes locked on the spot between my thighs.

"I want you to fuck me."

He swallowed hard. "Well, that backfired."

With a groan, he pushed off the wall and drew close. His erection pressed against my belly, his pale gaze capturing mine and stealing my breath. "Any requests?"

Anything. Everything. Steady me. Make me feel something other than this heartache.

Except— "I'm not up for anything too strenuous. Or rather I won't be in a second, and neither are you."

He frowned, and I pressed my palm against his chest and released a soft stream of magic into him, healing his scars a little more, until all that remained inside me was my core spark of power again.

Exhaustion flooded me, and I leaned into him, laying my cheek against his collarbone and savoring the feel of his slick, naked flesh against mine.

"Oh, sweetheart," he murmured, wrapping his arms around me and helping me stand. "Stop draining yourself. You're going to give Hawk a mental breakdown."

"One more session and you'll be pain free. Scarred, but no longer in pain." I slid my hand over his pecs. He wasn't close to being as bulky as Titus or even as built as Cassius—

I'd run my hands over Cassius's chest like this, appreciating his well-developed musculature, before he— before we— my throat tightened. "Everything I do makes me think of him."

"I know," he said, his voice strange and husky.

"Make me forget, Sebastian." My gaze dipped to my hip and the shimmering gold lines swirling over my skin. "Make me forget everything."

He hooked a finger under my chin and lifted my gaze to his. He had the strangest expression, a mix of sadness and regret and frustration and anger and that same shocking love I'd seen in Titus's eyes.

Then he captured my lips in a tender kiss and I shoved all other thoughts aside. I focused on the feel of his mouth against mine, of his arm around my waist holding me against his wet body, and the straining weak pulse of his cool bright life force.

If we didn't deal with the demonic infection soon, I was going to lose him as well.

Except I couldn't extract foreign magic from someone and even if we could go to Operations, there wasn't anyone there who could do it either. We'd have to call in a specialist.

"Don't go there," he murmured against my lips as if he knew my thoughts had wandered. "You're supposed to be forgetting. You're supposed to be letting me make you feel good."

He turned us, so I could lean against the tiles, and kissed me with a surprising tenderness, exploring my mouth and letting me explore his. It reminded me of having sex with Cassius and how, unbeknownst to me, he was taking his time, memorizing the moment because he didn't think we'd ever have sex again.

He'd thought it was because his fire magic would come back and he wouldn't be able to touch me again. Neither of us had thought it would be because he was dead.

Tears slowly leaked from my eyes, mingling with the mist on my face from the shower's spray. I deepened our kiss, letting Sebastian feel my desire and heartache.

The barely-there wisp of magic left within me connected with him and his life force, adding to my ache.

He was struggling but still alive and fighting.

So was I.

We'd get through this together. All of us—

The *rest* of us.

He cupped my breasts like I had moments ago and kissed his way down to my nipples. I grasped his shoulders to keep my balance, tipped my head back, and closed my eyes. In this moment there was just the feel of his tongue rasping against the sensitive bud and then the gentle pull as he sucked me into his mouth, connecting my peaked nipple to the softly building desire in my core.

He slid his other hand down between my thighs, his fingers skimming the edge of my brand and sending a flicker of cold magic through the swirling lines. My pulse stuttered, but he teased my folds, just a whisper of a touch, and kept my focus on him and what I wanted before I could really think about the mate I didn't want.

His pace was languid, sensual, and exactly what I needed. He brought me to the edge of a gentle climax with his fingers, his mouth paying homage to my breasts, then returned to my lips and urged me to hook a leg behind his waist.

With a low masculine groan, he pushed into me with a delicious, slow, friction until he was fully sheathed.

His life force surged against my senses for a second, bright and cold like it was supposed to be, not barely lit and straining against the darkness. That thing in my soul that needed him, needed all my guys, clicked into place. I was stronger and steadier, and a hint of power, more than what I'd had before, warmed my palms, as if I'd been ever-so-slightly out of alignment and hadn't realized it, and now, with him inside me, I was properly connected to my magic.

Sebastian met my gaze, giving me a glimpse of that sparklingly powerful universe inside him that I'd noticed back in the Winter Court and the calm, powerful stillness newly awakened in my soul grew stronger.

He held my gaze as if he couldn't look away and started to move inside me, the desire in his eyes growing. I let those icy blue orbs hold me captive. My soul might be strong and still at the moment, but it was still fragile and even if I wasn't safe anywhere else, I was safe in those sparkling depths.

He built my need even higher, changing pace and rhythm and force to bring me to a beautiful high before letting me fall over. For a glorious moment there was just the bliss of my muscles contracting around him, the low groan of his own soft release, and whatever it was that aligned our souls. He was the lover I hadn't known I wanted, who lifted me body, mind, and soul. I could face what lay ahead with him, Hawk, and Titus, even mourning Cassius, even being soul bound to a stranger, even facing the Winter Queen and Deaglan.

My skin radiated a brilliant light, signifying my satisfaction, and so did his. This was the first time I'd seen him light up like that and his life force thrummed stronger, more powerful, pushing back some of the darkness inside him.

"You will never cease to amaze me," he murmured as I closed my eyes and gave in to the exhaustion of having drained all my power along with the heartache of losing Cassius and the eventuality that I'd lose Sebastian and Hawk as well.

Sebastian helped me dry off, wrapped me in a new clean towel, and brought me back to Titus and Hawk, snuggling under the covers with me — putting Titus on the outside of our foursome.

Hawk rolled over and gave me a long sensual kiss. It felt like he was saying he loved me, which I knew was impossible. Whatever that strange awe was that filled his expression every time we made love, it wasn't love. And it wouldn't last.

"Everything will be better when you wake up," he murmured. "I promise."

"Even if it isn't, I'll still love you," I mumbled back and once again let myself drift to the edge of a gentle darkness where my heartache and worry was blanketed by blissful nothingness.

"Your fae magic has gotten stronger," Hawk whispered.

His words flittered through me. I hadn't noticed if the foreign magic infused in my cells had gotten stronger or not, I'd been too distracted by everything else.

"And you're glowing just like she is," Hawk added. "I didn't think you were one of the fae who lit up with an orgasm."

"I'm not. Usually," Sebastian whispered back. "It was all her. When she came. It was like she was pushing her healing magic inside me, but instead of angelic magic, she gave me fae magic. I've never felt anything like it."

"Maybe you don't have to go to Sargos." Hawk brushed a warm finger across my cheek and hooked a lock of hair behind my ear. "Maybe she can help you hold the infection at bay."

"That's not a real solution and we both know the second I start channeling magic the infection will grow again."

"But maybe it will be enough to buy us time to find someone else."

"Do you honestly think I won't have to use magic in the next couple of days? Hell, probably the next couple of hours, what with my mother and Deaglan looking for us." Sebastian pressed his cool lips to the back of my neck and his grip around me tightened. "I have no choice. I have to go to Sargos and pay whatever he wants. It's the only way to keep her safe."

His words made my heart tremble and my stomach churn. He was going to sacrifice something, pay a price he didn't want to pay to keep me safe, and I didn't want to be responsible for any more suffering. It was bad enough I selfishly wanted to keep all of them even though my mating brand was going to make me fall in love with the hybrid... if in fact my brand was real.

I drifted to sleep with the churning fear and hope that my brand wasn't real. If it wasn't, Sebastian, once he was well, could remove it, and I wouldn't have to give him up... not until he decided to move on.

I woke in Hawk's warm embrace, lying half on top of him, using his chest as a pillow, with the comforting crackle of his dark, demonic life force stronger than the last time I'd sensed it, sliding against my bright angelic essence. Both Sebastian and Titus were gone, their life forces beyond the bedroom, but still in the apartment, and I was overflowing with power.

The fae magic in my cells still radiated brilliant light as if I'd just orgasmed, and my healing magic heated my palms and rolled up my forearms.

Except this time I faced the window and could see bright slightly purple bands of light cutting around the curtain. Meaning even though the room was still dimly lit, it was clearly daytime. I couldn't have been out long enough to have regained so much power.

"Good morning, gorgeous," Hawk purred. "Or rather, afternoon. I think."

"You're feeling stronger." I shifted so I could look him in the eyes.

His hellfire was banked, small red pinpricks in his unusual blue-gray eyes, but it pulsed in time with his slow, steady heartbeat, strong and sure. He wasn't at full power, but he was definitely better.

"You and Bane gave me a nice little boost," he said, making me think of having sex in the shower with Sebastian... which made me think of Cassius.

My throat tightened.

"Hey." Hawk brushed a strand of hair out of my eyes. "It'll be okay."

It wasn't ever going to be okay. Not completely. But I could give Hawk more power and ensure he survived this mess.

I pressed my lips against his and released my heartache and desire. He couldn't do anything with my grief, but my desire would make him stronger.

With a groan, he returned my kiss, but let me stay in control. Even with just our lips connected, the sense of his life force grew stronger, teasing me with the promise of being fully connected and properly aligning my soul again.

I pushed the comforter back and straddled him, keeping our lips connected and rubbing myself along his hard erection. I wasn't completely ready for him, but I knew he'd easily get me there. He slid his hands down my body and captured my hips.

A crackle of heat swept through my brand and he froze.

"Please don't stop," I said against his lips. "I'm not his. It might not even be real."

"It's real," he replied, his voice husky. "You can't get rid of it. He's your soul mate."

It couldn't be real. I didn't love him. How could the hybrid be my soul mate when I *knew* I loved Hawk? When I needed him and Sebastian and Titus?

I drew back, an icy sliver of fear unfurling in my gut. "Are you ending this?"

"Never. I'm yours until your brand makes you fall in love with him," he said, his hellfire sparking. "But you should know everything before we continue. I've fallen in love with you."

My thoughts stuttered over his words. He couldn't be in love with me. Incubi didn't fall in love.

And yet I knew an incubus madly in love.

Except his bond with Essie made their love possible. With her other mates, he'd never kill her or starve and he wouldn't have to look elsewhere for sustenance.

"Are you sure?" Perhaps it was an infatuation. Incubi didn't become infatuated or jealous either, but that seemed more likely than falling in love. Falling in love was just too dangerous for everyone involved.

"I'm positive." He cupped my cheeks in his warm palms. "That connection you need from us? I need it too, from you. And I'll take it for as long as I can."

Because it didn't matter how much I needed him or cared for him. Eventually there'd only be room in my heart for the hybrid.

Unless...

My pulse picked up with a mix of hope and fear. "Would you want this forever? With him?"

Hawk's hellfire sparked again, the smoldering embers turning into miniscule flames, and my heart pounded. I knew in my soul that I needed them, but they didn't need me and asking him to join an already complicated relationship was asking a hell of a lot.

"Sebastian might not be able to break the bond," I forced out, "but maybe he can add to it."

"I don't know if that's possible."

"Neither do I. But if it was, when this is over, would you want your soul permanently bound to mine?" *Please say yes. God, please.*

I couldn't believe trapping myself in a second soul bond was the best solution. I hadn't wanted any soul bonds, hadn't wanted the horror of feeling my mate in danger, of possibly being torn into two between my mate and my magic. But if it was that or losing Hawk, I'd take Hawk.

Except he stared at me, his expression strange, and I couldn't figure out what it meant.

Then he rolled us over, pinning me to the bed, and captured my mouth in a breathtaking kiss that made my whole body tingle with need. "I think you just asked me to marry you."

"I did?"

And I wasn't going to think about the possibility that my desperate need to keep Hawk came from my heartache over losing Cassius.

The idea of being permanently bound to Hawk didn't terrify me. Not like I thought it would, not like being permanently bound to the hybrid. My bond was real and I was about to be living in my worst nightmare. I wasn't ever going to be free. I was trapped—

Trapped trapped trapped.

But not with Hawk. I could do this if he was with me. I'd never have to doubt if my love for him was real. With him, I could get through this.

Oh, God.

I. Could. Do this.

"I think I just did." I ran my fingers into his jaw-length sandy-blond hair and teased them along the base of his horns, making him shudder and his eyes roll back in pleasure.

He flashed me a brilliant, heart-stopping smile. "This deserves a celebratory orgasm."

"I can't complain with that." If sex was how he celebrated, I was more than in.

"But a quick one. Bane is making lunch... or dinner... or whatever time it is." He dipped in and kissed me, releasing a soft, sensual curl of magic inside me.

I moaned as it swelled around my heart and slid down to my core. He traced its path with his hand, plucking my left nipple then trailing his fingers down my belly and into my folds.

He expertly worked me up, teasing my clit, dipping a finger then two inside me, releasing more glorious magic, until I was panting and aching and on the verge of climax. I squirmed beneath him, my breath fast, my mind wonderfully empty.

Just like with Sebastian in the shower, I focused on just this moment, on the feel of Hawk's body pressed against mine and the amazing crackle of his life force.

And just like Sebastian, he slowly pushed inside me, releasing a little more magic and allowing my body to relax and fully take him without pain. That thing inside me clicked again and that awe, that *was* love, filled Hawk's expression.

"I can't believe you always look at me like that when we join," he said.

"Look at you like what?"

"Like you see me. All of me. Not just my body or how I can make you feel."

"Because you're more than just that." I curled my hips up, taking him deeper inside me and savored the delicious surge of his life force. "You're strength and compassion and fire and need. You're incredible. Your soul is incredible."

"And so is yours." He slowly pulled out then pushed back in, igniting every sensitive nerve in my channel.

Oh, God, yes.

I locked gazes with him, letting him see how much I loved and needed him, and we started a rhythm that quickly picked up speed. I couldn't deny that I did also love his body and how he made me feel — and the feeling was incredible. My high fae glow undulated with our movement, its waves growing, sweeping higher and faster through my skin as Hawk twisted my need tighter and tighter, until every muscle in me contracted, my eyes rolled back, and glorious sensation exploded within me.

My glow burst into a brilliant light and my connection with Hawk surged into my soul. I cried his name and he tensed with his own release, sending another powerful orgasm crashing through me.

"Oh, Hawk," I gasped, clinging to him, feeling his life force and his erection throb inside me. "Oh, wow."

I was never going to get tired of that, and if Sebastian could figure out how to add to my unwanted soul bond, I'd never have to give him up.

AMIAH

I passed out of course, but Hawk woke me, and we had a sensual — and unfortunately quick — shower and changed into clothes Sebastian had set out for us. For Hawk, a set of Sebastian's loose workout clothes, and for me the scrubs Chris had brought over from Operations when this mess had first started.

Everyone in the apartment had to have heard me call out Hawk's name and known I'd orgasmed, and I didn't care. Life was too short and I was done hiding the fact that I wanted sex. That, and I wouldn't have been able to hide it anyway with my new fae glow. And now that I'd recovered all of my magic — and much to my surprise every last drop — I was ready to connect with Titus.

A shiver of desire swept through me and Hawk chuckled.

"You're insatiable."

"Don't tell me you're complaining," I said, reaching to open the door, but he pressed his hand against it, leaned close, and gave me a quick, passionate kiss.

"Nope. And I've got something that's going to make you really happy."

"Pretty sure you just gave me something that made me really happy." Or as happy as I could be still knowing Cassius was dead.

My thoughts must have shown on my face because Hawk's expression softened.

"I told you it'll be okay, and it will be." He interlaced his fingers with mine and tugged me out of the bedroom. "We're going to your office," he called out.

Sebastian rushed into the archway between his living room and kitchen, wiping his hands on a dishcloth. He looked more like himself than he had since we'd been abducted into Faerie even though the glamour that I'd originally thought was his real appearance was still down. He was still the stunning Winter Court prince, a full high fae and not the not-quite-as-handsome faekin glyph witch everyone thought he was. But he wore a pale blue button-down, the sleeves rolled up to his elbows showing off the heartbreaking mix of black tattoos and scars, and loose beige slacks, and for some reason that made me feel like I was seeing the real him. Not Prince Seireadan and not Sebastian Bane semi-illegal magical items dealer. Just Sebastian. "It she—?"

"She's got more power than I've ever seen her have," Hawk replied before Sebastian could finish.

"Oh, thank God." He tossed the cloth onto the counter beside him and hurried to meet us as Hawk opened the door and led me into the office.

I knew the room had floor-to-ceiling bookcases stuffed with old, rare, and magical books, and that Sebastian had a large sturdy desk at the back by the window, a dark blue leather couch, and a wood-burning fireplace, but the only thing I could focus on was Cassius's body.

My heart leaped into my throat and tears burned my eyes.

The guys had cleaned him up, stripped him, and wrapped his hips in a towel. His complexion was pale and the laceration across his neck was shockingly deep, but somehow it still only looked like he was just asleep.

A tear rolled down my cheek.

That was just what I wanted to see. I'd lost my connection with his life force and couldn't sense it now.

I dropped to my knees beside his head and pressed my palms against cheeks that should have been room temperature but weren't. They were warmer. More like his natural body temperature as if he were still alive.

My pulse stalled and I jerked my attention from his face to his neck. It looked like blood welled in the wound ready to spill free but wasn't. Same with the wound at his ribs.

"I managed to get him into hibernation just before he died," Sebastian said, crouching beside me.

Hawk crouched on my other side. "He's not dead. You can still save him."

He wasn't dead?

He wasn't dead!

My breath turned sharp with a whirling mix of relief and joy and anger. "You let me think he was dead."

They'd held me while I'd cried.

We'd made love and they'd known Cassius had been alive all this time and hadn't told me!

My heart had broken. Even with this revelation it still hurt. I'd thought he'd died without knowing I loved him, thought there was always going to be an empty spot in my soul that would never be filled.

I'd lost my best friend and they'd known all along I hadn't.

"You let me think he was dead! You *all* let me think he was dead." How could they!

"It was my call," Sebastian said. "Don't blame Hawk or Titus."

"Hawk and Titus could have said something." I turned my glare to Hawk and he met my gaze head on. The awe— no love that I saw in his eyes was edged with fear.

"You were barely alive," he said. "You couldn't even save yourself."

"You've proven time and again that you have no sense of self preservation," Sebastian added. "I wasn't prepared to lose you."

"Right. Because I'm the healer. Everyone else is expendable." God, I hated that they all thought that, that all I was good for was keeping them alive. But it was true and that hurt even more. I couldn't defend myself in a fight and I kept getting hurt and putting them in danger. I'd become that person who drove me crazy and I had no idea how it had happened.

"You know that's not true." Hawk pressed his hand against my back giving me space by not holding me but comfort with his touch.

"Because there was no reason for you to sacrifice yourself. Cassius will keep. If my spell isn't removed, he'll keep forever," Sebastian said. "Don't tell me you wouldn't have drained yourself to death trying to save him,"

I opened my mouth to disagree. I'd already been drained, my magic wouldn't have locked onto Cassius, but my compulsion to save him would have been overwhelming. And it was Cassius. I would have given everything to save him. I'd already stained my soul by killing people, I would have given what was left to keep him alive.

"Yeah, thought so," Sebastian said, taking my lack of response as an admission of guilt.

"Bane knows I can't lose you like that," Hawk added.

"Neither can I," Titus said from the doorway, his shaggy red hair wet and dripping onto his bulky, muscular — and completely bare — shoulders and chest, his hips wrapped in a towel.

I wanted to yell at all of them, scream all of my frustration and anger and fear, but if the situation was reversed, I'd have done the same thing.

God, I hated the part of myself that saw reason. They'd lied. They'd hurt me.

And I knew in my heart I'd lie to them, let them believe the most horrible things, make them hate me if it kept them alive. I'd do whatever it took.

"Don't make us give you up before we have to," Sebastian said, shocking me, his voice strange and soft and making my heart ache.

I knew there was something between us. He wouldn't have kept having sex with me if there wasn't. But I didn't think it was so deep that he'd want to hold onto what we had for as long as possible.

I opened my mouth again but didn't know what to say. I wanted to be mad. I *was* mad. But I was also in love with them and a century of striving to be practical made me understand why they hadn't said anything.

"Now what are the odds I can convince you to eat something before you save Sparky?" Sebastian asked.

Just the thought of walking away without healing Cassius made my insides churn.

Sebastian sighed. My thoughts must have been clear in my expression yet again. "Didn't think so."

Hawk leaned closer and this time did draw me into an embrace. "What do you need?"

And just like that, he had my back. Like he'd had it from the very beginning of all this... which was the whole reason he'd lied to me about Cassius. He'd support and protect me. Even if that meant protecting me from myself and my magic that compelled me to sacrifice everything to save lives.

I shoved those thoughts aside and focused on the medical problem. "Lots of towels. I don't know how much blood he's lost, but the moment the hibernation spell is gone, he's going to start bleeding out again. I'll also have to heal him quickly, which will be painful and might set off his fire." I glanced at all the flammable books surrounding us and so did Sebastian.

"We should move him into the clean room," Sebastian said. "The protections on that room are strong enough his fire won't get out. If we put him in the corner there'll be enough space to keep Rin locked up while Amiah works."

Rin?

Right.

That was what Deaglan had called the hybrid.

Which meant the guys had already had a conversation with my unwanted mate and learned his name—

And there'd be time to ask about that later. Right now, I could get Cassius back. That was what I needed to focus on.

"Do we think it's wise?" Hawk asked. "If Deaglan actually did starve him for a long time, any amount of blood might send him into a feeding frenzy."

"I'd rather have Rin lose his shit behind a barrier than have Cassius burn down the building." Sebastian's gaze slid to me and just like his tone before, his expression was strange. "Better to find out now that he'll be unable to control his hunger than let him out and Amiah get a papercut."

"He's not getting out," Titus growled. "Ever."

"Really? And how's that going to work?" Sebastian jerked his attention to Titus, frustration sweeping through his expression. "He's her fucking mate."

Titus's canines extended and he snarled at Sebastian.

A new horrible realization flooded me.

I'd branded him.

I was going to have to seal our bond or both of us would go crazy.

Oh, God. I was going to have to sleep with him whether I wanted to or not.

Hawk's embrace tightened.

"Hey." He shot a dark look at Titus and then Sebastian. "Not what we should be talking about right now." He turned his attention back to me. "We need towels and we need to move him. Anything else?"

I was going to have to have sex with the hybrid. I'd seen what happened when an angel tried to ignore the bond and it hadn't been pretty. How could I have possibly thought being made to fall in love with him was the worse part about the brand?

"Amiah." Hawk hooked a finger under my chin and lifted my gaze to his. "Let's get Cassius back. We can deal with everything else later."

Because everything else was inevitable. This was my fate and I had no say in the matter. The only things I did have control over was how I faced my new mate and saving my best friend.

So I'd do that. I'd save Cassius, tell him that I loved him, and then have sex with the hybrid before I went insane.

I'd steeled myself to have sex with Sebastian with everyone watching. I could steel myself to have sex with the hybrid.

I sucked in a sharp breath.

Focus on saving Cassius.

"He'll be in shock from both the injury and the rapid healing." I made myself meet Sebastian's gaze and face the pity in his eyes. I wouldn't be ashamed of what I had to do. "Do you think you have enough magic to use your sleep glyph?"

"I do, but it would be best if you used it," Sebastian replied. "We've bought ourselves some time by coming here, but eventually my mother will recast the tracking spell, and she and Deaglan will figure out we left Faerie and catch up to us. Better if I save what I've got left for that."

"And I can still use it?" I'd used his glyph on him after we'd escaped the Winter Court, but it hadn't occurred to me that I could do it again, let alone in the mortal realm or on someone else.

"You still glow, so you're still high fae," Sebastian replied. "You just need to press one hand on the glyph and the other over Cassius's heart, think about pushing power into the glyph, and say ignite."

"Okay then." Hawk stood. "I'll get the towels."

He hurried out of the room, and Titus entered, picked up Cassius, and slung him over his shoulder. The towel dropped to the floor, but Sebastian grabbed it before I could.

"You're eating after this," he said. "I don't care what else happens, you haven't eaten in over a day."

"I'll eat. But on the roof." A shudder swept through me at the memory of being attacked on the roof by Balwyrdan, and I shoved it aside. We were limited in where we could go and I'd recover my magic faster if I could see the open sky. I'd just have to deal with the memory. Sebastian had been right. We could be in a fight again soon. I had to get my magic back as fast as possible. In the very least, I had to get enough back so I wasn't exhausted and dizzy and a liability.

"Sweetheart, I don't care where you do it, so long as you do it. And I will shove it down your throat if I have to."

"I'll hold you down while he does it," Titus said heading down the hall toward the clean room.

Jeez. Overprotective much? Just like my safety back in the aerie, it looked like they all agreed on me eating, too. "That won't be necessary. You may have to keep shaking me to keep me awake, but you won't have to force me."

And they wouldn't have to force me to have sex with the hybrid. I couldn't run away from that reality, so I'd face it head on.

I would.

Really.

Titus opened the clean room door and strode in. I followed, but my attention jumped to the hybrid kneeling in the middle of the enspelled circle.

My mouth went dry with fear even as something inside me warmed at the sight of him and drew me a step closer to the edge of the barrier. I was going to have to sleep with him.

The thought was horrifying. And it was even more horrifying that the warmth inside me sank low and started to softly throb.

God. This was a nightmare. I didn't think I'd feel the pull of the brand so soon, and not only was my life not my own anymore, neither, it seemed, was my body.

Had he realized he was going to have to sleep with me as well? Did the brand make his body desire mine like mine desired his even though the rest of me was furious at the thought? Was this situation just as terrible for him?

His hellfire smoldered, red pinpricks in black eyes that were locked on me, and the expression on his sharp, sculpted face was flat, no indication about how he felt about me or his situation. Just like it had been when I'd staggered in earlier.

Would he look less intimidating if he let any kind of emotion through? If he smiled, he might almost be as handsome as Cassius. Funny how I could notice something like that now that he wasn't trying to kill me.

Or was that just my brand making me find him attractive?

His long black hair had been pulled back into a ponytail, but a few shorter locks had escaped framing his face, drawing my attention to the white scar across his neck. He'd had his throat slit before he'd been turned. Most likely he'd been killed, not just drained, before his sire had performed the ritual to turn him into a vampire, suggesting he hadn't become a vampire willingly. His strange life force seethed against my senses, hot and cold, alive and dead, and always with the pain that had been permanently imprinted in his cells.

Now that I was fully conscious, it was clear to my magical senses that he was starving. He hadn't properly eaten in a long time and I could only assume that was Deaglan's doing. Just like the pain permanently imprinted in his cells. Bringing Cassius in here and letting him bleed even into a handful of towels was cruel, but we didn't have any other options.

The hybrid—

No. Rin.

Rin didn't say anything and didn't move, only followed us with his eyes, as Titus set Cassius on the floor in the corner where there was enough space for all of us to gather.

"How fast can you get bagged blood up here?" I asked Sebastian as he wrapped the towel back around Cassius's hips, giving him the modesty he wouldn't know he had but would undoubtedly appreciate. Which was silly, since everyone now, including the hybrid, had seen him naked.

"He needs more than just blood," Sebastian said. "He's half sin eater."

Well that would explain why Deaglan would have wanted him... although it didn't explain why he was still behind the barrier. There wasn't a spell a sin eater couldn't consume. It was why Michael had slaughtered every last one of them — or so everyone had thought — fearing that they'd be able to destroy his magically created army.

Of course, he was only half sin eater. He might not have inherited all of his sin eater parent's abilities.

And that didn't address the problem of him needing to feed on magical energy to survive. That wasn't something that could be easily bagged like blood, and I doubted Sebastian would want to sacrifice one of his rare, magical books to feed the hybrid.

We were going to have to figure out something else that kept everyone safe, and the first, easier, step was dealing with his vampiric hunger. Right now all of him was starving and he was certain to go into a feeding frenzy the second he smelled blood. It was a miracle he hadn't lost it when I'd staggered in earlier still bleeding. Perhaps if one of his hungers was satiated, he might be able to control his other hunger enough to not kill someone while he fed on their magic.

"Blood will still help," I said as Hawk hurried into the room with a pile of white towels — I was pretty sure Sebastian only had white towels — and set them by Cassius's head.

"I've ordered some blood along with clothes for everyone, since the only changes of clothes Titus and Cassius had are still in the trunk of my car where we left it when we—" Sebastian snapped his mouth shut.

But I knew what he was going to say. *When they rescued me from Balwyrdan.*

I shuddered, the memory of that horrible night rising to the forefront of my mind, and I shoved it back down. I wasn't going to think about what Balwyrdan had done to me. Not ever again if I could help it. "When will the blood and clothes arrive?"

"We agreed putting in a rush order would draw attention. It won't get here until at least the morning," Sebastian finished.

I glanced at Cassius. Could I resist my need to get him back until the morning? "What about getting blood from the club downstairs?"

Sebastian's apartment was above the most popular vampire nightclub in town. There was blood aplenty just three floors down.

"I don't want to risk my landlord finding out I bought blood from her club. Victoria and I might have come to an arrangement since the last time I had angel visitors, but I trust her even less than I trusted Mavis."

And Mavis had sold us out to Balwyrdan.

Not going to think about it.

"Okay, then we wait."

But the moment I said that, the compulsion to heal Cassius twisted in my chest and my magic swelled into my palms. I hadn't locked onto him, but I was one step away from that even though he felt dead to all my magical senses.

"I'm not sure it's wise to let Cassius stay down. Even until just the morning," Hawk said. "We keep having our asses handed to us *with* Cassius in the fight. We're going to get squashed if Deaglan finds us and he's still down."

"Except Deaglan can take Cassius's fire." And the last time that had happened, Cassius had almost died.

"And that's one of the many items at the top of my things to deal with list," Sebastian replied. "Just as soon as I deal with this." He jerked his thumb to his chest, indicating the demonic magic trapped inside him.

Titus huffed. "Even without his fire, it's better if he's awake and defending himself than one of us having to protect him or carry him around."

Which was something I couldn't argue with.

But jeez, I didn't want to be cruel to Rin. He might have almost killed me, and I didn't want to be soul bound to him — and I most certainly didn't want to desire him — but I wasn't Deaglan. I didn't purposefully try to hurt people. And without a doubt, the pain imprinted in his cells was because Deaglan had hurt him. With him trapped behind a barrier and starving, healing Cassius was going to be torture.

Not to mention, Sebastian was right. At some point we were going to have to let Rin out and taunting him with blood was no way to build trust. And I doubted we had the time to wait for the brand to make him love me. That could happen in a few days or a few months. It was different for every brand.

Except with his current state of hunger, it wasn't safe to let him out. Even if the brand made his body want me like it was making me want him, that didn't mean he trusted us or wasn't going to hurt us.

I crouched at the edge of the barrier, my pulse pounding. With my rushing blood and my magic heating my palms, just being in the room was probably taunting him.

But he gave no indication he was hungry or angry or feeling the same frustrating attraction I was. He didn't move, didn't breathe — he didn't have to because he was already dead — and he gave no indication about what he was thinking. Not even a flicker of hellfire to show he had any kind of emotion at all.

He just watched me.

His lifeless essence oozed across my senses before his unusual life force overwhelmed it. He was just so strange. He wasn't alive and my magic couldn't fix that. His undead nature made my magic shrink away from him.

But the part of me that sensed life forces didn't care that he was dead, which meant that power was a different, separate ability from my healing. He had a life force and I could connect with it. Just like I'd been able to connect with Deaglan's and his men's.

"You heard our conversation," I said. "We have blood coming for you, but I need to heal Cassius and that's going to involve blood."

His expression didn't change. He didn't even blink.

"I know you're hungry and I wouldn't do this here if we weren't afraid Cassius's fire would burn down the building."

Still nothing.

I glanced at Sebastian. "Is there a sound block on the barrier? Can he even hear me?"

"He can. Do you understand what Amiah is saying?" Sebastian asked him.

"I do, your highness," Rin replied in his barely-there soft voice as he bowed his head.

Except I wasn't sure he understood that I didn't mean to be cruel, and he'd looked down awfully fast when Sebastian spoke... although I didn't get the sense he was being completely submissive to Sebastian. More like he was going through the motions he thought Sebastian wanted to see.

But I had no idea why I thought that. His expression hadn't changed. There hadn't been fear or anger or anything else in his eyes.

Maybe he couldn't have emotions. Unlike Cassius, who struggled to keep his contained so he could control his fire, maybe Rin didn't have any at all.

Would that make it easier to have sex with him? Would I be able to just satisfy the brand's needs and go through the motions like he was now if there wasn't any emotion involved?

Would the brand even be able to make him love me?

The thought broke my heart, because I could have emotions and the brand would make me love him. I'd spend the rest of my life with an unrequited love that I hadn't wanted in the first place.

And there wasn't anything I could do about it.

AMIAH

I COULD, HOWEVER, GET MY BEST FRIEND BACK, SO I TURNED AWAY FROM Rin to focus on saving Cassius. I'd need to work fast. For once, I wouldn't have to hold my magic back. The faster I could get it into him, the better. Except if he was too close to death, it wouldn't matter how fast my power rushed in.

Which was something I wasn't going to think about. This was my second chance to save him and I wouldn't fail.

I knelt beside him, grabbed one of the towels, and pressed it against the laceration in his side.

"Titus, can you hold this?"

"Sure." Titus nudged Sebastian out of the way and knelt beside me.

I handed him a couple more towels just in case as Hawk sat on my other side, and without being told, pressed a towel against Cassius's neck.

I turned to Sebastian. "Can you release the hibernation spell without touching him?" Out of all of the guys, he was the least able to handle Cassius's fire. Titus was immune and Hawk could rapidly heal serious injuries.

"I can," Sebastian replied. "You want me on the other side of the room?"

"No, I want you behind me. I want to use your sleep glyph the second he's healed. Hopefully that will contain most of his fire. But the fastest way to do that is to heal him while having one hand on him and one hand on your glyph."

"Will touching both of them affect your magic?" Hawk asked.

"Cassius has the more serious injuries so my magic will heal him first, but," I gave Sebastian an apologetic grimace, "if I try to control my power, I might not be able to save him."

"Which means any extra is going to go into my scars and it'll be painful." He unbuttoned his shirt and tossed it on the floor by the door, making Hawk raise his eyebrows in question. "Hey, I like the shirt. I don't want it to go up in flames."

"Yeah, and that little gleam in her eyes just now when she saw all your bad boy tattoos had nothing to do with it," Hawk said.

Sebastian flashed Hawk a lopsided grin. "Well, maybe there's a bit of that, too." He crouched behind me, grabbed the back of my scrubs, and twisted the fabric around his fist. "I'll try to pull you away after you cast the sleep spell, but if your magic is too strong, I can't make any guarantees."

"I've got both of you," Titus said.

I adjusted my position so I could place one hand over Cassius's heart, his bare skin strangely warm even with my power heating my palm, and the other on Sebastian's small, swirling sleep glyph on his shoulder.

"Don't pull me away until I say I'm done or you sense the glyph has been activated. No matter what. I don't know if I have enough power to save Cassius without touching him." Not without killing more people, since healing from afar required a lot more magic than healing while in contact with someone. God, I hoped I never felt I had to take someone's life to save a life again.

"I'm not losing him."

"You won't," Hawk said, and Titus grunted.

"Remember to push power into the glyph and say ignite." Sebastian tensed, ready to jerk me away. "You just say when and I'll release the hibernation spell."

I drew in a deep breath and focused on my palm pressed against Cassius's bare chest. It rested over a heart that wasn't beating which made my heart twist with grief, even though I knew he was in hibernation and not actually dead.

Please don't be dead. Please let Sebastian be right about freezing him before he passed.

The power in my hand flared to life, creating a brilliant white nimbus, brighter than my unnatural fae glow. It burned under my skin, racing up my forearms and past my elbows, eager to be released.

I could do this. I had more than enough power to heal the cut in his side and neck and restore his blood... but only if he still had a life force.

"Okay."

Sebastian hissed a soft sibilant word and the pain in his life force surged against my senses.

But so did a small, flicker of fiery life force.

It whispered inside me then went out, making my soul stutter. Cassius. My whole essence snapped to a pinpoint focus on him, jerking away from the pain in Sebastian that I couldn't heal. There was only Cassius and my magic's desire to save him. Now. If I didn't do something now, I'd lose him.

Save him. Save him. Now.

My pulse leaped into a rapid tattoo and my magic exploded out of me before I even thought to release it. It slammed into Cassius, surging into the lacerations now gushing blood and filling up the towels, as well as seizing onto the last bit of his life force and clinging to it, forcing it to stay lit — something my magic had never done before.

In the blink of an eye, my power tore into the cells of his damaged flesh, wrenching them back to the way they'd been before his injury, and reignited the spark of life in the core of his being.

Every muscle in my body contracted as my power roared out of me in a violent rush, and then every muscle in Cassius's body seized as well.

His eyes snapped open, his angel glow so bright I couldn't see his pupils, and he released a great, heart-wrenching howl.

My connection with him shattered with a sharp, painful *snap*, all of his injuries fully healed, and my power slammed into Sebastian. He screamed as well, and then Cassius's fire exploded from his body and I was in the middle of an inferno.

Sweat burst over my skin with the sudden ferocious heat, and my healing magic stuttered and went out, completely spent in the blink of an eye. The towels Hawk and Titus held and the one around Cassius's hips burst into flames because Cassius was in shock and wasn't conscious enough to control his magic.

Flames raced through Hawk's pantleg and he scrambled back as Titus reached for me and Sebastian.

Fire scorched my hand pressed against Cassius's heart with an agonizing pain, turning my skin red when his remained perfect, and the flames caught in my scrubs.

Crap. I thought I'd at least have a second.

I mentally yanked at the fae magic in my body and shoved whatever I could into Sebastian's glyph.

"Ignite," I screamed, hoping the force of my word would ensure I properly powered the spell.

Cassius's eyes rolled back and his flames went out. Titus yanked off his burning towel, ripped the fiery end off with a quick jerk, and Sebastian shoved me to the floor so Titus could smother the flames in my scrubs.

"Fuck, now I know why Cassius is always on the verge of a mental breakdown," Hawk groaned. Both of his pantlegs were scorched — one burned all the way up to his knee — but his flesh underneath, while bloody, was back to normal.

Unlike mine. Titus had managed to put out the fire in my clothes so I hadn't been burned there, but my hand that had been over Cassius's heart was bleeding, and the pain was almost as bad as when I'd taken too much of Hawk's power. Much to my surprise, the damage was mostly first-degree burns with a little bit of second — which was why it hurt so much.

"Do you have anything left?" Sebastian asked, gathering me in his arms, careful not to touch my burned hand and forearm.

His life force thrummed against my senses and so did the pain of his demonic infection. It wasn't as bad as it had been before we'd had sex in the shower, but he wasn't getting a complete reprieve from it either.

Titus's life force joined Sebastian's, drawing my attention to him. His pupils were slitted and his canines extended, his dragon on the verge of taking over. He growled low in his throat and brushed aside a strand of hair that was pasted to the side of my face with my sweat then cupped my cheek with his large palm.

The ferocity of his life force surged with the contact, wild and primal and furious.

I was wrong. His dragon was the one in control right now and was barely holding it together.

Hawk crouched beside me and grabbed my good hand, clinging to it as if he were afraid to let go. His eyes were too wide and filled with fear, and his life force crackled with desperate fiery darkness, matching his rapid pulse.

My magical senses added him to the mix with Sebastian and Titus then reached out and connected with Cassius's strong, sure blazing life force, and Rin's strange alive yet dead force.

I let their swirling mix of life, hot and cold, bright and dark, fiery, ferocious, and wild, whirl inside me. They were *all* alive — or in Rin's case, undead — and Cassius was perfectly healed. So, too, were Sebastian's burns. My magical senses told me there wasn't a hint of physical damage left in either man's body.

Thank God, they're all alive.

And all I'd had to pay was the exhaustion of having drained myself and some excruciating pain. But I didn't have a life-threatening injury or any broken bones, which meant that in a few hours, I might have enough power to turn the burns into sensitive scars.

And strangely enough, I did have a little bit of magic left.

Hunh.

I'd thought I'd spent it all. Just a few seconds ago, it had felt like I had.

I pushed my remaining power into my burns, easing some of the pain, and the exhaustion of really having spent all of my magic this time swept through me... again?

My lids drifted shut and I savored the feel of the guys' life forces pulsing against my senses. It almost felt as if they pulsed inside me, like when we joined during sex. Except the sensation wasn't nearly as powerful as what I felt during sex.

And now all I could think about was having sex.

With my guys.

All of my guys... including Rin.

No. Not Rin. I didn't love him. Only my body wanted Rin because of the brand, not my heart or soul.

"Wake up, Amiah." That was Sebastian, and his words tugged my thoughts back to where I actually was. In his clean room, exhausted and in pain.

"Maybe we should just let her sleep," Titus growled.

"She hasn't eaten in over a day," Hawk replied. "She'll recover her magic faster if she eats something before passing out."

I forced my eyes open. "I'm okay. I just need a minute and then I can eat."

The exhaustion and dizziness would pass. Slowly, but it would pass enough for me to move around a bit, certainly eat something.

The hellfire in Hawk's eyes flared. "Don't you ever do that again."

God, I wish I could say I wouldn't. "Like I tell Cassius, I make no promises."

"This being in love thing sucks." He rubbed his face, smearing blood down his cheek but didn't seem to notice.

Behind him, Rin still knelt in the middle of the circle, his expression tight with pain. His hellfire writhed in his eyes and his fangs had fully extended, and he stared at me with a desperate hunger. I had no idea how he was still kneeling. His force of will was extraordinary, but it was clear his hunger was starting to overwhelm him and if it did, there was a chance he wouldn't be able to get it back under control until he'd fed.

"We have to feed Rin," I said.

The desire that I didn't want and couldn't do anything about because I was exhausted swelled, along with my need to heal even though all of my magic was gone. Which was ironic since I couldn't *heal* him. And yet it still urged me to go to him, release him from the circle, let him feed, and ease his suffering, something I'd never felt before for a vampire. If I pressed my palm against the wide thick glyph at the top of the circle, the barrier would come down.

I started to sit up before I fully registered what I was doing, but Sebastian held me tight. "Don't you dare. It's too dangerous."

I knew that, and yet the pressure of my healing compulsion mixed with my unwanted desire for Rin only grew stronger. And God, if we kept him in there starving, we were probably just as cruel as Deaglan. "We can't treat him like Deaglan did."

"We aren't and he knows that," Hawk said. "Blood is coming. He'll be okay, but I'm not willing to bet your life by assuming your brand will stop him from killing you while in a frenzy."

He was right. But it took everything I had to ignore my need to help him and focus on what I needed to do next.

I turned my attention to Cassius, beautiful, completely naked, and outlined with the charred remains of his inferno. The white floor, walls, and ceiling around him had been scorched black, and he was surrounded by burned and bloody towels and a lot of ash.

"In the very least, we should clean up this blood and get him into a bed," I said.

"Will his fire go off again when he wakes?" Titus asked.

"No, he's fine now." I'd never healed Cassius from so serious an injury, but he wasn't in shock or pain anymore. When he woke, he'd have full control of his power like normal... or as full control as he could get with it tied to his emotions — which was something else we were going to need to deal with on top of everything else.

"Okay," Sebastian said. "Who's getting Amiah food and taking her to the roof and who's cleaning up and moving Sparky."

"Not me," Titus huffed, smoke curling from his still-human nostrils. "My beast is getting tired of waiting. I'm not sure how much longer I can control it before it doesn't care if it hurts you when we mate."

"As soon as I get some power back," I promised.

Hawk glared at me. "And you've healed this burn."

"All right. Hawk, take Amiah. We'll meet you on the roof so we can talk about what were going to do about—" Sebastian ran a hand over his spikey white and silver hair. "Fuck, about everything. We seriously need a plan."

Hawk gathered me in his arms, even though I insisted I could walk. My pace would have been slow and I would have needed his help to balance, but I could have walked, except he wouldn't listen.

I kept my gaze off of Rin and prayed that eventually my need to heal his suffering would go away. He'd get blood in the morning. He'd be okay until then.

He would.

Really.

Hawk carried me to the kitchen where Sebastian had plates of penne primavera with generous amounts of freshly grated parmesan on top already doled out. After a quick reheat in the microwave — where I almost fell asleep while we waited despite the agony in my hand — we headed out of Sebastian's apartment, Hawk with a blanket slung over his shoulder and still carrying me, and me balancing my plate of pasta on my stomach and holding it with my good hand.

Outside, the hall was just as opulent and white as Sebastian's apartment with a marble floor and gilded frescoes on the ceiling. A part of me still couldn't believe the excess even though I now knew he was a Faerie prince. It just seemed so unnecessary, and the theme carried into his private stairs that led all the way down to the ground floor without entrances to any of the other floors, and up to the roof.

The last time I'd climbed these stairs, I'd just had sex with Sebastian, and then Hawk had made me come again with his fingers. I'd been so confused, had thought I'd just made a horrible mistake, and yet I'd loved it, craved more of it. Having sex with Sebastian had been amazing and it still was, even in comparison to Hawk — who was mind blowing, like an incubus was supposed to be.

Sex with all of my guys so far had been special, and I had no doubt Titus would be just as amazing. Even if he didn't have the experience Hawk and Sebastian did, our connection made it special and always would.

Would I feel that way about Rin? We supposedly had a deeper connection, our souls were now permanently bound together. We were supposed to be fated for each other.

Except I didn't love him.

I loved Cassius and Hawk and Sebastian and Titus.

Which, if I really thought about it was crazy. The only one who I'd spent any real time with was Cassius. But it didn't matter. I'd fallen in love with them, like a real person, not forced to love them by a magical bond. I didn't want to love Rin. And I certainly didn't want my body to desire him like it currently did.

We stepped out onto the roof and were instantly enveloped in late-afternoon heat. The air was thick with humidity and filled with the familiar rumble of vehicles on the streets down below. In front of us, the UV-blocking canopy that protected Union's vampire citizens from the sun for this one section in the Quarter, connected with the edge of the building, blocking us in, and only rose seven feet overhead before stretching to the building across the street. But it was enough to ease the pressure from around my heart because everywhere I looked I could see sky, the Supernatural Quarter's beautiful skyline, and the beginnings of a brilliant summer sunset.

Hawk set me on my feet by the security door so I could lean against its sun-warmed concrete blocks while he laid out the blanket on the roof's rough surface. Then he helped me settle with his legs on either side of me, letting me lean against him to keep upright so I could eat.

The memory of Balwyrdan finding me up here, confused and even more sexually frustrated than before, shivered inside me, and I shoved it back down. Again.

I couldn't leave. I needed to see the sky and I needed to be with my guys and let their life forces thrum against my senses. And I knew the tension in my body would only ease more once Sebastian and Titus came up. Already I felt lighter, more powerful — although the power was just in my mind. I couldn't have regained any amount of magic in the short time it had taken us to get up there.

Hawk held my plate so I didn't have to lean too far forward to eat, and I obediently ate while trying to not fall asleep. And the moment I took my first mouthful, I realized I *was* starving. Too much had happened—was *still* happening, and I'd somehow managed to ignore the fact that I hadn't eaten much of anything in far too long.

That was probably why I thought the pasta was the most incredible thing I'd ever eaten. Sebastian might be a good cook, but I doubted he was that good.

We sat in silence for a long time while I tried to stay awake and eat even with Hawk's raised demonic body temperature making me far too warm with the summer's heat to properly relax. But I didn't care about being too hot. I needed his arms around me more than I needed to be comfortable—

Which made me think of the Winter Court. I hadn't felt its chill since we'd returned to the mortal realm, and I suspected that was because of something Sebastian had done and not because I was no longer in Faerie... except hadn't Sebastian said he couldn't form a portal?

"How did we get out of Faerie?" I asked, taking another bite of pasta, even as my lids drifted shut.

"Bane summoned this short guy and said he owed you," Hawk replied. "Said you paid him to remove your brand."

And just the mention of my brand made my body ache for Rin.

I gritted my teeth, fighting the desire swelling within me. I didn't want him.

But my brand didn't care. Fate said we were meant to be and I had no say in the matter.

Hawk pressed his lips against the top of my head. "You're already feeling the pull of the bond, aren't you?"

There was no point in denying it. Hawk could sense sexual desire. He knew exactly what my body wanted even if my heart and mind were screaming in defiance.

"It's just my body. It's so frustrating. I don't love him. I don't want him. And yet the minute I look at him or think about him, all I want to do is have sex with him."

And while yes, I'd desired my guys almost as quickly as I desired Rin, this was different. With them, I'd had a choice. I could have resisted my desire, slept with only one of them, done any number of things.

But with Rin, if I resisted for too long, I'd lose my mind or die just like if someone killed him.

It wasn't fair that my body wanted sex before my brand had made me fall in love with him.

"I don't know how I'm going to get through it," I said, my voice frustratingly small even though I'd told myself that I'd face my situation head on. "I don't know how I can have sex with him if the brand hasn't forced me to love him."

Hawk tightened his embrace. "I can be there with you and use my magic to help you through it. You don't have to do it alone, do you?"

No. I didn't. There wasn't anything that said a bond had to be sealed with just the branded mates doing the act. Except I wasn't sure how Rin would react to that. Hawk was up for anything, but Rin might not be and he was just as stuck in this mess as I was. Was that really the right way to start our relationship? And did it really matter if having Hawk join us was the only way I could get through it? Our bond had to be sealed. There were no ands, ifs, or buts about it.

AMIAH

"We'll work something out after he's properly fed," I said to Hawk, even as the fear of having sex with Rin and my need to ease his suffering surged, battling inside me.

He'll feed soon and I don't have to do it alone. He only needs to last a few more hours and then Hawk will help me seal my bond. And then...

I had no idea what would happen after that, and I was just too tired to try to figure it out.

"Work what out?" Sebastian asked as he stepped onto the roof with Titus — who had a new towel around his hips — both men carrying a plate of pasta.

"Sealing my bond with Rin."

"That's not something you have to worry about right now. You've got at least a few weeks." Sebastian sat beside me and dug into his pasta.

"I don't." Which made me want to scream with frustration. "The brand isn't making me love him, but it is making me desire him. I don't know how long I can resist."

Sebastian shot Hawk a surprised look. "Already?"

"Yeah," Hawk said. "I can help her through it, but whoever said an angelic mating brand was a beautiful thing was fucked up. No one should have to have sex if they don't want to."

"We should put him in hibernation," Titus said, sitting on my other side, his plate piled high, easily double Sebastian's serving.

"Already had this discussion with lover boy," Sebastian said, pointing his fork at Hawk. "Amiah and Rin still have to seal the bond."

"If the bond hasn't made her love him, then it hasn't made *him* love *her*." Titus's pupils slitted. "We all know how vampires have sex. He's going to bite her and there's nothing stopping him from hurting her even if he isn't in a feeding frenzy."

"Which is why I'm going to be there," Hawk said.

"We should all be there," Titus growled back.

The idea sent a shiver of desire racing through me, although I was pretty sure Titus hadn't really meant for us to all have sex together.

"God, I love you," Hawk said.

Titus frowned, Sebastian snorted, and then Titus realized what he'd said and his eyes went wide.

"You know what I meant," Titus said, his voice gruff.

"I did," I said, my lids drifting closed again.

"We all did," Sebastian chuckled, bumping my shoulder with his and waking me up. "Eat."

I speared a piece of penne and made myself eat it, but the weight of having spent all my magic — again and again and again — was stronger than the strengthening thrum of the guys' life forces or even the pain burning through my hand, and I wasn't going to stay awake much longer. Except if I passed out, they were going to go ahead and make a plan without me. Again.

"So what's the plan?" I asked.

"We can't do much of anything until you've gotten the demonic magic out of you," Hawk said to Sebastian.

"Yeah, but I haven't been able to get ahold of Sargos," Sebastian replied.

Titus huffed. "How long have we got until your mother can recast the spell tracking Amiah's connection with the Winter Court?"

"Karthick blocked Amiah's connection to the Winter Court and we've left Faerie." Sebastian frowned at me and I realized I'd been pushing a piece of penne around the plate without actually spearing it. "If we're lucky, that will buy us a few more days. But even if I can get to Sargos before then, my mother is still going to come after us."

"And she and Deaglan are cozy," I said, giving up on eating and leaning back into Hawk's embrace. "How much do you want to bet he's offered to help find us?"

"It wouldn't surprise me if she lets him and his team come after us instead of risking more of her harem and her constructs," Sebastian replied. "And really the only thing I can do is keep breaking her spell after she's found us and then move us to a new location."

"That isn't really a solution," Hawk said.

"No shit." Sebastian rolled his eyes at him. "As long as the Winter Court has such a strong claim on Amiah and my mother remains Queen, she'll always be able to find us. No concealment spell will be able to hide her, not like it hid me." Sebastian set his plate on the rooftop and stared through the purple glass canopy at the Quarter's skyline. "I can't believe I'm saying this, but Cassius was right from the beginning. There's nowhere we can go. Getting the Heart is the only solution. We'll be more powerful than anyone else and we could use it to get the Winter Court to relinquish its claim on Amiah."

"But we don't know when the final key will be empowered," Titus said. "And Deaglan has the other keys."

"Which is why I need to get rid of this infection." The muscles in Sebastian's jaw flexed, the only indication of the now-constant pain he was in. "If I'm at full power, I can prevent Deaglan from taking Cassius's fire *and* get his keys. Deaglan thinks I'm weak and has no clue how powerful I've become in the three hundred years since he tried to kill me. We'll use that to our advantage."

"So we what? Hope you can get to Sargos before your mother and Deaglan find us?" Hawk asked. "That's a terrible plan."

"I'm not going to stop looking for a better option, but even if I find a way to hide us or break the Winter Court's claim on Amiah, I'm still going to need to get my power back." Sebastian sighed. "Which means I should get back to my books to find our option B."

Something he shouldn't have to do alone. "I'll help," I said, struggling to sit up.

Sebastian leaned in and gave me a tender kiss, using it to push me back against Hawk's chest.

"You're going to fall asleep before you've finished reading a single sentence. We still have time, probably a few days before my mother finds us. For God's sake, rest," he said, worry flashing in his eyes and not saying what I knew he wanted to. Rest so I had all my magic back, because we were going to need it.

Sebastian stood and Titus took his place, capturing my mouth in a hard kiss that stole my breath and left me reeling, before jerking back.

His body trembled, need darkening his eyes, and his erection tented his towel, but he managed to stand and step away.

"I'll help you," Titus said, his voice gruff.

Sebastian and Titus left, and I drifted into a half sleep in Hawk's embrace unable to keep my eyes open any longer.

The sun slowly sank below the Quarter's skyline, the sky darkened, and the streetlights turned on. Below, the *thump thump thump* of loud music pounded from the club beneath us in a primal, rhythmic beat, and more activity sounded from the street below as most of the vampire section's residents started their day even though the area was protected from the sun.

Hawk didn't say anything and didn't ask to change positions. He just held me as his heat and life force sank through my skin, into my veins, and swelled around my heart. Somehow, it connected with the core of my power there even though I always felt the source of my power in my palms.

But this wasn't my healing magic he was connecting with. It was whatever was inside me that connected with someone's life force. And whatever power it was, it loved the feel of Hawk. It yearned for him, strained to be wrapped in his life force, was strengthened by it without taking anything from him, not like how I'd used my magic to steal the life forces of Deaglan's men to power my healing.

I let it sink into my soul and savored the feel of it, fiery and dark, caressing my light. Somehow our life forces aligned. I didn't know how Rin was my soul mate and Hawk wasn't when we fit together so perfectly. But it was just more proof about how wrong everyone was about the angelic mating brand. Everything about it was a lie. Rin wasn't my soul mate, he was just the soul I ended up bound to when my brand finally awoke.

And I was going to have to figure out how to make the best of this horrible situation.

Everything in my soul said he wasn't a monster. Except I had no idea if that was the brand making me think that or not—

No, I'd felt his pain and, if I concentrated, could feel it now. Someone, most likely Deaglan, had hurt him for a long time, and he'd spoken up when he knew biting me would hurt me. I had proof that Rin wasn't a monster.

But that didn't mean he was my soul mate or that without the brand I would have naturally fallen in love with him. And while my body was drawn to him, I didn't feel that tug inside me that said he had what I needed like the tug I felt for Hawk, Sebastian, Titus, and Cassius.

We were trapped. Both of us.

God, there had to be a way out of this.

Except a bond once formed couldn't be broken... or could it?

Faerie's Heart was so powerful it could do anything. If we had the Heart, both Rin and I could be free.

I jerked awake with a gasp.

"You okay?" Hawk asked.

"I can get free," I said. "The Heart can do anything. I don't have to be trapped."

"It might not be able to break the bond."

"But out of everything, it's got the best chance." I grabbed my plate that sat by the edge of the blanket — where Hawk must have put it after I'd fallen asleep — and hurried for the door. I had to ask Sebastian if he thought it was possible.

"Amiah, wait a second. You might still be dizzy. You haven't been asleep for that long."

I turned back to Hawk and his eyes widened, and that's when I realized I had power and it must have been brightening the angel glow in my eyes. It wasn't a lot of power, but like the last time I'd woken, it was more than I should have had for only being out for a few hours. That, and my hand didn't hurt like it had before, as if I'd somehow healed my burns to a low throbbing ache while I'd been asleep. Which should have been impossible. I needed to concentrate to heal anyone, including myself, I couldn't do it while unconscious.

Except I was imbued with fae magic and had one of the keys to unlocking the Heart. I could use Sebastian's glyphs when I shouldn't have been able to power them at all.

"It's the key," I said, "or the Winter Court's claim. It must be affecting how fast I can get my magic back."

"We should tell Bane." Hawk grabbed the blanket and we hurried into the stairwell. "He might know for certain."

"And hopefully he'll know if the Heart can break my soul bond."

I could be free. For real this time.

God, free!

We rushed back to Sebastian's apartment and were halfway across the living room when Hawk glanced behind us and swore.

The air between us and the front door burst into a shimmering liquid mirror that rapidly swelled into a portal big enough to let at least two of the Winter Queen's guards to step through at the same time.

"Bane, a portal," Hawk yelled as two large ice guards indeed stepped through.

Hawk turned to face them and I scrambled to get out of the way. As much as I could rip out someone's life force, that was a last resort... although given our situation, we might already be at our last resort.

I focused on my magical senses, connecting with Hawk's dark, fiery life force, Sebastian's cold, barely-bright straining life force, Titus's wild ferocity, Cassius's fire, and even Rin's dead-not-dead life force. But I felt nothing from the ice guards—

Because — *crap* — they were constructs, made of ice and magic. They weren't alive and didn't have life forces.

Sebastian rushed out of his office with Titus close behind. "Fuck. Already?"

One of the guards swung its large ice spear, knocking aside Sebastian's couch and flipping over his coffee table, sending the marbles that had been in the bowl on top of the table bouncing and rolling across the floor in all directions.

The other guard lunged toward me, but Hawk shoved Sebastian's grand piano in its way. The construct batted it into the wall. One of its front legs broke and that side crashed down with a dissonant boom.

With a roar, Titus barreled past me — losing his towel and not seeming to care he was naked. He tackled the guard and they crashed into the piano, shattering it.

"Hawk, get Amiah out the door," Sebastian said. "I'll grab Cassius."

But another guard stepped through the portal, along with two shadow fae. Behind them were Deaglan's nightmare and female werebear, the Winter Queen's werepanther, and Sebastian's sister, Padraigin.

"Jeez, overkill much?" Hawk said.

"You murdered Her Majesty's most powerful sorcerer, and the Winter Queen wants my brother, the dragon, and his murderous wife alive." Padraigin's hard gaze landed on me, filled with a rage so cold it sent a shiver racing down my spine. "She's not going to take any chances."

"Most powerful sorcerer?" I asked.

"Noaldar," Padraigin spat. "You murdered Noaldar, you bitch."

Except we hadn't killed him. Deaglan had.

But with Deaglan's nightmare and werebear beside her and two shadow fae crouched in front of her, my guess that Deaglan had *graciously* offered to help the Winter Queen apprehend us had to be correct.

"So please, don't come peacefully," the werepanther snarled as he flexed his hands and extended his claws from his fingertips. "The only one we really need alive is the dragon."

Titus smashed his fist into the ice guard's head, shattering it, and the rest of its body collapsed, a puppet with its strings cut. "I won't be Deaglan's prisoner again. I won't be anyone's."

Two of the guards lunged for him as everyone else — except Padraigin — rushed toward the rest of us.

Sebastian grabbed my wrist and frozen magic exploded inside me. The pain in his life force flared, his full-body glow dimmed, and he groaned in pain. "I've broken the tracking spell. Get to the circle."

Right. We couldn't leave without Rin. Even if I didn't trust him, we were soul bonded and he'd eventually be able to find me through the bond — and with my luck, that would be sooner rather than later.

"Hawk, get Cassius." Sebastian grabbed his left forearm and hissed a sibilant word. His glow dimmed again for longer this time, his complexion terrifyingly gray. A force-wave slammed into the group in front of us, sending them, the furniture, and the dozens of marbles tumbling to the far side of the living room.

He sagged to his knees, gasping for breath, his expression tight with an agony that made my heart and soul scream. I had to help him and yet there wasn't anything I could do.

I reached for him on instinct and he slapped my hand away, but the contact sent a frozen spark slicing from my hand to his and his glow flickered a little stronger for a second.

Somehow I'd given him fae magic like I had when we'd had sex.

His eyes widened.

"I can give you more."

"No." He jerked back to his feet. "Later. There's no point if they kill you. Get to the circle. I can get us out of here using the circle. Everyone to the circle. Titus and I will cover you."

Deaglan's assassins, Padraigin, and the werepanther scrambled to stand, and Titus tossed one of the ice guards into them, knocking the shadow fae and the werebear back down again.

Padraigin leaped out of the way and raised her hands. A thick stream of water shot out of the kitchen — from the sink? — across the living room, and swept around Titus, encasing his head. But Sebastian sent a gust of wind and blew it apart before Titus could suffocate, spraying water in a fine mist across the floor and making the marble slick.

Both of the shadow fae — a man and a woman with shadows undulating under their pale skin — melted into the wildly shifting shadows around them created by Sebastian's swinging crystal chandelier, and lunged out of the shadows beside Sebastian.

"Behind you," I yelled and my senses snapped to their life forces ready to yank it out of them. But my power slammed against a wall like the wall Deaglan had made during our fight in the cavern and I couldn't grab hold.

Sebastian shot a force-wave at them, throwing them back. They crashed through the window and Sebastian snatched the shattered purple-tinted glass from the broken window in a wind gust and shot them at the shifters and the nightmare. But his glow stuttered again, the little bit of magic I'd given him already consumed by the demonic infection, and I could sense heat building under his skin. He wasn't just using his glyphs, he was channeling extra magic to weave spells on the fly with his sorcerer's ability.

He wasn't going to last long and there was no way we could win. Not even if he sacrificed himself. Which wasn't an acceptable option. We had to get out of there. Now. Except Sebastian wouldn't leave until I did.

I wrenched my attention away from him just as Hawk grabbed for my wrist, ready to pull me away.

"I'm okay. I'll meet you in the clean room." I couldn't help Hawk carry Cassius, and if I couldn't wrench out someone's life force, I couldn't fight back. Best to stay out of the way and not distract anyone. No matter how much that frustrated me.

I bolted to the end of the hall and rushed into the clean room.

Rin's gaze instantly leaped to mine and everything within me stalled at the sight of him, my mind, breath, and soul. The aching need that I didn't want roared into an insistent throb, urging me to go to him, embrace him, join with him, and complete the bond.

No. No no no no.

I wanted Hawk and Sebastian and Cassius and Titus. *They* were who I wanted, not Rin. And when we got the Heart, I'd break my bond with Rin and be free.

And I still had no idea if he was fighting the same compulsion. His expression and body language didn't change. Nothing about him changed. He still knelt in the middle of the circle. His hellfire was back to smoldering red pinpricks in his black eyes and he'd retracted his fangs. Just looking at him, I wouldn't have known that he was starving and on the verge of succumbing to a feeding frenzy or anything else.

Outside in the living room, Titus roared and something crashed, the *boom* so powerful it reverberated around me. Rin's gaze jumped past my shoulder and his hellfire snapped. It was just a flicker, but it was a change, a reaction.

Except at what?

I jerked around and came face to face with the nightmare. The icy fear of the nightmare's power seized me, darkness surrounded me, and Balwyrdan's fist smashed into my face sending me reeling.

AMIAH

MY KNEES HIT A COLD FLOOR AND THE NIGHTMARE'S FACE MATERIALIZED out of the darkness. His hellfire hair hissed and snapped, writhing over his head and between his tall thick horns as if caught in a wild storm, and the hellfire in his eyes blazed bright.

He grabbed the front of my scrub top and jerked me close. "Since you're still alive, His Majesty of the Shadow Court has changed his mind, Ms. *Healing* Angel," he said. "You're going to give him your key and serve him in every way he desires." The nightmare sneered at me. "But I'm allowed to try to break you first. Want to join in, Rin?"

I glanced back at Rin, who hadn't moved and still wasn't showing any kind of emotion. A small spark *popped* from the hellfire in his eyes, but the darkness swept around me again before I could figure out what that meant and Balwyrdan punched me again.

This time my nose broke with agonizing pain and a sickening crunch. Stars burst across my vision and fear clenched frozen around my heart. Tears streamed down my cheeks and I fought to breathe past the agony of my broken ribs.

Please, no. I never wanted to think about this again, let alone relive it. I had to break free of the nightmare's magic.

I searched my mind for his sour, nauseating darkness, but Balwyrdan grabbed my hair and wrenched my head back up.

I tried to bite back my cry of pain, but it still escaped as a pathetic mewling whimper. God, I needed to be strong. I could survive this if my guys came for me—

Except they had.

I mentally heaved against the nightmare's magic. I couldn't feel it, but I knew it was there.

A crack of light cut through the darkness.

"You know you want this sweet ass with her sweet blood and magic," the nightmare mocked. "You think you're so perfect. King Deaglan's favorite. Well not anymore."

The nightmare yanked me up and slammed me face-first against the barrier, its invisible magic biting my skin and as hard as any wall.

Rin remained kneeling, which made the nightmare snarl, yank me back, and slam me against the barrier again, this time breaking my nose for real with a blinding flash of agony and a sharp *crack*.

Blood gushed over my lips and dripped off my chin, and the nightmare jerked my head around, smearing my blood on the barrier.

Rin's gaze locked on it and his hellfire grew from smoldering pinpricks to miniature flames.

"I'm going to fuck her and make her bleed and watch you lose your precious control, you high and mighty asshole."

The darkness swept through my vision again and my pulse pounded. I wouldn't be able to fight back if I was trapped by the nightmare's magic. I had to get free, had to at least call out for help.

But Balwyrdan punched me in the chest, cracking my ribs, sending agony screaming through me and scattering my thoughts. A massive weight crushed around my heart and the air around me vanished.

I gasped, unable to help myself, knowing it was useless, that I wouldn't be able to breathe through the activated leash spell, but unable to stop my body's reaction.

My lungs burned and somehow the already dark world darkened even more and started spinning despite not being able to see anything.

I knew I was in an abandoned reception hall—

No. I was in Sebastian's clean room and the nightmare had me. Not Balwyrdan.

My air returned with another *crack* of Balwyrdan's fist in my face, this one sending agony exploding through my cheek.

I hit the floor again—

Except I knew I was still standing.

Balwyrdan grabbed the front of my dress, lifting me up, and my neck strap broke, the metal catch slicing my neck. Cold air rushed over my skin and I fell back to the floor, everything spinning. I couldn't breathe, couldn't think. *Please stop. God, stop.*

Balwyrdan yanked me back up by my hair again and howled with pleasure... or was that the nightmare? Balwyrdan had enjoyed beating me, knew exactly how to extract the most pain while keeping me alive, but I didn't remember the howling laughter.

He pounded his fist into my face again and shoved his hand down my pants... but I'd been wearing a dress... and Balwyrdan had gotten off on my pain, nothing else.

This wasn't real. It was the nightmare.

It. Was. The. Nightmare.

I mentally shoved with everything I had.

Get out.

Get out get out. "Get out."

The darkness exploded and I was back in the all white clean room, my face painfully pressed against the barrier and blood oozing from my nose. It also flowed from a deep cut in my neck, soaking into my scrub top, and had Rin's avid attention. He still hadn't moved, but now his hellfire raged and his fangs had extended. The nightmare had one hand on the back of my head pinning me to the barrier and was unlacing his fly with the other.

No. No no no.

Fear clenched my chest and my magic pounded and clawed at the wall surrounding his life force, desperate to find a crack, anything that would let it in and save me.

"Hawk! Sebastian!" I bucked against the nightmare's grasp and he pressed harder against my head.

"That's it, little angel, fight me," he said with a dark chuckle.

No. No!

I scratched deeper rents in the wall surrounding his life force.

Nothing. No way in.

God, there had to be a way in, a way to save myself. I had to do something.

"Titus—" I twisted and tried to scratch the nightmare's face, but he rammed his free hand into my ribs, cutting off my cry and shooting agony screaming through my chest as if my ribs were broken even though my magic told me they weren't — which was one of the horrifying powers of a nightmare so he could better feed on his victim's fear.

Out in the hall, the screams and yells and crashes of the fight were still happening. It had felt like an eternity trapped in the nightmare's magic, but I doubted it had been more than a few minutes.

"Sebas—"

The nightmare slammed my face back into the barrier making the room spin.

This wasn't happening. It couldn't be happening.

I renewed my mental clawing at the wall protecting his life force. I had to get in. Please. God. Let me in.

"You're supposed to be screaming my name. I want you begging, little angel. Beg me not to hurt you."

But I wasn't stupid enough to think begging would stop him.

"Come on. Beg," the nightmare said.

My magic ripped a hairline fissure in the wall and a trickle connected with the nightmare's fiery sour life force, but it wasn't enough to take hold and rip it out of him.

"Please, Nezener, make me bleed," he said in a mocking singsong, rubbing his now-freed erection against my rear, sending terror — no matter how hard I tried to fight it — rushing through me and feeding him, giving him strength.

I heaved at the fissure, desperate to make it bigger, to shove my power past the wall, but the nightmare slammed my face against the barrier again, shattering my concentration and making the room spin.

"Make me scream and bleed. Fuck me, Nezener."

My magic wasn't going to save me.

"Go fuck yourself," I spat.

The nightmare, Nezener, froze.

Yeah, didn't expect an angel to swear like that.

Which was exactly what I'd hoped for. He'd stopped for just a second, but it was more than enough time.

I jerked in his grip, grabbed his erection, and wrenched on it with all my might.

He howled in agony, his erection instantly going flaccid, and his pain exploded across my senses. My healing magic snapped into him, somehow not deterred by the wall protecting his life force, and connected with the membrane in his penis that I'd purposefully torn. But he backhanded me and my connection disconnected from him for a second.

My not-broken cheek hit the barrier, shooting pain through my face as if it were broken, and I crumpled to the floor... right beside the glyph that let the barrier down.

Rin's gaze was still locked on the blood leaking down my neck, and his hellfire now licked across his cheeks. The emotionless expression from before was gone, replaced with a ferocious, desperate hunger.

If I let him out, would he kill me even though we were soul bonded?

Did he even know we were bonded?

"You fucking bitch," Nezener screamed. He grabbed my face and smashed the back of my head against the barrier again.

The room darkened and spun. Real agony screamed through my skull and my magic stuttered, connecting and disconnecting with him — since his injury couldn't be fixed without surgery and my magic had decided it was more serious than the cut in my neck, my concussion, or my broken nose.

"You God damn fucking bitch." He smashed my head again and the room went dark.

One more and I'd be unconscious. He was no longer able to get an erection, but that didn't mean he couldn't hurt or permanently maim me.

He jerked my head forward to smash it a third time and I slapped my hand against the glyph and released the barrier.

I fell back onto the floor, Nezener lurching forward with me, and Rin launched himself at us. One second he was kneeling, the next he was a wild, frenzied monster coming at us.

Nezener scrambled off me and shoved me toward Rin, but Rin kept going. He tackled Nezener, flipped him, and smashed his face on the floor, stunning him.

With an animalistic snarl, Rin ripped open the side of Nezener's neck, sending arterial blood spraying across his face and clothes, and over the white walls and floor. He latched his lips over Nezener's carotid artery and started feeding with the desperation of a starving man.

My magic instantly locked with Nezener and surged, heating my hands and making them glow. The urge to go to him and save him squeezed inside my chest.

Save him. Save him.

No way in hell.

I crossed my arms, shoved my hands into my armpits, and tried to make my power turn inward to heal my broken nose and the cut in my neck. But I couldn't get it to leave my hands. I *had* to use it to save

Nezener, and if I didn't go to him — *now now now* — it was going to heal him from a distance.

Nezener moaned and thrashed, his fiery sour life force straining, desperate to stay lit. The agony in his neck blazed through me, consuming all my other pain, and I could feel his heart pounding, desperate, gushing his blood into Rin's mouth and onto the floor.

Save him.

No. I won't. I can't.

It wasn't even a matter of not wanting to, although I really didn't want to save him. It was a waste of power. Rin was going to kill him. Using my magic would just prolong Nezener's suffering and waste my magic when any one of my guys could be hurt and need me.

Except the need to heal twisted tighter, wrenching me forward onto my hands and knees to crawl closer, even as my magic surged through the connection it had already made with Nezener.

No. Absolutely not.

I heaved my magic back, fighting the burn and pressure, and the promise of an excruciating backlash.

Save him.

No.

Nezener's life force and heartbeat stuttered.

Save. Him.

Another stutter and the pressure of my power howled inside me.

"No."

With a whoosh, Nezener's sour life force vanished and my magic slammed into me, the backlash stealing my breath and igniting every cell in my body with a pain so powerful I prayed I'd just pass out.

Except I couldn't pass out. The guys might need me. Even if I couldn't access my magic until my backlash subsided, I still had non-magical medical knowledge.

That, and I was still in the room with a man who'd tried to kill me more than once and was in the throes of a feeding frenzy.

I tried to drag my attention to the door to look for help as Rin jerked his head up, his gaze zeroing in on me. Blood splattered his forehead and upper cheeks, and fully covered the lower half of his face. His hellfire was a wild ferocious fire with sparks snapping free and hissing when they hit the floor, and his lips were curled back in a vicious snarl. Nothing about him looked human. Even Titus when his beast took over looked more human than Rin did right now.

He lunged at me.

I tried to scramble back but my muscles seized with the sudden movement and I collapsed to the floor instead of getting away. Not that there was anywhere to go. He was between me and the door.

Rin straddled me, pinning me with his body, grabbed my jaw, and jerked my head to the side, giving him better access to the cut in my neck.

"If you kill me, you kill yourself," I gasped, the agony of my backlash screaming through me even as my body thrilled at his touch.

God, this was such a mess.

I was in excruciating pain and I *still* wanted him to unlace his pants and take me. My body didn't care that he was going to kill me. I needed him inside me, needed to seal our bond.

I grabbed his wrist, trying to move his hand enough to turn my head and properly meet his gaze, but I couldn't make him budge. "We're soul bonded. I die, you die."

"Maybe I'm done being someone's slave," he snarled, his voice still barely above a whisper and filled with menace. He trembled, every muscle in his body tight, his hunger only partially satiated from killing Nezener. "You're worse than King Deaglan, making me desire not just your blood and magic, but your body, too. I'm not dumb. You're going to make me watch you sleep with your husband while your magic twists up my insides, that's how you're going to make me obey you. Be a good boy and you won't have to watch. You just have to live with this... this need."

Oh, God. Did he think I'd branded him to torture him like Deaglan?

"King Deaglan denied me, made me watch when I disobeyed, but he never went so far as to make me *need* someone like I need you." His grip on my chin tightened, his sharp small vampire claws digging into my cheeks, and some of the wildness bled out of his expression, turning into a hard darkness. "Your chains are worse than King Deaglan's, and this is the only time I'm going to get to touch you, isn't it?"

My pulse stuttered with fear even as my body screamed with the agonizing burn of backlash mixed with throbbing insistent desire.

"I'm just as trapped as you are," I said, fighting my hips from rocking forward and telling him what my body wanted. Tears of pain and frustration burned my eyes. I didn't want any of this. For either of us.

Just knowing that he thought this was done on purpose to torture him broke my heart.

And while I might not trust him, I didn't think he trusted anyone.

He'd been a slave, tortured physically and psychologically, and I was sure being starved and denied sex was just the tip of the iceberg.

"The bond makes me want you too, and I have no control over it," I continued. "All I can hope is that we can get Faerie's Heart and it'll be able to break it."

He glared at me and I prayed that he'd somehow be able to know I was telling the truth.

"You didn't do this on purpose?" His grip on my face eased enough so I could look him straight in the eyes. His hellfire had shrunk to small flames, but he still trembled. "Why do I want to believe you?"

"Because it's the truth. Angels can't control when or with whom their mating brands bond them with. And if I had a choice, I wouldn't have picked you. If we don't find a way to break the bond, it's going to make me fall in love with you and I'm going to fall out of love with them." My desire and backlashed surged, making me groan half in pain and half in pleasure and my eyes roll back. "I don't know what your history is or what Deaglan did to you, but no one deserves to be tortured or forced to desire someone. You're not my slave or Sebastian's or anyone's anymore. And I'll be damned if we're both slaves to this stupid brand."

Please believe me. We couldn't keep him locked up and if the next key didn't become empowered soon, I'd have no choice but to sleep with him.

And I couldn't have sex with someone who I feared was going to kill me, even if Hawk was with me to help me through it.

Rin opened his mouth to say something when Titus — still naked — barreled into the room, wrenched him off me, and slammed him face-first into the floor.

"Get off her," the dragon snarled.

Sebastian staggered into the room, his fae glow completely gone, and Hawk rushed in behind him with a naked Cassius slung over his shoulder.

"God, Amiah." Hawk hurried to my side and I curled into a ball unable to stop myself.

"I'm okay," I gasped, as Hawk set Cassius down and reached for me.

"Never touch her again." Titus wrenched Rin up and slammed him back down, not even drawing a grunt of pain from the hybrid.

Was he going to take the beating without saying anything or crying out? Was that what he'd learned from Deaglan?

"Titus, I'm okay. I swear."

Titus snarled. Yeah, given how I looked with my nose broken, blood oozing from my neck, and curled up in pain, I wouldn't have believed me either.

"Rin didn't do anything. He saved me from Deaglan's nightmare," I said, and Titus's gaze jumped to Nezener's corpse, his blood painting the all-white wall and floor around him.

"Get your beast under control. You can't kill him and we can't stay here," Sebastian gasped. "Now everyone get in the fucking circle."

He sagged to the floor beside me and pulled me into his arms and pressed my hand against his inner left thigh over his pants. "Amiah, push power into the glyph under your hand and say ignite. It'll activate the teleportation spell I have embedded in the circle."

Titus jerked Rin up to his feet so all of him was inside the circle and Hawk pulled Cassius closer even though he didn't have to.

My magic connected with all of them. Sebastian had a deep laceration in his side that needed healing that I couldn't give him with my magic raging out of control inside me, and Hawk was low on magic. Titus had broken ribs — that, with his rapid healing, were already knitting back together — and Cassius was still out, his body feeling like he'd been given a strong sedative even though I knew he hadn't. And Rin was still hungry.

Footsteps clattered down the hall and the werepanther rushed into the doorway. Behind him were more shadow fae.

"Amiah, please," Sebastian gasped.

I wrenched my thoughts from my guys and imagined shoving as much of my fae magic through Sebastian's pants and into the glyph under my hand. "Ignite."

Sebastian cried out in pain and blinding white light blazed around us. The light shot into my body, the pain of the spell overwhelming everything else inside me including the agony of my backlash, and it ripped my cells apart in a way I'd hoped never to experience again.

HAWK

Agony screamed through me as Bane's teleportation spell ripped me apart then put me back together again. My hellfire flared out of my eyes and I completely lost my hold on my magic. At the same time, something heavy crunched, shattering glass and making metal squeal, and a white-feathered wing slapped me in the face.

Everyone moaned with desire, and I yanked my magic back under control as quickly as I could. I'd never been teleported before and I hoped to God I never would again. I was only grateful Bane had the spell already preset on his circle, because in his condition he wouldn't have been able to teleport just himself let alone all six of us. He'd have just burned himself to a crisp and we wouldn't have gone anywhere.

And he still, even with Amiah powering his glyph, looked like shit.

He lay on his back on the cool damp concrete of his underground garage in a growing pool of blood, his expression stunned, and only a hint of white aura flickered through the writhing black darkness and angry red spikes inside him.

Amiah had heaved forward, her wings fully extended. Her unnatural fae glow blazed bright as her aura, now flecked with gold — likely from the mating brand because the gold hadn't been there before — snapped and churned inside her. Every time it flared, she tensed and her expression pinched tighter with pain, as if her power had been released without focus, was raging inside her, and couldn't escape from her body.

Cassius lay beside me — the reason a wing had slapped me in the face — his aura burning bright again with his fire magic, while Rin with his strange seething black aura, had dropped to his knees. His hellfire roared from his eyes like mine had and his fangs were fully extended.

Titus, in his massive dragon form, sat fifteen feet away from us. He was half on a flattened blue sedan as well as the flattened front of a brown pickup and crammed between a concrete pillar, and a minivan that had been squished against a second concrete pillar.

His gold-red aura heaved with his beast's rage and I couldn't blame him. Everything within me had frozen in horror when we'd run into the clean room and seen Rin straddling Amiah, her nose broken and bleeding and a bleeding gash in her neck. And worse, I'd felt a desperate, painful desire radiating from both of them.

They were fighting it. Both of them. Neither of them wanted to feel what they were feeling, and yet they couldn't help themselves. The ache was almost as strong as the overwhelming need I'd felt from Amiah when she'd first entered my tent. It was filled with power and too much pain.

She was going to fall in love with him and hate herself for it.

And all I could do was be by her side, help her through it, and pray the Heart could free her... or add me to their bond.

Except to do that, we needed to get as far away from Bane's apartment as possible.

Even if Padraigin wasn't a sorcerer and hadn't brought one along, she was going to figure out that in Bane's condition we wouldn't have been able to teleport very far.

Titus huffed smoke from his nostrils and smacked his head on the low ceiling then, with a grunt, shifted back into his human form — not seeming to care that he now stood barefoot on the shattered glass from the vehicles.

"Get me to the SUV," Bane gasped, pointing to a full-sized expensive black SUV that was lit up like the sun with all the spells on it — one of which being a lock spell that kept the vehicle locked until the owner deactivated it. "I need to touch it to unlock the protection spell on it."

"Does it need a key?" I helped him stand and stagger to the SUV.

He pressed his palm against the door, his touch releasing the lock spell with a flash of magic that only I could see, then passed out, going completely limp in my hands.

Fuck.

He was the one with the better contacts... and the money... and hell, given that he'd had a teleport spell already in place — not to mention a spell on his library that sent his entire office into an interdimensional space only he could get to — this was clearly his escape plan. He probably already had a safehouse set up. If he was unconscious, he couldn't tell us where to go. And my place was a terrible alternative. I lived in my tent in Left of Lincoln. Even if it hadn't been sliced open, Lincoln wasn't a safe place to hide.

"Come on, man. Wake up." I gave him a shake, but he didn't even groan.

"He's drained himself too deeply and he's losing too much blood," Amiah said. "Even if I give him my fae magic, he'll still be exhausted and won't wake for a while."

"How long is a while?" Titus asked.

"More than a few minutes," she gasped, her power slicing deep inside her. "We need to get him some place where I can stitch him up."

Titus stalked the fifteen feet back to us. "But you have power."

"I can't access it." Another slice made her squeeze her eyes shut and hug herself.

God, she looked just like Bane with his demonic infection.

"My power locked onto Deaglan's nightmare and I refused to heal him," she said. "My power turns in on me when I don't release it. I won't be able to connect with my magic until the backlash passes."

"Which will be when?" Titus growled.

"It's bad," she said, biting back a groan. "Could be a couple of days."

A couple of days?

Fuck.

God damn fucking hell.

And there wasn't a damned thing I could do about it.

Fine.

The first order of business was to get everyone out of here and given that Amiah was in pain, Cassius unconscious, and Titus and Rin knew next to nothing about Union — not to mention, I didn't even know if we could trust Rin — that left me in charge.

How the hell did I end up in charge?

I yanked open the SUV's door, put Bane in the closest seat, and buckled him in.

The SUV was luxurious, spacious, fully loaded, and smelled like it was new. The back seats were down — which was perfect for Cassius and his wings — and a large duffle bag, glowing with spells only I could see, had been shoved half under the driver's seat.

This was definitely Bane's escape plan.

"Everyone in the car."

Titus jerked toward Amiah, his expression filled with his need to hold her, but he grabbed Cassius instead without me having to ask him. Which was good, because with Titus's greater strength it'd just be easier for him to get the angel with his released wings into the SUV.

"The last row of seats is down, you can put him in there," I said, then bent to pick up Amiah.

But she pulled her wings in and, with a strength of will that made my heart ache, stood before I could lift her.

I grabbed her before she fell and slid a thread of what little magic I had left into her to help ease her pain.

She clung to my shoulders, panting and trembling, and turned to Rin.

"You can go," she said. "You're not our slave or prisoner. But until our bond is broken, it'll keep drawing us back together no matter what we want."

Rin stared at her.

I couldn't read his expression and had no idea what he was thinking. I could only hope feeding on Deaglan's nightmare had satiated some of his hunger. He'd regained control of his hellfire and retracted his fangs, but still looked ferocious with blood covering most of his face while still radiating his unwanted, painful desire.

"It's your choice," she added.

A spark popped from his right eye.

"I swear."

Except it wasn't his choice. Not really. Fate had already taken away their choices and if they separated now and Rin was recaptured by Deaglan, or worse, went back to him willingly, Amiah would get hurt.

He continued to stare at her.

For fuck's sake!

"We don't have time for this." I helped Amiah climb into the SUV then glared at Rin. "Get in the fucking car."

His gaze jerked to me and another spark popped from his eye.

Jeez, this man had a crazy amount of control. I'd never seen any demon able to control his hellfire like that.

"If Deaglan gets his hands on you, that's going to hurt Amiah." My hellfire flared with my fear and anger and frustration, licking across my cheeks, and I didn't bother to control it. I *wanted* him to know I was serious. Deadly serious. "I won't let you hurt her."

He was getting in the SUV whether he wanted to or not. Except I had no idea how I was going to force him in. I was decent in a fight, but he was stronger than me and had claws. His vampire claws were small, not like a shifter's, but he still had natural weapons and I didn't. The only chance I had of overpowering him was if he were into guys, then I could use my magic on him, but I wasn't going to bet Amiah's life on that. Especially since I already knew he was into women, which lessened the odds that I'd be able to seduce him.

He dipped his gaze, the only indication that he accepted my order, and climbed into the SUV following Amiah, who knelt between the seats and had started unbuttoning Bane's shirt.

I hurried around to the driver's seat, Titus got into the front passenger seat, and Rin settled in the seat behind me with the duffle bag at his feet.

The SUV's key, one of those fobs that you didn't have to put into an ignition sat in the cup holder. Thank God. I pressed the button to start the car and drove to the ramp on the far side of the garage.

Once on the street, it took everything I had not to speed away, but I knew speeding would draw more attention than anything else. No one knew we were in an SUV and everyone's concealment charms were still active — including Titus's, much to my surprise, since he'd broken the glamour hiding his identity and the two spells had been tied together. Even if Padraigin had someone who could track us by the blood Titus, Bane, and I had lost during the fight, the charms would keep us hidden—

Except Rin didn't have a concealment charm, and he'd been Deaglan's slave.

Crap.

"Rin, can they track you?"

The light ahead turned red and I turned right so I could keep moving away from Bane's apartment. I didn't have a goal in mind, I just wanted to get us as far away as possible.

"No," he replied, surprising me with his quick response. Of course, he didn't elaborate, but I supposed I didn't need to know anything else.

If he couldn't be tracked, that meant they could only track Amiah through her connection to the Winter Court, and Bane had already broken the tracking spell when they'd first arrived. They were going to have to return to Faerie to get the Winter Queen to recast it and that meant we had a little bit of time. Not much, certainly not as much as we'd expected, but still some.

Titus squirmed in his seat, his dragon's head superimposed over his human one, a sign his beast was starting to regain control.

"Move faster," he growled.

"I don't want to draw attention." I stopped at a red light, my insides churning, everything within me screaming to move, go, escape. But we were barely out of the vampire's section of the Quarter and the streets were busy with vehicles as well as pedestrians. That was a lot of people who'd notice if a black SUV started driving erratically. I also didn't want to take another right. That would take us back toward Bane's apartment. Which meant as much as it made my pulse pound, I *had* to stop. "But we do need to figure out where we're going. We can't drive around forever."

I caught Amiah's gaze in the rearview mirror, my heart clenching at her appearance. Blood trickled down her neck and seeped into her scrub top and leaked from her broken nose, and bright red bruises had formed under her eyes and were starting to swell. Her expression was tight with pain and worry, her gaze slightly out of focus — probably from a concussion — but there was also determination in her eyes. She was going to get us all out alive if it killed her, and I'd be damned if I let her sacrifice herself.

"As much as I want to go to Operations, Cassius would say no," she said, bunching up Bane's shirt and pressing it against the deep gash in his side.

"I agree." The light turned green and I calmly — so fucking calmly it was driving me crazy — continued down the street then took the next left away from the Joined Parliament Operations Building. "If Deaglan or Padraigin know anything about the mortal realm, they're going to know every angel in town lives in Operations. That's the first place they'll look for us."

And while there were people and weapons at the Joined Parliament Operations Building, we didn't know how many people Deaglan and the Winter Queen would send after us the next time.

Three ice guards, two shifters, a handful of shadow fae, the nightmare, *and* Padraigin had already been overkill. Sure, we'd managed to get away, but barely. And while I'd heard that Union City's primary JP team was powerful — especially since they added the world's only archnephilim, a being who was half powerful archangel and half powerful hellfire queen to the team — there were also a lot of civilians living in the Operations Building, it being a significant JP research center.

Which was likely one of the reasons Cassius hadn't wanted to take the fight to Operations when this whole mess had started.

And that left us with what?

Fuck. I had no idea.

Amiah couldn't heal Bane and we couldn't just take him to a hospital. Wherever we went, we were going to get noticed. Amiah was clearly an angel and yet clearly had a fae glow. Bane even without his glow was still obviously high fae with his sharp facial features, strange white and silver hair, and delicately pointed ears. Titus was huge. And naked. And Rin, just as a demon-vampire hybrid without anyone knowing he was half sin eater, was almost as rare as an archnephilim.

Even Cassius was naked, something an angel would never do in public, and while we could probably find him clothes, angels also didn't spend a lot of time with demons. Just being in our odd group would draw attention to him.

Which meant somehow me, with my non-demon-like blue eyes and my magic that made most women and a good handful of men look my way, was the one who stuck out the least.

"Do you know of a vet's office? Ideally not in the Quarter?" I asked. There was probably at least one vet in the Quarter, and dozens in the city proper, but I'd never had a pet, so I didn't know where to go. "Will your angel nature let you break in so we can stitch him up?"

"We're still going to need some place to go so he can rest," she replied.

"*You* need to rest," Titus growled.

I turned onto a less-busy narrow side street and realized I was headed toward Squatters' Row, an area of the Quarter that had yet to be redeveloped. And while it had a lot of abandoned buildings where we might be able to find a place to hide, there were still too many people illegally living there who could notice us.

"There's a duffle bag under my seat by Rin's feet," I said, glancing in the rearview mirror confirming that we weren't being followed then pulling to stop at the curb. "Maybe Bane left an address to his safehouse in there."

I doubted it. He wasn't that stupid. Even though a magical lock was hard to pick, it could still be picked. But hey, I could hope.

Rin tugged the bag free and Amiah unzipped it. Inside was a magical book, a change of clothes, and two packets of hundred dollar bills.

Amiah's eyes widened. "Is that—?"

"Twenty thousand dollars?" I said. "Yeah. That'll buy us some discretion."

"If we can get there without being noticed," Titus added.

"And it still doesn't solve our medical needs." The magic in her aura snapped and she drew in a sharp breath. "We have to go to Voth's. He has a clinic in the back of his hotel."

"Are you sure?" Voth was a greater demon who was known to not like angels. Yeah, he'd fought in the war for the Angelic Defense and had accepted an angel medic as part of his team when they'd started getting the worst of the worst assignments, but that didn't mean he *liked* angels. "And how do you know he has a clinic?"

"Long story." Another snap, and her hands, still keeping pressure on Bane's wound, started to tremble. Her swollen eyelids fluttered closed for a second before she wrenched them open and the muscles in her jaw tightened.

She wasn't going to last, although because of her concussion we had to keep her awake for—

Hell, I had no idea how long we were supposed to keep her awake, just that we had to.

However long it needed to be, it would be better if she was only fighting to stay conscious and not also trying to take care of Bane at the same time.

"Offer Voth the money," she said. "And if that's not enough, tell him he can meet another bonded couple."

I wanted to ask why that might be the currency that got us into his clinic, but another snap of her magic had me putting the SUV back into gear and heading toward Voth's hotel on the outskirts of the Quarter.

It didn't matter what got us someplace safe, so long as she was safe.

God, nothing else mattered.

Why couldn't she have branded me? I was already hers, heart and soul, and if we couldn't free her or add me to her bond with Rin, I was forever going to be on the outside looking in.

AMIAH

Hawk drove through Squatters' Row to Voth's luxury hotel on the far side of the Quarter. The greater demon had been a barely controlled deadly powerhouse during the war, and the Angelic Defense commanders had basically pointed him and his team at a target and let him go at it, which had ended up giving him the moniker Angel of Death. After the war, his team had been instrumental in hunting down and killing most of Michael's magically made monstrous army, but for some reason that I couldn't figure out, he'd stopped hunting nephilim, bought the 19th century hotel, restored it, and settled down.

Or at least I'd thought he'd settled down until a few months ago when Essie and her guys, along with me, Cassius, and Sebastian, had fled Operations seeking protection from the Director of the Joined Parliament Bureau of Supernatural Law Enforcement, and we'd ended up in the small, fully stocked clinic at the back of Voth's hotel.

During that time, I'd had almost no interaction with Voth and I doubted he'd remember me well enough to just help me if I asked for it. Which is why I'd suggested money and the information about a bonded couple. I'd kept to myself, had probably looked like an angel who'd wanted nothing to do with her demon host while I'd helped Marcus through yet another horrible shifter transition and had my heart shattered. It had been Essie, not me, who'd gotten him through his transition from werewolf to hellhound, his beast responding to her and not me and confirming without a doubt that even though she hadn't branded him like she had the others, she was his mate.

That had been the final nail in the coffin of my dream. There hadn't even been a glimmer of hope left. The man I'd been so certain was my mate, that I'd secretly fallen in love with and had patiently waited for him to do the same with me, wasn't mine, had never been mine, and never would be.

Add the horrible realization that the mating brand wasn't the wonderful beautiful thing I'd been led to believe, and everything I thought I knew about myself and my destiny had been shattered.

Essie had branded Marcus shortly after that. I'd finished healing Sebastian, who'd been critically wounded during that whole mess, and quietly left Voth's hotel, returning to Operations a broken and lost angel.

Except going to Voth was our only option. I could only hope that the money would be enough for Voth to let us use his clinic, no questions asked. I didn't want to deal with the potential pity, or worse the congratulations I'd get for being one of those rare angels with an angelic mating brand. And I didn't know how Voth would respond. He'd demanded to see Essie and Gideon, the newly mated couple, as a non-negotiable part of the payment for a rare magical item that they'd needed. Had it been morbid curiosity since mating brands were so rare? Or was the Angel of Death secretly a romantic?

Regardless, if the only way we could get to his clinic was to show my brand, I'd do it. Whatever it took to save Sebastian and give us a moment to figure out what we were going to do.

Voth's large hotel sat sprawled on top of a gently sloping hill with a long circular driveway leading to a grand front entrance that was fully lit against the evening's darkness so everyone could clearly see its grandeur.

I'd never been through the front doors, but I knew — everyone knew — that Voth had beautifully restored the yellow-brick, ten-story building, sparing no expense on the lavish details.

It was still early evening and lights were on in many of the rooms, the glow warm on the top five floors, and slightly purple on the bottom five from the UV-blocking glass. The light was welcoming, and also a reminder that there were a lot of people awake and moving around the hotel who could notice us.

"Front door?" Hawk asked, pausing on the road instead of heading down the driveway.

"No, go around to the side. There's a parking lot and another way in," I said. That was how we'd arrived the last time.

Cassius had marched through the almost-as-grand side door, somehow convinced Voth to help us, and we'd been directed around back to the loading bay.

The parking lot was only half full, which hopefully meant Voth didn't have anything big going on in his theater at the moment and we'd be able to sneak into his clinic without anyone but Voth noticing us.

Hawk parked as far back in the lot as he could while still having a few cars around us so the SUV didn't draw attention. Then he quickly stripped out of his bloody and burned clothes and changed into the clothes that had been in the duffle bag.

"Titus, take over holding Bane's shirt," Hawk said, hopping out of the SUV. His gaze shifted to me. "I don't like the idea of you driving with what I'm sure is a concussion and barely able to see, but I'm pretty sure Titus and Rin don't know how to drive."

I didn't like the idea of driving in my condition, either, and while Titus had spent the last five hundred years in Faerie as Deaglan's prisoner and probably had no clue how to drive, Rin had been Deaglan's assassin. He might have had an opportunity to visit the mortal realm and learn.

I glanced at him and he gave a slight shake of his head. No.

Great.

"If the money doesn't work, telling him he can meet a bonded couple will," I said. It had to work. We had nowhere else to go and Sebastian was losing too much blood.

Hawk headed across the parking lot and entered the hotel while Titus climbed into the back and took over keeping pressure against Sebastian's side.

I slid into the driver's seat, gritting my teeth against my magic writhing inside me. I just had to stay focused enough to stitch up Sebastian and then awake long enough to ensure my concussion wasn't going to be a problem. Then I could collapse.

Sebastian moaned, making my heart squeeze, and I glanced back at him. He was still unconscious, and even without access to my magic, I could tell by the tightness in his expression and body that he was still suffering a pain deeper than just the laceration in his side.

God, we just needed to get through this. I just needed all of them to survive this.

Was that what Essie had been thinking when we'd driven, bleeding and broken, to this very spot?

No. The fear and desperation induced by her brands had to have made it worse. I was only bonded with Rin who was, more or less, fine. She'd been branded to three of her four men and they'd all just barely escaped with their lives.

I couldn't imagine what it would be like to be soul bonded to all of them. My soul was already furious and terrified for Sebastian, and still broken over Cassius even though I *knew* he was alive. I didn't want to be the one lying on the floor screaming in terror. And yet even without the bonds, a part of me felt I already was. At least if I was bonded, I'd not just get the detriments, but the benefits as well. Bonded angels' abilities were stronger, some developed new powers, and they could share life forces with their mates and possibly save them from dying.

God, I couldn't believe I was actually hoping for more bonds.

Although with my luck, I'd be one of those angels who didn't have anything enhanced no matter how many mates I claimed.

And yet, in the very least, I had to find a way to brand Hawk. If he was part of my bond, he wouldn't go crazy or starve ... and I wasn't going to think about how not giving Rin a say in the matter would be unfair to him.

We were just going to have to get Faerie's Heart. That solved everything. I bet it could even cure Sebastian's demonic infection.

My thoughts ping ponged between hope and fear and desire while my magic sliced into me, muting my sense of the guys' life forces. Blood still oozed from my neck and my whole head hurt, but I was determined. I was going to get Faerie's Heart. I'd do whatever it took—

Except as soon as I thought that, I realized I wouldn't do whatever it took. No matter how much I wanted the Heart, I wouldn't sacrifice any of my guys to get it, and I could only pray it wouldn't come down to that.

Movement by the hotel door caught my attention and I dragged my gaze from the steering wheel to look out the window and saw Hawk running toward us.

"We've got a deal," Hawk said, opening the driver's door. "I got him to give us full access to his clinic and his private suite with its private elevator, along with complete discretion, but..." His expression turned grim.

"But he wants to see the bonded couple." At least Hawk had gotten us a lot for the deal. I hadn't even known Voth had a private suite.

"Yeah," Hawk said as I moved over into the passenger seat and Hawk started the SUV. "You knew that would seal the deal. Do you know what he'll do about that?"

"No." No one on the primary JP team had talked about what had happened with Voth when they'd first visited him, and I hadn't asked.

Hawk drove down the sloping parking lot to the big modern addition at the back of the hotel where Voth had his massive stadium style theater. The loading bay door was already open and the bay empty, and we parked near the concrete steps at the back that led into the hotel.

"The clinic is the second door on the left," I said, trying to focus on what needed to be done before I passed out. Stitches for Sebastian and a little more blood for Rin would be ideal. "Titus, you get Cassius. Hawk, take Sebastian." He was going to get blood on his clothes, but I suspected it would be easier for Titus to manhandle Cassius's limp form with his wings out than Hawk.

I pushed open the door and climbed out of the SUV. The loading bay darkened and lurched, and I sucked in deep breaths, trying to stay focused.

All I needed to do was get to the clinic, stitch up Sebastian, and then Hawk could take over and get us into that suite.

With that held firmly in my mind, I staggered to the steps, but before I could climb them, Rin swept me into his arms and cradled me against his chest.

Everything within me froze with fear… *and* with desperate need.

His strange life force snapped across my senses, the physical contact allowing my magic to sense him past the backlash firestorm blazing inside me, and all of me strained for more. More of his life force, more of him.

His black gaze caught mine and my brain stalled again. Then he jerked his attention away, giving me no indication why he'd decided to help or if he was barely holding himself together against the same aching yearning or really anything. Had he decided he was safe with us? Or was it the brand forcing him to help me? Because the brand would do that. It would twist up a mate's insides until they couldn't do anything but help.

A spark of hellfire popped from his eye and he hurried us inside.

"The clinic's there," I said, pointing at the door.

He strode into the small room that was barely big enough to hold all the medical equipment Voth had packed in there along with the two gurneys. Rin set me by the first gurney, hesitated as if he wanted to stay close — and God, I wanted him to stay close — then moved as far away from me as the small room would allow. I guess he'd come to the same conclusion I had. The need to be close was the bond. It wasn't really how we were feeling.

"There's blood in the fridge," I said to him, pointing to the small fridge under the counter, thankfully close to him. "I can't do anything about feeding your magic right now, but we can end your hunger for blood."

Another spark popped from his eye, and I turned my attention to the sink, not waiting to see if he'd get the blood or not. I had other things to worry about. Like stitching up Sebastian before I passed out.

I scrubbed my hands clean as Titus and Hawk entered and set Cassius and Sebastian on the gurneys. Both men drew close to me, but gave me space to work, as if they wanted to be near me like Rin did but also didn't want to get in my way.

From the last time I'd been here, I knew the suture kits were in the cupboard over the counter to my left, and I pulled one out and set it on the counter by Sebastian's gurney. Then I turned to the cupboard on the other side of the sink where Voth kept his drugs. Sebastian didn't need a sedative, but it would still be good to numb the area around the laceration, or better yet, give him a strong analgesic that might help with *all* of his other pain until the shock and exhaustion of having used all of his magic had passed.

Except I was having trouble focusing on the small text on the vials.

Hawk inched closer to me so he could place a warm hand on my back while still holding Sebastian's bunched up shirt against his wound.

The fiery darkness of his life force slid across my senses and I leaned into his touch. It wasn't enough to completely steady me, but it helped.

"What do you need?" he asked.

"An analgesic, like morphine or—" My magic snapped inside me, stealing my breath and making me clutch the edge of the counter.

Oh, jeez. I needed more of my guys touching me and adding their life forces to Hawk's if I was going to get steady. And even then, given the backlash raging inside me, I wasn't sure it would help.

"Maybe you should talk me through stitching him up," Hawk said, moving my hand to Sebastian's shirt to take over applying pressure and grabbing a vial from the shelf.

Yeah, maybe I should. "Wash your hands first. There are syringes in the drawer below the drug cupboard, and saline in that one." I pointed to the next cupboard over. "And you'll need gauze, and—"

Hawk's attention jerked up to the doorway. "What the hell?"

My thoughts stuttered, but I didn't have to look to see who'd arrived. Even with the backlash muting my ability to sense life forces, I could feel Voth's massive dark, burning force the moment Hawk had spoken, and I was pretty sure if my magic hadn't been slicing through me and my head pounding in agony, I would have felt the greater demon from all the way down the hall.

Except with him, just at the edge of my senses, was also a warm, bright life force that I didn't recognize... and likely the cause of Hawk's reaction.

I dragged my attention up to the doorway, the room around me twisting out of focus with the movement. We'd been promised discretion and a second person wasn't discrete.

Voth, an enormous man — as tall and broad as Titus — stormed through the doorway, radiating darkness and danger, and with him was my fellow healing angel Priam, a warm-natured, boy-next-door kind of guy, and the source of the other life force.

"Amiah!" Priam's eyes widened and his angel glow flared. He grabbed a stool on wheels by the door and rushed to my side, urging me to sit. "You're glowing."

"Priam?" My sluggish thoughts lurched. He couldn't get involved in this. And why was he here? Not enough time had passed for Voth to call Operations and for Priam to get here... had it?

And that wasn't the point. Only Voth was supposed to know about us. Everyone else was in danger. That, and in that moment, I realized I hadn't wanted anyone to know I'd been branded. I'd hoped the Heart would get rid of it and no one but my guys — and Voth — would need to know the truth.

Priam's gaze flickered to Hawk, then he cupped my cheeks between his palms, forcing me to look him in the eyes, and a trickle of his healing magic slipped into me. But my magic lashed out at it, making him jerk his power back.

"What happened? I've never seen your backlash this bad or you hurt like this." He swept an appraising gaze over the rest of my guys, looking for anyone else who was injured like a good triage doctor, and I couldn't begin to imagine what he thought of us.

Titus was completely naked, but at least he gave off a shifter's essence, so his nudity could be explained — since a shifter's magic destroyed his clothing when he shifted — but Cassius's nudity couldn't be. While Rin's face was crusted with blood and Hawk still had a hand on me — something that, as an angel, was supposed to make me uncomfortable.

"Is Mr. Bane—?" Priam frowned.

Guess he'd finally looked past the tattoos covering Sebastian's chest and arms and realized that he didn't look like himself, or rather, he didn't look like the glamour he'd used to hide his identity while in the mortal realm.

"Sebastian is worse than I am and Cassius is just unconscious from a sleep spell."

"And you promised discretion," Hawk said to Voth.

Priam's gaze slipped to Hawk again before he nudged my hand away from Sebastian's side and looked at the fae's wound.

"You promised a bonded couple," Voth shot back, his voice low and gravelly like far-off thunder, and I couldn't tell if he was angry at thinking we'd lied to him or not.

God, would he throw us out?

Priam might solve our healing problem — because he wouldn't abandon us if Voth kicked us out — but we still needed a safe place to rest and hide.

I tried to meet the demon's gaze through my swollen lids. Right now, he looked human, with the exception of his size and his all black eyes with their simmering hellfire. That was one of the things that made a greater demon a greater demon. They, like angels, could keep their wings — and in Voth's case his fangs and horns — inside their bodies and release them at will. But no one would ever mistake him for a human. Even if he hadn't been huge, he still radiated a ferocious heat from his increased demonic body temperature, revealing just how magically powerful he was. And right now, he looked more intimidating than I'd ever seen him.

"I don't like being lied to," Voth growled to Hawk. "You should have just said it was for the doctor."

My thoughts stuttered at that. "You remember me? But would you have helped us even though I'm not here with Essie?" I didn't know why Voth liked Essie, but he did and had gone out of his way to help and support her even though she was a nephilim — a being that up until a few weeks ago had been enemy number one to the whole world. I'd just been the angel who'd come along and patched everyone up. I was the angel who'd tried to stand between Essie and Marcus and hadn't been very nice about it.

At the time, I'd thought I was protecting him, thought that she was going to shatter him because she'd branded the others and not him and she was being selfish for stringing him along. I'd thought he was my mate.

I'd thought a lot of foolish things.

"Of course I remember you," Voth said, leaning against the doorframe. "I'd know you even if you hadn't shown up with Essie. Priam hasn't stopped talking about you for twenty-five years."

"What?" That didn't make sense.

I dragged my gaze to Priam. His eyes were closed and his hands pressed against Sebastian's laceration, blood oozing between his fingers and light radiating from his palms.

"I talk about other things than just Amiah," Priam said, releasing his magic.

"You talk about—?" I tried to focus my whirling thoughts. My good-natured friend talked to Voth? How did he even know the greater demon and— "What are you doing here?"

"It's poker night," Priam said, turning to the sink to wash Sebastian's blood from his hands.

"You play poker?" Voth's hotel had a casino, but I didn't know any angels who gambled. In fact, I wasn't sure any angels ever visited Voth's hotel. It just wasn't our style.

"He doesn't play poker. He *loses* poker," Voth said, rolling his eyes at my friend. "He's so bad we've stopped asking him to buy in and just give him chips."

I frowned. None of that made sense.

"Remember when I took that medic position close to the end of the war?" Priam said, cupping my cheeks again, and making both Hawk and Titus inch protectively closer to me. "I was Voth's medic. Those of us from the squad who are still alive get together once a month and play poker."

How had I not known Priam had been Voth's medic? We'd spent a lot of time working together during and after the war.

He shot a spike of healing magic through my neck sealing the laceration shut, making me gasp before I could clench my jaw and hold it in. Fast painful bursts were the only way he could heal me with my backlash raging inside me, and my concussion and nose were going to hurt worse than that. I just needed to grin and bear it until it was done.

But another spike, this one exploding in the back of my head, made me whimper, and Hawk stiffened and Titus growled.

"It's okay," I gasped. "It's the only way he can heal me with my backlash."

Titus huffed and Hawk didn't relax, and Voth straightened, his hellfire flaring.

"Well that's interesting," the greater demon said. "Maybe you didn't lie about a bonded couple. Or is it a bonded trio?"

"We've all just been through a lot," I said. God, I didn't want to confess anything about my bond in front of Priam. He'd never understand.

"It's more than that," Voth replied. "Both the incubus and the shifter had a rise in power at your pain. They wouldn't have had that reaction if you were just a normal angel to them."

Priam sent another spike of healing magic snapping through my head.

"I don't want to talk about it," I ground out, as Titus and Hawk drew closer, their bodies tenser.

"Amiah, if you're branded, that's amazing," Priam replied, his eyes wide with an awe that made my stomach churn. "First Essie, and now you—"

"I said, I don't want to talk about it."

"But that was the deal." The hellfire in Voth's eyes flared.

God, was he really going to attack us because I didn't want to tell him I was bonded? "The deal was I talk to you and *only* you."

"So you're ashamed to be bonded to a demon." The danger radiating from Voth grew as if the idea of me not wanting to be bonded to Hawk was a personal slight.

"That's not it."

"Then you're ashamed he's an incubus." More fire sparked from his eyes. "He should be the one who's upset, fated to a lifetime of boring angel sex."

"Hey." Priam sent another painful spike into my head, this one wrenching my broken nose back into place, making me cry out in pain and my eyes water.

"Prove it isn't true," Voth said to Priam. "Prove angels are more adventurous than the rumors say. Show me."

Priam rolled his eyes at Voth not seeming to care about the danger radiating from the demon. "I'm not letting you watch me have sex, and I doubt Amiah will let you watch, either."

"My point exactly," Voth replied.

"I'm not ashamed to be bonded to an incubus. I wish I was bonded with Hawk."

Voth's eyebrows raised at that. "Then who are you bonded with?"

"Does it matter?" Hawk asked.

"I'm just surprised an angel doesn't want to tell everyone how special she is," Voth said, his gaze locking on me and his eyes narrowing.

God, he wasn't going to give up, and I had no idea why.

And in the end, it didn't really matter. We needed his help. "Because I'm in love with someone else."

Hawk added his other hand to my back, adding another point of contact even though it was through my scrub top, and his life force swelled against my senses, steadying me a bit, as Voth's expression turned sad.

"You might love him now," Voth said, "but I've seen the truth of the soul bond. You're meant to be with your mate. You always have been."

Except I didn't want to accept that. It couldn't be true. I *knew* I needed Hawk, Sebastian, Titus, *and* Cassius. I didn't feel that way about Rin... at least I didn't think I did.

No. I didn't. It was just the soul bond messing with my emotions.

Priam sent another painful snap of magic into me and the agony in my face vanished. I still had the pain of my backlash, but there wasn't anything he could do about that.

"Okay," Priam said, turning to the sink and washing his hands again. "You're good to go."

Hawk grabbed Priam's arm. "She's still in pain."

Priam blinked, as if his thoughts had stalled, then gave his head a sharp shake and jerked his attention away from Hawk as if he couldn't look at the incubus and speak at the same time. "I can't heal her backlash. Just like I can't get rid of whatever is causing Mr. Bane's pain. It's magical, not physical."

"It's okay." I turned my attention to Voth, who was still looking at me with pity.

It felt like he knew the hurt caused when an angelic brand formed but not between the people who were in love. Except I wasn't sure exactly how I knew that.

"Is there any way our deal could involve clothes as well as the place to stay the night?" I asked.

Although given that I hadn't told him who I was mated with, I wasn't sure if we still had a place to stay.

"I'll have clothes sent up to the suite," Voth said.

Guess not knowing everything was okay with him. Thank God.

"It doesn't have to be a suite," I quickly added. "It can be the same rooms as last time."

Those had been the plain rooms at the back of the hotel that he gave to his visiting performers. And while I'd have liked to have kept everyone together, beggars couldn't be choosers.

"I have a show moving in later tonight. You can have those rooms, but you'll get noticed, and the incubus made it clear you wanted discretion."

"The less people who see us, the safer everyone is," Hawk said, and Titus huffed his agreement.

Voth heaved a heavy sigh. "It must be something serious if you're not going to Operations."

"It is." I turned back to Priam. "Do Cassius and I even have jobs anymore?"

We probably didn't, given that we were on probation from the last time we'd run to Voth's hotel and had abandoned our jobs again.

"Chris has kept your disappearance a secret from head office, but he doesn't know how much longer he can do that," Priam said.

My throat tightened. Neither Priam nor Chris were obligated to protect us. In fact, if head office found out they'd been withholding information, they could lose their jobs, too.

"If head office presses, tell them the truth. Don't lose your jobs over this."

"It won't come to that," Priam said.

God, I hoped not. I'd miss working for the JP, but I could handle having to work — and possibly live — somewhere else. Cassius's whole world had been the JP since the war had ended, and I had no idea how he'd handle losing his job.

Of course, if we didn't survive what was coming, or if I couldn't get the Winter Court to release its hold on me, it wouldn't matter if I had a job or a home to return to.

AMIAH

Voth sent a quick text then led us — with Titus carrying Cassius, Hawk carrying Sebastian, and Priam supporting me — down the hall deeper into the hotel to a plain door marked EMPLOYEES ONLY.

Inside was a narrow gray cinderblock and concrete hall that led to a small vestibule with a metal security door that presumably led outside, and an elevator door that was locked by a card reader.

Voth pulled two cards from his pocket. "Both of these will open all the doors, the suite's door, the elevator, and the outside door in case you need to leave and come back." He used one to open the elevator then handed both of them to me. "Your clothes will be sent up in the dumbwaiter in the kitchen. And that's how your room service will arrive. Try to order the most expensive things on the menu. That will draw the least amount of attention."

"How much will that cost us?" Hawk asked.

The door started to close and Voth pressed his big hand against it, holding it open. "Nothing more than you've already paid. I'm taking a loss, but you're Priam's friend and someday I might need your help."

"You know if you asked, I'd help you regardless," I said.

"Not all angels would." His hellfire flared. "You helped Essie and her mates even after you knew what she was, even after the Director had proclaimed her a criminal, and even when it was clear you were unhappy. I've met angels with healing who aren't so generous. Your kind doesn't make the same vows as human doctors and I had real trouble finding one to join an all demon squad during the war."

Which was how he'd ended up with Priam. Because Priam had almost as hard a time saying no to someone in need as I did. I'd met a few of those angels who were selective in who and how they healed, but they didn't have the same compulsion that I did that forced them to heal whether they wanted to or not. Of course, they also weren't as powerful as me. Priam had a bit of the compulsion, but not to the same degree, and his power was somewhere in between them and me. But Priam was also a good man. He understood that any demon who'd decided to join the Angelic Defense was just as good as any shifter or human or angel — and because of Michael, I couldn't understand how any angel could still claim to hold the moral high ground just because they were angels.

"The steak with the truffle sauce is amazing," Priam added, helping me shuffle into the elevator.

Hawk snorted, following us. "You might regret that offer. Titus could probably eat a horse."

Titus rolled his eyes at him. "Two if I shift."

"How does that work?" Hawk asked as Rin stepped in, again moving as far away from me as he could in the small space. "Your human stomach isn't big enough to hold a horse, let alone two."

Titus shrugged, making Cassius's wings brush against the back of the elevator. "It's a shifter thing. We lose our clothes, but we don't have to worry about overeating in our beast form."

Voth rolled his eyes at my guys. "The suite doesn't have a booking until late next week."

"And you can call me if you need anything." Priam leaned me against the elevator wall and joined Voth back in the vestibule. "Get rest. All of you."

The greater demon let the elevator door close and, without us pressing a button, it took us up to the suite's small but lavish vestibule. Not that we could have pressed a button. There weren't any in the elevator.

The vestibule had a gold and crystal chandelier that brightly lit cream-colored walls and reflected in the black marble floor. Both the suite's door and the elevator's door were black, and the black, cream, and gold theme carried into a suite that was the size of Sebastian's apartment.

Actually, it was probably bigger. The suite had a formal entrance with a coat closet. To the right was a full kitchen and a formal dining room with a table that sat eight, and ahead and to the left stretched a luxurious living room with a large bank of floor-to-ceiling windows taking up the far wall. Beyond, lay a large patio with potted trees and shrubs and an amazing view of the city's Supernatural Quarter, while stairs at the back of the living room led up to three bedrooms — presumably all with en suites — and an office.

Warm soft light emanated from all of the bedroom doorways, and when I glanced into the closest one, I confirmed that the bedside light had been turned on and the crisp white sheets and black comforter on the king bed had been folded back, ready and waiting. And God, I just wanted to fall into one of them and pass out.

Except I was in burned and bloody clothing. The only one of us who wasn't filthy was Cassius.

"Let's get Cassius and Sebastian in bed," I said. I'd managed to make it up the stairs by clinging to the railing with Titus behind me to stop me if I fell, but I was running out of strength. Sure, with my concussion gone, I was no longer dizzy, but my backlash was still slicing through me, and I was exhausted.

"You need to get in bed, too," Hawk said, setting Sebastian on the black comforter of the closest bedroom and pulling it over him instead of tucking him in while he was still filthy.

"I will. I just want to clean up and then be with Cassius when he wakes." We'd been in Faerie the last time he'd been fully conscious, and I didn't want him to wake alone and naked in a strange place.

That, and I wanted to tell him about Rin before he saw Rin to avoid burning down the hotel.

"Titus, if you and Rin are hungry, order something from room service." I didn't doubt given that Voth catered to every known super, that he'd have food as well as blood. Voth probably had a license to house blood bunnies for those vampires who wanted to drink straight from the vein.

I dragged my gaze back to Hawk. "I won't be able to help you for a bit." And really, I needed to have sex with Titus before I had sex again with Hawk. It was a miracle Titus was still managing to control his beast, and I needed to help him mend that connection even if I wasn't at full strength. He wasn't going to last much longer, especially if I kept sleeping with the others and not him.

Hawk dipped in and brushed his lips against mine with a whisper of a kiss that sent soft heat unfurling within me. It wasn't strong enough to set off my desire — or rather make my desperate need for Rin any stronger — but it did help ease a bit of my pain.

"I'm fine," he said. "You take care of you for once."

He wasn't fine. His life force wasn't as strong as it should have been, but none of my guys were fine, and neither was Rin.

"The first time Bane broke the Winter Queen's tracking spell it was a little more than twenty-four hours before Padraigin showed up in his apartment," Hawk said. "We have a day. We have time to catch our breaths." His gaze slid to Rin and went slightly out of focus, a sign he was using his magical sensitivity to check for something, probably spells. "It's easier for me to restore my magic than the others, so when Amiah gets me back up, I'll let you feed on me."

Which meant Rin was going to have to wait to satisfy his sin eater's hunger. The question was, did he trust Hawk to keep his word?

Except there wasn't anything I could do about it if he didn't. I could only hope he wasn't going to attack us while we were down since there was no place to lock him up. That, and I didn't really want to lock him up. He'd had a chance to kill me and he hadn't. He might not be a perfect match for me, but a part of me, the part that even now with my magic raging inside me could still sense that whisper of pain forever trapped in his cells, wanted to believe he wasn't evil like Deaglan.

My magic sliced deep, making me gasp, and all of their gazes leaped to me. Hawk with heartbreaking worry, Titus with worry and need, and Rin with... nothing. But he *had* looked and I couldn't help thinking that just looking meant something.

Titus put Cassius in bed, on his back with his wings spread out behind him and the black comforter pulled up to the middle of his chest, then went back downstairs.

The tension in his body twisted at my heart even though there was nothing I could do about it right now. He needed me. Out of all of them, he was the one who needed me the most, and I was too weak to help him. I could only hope whatever rest I got while I waited for Cassius to wake up would be enough to make me look strong enough for Titus to think it was safe for us to have sex.

I went into the en suite of Cassius's bedroom to clean up, turned on the shower, and stared at myself in the mirror while I waited for the water to warm up.

Priam, as usual, had healed everything. My nose was back to normal, my eyes no longer swollen, and I knew once I cleaned away the blood on my neck, there wouldn't even be a scar where the cut had been. He'd even finished healing my burned hand. I still, however, looked like a mess. Blood crusted my lips and chin, my right cheek, and down my neck, and had soaked into my burned scrub top.

Groaning, I peeled off my top and stepped out of my pants, leaving them in a heap on the floor that I'd deal with later, and stepped into the shower.

As much as I wanted to just stand there and soak, Cassius could wake at any time. It was actually a little surprising he'd slept through the fight. Although given that I'd pumped too much magic into Sebastian's sleep glyph the last time I'd used it, and had been in a panic when casting it on Cassius, it wouldn't have surprised me if I'd used too much magic on him too.

I quickly showered, my backlash surging and snapping through me, dried off, and wrapped myself in one of the thick plush robes hanging on the back of the bathroom door, then dragged a heavy chair from the corner of the room to the bed.

My soul ached at just sitting there. I wanted to crawl under the covers with Cassius, but we'd only had sex once and hadn't had time to figure out our relationship, not to mention the last time we'd woken up together, he'd nearly lost control of his magic, something I really wanted to avoid.

That, and once he learned I was soul bonded with Rin, we wouldn't have a relationship.

The thought made my heart ache. I loved Cassius. I wanted a relationship with him and all my guys. But he, like everyone else, knew that the mating brand would make me fall in love with Rin and fall out of love with him. And while I desperately wanted to have as much as I could with Cassius for as long as I could, he wouldn't want that, not knowing I belonged with someone else.

And while I could try to keep Rin a secret from him, that would only make things worse. Even if I could somehow hide my brand from Cassius, the others knew the truth and it wouldn't be fair to them to ask them to hide it.

No matter how much it hurt, Cassius had to know, and it was best if he heard it from me.

I curled up in the chair, letting Cassius's strong fiery life force thrum against my senses, thrilled and sad that he was alive but no longer mine, and closed my eyes.

Despite the backlash, I dreamed of cold and darkness, and of being trapped, unable to move, and forgotten. No one was coming to save me. No one knew I existed. But I did exist. I *wanted* to exist. I didn't understand how they couldn't remember me. They needed me just like I needed them, but the darkness was too thick, my cage too strong, no one could hear my screaming, my begging, and I was never going to be free.

And then the cold deepened, crackling like a fast-moving frost through my essence. The Winter Court. Yet another prison. It called to me, had forced itself into my soul, and was never going to let go. I couldn't hide from it forever. It would find me. It would possess me. I'd be imprisoned in its icy essence.

That was the deal I'd made to save my guys.

I belonged to it, and my soul bond with Rin was nothing compared to the chain the Winter Court had wrapped inside me.

A blast of ice sliced through me, stealing my breath and jerking me awake.

Except it hadn't been ice. It had been my backlash.

"Amiah?" a groggy tenor asked, making my heart soar.

I'd heard that voice for over a hundred years, loved that voice, and I loved the man it belonged to.

I raised my gaze to meet Cassius's. His blue eyes — so like mine — were filled with life and light and love and desire. He was alive and well and he was at full power. He sat up, pulling in his wings with a flash of white angelic magic and giving me a perfect view of his beautifully muscled chest and arms. The memory of him naked, his stunning physique moving on top of me, rushed through my mind's eye and sent a tremor of desire racing to my core.

He'd be furious to know we'd thrown him into the back of the SUV without any clothes and mortified at being naked in Voth's clinic. Having spent most of that face-down didn't make it any better... only gave me really good memories of his tight glutes and how much I wanted to clutch those glutes when we—

"Hey," I said, suddenly feeling awkward. And while yes, I wanted to have sex with him again, what I really wanted in this moment was to wrap my arms around him, never let him go, and tell him how much I loved him. But that wasn't fair to him, not until he knew the truth.

His angel glow dimmed with worry and his expression darkened. "Who did we lose?"

"Lose?"

"I can see it in your eyes." A hint of smoke curled around him and the muscles in his jaw flexed. "You're upset. Who didn't survive the fight with Deaglan?"

"Everyone is alive. You were the worse and—" My throat tightened and another snap of backlash sliced through me.

More smoke curled from his skin and he clenched his hands. "God, I want to hold you, but…"

But he couldn't control his magic if he held me. Before he'd been injured, he'd barely been able to control it just being near me.

In fact, I needed to make this as emotionless as possible for his sake.

I drew in a sharp breath and tried to draw on my professional persona, but too much had happened. That Amiah was gone. I was never going to be her again. Everything I'd thought and believed had been wrong. I could never have enough control over my life or be careful enough to guarantee I'd be safe. I'd been taken again and hurt worse than the first time. I belonged to the Winter Court and without a doubt it was looking for me, determined to take me back to Faerie.

And really, I didn't want to be that cold, desperate-to-be-in-control woman anymore. She'd only hurt me, made me ignore a part of myself that I hadn't realized I needed.

Except who I needed were Cassius and my other guys, something I didn't know how to keep while I was soul bonded with Rin.

"Whatever it is, we can get through it," he said.

"I don't know if we can. My mating brand formed."

Another burst of smoke swept around him. "I thought you got rid of it."

"I thought I had."

"Oh God, Amiah. I'm so sorry." The light in his eyes flared. "Maybe it won't be the prison you're afraid of. Just because you're bonded doesn't mean you're trapped. You were already feeling a connection with us—" His eyes widened and realization flashed across his expression. "It's just with one of us, isn't it? And it isn't with me." His voice turned hard and his expression icy. But I knew now that wasn't because he was angry. It was because he was trying to control his emotions and not let his fire escape his body. "Who is it? I hate that it isn't me, but all of them have proven that they're worthy of you."

"The demon-vampire hybrid," I forced out.

"Deaglan's hybrid?" Flames burst around Cassius's hands, lighting the comforter on fire. "Shit."

He clenched his jaw and the flames swept back under his skin, but now he was so tense, he trembled.

I jerked forward to help him — which was stupid because there wasn't anything I could do to help — and managed to force myself to sit back before touching him and making the situation worse. Going to him would just make everything more difficult. "You still think this is okay?"

"There's got to be a reason you branded him."

"Because fate is cruel and the brand is a lie. Everything about the mating brand has been a lie." I bit back a bitter laugh. "How is being soul bonded with someone I don't love beautiful? Fate had four guys to choose from. Four guys who I *know* I love."

His eyes widened at that.

"Yes. I love you. I thought you'd died and it killed me knowing I'd been too afraid to tell you the truth because I also love Sebastian and Hawk and Titus. And even though you said you'd wait, that still meant you were going to ask me to give them up. Now I have to give all of you up." Tears of frustration burned my eyes. It wasn't fair. And while I knew life wasn't fair, it just made me so angry that I'd finally figured a part of myself out and was finally starting to accept who I was, and now fate had taken that away. "I know in my soul I need all of you and I refuse to let the mating brand change how I feel."

"So how do we fix this?" he asked.

My thoughts stuttered at that, but only for a second, and then my heart soared. God, I loved him. He hadn't said it couldn't be fixed, even though everything we'd been taught said it couldn't be. This was the man who'd had my back from the moment he'd rescued me from that faith healer's tent... well, from the moment he decided I wasn't going to emotionally fall apart and had stopped looking at me like I was weak and pathetic. This was my best friend. This was the man who'd been missing since the war, the one I'd been desperate to get back.

Who I was *going* to get back.

"I'm hoping Faerie's Heart will be able to break the bond."

"Then we'll get Faerie's Heart," he said.

My backlash surged, slicing deep, and I gasped, making him frown.

"Backlash?" he asked.

"Yeah."

His frown deepened, but he didn't ask me what happened. He knew if I'd fought my magic and refused to heal someone I'd had a good reason. "You'll get rid of it faster if you sleep."

"I know, but I wanted to tell you about Rin—"

"Rin?"

"The hybrid. His name is Rin. He's here with us. The others dragged him into the mortal realm with us when we fled Faerie," I said, realizing I still had a lot of explaining to do. Cassius might not have known that we were back in the mortal realm until I'd just off-handedly mentioned it. "You needed to know about him and I wanted you to hear it from me."

"Do we trust him?"

"I want to, but I don't know if that's the brand making me feel that way or not," I said. "I haven't had a chance to really talk with him, but I know he was Deaglan's slave, was tortured, and is angry about that."

"Which will either make him more dangerous or an ally." Cassius drew in a deep breath and reached to push the comforter and sheets back but paused, probably realizing he was naked. His expression grew pained and more fire sparked over his hands, but he managed to suck it back before lighting the comforter on fire again. "It'd be best if you left. Give me a few minutes to get into the bathroom, then you can have the bed."

"Right." I stood.

His gaze dipped to my breasts and I realized the robe had slipped open a bit. Not enough to be indecent, but enough to show an enticing amount of cleavage.

I tugged the fabric closed. "There are other rooms. You can keep this one. No one will make you share."

"But you'll share," he said, his voice suddenly low and dangerous, smoke curling from his arms. "How many more beds are there?"

"Two others." Which meant I was most likely going to share with more than just one of the guys. "Does that upset you?"

I wasn't sure I wanted the answer, but a part of me needed to know. I'd really liked falling asleep with all of my guys, but I only had two sides. Not everyone would get to sleep beside me and while Hawk didn't care who he slept with, and Sebastian didn't seem to mind either so long as I was present, I still wasn't sure about Titus or Cassius.

"Only if they don't give you what you need," he replied, and I realized his tone wasn't anger, but desire.

Another flame licked up his forearm and the comforter caught on fire again.

"Fuck." He wrenched his gaze away from me and the flames

vanished. "You need to leave before I accidentally hurt you, and I need to get someplace less flammable."

God, I wanted to stay. We'd only just begun to explore our desire for each other, but he was right. Until he could get his magic under control, I needed to keep my distance.

I hurried into the dimly lit hall, closed the door behind me, and stood there, not sure what to do. Yes, I needed to go to bed, but a part of me didn't want to go to bed alone.

Somewhere downstairs, I heard Titus say something, but his voice was just a little too quiet for me to make out his words. Given that the light in the living room was on, he was most likely talking with someone, and since Sebastian was probably still unconscious, Cassius was in the room behind me, and Rin practically mute, Titus had to be talking with Hawk. And while it wouldn't be fair to Titus to ask him to just sleep with me and not have sex, I could ask Hawk.

I turned to head downstairs but stopped at the sight of Rin kneeling on the office floor with his eyes closed.

The only light in the room came from the weak illumination in the hall, but with my night vision it was clear he'd washed the blood from his face. He still wore the same calf-length wrap tunic and leather pants as before, and while I couldn't see the blood on his black clothes, I had no doubt it was still there. A part of me wanted to believe that made him a monster. That would make it easier to hate him and resist our bond. He'd tried to kill me. He'd killed that man in Left of Lincoln without any emotion. But that silvery scar across his neck and the pain imprinted in his cells said he'd only done whatever it had taken to survive captivity at the hands of a real monster.

My desire for him swelled, overwhelming the pain of my backlash for a second, and I gritted my teeth against my aching need. That was just because of my brand. And yet, my body still took a tentative step toward him before I realized what I was doing.

AMIAH

RIN OPENED HIS EYES. HE MUST HAVE HEARD ME STEP CLOSER. HECK, WITH his vampire-enhanced hearing, he'd probably heard my pulse pick up with my yearning.

Be mine. Seal our bond.

Tears burned my eyes.

I didn't want him. I wanted them. Why couldn't fate have bound me with them?

"You love all of them? Not just your husband?" he asked, surprising me. Not because his voice had changed — he'd still spoken in that intense whisper — but because he'd spoken first and more than a single word.

And then my thoughts stuttered on that. "My husband?"

He'd said that before when we'd been in Sebastian's clean room, but there'd been more important things to talk about.

"Prince Seireadan," he said.

Oh. He thought—

But of course he did. He didn't know we'd lied to the Winter Queen so Sebastian wouldn't have to marry a stranger on the spot, and everyone thought because the Winter Court's wind responded to me that I was Sebastian's wife.

A part of me wondered if maybe that was true, if somehow we *were* married. Except even if it was, Sebastian would never accept that. He'd sworn he'd never be bound to anyone like that and as much as the idea of letting him go hurt, I wouldn't keep him when he said he wanted to end whatever it was between us. Besides, if I couldn't resist my bond with Rin, none of that would matter.

"He's not my husband," I said against the lump in my throat.

Jeez. Couldn't I just be strong for a minute? But grieving over the loss of someone wasn't a weakness. Not doing anything when there were things I could do, was.

And I hadn't given up. I was going to get the Heart and keep my men... those who wanted to stay with me.

A spark snapped from Rin's eye. "But you love him."

And I was going to free Rin from this mess as well.

"I do." I didn't know how. With the exception of Cassius, I barely knew the men I'd fallen in love with, but I loved them and knew I needed them. "I love all of them, and I promise, I'll find a way to remove our bond."

I took another step toward him, my unwanted desire throbbing between my thighs even as my backlash sliced through my body.

Rin's hellfire swelled into miniature flames and a hint of hunger bled into his expression before quickly vanishing.

"Did you get more blood?" I asked.

"Do all vampires in the mortal realm drink blood in a bag?"

If he was asking that, it meant he hadn't had much experience with this realm. Although maybe he just hadn't had mundane experiences. He'd been Deaglan's assassin and had probably spent most of his time hiding in the shadows — even though I was sure his demonic nature made him immune to sunlight, unlike most vampires.

"No," I said. The memory of him biting me and his seductive magic swelling inside me rushed through me, making my voice breathy.

I swallowed a moan and struggled to stay where I was. I did *not* want him. I didn't. "Most vampires don't drink bagged blood, but you need consent."

"And that's hard to get?"

"No." God, I needed him.

I took another step toward him, but my backlash surged, thankfully cutting through my need, and I forced myself back to the doorway.

If I was smart, I'd just leave him until I could get myself under control, but I also wanted to earn his trust. Everything would be easier if we weren't watching our backs or chasing after him.

"There are people who look for vampires to feed on them and people who've made that their profession," I said. "They're called blood bunnies."

"Are there magic bunnies?"

"No. There aren't any sin eaters left in the mortal realm." I hadn't thought there were any sin eaters left in any of the realms.

His hellfire sparked then shrank back to smoldering red pinpricks.

"But don't worry," I added, praying that him shutting down what little emotion he'd shown wasn't because he thought we were going to let him starve like Deaglan had. "Hawk said he'd let you feed on his magic just as soon as I can restore it for him."

My magic surged with a painful burst, tearing at my insides and drawing a pained gasp before I could stop it. "I just need to get through this backlash."

Another spark snapped from his eye. The smoldering red ember drifted to the floor and hissed when it hit the marble before going out.

"I'm sorry, but that'll probably be a few days," I added.

Except we didn't have a few days, not before the Winter Queen recast her tracking spell on me and we had to run again.

He continued to stare at me, no indication he understood what I'd said or that he'd done the same math and knew that he wouldn't be able to satiate his sin eater's hunger until after we'd run for our lives again, something we needed to figure out how to stop doing.

But we'd been reeling since this whole mess had started and every time we seemed to figure something out, something else threw everything into chaos.

My backlash snapped again, this one so sharp it made me whimper.

And if I couldn't get my magic to calm down and regain control of it, I wouldn't be able to save any of my guys if we ended up in a fight again.

"I need to get something to eat and some rest."

With Rin.

My desire for him surged again, and I gritted my teeth and forced myself to stay where I was.

No. I needed to do it with Titus or Hawk or both of them.

No. I needed to go to bed. Alone. At least until my backlash was gone.

"Rest will help with the backlash," I said. "With luck it'll pass within the day."

Except my luck lately had been terrible.

"I can ease your backlash," he said, with still no indication of an emotion in his expression. "If I take some of your magic, the storm inside you will dissipate."

"And by take you mean feed on me."

"Yes."

My pulse picked up with a horrifying mix of fear and desire. Feeding meant he'd have to come close. And God, I *wanted* him close.

No. I want the others. It's just the brand. It isn't real.

"I can't afford to lose too much magic," I said, my voice back to frustratingly breathy. If I could access my magic, I could save my guys, but only if I had enough left.

Was it worth the risk?

Did I really have much of a choice?

No.

If letting Rin feed on me meant I'd never have to go through thinking one of them was dead again, I'd do it.

"Can you control your hunger?" I asked.

"Yes."

"Can you control your desire?" Could I control mine?

His hellfire swelled into miniature flames for a second before returning to smoldering pinpricks. "Yes."

"Okay."

He stood and my pulse throbbed. My whole body throbbed. God, I needed him, needed to connect with him, seal our bond—

I gripped the doorframe as if that would help me stay where I was as he drew closer. For a second his hold on his essence slipped — I hadn't even realized he'd been holding it back — and I saw who he really was, felt the full intensity of his demon-vampire nature, alive yet dead, dark, and completely dangerous.

But then my magical senses connected with his life force and I felt his pain. Yes, he was a predator, a creature of the night who fed on blood and magic, but he was also a man who'd suffered greatly. That, and he couldn't do anything about his nature. He was who he was and the sense from his essence wasn't a sense of *who* he was, only *what* he was.

Then he pulled his essence back and returned to the dark, silent man who'd been kneeling alone in the office.

"I'll have more control if we connect with our lips," he said.

"You mean kiss." The idea sent a shudder of desire racing through me that sunk hot and sultry into my core.

"Yes." His gaze dipped to my lips.

A small part of me screamed that I should get one of the other guys, have them chaperone this... feeding, but the rest of me was possessed by the brand, and it was all I could do to not throw myself at him.

"Make it quick." I didn't know how long I'd be able to hold my desire at bay.

"Yes, your highness," he breathed, using the title I'd have had if I really were Sebastian's wife.

I opened my mouth to argue, tell him I wasn't a highness, or princess, or whatever I was, but he slid a cool hand over my cheek, tangling his fingers into my hair, and pressed his lips against mine.

Any words or thoughts I might have had vanished. His strange life force surged against my senses, and my need for him twisted in my core, an insistent throbbing, urging me to complete the bond. I tried to swallow my moan of desire, but a soft, breathy sound still escaped my mouth.

His grip tightened and he deepened the kiss, turning it into something more than just touching our lips, and yet it was still soft and sensual, a strange contrast with his life force and essence.

I wasn't sure what I'd expected. But it hadn't been tenderness. It made my unwanted desire billow, drawing another moan and making my knees weak.

Then a crackling thread of magic shot into my mouth, down my throat, and wrapped around my heart. It sliced into my backlash, even as my desire for him grew.

I gasped at the sudden pain and Rin cupped my other cheek, fully capturing my head. His magic grabbed something inside me, deep in my heart, and started pulling it up my throat and into his mouth.

Panic seized me and I tried to wrench away from him—

Or was I trying to get closer?

No, get away. *Get away!*

But he held tight, his lips still capturing mine, making it impossible to call for help. I could feel my magic pouring out of me, warm and viscous like how it felt when I pushed it out of my palms. Except this was rushing up my throat, making me gag.

My backlash sliced and heaved, still a wild storm raging inside me, but the core of it was weakening, sucked up by Rin, and was being replaced with my desperate, burning need for him.

I clutched the front of his tunic, caught between wanting to get away from him and wanting to get closer, and my breath turned ragged.

Then Rin's crackling magic snapped free and shot out of my mouth back into him and my backlash suddenly shattered, my desire surging to fill the void.

With a low soft groan, he shoved me against the doorframe, pinning me there. He slid his tongue into my mouth, returning our lip lock to a kiss that was anything but soft. It was hard and desperate and made the brand on my hip blaze bright with a golden heat that shone through the bathrobe.

Everything within me cheered. *Oh, yes. Yes!* This was what I wanted.

But it wasn't. God, why was that so hard to remember?

I. Didn't. Want. This.

"No," I gasped, tensing at the same time Rin tensed, and he pulled his lips away as if he too had remembered his desire for me wasn't real.

Gasping, he pressed his forehead against mine. "I'm not feeding on you again."

"Not until the brand is gone," I said, trembling with need and fear and frustration at the brand's control over my body.

"You'd let me feed on you after we're separated?"

"If you're still caught up in this mess. Yes," I said. "I'm not going to let you starve."

"What will your lovers think?"

"It's my body. My choice." Although I was pretty sure that was going to be a huge argument with all of them. But it didn't matter what any of them wanted. No one deserved to be starving, and the pain imprinted in Rin's cells made my healing compulsion twist in my gut. I might not be able to do anything about it, but I could deal with his current suffering.

Except a part of me screamed that I only felt that way because of the brand. I didn't know him. Yes, Deaglan had treated him badly, but that didn't mean he wasn't also a bad person. For all I knew, he enjoyed killing people.

"It'd be better if I didn't," he said, as movement in the hall caught our attention.

We both looked up as Titus, dressed in a pair of beige shorts and nothing else, snarled and lunged at Rin.

Rin jerked away from me, sidestepped Titus's punch, and used the big man's forward momentum to toss him face-first to the office floor.

Titus hit with a hard thud, crashing into the heavy dark-wood desk at the back of the room, but leaped to his feet and curled his lips back, flashing his extended canines at Rin. He flexed his hands and claws grew from his fingers, while his pupils slitted and his life force writhed in a wild, ferocious frenzy. His beast was taking control.

Oh, crap. I'd put off having sex with him for too long.

"I said you're never touching her again," he growled, his muscles bunching, ready to attack.

"Stop." I jumped between him and Rin before he could strike, and raised my hands to him. My pulse roared in my ears, a mix of fear and frustrating desire, and I prayed Titus still had enough control over his beast that he'd listen to me. "I said he could. He's calmed some of my backlash."

Footsteps pounded from down the hall as well as up the stairs and Cassius — in a robe — hurried into the study, smoke billowing around him. Hawk — in a light blue T-shirt and beige shorts — was right behind him, his hellfire blazing.

"It's okay." God, this could get out of hand quickly. "I'm okay."

Red-gold scales rippled up Titus's neck and along his jaw, and his trembling increased. He was trying to fight his beast's instinct to protect me, but he'd spent too long in Deaglan's captivity without being able to shift or having the flesh-to-flesh contact that his shifter's soul needed.

"Titus." I took a step toward him and held out my hand in invitation for him to take it. My soul ached for his pain even as my desire for Rin still throbbed inside me.

No, I wanted Titus.

Except I wanted both Titus and Rin. If I was being honest with myself, I wanted all of them.

"Let me help you. Let's heal your two halves." That would go a long way to helping him think straight. Logically he *knew* he couldn't kill Rin, but his beast wasn't logical. It was wild primal emotion, and I didn't know if right now it was thinking beyond believing that I was in danger.

"Amiah, please," Cassius begged. "Wait until your backlash has passed."

"Her backlash is a fraction of what it was before," Hawk said. "You're magically weaker, but not drained."

"Not helping," Cassius snapped. "At least let Titus regain control of his beast."

Titus snorted and smoke curled from his nostrils. His life force grew stronger as his human nature battled with his beast's, neither able to accept each other or properly reform their connection.

And it was worse than before. There'd been a time in the Winter

Court where I'd thought he was on the mend, that just flesh-to-flesh contact and being able to shift might be enough, but now it was clear he needed more, and I could only pray I'd be enough.

"He's not going to be able to regain control without help. We've waited too long." I took another step toward him. One more and I'd be able to press my palms against his bare chest. Hopefully, even though I wasn't a dragon or his mate, I'd be able to help him. God, everything within me yearned to help him.

Except he needed so much more than just steadying now. He needed to re-find that balance between the two halves of his soul, he needed to trust his beast.

"I can get control," he said through gritted teeth. The scales melted back into his skin, but his chest heaved with rapid breaths and his expression was tight with pain.

"You don't have to do it alone." I took the final step and pressed both of my palms to his broad muscular chest and a part of me thrilled at the contact even as my need for Rin throbbed stronger.

Titus stiffened instead of relaxing like I'd hoped and the scales swept back up his neck, but his frenzied life force whirled into a more cohesive storm, both parts of him sharing a desire for me.

Yes. Complete our connection. Make me forget about Rin, just for a little while.

He wrenched his attention past me to the others. "Get out."

"No." Cassius jerked forward a step, fire curling up his forearms.

Titus wrapped an arm around me and yanked me tight against his body, sending desire rushing to my core as my gaze flickered to Rin.

No. I heaved my attention back to Titus who bared his teeth and snarled, his beast fully taking control. "Get. Out."

"Not until I know she's safe," Cassius said, surprising me. He wasn't saying no to me being with Titus like I — and probably everyone else — expected, he was saying I could when Titus got his beast under control.

Except Titus wasn't going to get his beast fully under control until I helped him, and to do that, I needed to trust and accept him. All of him.

And even then it was a longshot to healing his soul. Yes, we had a connection, but given how broken his connection was with his beast, it might not be enough... or it might confirm what he believed, that I was his mate, since connecting with a mate's soul was the most powerful and steadying connection a shifter could make.

Which excited and terrified me at the same time. I needed him. I needed all of them. But if I was his soul mate and I couldn't break my bond with Rin or add to it, Titus, along with Hawk and Cassius, was going to get hurt.

"Titus, let her go," Cassius repeated. "At least until you've gotten your beast under control."

"No," Titus— or rather his beast growled.

"Cassius. I'm safe." I reached up and urged Titus to press his forehead against mine, adding another point of contact and drawing his focus away from Cassius and back to me. "Your beast isn't going to hurt me."

I need you. I don't need Rin.

Titus shuddered and closed his eyes, his whole body tense and trembling. "I don't know that he isn't."

"I do," I said. God, the others had to get out of there so I could take off my robe and press more of my flesh against his... to have him inside me and complete the circuit that I knew we shared just like I shared with the others. "We have a connection. I know it in my soul, in the core of my being, and branding Rin isn't going to change that." *Please, God, don't let it change that.* "You know that, and so does your beast. He's not going to hurt me."

"But you're not a dragon. I'm too strong. I need to be careful."

"And your beast knows that as well." I wasn't interested in mixing pain into my sexual experiences, but that didn't mean the guys had to treat me like I was glass. I could handle a bit of roughness. In fact, the idea made me ache for it, for a repeat of my first time with Sebastian or my first kiss with Hawk where both men had completely taken control, overwhelmed me, and sent me reeling in the most amazing way.

I turned to Cassius and Hawk in the doorway, but my gaze slid past them to Rin, standing in the corner, his expression revealing nothing about how he felt.

My desire for him churned stronger and I struggled to force it into my desire for Titus. What I felt for Rin wasn't real. My need for Titus was.

"I'm helping Titus heal his soul," I said, dragging my attention back to Cassius and Hawk. *I'm helping me forget about Rin.*

Cassius's eyes narrowed and fire rippled past his elbows, but Hawk gave me a tight nod.

"You want me to help?" he asked, his gaze dipping to Titus's crotch, reminding me that I was still inexperienced and Titus was a big man. If he didn't get me worked up enough and take it slow — which I doubted he'd do either — this first time was going to be painful.

"This mating is mine," his beast snarled.

A whisper of fear cut into my desire, but my eyes found Rin again and my need swelled.

God, this was such a mess.

Hawk raised his hands in defense. "Hey man, if you're worried about hurting her, maybe having someone there is a good idea."

"Mine." He curled his lips back and growled.

He wasn't going to say yes. It had to be difficult enough for Titus to share me with the others, asking him to open up his bed was clearly too much.

"It's okay," I said, leaning my cheek against Titus's bare chest, giving him more flesh, savoring the feel of his hard muscle and concentrating on my desire. To hell if it was for Rin. "Titus needs this."

And I could deal with a little pain to help him and to make me forget, just for a moment, that I wanted Rin. I wanted to feel our completed connection more. If I focused past my desire and the remnants of my backlash, my soul begged to connect with Titus's life force. God, it hadn't even been a day since I'd connected with Sebastian and Hawk, and my soul needed to feel that completed circuit again.

"Okay." Hawk ran a hand through his jaw-length sandy blond hair, not looking happy about agreeing. "The moment it's anything other than desire, I'm coming up and stopping it."

"Agreed." Cassius yanked his fire back under his skin.

"Now get out," Titus growled.

Hawk rolled his eyes at him. "How about taking her to a bedroom, big guy."

Titus blinked as if he didn't understand Hawk, then his dragon huffed. "Right. Yes."

He swept me into his arms and shoved past Cassius and Hawk, and I pushed aside everything but the core of my desire. I wanted this, I ached for this, I needed this.

AMIAH

Titus carried me to the empty bedroom at the end of the hall, used his heel to knock the door closed with a heavy thump, and sat me on the edge of the bed.

My thoughts slipped to Rin, and I wrenched them back to Titus and the throbbing between my thighs.

"The moment you think I'm going too far, stop me. Don't wait for Hawk," he said, kneeling on the floor in front of me, his golden gaze capturing mine, his body trembling with the effort to control the wild desire he'd had in the office, making my heart ache.

The warm light from the bedside lamp caught in his eyes and reflected back like a cat's eyes, but it didn't hide the turmoil that I could see there. A battle between man and beast raged inside him, and it made my soul weep.

God, he'd been so close to just letting it out. A quick walk down the hall and he was back to fighting himself.

I cupped his cheek with my hand and the sense of his life force swelled, a wild, ferocious, desperate storm. This wasn't the way it was supposed to be. He was powerful and amazing and his beast was a majestic creature. He hadn't deserved what Deaglan had done to him—

Just like Rin didn't.

I shoved that thought away.

Focus on Titus. He needs this, just as much as I do.

"You won't go too far."

Please fill me, please make me forget Rin and how this is probably going to hurt and how I almost lost Cassius. Make me forget everything. Please. Just for a moment.

I knew it wasn't healthy to keep using sex as a distraction. But right now, if I didn't find a way to let everything go and focus on Titus, he might not be able to mend his connection with his beast.

"Promise me you'll make me stop," he— no his beast growled.

"I promise." I knew neither he nor his beast would go too far and seriously hurt me beyond what I could heal. From the tension in his body, I was afraid he wouldn't go far enough.

Proving my fears right, he dipped in with a barely-there kiss. It was nothing like the wild forceful one we'd had before in the aerie, and it wasn't going to do anything to heal the damage in his soul, or drive everything out of my mind... or satisfy my aching desire inflamed from kissing Rin.

Before my mind could jump back to Rin, I brushed my fingers across the rough red-gold stubble dusting Titus's cheeks and tangled them into his dark red hair so I could draw him closer and deepen our kiss.

He rumbled low in his throat, the sound deliciously primal and masculine, but he didn't take my cue and his body remained tense with the effort to hold himself back.

"Titus," I murmured against his lips. "You have to let go and stop fighting your beast."

"I know but—"

"No buts. You're not going to break me, I'm not glass, and I'm not afraid of him."

His life force heaved against my senses, sharp, desperate, wild, and scales slid up his neck again.

"You should be." He sucked in a quick breath, forcing the scales back under his skin then cupped the back of my head and pressed his forehead to mine. "He's angry. Angry at being locked way inside me and angry that you need *them* as well." His trembling increased, the extra point of contact with our foreheads not helping to calm his soul. "And he's angry that you branded Rin and not me."

My throat tightened, even as my need for Rin rippled through my core. "I'm angry about that too. But we'll get the Heart and fix that."

I drew back just enough so I could look him in the eyes. I let him see how much I desired him, all of him, how much I needed that something in him that I also needed from the others, and how determined I was to make this right.

"Stop fighting your beast and stop holding back," I said. "I've been fantasizing about this from the moment I first saw you. Thinking about our kiss back in the aerie has been driving me crazy."

I captured his lips, releasing my desire for him, determined to show him how much I wanted him and that I wasn't afraid, despite my concerns for his size.

He rumbled again and — finally! — kissed me back. His hand on the back of my head held me close as he raked his tongue against mine, making my whole body throb with need. He kissed me with the same wild, desperate passion he'd had when we'd been back in the aerie and when we'd been attacked in the Winter Court, and I gave in, letting it overwhelm me.

There were no thoughts of Rin or fear about Titus entering me. There was just pure need, surging and whirling, sweeping through the remnants of my backlash and mixing with my life force.

This was what I wanted, what I needed.

God, yes.

But Titus jerked back, making my thoughts stutter and my fears start to rush back in.

No. Don't stop.

He groaned, his expression was tight with pain and his body tense. He was still fighting his beast when he should have been accepting it and trusting it, still trying to control it.

"Let him out. It's okay." *You need him to heal and I need him to forget. Please.*

"I know." He squeezed his eyes shut and took in a deep shuddering breath, but it did little to ease the tension in his body.

"So what are you waiting for? It's the only way you'll be able to properly reconnect your soul." Well, not the only way. Having sex was the way shifters of the same species helped each other. For vastly different species, those with no sexual desire, or those rare patients who'd been newly infected with lycanthropy, the alternative was slow and steady. A process that took weeks, sometimes months or years.

We didn't have that kind of time, and Titus and I shared a sexual desire. I could help heal his connection with my body.

And he could help steady my soul, something that, as an angel, I wasn't supposed to need.

"Just let him out."

He snorted, smoke curling from his nostrils, but his body remained tense.

Nothing I could say was going to make him let go. He'd been holding his beast in for so long, he feared that part of himself. Which meant I was going to have to force his beast to take control, show the man that his beast wasn't just mindless and wasn't going to hurt me.

Please, God, let his beast still have some kind of control.

"For goodness sake. If you're not serious about having sex, I'll go back to Hawk," I said, trying to get a rise out of his beast — not the safest thing to do but really my only option.

His eyes narrowed, and a hint of his red-gold scales reflected the lamp light along the side of his neck, but his body remained tense, his will still keeping Titus the man in charge.

Damn. Hawk wasn't enough of a threat to make his beast seize control. He'd already accepted that I needed to be with Hawk as well as him.

My heart twisted. I didn't want to push the matter, but it seemed he'd left me no choice.

I slowly ran a hand down my neck, into my robe, and cupped my breast, hoping, with my inexperience with seduction, that I still looked sort of sexy.

His gaze followed the movement, his pupils dilating, and my breath picked up with a mix of desire, fear, and regret at what I had to say next.

"Actually, I ache for Rin." Which, God, I did. *And I'm not going to think about.* "I'm going to go to him."

I stood, but Titus snarled, grabbed my wrist, and yanked me back down to the bed. Scales rushed up his entire neck and into his stubble, and he bared his elongated canines at me.

"No," his beast growled, his tone sending an inappropriate shiver of desire racing through me.

Yes, let it go.

"You're mine."

"Prove it," I growled back, shoving him with all my might.

Don't fight him. Let him take over. Trust him. Trust me.

He toppled onto his back, only because I'd caught him off guard, and his eyes widened in surprise.

I straddled him, digging my fingernails into his chest, and leaned close, my lips almost, but not quite, brushing his. "Prove it," I repeated.

His beast rumbled at my challenge, grabbed the back of my head, tangled his fingers in my hair, and smashed our lips together.

He fully controlled the kiss, tilting my head to get the angle he wanted so he could completely possess me. My body ignited, every nerve suddenly sensitive, and my mind went gloriously blank. There was just the sensation of being overwhelmed and my desire fueled by the ferocity of his shifter's life force. And his life force was wild and strong, man and beast surging, blending, breaking apart.

Titus the man wanted control, but his beast right now was too strong.

He wrapped his other, powerful arm behind my back, yanked me close, and rolled us over.

"Mine," his beast snarled, pinning me with his pelvis, his large erection grinding against my clit and sending the whisper of a climax through me.

Oh, yes.

I tried to rock my hips in response, but I couldn't move against his weight. He pulled back and looked down at me, his expression pure sexual hunger, making me shiver in anticipation. Scales now ran across his collarbone, over his shoulders, and across the tops of his pecs. I scratched my nails across his skin, the scales still soft like flesh, and drew another rumble of desire.

"Mine," I snarled back.

At my word, his life force swept into a whirling vortex inside me, his battling threads merging into a blazing, ferocious power for a second before breaking apart again.

Crap, he'd had it.

He just had to trust himself. Something he used to do. He'd been born a shifter, his soul had always had those two halves and, like all born shifters, he had a natural connection between them.

Did that mean our connection was strong enough for me to help him heal? If it wasn't, it wouldn't matter if I slept with him or not.

Except everything within me screamed that wasn't true. That I could heal him. That there wasn't just something in his life force that I needed. That he, like the others, was mine.

"Mine," I snarled again, and with an instinct I didn't know I possessed, I sat up and grabbed his head, but instead of kissing him, I bit him between his neck and shoulder. Hard.

His life force snapped back into that merged vortex, both man and beast joined in reaction to me biting him, because by doing so, I'd claimed him like many predatory shifters claimed their mates.

With a growl, he grabbed my hair at the scalp, jerked my head back, and captured my mouth again in a bruising kiss that shattered all breath and thought. His other hand pushed inside my robe and roughly kneaded my breast as his erection ground against me with the hard promise of where we were headed.

And God, that was exactly where I wanted this to go.

My body was on fire with sensation. Every nerve turned on, all my senses locked onto him, his merged wild life force, his hand in my hair, and his other hand rough against my nipple. His hot breath rushed into my mouth and washed over my cheeks, and all I could do was let go, like I'd told him to do, and give in to it all.

"I knew you were my soul's mate," he snarled against my lips, and he shoved a thick finger into my already slick heat.

I gasped and bucked at the sudden invasion. But he didn't let up, possessing my mouth with a ferocity that sent me reeling and pumping his finger inside me, hard and fast, twisting my need tighter and tighter.

Oh God, yes.

My breath grew ragged and he shoved in a second finger, adding to the pressure and friction, then a third, stretching me. His thrusts were hard and fast, verging on painful. Then he ground his thumb against my clit, and my muscles clench tight around his fingers, my orgasm sudden and powerful, drawing a cry of pleasure.

"Mine," he growled, and he withdrew his fingers, opened his fly, and pushed his large erection inside me before I could fully register what he was doing.

My whole body tensed at the sudden bite of pain. Oh God, he was too big. I needed more time. Then his life force blazed inside me, and that piece of my soul that needed him clicked into alignment. It sent an aftershock of my orgasm rippling through me and relaxed my muscles to better accommodate him.

Titus gasped and jerked his golden gaze to mine. His pupils were fully dilated like a human's, but both man and beast were looking at me, his eyes filled with shock and awe and desire.

Then his desire overwhelmed everything else, and his life force inside me surged. I was wild and ferocious, just like Titus. My desire for him was stronger than my worry or pain or anything else.

I locked gazes with him, snarled at him, and dug my nails into his chest, drawing blood.

He snarled back, grabbed my hips, jerked himself out, and thrust back into me in a forceful stroke. Glorious friction and pressure filled me, and he did it again and again.

I cried my pleasure, dug my nails into his forearms, and bucked into his powerful strokes. His breathtaking, powerful life force roared inside me, and my full-body glow writhed around my body like a sea caught in a powerful storm. We crashed together, two primal beings, connected in spirit, our souls aligned, gasping and moaning and growling, and our gazes locked.

His pupils slitted again and his canines extended, the wild desire in his eyes feeding my own need. He was mine. This was right. And oh my God, it felt amazing.

My whole body roared with a consuming rush of wild life force and sensation. I couldn't catch my breath and I didn't care. This was the passion I'd ached for, and this was Titus fully embracing who and what he was.

God, he was mine. Just like the others were.

Mine mine mine.

The muscles in my core seized and another climax tore through me. It ripped a scream from my lips. My glow burst into a brilliant white light that lit up the entire room, my eyes rolled back, and stars exploded behind my lids.

With a final, powerful thrust, Titus roared his own release and sank his teeth into my shoulder, making my soul sing. He'd claimed me, marking me as his, and I was going to bare his mark with pride...

And not think about what might happen when my brand made me fall in love with Rin and Rin alone.

CASSIUS

My fire seared through my veins, boiling my blood, as my desire and fear and anger raged through me. Flames poured from my hands onto the concrete patio around my bare feet and I didn't bother trying to hold it in.

I wouldn't have been able to no matter how hard I tried.

The best I could hope for was to contain it enough to not burn down Voth's hotel... which somehow we'd gotten to.

I was afraid to ask what had happened. The last thing I remembered, I'd been injured and Amiah had been screaming and running into the middle of the battle with Deaglan's shadow fae, and then a blazing agony had sliced through my throat and my life had gushed from my severed arteries. I'd collapsed and all I could think about was protecting her and that I'd failed. I'd had one job and I'd failed.

It didn't matter that I was still alive to continue fighting for her. Deaglan was still out there and she was still in danger. That, and everything within me was screaming that Titus wasn't in control and he was going to hurt her. I shouldn't have agreed to them having sex.

Why the hell had I agreed?

Except she'd had that look in her eyes, the one that said it didn't matter what I said. She was going to do what she wanted, regardless of the consequences, and the only way I'd be able to stop her was if I tied her down.

She'd had the same look when she'd run into the fight and I'd told her to get back to safety, and again in the office when she'd walked right up to Titus, who'd been shaking with his beast's fury, and had pressed her body against his.

Still, I should have tried harder to make her see reason, forced her to wait until he was at least in control.

God, all I wanted to do was wrap my arms around her and protect her.

Except that wasn't *all* I wanted.

I bit back a scream of frustration and my fire surged around me, shooting high above me before I could hold it back.

Shit. We were supposed to be hiding. I had to hold it together, or at least hold it together enough that I didn't give away our position.

But God damn it, I couldn't just accept that I'd never be able to give her what she needed like Titus could— like he *was*. Right now. Only the odds weren't good that I'd even be able to touch her again. Not unless I could fix whatever inside me was broken or my magic was permanently taken away from me.

That was what really made me angry. It should have been me up there with her. I was the one who'd been in love with her for a hundred years. We weren't just friends anymore, we were lovers, and I'd treat her the way she deserved, with reverence and adoration.

But I couldn't. I couldn't even get close to her, and I knew she also desired passion. It had been obvious in the way she'd melted into Titus's ferocious kiss in the cavern in the Autumn Court.

But even if I was mistaken and she didn't want the intensity of a shifter's passion, she still would have had sex with him. It wouldn't have mattered what she wanted at all. He needed her. Even I could see his connection with the beastly half of his soul was broken and knew that the best and fastest way to heal that was through sex.

And, as much as I wanted to pretend it wasn't true, I also knew she needed him, needed to make her own connection with his soul... or — how had she put it? — his life force, just like she'd connected with me.

Which, if I couldn't get my magic under control or get rid of it, was never going to happen again. And none of that mattered if we couldn't get the Heart and remove her mating brand.

I was going to lose her forever.

I'd already lost her.

The brand she'd said she'd had removed, that she hadn't wanted and had been afraid of, had already taken her from me.

Fuck.

My fire roared around me again and ignited my robe.

Fuck!

Fuck fuck fuck.

I heaved at my power, yanking the flames out of the fabric before I ended up naked. Again.

This was a nightmare. My only hope of getting Amiah back was getting the Heart and given that Deaglan had nearly killed me, I had serious doubts all of us were going to survive another confrontation. Not to mention, I was losing the instinctual control over my fire that I'd been born with that protected my clothes, which made me less than useless to Amiah. It made me dangerous.

I needed Bane to freeze or pull out my fire. It was the only way. Just for a little while, just until we could figure out how we were going to deal with Deaglan, because without my fire I couldn't protect Amiah.

God, I'd never wanted to be the Salamander again, but it seemed he was all that was left of me, the wild, angry force of nature bent on brutal justice for the murder of my youngest brother. Once we had a plan, I could point myself at the Shadow King and stop fighting my magic.

A part of me was relieved at the thought. My battle with myself would finally be over. It had been twenty-five years of struggling, my hold getting weaker and weaker, and I couldn't hold out much longer. I was broken and no one could fix me. This, at least, was a way to protect the person I held most dear.

We'd still need to figure out a way to stop Deaglan from taking my fire... although I had a horrible suspicion that if I truly gave in to the firestorm raging inside me, Deaglan wouldn't be able to take all of it.

My flames billowed around my feet, rolling toward a potted tree, and I heaved it back in.

Please, God, let Bane have figured out what Deaglan had done to take my fire and be able to repeat that. I just needed to hold out long enough for one last confrontation with that monster.

Except I hadn't seen Bane in the office when Titus and the hybrid had been fighting over Amiah.

The hybrid.

Her mate.

My throat tightened and a gust of wind swept sparks from my fire drifting into the night sky. Bright angry specks against the darkness.

Why couldn't it have been me?

Hell, why couldn't it have been any one of us? I'd even have accepted Bane as her soul mate.

But not a complete stranger who'd tried to kill her the instant he'd seen her back in the park ring when we'd first found Titus. She didn't deserve that. She hadn't deserved anything that had happened to her in the last few days.

Except if her magic hadn't locked onto Titus and she hadn't been accidentally leashed to him, she never would have realized the truth about herself.

I'd never heard of an angel needing to connect with someone through sex, which meant she never would have even known to ask until she realized what was happening, and even then, she might have been confused. She wouldn't—

My thoughts stuttered. Could she make her connection with anyone? She'd said she'd been waiting for her soul mate and hadn't realized she'd needed to connect through sex.

Did that mean she hadn't had sex until we'd fallen in with Bane and Hawk?

I had no idea if that made things better or worse. If she could connect with anyone then my death wouldn't affect her nor Bane and Hawk going their separate ways. She could happily carry on with Titus or replace us. But if it was just the four of us, she was fated for more heartbreak. Even if I survived, she'd still lose Bane and Hawk—

And none of that mattered because her soul was bound to the hybrid.

God, I couldn't allow that. I had to get Faerie's Heart and fix this for her... maybe it could even fix me.

Hope squeezed around my heart and I shoved it as deep down inside me as I could. I couldn't afford any doubt, anything that made me hold back. That could mean Amiah's death. I had to fully embrace my power and let it consume me if that's what it took to keep her safe. If I survived what was coming, then I could hope.

And the first step to saving Amiah was coming up with a plan, which meant I needed to gather the others. I couldn't do this alone and they *were* going to help Amiah even if I had to force them to.

Except even if everyone agreed to have that conversation on the patio, I still needed help with my fire, and that meant finding Bane.

I sucked in a steadying breath and imagined myself surrounded by ice, but that did nothing to cool my flames.

My fire snapped and hissed. The breeze picked up more sparks, twirling them into the sky, and a pillar of flame shot up, following it.

God damn it. Ice. Cold. God damned frozen things.

I wrenched the pillar back into me, making the inferno inside me burn hotter, and clenched every muscle in my body, determined to keep it in. I could do this. I had to do this.

I mentally seized the fire rolling across the patio and dragged it back inside me, adding to the inferno burning my skin then yanked in the flames around my hands.

The effort left me panting with a searing pressure that threatened to tear out of my chest, but now only smoke billowed around me. And that was going to have to be enough. I was barely holding the flames in, gathering up the smoke was going to be too much. I could only pray I wouldn't set off any fire alarms.

Better yet, I should just open the door and call for Bane, get him out here on the patio and relieve some of this pressure. Then I could sit inside like a normal person and have a non-normal conversation about the nightmare Amiah was caught up in.

I opened the door to go back into the suite and was met with moaning and grunting punctuated with cries of pleasure.

Good Lord. Was that Amiah having sex?

My pulse leaped in a wild tattoo and my heart squeezed at that thought with a churning mix of fear for her and jealousy directed at Titus, and my fire exploded over my hands.

God damn it.

I jerked back onto the patio, letting the door close and shutting out the sound — the lack of noise an indication that a sound block spell had been cast on the suite.

I fought to heave my fire back under my skin, but I couldn't concentrate. All I could think about was how it sounded like he was hurting her and—

Movement through the bank of floor-to-ceiling windows caught my attention as Hawk strode into the living room from the kitchen. He held a full, white, plastic bag and was headed for the stairs, but his gaze met mine and he changed directions.

"A change of clothes," he said, opening the patio door and holding out the bag.

Amiah screamed again and I couldn't tell if it was pleasure or pain.

Except Hawk had said the moment she stopped enjoying sex with Titus he'd put an end to it. And I trusted him to take care of her. He might have been a lot of things, but he'd proven I could trust him and he'd sworn he'd protect Amiah.

So if he wasn't running upstairs, that meant he was still getting sexual energy from them and she was all right... or at least emotionally all right. I wasn't sure about physically.

My fire flared and I backed away from him, not taking the bag, afraid I'd set the clothes on fire before I had a chance to change into them. "How can she be enjoying that?"

Hawk's expression darkened and he stepped fully onto the patio, letting the door close behind him. Guess he wasn't happy about what he was hearing, either.

"It feels like she's riding his essence," he said. "I don't know how she's doing it. That's an incubus or succubus thing, but her desire right now has the same edge that a shifter's does."

Of course it did. Because if she needed to connect with him, whatever it was that was inside her would help her do it. It was the only explanation... since I didn't want to accept that she wanted that kind of sex. If she did, I'd never be able to give it to her even with my magic controlled or gone.

I sagged to my knees in the middle of the patio, needing to sit but not trusting that I wouldn't destroy the patio furniture. "Whatever it is she needs from us is helping her."

"That would be my guess," Hawk said. "It's making this first time with him and his larger-than-she's-accustomed-to cock enjoyable."

My fire surged, rushing up to Hawk's feet and making him jerk back with a yelp. I didn't know if he meant that to also mean that she didn't have a lot of sexual experience or just that Titus was big and she probably hadn't ever had sex with someone as... well endowed — and thanks to his shifter magic destroying his clothes, I'd seen him fully erect, and he was very well proportioned.

I gritted my teeth and heaved my fire back as best as I could.

I couldn't do anything for Amiah right now. I couldn't even touch her. I needed to get my God damned fire under control, and then I needed to stop Deaglan for good.

"Where's Bane?" I asked through clenched teeth. "I need him to try to rip out some of my fire before I burn this place down."

Hawk's expression darkened even more, and he dropped onto the edge of one of the three black couches and rubbed his face. "He's down for the count until we can deal with his demonic magic infection."

He's what?

"He's infected with demonic magic? When the hell did that happen?" Although that would explain why he wasn't as magically powerful as he should have been. A man who I knew had teleported an astounding ten people shouldn't have been struggling in the last couple of fights as much as he had been.

"He said something about the Hellfire Queen and an archnephilim."

That had been my brother and his mate's last battle, where I'd been next to useless in protecting him. That also meant Bane had been struggling since before this whole mess had started.

"Every time he uses magic it gets worse and that last battle with Deaglan and then escaping his apartment—" Hawk ran a hand down his face again. "I know you're struggling, but we can't do anything until we can get that shit out of him."

Movement inside the suite caught my attention again as Bane, wrapped in a fluffy white robe, staggered to the top of the stairs. He looked horrible. His complexion was gray and I could see him shaking from all the way out on the patio.

He clutched the railing and took a trembling step down, but his leg didn't support him and he crumpled, tumbling forward.

Hawk and I jerked to our feet, but we weren't going to be fast enough to stop his fall — and I was now fully engulfed in flames again and more likely to set the suite on fire if I ran inside.

Then a dark figure swept up behind him and grabbed his arm. He yanked Bane up, jerking him to his body, and wrapped an arm across his chest to support him.

The hybrid.

Hawk bolted inside and the hybrid's gaze snapped to him.

"We should get him back in bed," Hawk said before the patio door slid shut.

Bane raised a trembling hand and shook his head.

The hybrid didn't say anything and didn't move. His expression was hard and void of any kind of emotion, and it made my fire heave and blaze hotter.

This was who fate had bound Amiah to. This emotionless monster—

No. Amiah didn't think he was one. She'd said he'd been tortured by Deaglan, had been his slave, and he did just save Bane from falling down the stairs.

Except that didn't make their soul bond right. She didn't know him. She didn't love him.

And I wouldn't be able to free her from him without Bane, and Bane was in serious trouble.

TITUS

I clung to Amiah, my cock buried inside her, my teeth in her shoulder, and a wild new energy rushing through my body. It snapped through my soul and wrenched at my two disconnected pieces, a mix of my own shifter nature and the strange powerful magic that had flooded me the moment Amiah had screamed her release.

I hadn't thought her power could get stronger. I'd entered her and whatever it was that she needed from me — from all of us — flooded me, connecting our hearts and souls. It had filled me with absolute certainty that she was mine and I was hers, and nothing else in that moment had mattered.

And then she'd come and my soul had ignited. I was on fire, filled with strength and power. Her power. My power. A power from someplace else, someplace that called to both halves of my soul and wove both man and beast back together into a balance that had been missing for centuries.

This. This was how I was supposed to feel.

I'd forgotten how steady my soul used to be, how strong. Now, even in my human form, I could feel my dragon's fire warming my throat, a sensation I'd lost when my soul had started to separate.

I wanted to shift, spread my wings, soar into the sky, and roar the news of my mate for all to hear. I'd never felt stronger than in that moment, our bodies and souls joined. I'd never been more certain of who and what I was, and I knew exactly what my purpose was: protect my mate.

Mine.

Forever and always. And all of me, not just my beast, was positive she was more than just my mate, more than what I could give her soul, she was my soul's mate. We were fated for each other.

It was the only way she could have mended my soul so easily. Because she hadn't just eased my turmoil, she'd face my raging beast without fear and completely steadied him. Only my soul's mate had that kind of power.

And even though she wasn't a dragon, I'd been unable to stop myself and had marked her as mine.

Of course, much to my surprise, she'd tried to mark me as well... which was what had gotten the whole thing started.

I didn't know what had possessed her to try — and I didn't want to accept it was just to make my beast take over, even if it had been. Pushing me over and drawing my blood with her nails would have been enough for him to seize control of our body, especially given how tenuous my hold had already been. But then she'd bitten me. I hadn't stood a chance.

My control had shattered and my beast had fully taken over, his passion without restraint, not caring that she wasn't a dragon and couldn't withstand a dragon's full strength.

And now I could only pray I hadn't hurt her too badly... since I wasn't even sure exactly what I'd done.

This hadn't been what I'd wanted for our first time. I'd wanted to draw it out, bring her to climax again and again, and when I couldn't take it any longer, I'd wanted to savor the feel of slowly sliding into her slick tight sheath and watching her eyes roll back in pleasure

But my beast had wanted to claim her, *needed* to claim her, and it had been denied for so long, our passion made anything other than ferociously taking her impossible.

"Oh wow, Titus," she moaned, and another, smaller, orgasm swept through her, making her muscles clench around my cock again and her full-body fae glow flare even brighter.

A pressure in my chest, the fear that I'd seriously hurt her, that she was now afraid of me, and that she hadn't enjoyed that, released, and my beast rumbled against her shoulder, her blood trickling between my lips. *Mine.*

Oh yes, mine, I agreed and the power in my soul surged.

She was amazing. I couldn't believe she'd enjoyed that, wasn't crying in agony from how rough I'd been.

My thoughts tripped at that. My teeth were still in her shoulder.

Shit.

I shouldn't have bitten her, not sinking my canines in all the way. She wasn't a dragon. She didn't heal like a dragon.

Shit shit shit.

I drew my teeth from her flesh and raised my head, my gaze instinctually jumping to hers, and I was drowning in her stunning blue eyes.

Her angel glow blazed bright, brighter than when I'd carried her into the bedroom, although that was probably my imagination since she hadn't had enough time to recover her magic, and she captured my soul, my whole healed soul.

The love and warmth and acceptance in her gaze wrapped around me and my heart thrilled. There was no fear or pain and anger at the fact that I'd hurt her. She embraced all of me, my large, dangerous body and my wild primal soul. She was incredible.

And the pain I'd seen in her eyes back in the aerie, that fear that there was something broken inside her that she didn't understand, was gone. It was replaced with certainty and strength and I could sense something deep inside her starting to awaken, something empowered by connecting with me... and the others, and—

My pulse skipped a beat. Crap. I'd claimed her. Would my beast accept her having sex with the others even though I *knew* she needed them, or would he see that as a challenge to his claim?

But my primal nature huffed at me. She needed them as much as she needed me and that made them a part of her. That was who our mate was.

The love in her eyes deepened as if she saw me come to that shocking realization, and she raised her hands to cup my cheeks, but stopped before making contact and frowned. Her fingers were bloody.

Her gaze jumped to my shoulders then my arms and my chest, taking in the marks she'd scored in my flesh, and her expression turned shocked. "Did I do that?"

I chuckled and my beast turned the sound into a satisfied rumble. "Oh, yeah. It could only have gotten better if you had claws." And much worse because I did have claws.

I slid my gaze down her stunning body, taking in her delicate figure, and my cock, still inside her, started to harden again.

But a whisper of fear chilled my desire as I reached the swirling gold lines of her mating brand on her hip. It pulsed with power, proclaiming that she wasn't mine, she wasn't even Seireadan's, Hawk's, or Cassius's. It didn't matter what I knew to be true in my soul. Her brand said otherwise.

And there was no way I was going to accept that. She was mine and I'd never let that monster touch her again... even if he had helped her ease her backlash... which meant maybe he wasn't a monster?

I bit back a growl. I had no idea what to think about the hybrid, and really, that was a worry for later.

"Are you okay?" I asked, my voice gruff. I couldn't see any bruises or scratches, save for my bite, and she wasn't crying, but that didn't mean I hadn't hurt her.

She shifted as if testing her body, taking more of me inside her and softly groaning with pleasure. "I'm good. I don't know how. I should be black and blue and very raw because... well..."

A gorgeous soft blush blossomed on her cheeks and I grew harder, drawing another soft moan of desire from her.

"Because?" I prompted.

"Because you're bigger than I'm used to," she said, her voice breathy.

I slowly drew myself halfway out of her and her eyelids fluttered shut, her lips parted on a soft moan, while my dragon preened at the thought that I had something the incubus didn't.

"But—" she groaned.

"But what?" I leisurely pushed back in. She felt incredible, better than I could have imagined and my five hundred year drought had nothing to do with it. She was mine. This was right, the way we were supposed to be, and this time I was going to give her the slow, sensual lovemaking that she deserved.

She gasped and dug her nails into my forearms, making my beast rumble in pleasure.

"But my body is fine and some of the power Rin took to relieve my backlash has already been restored."

I drew halfway out again and she bit her bottom lip, only partially keeping in another moan.

"Just give me a minute to stop my bleeding," she said, even as her hips curled up, urging me to push back in.

My beast snarled at that, half in anger at itself for biting her and half because it didn't want to stop, even for a minute.

Somehow, I resisted the urge to push back in until she told me she was ready. She'd already made love with me for me. This time was all for her. But my instincts urged me to dip forward, making me tremble with the effort to hold my cock still, and I gently licked her front puncture wounds and cleaned away her blood.

It was pure dragon instinct, although I was sure there were other shifters who had the same compulsion, and as weird as it might have seemed to an angel, I reveled in the action. Licking her wounds without thinking meant my beast and I were one again, that I was in touch with all of my soul not just fractured parts of it.

Her magic warmed her flesh under my tongue and the power of the connection she'd made with my soul flared again.

"God that feels so good." She opened her eyes and captured me body, mind, and soul again. "You make me feel incredible, and strong, and ferocious."

"Because you are." I couldn't understand how she didn't think she was strong. She was one of the strongest people I'd ever met. She was willing to do anything to protect us despite the dangers. She hadn't hesitated to heal Cassius even though I was certain she knew she'd get burned and that she wouldn't have any magic left to heal herself. She gave and gave and gave to anyone and everyone from her soul and heart, from the very essence of her life force.

And somehow fate had decided I was hers.

Because I would give everything to protect her, to bring her joy and pleasure.

I pushed back inside her, drawing a low throaty moan, as someone — soon to be a dead man if he didn't leave right now — knocked on the door.

I dipped into kiss her, my lips a fraction from hers, when whoever it was knocked again.

"Hey, guys," Hawk said through the door.

"Go the fuck away. If you know what's good for you, you'll leave," I snarled, my lips curling back and my canines extending even though he couldn't see me.

"Oh, I'd love to keep riding your sexual energy, but Bane is up," Hawk replied. "He doesn't look good and I don't know how long he'll remain conscious. If you want to participate in the plan to get us out of this mess, now's the time."

"Tell him to suck it up. We're not done." I glanced at Amiah, who gave me a soft smile. "I want to make you feel strong all night."

"I want you to," she whispered, cupping my cheeks between her small palms and drawing my gaze to hers. "God, I want you to. But Sebastian knows this situation better than any of us, and I won't allow Deaglan to hurt any of you again. You deserve to be free."

She gave me a sad soft smile and my heart clenched. She wasn't free. She was trapped in a soul bond with the hybrid and claimed by the Winter Court.

And Seireadan was the only one who could possibly fix that.

"Okay," I said, my voice gruff.

"Guys?" Hawk asked. "You in on the planning or not? Cassius will be pissed if he thinks I didn't invite Amiah."

"We're coming," Amiah called out, even as she shifted her hips taking me deeper inside her and drawing a soft moan of pleasure. "We just need a few minutes to clean up."

"Well you're not *coming*," Hawk said, his tone turning playful. "And I'd hate to leave you hanging. Let me give you a hand so you can finish off... again quickly."

"No!" I wasn't going to have him take over when it was finally my turn... even if my turn was being cut short. And hell, I could be quick without the incubus's help. She'd get at least one more orgasm before we left this bedroom. I captured her lips in a hard, fast kiss that made her dig her nails into my shoulders. "You're not coming in here. I'm perfectly capable of satisfying my mate."

"Oh yes, you are," she breathed.

"Hey," Hawk said, "it wasn't a criticism. I bet you she's lit up like the sun she's so satisfied. It was an offer. For both of you. You need to wrap it up quick. She's ready to go, but you could use a boost if you're going to come again. And after half a millennium of celibacy— You deserve to come again."

Well, I did, and it sounded like a great idea, but— "You're just trying to share my time with Amiah." It was bad enough I had to share her body with them. I wasn't going to also share the time I got to have sex with her.

"Nope. Although don't get me wrong. If you want to share? I'm game for that."

Amiah bit her lip on another moan, but I couldn't tell if it was Hawk's words or her slowly moving hips, inching me in and out of her channel that was heightening her arousal... although I had found her with Hawk and Sebastian when the second key had been empowered, and she'd been glowing with satisfaction, so I know she enjoyed having more than one of us at the same time.

"Right now, though," Hawk said. "I just need to touch you, give you a boost, and leave."

"Would you like that?" I asked her, but I wasn't certain if I was asking about just getting a hit of Hawk's magic or having sex with her and Hawk. And could I do that?

Her muscles trembled around my cock and she stilled and sucked in a breath, trying to control her climax. "I don't care if you want to have sex with me and the others at the same time, but let Hawk give you another orgasm. I want to feel you come inside me again."

Her words made my balls tighten. That was a request I desperately wanted to honor.

But I didn't want Hawk in the room and I certainly didn't want his help. She was mine and this was my time with her.

"Tick tock, guys," Hawk said.

"Let him help you," she said, capturing my gaze with hers, her love and need clear in her eyes. "Come again for me, Titus."

I bit back a growl. How could I say no to that?

"Fine. But know that I don't need your help getting off," I called out to Hawk.

"Again," Hawk said, "not a criticism on your prowess, merely a comment on your limited time."

He opened the door and his gaze leaped over us lying on the floor, me pinning Amiah's small fragile body beneath me and blood from Amiah's scratches streaking my body. For a second I was afraid he was going to be furious that I'd hurt her, then he flashed his wicked smile, making Amiah softly moan with his power.

"Hey, gorgeous," he purred, crouching by her head. "I see you've figured out what really gets a predator shifter going. Are you okay?"

"Really? You're going to ask me that?" she said, her voice breathy. "You already know I'm better than okay."

He rolled his eyes at her. "Yeah, and I have no idea how you are from all the racket you were making. I'm surprised the room isn't destroyed what with dragon boy here finally releasing his beast."

"Ha ha. I have some control," I said since there was no way in hell I was going to admit I'd been terrified that I'd hurt her. "Now can we get on with this? I have a mate to satisfy."

Hawk's expression heated. "Yes, you do."

He grabbed my shoulder and without warning sent a blast of hot sensual magic exploding inside me. It roared through every cell in my body then shot into my cock. I was instantly hard, so hard it hurt, and before I realized what I was doing, my hips thrust forward even though I was already buried inside Amiah.

She took it with a quick gasp, her blazing fae glow rippling up her body with the impact and her eyes widening just before they rolled back and she released a deep moan that made my balls even tighter.

"God, you're gorgeous," Hawk said, the desire in his eyes deepening as he slid his gaze down her body to where we were connected. But instead of looking upset, his need deepened and his hellfire swept across his cheeks. "Man, I know joining in is out, but you sure I can't watch?"

"Hawk—" His magic inside me surged and my attention snapped back to Amiah as I slid myself out to the tip and thrust back into her. She was so tight and slick and felt so good and Hawk's magic had me already on the edge. And as much as I'd wanted slow and sensual for our second time, I was going to come hard and fast. Again.

Another surge and I slid out and thrust back in. This time Amiah curled her hips to meet me and we crashed together, my hold on myself starting to slip.

I gritted my teeth. I needed to hold it together long enough to make her come first. Whatever I did, she had to come again. This time was supposed to be for her, and it didn't matter what Hawk did. He could stay or leave or, hell, join in, so long as he didn't get in my way.

A growl rumbled in my throat and I thrust again, harder this time, and once again she met me, moaning her pleasure, and fueling my shifter's passion.

Mine.

Mine mine mine.

I thrust again and again, our pace leaping from fast and steady to frantic. Amiah met me every time, gasping and moaning and bucking beneath me, just as wild as me, and Hawk's magic twisted me tighter than I'd ever been before.

I pounded into her, barely conscious of ensuring my grip wasn't too tight and my claws didn't extend. My own need to release raged through me, but I hung on, clinging to the need that I needed to hear and feel her release first.

And then she cried out and tensed. A look of pure bliss filled her expression and her fae glow blazed so bright it was almost blinding. Her contracting muscles clenched tight around me and I released my hold on myself.

Stars exploded behind my lids, and every muscle in my body contracted with a powerful orgasm fueled by Hawk's magic that filled me with sensation all the way down to my soul.

Mine.

Amiah's connection within me surged, and Hawk's magic sent another eruption screaming through me, and my soul roared its certainty.

She. Was. Mine.

And it didn't matter that Hawk was still in the room, that his hellfire licked across his cheeks with his desire for her or me or both of us, or that I'd ridden his power to pleasure Amiah. He was a part of my mate.

He was mine, too.

They all were.

I didn't want to have sex with them, not without Amiah, but my beast had made up its mind and that shocked the hell out of me.

They were mine. They were also my soul's mate.

SEBASTIAN

Sweat dripped down my back, coming, only in part, from the muggy night air, and I huddled on a couch on the patio, the demonic magic inside me slicing deep into the very essence of my being.

God, I shouldn't have gotten out of bed.

Hell, I wished I hadn't even woken up. Except if I'd waited for the agonizing acidic burn of the demon magic inside me to ease up, I'd have never woken, let alone moved again.

Which, at the moment, seemed like the best idea ever.

Except if we were going to get out of this mess, we needed a plan, and I was the one who knew the most about what the hell was going on.

"Hawk said they were done," Cassius growled from the far side of the patio, fire dripping from his hands onto the wide concrete tiles as if he'd given up on trying to fully contain his magic. "How long does it take to get someone?"

The demonic magic surged, making me suck in a sharp breath. "Give them a minute to clean up."

And for Amiah to heal herself.

Which I wasn't going to say out loud, even though I was sure he was thinking the same thing. From the moaning and crying and roaring that had been coming from the bedroom when I'd woken, Titus's beast had to have been fully released, and even if by some miracle Cassius had accepted that Amiah wanted to have sex with all of us and he had no right to stop her, he'd never accept sex that hurt her.

Hell, I was shocked by it as well because I was pretty sure she didn't get off on pain.

And maybe she didn't.

She knew the fastest way for Titus and his beast to merge back together was through sex, and that he needed to release his beast and trust it on a soul deep level. She'd do whatever it took to heal him, even if that meant enduring some pain. And even if she didn't make the same connection with Titus that she did with me and Hawk, she'd sacrifice her body to save him.

Although I was pretty sure she'd connect with Titus, and that she'd connected with Cassius when they'd had sex.

Except if she did need something from the four of us, how did that explain her mating brand awakening and forming a bond with Rin? Was that fate just being fucked up? Or did she need him as well?

And why.

That was what really bothered me.

I had no idea why. Why did I want to be bonded with her despite still being certain that I never wanted to be soul bonded with anyone? Ever. There was something about her, something that was fucking with my mind, and I really hated when things fucked with my mind.

The demonic magic surged again, and I bit back a groan.

Jesus. I also hated things that fucked with my body.

All I'd wanted was to be left alone. No Winter Court, no fucked-up head games, and no expectations. I didn't want the throne. I never did, and things had been great. I'd made a good life, had no obligations, and could buy all the books I'd wanted.

And then I'd gone and helped.

I was such a fucking idiot. If I hadn't stuck my nose in where it didn't belong, if I hadn't cared so damned much about this realm, I wouldn't have been infected.

But I did give a shit and letting the Hellfire Queen take over would have ruined my perfect life.

Which had really just been a fantasy, because Faerie had always been fated to shove its way back into my life. I was a royal and that's what Faerie did to royals. I'd been an idiot to think I could have escaped it. And yet the idea of dealing with this mess with the Heart and Deaglan

— because the only way out was through — and leaving all this shit behind made my pulse race.

Because it wasn't the mess I didn't want to leave. It was *her*.

I liked what she, Hawk, and I had. Hell, I didn't care if Titus and Cassius wanted to join in, just as long as I could keep her. I loved her.

Which was probably more of whatever she was that was fucking with my mind.

The demonic magic flared again and my vision darkened, forcing me to suck in ragged breaths to stay conscious.

And yet a small part of me said it wasn't, that I wasn't being influenced by her magic, that I was genuinely in love with her and my behavior was perfectly normal for an idiot in love, while another part didn't give a shit. The connection she made with me when we had sex didn't just go one way. I'd felt it too and every time we had sex it got stronger and made me feel stronger in spite of my demonic infection.

I still didn't want her brand. Really. But I certainly didn't want to give her up.

I glanced at Rin.

Why the hell couldn't it have been me?

I clamped down on that thought. I didn't want it to be me. But if it hadn't been me then what we had would still be gone.

A spark of hellfire popped from Rin's right eye, the only indication he was alive and conscious... well, undead and conscious. He still wore his all black assassin's garb that was probably still coated in blood, and stood at the edge of the patio's conversation area, staring into the living room. Except I couldn't figure out if he was watching for Amiah or not... like Cassius and I were.

I also had no idea what to make of him. He still showed no emotion. I think the most I'd ever seen from him had been when he'd been straddling Amiah in my clean room and that had been pure desperate hunger. I hoped to God, for her sake, that he'd open up. Amiah might have been cold and in-control when we'd first met, but now her heart was fully exposed, her emotions clear, and she lit up with passion. All that wonder and confidence was going to vanish if Rin couldn't muster any outward desire for her.

I also had no idea if any of us trusted him, and wandering around free didn't mean anything. There wasn't any place in the suite to lock him up. And hell, from his body language and the fact that he stood halfway across the patio from me, it was clear he didn't trust us, either.

Except he hadn't had to catch me before I fell down the stairs. Which didn't necessarily mean anything. It could have just been a moment of weakness when Amiah's brand had overwhelmed him and forced him to do the right thing, or his hope of lulling us into trusting him before he killed us and dragged Amiah to Deaglan.

God. And at some point, Amiah was going to have to sleep with him.

The thought made my insides churn, increasing the demonic magic's burn.

Of course, I didn't know what had happened between Amiah activating my teleportation spell on my circle and waking up here — which from the Quarter's skyline had to be Voth's hotel.

Maybe Rin had opened up. Maybe one of the others had gotten a better read on the man.

"They're taking too long," Cassius said, drawing my gaze away from Rin and the living room and back to him. "I'm going to get them."

The angel's expression was tight with a pain that almost looked as bad as mine, and his fire roared around him, shrinking and billowing as if caught in a wild storm. I had no idea how his robe or the plants around him hadn't caught fire.

He sucked in a noisy breath and most of his fire vanished, leaving only tiny flames flickering from the back of his hands and smoke curling around him. Except his body shook so hard, likely in his attempt to control his fire, the smoke around him undulated.

He was one fucked up mess.

The demonic magic billowed again, stealing my breath for what felt like an agonizing eternity but was really only a second.

And so was I.

"Just wait," I gasped. "You're going to hurt yourself trying to control your power like that."

"Well I need to figure something out until you can deal with your demonic magic infection."

If I *could* deal with it.

Something else I didn't want to say out loud because everyone would freak if they knew there was a chance the demonic magic had already severed my connection to Faerie and I couldn't be saved.

Amiah most of all.

God, I hoped I was wrong. Except my fae glow was gone and I couldn't feel Faerie's magic inside me or sense my always-there connection to the realm.

Movement at the top of the stairs caught my attention and Amiah, wrapped in a fluffy white robe, stepped onto the first step.

She was radiant. Literally. I'd never seen her unnatural fae glow so bright before. It created a white nimbus around her like that of the angels depicted in the humans' art, and her expression was joyous... and a little dazed. She'd thoroughly enjoyed her time with Titus. Which was a relief, because Titus still needed more time with her to properly reconnect the two halves of his soul and she'd make herself do it even if she was now afraid of him.

But there was also something more to her glow. The power radiating from her that always pressed against my senses because of my magical sensitivity felt different, and I could sense it even with her on the other side of the suite. It had changed when the Winter Court had claimed her and now was ever-so-slightly different... or was it just that the Winter Court's power was starting to break free of the spell Karthick had cast to block it?

God. It was bad enough we barely had any time before my mother recast her tracking spell and found us again. I had no idea how she'd managed to recast it so quickly in the first place. But Karthick's spell on Amiah should have lasted longer than a few days. We should have had more time.

Titus, in a pair of beige shorts, and with water from his hair, glistening on his massive, muscular chest followed close behind her. His power was strong and sure again, not stuttering and fractured, and a pressure in my chest eased — and was quickly replaced with a painful surge of demonic magic.

His essence hadn't felt this steady since before the last time Faerie's Heart had awakened and he'd lost his kin. I was pretty sure his realignment was still fragile, but this was the first step he needed to take. A step I wouldn't have been able to help him with even if I hadn't been infected with demonic magic. No, he'd needed Amiah and fate had thrown those two together.

And was now tearing them apart.

Hawk stepped into sight — still wearing his beige shorts and blue T-shirt. His essence was back to full power as well. Except it hadn't been when he'd left to get Titus and Amiah, which meant he'd gotten more sexual energy while he'd been up there, he'd probably encouraged them along for a little more.

He was someone else fate was fucking over.

And God damn it, it pissed me off that even when I got rid of this infection, I wouldn't be able to help them.

Halfway down the stairs, Amiah's gaze landed on me and her angel glow flared, her joy sharpening into seriousness.

She hurried the rest of the way down and across the living room, moving as if she were in perfect health, and my heart skipped a beat.

She was okay, and with her power at full, Titus hadn't seriously hurt her.

Thank God.

Cassius jerked forward a step as she opened the door, his fire rolling up his forearms before he sucked it back in and backed up the step he'd taken.

Rin also shifted toward her then froze as another spark of hellfire snapped from his right eye and drifted to the patio, the only indication that she affected him as well.

"We have to deal with this infection," she said, sitting on the couch beside me, cupping my cheeks between her cool palms, and urging me to look at her as if she could do something about the magic trapped inside me... which she couldn't.

A weak flurry of frozen sparks rushed from her hands into my face and a hint of fae magic fluttered inside me.

Okay. Maybe she could help me.

Except she could only transfer magic. She couldn't remove the infection because as a being from the Realm of Celestial Light, she had no way of connecting with the demonic magic.

I slid my gaze to Hawk, who'd sank onto the couch opposite me, his gaze on Amiah, a strange soft yet still heated look in his eyes — another one of us who was also a fucked-up mess.

"Any word from Sargos?" I asked him as Titus picked up Amiah, pulling her hands away from me.

My heart stupidly clenched at the absence. Jeez. Yes, I was in love with her, but so was everyone else and Titus's realigned soul was still fragile. He needed to hold her more than I needed her touch.

But instead of moving away, Titus took Amiah's seat and settled her in his lap with his arms around her, and she reestablished contact with me, interlacing our fingers.

"You're going to Sargos?" Cassius asked, more flames rolling up his forearms. "Are you insane? He's responsible for the deaths of at least four JP agents."

"Then it's a good thing I'm not an agent." The demonic magic surged, but another small flurry of fae magic sparks rushed from Amiah's hand into mine.

Cassius glared at me. "We can also link him to human and super trafficking and the deaths of a dozen more supers."

"And he's the only one close enough to get here on time that can get this shit out of me." Another agonizing surge. "Trust me," I said through gritted teeth. "I'd rather not risk drawing his attention, but I have no choice."

I'm running out of time. If I haven't already.

Cassius's smoke thickened around him. "You don't know what Sargos will charge."

"Does it matter?" Amiah asked. "Sebastian can't carry on like this."

"It matters because Sargos could ask for one of us as payment, not just Bane." A burst of fire shot from his body into the night sky. "God damn it," he hissed and yanked his flames back into his body. "I will *not* let anyone take you again."

"Sargos won't know about her," I said.

"You honestly believe he won't find out about her?" More fire rolled up his body.

"He won't because the fucking brand is going to take her out of my life," I snapped back.

Titus rumbled and tugged Amiah closer to his body and the muscles in Hawk's jaw tightened.

Amiah squeezed my hand and she met my gaze. For a second, I was drowning in a glowing blue sky, my soul captured by hers and the hope I saw in her eyes. "Not if the Heart can remove it."

Out of the corner of my eye, I saw Rin shift a step closer.

The Heart could fix this.

Holy shit, the Heart could fix this!

I cupped her cheeks and captured her lips in a quick, hard kiss. "I'm an idiot. Of course the Heart can fix this."

"Which doesn't solve the issue of Sargos," Cassius said.

"Who hasn't even called back," Hawk pointed out. "Sargos or not, we're running out of time."

"How much time?" Amiah asked, fear creeping into her expression.

God, I wished she hadn't asked that. I didn't want to confess to her that there was no time. I needed to do something now if I still had a connection with Faerie. It had been torture watching her grieve Cassius.

I didn't want to put her through that with a real death. Of course, Amiah and I barely knew each other. Maybe she wouldn't be heartbroken over me like she'd been with Cassius... and I didn't know what made me more upset, the fact that she'd be all right if I died or that she wouldn't be.

"Not much," Hawk said before I could figure out an answer.

"There's got to be something we can do, some way we can buy you time." Amiah's angel glow flared, revealing her worry. "I thought I could help and give you fae magic like I did back in your apartment, but it doesn't look like I'm giving you anything, and your pain isn't getting any better."

I offered her a sad smile. "You're giving me some, just not very fast and the demonic magic is consuming it as soon as it enters my system."

"Then tell me how to give you more. I did it before. I don't know how, but I did. It was after we had sex. You said—" Her eyes widened. "You said you got it when I came. It has to be the connection I form when we have sex. It lets me transfer more magic to you faster."

Hawk sat forward. "If you don't cast anything, another transfusion could keep you going for a day, maybe more."

"How much do you want to believe I won't have to cast something in the next twenty-four hours?" I shot back.

"Maybe you'll get to Sargos in time," Titus said, his voice gruff. "How powerful is he? There are four of us and you were powerful five hundred years ago. I bet you're more powerful now."

"Alone, we could take Sargos," Cassius said, "but he has a small army. Even if we fight them off, he'll just send more men after us."

"Then we recall the main team," Amiah said, her expression grim. "Essie can pull demonic magic out of demons, and it's her magic. Surely she can pull it out of Sebastian. We'll have to turn ourselves in for a disciplinary hearing, but she can get back here in about twelve hours."

"Except if you turn yourselves in, you might not be able to go after the Heart," Hawk said. "What happens when the next key is empowered or when the Winter Court starts calling you back?"

Amiah shivered. "We'll deal with it. At least no one will be dead or one of Sargos's slaves."

Except I didn't know if she could deal with it. The last time a key was empowered she couldn't breathe, had been freezing, and Titus hadn't been able to find the key without her.

If we couldn't get the key, we couldn't get the Heart.

The demonic magic surged again and so did a trickle of her fae magic.

"You can't call the JP," I forced out.

"We have three options," Cassius said. "Nothing—"

"Not acceptable," Amiah interrupted.

The light in Cassius's eyes flared. "I agree. Which leaves us with going to Sargos or calling the JP."

Rin shifted a little closer and another spark of hellfire snapped from his eye.

"I can do it," he said, his voice so soft I could barely hear it.

Everyone stared at Rin and I mentally slapped myself. Of course Rin could pull the demonic magic out of me. That was what he did. Except—

"Can you pull out just the demonic magic?" I asked. It wouldn't be helpful if he also pulled out all of my fae magic. Although that might kill me faster than the slow fade I was looking forward to when my connection to Faerie was severed.

"Demonic magic is sticky. It'll take some fae magic with it, but I don't know how much." Rin's gaze darted to Amiah then returned to me. "Your highness will have to replenish yourself first."

Meaning I needed to sleep with Amiah.

RIN

I WAS FOOLISH TO HAVE AGREED TO HELP. I DIDN'T KNOW IF I TRUSTED Prince Seireadan or any of them, and I didn't trust the desperate aching desire I had for Princess Amiah, but I certainly didn't trust the Shadow King.

Even if the odds were good that Prince Seireadan would enslave me and that Princess Amiah couldn't free me from our unwanted soul bond, I had to take the chance. Because there was no chance anything good would come out of the Shadow King getting Faerie's Heart.

Except the only way for Prince Seireadan to get the Heart was if I removed his demonic infection. Something I was certain I could do. It just wasn't going to be easy, and I suspected it'd be painful. And that could incur the prince's wrath. Something I'd been trying to avoid since I'd realized escape while trapped in the soul bond was impossible. Right now was the freest I'd been since before I'd been murdered, and there was a slim chance that I'd be completely free. I wasn't going to screw that up by drawing the attention of one of Faerie's fickle royals.

"So I guess we should—" Prince Seireadan jerked his chin toward the lavish, black, white, and gold living room that was almost as opulent as the Shadow King's rooms. "You know. Get it on."

"Oh, how romantic." Princess Amiah rolled her eyes at him, adding to the evidence that even if they weren't married, they were close. No one rolled their eyes at a royal from Faerie. It was too dangerous, and I'd seen people pay with their lives for less.

"Sweetheart, you already know there's nothing romantic about me." He flashed her a wicked smile, but the sharp angry magic I could sense inside him snapped and his expression twisted tight with pain. "Fucking hell."

"Come on." Princess Amiah tried to pull out of the dragon's hold, but he held tight, and even if she fought with everything she had, she'd never be able to break free. With a sigh, she raised her gaze to meet his. "You have to let me go, Titus."

"I know." Titus heaved a heavy sigh.

"She's not just yours," the angel said, smoke billowing around him. We hadn't been introduced, but I'd overheard them calling him Cassius, just like I'd overheard them calling the dragon Titus. "At least you can hold her."

"*She* won't be any of yours if we can't get the Heart," she said, her gaze flickering to me, capturing my soul within their blue depths before she jerked her attention away.

Except looking away didn't release me. I burned with a need I'd never experienced before, a cruel unwanted yearning to pull her out of the dragon's arms and kiss her again even though I knew it would be a mistake that could enrage the prince.

It had been a mistake to kiss her that first time.

It had been a mistake to even offer to ease her backlash.

Now I knew what she tasted like, her lips and her magic, and I hadn't gotten nearly enough.

I shouldn't have said anything, shouldn't have spoken up when she'd stepped into the office.

But I'd been starving. I was still starving, and not just for magic. I hadn't been able to trust anyone since Deaglan had bought me, and while His Majesty had granted me a sexual release from time to time there'd always been strings attached to remind me of my place.

And everything within me said I could trust Princess Amiah, I needed Princess Amiah, I was lost without her. With her, I'd be free, even though we were trapped together.

Except that was just another prison. One she didn't want either. That much, at least had been clear. With my enhanced hearing, I'd heard her tell Cassius how horrible the brand was and that it hadn't been fair that she was stuck with me when she was in love with all of them. She hadn't lied to me back in Prince Seireadan's clean room when she'd said the brand would make her love me and fall out of love with them. I just had to hope she'd meant what she'd said in the garage, that I wasn't their slave or prisoner.

"So if any of you want to keep me, Sebastian needs to get rid of his infection." She gave the dragon a firm, fast kiss.

With a huff he released her and she slipped from his embrace and held out her hand to Prince Seireadan.

"Shall we... get it on?" she asked.

Now he rolled his eyes at her, making jealousy that I shouldn't have been feeling twist around my heart.

They were so comfortable together, so relaxed, something I was sure I'd never have with her... not that I wanted that. That was the brand making me desire a relationship with her. And yet it wasn't just her. They were all comfortable with each other, like close friends — something else I'd never had and never would — and none of them treated Prince Seireadan like they should and he didn't seem to care.

With a groan and a sharp surge of his magic that drew a strangled gasp, the prince stood and staggered into Princess Amiah.

She caught him, wrapping her arms around him and letting him lean into her. "God, I wish I could take your pain," she murmured into his ear.

"I wouldn't let you," he whispered back. "You already carry too much."

My hellfire heaved inside me and I mentally knuckled down, holding it back. I couldn't show how I felt. That was a weakness that could be used against me. But it was clear he was in love with her. If they weren't already married, something I still questioned even though she'd said they weren't, they would be soon. They already had the Winter Court's blessing.

"I don't carry enough," she replied. "You guys keep doing things for me."

"Yep, and going to keep on doing it," Hawk said, pulling Prince Seireadan out of her arms and supporting him. "Let's get him up to bed."

Princess Amiah held open the patio door for Hawk and the prince, then followed them across the living room, taking a part of my soul with her, while I fought the rest of me that urged me to follow.

"I'm ordering food," Titus announced. "You want anything?" He glanced at Cassius, who frowned at him.

"Didn't you already eat?" Cassius asked.

Titus flashed his canines at him, his expression pure male satisfaction. "I worked up another appetite."

"Really? You're going to push my buttons, too, like Hawk and Bane?" Cassius glared at him then dipped his gaze to the fire rolling over his hands, making Titus's cocky expression vanish. "Can you guys please stop rubbing it in?"

"When Seireadan gets his magic back, I'm sure he'll be able to help you," Titus said. "And then *you* can work up an appetite."

Cassius's eyes widened in surprise and his angel glow flared. "You mean that? You don't see that as a challenge for her?"

"She's my mate and she needs you. So you're my mate, too," Titus huffed as if it was obvious, which it definitely wasn't. "Do you want food?"

More smoke billowed around Cassius and he narrowed his eyes. "I'm not having sex with you."

"Good, because I'm not having sex with you. Food?" Titus asked again.

"Don't bother. I'm just going to end up burning it right now."

"Okay." Titus opened the patio door, and his gaze slid to me despite me trying to stay still and unnoticed, and his expression grew sober. "There's a change of clothes waiting for you, too. Deaglan has a new shifter on his team and it would be better if you weren't smelling like blood."

I gave him a slight nod and followed him inside. I couldn't tell what the hierarchy was between the other men and didn't want to risk pissing off Prince Seireadan's right hand, not until I had a way to escape — which wouldn't happen until I was no longer bound to Amiah. And while Titus might have just escaped the Shadow King's prison and was the least likely to be in charge of this group, that didn't mean he wasn't.

He led me back to the kitchen and handed me a white crinkly bag with black material — presumably clothes — then opened the room service menu and scanned the listings.

I didn't wait to see if he'd offer me more blood. He hadn't been the one who'd done it the first time. That had been the incubus... who I also couldn't figure out. Princess Amiah had said she loved him, but the prince had kissed him to save him back in the cavern. Was Hawk the prince's right hand? He'd taken over when Prince Seireadan had passed out.

So far, with the exception of Princess Amiah, who was being influenced by our bond like I was, Hawk had been the most welcoming, and Titus the least.

The dragon had barely looked at me since we'd arrived, and I didn't know if that was because I reminded him of the Shadow King and his imprisonment or because his beast had chosen Princess Amiah as his mate, which made our soul bond a huge problem.

It was actually shocking that he'd given Cassius permission to sleep with her or that he hadn't fought harder to keep her from having sex with the prince. Sure, she'd said she was in love with all of them, but that didn't mean it went both ways, and I'd heard that dragons were extremely possessive.

Another sour band of jealousy wrapped around my non-beating heart. I wanted that acceptance with them... with *someone*. I wanted someone I could trust, who I could finally, after five hundred years, let my guard down with. But it didn't matter that my soul was saying I could trust them.

That was the brand.

Because *she* trusted them.

The best I could hope for in the situation was that I could stay unnoticed until all of this was over and then sneak away.

Except that was only if they could get the Heart.

Which meant it was in my best interest to do whatever it took to ensure the Heir to the Winter Court's throne got the Heart and the Shadow King didn't.

With a new determination that I hadn't felt in a good couple hundred years, I headed up the stairs to take a shower and change. But the moment I reached the top step, my gaze was drawn to the door at the end of the hall.

It was slightly ajar as if someone hadn't been paying attention when they'd shut it and the latch hadn't caught.

"You sure this is a good idea?" Hawk asked, my heightened hearing easily picking up his soft words. "He hasn't tried to kill us or summon Deaglan, but that doesn't mean he won't. I'm not comfortable with him feeding on you."

I tried to go into the first bedroom, not caring who'd been in it last, but I couldn't stop myself from creeping toward the end of the hall.

"You were going to let him feed on you," Princess Amiah said.

"He can feed on me because I can take it," Hawk replied.

"Yeah right," the prince said. "He needs to feed and you think it doesn't matter if he kills you because you're not as useful as I am."

I reached the door, peered inside, and my essence stuttered.

There she was, a radiant goddess, standing perfectly framed in the crack with her back to me, her fae glow so bright I couldn't tell if there were lights on in the room or not. Her long blond hair, still damp from the shower she must have taken after sleeping with Titus, hung loose, the ends just starting to curl, and her magic, still a little wild, her backlash not fully calmed, rushed inside her like waves in a light wind.

I knew peeking in was a bad idea, that I'd be punished if they caught me, and with Prince Seireadan lying on the bed, his head in sight, there was a good chance I'd be caught. All it would take was a glance at the door. But I couldn't help myself. I was drawn to her whether I wanted to be or not. My soul cried to be with her in every way possible, spiritually, emotionally, and physically.

And God, I wanted to be in the room with her, to feel her mouth against mine, her pulse racing with the same aching desire that raced through me. I didn't care how she took me. She could keep her relationships with the others. I wasn't possessive like a dragon. I'd sleep with her alone and I'd sleep with her with them. I just needed to be with her.

The thought made my cock start to stiffen and, with far too many years of experience, I focused on the still nothingness in my heart and relaxed my body's reaction, making my burgeoning erection slip away.

"Is that true?" the princess asked, opening her robe and letting it slide to the floor, pooling around her feet.

Oh, God.

My cock went instantly hard again and the urge to storm into the room and take her squeezed in my chest. I *had* to join with her. Everything in my soul screamed at me to be with her, finish what fate had started and seal our connection.

Because of the brand.

I struggled to get myself back under control. The Shadow King would have devised a cruel humiliation if he'd seen me get hard without permission while he was having sex.

Hawk stepped into sight behind her, brushed her hair aside, and pressed his lips against the back of her neck.

My hellfire heaved inside me and heated my eyes.

I dragged my thoughts back to my inner stillness. I was dead. I was perfectly still. I was a calm pond, its water still like glass.

A ripple shuddered through my mental pond.

Calm. Like glass. I had to regain control of my body. The incubus might know how I felt — and he'd probably tell the others — but I couldn't let it look like I was going to act on my desire.

Because they weren't *my* desires.

"If we can get rid of Bane's infection, he can fix everything for you," Hawk murmured, his lips teasing her skin and drawing a soft sigh. He glanced past Princess Amiah at Prince Seireadan. "And I can take it. You can't. I've got more magic between taking too much and being dead than you do."

"Which is why you're going to watch him and my magic levels and the second it looks like he's taken too much of my fae magic or he actually gets rid of the source of the infection and is still feeding, you make him stop." The prince propped himself up on his elbows, his expression serious. "And I don't care how, so long as you don't kill him."

Which meant I was going to have to be careful... or expect an attack that I wouldn't be able to defend myself from, because fighting back would only make them think I still meant them harm. I'd already made the mistake of fighting back when the dragon had attacked me after my too-brief kiss with the princess. Instinct had kicked in and I'd just reacted. And while there hadn't been an immediate punishment, that didn't mean there wouldn't be one.

And it would be worse if Prince Seireadan saw me hard for his wife.

I had to leave. Get into one of the bedrooms and lock the door.

But I couldn't make myself move or even look away. My essence was locked onto her in a way that terrified me. My desire hadn't been this intense when she'd accused me of killing Cassius and collapsed. I'd seen her naked body then and hadn't gotten hard.

Except then I hadn't kissed her or tasted her magic. Now I'd had a torturous tease of her that only added to the pressure of our unwanted bond.

"Maybe it won't come to that," Princess Amiah said, sitting on the edge of the bed and laying a hand on Prince Seireadan's ankle. "I don't know if the brand is affecting him in more ways than desiring me, but he didn't have to help me with my backlash."

More ripples undulated through my mental pond.

"Don't forget he got something out of that, too," the prince replied.

I tried to close my eyes, but I couldn't stop watching.

The demonic magic in the prince snapped, sharp and hard against my senses, and he collapsed back on the bed with a groan.

"Fuck." He squeezed his eyes shut. "I don't want to admit that I'm not up for this, but—" Another snap that twisted his expression. "I have no idea if I'm up for this. It certainly isn't going to be anything to brag about."

Princess Amiah gave him a sad, soft smile. "You don't have to worry about impressing me." She slid her hand up his calf and past his knee, pushing aside the edge of his robe and revealing the curl of a thick tattoo running up his thigh.

So the prince hadn't just inked glyphs into his arms and torso. He was completely covered. I didn't know if that meant he wasn't as powerful as everyone believe because he needed the spells already set on his body, or if he was that powerful and wanted to use his magic as efficiently as possible. Efficient magic use meant he could go longer and cast more complicated spells, and that would make him incredibly dangerous.

"You've already impressed me," she said, her voice turning husky.

A wave swept through my mental pond and my cock grew harder.

Calm. Still. I am the nothingness inside me.

"I know what you're capable of and I know once we've treated this infection, we'll go back to our—" She caught her bottom lip in her teeth for a second, sending another wave sweeping through my stillness. "We can go back to our arrangement."

"Yeah," he replied, as the demonic magic inside him surged. He clutched the comforter beneath him, clenched his jaw against a groan, and squeezed his eyes shut.

"Now." She straddled his legs and tugged open his robe. He wasn't fully erect but I was sure that had more to do with the pain and not how he felt about the princess. "Let's get some magic in you and relieve a bit of this pain."

He reached for her, urging her to come to him, but instead of crawling up his body, she dipped down and ran her tongue slowly up his cock, making it rise to attention.

Any hope of controlling my erection shattered. She'd just dropped a massive boulder in the center of my pond, sending the water crashing inside me. My cock throbbed for her attention and it took everything I had to just stay where I was.

That was what I had to focus on now. Staying put. I wasn't going to be able to control my body's reaction and I wasn't going to be able to turn away.

But I sure as hell couldn't go into that room. I just had to endure. I'd endured worse. I could endure it now. Because if I didn't screw this up, there was a chance I could finally be free.

AMIAH

I ran my tongue up Sebastian's erection again and focused on the anticipation of driving him crazy. I couldn't think about his pain even if it sliced against my senses. The only thing I could do to help was give him an infusion of my fae magic.

Except the small connection I now had with him just by touching him wasn't enough. We needed to be fully connected and to do that, we needed to have intercourse, and neither of us were ready for that.

"Oh, fuck," he gasped. "That really wasn't a one time deal."

I glanced up at him, the pain in his eyes making my heart clench. "Are you really surprised?"

"Sweetheart, you're still an angel and this is very unangel-like behavior," he said.

His pain surged again, slicing into both of us, and I fought to not show how it was affecting me. He wasn't Cassius, but I didn't want to risk him trying to stop this. It was the only way I could help him.

He drew in a ragged breath as the surge passed. "I keep waiting for you to come to your senses."

Still? Really? Was he trying to push me away?

That didn't make sense, not with what he'd said before I'd healed Cassius. He'd implied there was something more between us than just our arrangement.

But then that had been before he'd seen Rin straddling me in his clean room and had been reminded that there couldn't be more between us — at least not until we got the Heart. And even if we got the Heart, there was still a chance I'd never be free.

My pulse stuttered with the realization of what he was doing. He was trying to push me away to protect me.

Being in love with him and the others would only make everything harder for me. It was already tearing me up that my body desired Rin, and I knew it was going to shatter me when I realized I'd fallen out of love with them.

But his plan was stupid. I wasn't going to stop loving him or any of them because of the fear that my brand would make me fall out of love. I wasn't ever going to stop fighting for us until I'd tried everything possible to keep them. Even knowing that eventually Sebastian would want to go his own way. But our separation had to be his choice, not because of the cruel fate forced upon us.

"You're not going to get me to take it back. I love you just as much as I love Hawk and Cassius and Titus." I wrapped my hand around his now full erection and drew it up to my lips. "I know you can't make a commitment. I don't expect you to and I don't expect you to love me back."

"Amiah—" he started, but I captured his gaze, stopping whatever he was going to say. He didn't have to apologize for who he was. I'd been trapped before — I was trapped now in my bond with Rin — I wasn't going to force that on anyone, no matter how much I loved them. *Because I loved him.*

"We have an arrangement. And until you say we're done, I'm going to enjoy you in every way that excites us." I slid him into my mouth, savoring his low throaty groan, this one clearly from pleasure.

His pupils dilated, and I gave myself to the sensation of him in my mouth. He was harder than when I'd first grasped him, full and thick, and his life force, weak and straining against the darkness, thrummed against my senses.

I slowly slid him out, my hand following my lips, then pushed him back in. His groan deepened and the sound rolled through me, making me wet.

God, I loved that sound, loved that look in his eyes. I didn't know how he did it, but I always felt as if I was the only woman in the world for him when we made love. I knew it was a lie, that there'd been lots of women and there would be a lot more, but I didn't care. It made me feel as if I was free to do anything, that he wouldn't laugh at me if I made a mistake or didn't know something, and I didn't have to maintain any kind of control. I could just be me with him.

"Next time you slide him out, swirl your tongue over his tip," Hawk said as he climbed onto the bed and knelt beside me.

Sebastian's gaze jumped to him, and I obeyed, teasing him with a fast flick, making his gaze snap back to me and his erection flex beneath my hand.

Hawk leaned close, his lips against the divot behind my ear, his warm breath sending a shiver of need racing through me. "Harder."

Sebastian's erection flexed again at the suggestion.

I slid him out and roughly swept my tongue over his tip. Sebastian's eyes rolled back as his hips rose, telling me what he wanted.

"Now relax your throat so you can take him deeper," Hawk murmured, his breath sending another shiver racing through me as he slid in a curl of his seductive magic. It unfurled, soft and small, in my core, just a whisper of what I knew it could be, and melted away some of the tension still in my body, reminding me that I needed to relax not just my throat.

I dipped in, taking Sebastian deeper than he'd ever been before, drawing another throaty groan, but his demonic magic infection snapped, turning his groan into a strangled moan.

My heart clenched, and I struggled to concentrate on feeling good, on the sounds he was making, on the heat building within me. If we couldn't get the Heart or it couldn't free me, my time with him was limited, and I didn't want fear ruining what could be one of our last times together.

Not to mention if I couldn't transfer enough fae magic to him, Rin might not be able to save him.

My pulse stuttered with fear, and I slid him out, raked his tip with my tongue, and took him back in, trying to distract him from the pain and myself from my worry.

Sebastian's breath picked up and he clenched the comforter. The icy brightness of his life force grew a little stronger, and I clung to that. It was proof I could help him, that I could give him enough magic to survive.

"Amiah," Hawk murmured, jerking me from my thoughts back to the bedroom. "Stop concentrating. You get to enjoy this too."

The curl of his magic grew a little stronger and he teased his fingers over the invisible seams between my shoulder blades where my wings emerged.

Hot, sultry need burst in my core, overwhelming any other thoughts. God, it was just a whisper of a touch. It could have been an accidental brush if I hadn't been positive Hawk had known exactly what he was doing. But it was as if he'd sucked on my clit and shot a blast of magic into me, making that sensitive bud throb and activating every nerve in my body.

I released a deep throaty moan around Sebastian's erection, I wouldn't have been able to hold it back if I'd tried, and he slipped in a little deeper.

"Oh fuck," Sebastian groaned.

"Not quite yet," Hawk chuckled. "But if you want her to keep going, you're going to need to give her a hand because I plan on seriously distracting her."

My pulse lurched in a rapid tattoo, his words skyrocketing my anticipation, and he brushed my wing seams again, twisting my need tighter.

Sebastian tangled his fingers in my hair and I realized I'd stopped what I was doing, all my thoughts lost to the aching need inside me.

"Do you want to keep going?" he asked, his gaze dipping to his erection in my mouth. "With me, I mean."

I rolled my eyes at him. Of course I wanted to keep going. This was on my list of things to try. I wanted to know what it felt like to pleasure him with my mouth while I was being pleasured, wanted the press of bodies and the thrum of their life forces. I just hadn't expected it to be so... distracting.

Hawk teased my wing seams again, and another moan escaped me, but I managed to maintain enough thought to answer Sebastian by sliding him out and back in again.

I could do this. I just needed to concentrate.

"Jeez, gorgeous. Stop thinking," Hawk chided, giving my seams a firm rub, shooting more sensation straight to my core. "You're supposed to be enjoying this. Trust us. We've got you."

Sebastian's gaze jumped to Hawk and he gave a tight nod. They'd agreed on something and I had a feeling it was to blow my mind and make me come screaming.

And I had absolutely no problem with that.

"Now let go, and let us make you feel good," Hawk purred.

He rubbed the seam behind my right shoulder blade again as he swept his other hand over the swell of my rear and traced a finger through my wet folds.

Oh, yes. I just needed to let go. Every time I gave in to them during sex, I'd felt amazing. They had me. I was safe with them. If I really thought about it, I'd always felt safe with them.

A pressure in my chest released and I let go. I could worry about my bond, about getting the Heart, about facing off against Deaglan, about keeping my guys alive, about all of it later. Right now, there were just the three of us and the amazing sensations rushing through me.

Sebastian's grip in my hair tightened, holding me steady and drawing my attention back to him, his pale gaze capturing me. The desire burning in his eyes turned me on even more. This wasn't an act. He craved me as much as I craved him, and he drew himself halfway out of my mouth then pushed back in again. His expression and the friction against my lips and tongue were unbelievably erotic. I wanted him to make love to my mouth, wanted to watch him lose control and shatter, and I wanted to taste him.

My muscles clenched at the thought, and Hawk pushed two fingers inside me, adding another point of erotic sensation. All fear of Sebastian's condition, all sense of pain vanished. There was just him and Hawk, their hot and cold, dark and bright life forces thrumming against my senses, and my throbbing desire. I reveled in the feel of Sebastian's fingers in my hair, his body trembling as he slowly pumped into my mouth, and Hawk's fingers sliding in and out of me.

My need twisted tighter and my breath grew ragged. God, it felt amazing. I wanted to be like this forever.

Then Hawk swept his other hand from my wing seams over the swell of my rear and teased a suddenly slicked fingertip around my anus.

My breath stalled, everything within me stalled, focused on that one point. I'd read about this and the sensitive nerves there, and I ached to try it, just like I'd ached to have Sebastian in my mouth, to have both of them capturing me between their bodies. So far everything about sex had been so much more than I'd imagined and my body vibrated in anticipation. Then Hawk slowly pressed his fingertip inside me, sending a heated pleasure rippling through me that had nothing to do with his magic.

Oh, wow. Oh, yes. I released a long low moan around Sebastian's erection.

"Fuck me," Sebastian groaned, slowly pumping back into my mouth.
No. Fuck me. Please.

I pushed my rear back, encouraging Hawk, trying to tell him — as if my moan and his ability to sense sexual energy wasn't already enough — that I wanted him there, wanted more, wanted what it meant, both of them at the same time.

I dipped my head down, bumping Sebastian against the back of my throat, and Sebastian's fingers dug into my scalp, his body shaking.

His erection was as hard as steel in my mouth, but somehow he managed to keep his slow pace, in and out. Hawk matched it, sliding his fingers in and out of my rear and folds. The sensations were overwhelming, hot and tight and building an incredible pressure inside me as their life forces grew stronger and whirled around my heart.

Sebastian's thrusts grew faster, his breath just as ragged as mine, his control starting to slip. "I don't know how much longer I can hold on," he moaned.

"Just a little bit more." Hawk slipped the fingers between my folds up to my clit. He stroked the sensitive nub as he slid a second finger past the tight ring of muscle in my rear, joining the first, stretching me,

Oh, yes.

Need snapped through me, and my muscles started to contract with the promise of an orgasm, and cruelly, wonderfully, breathtakingly, Hawk captured my release with his magic and held me on the edge, torturously close but not able to fall over.

"Not yet," he purred. "Neither of you."

Sebastian's breath hitched and his head tipped back. "You're fucking cruel."

"Am I really?" Hawk asked, working his fingers inside me and teasing my clit, twisting me so tight I was going to shatter the moment he released me. "I don't believe for one second you're not enjoying this."

"Asshole," Sebastian groaned, and he pulled himself out of my mouth, and tugged me up his body. Hawk shifted in behind me, his fingers still stretching and teasing, and making me tremble with need, trapped on the verge of an explosion.

I fought to keep my gaze on Sebastian, but my eyes kept threatening to roll back, my body desperate for the mind-blowing release twisting in my core.

"Oh, sweetheart," he murmured, brushing a lock of hair out of my eyes, the touch tender and warm even though his gaze was still scorching. "I don't think I'll ever get tired of watching you fall apart."

He captured my lips in a searing kiss, one hand tangled in my hair, holding me close, and the other aligning himself with my opening.

He buried himself inside me with a slow, glorious thrust, and the icy brightness of his life force flared inside me. My soul clicked and his magic swelled around my heart, more powerful than the last time we'd joined. This time I was the ice and the vast power. Just like I'd been the wild ferocity when I'd connected with Titus and an inferno with Cassius.

His eyes widened as if he felt the new strength in our connection, then the tip of Hawk's thick erection pressed against my rear, and my thoughts scattered. All I could think about was how Hawk was going to make this feel amazing, and with a seductive swell of his magic to turn the bite of pain from his size into a breathtaking hot throbbing, he slowly breached my entrance.

This time my eyes did roll back. I couldn't stop them. The sensations were overwhelming.

Beneath me, Sebastian's trembling increased, but he managed to hold both of us still, waiting for Hawk to fully enter me.

And slowly, oh so slowly, Hawk pushed inside, using his magic to help me adjust. He felt enormous, both of them did, and every nerve ending inside my body ignited as he sank in deeper and deeper until his flesh was pressed tight against mine.

God, it felt so good. I was panting and mewling for release and they hadn't even done anything yet.

That thing in my soul clicked again, and Hawk's fiery darkness surged through my veins and entwined with Sebastian's life force around my heart. I was darkness and sex and ice and power. My already bright fae glow grew brighter, rolling up and down my body with my pent-up need.

Then they started to move, slowly, finding their tempo, the friction and fullness twisting me tighter and tighter. I panted and moaned, my fae glow rushing around me, a lake in a wild storm, revealing just how much I was enjoying myself.

Sebastian's grip in my hair tightened, twisting my head to the side, and I caught a glimpse of Hawk driving into me, which would have made me come if his magic hadn't been holding me back. His hellfire licked his cheeks, his expression was a mix of awe and bliss.

The guys' breaths quickly grew as heavy as mine and each thrust became stronger. Their life forces swelled, roared around my heart and through my veins, and I knew in my soul that they were mine. I didn't know why I hadn't branded them, but I knew without a doubt they were mine. Even Sebastian. There weren't going to be any other women in his future, not because I'd force him to make a commitment to me — I doubted he would regardless — but because we were fated for each other. It didn't matter how much I'd wanted to control my fate, meeting him, meeting all of them had been inevitable.

They were mine. Always.

"Oh, God, Amiah," Sebastian cried as he thrust hard and tensed. His fae glow ignited as brightly as mine, his eyes rolled back and his hips arched off the bed, burying him deeper inside me as his orgasm tore through him.

Hawk released his hold on my desire, and a tsunami of bliss pounded into me. Glorious sensation tore through every cell in my body, ripping a scream of pleasure from my lips and tensing every muscle. Stars exploded behind my lids and the sense of Hawk and Sebastian's life force overwhelmed me, powerful, entwined light and darkness, ice and fire.

Far away, I felt Hawk tense behind me, crying his own release, but the waves kept crashing over me, again and again, spinning me until I melted into an amazing, boneless, darkness.

I didn't know how long I drifted, but when I woke, my cheek was against Sebastian's chest, his white flesh, marked with all his mesmerizing tattoos, radiant.

We'd separated, all three of us, but he had his arms around me in a tight embrace, and Hawk was pressed against my back. Cold in front, hot behind, and the memory of them driving into me.

Another smaller orgasm rushed through me, drawing a moaning sigh of pleasure.

"No kidding," Sebastian said. "I'd thought holding back an orgasm was something only fucked up incubi or succubi did, but damn. I don't think I've ever come that hard, and from your scream," he said to me, "I don't think you have, either."

"I don't think I've ever gotten a hit that strong," Hawk murmured, his words slightly slurred as if he'd gotten too much sexual energy.

I shifted in Sebastian's embrace so I could check Hawk's eyes.

He gave me a heart-stopping smile and kissed me before I could get a good look, but it didn't seem as if he were ODing, just a little intoxicated.

His kiss made another rippling orgasm tease through me and I released a soft moan, savoring the sensation.

But as much as I wanted to just lie there in their arms, the whole point of this was to heal Sebastian's infection.

I turned back to him, concentrated past my orgasmic haze, and checked his life force. He still battled the darkness trapped inside him, but the spark of fae magic embedded in every cell in his body, just like it was currently embedded in mine, was stronger, brighter, and icier.

It called to the icy power inside me, urging me to open myself up to it.

A chill shivered down my spine and Hawk shifted closer, pressing more of his ever-so-slightly too-hot body against mine.

"We should check with Rin to see if I've given you enough magic," I said.

"A part of me really hopes you haven't." Sebastian pressed his lips against the top of my head, giving me a tender kiss. "But it would be best if I recovered what this demonic shit has been blocking before my sister and Deaglan find us again. I don't want to have to channel raw magic in our next fight if I don't have to, and it's going to take time for me to add power to my glyphs and replenish my internal well."

Another chill raced through me, this time setting off another soft aftershock of orgasm.

Oh, wow.

"We should give Amiah a little more time," Hawk said, his warm breath caressing my neck. "It's probably not safe to stand yet. You were barely out for a minute and my magic usually knocks you out for longer than that."

Except as much as I wanted to keep cuddling with them, Sebastian was right. It was dangerous to not heal him as soon as possible. So many things depended on his magic, the most important being his survival.

"If you two are fine, go without me. I can join you when I'm ready."

Sebastian glanced over my head at Hawk. "How much do you believe that? The moment we step out of this bedroom, you're going to try getting up."

I opened my mouth to deny that, but Sebastian cut me off with a hard, fast kiss.

"Don't bother denying it," he said. "You're too damned stubborn to not try."

"It's one of the things I love about you," Hawk added.

I shifted, squeezing in between them so I could prop myself up on my elbows and look both of them in the eyes, as another shiver swept through me.

"You're probably the only one," I said. "I have a feeling the rest of you have already sided with Cassius and have decided I'm too fragile to do anything."

Sebastian snorted and his life force surged against my senses sliding a thin thread of ice through my veins. "He did let you and Titus go at it. I have no idea how he managed to stay on the patio with all the noise you were making."

"Pretty sure we just made a lot of noise too," I said.

Another icy thread swelled inside me and Hawk was starting to get too hot to lie beside.

"Yeah, but they all know it's because of me," Hawk said as I carefully sat up so I didn't make myself dizzy. The absence of his body heat sent gooseflesh rushing over my skin, and I didn't know what was worse, being too hot or too cold.

Hawk put his hands behind his head and swept his gaze down my body, desire rekindling in his eyes. "I want you to have the best experience possible. First times only happen once."

"Yeah, but now she'll be expecting that every time," Sebastian said, his life force swelling again… except now I wasn't sure if the ice was coming from Sebastian, it seemed sharper, colder than he'd felt before.

"Pretty sure I won't notice if the next time is half as good. That was so much more than I'd dreamed it would be."

"You dreamed it, hunh?" Hawk's lips curled into a dark wicked smile. "Any other dreams you want to tell us about?"

"We'll there's—"

The ice inside me exploded into a ferocious storm, and God, it wasn't Sebastian, it was the Winter Court. With horror, I realized I hadn't just been feeling his life force, but his connection with the court as well. And through him, it had found its way into me.

"Amiah?" Sebastian frowned and something popped behind me.

"Oh, shit." Hawk jerked up and reached for me, but a powerful frozen wind jerked me off the bed and yanked me across the room into a portal.

Sebastian screamed and one of his glyphs lit up, but the air around me thickened with magic, plugged my nose and ears, and poured down my throat.

The Winter Court was taking me back to Faerie whether I wanted to go or not. And this time, I'd be without my guys.

FATED RESOLVE

ANGEL'S FATE, BOOK 5

AMIAH

TIME STUTTERED INTO HORRIFIC SLOW MOTION AND ICE SWEPT THROUGH my veins as the Winter Court's wind held me and the portal's viscous air started to engulf me. The glow in the glyph Sebastian had activated blazed brighter, lighting up his whole bare side, and Hawk scrambled to his knees, the sheets tangling around him as he started to lunge for me.

But neither of them were going to be fast enough to save me.

The portal was already closing and they were getting farther and farther away.

Then Rin, moving faster than both of my guys with his enhanced vampiric speed, leaped through the doorway into the bedroom and dove for me. Hellfire blazed in his black eyes, and his long black ponytail and black sash swept out behind him as he careened toward me.

For a second, his sharp facial features were a mask of terror, then he slammed into me, the portal fully engulfed us, and with a bone-jarring *pop*, spat us out.

We tumbled together across a cold slick surface and crashed to a stop. My head cracked against something hard and the impact of Rin's weight on top of me made the air explode from my lungs.

Gasping, I tried to get my bearings, but everything was white and freezing and I was spinning and spinning and—

Rin's gaze met mine and everything else vanished. There was just him and me, and I was drowning in his hellfire. His strange life force thrummed through me and my body throbbed with desire. My need for him— No, my need to seal our bond, not for him because I didn't love him, consumed me. It was all I could think about even though a small part of me was screaming that I needed to get up and see where we were in the Winter Court.

Because without a doubt, we were in the Winter Court.

But I couldn't look away. I was trapped in his eyes just like I was trapped in our soul bond and trapped by the Winter Court's claim.

Because you promised, the Winter Court hissed inside me.

Rin's gaze dipped down and his hellfire flared, licking across his cheeks, reminding me that he fought the same aching desire I did—

And I was naked.

Oh, God! I didn't even have a robe this time. I'd just finished having the most amazing sex with Sebastian and Hawk in order to give Sebastian enough fae magic so Rin could remove his demonic magic infection, and I'd been yanked out of bed. I hadn't even had time to recover. My unnatural full-body fae glow still blazed with what had been an incredible orgasm.

"Your highness," Rin said in his barely-there voice, his gaze jerking back to mine.

Not your highness. Your Majesty, the Winter Court howled and its cold roared through me, seizing every muscle in my body with a painful contraction.

I screamed, a desperate cry tearing from my lips, carried on a blast of frozen magic. Except the blast didn't expel the excess power from my system. The magic just kept growing inside me, its cold rushing through my veins, sinking into my bones, and invading every cell in my body.

I was frozen down to my soul, my limbs heavy and numb, my healing magic telling me I was already on the verge of hypothermia. I wasn't supposed to have the Winter Court's magic inside me and I didn't know how much more my body could take.

Rin scrambled off me, his hellfire and all sense of emotion vanishing from his expression. He swept his gaze around the room, but even without looking, I knew it was just the two of us. I couldn't sense any of my guys' life forces or anyone else's. There was just Rin with his strange alive yet dead, frozen and burning life force, edged with pain that had been permanently embedded in his cells, and me.

You let me in. You agreed. Whatever the cost. The Winter Court released my muscles, but its cold continued to consume me, pounding around my heart, a forceful second heartbeat. *You promised.*

"I did," I gasped through chattering teeth, and I curled into a ball, desperate to get away from the cold. But curling up did nothing to warm me or control my shivering.

I chose you and you lied. The court's wind picked up, stinging my skin. *You cut me off and left Faerie.*

"We needed to escape."

You promised. Its power sliced into my soul, drawing another scream and blast of frozen magic from my mouth. *You belong to me. You're my queen.*

Its wind seized me and wrenched me off the floor. We were in the center of the Winter Court's enormous throne room, its white semi-translucent walls, floor, and pillars glimmering like ice in the dim light of the glowing orbs floating overhead. Above, soared the vaulted ceiling, still partially shrouded in shadows, and in front, at the far end of the room on a wide dais, sat the queen's massive ice throne.

You promised. The court yanked me across the room and shoved me onto the throne. *Now take control from her.*

"Now?"

Rin bolted after me, leaping onto the dais without bothering with the three shallow steps. "Your highness."

Majesty, the Winter Court roared. Its frozen magic clenched my muscles again and its wind whipped around me, shoving Rin off the dais and back to the center of the room.

I can't be your queen. I'm not fae. Your magic will kill me.

I'll sustain you, but you have to take control of me from her.

Except my healing magic said that was a lie. It didn't matter how much fae magic the court pumped into me, I was a being from the Realm of Celestial Light. I wasn't supposed to have fae magic inside me, just like Sebastian wasn't supposed to have demonic magic inside him.

Please, the court begged. *She doesn't love me. Not like you will. I'm just a power to her. Something to be forced to her will.*

Now I was really confused. "But the courts kill high fae to find their monarch," I gasped, shaking so hard I could barely get my arms around my knees to hug them to my chest.

Rin stood and a spark of hellfire popped from his eye and was swept away in the Winter Court's frigid gale.

Faerie makes us, the court replied. *It takes back its magic until a high fae strong enough resists it. I don't know why, and I don't know why I can make a stronger connection with you than her, why I can actually communicate with you. But I won't be her slave any longer. I'm supposed to be her equal.*

Rin's attention jumped to the closed large doors at the back of the room as a blazing bright, frozen life force snapped at the edge of my senses.

Oh, no.

The Winter Queen was coming.

She'll kill you if you don't take me from her.

The heavy, intricately carved doors crashed open with a thunderous boom and a frozen blast of wind. The gust sent Rin tumbling back to the dais's shallow steps and the Winter Queen strode in.

My pulse pounded with a mix of fear from the fury in her eyes and the dangerous cold consuming my body.

The Winter Queen wore a black gown made out of layers of gauzy material that accentuated her pale, luminescent skin. The neckline was cut dangerously low, barely covering her breasts, and the skirt was slitted up both sides, revealing glimpses of her long legs as the pieces of her dress fluttered and snapped in the windstorm surrounding her.

The wind also swept through her long silver-white hair, and with the billowing dress and her hard glare, she looked like the powerful, beautiful, terrifying queen that she was.

Behind her towered two identical ice guards. They were broader and taller than Titus — which was saying a lot, since Titus was one of the biggest men I'd ever met — and each held a large long spear that I knew from our fight in the ballroom could seriously injure any of my guys.

"That's my chair," the Winter Queen snarled, and a ferocious wind seized me and jerked me up.

But another wind tore through it and yanked me back onto the throne, making the Winter Queen's eyes narrow.

Command me. Take me from her. The Winter Court's frozen magic thudded harder in my chest, overwhelming my heartbeat and slicing deeper into my soul.

"And this is my court." The Winter Queen raised her hands and an ice storm, spiked with sharp ice shards, roared around the room.

Its ferocious wind buffeted me, stealing the air around me before I could draw a breath. It yanked on my hair and whipped it against my face, neck, and shoulders. Blood welled on my arms from three shallow cuts and was swept away in the storm, the slices happening so fast — and my body so cold — I hadn't felt them.

Command me.

I clung to the throne's arms, fighting to stay seated as blood welled in another cut across my shoulder, this one deeper than the first ones. I had to take control. I'd given myself to the Winter Court to save my guys and now it was time to pay my debt.

And if I didn't win this fight, I'd never see my guys again. Even if the Winter Queen didn't kill me, she'd still lock me up in the depths of the court and never let me out.

Rin staggered to his feet, leaning into the storm, and turned to face the queen. The wind snapped and jerked on his long black ponytail, sash, and the slitted ends of his calf-length wrap tunic. His fate was tied to mine, more so than any of my guys. If the Winter Queen killed me, he died too.

I couldn't be responsible for that. I'd promised we'd get the Heart and set him free, and I had every intention of doing that. I was stronger than the Winter Queen. My guys and my determination to get back to them made me stronger. It had to.

No. It *did*.

I'd been stronger than her before. I'd be stronger now.

Except before when we'd fled the Winter Court's ballroom, my control had been momentary, and then she'd unleashed a storm that had almost crashed us into the side of a mountain.

If I wanted to keep control of the court, I had to break her connection with it and let the court fully take me. There wasn't any other option.

HAWK

A FROZEN WIND EDGED WITH THE COLD BRIGHTNESS OF THE WINTER Court's magic yanked Amiah off the bed and into the blinding white blaze of a portal, and my pulse stalled. I scrambled to grab her and pull her free while Bane activated one of the spells tattooed on his body. His magic flashed at the edge of my vision, but I refused to look away from Amiah to see what he was casting. It would take a second of concentration to determine what the spell was and I could lose her in that second.

And God, I couldn't lose her.

Horror filled her expression and the portal's brilliant light started to engulf her. Everything inside me screamed. *Save her! Now.*

She was strong, she could survive the Winter Court alone, but she shouldn't have to. I didn't want her to. I wanted to be at her side for everything, good and bad, because I knew in my soul, I belonged with her.

I didn't care if she'd branded Rin and not me. She didn't need to bind our souls together to have me. I was hers. Always. If I wasn't supposed to be hers, the connection we formed when we made love would have weakened as her bond with Rin strengthened. But our connection had been stronger this time than it had ever been, even without being able to make eye contact with her while we made love.

Except as I dove for her, I knew with gut-churning fear that it didn't matter what I did, I wasn't going to be fast enough to reach her before the portal pulled her back into Faerie.

And from the terrified look in her bright blue eyes, she knew it too.

Then her gaze leaped past my shoulder. Rin, who I'd known with my ability to sense sexual energy had been outside the door watching us have sex, bolted into the room. His hellfire roared from his eyes, licking across his cheeks in a shocking display of emotions, and he dove for her, too.

They collided as the portal closed and its blinding light — that only I could see with my magic sensitivity — vanished, leaving a large black blob in the middle of my vision.

I flew through the space where the portal had been and slammed head first into the wall. Pain snapped through my skull and neck and my internal magic flared hot, healing my concussion and cracked vertebra before I'd even hit the floor. I scrambled to my feet and lost my balance, falling against the wall and had to use it to keep standing. I was still high on the sexual energy the three of us had generated and the room was ever-so-slightly out of focus.

"Fuck!" Bane screamed, and I heaved around to face him, making the room lurch.

"Open a portal. Get her back," I begged. Yes, she could handle the Winter Court alone — *please be able to handle it* — but she wasn't alone, and while the portal had the icy white light of the Winter Court I had to remember that didn't mean it had actually taken her to the Winter Court. "We don't know Rin's intentions. For all we know he's been waiting for this moment so he can take her to Deaglan."

"You know I can't make a portal," Bane snapped. He'd made it to the foot of the bed before the portal had swallowed Amiah and stared at the spot where she'd been with a raw, desperate look in his eyes.

Shit. Right. I knew he couldn't make a portal. Even if he hadn't been infected with demonic magic, he still wouldn't have been able to make a portal. I didn't know why someone who could access and weave the raw magic of Faerie into anything he wanted couldn't make a portal, but magic was funny like that, filled with surprising — and at times frustrating — inconsistencies.

Except I still had to get to her. Even if Rin wasn't intent on taking her back to Deaglan, she was still fighting her desire for him, and it would break her if their soul bond overwhelmed her and she had sex with him.

"We have to—" I jerked my gaze around the blurry room. We

couldn't do anything trapped in the human realm. Who did I know who could form a portal?

No one. I didn't know anyone who could form a portal. I only knew people who could open one of the many natural portals to the various realms scattered throughout the world. I jerked my gaze back to Bane. "Where's the closest portal to Faerie?"

"For fuck's sake, bleed off that excess magic," Bane said. "*You* can summon a portal."

My thoughts shuttered.

I *could* summon a portal. Sort of. Karthick, the strange fae sorcerer who'd helped us return to the mortal realm, had imbued me with a spell that alerted him to our desire to return to Faerie. He'd said when the Winter Court's call was too much for Amiah, he'd form a portal so we could return.

I bit back a bitter laugh.

She hadn't even had a chance to fight it. The Winter Court had just yanked her back without warning.

All we'd needed was a minute, long enough to gather the others — to hell with getting dressed — and then a second for me to think about activating the spell that contacted him.

A flicker of the sorcerer's strange magic teased the back of my mind, and Bane's eyes flashed wide.

"Don't. You're the one with the spell. Karthick won't be able to find Cassius and Titus if he pulls us back into Faerie without them." Bane released the magic he'd pushed into his glyph, but his full-body fae glow remained bright, even though the demonic magic still writhed and snapped inside him.

Which wasn't a good sign.

Yes, Amiah had given him an infusion, but it hadn't pushed back the infection only added to the magic inside him, and I didn't know if that meant he'd be strong enough for Rin to remove the infection or not.

Except now he was going to have to cast more spells to get her back and we'd be back where we started with him on the verge of dying — and it was now up in the air if Rin was actually going to help him.

Sure, Deaglan had tortured the demon-vampire hybrid, but that didn't mean Rin wouldn't take Amiah back if he thought the Shadow King was going to get Faerie's Heart. He might think handing her over was the only way to protect himself.

I reached for my shorts on the chair where I'd tossed them when I'd stripped to join Amiah and Bane in bed, missed, and stumbled forward.

Shit. Bane was right. I couldn't save her like this, and as much as I wanted to keep every little last bit of her energy and essence inside me, it was just going to get in my way.

I shoved the excess out of my body, not bothering to focus it, and made Bane groan and his cock rise.

"Fuck, really?" he asked, pulling on his robe.

"You said get rid of it." I grabbed my shorts, the room more in focus, if still a little fuzzy at the edges, yanked them on, and didn't bother with my T-shirt. "I'm not wasting time by being careful." The need to save her squeezed my chest and I fought to breathe.

"We'll get her back." Bane's expression hardened, sending a chill racing down my spine as he strode from the room.

This was the man I'd met during the war — even if he only possessed a fraction of the power he'd had back then. This was the man who did whatever it took to save lives... and in the case of those children, ease their suffering.

God, he'd been terrifying. Cold, hard, determined, and powerful. Completely unlike who he was now. I hadn't known what true power was until the first time he'd let down his shields and I'd looked at him with all of my magic sensitivity. He wasn't just a faekin with a deep personal well of magic. He was magic itself. A direct conduit to the Realm of Faerie with the strength of will to harness so much power that it had to be like holding the sun when he did.

"I promised I'd free her from the Winter Court and I swear I will if it's the last thing I do."

Which was exactly how I felt. Amiah connected with something inside me that I hadn't known existed. I didn't want to go back to the way I'd been before. I couldn't. I wasn't supposed to be able to make a connection with someone. It was against my nature. And yet it was like I'd always been craving that connection, needed that connection, and just hadn't realized it.

I didn't know what she gave Bane, how he, like the rest of us had fallen in love with her, but if he even felt a fraction for her of what I did, he couldn't do anything but save her.

And from the way he'd looked at her when she was captured between the two of us, he was all in with her.

He might think he was angry about desiring to have a soul bond with her, might think that because whatever he believed she was — which he still hadn't figured out — was influencing him, but I knew he wanted her brand because she gave him something he hadn't known he'd needed, just like me.

I followed him into the hall, past a white bulging plastic bag sitting by the door. That had to be Rin's change of clothes. He'd still been wearing his bloody wrap tunic, black leather pants, and boots when he'd leaped into the portal with Amiah. He must have come upstairs to change and been drawn to her like all of us were drawn to her.

Except his compulsion was stronger than ours. I'd felt it in his sexual energy, a gnawing, desperate need that he had barely any control over. He wanted her, burned for her, but his desire was filled with pain and anger. He wanted to resist the pull of their bond as much as she did, but it was overwhelming.

I was actually shocked he'd managed to stay in the hall while we were having sex. Of course, if he'd come into the room, I didn't know if he would have begged to join us or fought to take her from us. And I prayed I'd never have to find out if he was open to group sex or not.

I didn't want Amiah to have to seal her bond with him. Even if she had asked me to help her get through having sex with someone who was pretty much a stranger, I didn't want her to do it. In part because being forced to have sex was horrible, and, as selfish as it was, because I feared sealing her bond would mean it would be the end for us.

I raked a hand through my jaw-length hair and hurried down the stairs after Bane. Titus sat at the large island in the center of the kitchen with a room service tray in front of him and three empty plates.

He jerked to his feet the minute he saw us, a ghostly dragon head forming over his own head in his red-gold aura, a sign his ferocious, primal nature was rising to the surface. "Where is she?"

"The Winter Court took her," Bane said, his tone sharp. "Are those my clothes?" He pointed to a white plastic bag sitting on the kitchen counter behind Titus.

"The court took her?" Titus growled. "How did the court take her?"

"It formed a portal and yanked her through," I said, my insides churning. We had to go. Now.

"But the court can't form a portal," Titus replied.

"No shit. Which means it's gained a new power or someone else made the portal." Bane reached for the clothes, but Titus grabbed the bag and stormed toward the patio.

"You can get changed when we get there." He shoved open the door with so much force it swung all the way open, snapped off its hinges, and hit the floor-to-ceiling glass window beside it, shattering the glass in both the door and the window.

"Fuck. Titus!" Bane hissed as Titus stepped through the broken glass, not seeming to care that his feet were bare. "Voth is going to kill me for that."

Cassius, who'd been standing at the far end of the patio, staring at the Quarter's skyline, wrenched around at the noise, his fire billowing around him, sending smoke and a flurry of sparks rushing into the night sky.

"Control your fire," Titus snarled at Cassius as he grabbed a plastic bag from one of the patio couches and tossed it at the angel.

Cassius caught the bag. It caught on fire and with an effort that made his blazing red aura snap and seethe, he wrenched his flames under his skin. "What the hell?"

"The Winter Court took Amiah. We're getting her back," Titus said.

The angel glow in Cassius's eyes flared. "We need a portal."

"We have one. Hawk can contact Karthick and he can pull us back into Faerie." Titus drew close to Cassius and glared at us, his message clear: join the group and contact Karthick. And I couldn't agree more.

I marched across the broken glass, my body healing the cuts in my bare feet as fast as they formed, while Bane followed, carefully picking his way through the mess.

"I'm going to pretend that made sense," Cassius said, as I took up position beside him.

Guess no one had filled Cassius in on what had happened while he'd been on death's door frozen in Bane's hibernation spell.

I open my mouth to explain, but fuck it. Cassius was smart, he'd catch up and it would be better if I just used the spell Karthick had put in my head. Except—

"When Karthick makes this portal, where in Faerie will we end up?" I doubted he'd be with Amiah, and I wasn't sure if someone could create a portal and not be standing at one of the ends.

"Probably the Wilds," Bane said. Which was the worst place for him to end up, since I doubted he'd have much time before Faerie started pulling out the fae magic Amiah had just given him. "Which means I'd appreciate it if we hightailed it to the aerie the moment we're through."

"We're going to the Winter Court," Titus said. "I'm not wasting time going to the aerie."

"And find her how?" Bane shot back, grabbing the bag with his clothes from Titus, but the dragon didn't let go. "Last time I checked, her concealment spell was still active, which means I won't be able to find her through magical means, and we sure as hell can't just walk into the Winter Court. Aside from the fact that none of us want my mother to get her hands on you so she can get the Heart, Amiah would kill herself trying to save you if you were captured."

"If any of us were captured," Cassius said, pulling on a pair of bright red, yellow, and green board shorts that were so completely out of Cassius's character it would have been comical if the situation hadn't been so serious.

Bane tugged on the bag again but Titus still held tight. "Let go. I'm not going into Faerie in a robe. I have no idea what we're going to be walking into."

"We're walking into nothing if we waste our time going to the aerie," Titus snarled. "We know she's at the Winter Court—" Titus frowned. "Where's the hybrid?"

"He went through the portal with her." Bane yanked harder, ripped open the bag, and pulled out a pair of tan shorts and a black T-shirt. "And no, we don't know that she's in the Winter Court. For all we know Rin has decided to take her to Deaglan."

"He's what?" The dragon head in Titus's aura grew brighter and actual scales slid up his neck. "If the hybrid hurts her— If Deaglan even thinks about touching her—"

"It's more likely the brand compelled him to go through with her," Cassius said, shrugging into a pink, blue, and purple Hawaiian shirt, not looking at all confident about his statement. "Even if he wants to take her to Deaglan, he has to know what will happen to her. He'll have to fight the brand to do it."

Which I prayed was true.

"That assumes the brand is powerful enough," Titus snarled back.

"It's powerful," I said, fear and hope churning in my stomach. He'd barely been able to resist his desire for her. I could only pray he'd be unable to resist protecting her.

AMIAH

I GRABBED AT THE WINTER COURT'S FROZEN MAGIC INSIDE ME, EVEN AS everything within me screamed that I couldn't take much more and I wouldn't survive. My body was already too heavy and I couldn't feel my fingers and feet. But I couldn't let the Winter Queen kill Rin and I had to — *please, God! I had to* — get back to my guys.

Command me.

Mine. You're mine. Your wind is mine.

I seized the wind from her, but a force snapped inside me and the gale burst out of my mental grasp.

The Winter Queen sneered. "This is my court and my throne, and he's my heir. I don't care how good a fuck you are. You won't take him from me and you won't stop him from doing his duty and giving me a grandchild."

A barrage of ice shards hurtled toward me and Rin leaped onto the dais in front of me.

My pulse stuttered. He didn't know me. He couldn't be throwing himself in front of danger because he wanted to protect me. It had to be the bond, either because it was forcing him to protect me or because he thought he'd be better able to take the attack so both of us could live. And neither option was acceptable.

I wrenched my hands up and clenched at the ice in my heart. "Stop."

The ice shards clattered to the floor and the wind vanished as the frozen magic inside me screeched against my soul.

Let me in.

You are in.

Deeper. I need to be deeper.

I strained to relax, to let it in fully, but the screeching turned to howling and the court's powerful second heartbeat pounded through my whole body, stealing my breath.

Let. Me. In. It sliced a deep gash in my soul and heat exploded in the delicate gold lines of my mating brand with Rin. Light blazed from the intricate pattern that trailed from the middle of my left thigh, over my hip and waist, and curled around my bottom ribs to my back, and a matching glimmer of gold light, too weak to notice unless you were looking for it, bled through Rin's wrap tunic.

"The marriage vow wasn't good enough? You branded him too?" the Winter Queen snarled, and she blasted more ice at me and Rin.

I shot my own blast of wind and slammed the shards to the floor, but the effort left me gasping and trembling.

Let me in. You have to let me in. Now. She'll kill you if you don't.

Except it wasn't me blocking the court. It was my angelic mating brand.

Oh, God.

My stomach bottomed out with horrific realization. The brand wasn't letting the court in because it wouldn't allow any other bonds. My soul belonged to Rin's and his to mine.

Which meant we had to get the Heart no matter what. It wasn't just the only possible way to break my bond with Rin, but the only way I might be able to add Hawk. And if I couldn't add Hawk or get rid of the brand, it would make me fall out of love with him and he'd starve himself to death or go crazy.

"I will have my heir back," the Winter Queen said, and she strode toward me with her guards at her side. "And I *will* have that dragon."

Two more ice men stepped into the doorway and Rin grabbed my elbow. He jerked me to my feet, but I was shaking so hard I had to cling to him to keep standing.

"The Shadow King can't have her," the Winter Queen said as the two guards in the doorway entered, following the first pair, and another pair took their place, making it six guards and the Winter Queen against the two of us.

Please, you have to let me in. You have to take me from her.

I can't control my soul bond. I can't be your queen. And I wasn't going to tell it there was a chance I'd be able to be its queen once we had the Heart. I didn't want to be queen and getting the Heart didn't guarantee anything no matter how much I placed my hopes in it.

You have to be queen. The court clawed at my soul with a wild desperation. *You have to be.*

"Give her to me, hybrid, and I'll give you a place in my court." The Winter Queen's lips curled back in a wicked smile. "I have an opening in my harem. There are many pleasures for those who are close to the queen. Leave the Shadow King and join me."

"Except he's no longer with the Shadow King," a feminine voice said from the small door that stood behind and to the right of the dais, and another icy, bright life force thrummed against my senses seconds before Padraigin stepped into the throne room. "Isn't that right, hybrid?"

She wore a white leather jerkin and pants similar in cut to the clothes Deaglan wore, and her long black hair was pulled back in a tight braid. A large vortex of water whirled around her, skimming her clothes and tugging on her hair but never leaving a drop.

With a hiss, a liquid rope snapped out from the vortex, seized me, and yanked me out of Rin's arms and off the edge of the dais.

I hit with a bone-jarring *thud* and barely managed to get my hands up in time to protect my face from smacking against the floor.

Rin leaped for me, but a blast of water hit him in the chest, shoving him off the front of the dais and sending him skidding across the floor to the middle of the room and to the feet of the original set of ice guards. Both guards jabbed down with their spears and Rin jerked to one side, grabbed the shaft of the closest spear, and used it to wrench himself around and ram both of his heels onto the other guard's knee.

That guard lost his balance and his spear swung wildly off target, giving Rin an opening to race back to me.

But the Winter Queen seized him with a wind whip and wrenched him back. He twisted instead of falling and cut through the wind with his small sharp claws.

Let me in, the Winter Court begged.

I can't. My soul bond won't let me. But I still had to do something. I'd seen Rin in battle and knew he was terrifyingly deadly, but he still couldn't win against six ice guards, Padraigin, *and* the Winter Queen.

The odds weren't even good that we'd be able to get away.

But capture wasn't an option.

I had to get back to my guys. My soul already ached with the absence of their life forces and the connection I needed to make with them.

The Winter Queen swept another wind whip around Rin as the closest ice guard stabbed at him while the second set of guards hurried to join the fight, and the third set blocked the doorway at the back.

I seized the Winter Court's cold inside me. I might not be able to let it in and sever her hold on it, but if I fought hard enough, I still had its wind.

The cold thudded through me, and I sent a blast of ice and air at the guards, trying to aim high enough that I wouldn't also hit Rin.

But a water whip wrapped around my neck and wrenched me to face Padraigin before I could see if I'd helped.

"I can't kill you with my mother watching," she said, "not until she's gotten the dragon. But I can make you suffer for killing Noaldar."

The water whip gushed up my neck and swept over my face. Fear squeezed my heart. She was going to surround my head with water.

I tried to take a quick breath and buy myself more time, but wasn't fast enough and ended up gasping in water. My throat constricted and I fought the urge to cough and lose what little air I had.

Inside me, the Winter Court howled, desperate to gain hold of my soul, to free itself from the Winter Queen, and its frozen power turned the water to slush, stinging my eyes.

On instinct, I clawed at the liquid, even though I knew it was useless, my fingers passing through it, not even making a break long enough for me to draw in a small breath.

My lungs burned and my reflex to cough won out. Water sprayed across the floor with my cough and I gasped in another lungful of water. My pulse pounded with a too-familiar fear and the memory of Balwyrdan alternating between beating me and suffocating me with the leash spell swept through me.

God, I'd sworn I'd never be helpless again—

And damn it. I wasn't going to be. Ever.

I strained to form a blast of wind and blow apart the water, but the Winter Court's magic kept slipping out of my mental grasp. Everything within me was howling and cold and the room was growing darker. I couldn't concentrate, couldn't breathe, and was about to pass out.

Help me, I begged the court.

Let me in.

I can't.

Behind me, only partially muffled by the water, something crashed with a resounding boom, and I prayed that was one of the ice guards going down.

If you can't let me in, the court replied, *I can't help.*

You're seriously going to refuse? It's not that I don't want to let you in. I can't.

Padraigin crouched and glared at me, her pale icy gaze so much like her brother's and yet so different, filled with rage and pain.

Except Padraigin's pain wasn't the physical pain that Sebastian suffered. It was emotional. A deep, consuming heartache that reminded me of the pain I'd felt when I'd thought Cassius was dead.

"I was going to disband the harem when I became queen," she said. "It was just going to be me and him."

Her grief tore at my heart. I knew how she felt, knew the complete emptiness, the aching hole in her soul left by the death of her lover, and I knew the rage and desperate need to find justice. And while I hadn't killed Noaldar — Deaglan had — with the water surrounding my head, I couldn't tell her the truth, and I wasn't sure she'd listen if I could.

"I hadn't thought I'd find love again after my husband died." She clenched her fist and the water squeezed my skull with an agonizing pressure. Black specs swarmed across my vision and the white room grew darker.

Please. Just a little wind, I begged the Winter Court.

Make me.

"You took that from me," Padraigin said.

My body screamed for air and the darkness deepened. I had to do something. Now.

I clutched at the icy magic inside me. *I. Said. Wind.*

The Winter Court's wind lurched and stuttered and a trickle of air cut through the water around my mouth. I greedily sucked it in, but it didn't last, and my hold on the Winter Court slipped out of my trembling mental grasp again.

Wind.

Another stutter of air, this one not even strong enough to cut through the water.

"I'm supposed to be queen," Padraigin said. More water flooded around my head, weighing it down until I couldn't hold it up, and I sagged forward, forced to bow to her. "I know I am. I'm supposed to be with Noaldar. But the court abandoned me, just like Seireadan did. And because of you, I'm alone."

Wind.

Nothing.

Please.

Out of the corner of my eye, I saw Rin crash into the throne, stagger to his feet then sag to one knee. His life force crackled against my senses, sharp, fiery, dark, and frozen cutting through the Winter Court's cold.

My pulse lurched. I had to save him. I couldn't lose him.

And while I knew that was just our bond compelling me, I also knew the only way I'd survive Faerie without my guys was with Rin — so long as he didn't betray me and hand me over to Deaglan.

Padraigin grabbed my hair, her life force bright and frozen, joining Rin's snapping and crackling inside me, and she yanked my head up, forcing me to look at her. "You took everything from me."

More dark specks swarmed my vision and my lungs burned. The little gasp I'd taken was already gone.

Let me in, the Winter Court hissed.

I can't. Why couldn't it understand that? If I could let it in, I would. Whatever it took to survive and get back to my guys.

It's the only way.

I can't.

"When my brother comes for you, I'll take everything from you, too." Padraigin's life force snapped stronger, overwhelming everything else, the threatening darkness, the Winter Court's cold, and my body's desperate, screaming need for air. There was just her and she was a frozen power like her brother. Except instead of a vast universe of sparkling magic like Sebastian, she was a heaving, raging sea.

A gust of wind hit my back — doing nothing to dislodge the water — and my senses jerked to the Winter Queen. She was a frozen rage, straining to stay in control of a power that wasn't hers and was constantly fighting her. Her life force joined Padraigin's slicing and heaving inside me.

The connection wasn't the same as the connection I made with my guys or even Rin, but it was a connection and there wasn't a barrier in my way like the last time I'd tried to seize Padraigin's life force. This time, I could grab onto her soul and yank. I could kill her and the Winter Queen in an instant.

But then I'd really be the monster Padraigin accused me of being... again.

My throat tightened at the memory of taking the life forces of Deaglan's assassins in my desperate attempt to save Cassius.

I wasn't just the embodiment of life anymore.

I was now also death.

Something I swore I'd never be, something I thought I couldn't be with my compulsive need to heal.

And if I killed Padraigin and the Winter Queen, more Winter Court high fae would die because the court would tear through them, taking their magic — and as a result their lives — until it found someone strong enough to control it.

Except I swore I'd never be someone's prisoner again, and I would die first before I let Padraigin, let alone the Winter Queen or Deaglan, get their hands on Titus or any of my guys.

I seized Padraigin's life force and yanked. I didn't want to kill her, I just wanted to break her concentration, but her life force flooded into me, burning through my veins, and with a scream, she dropped to her knees and clutched her chest, her eyes wide with fear.

The water around my head splattered to the floor, pooling at my hands and knees, and I gasped in a desperate breath and shoved her life back into her, drawing another howl of pain.

"Enough," the Winter Queen yelled and a blast of wind slammed me face-first to the floor.

Sparks exploded in my vision and the world whirled around me. Before I realized what I was doing, my power seized the Winter Queen's life force and yanked, drawing a scream of agony from her.

Her life flooded into me, rushing through my veins, and started to heal my court-induced hypothermia.

Yes, the Winter Court hissed, its joy at her death and its freedom flooding me, weaving around my new ability to take life and seizing control of it. *Finally. Now let me in.*

I can't. Even if I wanted to. And as much as the Winter Queen was a monster, I couldn't kill her.

I heaved at the Winter Court's hold on my magic. I should have been able to take control. The Winter Court didn't completely possess me. But its hold on me was strong and it was desperate. It needed to be free. I understood that need. I also understood that the deaths wouldn't stop with the Winter Queen, and I couldn't be responsible for all those other lives.

But the Winter Court didn't care. It was going to kill the Winter Queen and I was going to be its weapon.

AMIAH

With a scream, I wrenched my power out of the Winter Court's control and shoved the Winter Queen's life back inside her.

The Winter Court howled, its frozen magic slicing inside me, the hypothermia I'd started to heal returning.

Why? I could have been free.

But I can't control you. You would have killed the high fae in your court until someone else took control of you.

But I have to be free from her, it cried. *Please.*

Rin's life force snapped against my senses, and he picked me up and bolted out the small door at the back of the throne room.

Please, the Winter Court begged. *I can't be trapped with her. I won't let you leave me like Seireadan and Padraigin did.*

Which didn't make sense. Yes, Sebastian had abandoned Faerie when his best friend and his fiancé had tried to murder him, but Padraigin was still there. *Padraigin didn't leave you.*

She did. Her husband died, Seireadan left, and she faded out of reach.

Faded? If you could connect with Padraigin, would you accept her? I didn't like that she was trying to kill me, but she'd been told a lie and I understood her pain. The question was, had she been behind Noaldar trying to stab me with a poisoned knife and almost killing Hawk? Did I really want someone in control of the court who'd used a poison so deadly not even an incubus's rapid healing would have been able to save him?

If she hadn't been involved, she would certainly be a better option for the Winter Court than its current queen.

I can't reach her.

If you could?

I can't and I won't let you go.

I can't let you in. I had to find a way for it to connect with Padraigin. Except if it couldn't, I'd have to find someone else, and I wasn't going to force the court on Sebastian. He'd made it clear he didn't want to be king.

I'll find someone. I promise, I thought at it, my body shivering uncontrollably, icy water dripping from my hair and sliding over my bare skin. I had no idea how I'd free it, but I knew what it was like to be trapped with no hope of escape, and no one, not even a magical court, should have to suffer like that.

Rin raced down the narrow white hall, the walls, even in what had to be a servants' hall, carved with intricate swirling patterns. I clung to him, desperate for even the little bit of heat in his undead body. He wasn't even as warm as Sebastian's cooler-than-normal body temperature, but he was a lot warmer than the Winter Court's frozen power.

He reached a T-intersection, ran right, then took the first left. I prayed he knew where he was going, since I had no clue how to get anywhere in the court.

Up ahead, three female ice servants, all petite women who looked identical in every way — face, hair, build, and clothing — dropped their baskets and serving trays and leaped at us.

Rin jerked out of the way, but icy fingers clawed at my arm, digging deep painful rents in my flesh.

Another woman grabbed my ankle, but Rin twisted and kicked her into the third woman, slamming them into the wall. The impact shattered the torso of the one Rin had kicked and she broke apart without uttering a sound.

The third servant didn't give the broken one a second look and lunged at us, but Rin bolted away before she reached us, racing down the hall to another T-intersection.

He turned right into a much wider hall and stopped. Four large ice guards stood at the far end, guarding a set of large, intricately carved ice doors.

"Can you control them, your highness?" he asked in his soft, barely-there voice.

One of the guards barreled down the hall toward us, and I wrenched at the Winter Court's magic inside me.

A gust of wind stuttered around us, freezing the water on my skin and in my hair, then vanished.

The guard swept his spear at us and Rin twisted to the side just enough so the spear tip plunged past us.

I strained to summon more wind as the guard jerked his weapon to the side and Rin twisted out of the way again.

Another stuttering gust of wind that quickly sputtered out.

Please. I promise I'll free you, I told the Winter Court.

Her hold is too tight. She won't let me help you.

"I can't control them," I gasped, as a second guard hurried to join the first, and the first thrust his spear at us again.

Rin jerked back and the two ice servants who we'd just run from hurried into the hall behind us while the icy bright life forces of the Winter Queen and Padraigin drew closer.

"Can you stand?" His gaze swept around the hall as if he were searching for an out-of-the-way place to put me so he could fight.

Except even if he could fight the ice guards and the servants, the Winter Queen and Padraigin were coming. We'd just end up in the same situation we'd run from in the throne room.

"Just run. The Winter Queen and Padraigin will be here soon."

A spark of hellfire snapped from his eye and he tightened his grip on me. "All the other exits will be guarded like this one. If we wait, she'll add more men."

"If we don't, the Winter Queen might not care if Padraigin drowns us."

Rin twisted, dodging another spear thrust, but the second guard also jabbed, forcing Rin to heave out of the way and step into the hands of the servants.

One grabbed my arm, digging her sharp fingertips into my flesh and the other seized Rin's tunic. They yanked him off balance and wrenched me out of his arms.

He scrambled to grab me, but a guard seized his ankle and slammed him into the hall wall.

He hit with a heavy *thud,* fell to the floor, stunned, and the guard stabbed at him.

My pulse skipped and the Winter Court's pulse took its place with a crushing beat in my chest. Its wind rippled around me, its cold freezing into every cell in my body and yet still not completely in my control.

Because I couldn't let it in.

There was only room for Rin. My brand made sure of that and it howled at me to save him.

Save him. Save him. Now now now.

My desperation clenched at the Winter Court's magic and a burst of air hit the spear. The sharp tip dug into the floor, narrowly missing Rin's chest. He scrambled toward me, but the ice maid who wasn't holding me lunged at him.

Without losing his stride, he hit the maid in the center of her chest with a powerful open-hand strike, shoving her into the wall and shattering her body then snapped a hard, fast kick to the other maid's head. Her skull broke in half with a sickening *crack*, the pieces tumbling to the floor, and her body collapsed on top of me.

I rolled her off me and Rin yanked me back into his arms. But two of the ice guards swung at him and even with his faster-than-human speed, he wasn't going to be able to dodge both strikes and secure his grip on me.

My heart skipped another beat and the Winter Court's pulse took its place again, this time with a frozen surge of power that blasted wind at all four guards, slamming them against the large doors. One guard's arm cracked and fell off and another lost a chunk out of his side.

A flicker of hope cut through my fear. I just needed another blast like that and we could escape.

I mentally seized the Winter Court's magic, willing everything I had into it to control it just one more time. But that other force snapped through my control again, and just like the last time, the Winter Queen took her power back, and a massive wall of ice shot up from the floor, blocking off the door.

I strained to wrench the court's power back, but the Winter Queen held on tight, even as the Winter Court's heart pounded inside me, slicing into my soul, desperate to join with me.

You're mine. I command you. I heaved at the cold, but the queen's grip tightened and her life force drew closer. I tried to seize her life force again but couldn't reach her. She was too far away for my magic to do anything more than sense her, and it was a terrible idea to risk capture to wait for her to get closer.

"I'm not going to break the wall in time. We have to run," I gasped through chattering teeth. "We can figure out how to escape once we're out of immediate danger."

The hellfire in Rin's eyes flickered to miniature flames then snapped back to smoldering red pinpricks and he ran to the closest hall — which happened to be between us and the guards.

All of the guards lunged at us, and Rin twisted, dodging a spear thrust then jerked to the side to avoid another. His shoulder hit the wall and so did the back of my head, making the world lurch and darken, but he didn't hesitate... or ask me if I was okay, since a concussion was nothing compared to being captured or killed. He just kept running down hall after hall.

The Winter Queen and Padraigin's life forces grew farther away, but for every hall that didn't have one of the queen's constructs, two more did, and while Rin chose running over fighting when possible and didn't look like he was getting tired, eventually it wouldn't matter how little he fought. Neither demons nor vampires had unlimited strength. He'd get tired and we wouldn't be able to make a stand.

We had to get out of the Winter Court.

Except Rin was right. All the exits would be guarded... if the Winter Queen didn't just block them all off, trapping everyone inside until she captured us.

Unless, of course, there was a way out that she didn't know I knew about.

"Do you know how to get to the ballroom?"

Please, God, let him know where we are and how to get there.

"Yes." He jerked around and ran back to the last hall we'd passed.

Thank, God.

"There's a hall that leads to the Winter Forest. There's a door just before the barrier. It's for the catacombs and a way out of court."

Going through the catacombs had been our original escape plan the last time we'd been trapped in the Winter Court. Only a select few could cross the barrier into the Winter Forest, so the hall to the catacombs — and what Sebastian had said was a forgotten way out of court — was never guarded.

And I could only hope nothing had changed since we'd been there last.

AMIAH

WE REACHED THE BALLROOM'S MAIN FLOOR WITHOUT RUNNING INTO MANY more servants, and Rin paused at the entranceway in the dimly lit hall, made darker by the shadow of the wide balcony that ringed the large dark room.

Unlike the last time I was there, there weren't any glowing orbs lighting the space, and the buffet tables piled with food that had sat against the walls under the balcony were also gone. So, too was the massive bed with red silk sheets that had dominated the center of the room where Sebastian and I had been forced to consummate our fake marriage.

I shuddered at the memory of him yanking my hair, hurting me, kissing me like he was angry, and pushing into me before I was ready, all to put on a big enough show so his mother wouldn't demand we have sex with her entire court watching ever again.

A spark of hellfire popped from Rin's eye, the only indication he had any kind of emotion.

He'd bitten me that night at Deaglan's command, had sent his seductive vampiric magic sliding through my veins, and then had watched me and Sebastian.

Another shudder swept through me.

Did he think that's how I liked to have sex?

God, I hoped not. If we didn't get the Heart soon and break our soul bond, I was going to have to have sex with him or go crazy, and I was nervous enough about having normal sex with him.

And with my body starting to ache for him again despite the Winter Court freezing my very essence, I didn't know how much longer I could resist my unwanted desires.

"Which hall?" he asked, his soft voice twisting my desire tighter.

Come on. Think of something else. Anything other than sex with Rin.

But that made me think of sex with my guys, of their kisses and caresses, how they made me feel incredible. The memory of both Sebastian and Hawk moving inside me flooded me and my aching desire swelled. I wanted more of that, more of the connection we formed that kept getting stronger, more of the amazing sensations, and more of the certainty that I could let go with them, that I didn't have to be in control, that I was safe.

Jeez. And right now to be safe, I shouldn't think about sex at all.

"Your highness," Rin murmured and I bit back a moan.

Jeez. You're freezing. How can you possibly be turned on? You're running for your life for goodness sake!

I heaved my attention to the hall on the other side of the ballroom and pointed with a trembling hand. "That one."

He hurried across the room, passing through the wide patch of moonlight pouring through the large skylight in the center of the room where the bed had been.

I forced my gaze up, my heart yearning to be outside and free, not trapped in the Winter Court's mountain, and took one last look at the sky. We were heading deeper into the court, farther away from the sky, and I had no idea when I'd see it again.

The thought squeezed in my chest. Not knowing when I'd see the sky again was just something else I needed to ignore. I couldn't let my fears or my desires control me. I had to focus, keep an eye on Rin for any indication that he was going to betray me, and get back to my guys. It didn't matter that everything within me said I could trust him. That was just the brand influencing me, not the truth.

We reached the narrow hall. Strangely these walls weren't carved with the swirling design that covered every other wall in the Winter Court. They were smooth and solemn, fully opaque and there wasn't a door in sight.

A frozen breeze swept over us, drawing my gaze through the gloomy darkness to the rectangle of moonlight at the far end and the vast swath of glimmering snow between the end of the hall and the edge of the Winter Forest.

Rin strode down the hall and the breeze grew stronger. My shivering increased, my breath misting, not because the air around me was cold, but because the air *inside* me was.

God, I hadn't even been this cold when the keys to unlock the Heart had become empowered.

My thoughts stalled, and between one blink and the next, we were a lot closer to the end of the hall and the square of moonlight than we'd been before. Which meant my hypothermia was getting worse — and I didn't even need my magic to tell me that.

I was already heavy and numb, and despite my shivering, my pulse was starting to slow. I wasn't going to last much longer, not without expending my healing magic, which was the last thing I wanted to do. It took a lot more magic to heal myself than to heal others and I wanted to hold on to what I had for when my guys came for me. Because they would come for me.

Please. You need to let me go, I mentally gasped at the Winter Court.

No. Not until you find me a new monarch.

I can't do that if I die from hypothermia.

If I release you, you'll betray me. The Winter Court's icy power surged and the hall vanished. Frozen darkness surrounded me, squeezing me so tight I couldn't move, couldn't breathe.

I blinked and lost more time. Now we were almost at the end of the hall and it was getting harder and harder to focus. It was as if I was thinking in slow motion. My thoughts stalled, lurched then stalled again, and all I really wanted was to go to sleep.

I wasn't going to be able to take much more. *I won't betray you.*

The Winter Court heaved and snapped inside me, and snowflakes twirled out of my mouth with my next breath.

I fought to keep my eyes open and reached for my healing power, but my thoughts were too sluggish, and it kept slipping out of my mental grasp. I'd waited too long and was no longer able to concentrate enough to push my magic inward and heal myself.

Please.

Fine.

I released another breath filled with more flakes. They sparkled in the moonlight, the unnatural fae glow radiating from my body, and with the fae magic I wasn't supposed to be able to see as a being from the Realm of Celestial Light.

More flakes flew out of my mouth, and a whisper of heat unfurled around my heart.

Some of the cold that had been inside me was leaving. But not all.

I could still feel the ice in my veins, knew if the Winter Court wanted to it could flood me with its power again and kill me.

Find me a monarch, it hissed, its threat clear. If I didn't find it a monarch, it would take me whether I could fully command it or not.

Rin reached the end of the hall and there, barely visible even while standing directly in front of it, was a plain, narrow door. It opened into a plain passage, and Rin hurried into the narrow space before I could get a good look at what was inside and closed the door behind us.

There wasn't any light, but my fae glow, still radiating light from my orgasm, offered more than enough illumination to tell we were at the top of a narrow staircase.

"Put me down," I said. I couldn't sense the Winter Queen and Padraigin's life forces and didn't want Rin carrying me all the way out of the Winter Court. Of course, even though I wasn't shivering nearly as much as before, I still had no idea if I could walk, but since I wasn't about to pass out from the cold, I wanted to at least try to stand on my own.

"Yes, your highness." He set me on my feet, close to the door so I could lean against it to keep my balance and turned his back on me.

"Rin, you don't have to call me your highness. I'm not a princess."

He untied his sash and my pulse picked up.

"I ah... I'd rather you call me Amiah," I said, my voice breathy as my unwanted desire surged.

Oh, God. I knew our bond made him desire me as well, but was he struggling as much as I was? It was so hard to tell with his emotionless demeanor.

"We should probably think about this." And pull ourselves together.

He shrugged out of his wrap tunic and held it and the sash out to me, still keeping his back turned.

I stared at his naked torso, my thoughts stalled on his body. I'd seen him without his tunic before. He, like my guys, had been forced to only wear pants to the Winter Queen's party, and I knew what his beautifully sculpted chest, abs, and arms looked like.

Then my thoughts tripped. He was holding out his tunic.

I didn't have to be naked.

"Thank you." I took the tunic, my hands still trembling with the cold, and pulled it on. It wrapped across my chest and almost all the way around my back and hung to my ankles. It was also still crusted with blood from when Rin had ripped out the throat of Deaglan's nightmare, but at least it covered my body... more or less. Less, because if I moved the wrong way the slits would flash everything to anyone looking, but it wasn't any more revealing than the dress the queen had made me wear at my marriage consummation party... and once again, I didn't have shoes.

"We should put more distance between us and them. Can you walk, your highness?"

"I said call me Amiah." I reached for the sash and my fingers brushed his, sending a shock of need sweeping through me and making me gasp.

His gaze jerked to mine, and once again I was drowning in his hellfire, the warmth of my desire bleeding through the Winter Court's frozen magic. Everything within me cried to draw closer, tease my fingers across his back, kiss him again. All I'd need was a single step and I could press my body against his.

"Please," I gasped, forcing myself to stay where I was. "I've already told you, Sebastian and I aren't married."

He didn't move, didn't breathe, didn't even blink. Not that he needed to breathe or blink — he was undead — but most vampires never lost those living reflexes.

"I'm just Amiah."

The silence dragged on between us with our gazes locked, his life force thrumming against my senses and our bond throbbing inside me.

"And even if Sebastian and I were married—" Which would never happen. "—I'd still just be Amiah."

A spark popped from his eye and the pain imprinted in his cells from his centuries of suffering at Deaglan's hands whispered through me.

That pain had been excruciating when Rin had questioned Deaglan's command to bite me, and it made me furious every time I thought about it. Deaglan had hurt Rin again and again on a level I wasn't sure I'd ever fully understand. And while I knew the terror of being held captive and of doing whatever it took to please my captor to avoid punishment, I'd barely suffered compared to Rin's five hundred years. What had he done to survive? What was he willing to do?

My heart broke for him.

God, just like with Cassius and Titus and all of my guys, I yearned to heal Rin. But his emotional and psychological injuries weren't something I could heal.

Essie, with her archangel empathic healing magic might be powerful enough to heal his soul. She connected with peoples' emotions and healed psychological wounds, but I wasn't sure if she could truly mend a broken soul. I hadn't heard of anyone being able to do so.

Regardless, she was his best bet, and when we got through this — because all of us *were* getting through this — I'd give Essie my long overdue apology and beg her to help him whether our souls were still bound together or not.

But until then, all I could do was try to convince him he was free and he didn't have to placate me or anyone else.

"You're free. I swear it." Or as free as he could get with his soul bound to mine. "Free to use my name, and Sebastian's, and anyone else's, and free to say what you think."

Still nothing.

Did he think this was some kind of trap? That I'd tell him he could do something then punish him for it?

Dread tightened in my gut. "Oh, God. Did Deaglan hurt you for things he said you could do?" No wonder Rin didn't trust me. He probably didn't trust anyone. I couldn't imagine what five hundred years of always being on guard, always being in pain, did to a person.

I'd only spent a hundred years desperate to be in control so I'd never be taken again. It had been exhausting and soul-crushing and I'd been free, not someone's slave. I hadn't even known the truth of how exhausting it had been until I'd found Sebastian and Hawk and trusted them enough to just be myself with them.

I stepped close, the need to go to Rin overwhelming me. I cupped his cheeks, his undead skin unnaturally warm against my cold fingers, and drew his forehead down to mine. My desire for him swelled, but my need to steady his soul as if we were both shifters was stronger, and while I knew my feelings towards him were only because of the brand, in that moment I didn't care.

"Please believe me. I will never purposely hurt you," I said.

Please, God, believe me. You shouldn't have to be on guard all the time.

"Even after we're free of each other, I won't hurt you. None of the guys will, either."

"You can't promise that," he said.

"You're right I can't."

Please trust me.

Please don't betray me.

Because there was still a chance he'd think delivering me to Deaglan was the best way to survive.

"I suspect they wouldn't react well if you hurt me," I said.

"I'm not sure I can hurt you. The bond is..." Another spark popped from his eye, brushing my cheek with a glorious kiss of heat before vanishing. "...compelling."

That was an understatement.

I huffed and eased back so I could look him in the eyes. "How very diplomatic of you. It's driving me crazy and I only branded you two days ago. It's only going to get worse until we seal the bond or get rid of it, and it tells me I can trust you, that you won't betray me to Deaglan." The words slipped out before I could stop them. I shouldn't have confessed that. If he was lying about how the bond was influencing him, he could use that information to hurt me.

But God, I wanted him to not hurt me, wanted him to not be the monster I'd thought he was when we'd first met, the monster that my brand assured me he wasn't.

RIN

I STARED AT HER, FIGHTING TO FIND MY STILLNESS, BUT THE POND INSIDE ME had been roiling since the portal had spat us into the Winter Court's throne room—

No, I'd been roiling since I'd met her and was still a raging storm from watching her have sex with Prince Seireadan and Hawk.

It had been an exquisite torture. The sounds she'd made still rang in my ears, every moan and gasp teasing me, urging me to be the one to bring her such pleasure. She even still glowed with the light that had undulated through her body, growing brighter and brighter as her pleasure grew.

And now here she was, her delicate hands still on my cheeks, her fear and need and hope exposed and raw in her eyes.

She wanted to trust me, had come out and said what terrified her — although from the way her eyes had flashed wide, she hadn't wanted to confess that.

She needed my help to get out of the Winter Court and was smart enough to realize that, but she didn't trust what our soul bond was telling her.

Well I didn't trust it, either.

Except my desire aside, the rest of me *knew* she wouldn't hurt me even if we hadn't been soul bonded. She was an angel with healing magic. I wasn't sure she was capable of taking a life.

Of course, that didn't mean Prince Seireadan wouldn't hurt me. He didn't behave like any other Faerie royal I'd ever encountered, but that didn't mean anything. Princess Amiah and the others were clearly close to him, his trusted confidants. He'd already told Hawk if I took too much fae magic while sucking out his demonic magic infection, the incubus could do whatever he wanted to stop me so long as it didn't kill me and endanger the princess.

"Rin?" Fear crept into Princess Amiah's eyes and she shifted back a step, sending more waves crashing through my mental pond.

I'd taken too long to reply and had broken the tentative trust she'd been trying to build by assuring me I was free.

"I can't return to the Shadow King." Not that I ever wanted to, and I wasn't stupid enough to think bringing him the princess would stop him from killing me. I'd broken free. Even if it hadn't been my doing, I'd still escaped. That was unforgivable.

Princess Amiah's eyes narrowed. "Can't? That doesn't make me feel better."

My only option was to help Prince Seireadan get the key and hope he'd use it to break my soul bond with the woman he loved.

And the prince would never forgive me if I let anything happen to her. While it was clear the Winter Queen didn't want Princess Amiah dead — or at least not right away — that didn't mean she wouldn't torture her. We needed to get moving, get out of the Winter Court and into the Wilds. It would be harder for the Winter Queen to send constructs after us and dangerous for her to send high fae. I wasn't sure how the Wilds would react to the princess since she had the high fae's full-body glow but wasn't really high fae, but it was still our best bet.

"Can you walk?" I asked.

Given her condition, if she could walk she'd still be slow, but that would mean my hands would be free if we ran into trouble again, and I wasn't going to assume there wouldn't be trouble again. As much as it had seemed that the Winter Court was trying to force the princess to take the throne, this was still the Winter Queen's court. That, and it was getting harder and harder to concentrate with her in my arms, and I doubted her putting my tunic on would change that. I had the memory of her naked body seared into my mind.

The princess's angel glow flared in her eyes. "Yes, I can walk."

She pushed past me, her body still trembling from the cold, and started down the steps.

I rushed to stay close so I could catch her if she fell.

"Just because you can't return to Deaglan doesn't mean you don't want to," she said.

Did she honestly think I wanted to go back to that monster?

A million responses popped into my mind, all dangerous to say out loud to a royal, and instinct shoved all of them deep down and kept my mouth closed. It was always better to not say anything. Yes, sometimes I was punished for that too, but speaking my mind had always been worse.

She reached a wider step and looked back at me. I jerked to a stop before I ran into her. We were so close. Another inch and our bodies would brush. And God, everything within me wanted that and more.

Except that was the bond... well, maybe not completely the bond. She was sexy and passionate and my soul said I could trust her. I hadn't had sex with someone I'd been able to trust since I'd been killed and the Shadow King had bought me.

She captured my soul in the bright blue depths of her eyes, sending waves churning through my last hope of inner stillness, her expression questioning.

She was still waiting for an answer.

But did I dare speak my thoughts?

Just because she said I could, didn't mean that was true.

My soul screamed at me. Just speak. Just say what I thought and felt. She wouldn't judge me.

But if I said the wrong thing, I could ruin this. This was the closest I'd been to being free in five hundred years. I couldn't afford to make her, Prince Seireadan, or any of his trusted men angry. There was just too much to lose.

My mental pond heaved, the storm raging inside me and a spark of hellfire escaped my control.

Her eyes narrowed and I watched the raw hope in her eyes shift to disappointment then harden into determination.

I'd taken too long to respond again.

"If you only believe one thing I say, believe this," she said, "I'll kill myself before I let you hand me over to Deaglan." Which meant she'd kill me because of our soul bond. "I won't let him get my key and I won't let him get Faerie's Heart."

I knew she'd do it, too. I'd seen her in action and knew she'd sacrifice herself without hesitation to save lives. She'd healed the prince's burns before she'd healed herself like a typical angel with strong healing magic. And anyone with half a brain knew that if the Shadow King got Faerie's Heart, lives would be lost. Except I had no idea why she was telling me this.

"I know you're a survivor and know you'll do whatever it takes to stay alive." Pain leaked into the determination in her eyes.

God, she was pitying me. But the moment I thought that, I realized the look wasn't pity but understanding of the difficult choices I'd had to make, the stains I'd put on my soul for the sake of survival. Because that had been my only choice. With the king's leash spell on me, it had been impossible to escape or even kill myself.

Her angel glow flared and her determination returned. "No matter how much I want to trust you, I know you'll say whatever you think I want to hear. Our bond might be driving me crazy with the need to sleep with you, but it hasn't turned me into a fool, and I doubt it's made you fall in love with me yet. So I want to be clear. Your odds of surviving this mess aren't better with Deaglan."

I already knew that. She didn't need to threaten me.

So tell her. Say something.

"Yes, you're free," she continued. "You won't be punished for saying or doing as you please, and once I reunite with the guys, you're not obligated to help us, not even to get the Heart and your full freedom. But I want you to know that I'll do whatever it takes to protect the men I love and all the lives in this realm."

I know that. If it brings the Shadow King down I'll help. My mouth and throat tightened with words I wanted to say, had to say, but couldn't.

God just say them!

But a ghostly snap of the agony from the Shadow King's leash spell sliced through me, reminding me of the cost of opening my mouth. I'd been foolish when I'd questioned his command to bite her at her wedding party, and after the party, King Deaglan had seen to it to remind me of the cost of speaking up. I didn't know why I'd slipped. I hadn't slipped like that in a long time, but she'd been so weak, her life drained and if I'd taken too much I could have killed her, and there'd been— *still was* something about her that made me need to protect her.

And yet she said I was free. She was a healing angel for goodness sake. She wouldn't hurt me.

"I—" *Come on. Test her. Her reaction, even Prince Seireadan's reaction, couldn't possibly be worse than the Shadow King's.*

But God, I didn't want to lose my chance to finally be free.

Just say it.

"I will be clear, too," I forced out. "I will never have another master." I snapped my mouth shut on the rest of my statement, that I'd kill myself and her, too, before I became anyone's slave again. Saying that was too dangerous, especially if she told the prince and he thought I'd actually go through with it. He could cast a spell that could trap me just like the Shadow King had. It was bad enough I'd given her the same poorly veiled threat that she'd given me.

But her expression grew sad, and not angry as expected.

"You shouldn't have had one in the first place." She turned her back to me and resumed heading down the stairs. "No one should," she murmured, talking again as if she had first hand knowledge of what it felt like.

More ghostly pain whispered through me, and I gritted my teeth, letting it swell through my mental pond and dissipate.

She released a frustrated huff, making me tense. "God, what Deaglan did to you makes me so angry."

"Why?" Why would she care? She didn't know me, didn't know what I'd experienced, and just like our bond hadn't made me fall in love with her yet, I doubted it had made her fall in love with me.

Another whisper of pain sliced through me and I fought to just let it pass. I didn't know why it was acting up. It hadn't been this bad when she'd first freed me. Of course, my body also hadn't been burning for her when she'd first freed me, either.

"That's why. I can feel your pain," she said without looking back. "But even if I push past my magic's resistance to connect with the undead, it's still not something I can heal. Which is frustrating because I know how much you're hurting and I can't do anything about it."

I didn't know what to say to that even with the new freedom to say whatever I wanted, so I made a non-committal grunt which seemed to satisfy her.

We continued down the staircase in silence, the steps — looking like they were made from ice even though they weren't slippery — twisting around and around into the darkness below.

But the silence was even more uncomfortable than trying to speak my mind, because my mind was whirling and I couldn't get it to stop.

I hadn't understood our conversation. I mean, I had. But I doubted it was that simple. There had always been a trap for me to stumble into for the Shadow King's entertainment, there had to be one now.

Except she wasn't the Shadow King.

I slid my gaze down her body, taking in her curves wrapped in my tunic, and her still-glowing skin, reminding me of what I'd witnessed. The tenderness and passion between her, the prince, and Hawk was unlike anything I'd ever seen before. The Shadow King had never taken a lover that way. No one who I'd been forced to watch had, and I certainly hadn't. I hadn't loved anyone I'd been allowed to have sex with. My release was a duty to please the Shadow King. It was never just for me.

And now I had no idea what to think of her. I hadn't been surprised that the prince had aggressively dominated her when they'd consummated their marriage in the ballroom. With my experience with the other Faerie royals, I was surprised blood hadn't been drawn and there hadn't been more screaming.

Which did she prefer?

I didn't know if I could continue performing in the way the Shadow King liked.

And God, it didn't matter because I was never going to sleep with her.

Jealousy that I didn't want, that was a product of our unwanted bond, squeezed around my heart. I'd never gotten a chance to find someone who loved me like she, the prince, and Hawk clearly loved each other. I'd barely managed to have the comradery they all had with each other before I'd become the Shadow King's slave.

And I wanted that.

Because of the bond.

Except the ache was so deep, I feared my desire to belong, to be loved, wasn't because of the bond, that the bond was just another torture, a way of showing me a yearning I'd repressed for five hundred years that I was never going to have.

AMIAH

I LEANED AGAINST THE WALL DETERMINED TO KEEP MY BALANCE AND MOVE quickly down the stairs despite my still partially numb hands and feet.

As much as our bond said I could trust Rin, I couldn't bring myself to fully believe it. And not clearly stating that he wasn't going to betray me didn't ease my fears.

Of course, I hadn't realized until he'd given me his own ultimatum about never having another master just how difficult it was for him to speak out.

Just saying those words had awoken his cells' memory of the agony Deaglan had inflicted on him.

Which made me furious, both at Deaglan for what he'd done and myself because I shouldn't have threatened him. That hadn't helped to build trust either, but I'd wanted him to be clear on what his situation was.

And now, we were back to an uncomfortable silence where I was hyperaware of just how closely he followed me, how I was wearing his tunic and nothing else, and how much our bond wanted to be sealed

Except I didn't know what else to say or if he'd even engage me in conversation.

His last response had been a grunt, which hadn't felt like an invitation to keep going. But then, his mind could be whirling just as frantically as mine, and if he felt even half of the desire I did, he was probably finding it hard to concentrate, too.

I hurried down two more steps, and the stairwell changed from the ice-that-wasn't-ice to stone, merging seamlessly from one material to the next.

Another dozen steps after that we reached the bottom, stepping into a small antechamber, its diameter about ten feet and its stone walls smooth without ornamentation or cracks or tool marks like the ice stairwell.

In front of us, two man-sized stone statues stood on either side of a wide archway. The statues wore simple robes, the stone carved to look like flowing fabric, and they hid their faces in their hands as if they were crying. Ahead, the light emanating from my skin — and still our only source of illumination — cast a long, pale rectangle on the floor beyond the arch and lit two more weeping statues.

I didn't know exactly where the exit out of court was — Sebastian had only mentioned it was in the catacombs — but there was still only one direction we could go, so I staggered forward, heading down the passage, hugging myself, unable to hide just how much I was trembling now that I didn't have a wall to lean against.

But Rin didn't offer to help me. He just kept a little too close, and I wasn't sure if that upset me or not. My guys wouldn't have given me a choice. All of them, even Sebastian, would have picked me up whether I wanted to be carried or not, and that part of my soul that needed them ached for that contact.

Except Rin wasn't one of my guys.

I had to remember that, no matter what my brand told me.

Besides, it was already difficult to ignore my desire with him in my personal space. It would have been even more challenging if he held me again.

Determined to stay in control and not throw myself at him, I forced my attention forward and kept moving as fast as I could. Wide alcoves, guarded by more weeping statues, lined both sides of the passages, and inside were large sarcophaguses made of ice. These were covered in the same swirling ornamentation that decorated the rest of the court, the grooves catching my light and reflecting back as icy shimmers. Ahead, the passage stretched into darkness and without any other light, it was impossible to tell where it ended... if it ended. For all I knew, we were walking into a dead end.

God, there had to be a way out. Sebastian had said there was.

Except Sebastian hadn't lived in the Winter Court for three hundred years. A lot could have changed in that amount of time.

My chest tightened, and the stone and the darkness crowded around me. I couldn't be trapped beneath this mountain. I needed to see the sky, needed to be free. Now.

Now now now.

I gritted my teeth. There *was* a way out. Even if we had to go back and face the Winter Queen and Padraigin again, I could get out. I could be free. I was okay.

But that thought didn't ease the panic building inside me. If I couldn't see the sky, I couldn't escape. And I *had* to escape. Everything. This mountain, the Winter Court, my bond with Rin. *Please. I can't be trapped again. I swore.*

And damn it, falling apart wasn't going to help me. I was stronger than this. I'd survived worse. I'd survived being beaten by Balwyrdan and I *would* survive this.

I squared my shoulders and picked up my pace. Moving faster would get me out of there faster and hopefully warm me up a bit more.

I would get out. I would get back to my guys. I would. I would—

Ahead, a flicker of weak light sparked then vanished.

It happened so quickly that I wasn't sure I'd actually seen it. Then it sparked again and grew as I drew closer, until I could clearly see an opening with a glowing fae orb floating near the ceiling.

Some of the pressure in my chest eased.

Thank God. I was free. I was—

I reached the opening and swept my gaze over a vast cavern. More glowing orbs hovered in the air, revealing a fully enclosed space with a craggy ceiling, and a chasm that disappeared down into darkness, was at least a hundred feet across, and stretched in either direction as far as I could see.

I was still trapped.

Hugging myself against my internal cold, I stepped out of the passage, passed between two enormous stone statues, and walked to the edge of the ledge.

There wasn't a railing to stop me from falling, but if I did, there was more than enough space for me to release my wings and fly — not that there was anywhere to fly to. Although the other side was riddled with ledges and caves. Perhaps there was a way out over there.

To the right of the ledge sat a set of stairs. They'd been cut into the chasm's wall and led down into the darkness, suggesting the only way out was to go deeper into the mountain.

A shudder swept through me and I turned to head down the stairs.

But as I moved, so did the statue closest to the steps. It broke away from the wall with a resounding *crack* that echoed through the cavern and blocked my path with its enormous body.

Another *crack* boomed from behind me and I jerked around to see the other statue step forward as well. Both of them were twice as big as the Winter Queen's ice guards, but they still wore similar looking armor and clothes — even though all of their clothes and armor were stone — and each carried a large stone spear.

"She can animate stone too?"

I'm more than just ice and wind, the Winter Court said, its voice a barely audible whisper, as if it was trying to communicate from far away.

If you're also the stone, can you make us a way out of here?

I could if you were my queen.

Which still wasn't going to happen, and without a doubt, these stone guards hadn't woken up to show us the way out. We needed to get out of there, and while I could just release my wings and fly, Rin couldn't. And even without our bond compelling me to help and protect him, I wasn't going to abandon him.

More *snaps*, smaller and sharper, sounded from inside the passage and the closest weeping statues dropped their hands from their faces and turned to look at us.

"Run," Rin said, reaching for me.

Except the best thing for me to do was get out of the way.

"You run. I'll fly."

I leaped off the ledge before he could grab me and pushed power into my back, releasing my wings through Rin's tunic then glided up and away from the ledge.

A spark popped from his eye and he bolted for the statue guarding the stairs. With his faster-than-human speed, it was clear he was aiming to dart around or between the statue's legs. But the statue moved faster than I thought possible given how slowly it had stepped away from the wall, and swiped its spear at Rin.

Rin jerked, and the spear sliced his side instead of impaling him and sent him tumbling toward the wall by the archway.

He hit with an *umph*, but didn't utter any other sound, and managed to stay standing. Except before he could try again, one of the weeping statues lunged out of the passageway and grabbed his arm.

Rin punched the statue's wrist with his free hand, shattering the stone, its hand falling away from his biceps, and he shoved the rest of it over the ledge. It plummeted into the darkness below, also not uttering a sound, which made me even more furious at Deaglan, since I was certain that Rin trying to control the sounds he made in the fight was because of Deaglan.

The second statue jabbed his spear at Rin. He twisted out of the way and leaped for the stairs again, but the first statue swept out his spear, blocking Rin's path.

Rin dodged the swipe, jerked out of reach of another weeping statue's hands, and leaped at the wall. His foot hit that wall above the weeping statue's head and he pushed off, diving for the space between the wall and the first statue's thigh.

But the second statue jabbed again and caught Rin in midair. The point pierced through his back and exploded out of his chest with a spray of blood.

My healing magic stuttered, recognizing his injury but shying away from his undead nature, as he started to scream then clenched his jaw, swallowing it.

With a grunt, the statue jerked his spear and flicked Rin off the tip

He sailed over the edge of the ledge into the middle of the chasm, and everything within me froze.

Oh, God.

I had to save him. I couldn't lose him. I might not want him, but I needed him. I wasn't sure if I needed him like I needed my guys or if I just needed him because of our soul bond, but everything inside screamed he was mine and I was his. To protect. To love. The universe had spoken. He was my fate... because of the damned bond.

I dove for him. I wasn't strong enough to fly with him, I wasn't even sure I could slow our descent enough or glide far enough with him to avoid crashing to our deaths, but I had to try.

I grabbed Rin's wrist. His weight yanked my wings back, and I strained to flap them, keep them spread, anything to slow our fall.

We hurtled down, the rough walls of the chasm flying past us, my full-body glow casting wild flickering shadows in the caves and crevasses, my efforts twisting and jerking us.

With a yell, I flexed my wings and caught air. Pain tore through my back, but I managed to keep them open, and we careened toward the far side of the chasm and slammed against the craggy wall.

The impact made me instinctually yank my wings back into my body to protect them, and more pain sliced through my chest as we crashed in a tangle of limbs with me mostly on top of Rin.

We'd landed on a narrow ledge at the mouth of a cave with the stone guards' ledge across the chasm and above us.

Both statues released a deep, primal yell that roared through the cavern as they threw their spears at us. The massive stone weapons hurtled across the chasm and Rin seized me. He rolled us into the cave as one spear slammed into the side of the cave's mouth and the other hit the mouth's top.

With a boom, large chunks of stone broke free and dust thickened the air. A heavy stone hit my temple and the cave spun... or was that Rin still trying to roll us to safety.

For a second I was shrouded in darkness, my head pounding, and I couldn't remember where I was or why my body hurt, just that I was trapped, unable to move, and forgotten.

Help!

Then my eyelids fluttered open, yanking me back to consciousness and the cave. Both my healing magic and my new life force magic snapped to Rin, connecting with him and flooding me with his pain, even as my healing magic writhed inside me, wanting, but not wanting to heal him.

I knew instantly that the laceration on his side was deep, but his vampiric healing could take care of it. His chest wound, however, was too big for his vampiric healing, and he was losing too much blood too quickly.

Even with his better-than-most-supers healing capabilities, the injury was too severe for him to heal it without feeding. And he needed to do that now before he passed out.

I dragged my wavering gaze to him. He lay a few feet away from me, his expression tight with pain and his hands pressed over the hole in his chest. His eyes were wide, unfocused, and his hellfire flared then jerked back to pinpricks then flared again as if he were trying to control it and couldn't. His torso also heaved with breaths he didn't need to take, the shock of his injury making his body think it was still alive and needed air. Blood oozed between his fingers and pooled on the ground beneath him.

The panic that had seized me when he'd been thrown off the ledge surged.

Save him. Save him.

"Rin." I crawled to him and offered my wrist. "You need to feed."

His fangs started to extend, but with a groan, he pulled them back in, clenched his jaw, and squeezed his eyes shut.

"Rin, please." I pressed my wrist against his lips, praying instinct would kick in. "You have to feed." The need to save him squeezed in my chest. I could force my magic to connect with him, I'd managed to do it a few times in the past for other vampires even though their undead nature repulsed my power. But vampires were harder to heal than incubi or succubi and it was always better to just give them blood. And without a doubt, healing Rin's wound would drain me to unconsciousness and I still wouldn't be able to completely heal the injury. "I don't want to have to find something to cut my wrist. Feed before you pass out."

"I will," he gasped as flames flickered from beneath his lashes. "Just give me a second to focus. I don't want to take too much and make you weak."

"Just bite me." His life force was weakening, leaking out of him onto the ground. We were running out of time. "It's infinitely easier to heal myself from blood loss than it is to heal you."

His lids snapped open and his gaze captured me. He was filled with such pain — and not just physical pain. He was angry and wary, and, if everything with Deaglan had been a trap, his emotions were justified. Then he grabbed my hand and sank his fangs into my wrist.

The bite hurt, but my pulse still picked up in anticipation.

I'd only been bitten once by a vampire, by him, but I'd never forget the feeling of his sultry magic sliding into me. The sensation had been everything I'd heard about and more, and I now knew why people sought out vampires and begged them to feed on them.

Then he took a strong pull on my vein and that magic rushed into me, hot and needy, racing through my veins and instantly inflaming our bond's desire into a desperate screaming need.

Oh, God.

A long throaty moan escaped my lips and my breath turned ragged. Moisture pooled between my thighs and my whole body throbbed. I needed a release. Now. I needed to seal our bond. Now.

Rin's eyes widened with surprise, and I pressed my wrist harder against his mouth. He hadn't taken nearly enough blood to heal. He couldn't stop, and if my wrist was against his lips, my mouth couldn't be.

"Don't stop." My gaze leaped to his crotch. I'd have to twist to get my free hand to his lace-up fly but—

No.

No no no.

I wrenched my eyes back to his. "And don't let me have sex with you," I begged. "Please."

I didn't want to put my complete trust in him, just like he didn't want to trust me, but I wasn't going to have a choice. Even if Rin's sensual magic didn't get stronger while he fed — and I feared it would — I didn't know if I'd be able to control myself, not until he'd stopped feeding and his magic wore off.

His expression turned solemn. I didn't know if that meant he understood just how much trust I was putting into him or not, and with another strong pull, my thoughts scattered and I didn't care.

My core throbbed and every nerve turned hyper-sensitive. Everything twisted my need tighter: the air rushing in and out of my lungs with each rapid breath, every miniscule movement that brushed his wrap tunic against my skin, the rough stone beneath my bare legs, and his mouth. God, his mouth! The pull on my vein, the feel of his teeth in my flesh, his hand gripping my wrist. This was so much more than when he'd bitten me before. Of course, I'd been weak and had passed out before and I hadn't been soul-bound to him.

"Rin," I breathed. *Take me, satisfy me, please, God.*

I gritted my teeth and squeezed my eyes shut, fighting to stay where I was. I could withstand his magic. I had to. I didn't know if Faerie's Heart would be able to break our bond once we'd sealed it, but I was certain it would be easier to break if it wasn't sealed.

Rin took another long pull, twisting me tighter and sending me spinning.

Far away, in the back of my mind, I knew the spinning was because of blood loss. He was taking a lot, and he needed to. Once his magic healed his chest wound, he'd need more to regain his strength. And he had to regain his strength. He was the one who could fight. It would be better for him to be strong than me.

My healing magic fluttered inside me, and I fought it, too. I didn't want my body to work against Rin and close the punctures in my wrist. I just needed to hold on. Just a little longer.

Then Rin retracted his fangs, pressed his lips against my skin, and a whisper of the miniscule healing magic that all vampires had closed the wound in my wrist.

My healing magic surged and I released my hold on it. I didn't want to waste a lot of magic healing myself, but I was out of willpower and something had to give.

Except releasing my hold on my magic also released my hold on everything else, and before I fully realized what I was doing, I'd tangled my fingers in Rin's hair and I smashed my mouth against his.

He groaned and kissed me back with the same desperate ferocity, his lips and tongue tasting of blood, which made his magic inside me swell.

I shifted to straddle him, but he grabbed my wrists and drew back, putting me at arm's length.

"You don't want this," he murmured, his hellfire raging in his eyes, his breath as ragged as mine.

Of course I did—

No.

I didn't.

God. My need for Rin wasn't real. It was just fate being cruel and this heightened desperation for a release would pass. I just needed to wait for his magic to dissipate. Which I prayed was soon, because if it didn't or I didn't have sex, I was going to lose my mind.

AMIAH

Rin left to explore the cave to see how far back it went — or at least to see if it didn't stop before he ran out of light. And thankfully with his night vision, it meant he could put a good distance between us and give me a much-needed moment to pull myself together.

Which wasn't easy. My body still burned with my need for him. Thank God he didn't want our soul bond either and had managed to maintain some self-control. If he hadn't, I would have had sex with him on the hard ground while he lay in a pool of his blood.

I sucked in a deep breath that did nothing to ease my aching desire and shoved that thought as far down as I could. I needed to focus and heal myself. I was bleeding from the fight with the ice maid as well as from a cut on my temple when the mouth of the cave had collapsed, not to mention I was low on blood from Rin's feeding.

I drew in another breath, which didn't help, and pushed my healing magic into my body. It healed the lacerations first then slid into my circulatory system to help restore the blood Rin had taken.

I was mostly healed and not as weak as I feared I'd be from using my magic when he returned. But I was also still aching with need.

"It widens up ahead," he said, his soft voice sliding through me, drawing a shiver of desire.

God, even the constant thrum of his hot-cold, alive yet dead life force turned me on.

"It would be safer to follow this passage instead of digging our way back out to the cavern," he added.

Of course, going deeper into the mountain meant the possibility of reaching a dead end and having to come all the way back. But there was no guarantee the statues weren't making their way across the chasm instead of returning to their positions, or if they had returned, that they wouldn't reanimate the moment we stepped out of the cave.

If we were really lucky — which I wasn't going to hold my breath on — they'd believe we were dead and the Winter Queen would stop coming after us.

"Okay." I staggered to my feet, using the rough cave wall to keep my balance. I was still a little lightheaded and still throbbing with need.

Rin's eyes narrowed, his hellfire back to smoldering red pinpricks. "Do you need help?"

Being satisfied? God, yes!

I bit the inside of my cheek. *Not a good idea.* In fact being within arm's reach of him was probably a bad idea. "We should keep our distance until your magic leaves my system."

A spark of hellfire popped from his eye. "You commanded me not to have sex with you. I won't."

"I didn't command. I asked. And I believe that you won't." And not giving into our bond, only added proof to our bond's insistence that I could trust him. "But I don't want to make this harder on either of us, and if you touch me right now, I'm not sure I can control myself."

Which was frustrating and embarrassing, and while I now knew it was impossible to control everything, this was one of those things I had to stay in control of.

He gave me a tight nod and led the way deeper into the cave.

I followed, trying to focus on the rough, cold stone beneath my bare feet and the still-present chill of the Winter Court's magic inside me. But it wasn't enough to distract me. Every little movement turned me on, and I had to keep wrenching my attention from his naked back and how I wanted the rest of him naked.

As promised, the cave did open up, becoming wider and taller, although not by much. It certainly wasn't enough to ease the sense of being trapped that I felt with all this rock crowding around me, which only made it harder to ignore Rin's magic coursing through me.

We walked in silence for what felt like an eternity, with Rin keeping his distance, not even glancing back at me. If I hadn't been desperately trying to ignore my desire for him, that would have upset me. But as it was, I feared even just making eye contact with him would have been too much.

After a while, the passage narrowed, barely wide enough for us to get through sideways, and my pulse grew faster as the fear of being trapped swelled.

Rin turned sideways and shuffled inside.

I gritted my teeth, turned, and followed, determined to fight my fear. But the second I started moving, my fear vanished completely. Each sliding step through the narrow passage made the rough stone push Rin's tunic against my sensitive skin, twisting my desire achingly tight. I couldn't breathe without my desire swelling, couldn't think without thinking about sex with him, even trapped between all that stone.

I was going to lose my mind and we weren't going to be able to get the Heart in time. I needed him now. Had to have him. God, please.

He reached the end of the crevasse and skidded a few feet down a slope. I shuffled to the opening after him as warm air, filled with a fresh evergreen scent, washed over me.

My thoughts stuttered at the sight in front of me, and for a second I was unable to comprehend what I was looking at.

A grotto?

We'd reached a grotto.

It was similar to the grotto in the Winter Court with the healing pools. Moonlight shone through a large opening in the stone above us, shining down on a central pool, while a dozen small glowing orbs floated near two other pools on raised shelves on the left-hand side. I didn't know where the water for those pools came from, but it trickled over and around the rocks and tree roots into the pool below, sending gentle ripples lapping against its edges.

Like the healing grotto, parts of the ground had been smoothed, creating a path around the pools, while the rest of the stone had been left rough. There were also evergreen bushes and narrow trees, although these were mostly around the cave's edges and didn't offer as much privacy for those in the pools like the foliage in the healing grotto in the Winter Court had.

Rin turned to me and held out his hands to help me down the slope.

All thoughts of the grotto vanished, and my breath hitched. There was just him and my need and—

Come on. Get a hold of yourself.

Except to do that, I couldn't get close... or look in his eyes... or, hell, just look at him.

I avoided his gaze and ignored his hands and carefully slid down the slope, determined to keep some distance between us.

Out of the corner of my eye, I watched a spark of hellfire pop from his eye, and he dropped his hand.

"I just need a moment." I'd be okay. I just needed to resist until the sensation passed.

And it would pass. Please.

My gaze landed on the central pool and the soft steam curling from its surface. A moment to gather myself and regain my bearings wouldn't hurt either. We hadn't stopped running since we'd been yanked back into the Winter Court.

And while I knew we weren't completely safe, there was no sign that anyone was following us at the moment. This might be our only chance to catch our breaths.

I wasn't sure how I felt about taking off Rin's tunic so I could properly bathe with my desire still screaming through me, but I could at least sit and put my legs in the warm water and try to regain my bearings.

Except if I said I wanted to take a bath, that might ensure he'd keep his distance from me and give me the space I needed.

I glanced down at the blood on my arms where Rin had held me with his blood-covered hands when he'd fed. "I'd like to take a moment to clean up."

"Do you need help?"

Yes, God, yes!

"No." Although the most private pool was up a set of uneven stairs that didn't have a railing—

No. If I leaned against the wall as I climbed, I'd be fine.

"I'll be okay." I tried to give him a pointed look to make him notice the blood on his torso.

But that was a serious mistake and I ended up raking my gaze over his sculpted chest, sending more desire rushing through me and bringing me to the edge of a climax again without actually taking me over and giving me a release.

"You should probably clean up as well," I choked out as I wrenched my attention from him and headed to the stairs.

Don't look. Just don't look.

God. I'd just decided looking was a bad idea and then I'd looked.

What was wrong with me?

Clinging to the rough stone wall to keep my balance, I carefully climbed the steps and shuffled behind an outcropping that hid me from Rin. I didn't know if Rin was going to take my advice... or if he'd strip down too—

God, I hoped he did.

No!

No, I didn't.

Jeez. And it didn't matter if he did or not. What I was feeling wasn't real. It was our bond and his magic, and I just needed to relax and let it pass.

I untied his sash and shrugged out of his wrap tunic, ignoring the slide of fabric against my too-sensitive skin.

It would pass. I didn't know why it hadn't passed already. Surely enough time had gone by... although he had needed to feed deeply. That increased the duration a vampire's magic remained in the donor's system.

I eased into the water, submerging myself all the way up to my chin. The water was ever-so-slightly too warm, but I didn't care. I needed the heat, needed its relaxing warmth to seep into my muscles. Needed to use that to relax and release my throbbing desire.

I rubbed away the blood on my arms.

My desire throbbed with my pulse... which was getting faster.

I swept my hands up my arms to my neck.

I'd had a shower after having sex with Titus, but I hadn't had a chance to clean up after having sex with Sebastian and Hawk.

I trailed my fingers to my breasts. The memory of them inside me, the pressure and pleasure and connection flooded me, and the ache in my core grew stronger.

Maybe if I gave myself an orgasm, Rin's magic would dissipate faster.

I slid a hand between my legs and brushed my clit. I was already so close that sensation instantly shot through me, bringing me to the edge again.

I swallowed my moan, not wanting Rin to hear.

It shouldn't take much to push me over and then everything would be fine. Or as fine as it was going to get with my soul bound to Rin and my heart bound to my guys.

I teased my finger over my clit again, focusing on my need and letting it sweep through me with the powerful release that was promised within it.

But I couldn't get my body to let go. My breath grew faster and my need turned desperate as Rin's magic just kept growing. I yearned for him to push inside me and join our bodies like our souls were joined. I burned for him and that just made my need burn hotter—

I bit back another moan, every nerve in my body twisted tight. It was like he was still feeding, his magic rushing through my veins, growing stronger and stronger, promising a glorious climax that wasn't God damned coming.

Which didn't make sense. His magic should be fading. The only time a vampire's magic remained was if the blood donor was bite-locked—

Crap.

Was I bite-locked?

I couldn't be bite-locked. Rin would have needed to claim me by wrapping his essence into mine and I was sure I would have felt that—

Okay, given the desperate need coming from our bond when he'd fed, maybe I wouldn't have felt it, but he'd still have needed to place his hand over my heart to gain entrance to my essence... unless his sin eater ability gave him access to my essence without that physical contact.

Except I couldn't be bite-locked. I just couldn't, and I couldn't make my mind work past that denial. A bite-lock happened when a vampire had a strong claim on a super, or an extremely strong claim on a human. It was considered an added bonus since a vampire's feeding usually involved sex as well as blood, and the bite-lock allowed the vampire's magic to continue to grow until it was released with a powerful orgasm.

My pulse stalled altogether.

An orgasm brought on only with the help of someone else.

Oh, God.

If I was bite-locked, it didn't matter how much I rubbed myself, I wasn't going to be able to release Rin's magic. And I had to be bite-locked. There wasn't any other explanation for why I couldn't make myself come. I knew what worked for me, had spent many years more or less satisfying myself while I'd been foolishly waiting for my soul mate — and after sex with Hawk I now knew how less my satisfaction had actually been.

My breath turned ragged and I bit back another moan.

I couldn't believe Rin would do that to me, couldn't believe he'd claim me without my consent.

I heaved my attention inward to see how strong the claim was. Once his essence was out of my system, the bite-lock would go away. It wouldn't help me right now, but it would tell me how long I needed to be careful around him.

Except I couldn't find his essence inside me. I could feel his life force, strong and sure thrumming against my senses and pulsing in our brand, but his essence wasn't woven into mine. Which meant I shouldn't have been bite-locked.

Unless...

My stomach bottomed out with horrific realization. I only knew of one other angel, or rather archnephilim, who was bite-locked. I'd assumed it was because her vampire mate had claimed her before he'd known she was really a super. But what if it wasn't because she was a super? What if it was because they were branded mates?

Rin's magic surged, and my moan escaped before I could think to hold it back.

This was a serious problem. Rin's magic was going to just keep building inside me until I lost my mind and my heart stopped. And because it was magic, my healing magic couldn't get rid of it.

I climbed out of the pool and pulled on Rin's tunic even though I was still wet. I didn't have a towel and I couldn't wait until I'd dried off. As much as I really wanted to wait until we'd met up with the others, there was no guarantee we'd meet up with them anytime soon. I wasn't going to last — I wasn't sure I was even going to be able to get back down the stairs — and I had no other options. I had to ask Rin for help.

I staggered to the stairs, my body trembling, desperate for a release that wasn't coming. "I think we have a problem," I gasped.

Rin's gaze jumped to me and my core throbbed. He knelt in front of the pool, his pants still on, with water dripping down his now blood-free chest. Relief and disappointment churned in my gut over the fact that he was still clothed, while the rest of me zeroed in on the water trailing over his beautifully sculpted muscles.

And now all I could think about was licking that water off him.

I sucked in a ragged breath and stepped down the first few steps, but my need made my legs weak, and I stumbled down the next two.

Rin's eyes widened in surprise and he rushed to the stairs and caught me.

I half landed in his arms, our chests colliding, the impact sending a shock of climax racing through me before it vanished, leaving me even more desperate.

"Your highness." He wrapped an arm around my back and held me close, steadying me. Except that only made my need throb stronger.

"I told you, I'm not a princess," I moaned. "And we've got a serious problem."

CASSIUS

I HELD ONTO THE OUTSIDE OF THE SPINDLY STONE RAILING IN FRONT OF THE wall-to-wall, floor-to-ceiling opening in the sitting area in our original suite in Titus's ancestral home. My fire rolled off me and my wings like lava and fell, bright against the night's darkness, into the Wilds far below, but I didn't bother trying to control it. That would just wear me out for when we found Amiah and I really did need to control it.

We'd been on the patio in Voth's hotel and a portal had formed and sucked us into Faerie before I could point out that none of us had boots and Hawk didn't have a shirt.

The portal had spat us out of its shimmering air into the middle of the Wilds without the aerie's mountain or any of the courts' protective domes in sight. There was just desolate nothing as far as I could see in either direction, and even when I pushed my wings through my ridiculous Hawaiian shirt and taken to the air — once we'd convinced Titus going to the aerie was our only option — there'd still been nothing in sight... at least not until Titus had tossed his clothes to Hawk, shifted, and flew up to join me. Then the aerie's mountain appeared a couple hundred feet away as if it had always been there, which Bane had taken to mean that *that* was where we needed to go — much to Titus's frustration.

Everyone else — including a short squat man who'd been standing on the other side of the portal when we'd come through — had climbed onto Titus's back. Bane had introduced him as Karthick and we'd flown to the aerie. Titus took us directly to the suite where we'd recovered from the horrific events in the Winter Court, where Amiah had cuddled with Hawk, desperate to use his body heat to warm the Winter Court's chill inside her, and where she'd yelled at me that they were having sex.

I'd been so mad and so certain that she hadn't realized what she'd been doing and that she hadn't been thinking straight. Because the Amiah I knew, the woman who'd fought with everything she had to stay in control, would never have succumbed to an incubus's charms... or Sebastian Bane's charms for that matter.

Except she hadn't succumbed to anyone's charms. She'd said she needed them, needed us. All of us.

And I couldn't deny that.

I needed her too.

I blasted a ball of fire at the ground, desperate to relieve the pressure, but just like letting it loose, pushing out more magic still did nothing to release the power roaring through me, threatening to explode into a firestorm that would burn me up.

But that wasn't going to happen until this mess with Faerie's Heart was over... if there was anything left of me.

My fire already raged through me and I'd already decided I would become the Salamander again to protect her. I'd become more than the Salamander if I had to. Whatever I had to do to protect her. I wouldn't fail her like I'd failed Dominic. We just needed to get her back first.

The thought made my fire burn hotter.

I didn't know how I should have protected her from the Winter Court, but I should have. I should have foreseen that it would take her. I'd known before Deaglan had almost killed me that the court was also a threat. I should have been thinking about that along with everything else and come up with a plan the moment I'd woken in Voth's hotel.

But I hadn't been able to think past the need to keep her safe or the fact that the mating brand she hadn't wanted, had thought she'd gotten rid of, had manifested and bonded her with Deaglan's demon-vampire hybrid.

I still couldn't make my mind work past the fact that he was her soul mate.

It wasn't right.

If it couldn't have been me, it should have been Titus. His dragon had claimed her as his mate. Or even Bane or Hawk. They cared for her. They connected with her during sex just like I did.

And God, I didn't want her to find out if she connected with Rin.

Which was selfish. If she wanted to have sex with him, she could. It wasn't my place to say she couldn't, something she'd made perfectly clear in this very room. But I feared the angelic mating brand would force her to have sex with Rin and that wasn't something I could protect her from... unless we got Faerie's Heart and broke her bond.

I gritted my teeth and focused on the others. Titus glowered at Bane, smoke pouring from his human nostrils. He'd put his shorts back on but hadn't bothered with his shirt, while Bane, who'd barely managed to get dressed before the portal opened, sat on one of the many cushions in the room looking anything but at ease.

"You were supposed to contact me when the Winter Court's call grew too strong," Karthick said.

"And your spell to block its power should have lasted more than two days." Bane ran a hand over his spikey white and silver hair.

His full-body fae glow radiated from his pale skin, brighter than I'd seen it since we'd last been in Faerie. Having sex with Amiah — and given that Hawk hadn't come down right away, Hawk too — had worked. She'd managed to transfer enough fae magic into him to help him out and he no longer looked like he was dying.

Of course, if what I'd been told was true, the moment he cast anything, his demonic infection would grow again. And as much as I wanted him to use his newly regained strength to help me control my fire, protecting Amiah came first. He needed to save everything he had for her.

"I know you said her concealment charm is still working," I said to Bane, "but are you sure you can't use magic to find her?" He was a sorcerer, able to weave magic into almost anything he wanted so long as he had the willpower to control it.

"I'm sure." Bane jerked his thumb at Karthick. "Even Karthick wouldn't be able to find her."

Which created a serious problem. Being unable to pinpoint her location meant we'd have to physically search for her, which meant a greater chance one or all of us could be captured. And while I was sure all of us would be willing to make that sacrifice for her, I doubted she'd agree.

Titus huffed, sending a blast of smoke billowing around his head. "We know she's in the Winter Court. We're wasting time."

"Unless Rin has already taken her to Deaglan," Hawk said, staring at the cushion beside Bane and shifting from one foot to the other as if he couldn't stand the thought of sitting.

He looked just as desperate as Titus, but also a little stunned, and I didn't like the idea of him coming along on a rescue mission if he wasn't completely focused. It didn't matter that Hawk, because he was an incubus, couldn't return Amiah's affection. She loved him. And if I let him come along in his current state and he got hurt, Amiah would be crushed.

"Rin would have to get out of the Winter Court first," Bane said. "We have time to figure something out before he can reach the Shadow King."

"Only if Deaglan wasn't the one who created the portal," Hawk said. "You said the Winter Court couldn't make one. Well someone had to have made one to have dragged her into Faerie."

"The court can make a portal if it's determined enough," Karthick said, adjusting the thick leather bandolier slung across his dark green shirt and then sitting on the cushion beside Bane. "I just haven't seen one make a portal in a long time. It has to really want something or the monarch's will has to be incredibly powerful."

Titus snarled and more smoke poured from his nostrils. "So she might not even be in the Winter Court?"

"No, the portal took her there," Bane said. "I felt its power."

"But we're not just storming into the court," I said before Titus could shift and fly away. "We need to be smart about how we get her. Hell, in the very least we all need boots." As much as my soul cried to go to her and protect her, I wasn't an idiot. Right now I was a walking weapon — and almost as much a danger to the guys as our enemies — and Titus was also a walking weapon, but Bane had limited power and Hawk had nothing.

"I'm not going to sit here while our mate is in danger," Titus growled.

"She's not helpless and Rin is with her." And I could only pray I was right that their bond was strong enough and it had compelled him to jump in the portal with her to protect her.

It had to be.

An angelic mating brand might not be the beautiful sacred thing all angels had been told it was, but it still compelled the bonded mates to protect each other. Amiah had said Essie had been on the floor desperate when my brother, Gideon, had been seriously injured. If Rin was even dealing with a fraction of that compulsion, Amiah was safe... or at least safe from him.

Which meant we didn't need to run headlong into danger. We had time to figure something out.

Red-gold scales swept up Titus's neck to his jaw and his canines partially extended. "I'm not going to bet her life on him keeping her safe."

My fire flared in response and I forced it behind me instead of blasting it into the living room. "And I'm not letting you get yourself killed because you can't think straight."

Titus heaved toward me and Hawk leaped in between us.

"We're talking in circles!" Hawk snapped. "Cassius is right we need a plan." Titus growled and Hawk glared at him. "And you're right, too. We need a plan *now*. We can't track Amiah because of the concealment charm, but Rin doesn't have anything hiding him."

"If the angelic mating brand is compelling him to protect her, then they're together," Bane said. His gaze slid to Karthick. "We have nothing of Rin's for a proper tracking spell, but I doubt there are any other demon-vampire hybrids in Faerie. Will the realm tell you where he is?"

The short man grimaced and the muscles in his jaw flexed.

"I wouldn't ask if it wasn't important," Bane said. "Right now you're the only one who can make the connection. I wouldn't survive channeling the power needed to ask. I barely survived summoning you."

"I know." Karthick's expression grew darker. "And I know getting her back isn't just because of how you feel about her. She has a key to releasing Faerie's Heart and Deaglan can't be allowed to get it. But if I do this, I won't be able to help you fight him. Faerie won't willingly let me go."

"Maybe it will," Bane said, but he didn't sound confident.

"You know it won't. But I've been avoiding it for over seven hundred years. It's going to hold me again soon," Karthick said. "It might as well be on my terms."

The idea of this man being held by Faerie to find Amiah made my stomach roil. She wouldn't want anyone to sacrifice anything for her. But the rest of me didn't care so long as she was safe.

Which was shocking... and not at all surprising.

I was done being the angel who followed the rules and maintained law and order. I'd stopped being that angel the moment I learned Amiah was leashed to Titus and had started my journey back to becoming the Salamander. I just needed to hold myself together until we faced Deaglan. Then I could embrace who I'd always been—*what* I'd always been, a primal fire fed by primal emotion trapped in an angel's body.

TITUS

My beast heaved inside me, furious that my mate had been taken, that she was in danger, and that Cassius was right. We didn't know where she was and we couldn't just storm into the Winter Court to get her.

I snarled and my claws extended from my fingertips. I had to do something. The others might believe that Rin wouldn't hurt her, but every time I closed my eyes, I still saw his sword in her chest, her eyes wide with shock and horror and pain. It didn't matter that their soul bond might be getting stronger and compelling him to protect her. There was still a chance that he'd hurt her or, worse, take her to Deaglan.

Karthick, the squat, bulky Summer Court sorcerer stood and readjusted his bandolier.

"Let's get this over with. I'll need someplace green." His gaze jumped past me to look out the window. "I can't do it in the Wilds. We'll have to risk going to the Summer Court."

Which would waste even more time.

Seireadan turned to me, and from the look on his face he was going to ask me to stay in the aerie and not risk being captured while they went to the Summer Court.

Which was smart and completely unacceptable.

"No," I snarled at him before he'd even said anything. I wasn't hanging back and hiding. I'd never hung back and hidden, and I wasn't going to start now, not with my soul's mate in danger.

"There's a small forest, a meadow, and a lake in the center of the aerie." I glared at Karthick, my fire burning hotter in my throat, sending smoke curling from my nostrils. "That green enough for you?"

"And better than returning to the Summer Court," Karthick replied in his low, gravelly voice. "Lead the way."

I stormed to the hall leading out of the suite without waiting for the others. They'd follow. She was their mate, too, and even though they were managing to appear calm and think rationally, I could still smell their fear.

"I'll meet you there," Cassius said, making me stop and jerk back to face him.

"We're not waiting for you," I growled.

"I wouldn't want you to. But if we don't want to draw attention when we sneak into the Winter Court or wherever we're going to end up, then I should change into something less... loud." He glanced at his bright, gaudy clothes. "And everyone needs boots."

My beast huffed at him. "Fine." Out of everyone, he had wings and wouldn't need my help to get down to us or waste time trying to find the stairs, so I could stay with Karthick and find out where Amiah was. "But make it fast. The second we know where she is—"

"You don't need to tell me," he said as he pushed off from the railing, caught the wind with his wings, and soared down three levels to the storeroom where the human clothes were kept.

"How long will this take?" Hawk asked, drawing my attention.

My beast started to snarl at him, and I yanked it back under control and continued down the hall to the landing in the center of the aerie. Beating the shit out of him for not protecting our mate wouldn't accomplish anything. It wouldn't even make me feel better because I knew it would upset Amiah.

And really, Hawk looked just as angry and lost as I felt, as well as slightly stunned. He had a hint of that glazed look that he'd had when the Winter Queen had flooded the court with magic to make Seireadan and Amiah have sex which had caused him to overdose on sexual energy. He'd probably been close to full or at full after he'd watched me and Amiah have sex. Joining Amiah while she had sex with Seireadan to give him a transfusion of sexual energy had to have been a little too much for him.

If I was going to be angry at anyone, it was Seireadan. He was a sorcerer. He could have cast something to prevent Amiah from getting sucked into the portal.

Except Karthick had said that the Winter Court could create a portal if it was determined enough, something I hadn't thought possible. I wasn't sure if there was anyone, other than the court's monarch, capable of stopping a court when it was determined. Which meant I couldn't be mad at Seireadan, either.

We stepped onto the landing at the end of the hall and my beast jerked inside me, sending more scales rippling over my chest and slamming my fist into the side of the mountain.

A chunk of stone cracked off, bounced off a landing two levels down, ricocheted off a thick tree branch, and clattered into the jagged rocks below, while a sudden breeze swept down through the large hole in the top of the mountain. It rustled the leaves of the small forest on the cavern floor, made the long grasses in the meadow wave, and sent rippling waves through the usually calm lake on the far side.

I should have protected her.

But that meant I should have been there, watching her have sex with Seireadan and Hawk, and I wasn't sure if I'd have been able to just sit there and let that happen. Sure, it hadn't bothered me when Hawk had watched me satisfy her. But I'd been the one pleasing her, using my cock to bring her satisfaction. Would my beast— hell, would any part of me be able to sit back and watch any of the others do that? Would I be able to watch while she lit up with her release and gasped their names?

Fuck.

I punched the side of the mountain again, sending more pieces of stone tumbling to the ground far below.

With a snarl, I pulled off my shorts, tossed them to Hawk, and shifted before my beast completely took over and I punched one of the others instead of just the mountain. They climbed onto my back and I soared over the forest and landed in the meadow.

Karthick waded through the long grasses that came up almost to his chin to the edge of the forest and stopped at the base of a large old tree. Its thick, gnarled branches twisted around each other and stretched wide, creating a canopy that would protect him from the elements while Faerie held him.

The last time we'd seen Karthick, he'd mentioned that Faerie wouldn't let him leave. And now he was certain Faerie would deepen its connection with him, merging him with the realm for who-knew-how-long just for asking it where Rin was. That was something the realm did to monarchs who didn't have heirs.

Except Karthick wasn't high fae, and all the courts had monarchs. Which meant there had to be another reason the realm wanted him. He'd said the realm had been after him and he'd been avoiding it for over seven hundred years.

"You sure about this?" Hawk asked, as Karthick flicked his fingers and used magic to flatten the grass around the trunk.

My beast wrenched my attention to Hawk and growled. I bared my teeth at him, my dragon-form's canines as long as his forearms, and let fire lick over my tongue. It didn't care who it sacrificed to get our mate back, even though it knew Amiah would have asked the same question.

We get her back. Whatever the cost, it snarled in everyone's head.

"Hey," Hawk raised his hands — still holding my shorts — and retreated a good dozen feet away from me. "We all know Amiah is going to beat herself up knowing we let Faerie imprison him to help her."

"There's more at stake than just finding her," Karthick said, as he settled his squat body between two large gnarled roots. "Deaglan can't be allowed to get the Heart, which means he can't be allowed to get to her and her key. If I have to go into forced hibernation for a couple hundred years then that's a price I'm willing to pay. It's not like I'll be suffering or anything. I'll just be asleep for an indeterminate amount of time."

"Agreed," Seireadan said. "She won't like it, but she'll understand it."

I huffed my agreement, sending a cloud of smoke billowing from my nostrils, and shifted back to my human form. Hawk tossed me my shorts, and I put them back on as the others gathered around Karthick.

He took off his bandolier and handed it to Seireadan. "Keep it safe for me."

"I will," Seireadan replied. "I'll leave it in the suite's sitting room so you know where to find it." His expression turned grim, but he didn't say what we were all thinking. That he couldn't keep Karthick's bandolier with him because there was a chance we'd get caught trying to rescue Amiah or that we'd lose our battle with Deaglan.

"There's a set of stairs over there that you can take to get you back up to the suite," Hawk added.

"Thank you." Karthick turned his attention back to Seireadan. "You'll need to make the connection with me, so you can get the hybrid's location. If *I* make the connection, I might not be able to release you and you'll end up trapped as well."

Light flared in the tattoo around Seireadan's neck as he sat at Karthick's feet just inside the circle of flatten grass, and the Summer Court sorcerer raised his eyebrows at him.

Seireadan glared back at him. "I'm not wasting more magic than I have to by weaving this spell from scratch. Especially if we have to fight my mother or Deaglan to get Amiah back."

"Not what I was going to comment on," the Summer Court sorcerer said, his expression turning grim.

"We're not going to talk about *that*, either," Seireadan replied. "The only person in Faerie who can do anything about it might be the hybrid—"

"And we're not sure we trust him," Hawk added, figuring out about the same time that I did that Seireadan and Karthick were talking about his demonic magic infection.

And all of this talk was wasting time. For all we knew Amiah was being held prisoner in Deaglan's court right now, reliving her worst nightmare, something I'd promised myself, I'd never let happen again.

"Get on with it," I growled.

"Right." Seireadan ran a hand over his spiky white and silver hair. "Whenever you're ready."

The Summer Court sorcerer drew in a heavy breath and closed his eyes. A hint of the high fae full-body glow flickered in his hands and face, which was odd because he wasn't high fae and he shouldn't be glowing. As I watched, the glow grew brighter, rolling up his bare forearms and radiating through his dark green shirt. Then the glow seeped into the ground around him, undulating out from his body and also up along the tree's thick roots toward the trunk.

Seireadan rolled his shoulders, sending his own glow rippling down his body, and closed his eyes as well. Hawk squinted, trying to keep watching even though he was trying to see past their brilliant body glow along with the light that only he could see with his magical sensitivity from the magic they were channeling.

The wind gusted through the hole in the mountaintop again, this time stronger than before. The grass whipped around my and Hawk's legs and against Seireadan's back and made the tree branches sway above Karthick, fluttering the leaves. The light swelled up the trunk and flickered in the branches and then the leaves. Sparks of light flashed around us, like a spinning crystal catching the sunlight, forcing me to squint as well.

Karthick's breath picked up and sweat beaded on his forehead. He clutched the roots on either side of him, the thick muscles in his forearms tensing and his biceps bulging, straining against his shirt.

"Please," he ground out through clenched teeth.

The gust turned into a gale, wrenching on the tree branches, sending a flurry of leaves into the air, and flattening the grass around us. Hawk staggered to the side before catching his balance and turning to lean into the storm, and Seireadan bent forward and pressed his palms against the ground to steady himself.

I widened my stance a little and released some of my dragon's weight into my human form, making me too heavy to blow away, so I could stay put and not have to look away.

"You know I will," Karthick gasped. Tears formed in his eyes and the wind whipped them away. "I always will."

The wind vanished suddenly, sending Hawk staggering forward, and the light swept out of the leaves, down the trunk, and into the ground. It then pushed out of the dirt around Karthick as glowing, white vines. The vines swarmed around his legs, arms, and chest, and climbed up his neck.

The Summer Court sorcerer groaned as the vines partially covered his face and threads of white magic that pulsed like a heartbeat wove through what little skin remained visible under the vines.

"Did we get the hybrid's location?" Cassius asked, landing beside me, with an armful of boots that he tossed into the grass in front of him.

Thankfully he'd pulled in his magic so he wouldn't set the meadow on fire, but it was clear from the tension in his body and the sudden gusts of smoke billowing around him that he was struggling to hold it back.

"Not yet," Seireadan said, his body still bowed forward and his eyes squeezed shut. "Rin is under the Winter Court's main mountain and there are two ways he can get out. We need to wait until we know which way that will be."

We had to wait?

My beast heaved inside me. It didn't want to wait. It couldn't wait. Amiah was in danger and I couldn't just stand there.

"We should just go," I growled.

"If we pick the wrong exit, we might never be able to find her," Seireadan replied. "I won't be able to reconnect with Karthick again. This is the only chance we've got."

"And we still don't know if Amiah is with him," Hawk said.

Fire rippled over Cassius's arms and he sucked it back into his body before it fell into the long grass. "She'll be with him."

Except the question was, would he be with her because he was protecting her or because he was trying to take her to Deaglan?

AMIAH

I leaned into Rin's embrace, my body desperate for a release only he could give me, begging me to unlace his pants and have him push inside me. I needed him. I was going to shatter without him.

God. I'd thought my brand making me desire him was bad enough.

"I'm bite-locked," I said, my voice breathy.

My hands slid up his sculpted chest, his flesh wet from having cleaned himself off, and his hellfire burst into miniature flames.

"I didn't claim you," he whispered. "I swear."

My gaze dipped to his waist, and I traced my fingers along the delicate golden swirls curling out of his pants, up to his ribs, and around his back that were a match to mine. "But I claimed you."

A spark popped from his eye. Its heat teased my cheek, sending another swell of desire straight to my core, drawing a desperate moan, which made him tense, his body trembling against mine.

"Did you know?" he asked.

"That my brand would bite-lock me?"

Another spark popped from his eye, and I couldn't tell if he was trying to accuse me of putting us in this situation or genuinely asking if I didn't know.

"I didn't, but even if I did, we didn't have much choice. You were dying, and my healing magic wasn't going to be enough. You needed to feed."

"Because if I die, you die."

"Because I had the ability to save you." Even if our souls hadn't been bound together, I still would have given him my blood. "You didn't deserve to be Deaglan's slave and I need you to get back to my guys."

I need you in me, satisfying me. Please.

I squeezed my eyes shut and clung to him. I didn't have to have intercourse with him, not like what our bond wanted. I just needed him to give me an orgasm.

"Okay," he murmured, his grip on me tightening. "How would you like me to release you?"

Any way. Every way.

"Whatever you're most comfortable with as long as we don't seal our soul bond."

"Understood."

He grabbed my hips and sat me on the edge of a step on the staircase behind me, his expression flat, his hellfire pinpricks like always as if he weren't just about to make me come.

God, this is so awkward.

And there wasn't anything I could do about it.

I spread my legs so he could step close, and his hellfire grew into flames again, flickering in a mesmerizing dance, making his magic inside me burn hotter.

"If you need any more blood," I said, my voice husky, my body trembling, "this would be the time to take it."

I didn't want to put either of us through this again, but I also didn't want him weak. If the brand made Rin feel like I had even before his magic had made my desire go crazy, asking him to give me an orgasm without having one himself was cruel. Donating more blood now meant we'd only have to do this once.

"Thank you." He cupped the back of my head and dipped in.

My pulse pounded, and my breath became sharp, desperate pants.

His lips brushed my neck, sending a taunting whisper of an orgasm through me, and then his teeth sank into my skin with a flash of pain and a wild rush of need.

Oh, God. Oh, yes.

I tipped my head to the side, giving him full access to my neck, and tangled my fingers in his long black hair.

He took a bone-melting pull that sent me spinning, and my panting grew heavier, making my breasts heave against his tunic, my nipples aching for his touch. But he slid his free hand under the hem of his tunic and up my inner thigh instead, his fingers drawing closer and closer to where I desperately wanted him.

Another hard pull on my vein and another whisper of a climax that wasn't going to fully manifest until Rin released me twisted in my core.

The thought was terrifying. I was helpless. If Rin changed his mind, he could leave me hanging, letting his magic build until I went crazy or died. It was already twisted painfully tight in my whole body. Much more and I'd be in agony.

Please let our bond be right about him. Please let me be able to trust him.

Then, with a soft moan that feathered his breath against my inflamed skin, he teased his fingers through my slick folds and all thought and fear vanished.

Every nerve within me ignited and my need roared through my veins, through the Winter Court's chill, and burned into every cell. I was overflowing with sensation that I couldn't contain. It filled me with a radiant golden power, the magic that bound our souls together, and the glorious thrum of Rin's strange life force.

He slid a slickened fingertip to my clit and with barely a touch because I was already teetering on the edge, my orgasm tore free.

Every muscle in my body contracted painfully tight, and I released a cry half in pain and half in pleasure, and clung to Rin's head. His magic crashed through me, momentarily stealing all breath and thought. My unnatural full-body fae glow blazed around us while both of our brands burst into brilliant golden light at the same time.

Our bond, while still not sealed, had just gotten stronger, and my soul sang with certainty. Rin was my fate. He was the one I was supposed to be with.

Except the rest of me cried for the others and fate could be damned.

I wasn't going to let it make me fall out of love with them and I wasn't going to trap Rin in a soul bond he didn't want.

There had to be a way for all of us to get our happily ever after, and I was going to do everything in my power to get that. We just needed Faerie's Heart and we all needed to survive.

He waited, as I clutched his head, keeping his mouth pressed against my neck, until his magic weakened enough that my painfully contracted muscles started to relax.

With a groan, he pulled his fangs from my throat, healed the wound with the whisper of his healing magic, and held me as my body shuddered with more tremors as his magic slowly left me.

God, having his arms around me felt so right, even though my mind was screaming it was wrong. Even still in pain, my body craved more, craved to give him the release he probably ached for but hadn't been given.

Then he tensed as if he realized what he was doing and eased out of my embrace, leaving me cold and aching and frustrated, both emotionally and still a little sexually.

"I'll see if there's a way out," he murmured without looking at me and he marched to the other side of the grotto.

Hugging myself to keep myself where I was, I wrenched my gaze to the craggy ceiling to stop from looking at his bare back and tight glutes wrapped in black leather. Except I'd gotten a good enough look when he'd been walking in front of me that the image easily jumped into my mind's eye.

God, I wanted to call him back even though he'd just given me an orgasm.

I sucked in a steadying breath.

I could resist him. I just needed to hold out just a little longer. Just until we got the Heart.

Except I had no idea when the final key would become empowered. It could be in a few seconds, a few days, or a few months. And even after that, we still needed to get the other two keys from Deaglan then do whatever it was we were supposed to do to unlock the Heart.

The thought made my pulse leap. There were still too many things left to do, too much potential waiting, and too many opportunities for something to go wrong.

Sure, I could last a few more days, maybe even a few more weeks if I managed to keep myself away from Rin. But months? And then what about facing off with Deaglan? The last time we'd done that, Cassius had almost died.

A chill raced through me and I was suddenly aware of the Winter Court's cold. It wasn't nearly as strong as it had been when the court had first yanked me into Faerie, but it wasn't gone, either. I just hadn't been noticing it with Rin's magic screaming through my body.

"I found a way out of the grotto," Rin said, his soft voice making my pulse skip a beat and jerking my attention to him.

He stood about ten feet away as if he didn't want to go near me, but his hellfire had returned to their usual smoldering pinpricks and his expression was flat as if he didn't have the same aching need as I did and hadn't been affected in any way by releasing me from the bite-lock.

"Can you stand?"

I slid off the step, holding onto it just in case my knees gave out. Even after experiencing Hawk's magic, I'd never felt anything like the build up of Rin's magic or its release.

Thankfully, I managed to stay standing, and while I still trembled a little bit, I walked with confidence across the uneven ground to his side.

We left the grotto in an awkward silence, following a narrow, rough-hewn passage, the glow from my skin once again lighting our way.

I wasn't sure how long we walked. With the silence and the long passage, it could have been an eternity or just an hour.

Given that my glow hadn't faded, it was probably only an hour or so, but God, it felt like an eternity.

I had no idea what to say to Rin. I could ask him about where he was from or what he was going to do once free, but he hadn't looked at me since I'd proven I could walk without assistance and I wasn't sure if he'd even answer my questions... or if he'd see the questions as an interrogation that he was required to answer.

And really. We didn't need to become friends. A part of me hoped he'd help us get the Heart since we'd need all the help we could get to get Deaglan's keys away from him, but I'd made it clear he wasn't obligated to help. Even if he did, once he was free, he'd want to get on with his life and I doubted I ever see him again. There was no point trying to force a conversation on him if he didn't want to talk.

I released a heavy breath that misted around my head from the cold air surrounding me and surprisingly not from the frozen air *inside* me.

My pulse picked up. That hadn't happened our entire time in court. Did that mean we were getting close to the outside?

I peered into the darkness ahead of me and caught a faint flicker of light up ahead. Except I wasn't sure if there'd be light outside, which meant we could be approaching another chasm with statues that would attack us, and I shouldn't get my hopes up of finally escaping from beneath all this rock.

But the light didn't brighten into the white glow of the fae orbs that had illuminated the chasm. The pinprick kept getting bigger and bigger until it was the size of the passage, and I realized that I was looking at the shimmering opalescent barrier outside that protected the Winter Court from the Wilds.

Oh, thank God.

I hurried past Rin to the end of the passage and turned my gaze skyward.

A vast expanse of opalescent barrier bright enough to block out starlight but not moonlight stretched out before me. I knew if I looked up and back I'd see the mountain towering over me, so the expanse of sky wasn't as vast as I wanted it to be, but still, it was enough for the pressure in my chest to release.

I breathed out another heavy breath, sending more mist rushing around me, and another.

Free. Thank God, I was free... sort of.

I shoved that thought aside.

One problem at a time, and the first had been to get out of the mountain. Next was to get out of the Winter Court.

I pulled my gaze down from the sky to the rocky, uneven, snow-covered slope that lay between the passage's mouth and the barrier. Not much more than the length of a football field stood between us and the court's boundary. We were almost there.

Rin stepped out of the passage into the snow and sunk halfway up to his calves

Swell.

I had no shoes and no pants.

This was going to be cold and even though I could heal any frostbite I might end up with, I still needed to walk through that first.

Hopefully once we got into the Wilds, I could take a minute to heal myself. With luck, we'd eluded the Winter Queen and Padraigin and they wouldn't be able to find me until they'd recast the spell that tracked my connection to the Winter Court.

And I was going to pray that the Winter Queen was on the same kind of schedule as before, and I still had at least a day before she finished the spell and found me.

I drew in a steadying breath, ready to brave the snow, but Rin turned to me, his attention on my bare feet and legs — his gaze never reaching my eyes — and he held out his arms in an invitation to carry me.

"Your highness," he murmured.

"Amiah," I corrected, my voice breathy with our bond's desire, and drew close so he could pick me up. "And thank you."

With one quick motion, he swept me into his arms and cradled me against his bare chest. I leaned into his embrace, unable to resist the bond with his arms around me.

Jeez. We couldn't get back to my guys soon enough.

But the second he stepped away from the passageway's entrance, a water whip snapped from somewhere above us and seized my leg. It wrenched me out of Rin's arms. I tumbled down the slope, the deep granular snow engulfing me and stinging my skin, and crashed into a large chunk of rock.

Rin lunged for me, but the water whip snapped toward him, forcing him to twist out of the way and defend himself from Padraigin who stood on a ledge jutting out from the mountain face above the opening where we'd exited the mountain.

"Run," Rin hissed.

I heaved myself to my feet ready to run when our soul bond clenched around my heart, stealing my breath.

I couldn't abandon him.

No matter what he'd commanded, I couldn't leave. That, and I had the ability to save him. I just had to be willing to kill Padraigin.

The thought made my magic latch on to Padraigin's life force and I was suddenly hyperaware of her. Icy and liquid. Her life force was an ocean in a wild storm filled with power, a power that could fuel my magic just like the life forces of Deaglan's assassins had powered my healing magic when I'd tried to save Cassius. I just needed to pull.

Except Padraigin wasn't really the enemy. She was grieving and wanted revenge, and she'd been told a lie about Noaldar's murder. That and she was Sebastian's sister and my possible salvation from the Winter Court. If I killed her, it would be harder to find a new monarch for the court, maybe even impossible.

AMIAH

Padraigin's water whirled around her in a powerful vortex as she glared at me, her eyes filled with rage.

"Go ahead." She pressed a hand over her heart as if she could feel the pressure of my magic inside her and knew I could kill her with a thought. "Kill me like you killed Noaldar. But know killing me won't stop *them*."

The glassy shimmer of portals burst to life in the air around me and half a dozen ice guards stepped through.

Hellfire snapped from Rin's eyes. He leaped to my side and tossed me over his shoulder, the sudden jerk into his arms shattering my concentration on Padraigin's life force.

He bolted for the barrier, aiming for an opening between two of the guards.

They slashed their spears at us, forcing him to jerk out of the way, and Padraigin seized Rin's wrist with a water whip. She wrenched him off balance, and he stumbled but kept hold of me, his grip painfully tight.

"Please," Padraigin said, her voice dripping with menace. "Keep trying to escape. I'll just tell Mother you put up a fight. She won't care how damaged you are so long as you're alive."

She turned her whip into a ball of water and shot it at Rin.

He dodged the blast, but she quickly shot another one and he couldn't get out of the way in time. It caught his shoulder and sent him stumbling into an ice guard.

The guard grabbed him and Padraigin seized me with her whip again.

But before she could yank me out of Rin's hands, Titus, in his massive red-gold dragon form flew through the barrier with Sebastian and Hawk on his back, clinging to his spine ridges. Their life forces, wild, icy, and sensual rushed across my senses and my soul greedily clung to them, steadying me, making me suddenly aware of how unbalanced I'd been feeling without them.

With a flick of his tail, Titus knocked off the head of the guard holding Rin then opened his mouth and blasted fire at another guard.

The guard holding Rin collapsed, the rocky slope thankfully making it fall away from us and not on us, while the guard caught in Titus's fire lunged for me. But his ice body had weakened and his leg snapped with the sudden movement, unable to hold all of his weight, and dumped him on the ground. He jabbed his spear at me, but Titus slammed his foot down on it, shattering it, seconds before his fire melted the guard enough that it lay still, no longer animated and now just a chunk of ice.

Are you okay? Titus roared in my head. *Did he hurt you?*

I'm okay, I replied as Cassius flew through the barrier.

His entire body and his wings were covered in flames, and his fiery life force added to the bright and dark, hot and cold, wild and ferocious mix whirling inside me.

He dropped two pillars of fire on two more guards. Both pillars were blazing hot, radiating heat that was almost too much to bear just like the pillar that had turned Balwyrdan to ash. Large cracks formed in the guards' ice bodies, and they fell apart and melted.

Padraigin seized their water before it evaporated and shot a blast at me and Rin.

Rin tried to jerk out of the way, but the water swept around my head before I could gasp in a breath.

"Your highness." Rin's hellfire flared, and he dropped to his knees, dumped me into the snow, and madly swiped at the water suffocating me. But his fingers kept passing through the liquid, not making enough of a break for me to draw in the smallest gasp.

"Leave or she suffocates," Padraigin said, her voice partially muffled by the water.

Titus roared and sent a blast of fire at her, making my pulse lurch.

If Padraigin died, the Winter Court might never free me.

Titus, no, I mentally gasped, even as my lungs started burning for air.

I joined Rin clawing at the water around my head, unable to stop myself even though I knew it was useless.

One of the two remaining ice guards leaped in front of Padraigin and took Titus's blast. Its feet hit the uneven slope and its legs shattered, weakened by the flames, sending it tumbling toward me and Rin.

Titus slapped it out of the way with his tail, sending the pieces hurtling back toward Padraigin.

Her water swept around the pieces and tossed them back at Titus, Sebastian, and Hawk, but Cassius melted them with his fire, turning the projectiles into a fine mist before they struck.

Stop. Please. She might be able to free me from the court. If she didn't kill me first.

Dark specks flooded my vision and I fought the screaming instinct to open my mouth and breathe.

Titus landed in the snow between me and the remaining ice guard. *She what? How can she free you?*

I don't— I need—

To breathe. God, please.

I strained to connect with the Winter Court's magic. Even a whisper of wind might be enough for me to gasp in a breath, but I couldn't tell the difference between the regular cold consuming me and the court's frozen magic.

"Padraigin, don't do this," Sebastian said, his full-body fae glow strong, although I could still feel his bright icy life force straining against the painful darkness writhing inside him. "Amiah isn't a threat to your claim to the throne."

Two of his tattoos lit up and the water around my head sloshed but didn't pour away.

"You might be a sorcerer, but you were never stronger than me at water magic," she snarled. "Leave and I'll let her live. Which is more than she deserves for killing Noaldar."

The darkness in my vision grew and the world started to spin. The urge to breathe twisted inside me as I continued to claw at the water. I wasn't going to be able to resist the reflex.

Rin grabbed my face, jerking my dimming focus to him. His hellfire blazed, with full, wild flames, revealing his fear, and he sucked in a quick deep breath then shoved his face into the water and pressed his lips against mine.

My thoughts tripped, my air-deprived brain unable to understand why he was kissing me. Then realization hit me. He was trying to give me air, just like Sebastian had when the leash spell had been suffocating me in Left of Lincoln.

I opened my mouth and gasped in his breath, and he pulled his head out of the water and sucked in another breath.

"I don't think so." Padraigin's water heaved around me and shoved his hands away from my face and wouldn't let him pass through to reach me again. "Leave."

"For fuck's sake," Sebastian snapped, and the light in the two lit-up tattoos blazed brighter.

The water around my head burst away, spraying Rin and freezing against his skin. I sucked in ragged breaths and hugged myself, my teeth chattering as the water on me, no longer in Padraigin's control, instantly froze as well.

"I wasn't better than you *three hundred years ago*," Sebastian said. "I've gotten a lot stronger since. Back off and you won't get hurt."

"Won't get hurt?" She barked a bitter laugh. "You couldn't hurt me any more than you already have. She killed Noaldar."

"And you tried to murder her at her wedding celebration," Hawk said.

I shuddered at the memory. If it hadn't been for Hawk stepping in the way and taking the strike from the poisoned blade meant for me, I would have died. As it was, even with his rapid healing, I'd nearly lost him.

Padraigin glared at me. "So you make up a lie to justify what you've done? They all believe you, don't they? They'll all do anything for you not knowing what a monster you are."

"If you're so sure she killed your lover then demand the blood price," Sebastian said. "You're a royal. You can make Faerie give it to you."

Padraigin's expression grew even more bitter. "Faerie has abandoned me, just like you did. I could demand all I liked. It would never give it to me."

"Then I'll demand it for you," Sebastian said.

"What the fuck?" Hawk hissed, as sparks snapped from Cassius's body.

The blood price won't hurt her. She's not guilty, Titus said in my head and, from the way Cassius's fire stopped sparking, in everyone else's head as well.

Padraigin raised her chin in defiance. "You're bluffing. You'd never endanger your wife."

"She's only in danger if she murdered your lover," Sebastian replied. "I was there. Deaglan ripped out one of the keys to unlocking the Heart and all of Noaldar's fae magic with it."

"That's a lie. Noaldar didn't have a key. He'd have told me if he did."

"And yet I'll demand the blood price against Amiah on your behalf." Sebastian slid off Titus's back, knelt, and shoved his hands into the snow.

His fae glow flared brighter and the painful darkness trapped inside him burned against my senses. But before he could do anything, the air around us exploded into more shimmering portals and more ice guards raced through and swung their weapons at us before Padraigin could command them.

"Get Amiah out of here," Cassius said. He melted three more guards with pillars of fire that he shouldn't have been able to cast given how much magic he'd already expended. And yet even after that his fire still roared around his body.

Titus took out two guards with a single swipe of his tail then grabbed Sebastian in one large front claw and me and Rin in the other, squishing us together chest to chest.

My gaze locked on Rin's as Titus flapped his large, leathery wings and leaped back into the air, and I was once again drowning in hellfire.

God, I need him.

No. I don't.

Titus flew out of the barrier and I wrenched my attention past Rin's shoulder, desperate to focus on anything other than how much I wanted him.

The dragons' flat-topped mountain stood on the horizon ahead of us, and Titus barreled toward it, not slowing down even though we were out of the Winter Court and I desperately needed to get away from Rin.

Below, the Wilds was a patchy mix of jungle and desolate wasteland as if it couldn't make up its mind what it wanted to be, and the jungle's heat, already steamy and hot even though the sun was just starting to lighten the horizon, melted the ice on my skin and in my hair and warmed me up a little... while my body, pressed tight against Rin's, warmed me even more.

But despite the increased temperature around me *and* inside me, I still wasn't as warm as I should have been.

The Winter Court's magic still flowed through my veins, and while I wasn't shivering uncontrollably anymore, I had no doubt that the Winter Court wouldn't wait for long before it tried to make me its queen. It had been desperate to be free of the Winter Queen, and I didn't think it cared if it killed me so long as it could use me to break free of her.

For now, however, I was safe with my guys, and once we were back at the aerie — and I put some distance between me and Rin and could think straight — we could regroup and figure out what to do about everything.

The desire from my brand swelled, and I clenched my jaw and forced myself to keep my gaze on the mountain and not look at Rin.

I wouldn't look, and I wouldn't think about my body against his, my breasts squashed against his chest, and his erection digging into my thigh.

Oh, God.

If I turned my head, just a fraction, I could kiss him—

And now all I could think about was kissing him, and how I kissed him after letting him feed on me and fill me with his sensual, throbbing magic—

Focus. We were almost there. I could hold out.

I made myself study the mountain as we drew closer. It towered over everything, the land around it flat, as if it had been dropped and left in the middle of the vast plain. Even with half of the area dense jungle, it was still clear there weren't any other mountains or even hills nearby.

Of course, the fact that a mountain was sitting in the middle of nowhere wasn't the strangest thing I'd seen in Faerie. I'd seen a whole court torn apart, pieces of land floating every which way, water flowing up — or down or sideways depending on how you looked at it.

And really, the mountain wasn't a mountain. It was a city with rooms for dragons in their dragon form as well as their human form that had been made to house hundreds.

Except now there was only one dragon left.

The last time we'd been to the aerie I'd been in shock over the events in the Winter Court's ballroom and then a key had become empowered. I hadn't really thought about how horrible it must have been for Titus to return to an empty home, knowing it would never be full again.

And then he'd asked me to be his mate and I'd turned him down.

You just hadn't realized the truth yet, Titus said in my head.

You know it's rude to spy on someone's thoughts, I replied, but I wasn't really upset. I was relieved. Having him in my head strengthened our connection, and I needed that, needed him to steady my soul just as I sensed he needed me.

Sebastian, hanging in Titus's other claw, gasped and pulled my attention away from Titus's life force to his. A white spark of fae magic popped out of his cheek and flew into the jungle below, and the pain of the seething darkness inside him burned hotter than it had only a few minutes ago. Using his magic to save me had already erased some of the magic I'd given him and the longer we were in the Wilds, the more magic Faerie would rip out of him.

And while I could have sex with him again and give him another transfusion of fae magic, that wasn't a permanent solution.

We had to get him back to the aerie and we had to get the demonic magic infection out of him before it was too late.

AMIAH

WE REACHED THE MOUNTAIN JUST AS THE SUN ROSE ABOVE THE HORIZON and as Faerie started ripping out the fae magic I shouldn't have had inside me with sharp burning snaps.

Thankfully, I only suffered a few quick pops before Titus barreled into the wide cave sitting almost at the top of the mountain. It was the same cave where we'd entered before, and just like the last time, for a heart-stopping second, we flew in absolute darkness before small red flames burst to life near the ceiling to light the way.

A moment later, we were out the other side in the enormous, partially covered cavern in the middle of the mountain, and Titus set me, Rin, and Sebastian on the same outcropping as before with its human-size passage that led to our previous suite.

Rin jerked away from me before I could move, but even the distance didn't ease my body's throbbing.

God, I had to think of something else. Anything else.

But his strange alive yet dead, fiery yet cold life force thrummed against my senses, along with his pain, so much pain—

I shuddered, and that whisper of pain swelled, yet for a second it didn't feel as if it came from Rin but from below me.

Then Titus landed beside me with a whoosh of air. He barely gave Hawk enough time to scramble off his back, before shifting and wrapping me in a crushing, warm embrace.

His life force overwhelmed Rin's as his beast's ferocious nature flooded me — his beast still in control of their body even though he'd shifted back to his human form.

I focused on his ferocity, forcing it to overwhelm my brand's desire for Rin. This was who I was supposed to be with, along with Hawk, Cassius, and Sebastian — for as long as he wanted to stay with me.

"Tell me how Padraigin can free you from the Winter Court," Titus said, his voice rumbling through me.

"I'm not sure," I replied, not even trying to get him to loosen his hold. His connection with his beast, while not as fragile as it was before, still wasn't perfect. Even if it had been, he still wouldn't have released me until it had calmed down, and the only way to get him calm was flesh-to-flesh contact to steady his soul.

And really, I needed the contact as well.

My soul was out of alignment. And now that my throbbing need for Rin was receding a bit, I could feel my soul wavering, its thrum more unsteady than it had ever been before, which worried me. It was only dawn. That meant it couldn't have been more than five or six hours since I'd last had sex. If my imbalance kept growing, I was going to need to have sex all the time just to be able to concentrate, and as much as I loved having sex, that wasn't conducive to having a normal life.

"Padraigin can free you?" Cassius asked. He stood on the edge of the landing as far away from all of us as he could. Flames still rolled over him and dripped over the ledge, breaking apart as it hit one outcropping then another before showering a patch of jagged rocks at the bottom with sparks. The fire wasn't as powerful as it had been when he'd first flown through the Winter Court's barrier, but given how much magic he'd expended during that fight, he shouldn't have had any left. He shouldn't have even been smoking. "What do you mean Padraigin can free you?"

"I'm not sure. The Winter Court said it couldn't reach her—"

"So *that's* what I was looking at," Hawk said, as if he should have known all along. "She's enspelled."

He drew close to me, his demonic body heat billowing over my still unnaturally cool skin. He pressed a hot hand against the back of my neck, adding another point of flesh-to-flesh contact and entwining his life force with Titus's. Together, their life forces tugged my soul a little closer toward proper alignment and helped me lock down even more of my desire for Rin.

"I thought there was something wrong with her." Sebastian ran a hand over his spiky white and silver hair. "There are only two people in Faerie powerful enough to cast a spell that subtle, and I doubt Karthick enspelled her."

"Let me guess. That leaves Deaglan." Cassius jerked his chin to the passage leading to the suite we'd used the first time we'd been there. "We really should be discussing this while we eat. I'll meet everyone in the dining room." He leaped off the ledge and spread his wings with a burst of fire, and flew back up to the opening in the top of the mountain.

"Sparky is right," Hawk said. "Titus and I and Rin—" His attention jumped to Rin, making mine slide to Rin as well despite my determination to not look at him. "We're the only ones who've eaten recently."

A spark of hellfire popped from Rin's eye, but his expression remained flat, and I couldn't tell what he was thinking. He'd moved to the side of the ledge by the wall, as far away as he could get, and while his distance was necessary, his flat expression made my heart ache. He'd been opening up — if only a little — and now had completely closed himself off again.

And while I knew it was foolish to think that because he was opening up to me, he'd also open himself up to the others, a part of me still hoped he would.

Titus swept me up into his arms and cradled me against his massive chest. "Food is a good idea."

"I'd really rather deal with Sebastian's infection then have a shower and go to sleep," I said, pressing my ear against Titus's chest and listening to his strong, solid pulse while savoring his body heat. I didn't bother reminding him that I was perfectly capable of walking. No matter how much I argued, his beast wouldn't listen right now, and really, it wasn't a fight I wanted to have.

Sebastian rolled his eyes at me and headed into the passage. "Haven't you learned anything? Cassius isn't going to let you do anything until you've eaten."

"And I want to know how Padraigin can free you from the Winter Court," Titus said, following Sebastian.

Hawk fell into step beside him, and Rin trailed behind, keeping back, clearly not a part of our group.

Titus carried me into the kitchen, a large room with an old-fashioned metal stove and sink, and stone counters that wrapped from the door around the wall and jutted out creating a separation between the kitchen and the dining room.

He headed straight into the dining room with its long stone tables and benches, as Sebastian went into one of the two pantries, and set me on my feet beside the closest bench then glanced at the kitchen and back to me as if he wanted to get me food with Sebastian but at the same time didn't want to leave my side.

A chill shivered down my spine at the loss of his warmth, but Hawk stepped up behind me, replacing Titus's missing heat.

"Go find her something," Hawk said, handing Titus a pair of shorts then wrapping his arms around my waist. "You're not the only one who needs a little physical contact."

Titus huffed in agreement, his dragon surprising me at accepting Hawk's request, and he returned to the kitchen.

I leaned back into Hawk's embrace, savoring the heat radiating from his body, the sensual thrum of his life force, and the soft caress of his magic unfurling low within me. It wasn't strong enough to make me desperate, and thankfully it didn't break my determination to resist my soul bond's desire. It was just enough to relax me.

And yet a part of me wished it was more, wished I could just melt into his magic and connect with him, with all of them, and forget about Rin and everything that was going on.

But we needed to have a serious conversation about how we were going to free me from the Winter Court and how we were going to get the keys to free the Heart that Deaglan had away from him, and that was just as important as properly aligning my soul.

"You're glowing," Hawk murmured in my ear so none of the others could hear — at least no one but Rin with his heightened hearing. "And I'm pretty sure the glow from me and Bane would have worn off by now." Meaning he knew I'd had another orgasm since we'd been separated. Everyone probably did, and Hawk had just gotten around to asking me first.

I tipped my head back on his shoulder and pressed my lips against his jaw. "I'm bite-locked," I whispered. I didn't know why I didn't want the others to know. If I ever fed Rin again, they were going to find out, but I didn't want to derail the conversation from what was really important, getting the Heart. Because getting the Heart solved everything.

"Did you...?" Hawk's warm breath caressed my cheek, drawing a shiver of need, and my gaze jumped to Rin who stood by the counter separating the dining room from the kitchen.

Just looking at him stole my breath, just like looking at all of my guys—

Except he wasn't one of my guys.

And yet my mating brand claimed he was my *only* guy.

The throbbing need to seal our bond broke through my mental hold, and the memory of him releasing his bite-lock flooded me.

I bit back a moan. I wanted more of his seductive magic rushing through my veins, wanted him to explore my body with his lips and hands, wanted to explore his body with mine. I wanted him in me. I needed him. Needed to solidify our connection and accept my fate.

"Amiah?" Hawk's grip on me tightened, yanking me away from my thoughts. "I can't tell from your desire— Did you seal your bond?"

"No," I breathed, but it was getting really hard to resist, and now I wasn't so sure I'd last a few weeks let alone a few days. "I'm still hoping we can hold out until we get the Heart, but Rin was hurt and needed to feed."

"God, I love that look on your face," Sebastian said, interrupting our conversation and drawing my attention away from Hawk. He stood in the kitchen with a heated look in his eyes, holding a basket of strangely colored mixed... fruit?

"Hers?" Hawk purred not indicating he knew my look had really been for Rin. "Or mine?" He slid his hand over my hip, found one of the slits in Rin's tunic, and teased his fingers across my bare thigh. All of my attention snapped to him and a curl of his sensual magic unfurled low within me.

Sebastian's eyes lit with a wicked smile. "Well gee, I don't know. I suppose I'll have to watch a little longer to make up my mind."

"Can we keep it in our pants long enough to let Amiah recover?" Cassius snapped as he flew in through the large window that took up almost an entire wall in the dining room and landed at the back of the room, keeping his distance from us.

Fire still dripped from his body, now sudden bursts instead of a steady stream, and he looked exhausted. Gone was the hard, icy angel determined to control his emotions and his magic at any cost. Now he was a worn-thin version of the man who'd been my best friend.

Sebastian's expression turned sober. "You're right. Titus said you were okay. Are you or did you just tell him that so he wouldn't lose his shit on Padraigin?" he asked, as he crossed to me and captured me in his pale blue, almost colorless gaze.

A sense of enormous power flickered in those icy depths, just for a second, before the swell of painful darkness overwhelmed it, reminding me that we shouldn't just be standing there.

"We should deal with your infection," I said, and his expression shifted into that same awe that I'd seen in all my guys when we made love, the expression he'd had the last time I'd taken both him and Hawk. And while I knew it meant he cared deeply for me, I also knew he'd eventually walk away from what we had. He'd been adamant about his desire to never commit to anyone and I had to respect that.

Which meant I needed to cherish the moments we did have.

I held out my arms and he set the bowl on the table and leaned into me, letting me hug him captured between him and Hawk, cool and hot, sensual and bright, and exactly where I was supposed to be.

"Don't avoid the question, sweetheart," he murmured. "Are you okay?"

"I'm just tired and hungry and in desperate need of a shower," I said, my lips brushing against his neck and sending a frozen spark of fae magic into him.

"Thank God." He drew back enough so he could kiss me.

The kiss was soft with the same heartbreaking tenderness that he'd kissed me with just before we'd been forced to consummate our fake marriage in front of everyone in the Winter Court. It made my soul sing and break at the same time. I needed him. I loved him, and my soul bond was going to make me fall out of love with him, with all of them.

I shoved that hurt aside. I would find the Heart and I would keep my guys... for as long as they wanted to be with me.

"Now that everyone's gotten their hugs in," Cassius said, "Let's talk Padraigin. Deaglan enspelled her. Why?"

"We should deal with Sebastian's infection first," I insisted.

Cassius glared at me. "Bane can wait ten minutes while you eat."

I opened my mouth to argue with him and his glare deepened.

"No," he said before I could reply. "Whatever you're going to say. No. Every time we think we've a moment to catch our breaths, something happens. I doubt you've eaten in the last twelve hours— hell, knowing you, you probably haven't eaten in the last twenty-four hours. We can't afford to have you collapse because you're starving."

"He's got a point, gorgeous," Hawk said.

It had only been about twelve hours since I'd last eaten that bowl of pasta on Sebastian's roof, but there hadn't been much more before that, and even if they didn't need me to heal them, all of them could be dangerously distracted if I collapsed.

"I doubt we have enough fresh food right now for a proper meal, but we can still eat something, and while we do that, we should discuss Padraigin." Cassius gave the bench in front of me a pointed look, but when he raised his gaze back to me, it was filled with worry. "Bane has lasted this long. He can wait ten more minutes."

The thought of letting Sebastian continue to suffer twisted inside me.

"Please," Cassius said, his voice tight with worry, and I realized all of them, including Sebastian, were looking at me with the same concern.

Sebastian eased out of my embrace. "I'll be fine for ten."

My need to heal him twisted stronger and I fought to control it. Even if I wanted to, my magic couldn't heal him, and getting something to eat was the smart move. But I didn't know how much longer I'd be able to hold out against my compulsion. I was already trying to ignore my soul bond's desire with Rin. Now I also had to ignore my healing magic.

I forced myself to sit on the bench in front of the bowl of fruit, grabbed a bunch of what looked like orange grapes still on the vine, and popped one into my mouth — yep, it tasted like a grape. "The Winter Court said Padraigin faded out of reach."

I quickly ate five more *grapes* as Sebastian sat beside me. The faster I ate, the faster we'd get to healing him.

"If it happened shortly after I left," he said, as Hawk slid onto the bench on my other side, "it was probably to make my mother use her resources to search for me. I'm pretty sure Deaglan was royally pissed that I survived his assassination attempt."

"I'm not sure how the court determines time. It said you left and then she faded," I replied, shoving more grapes into my mouth.

I reached for another bunch but Sebastian grabbed it before I could and held it for me so he could interlace the fingers of our other hands under the table. Small icy sparks of fae magic snapped across my skin and sank into Sebastian. I didn't even need to concentrate, which worried me even more and made my healing compulsion twist stronger.

"Do you know when Deaglan might have enspelled her?" I asked Rin, glancing his way but trying not to fully look at him. I knew if I did, with everything I was struggling with right now, I'd end up throwing myself at him. But out of everyone here, he was the most likely to have overheard something about Deaglan's plans.

And while both he and Titus had been Deaglan's prisoner, he'd had more autonomy than Titus. Of course, that autonomy had come at a painful price. Titus just had scars from the chains holding him that he'd tried to break every day. Rin had agony imprinted in his cells.

"No," Rin said.

"Or why he might have enspelled her?" I asked, my attention slipping to him and my desire straining my control.

His gaze shifted to Sebastian then back to me, and a spark of hellfire popped from his eye. "No."

I waited a second— we all did, but the pain in his cells flared and he kept his mouth shut and his expression flat.

"It's okay if you don't know," I said, dragging my attention away from him and popping three more grapes in my mouth.

"Yeah," Sebastian added. "Deaglan's an asshole, but he's not a dumb asshole. If enspelling Padraigin is important to his plans, I doubt he'd tell anyone about it. Unless he could use it to hurt someone."

"And why or when isn't important," Titus added, returning to the dining room wearing his shorts and carrying a platter of cheese and dried meat. He set the platter on the table and sat on the bench across from me. "The only thing that's important is figuring out if breaking the spell on your sister will free Amiah."

"Do we really want Padraigin to be queen?" Cassius sucked in a deep breath and clenched his jaw and his fire sank under his skin. "She tried to kill you."

"Because she didn't know that Deaglan really killed Noaldar," I said.

"She does now," Titus replied, as Cassius drew near the table, grabbed a handful of meat strips off the platter then retreated back to the end of the room and released his hold on his fire again, letting it drip around him.

"But even then," Hawk added, "do we honestly believe she didn't know that Noaldar tried to murder Amiah?"

"I don't care if she did or didn't know or who sits on that throne." Sebastian squeezed my hand and more icy sparks of magic snapped from my skin into his.

God. I had to heal him.

No. I had to eat just a little more so they wouldn't worry.

"Right now," Sebastian said, "the court wants Amiah and there's a chance we can convince it to take Padraigin instead."

"But if she's just as bad as your mother—" Cassius said.

"Then not much will have changed except Amiah will be free." Sebastian gave Cassius a pointed look as if daring him to argue with him. "We get the Heart, separate Amiah and Talkative, and get the hell out of Faerie."

My gaze slipped to Rin, and my resolve to resist my desire weakened, letting it swell through me with sudden aching need.

Crap.

I seized it again, shoved it back down, and yanked my attention back to the guys.

Smoke billowed around Cassius. "That doesn't deal with the fact that all of Faerie will still be after us. The whole plan was to get the Heart so we had leverage to protect ourselves. We're still going to need to make alliances."

"If Padraigin is as crazy as my mother, there are still four other courts we can make deals with," Sebastian said.

"Three," Hawk corrected. "I don't care that Balwyrdan is dead, I'm not making a deal with the monarch who had that monster in his employ."

"Fine, three," Sebastian snapped. "Let's not forget the whole point is to get the Winter Court to release its claim on Amiah. If it'll take my sister then fan-fucking-tastic."

"I agree," Titus growled. "So long as Amiah is free."

"I'm not arguing that point," Cassius said, his fire and smoke surging for a second before he yanked it back to its new dripping normal. "I'm just wondering if there are better options than Padraigin."

"There might be, but I'd rather not waste time trying to find someone." Sebastian handed me a large chunk of cheese, and I realized I'd finished off all the grapes in the bowl. "We've got more than enough to handle at the moment. We don't know when the final key will become empowered and the only way I'll have a chance at taking Deaglan's key is to get this demonic shit out of me."

His words made my healing compulsion twist tighter, stealing my breath. I had to heal him. Now. *Now now now.* I couldn't eat another bite. I was going to do something whether I wanted to or not and my two options were sealing my bond with Rin or healing Sebastian.

And healing Sebastian was really the only option.

I shoved up to my feet, using our joined hands to urge Sebastian to stand as well. "We're dealing with that right now."

"Amiah—" Cassius started, but something — probably the strain in my expression — stopped him.

"Rin, are you up for pulling the demonic magic out of Sebastian?" I asked, clamping down on my desire so I could look at him.

Rin's gaze slipped to Hawk for a second, and I couldn't help but wonder if he knew that Sebastian had asked Hawk to stop him by whatever means necessary if it looked like he was taking too much fae magic and endangering Sebastian's life — since a fae couldn't survive without the fae magic wrapped into his essence.

Then Rin's gaze jumped back to me and my pulse stalled.

Oh, God. Please.

"Yes," he whispered.

"Are you?" Sebastian asked me, and I heaved my attention to him. "I'd like you with me. Depending on how sticky the demonic magic is any little bit of fae magic you give me could make the difference." He squeezed my hand and a flurry of fae magic sparked from me into him.

"Of course I'll be there."

"You'll want to lie down," Rin said. "This could be painful."

"I have no doubt it will be." Sebastian released a heavy breath. "Let's get this over with."

SEBASTIAN

I didn't care anymore if whatever Amiah was, was fucking with my mind. That portal had opened and yanked her away, and I'd felt as if it had torn out my heart. It didn't matter if my feelings for her weren't a hundred percent mine. That still meant the feelings that *were* mine were certain that I loved her, loved her spirit and determination and trust. God, no one had ever trusted me like she had. She gave me everything, her body and heart, even though she still expected our arrangement to come to an end.

And the moment she'd been taken from me, I knew I didn't want it to end and I was damn well going to do whatever it took to give her what she wanted. She wanted to be free of the Winter Court? I'd take the throne if I had to. She wanted to be free of her soul bond? I'd get her the God damned Heart. She wanted me? I'd take the sacred vows with her.

Fucking hell.

I was well and truly screwed.

And I didn't care. The idea of losing her forever had solidified my certainty and it didn't matter how that had come to pass.

We left the kitchen and headed down the hall, a whole fucking processional with everyone — including Cassius with his fire barely contained and smoke billowing around him. The flickering magical flames dancing near the ceiling cast shadows on the wall around us, and

I watched my shadow heave and twist, as if the battle inside me was being portrayed on the walls.

As much as Amiah had given me a boost of fae magic when we'd had sex, my insides were still on fire. And connecting with Karthick and then breaking Padraigin's control of the water around Amiah's head had only made it worse.

And while my fae glow was still strong, it hid the truth. That I was weak and my ability to connect with Faerie's primal magic was still seriously damaged. I just hoped to God the damage wasn't permanent. If it was, I had no hope of taking Deaglan's keys and then Amiah would have no hope of being free of Rin.

I also wasn't going to think about the fact that her unnatural fae glow was bright again when the glow from having sex with me and Hawk should have already faded. If she wanted to tell me what had happened between her and Rin, she would. As it was, she was making a determined effort not to look at him which meant she was still trying to resist the compulsion of the angelic mating brand to seal their bond... and that the compulsion was getting stronger.

We headed into the suite at the end of the hall, the sitting room bright and airy with the morning sunlight, and stepped into the first bedroom. The bed had been magically remade. In fact all the rooms in the aerie had reset to a clean and waiting state when we hadn't returned within a few days of leaving. Which was good, because we all needed to rest and none of us were up to doing any housework.

This bedroom was where Amiah had propositioned me to join a threesome with Hawk. I'd been shocked. I'd thought the threesome in the Winter Court had been a necessary evil to save Hawk — since I knew Amiah would do anything to save a life. I hadn't expected her to be so sexually curious... and holy fuck was she curious.

My thoughts leaped back to the last time we'd made love. She'd taken both me and Hawk at the same time, and her pleasure had lit her up so brightly it had been hard to keep looking at her. But I hadn't wanted to look away. I loved seeing her come, loved the look of absolute bliss and complete trust that filled her expression, and loved the thrumming connection that formed between us.

It had been even better being able to watch both her and Hawk together. He'd only had eyes for her, and as much as it had been sexy as hell watching them come, it had been breathtaking seeing his love for her. There was no one else for him and there never would be anyone else.

And I was damn well going to make sure whatever happened, she and Hawk — and I guess Titus, too, since he'd claimed her as his mate — had their happily ever after.

To do that, I needed to get rid of this infection, pray the connection that made me a sorcerer healed in time, and then make sure my ex-best friend didn't get Faerie's Heart.

I sat on the bed, suddenly hyperaware of the demonic magic consuming me.

This was going to hurt.

Rin had said it *could* be painful, but I knew it was going to be excruciating. The demonic magic had invaded every inch of my body, lined all of my magical channels, and had crept into my cells. Ripping it out would rip out most, possibly all, of my fae magic with it.

Except only removing part of the infection wasn't an option. Amiah's transfusion had only added more fae magic to my system. It hadn't shrunk the infection, and soon it wouldn't matter how much magic she gave me, there wouldn't be room left for it inside me.

Amiah squeezed my hand, sending a flurry of icy fae magic sparks rushing into me that were quickly consumed by the infection. Her expression was tight with worry and it made me want to lie and tell her everything would be okay... which was ridiculous. She wasn't an idiot. She might have a limited understanding of fae physiology — since I was the only full fae in the mortal realm and I hadn't let any physician study me — but even without Hawk mentioning it, she knew if Rin pulled out too much fae magic, I'd lose my connection to Faerie and die.

"All right," I said, lying back. "Let's do this."

Amiah released my hand long enough to go around to the other side of the bed, climb on, and kneel beside me. Then she reclasped my hand between hers, her cool palms a sign that the Winter Court's magic still flowed within her and that her body wasn't completely handling the extra power, since between us, I should have had the colder body temperature.

Rin sat on the edge of the bed opposite her. For a second, his hellfire flared into miniature flames with a surprising show of emotion before it snapped back to smoldering pinpricks. But the sudden flare was strong enough to activate the intention glyph tattooed on the inside of my right thigh, which meant whatever he said next, I'd know if he was lying or if he intended me harm.

The hybrid's gaze flickered to my lips then back to my eyes. "I'll have more control if I can connect through your mouth."

Truth with no intent to purposely hurt me. Not that his intention really mattered. Even if he meant no harm, there was still a chance removing the demonic magic would kill me.

"So kiss," I said.

"Yes, your highness."

"Swell." First Hawk and now Rin. "This is becoming a bad habit."

"It's only bad if you don't enjoy it," Hawk drawled as he sat at the foot of the bed. His hellfire had blossomed to miniature flames as well, and his expression was tight, as if he were worried, but didn't want Amiah to know how worried. He, out of everyone — except for maybe Rin — with his magical sensitivity and his work with witches, knew exactly how dangerous this was.

I rolled my eyes at him. "Kiss a guy once and he thinks you're into that. Pretty sure I'm not going to enjoy this." I turned my attention back to Rin. "Whenever you're ready."

Because there was no way *I* was ever going to be ready.

Rin gave me a tight nod, grasped my head, and dipped close.

My pulse pounded, and I strained to look at Amiah from the corner of my eye to help steady my nerves, but her angel glow blazed bright in her eyes, revealing her fear, which made my chest tighten. I hated seeing that look in her eyes. I wanted those seductive bedroom eyes, the eyes that had looked up at me while she'd sucked my cock. Hell, I'd even take the frustrated uptight glare she used to give me when I teased her.

Rin pressed his lips against mine in an open-mouth kiss and released his hold on both his vampire and demon essences, letting me fully sense them with my magical sensitivity. The sudden weight of his power roared against my senses, giving me no time to really register that I was kissing a man... again.

Holy fuck.

I hadn't realized just how powerful Rin really was. His tight control on his emotions had also extended to his essence, and now he radiated just as much power as Cassius — now that Cassius had given up on controlling his magic.

Rin might not be able to consume magic once it had been woven into a spell, but his capacity for raw magic was enormous... and a small part of me couldn't help but wonder if Deaglan had known exactly what he'd had. Rin could kill a super who possessed magic by consuming that magic without leaving a mark, and all that magic could be channeled out of Rin by a sorcerer if he or she could make a proper connection to Rin and had the willpower to control that much raw power.

Then a crackling thread of energy shot down my throat and engulfed my heart, and all thoughts of Rin's potential vanished. Blinding agony tore through me and I screamed into Rin's mouth.

The demonic magic was no longer just an acid inside me, it was acid all around me as if I'd been dumped into it and completely submerged. I was sure my skin was bleeding and blackening as if I'd been lit on fire, and every gasping breath burned down my throat and into my lungs.

I heaved against Rin's grip, kicking and clawing, my body taking over, desperate to end the agony, while my mind just screamed.

Oh fuck. Fuck fuck fuck.

It was all I could think of. Over and over again. All other thought was gone. There was just my howling curse and Rin's power shooting through my veins and shredding my insides.

"Grab his legs," Amiah said, her voice sharp and commanding, momentarily cutting through the howling in my head. "Titus, grab his other hand."

Someone pinned my legs and a big hand yanked my free hand away from Rin's throat.

"You can do this," Amiah said, and I heaved my gaze back to her as best as I could with Rin immobilizing my head.

Her eyes, while still bright with fear, were also hard with determination. This was the angel who commanded the medical team in the JP Operations building and who'd probably faced worse and had to make impossible choices as a physician for the Angelic Defense during the war.

The pressure of Rin's magical strength crushing against my chest grew, and the lightning dug in deep, fusing with the demonic magic and tearing it out of me. I tried to separate my mind from my body and just endure it, but my once strong willpower had been weakened by weeks of agony and I couldn't focus.

Then the hellfire in Rin's eyes flared, bursting into flames that licked across our cheeks and the demonic magic pouring up my throat thickened.

I gagged and gasped, desperate to catch my breath, choked on my magic then gasped some more, but the oozing stream wouldn't stop long enough for me to draw in a proper breath.

God. I just had to hold on, get through this.

Except the moment that thought swept through me, I realized this wasn't going to be enough. Even with my body on fire, I could still feel the demonic magic clinging deep inside me, wrapping itself around my fae magic.

I tried to capture Rin's gaze to somehow convince him he had to push his magic in deeper, and, as if he could read my thoughts — and really, he'd probably just figured out the truth at the same time I had — his power surged. It flooded my entire body and tore into every cell with excruciating agony, ripping at both demonic and fae magic without hesitation.

Now oozing acidic darkness and bright icy power poured up my throat in equal amounts, and everything started to go dark and fuzzy. Even the pain.

Thank God. Finally I could close my eyes and separate myself from the pain. I could float in the thick darkness, give in to it and—

"Sebastian, stay with me."

Amiah's words shot through me and I tried to open my eyes. But they were just so heavy and I could barely breathe and for the love of God, please just let me pass out.

"Sebastian, please. Hold on." A flurry of icy sparks sliced into my hand, raced up my arm, and was enveloped in demonic magic without having any chance of reaching my heart... which was slow... and heavy.

"I can't give him enough this way," Amiah said. "He's losing too much fae magic."

"We have to stop." That sounded like Hawk. "We'll find another way."

I tried to shake my head and tell them not to stop. Rin had to get rid of all of it. Now. If he left some, even a trace, because I was so low in fae magic, the demonic infection would regain strength. This was my only chance to stop Deaglan from murdering thousands because it amused him and to free Amiah. But Rin wouldn't let me move, his fingers dug into the sides of my head, his grip like a vise, and all I could do was gasp and gurgle.

"He's the only one of us— getting the— keys from Deag—" Cassius said, my thoughts stuttering, the agony yanking me between consciousness and unconsciousness and only letting me catch some of his words.

"He won't be able to if he's dead," Titus growled.

"I'm ending this," Hawk said. "We'll find another way."

"No," Amiah commanded in her in-charge physician's voice. "This is the only way— might not get another— stop now, he could still die. Keep go—"

Rin's power surged, digging into already damaged cells, yanking me back to the burning, blinding agony.

"He needs a stronger infusion." Amiah released my hand and I clawed at Rin's face, my body still thrashing until someone grabbed my wrist and yanked it away. "Hawk, get him up and get me ready."

Someone straddled my legs — Amiah? — and tugged at the front of my shorts. A blast of seductive magic burst through the agony, and my cock was instantly hard, so hard it hurt.

"Just hold on, Sebastian," Amiah said, and her slick, tight heat slid around me.

Oh, fuck.

Everything within me zeroed in on her. All the pain and fuzzy darkness fell away, and there was only her, my need for her, my awe of her, my shock that she was the one I'd fallen in love with.

She started to move, slowly rocking her hips, sliding me along her channel, and the connection that formed between us when I entered her swelled, filling me with heat. It was like the heat of her healing magic — when she wasn't just blasting it in me — sensual and thick, and yet it wasn't her healing magic.

Except I didn't know what it was. I'd never experienced anything like it before, had no frame of reference to identify it when I used my magical sensitivity. It was like our souls were entwining, which strengthened both of us like a miniature soul bond that ended the moment we separated.

At the edge of my senses, I could still feel the agony screaming through me, but it couldn't break through our connection, couldn't diminish the feel of her riding me, using Hawk's magic to build up her desire along with the blazing fae power she was going to give me with her release.

I reached out to her, unable to see her with Rin's face blocking my view. I needed to touch her, connect with her with more than just my cock.

She laced her fingers in mine and the connection between us surged, weaving around Rin's magic, the demonic magic infection, even my own fae magic, and connected with something deeper inside me.

It was the most incredible sensation, powerful and wild despite the pain. It made my balls tighten, and Hawk's power surged. My body bucked into her, my thrusts coming faster and faster. She matched my pace, her grip on my hand tightened, and beyond the roar in my head, I could hear Amiah's gasps and moans.

God I wanted to see the look on her face, wanted to see that raw, honest expression, the real her embracing her bliss, and then I wanted to watch her eyes roll back with her release.

The memory of her impaled on my cock, with Hawk in her ass, and the amazing look on her face swept through me. Absolute trust. Absolute love. Absolute pleasure. Fuck. I never wanted what we had to end. I wanted to keep making love to her, wanted to watch the others make her come, wanted it all with her.

Fuck. My hips bucked up as she came down, crashing us together, and I came hard.

She cried out her own release, letting go of my hand and grinding down on me, and the tidal wave of fae magic that had been building inside her crashed into me. It sparked and snapped, igniting the magical thread of our connection that had woven through me, and consumed the remaining demonic magic. Then the power of the connection sank deeper, whirling through my essence and imbedding into my soul.

Rin gasped. His magic and the remaining demonic magic rushed out of me and he fell off the bed, revealing Amiah still on my cock, her expression dazed and shocked as she clutched her left side. Hawk knelt behind her, straddling my legs as well, with one hand shoved inside Rin's tunic cupping her breast and the other between her thighs.

Gold light radiated through Rin's tunic and between her fingers at her left hip and up her side where her brand with Rin was... where my body still burned despite the rest of me being pain free.

My magic senses lurched to the golden threads now woven into my soul connecting us then snapped to the golden power blazing from the top of my left hip and curling up my ribs.

Oh fuck.

She'd branded me.

AMIAH

Sebastian stared at me, his eyes wide as I clutched my side. I'd orgasmed and released the fae magic I'd been gathering inside me to give to him and my mating brand had burst to life.

Fiery pain radiated from the middle of my left thigh, past my hip and waist, and halfway up my ribs, and golden light blazed through the heavy fabric of Rin's wrap tunic and between my fingers.

"You branded me," Sebastian gasped, and my gaze dropped to his side where brilliant golden light shone through his T-shirt.

Oh, God. I *had* branded him. Except I wasn't supposed to have branded him. He didn't want a permanent relationship. He'd made that very clear. This was a mistake. A terrible, terrible mistake.

"Sebastian, I'm sorry. I'm so sorry. I didn't mean to." I tried to reach for his hand, but just moving sent the room spinning, and Hawk tightened his grip and held me firmly against his chest. "I'll make this right. I promise. I know you don't want this. We'll get the Heart and I'll free both of you. I—"

"You branded me," he gasped again and his eyes rolled back and he passed out.

"Sebastian." My body started to tremble and I couldn't get my mind to get past those three words. I'd branded him. Sebastian Bane. The man who swore he'd never be foolish enough to be caught in a soul bond.

And God, I didn't know if I'd be able to free him.

Unlike Rin, my bond with Sebastian had formed while we were having sex. Which meant our bond had sealed the moment the brand had flared to life.

My trembling grew stronger and I couldn't get the room to stop spinning, couldn't catch my breath, and couldn't get my thoughts to focus.

I'd. Branded. Him.

I'd ruined his life.

There had to be a way to fix this. I had to fix this.

God, Please.

But the room just wouldn't stop spinning, and it was getting darker and darker, and I struggled to focus on anything other than having another unwanted bond.

A far-off part of me said that was because I was going into magical shock. Which didn't make sense. I never went into shock. Shock was something that happened to human witches if they channeled too much magic too quickly or channeled all of their internal magic in one powerful blast. It didn't happen to angels, and it certainly didn't happen to angels with healing magic.

Except I hadn't been channeling healing magic. I'd channeled fae magic, something I wasn't supposed to have, along with something else, something even more powerful.

Because Sebastian had been dying.

His life force had been pouring out of him along with the demonic magic and most of his fae magic, and the power within me that connected with life itself and joined with my guys when we had sex, had connected with Sebastian before I'd even thought of saving him with sex.

And that life force power had surged stronger the second he was buried inside me — just like it always did. It had seized his draining life force, locked what was left in his body, and started to heal it.

It had been just like how I'd kept Cassius's life force in his body while I healed him after Sebastian had taken him out of hibernation.

And when I'd come, the final wave of fae and life force magic had crashed into Sebastian, strengthening his weakened life force and restoring enough of his fae magic to keep him alive.

My gaze slid to Rin, who sat on the floor slouched against the wall. My need for him swelled, and my breath picked up despite still having Sebastian inside me and being unable to stop my shaking. I needed Rin, needed to seal our bond like I'd sealed it with Sebastian.

But more, I needed to comfort and heal him — even though what was wrong with him wasn't something I could heal. He didn't look as bad as I felt, but his complexion was gray and his breath was short and ragged.

"Rin, look at me." He'd consumed a lot of magic and his complexion and rapid breathing could be a sign he was ODing.

God, I should have thought of that before we'd started. I'd just been so desperate to save Sebastian so we could get the Heart.

Of course, I hadn't thought it was possible for a demon who actively consumed magic to OD through consumption. Usually them overindulging was like the average person overindulging. The only instances of ODing I'd ever come across were with demons like incubi, who could not only consume magic but passively absorbed it as well and had had too much energy get through their natural shields.

"Rin, look at me."

A spark of hellfire popped from his eye and he shuddered but didn't look up, which didn't tell me anything about his condition. He could be in trouble, or he could just be trying to get himself under control, not wanting to show us any weakness.

"Rin."

Another spark of hellfire.

Fine. If he wouldn't look up, I'd make him. I tried to pull out of Hawk's embrace, but he held tight, and just the effort of trying to move sent the room spinning. "Hawk, please. Help me."

"You don't look well," he said.

"I don't feel well, either," I said through chattering teeth, "but Rin could be ODing, and I can manage for a few minutes with my magical shock. I want to check him first."

"I'll get him," Titus said, starting to crouch, but Rin stiffened and wrenched his head up to look at me before Titus could touch him.

His gaze was unfocused, but his hellfire was tightly contained in his usual smoldering pinpricks with no hint of flickering flames.

"Hawk, please." I leaned toward Rin and Hawk helped me off Sebastian and onto the floor in front of Rin.

He watched us, his attention dipping to Hawk's arms around me, then jumping to Titus as the dragon straightened and pulled the bed's blanket over Sebastian, then jerking back to me. The muscles in Rin's jaw were tight as if he were desperately trying to hold himself together, and the pain in his life force was as strong as it had been when he'd tried to speak his mind.

I cupped his cheeks with trembling hands, but I couldn't tell if his temperature was off or not because my own temperature was too cold and it was hard to concentrate past the whirling room and the encroaching darkness. All I had to go on was his hellfire, and that remained stable, which meant he wasn't ODing just severely intoxicated.

"We need to get you in bed," I said. We needed to get *me* in a bed too—

But not with Rin or Sebastian.

My gaze slid back to Sebastian. Everything within me begged me to stay with him. Him and Rin. But I'd just done the one thing Sebastian had been adamant he never wanted, and while the brand would eventually make him fall in love with me, that didn't mean he wouldn't be furious for a very long time or that branding him was right.

I dragged my attention back to Rin and the need coming from our bond surged, despite how awful I felt.

"Can someone help Rin to a bed?" I asked through gritted teeth.

"I'm fine." Rin cupped his hands over mine, capturing them against his cheeks, a hint of need and desperation creeping into his eyes then vanishing.

Cassius huffed. "You don't look fine."

"You look like you're going to puke," Hawk added.

A spark snapped from Rin's hellfire and the pain in his life force grew stronger.

God, it broke my heart thinking he could have this agony for the rest of his life and there was nothing I could do about it.

I pressed my forehead against his, needing to get closer, to comfort him even with something as small as a brief touch as if I were a shifter, and a thread of my life force magic connected with him.

It whispered through his life force, a barely-there presence, softly seeping and easing his pain. I didn't know how I was doing it, and I could feel my magical shock growing as I let my magic trickle into him, but I didn't care. I could use my healing magic on my shock and my suffering was nothing compared to his.

"Your highness," he murmured and his hellfire licked against my skin before he yanked it back under control. "Stop. You're weak."

"Yeah," Hawk said, tugging me away from Rin, breaking our connection, and making the room lurch.

"I'll be okay. I can heal this." I focused on my healing magic in my palms.

I was brimming with power. The magic I'd used to heal myself after Rin had fed had already been restored. In fact, it was stronger than it had ever been, rolling around my hands and up my arms, ready to be used, *eager* to be used. Which was going to be a problem if I didn't use it soon.

It had been a long time since I'd had so much power that I needed to find someone to heal to release the pressure. All of the fights and trying to stay alive had kept me drained and I hadn't had a chance to think about what would happen if my internal well filled up and I didn't have a safe outlet to release the pressure.

I tried to concentrate and push some of the power into me to strengthen my heart, warm my body temperature, and weaken the effects of magical shock. I technically couldn't heal the shock since it was magical, but I could deal with most of the symptoms.

Except I couldn't focus. Just like the room was whirling around me, so was my mind. I was heavy and cold and spinning in darkness, around and around and around and—

I closed my eyes, but that only made it worse, and the darkness started to crush around me. I couldn't breathe, couldn't move. I was trapped and forgotten.

"Fuck, Amiah," Hawk said, his voice sounding far away.

I jerked— no, someone jerked me and my eyes snapped open. Rin stared at me, his complexion still gray, his eyes wide with fear and his hellfire small flames. Titus was also close, clasping my hand between his big palms, while Cassius stood behind him, his angel glow blazing and smoke billowing around him.

"You can't reach your magic," Hawk said.

"I can—" I didn't know why I insisted — old habits I guess — because it was clear I was just too tired to concentrate and couldn't.

"No, you can't. I can see you trying to grab hold of it and it's slipping away." Hawk pressed his lips against the top of my head. "We've got you and we've got Rin."

"I'm still going to need to burn off some of this healing magic," I said, my words starting to slur.

"I have no doubt we'll get the shit kicked out of us soon enough," Hawk said. "Cassius? You want to help Amiah?"

"I can't. It isn't safe. I'll get a bowl for Rin in case he does vomit." He sighed. "I'd offer to get him and Amiah clean clothes, but I don't know if I can control my fire long enough to not burn them."

"Get the bowl, there are enough of us to take care of the rest," Titus said, his gaze sliding behind me to Hawk. "I—" His pupils slitted and scales curled up his neck. "I need contact."

I placed a trembling hand against his cheek and he closed his eyes and leaned into my touch just like Rin had. We'd managed to heal the connection between the two halves of his soul, but it was still fragile. I couldn't imagine what he'd been feeling when Hawk and Sebastian had told him I'd been taken to Faerie. God, what was he feeling now that I'd branded Sebastian and I still hadn't branded him?

"We'll take a bath and clean up, that might help your shakes," he said, his voice gruff. "Then bed."

A shiver rushed through me and my gaze slid back to Rin of its own volition, making my throat tighten. I didn't want him. I wanted Titus. I wanted the others. And I was in no condition for anything with any of them.

"Come on." Titus gathered me in his arms and carried me out of the bedroom.

He headed straight to the bathroom and around the ninety-degree turn in the hallway, the only thing that made the bathroom private since it didn't have a door — none of the rooms in the aerie did.

Inside, he set me on the floor beside the large tub then headed back to the rack by the door and grabbed a handful of towels off the rack. The tub had been carved into the stone floor and was fed by a stream of water that flowed into a trough through a hole in the wall near the ceiling that split and fed the shower and the tub.

I stared at him as he returned to me, taking in his large muscular body. He wasn't beautiful like Hawk or Sebastian, but he had a rugged, raw handsomeness that always made my heart flutter when I looked at him.

Right now, red-gold scales teased across his collarbone and up his neck, drawing my gaze up to his stunning golden eyes. His pupils were slitted, his beast close to the surface, but the look in his eyes wasn't rage, but a ferocious, protective love.

It made my heart ache because I felt the same love for him. But the only thing that could keep us together was getting Faerie's Heart... and even then there was a chance the Heart wouldn't be powerful enough to add or remove anyone from my soul bonds.

With a dragon-like huff, he unzipped the fly on his shorts and let them drop to the floor.

A whisper of desire seeped through my cold and exhaustion, making me ache and reminding me of the first time we'd had sex. And while yes, I wanted to have sex with him again, what I really wanted right now was to fall asleep in his arms with his life force thrumming against my senses steadying my soul.

He slipped into the water, drawing close to me, and helped me untie Rin's sash and open up the wrap tunic.

I let the heavy fabric slide off my shoulders and pool around my hips, and Titus's gaze followed the fabric down. More scales crept over his jaw to his temples. He was looking at my new brand. The brand that made my heart sing because I was in love with Sebastian and cry because I'd trapped him and hurt the others by not branding them.

"It doesn't mean anything," I said, my voice small and trembling. "It's a mistake, just like my bond with Rin."

"It's not a mistake. Seireadan loves you." Titus traced the new golden lines with his thumb.

The brand was interwoven with the top half of Rin's brand but not joined, indicating that Rin and Sebastian didn't share any part of each other's brand. The delicate lines curled from my waist and up my left side to the middle of my ribs and shimmered with power, cutting through my dimming wavering vision, strong and bright and permanent.

So very very permanent.

Which I hoped to God it wasn't, because that would mean I wouldn't be able to free him or Rin.

"He feels deeply for me," I said. "But I'm not sure he loves me, and that's still no excuse for trapping him in a soul bond."

Titus hooked his thumb under my chin and gently urged me to meet his gaze somehow managing to keep the room at its slowly spinning speed and not making it lurch.

"He loves you. We all love you. Just because we all don't have a mark to show it—" His gaze slid to my shoulder where he'd bitten and claimed me when we'd had sex, and his expression softened, his love brightening his eyes again. "You kept my mark. You didn't fully heal my bite and you're letting it scar."

I smiled back at him. "Of course I kept it. We're mates."

That was one thing I was sure about. Titus was my mate and so were Hawk and Cassius. A part of me believed Sebastian was too because I made the same connection with him that I did with the others, but that still didn't make it right for fate to force a soul bond on him.

I slid my fingers over Titus's shoulder where I'd tried to bite him. Even if I'd had fangs, his rapid healing would have made it impossible for him to keep my mark. Which I guess meant dragons didn't bear mating marks like other predator shifters and I hadn't needed to control how I healed it... which didn't make sense because he'd been thrilled that I'd kept his mark.

The love in his expression deepened and he turned as if he knew what I was thinking, showing me a set of silver white scars on his left biceps. "I knew you were my soul's mate all along and the fact that one of your marks on me scarred proves it."

He drew me into the magically warmed water, sat on the bench that was submerged halfway down, and cradled me against his chest.

"I don't need your mating brand to know we belong together," he said. "You heal and settle my soul, you always will."

"Until my mating brands make me fall out of love with you." And the only way to stop that from happening was to remove both of my brands.

"They won't. You've marked me." He cupped my cheek and urged me to rest my head against his chest, adding another point of physical contact. "My soul's mating magic is just as powerful as yours."

I closed my eyes and let the heat of the tub and the thrum of his ferocious primal life force seep into me. It slid against my senses, passionate and sure, and something inside me sighed and started to relax. This was right. This was where I was supposed to be. With him. With them. All of them... including Rin?

RIN

I LAY IN A BED LARGER THAN ANY BED I'D EVER SLEPT IN — AT LEAST SLEPT in willingly by myself — my eyes closed, my world reeling. It didn't matter how hard I tried to focus on my inner stillness, how much I yearned to retreat back to the calm clear pond inside me, I couldn't think of anything but her. Even the churning discomfort of having consumed too much magic couldn't distract me.

I hadn't even watched her have sex with Prince Seireadan to give him the necessary transfusion of fae magic that saved his life, and yet that was all I could think about. She'd been radiant when I'd finished removing the prince's demonic magic infection. So sexy it made my soul ache and my cock throb. She'd thrown her head back with her release, resting it on Hawk's shoulder and giving me an erotic view of his hand shoved inside my tunic cupping her breast, and his other hand buried between her thighs. Which had made me think of watching her make love to the prince and Hawk in the mortal realm, her body moving to their rhythm, both of them driving into her until she'd cried her release and her full-body fae glow blazed bright.

God. I wanted that. And right now.

I didn't care that it was our unwanted soul bond making me burn for her, and it took everything I had just to stay where I was.

I wanted to taste her blood and magic again, wanted to push my cock, not just my fingers into her, and make her light up. I wanted to hold her like I'd held her after I'd released my bite-lock, wanted for her to cup my face with her soft hands and press her forehead against mine, and to feel her trusting me with her body and heart.

I wanted her to accept me.

And for a second, I'd thought maybe she had. She'd been so concerned for me after healing Prince Seireadan, had even foolishly given me more magic — a strange kind of power that I didn't recognize — and had eased some of the agony in my cells. Agony that I thought would never be eased.

But she was an angel with a strong healing magic.

I had to keep reminding myself of that.

She'd treat anyone who was suffering. Her magic compelled her. She'd probably treat King Deaglan the way she treated me if he'd been in my condition.

Except my soul couldn't accept that. What we had was special, fated—

And not real.

We were both being influenced by a soul bond neither of us wanted, and now she'd branded one of the men she really loved and would be able to forget me.

That thought made my soul ache with a pain that I didn't want, that, no matter how hard I tried, I couldn't convince myself wasn't real.

God, I had to pull myself together. Now that they were soul bonded, Prince Seireadan could become even more protective of Princess Amiah, and with his power freed, it was just a matter of time before he regained enough magical strength to leash me like King Deaglan had. I couldn't let myself think that these people cared for me because they'd helped me to a bed. I was just the man whose life was accidentally bound to the woman they loved. I didn't belong. They'd never accept me, and the only way I could truly be free was if I helped them get the Heart and then trusted that they'd keep their word and break the bond between me and Princess Amiah.

And none of that sat well with me, not trusting them to free me… nor being freed from the princess.

I drew in a slow breath even though, being undead, I didn't need to and focused on the pond inside me and its raging water, but the sound of footsteps drawing close jerked me to high alert, and everything, including my yearning for the princess and my churning stomach got shoved aside.

With my heightened hearing, I could tell the steps stopped at the doorway to my room, and from the rich, deep smoky scent curling around me and the hint of heat radiating across my skin, I knew it was Cassius. Of course, even without the smoke and heat, I would have recognized Cassius from his painful magic writhing against my sin eater senses.

Which completely astounded me. His personal well of magic should have been dry. Even if he'd managed to control his fire and not let it drip free while Princess Amiah and I were in the Winter Court, the massive pillars of fire that he'd dropped on the ice guards should have drained him.

But it was as if he had an endless supply of power, a connection to a source of magic outside of himself as if he were a fae sorcerer. Which was impossible. Angels could only draw on the power stored inside themselves, their connection to their primal realm was only a pinprick that allowed a trickle of power back inside them and refilled their well. They couldn't actively draw raw power from the Realm of Celestial Light. The only beings able to actively draw raw magic from their primal realm were the fae, and there were very few who could do that.

Except it didn't matter where he got his power from. From the way it heaved against his control, he was going to have to figure out a way to shut it off, or, just like a fae sorcerer, his willpower was going to falter and he was going to burn up.

His footsteps resumed, softer and slower this time, drawing closer. He was sneaking up on me.

I whipped through my options. I could continue pretending I was asleep until he was close then attack before he attacked me, catching him off guard. Except that would ruin any chance of staying on Prince Seireadan's good side.

No. I had to just take whatever he was going to do to me, like I took it with King Deaglan.

And if I was going to do that, then I wanted to see it coming.

I opened my eyes, catching Cassius halfway between the doorway and the bed, but he didn't pause, didn't even act as if I'd caught him sneaking up on me, and continued to the bed.

"Didn't mean to wake you," he said, holding out a metal bowl to me. Smoke curled over his hands and wrapped around his forearms and his body trembled with tension. Except it wasn't the tension of a man on guard, but one straining to hold back an endless, roaring power.

His gaze dipped to my side where Princess Amiah's brand curled out of the waistband of my pants then jerked back to my face, as if he hadn't wanted to look at the proof of our soul bond but couldn't help himself.

The princess had said she was in love with him, too, and from the conversation I'd overheard between him and Titus on the rooftop patio in the mortal realm, he felt the same way about her, and the dragon recognized him as another of Princess Amiah's mates. He, as an angel, knew better than the others that he couldn't get rid of me because of the angelic mating brand, but that didn't mean he didn't want to and that didn't stop him from taking his frustration out on me. He just couldn't kill me.

"Amiah told me you weren't Deaglan's servant willingly and you're angry about that." Now his gaze dipped to the scar across my neck where my throat had been slit when Deaglan's assassin had murdered me so I could be turned into a vampire. "I'm hoping you've already figured out that your best bet at getting justice is by working with us."

Except the princess had said I didn't have to, that I was free. I could help or not. It was my choice.

The urge to speak up and question his statement to find out just how true the princess's words had been tightened in my throat. But the pain in my cells fluttered stronger, reminding me of the cost of saying anything.

Which in turn reminded me of everything I had to lose if the Shadow King got Faerie's Heart. He wouldn't hesitate to take the princess and break her, and if he found out we were soul bonded, he wouldn't hesitate to hurt me in order to control her. I couldn't let that happen. Even if we hadn't been permanently bound together, I wouldn't have been able to just walk away and let King Deaglan hurt her.

CASSIUS

MY FIRE HEAVED AGAINST MY CONTROL, AN INFERNO BURNING THROUGH MY veins, through my whole body. It strained to break free while smoke that I couldn't completely hold back billowed around me. I wasn't going to be able to contain it for much longer and needed to get outside, but I couldn't just give Rin the bowl that I'd gotten for him from the kitchen, not without confirming that he wasn't going to endanger Amiah.

Which was ridiculous. I had no way of knowing if whatever Rin said was the truth. The only thing I had to go on was that the brand would compel him to protect her — and I had no doubt it was compelling him from how he'd protected her against Padraigin.

I ran a hand over my short-cropped hair, exhausted from having to constantly fight my fire. Seeing her have sex with Bane, not caring that we were all watching, had almost been too much for me. My fire had leaked past my control, burning my clothes and searing a painful strip up my ribs before I'd managed to pull it back — and the fact that I'd burned myself was a sign that I was starting to lose all control, even the instinctual control I'd been born with that prevented my fire from burning me.

But I'd been shocked at seeing Amiah ride Bane, and that had shattered my control for a second.

I'd also been turned on. Something I didn't want to admit to anyone.

Not the others and certainly not Amiah. And on top of all of it, I'd been bitterly jealous.

Amiah and I had only made love once and the odds that I'd be able to control my fire before I used it to end this mess by burning myself and Deaglan up were slim. We were never going to have sex again and watching her and Bane had been agonizing.

Then she'd cried her release, the light in her body had blazed brighter, and she'd infused Bane with fae magic and branded him.

That made my fire burn hotter and my heart ache even more.

I wanted to be happy for her, happy that she'd found someone else. Because if we couldn't get the Heart or it couldn't break her soul bond with Rin, she and Rin were permanently bound to each other. At least now she'd have someone else in the relationship, someone she'd told me she loved.

And yet I wanted with every fiber of my being for her to have branded me, even though I already knew my fate was to embrace my fire, let it burn away Cassius leaving only the Salamander, and then take Deaglan down with me so she and the others and all of Faerie were finally safe.

I heaved my thoughts back to Rin, who lay on the bed, watching me. His complexion was gray and I had no doubt it was going to take more than a few minutes for him to recover from consuming all the magic he'd had to consume to save Bane. But other than that, he gave no indication that anything was wrong with him. His expression was neutral, his hellfire tight, controlled pinpricks in his black eyes, and his body was relaxed — as if he weren't on the verge of vomiting, like his complexion implied.

But I knew he was anything but relaxed.

He'd hung back when we'd arrived at the aerie and had barely spoken more than two dozen words even when Amiah had asked him a direct question. He didn't trust us and I couldn't blame him for that. He didn't know us and even with the brand compelling him to trust and protect Amiah that didn't mean he thought he was safe with us. Up until two days ago, we'd been the enemy, someone his king had commanded he kill, and he had no idea how the rest of us felt about him.

And in truth, I wasn't sure how any of the others, let alone myself, felt about him. Fate said he was Amiah's mate — or rather one of her two mates now that she'd also branded Bane — but if Amiah was right about the brand being a nightmare and about it being wrong about her and Rin, then I couldn't trust him.

Except she'd also said Deaglan had tortured Rin, which gave us a common enemy... but only if Rin didn't think we'd lose.

"You know if Deaglan kills Amiah, you'll die, too," I said, offering him the metal bowl.

"Yes." He glanced at the bowl but didn't move to take it.

My flames snapped under my skin and black smoke curled up my arms.

Rin's attention flickered to the smoke then returned back to my gaze with no sign of what he thought about my smoke, me, or this situation. Was he angry that she'd bound his soul to hers? Was he happy that she'd freed him from Deaglan?

And really none of that mattered. The only thing that mattered was making the situation clear to him. "There's no going back. Even if Deaglan would take you back, you'd be his slave again, and I doubt he'd bother to free you from Amiah."

For a second it looked like the smoldering red pinpricks in his eyes grew slightly bigger.

Except it hadn't been enough to tell what he was feeling and had probably just been my imagination, my desire to see some kind of emotion from him. He was bound to Amiah, and I wanted to believe that fate wouldn't have forced an emotionless monster on her, that he was an ally. He was a quick, strong, skilled fighter and we were going to need all the help we could get if we were going to get the last key and take Deaglan's two other keys.

My gaze dipped to Amiah's brand etched into Rin's skin. God, I wanted her brand, wanted her to have claimed me instead of Bane and certainly instead of Rin.

My fire snapped and heaved, burning through my veins and straining my control. More smoke billowed around me, heavy and thick, and I shook with the effort to hold it back.

I couldn't stand there any longer. I had to get outside and release it before I burned my clothes and more of my body.

"Your only chance of surviving this and being free is by helping us." I set the bowl on the bed beside him and strode to the doorway.

"Only if the Heart can break the soul bond," he whispered in his barely-there dispassionate voice, making me stop in my tracks.

My fire roared stronger, and flames broke through my control and rolled up my arms, burning more of my cotton tunic.

"It'll break it," I ground out.

It had to. It didn't matter that every angel knew a mating brand was permanent and that the soul bond couldn't be broken. Amiah couldn't be bound forever to this emotionless stranger. She deserved all the passion and love that she craved, that I desperately wanted to give her and couldn't. I wouldn't allow Rin to be her fate.

AMIAH

I DRIFTED IN AND OUT OF CONSCIOUSNESS, STILL COLD AND REELING FROM my magical shock, as Titus gently washed me, wrapped me in a towel, and carried me to a bed.

A bed without Rin or Sebastian.

Which was for the best, despite what my soul bonds were telling me.

Together, we curled up under the blankets, Titus still holding me close, steadying both my soul and that thing I needed from him when we connected, and I drifted off into a frozen darkness.

The Winter Court still possessed me. Its magic still clenched around my heart, trapping me, freezing me. I couldn't move, couldn't breathe, and everything within me screamed.

Help me. Hear me. Someone.

But no one was coming. Because no one remembered I existed.

But I do exist. I'm more than darkness, more than cold. I need to move, to be free. Let me out.

Let me out let me out let me out—

I gasped and jerked awake, sending the room lurching despite the bright sunlight streaming through the doorway. I still shivered with magical shock and couldn't have been asleep for very long, while my heart raced with the fear of being imprisoned again, this time in darkness forever, completely forgotten.

Titus stared down at me, his eyes wide, his pupils slitted, and scales covering his neck and the top half of his chest. His ferocious life force surged against my senses, on alert, ready to fight and protect, and I clung to it, desperate to steady myself.

I wasn't trapped. I wasn't forgotten. I was fine.

Except I couldn't make myself completely believe that. There was something...? Someone? In pain.

I shoved that thought back. I knew where the pain came from. Rin. And there wasn't anything I could do to help him... or was there? I thought I'd eased some of his pain with my life force magic, but I wasn't sure how or if that had even happened.

"Are you okay?" Titus asked, his voice gruff. "You were begging to be free and crying."

Hawk rushed into the doorway, and his sensual fiery life force joined Titus's. "What's wrong?"

"Nothing." A tear leaked from my eye, and I wiped it away, realizing my cheeks were wet from more than just that tear. "It was just a dream."

God. A really bad dream.

Except it hadn't felt like a dream. It had felt real. I'd been trapped. I'd needed help. And no one was coming. Ever.

I shuddered and shifted closer to Titus, who wrapped his arms around me again, drawing me back into his warm embrace.

Hawk, his expression still tight with worry, sat on the edge of the bed and brushed a lock of hair out of my eyes. "I really want to cuddle with you, too, but I'm the only one who can watch Bane and Rin while Cassius burns off more fire."

"He's still releasing it?" Titus asked.

"Yeah." Hawk skimmed his thumb over my cheek, wiping away the rest of my tears. "It's not good. He dumped infernos on those ice guards and it barely put a dent in his power. And we won't be able to help him until Bane recovers his magic."

"How long has he been dripping flames?" Fire had been pouring off Cassius when the three of us had come down after healing Titus's connection with his beast.

"He's been going pretty steady since you and Titus had sex."

Desire shivered through me at the memory of being with Titus, despite the fact that I was worried about Cassius and still cold and trembling and spinning with magical shock. Hawk's lips curled into a wicked grin that made my unsteady thoughts lurch away from Cassius and turned me on more — which was probably what he'd intended since there wasn't anything I could do to help Cassius.

And boy, it was hard not to think about sex with Hawk or Titus or Rin—

I heaved my thoughts away from Rin and focused on the two men in front of me who I did love.

Sex with Titus had been wild and passionate. I wasn't sure what had gotten into me, but letting go like that and embracing the ferocity of Titus's life force had been incredible and freeing. It had also been incredible when Hawk had given Titus a boost so round two could quickly follow round one.

My cheeks heated at the memory and Hawk chuckled.

"I can't believe you still blush when you think about sex. We all just watched you ride Bane to save his life." A hint of darkness swept through his expression.

Out of all of the guys, Hawk was the one I needed to bond with. Not Sebastian. Hawk wasn't supposed to fall in love, but he had, and if I fell out of love with him, he'd suffer more than any of my other guys. I couldn't imagine how much it must have hurt him to see me brand Sebastian.

I took Hawk's hand and interlaced our fingers. "We'll get the Heart and fix this. If I could, I would have branded you instead of Sebastian."

"I know you would have, gorgeous." His smile turned soft. "We all know you can't control who you brand."

I huffed a bitter laugh. "So much for fate binding soul mates together. So far I've branded two men who don't want a permanent relationship with me. One of which I don't even know let alone love."

"You honestly think Bane is going to be upset you branded him?" Hawk asked. "Didn't you see the way he looked at you when we made love at Voth's?"

"I know he doesn't want to be trapped and I just trapped him. He might care for me or even love me, but he's going to resent that I've taken away his choice." And yes, Titus had already assured me that wasn't true, but I couldn't seem to make myself believe that.

"Silly, angel," Hawk murmured and he dipped in and captured my lips in a slow sensual kiss that warmed my desire for all of my guys. "He already made his choice. We all have. Now it's just a matter of adding us to the bond and freeing Rin."

My bitterness grew stronger and tightened my throat. "We won't be able to do that without the Heart," I said. "The Winter Court tried to make a bond with me and my brand wouldn't let it."

Hawk's expression turned serious, clearly coming to the same conclusion I had, that Sebastian without help from the Heart wouldn't be able to add him to my bond with Rin... and now, I guess, the bond that included Sebastian as well. "I really hope the Heart is as powerful as we believe it is. Everything is riding on us getting it."

"Dragonkind wouldn't have locked it away if it wasn't," Titus said.

"Yeah, but did they know at the time they were also risking everything?" Hawk asked. "Maybe it was only mostly powerful and if they'd known they'd get linked to it they wouldn't have done it."

"The lore says they knew there was a good chance the binding spell would link our species to the Heart." Titus's grip around me tightened. "But I doubt they expected the Summer Court's king to try to exterminate us to prevent the other courts from getting it."

Which was the horrible reality that Titus had been forced to live through. He'd lost everything the last time the Heart had awakened. His mate, his family, his friends. He was alone, the last of his kind, and while his soul had picked me to be his mate, there were aspects about him, about being a dragon, that I'd never be able to fully understand. And there wouldn't ever be anyone who would understand, because even if I wanted to, I'd never be able to have children with him. Angels could only have children with other angels.

Another tear trickled down my cheek and Hawk wiped it away.

"If dragonkind knowingly risked themselves then it means the Heart will be powerful enough to free Rin and add the rest of us," he said.

We all knew that wasn't a certainty, but it was all we had to hang onto. The only other option was that fate was finally kind to me and I'd brand the others. Which still didn't help Rin.

And I doubted fate would ever be kind.

I'd done everything I could. I'd had Karthick rip out a part of my soul — a part that had now healed when souls didn't just heal by themselves — and my brand had still awakened. I'd spent a lifetime running toward that fate only to realize I didn't want it, and when I'd finally gotten what I'd wanted, finally found men I loved not because fate made me but because of who they were, fate had stepped in and forced a stranger on me.

I'd been a fool to think I could have fought it. I would have been better off guarding my heart, because as much as Titus believed his mating magic was just as strong as mine, I feared it wasn't. And every time I thought about that, it tore out another piece of my heart. If Titus was right, it also meant that Rin and Sebastian were the mates I was supposed to have had all along.

And if I believe that, that meant no matter what I tried, even when we'd gotten the heart, I wouldn't be able to free Rin. I was going to have to break my promise to him, and that sent another tear trailing down my cheek. No one deserved to be trapped and manipulated. And that was exactly what the brand was doing to Rin.

Of course, maybe he was my soul mate and even if the brand hadn't formed we'd have fallen in love.

Hawk dipped in and gave me a tender kiss on my cheek. "We can't do anything until Bane gets better, so go back to sleep. You've barely been asleep for an hour and you haven't rested nearly enough to recover from —" He ran a hand through his jaw-length sandy-blond hair. "Hell, from everything, and you're still in magical shock." His gaze slid to Titus's and he gave him a tight nod then left.

"Hawk is right. You need more rest," Titus murmured. "Let my soul steady yours, like you've steadied mine."

I fell back asleep, but the dream of being trapped in a frozen darkness, forgotten and in pain continued to haunt me.

Please help me. Please free me. Remember me.

I gritted my teeth. I wasn't forgotten and I wasn't trapped. This was just a dream.

Make it stop.

The pain swelled, and the frozen darkness whirled around me. I needed to heal myself—? Rin—? Someone else—?

Find me.

This is just a dream.

Except it didn't feel like a dream. It felt like something more. And it was. I was connected to Rin through my angelic mating brand and my soul was desperate to heal him. I had to heal him. That was where the dream was coming from.

My healing compulsion flooded me and jerked me awake again.

Except waking didn't ease the pain or the desperate need to stop the suffering this time.

Beside me, Titus, his breath heavy with sleep, lay on his back, one arm underneath me and the other on his chest with his hand over his heart. Red-gold scales covered his neck and the top half of his chest, as if even asleep his beast was taking over, and his ferocious life force thrummed through me.

I clung to the sensation, trying to steady myself, but couldn't make my mind work past the pain.

Sunlight still poured through the doorway and I still trembled with magical shock. I doubted I'd slept for more than another hour and from the pressure building in my chest and the blazing heat in my palms from my healing magic, I knew in my soul I wasn't going to get any more sleep until I'd dealt with Rin's pain.

Except the second I thought that, I realized this pain wasn't Rin's. My senses told me his life force was in the room beside me, just like Sebastian and Hawk were in the room on my other side, and Cassius was high above me, likely perched on top of the mountain.

And while yes, Rin was still in pain, the pain inside me twisting my healing compulsion and urging me to go and heal came from far below.

Help me. Please. Make it stop.

My pulse lurched with realization.

There was someone else in the aerie and they were in agony.

My healing magic swelled up my forearms, my power overflowing, and before I realized what I was doing, I'd gotten out of bed and wrapped a towel around my body.

I turned to tell Titus about the stranger in the aerie—

Except I didn't.

I was pretty sure I thought about it, pretty sure I opened my mouth to speak, but I blinked and the next thing I knew, I was heading across the sitting room to the long hallway that led to the center of the mountain.

It was like I was still trapped in the dream... and maybe I *was* still dreaming. The voice that called for help and begged to be set free whispered inside me, along with the pain and the cold and the darkness.

Please, I couldn't be trapped—

But in *this* dream, *I* wasn't trapped. I was going to free whoever it was who was trapped and forgotten... and yet I had a horrible feeling when I found whoever it was, I was going to end up staring down at myself, trapped and in pain.

I tried to turn around, to wake up. Anything. But the call for help was overwhelming, and despite needing to lean against the wall to keep my balance, my healing compulsion still pulled me forward.

Help me. Free me. Please. It has to stop.

I reached the landing and swept my gaze over the partially covered cavern in the center of the mountain. The sun sat high in the sky and streamed through the large hole in the top, shining on most of the forest, all of the meadow, and half of the small lake. It looked so real with the sunlight sparkling in the gentle waves and catching in the dust and pollen lazily drifting over the meadow's long grass. Even the breeze, warm against my still-too-cold skin, felt real.

The pain came from the ground, close to the forest... in the forest?

I wasn't sure, but that didn't matter. If this was a dream, I'd end up where it wanted me to end up, and if it was real, my healing compulsion would still force me to where I needed to be.

I released my wings through the towel and glided to a large tree at the edge of the forest where a mass of glowing white vines curled around something at the tree's base and trailed up its trunk.

No. Not something. *Someone.* A man.

I could see one closed eye and part of his cheek and mouth, and I could feel his life force, weak and thready and overwhelmed by another more powerful life force. Threads of glowing magic pulsed in his skin in time with the light pulsing in the vines like a slow and steady heartbeat despite the pain radiating from him.

I secured the towel around my chest to free both of my hands, hurried to his side as fast as my trembling body could manage, and grabbed one of the vines covering his head.

My pulse tripped, and my healing compulsion twisted tighter, my magic burning up my forearms, ready, eager to be released, and, much to my surprise within my control as if enough of my magical shock had eased that I could connect with my power, but not enough to steady and warm me.

The man in the vines was Karthick. I had no idea how he'd gotten into the aerie or ended up covered in vines, but I had to help him.

I wrenched on the vine and pushed my healing magic into him, but the vine clung tight — it didn't even budge — and my healing magic slid through him unable to connect with anything inside him because there was nothing physically wrong with him.

Even my life force magic couldn't properly connect with him, as if his life force wasn't really there, either.

Please. Help me.

I dug my nails into the vine to get a better grip and heaved, making my trembling worse and the world darkened and lurch, but I couldn't get it to move even a fraction of an inch.

Help me. Make it stop.

"I want to." But I couldn't. Not by myself. I had to get help. Of course, if this was a dream, then nothing would make the vines move and I'd likely end up running in circles unable to find help.

Except the more I thought about it, the more this didn't feel like a dream.

My healing compulsion twisted tighter, making it hard to breathe, screaming at me to help him, ease his pain, do something. Now now now. But it didn't matter how hard I pushed. I couldn't make it connect with him. *He* wasn't the one in pain. And yet he was. My compulsion said the pain came from him... or did it come from the other massive life force overwhelming his? Even if it wasn't his pain, my compulsion wasn't forcing me to go anywhere else in the aerie, and I had a feeling if I tried to leave, it wouldn't let me.

Which was going to become a serious problem if I couldn't heal whatever it was that was driving my compulsion crazy.

He groaned and his eye opened, his bright green iris cloudy with white fae magic.

Make it stop, he gasped. Except his mouth didn't move. *Please. Remember me. Why can't anyone remember me?*

God. So much pain. So much fear. I had to do something. I couldn't be trapped— No. He— It?

I had no idea who or what I was sensing. Whatever it was he or it couldn't go on with things as they were.

"I'm not strong enough. I have to get help." I tried to stand, but my compulsion kept me rooted to his side, clinging to the vine. I couldn't move, my effort making dark specs flood my vision.

"Don't," Karthick gasped out loud this time, his voice tight with the pain my magic insisted wasn't his. The pulsing in the vines grew faster and brighter, drawing another groan and some of the magic clouding his eye cleared.

"Sebastian will know what to do. He can help," I said.

I tried to blink the darkness from my vision and move, but was now trapped as much as he was, locked in place as the cold inside me swelled and my trembling increased.

"Seireadan can't help," Karthick replied. "And neither can you."

"I have to." My compulsion wouldn't let me ignore him. "You're in pain."

"Pain?" Confusion darkened his expression. "What pain?"

"You don't feel it?"

Heal me. Help me.

Free me.

The strange life force surged stronger.

Make it stop.

I can't. I don't have the power.

I strained to connect with the pain, find its source within him. Because it had to be there and I had to be able to do something. I just had to.

But the deeper I searched, the more the source of the pain slipped farther out of reach, and the faster the world spun around me.

God, it didn't make sense. How could the pain be his but not his?

"It's okay," he groaned. "This is the deal."

"The deal?"

He drew in a ragged breath and slowly released it, letting his eyelid flutter shut, and the light in the vines pulsed brighter.

His breath turned slow and steady with sleep, and the sense of pain and powerful life force suddenly vanished.

"Karthick, what deal?" For a second my magic fully connected with him, told me he was in a deep sleep and nothing was wrong with him. Then my healing compulsion released me and my magical shock swelled, sending me reeling.

I sagged back onto my rear and squeezed my eyes shut, trying to stop the world from spinning.

What were the odds that the guys would tell me about the deal? And did it really matter? There wasn't anything I could do about it, and Karthick had insisted Sebastian couldn't help, either.

"The deal was to find you," Hawk said from behind me.

My senses jerked away from Karthick and connected with Hawk's dark, seductive, fiery life force, sending a shiver of desire rushing through me despite my shock.

He stood a few feet away in the meadow, the sunlight catching in his sandy blond hair and making his gray-blue eyes seem pale, almost as pale as Sebastian's. He wore only the pair of beige shorts that he'd gotten from Voth — since the fabric and style didn't match anything I'd seen in Faerie — giving me a perfect view of his beautifully sculpted body. He looked breathtaking and exhausted, and my heart and soul ached for him.

God, I ached to connect with him, to have his life force thrumming inside me, and I ached because fate had bound me to Rin and now Sebastian and not him.

AMIAH

"I'm surprised you told me," I said to Hawk. Normally the guys wouldn't have said anything, as if I wasn't capable of handling hard decisions. Which drove me crazy. Except I knew it wasn't because they thought I couldn't handle it, but because they were trying to protect me, saving me the grief of feeling bad about a difficult situation.

"It's not a secret, although I'm sure the others wouldn't have wanted you to worry—" He offered me a soft, sad smile. "Or feel guilty."

Which was the real reason the guys didn't tell me things.

Except I did feel guilty. Karthick had sacrificed himself so the guys could rescue me. That wasn't something I wanted to be responsible for.

"This is my fault. He let this—" I waved a hand over the vines. "—whatever this is, capture him so you could find me. He shouldn't have done that."

"We had no other way. The concealment charm Mavis gave you is still working, so even if Sebastian had been able to cast a location spell, he wouldn't have been able to find you." The hellfire in Hawk's eyes flared, and he waded through the tall grass to me and held out his hand to help me up.

I took it, and he tugged me to my feet, sending the world spinning. I leaned into him and he wrapped me in a firm embrace.

The feel of his sculpted muscles, the fact that I only wore a towel, and his body heat sent another shiver of desire rushing through me. God, I needed him on a soul-deep level and he needed me.

My throat tightened. Why hadn't I branded him instead?

"Letting Faerie hold him was our only choice. We had to find you," he said, pressing his lips against my forehead. "We were afraid Rin was taking you to Deaglan."

Rin's name turned my shiver into a throbbing ache between my thighs, and I clung to Hawk, fighting the urge to stagger back into the suite to find Rin.

And now that my healing compulsion had eased, my soul felt even more out of alignment, even though it hadn't been very long since I'd had sex and connected with Sebastian in order to save him.

"Rin can't hurt me. The brand is too strong," I replied, his name on my lips making my need burn hotter. And even if the brand wasn't as powerful as I believed, I'd made it perfectly clear that siding with us was his only chance of surviving this mess.

Except the moment I thought that, I knew he wasn't just siding with us because I'd threatened him. And while yes, the brand had to be compelling him, so too was his distrust and hate for Deaglan.

"I know you didn't know Rin wouldn't hurt me, but to let Faerie trap Karthick like this." I shuddered at the memory of all that pain, determined to focus on that and not Rin.

But God, I needed to seal my bond with Rin. Now!

No. Focus on the situation. Focus on how Karthick sacrificed his freedom for yours.

Even if the pain was somehow gone, I didn't want to be responsible for Karthick being trapped like that. "How long will Faerie hold him?"

"He didn't know how long," Hawk replied. "Is he really in pain?"

"I thought he was. My healing magic compelled me here, and there was an enormous pain radiating from him. But my magic couldn't connect with him." I glanced at him, barely visible beneath the white pulsing vines. "And now there's nothing."

Hawk's embrace tightened. "He agreed that keeping your key from Deaglan was more important than his freedom or anything else."

A part of me hated that thought, hated that someone had willingly given up his freedom for mine, while the logical part of me understood. There was more at stake than just me and my guys.

Even if the Heart was only half as powerful as I believed, it was still too powerful to let Deaglan have it. He'd torture and kill thousands.

Sacrifices had to be made and I could only pray this was the worst of it.

My soul shuddered and fear unfurled cold and hard in my chest. Even if we did get the Heart there was a chance I was going to lose everyone except Sebastian. The only way to guarantee that I didn't lose the others was to brand them.

Except I couldn't just brand them—

Or maybe I could.

I'd reached deep inside myself to give Sebastian everything I had to save him and I'd ended up branding him. If I had sex with Hawk and did the same thing — even though I couldn't actually give him fae magic — maybe I could brand him too.

Everything else about the angelic mating brand had been wrong. Maybe not being able to control who I branded was a myth as well. And while I didn't have to have sex with Hawk to brand him, adding the connection that I made with him and the others during sex could only help.

It had to.

"Hawk," I said, my voice breathy even as my thoughts jumped to Rin and how much my body ached to have sex with him.

Hawk slid his hands to my cheeks and urged me to look up at him. "You're not going to be able to resist your bond with Rin for much longer."

"I can last until we get the Heart." *Especially if I brand you.*

And really, branding him solved two problems. It didn't just save Hawk from losing his mind and starving to death, but would also strengthen my soul. I'd have two complete soul bonds to help me withstand my incomplete bond. Surely that would be enough to help me last until the final key was empowered and we'd gotten the Heart.

My desire surged stronger and the hellfire in Hawk's eyes flared.

"Help me relieve the pressure and forget." I should have just told him the truth, that I wanted to have sex with him to brand him. But I feared I'd break his heart even more if I told him my plan and it didn't work.

Except it would break *my* heart if it didn't work. I'd felt broken and empty, like a piece of my soul was missing when I'd thought Cassius was dead, and I knew I'd feel the same way if my bonds made me fall out of love with Hawk.

He brushed his lips against mine in a brief and tender kiss, sending his dark and fiery life force thrumming against my senses and making my need pool hot and wet between my thighs, the reaction stronger than it should have been for such a chaste kiss.

"Hawk, don't tease me," I groaned as I tangled my fingers in his hair, tugged his mouth back to mine, and kissed him with all my desire, frustration, heartache, and determination. I loved him and I was not going to lose him.

"That wasn't intended as a tease," he said against my lips, turning us so he could pin me against a tree trunk.

He kissed me like the first time he'd kissed me in the abandoned bathhouse with everyone watching. Hard and hot. It had shocked me that he'd taken control, grabbed my hair, and tugged my head back to deepen our kiss. And it had shocked me even more how much I'd loved it.

Now I couldn't get enough. I loved all the ways Hawk made love to me, soft, reverent, playful, informative, and passionate. He wasn't as ferocious and out of control as Titus, although if I asked him, I'm sure he would be, but there was still a delicious hint of dominance to his kiss this time.

I moaned into his mouth, letting him know, even though he could feel my desire, how much he turned me on.

And I wasn't going to think about how a good chunk of my need came from my incomplete soul bond with Rin.

No. This was for Hawk, and I was going to use my power to brand him like I'd branded Sebastian.

I tangled my fingers in his hair and rubbed my thumbs against the base of his horns, drawing a low, sensual moan from him, that vibrated straight to my core and mixed with his thrumming sensual life force. God, I loved that sound and that feeling. I wanted it forever, wanted him to show me everything I'd read about and more.

I gave into the feel of his mouth possessing me, his body, hard and hot against mine. He dominated because I'd asked him to help me forget and he was overwhelming me with sensation: his lips and tongue, his grip in my hair, his body against mine pressing me against the tree trunk, its bark rough against my bare shoulders.

I let him sweep me away from my fear of losing him and of losing all of them. In this moment there was just Hawk and our desire.

My thoughts lurched. It wasn't just our desire. I had to remember the whole point for asking him to make love to me. I couldn't just let him help me relieve the pressure of my incomplete soul bond with Rin or forget my worries. I needed to gather my power and brand him like I'd branded Sebastian.

But God, it was so hard to remember that with my mind still whirling with shock and his seductive magic blossoming low within me.

He tugged open my towel and roughly palmed my breast. The soft fabric draped at my sides, held against my body by my still-released wings protruding through it.

I arched my back, pressing my breast into his hand, eager for him even as I struggled to concentrate on my power and our connection.

I could do this. I could brand him. I just needed to stay focused on his life force and gathering my magic to release it when I came.

He plundered my mouth, stealing my breath and making my breasts heave into his rough touch, then pinched my nipple, making me gasp at the sharp bite of pain. But he quickly melted it away with his magic, making me release my breath with a throaty moan and my thoughts stutter.

"You're not supposed to be thinking," he said against my lips and he pinched my other nipple, the touch of pain and flood of magic sending me whirling and throbbing.

His life force surged against my senses, and my soul shifted closer to its proper alignment as I strained to focus on that, on taking his life force and merging it with mine.

"Stop thinking." He dropped his hand between my thighs and pushed two fingers into me, sending a shockwave of pleasure rolling through me at the sudden invasion.

"I'm the one making love to you. Be here with me. Don't let him share this moment," he said, thinking that my thoughts were on Rin because he didn't know I was trying to brand him.

He withdrew his fingers and pushed them back in, plunging them in and out of me, working me up and scattering my thoughts, not needing an ounce of his seductive magic to get me panting and desperate for him. I hooked my leg around his waist to give him easier access, and he brought me right to the edge, my muscles trembling with the promise of an amazing release, then he flooded me with magic and cruelly, wonderfully, breathtakingly jerked me back.

I clung to his horns, having completely forgotten to keep rubbing them, panting into his mouth, my body trembling on the edge of a climax that he controlled.

With one hand, he flicked open the button on his waistband,

unzipped his fly, and let his shorts fall to the ground, freeing his full thick erection. Pre-ejaculate glistened on his tip, and I tilted my hips, sliding my wet folds against his hard length.

"Hawk," I moaned, as he pushed inside me.

His life force blazed across my senses and swirled around my heart, and my soul shifted, clicking closer into alignment, powerful and strong and almost properly aligned.

I hooked my other leg around him and he grabbed my hips, trusting me to keep my balance against the wide tree trunk, his incubus strength more than enough to hold me up, and thrust into me with powerful strokes, as if he weren't just trying to make me forget about Rin and all my worries, but also trying to forget about his worries as well.

Our bodies crashed together, glorious shockwaves that rolled from our impact up my whole body. He twisted my need, already on the edge and held back by his magic, amazingly tight, making the world spin not with magical shock but with stunning pleasure. Each thrust was a claim to my body and soul, like how Titus had ferociously claimed me, and a promise that he was mine and always would be.

And I wouldn't let my soul bonds with Rin and Sebastian forsake that promise. I was his, too. I'd fallen in love with him like a normal person, in the way I'd wanted to, and I wasn't going to let a mating brand I didn't want take that away from me.

I wrenched at my magic, the healing power still overflowing, hot and sticky in my palms and curling up my forearms, the fae magic embedded in my cells that chilled me despite the aerie's warm temperature and Hawk's demonic body heat, and the strange new life force power that I still couldn't properly recognize.

Hawk pounded into me, his magic swelling, my need so tight I was sure I'd explode, and still I clung to my power. I'd release it when I came, just like when I'd saved Sebastian. I just needed to hold on and ride the amazing wave that I knew was coming.

Then he thrust hard and tensed and let go of his hold on my orgasm, making us come together.

I crashed over the edge and released my own magic. I wouldn't have been able to hold onto it even if I tried. I shoved it into him, feeling its heat unfurl around my heart and warm my left side, before the pleasure of my release and the power of his life force swept through all other sensations. I was darkness and fire and sensuality even as my unnatural full-body fae glow burst to life. Lights flashed behind my lids and I was spinning and spinning and spinning on a wave of amazing, overwhelming, glorious sensation, my body thrumming with power—

But not the right power. My side was warm, but not burning like it had been when Sebastian's brand had formed, and Hawk had a soft bittersweet expression, as if he'd figured out what I was trying to do and it had failed.

I had failed.

I hadn't branded him and it didn't seem to matter how much I loved him. Fate didn't think he was mine.

My throat tightened with tears. "I thought it would work. I *wanted* it to work." Why hadn't it worked? "I love you."

I sagged into his embrace, the release of his magic tugging me toward unconsciousness like it always did.

"I know you do, gorgeous," he murmured against my temple. "I love you, too."

HAWK

Amiah passed out, her skin blazing with light and her expression soft with bliss from her orgasm. I set her down long enough to pull my shorts back on and resecure her towel then carried her — mindful of not letting her wings drag on the ground — along the edge of the forest to the stairwell in the side of the mountain to take her back to our suite.

And while yes, she could fly herself back up there, I didn't want to wait for the side effects of my magic to wear off — since I'd promised Cassius I'd keep an eye on Bane and Rin while they were unconscious — and I didn't want to wake her.

Her aura had still been trembling with magical shock when I'd realized her painful sexual energy was out on the ledge at the end of the hall, and it was still thready now. She hadn't had much sleep in the last few days, and letting my magic give her hopefully half an hour of sleep, maybe more, was the least I could do for her.

Especially after letting her see my disappointment when I'd finally realized what she'd been trying to do and it hadn't worked.

God, I'd thought she'd been distracted by her desire for Rin and she'd specifically asked me to help her ignore it. It had only been when she'd come and released a massive wave of magic into me that had caressed my soul and wrapped around my heart that I realized she'd been trying to repeat what she'd done with Bane and brand me.

There'd been a second when I'd thought it had worked. The connection we made during sex, the sense that she *saw* my whole soul, had never been stronger. Hope had filled her expression and my heart had swelled with the impossible love I felt for her.

And then the magic had dissipated instead of sinking into me.

Her expression had fallen, the look in her eyes complete heartbreak, before my magic swept her away and overwhelmed all other thoughts and feelings.

I reached the wide entrance to the stairwell and started the multistory climb back up to the suite, my heart heavy. I wanted to give her my life, wanted to have my soul bound to hers. With Bane's soul also bound, there wouldn't be any worry about me starving or feeding too deeply from her.

The thought made my chest tighten with jealousy. Why couldn't she have branded me instead? He didn't need her brand like I did. He'd have been fine if she fell out of love with him.

Except I knew that wasn't true.

He wouldn't end up crazy like I would, but he'd be just as shattered when her soul bond made her fall out of love with him.

It was stupid of her to think that Bane would hate her for branding him. Sure, he'd said he didn't want to be bound to anyone, but that had been before he'd fallen in love with her, and from the way he'd looked at her while we were having sex at Voth's, he was completely in love with her.

And really, I should be happy for him and her. If everything went sideways and she couldn't remove her soul bond with Rin, at least she'd have Bane to help her through it.

But that thought made me think of the promise I'd given her about being there for her when she had to have sex with Rin.

She'd said she'd be able to hold out until we'd gotten the Heart, but from the strength and pain of her desire for Rin, I didn't know how much longer that would be, and we had no idea when the final key would become empowered. It could be hours, days, or weeks. If it took too long, she'd have to seal her bond with Rin or go crazy.

Would she want Bane to help her through that instead?

Her brand proved she was in love with him and that she'd been fated to be with him from the very beginning.

I shoved that thought aside as I reached the landing for our floor and headed to the long hallway leading to our suite.

She was still in love with me. She was so in love she'd tried to twist fate to her will and brand me even though angels couldn't control who they branded.

Just because she'd tried and failed didn't mean she wouldn't eventually bind our souls together. Trying to repeat what she'd done when she'd accidentally branded Bane and failing to brand me didn't mean *never*. It just meant right now wasn't our time.

Which was something I had to hold on to or I'd lose my mind. We connected when we had sex. I gave her something she needed, just like the others did. That meant she needed me as much as I needed her—

Except I didn't know if having a complete soul bond changed that. Maybe she didn't need me or the others anymore. Which, knowing her, would break her heart as much as it broke mine.

I didn't want to believe that fate was as fucked up as Bane believed, or that the angelic mating brand was the complete nightmare Amiah thought it was. She'd branded Bane. It couldn't be a nightmare. And yet it was going to force her to have sex with Rin even though neither of them wanted that.

She murmured in her sleep, her breath unnaturally cool against my bare skin, and her hand slid up my chest to rest over top of my heart, making my soul sing and weep at the same time.

I didn't want to hold out hope that fate or the Heart would fix this, and yet it was the only thing I had. I wasn't going to leave her and I wasn't going to stop loving her. She knew that and if she didn't brand me, falling out of love with me was going to hurt her as much as it would hurt me. Just as much as having sex with Rin and being stuck in their unwanted soul bond would hurt her.

And none of that would matter if she didn't survive getting the Heart.

Which I couldn't protect her from even if I wanted to. Titus wouldn't be able to find the next key when it became empowered without her, and we were going to have to drag her along.

The thought made my pulse race. We'd barely been able to protect her from Deaglan in our last encounters— hell, we'd almost lost her when Rin had stabbed her. Now I knew why Cassius always looked like he was on the verge of a mental breakdown.

I carried her into the bathroom and gently cleaned her up — my magic and her exhaustion from what had been a horrific week keeping her asleep — and was halfway across the sitting room on the way to her bedroom when Titus rushed out of the doorway.

Scales covered his jaw, neck, and most of his chest, and his aura blazed bright, his dragon's head superimposed around his human head.

His attention jumped to us, and his gaze slid over her body wrapped in nothing but a towel and glowing brightly from her orgasm.

With a snarl, his aura blazed brighter, his pupils slitted, and his canines extended, and for a second, I was sure his beast was going to take over and beat the shit out of me. I'd clearly had sex with her. Even if she hadn't been glowing, I hadn't cleaned either of us up enough to completely remove the scent of our arousal.

But then some of his scales melted back under his skin and he released a heavy breath, sending smoke curling from his human nostrils.

"Is she okay?" he asked, his voice gruff.

"Just sleeping off my magic."

"Good. She needs to rest," he replied, his acceptance that I'd slept with his mate still surprising me even though he'd made it clear he believed we were all her mates.

"That's going to take some serious getting used to," I said, continuing to the bedroom.

Although his dragon's head was still clear in his aura, his pupils were still slitted, and his canines extended, which meant his dragon was straining for control or *in* control.

Titus the man might have fully accepted that Amiah slept with all of us, but Titus the beast was probably still coming to terms with it. And really, it hadn't even been twenty-four hours since Amiah had mended his soul. The connection between his two halves had to still be fragile, and the more time he had with her the better.

Which meant it should be him and not me who got back into bed with her.

"You want to get in first so you don't hurt her wings when you get back into bed?" I asked.

"You sure you don't want to sleep with her?"

I did, God, everything within me begged to stay with her. And while a part of me wanted to make love to her again the moment she woke up, another part just wanted to hold her close.

"Your soul needs contact with her more than I do." The words stung. They were true, but that didn't mean they didn't hurt. I *did* need her and didn't want to be without her. But neither did Titus, and if she didn't brand him, he was facing the same fate I was.

And if we all weren't at our best, if he was still fighting his dragon nature, then something could go wrong and we could all lose her.

SEBASTIAN

I WOKE WITH A START, AGONY BURNING THROUGH MY BODY AS IF I'D BEEN dunked in acid. It was all I could feel. I couldn't sense the demonic magic infection or my fae magic or the blaze of golden magic that had branded my left side and filled my soul.

Had I just imagined being branded?

I'd been delirious with pain and barely conscious when Amiah had come and flooded me with fae magic. Maybe I'd been wrong. Maybe I was just so desperate to keep her, still so terrified that I'd lost her when the Winter Court had taken her that I'd imagined her branding me.

The thought made my pulse race. But instead of racing with the fear of being trapped, it was with the fear that she hadn't bound our souls together, that no matter what I did, I was going to lose her when her soul bond with Rin made her fall out of love with me.

I shoved aside the blanket someone had covered me with and yanked up my shirt to stare at the delicate gold threads woven into my skin, the intricate design twisting around the thick black lines of my circle of power glyph tattooed along my ribs.

"Oh, thank God." I hadn't imagined it. I just couldn't feel the power in the bond because the rest of me was still raw from weeks of suffering with the demonic magic infection and then having Rin rip it and my fae magic out of me.

"It's sealed," Hawk said, drawing my gaze to him. He sat on the floor by the doorway so he could keep an eye on me and the sitting room at the same time. "It formed during sex so it sealed right away."

I knew that, and Hawk knew that I knew that, but Hawk, with his magic sensitivity could also see how much of a fucked-up mess I was and that I probably couldn't sense the brand, let alone sense if my soul bond with Amiah was fully sealed or not.

The memory of her face and the horror in her eyes when she'd realized what she'd done rushed into my mind's eye, and my pulse lurched. She'd said she'd make it right, that she hadn't meant to brand me, that we'd get the Heart and she'd free me like she was going to free Rin. She thought I didn't want her.

With a jerk, I sat up, sending agony screaming through me and turning my breaths into sharp, shallow gasps as I fought to stay conscious.

"Hey." Hawk rushed to the bed, sat beside me, and grabbed my shoulders. But I wasn't sure if it was to steady me or keep me where I was.

Probably a bit of both.

Except my soul cried that I had to go to her, reassure her that I was okay, that I wanted her.

And the need only partially came from our newly formed bond. The rest came from the fact that I loved her and I'd fallen in love with her before she'd branded me.

"She's okay," Hawk said, but his expression turned grim and I didn't know if it was because she wasn't okay or if he was acutely aware that she hadn't branded him.

I grabbed Hawk's wrists and met his gaze. We hadn't been friends during or even after the war, more like business associates. He had a magical talent I sometimes needed for my business and I trusted him. And while he knew my secret, that I was actually a full fae sorcerer, it was only because I'd desperately hoped by working together we could have saved those children, but I'd never allowed him or anyone to get close enough to become a trusted friend. The last friend I'd trusted had fucked my fiancé and convinced her to help him poison me.

But now I didn't want to lose Hawk almost as much as I didn't want to lose Amiah. I wasn't in love with him, not like I was in love with Amiah, but I loved what the three of us had together, loved watching him make love to her, loved the sounds she made when we worked together, loved how she lit up, both emotionally and with her full-body fae glow when she came, or hell, even just looked at him. He was the first of us to accept her for who she was and what she wanted... because I'd been an idiot and had been so sure she and Cassius were meant to be together and had been afraid of Cassius losing his shit on me—

Which wasn't completely true. If I was being honest with myself, I was afraid to fall in love with her. Just like having a friend, the last time I'd been in love, I'd been betrayed. And while I knew Amiah wasn't capable of trying to kill me like Enowen had, I'd been afraid she'd come to her senses and realize she was supposed to be with Cassius.

Except fate said she was supposed to be with me.

I pressed my hand against her brand etched in my skin even though the only thing I could feel was the pain wracking my body.

Fate also said she was supposed to be with Rin.

Were we both mistakes?

I didn't want to be a mistake.

I'd known the moment Rin had stabbed her in the Summer Court's luminous cave garden that I was in love with her. Hell, I'd known before then, I'd just been too stupid to accept the truth. And I *knew* she loved me. She'd said so, and had been so sorry that she'd broken our agreement to just have sex until it was no longer fun.

But if I wasn't a mistake, did that mean Rin wasn't either?

I wasn't sure what to think of that. He'd protected her from Padraigin when they'd been trying to escape the Winter Court, had even given her air when she'd been suffocating, just like I had back in Left of Lincoln, but that didn't mean we could fully trust him. Yes, he'd helped when he didn't have to, but until we released him from his soul bond with Amiah, he was stuck protecting her because their lives were tied together... just like mine was now tied to hers as well, and how Hawk's should be.

"When we free Rin, we'll add you," I promised. "It probably won't even come to that. She's more in love with you than any of us. I'm sure she'll brand you, too."

"Yeah." Hawk flashed me a smile but it didn't reach his eyes.

He didn't believe that, and as much as I wanted to reassure him that it was true, I couldn't.

Love didn't mean anything as far as angelic mating brands were concerned.

Which meant I was just going to have to pull my shit together and bend fate to my own will. Amiah and Hawk belonged together, and just like I was going to do whatever it took to free Amiah from the Winter Court, I'd do whatever it took to add Hawk to our soul bond.

AMIAH

When I woke again, the light coming from the sitting room wasn't as bright, but it was still light out which meant the sun was still up and on the other side of the mountain. The heaving, lurching darkness of my magical shock was gone, so I'd been asleep long enough for it to finally pass, but I was still cold and shivering with the Winter Court's magic.

I lay on Titus's chest, my wings spread out on either side of me, the towel still wrapped around me, with Titus's arms holding me tight. His warm breath, heavy with sleep, caressed the top of my head with glorious warmth, and his ferocious life force sang against my senses—

No, it sang within me, entwined in my essence in perfect harmony, strong and sure, and even though he wasn't inside me, it felt as if my soul was closer to being properly aligned than it was when we were in contact.

It felt right to be in his arms, just like it always felt right to be in Hawk's and Sebastian's. Just like it felt right in those rare moments when Cassius held me.

My throat tightened at that thought. I'd tried to brand Hawk and had failed. I didn't want to accept that how I felt when he held me was wrong, that we weren't meant to be together.

And even if it did, fate could be damned. Hawk made me feel loved and safe. He made me feel strong and sexy, and I knew in my soul that I needed him. Just like I needed the others.

If I couldn't brand him like I'd branded Sebastian then I'd get the Heart.

My pulse picked up with fear and I tried to shove it aside. I didn't want to bet everything on getting the Heart. No matter how powerful everyone thought it was, there was a chance it wouldn't be able to break my bond with Rin and that it wouldn't be able to add Hawk, Cassius, and Titus to my bond with Sebastian.

And there was a chance that some of us, or all of us, wouldn't survive the fight with Deaglan to get it.

I pulled in my wings and eased off Titus's chest to lie beside him with his arms still around me. Out of all of my guys, he was the most rugged. He wasn't as gorgeous as Sebastian or Hawk or even as classically handsome as Cassius, but he was still beautiful. There was a pureness, an honesty to his appearance. He was a predator, powerful and wild in nature and fiercely protective, and he made no apologies for that. I teased my fingers across the red-gold scruff along his jaw, and his lips curled back in a soft smile.

"That feels good," he rumbled, his eyes still closed.

"Yeah?" I tangled my fingers into his shaggy red hair and brushed my lips against his. It was just a whisper of a touch, but it drew a low, longer rumble, and his stunning golden eyes fluttered open.

"That feels even better." He slid the hand beneath me up my back and cupped my head then dipped in for a deeper kiss. It was slow and sensual and filled with his powerful passion as if he wanted to draw it out for as long as possible.

The part of my soul that needed him shifted closer to alignment and his life force inside me strengthened.

He tangled his tongue with mine, exploring me, savoring me, filling me with a soft, comfortable desire. A desire that was all for Titus. It wasn't the desperate, aching need that my angelic mating brand made me feel for Rin, this was a desire that started in my heart, filled my chest, then, after infusing my essence with my love and the love I saw in Titus's eyes, it sank, warm and achingly soft, between my legs. I loved him. Mating brand or not, we belonged together, and I knew that in my soul.

My towel had fallen open, and Titus skimmed his free hand over my branded hip and up my ribs, making power flicker through the golden threads woven in my skin. But Titus either didn't notice or didn't care, and he swept his palm up to my breast and brushed his thumb across my nipple, drawing a soft moan, which in turn drew another low rumble of pleasure from him.

His touch was more than enough of a distraction that I could easily push my worries aside and embrace the present, and warm enough that I could ignore the Winter Court's frozen magic still chilling me from the inside. I was in bed with a powerful, amazing man. A man capable of ferocious passion who was now showing me his soft, sensual side. Each brush of his thumb tightened my nipple, making me ache for more, and slowly built up my desire.

This morning — or whatever time of day it was — I was going to have sex with Titus the man, and it seemed he wanted to draw this out. Which I had absolutely no problems with.

I arched my back, pressing my breast against his palm in encouragement, and savored the sensations.

His touch grew firmer, and he trailed kisses down my neck and across my collarbone to the silvery scars that I'd left in my skin after he'd bitten me.

"Mine," he rumbled, sending a shiver of need and joy rushing through me.

A hint of red-gold scales curled up his neck, but his beast didn't take over, and I could sense a completeness in his life force. The connection between the two halves of his soul was still fragile, but letting Titus the man have this moment was a demonstration of trust, just like letting his beast have sex with me the first time was.

"Always," I murmured back, and I would do whatever it took to keep him.

He worshiped my body, replacing his thumb with his lips and flicking and sucking my nipple into an aching tight bud, while the hand that had been on my breast, slowly inched down my belly.

The tip of his fingers brushed the edge of one of my brand's swirls, and a small part of me felt more power flicker through the golden threads, but I was so focused on the sensation of his mouth and hand on me that I didn't care. And really, there wasn't anything I could do about it right now, and I wasn't going to let it get in the way of joining with my dragon.

And then he roughly swiped his tongue against my nipple, and any remaining thoughts of my brand and my mates and the fate I didn't want vanished, swept away on a shiver of desire that rushed hot to my core.

My breath picked up despite Titus's pace, and I dug my fingers into his scalp and pressed my breast against his mouth. I needed more, needed it all, needed to feel our life forces fully entwined, our souls aligned and in perfect harmony.

But my urging only drew a low, sensual rumble, a mix of dragon and masculine satisfaction.

"This time is for you." He turned his attention to my other nipple and gave it a quick flick with his tongue that made me gasp and snapped sensation straight to my core. "This is what I wanted for our first time, but my dragon had other plans."

He sucked on my already tight bud, slowly building the pressure, the tug reaching deeper and deeper inside me, the passion and ferocity of his life force growing with a glorious, slow pressure.

I squirmed, my core throbbing and moisture pooling between my legs. He might not have the same kind of experience or sensuality that Hawk did, but that didn't matter. I could *feel* his passion, his love for me. He hadn't been able to control himself the last time we'd made love and I hadn't wanted him to. But now, even though I could sense his growing passion, he was all control. This was, as he said, all for me.

He slid his hand from my belly to my thigh, his fingers following the bottom swirl of Rin's mating brand, sending more power flickering through it. This time the power stayed, adding to the aching need starting to twist within me. For a second I feared it would wrench my desire from Titus to Rin, but it didn't, it merely added to the glorious pressure building inside me. I ached for both of them and right now, my soul needed Titus as much as it needed to seal its bond with Rin.

Then Titus slid his hand down my thigh to the inside of my knee, pressing on it and urging me to open for him. My pulse grew faster, my desire tightening and growing hotter in anticipation.

His pace as he kissed his way down my stomach was still slow and reverent, very much like how Cassius had kissed me. Except Cassius had been trying to draw the moment out for as long as possible and memorize every detail because he'd thought we'd never be able to make love again. Titus believed we'd have a lifetime of having sex — if he was right about the power of his mating brand — and this was him professing his love. Every kiss and touch and rumble of satisfaction was an *I love you. You're special, you're cherished, you're mine.*

It made my soul sing, and when he nudged my other knee, I happily opened my legs in invitation, my need for him and to complete the circuit of our souls turning hot and tight. And I wasn't going to think about how my desire to feel properly aligned was like a drug that I needed to have more of and more frequently. Once everyone was safe, I'd figure it out— *We'd* figure it out.

He lifted his gaze to mine, his stunning golden eyes filled with love and desire.

"I love you too," I murmured.

That drew a low rumble of satisfaction, even as the desire in his eyes grew, and he settled between my thighs, his broad muscular shoulders and his massive biceps bunching with the movement.

God, he was so powerful. Even without being able to sense his predator nature, I'd have known he was a predator, just by how he moved. And yet I felt completely safe with him. Even if his beast took over and we had the same aggressive sex as before, I knew he wouldn't purposely hurt me. He might bang me up a bit, stretch me beyond what my body could easily handle, and mark me again, but my life would never be in danger.

But right now, Titus the man was fully in control, and he teased his tongue with a barely-there touch up my inner thigh to the crux between my thigh and torso. Close and yet so far away from where I wanted him.

His hot breath teased my sensitive flesh, and I squirmed, trying to move that fraction of an inch so his breath hit just the right spot. But he captured my hips in his large hands and held me still with his incredible strength.

"You don't get to rush this," he growled, sending desire shivering through me.

"You're going to drive me crazy."

He raised his gaze, his lips curled back in a lopsided smile but his eyes were dark with desire. "That's the point. All I did was take last time."

"If it hadn't been obvious, I can assure you, I enjoyed myself, too."

"Then you're really going to enjoy yourself now."

He dipped his head back down, still holding my hips in an iron grip, and was absolutely true to his word. He tormented me with his tongue and lips, slowly — so damned slowly — licking and sucking, drawing out every glorious sensation until my breath was ragged and my need achingly tight. It was wonderful. I reveled in the feel of his powerful body between my legs, his large hands on my hips controlling my body, and the growing power of his life force inside me.

Then he picked up his pace and slid a finger inside me. His life force surged, and my need grew blazingly hot before sweeping through me in a long, sensual, bone-melting climax.

It wasn't hard like the climax I'd had with Hawk when I'd tried to brand him or with Hawk and Sebastian when they'd both filled me, or even the last time I'd had sex with Titus. But it was still powerful, and a long low moan of satisfaction escaped my lips as I rode the wave, letting it seep into and relax every muscle in my body.

TITUS

The light in Amiah's skin grew, slowly building in intensity as her orgasm swept through her. It was stunning to watch. Unlike the last time we'd made love when her fae glow had burst into a sudden brilliant light, this was like a cloud leisurely drifting away from the sun. It started small, barely brighter than her usual glow and swelled with a beautiful crescendo as she moaned her release.

"Oh, wow," she sighed, her words soft and slurred.

I slid my gaze up her stunning, delicate body, my beast preening at her praise. *Oh, wow*, had been my goal, and so too had been her currently relaxed state. And while I knew she was sturdier than she looked, and had clearly enjoyed my beast's ferocious sex before, this time I wanted to do things right. I'd nearly killed Seireadan when he'd shoved his cock into her in the Winter Court before she was ready, and then my beast had gone and done the same thing. She was smaller than I was used to and needed to be fully relaxed and wet before we joined, and even then I needed to hold my beast at bay and take it slow.

And while my beast had agreed this was my turn and loved the feel of her against my mouth and her taste and the little sighs and gasps and mewling sounds she made as I was working her up, it was eager to get to the joining part, the part where our souls connected, the part that she needed from me and the others.

I just needed to remember to be slow. This wasn't something I should rush. I crawled up her body and captured her lips in another long, sensual kiss as she curled her hips, catching the tip of my cock at her entrance in invitation.

"Mine," she breathed, that one word on her lips making my soul sing and my already hard cock harder.

I slowly pushed into her, pausing, barely inside her, waiting for her body to adjust to me, savoring the delicious torture of drawing it out. Even with her satiated and relaxed and slick from her orgasm, she was still incredibly tight, and I didn't want to hurt her.

My beast rumbled low inside me in agreement, surprising me that it loved the agonizingly slow push into her, the pressure and heat around my throbbing cock, and the slowly building power of her magic connecting with my soul.

She moaned, and her glow undulated in soft waves up to her head then down her body to where I was partially buried inside her. I inched a little farther in, drawing another moan and ripple through her glow, and she gripped my forearms as her head tipped back on the pillow.

It was like the fantasy I'd had of her from the moment I'd first met her, and yet so much more. Her blond hair was splayed around her in a golden halo, and her lips were parted on a soft, sensual moan.

And then I sank in all the way, finally fully sheathed, and the connection between us roared into me, seeping through my veins and weaving into my essence. I was steady, with no doubt in my soul, and I knew we were each other's soul's mate. She might have branded Rin and Seireadan, but she was also mine, and the scars from the shallow marks she'd scored in my flesh when my dragon had claimed her were proof. If she hadn't been my mate, her marks would have vanished, probably even before we'd finished mating the first time.

And then she looked at me between lids partially lowered in pleasure, and the light radiating from her body, already glowing brightly from her first release, surged stronger. She curled her hips, the miniscule movement pressing her pelvis against mine, urging me to start moving, and sending powerful ripples through her fae glow.

It was breathtaking and despite my certainty, a part of me still couldn't believe that I belonged to this stunning, brave, powerful woman.

Just like the others did. Hawk had been right. We were all Amiah's mates, and — probably to everyone's surprise — that felt right to my beast. This was the way it was supposed to be. They were who I was supposed to be with. They were my new pack and she was our queen—no, our goddess, and I was at her altar worshiping her.

I slowly pulled out and just as slowly pushed back in as her eyes opened a little wider and she captured my soul, like she always did, in her stunning blue depths. Even if her powerful magic hadn't been singing in my veins, I would have known she loved and trusted me. It was clear in her eyes.

I worked her back up, savoring the feel of her around me and all the amazing sounds of pleasure she made. She rocked her body in time with mine, meeting me with each thrust, her moans coming faster and getting louder, announcing her rising desire without any hesitation. It filled both me and my beast with possessive, masculine desire, knowing she trusted me and had completely let go of any inhibitions. Not to mention it made my beast revel in the knowledge that everyone in the suite could hear how I was satisfying our mate.

I picked up our pace and carefully teased my thumb over her clit. I wanted to bring her the most pleasure I could, but I didn't want her to come just yet — and unlike an incubus, I couldn't control her orgasm.

She gasped at my touch and dug her fingernails into my forearms, making my beast rumble with pleasure.

Mine.

Another tease, and she thrust her hips up, taking me in as deep as I could go. Her breath was ragged, making her breasts heave and her glow writhe, and I could tell she was on the edge.

"Oh, Titus," she moaned, making my balls ache, forcing me to fight my own release. She was going to come again and she damned well was going to be first.

I pumped faster, unable to hold back my release *and* keep my pace steady, and rubbed my thumb over her clit.

"Oh," she cried. "Oh, yes."

The ripples of her orgasm started to flutter around my cock and I increased my intensity. My beast surged, its power swirling into her magic entwined inside me, and I brought her crashing over the edge again.

With a long loud cry, her hips bucked off the bed and her muscles clenched tight around my cock, making me come as well.

Her glow burst into a blinding light and her power flooded into my soul. My beast roared. She was mine. I was hers. And together we were powerful.

I waited until her breath steadied and her body relaxed beneath me then tugged her into a firm embrace and watched as she drifted back to sleep, fully satiated and relaxed. I wanted to hold her like this forever and keep her safe. But I wasn't the only one who needed to hold her and I didn't know if I'd be able to fully protect her.

We still needed one more key to become empowered and I wasn't going to be able to find it without her. Which meant she had to come with me to get it and that meant taking her into a fight with Deaglan, because without a doubt as soon as the last key became empowered Deaglan would go after it too. Of course, if Seireadan had finally regained his magic when that happened, we might be able to get Deaglan's keys and then the Heart and Amiah would be free of Rin.

Except that still meant taking her into danger and that made both me and my beast furious.

I held her, half-asleep myself, and listened to the heartbreaking quiet in the aerie. The last time I'd been there for any amount of time had been before the Summer Court's king had slaughtered my people. The aerie had been full of life with children laughing, playing, learning to shift and fly and release their elemental breath. There'd been separate packs, even among the elements, but earth, fire, water, and air dragons all lived in harmony — or as well in harmony as predator shifters could — when we returned to the aerie. For some, like me and my pack, it was a yearly pilgrimage.

I'd been newly mated and the pack had come for the elder to bless our union. Now I had joined with my soul's mate and there was no elder to bless us, no family to celebrate and spit fire into the night's sky. There'd be no fire or pilgrimage or blessing for our children, either.

There would never be any children because angels could only conceive with other angels.

Amiah sighed in her sleep and a hint of her power whispered soft and warm inside me even as she snuggled, pressing more of her flesh against me, steadying my soul.

I didn't need children to be fulfilled. But what made my heart hurt was knowing I was it. Once I was gone, dragonkind would be gone as well, and a part of Faerie would be lost forever.

I hadn't thought I'd ever wanted to return, and then I'd met Amiah. The look on her face, the awe and wonder when I'd taken her to that balcony in the Winter Court and showed her how stunning the court was, had been breathtaking, and I wanted to share all the things I loved about Faerie with her. Except one of those things had been the life and joy in the aerie.

She sighed again and her eyelids fluttered open, releasing her radiant angel glow.

"I could lie like this forever," she said, "but..."

But we didn't have the luxury of lounging around all day. We needed a plan for fighting Deaglan, for dealing with Cassius's magic, and for freeing Rin from their soul bond. And she'd want to check on Seireadan. Her new mate.

I pressed my lips to the back of her head and inhaled the sweet scent of her body and our lovemaking. "Go get cleaned up and check on the others. There was a set of clothes for you on the rack in the bathroom when we'd bathed last night."

"I'm glad you didn't bother to grab them," she murmured. "I like sleeping like this." She turned in my arms, captured my lips with hers, and pressed her body against mine.

My beast rumbled at the feel of her flesh sliding against mine and my cock grew hard again.

"You need to stop doing that," I said, my voice gruff with my rising desire.

"What?" she asked batting her eyelashes at me in mock innocence.

Yeah, she knew exactly what she was doing to me.

I rolled on top of her, sliding one leg between hers and pinned her to the mattress beneath me. "You know it's dangerous to tease a wild beast."

Her hips rolled up, rubbing her thigh against my cock, as her head tilted back and she released a frustrated moan. "I'm never going to get anything done. You're too sexy and I already feel out of alignment. We just had sex. How could I possibly want more sex?"

I flashed her a wide grin, my beast preening. "So you're saying you can't get enough of me."

"Yeah." She rolled her eyes at me, her expression playful, but her angel glow still dimmed with worry. "At the rate I'm going I'm not going to be able to walk, let alone get out of bed without healing myself for all the sex I crave."

But that wasn't what she was worried about. If her need to join with us was growing more insistent then that was a sign that something wasn't right. Sex alone wasn't enough anymore.

"Seireadan will know what's going on with you," I said. He was the smartest person I knew and had always had his nose in a book when we'd been young. His office back in his apartment had been filled with books. There'd even been a stack of books in his kitchen tucked into a corner, so I knew in the five hundred years we'd been apart, he hadn't lost his thirst for knowledge. "He just needs time to figure it out."

"Time I doubt we have right now." Amiah drew in a heavy breath and released it. Her angel glow flared, and a renewed determination filled her expression. "And there are more important things to worry about right now. Things I should probably shower and get dressed for."

I rolled off her, my beast disappointed that we weren't going to have sex again, and let her get out of bed. "We should also eat. We shouldn't face any kind of battle on an empty stomach."

"Meet you in the kitchen?" she asked, tugging her towel back around her stunning body. "I want to invite you into the shower, but that's just as bad as staying here."

"Take your time," I said— or rather, my beast said. "There are some dragon compulsions I just can't resist and I need to catch you something fresh."

She raised her eyebrows at that.

"You're my mate, but you can't hunt." I didn't say the only time the urge to hunt for a mate kicked in was if a dragon was sick or in the last stages of her pregnancy. Why I needed to hunt for her didn't matter. I needed to and that was just the way it was. "I'll be quick."

"Will you prepare it as well?"

I snorted and offered her a wicked grin. "That's what our other mates are for. They need to prove themselves to you, too."

She chuckled and headed out the doorway. "Yeah, I'm sure Hawk, who I doubt has ever cooked a day in his life, would love to learn how to butcher a whole animal."

"He or Seireadan are going to have to. Cassius clearly has the job of cooking it."

She shook her head, her shoulders gently shaking with her laughter.

I watched her as she walked into the sitting room, picked her way around the cushions and low tables, and headed to the bathroom. When she stepped out of sight, I got out of bed, not bothering to grab the other towel to cover up since I was going to shift and that would ruin a perfectly good towel, and moved to the doorway to keep her in sight.

She was so beautiful and kind and warm and ferocious. Yes, she wasn't wild like a dragon, but she had a strength of will that I knew was going to drive all four of us crazy. And I couldn't wait.

I turned to the large window stretching from one side of the sitting room to the other, but Rin, kneeling in the corner by the railing, caught my attention. He was as far from the bedrooms, the bathroom, and the doorway out of the suite as he could get, as if he were trying to keep himself apart from us... or perhaps trying to stay unnoticed. But his gaze was locked on Amiah and remained on the doorway to the bathroom even after she'd disappeared around the corner.

"That's my mate," I said.

"Yes," Rin replied in his harsh whisper, his attention never leaving the bathroom.

"*My* mate," I— or rather my beast insisted, as I strode to the railing to stand between him and the bathroom's doorway. Before me, beyond the large window, stretched the Wilds. It was a lush, verdant jungle that would be packed with prey as if Faerie knew I needed to hunt for her. Scales rippled down my neck and across my chest and my fire warmed my throat. "She's incredible."

"Yes."

He glanced at me, his black gaze meeting mine for a second, before it jumped past me again, as if he couldn't stop looking for her.

Which made my beast furious. It didn't care that Rin probably couldn't help himself because of his soul bond with her. He was looking for her and he had no right. "You almost killed her."

"Yes."

He didn't move. He didn't even blink. And his gaze never shifted back to me.

Snarling, I jerked forward a step, putting myself back in his line of sight. "That's all you have to say about it?"

Rin still didn't react. He just sat there as if nothing in the world affected him. But I wondered if that was really the case. He'd still been expressionless when we'd found him and Amiah in the Winter Court, but he'd been holding her, protecting her from the ice guards. And when Padraigin had tried to drown Amiah, Rin had given her his breath.

"So?" my beast pressed. I didn't know why I wanted an answer. Yes, he owed it to me and the others, but I doubted I get it.

"My master commanded and I obeyed."

I glared at him. That was all? He'd been given an order?

She'd been bleeding to death on the hard stone. She had to have been in agony and terrified.

And now I wanted to rip something apart.

Except I couldn't rip into him. He was her mate right now whether I liked it or not, and if I hurt him, I hurt her.

"So you don't feel bad at all?" my beast snarled.

"How I feel won't change what I've done." A hint of hellfire flickered in his eyes then disappeared. I wasn't even sure I'd seen it. But if I had, did that mean he actually felt something? Something other than the hunger I'd seen when we'd run in on him covered in blood straddling Amiah in Seireadan's clean room?

"But you *do* have feelings?" I wasn't sure I wanted to know the answer. If he wasn't the cold, unfeeling hybrid who'd stabbed her, if he was really someone who'd been forced to do things he hadn't wanted to do, then did that mean he was another of Amiah's mates? Fate had bound their souls together. What if that hadn't been a mistake?

I'd told Amiah that I was certain my mating magic was as strong as hers, but I couldn't squash that little nagging doubt that said I was wrong. My soul didn't and never would join with Amiah's to the same degree as hers had joined with Seireadan's and Rin's because she hadn't branded me. I didn't know much about angelic mating brands, only what Seireadan had shared many years ago when he'd stumbled across it in a book. So all I really knew were that they were powerful forces of nature that entwined the recipients' souls together.

And while Amiah was in my soul and my beast *knew* she was mine, the magic in our souls would never entwine. We were still separate. We couldn't connect with the power in each other's souls like she could — or rather soon would — connect with Rin's and Seireadan's.

I heaved my attention back to Rin who was still staring past me. He was so intent on *my* mate — *mine* — I doubted he'd even noticed I'd stopped focusing on him for a second.

"Do you have feelings?" I snarled.

He couldn't be one of her real mates. She deserved so much more. She deserved knowing every day with every touch and kiss and look that she was loved.

A spark of hellfire popped from his right eye and the muscles in his jaw flexed.

"Yes," he said, his voice barely audible, filled with longing and pain and sorrow. "I have feelings."

Fuck.

I leaped out the window and shifted, spreading my wings and catching the wind as I plummeted to the ground. My beast heaved and snarled inside me. Mine. She was mine and Seireadan's and Hawk's and Cassius's. My beast and I could accept that. *We'd* never purposely hurt her. We'd certainly never come close to killing her.

Except from the heartache in Rin's voice, it was obvious he had feelings for her, not just those forced on him by their soul bond. He was drawn to her, her power and vitality and kindness just like the rest of us.

What if, when we got the Heart, he convinced her not to remove the brand? What would happen to those of us she hadn't branded, who didn't have their souls entwined with hers?

I spat fire into the sky. My mating magic was strong enough, and when we got the Heart, whether she kept the man who'd tried to murder her or not, we could convince her to use it to brand the rest of us.

Now we just had to face Deaglan, the monster who'd held me captive, unable to shift, in a windowless dungeon for the last five hundred years.

My beast spat more fire. Yeah, I wasn't strong enough to defeat him by myself, but with Seireadan's help, I was going to eat the bastard and ensure Amiah's safety.

AMIAH

I took a quick shower even though I suspected Titus wouldn't be back right away. Yes, he'd said he wanted to hunt for me, but given that he was still mending his connection with his beast, he probably also needed to shift and spread his wings for a while.

Of course, I also had compulsions I didn't want to fight, which was why I'd given in and only had a fast shower. And while I needed to ignore my desire for Rin and the yearning to properly align my soul again, I didn't have to fight my need to ensure everyone was okay. And the last time I'd checked, half of us weren't.

I quickly dried off and changed into the slightly-too-big leather pants, but paused before pulling on the really-too-big cotton shirt to stare at my brand and confirm that Sebastian and Rin only shared a brand with me, not each other. Which meant they weren't soul mates. They only *shared* a soul mate and the brand wasn't going to make them fall in love with each other — or rather they only *temporarily* shared a soul mate since I was freeing Rin as soon as I got the Heart.

And the only way to do that was to check on the guys and come up with a plan. I pulled on the shirt as well as a pair of boots that had been left under the clothes rack even though we were inside. I had no idea when we'd have to run out or if the Winter Court would yank me away again, and I wasn't going to do any of that again without boots. With a sigh, I raked my fingers through my long blond wet hair and checked my reflection in the mirror above the sink.

I looked normal.

Which was good.

Normal wouldn't worry the guys.

I didn't have any scratches or bruises and the glow in my eyes was bright, indicating I was at full power — fuller actually. I'd never had so much magic before and even without concentrating on using it, I could feel it seeping through me, staving off some of the Winter Court's chill.

It wasn't enough to get rid of all of the cold, I still shivered and was going to go back to the bedroom to grab a blanket, but my power was healing me enough to prevent what should have been inevitable hypothermia. And that, thankfully, also released enough magic to avoid the pressure that compelled me to heal someone, anyone, when my power was overflowing.

Which was shocking. My magic shouldn't have been doing anything without me having to concentrate. And while there'd been that other time on Sebastian's roof where my magic had seemed to work while I'd been dozing, I hadn't been certain.

Now I was. Somehow, perhaps because of my new soul bonds, I was able to use my magic on a subconscious level.

Of course, if I didn't need to concentrate, what would happen when we were in a fight and someone got seriously hurt? I could now connect and heal someone from a distance. Would my magic just heal that person whether I wanted it to or not? And what if that person wasn't one of my guys? What if it was Deaglan?

I shuddered at the thought. I didn't want to have to heal him or any of his men, and with my healing compulsion and the threat of backlash, it was already a struggle to hold back my magic. If I subconsciously connected and healed Deaglan, I could end up helping him and endangering my guys and everyone else in Faerie.

Which was unacceptable.

My magic was *my* magic. I wasn't going to let it control me, just like I wasn't going to let my soul bonds control me.

I sucked in a steadying breath and mentally gathered my magic, pulling it back into my palms.

It tugged against my hold, straining to remain within my veins, quietly and constantly working against the Winter Court's cold.

No.

I tightened my mental grip and wrenched it free, letting ice rush in and replace it.

God, I hadn't realized just how much it was protecting me from the Winter Court's frozen power.

My magic heaved, hot and sticky around my hands and up my forearms, but I held tight, even as my breath misted and my shivering forced me to grip the counter to keep standing. I needed to prove I could still control it, that if I had to, I could choose my guys over Deaglan and his assassins.

And I could. I *would*.

But God, it was so cold.

My teeth started to chatter and my lips grew blue. I fought to hold on a little longer, but even with my magic burning my hands, I couldn't feel them or my feet. It had barely been a minute and my extremities were already numb. I had to hold on for longer than that if I was going to control my power enough to determine who I healed. And God, I was just trying to hold on to it. I wasn't trying to push it into someone else.

My eyelids drifted shut and my thoughts stuttered. It was just for a second — or at least I thought it was for a second — but it was enough for my magic to yank free of my control and flood back into my body.

This was going to be a problem.

But it was a problem I could deal with... I hoped. At least I didn't have to deal with it alone. Sebastian might be able to help me and Hawk with his magical sensitivity might be able to tell what exactly was going on.

My heart clenched at the thought of Hawk and not being able to brand him.

Come on. I had to think of something else. There wasn't anything I could do about keeping him until I'd gotten the Heart.

Which meant I had to stick to my original plan of checking on the guys and then all of us coming up with a plan.

Determined to stay focused on something that I *could* control, I strode out of the bathroom to head to the bedroom and grab a blanket before checking in on the others, but the second I stepped into the sitting room, my gaze landed on Rin.

He knelt on the far side of the room by the railing, his gaze locked on me, and everything within me stalled. Thoughts of my guys, feeling the cold consuming me from the inside, and my need to get everyone through this alive. There was only Rin and my desperate aching desire to seal our bond.

His black eyes captured me even from across the room, dark, emotionless depths, and I headed toward him before I fully realized what I was doing.

A spark of hellfire popped from his eye — which I was almost certain was a sign he was struggling to contain his emotions — and I grabbed the railing to stop myself before I got any closer. If he felt even half of what I was feeling, drawing close to him was cruel because I wasn't certain I'd be able to control myself and that would mean it would be up to him to stop us from having sex.

I tried to move my attention to the jungle outside, tried to think about Titus shifted into his majestic red dragon, soaring over that dense canopy, but I couldn't take my eyes off Rin. And it seemed he couldn't take his eyes off me.

We stared at each other, the silence growing heavier and heavier between us, my body throbbing with a need I was *not* going to satisfy.

I shifted my attention to his body. I might not be able to look away, but I could at least not be drowning in his eyes.

At some point while I'd been asleep with Titus, he'd changed and showered and now wore the same brown leather pants and cotton shirt that we'd all worn the last time we'd been in the aerie. It was strange to see him in anything other than his black assassin's garb. He still looked dangerous, which was terrifying because I knew he was holding in most of his essence that revealed just how dangerous he really was, and yet he also looked uncertain.

I wasn't sure why I got that impression. His expression wasn't any different than it usually was and neither was his posture. Perhaps it was because he was kneeling in the corner as far away from the rest of us as possible.

Of course, if he didn't trust me when I'd said we weren't going to hurt and betray him, then keeping his distance and keeping quiet, especially since our bond made it impossible for him to leave, was his safest option.

Which made me furious and frustrated. At Deaglan, at myself, and at Rin.

I knew it wasn't fair to expect him to trust me or any of the others. I suspected he, like me, was fighting our bond and questioning the feelings coming from it — like believing I could trust him. Deaglan had held and tortured him for five hundred years. That wasn't something someone just got over. And even though I'd broken the spell Deaglan had used to keep him captive, that didn't mean I was automatically better than the Shadow King.

And the only thing I could do was be patient and continue to show Rin that I could be trusted, that I wasn't going to hurt him, that I did, indeed, want to set him free.

My gaze lifted back to his face and his flat expression. A part of me yearned to see him smile, but the rest of me, the logical part of me knew that wasn't going to happen before I freed him from our soul bond and after we'd gone our separate ways, which meant I was never going to see him smile.

And God, it was so hard right now to keep in mind that we were going to part ways. Remembering that was harder than it had been before, which meant our soul bond was getting stronger.

And that also meant if we didn't seal our bond soon, one or both of us would start feeling the effects of resisting it.

That thought sent a shiver racing through me. I'd seen some of the effects of someone resisting the bond, seen the growing desperation and frustration, and how it stole focus, making it impossible to concentrate.

I also knew what I'd seen had only been a glimpse and that it could be much worse. The symptoms were the same as if one part of the bond died, and I'd seen that firsthand. Dying together would have been the preferable option.

I'd spent months helping an angel survive the death of his human mate. Their bond had been relatively new, so he'd managed to survive, but there had been many days when he hadn't wanted to, and many days where I feared his mind was too broken to recover and I'd have to permanently put him in an institution.

Another spark of hellfire popped from Rin's eye and he stood.

My pulse stuttered with the hope and fear that he'd come to me, reassure me that that wasn't our fate. But we were running out of time if we didn't want to seal our bond and we had no idea when the next key to releasing Faerie's Heart would become empowered.

I tightened my grip on the railing.

Please come to me.

Please don't.

"You look better," I blurted out. Maybe if we weren't staring at each other in silence, I'd be able to get a hold of myself. At least I'd have something to distract me from my thoughts.

And he did look better, his complexion was back to normal and his life force felt steadier—

In fact it almost felt as if some of the pain permanently imprinted in his cells had eased up.

"I am," he replied.

I waited for him to say more, to tell me about how he felt because with my healing magic shying away from his undead nature it was difficult to tell if he was where he should be health wise or not.

But his gaze dipped to my hands clutching the railing, and he remained silent... because there was no point in saying anything. No one in the last five hundred years had cared how he'd felt or that he might have risked his life removing Sebastian's demonic magic infection.

"The others might be distracted by trying to figure out what to do about the Heart and Deaglan," I said, "but we're all grateful that you saved Sebastian. Thank you."

His gaze lifted again to meet mine. "Yes, your highness."

I bit back a sigh. Still? I thought we'd been over this. "I told you to please call me Amiah. I'm not a princess."

"You branded Prince Seireadan." His hellfire flared into miniature flames. "Unless you're going to break your bond with him, too."

"If he wants me to," I said, my throat tightening at the thought despite the fact that both Titus and Hawk had assured me he wouldn't. "I won't hold anyone against their will."

Another spark of hell fire popped from his eye as he stared at me and my insides twisted with the awkward silence between us.

"Did you know helping Sebastian would make you sick?" I asked.

"No," he said. "The demonic magic was stickier than I expected. I didn't anticipate consuming so much fae magic."

"But you didn't stop when it became too much."

"You didn't command me to stop."

He said it so matter-of-factly that for a second I wasn't sure I'd heard him right. *I* hadn't said stop. "Would you have killed him?"

His hellfire grew into miniature flames and a hint of something I couldn't recognize flickered across his expression then vanished. "You wouldn't have let me. You're a healing angel and you love him."

Which was true on all three accounts, except I'd unknowingly hurt Rin in the process. That was something I couldn't let happen again. Which meant I needed to know more about sin eaters since I knew next to nothing about them. Michael had hunted them down in secret, exterminating the race before he'd even started his war, and by the time anyone had noticed, it was too late. Because of that, I'd never had to treat one, and I'd had more than enough on my plate learning about all the other types of demons who'd stepped up and joined the Angelic Defense.

But the most important question I needed to know from Rin was— "Can you overdose?"

A hint of a frown furrowed his brow. "I don't understand your question."

Which didn't necessarily mean he couldn't because he didn't know what I was talking about, only that he had limited experience with mortal realm terms. For all I knew, he called it something else.

"Overdosing is where you've consumed so much magic it endangers your life."

His hellfire snapped back to red pinpricks and his expression went flat again, shutting me out again. "King Deaglan never asked that of me."

I bit back a frustrated sigh. "You already know I'd never ask that of you. Ever. I just don't know anything about sin eaters and I don't want to ask you to do something that will hurt you." Especially since it was clear he still thought obeying my requests was his only way out of this mess.

His gaze dipped back to my hands. "I know that. Because of the bond and because of what you are. I just—" Another spark popped from his eye and the pain in his cells surged stronger.

God, even just saying that awakened the memory of what had to have been thousands of punishments for speaking up or asking a question.

"You just don't trust what you're feeling and old habits are hard to break." I took a step toward him before managing to tighten my grip on the railing and stopping myself. "You've spent centuries not trusting anyone, believing everyone is going to hurt you or trick you or trap you."

"You speak as if you know," he said, his voice barely more than a whisper.

"I don't know like you or Titus do." I didn't think I'd ever be able to fully understand the physical and psychological pain they'd suffered.

"But you know more than just your experience with Balwyrdan."

"Yes." My throat tightened. I'd thought the faith healer had taught me what fear was, but I'd been wrong. Balwyrdan had taught me real fear, the faith healer had taught me hopelessness. "I made a mistake when I was young."

Rin slid his hand across the railing, his fingers drawing closer to mine and yet still so far away. "So did I."

My heart ached for him and me. It ached for all of my guys. Titus and Sebastian had been betrayed by a friend, Cassius had lost his brother, and Hawk was going to be shattered if I couldn't figure out how to remove all of my brands or brand him.

Somehow I managed to drag my gaze out the window and stare at the jungle stretching all the way to the horizon. There were no patches of wasteland like the last time I'd seen it as if the Wilds knew what it wanted to be right now, without any doubts.

God, I wished I had no doubts. It had been so long since I'd been certain in who I was and what I wanted, and having my bond with Rin twisting inside me, urging me to step closer, complete the connection with our fingers and complete our bond wasn't helping.

But I'd been a mess long before Rin, before any of the mess we were now caught up in. I'd been in love with someone who didn't love me back. I'd thought if I just waited he'd notice me and that the fate of my mating brand was beautiful.

Which it wasn't. I was now bound to a stranger who I didn't know or love...

Except the longer I stood there, aching for Rin, thinking about his anger and hurt and mistrust, the more my heart broke for him.

He wasn't the nightmare I thought he'd be, and he certainly wasn't a monster, and I was starting to doubt my concerns about him. He'd protected me in the Winter Court, he'd saved Sebastian when he knew if he kept going it would make him sick. He hadn't had to do any of that. He could have sat back, watched, and waited. I'd already made it clear that he didn't have to participate and yet he'd volunteered to help.

And while I could argue that he'd done what he'd done because Sebastian was his best bet for getting the Heart and being free, I couldn't shake the sense that he would have made the offer regardless.

"So... ah... What will you do when this is done?" I asked, determined to break the awkward silence between us that was growing more awkward by the second. "When you're free?"

A warm moist breeze swept through the window, carrying the rich scent of flowers and greenery, and ruffled through my wet hair.

"I don't know," he replied, and from the corner of my eye, I saw him turn his gaze to the jungle as well. "I stopped thinking about that when I realized escape was impossible. I'm not sure I even know who I am anymore."

My hand inched closer to his— No, my whole body did.

"When this is done, I can help you figure that out," I said.

"Wouldn't that upset your lovers?" His gaze remained on the jungle, but his hand slid closer. Now barely an inch lay between our little fingers.

"I'm pretty sure we've already established that it's my decision," I replied, my voice breathy and my desire swelling with just the closeness of our hands. "Besides, helping you figure yourself out is easy compared to everything else. I have to figure out how to add Hawk to a bond I can't just add someone to and how to help Cassius regain control of his fire. I'm also pretty sure there's a disciplinary hearing waiting for me and Cassius at work, and I'll probably have to look for a new place to live and a new job."

"I suspect the prince will be able to assist with a lot of that," Rin whispered.

"I suppose he would—" If he wanted to keep our bond. Although there was no way I was going to be a kept woman and rely on Sebastian for my wellbeing, regardless of how much money he had. That would drive me crazy.

Not to mention whatever I did, I'd also need to find a way to release my healing magic. Which was something Sebastian couldn't help me with. And there was no way I was going to let him or the others purposely hurt themselves so I could relieve the pressure.

"I'd still need to find a job or charity work or something," I said. "My healing magic builds up and if I don't release it, I end up running into dangerous situations."

"Like chasing after a dragon falling from the sky."

"Yeah."

That had been the first time Rin had tried to kill me. Of course, now that I'd seen more of him in action, I wondered if he'd actually been trying to kill me. He wasn't as fast as a master vampire, he wasn't even as fast as a full five hundred-year-old vampire because he was only half vampire, but he was still faster than the average human.

Far off in the distance a flock of birds burst from the jungle canopy, scattering this way and that, dark specs against the brilliant blue sky.

A part of me wanted to ask him if he'd been holding back, but knowing wouldn't make a difference. If he said he'd purposely been slow that only confirmed what our bond told me, that he wasn't a monster and I could trust him. And if he hadn't been, he'd still been under orders and would have likely faced a serious punishment if he disobeyed.

A whisper of pain fluttered through my chest where he'd stabbed me, and I pressed my hand over my heart, despite it just being a phantom sensation.

"I didn't want to hurt you." More hellfire sparked from his eye.

"But Deaglan would have hurt you if you hadn't."

"Yes," he said, that one word, barely audible but still heavy and solemn. "I'd hoped you could have healed yourself. I didn't know you could heal someone from a distance and that you were draining yourself to save Cassius. I didn't know angels could heal someone from a distance."

"I didn't know we could, either. I think it has something to do with my new magic, the one that lets me connect with someone's life force."

The birds vanished back into the jungle, leaving a solitary one, gliding on the thermals.

"King Deaglan knows you have healing magic and Nezener said he wants you for more than just your key," Rin said. "Your lovers are right to fear him taking you."

I shuddered at the memory of Deaglan's nightmare attacking me and Rin ripping out his throat. The shudder sank into a frozen stone in my gut at the thought of Deaglan. I'd barely seen a glimpse of how sick and twisted he was and that had been more than enough for me. "Yeah, I fear him too."

The solitary bird banked, soaring closer to the mountain, then it pulled its wings back and dove beneath the canopy.

"Amiah," he whispered, shocking me by using my name.

My gaze leaped to him, and I was captured in his black eyes, drowning in darkness and simmering hellfire and aching desperate need.

God, I needed him. Now. Please. He was mine. We were meant to be. It was the fate I'd been so sure I hadn't wanted, the worst possible thing that could happen to me, and now it was all I wanted, all I could think about.

"I'll protect you, too."

"You're not obligated to do that," I forced out.

"You've made that quite clear."

Go to him. Kiss him. Join with him.

I gritted my teeth. It was just the bond. It wasn't real, and if Rin was feeling anything close to what I was feeling, his need to protect me was because of our brand. "The brand is compelling you. Maybe Sebastian can help you fight it."

"It's not the brand." He dragged his gaze away from mine to stare out the window again. "All right, it *is* the brand. In part. But even before you branded me, I knew what your magic was and that if Deaglan ever learned about it, he'd want you." His grip on the railing tightened, his knuckles turning white, and a chunk of stone broke free and tumbled over the edge, disappearing into the jungle far below.

"I won't let him have you. I won't let him—" The pain in his cells roared to life, ripping a strangled groan from his lips. "I won't let him—"

Another painful explosion cut him off and my magic connecting me to his life force flared, pushing more of my strange new magic into him, desperate to ease his pain.

Somehow he sucked in two quick ragged breaths that he didn't need and then dropped his emotionless mask back into place, as my magic eased some of his pain.

"I will fight with you and I will win the freedom you've tried to give me when you broke King Deaglan's leash spell on me," he said, his voice back to a barely-there whisper. "I promise."

His little finger brushed against mine, sending a shock of sensation shooting through me.

My breath hitched at the contact and my gaze dropped to where we were connected. It was barely a touch, just the tip of his little finger against mine, and yet it shot liquid need rushing through my veins. Then my gaze leaped up to his and all of me, my body, my mind, my soul stalled again. I was lost in his eyes, in his writhing, confusing life force, and in our bond.

AMIAH

Rin's hellfire sparked then burst into full flames that licked across his cheeks and his eyes widened.

"I'm sorry." He jerked his hand back, but his gaze remained locked with mine, twisting my desire tighter.

"I should leave. Check on Sebastian and…" I tried to glance behind me, but couldn't pull my gaze away from him.

This was becoming impossible. I needed space to focus. Surely if I could get away from him I could get this desire back under control.

"I'll go," he said also without looking away.

But neither of us moved. We were trapped in the vortex of our incomplete mating brand.

"This is a serious problem," I forced out.

"Yes." His hellfire surged and sparked as if he were fighting to get it back under control.

Come on. Just leave. Turn around and walk away. But I couldn't. I was going to shatter if we didn't seal the bond. Life wasn't worth living. I couldn't live without him—

Which was the bond. It was just the bond making me think that. It wasn't real.

Think about the others. Think about Sebastian. He was one of my mates, too. Surely I could redirect my need to him. Except I'd already sealed my bond with him. I wasn't going to lose him.

Unless he wanted to leave.
But he's hurt... or he was hurt. He's definitely unconscious.

My magic that connected with life forces swept out of me, shot past the bedroom where he'd been and down the hall to reach Sebastian's icy brightness. His power wasn't anywhere near the vast universe I'd glimpsed before, but all hint of the demonic darkness was gone. He was weak but healing.

He was also fully awake and in the dining room. And didn't immediately need me.

My magic leaped to Hawk's fiery darkness. He, too was in the dining room and overflowing with power. Also not in need of help.

"Command me to go," Rin said, shifting closer to me again. "Make it an order."

"I don't want to give you orders. You're not my slave or soldier, you're my ma—" I stopped myself before I could say mate. "You're free."

"Neither of us are free with this bond," he murmured. "I have centuries of obeying. It's been burned into my soul. Tell me to leave." He shifted forward another step. "Please."

God, I hated that this was the only way. And while maybe it wasn't, I couldn't think past my desire to come up with anything better. "Go—"

"Yes?" He drew even closer, his body language clear he was fighting his need, while his eyes begged me for an order, begged me to accept him, and begged me to love him.

Except it was so shocking to see a full emotion on his face that I couldn't resist the bond's compulsion. I closed the last few inches between us before I realized what I was doing, cupped his cheeks in my palms, and brushed my lips against his.

With a groan, he deepened the kiss for a second then pressed his forehead against mine, captured my own cheeks with his hands holding me steady, and heaved his lips the fraction of an inch necessary to separate our mouths. His body trembled with his force of will to resist our bond, and it took everything I had just to stay where I was.

"Please," he gasped.

But I couldn't just tell him to leave. I wanted to keep him. He'd already offered to protect me, to help—

I strained to stay focused on that. The only way he was going to help was if we had a plan and we all needed to gather to come up with one.

"Sebastian and Hawk are in the kitchen," I forced out. "Join them."

Join me.

No.

"I'll find Cassius and we can brainstorm plans while we wait for Titus."

And I could only pray that putting some distance between us and giving myself time to regain my composure would be enough for me to continue resisting our bond.

"Yes." The pain in his cells flared and he drew away, releasing me at the very last second, and bowed. "Your highness."

I hugged myself, fighting to stay where I was as he hurried out of the sitting room.

The final key couldn't become empowered soon enough, but even then, it was becoming clear we weren't going to last. We were going to need help and Sebastian was the only one who might be able to lend a hand. Which just added more to the list of things Sebastian had to do... if he could even do it.

I tried to push that thought aside. There wasn't anything I could do about it right now and we really did need to get together and come up with a plan. Hadn't that been my original goal when I'd come out of the bathroom?

And to do that, I needed to find Cassius.

I closed my eyes and concentrated on my ability to sense life forces. I'd sensed Sebastian and Hawk — and I could still sense them in the dining room with Rin heading down the hall — maybe I didn't have to go searching through the enormous aerie, maybe I'd be able to tell where Cassius was by just standing where I was.

My magic swelled, tugging me toward Rin and Sebastian, but I heaved it away and concentrated on Cassius's blazing hot, fiery life force. His life force was in just as much turmoil as Rin's, writhing and snapping, but it was also raging out of control... which it might not be right now if he'd managed to expend all of his fire magic.

But as soon as I thought that, my magic leaped up to the mountain's flat top and connected with an enormous firestorm. He still had power. A lot of power. And I had no idea how.

Worried, I pushed a little magic into my back, released my wings, and flew out the window. I caught a gloriously warm air current and soared up the last few stories to the top of the aerie, letting my magic draw me to him. Except even without my magic, I would have been able to find him.

He sat a quarter of the way around the mountain from our suite on the edge of an outcropping with fire spewing off of him. It rolled around him like a burning river and poured off the ledge in a flaming waterfall into a pond far below, sending up billowing steam clouds that curled halfway up the mountain before being pulled apart by the breeze.

He watched as I landed, pulled in my wings, and settled with my legs hanging over the mountain's edge, close enough for a conversation, but not so close that he'd have to work too hard to keep his fire away from me.

Heat radiated from his flames, drawing a shiver and making me aware that I was still too cold and had been meaning to grab a blanket before being sidetracked by Rin.

I crossed my arms, trying not to look like I was hugging myself in an attempt to warm up, and turned my attention to Cassius.

He looked haggard, even with his angel glow still shockingly bright — indicating that he was still overflowing with magic — and his clothes, a bright Hawaiian shirt that clashed with equally bright board shorts, were singed, a sign that he'd almost lost all control.

My compulsion to heal surged, urging me to ask about his health. But asking would probably just start a fight and I didn't want to fight with him anymore. I just wanted to be with my best friend, like we'd been before the war.

Except too much had happened for us to go back to that... which, in truth, I didn't really want anyway. I wanted our new romantic relationship. Something that was impossible at the moment with my soul bonds with Rin and Sebastian and his fire raging out of control.

"Where did you get those clothes?" I asked instead. "And were you wearing them when you rescued me from the Winter Court?"

I was sure I would have remembered something so gaudy... but I'd also been struggling with the Winter Court's cold and my desire for Rin and just relieved that my guys had found me that maybe, somehow, I'd missed seeing them.

"I wasn't. I've already burned through those and I didn't want to ruin another perfectly good set of clothes." He glanced at his shirt. "This is Voth's idea of a joke."

"Ah." I was sure Voth had bought everyone else something reasonable but couldn't help himself when it came to picking out something for Cassius. "I have no idea how Priam is still friends with him now that he's no longer his medic."

"He and Priam are friends?" Cassius asked.

Right. Cassius hadn't been awake for that. There was probably a lot he needed to be caught up on. "Surprisingly, yes. Priam even plays poker."

Cassius raised his eyebrows at that.

"That was my reaction, too. So, to catch you up," I said, "Sebastian was conscious just long enough to get us into his SUV when we fled his apartment, but he passed out and we didn't know where to go."

"So you thought you should go to Voth." Cassius rolled his eyes at me. "The world really has turned upside down."

"Well we were short on options. You were unconscious, Sebastian was barely alive, and I couldn't help him with my backlash." The breeze teased through my thin cotton shirt, just a little too cool despite the fact that we were surrounded by jungle, and I shifted closer to Cassius and his fire. "Voth helped Essie when she and the team were in need. That and we found a bag of Sebastian's money in the SUV and figured we could pay him for the use of his clinic."

"Ah, didn't think he'd have helped out of the goodness of his heart. How much is Bane going to charge the JP this time?" Cassius asked, his expression turning grim.

Except I had no idea over what. There was a lot to be grim about at the moment, the least of which was whatever bill Sebastian was going to try to get the JP to pay.

The urge to ask Cassius about his health twisted tighter inside me as the breeze made me shiver again.

Cassius's fire flared, sending a wonderful wave of heat washing over me and shooting a flurry of sparks into the air that were picked up by the wind and tossed around him. "We nearly lost him. If you hadn't— You didn't even hesitate to have sex with him." He shook his head and released a heavy sigh. "But of course you didn't hesitate. You never hesitate when you're saving a life. You ran into the middle of a fight for goodness sake to save me."

And I'd do it again. Always. Especially if it meant saving one of my guys.

He ran his hand over his blond buzz cut, looking even more exhausted, and more sparks burst from his flames.

I fought another shiver and bit back a sigh. There was too much I was trying to ignore. Something was going to have to give and the best thing to stop resisting was my compulsive need to heal.

"When was the last time you slept?" I asked. According to my magic it felt like he was running on fumes, but I wasn't sure why. Surely I hadn't been asleep with Titus for that long... although if Cassius had been fighting his magic non-stop since before the Winter Court yanked me back into Faerie, I wouldn't have had to have been asleep for a long time for Cassius to now be exhausted.

He shot me an exasperated glance. "Not sure that's the most important thing we need to talk about."

"And that wasn't an answer." Which was the typical response I'd expected.

His glance turned into a glare, trying to silently get me to change the topic — also typical of him — and I glared back, giving him my driest, no-nonsense look.

"How long, agent?" I asked.

He huffed. "Not sure you can pull that one anymore."

"Priam assures me I can. He and Chris are covering for us." Although I didn't know how long they'd be able to keep it hidden that we'd abandoned our jobs, again. "So don't change the topic."

"That means I'm still the senior agent-in-charge then."

I rolled my eyes at him. "When has that ever worked for you? Trauma trumps agent-in-charge and you know I'm going to hound you until you tell me what I want to know."

"You're not going to be able to do anything about it."

I was well aware of that. "Stop telling me what I can and can't do. You already know you can't and you already know it's easier for me to ask you than to fight my magic."

His expression turned strange and he jerked his attention away from me to stare at the Wilds. "It hasn't even been a whole day since I woke in Voth's hotel. But that's not the problem. I can't get my magic under control and it isn't running out. It's exhausting just trying to keep myself clothed."

Which was what I'd feared and it made him right. There wasn't anything I could do to help him.

"You just need to hold out for a little longer. Sebastian is awake, but it looks like he's still magically weak."

"Looks like?" Cassius's attention slid back to me, his expression worried. "You've never been that vague before when discussing someone's condition."

"I haven't had a chance to confirm it. I've only sensed it," I replied.

"His life force is on the mend and it tells me he's in the kitchen with Hawk." And now Rin.

"And you know all that with your magic now? You don't have to look at him or touch him?"

"Yeah." The cold inside me swelled and I shifted closer to Cassius. Now only a foot lay between me and his flames. "And I can sense Hawk and Rin are with him."

"Well that'll be useful if we still have our jobs." He turned his gaze back to the clear, blue horizon.

"You know we'll figure it out. We always do." Although I didn't think we'd ever gotten into trouble this deep before. There'd been a few times during the war when we'd found ourselves in some difficult situations — like the time Cassius's unit had helped me, Priam, and two human physicians evacuate a group of children suddenly caught in the middle of Michael's war. But that hadn't been nearly as bad as now. We'd had more information then *and* we'd had backup. Right now it was just the five—

No, Rin was now a part of this, too.

Still, that only made it the six of us against Deaglan and all his men.

"Titus is out hunting, but the others are in the kitchen," I said. "Let's come up with a plan." The cold swelled again, and I hugged myself tighter, afraid if I got any closer to Cassius it would add more strain to his control. It was bad enough he was struggling to keep his clothes from igniting, adding the worry that he was going to burn me wouldn't help.

"I'm not sure we can come up with a plan," he replied, thankfully not glancing back to see how close I was to the molten flames pouring off his body.

I stared at him, not believing what he'd just said. "It's not like you to give up."

"I haven't." Another flurry of sparks swept around him. "The situation is too fluid. We don't have enough information and things are changing too quickly. We don't even know when the next key will become empowered. We could be waiting like this for days... or months."

I didn't want to have to wait months, but that at least would give us time to recover and come up with a strategy or two. Every time we'd faced Deaglan he'd beaten us, and the last time he'd almost killed Cassius. "We can at least figure out a way for Sebastian to prevent Deaglan from taking your fire."

"Only if Bane has regained enough of his magic in time to do that." He glanced at his hands and the fire pouring off of them. "And he's going to need a lot of power to stop this. On the bright side, it'll also take Deaglan a lot of power to pull all of this out of me, so perhaps that'll weaken him enough for us to get his keys."

"Well maybe that's the plan," I replied, the breeze sending another shiver racing through me. "Maybe we don't have Sebastian help you control your power, we force Deaglan to use up his magic protecting himself from you."

"I've been thinking the same thing." He rolled some of his fire into a ball in his palms. It heaved and writhed against his control, something I was seeing far too often recently. "That's what I did when I left special operations and joined the front line. I was pointed in the right direction and forced Michael's nephilim to expend their magic so the rest of the division could take them out."

"So you walked to the front of the line and put a bullseye on yourself?" I'd known he'd been furious when his brother had stopped contacting the Angelic Defense and the other spy we'd had in Michael's army had confirmed Dominic was dead, but I hadn't known he'd done something so foolish. "You could have been killed."

"At the time, that was the point," he replied, his voice strangely void of any emotions. "I was going to take out as many of them as I could until they stopped me. But Gabriel managed to kill Michael and Rafael, ending the war before that happened."

God, Dominic's death had made him suicidal and I hadn't even realized it. The thought made me heartbroken and furious. My best friend had been hurting and he hadn't said anything. And I'd been too caught up in the unending stream of injured soldiers and civilians to notice. "You should have told me. I could have done something."

"I didn't want you to do something. Dominic died because of me. He came to me eager to join the fight and told me about the mission. I told him to take it. Told him he was perfect for it with his rare dual magics." The fire in Cassius's hands exploded, showering flames and sparks around him. "I failed to protect him. I should have told him to join the regular forces. He'd at least have had a team to back him up. But no, I told him to take the mission where he was in the middle of Michael's army alone. We couldn't even recover his body to give him a proper burial."

"Cassius, you didn't kill your brother. Dominic was even more headstrong than you and Gideon. I have no doubt he wasn't asking for your permission to take the mission but to inform you of his decision." I hadn't spent a lot of time with Dominic, he'd kept his distance from everyone probably because of his ability to read minds, but when he'd made up his mind about something, he'd been worse than Cassius.

"I just wish I could have protected him." Cassius ran his hands over his head again, dripping fire onto his shoulders and making his Hawaiian shirt smoke. "I swear. I'll do whatever it takes to keep you safe."

"That better not involve you dying. I already thought you were dead once and I swear—" A shiver rushed through me and the cold sank deeper inside me. I couldn't get closer to Cassius's fire without endangering myself and I couldn't hug myself any harder — not that it was helping. I really should have grabbed that blanket before looking for Cassius. "I swear I'm never going through that—"

I pushed more of my magic into me to keep staving off my hypothermia, but the cold exploded, shattering my connection with my magic and stealing my breath. I struggled to regain control of my power and push it back into my body, but it whirled through me, slipping through my mental fingers, as if I was experiencing backlash. Except I hadn't done anything for my magic to turn against me.

"Amiah?" Cassius jerked to his feet and his fire flared, suddenly too hot.

I scrambled back, lost my balance, and fell back onto my rear as a wave of frozen pressure crushed around my heart. It was like I was experiencing the leash spell all over again—

No. I could still sort of breathe and I was freezing... which was what had happened the last two times we'd needed to go after a key.

The final key had become empowered and we weren't even close to being ready to face Deaglan again.

FATED HEART

ANGEL'S FATE, BOOK 6

AMIAH

CRUSHING COLD FILLED MY CHEST AND STOLE MY BREATH, AND I KNEW THE final key to releasing Faerie's Heart had become empowered.

"Amiah!" Cassius's fire writhed, sending painful heat radiating across my suddenly too-cold skin, and his body tensed as if he were fighting to get control of his magic but couldn't. Which was terrifying. His chiseled facial features already looked haggard, and he had dark circles under his eyes despite the still-powerful glow radiating from them.

I couldn't understand how he could still be at full power. He'd been dripping flames since yesterday, and now even his clothes were burned. He should have been completely out, without even a hint of smoke.

"Amiah," he pressed, yanking my attention back to myself and the ice crushing inside me.

"It's the final key," I gasped, struggling to my feet. "It's become empowered. We have to get to the others."

I glanced around, looking for a way off the top of the dragon's mountain, and while there were craggy outcroppings jutting up that could have hidden a passage back into the aerie, my soul screamed that we didn't have time.

I pushed power into my back and released my wings. We had to get the key. Deaglan already had two of the four keys, and even if we weren't ready to take his keys from him, we couldn't risk him getting another one. He was a powerful fae sorcerer and another key, even without being able to find the Heart, still made him more powerful.

"Don't you dare try flying in your condition," Cassius said through gritted teeth. His fire stopped pouring from his body, but it still roared around his hands and up his forearms.

"I can make it to the kitchen." I was going to have to make it. That was where Sebastian, Hawk, and Rin were. And then I was going to have to make it to wherever the key was, because I couldn't touch Titus and, given how much Cassius was struggling to control his flames, he was going to kill himself trying to hold it back long enough to carry me to where ever the key had become empowered.

"Amiah, just give me a minute. It's too dangerous for you to fly."

I opened my mouth to argue, but the frozen pressure inside me surged and a groan of agony escaped instead. For a second I was surrounded by darkness, trapped and crushed and forgotten.

No, please.

Save me. Remember me. Free me.

Panic seized my heart, and my soul screamed, the cry yanking me back to the flat-topped mountain. I had to go. Now. I had to get the key, had to be free, and I couldn't wait.

Cassius's fire weakened, turning into thick billowing smoke, then burst over his hands again. He trembled with the effort to get it back under control and his breath turned ragged.

"You need Sebastian," I said. He wasn't going to be able to get it under control, not without help, and the only way to get help was to go to Sebastian. Which meant as foolish as it was, I needed to fly on my own.

I spread my wings and stepped off the mountain's edge as the pressure swelled and snapped, sending frigid shockwaves crashing inside me.

Both mind and body seized, and I missed catching the wind.

"Amiah!"

I plummeted toward the ground, the humid jungle air blazingly hot against my frozen skin.

Cassius leaped off the mountain after me, fire exploding from his body as he released his wings and streaming behind him like a writhing red-orange banner.

Desperate, I stretched my wings and caught air, but my shivering made it hard to keep gliding and the pressure in my chest made it impossible to catch my breath. There was no way I was going to be able to fly to the newly empowered key. I wasn't even sure I was going to make it to the kitchen.

Except Cassius was fully on fire — including the hem of his gaudy, ridiculous Hawaiian shirt — and with the ferocious inferno heaving in his life force, he wasn't going to get it under control anytime soon.

I had to get to Sebastian. Sebastian would be able to help—

Except if he used what little magic he'd managed to recover since we'd cured his demonic magic infection, he might not have enough magic to fight Deaglan. Which meant I had to hold it together until we'd won and so did Cassius.

Gritting my teeth, I searched for the dining room window. I wasn't sure which of the many openings in the mountain's face was our kitchen-dining room area, but the moment I realized I wasn't sure where I was going, my magic that sensed life forces connected with Sebastian, Hawk, and Rin, who were all still in the dining room.

Their life called me like a beacon, and I careened toward their icy brightness, fiery darkness, and alive-yet-dead essence, not caring how fast I flew or how much I struggled to keep my balance. I didn't have to look good getting there. I just had to get there before I lost all breath or the darkness overwhelmed me again and I fell out of the sky.

The heat from Cassius's fire grew stronger as I reached the large window to the dining room. Much to my surprise, all three of my guys sat together at the long stone table closest to the window's spindly stone railing. Hawk and Rin had their backs to me, but Sebastian faced them and saw me coming.

"Hawk, behind you," he said as he scrambled over the table.

Both Hawk and Rin jerked to their feet and turned to face me, and I crashed into Hawk's arms. Our chests hit with a heavy thump that stole what little breath I had left. For a split-second, his life force rushed through me and my soul sang at the contact. Then my body screamed at his hotter-than-a-human's body temperature, his touch burning even through our clothes, and I tried to push out of his embrace.

"Too hot," I gasped. But my legs were unsteady and I couldn't keep my balance let alone push away from him.

His unusual gray-blue eyes widened, and I knew he'd instantly figured out what was wrong. He grabbed my shoulders to steady me and stepped back as Sebastian's arms, which should have been cool because he was winter fae, but were gloriously warm and not too hot, wrapped around me. His life force connected with Hawk's fiery darkness and the song in my soul grew stronger.

"What the hell is wrong with you?" Cassius demanded as he landed a good twenty feet away, his inferno roaring around him.

"The final key— empowered," I said through chattering teeth to the others, ignoring his question.

"Shit," Hawk hissed.

"And *not* what I was talking about," Cassius said as he glared at me. He heaved his wings in, sending sparks showering around him, and slapped his hands against the hem of his still-burning Hawaiian shirt to put out the flames. "Still, I was hoping we'd have more time."

"Yeah," Sebastian said, his voice strange and soft.

I dragged my gaze up to his, and for a second was captured in the vast pale-blue depths of his eyes and glimpsed a hint of the endless universe of power within him. Regret and fear churned with the frozen pressure inside me. I wanted to believe that Titus and Hawk were right and that Sebastian wasn't furious that I'd permanently bound his soul to mine, but the look in his eyes was strange. It was a mix of... I had no idea what it was, and I was too cold and suddenly too exhausted to figure it out.

"I'll fix this. Just like I'll fix it with Rin," I promised. If Sebastian wanted the bond gone, I'd do whatever it took to free him, no matter how much it hurt me, or how impossible it might be because the bond was fully sealed.

"Don't be an idiot." He slid his hand to my side and pressed his palm against my ribs where our bond lay hidden beneath my thin cotton shirt, its golden threads permanently etched into my skin. "Fate might be fucked up, but this isn't a mistake."

"You don't know that. When this is over you're going to regret not being able to move on and return to the life you had before all this."

"The only thing I regret was not being able to see Sparky's face when you sank onto my cock and got Hawk to make you come."

And a part of me couldn't believe I'd done that, either. But Sebastian had been dying and the only way to save him was to give him as big a transfusion of fae magic as I could while Rin pulled out the rest of the demonic magic infection.

"You didn't miss much," Cassius said, his voice gruff.

"Turned away and couldn't watch like a typical angel then," Sebastian teased. "You could have picked up some pointers."

The fire pouring off Cassius thinned to a trickle. "I don't need pointers."

"You sure? She's been sleeping with an incubus. She has higher expectations now." Hawk batted his eyelashes at Cassius and flashed his heart stopping wicked grin. "I should probably show you a thing or two so you can keep her satisfied."

"You want to suck my cock, fine," Cassius huffed, his statement shocking me. I didn't think I'd ever heard him say anything like that before, but then I'd heard him swear more in the last few days than I had during our entire time together. Clearly my other guys were a bad influence on him... not to mention he was under a great deal of stress. "But I'm pretty sure *that's* not going to satisfy *her*."

"Hey if that's where you want to start," Hawk drawled, "we can certainly work up to the more complicated lessons."

Cassius's fire sparked and then shrank some more as if Hawk and Sebastian's teasing was actually helping him control his power. Now flames only danced over his hands and arms.

He sighed and rolled his eyes at Hawk. "Can we deal with what's important?"

"Pretty sure Amiah's satisfaction is important," Hawk said.

"Yes," Sebastian whispered, his grip around me tightening, and his life force surging, overwhelming the frozen pressure for a second. "You and Hawk weren't the only ones to break our agreement. You astound me, Amiah, and frustrate me and surprise me. When we get the Heart, free Rin and keep me."

"That's just the bond talking," I whispered back.

"You know it isn't. It's too new. I can feel the potential power in it, but it's barely formed. Even your bond with Rin didn't influence your feelings this quickly," he said, pressing his lips against the top of my head. "I'm just relieved I won't be forced to give you up."

Hawk's back stiffened — because if we didn't fix this mess, he *would* have to give me up. The thought made my heart squeeze. "I'm not giving up any of you."

Rin stepped up beside me and held out a blanket. I hadn't even noticed that he'd left the dining room and returned. His hellfire was tight, simmering pinpricks in his black eyes and the expression on his sharp sculpted features was flat, but somehow I could tell he was hurt and worried.

"Only those who want to stay," I said, taking the blanket. His strange life force joined Sebastian's and Hawk's and the frozen pressure weakened again for a second before flooding back in and stealing my breath. "I made you a promise and I intend to keep it."

"Yes, your highness," he murmured. Except it sounded as if he didn't want me to break our bond.

Which was ridiculous. It was just the bond making me see things that weren't there.

The urge to be with him swelled—

Although if I really thought about it, it hadn't gone away. I'd just managed to distract myself by talking to Cassius and now with the freezing weight from the empowered key. My need for Rin hadn't diminished like I'd hoped. It was still just as powerful as it had been when we'd talked a few minutes ago in the sitting room and I'd barely been able to resist it. I'd had to command him to go, which had torn at my heart but had thankfully managed to get us to part before we'd given into the screaming need to seal our bond.

I clutched the blanket to my chest, determined to fight everything, the cold, the darkness, and my desire for Rin. Except there were too many things to fight and I'd been fighting for so long. Something inside me was going to break and sealing our bond was the better of the bad options. That, at least, wouldn't kill me. Everything else could.

I dragged my attention away from Rin, only to meet Hawk's gaze. His hellfire had grown into miniature flames and his expression was pinched with worry and heartache, and my throat tightened with grief.

I loved him so much. I didn't want to spend the rest of my life without him. Except when I'd tried to brand him like I'd branded Sebastian by gathering all the power within me and releasing it when we'd had sex, it hadn't worked.

And because fate was cruel, with his ability to sense sexual energy, he knew I desired him and also knew that I wasn't going to last much longer against the urge to complete my bond with Rin. I was going to have sex with Rin when I really wanted to form that bond with Hawk.

I bit back a bitter huff. All the guys probably knew I wasn't going to last much longer against my bond with Rin.

Which meant we needed to get moving so we could get the final key, take Deaglan's keys, get the Heart, and break my bond with Rin... except we couldn't do any of that without Titus who was flying over the Wilds somewhere, hunting for food so he could bring it back to me and prove his dragon's mating magic was just as powerful as my angelic mating brand.

And I hoped to God it was because he was another one who was going to be heartbroken if we couldn't get the Heart and fix this mess so that I didn't fall out of love with him.

"We need to get moving," I forced out between chattering teeth. "And we need a plan."

"We need Titus to get his ass here," Sebastian said. "We can't come up with a solid plan until we know where the key is."

"What we need is to figure out how we're getting Amiah there. And no," Hawk said, glaring at me. "You're not flying."

But that left Cassius, who, while he looked like he was mostly in control of his fire right now, could lose it just by holding me, or riding Titus, who would increase the key's frozen pressure inside me when we touched.

At the thought, my magical senses shot out of the aerie and connected with Titus's fierce, primal life force. He was on the other side of the aerie, barreling toward us, and would arrive within minutes. The pressure in my chest grew tighter, making it difficult to draw even the shallowest of breaths then snapped with an explosion that swept ice through me.

Oh my God.

The blanket slipped from my numb fingers and my shivering shook me so hard I knew the only reason I was still standing was because Sebastian was holding me.

"Either way, you have to use your magic," I said, clutching at Sebastian's arms around me as if that could somehow warm me up. "Which is easier for you? Helping Cassius control his fire or staving off some of the key's effects so I can ride Titus?"

"Doesn't matter," Cassius said before Sebastian could reply. "Use your magic on Amiah. I want everything I've got to dump on Deaglan."

"Don't be an idiot. We need to think about this, and we shouldn't unnecessarily waste Bane's power." Hawk turned his attention to Sebastian. "You've barely recovered a fraction of the magic you lost fighting that demonic magic infection, and I bet your magical channels are still damaged and fragile. You can't risk burning yourself up by channeling too much raw power, and you certainly can't channel the same amount of power that you used to be able to. Not yet."

Well make a decision, Titus said in my head — presumably all of our heads — as he soared into sight and landed with his enormous back feet on the spindly stone railing and his front feet on the long stone dining room table beside us.

He was stunning in his dragon form with his red-gold scales catching in the afternoon sunlight. He huffed smoke from his massive nostrils and blinked his large, golden eyes at us as the smoke curled around horns that swept up and back from his temples.

We have to go. Now.

His wild life force surged against my senses, and for a second I was strong, powerful, ferocious. Then the key's connection that bound us together snapped, pounding into my chest and stealing my breath.

And as much as I wanted to argue and say that was just the key compelling him to rush into battle and it would be smart of us to come up with a plan first, I couldn't. Deaglan could find the keys without Titus. He was probably already on his way... if he wasn't there already. We didn't have any time to waste.

"It isn't much of a decision," Sebastian said. "We have to bring Amiah, and Cassius is more useful in a fight right now. And just for the record, I have no idea how much power either option will take."

"Fine," Hawk said, not sounding happy about the decision but thankfully not wasting more time by arguing. "Then do your thing and let's get going."

A flicker of icy magic tingled through me, somehow colder and definitely brighter than the frozen power crushing me, and the cold and pressure inside me eased. It wasn't a lot. It still felt like someone was sitting on my chest and I was still too cold, but it was better than before.

"Done," Sebastian said.

Great. Now let's go, Titus growled.

"One second," Cassius said. "Rin, you're the fastest of us. Grab some pants and boots for Titus. They'll be the biggest sets on the bottom shelf in the bathroom. I don't want to have to watch him fight naked ever again."

"You know he's just going to end up shifting and destroying them," Hawk said as he climbed onto Titus's back, settled between two of his spine ridges, and reached down to help me up.

I took his hand, his skin painfully hot against mine, and placed my other hand on Titus's side. Sudden crushing power slammed into me, throwing me into darkness. My pulse leaped into a wild tattoo and I fought to breathe. I was trapped. Again.

Not again. Please. No one knew where I was. No one was looking for me. I was forgotten, trapped forever in this crushing darkness. Unable to move, to cry out, to do anything. *Please.* I couldn't stay like that. I had to be free— No Karthick had to be free— No...? *Please. Someone. Anyone. Help me!*

"Please," I gasped.

"Fuck. I've got you," Sebastian said, his voice small and far away.

A cold blast of icy magic roared into my body. It yanked me back, making the dining room lurch around me, but the pressure and cold remained. They didn't even ease up like they had when Sebastian had first used his magic a few seconds ago. Now I could barely draw in a breath and I couldn't feel my hands and feet at all.

Hawk stared at me, his hellfire full flames in eyes wide with fear. "This is a terrible idea."

"There isn't a better one," Sebastian said, grabbing my hips and steadying me, while Rin knelt, laced his fingers together, and held out his cupped hands by my knee in an offer to help me up.

"Thank you," I gasped, putting my foot in his hands.

A hint of fear, so subtle I probably would have missed it if I hadn't been determined to better read Rin's body language, tightened his expression. Whatever they'd seen, it had terrified both Hawk and Rin.

It scared all of us, Titus said in my head as Rin lifted me into Hawk's too-hot embrace. *You were screaming for help.*

Out loud?

Yeah, he said, his mental voice dark with worry as his life force snapped again inside me, crushing around my heart

I gasped and Hawk leaned back, putting as much distance between our torsos as he could while holding me steady, probably thinking it was his body temperature that had made me gasp, while Sebastian scrambled up behind me. He took over supporting me and pulled me around to sit in front of him, putting himself between me and Hawk.

Another flurry of icy magic rushed through me, easing even more of the pressure and cold, and I had no idea how much magic it had taken to do that.

"Stop using your magic," I said. "I can handle this. Cassius might be more useful in a fight, but you still need your magic to get the other keys out of Deaglan."

"And you need to make it to wherever we're going alive, sweetheart,"

Sebastian said, taking the blanket from Rin and wrapping it around me. "You now take out two of us if you bite the dust."

Because my souls were bound to both Rin and Sebastian, and if I died, they died or went crazy.

"Really didn't need that reminder right now." I clutched the blanket and leaned back into Sebastian's embrace. His life force swelled against my senses, adding to Titus's ferocity, and warmed most of my chill for a second before the key's connection between me and Titus snapped again, ricocheting more ice through my veins.

"You're the priority," Sebastian whispered in my ear, his breath hot against my cheek and neck when it should have been cool. "I don't care what the others say."

"But if we don't get the Heart—"

"Then we'll deal with it," he said as Rin climbed onto Titus's back and settled between the ridges ahead of me. "Rin, get closer. Your essence is strong, which means your body temperature is about the same as mine and she needs all the heat she can get."

Rin glanced back at us, his gaze jumping from me to Sebastian, and he shifted over the spine ridge to pin me between them, sending a whisper of desire rushing through me despite the crushing cold.

"That wasn't an order," I said to him, my voice frustratingly breathy. "I meant what I said. You don't have to help us."

"I know," he replied in his barely-there voice, making no indication that he wanted to get off and stay behind in the aerie. "And I meant what I said, too."

He didn't repeat himself, because when we'd talked about it a few minutes ago in the sitting room, the pain in his cells had flared up, making it hard for him to speak. But he'd vowed that he'd fight with us and that he'd protect me, and I believed him... and not just because our bond was telling me that I could trust him. He'd made a point to tell me even though it had caused him pain, which meant he was serious about it and had felt, whatever the consequences, it was worth saying.

"Now that we've got that sorted, let's get this key and beat the shit out of Deaglan." Cassius released his wings with a burst of fire that hissed when it hit the stone tables, benches, and floor, and he leaped out the window. "Where are we going?"

The Winter Court, Titus said in our heads as he turned and leaped after him, spreading his massive leathery wings and soaring out of the aerie.

"Well that's just great," Sebastian huffed, his voice thick with sarcasm. "Because we wouldn't want to make getting this last key easy."

My pulse picked up and the ice inside me tightened in my stomach. I didn't want to go back to the Winter Court. I'd promised that I would find it a new monarch. That had been the only reason it had pulled some of its power out of me. But I feared that if I returned without having someone else to take my place, it would try to take over my body again. And I was afraid that if it did, it would completely incapacitate me.

I was barely holding on as it was. Even now, I could feel the effects of Sebastian's magic inside me weakening and the call from the key growing stronger. And there was no way I was going to admit any of that to the guys because I had a feeling we were going to need every ounce of magic and concentration that we had to beat Deaglan.

CASSIUS

Titus led the way, flapping his massive wings, building up speed, and soaring over the Wilds, while I followed. My fire — that I'd somehow managed to pull back under control while Hawk and Bane were giving me a hard time about sex — burned through my blood, straining what little control I'd managed to regain in the dining room, and I had no idea how much longer I'd be able to hold it together.

This was the worst possible time for us to face Deaglan. We hadn't talked about possible strategies to use against him and even if Hawk hadn't said that Bane was still magically weak, I would have known from how dim his full-body fae glow was and the exhaustion in his expression.

Amiah hadn't noticed how tired he was, which spoke to how tired *she* was and how dangerous it was dragging her into a fight.

Hell, we were all tired. The others might have slept for the morning, but that wasn't enough to make up for almost a week of constantly being on the run.

The only one of us who might possibly be okay was Rin, and I still wasn't sure he was one of us.

And while Amiah's brand was compelling him to protect her, that didn't mean he'd do anything for the rest of us.

Which frustrated me and made my fire writhe and snap under my skin. I wanted to be able to count on him as a member of our team. He was a fast, strong, skilled fighter even without his katana. But I wouldn't know how much he'd follow orders or if he'd even follow them at all until we ended up in a fight.

And without a doubt, we were going to end up in a fight.

Deaglan had been seconds behind us the last two times a key had become empowered. He was going to show up for this key.

I could only hope I'd be able to do what needed to be done.

I glanced at Amiah huddled between Bane and Rin, wrapped in a heavy blanket and still shivering despite the hot, humid air, wafting up from the jungle below.

Her lips were blue, her complexion pale, and Bane had his arms around her.

My throat tightened and my fire flared stronger and slipped past my mental hold, showering sparks into the jungle and sending up a large gust of heavy black smoke.

I thought I'd have more time with her.

In the very least, I thought I'd get a chance to really talk with her like we used to in the early days after I'd rescued her from that human faith healer. Certainly more than the brief conversation we'd had on top of the aerie while I was still angry and jealous that she'd branded Bane and not me.

But if my fate was to become the Salamander again, burn myself up and take Deaglan with me, then it made sense that she wouldn't brand me. Not branding me was for the best. It made it perfectly clear what my fate was.

If we were bound, my death would mean her death or, in the very best situation, her going crazy.

Besides, even if she had branded me, with my fire raging out of control, I'd have ended up burning her when we sealed our bond. And just like she was going to have to seal her bond with Rin soon or suffer the same effects of one half of the bond dying, she would have had to seal her bond with me.

Or break it with the Heart.

Like she planned to do with Rin... if the Heart would even be able to break the bond. Even then, we'd be back to where we started.

Me without her.

On the horizon ahead of us and quickly getting larger, rose the Winter Court's opalescent dome. Thankfully, at our pace, it wasn't very far away and, from all the offhand comments I'd heard Bane and Titus make about Faerie expanding and contracting the Wilds as it desired, it looked like Faerie wanted us to get there.

Which made me wonder if Faerie would place the Winter Court farther from Deaglan. Of course, with our luck, Deaglan could have found someone able to make a portal that could just transport him instantly wherever he wanted. Even if he hadn't found someone, he was still going to show up and we still hadn't talked strategies.

And while I didn't want Amiah to know my plan, I needed to tell Bane so he didn't use his magic to stop me.

Out of all of the others, he was the only one who might be powerful enough to stop me. Thankfully he was also the most pragmatic. He understood that sometimes terrible choices needed to be made and this was one of those times.

But it was too late to say anything. I couldn't very well pull Bane aside when we landed wherever we landed and have a private conversation. Amiah and the others would want to know what we were talking about and they'd make a big deal about it until they knew.

No, I had to just find the right moment after Bane took Deaglan's keys, and end this.

And if it looked like Bane wasn't going to get Deaglan's keys... I'd still end it.

Sure, Amiah would be stuck with Rin forever, but she'd be alive. They all would, and whatever I did, I would ensure Amiah's safety and protect her and the men she loved like I hadn't done for my brother—

My thoughts tripped on that. Amiah had said Dominic's death hadn't been my fault, that he was stubborn and would have taken that assignment whether I'd told him to or not.

That was true, and maybe if I had the time, I'd accept that.

But I was out of time, and this time if Amiah or any of the others died in this fight it would be my fault. Which I wasn't going to let happen, even if it meant I had to sacrifice everything.

AMIAH

We barreled toward the Winter Court's opalescent barrier, the rushing wind cold and stinging against my skin despite the fact that we flew over a humid jungle and that I'd tucked my head down and used Rin as a shield.

The new key wrenched on my soul, twisting with the other key inside me adding to the strain and I fought to hide my shivering and my strained breathing.

I just had to hold on.

We were almost there.

Once I got off Titus some of the cold and pressure would ease up.

I just couldn't let the guys see how much I was struggling.

Especially Sebastian, because he'd use even more magic to help relieve the cold and pressure, and if he didn't have enough magic to pull the other two keys out of Deaglan, we'd have to retreat. Which meant facing the Shadow King a second time, which increased the chances that one of my guys wouldn't survive, and that was unacceptable.

Thankfully, we reached the barrier before Faerie started to rip its magic out of me or Sebastian, and Titus soared in without hesitation, flying right into a ferocious snowstorm that had been invisible and contained within the court's barrier.

The frozen wind filled with ice pellets jerked us this way and that, and I couldn't see anything around me. I could barely see the back of Titus's head.

"Fuck," Sebastian hissed, huddling closer and using his arms and Rin's body to protect me from the storm. "My mother is pissed. Please, T, tell me the key is somewhere indoors."

The Queen's Falls, Titus said. *At least it'll be—*

A new cold exploded inside me, tearing at me from the inside out. It rushed through my veins and into my cells, and howled in my ears, cutting off Titus's words. I couldn't breathe, couldn't think, and I was cold. So damned cold.

You promised, the Winter Court wailed, and I could feel its agony whispering against my senses as if it were a person with a life force. It, too, was being torn apart by the Winter Queen's fury and while the queen couldn't kill it, that only meant the court's suffering would never end. *Please. Let me in. Become my queen.*

Its cries tore at my heart as its magic tried to rip into my soul. But the barrier between us was even stronger now that I belonged to both Rin *and* Sebastian. It was never going to get in. It was only going to make me suffer with it.

You know I would if I could, I mentally gasped at it. *I said I'd find someone for you and I will.*

Behind me, Sebastian tensed and groaned. Heat flared through our brand etched along my ribs and my connection to Sebastian's life force swelled, making my pulse skip a beat.

Oh, God. The Winter Court couldn't have me, so it was trying to take Sebastian. Except Sebastian didn't want to be king. He didn't want the commitment, just like he hadn't wanted a relationship, and even though he'd accepted our soul bond, I was certain he still didn't want to be king.

Titus lurched, wrenching to the side to avoid crashing into a sheer cliff face that was suddenly in front of us, making my stomach heave and the world spin. There was too much pressure, too much movement. I needed to stop. I needed to breathe. I wasn't going to last much longer, but I didn't want to ask Sebastian for help. I wanted him to use every ounce of magic he had to end this and free me and Rin.

Titus dove into a deep gorge, and Cassius yelled something that I couldn't make out with the wind roaring in and around me. He plunged down after us, his fire a writhing beacon, still enormous and brilliant despite the wind and ice tearing at it, and despite the fact that he shouldn't have had any magic left.

A part of me feared he'd be completely out of fire when we finally faced Deaglan, but a stronger part of me feared this was his new horrible existence, unable to control an inferno that had no end. I didn't have the power to heal an angel's magic. The only angel who had been able to heal someone's magic was dead. And it broke my heart thinking that Sebastian might not be able to help him and if we couldn't get the Heart or it couldn't help him, either, the only way he'd ever be able to have a normal life again would be to give up his magic completely.

The narrow gorge thankfully blocked the wind and I managed to draw in a marginally deeper breath now that the wind also wasn't tearing the air out of my mouth. Titus raced along its path, skimming the bottom, partially turned on his side because the gorge wasn't wide enough for his wing span, forcing me to cling to Rin as he clung to Titus's spine ridge in front of him to keep seated.

But the lack of wind stinging my skin made me hyperaware of the pressure and cold crushing and tearing me and the now-almost painful heat radiating from my brand connecting me to Sebastian as the Winter Court fought to gain purchase in his soul.

"Holy fuck, Amiah," Sebastian gasped. "Is *that* what the Winter Court's been doing to you?"

"Trying to take over?" I turned my head just enough so I could catch his gaze. Anger had turned his pale blue, almost colorless eyes hard, but I couldn't tell if he was angry because the court was trying to control him or because I hadn't mentioned how difficult it had been to fight it. "Only since it pulled me back into Faerie and the angelic mating brand won't let it in."

Please, accept that, I thought at it. *There's nothing I or Sebastian can do about it, but I'll find you someone. I promise.*

No. You have to take me from her. Now. The court heaved and clawed, digging deeper into my soul — and from Sebastian's tightening expression, his as well. Except that only added to the pressure inside me, and I jerked my face away from Sebastian before he realized I was once again fighting to draw in even the shallowest of breaths.

"Well, I guess now I really can't become King. Thanks for that." A flurry of Sebastian's icy magic swept through me, easing some of the pressure and weakening the Winter Court's voice inside me.

"For the love of— Stop using your magic," I snapped at him.

Titus barreled around a curve and into a section of the gorge that was wide enough for him to level out. Ahead lay an even wider area still protected from the storm by the towering sheer mountain walls. A dozen, mostly-frozen waterfalls of various heights and widths filled the area, with an enormous one at the very back. Trickles of water trailed over their frozen surfaces, dripping from long icicles and rough edges. Inside the ice, small flecks of light sparkled within them as if they were reflecting sunlight despite the fact that a storm raged above us, glimmers of the Winter Court's magic that I could only see because I still had its power slicing into my body.

Titus landed at the edge of a large pool that was frozen except for a small area by the waterfalls. The ground beneath his feet was a mix of ice and stone with hundreds of tiny blue flowers poking up between the cracks. They, too, pulsed with power that I wasn't supposed to be able to sense and tinkled like hundreds of small bells when the wind from Titus's wings brushed them.

I scanned the area, searching for the key's bright blue pinprick. I should have noticed it right away. The keys had blazed like miniscule suns the last two times we'd gone after them and they'd yanked on my soul, drawing me to them whether I wanted to go or not. And while I could feel the yank, calling me to a thin waterfall beside the largest one, I couldn't see the key's light.

Get off, Titus said in my head, his mental voice sounding tight and labored as if he, too, was struggling with the pressure of the empowered key. *The key is in the passages behind the falls.*

"This just keeps getting better and better," Sebastian groaned as Rin hopped off Titus's back then held out his hands to help me down. "If the key is in the tunnels, you can't stay in your dragon form."

"We'll manage," Cassius said, his expression grim as he yanked his wings into his body with a snap of flames and swept his gaze over the area.

His fire dripped around him, hissing against the ice and releasing clouds of billowing mist that partially obscured him. "At least he's not doing it naked this time. Hawk. Bane. Do either of you sense anyone?"

"The magic in the waterfalls is fucking with my sensitivity," Hawk said, also hopping off. "This whole area is lit up like the sun. And the shield Bane gave me the first time we were here to help me see properly is still up and working and I *still* can't see the magic in the key. The last time we ran into one, it was blinding, more powerful than anything else around it."

"I'm not much better," Sebastian said, helping me slide off Titus into

Rin's arms.

Trembling, I collapsed into Rin's strong embrace, and even with the cold and pressure crushing me, stealing my breath, and a heavy blanket between us, the contact made my need to seal our bond surge.

"I don't hear anyone," Rin said, surprising me that he was offering information without anyone asking for it.

One of his hands slid up my back, the movement drawing a shiver of need, and I leaned into him, unable to fight my desire along with everything else.

"The Shadow King is powerful," Rin added, surprising me even more, "but he doesn't have easy access to someone who can create a portal."

Which didn't necessarily mean that Deaglan wasn't already there, but there wasn't any other way we could check. And while I might be able to tell if there was someone around with my ability to sense life forces, I doubted with the key's frozen pressure inside me, that I'd be able to concentrate enough to tell. As it was, I could barely sense my guys standing beside me, and that included Rin who held me.

"Well, hopefully we've gotten here first. Which waterfall?" Cassius asked, thankfully not glancing back and seeing me in Rin's arms. I didn't think it would start a fight. Cassius knew an angelic mating brand was a powerful thing. But I knew it would upset him. It was a reminder that the brand wasn't the perfect sacred thing that we'd been taught to believe, that it was messed up and confusing and, in this case, just wrong. It was also a reminder that he couldn't hold me, and unless we could figure out how to deal with his magic, he never would.

Then Rin's fingers reached the back of my head and he stiffened as if he'd suddenly realized what he was doing.

"Your highness." He shifted both of his hands to my shoulders and stepped back, holding me at arm's length. Sebastian slid off Titus and, with a tight nod to Rin, wrapped an arm around me and drew me close to his side.

"Which waterfall?" Sebastian asked me.

"That one." I pointed in the direction of the key's persistent yank, as Titus shifted and quickly pulled on his pants and boots.

Cassius ran a hand over his blond buzzcut. "I really want to tell someone to stay here with Amiah. But it's the same situation as the caves in the Summer Court and I'm not going to risk Deaglan or his men catching her with only one of us to protect her."

"Especially since he knows she has a key," Titus growled.

"And he knows she has healing magic," Rin added.

The thought made my stomach churn. I would never be someone's prisoner again.

Except if Deaglan got his hands on me, my options were limited. He could block my ability to connect with his life force so I couldn't fight back, and now I couldn't kill myself because that would kill Sebastian and Rin.

"I'm the least capable in a fight." The hellfire in Hawk's eyes flared, but I didn't know if it was because he'd been forced to admit that out of all of my guys he was the least dangerous or if it was just from worry over the situation. "I'll hang back and protect Amiah and Bane while you guys get the key and kick the shit out of Deaglan when he inevitably shows up."

"Agreed." Cassius turned an icy glare on me. "Whatever happens, don't you dare run into the middle of a fight."

"You know I can't promise that." The frozen pressure inside me twisted tighter and I bit back a whimper, making Cassius's eyes narrow and his angel glow flare.

"Right." He turned his attention to Sebastian and Hawk. "Her magic is at full so if anyone is seriously wounded, she'll be compelled to heal them even if they're Deaglan's men or Deaglan himself. Sit on her if you have to, but don't let her run headlong into danger."

He strode around the edge of the pool toward the frozen waterfalls, his footsteps crunching in the gravel and ice and making the flowers tinkle. Dark, thick smoke billowed around him, but somehow, he managed to keep his fire contained.

Titus, now dressed in leather pants, boots, and nothing else, hurried to catch up with him, while Rin, after a quick glance at me, followed.

"He really didn't need to give that order," Hawk muttered, falling into step on my other side.

"He can't help himself," Sebastian replied, as he helped me hurry across the uneven slippery ground, our footsteps also making the flowers chime. "And I'm not a fan of his fire in the ice tunnels. That's real ice, not like the ice that the court is made out of. There's a good chance we could all drown if he isn't careful."

"I heard that," Cassius said. "And I'm painfully aware of the effect my magic will have on all this ice."

The way into the passages was a narrow opening between a short, wide waterfall and the mountain, and up a steep incline that was as tall as I was. Ice covered the incline's rough surface and with all my shivering, I had no idea if I was going to be able to climb up it. I certainly wasn't going to be able to manage while clinging to the blanket.

"Can you resist the call of the key long enough to stand guard?" Cassius asked, turning to Titus. "I'd rather someone who can fight without taking the tunnel down around us go up first."

"I've resisted this long," Titus growled. "The only way to protect our mate is to be cautious."

He flexed his fingers as if to accentuate his point and his unusual thick dragon claws extended from his fingertips. He turned sideways — because his chest and shoulders were too broad to fit through the space — and shuffled into the opening then used his claws to quickly climb up the slope as if it weren't covered in ice.

Cassius followed, his chest and shoulders also too broad, forcing him to turn sideways. With a degree of control I'd thought he'd lost given how singed his clothes were, he melted away small patches of ice, exposing the stone to create hand and footholds that would make it a little easier for me to climb up — so long as I had some help. But by the time he reached the top, he was trembling with the effort to use his magic so precisely and flames started snapping over his hands.

"We need to do something about that, Cassius," Sebastian said as Rin climbed up then held out his hand to help me.

"I can manage," Cassius ground out. "I want access to everything I've got for this fight, so let's just get this key and get the hell out of here so we can face Deaglan out in the open."

"Yeah," Titus growled, his attention turned toward whatever lay beyond the incline, his large chest heaving with strained breaths, and his body trembling as much as mine and Cassius's. "I can see it. The sooner we get it, the sooner we get out of here."

I couldn't have agreed more. The longer it took to get the key, the longer I'd be unable to breathe. I tossed the blanket up to Rin since I wasn't going to be able to climb up with it, then I took his hand and let him and Sebastian help me up.

The space behind the waterfall was larger than I expected, opening into a long narrow ice cave almost wide enough for Titus in his dragon form to spread his wings, but with a low ceiling that was only about a foot taller than him in his human form. The walls, floor, and ceiling were mostly ice, with hints of stone peeking through the blue-white coating, and were riddled with holes, some big enough for Titus — in his human form — to pass through, others barely the size of my fist.

The thought of all that ice and stone surrounding me pressed against my senses and my chest constricted even more. I tried to focus on my surroundings and not the sudden panic racing through me at the thought of being trapped and unable to see the sky. I concentrated on how clear and blue the ice was, how the magic that I'd noticed when we'd first arrived was now stronger, the glimmers bigger and brighter, and how there were trickles of water sliding down the back side of this waterfall. I even tried to focus on the cold and how behind the waterfall it was almost as deep as the cold inside me, and now the guys' breaths misted as well as mine, but it was just so hard to push aside my claustrophobia.

Then my attention jumped to a series of holes at the back — the ice an uneven lattice partially obscuring the other side — and the pinprick of brilliant blue light beyond it.

Everything within me jerked toward it, my thoughts, my soul, even my body took a step closer, and my fear of being trapped was overwhelmed by the call of the key. I had to have it, had to take it inside me and become one with it. If I claimed it, the pain and pressure inside me would go away. I'd be free. I'd be remembered, I'd be—

Rin held out the blanket, but I ignored him and took another step toward the empowered key. I needed to be free. Please. *Free me. Help me. Please.*

"Hey." Sebastian grabbed my wrist, stopping me.

A burst of searing heat swept through our brand, shattering the key's call and sending burning agony racing up my side to my heart and making me moan in pain.

Rin grabbed me before my legs gave out, wrapping me in the blanket, and his hellfire burst into miniature flames before shrinking back into red pinpricks. For a second I was drowning in his black gaze, then he pushed me back into Sebastian's embrace, and turned his attention to the cave.

"What the hell was that?" Hawk asked, inching closer, the heat radiating from his body almost too warm even though he still stood a good two feet away.

"The key." I tugged the blanket tighter around me.

"It's the last one. The call has gotten stronger," Titus added, heading to the back of the cave and peering through the holes.

"Can you see a way in?" Cassius asked, joining him, his gaze jumping to the closest opening that was big enough for us to pass through. Except it looked like the passage turned away from the area where the key lay and I doubted he, or any of the others, wanted to wander around these passages hoping that they'd end up at the key.

"If you can control your fire a little longer, just melt an opening and let's go," Sebastian said. "As soon as it's big enough, I'll refreeze it to keep it stable."

I opened my mouth to tell him not to waste his magic, but he gave me a pointed glare, cutting off my words.

"Don't argue." He leaned me against the cave wall to help me keep my balance without him. "It's worth the power if it gets us out in the open before Deaglan arrives."

"Agreed," Cassius said, pressing his palms against the icy lattice separating us from the key.

Sebastian hurried to join him and Titus, while Rin took up position in the middle of the room and Hawk shifted closer to me. All of them moved as if the five of them had been working as a team for years and not just a few days.

With a quick glance to Sebastian who nodded that he was ready, Cassius released his fire. It surged around his hands and water rushed down the wall in quick-moving runnels and pooled around his feet. The ice melted and crumbled, creating a hole the size of his head that quickly grew into an opening big enough for Titus to go through if he turned sideways.

"That's good," Sebastian said, swiping his hand through the air in front of him. A glyph on his back flared to life, glowing through his thin cotton shirt, and a frozen blast of air swept around us and flash-froze the water.

Titus rushed through the opening before the light in Sebastian's glyph had faded, indicating he'd finished, and the big dragon half slid and half ran the remaining fifty feet to the key. But as he reached it, the shadows in the crevasses of the uneven walls, floor, and ceiling, made deeper and darker by the key's light, shot toward him.

They slammed into his chest, knocked him over, and sent him crashing back to the edge of the newly-made doorway.

"It took you long enough to get here," a dark voice purred. The voice twisted my nerves, and my pulse lurched. We were too late. The Shadow King was already there.

AMIAH

THE SHADOWS MERGED INTO ONE GIANT SHADOW BESIDE THE GLOWING KEY then melted away— or rather sank back into Deaglan where they writhed and swirled under his pale skin. He wore the same black leather jerkin and pants that he had before and had the same dangerous gleam in his eyes that made my stomach tighten even more with fear.

"It looks like my guess was correct. You didn't—" His lips curled back into a sneer. "Or perhaps you *couldn't* leave your pretty, *powerful* wife behind. Thanks for that. Now I don't have to work to get the final key." His gaze jumped to Rin and his eyes narrowed. "You, however, are unexpected. You know the price for betrayal. I would have thought you'd have run when the leash spell broke, not been stupid enough to side with Seireadan."

Rin shifted his feet, widening his stance ever-so-slightly, the only indication he'd heard Deaglan's words.

"I won't let you touch her," Titus roared. He lunged for Deaglan and Cassius rushed after him, snapping his fire whip at the Shadow King, unable to release anything more powerful because that could weaken the ice and bring the cave down around us.

But the Shadow King released a powerful blast that consumed Cassius's fire whip and knocked him to his knees while tossing Titus completely through the icy lattice this time.

The ice in the ceiling and walls cracked, and a large chunk above

Sebastian broke free, forcing him to wrench out of the way or be crushed.

Everything within me stalled, locked on Sebastian and Rin— no, *all* of my guys. They were in danger. I had to protect them, keep them safe. It didn't matter that I couldn't fight, that if I tried anything I'd just make everything worse. My soul said I had to. They were mine and I couldn't lose any of them.

And the best way to do that, was to get out of danger as best I could and hold onto my healing magic for when they needed it.

"This key is mine and so is your pretty little healing angel," Deaglan snarled and he grabbed the key.

Its blue light flared blindingly bright then sank into his skin like the shadows had and the frozen pressure stealing my breath and body heat vanished.

I gasped in a deep breath and my magical senses surged, flooding me with life. I could feel my guys, strong and sure, their power surging through my veins and giving me strength.

And I could feel dozens of other life forces all around us. Dark and thick just like Deaglan's, and all protected by the same shield as before.

We were surrounded, Deaglan's shields prevented me from using my new power to incapacitate them, and now the only thing stopping Deaglan from getting the Heart was the single key inside me.

"Hawk, get Amiah out of here," Cassius said, leaping back to his feet and snapping his fire whip at Deaglan.

Hawk grabbed my wrist, his touch hot, but thankfully not painful anymore now that the key had been claimed, and yanked me back toward the incline and the narrow passage behind the frozen waterfall. But half a dozen shadow fae stepped out of the shadows between us and our exit and rushed toward us.

"Shit." He wrenched me behind him and Rin bolted toward us.

"No, Rin, protect Bane," Cassius commanded.

Rin's gaze locked with mine and his hellfire flared. I knew he wanted to come to me. I wasn't sure how I could tell. His expression didn't change, but my soul said he, like me, was compelled by our bond to protect each other.

Then his gaze jerked to Bane and I could sense a strange need through our partially formed connection to protect him as well... and while I was sure it was my need from the bond to keep Sebastian safe that was influencing Rin, it felt like a part of the desire was also Rin's.

Of course, while Sebastian and Rin weren't mates and they didn't share any part of my brands, Rin was aware that if Sebastian was in danger, so was I.

With another strange flare of protective emotion through our bond, Rin jerked away from me and grabbed an assassin rushing toward Sebastian. Whether he was helping to keep himself alive and free or not — and I was having serious doubts that that was the only thing motivating him now — he'd committed to helping us. Attacking one of Deaglan's men in front of Deaglan was a clear defiance to his old master and there was no turning back for him now. And if Deaglan didn't outright kill Rin, he could face another five hundred years or more of torture.

We all would.

And all of Faerie might too if we couldn't get the keys from him.

Which meant we had to win this fight.

Except if Sebastian was going to take Deaglan's keys, he wouldn't have enough extra power to cast a light spell like he had in the Summer Court's luminescent cave garden and prevent the shadow fae from jumping in and out of the shadows.

"Amiah, how many are there?" Cassius asked, reminding me that with my ability to sense life forces, I could at least get a head count for them.

"There's—" I focused on my new power. It swept out of me and whirled around all of Deaglan's assassins unable to fully connect with them because of the shields protecting their life forces.

They were a mix of men and women, all shadow fae and I had no doubt all skilled fighters. There were six in front of me and Hawk, at least a dozen around Deaglan, and almost two dozen more lining the cave between the waterfall and the lattice.

"There's about four dozen," I said.

"Not a problem," Titus growled and someone screamed.

My healing magic surged, yanking my attention behind me to the man Titus had just critically wounded, then the compulsion stuttered and vanished as the man died. But Titus tore out the throat of another shadow fae with his sharp claws and my magic surged again, making me take a step toward him before I realized what I was doing.

No. I gritted my teeth, fighting the compulsion. My urge vanished again, thankfully without compelling me further into the fight, but it was a serious reminder that I had to get out of there before I did something stupid.

I started to turn away but Cassius snapped his whip at Deaglan, who sent a flurry of shadow spears at him and the memory of Deaglan's shadow spear tearing through Cassius's side froze me in place.

That had been the first serious injury he'd taken before Deaglan had ripped out his fire and then an assassin had slit his throat. And while I knew Cassius was a skilled fighter, everything within me still screamed. I couldn't lose him. I couldn't lose any of them. Yes, my guys were capable of handling themselves in a fight, but we were just as outnumbered as we'd been before and Deaglan was just as powerful.

The ice inside me surged — even though the empowered key's magic no longer crushed around my heart — and a flurry of snowflakes danced out of my mouth as the Winter Court's voice grew stronger, fighting to break through whatever Sebastian had done to mute it.

I mentally seized the cold inside me and jerked my hand up.

Please, God, let this work.

A blast of frozen wind exploded from my hand. It tore through the lattice between me and Deaglan, breaking away more chunks of ice, and ripped Deaglan's shadow spears apart before they reached Cassius.

The wind knocked everyone between me and Deaglan to their knees, including my guys, and crashed into the Shadow King, slamming him into the wall behind him.

His head snapped back and my healing magic surged again, rushing hot and sticky over my hands and up my forearms. It overwhelmed the Winter Court's cold, shattering my mental hold on it and forcing me to connect with Deaglan.

He was injured, two cracked ribs, a mild concussion, and a laceration in his scalp. I had to go to him. Heal him.

And if I didn't, my magic would drain me and heal him where I stood. It wasn't going to leave me a choice. It didn't matter that it wanted to heal someone who was trying to kill us. All it knew was that someone needed to be healed.

I heaved at my power. I didn't care how injured he was or what kind of backlash I'd suffer. I. Would. Not. Heal. Him.

Deaglan's gaze jumped to me and his shadows whirled into a wild vortex around him. "You're not supposed to be able to do that."

"She's my wife," Sebastian said, scrambling to his knees and grabbing his left forearm. He shot a force-wave into Deaglan's face and snapped his head back against the icy stone wall again. "Of course she can control the court's wind."

My healing magic twisted tighter, the pressure in my chest was almost as powerful as the key's before Deaglan had taken it, and I hugged myself as if that would keep me in place and control my power.

Sebastian jerked around to face me and shot another force-wave into a shadow fae rushing toward me, as Rin seized another one lunging at Sebastian's back and tossed him against the wall with a heavy thud. That shadow fae crumpled to the ground, and small chunks of ice broke off from the wall, showering around him.

My magic surged again, this time to the man on the ground.

No. I clenched my jaw, and hung on to the blanket as if not releasing it would ensure I didn't release my power.

Another shadow fae lunged at me, his long knife reflecting the flickering magical light trapped in the icy walls. I scrambled out of the way, forcing myself to go toward the frozen waterfall and its frigid trickling water and not toward Deaglan or his fallen men like my power wanted. I needed to leave. Once we were outside, Cassius would be able to fully release his fire and Titus would be able to shift.

"No one but the queen should be able to reach it right now," Deaglan said, sending a flurry of shadow spears at Sebastian. "She's determined to control her court, whatever the cost."

Cassius tore the shadow spears apart with his fire whip, and Titus lunged at Deaglan, who created a wall of shadows, deflecting Titus's claws, and dove out of the way.

"And let me guess—" Sebastian pressed his hands over his heart and ignited an enormous— no, not just one, but two large glyphs on his back and another one that curled around his right biceps, using a mix of his sorcerer's ability to control raw magic and combine whatever the spells were in the glyphs tattooed in his body. "You had something to do with that?"

Deaglan sneered. "It's not my fault she's already paranoid. She barely needed a push."

Cassius snapped his fire whip at an assassin, grabbing her leg and tossing her at Deaglan as Titus lunged at him again. But Deaglan shoved his assassin into Titus with his shadows, shooting a spear through the woman's chest, drawing a scream of agony, and sending the spear all the way through her into Titus's torso.

My magic heaved me forward and I wrenched back, pressing my shoulder blades against the waterfall. The water trickling down the ice seeped into the blanket, and I struggled to stay where I was. I had to stay put—

No. I had to get outside. There was no way I was going to withstand my healing compulsion, not when I could now heal from a distance.

Titus roared, tore the shadow spear apart with his claws, and tossed the dying woman into another assassin, sending them tumbling across the floor to crash against the wall. Her life force heaved against my senses then went out and my compulsion released me again.

"Hawk," Cassius yelled. "Get Amiah out of here."

"Trying," Hawk gasped, sidestepping an assassin's lunge, seizing the man's wrist, and wrenching the knife from his hand. "Just needed a weapon."

The magic trapped in the icy walls flared, along with the Winter Court's chill inside me, and two shadow fae assassins popped out of the thin shadows created by the edge of the ruined lattice behind Sebastian.

Time stuttered into horrific slow motion. Rin was only a few feet away, but he fought with three other shadow fae, and the side of his beige cotton shirt was stained with blood. He'd been cut and from the way the assassins were dodging and deflecting his attacks, it was clear they were almost as skilled as he was. He wasn't going to be able to disengage from them and get to Sebastian in time. No one was.

Everything within me froze, and I seized the Winter Court's cold inside me again with everything I had and released another powerful blast of wind. Except a force snapped inside me, just like the last time the Winter Queen had taken back control of the court, and the wind sputtered. It shoved the assassins half a dozen steps away from Sebastian but didn't knock them over like the last time.

I strained to regain control of the wind and send another blast, but it kept ripping out of my mental gasp, stuttering shocks of frozen magic around my heart that made me tremble and forced me to clutch the waterfall's rough, wet ice to stay standing.

"That's better," Deaglan said. "Looks like Mommy Dearest just needed a reminder that your little bitch was trying to take over."

Rin grabbed one of the fae he was fighting and shoved him into one of the men who'd tried to attack Sebastian, while Cassius seized the other with his whip and yanked him to the back of the cave.

"No one is taking over." The light in Sebastian's glyphs flared brighter, consuming all of the shadows around him. He closed his eyes, his body trembling with the effort to control his magic, and pointed a finger at Deaglan. "Especially not you."

Blinding white light shot from Sebastian's hand and slammed into Deaglan's chest. The Shadow King tensed and his eyes widened, then his lips curled back in a dark sneer and he heaved forward a step, pushing into Sebastian's stream of magic.

"You're not powerful enough to stop me," he snarled. "You weren't three hundred years ago and you aren't now. I'm going to have your wife just like I had Enowen and she's going to beg and plead and I'm going to make you watch."

"Not happening," Cassius growled as he shot a small fireball at Deaglan, then, with his fire whip, seized the wrist of an assassin who had his hand raised to slash at Sebastian's back.

He yanked the assassin away, but Deaglan formed a shadow shield that consumed Cassius's fireball and shot a shadow spear at him, despite Sebastian's magic still pouring into his chest.

"You're weak," Deaglan said. "You're all weak. You should have bowed to me, Seireadan, accepted me as your rightful king. You could have been my right hand. We could have ruled Faerie together not just our small little courts."

A thread of darkness shot through Sebastian's light and into his hand. Shadows exploded under his skin and every muscle in his body contracted. His mouth opened in a scream he couldn't release and his life force flared against my senses, wild and desperate. Then a darkness, deeper and more painful than his demonic magic infection had been, tore into him and made my healing magic roar all the way up my arms and burn around my heart.

I gasped, my soul screaming to save him, to do something, anything. He was my mate. I *had* to save him.

Except I couldn't heal what Deaglan was doing to him. Even if I ran into the middle of this fight — which as much as I told Cassius I couldn't promise, I knew it was a beyond foolish thing to do — my healing magic wouldn't be able to save Sebastian.

AMIAH

Sebastian's scream tore free, a desperate, strangled cry that made Deaglan's sneer deepen. The Shadow King straightened and took another stronger, steadier step toward him. All of Sebastian's white threads turned black, completely taken over by Deaglan, and the shadows inside him billowed, blotting out his pale skin and full-body glow for a heart-stopping second.

"What do you think?" Deaglan asked. "Should I block your connection with Faerie and watch you fade? Once I have the Heart all those who refuse to bow to me will face that long, slow death."

Titus roared and my healing magic flickered to another critically wounded shadow fae before my soul bond yanked me back to Sebastian. His life force blazed against my senses, his icy light desperately fighting Deaglan's consuming darkness.

Cassius snapped his fire whip through the darkness pouring into Sebastian's chest, breaking the connection, but Deaglan's shadows were already in Sebastian, devouring his magic and his life.

"No." I jerked forward a step and Hawk grabbed my arm and wrenched me back. "I have to save him."

I dropped the blanket and clawed at Hawk's grip, but he wouldn't let go, which forced him to shove me back against the frozen waterfall and twist out of the way of a shadow fae's knife to avoid getting stabbed without releasing me.

"I don't think so," Sebastian gasped, and his glow flared. Two more glyphs burst to life, joining the others, and his life force strained against Deaglan's darkness.

My soul screamed. I wrenched harder against Hawk's grip. I had to do something, had to help somehow. I couldn't just stand there and watch Deaglan kill him.

Then my power that connected with life forces, that had been connecting with him and my other guys before I'd formed a soul bond with him, exploded inside me, overwhelming my healing magic and its compulsion to heal Deaglan and his dying assassins.

It shot out of me and into Sebastian and wove into his life force. His gaze jerked up to me, his eyes wide, and his fae glow blazed, now almost completely fueled by my life force magic, as if I was giving him fae magic even though we weren't having sex.

Deaglan snarled and shot another shadow spear at Sebastian. I opened my mouth to yell a warning, but Sebastian wrenched his attention away from me, jerked his hand up, and released a force-wave from his palm without releasing the power in his already activated glyphs or even bothering to activate the force-wave glyph on his left arm.

The wave tore through the shadows, slammed Deaglan back against the wall, and shattered the connection between them — including Sebastian's original connection with Deaglan where he'd tried to take the keys.

My healing magic surged but didn't go to Sebastian, instead snapping to Deaglan. Two more broken ribs and his concussion was worse.

Sebastian collapsed to the ground, his glow barely visible, his personal store of magic almost completely gone. With a groan, he heaved himself back to his knees and raised his hands again.

"Don't you fucking dare channel more raw magic," Hawk yelled. "You'll burn yourself up and that'll kill Amiah."

"Rin, grab Bane," Cassius commanded. "We're getting out of here."

"I don't think so," Deaglan snarled. "You still have something I want."

A flurry of shadows slammed into the ceiling and walls around the exit, shattering the ice and stone. Large chunks broke free with a resounding boom and blocked our way out.

I wrenched my gaze around the cave, searching for another exit. Even if I hadn't noticed one when I'd first entered, there had to be something.

"Fuck," Hawk hissed and he yanked me out of the reach of another assassin, but a second one jumped out of the shadows. He wrapped an arm across Hawk's neck and rammed his knife into Hawk's back, drawing a scream of agony that jerked all of my guys' attention to Hawk and me for a dangerous second.

My magic stuttered, needing to heal Hawk even as his own magic rapidly healed his injury as best it could with the knife still buried in his body.

He stabbed backwards with his stolen blade, trying to get the fae holding him to let go, but the fae twisted out of reach and tightened his grip around Hawk's neck.

I mentally grasped at the glimmer of cold inside me, desperate to take control of the Winter Court's wind again. But before I could even figure out if I could wrench control away from the Winter Queen, Rin sidestepped a jab from another shadow fae, and in one fluid motion, seized the man's wrist, broke his elbow, took his knife, and threw it at Hawk. The blade skimmed Hawk's cheek, drawing a cut so shallow it didn't even bleed before it healed, and landed with a heavy, wet *thunk* in the eye of the shadow fae choking him.

The shadow fae screamed and collapsed, and Hawk shoved him aside and jerked out of the way of another attack.

"Bane, is there another way out?" Hawk gasped, lunging in and sliding his blade into his newest assailant's chest.

"Yeah," Sebastian gasped as Rin grabbed his arm and wrenched him to his feet. "But—"

"Don't bother." Cassius blasted a large fireball at the far side of the waterfall. Its heat licked hot against my skin as it tore through the thick ice and exploded out the other side. With a resounding boom, massive chunks of ice broke free and released a veil of rushing water where the ice had been. "Get her out of here."

Cassius sent another fireball, almost as big as the first one, at Deaglan. But Deaglan absorbed the fire with a shadow shield and shot it out of another shadow in the wall beside Cassius.

"He can redirect magic, too?" Hawk yelped, wrenching out of the way of another shadow fae. "That's just fucking great."

"Hawk!" Cassius pulled his fire back under his skin, but his Hawaiian shirt ignited, the flames rushing up his right side before he extinguished them, revealing he was dangerously close to being mentally and physically exhausted and about to lose control. "Go. All of you."

Rin tossed Sebastian over his shoulder and started running, as Titus killed two more assassins.

"You, too, Titus." Cassius swept up a wall of flames between him and Deaglan.

"And you," I said to Cassius as Hawk grabbed my wrist again and yanked me toward the rushing water and our way out.

"I'm right behind you," Cassius said over his shoulder, taking a backward step in our direction, his body language indicating that thankfully he wasn't going to do something stupid and stay behind, that he really was just covering our retreat. "Now, go."

Hawk released me at the last second and we leaped through the frigid water. My feet hit the thin ice at the unfrozen edge of the pool, sending cracks racing through its surface, then they slipped out from beneath me and tossed me forward, sending me skidding — thankfully — away from the open water. I bumped to a stop against a large rock protruding from the ice and, wet and shivering uncontrollably, grabbed the rock and used it to help me scramble to my feet.

A few feet away and closer to the waterfalls, Hawk also staggered to his feet, somehow able to keep his balance on ice that now had a thin coating of water on it making it even more slippery.

Behind him, Rin leaped through the waterfall with Sebastian slung over his shoulder. He landed on his feet — he didn't even slip — and bolted toward us, while Titus followed a second later, shifting as he exited, not bothering to try to land on the pool, the shift beautiful and fluid, as if his body was a red-gold liquid that rapidly expanded then hardened into his stunning dragon form. His wings clipped the edge of the opening, sending more chunks of ice crashing onto the pool and making the ice beneath me crack and heave.

Hawk's eyes flashed wide as the ice broke apart beneath his feet. "Oh, fuck."

He toppled over and fell through the shattered ice.

I screamed and jerked forward, but Rin shoved Sebastian at me, and, with a sudden twist, turned back to the hole and dove in after Hawk.

Sebastian lost his balance and skidded into me, and I grabbed his arm and heaved him to his feet as the ice beneath him broke apart.

With a yelp of surprise, he lurched forward, pinning me against the rock.

I clung to him with one foot on a narrow ridge just under the water beside Sebastian's foot and the other on a chunk of ice still attached to the rock. His life force whispered against my senses, weak, but still alive, just like his fae glow, but it didn't ease the pressure building inside me.

We still had to get away from Deaglan — since escape right now was our only option — but Hawk and Rin were under the ice, and Cassius was still inside the cave with Deaglan.

"Are you fucking kidding?" Sebastian groaned. "There are more?"

I glanced behind me to the row of shadow fae and shifters standing at the edge of the pond.

Not for long, Titus said in my head, and he swooped at them, blasting fire from his mouth. They scrambled out of the way, screaming as their clothes caught fire. My healing magic clenched around my heart, and three threads of magic shot out of me, connecting with three different people.

Oh, God. Now I could heal multiple people at the same time from a distance?

I yanked my healing magic back inside me, making it burn around my chest desperate to be released, desperate to heal those who needed healing.

"I have to get out of here," I gasped to Sebastian.

"Not before I take what's mine," Deaglan said, his shadows sweeping around him, keeping him aloft and protecting him from the water. He tossed Cassius, bloody with burned clothes, into the pool, and my pulse stalled as he disappeared beneath the water, while my magic still heaved against my control, still connected with Deaglan's men, their injuries more serious than Cassius's.

Come on. I mentally yanked with everything I had. My connection with Deaglan's three assassins snapped, making my power crash into me, and I shoved it into Cassius, not even trying to regain any control, using my connection with his life force to guide me. It flooded into him and yanked his cells back together in what I knew was an excruciating instant.

Titus dove after Cassius, shattering more of the pool's ice with his feet, and seized Cassius with one claw and Rin and Hawk with the other, as Deaglan shot a flurry of shadows at me and Sebastian.

Two shadow spears plunged through Sebastian's chest, drawing a strangled scream, and Deaglan tossed him off me into the pool's frigid waters. But before my magic could connect with him, another shadow wrapped around my throat and yanked me off my precarious perch, and Deaglan's dark power poured into me.

I gasped and clawed at the shadow, but my fingers kept passing through it even as it grew tighter, cutting off my air.

"Give me the key," Deaglan said, his shadow sinking into my skin and infecting the brilliant white fae magic embedded in my cells. "It'd be a shame to have to kill you like I did Noaldar. He was rare. Even a weak sorcerer like him is rare in Faerie. But with your healing magic, you're invaluable."

"I won't let you have me." Everything within me screamed. I couldn't be taken. I couldn't let my guys suffer. I had to break free.

Please, God. I won't be taken again. Never again.

My life force magic surged, weaving into Deaglan's power. The shadows tearing at my insides weakened for a second, and a flicker of hope swept through me. I'd used my magic to help Sebastian break free of Deaglan's power. I could use it to free me.

I shoved more of my magic into Deaglan's. His shadows weakened again and my magic brushed up against a crack in the shield protecting his life force.

My pulse skipped a beat. I could feel the other three keys inside him, calling to the key inside me and calling to something else, something barely within reach and incredibly powerful. The kind of power no one, not even the most generous and honest soul should possess. The kind of power that warped everything, even the best of intentions, and I had no idea if I would be strong enough to just use it to free Rin and then destroy it.

But I knew without a doubt, I couldn't let Deaglan get his hands on it

Even if I couldn't use the Heart and had to just destroy it, I still had to get the keys.

I shoved my magic through the crack in the shield protecting his life force and seized them, but my ability to connect with life forces also grabbed his life and his eyes widened in horror.

"Not a chance, bitch," he snarled. "Give me the key and maybe I won't kill you."

His power exploded inside me as he used his sorcerer's ability to connect to Faerie's raw magic to increase his power. It tore into my magic as if it was nothing, freeing his life force, then shot into my heart. He seized the key, my magic, and my life force just like he'd done with Noaldar, and yanked, sending agony tearing through my body and soul.

Screaming, I mentally clutched at the key and my life force, fighting to gather as much of my magic around them as I could, but his magic was too ferocious, and the world turned into an agonizing darkness as my life force stuttered and my pulse stalled.

I fought to breathe, to stay conscious, but he consumed every ounce of power I pushed into my life force to keep it lit. I wasn't going to last.

I had to give him the key.

Except even if I gave in and let him have the key, I knew he wouldn't stop. He couldn't take me prisoner and he couldn't let me live. I was too dangerous. I'd threatened his life and despite my healing compulsion, I could rip out his life force the second he let his guard down.

Someone behind me screamed and a blast of hot air swept over me as a fireball slammed into Deaglan, but his power didn't release me, even as he used more magic to protect himself from Cassius's fire.

The agony inside me swelled, a dark slicing power that cut into my heart and consumed me. I fought to hold onto a glimmer of my life force. I didn't need it all. I just needed enough to survive, but every time I tried to hold on, more darkness flooded into me.

Please. God. I had to stay alive. If I died. Sebastian and Rin died, and Hawk and Titus and Cassius would be shattered. *And* Deaglan would have won.

But I was getting weaker by the second and unlike Deaglan, I could only access my personal supply of magic and was only able to focus it to my two magical abilities. I couldn't connect and channel raw magic and make it do whatever I wanted. No angel could. Only the fae with their realm's magic embedded in their cells could access an infinite supply of power and even then, only a handful like Sebastian and Deaglan had the strength of will to harness that ability.

Except, I could *not* let him win. I had to survive long enough for my guys to save me... if they could save me—

No, they would. I just had to hold on. Somehow.

The magic around my heart where I felt the core of my new life force ability flickered and went out, and its protection against Deaglan's attack vanished, letting his darkness swarm into my heart and seize my life force and the key.

Oh, God.

I strained to shove my healing magic into my heart, push Deaglan's shadows back, and keep my life force lit and the key buried inside me, but my healing power couldn't connect with my soul or the key. It healed bodies, and holding onto Cassius's and Sebastian's life forces when I'd healed them had been my new magic working with my original power to keep them alive while I healed their injuries.

The darkness deepened and my life force faded to a barely-there pinprick. Then a flicker of heat cut through the agony and a glimmer of gold sparked in the darkness. Sebastian's icy bright life force whispered against my senses, and a trickle of power bolstered my fading life.

My soul snapped to his life force and the trickle grew stronger. Somehow, even though my bond with him wasn't even a day old and I shouldn't have been able to, I was taking strength from him and using it to support my dwindling reserves.

Except I could already feel that it wasn't going to be enough. The brand wouldn't let me drain him to death — the connection would break before that happened — and Deaglan's shadows were still devouring my life force and trying to rip the key from my soul.

I couldn't hold on to both of them and I could only pray that if I gave Deaglan the key I'd be able to push out his shadows with Sebastian's help and survive.

AMIAH

I WRAPPED MY AND SEBASTIAN'S STRENGTH AROUND MY LIFE AND RELEASED my mental hold on the key.

Please, God, let this work.

But Deaglan burst into wicked laughter as his shadows tore out the key then surged stronger inside me, slicing and burning and consuming my life force.

"Did you really think giving up the key would save you, little angel?" Deaglan sneered.

I screamed and yanked on Sebastian's icy sparkling life force, drawing it in as fast as I could.

But Deaglan's magic just kept growing, fueled by Faerie's unending supply of power, and Sebastian's life force wasn't his magic or his connection to Faerie. It was the power in his body and soul and I needed more than what he had if I was going to shove Deaglan out and keep him out before I'd taken too much from Sebastian and our bond broke off the flow of strength.

God, I might need more just to keep Deaglan at bay inside me.

Desperate, I searched deep within myself for something, anything, the smallest flicker of power that could save me.

There. Another golden glimmer, flickering and weak and not fully formed. My soul bond with Rin.

We hadn't sealed our bond so our connection wasn't as strong as the one I had with Sebastian, but I still could feel Rin's life force, writhing hot and cold, alive and dead against my senses, and even if it was a fraction of Sebastian's strength, it would still help. It *had* to help.

I grasped my weak connection with Rin and added it to Sebastian's, wrapping the golden threads around my life.

Deaglan's power stuttered, and my hope swelled.

I was doing it. I could get free.

I shoved at his darkness, determined to get him out, but somehow he opened his sorcerer's connection even wider — God, it had only been partially opened! — and he channeled so much magic so quickly, I knew he was risking burning himself up just to end me.

But he was probably betting that I'd break before he did, and with the agony screaming through me, there was a good chance I would.

I could already feel Sebastian growing weaker, knew if I didn't heal the wounds in his chest he'd bleed out, and knew my angelic mating brand would separate us or reverse the flow of strength to save his life, and what I was getting from Rin right now wasn't enough to compensate.

Except I hadn't branded anyone else. There was no one else I could draw on—

No. That wasn't true. I'd marked Titus. My scratches on him had scarred, despite his incredible healing powers, indicating that we were soul mates, and he was certain a shifter's mating magic was just as powerful as an angel's. Shifter mates couldn't share strength like angelic mates, but if I was going to be able to draw strength from any of my other guys, it was going to be Titus. He had a closer connection to my soul than Cassius and Hawk.

I reached out, using a bit of Sebastian's strength to fuel my life force magic, and connected with Titus. His wild ferocity flooded me and the golden light within me exploded. It roared into every cell in my body and tore Deaglan's shadows apart, yanking me out of the darkness.

Deaglan screamed and clutched his chest, his eyes wide. My unnatural fae glow blazed around me, tinged with gold, and my whole left side, from the middle of my thigh up to my armpit, burned with the now-familiar fire of a forming brand.

Mine, Titus roared in my head.

"You're not strong enough," Deaglan spat at me. "You're not a sorcerer."

The shadow around my throat tightened, cutting off my air, and I thrashed, unable to break free. Behind me, my guys screamed and strength from my newly formed bond with Titus surged, desperate to save me.

Then a blast of water shot up from the pond, severing the shadow holding me and I fell into the frigid water.

The sudden shocking cold stole what little breath I had left, and I gasped in a lungful of water before it — the water — heaved me up and threw me onto the ice. I skidded halfway to the shore, soaking wet, gasping in ragged breaths, and shivering so hard I didn't even bother to try to control it.

Then my connection with Sebastian jerked taut and the flow of strength surged out of me and into him. He'd reached his limit and now was in more danger than I was.

I tried to raise my head and look for him. I knew he was on the shore, but I couldn't make my body move. I was too cold and tired, and really, I didn't need to see him. All I needed was to release my overflowing healing magic into him like it wanted, like *all* of me wanted, and save his life.

My power swelled at the thought and tore free of my mental grasp. It flooded into Sebastian, drawing a strangled scream and I fought to slow it down. I didn't need it to work in an instant. There was no need for this healing to be painful.

But I didn't have the same kind of control over my power when healing from a distance as I did when touching someone, and it yanked his cells back together, closing the wounds into tender scars before I managed to get it under control.

"So that's how Noaldar died," a feminine voice said. "You said the angel killed him, Shadow King."

"Oh, did I?" Deaglan asked with mock innocence.

With my magic now under control, it softly mended Sebastian's scars into perfectly smooth flesh and disengaged from him, leaving me shivering and gasping with only a quarter of my healing magic left.

I dragged my gaze up to look for him, but my attention landed on Padraigin. She stood in the mouth of the gorge, her water whirling around her, creating a wind that swept her long black hair around her.

"You killed him!" Padraigin yanked water from the pool and blasted it at Deaglan.

Deaglan threw his head back and howled with laughter as his shadows tore the water apart, sending it showering back to the pool like rain. "And what are you going to do about it? You're not as powerful as me and even Faerie has abandoned you."

"I might not be able to demand the blood price, but I will make you pay. You don't get to take something I never thought I'd have again," Padraigin screamed, her voice cracking with heartache and rage, and the water around her formed into droplets and shot toward Deaglan like bullets.

He swept up a shadow shield, but the droplets tore through it, and his eyes widened in surprise. With a gasp, he jerked to the side, and the shadows keeping him aloft dropped him beneath the barrage.

But Padraigin raised her hands and more watery bullets flew toward him, flying faster than before. "I don't care if Faerie won't answer my call. I'll take my blood price without its help."

The bullets tore his shadows apart and sliced into his body, making my healing magic snap to him. He plummeted toward the pool, his agony rushing into me, my healing magic screaming at me to heal him.

"You don't get to win!" she cried and a massive wave of water surged up and slammed Deaglan into the rough ice of the frozen waterfalls at the back of the gorge.

With a scream, his shadows exploded out of the water. Half whirled protectively around him, while a flurry of spears slammed into the gorge wall above Padraigin, tearing out massive chunks of ice and stone.

One of my guys yelled and a blast of fire flew toward Deaglan. He blocked it with more shadows as Padraigin swept up a water shield to block the landslide, but Deaglan shot a shadow spear through her chest, breaking her concentration, and the stone and ice crashed through the shield onto her.

My healing magic jerked to her. Her back was broken, so were half of her ribs and numerous other bones, and both of her lungs were pierced. The compulsion to heal her squeezed in my chest, but I fought to control it. After healing Cassius and Sebastian from a distance, I only had about a quarter of my healing magic left and I didn't know if that would be enough to save Padraigin from a distance. I also wanted to have some left over in case Cassius had sustained more injuries while fighting at the pool's edge, not to mention I was going to need to do something about my rapidly developing hypothermia.

Deaglan shot more shadows at me, and I tried to scramble out of the way, my hands and knees slipping out from under me on the wet ice. Titus roared and flew toward me. He spat a stream of fire at Deaglan's shadows as Cassius sent another fireball at the Shadow King, but Deaglan's shadows wrenched him out of the way and swept him up into the winter storm raging above the gorge.

In one fluid movement, Titus shifted, landed on the ice, and grabbed me, clutching me to his massive muscular chest. Heat radiated from his naked body and I leaned into him even as my compulsion to heal Padraigin twisted tighter.

"Get me to Padraigin," I said, shivering so hard it was difficult to speak, let alone hold back my magic.

"Titus," Sebastian said, scrambling to the rockslide covering Padraigin and pulling away a large piece of ice. "Help me."

Cassius rushed to his side and started heaving rocks and ice off the pile. His clothes were burned, barely more than soaked scraps pasted to his body, and blood trailed from a laceration in his left biceps and dripped from his elbow.

I tried to pull my magic from Padraigin to Cassius to determine how injured he was, but I barely had the strength to keep it from pouring into Padraigin let alone move it to Cassius. I could only hope that the healing I'd given him when Deaglan had tossed him into the water had been enough and he hadn't taken anything else that was serious during the fight by the pool… because even injured, Cassius would help Sebastian save his sister.

"Titus," Sebastian gasped, his chest heaving and his fae glow dangerously weak. He grabbed another chunk of ice the size of his head and shoved it aside, as Rin and Hawk joined the effort. "Please."

Titus's grip on me tightened and he growled— no, from the ferocity radiating from his life force his beast was in control and *it* was the one who'd growled low in his human throat. And from the tightness of his grip and his still rapidly pounding pulse beneath my cheek, his beast was still in protection mode.

"I'm okay," I said, pressing my palm over his heart and raising my gaze to meet his.

"You're not. You're struggling," he replied, his voice gruff. "You need comfort and protection."

"I'm safe." For now. "Deaglan's men have fled." Those still alive had run when Deaglan had. "What I need is for Padraigin to be uncovered so I can heal her and break my compulsion."

"I know," he replied. "I'm just trying to get my beast to realize that as well."

"Hey, man," Hawk said, heaving aside another large chunk of ice. "We really could use a hand."

"Yeah." With a growl, Titus set me on my feet a safe distance from the rockslide but still close to the gorge wall so I could lean against it, and stormed to Hawk's side. He picked up a massive piece of rock by himself and tossed it aside then reached for another.

TITUS

I HEAVED A LARGE CHUNK OF ICE ASIDE AS MY BEAST SNARLED INSIDE ME. It knew uncovering Seireadan's sister was the best way to help our mate, that her healing magic wasn't going to release Amiah until she'd healed Padraigin or it turned inward and made her suffer with its backlash, but it still hated the idea.

Padraigin had tried to kill Amiah and couldn't be trusted, and our mate needed to be held, her soul steadied, and right now.

Not to mention my soul needed steadying right now, too.

Deaglan had almost killed her, which had terrified me and still did, and yet my soul was also thrilled that she'd branded me. She'd made another connection between us, easing any fear that her soul bond with Seireadan would make her fall out of love with me.

And while I'd said I was confident that my mating magic was as powerful as hers, I hadn't been able to squash that little voice of fear that asked what if it wasn't?

Now there was no doubt. Fate agreed with my beast, that she was my soul's mate and all that remained was fate branding the others and confirming what my beast also knew was true. That Cassius and Hawk, as well as Seireadan, were also her mates, that they were my new pack.

My beast growled at that and I yanked another large piece of ice — bigger than what any of the others could move by themselves — off the pile, while Cassius helped Hawk to move a slightly smaller chunk.

They didn't look good. Their breaths were heavy with exertion and I could smell their blood and the blood of Deaglan's assassins on them as well as their fear. They'd fought with everything they had when we'd landed back on the beach and faced more of Deaglan's men, but they, like me, had watched with horror as Deaglan had nearly killed Amiah and Seireadan had been bleeding to death.

My gaze shifted to Seireadan who worked beside them, still trembling and weak and covered in his own blood, as he desperately hauled chunks of ice and rock off the pile to save his sister.

He hadn't been strong enough to pull out Deaglan's keys or to protect Amiah, and while a part of my beast was furious at him, the rest of my beast and all of my human soul knew this fight had come too soon. It had only been half a day since Seireadan had been in agony with the demonic magic infection consuming him, and he hadn't been given enough time to recover from having that removed.

Except now that the fourth key had become empowered, the Heart and the temple where dragonkind had locked it away, would manifest in the Wilds at dawn. And even if he hadn't depleted his internal magic and weakened his willpower that kept him from burning up when he channeled raw magic during this fight, we still wouldn't have had enough time for him to become as strong as Deaglan by dawn.

Which left us with what? We weren't strong enough to get Deaglan's keys from him, but we couldn't just run away. Even if I didn't care about the rest of Faerie — and my beast didn't — Deaglan would still come after us to get revenge on me, Seireadan, and Rin, and to take Amiah.

Even with Rin's help, we weren't strong enough to win this.

I heaved off another chunk of ice and glared at the demon-vampire hybrid.

He, too, was helping to dig out Seireadan's sister and was also in rough shape.

It hadn't surprised me that he'd come along to get the final key. His life was tied to Amiah's and anyone with a glimmer of survival instinct would have joined us to ensure she stayed safe. What surprised me was that he'd trusted Hawk to protect her and worked as part of our team to protect everyone.

And while a part of that could be attributed to Amiah branding Seireadan, as well as Rin not wanting to become Deaglan's slave again, I knew from our conversation at the aerie that most of it came from the fact that he wanted to stay with Amiah. And staying with Amiah meant making friends with the rest of us.

I hadn't wanted to believe my instinct that his feelings for her went deeper than what the brand was compelling him to feel.

After he'd told me that he did have feelings and I'd realized the truth, I'd soared over the Wilds, furious that he was in love with her — he'd almost killed her for goodness sake! But everything he'd done in this last fight with Deaglan had been for Amiah.

He'd outright defied Deaglan by killing his men and he'd pulled Seireadan out of the ice passage then had jumped into the pool's freezing water to save Hawk.

My beast snarled and I hurled a chunk of rock behind me. It landed in the middle of a patch of bluebells that hadn't been trampled or burned during the fight, making them tremble and chime.

I'd wanted to show Amiah this gorge and watch her face light up when she swept her wings and made the flowers chime. Then I'd wanted to soar with her through the maze of larger tunnels behind the Queen's Falls and show her the amazing beauty of its ice and how it glimmered from shafts of sunlight.

Now this place, one of the places I loved in the Winter Court, was the site of our greatest defeat, and I could only hope the fight at my peoples' temple wouldn't be worse.

Except I had no idea how we could possibly survive the final battle let alone win.

AMIAH

I CLUNG TO THE WALL, WATCHING THE GUYS WORK, THE HEALING MAGIC I had left glowing around my hands, sticky and too hot against my chilled skin. My whole body trembled with the cold and water dripped from my hair and clothes and started to freeze on the stones around my feet. Above, the winter storm still howled, pelting snow against the wall on the opposite side of the gorge and drifting onto the shore and the still-frozen side of the pool. I tried to be grateful for the fact that Padraigin had been trapped on the leeward side of the gorge and we weren't being showered with snow and ice pellets, but it was hard to focus past the cold and the twisting need to save her.

I heaved my attention to my guys' life forces, hoping that might distract me. I could still feel them like ghostly whispers of wind against my senses, but that wasn't because their life forces were weak, but because my power was and I wasn't in physical contact with them.

Then my senses lurched back to Padraigin, her bright, icy life force stuttering and desperate to stay lit. My healing magic twisted tighter around my heart and I gritted my teeth.

Save her. Now. Now. All I had to do was let go and the worst of her injuries would be gone without me even moving.

Except as much as my magic claimed that, I didn't know if it was true. I still didn't have a good idea how much magic it took to heal someone from a distance instead of healing them while touching them, I just knew that it took more.

Titus tossed off another massive stone, revealing a pale hand covered in blood, and my healing compulsion clenched in my chest and jerked me forward. But my legs were too weak and I stumbled, unable to keep my balance with my shivering and my numb limbs.

Rin, the closest of my guys— no, *the* guys, not *mine*, he wasn't mine, leaped forward and caught me. He wrapped me in a firm embrace, and my senses locked onto him, my soul singing with the contact while my body throbbed with a sudden, desperate need, determined to defy what I knew was right and claim him as mine instead of freeing him.

God, the urge from our bond was stronger than before. It was almost stronger than my healing compulsion, something I hadn't thought possible, especially when my healing magic had locked onto someone who was in critical condition. I was supposed to be with Rin. Just like I was supposed to be with Sebastian and Titus. Just like I knew I was also supposed to be with Hawk and Cassius.

No. I only *thought* I was supposed to be with Rin because of the bond, and because I'd made a horrible mistake by deepening our connection when I'd seized his golden thread inside me and pulled on his strength so I could fight Deaglan's magic.

Except it was getting harder and harder to believe that it was just the bond influencing me.

I tried to shove those thoughts aside, but that only made me hyperaware of the crushing compulsion from my healing magic. It yanked me toward Padraigin, forcing Rin to tighten his grip to keep me in place.

"It's still not safe," he whispered with his barely-there voice, his breath feathering across the back of my neck, warm against my skin. "Some of the rocks are still unstable."

Everything within me jerked back to him, my thoughts, my soul, and, much to my surprise, my healing magic.

He had multiple lacerations on his chest, back, arms, and one down his right thigh, and half of them were still bleeding, indicating that he was low on magic and couldn't properly heal.

"You need to feed," I said, shifting in his arms to meet his black gaze, my soul and body aching for him.

"Not on you." His soft voice shivered through me, adding to the growing heat pooling between my thighs despite the cold, and my breath picked up with need.

I wanted to agree with him, but couldn't force out the words, because what I really wanted was his bite and his magic. I wanted everything that went with being his soul mate. He wasn't the monster I'd first thought he was. He'd kept his vow to protect me and even protected Sebastian and Hawk during the fight.

Hellfire sparked from his right eye and a strange mix of need and frustration and heartache whispered through our bond as he stepped back, putting space between us. He held my shoulders to keep me steady and Hawk hurried from the landslide to my side and tugged me into his embrace. His demonic body temperature was too hot for comfort — but not painful like it had been when the key had become empowered — and I leaned into him, needing his touch right now as much as I needed Titus's, Sebastian's, and Rin's.

"You can feed on me," Hawk said to Rin. "I can handle your magic. The others can't and they know it, which means they'll try to fight it or do something stupid like demand you don't use it."

My magical senses flickered to Hawk then back to Padraigin. He, too had injuries that were still bleeding, indicating that he was also almost out of power, too. "You're hurt and magically weak. You won't be able to give him much."

"That'll be fixed soon enough." He brushed his lips against mine in a quick, barely-there kiss, then slid his gaze back to Rin. "You two need to seal your bond before one of you goes crazy. You can't wait much longer." His expression turned grim. "Even if we'd gotten Deaglan's keys, I don't think you'd have been able to wait to get the Heart, not unless we could have gotten it right away."

"Which we couldn't," Sebastian said. "The Heart won't reveal itself until dawn. So bad for you and Rin, but also bad for Deaglan. We still have one last chance to stop the bastard."

"I can hold out until dawn. I don't want to trap Rin," I said. "If we seal our bond, I don't know if the Heart will be able to break it."

"Gorgeous," Hawk said, drawing a wet strand of hair out of my eyes and tucking it behind my ear. "We both know if you wait too long the psychological damage will be permanent. Your bond with Bane and now Titus might save you, but it won't save Rin."

My heart clenched with a mix of emotions. Rin didn't deserve any of this. He didn't deserve to go crazy or die or be trapped in our bond. But Hawk didn't deserve this either. I'd branded another one of my guys, but it wasn't the one who I really needed to brand.

Titus and Cassius shoved aside another large piece of stone and Sebastian pulled Padraigin free from the rest of the debris.

My healing compulsion surged and my magic flared brighter around my hands, its heat painful, as if I'd put my numb hands into water that was too hot.

Save her. Save her.

Fine. "We'll discuss this when we're back at the aerie," I said, trying to push out of Hawk's embrace even though I was pretty sure my legs wouldn't hold me. I couldn't do anything about the situation with Rin or Hawk right this very minute, or the heartache and frustration that came with being helpless. "Whoever thought an angelic mating brand was beautiful was an idiot."

But my heart clenched the moment the words had left my lips. What I had with Sebastian and Titus *was* beautiful. I loved them and being soul bonded with them felt right.

Except I couldn't shake the thought that being bonded with Rin also felt right, no matter how hard I tried. And I wasn't sure anymore if I was fighting the feeling because the bond was influencing me or if I only *thought* I was being influenced.

Rin shifted away from me and a strange flicker of emotion passed through our bond, but I couldn't tell what it was.

Fear? Heartache? Grief? Whatever the emotion, it had to be because we might be forced to seal our bond.

And yet a part of me couldn't help wondering if it was because I was still fighting our connection.

Which was ridiculous. We were strangers.

Except that had nothing to do with whether we were soul mates or not. Not knowing each other didn't mean we weren't fated for each other.

I shoved that thought aside. There was too much piling up on me, the bond, my fears, and the twisting compulsion to heal Padraigin. Something had to give and the easiest and best something for everyone was to release my hold on my healing magic.

"I need to heal Padraigin," I said through my chattering teeth.

"Then we need to get you back to the aerie and warmed up," Cassius replied, stepping away from us.

His fire flared stronger, surprising me. I hadn't realized he'd been holding it back while digging Padraigin out of the rubble, and I certainly hadn't realized that he still had so much magic left.

Hawk helped me onto the cold, rocky ground beside Padraigin, and I placed my hands over her heart and released a thread of magic. It rushed into her, a sudden flood that shattered my control, turning the thread into a torrent that didn't just go to her worst injury first like my magic should have. Instead, it poured through her veins, infusing into her flesh and bones like a sticky, hot mist that went everywhere.

I fought to control it, to focus it since I didn't know if I had enough power left to heal all of her injuries, but it was like trying to hold onto smoke. My magic kept slipping out of my mental fingers. It sank into every one of her cells, mending them, drawing them back together, all of them, healing every injury at once in a way my magic had never healed before.

I tried to cut off the stream, but my power had a hold of me and the only thing stopping it from instantly wrenching her body back to the way it was before, was my weakened condition.

Even then, it happened faster than I knew was comfortable, making her moan and whimper before she'd fully reached consciousness.

Then my magic stuttered and the sticky heat pouring from my hands into Padraigin cooled then went out without even disconnecting from her. It was just gone and all that remained was the always-there miniscule spark in my palms.

Exhaustion swept through me and the world dimmed, and I forced myself to sit back on my heels and not collapse on top of Padraigin. Hawk gathered me into his too-warm embrace, drawing me back even farther, and his fiery darkness whispered against my senses, as Padraigin heaved in a sharp breath.

Her pale eyes — so much like Sebastian's — snapped open and locked on me.

"You have healing magic," she gasped. "Powerful healing magic." Her gaze jumped to Sebastian. "It's no wonder you and the Winter Court picked her."

"I picked her because I'm in love with her." Sebastian knelt beside me and interlaced our fingers, adding his icy life force to Hawk's. "She could be powerless and I'd still have fallen in love with her."

The spark of magic in my palms that was also there fluttered a little stronger. That was weird... or had it always been that strong and I was just too cold to have noticed naturally disconnecting from Padraigin?

Regardless, I'd been wrong. I still had a little power left, and I could give it to Cassius and stop all of his bleeding. Barely, but at least it would be stopped.

And the minute I thought it, I had to do it. The urge twisted inside me as powerfully as my compulsion to heal Padraigin despite the fact that I had almost no magic left.

"Cassius." I held out my hand to him.

His eyes narrowed and the muscles in his jaw clenched.

"Don't argue with me. You know I have to," I said. "I'm too tired to fight it. Just come here."

He released a heavy sigh and heaved his fire back under the skin of his right hand. His flames still curled over his left arm, the sparks hissing as they hit the icy ground beneath us, and he knelt as far away from me as he could while still being within reach. "I hate when you drain yourself."

"I know. You all do." I took his hand and released my power, letting it pour into him, not bothering to control it. I was too weak for it to be painful, and as expected the most I managed was to seal all of his lacerations shut, turning them into painful, barely healed wounds.

This time my power did vanish. Even the spark in my palms went out and exhaustion dragged me into darkness. Except instead of blissful unconsciousness, I was once again trapped in that frozen nothingness, forgotten and helpless and no one was coming to save me.

Then a fiery darkness bled into my icy prison, making the nothingness stutter, and my consciousness jerked back to the gorge.

"—shouldn't have let her heal you," Titus snarled.

"She would have done it anyway. Her magic compels her," Cassius said, sounding exhausted and frustrated. "Now let's get out of here before we all catch a cold and she has to heal that."

"Not before we break Deaglan's spell on Padraigin," Sebastian said, making my pulse leap, fear trying to make my heart race but my exhaustion dragging it down.

Hawk and Sebastian had figured out that Deaglan had used his sorcerer's ability to block Padraigin's connection to the Winter Court, but none of us knew how powerful the spell was or how much power Sebastian would need to break it.

"Spell?" Padraigin asked. "What are you talking about."

"Don't you dare," I gasped, tightening my grip on Sebastian's hand and forcing my eyes open to look at him.

Even without my magic, I could tell he was as exhausted as I was and without a doubt, his connection to Faerie's raw magic was still weak. That wasn't something I could heal, and I knew normal magical channels for supers with an internal magic source, didn't heal right away. They needed time, and I suspected, since I — and everyone else — knew next to nothing about fae sorcerers, that his magical channels were the same. Which meant he was in serious danger of burning up if he used his magic right now.

AMIAH

"We can wait, Sebastian," I gasped, the exhaustion from having used all of my healing magic threatening to drag me into unconsciousness again. "You don't have to use your magic right away."

"No." Determination hardened his eyes. "I'm not leaving here until the Winter Court has released you. Hawk, show me where the spell in Padraigin is. That will help lessen the amount of magic I'll need to channel."

"I don't think so," Padraigin said, pushing herself against the rock behind her and raising her hands. Water swept out of the pool and whirled around her head in a rushing vortex. "No one is doing anything."

Sebastian's attention jumped to Padraigin but the determination didn't leave his eyes. He was doing this whether she wanted him to or not. "You're enspelled. Deaglan blocked your connection with the Winter Court. That's why it feels like Faerie has abandoned you."

"That's why I can't demand the blood price for Noaldar's murder?"

"Yes. Although Deaglan isn't an idiot and he's powerful." A hint of sadness crept into Sebastian's expression. "Even when we restore your royal connection with Faerie, he'll have cast protections around himself. You still won't be able to demand the blood price."

A water droplet fell from the vortex onto her face and rolled down her cheek like a tear. "So, breaking the spell is useless."

"No. You're a royal. Your connection with Faerie is your birthright," Sebastian said, surprising me by not coming out and telling Padraigin that if her connection was restored there was a good chance the Winter Court would make her its queen.

Of course, if Sebastian didn't completely trust her, then it made sense not to tell her that she'd possibly become more powerful *and* that she was helping to free me. It was bad enough that she knew I had healing magic. Although even if I'd thought about trying to keep my power a secret, I still would have made the same choice and saved Padraigin.

"Hawk," Sebastian said.

Hawk shifted me out of his lap into Titus's waiting arms and rose on his knees so he could reach Padraigin.

"Bane," Cassius said, his voice dark. "You and Hawk can't just push your magic into her without her consent."

"Amiah doesn't need consent when she heals someone," Sebastian said.

Cassius's angel glow flared. "This is different. Amiah's magic won't affect her like Hawk's will."

"I don't care," Padraigin said. "Just do it." Which ironically was the consent Cassius had been looking for.

Hawk placed one hand over Padraigin's heart and the other on Sebastian's shoulder and closed his eyes.

"Just take a breath," Hawk said, just like he had the first time we'd met and he'd pushed his power into me. "It'll be easier and faster if you don't fight me."

Padraigin tossed her water vortex back into the pool, drew in a deep breath, and released it on a low, soft moan, sending a sympathetic shiver of need whispering through me.

I'd been overwhelmed the first time Hawk had pushed his magic into me, and had almost undone his fly and straddled him with the others watching. A thought that had turned me on even more.

A thought I was already starting to explore and wanted to keep exploring.

With *all* of them.

Padraigin released another low moan and her breath picked up.

"Almost there," Hawk murmured.

"Just a little farther." Sebastian closed his eyes and placed his hands over Hawk's on Padraigin's chest. "The bastard hid it deep. Even if I had figured out what it was, I wouldn't have been able to pinpoint it."

"Just get it out," Padraigin gasped, clenching her hands in her lap and trembling, likely with the effort not to touch Hawk in a sexual way.

"Reaching it is the first step," Sebastian said and the muscles in his back tensed. "Now I've got to pull it out."

His life force flared against my senses, and his brand along my ribs grew warm. Strength seeped out of me into him and I could feel him trembling on the edge, fighting to stay in control of Faerie's raw magic and not let it burn him up.

"Almost have it," he said, the tension in his body growing, making him shake.

Hawk started to tremble as well and his life force joined Sebastian's writhing against my senses. "Bane—"

"I almost have it." Mist curled from Sebastian's forearms. "I just— need— a little more— power."

The pull of strength increased, making the world darken and slowly spin, and his full-body fae glow blazed around him.

I fought to keep my eyes open. If I passed out, Sebastian could lose his concentration and all that magic he was channeling could turn in on him and burn him up in an instant.

"Bane, it's too much," Hawk said. "You have to release it. Try again later."

Padraigin whimpered and clutched the front of Hawk's shirt, trying to pull him closer. Her breath turned into desperate pants and her expression twisted in a terrible mix of desire and pain.

Sebastian's breath turned ragged as well but for an entirely different reason, and more mist whirled around him, rising from his head, shoulders, and back, his rising body temperature heating the water in his clothes and hair and the cold air rapidly chilling it around him. "I'm not stopping until Amiah is free."

"Bane." Hawk tried to pull his hand out from under Sebastian's, but Sebastian shoved forward pinning Padraigin against the rocks behind her and keeping Hawk's hand trapped beneath his.

"No. Not until she's free," Sebastian gasped.

Which was unacceptable. I could last a little longer with the Winter Court's magic inside me. I couldn't lose him and I couldn't let him hurt himself like this, not when this wasn't an emergency.

"Just stop," Hawk said, heaving against Sebastian's grip, but still not able to pull free. "You still need power to fight Deaglan and this could permanently damage your magic channels."

"If you'd stop forcing me to fight you too, I'd be done," Sebastian snarled, "I almost have it."

The flesh on his forearms turned an ugly red. Even with my healing magic gone it was clear he was going to burn himself up before giving up.

"Sebastian, please. We can try again later." I pushed out of Titus's embrace and grabbed Sebastian's arm to draw him away. He might fight Hawk but maybe if he saw my fear, he wouldn't fight me. After all, he was doing this for me.

But a sudden, ferocious cold exploded inside me. Every muscle in my body clenched painfully tight and my whole body went numb. I tried to draw in a breath, but it felt like I was breathing in ice. The air around me was suddenly frigid— no, everything around and inside me was frozen, and it came from the tiny bit of fae magic that had been embedded into every cell in my body the moment the Winter Court had claimed me.

You promised, the Winter Court hissed. *A new queen or you. That was the deal.*

"Amiah!" Sebastian let go of Padraigin and the cold tore into me.

Her or you. I won't wait any longer.

No. Please. We can break the spell later. You just need to wait a little longer.

"Amiah." Sebastian reach to cup my cheek, but his skin was excruciatingly hot and I flinched away from his touch and whimpered.

"She's freezing. We have to get the Winter Court's magic out of her," Titus said. "It's killing her."

Sebastian jerked back to Padraigin who'd sat up and stared at us, her eyes wide with shock. He slammed his palms against her chest, shoving her back against the rocks and drawing a scream of agony.

"Sebastian, no," I gasped.

"The only way to save you is to break the spell." His life force heaved against my senses. Blisters formed on his hands and forearms and burst, and my weak healing magic flickered to him. But I didn't have enough power to heal him even if I could touch him and concentrate past the frozen agony consuming me.

Then Padraigin's full-body fae glow blazed so bright it was hard to look at her, and the Winter Court's cold sliced deep into my soul. It tore a scream from my throat, releasing a frozen breath filled with a flurry of snowflakes along with the court's sparkling white magic.

"Got you," Sebastian hissed. He yanked a black mist out of Padraigin's chest that shuddered then burst apart, then he collapsed on top of her.

My unnatural full-body fae glow blazed as brightly as Padraigin's had and another flurry of snowflakes and magic rushed out of my mouth. The cold inside me and my glow flickered like a candle in a storm, then went out, leaving me still cold, but not shockingly so, and still exhausted and now extremely weak. I hadn't realized how much power the Winter Court had given me and now I was myself again, a regular angel with healing magic. Nothing more.

A flicker of my new life force magic unfurled in my heart, and I could feel my guys' life forces whispering against my senses, proving I wasn't *just* an angel with healing magic anymore. And when I wasn't so tired and could think straight, I'd think about what that meant and who I now was.

Padraigin's eyes flashed wide with surprise and then a low, sensual moan escaped her lips. "Oh, yes. This is how it's supposed to be."

The Winter Court's wind poured out of the storm raging above us and swept around her. "I knew I was supposed to be queen."

She pushed Sebastian off her and stood. Water joined the wind, whirling around her, the elements tugging on her hair and clothes making her look as ferocious as her mother had when I'd last seen her storm into the throne room.

"You have your connection," Hawk said, pulling Sebastian away from her, as Titus clutched me protectively against his chest.

"And *you* have an angel with healing magic," Padraigin said.

"This isn't a fight you want to start," Cassius said, his fire roaring around him as Rin stepped between Padraigin and my guys and let his small vampire claws extend from his fingertips.

"I'm the new Winter Queen. With Seireadan drained, you can't stop me from taking her."

"Really?" I forced out through chattering teeth. "We just saved you. Twice."

I couldn't believe that the second she had the Winter Court's power she'd turned into her mother. But then I didn't really know her and I couldn't even begin to imagine what it had been like to live for centuries with the Winter Queen, especially since Deaglan had blocked her connection to the Winter Court, making it look like she wasn't even a second choice for the court's heir.

"And with your magic, you'll continue to save me." Her eyes

narrowed, filled with a dark, dangerous light, and the wind and water vortex whipped around her, picking up pieces of stone and ice. It wasn't even a veiled threat. She was arming herself, ready to fight my guys to take me.

How dare she!

"You don't want to do this," Sebastian gasped.

The force-wave glyph on his left forearm lit up and my pulse stuttered. Using his glyph still meant he had to channel magic. He was just as exhausted as I was, and blood oozed from his cracked and blistered hands and forearms. I had to stop this before it went any further.

I pushed past the cold and exhaustion threatening to pull me into unconsciousness and grabbed the glimmer of life force magic in my heart. Deaglan had drained me during the fight, but I didn't need much. And by God, I was going to have enough to make her back off.

I shot my magic into Padraigin and seized her life force. I didn't want to kill her. If she died, the Winter Court might reclaim me and then we'd be back where we started, but I needed her to know in no uncertain terms that I would do whatever it took to protect myself and my guys.

I yanked on her life force, making it *snap* and drawing a shocked gasp that made her gaze leap to me.

"Back off," I snarled. "I won't let you take me or hurt my guys."

Padraigin sneered at me. "Don't bother bluffing. You fooled me once in the throne room, you won't fool me again. You're a healing angel. Your magic won't let you hurt me."

I gave her life force a harder *snap,* drawing a strangled scream. Her eyes rolled back and she tipped to the side as if she were going to pass out then gasped in a deep breath and jerked upright, her eyes wide with shock.

"I've already killed to protect the men I love. You'd just be one more." I glared at her, hoping that even though I was exhausted and still shivering uncontrollably, she'd see just how serious I was. I'd feel bad for killing Sebastian's sister, but if it meant saving my guys, I'd kill her in a heartbeat.

Padraigin's gaze jumped from me to Sebastian then slid over the other guys. With a huff, she stood and her wind and water swept her out of the gorge.

I sagged back into Titus's embrace and pressed my body against his as if that would ease the cold making me shiver uncontrollably. And while I wasn't as cold as I'd been with the Winter Court's magic inside me, I was still wet and we were still in freezing temperatures.

"Holy fuck, Amiah," Sebastian gasped.

"Yeah, I didn't know angels could bluff like that," Hawk added.

Cassius sagged to his knees, his fire pouring around him. "I didn't know you could bluff at all."

"It wasn't a bluff," Rin whispered, making them stare at him while he stared at me.

My pulse stuttered again, this time with the aching need that swelled inside me every time Rin and I made eye contact.

"I won't be taken again," I said, my voice breathy. "And I won't stand by and watch someone hurt or kill any of you. Never again." And I didn't want to think about how I might be forced to watch exactly that when we confronted Deaglan again. I couldn't seize his life force like I could Padraigin's. And even when I'd managed to push through the magic protecting him, he'd still been too strong for me.

No. I would find a way. I wouldn't just stand there and watch him kill them. I would fight with everything I had. I would do whatever it took to keep all of my guys alive and make sure Deaglan didn't get the Heart.

SEBASTIAN

I released the power I'd pushed into my force-wave glyph, fighting not to show just how much my raw magical channels and my burned and bloody hands and forearms hurt. Even though it was clear by the barely-there glow in Amiah's eyes and the now completely gone glow in her body that she was out of both angelic and fae magic, I still didn't want to risk her magic making her do something foolish.

I could at least protect her from that.

It was bad enough I hadn't been strong enough to pull out Deaglan's keys and finally end this nightmare, but I hadn't even been able to do anything when Deaglan had been ripping out her key along with her magic and life.

My attention lurched from my hands to the heat radiating from our mating brand and I sucked in a ragged breath in a pathetic attempt to steady my nerves.

The magic connecting us had grown stronger. I could feel it woven deeper into my soul and I knew with absolute certainty that we were fated for each other. But I also now knew why Amiah had been so afraid of her mating brand.

Fear from the mating brand had almost paralyzed me when I'd realized Deaglan had given up on capturing her and was just going to kill her to take the key. Even knowing I was bleeding to death from the holes

Deaglan's shadow spears had punched into my chest, I still had only been able to think about saving Amiah.

And then she'd somehow grabbed the magic connecting us, grabbed the magic connecting her and Rin, *and* empowered a barely-there connection between her and Titus. I hadn't even known that connection had been there until I'd sensed her pushing a strange magic that I didn't recognize into it, or couldn't recognize because I couldn't think straight from the pain and panic and blood loss.

Now she'd branded another one of us and while I was thrilled for Titus, the situation was still a fucked-up mess because she hadn't branded Hawk.

And I had no idea how I was going to fix that.

God, I had no idea how I was going to fix any of this. I hadn't been able to take Deaglan's keys and we were now in worse shape than before. I wasn't going to be able to recover much more magic or heal my magical channels before dawn and Amiah, drained of power, wasn't going to be able to heal all of our injuries, either.

At least the Winter Court had released Amiah. I couldn't sense any fae magic inside her and while she was still shivering and her lips blue, that was because we were outside in the cold and she was soaked.

Cassius's gaze shifted to Amiah and his expression grew darker. Except I wasn't sure what he was thinking. That she was a mess? That Deaglan had almost killed her? Or that she'd threatened to kill Padraigin and hadn't been bluffing?

Did he know she'd taken the lives of Deaglan's assassins back in the Summer Court and used them to save his life?

Without a doubt, she wasn't the same angel he'd known before this mess had started, and I couldn't tell from his expression how he felt about that. Would he break her heart by renouncing her because she was no longer the angel he'd fallen in love with?

A flurry of sparks snapped from Cassius's flames and the enormous pressure from his power swelled against my magical sensitivity as his hold on his power started to slip — which was crazy, because he was already dripping fire and looked out of control. If he was still *in* control, I wasn't sure I wanted to see what out of control looked like.

His expression had softened for a second with that surge of power then hardened again as he yanked his power back. He didn't look the way he did because he was upset with Amiah or wasn't in love with her, but because he was on the verge of being burned alive by his own power and whatever emotions he had threatened his control.

"We should get out of here," Cassius said his voice gruff as he marched farther away from us and released his wings with a burst of fire. "I don't want to bet that your sister isn't going to come back."

"She's a real piece of work, that one," Hawk added.

Titus huffed his agreement, slid out from beneath Amiah, and marched away from us in the opposite direction Cassius had so he had enough room to shift.

"Well I'm not going to argue with you," I gasped. I was still shocked that the second she'd gained the Winter Court's power she'd tried to take my wife. I hadn't wanted to completely believe that she was cutthroat enough to have been involved in Noaldar's assassination attempt on Amiah, no matter what the others thought. Padraigin hadn't been bloodthirsty when I'd fled Faerie three hundred years ago.

Of course, three hundred years was a long time and her connection to Faerie had been blocked, not to mention our mother hadn't accepted her as the new heir. Even a hundred years of that along with all of the other court machinations, and I might have turned out the same. What was a sibling's happiness and someone's freedom, compared to having an angel who could save you from almost every type of assassination attempt?

God, I'd never been more glad to have turned my back on my family, my birthright, and my realm. Good fucking riddance.

Now all I had to do was to somehow stop Deaglan from getting the Heart — because that was the right thing to do and I was an idiot who did the right thing — and get Amiah and the others as far away from Faerie as possible. And to do it all in my current condition.

HAWK

I pulled Amiah into my arms, taking Titus's place and helping to keep her warm while Titus shifted.

God, I wanted to hold her like this forever, and yet it was starting to look like that wasn't our fate.

Now she'd branded Titus, and even if I hadn't felt the explosive power of their bond forming in that desperate instant, I would never have been able to miss the delicate gold lines swirling up the left side of Titus's human ribcage to his shoulder. That and the magic in his brand was brighter than anyone or anything else around me even with Faerie's magic hanging in the air making everything just a little too bright.

It made sense for her to brand him, especially since I'd felt her magic desperately searching for a way to push Deaglan's power out of her and she'd needed help. His dragon had already claimed her as his mate. They already had a connection, even if that connection had been a fraction of the strength that they now had with Amiah's brand.

But that didn't mean it didn't sting knowing that her soul hadn't picked me next.

She leaned into me, still cold, but thankfully not so cold that my demonic body temperature was too warm for her. Her power was terrifyingly low, the glow in her eyes almost completely gone, the magic in her aura so weak I had to concentrate to see it, and she wasn't trying to hide her exhaustion. Which spoke to just how exhausted she actually was.

I had no idea how she was going to continue resisting her bond with Rin in her condition, and even if she did, with the ferocious desperate desire radiating from both of them, waiting was dangerous. They could insist all they wanted that they could last until we got the Heart, that they only had to make it until dawn, but I doubted either of them would, not without hurting themselves, and we still had to get through a fight with Deaglan first.

Which broke my heart. She didn't deserve this, and while the bond's influence would probably make having sex with Rin easier than she first feared, that didn't diminish the emotional toll something like that took. I wasn't sure she'd ever be able to forgive herself for sleeping with someone she wasn't in love with and for possibly destroying Rin's hope for freedom.

God, this was such a mess. Of course, it had been a mess since the very beginning and I had no idea how we were going to fix any of it.

Titus shifted into his incredible dragon form and Rin offered Bane a hand to help him stand.

Bane glanced at his own burned and bloody hands, sighed, and staggered to his feet without help, saving himself the agony of using his hands. Except I had no idea how he was going to get onto Titus without them.

Cassius must have been thinking the same thing because somehow he sucked his fire back, his body trembling with the effort, swooped over to Bane, grabbed him under the armpits, and flew him up to Titus's back. Then he flew back to the edge of the pool and released his hold on his fire with a sudden burst of flames.

His aura was just as red and angry as it had been when he was at full power... which he shouldn't have been. He'd been bleeding fire since he'd woken in Voth's hotel and we were well past twelve hours of constant flames, not to mention all of the fire he'd used during this most recent fight. It was as if he didn't just have a personal well of magic, but a direct connection to his primal realm, the Realm of Celestial Light.

Except that was impossible. Only the fae had a direct connection to their realm, which meant there had to be something else going on. I just had no idea what, and from the fact that Bane hadn't mentioned anything, he didn't know anything, either.

"I could have managed," Bane grumbled as Rin climbed up behind him and reached down to help Amiah.

"Sure you would have," I said, releasing her so she could climb up then settling in behind Amiah and drawing her back into my arms.

She sighed, snuggling close, but her gaze remained locked on Rin. He stared back at her, his expression stunned, and the desire radiating from both of them swelled stronger.

It hurt just sensing it with my magic, my insides twisting with need, begging me for a connection and a release, and I couldn't imagine how much it hurt for them to resist it.

This went beyond lust. Because of course, it wasn't lust. It was fate determined to make their souls collide, joining them whether they wanted to be joined or not. It was inevitable.

And maybe it was supposed to be inevitable. He hadn't had to save me during the fight. I wasn't soul bonded with Amiah like Bane was, so me being in danger didn't endanger him. And yet Rin had saved me once and given me a much-needed hand when I'd fallen into the pool.

It had also been clear during the fight that their bond had been urging him to protect Amiah, but he hadn't. He'd left it up to me — what little good I'd been — and had fought like he was a part of our team, like he'd always been a part of the team, a team that had only been together for about a week.

Except it felt like we'd always been a team. I hadn't even felt that way after eight months of fighting for my life during the war with the guys in my infantry unit.

A spark of hellfire popped from Rin's eye and he jerked his gaze away from Amiah. The desire radiating from him twisted tighter and he climbed in front of Bane, putting the fae between them, as if that would somehow make it easier to ignore their bond. Which it clearly didn't.

With a huff, Titus leaped off the ground, making Bane jerk to the side and forcing him to grab the spine ridge in front of him to keep his balance. He gasped in pain and Amiah started to lean forward to hold him.

I pulled her back then grabbed the back of Bane's wet shirt to steady him as Titus flapped his large powerful wings, and flew out of the gorge into a now perfectly clear blue sky.

"Move back so I can keep hold of you," I said to Bane.

"I'm fine."

"Yeah, and if we end up in a fight and Titus starts flying like a maniac?" I asked.

"Then I definitely don't want your puke on me," Bane shot back, but he shifted over the spine ridge behind him and tucked up tight against Amiah so I could wrap an arm around his waist to help steady him.

Amiah also clung to him, leaning against his wet back. Somehow, despite the fact that his wet shirt was cold and she still needed to warm up, she closed her eyes and her breathing slowed and grew steady as if she'd fallen asleep. Her aura, now with more gold flecks scattered within it, softened against Bane's and a gentle diffuse power seeped into him.

The power looked like Amiah's healing magic, but without its usual intensity — not to mention that I could clearly see that she didn't have any healing magic left.

Which meant the power had to be from the angelic mating brand. It was new, she shouldn't have been able to use it like that yet, but she'd connected with him when she'd been desperate to save herself from Deaglan. She'd drawn on Bane's strength and something else inside her to push Deaglan's shadows out of her, so it made sense that she was giving her strength to Bane now so he could make it back to the aerie.

Thankfully, Faerie was feeling kind, and let us reach the aerie quickly, and Amiah didn't have to sacrifice strength that she couldn't afford to give up.

With a groan, Cassius landed on top of the flat-topped mountain and pulled in his wings. He sagged to his knees in the middle of a river of molten fire that poured off his arms and hands, not even bothering to tell us to stop with him or wave us on or give any kind of command. While Titus flew us back to the dining room and landed with his front feet on a table and his back feet on the spindly stone railing.

Rin hopped off before Titus had completely settled. The hybrid landed on the floor, skipping the table altogether, and staggered forward a few steps with one hand pressed against his side, before he caught his balance against the edge of another table. His strange black aura writhed around him and a thick drop of blood splattered onto the floor by his foot.

Shit. Amiah had said he'd needed to feed, but I hadn't thought he was so low that he'd still be bleeding by the time we got back to the aerie. Vampires might not have the same kind of healing incubi did, but they still had some of the best healing in the supernatural world.

I hopped off and helped Amiah onto the table. She sagged where she was, her legs unable to hold her, and my heart clenched. I wanted to pick her up, carry her to a bedroom, and hold her until she'd regained her strength, but Bane wasn't going to be able to get off Titus by himself and Rin was in no condition to help.

Except when I tore my gaze away from Amiah and reached up to help Bane, he was staring at his hands. They still look sore, but the blisters had mostly healed and he was no longer bleeding.

"She didn't have anything left when we got on Titus," Bane said, his gaze jumping to me. "You saw that right?"

"The bond is new, but I guess it isn't too new for you to draw strength from her."

"Except strength from a soul bond wouldn't have physically healed me." He swung his leg over Titus's side, grabbed the spine ridge in front of him, and slid onto the table beside Amiah. "It would have just kept me alive, not healed me. It can't do that."

"I must have recovered a little while we were flying and instinctually given it to you," Amiah said, dragging her gaze up to his.

"Yeah." He cupped her cheek and gave her a soft smile that was filled with the same kind of deep, overwhelming love that I felt for her.

I had no idea how she'd thought he'd be upset with her branding him. He was as in love with her as the rest of us were. He hadn't even blinked an eye when he'd woken after Amiah had branded him. He'd yanked up his shirt, pressed his palm over the delicate gold lines swirling between the lines of his circle of power glyph tattooed along his ribs, and breathed a sigh of relief. And with the brand forming during sex, it was already sealed. They weren't going to experience the same desperate torture that she and Rin were experiencing.

I dragged my attention to Rin. More blood splattered onto the floor by his foot and he still held a hand against his side, but he stood perfectly straight, with no hint in his expression of the pain he must have been feeling.

Jeez. Deaglan really fucked that guy up. He didn't have to remain standing and certainly not at attention.

"Hey," I said, stepping off the table and drawing his dark gaze to me. "You need to feed."

At the word *feed*, his attention jumped to Amiah and the desire from both of them twisted so tight I couldn't breathe.

Holy fuck.

Rin's hellfire flared and the muscles in his neck flexed as if he were trying to move his head and look away but couldn't.

"Tell me to go." He inched a step closer to Amiah, clenched his hands, and forced himself to stop moving. It was agony to watch and worse feeling it with my magical senses, and it made my stomach churn knowing that I was gaining strength, subconsciously feeding on their sexual energy, as we stood there.

"Please," Rin whispered.

Amiah squeezed her eyes shut, pressed her forehead to Bane's, and clutched the front of his shirt, her body trembling. Her desire screamed through her, demanding she look at him, go to him, seal their bond. Her aura, weak without a glimmer of her internal magic, trembled around her and a black fissure shot through it.

What the hell?

Another fissure sliced through her aura and horrible realization flooded me. I'd thought not sealing the bond was a purely psychological damage and the death of the surviving half of a broken soul bond was because they let themselves waste away with a heart so broken they just couldn't do what it took to stay alive.

But I'd been wrong. A fissure in her aura meant a fissure in her soul and that could kill her.

Rin took another lurching step toward her before making himself stop and I realized he had dozens of fissures in his aura. They were only visible from the corner of my eye because of the nature of his black aura that made the fissures almost invisible, and I'd only seen them for a second, but they were there. They couldn't wait any longer. Whether they wanted to or not, whether it ruined Rin's chances of being free of Amiah, they had to seal their bond. It was the only way they could survive.

AMIAH

My pulse pounded, throbbing in my chest and between my thighs, and my whole body ached with unfulfilled need. Everything within me screamed to seal my bond with Rin. Now now now. I was going to shatter into a million pieces even with Sebastian and Titus's bonds, and I was never going to recover.

God. I couldn't imagine what Rin must have been feeling. He didn't have any other bonds to help him.

"You have to seal your bond. Now," Hawk said, his voice sharp with fear, making me jerk my gaze up to him, but my attention jumped to Rin despite my determination not to look at him and not to get trapped in the vortex of yearning that was threatening to overwhelm me.

But I *was* trapped. I didn't even need to be drowning in Rin's black eyes to know there was no escape. It didn't matter what I wanted. We couldn't make it the remaining twelve or thirteen hours until dawn. I knew with every fiber of my being that we'd run out of time.

"Are you crazy?" Sebastian asked.

"Their souls are about to shatter," Hawk said hopping off the table, pulling me into his warm arms, and cradling me against his chest.

"Shatter?" I gasped.

"You can't wait until we've gotten the Heart, gorgeous," Hawk murmured as he pressed his lips against my forehead. "I'm sorry. But if you two don't seal the bond now both of you will die."

She's exhausted, Titus growled in my head. *She can't have sex.*

"This sex doesn't have to be anything amazing," Hawk replied, proving that Titus had spoken to all of us. "It just has to happen."

It's too— "dangerous," Titus said, half in my head and half out loud as he shifted, somehow landing on his feet between the table and railing without looking awkward.

"It's just sex," Hawk said, carrying me across the dining room without waiting for the others. "There's nothing dangerous about it."

"And if he loses control and feeds on her?" Titus growled back, hurrying after him with Sebastian and Rin close behind him.

"Stop talking about Rin as if he isn't here," I gasped, my neck craning around so I could look past Hawk, my body straining to keep my gaze on Rin. With the exhaustion dragging at me, making the room dim and my head spin, it was impossible to fight the bond.

Desire and heartache from Rin flooded through our connection, and yet he showed none of it in his expression. The only indication he felt anything was the hellfire in his eyes that had grown from their usual smoldering pinpricks to miniature flames.

The agony from his unhealed wounds whispered across my senses with healing magic that I shouldn't have had while his life force writhed and snapped almost as desperate as the desire coming from him through our bond.

On top of all of that was my desire, urging me, begging me. *Please.* He was mine. It didn't matter what I thought I wanted, that I didn't know him. I needed him and had always been meant to be with him, just like I'd always been fated to be with the others.

"Rin can feed on me," Hawk said as he hurried down the hall to our suite and into the closest bedroom. "I've already gained enough sexual energy to heal the few wounds that I couldn't heal back at the Queen's Falls. I'll get that and more back when you two have sex."

He set me on the bed as the others crowded into the room except Rin who hung back and stayed in the doorway.

"We need to think about this," Titus growled, shoving Hawk aside and crouching in front of me.

The room whirled around and around and yet my exhaustion did nothing to diminish my need for Rin, just made it impossible to look away from him. As much as I wanted to wait until we'd gotten the Heart, it was clear we'd run out of time.

"There's nothing to think about," I said, my words slurred and I started to tip over.

Titus caught me and held me upright. "You're practically unconscious."

I tried to drag my gaze to Titus, look him in the eyes to assure him it was going to be okay, but I couldn't look away from Rin.

"Rin won't hurt me," I said.

The hellfire in his eyes flared and blood oozed around the hand that he had pressed against his side and dripped onto the floor by his boot. He was in such pain, physically, psychologically, and emotionally. The bond was cruel. It was just something else forced upon him. And yet I couldn't sense any anger coming through our connection. Which might have been because I was just so tired and the bond's desire was overwhelming, and the emotions I felt from him through the bond weren't strong to begin with.

Except the second I thought that, my soul was adamant that what I felt from him was true. He didn't hate me and I could trust him. I'd always been able to trust him.

"This isn't your fault," he said, as if he could hear my thoughts. And with our soul bond maybe he could. An angelic mating brand usually enhanced a super's powers and gave him or her new abilities. Mates when they were separated could usually find each other just by thinking about them. Except that usually took time to develop. Of course, nothing about my bond with Rin had been usual.

"This is happening," Hawk said, standing between me and Rin, capturing my cheeks between his palms, and forcing me to look at him. "I'm not going to lose you."

Except there was a good chance he would. I hadn't branded him yet and I was terrified I never would. My throat tightened. I didn't want to lose him either. I didn't want to lose any of them, but the power of the brand was overwhelming. I'd been a fool to think I could have ignored it.

And really, I hadn't thought I'd be able to ignore it indefinitely. I'd just thought I'd have more time to make the situation right.

But my soul cried that this *was* right. I was fated to be with Rin and I had to stop fighting it.

I drew in a breath to say—

I had no idea what I was going to say, and Hawk smashed his lips against mine and sent a rush of hot sultry magic flooding down my throat before I could speak.

His life force rushed across my senses, fiery and dark, joining his magic, adding to my throbbing need for Rin. My breath turned ragged even as fear clenched cold in my chest. From what little I'd been told, incubi didn't have a lot of control over energy transfers which was why they didn't want anyone to know about it. It was too easy to just give the recipient everything and kill themselves. Something I couldn't allow. And whatever I did, whether I could add him to my bonds or not, I couldn't let him die.

I grabbed his wrist to pry his hands from my face and pull away. But he sagged to his knees first, breaking our contact along with the transfer of his life energy into me. The sense of his life force inside me dimmed, but thankfully didn't disappear completely and I clung to his fluttering fiery darkness, unable to use my power to strengthen him because that would just transfer the life force he'd given me back to him.

"Rin." He set his arm on the bed beside me, his wrist up in invitation for Rin to bite him.

"Hawk, stop." I cupped his cheeks just like he'd cupped mine, but struggled to hold his gaze and not look up at Rin.

"It's okay, gorgeous," Hawk said, and his life force fluttered a little stronger... or was I just imagining that?

"With the sexual tension between you and Rin, he's already regained a quarter of what he gave you," Sebastian added, confirming with his magical sensitivity what I'd hoped was true. "He'll be back up to full and good as new before you and Rin are done, and that's even if he doesn't join you."

"Which just leaves that final question." Hawk pressed his palm against my hand that was still cupping his cheek and leaned into my touch. His life force surged a little stronger, and that part of my soul that I never realized was out of alignment until it moved, shifted a little closer to where it was supposed to be. "Do you still want me to stay with you and help you through this?"

I opened my mouth to say yes, but the word caught in my throat. When Hawk had made the offer, I hadn't known Rin, hadn't trusted him, and was afraid having sex with him would be just as horrible as being forced to have sex with Sebastian with everyone in the Winter Court watching. But Rin had proven that the bond wasn't lying to me. I could trust him and he wasn't going to hurt me. That, and inviting Hawk to join us might not be fair to Rin, especially if he didn't like having sex with more than one person. Not to mention after branding

Sebastian and now Titus but not Hawk, it probably wasn't fair to Hawk either.

"Whatever your highness wishes," Rin whispered before I could ask if he minded if Hawk joined us.

Except the grief coming through our connection grew stronger and his hellfire snapped back to pinpricks, a sign he was closing himself off from me. He didn't want Hawk to join us, he—

Horrible realization flooded me. He'd been Deaglan's slave. The odds that he'd made love with someone during his five hundred years in captivity because he loved them were slim. Rin had said Deaglan had denied him sex. Had he even had sex in five hundred years?

"Did Deaglan let you...?" I wasn't sure how to ask something so personal, especially with the others standing around. Rin was so private, so closed off. And while it looked like he was starting to open up to me, it was clear he was still wary of the others.

"For his entertainment," Rin said matter-of-factly in his barely-there voice. "I can perform with an audience."

Which meant he hadn't had sex in half a millennium because he wanted to or without someone watching. Now he was once again having sex against his will. I couldn't force him to have an audience as well. That was beyond cruel.

"This might still be something we have to do, but this isn't a performance for anyone's entertainment." The desire from our bond was more than enough to get me through this without Hawk's help. That, and a part of me couldn't help wondering if all of my desire really came from the bond, if maybe some of that desire came from me without any of its magical help.

Rin was a handsome man with his sharp sculpted facial features and his beautiful honed musculature. He wasn't as breathtaking as Hawk or Sebastian, but then very few people were. If our situation had been different, I still would have been attracted to Rin, especially if he hadn't had his walls up. The glimpses he'd shown me of the real Rin were of a man with a quiet thoughtful determination who'd been hurt in unimaginable ways. He was afraid to trust and it broke my heart thinking how lonely he must have been surrounded by Deaglan and his other assassins and not able to trust any of them.

His hellfire flared then snapped back to pinpricks. "I don't want you to feel like you're in danger."

"I know you won't hurt me."

Rin's gaze jumped to Hawk then Titus and Sebastian before jerking back to me.

"And they know it as well," I added.

"Because of the brand," Rin said.

"Because you're smart enough to know hurting her won't help you. Not to mention you didn't hesitate to fight Deaglan's men," Sebastian said. "The only one who thinks you will is Titus."

"Just my beast," Titus growled.

"And it's just an overprotective asshole," Sebastian said with a shrug. "Come on, Titus. This has to be done."

Sebastian hooked a finger under my chin, drawing my gaze up to his. "We'll get the Heart and I'll break your bond even if it's sealed. I promise."

My pulse stuttered, my stomach bottoming out in sudden fear, the reaction shocking me. I didn't want him to break my bond with Rin. I wanted to keep it, keep Rin, keep all of them.

Sebastian dipped in and captured my lips in a deep kiss that made our brand flare. The icy brightness of his life force curled into Hawk's fiery darkness and together they sank into my chest and wrapped around my heart.

He stepped back and Titus took his place, kissing me just as deeply and adding his wild ferocity to Sebastian and Hawk's life forces and making his brand light up as well.

Then they left, drawing my gaze back to the doorway and Rin.

His hellfire blazed in his black eyes, the intensity of his demon-vampire hybrid nature fully revealed, and he captured me in those dark fiery depths. My need jerked taut, stealing my breath and making Hawk's life force flutter even stronger.

Rin crossed the distance between us and knelt beside Hawk, his gaze never leaving mine. He took Hawk's offered wrist, brought it to his lips, and sank his fangs into his flesh.

Hawk drew in a sharp breath then released a low throaty moan, the sound thrumming against my senses and sinking low and hot between my thighs.

Oh, yes. I knew what Rin's magic felt like. I wanted it again and again just like I wanted Hawk's.

The intensity in Rin's eyes deepened, capturing me in a vortex. I was drowning in desire, teetering on the edge of a release that I hadn't wanted and now desperately needed. And all I could think was, *yes. God, yes. Finally.* My reasons for joining with Rin might be different from my reasons for joining with the others, but they were just as powerful.

The hellfire in Rin's eyes flared stronger, licking across his cheeks. He took a long pull on Hawk's vein, drawing another moan from Hawk and my desire twisted tighter. It was as if Rin was feeding on me, flooding me with his magic and not Hawk, and it tugged the connection between us tighter, which made me inch physically closer.

I opened my legs, and both Hawk and Rin leaned forward, pressing their chests against the insides of my thighs. Their life forces crackled against my senses with teasing ripples of power, fire and darkness that were similar to each other and yet so different.

Rin took another pull on Hawk's vein and Hawk's groan deepened. He clutched the top of my thigh, sending a burst of his sultry magic straight to my core. I shuddered on the verge of a climax before he stole it away and yanked his magic out of me, leaving me gasping and breathless.

AMIAH

"I should leave," Hawk said, his voice low and dark with sexual desire, his body trembling as if he were trying to hold himself back.

Rin released him and Hawk's magic sealed the two small puncture wounds shut before Rin could heal them with the miniscule magic all vampires had.

Hawk's hand slid higher up my thigh and another swell of sensual magic made my pulse stall.

"Crap." He heaved himself to his feet and took a step away from me.

I dragged my attention away from Rin's bottomless black eyes and met Hawk's gaze. My heart ached for him and my soul needed him as much as I needed the others. I could see the hurt in his eyes and not just because I was asking him not to join us, but because I hadn't claimed him like I'd claimed Sebastian and Titus. But I could also see his love and hope.

"I *will* brand you." I didn't know when or how, but it would happen. And if it didn't happen naturally, I'd use the Heart. I wasn't going to let him wither and die and I wasn't going to fall out of love with him. "I—"

I strained to keep my attention on Hawk and not look back at Rin while everything within me cried to turn to Rin, take him inside me, complete our bond.

"Hawk," I breathed his name and his hellfire licked across his cheeks. "I love you."

"I love you, too." He gave me a soft sad smile, but I wasn't sure if it was because he didn't believe that I would eventually brand him, or because of our current situation. "Now seal your bond before both of you lose your mind."

He hurried out of the bedroom and my gaze wrenched back to Rin.

He was so close, his body still pressed against my thigh, and my legs were still wide open in invitation. We were finally alone, finally going to seal our bond, and all of me, body and soul, ached for him.

Our need hung heavy in the air between us as we stared into each others' eyes. Then Rin rose up on his knees, tangled his fingers in my hair, and captured my lips in a bruising, breathtaking kiss.

I kissed him back, letting the dam inside me that I'd been desperately holding together by force of will alone to contain my desire, shatter. I needed him on a soul-deep level and I had to have him. Now. God, please. Now.

The metallic tang of blood flavored his mouth and I didn't care. It wasn't the turnoff I'd thought it would be. In fact, it twisted my need tighter, reminding me of him feeding on me. His magic was delicious and hot, like Hawk's but sharper, less refined. And just thinking about it made me hot and achy and desperately needing it.

"Bite me," I gasped against his mouth. "Please."

But he pulled me off the bed onto my knees before him and plunged his tongue into my mouth, his kiss turning ferocious. His grip in my hair tightened and he urged my head back, deepening what had already been an overwhelming kiss. Desperate, hungry need swelled through our bond, and not just because of our bond. Rin's desires had been denied and controlled for five hundred years, and like the dam inside me that had shattered, so too had the dam inside him.

The intensity of his passion stole my breath and made my soul sing. My skin turned hypersensitive and every breath he released on instinct — that he didn't need to release because he was undead — every flex of his muscles, and every brush of his body against mine twisted me tighter.

I shoved my hands under his shirt and ran my palms up his sculpted abs as I pushed the wet fabric up, savoring the feel of his hard muscle under my hands and the thrum of his life force against my senses.

With a low growl, he pulled away, yanked off his shirt, then grabbed mine and yanked it off as well.

"Stand," he commanded in his barely-there voice, his gaze still never leaving mine even though I was now topless.

The need coming from our bond surged, focused and intense, just like his vampire nature, and yet it was also edged with the fiery darkness of his demon half. It made my breath hitch, my own need so tight I trembled.

"Please," he murmured.

I obeyed and he rose on his knees with me, unlaced the fly on my slightly-too-large leather pants, and let them fall to the floor. Then he finally broke eye contact, slowly dragging his gaze down my body with a look similar to the ones Sebastian and Hawk had given me. A look that said he thought I was beautiful, that I was the only woman in the world for him, that he desired me and would have desired me even without the brand forcing us together.

Except that last part, the part where he would have wanted me even if I hadn't branded him, was just *my* desire. It was what I wanted to see because, as crazy as it was, I didn't want to let him go and couldn't continue believing that fate binding our souls together had been a mistake.

He traced a cool finger over the swirling gold lines of our brand etched into my thigh. "I know you don't want this."

His words made my heart clench with grief even as heat rippled through my skin at his touch, miniature shockwaves that grew as they rolled through my body, crashed around my heart and in my core, and drew a soft throaty moan from my lips.

"Because I want you to be free," I replied. "Trapping you in our soul bond is as bad as Deaglan trapping you in your vampire sire's bond."

He dipped in and brushed his lips against my thigh, following the same path as his finger and sending more, stronger, shockwaves crashing through me.

Oh, God.

I tangled my fingers into his long black hair to keep my balance and he slid his hands to my hips to help steady me.

"Nothing you do could ever be as bad as King Deaglan," he said, his breath teasing my sensitive skin as he gently pressed down on my hips, urging me to sit. "I know you'll free me if you can. I know you won't forsake me if you can't."

I sank back onto the mattress and he slid his hands to my knees, then up the insides of my thighs, spreading my legs wide.

"I won't punish you for something that isn't in your control. You're kind and generous and caring. You're a goddess." He kissed the inside of my knee and sucked in a sharp breath, his body trembling. "You're *my* goddess and I won't let this brand tell me how to worship you."

He trailed kisses slowly, oh so slowly, up the inside of my thigh, his hand following a similar slow path up my other thigh, to the inner crux of my legs.

My breath turned ragged and my fingers found their way back into his hair. I clung to his head as he teased his hand closer and closer to my slick aching core and flicked his tongue over my femoral artery.

My pounding pulse had to be a siren's song to his vampiric nature, and yet he was drawing it out, somehow defying the screaming need from our bond to raise my desire higher before letting me fall over the edge with bliss.

Then he sank his fangs into my thigh with a delicious sting of pain and a surge of his life force against my senses.

I gasped and tensed, unable to stop my natural reaction to being bitten, but a long hard pull on my vein flooded me with his sultry, hot magic, and I released my quickly drawn breath on a long, low moan.

He took another pull, sending more magic rushing through me, as he brushed his fingers through my folds.

Oh yes. A shudder of climax teased me, pulling me closer to the edge, and I clung to his head, fighting to keep my eyes open as I watched him suck on my vein and slide two fingers inside me.

It was unbelievably erotic watching him, his fingers sliding in and out again. He teased his thumb through my slick heat, then pushed back in and brushed his thumb against my clit.

Another low moan fell from my lips and I squirmed, my hips rocking into his fingers taking them deeper inside me, and he increased the pressure on my clit. My breath turned into short, sharp pants, and my inner muscles started to tremble around his fingers.

"Rin," I gasped as he pulled his fangs from my thigh and healed the puncture wounds. "I'm going to come."

"Then come." He slid his fingers out, but instead of rising and freeing his erection, he pressed me back onto the mattress with one hand, pushed the fingers of his other hand back inside me, and swirled his tongue over my clit, sending sensation shooting through me.

Oh, God. I bucked into his mouth and he yanked his fingers out, and grabbed my hips, holding me steady in an iron grip. He teased and licked and sucked, his magic rushing faster and faster through me until it swept me over the edge.

My orgasm crashed over me, stealing my breath, even as the need to seal our bond grew stronger. I needed him inside me. I ached for him like I ached for my other guys—

Which was just my imagination.

And right now, it didn't matter.

Right now, even though all we needed to have was sex, he'd taken the time to give me an orgasm, which, if I thought about it, was his way of saying he wouldn't forsake me either if we couldn't break our soul bond.

He stood, drawing my attention back to him as he unlaced his pants, releasing a full thick erection, and pushed them off his narrow hips. Need and something softer, something that, through our brand, felt like love but couldn't be because we didn't know each other, filled his expression.

It made my heart skip a beat. The only time I'd ever seen him reveal so much emotion was back in Sebastian's apartment when I'd released him from the magic circle, and at that time his expression had been pure, wild hunger because Deaglan had been starving him.

"You're glowing again," he whispered, his body trembling, his need seeping through our bond just as strong as mine.

I glanced down at the soft glow radiating from my skin. It was barely visible since it was midafternoon and sunny outside and the bedroom didn't have a door, but without a doubt, I was glowing again. I'd been too exhausted after the fight with Deaglan that I hadn't thought to check to see if all of the Winter Court's magic had left me. I guess I still had a bit of Faerie inside me.

"Guess you won't have to worry about the guys asking if you satisfied me," I said, squirming, my body aching, my breath picking up again, as Rin grabbed my legs.

"That wasn't something I was worried about." He pulled me to the edge of the bed, lifted my hips, and slowly pushed into me.

Oh, God, yes!

He felt incredible, sliding against my sensitive nerves, reigniting a desire that had barely been satiated with my first orgasm, and making all of me, body, mind, and soul tighten in anticipation.

Then our pelvises connected and his life force surged inside me, cold and fiery, alive and dead, intense and writhing, and that thing in my soul that clicked with the other guys, clicked.

My soul snapped into alignment, strong and sure.

Oh, my God. "I connect with you, too."

Rin stared at me, his eyes wide, his body tight and trembling. Awe flooded through our bond... along with hope.

"Does that mean you'll take me as a real mate? That you won't try to break our bond?" he asked.

"You don't mean that."

Except I knew without a doubt now that he was mine.

He was more than just a mate fate had forced on me. He was just like the others and I needed him. I didn't understand how I hadn't realized that I needed him. I'd known I'd needed Titus before we'd had sex.

Of course, I'd been so certain branding him had been a mistake and so determined to resist the lure of the bond that it hadn't even occurred to me that I needed him like the others.

But then maybe I just needed sex.

Maybe I connected like this with everyone.

Except the second I thought that, I knew in my soul that wasn't true.

I needed *them*.

Their souls.

I just had no idea why.

Fear trickled into Rin's awe and my heart clenched. He wanted me to keep him and I had yet to answer him.

"Our bond isn't a mistake." He brushed his thumb across my clit, sending a shudder of desire rippling through me.

"It isn't," I gasped. "We're meant to be mates."

I still didn't know if the angelic mating brand was beautiful and sacred, but fate hadn't been wrong binding our souls together.

Whatever I needed from the others, I needed it from Rin, too. He was the final piece in the puzzle... but for what?

Relief and desire and love flooded through our bond, and, trembling to control his own need, Rin increased the pressure on my clit, twisting my desire tight again, while the thrum of his life force inside me grew.

I fully gave in to the sensations of Rin's hands on my hips, his thumb deliciously hard on my clit, and the feel of his erection sliding out and thrusting back into me.

God it felt so good. So right. This was how it was supposed to be. We were supposed to be together and I'd been a fool to fight it.

My breath turned ragged again and my soul sang. Heat warmed our mating brand and a golden light flickered in the delicate lines etched into Rin's skin, making me realize my brand was also glowing.

Rin's pace picked up and quickly turned wild, the emotions radiating from our bond telling me he was giving in to our bond and our joined bodies, too. I curled my hips up to meet each thrust, taking him in as deep as he could go, our bodies crashing together.

Each impact sent glorious heat shuddering through me, a heat that swelled, warm and sure and strong around my heart and along the bond that connected our souls. It spun my desire higher and higher with an incredible pressure.

I panted and moaned and matched his powerful pace, my nerves twisting tight, the incredible pressure building inside me.

Then light exploded in every cell in my body. My full-body glow blazed bright with a mix of white fae magic and a strange golden magic, and my orgasm crashed through me, stealing my breath, sending me spinning, and making stars flash behind my lids.

"Rin," I cried and he tensed with his own release.

Rin's powerful, intense stillness flooded me. That part of my soul that needed him and the others, that I'd thought was a separate connection from my soul bonds, shifted again, and a ferocious burning power exploded inside me.

RIN

Power exploded inside Princess Amiah, tearing a scream from her lips, and her body went rigid in my arms. She'd just cried out her pleasure, which had brought my own release, our soul bond had sealed with a blaze of golden light and a power that had flooded me with certainty and love then a wild, uncontrolled magic, had ripped through her.

It was as if a door or a wall inside her had shattered and she was drowning in a ferocious, burning power, so hot I could feel it radiating from her skin.

I had no idea where it was coming from. It wasn't hers. She'd never had a power that had felt or looked like that. And yet, her essence was entwined within it, marking it as hers.

Except it wasn't flowing through her. It was building up inside her, burning hotter and hotter, holding her muscle taut, her back arched off the bed, her mouth locked open in the cry she'd just released, and her nails digging into my wrists where she gripped me when she'd come.

"Princess, you have to release it." *You have to take a breath.*

But she didn't move, trapped in the agony of the power scorching inside her.

"Take a breath." *Please.*

Her pale flesh turned pink, flushed with the heat, so hot she wasn't even sweating. She was burning up as if she were channeling magic, except that was impossible. She wasn't a witch or a high fae. She didn't draw on magic outside of herself.

And it didn't matter. If I didn't do something, she'd suffocate or burn up. Probably both.

I screamed out for Prince Seireadan. I didn't care if he blamed or punished me. I couldn't handle this alone and out of everyone, he was the one most likely to know what was going on. I could only pray that in his weakened condition he'd be able to save her.

I tried to yank my hands free of her grip so I could lean close, press my lips against hers, and use my sin eater's hunger to remove the power roaring inside her, but her muscles were still locked, her hands painful around my wrists, and I couldn't wrench free even with my superior strength.

And she still hadn't taken a breath.

God, I had to do something. Now. It didn't matter that I would also take her healing magic and possibly some of her life energy without lip to lip contact. I had to start consuming the magic burning her up or I was going to lose her.

That thought sent panic racing through me, tearing through what little stillness I had left within me. Everything within me, every fiber of my being knew she was mine and I hers.

I wasn't sure when I'd accepted that what I felt for her was deeper than the desire radiating from our bond, and I had no idea how I had those feelings when we barely knew each other. But when I looked past the insistence of our bond, I realized that something had clicked within me the moment I'd seen her. At the time, I'd been trapped, unable to escape from King Deaglan so I hadn't allowed myself even on a subconscious level to recognize what had happened. After that, I'd been fighting the bond along with my fear of being trapped by another master.

But Amiah wasn't another master. She'd been determined to free me, had been kind to me, understood that I didn't react like the other guys, that I was hesitant to speak up, and had pain permanently etched in my soul because of my five hundred years with the Shadow King. She was the woman I was fated to be with... if she survived whatever was happening to her.

I seized my sin eater's hunger and shoved my power into her through the three points I had connecting me with her: my hands still gripping her hips and my cock still buried inside her.

The inferno inside her ripped at my magic and I fought to grab hold of it. I'd never experienced a magic that was as wild. Not even Cassius's fire that I couldn't get a hold of and would probably have to fight to keep a hold of it if he ever let me kiss him to gain access to his power wasn't as ferocious. Pushing my power into the princess was like shoving my hands into a fire filled with a million slicing blades.

And that was what was tearing my princess up from the inside and burning her up.

Her skin was now bright red and a cluster of blisters had formed over her heart, making my soul cry at her agony, while our newly sealed bond screamed at me, insisting that I had to save her. I couldn't lose her, not after I'd just found her.

With a snarl, I pushed more of my power into her, speared it into the wild magic, and made a connection.

The wild magic wrenched and writhed against my hold, but I held tight, and sucked a mental gulp of that power into me.

Amiah gasped in a deep breath — *thank God* — and released another desperate scream.

The power was still too much and still flooded inside her, the pressure inside her excruciating.

I sucked in more magic, drawing it into me as fast as I could, but it just kept pouring into her. And now the power was burning and slicing inside me, my sin eater magic fighting to contain and absorb it, and losing.

Footsteps pounded into the room, but I couldn't risk breaking my concentration and my connection with Amiah to see who'd come. I had to keep consuming the magic, keep relieving enough of the pressure so she could breathe, keep praying that whoever had shown up, he'd be able to help.

"Oh, fuck," Prince Seireadan gasped. "I know what she is."

Another set of footsteps rushing toward us.

"What the hell is going on?" Hawk asked. "There's so much power, I can't even see in the room."

"Get Titus and Cassius. Now. She needs them. She needs all of us," Prince Seireadan said.

He hurried onto the bed to kneel beside Amiah, and I sucked in more magic, straining to hold on against the fire and pressure and agony still growing inside her and now swelling inside me as well.

"Help her," I gasped, the world turning red, the ferocious power's roar filling my head, threatening my consciousness.

"Just hold on Rin," he said. "And whatever you do, stay inside her."

"Stay inside her?" Cassius said, his voice sharp as a wave of heat swept over my naked back and a cloud of black smoke billowed into the room.

"Right now, he's the only thing keeping her soul in her body. She's a divine channel."

"What the hell is a divine channel?" Hawk snapped.

"I'll explain after we save her. Everyone get your hands on her. She needs physical contact with all of us." The prince cupped her cheeks and pressed his face close to her. "Amiah, you have to close the door."

She moaned and gasped in another desperate breath before her muscles clenched tight again.

Titus hurried onto the bed opposite Prince Seireadan, making the mattress sink with his massive weight and Amiah slide closer to him. He reached to press his large hands against her shoulder, but hesitated at the sight of the blisters spread across her chest and shoulders and up her neck. Half of them had burst, and the flesh around her heart was dry and cracked and oozing blood, while the rest of her had turned a sickening dark red with the heat.

"She's burning up," Titus growled.

"Just get your hands on her," Prince Seireadan said, his gaze remaining locked on Amiah. "Come on, sweetheart," he begged, his voice tight with fear, his body trembling. "You have to close the door."

Titus searched her body for a safe place to hold her, while Hawk, his eyes barely open — all the magic and his extreme magic sensitivity blinding him — scrambled onto the bed beside the prince. The incubus pressed his hands against Amiah's side and her muscles released long enough for another soul-shattering scream to tear out of her.

The firestorm inside her shuddered and a flicker of life and power fluttered through our brand, before it swelled again, seizing her body, slicing into her and me and burning hotter.

"God, Amiah. Please," Prince Seireadan said. "Close the door."

But her mind was too far away and it didn't seem to matter how much power I pulled into myself, I couldn't clear the way for her to focus and do what the prince asked.

"Titus, Cassius, please," Prince Seireadan said. "You have to touch her."

Titus growled and shoved his hands against their brand curling over her upper ribs. Blood oozed around his fingers and red-gold scales slid up his neck and across his jaw.

The firestorm inside her flickered again, releasing her, letting her draw in short, sharp pants.

"That's it Amiah. Close the door," the prince said.

"Door?" she gasped, her eyelids fluttering open.

"Yes. A door inside you opened." The prince pressed his forehead to hers, adding another point of contact. "You have to close it, sweetheart."

"I have to—"

The firestorm heaved, snapped stronger, broke off, and snapped again. Each surge made her convulse and scream and sent agony tearing through my body and soul.

"She's not going to be able to do it herself," Cassius said. Out of the corner of my eye fire billowed around him and poured onto the stone floor around his feet. "Bane, you have to help her."

"I can't," the prince gasped. "I don't have enough magic and even if I did, blocking her divine connection would just postpone this. She needs to close the door herself."

"If we postpone, we could be better prepared." Cassius heaved at his fire, pulling it off the floor, but unable to fully draw it back under his skin.

"Yeah, until the block shatters when none of us are around or we're in the middle of a fight with Deaglan," the prince snapped. "Now get your fucking hands on her! She can't do this without you."

"I'll burn her if I don't get this under control," Cassius growled back.

"She's already burning up. Cassius, please." Prince Seireadan's voice cracked and a tear dripped from his eye onto Amiah's cheek, hissing from the heat of her skin and evaporating.

Cassius snarled and wrenched his fire under control. Black smoke billowed around him and he clamped his hands onto Amiah's thigh overtop of my brand.

The firestorm stuttered and more of my magic spurted into her, suddenly without resistance. I heaved at the power tearing up her insides, pulling it into me as fast as I could, not bothering to try to absorb it. I had no idea when the storm would gain strength again and I needed to get as much out of her as I could. I could deal with it later. I just needed to hold on against the storm that was now also raging inside me long enough to save her. God, I had to save her.

Amiah's eyes fluttered open again.

"Amiah, close the door," the prince said.

"What door?" she gasped. "There isn't a door."

"Then make one. Please. Imagine a large door in the core of your being." Another tear dripped from the prince's eye and evaporated when it hit her red and now blistered cheek. "Imagine closing it."

The firestorm fluttered again and I wrenched out more magic, letting the burning, slicing power pour into me.

"That's it, sweetheart," the prince said. "Push it closed and lock it."

I trembled, the pressure and agony of her magic straining within me. I'd taken too much, and because I had no way to release it, I had to just hold on and suffer until my body had absorbed it.

"Almost there," Prince Seireadan said.

She whimpered, as tears leaked from her eyes and her burned and bloody body shook.

"Just a little more," the prince murmured.

The firestorm sputtered and went out, and her eyes rolled back and she went limp and passed out.

Cassius heaved away from her back into the doorway and his fire exploded from his skin. And while I knew I should have felt the heat rolling off him, I couldn't feel anything except the blazing, screeching power slicing inside me.

Finally released from her grip, I sagged to my knees as Titus gingerly pulled her into his arms.

"What was that?" he growled.

The firestorm sliced deeper inside me, making my stomach roil, and I squeezed my eyes shut. Throwing up wouldn't help me. It would only expel the blood I'd consumed to feed the vampiric half of my nature. And while I'd healed the injuries I'd sustained during the fight with King Deaglan, I was still weak and hadn't had a chance to absorb all of the blood yet.

"That was a miracle," the prince gasped.

"How is *that* a miracle?" Cassius demanded. "She's worse than when Balwyrdan beat her to a pulp."

I strained to slow the breathing I logically knew I didn't need but still couldn't stop myself from doing. My inner stillness was on fire and seething.

It was too much. Too much fear clenched my soul at the thought that I'd almost lost her after I'd just found her, and too much pain.

I'd thought I'd known pain, that King Deaglan had thoroughly educated me in all the ways a body and mind could be tortured. But this was an agony that ate into my essence and soul.

"She can heal this," Prince Seireadan said.

My stomach clenched tight and bile burned my throat.

Oh, God.

I had to get to the bathroom. In the very least, get away from them.

"If the power had awakened without Rin, it would have killed her or taken her soul and left her comatose."

I lurched away from the bed, still on my knees. I knew I couldn't stand, but I also couldn't throw up with the prince watching. I'd be punished. King Deaglan would hurt me, make me lick it up, make me—

The agony surged stronger. I had to get out of there. Had to—

My stomach clenched tight, shooting an inferno through my body and drawing a scream I couldn't hold in as blood and bile choked me.

"Fuck, Rin." Hawk scrambled off the bed, knelt beside me, and pulled my long hair out of the way. "Stop trying to hold it in."

But I had to. The king—

Except Prince Seireadan wasn't King Deaglan—

The fiery agony roared stronger.

"Bane—" Cassius's fire rolled into sight then jerked back. "Do something. His life is linked to Amiah's."

My body heaved, expelling blood and bile, but that didn't alleviate the pressure inside me.

"He can't absorb all the magic he consumed," Prince Seireadan said. "But I can't—"

Icy white magic burst through Amiah's mating brand on my hip as I threw up more blood, my body shaking so hard I wasn't sure I'd be able to stay on my hands and knees much longer.

"I—" Prince Seireadan's magic snapped from my hip to my heart, a sudden ice storm that devoured the fire burning my insides, and tore it out of me.

I screamed—

And so did Cassius as a blast of white magic slammed into his chest and ripped out his fire.

The angel grabbed the doorframe but his legs wouldn't hold him and he sagged to his knees, his head bowed, and his breath ragged.

My body gave out as well, but Hawk grabbed me and pulled me away from my vomit, letting me collapse in his arms.

"Forgive me, your majesty," I gasped, my thoughts wild and disjointed. "Don't punish me, please. I didn't mean to. I— Please—"

Apologizing and begging had never worked with King Deaglan, but I couldn't help myself. I didn't mean any of this. I'd had no control over my body. I still didn't. Tremors tore through me and all of me still felt like I was on fire. It was like those early years, before I'd found the stillness in my soul, the calm pool where my mind retreated to when the Shadow King was being cruel.

"Rin," Prince Seireadan murmured.

Unable to help myself, afraid of what I'd see and unable to convince my lurching thoughts that Prince Seireadan wasn't King Deaglan, I dragged my gaze up to meet the prince's eyes.

There wasn't a hint of anger in his expression, only overwhelming relief. "Thank you."

Then a whisper of golden stillness unfurled around my heart. It wasn't enough to ease the pain in my body, but it filled my soul with certainty. I wasn't alone and I was no longer a slave. My soul was still bound, but I wasn't a prisoner. I was a partner, a lover, someone seen, someone cherished. Someone who finally belonged.

SEBASTIAN

Rin sagged in Hawk's arms, passing out, and I collapsed back on the bed. My magical channels burned from yanking all the magic out of Rin and then using it to craft a spell on the fly that ripped out Cassius's fire. But fuck, it was a second miracle that I was able to connect with Rin through Amiah's brands, especially since we were only linked through her, we didn't share part of a brand.

Even though I'd somehow already recovered some of the strength I used to have, I still wouldn't have had the magical strength to save him if I hadn't had an easy way to connect with him. And without a doubt, he would have died if I hadn't pulled all that raw divine magic out of him. Which, even if that wouldn't have killed Amiah or driven her crazy, was still unacceptable. He was the only reason she was alive.

And he was one of us.

We'd all just been too stupid to see it.

Fate had clearly figured out a long time ago the only way Amiah would survive coming into her full power was if she were near a sin eater, and the only way for that to happen, since Rin was the only sin eater left, was to break Deaglan's leash spell on him. Which had to be why she'd branded him, since an angelic mating brand was the only way to break a vampire sire's bond which had been the foundation of Deaglan's leash spell on Rin.

"If I get my hands on Deaglan, I'm going to kill that asshole. Slowly,"

Hawk snarled. "Did you see Rin's face? He was terrified for throwing up. For throwing up for fuck's sake!"

"No wonder he always hangs back and never says anything," Cassius said, staring at his hands with eyes that barely had any angel glow in them. Then his gaze slid to Amiah and my chest squeezed at the heartache in his eyes. This was a moment of reprieve for him, just like I'd intended when I'd ripped out and temporarily blocked his connection with his fire. Except from the look in his eyes, while he wanted to hold her, he was going to take the high road because she was bleeding and burned.

Yeah, well, I had good news for him... so long as he didn't think too hard about how we got into this mess.

"We should all get in bed with her," I said. "Preferably naked. She needs as much flesh-to-flesh contact with us as she can get right now."

"Really, Bane?" Cassius groaned. "If she needs flesh-to-flesh contact then only the two on either side of her need to take our clothes off."

"Come on, hot stuff. You know he only brought it up so he can see you naked again," Hawk teased, sliding his gaze over Cassius and letting desire darken his eyes.

But the hurt in Cassius's eyes deepened and didn't turn into frustration like it usually did.

Of course, the last time we'd seen him naked — or rather the last time we'd seen him naked that he'd been conscious for — had been after he and Amiah had had sex for their first and only time.

"Titus isn't going to let her go, but you should take her other side while your fire is out." Hawk's expression turned sober as he gave up on his teasing tactic to change Cassius's mood, and he turned his attention back to me. His hellfire blazed in his eyes and the power radiating off him indicated that Rin and Amiah had gotten him back to full before everything had gotten fucked up. "So what the hell was that?"

A mess and a miracle and one hell of a complication. And I had no idea if it was good. At least from the power entwined in Amiah's brand on Rin's body, they'd managed to seal their bond and weren't going to go crazy or die from that.

Thank fucking God!

Titus inched farther onto the bed, propped himself up with the pillows, yanked off his shirt, and gingerly drew Amiah up so she was tucked against his side with her head resting on his bare chest. She looked so fragile lying beside him, like a broken doll with her skin red and raw and oozing, and her breath was still short and sharp as if it hurt to breathe.

God! She'd almost died.

My soul still trembled at the thought and only partly because of the brand.

I'd fallen in love with her before fate had proclaimed we belonged together and I couldn't have been more relieved to be bonded with her. The only thing that had upset me about all of it, was that Hawk was still left out in the cold.

And while there was still a chance she wouldn't brand Hawk, the odds were now good that she would. Eventually.

Because she was a divine channel. And she needed all five of us.

Of course, maybe she wouldn't brand him. He was, after all, an incubus. Falling in love and commitments weren't part of his nature.

She slid a hand to Titus's ribs, her fingertips brushing the bottom of his brand, and light flickered in the delicate gold threads in his skin and then through all of hers.

A soothing, barely-there breath of warmth seeped through my brand and eased into my magical channels as if even unconscious she could somehow heal me… which her healing magic wasn't supposed to be able to do and could only be because of our soul bond or her connection to the divine magic.

Fuck, this was such a mess.

I raised my hands to rub my face but stopped, realizing that I had blood on them. Amiah's blood. Because I was a fucking moron and hadn't recognized what should have been blatantly obvious— or at least blatantly obvious to me.

It didn't matter that divine channels had only been mentioned a few times in the thousands upon thousands of books I'd read and briefly at that, or that there'd only been two mentioned in those books and neither of them had been angels, or that the last recorded channel that I knew about had died over six hundred years ago. I should have known what she was when she'd said she needed to connect with us.

Hell, I should have known what she was when I'd *felt* that connection when we had sex. No supernatural being connected like that. Not even succubi or incubi.

"You said she's a divine channel," Titus whispered, his voice low, likely in the hope that he wouldn't wake her. "What does that mean?"

"That she can connect to the raw magic between the realms," I said.

"There's magic between the realms?" Hawk asked, which didn't surprise me. Very few people knew that there was a power outside of the primal powers of each realm and even fewer people were able to sense it. Hawk, even if he could sense it with his incredible magical sensitivity — and he probably could — likely wouldn't know what he was looking at and assume it was something else.

But it was real and powerful, the magic of fate, the magic that bound angels' souls together — even though angels still believed magic from the Realm of Celestial Light created angelic mating brands.

I pulled off my shirt, tossed it to the floor, and slid my fingers over the golden swirls branded in my side. "It's this. The magic of life and souls. And Amiah now has a direct connection to it like I have a direct connection to Faerie."

Cassius frowned. "So she's now a sorcerer?"

"No. She can't weave spells like I can." Speaking of which—

I pulled on my connection to Faerie, drew in a painful swell of magic, and forced it to bend to my will to get rid of Rin's puke. The others frowned at me but thankfully didn't argue with me about choosing to use my magic to clean that up.

"I also doubt she'll gain a witch's ability to craft spells," I said. Although she still had that beautiful after-sex fae glow, which suggested that she still had a little bit of fae magic inside her even though it had looked like the Winter Court had pulled all of its magic out of her. She might still be able to power my glyphs... or her own glyphs, if she chose to get any tattooed on her body.

"She can't bend this raw magic to her will," I continued. "It's too powerful. She can only use it to augment her own magic. Although given that she took the lives of Deaglan's assassins to fuel her magic to save Cassius—" And that I could feel a small trickle of power soothing my magical channels. "—it looks like what her healing magic can connect with has expanded as well."

"So that's what she meant when she told your sister that she'd already killed to protect us." The hurt in Cassius's eyes deepened. But it didn't feel like he was hurt that he hadn't known what she'd done, but that he was hurt on her behalf for the choices she'd been forced to make.

"She wasn't going to lose you," Titus said.

"And they were trying to kill all of us," Hawk added.

"Yeah," Cassius replied, his voice gruff.

"I would do it again in a heartbeat," she whispered, her soft voice making all of us jerk our attention to her. "I've made horrible choices before and I'm sure I'll have to make more horrible choices in the future. I deal with life and death. That's just the way it is."

"Gorgeous," Hawk breathed.

Her eyelids fluttered open for a second and her gaze, with barely a hint of her angel glow, slid over us, drawing a soft smile before her attention landed on Rin's unconscious body in Hawk's arms, and her smile wavered.

"He's okay," Hawk said. "Just passed out."

"Thank God." Her lids slid closed again. "So I'm a divine channel. Is that why I feel like I've been lit on fire?" she asked, her words starting to slow and slur, exhaustion starting to pull her back under.

"Yeah," I said, unable to move my gaze away from her. My soul ached for her, yearned to be closer, but as much as I wanted to tuck up on her other side, Cassius needed that more than I did. "And even after you gain some control with how wide you open your new connection, you shouldn't use it without at least one of us with you. We're your soul anchors. The connection you form with us keeps your soul in your body so it won't be swept away by the divine magic."

"The only reason it didn't take my soul was because Rin was inside me when the door burst open, isn't it?" she mumbled, her lids fluttering as if she were trying to open her eyes again and failing.

"So it just burned her instead?" Cassius asked. "I don't like how that's the better option."

"No," Titus growled, and more scales rippled over his chest, his dragon still straining to take control even though Amiah was out of immediate danger. "It almost *did* take her soul. I felt that through our brand. She needed all of us touching her to keep her with us."

"Which is why the only two recorded mentions of divine channels that I know of are so short." That had been the worst part of realizing at the last minute what she was. "The first channel didn't survive her awakening because she hadn't found her fifth anchor."

The other one hadn't survived the death of one of her anchors. And that was even scarier. That channel hadn't even been channeling divine magic. She just hadn't been able to have regular sex with one of her five anchors and the magic had sliced through her mental barrier that had been holding it back.

And I could already feel more of her magic leaking into me and see hints that she was healing her burned flesh. I doubt she was even aware she was doing that, and even after I'd trained her, she might always be leaking just a little bit of magic. Which was a more terrifying thought because if she couldn't properly seal the door, there was always a chance her magic would be able to force it open.

I laid my hand on her ankle, trying to convince myself she'd be okay. She'd just made a door to a connection she hadn't had before and was weak. She hadn't had time to mentally build it up so of course she was leaking power. She could handle this. We just had to get her through the next few hours... maybe days. Even if she couldn't control the power when she opened the door, she'd at least have a more solid door with a better seal and could just keep it closed.

Except if things didn't go well against Deaglan and one of us died, she was going to die as well. It wouldn't even matter if she was soul bound to whoever died or not. Without all of us, the divine magic would eventually overwhelm her and take her soul.

"How do we know she needs five of us?" Hawk asked, his voice tight with worry. "What if it's six or seven or more? How do we find them? And can it be anyone?"

"No, it can't just be anyone," Amiah said, managing to drag her eyes open for a second before they fluttered shut again.

God, she should just let herself pass out. Except I knew she wouldn't because she didn't want us to discuss her or a plan or whatever the hell we were going to be doing next without her. She just wasn't remembering that we couldn't do anything until dawn and that none of us were in any condition to do anything other than come to terms with our new reality, that she was a channel for the most powerful, most wild magic in the universe.

"I know in my soul that it's the five of you," she said. "It's always been you."

"So," Cassius said, suddenly looking just as exhausted as she did.

The adrenaline from seeing her magic burn her up from the inside must have finally passed and almost a whole day of channeling his own magic had completely drained his strength. It was probably good that I'd ripped out and temporarily blocked his magic because if his willpower faltered, he'd end up burning himself up.

Which was also something else I had a feeling I needed to figure out sooner rather than later. I doubted my luck at remembering something important just in the nick of time would continue to save Cassius.

"So branding Rin and Sebastian and Titus...?" Cassius asked.

"Wasn't necessary," I said. "She needs all five of us whether she brands us or not."

"It was *completely* necessary," she corrected. "It was the only way to free Rin from Deaglan, to save you when Rin was removing your demonic magic infection, and to save myself from Deaglan when he took my key."

"But will that affect how you feel about Hawk and me?" Cassius asked.

"Never. I love all of you." She heaved a heavy sigh. "Okay, I don't know if I love Rin yet, but I know I will."

But Cassius turned his attention to me to confirm the truth of her words. Except I couldn't. I had no idea if the brands would make her love us more. She still needed him and Hawk and needed to have regular sex with all of us to keep her soul rooted in her body, but I had no idea how her emotions would be affected.

"So what does all this mean?" Hawk asked. "She has access to an enormous source of power but she shouldn't use it?"

Pretty much. Except I knew we wouldn't be able to stop her if someone's life was in jeopardy and she had no other option. "It means she needs to be careful."

Her eyes fluttered open and I gave her a stern glare.

"You'll be able to heal more people and more serious injuries at a time," I said, "but you're now bound by your willpower. If you get exhausted you're no longer just out of magic, but unable to control this enormous power."

"So I could burn up like you," she said.

"Yes." I slid my gaze over her blistered and burned skin, my throat tight even though she already looked better than before Titus had moved her to his side. The fact that she was burned at all was my fault. If I hadn't been a blind idiot, I'd have known this would happen. I could have helped her prepare and saved her and Rin all that pain.

"So... you know... don't open that door you just made inside you until I've helped you learn to control it." I flashed her my wicked smile — the one that always made her blush even though we were now in a sexual relationship — and let my desire fill my eyes. "Oh, and you have to have regular contact with us to keep your soul anchored."

"Gee," she murmured, her eyes sliding shut again. "How will I ever manage? I guess this explains why I need you guys near and touching me all the time even though I'm not a shifter."

"You need a little more than *just near and touching*," I said. She really had to be out of it to have completely missed my innuendo. She hadn't even blushed.

"You should probably show me what you mean, Sebastian." A hint of a smile curled her lips, proving she *had* understood and was teasing me back. Then she released a soft sigh and her expression grew slack, her exhaustion finally dragging her into unconsciousness.

"I will, sweetheart. I promise." I turned my attention to Cassius. "But first, she needs to rest and you need to strip."

Cassius rolled his eyes at me. "I'm not cuddling naked with you, Bane."

"No, you're cuddling naked with *her*. She's still leaking magic. Which so far is good for her—" I drew in another swell of magic from Faerie, which didn't hurt as much as the last one had — a result of her healing magic still seeping into me — and made the blood on her body and on the rest of us disappear, revealing that she'd already healed her cracked and blistered skin, and now it was just red and tender. "But until she can have sex again with one or all of us to better anchor her soul in her body, holding her will have to do."

"She's healing herself and she isn't even concentrating, is she?" Hawk said.

"Yep. Just like she unconsciously healed my hands while we were flying back from the Winter Court." Yet another sign that should have made me realize what she was. "Now come on, Sparky. I don't know how long the magical block I put on your fire will last, but if we're lucky, she'll wake while your fire is still out and you can offer her round two."

"With all of you in bed with us?" Cassius asked, unbuttoning what was left of his Hawaiian shirt. All of his clothes were tattered and burned and even if there hadn't been a chance for Cassius and Amiah to have sex and she hadn't needed flesh-to-flesh contact, I would have told him to take his clothes off before getting in bed.

I rolled my eyes at him. "If you're feeling shy you can ask us to leave."

"Maybe Amiah will be shy." He shrugged out of his shirt, revealing a nasty burn curling over his left shoulder and down his side.

God, if his own fire was burning him, he really was in trouble.

"Really?" Hawk gave me a sharp look at seeing the burn then turned back to Cassius. "I would have thought you'd have figured it out by now that she doesn't care if we see her naked or if all of us are with her while she has sex."

"Yeah, well," Cassius said, his voice gruff. "I'm not sure that's something I'm into."

But he still let his gaudy board shorts fall to the floor, revealing another burn curling around his left thigh, and climbed into bed. With luck, the physical contact with Amiah would help heal those burns, just like she was healing her own and healing me.

And I wasn't going to ask if he'd gone into the fight with Deaglan like that. He was a stubborn fall-on-his-sword angel. Of course he had.

Which, fuck, probably meant he was going to do something stupid to keep her safe.

"Just so everyone knows," I said, giving Cassius a pointed glare. "She needs all of us. She can't keep her soul in her body without regular contact from *all* of us."

And I could only pray we all survived this fight with Deaglan.

AMIAH

I WOKE IN BED IN A DARK ROOM WITH ONLY A HINT OF SOFT MOONLIGHT shining through the doorway. My magical channels and my body were still a little raw, but not nearly as raw as they'd been before, and the soothing thrum of fiery, dark, bright, icy, and alive yet dead life forces caressed my senses and whispered in my soul.

Hawk's seductive darkness was the strongest, stronger than it had ever been before, probably because he was tucked tight behind me, his chest to my back, with an arm across my waist holding me close. The others' life forces were also stronger than before. Not nearly as strong as Hawk's, but I wasn't in direct contact with any of the others. I could even feel Cassius's and Titus's life forces, even though I could also sense that they weren't in the bed with us let alone in the room. It was like a wall inside me had been broken and my magic was no longer just sensing them but had permanently connected with all of them despite only branding three of them.

But it didn't matter if I'd branded them or not. They were my guys. All of them.

The thought brought a smile to my lips. Mine. And now I knew I wasn't crazy. I *did* need them and I *did* need to have sex with them. They were my soul mates, a match to my soul to help anchor my soul in my body while I channeled my new terrifying power.

I fought to suppress a shudder at the memory of all that magic burning through me, consuming my body and soul.

God. If I hadn't been with Rin when my connection had fully formed and if the others hadn't reacted so quickly, I would have died in agony.

Another shudder swept through me and this time I couldn't hold it back.

"You okay?" Hawk murmured, his lips brushing the sensitive skin behind my ear, turning the shudder of fear into one of soft desire. It wasn't enough to instantly turn me on, but it was a good start if that was where I wanted to go.

"I don't know. I don't feel like I've been lit on fire anymore." I glanced at my chest, where the worst burns had been.

My skin was red and tender, but the blisters and cracked skin were gone and so, too, was the blood. If I concentrated past the thrum of the guys' life forces, I could feel a trickle of my healing magic slowly and softly mending my body and, much to my surprise my magical channels as well — something I hadn't been able to heal before. I could also feel a trickle seeping from Sebastian's brand into his magical channels and healing them too... at the same time. Also something I hadn't been able to do before.

I'd never heard of a healing angel capable of healing multiple people at the same time, and I couldn't help wondering how I was going to manage my healing compulsion with this new ability. Would I even be able to stop myself? I could heal from a distance. How far was my reach? The Joined Parliament Operations Building was a couple of miles from the hospital in the Supernatural Quarter. Could my power reach that far? Would I constantly be drained with my magic connecting and healing the sick and injured in the hospital?

Except Sebastian had said I couldn't be drained. I had access to an unlimited supply of magic. Now I became exhausted instead of empty and could burn up like he could. Unless, of course, the divine magic swept my soul out of my body.

"It's all just a lot to take in," I finally added.

"You're not doing it alone." He pressed his lips against the back of my neck, sending another soft shudder sliding from his lips to my core, reminding me that I was naked in bed with an incredible man — three incredible men, actually. I pressed back, sliding my body ever-so-slightly against his and confirmed that Hawk was also naked.

Hawk hummed low in his throat. He slid his fingers up my abs and teased the bottom of my breast, adding a soft flutter of sensual magic unfurling warm within me.

The heat caressed around my heart and sank slowly to my core. It relaxed me and turned me on at the same time, and I willingly embraced it, while trying not to think about the fact that the last time we'd had sex, I'd tried to brand him and failed.

"So you're confirming that I'm a lot to take in," he teased, his tone dark with innuendo.

"I don't know," I teased back, my voice breathy. "I should probably double check to make sure."

"How would you like to confirm?" He brushed his fingers up my throat and slid his thumb into my mouth. "Here?"

I swirled my tongue over the tip, reminding him of the instruction he'd given me when I'd had Sebastian in my mouth, then sucked on the digit. I'd happily take Hawk in my mouth. The thought of his gaze capturing mine, his hellfire blazing brighter and brighter as I brought him pleasure made my core clench in anticipation.

He hummed again, slid his hand down the length of my body, and teased his fingers into my curls. "What about here?"

My core clenched tighter. Having him push inside me and bring me to climax was just as appealing.

"Or what about here?" He cupped my mound, drawing my hips back, and pressed his erection against my rear, his length pressing into the cleft between my cheeks.

I gasped at the memory of him sliding into me while I'd already had Sebastian inside me.

Oh, yes,

"That's the one. Liked that, did you?" he said, his lips teasing the sensitive skin behind my ear again.

"Loved it." It had been the most incredible sensation, full and hot. Having both him and Sebastian moving inside me at the same time had more than lived up to the anticipation that had been building since I'd learned about the act.

With a groan, Hawk shifted his hips, slowly sliding his erection through my cleft, taunting me with the imitation of the act I wanted.

He teased his fingers up to my breasts again and worked one nipple then the other into a tight, aching bud. He licked and suck the oh-so-sensitive skin behind my ear, his hot breath rushing over my skin, turning every nerve hypersensitive, and the fiery darkness of his life force thrummed inside me, attuning my senses to him. Every flex of his sculpted muscles against my body as he moved his hips, inching his erection deeper between my cheeks, every brush of his skin, and every light flick and delicious pinch from his fingers on my nipples twisted my desire tighter.

He knew exactly how to work me up, turning my yearning into a beautiful, throbbing need. He didn't even need his magic, not yet, and I suspected the only reason its sultry power teased around my heart and in my core right now was because of his incubus's nature and he couldn't completely hold it back.

"I'll never get tired of the feel of your desire," he whispered, as his tip pressed against my entrance, making my breath hitch and the muscles in my core ripple in anticipation.

I squirmed, pressing back against him, urging him to enter me and flood me with that incredible sensation again.

"I know it was fate that brought us together, that our joining was inevitable because I'm one of your anchors, but being with you still stuns me," he said.

His sensual magic swelled, and with a soft, hot-as-hell groan of pleasure, he slowly pushed past the tight ring of muscle in my rear.

My pulse stuttered and all my senses locked on all the sensitive nerves that Hawk's invasion had ignited.

God, it felt so good. The pressure and fullness and that little lick of pain turned into an exquisite pleasure by his magic. His life force surged fiery and dark against my senses, strengthening my soul, sliding it closer to its proper alignment, and filling me with hot sensuality.

"I love you," he murmured against my neck, his hot breath making me shiver and inching him deeper inside me.

"I love you, too."

He slid his hand over my belly, brushing his fingers into my curls, but paused as Titus stepped into the doorway.

His large body filled the space and blocked out the dim moonlight, and his eyes met mine then slowly slid down my body, his beast rising to the surface and slitting his pupils as he looked at me.

"Like what you see?" Hawk purred, drawing my leg back and hooking it behind his, baring more of my body to Titus.

He rumbled low in his throat, his attention locked between my thighs. My pulse picked up with the eroticism of Titus watching Hawk pleasure me. I liked being watched by my guys, liked turning them on and in turn being turned on by them.

Hawk brushed a finger into my wet folds, sending glorious liquid sensation sliding through me. I fought to keep my eyes on Titus and not let them roll back with pleasure.

Scales swept over Titus's neck and jaw and his breath picked up, expanding his stunning broad, muscular chest.

"Are you just going to stand there?" Hawk asked.

The implication that Titus might actually join us instead of just watch made my pulse skip with sudden, aching need.

Hawk sucked in a sharp, sudden breath. "Fuck, Amiah," he groaned, sliding his slickened fingertip over my clit, the touch making me suck in my own sharp breath.

"That's what I'm hoping for," I moaned back, reaching a hand out to Titus.

Titus's gaze flickered to my eyes then back to where Hawk tormented me with his fingers.

"We're both... big," he said, his voice thick with desire. "I don't want to hurt you."

"Hawk will make sure that doesn't happen," I replied, my need surging. And given that I'd unconsciously healed my burns, I wasn't even sure if I'd end up sore afterwards even if Titus's beast took over and went all out.

I squirmed. Just having Hawk buried inside me, his fingers teasing me, opening me to Titus, wasn't enough. I needed him moving, needed that glorious friction. I needed both of them. Their bodies and their life forces. I could feel my soul close, but not quite fully aligned, and knew I could only get that with sex.

More scales swept down Titus's chest and he stalked to the bed, his beast fully revealed. This was Titus the powerful predator and even before he dipped in to capture my lips with a bruising kiss, I could feel the wild ferocity of his life force surging stronger against my senses and entwining with Hawk's inside me.

I gave in to the feel of his powerful energy and the crush of his mouth against mine. Hawk moaned low in his throat and rubbed slow circles on my clit, ratcheting up my desire, filling me with hot, throbbing need.

"Mine," Titus's beast growled against my mouth, making my soul sing with the certainty of that one word.

I was his. I was all of theirs.

And they were mine.

He pulled his lips from mine and dropped to my breast, sucking my nipple into his mouth with a tight pinch that Hawk turned into more delicious pleasure. I tangled my fingers into Titus's red hair and arched my back, pushing my breast against his lips, while Hawk's finger continued to torture my clit.

My breath quickly picked up and Titus turned to my other nipple, grazing it with a partially extended canine, sending a shudder rushing through me.

His gaze jerked up to me, his beast checking on me to confirm my reaction had been from pleasure not pain, and he captured me in his stunning golden eyes. His pupils were fully slitted, his beast in control, and the wild ferocity of his life force billowed through me, the waves coming faster and getting bigger.

I moaned my pleasure and squirmed against Hawk, shifting his erection inside me, giving me a glimpse of the incredible sensations awaiting me. The movement drew another moan from my lips and the whisper of a climax trembled through me before Hawk swept it away with his magic.

"Not yet," he breathed, flicking my clit, sending more pleasure rushing through me then torturously pulling it away in the best possible way.

Oh, yes. I didn't think I'd ever get tired of that. I'd thought before I'd experienced it that someone controlling my release would be cruel, but the build up was incredible and it meant I could revel in the amazing sensations of Hawk buried inside me, while Titus licked and sucked and built my pleasure to an incredible high before I crashed over the edge.

"Oh, gorgeous," Hawk purred, rolling us onto his back, and pulling my legs wide on either side of him. "You make the most incredible sounds."

Titus rumbled his agreement and dropped his mouth to my clit, sucking just as hard on it as he had on my nipples.

Oh, God! Sensation shot straight to my core and I bucked, but Hawk grabbed my hips and kept himself buried while keeping my desire hanging on the edge but not crashing over.

I moaned and heaved against Hawk's grip, my body needing to move, as Titus roughly swept his tongue through my folds and over my clit, before clamping down again on that sensitive nub.

My breath turned short and sharp and my eyes rolled back, and I feared I was going to come before Titus had even entered me despite Hawk holding back my release.

Then Titus climbed onto the bed, straddling Hawk's legs, locked gazes with me, and aligned his full thick erection against my opening.

I panted, all of me aching for the pressure of his invasion, my body still squirming against Hawk, Hawk's grip on my hips like steel holding me steady.

With a low, rumbling groan and his body trembling, Titus slowly pushed into me, stretching me to my limit, adding his girth to Hawk's. Hawk's sensual magic unfurled stronger within me, but I was so wet and aching and ready for both of them, he didn't have to do much.

It felt like it took forever for Titus to fully bury himself inside me, his patience as he inched in, letting my body adjust, was incredible. Especially knowing his dragon was the one in control. But the second he was fully sheathed, that part of my soul that needed them clicked into place and the wild ferocity of his life force roared through me, joining with Hawk's.

I felt powerful and strong, fierce and sexy and I could feel another layer of strength wrapping around my heart and securing the door inside me that I'd somehow managed to put up before I'd passed out. And yet I had the sense that if I opened it a crack with any of my guys buried inside me, the ferocious power I now had access to wouldn't instantly sweep me away

Then both Titus and Hawk slowly started to move, dragging themselves along my channels, finding a rhythm between them that made my desire soar. It was all I could do to hang on. But I felt safe letting them take control of my pleasure and build it up as they found their own. I trusted them and knew they'd make sure I was well and truly satisfied.

And God, the feeling of them inside me was incredible, full, amazing, and so was the rub of their muscular bodies against mine.

Titus's canines extended in full and red-gold scales slid over his chest to his abs. His breath grew as ragged as mine and his pace turned frantic. I clung to his forearms and dug my nails into his flesh. He snarled back, thrusting into me. Hawk buried himself deep in my rear and held me steady until Titus tensed and roared his release. His life force pounded through me, twisting my desire so tight it stole my breath. Then Hawk started to withdraw and thrust, plunging in deep with glorious pressure and friction.

With a groan, he released his magic that was holding me back, and I crash over the edge.

I cried out, stars flashing across my vision and my muscles clenching around both of my guys. It swept through me, an amazing wave that sent me spinning, filled with fire and darkness and ferocity and strength. I was powerful. I was wild. I was sensual. I felt incredible.

And my entire body blazed with light from the ghostly remnants of the fae magic that was still within me.

I rode the wave with the guys inside me, our quick breaths rubbing our bodies together, my hypersensitive nerves still all firing at once and making the sensation go on and on. God, I would never get tired of this feeling.

Then the soft, blissful darkness of Hawk's power swelled over me and I was floating, boneless and relaxed with the last few ghostly tremors of my climax rippling through me.

Oh, wow.

Titus slid out of me, and I dragged my heavy lids open and met his golden gaze as he sat back on his heels. He stared at me his expression slightly dazed, his love for me filling his eyes, and sending warmth through our brand and radiating around my heart.

"Like I said before," Sebastian purred, drawing my gaze to the other side of the bed. "That's one hell of a way to wake up."

He lay on his side at the far end, one hand propping up his head, the other slowly pumping up and down his erection. His lips curled back in a wicked smile as my gaze dipped to follow the movement of his hand then back to his face. "Wanna take over?"

I cocked an eyebrow at him as my desire reignited, melting away the last drowsy remnants of Hawk's magic. "Do I?"

Rin, who lay between us, his hips and legs covered in a blanket, his hellfire blazing in eyes filled with desire, lifted himself up on his elbows. "I'll get out of the way."

I rolled off Hawk, straddled Rin's legs, and brushed up against a rock-hard erection under the blanket. My desire swelled stronger, and I pressed a hand against his chest to stop him from getting up. He was one of my guys as much as any of the others. He didn't have to get out of the way. "Sebastian can wait his turn."

"Oh I can, can I?" Sebastian said, his wicked smile deepening as he pumped his hand down his erection.

"Pretty sure you'll enjoy watching this as much as Rin and I will enjoy doing it." I pulled down the blanket covering Rin's hips, letting his erection stand proud and tempting.

I licked my lips and Rin's erection bobbed in response. Oh, yes. If Rin was game, I wanted to make him come in my mouth.

"Princess," Rin whispered in his barely-there voice, and a hint of fear seeped through our soul bond. "His highness should go before me."

"Rin." Sebastian rose to his knees his hand still wrapped around his erection. "You're as much Amiah's mate as the rest of us. You never have to take a back seat."

"That, and Bane will probably get off watching." Hawk rolled his eyes at him. "I'm surprised our little threesome didn't make you come. You're awfully close."

"I'm hanging in there, pretty boy," Sebastian huffed. "I want to feel Amiah coming around my cock before I get off."

"That can be arranged," Hawk said, and Sebastian tensed and groaned, most likely as Hawk took control of Sebastian's release.

"Fuck, I really want to hate when you do that," Sebastian hissed.

Hawk flashed him his own wicked smile. "And yet you love it."

Sebastian rolled his eyes at Hawk, making the incubus chuckle, and I turned my attention back to Rin. He stared at me, his desire hot and raw, his love and need and certainty seeping through our soul bond.

If we were alone, I had no doubt he'd kiss me, or tell me to take him in my mouth, or say what he wanted. He *knew* we were mates, knew he belonged as a member of our sextet. But it was going to take more than a few days for him to unlearn the mistrust and caution that had been ingrained into his mind and soul over the last five hundred years. And it was cruel to try to push him so soon in his recovery. Except everyone but Cassius was in bed with us and the whole reason we'd sealed our bond without an audience was because Deaglan had made Rin perform in public.

"Do you care that they're here?" I asked.

"No," he said without hesitation or looking away from me.

I strained to sense any uncertainty about being intimate with me with the others sharing our bed, but there was only need radiating through our bond. The whisper of fear when he thought Sebastian would get upset because I wanted to have sex with Rin next, was gone, completely replaced with his quiet strength and stillness.

"Would you like me to pleasure you?" he asked, pushing against my hand and trying to sit up. But I kept pressure on his chest, urging him to stay where he was, and he didn't fight me.

"I was hoping I could pleasure you," I said, my voice husky.

I dropped my gaze back to his erection and licked my lips again.

"Fuck, you *are* going to make me come," Sebastian groaned.

The desire radiating through my bond with Rin surged stronger.

Without a doubt, that was a yes.

AMIAH

I trailed my hands from Rin's chest, down his sculpted abs, and teased my fingers around the base of his erection. The muscles beneath my fingertips flexed, making his shaft bob again.

My breath picked up in anticipation, and with my gaze still locked on his, I wrapped my fingers around him to hold him steady, slowly lowered my head, and teased my tongue over his tip.

He sucked in a sharp breath that he didn't need to take, and it brought a smile to my lips. God, I loved that sound. I loved when all my guys made it. But I loved more that low masculine moan, the one edged with a growl, that told me they loved what we were doing.

I swirled my tongue over his tip and slid him into my mouth. The hellfire in his eyes flared, licking across his cheeks, fully released, and the desire and love in his eyes and pouring through our bond grew breathtaking.

His life force thrummed against my senses and I slowly drew him out, sliding my hand up and adding more pressure than I could manage with my lips, teased his tip again, and slid him back in, relaxing my throat to take him deeper than before.

Another slow slide out and back in again, and the breath he didn't need grew faster. The desire in his eyes deepened, turned scorching, and heat swelled in my core, my desire rising again even though I'd just had an incredible orgasm with Hawk and Titus.

I picked up my pace, drawing him out and back in, savoring the feel of him against my tongue and brushing the back of my throat.

A low soft moan escaped his lips and his body started to tremble, his hips pressed against the bed, as if he refused to give in to his body's need to start moving.

"You can show her what you want," Hawk said, his voice soft and sensual.

The question flickered in Rin's eyes even as he dug his fingernails into the blanket in an effort to not touch me.

I hummed my agreement, roughly swept my tongue over him, making his eyes roll back, and took him in deep again.

A spark of hellfire snapped free from his right eye and floated in the air around him. He tangled a hand in my hair, and his hips slowly rocked up, slipping him in farther, making my throat tighten.

"Just relax," Hawk murmured, and a curl of his magic softened my gag reflex.

Rin tugged my head up and slowly urged me back down. I relaxed into him, keeping my grip and lips firm, sucking and stroking as best I could, as he showed me the pace he liked.

His other hand joined his first, his grip on my head tightened as his need scorched through our bond with a direct, hot, achy connection to my core. I gasped around him, keeping my gaze on his even as his eyes rolled back, and his pace picked up. He was completely letting go, giving in to the pleasure I was giving him and fully trusting me and the guys.

"Fuck me," Sebastian groaned as he teased his fingers over my rear and slid them up my back to the invisible, hypersensitive seams beside my shoulder blades where my wings emerged.

I gasped as Rin rocked in and Hawk stole my gag reflex. Rin's eyes jumped to mine and I sucked on him, assuring him I was fine and drawing another soft moan from him. His eyelids fluttered partially shut again and he urged me to resume our pace as Sebastian brushed and licked my wing seams, tormenting me until I was panting around Rin's erection and trembling on the edge of another orgasm.

Then Sebastian swept his hands back over my rear, grabbed my hips, and slid into my wet sheath, making his icy bright life force entwine with Rin's.

Oh, God. My core started to tighten, the sensation of him pushing into me with Rin in my mouth nearly tipping me over the edge toward an orgasm. But I didn't want to come until Rin had, and I didn't want Sebastian to distract me from finally feeling what it would be like to have a man come in my mouth.

I sucked in a breath, fighting my release, drew Rin out, and turned my head in his grip so I could shoot Sebastian a dark glare. "Rin comes first."

Tension rippled through my bond with Rin and I pulled my gaze back to his, letting him know how much it turned me on to have him in my mouth. I sucked him back in, fighting my climax as Sebastian pressed tight against me, holding still, every shift of my body to make Rin come brushing Sebastian against nerves twisted so tight I thought I'd explode.

But Hawk held my orgasm back and Rin relaxed and returned to rocking into my mouth, his breath becoming ragged again, the pressure and desire in our bond building into a firestorm until he tensed, holding my head down, and came with a rush of salty heat.

A shuddering moan escaped from his lips and bliss swept through our bond filled with his release but also love and trust and peace. He knew he was mine and I was his, and he knew he belonged with all of us. Yes, it was going to take time for him to heal, to stop reacting on instincts honed over five hundred years of physical and psychological torture, but I knew in my heart and soul that he would heal.

"Fuck that was hot," Sebastian groaned, his body trembling against mine.

He slid a hand to my breast, his grip deliciously firm, and urged me to sit up, his erection still buried inside me. I rose, leaned back against him, and laced my fingers behind his neck, giving him and the others full access to my body. Light blazed from my skin, pulsing in time with my rapid heartbeat, stronger than when it had blazed with the orgasm Hawk and Titus had given me.

Rin had a beautiful, stunned expression on his face, while Hawk and Titus looked hungry again. The intensity in their eyes as they swept their gazes over my body added to the throbbing need inside me but also filled me with awe.

They all had that look. The look Sebastian had first had when we'd made love, the look that made me feel powerful and beautiful and cherished. And now I knew they looked at me like that because they loved me and I loved them.

Sebastian inched himself halfway out of me, sending the tremble of a climax rushing through me and making me gasp. Hawk tightened his magical grip on my orgasm and Sebastian pushed back in, while Titus drew close and flicked his tongue over my nipple and Hawk laid in front of me, grabbed my knees to hold them open, and blew a teasing breath over my clit.

Oh, God. I started to buck, but Sebastian held me steady, keeping himself buried inside me, as Hawk's magic continued to hold me on the edge, aching for a release that only he would allow.

Having someone control my orgasm like that should have been terrifying. It went against everything I'd thought I was before this whole mess had started. I'd thought I wouldn't be safe if I wasn't always in control. I thought if I was careful, I wouldn't be hurt again. And both were wrong. Being careful hadn't protected me from getting hurt, and even though I had little control right now, I was completely safe. My guys would never hurt me and if I asked them to stop, they would. I was safe with them, safe to fully explore who and what I was, and safe to share my fantasies.

Rin sat up, his hellfire blazing, and joined Titus, sucking and teasing my nipples, while Hawk tormented my clit with his tongue. Sebastian pumped into me, his thrusts getting faster and more forceful.

They built my desire tighter than it had ever been before, tipping me closer and closer to the edge, but Hawk wouldn't let me fall. My body and soul begged for a release. But I had no idea what I was doing or saying only that I panted and moaned and writhed as miniature eruptions taunted me, my need on the razor's edge of painful.

Then Hawk released me and my orgasm tore through me, every muscle contracting, every nerve firing, my body clenching hard around Sebastian, making him half groan half growl his own release. His body tensed as well and we were locked together, bliss cascading through us, igniting our brands and turning our skin a brilliant white light as if we were both high fae.

Sebastian's life force blazed around my heart, icy and radiant and filled with an enormous universe of power, and the others' life forces joined his, sending a ferocious surge of power rushing through me and weaving into my soul. This! This was how it was supposed to be. This was how *I* was supposed to be. I felt solid and strong. I felt incredible.

My muscles finally relaxed, and so too, did the power rushing inside me, letting me float, boneless, filled with bliss, riding the wave of my orgasm mixed with Hawk's magic.

"Holy fuck," Sebastian groaned, his breath ragged. He'd leaned back on his heels a bit and wrapped his arms around me, supporting me against his body while I'd been momentarily unconscious from Hawk's magic. "I could get used to this."

"If we're going to keep doing this, I'll need better shields," Hawk said his words slurred. He still lay between my knees, his head butted up against my mound, but he'd rolled over and stared up at me with a happy, stunned expression.

His hellfire flickered and danced in his eyes indicating he'd taken in a little too much sexual energy, but not enough to OD, merely enough to make him the equivalent of drunk or high.

Titus rumbled his agreement, flopped back on the bed, and stretched out like an extremely satisfied enormous cat, while Rin fell back as well, his hellfire back to miniature flames and his expression soft with a small smile curling his lips.

Movement glimpsed out of the corner of my eye caught my attention, and I slid my gaze to the door.

Cassius stood in the entranceway, backlit by the soft moonlight shining from the sitting room behind him and wearing only a towel that was clearly tented by an erection. His life force crackled against my senses, his fire whispering around my heart, but there wasn't a spark of fire or curl of smoke coming from him. And while the angel glow in his eyes was weak, confirming he was low on power — thank goodness — it was still bright enough to illuminate an expression filled with sexual hunger that sent a shiver of desire teasing down my spine.

There also wasn't a hint of the icy hard angel or the sour look of admonishment I'd have expected for having been caught with all four guys making love to me at the same time. Not that I would have been embarrassed or apologized for any of it. I had three mates and five anchors. I wasn't a normal angel and I wasn't going to have normal angel sex — thank God! I'd still have sex one on one with my guys, but given that Rin and Titus didn't seem to mind joining Sebastian and Hawk, I was also going to have more amazing moments like this.

I released my grip around Sebastian's neck, but stayed where I was, naked and exposed with Sebastian still buried inside me and Hawk still within licking distance of my clit, and reached out to Cassius, inviting him to come to me. I didn't know when his fire would return, and I wanted to make love with him as well. None of us knew what lay ahead for us. The only thing that was certain was that we had to do everything in our power to keep the Heart away from Deaglan. Whatever it took.

"We'll leave and give you guys some privacy," Hawk said.

"Yeah," Sebastian agreed, placing his hands on my hips to help me get off him. "I don't know how long my block on your magic will last so now's the time."

"Don't," Cassius replied, his voice gruff. "Stay."

"So you *are* into this," Sebastian said, his tone turning wicked and playful as he slid his hands up to my breasts, cupped them, and brushed his thumbs over my nipples, making them tighten.

"This is who we are." Cassius's gaze dipped to where Sebastian fondled me before jumping back to my eyes. "I knew it the second I saw all five of you together. You were breathtaking," he said, striding to the bed. "So incredibly sexy."

He captured the back of my head with a firm hand and smashed his lips against mine.

I gasped in surprise, not expecting such a passionate start, and he slid his tongue into my mouth, turning the wild kiss into a breathtaking, scorching kiss.

He kissed me as if he were starving. And he probably was. If his emotions made it difficult to control his fire, then sex with anyone could have been challenging.

But the ferocity of the kiss was also a promise. This time he wasn't trying to draw everything out as long as possible and memorize each detail. He believed we'd do this again and he was fully embracing his passion, a passion he hadn't been allowed to express before for fear of hurting me. In this moment there was just us and our desire and nothing else, no fear of his fire raging out of control, no fear that this would be our only time, and no fear that things would go badly with Deaglan.

I kissed him back, letting his passion sweep away all other thoughts. His life force flared stronger, a whisper of fire sliding through my veins, and I welcomed it inside me, letting it solidify my soul's proper alignment, strong and sure within my body.

Sebastian, still inside me, groaned softly and continued to knead my breasts, rubbing his thumbs over my nipples, while Hawk teased the insides of my thighs, sending a curl of his sultry magic unfurling in my core. The guys made me ache all over again with a need that I wasn't sure would ever be completely satiated. They made my heart and soul sing as warm golden threads seeped between the cracks around the door inside me and brightened the brands etched into my skin.

My breath quickly picked up and so did Cassius's. With a groan, he lifted me up and laid me on the bed beside Sebastian. His eyes were filled with heat and need and love as he raked his gaze down my body, and somehow a trail of his fiery life force followed the same path inside me.

It caressed down my throat, around my breasts, and pooled between my thighs, making me gasp in pleasure, which brought a stunning brilliant smile to his face.

It had been a long time since I'd seen him smile like that, seen him look so free and at ease, and I knew in that instant that I'd been a fool to think he hadn't been my soul mate. He'd been by my side for years, helped me through those terrifying, heartbreaking early days after my rescue when I was afraid and angry. We'd always been at ease with each other, and I'd convinced myself that was because he was my best friend, and not because he was also my soul mate.

But then I hadn't been ready to accept the truth about myself or the desires of my soul. I'd needed to reach the end of my resistance and embrace that I was a sexual being. And I'd needed to meet Hawk and Sebastian. Nothing would have been possible without Hawk embracing my nervous request for him to make love to me or for Sebastian agreeing to join us.

Cassius tugged off his towel and settled his hips between my thighs, his erection brushing against my folds. I tipped my hips up, welcoming him in, and with a shuddering groan, he pushed inside me.

The power in my soul surged like it always did when one of my guys entered me, making me gasp, and his fiery life force flooded in.

God, I loved that feeling. I loved Cassius and all my guys.

We moved together, quickly building up each other's pleasure. More of the golden magic in my heart seeped around the edges of the door and more fire and darkness and sensuality from my guys swept in, securing me in my body.

But even as the guys' life forces steadied me, the light in Cassius's eyes grew brighter and started to flicker, indicating his magic that I'd thought had been drained was returning faster than possible and was starting to break through whatever Sebastian had done to block it.

His breath turned sharp and he gritted his teeth, fighting the sudden surge. But his hands on my hips grew hot and smoke curled up his forearms, the precursor to his fire breaking free. The fire in his life force blazed stronger and all of my senses snapped to him. His insides were on fire with a flame that couldn't be extinguished, fueled by a power that came from beyond him.

Which didn't make any sense. Angels had an internal well of power for their ability. And while a very rare few had a witch's ability to manipulate magic that had been saved in an external source like a glyph or a crystal, Cassius wasn't one of them.

Of course, up until a few hours ago, I hadn't known I could connect to divine magic like a fae sorcerer could connect to Faerie's raw magic.

At the thought, a large thread of golden magic swept past my door and rushed around my heart.

Flames snapped over Cassius's hands and he jerked his hands from my hips. "Shit."

"What the hell was that?" Hawk asked.

"I'm breaking through Bane's spell." He met my gaze, his body trembling with the effort to hold his magic back and with the desire that still made his breath ragged and his erection thick and hard inside me.

God, I wanted him to finish, wanted to give him the release he'd been denied for too long, but it was cruel to ask him to keep going. He wouldn't be able to enjoy it if he was also concentrating on not bursting into flames.

"I've got this," Sebastian said.

"Don't." More flames rippled over Cassius's hands and he sucked in a sharp breath and pulled them back under his skin. "It's almost dawn. You'll need everything you've got when we face Deaglan."

Cassius met my gaze. Grief and heartache filled his eyes, but there was also an edge of determination there. "We'll figure this out after we get the Heart. Maybe it'll be able to fix my problem."

He started to pull out of me and the golden thread inside me drew taut. All of my senses snapped to it and I followed it into Cassius's heart where it surged and heaved and turned into a roiling flame. Except my sense of whatever this connection was between us was growing fainter and fainter the closer he got to pulling out, while his fire continued to build.

My pulse stuttered as horrible realization hit me. He was taking my excess divine power. Power that would have swept my soul out of my body if left unchecked. Except he wasn't a divine channel and his body was turning the divine magic into fire.

God, I had to fix this, figure out how to pull my power out of him.

I mentally reached for the thread to follow it to where it was anchored inside him and hopefully disconnect it, but he fully withdrew and my sense of my magic pouring into him vanished.

"No." I grabbed his hips and bucked my own, pushing him back into me and re-establishing the connection.

My divine magic surged, sending flames racing up Cassius's arms, but also sending my senses rushing into him. My healing magic quickly assured me he was in perfect health, then my divine magic took over again, sweeping me through his heart up to his left shoulder and the source of our connection. An angelic mating brand.

The delicate gold lines were barely formed and threaded under his skin too deep for anyone to see, but they were there, and they matched a similar, barely-there brand on my shoulder that I hadn't realized had been there before.

The realization made my divine magic explode inside me and rush into Cassius, turning the thread between us into a massive channel, filled with a torrent of golden magic. It swept into Cassius's body, drawing a scream and sending fire racing up his arms. He tensed, his hips rocking forward, burying his erection deeper inside me, and deepening our connection. The magic roared around his heart then swelled up into his shoulder, igniting our mating brand and bringing it to the surface.

Golden light blazed from his skin and radiated from his eyes, and he came hard within me, his pulse pounding against my inner wall, his fiery life force flooding me. His gaze jumped to my shoulder and his eyes widened as a brilliant smile lit his entire face, even as smoke and flames still rolled over his skin.

My soul clicked into place and the power in his fully awakened brand threaded into the magic he was still drawing out of me. It pulled the excess magic deep inside him as if he'd developed a second personal well to store this new power, and the flames and smoke vanished.

CASSIUS

I stared at Amiah, my heart bursting with love and amazement and power. So much power. From her. Power that I suddenly realized I'd been taking from her for years as her connection to the divine magic had slowly awakened.

I was her first anchor and I'd been keeping her soul in her body while she'd searched for the others. And when her connection to the divine magic had grown, so, too, had the power pouring into me.

No wonder I'd been dripping flames for the last twenty-four hours. She'd been on the verge of fully coming into her new ability and had been leaking magic like a sieve.

"What the hell just happened?" Bane groaned. "It was like a pressure bomb of power just went off and then it disappeared."

Hawk squinted at me. "It didn't disappear. He's still got it, but the mating brand has given him the strength to store and control it." He groaned. "So *that's* what's been going on. I can't believe I didn't see it. You've instinctually been siphoning off her excess divine power, but you've been thinking too hard about controlling it. That's why distracting you or changing your emotions strengthened your control over it. It pulled your focus off the power and let your instincts take over."

"So the harder I tried to control my fire—?" I asked.

"The worse it got," Bane said.

Amiah cupped my cheeks, dragging my gaze back to hers. She was radiant, her skin brighter than before, and her eyes — filled with the soul deep love she gave the others — were focused on me. It made my heart swell and I dipped in and kissed her.

"You've been protecting me all this time," she said, "and I'd been too foolish and then too afraid to see the truth."

"I didn't see it, either." All I'd known was that I'd had to protect her — I still did — and that I'd fallen in love with her and I couldn't fail her like I'd failed my youngest brother, Dominic.

"I'm not sure either of you were ready for the truth," Hawk said. "This isn't your normal angel relationship."

Amiah's gaze slid to Hawk and she reached over Rin's legs and interlaced her fingers with Hawk's. He was the only one left, yet he was the one who needed to be branded the most.

But she'd branded her other anchors, so surely she'd brand him too. It was just a matter of time... and surviving the fight with Deaglan.

A new horrible realization hit me. I couldn't go all out on Deaglan anymore. I couldn't fully release my fire and burn both of us up. Amiah and I were soul mates, and I could feel in my soul that our bond was fully sealed. Not to mention Bane had warned us that she needed regular sexual contact with all of us to keep her soul anchored inside her.

Which meant if I was going to keep her safe, we needed a plan.

"You'll argue with me if I tell you to stay here while we fight Deaglan, won't you," I said to her.

She cocked her eyebrow and gave me her driest, no-nonsense physician's glare, the one that had been missing since Balwyrdan had beaten her to a pulp. "I can heal from a distance, but I'm not sure how far my magic can reach. I won't risk one of you dying if I have the power to save you. And I'll know if you're in trouble. I'll feel it in our brands."

She shuddered and I remembered what she'd told me, that the mating brand was a nightmare, that she'd seen my brother's mate, Essie, on the floor begging for help when her mates had been seriously injured and she'd been unable to go to them.

"God, I really want to say fuck it. Let's not risk it and let Deaglan have the Heart," Hawk said. "But I know even if the rest of you agree with that, it won't protect Amiah. He knows you have a powerful healing magic. Once he has the Heart, he'll still come after you. You're just too valuable."

"Getting the Heart from him is the only way we get through this," Bane said, his expression grim.

"How?" Titus asked, inching a little closer to Amiah even though Rin and Hawk lay between them. "Faerie will reveal my Ancestor's Temple within the hour. Is all your magic back, Seireadan?"

"I'm surprisingly close, thanks to Amiah," Bane said, "but my magical channels are still tender."

"If things go south, will you be able to teleport us out of there?" I asked as I reluctantly pulled out of Amiah and lay beside her, keeping her close, unwilling — in a very unangel-like way — to completely separate from her just yet.

Bane laid a hand on her ankle, as if he, too, needed to be in contact with her right now. "Depends on how much I've spent during the fight."

I was hoping that wasn't what he'd say but knew in my heart that it was the truth.

I'd seen Bane do incredible things, knew he was a magical force of nature and probably one of the most powerful supernatural beings who lived in the mortal realm. But Deaglan was also incredibly powerful and I had a horrible feeling that having all four keys only added to his magical strength.

"Okay," I said, wrapping my arm over Amiah's waist and holding her close. "Deaglan is probably going to bring a small army with him. Hell, he might even bring a large army. And he knows that Titus will be able to lead us to the temple." A whisper of fear churned in my gut. "It wouldn't surprise me if he also knows Amiah is a threat and can do more than heal."

"He does," she said. "He's been shielding his men's souls against my magic ever since I killed them in the Summer Court cave to save you. That's why I'm back to being useless in a fight."

"Except that isn't useless," Bane said. "Every person he shields uses magic and strains his willpower. If you keep trying to break through those shields, he'll either have to pour more magic into them or let you break through."

"And if I break through, I'll be able to kill them." A shudder swept through Amiah, making my throat tighten. Yes, she'd said she'd kill again if it meant saving us, but it broke my heart that she even had to make the choice.

I wanted to reassure her and tell her that it wouldn't come to that, but I wasn't a fool. This was war, and if we lost, many more people, not just us, would die — and given Deaglan's inclination toward cruelty, they'd die in horrible, painful ways.

"So Amiah can help deal with the army or help drain Deaglan," I said.

"Only if she doesn't get swept away by her power," Bane warned.

"I'll stay with her," Hawk said. "She doesn't have a soul bond with me so it'll be harder for her to use me to anchor her without touching me or being near me."

I turned my attention to Titus. "Will you be able to shift in the temple?"

"Yes," Titus said, his voice gruff. "It's my people's temple."

"But Deaglan knows that," Bane said. "He'll be prepared with a spell to keep you contained."

Which was the most frustrating thing about this situation. We'd gone up against Deaglan enough times that he knew what we were capable of. And while we also had a rough idea of what Deaglan and his assassins could do, he could also add anyone to his army, not just shadow fae. For all we knew, he held more supernatural beings captive like Titus and Rin. And just like Rin, he could force them to fight for him.

"Okay. So, we have my fire, Bane's magic, and Titus's dragon form." I slid my attention to Rin. He'd been a seriously dangerous foe when we'd been fighting him, and while he'd still been dangerous during the fight at the Queen's Falls in the Winter Court, he hadn't been quite as deadly without his swords. "Bane, is there any way to get Rin and Hawk weapons?"

"There aren't any in the aerie," Titus said." Dragon's don't need weapons."

"And I doubt we have time to go find something," Hawk added. "I'll just have to take someone's during the fight." He huffed. "And yeah, I'm regretting not keeping hold of the knife I took at the waterfalls."

"The one you dropped when you went under the ice?" Rin asked in his barely-there voice, shocking me that he'd said something that wasn't completely necessary.

"Yeah, that one. Funny how I wasn't thinking of keeping a weapon while being dunked in freezing cold water," Hawk said.

Which didn't surprise me. Yes, he'd served in the war, but he wasn't a career soldier and didn't have the century and a half of fighting experience I had or the five hundred years of experience Rin had.

He'd also been a canary, and there'd been so few with a strong enough magical sensitivity to be effective canaries — those able to notice hidden magical traps before they were activated — that those who'd signed up had only been given basic training before being handed a rifle and sent out with their unit. That said, he must have had a little more than basic training because he'd been able to hold his own against some skilled fighters and was even capable of disarming someone and taking their weapon.

"I can't get anything for Hawk," Bane said, sliding off the bed, kneeling on the floor, and turning his attention to Rin. "But I'm betting you've had your swords for a long time."

"My uncle gave them to me before I was turned," Rin whispered.

"Then you're connected to them. Having them for that long will have imprinted your essence on them. If they're in Faerie, as a royal and a sorcerer, I should be able to get the realm to return them."

"Except how much magic will that take?" Amiah asked as she sat up, the angel glow in her eyes flaring with her worry. "If your will breaks and your magic starts to burn you up, I'm not sure I'll be able to stop it."

I sat up with her, not wanting to lose the contact of her skin against mine, and drew her back into my embrace.

The others sat up as well, Hawk with his worry clear in his expression, Titus radiating dangerous ferocity in place of worry, and Rin with almost no expression at all—

No, that wasn't true. The hellfire in his eyes had become miniature flames instead of the usual smoldering pinpricks. And I had no idea if he was actively trying to hide his emotions or if keeping everything to himself was usual for him as a result of half a millennium of being Deaglan's slave.

"It'll take some magic, but not enough to put a dent in my control." Bane flashed her that wicked sensual smile that used to drive me crazy and now just made me roll my eyes at him, but his expression quickly sobered. "I'm acutely aware of what's at stake with this mess and what the cost will be if we fail. But Deaglan won't just overwhelm us with his power. He'll do it with men, too. He doesn't care how many shadow fae or conscripted assassins we kill and if we don't use every advantage we have, we won't be able to stop him."

He pressed his palms to the floor and closed his eyes. His full-body fae glow flickered under his skin and rushed down his forearms and around his hands. The air around him shuddered and the muscles in his back flexed, then the muscles in his arms and his jaw tightened as well.

He dropped his head forward and squeezed his eyes shut, and Amiah tensed, her breath picking up and her angel glow growing stronger.

"Come on," Bane groaned, his breath getting faster as well and his body trembling with the effort to make Faerie answer his request.

Then the light around his hands exploded, momentarily blinding me, and a wave of power swept around him, shoving Amiah into me and knocking Hawk and Rin to the head of the bed.

I wrapped my body protectively around Amiah, as my fire rose to caress just under my skin.

But it didn't burst through like it used to. I was fully in control again and I could feel its enormous pressure curled around my heart, filled with Amiah's golden radiance, waiting to be summoned to protect her.

Amiah had healed whatever had been broken inside me when Dominic had been murdered. I was now no longer the Salamander... unless I wanted to be.

Bane groaned again and I blinked the black specs from my vision. I didn't expect there to be trouble, but I wasn't going to risk it.

Before him, lying on the stone floor, were Rin's swords, clean and perfect and resting in their black sheathes as if the shorter wakizashi hadn't been lost in a swamp in the Autumn Court and the katana hadn't been lost— I had no idea where he'd lost the other one, only that it had been lost.

"My *daishō*," Rin whispered.

Amiah beamed at him and grabbed his hand, and he gave her a soft, honest smile.

It was small and quickly vanished behind his usual, calm expression, but it was like a sudden ray of sunshine peeking through the clouds after days and days of overcast sky.

A pressure that had been squeezing around my heart from the moment I'd learned he was her mate, eased. I doubted Rin would open up completely to me or the other guys, but that small smile assured me he'd open up to her.

And that was the only thing that mattered. We could make this relationship work. My brother, Gideon, happily shared his mate with three others, and — I wasn't sure when it had happened but it had — I was happy to share as well. It felt right, and as much as Bane and Hawk were going to drive me crazy, it was a good crazy, the kind of crazy that came with a close, loving family.

Now all we had to do was survive what was coming next.

RIN

Prince Seireadan set my *daishō* on the bed by my feet while Princess Amiah smiled at me and squeezed my hand.

No, not *princess*. Just Amiah.

Except there was nothing *just* about her.

I could feel her love for me radiating through our now sealed soul bond, along with a soft breath of magic whispering through my cells, easing the agony imprinted in them.

And while I knew she was healing me subconsciously, I had no doubt she wouldn't stop if she realized what she was doing. She'd add more power even if it meant weakening herself for this final battle with the Shadow King.

Which was why I wasn't going to point out what she was doing. She might need all the healing magic she had to get all of us through this, and I didn't want to risk her draining herself before the fight had even begun.

I also had no idea if her new power was connected to her healing magic or not and if she'd go so far as to try to use it to save us if her natural reserves were gone.

The memory of that wild magic slicing inside both of us sent a shudder rushing through me and I clamped down on it, not wanting her to see my fear. But she must have sensed my worry because a hint of concern flickered in her eyes, making my heart clench.

I could still feel that strange wild magic inside her. It was muted as if she'd managed to create that door inside of her that Prince Seireadan had begged her to make. But I could still sense the magic leaking into her and knew if she used it without training, it would kill her.

And that couldn't happen.

Not after I'd just found her.

I'd been lost for five hundred years, kept by my master because I entertained him, with nothing to live for and no way to die.

And now I had everything to live for and was facing almost certain death.

With Amiah, I belonged. I was trusted and could trust, was loved and could love back without fear. And while I was still wary of the others, I had hope. Something I hadn't had in a very long time. Prince Seireadan had said I was Amiah's mate just as much as the rest of them were, and none of them, not even Titus, had been hesitant to have me in their bed and share our mate.

"So," Cassius said, his arms around Amiah, holding her close, but not as if he wanted to protect her from me, but because he wanted her near.

I could relate. My soul sang with joy and certainty and all she was doing was holding my hand.

I dragged my focus back to Cassius. His magic was still enormously powerful to my sin eater senses, but now it was contained by that same strange magic I sensed leaking from Amiah. She'd healed whatever had been wrong with him when she branded him, just like she'd given me a new life and something to fight for when she'd branded me.

"You know Deaglan the best," Cassius said to me. "What kind of fight are we looking at? How many men could he bring to the temple?"

I turned to the prince. "How long can he wait to claim the Heart, your highness?" If the Shadow King had all day to get there, even if Faerie tried to keep him from the temple, he could march thousands of soldiers across the Wilds to get it.

Hawk groaned. "You've got to stop calling him that. It'll give him a fat head."

"Too late," Cassius said.

The prince huffed. "Yeah, well, Amiah loves my fat head," he shot back, his tone wicked, turning head into a sexual innuendo.

Hawk snorted at that. "I think she likes Rin's better. He let her finish."

The prince looked at me and I froze. Every instinct I had said this was a competition I didn't want to be involved in, not against a royal, while a small part of me urged me to say something, push back, see what happened.

"It was incredible," I forced out.

"I bet it was," the prince replied, not looking at all upset, "and you should drop the title. *Prince* Seireadan died three hundred years ago. I'm Sebastian Bane, sorcerer, magical items dealer, and mate to an angel."

"When this is done, we're going to have a talk about your magical items business," Cassius said, as if he were confident that we'd get through this — and I wasn't sure if he was or if he was pretending to be confident so he didn't scare Amiah.

"My business is your business. The only way this relationship is going to work is if we're all being honest with each other." The prince— no, *Sebastian*, chuckled at Cassius's shocked expression.

"He's going to be even more shocked when he learns your business isn't shady at all," Hawk said.

"Hey," Sebastian replied. "I worked hard to build up my shady reputation. Less people mess with you if they think you're dangerous."

His expression turned sober and an unsettled silence filled the bedroom.

We all knew what he'd thought and we'd all thought it when we saw his expression. The Shadow King was dangerous. The most dangerous man in Faerie. And the six of us were going to mess with his plans.

Sebastian raked a hand over his spiky white and silver hair. "Deaglan has to get the Heart at dawn. If he doesn't, the keys will dissolve and the Heart will go back to sleep. He'll then have to wait for it to reawaken and for the keys to become empowered again to get it."

"So we just hold him off until it's too late and the Heart goes back to sleep," Hawk said. "We can do that."

"But we'd just end up having to do this again when the Heart reawakens." Amiah's grip on my hand tightened and her gaze jumped to Titus. "This has to end."

"Agreed," Cassius said.

Hawk sat forward and glared at him. "Even if it puts Amiah in danger?"

"She's in danger either way," Cassius replied. "Getting the Heart now means not waiting for who-knows-how-many years for this mess to start again. And we have no idea when that would be. It could be a few years or it could be centuries. I don't know about you, but I'd like to start my life with Amiah knowing this is all behind us."

"Agreed," Sebastian said and the others nodded their agreement as well.

"That said," Cassius continued, "we have to remember that we're Amiah's anchors. If any one of us dies, she dies. So if it looks like there's no hope, we retreat."

If one of us dies, she dies? My pulse lurched at that and Amiah's attention jumped to me.

"It's my new power," she explained.

"To summarize, we need to have sex with her to keep her soul anchored in her body," Hawk said. "Pretty sure we can all manage that."

"So no self-sacrificing in the fight with Deaglan," Sebastian added, glaring at Cassius.

"You've already made yourself clear on that," Cassius replied. "Can we get back to figuring out what we're doing? It'll be dawn soon and I want to have at least the semblance of a plan and a chance to clean up and get dressed before we have to head out."

HAWK

WE CAME UP WITH A PLAN AND IT WAS TERRIBLE.

Sure, it was the best plan for our grim situation, but that didn't make me — or I'm sure any of the others — feel better about it.

The only upside in any of this was that Deaglan would have to rush to the temple when Faerie revealed it, and wouldn't have the time to march his whole army there. He'd choose to take his elite squad, which Rin assured us was a two hundred person unit of his fastest and most skilled fighters.

Two hundred was better than thousands, but the odds still weren't good, and with Amiah glowing and no one able to tell when she'd stop, we were going to have to put her in the middle of that mess. We couldn't hide her, and we needed everyone who could fight protecting the altar until we could either kill Deaglan or get the keys away from him. Which meant to keep Amiah safe, she had to be at the altar as well.

Rin had also said Deaglan had connections to at least two other sorcerers that he could convince or coerce into joining his fight. They weren't nearly as powerful as he was or Bane, but they could still cause problems. And while retreat was still a last-ditch option, no one really wanted it to come to that. Retreat would either postpone this mess for later or give Deaglan the Heart, not to mention since we were fighting in the middle of an open-air temple, we'd be surrounded which made retreating difficult. Especially if Deaglan's mages were holding Titus down and he couldn't fly us out of there and Bane couldn't teleport us.

So the plan was to try and trick Deaglan into thinking we were just going to hold the altar until it was too late for him to get the key. Bane would cast two spells on the altar. The first was a spell that prevented any shadow fae from hopping out of the altar's shadows — or mine and Amiah's shadows since we were going to be at the altar — which would force Deaglan's men to face us head on. But Bane would make the spell weak enough that Deaglan, with his superior magical strength, *would* be able to shadow hop to the altar. Hopefully that would be enough to hide Bane's real magical strength and to trick Deaglan into hopping to the altar and setting off the other spell, a containment spell, that locked Deaglan inside so Bane could take the keys.

And all of that depended on us getting to the temple faster than Deaglan and Bane casting the spells before Deaglan noticed, which Titus believed we could. All of which was one hell of a longshot that I didn't want to bet anyone's life on, especially Amiah's.

But we still had to face Deaglan. There wasn't any other option, and that was the best plan we had.

With that decided, we all headed to the bathroom to clean up and get dressed and wait for Titus and Amiah to sense the temple.

I hung back, letting the others go first, worry making my stomach churn. Worry over the fight and Amiah's survival, and worry about my relationship with her.

She needed me, and I needed her, and I didn't want to be afraid that she wouldn't brand me, that our relationship wouldn't be as complete as the relationship she had with the others. But I couldn't help myself, and it was all I saw when I looked at them.

The golden power of her angelic mating brands blazed up her left side from the middle of her thigh, up her ribs, and over her shoulder, and matching power radiated from the others: Cassius over his shoulder, Titus halfway down his ribs, and Bane from the middle of his ribs to his hip. Even the delicate golden swirls trailing over Rin's hip and thigh pulsed with the surety of a fully sealed bond.

Amiah stepped into the shower and turned her brilliant blue gaze to me, stealing my breath at the intense love in her eyes.

"Help me clean up," she said, extending her hand to me.

I took it and she gently tugged me into the magically warmed water. Our naked bodies brushed together and I captured her lips in a deep kiss, trying to show her how much I loved her, while not letting her see my fear — and if I was being honest, my jealousy, too.

This wasn't her fault. I knew she wanted to brand me. She'd already tried and failed. But I didn't want to accept that this was our fate, even if that fate made perfect sense.

God. I'd been an idiot not to see it by now.

I was an incubus.

I wasn't supposed to fall in love or get jealous. The others could. Branding them ensured a stable relationship with all five of them, but she had no need to brand me. I was supposed to be fine with having sex with her and not having our souls bound together.

"The Heart will make this right," she murmured against my lips, her eyes filled with a fierce determination. "I'm as much yours as I am theirs."

God, I wanted to believe her, wanted with every fiber of my being to believe that getting the Heart meant she'd stay in love with me.

I shoved that fear aside. I couldn't lose focus. I was going to enjoy all the time I had with her even if she fell out of love with me, and I sure as hell wasn't going to be so distracted that I let her get hurt during this fight.

Titus growled and I jerked my attention to him. He'd enjoyed sharing her with me, his sexual energy had been powerful and heady when we'd been making love, but there was still a chance some of his possessive predator nature would kick in.

But Titus wasn't looking at me and Amiah. His gaze was at the back of the bathroom.

"The temple has manifested." He leaped out of the bath and stormed, still naked and dripping water, out of the bathroom to the sitting room.

"Amiah, can you feel it?" Cassius asked.

She shook her head. "No. Not even a hint of cold."

Which meant we wouldn't have to worry about her being incapacitated and on the verge of hyperthermia.

"Thank God," Cassius breathed. "Now everyone, get dressed." He pulled one of the many sets of clothes off the rack by the doorway, handed it to Rin, and took another set for himself.

My pulse leaped into a wild thrum and I gave Amiah another hard, fast, passionate kiss.

This was it. The final battle that we couldn't run away from and couldn't lose.

TITUS

I MARCHED INTO THE SITTING ROOM AND SHIFTED, MY LARGE DRAGON FORM shoving cushions and tables aside to make room for me. A powerful heat had swelled in my chest and I suddenly knew where the temple of my people lay in the ever-changing Wilds.

Amiah had said she hadn't felt when Faerie had revealed the temple. And while she looked fine in the bathroom with no shivering or passing out like she had when the keys had been empowered, the second I took my dragon form, my telepathy connected with her and I could hear her thoughts. She was fighting her fear that something would happen to us, as well as fighting an almost overwhelming terror of being held against her will again, and it made me furious that she even knew what that fear was.

And yet when she hurried out of the bathroom with the others, her expression remained stern and determined. She would fight through her fear and would do what had to be done just like she always did.

I bit back a snarl. She shouldn't have to fight her fear. Hell, she shouldn't be in a situation where she was afraid, and every instinct I had, both man and beast, hated the idea of bringing Amiah into this fight.

I'd lost everything the last time the Heart had awakened, and I hadn't thought I'd ever have a pack again or that I'd find my soul's mate.

But somehow fate had given me this precious second chance, and it didn't matter that Amiah or the others weren't dragons. They were mine and I wouldn't let the Heart or Deaglan take that away from me again.

Except that meant we had to face the Shadow King as a pack. All of us together. No matter how much I wanted to argue with Amiah that she needed to stay behind.

Her healing and her ability to take the life force energy of Deaglan's assassins could be the deciding factor in this fight.

Except that didn't make me feel any better. My mate was going to be in the middle of a war. And while I knew she was as strong-willed as a dragon, she wasn't a warrior, she was a healer.

"I don't care if I get to kill the Shadow King," Rin whispered, as he attached his swords to his belt. "You," he said to me, "have as much claim to his life as I do."

Seireadan also has a claim, I said in everyone's head as Seireadan, Hawk, and Rin climbed onto my back, and Amiah and Cassius released their wings with a flash of angelic light. *Deaglan poisoned him and left him for dead here in the Wilds.*

"Well I don't care who kills that asshole," Seireadan said, "just so long as someone does."

"Should we worry about what the Shadow Court will do to the court's high fae when he dies?" Amiah asked, reminding us that when a court monarch died, the court tore through the remaining high fae to find someone strong enough to control it and take the throne. "Does Deaglan have an heir?"

"He doesn't," Rin replied, "but there are at least two shadow fae strong enough to hold back the court who are currently in hiding and who've eluded His Majesty's assassination attempts."

A shudder swept through the stillness coming from his mind, but I wasn't sure over what. I didn't naturally hear his thoughts like I could Amiah's, and I suspected I'd have to push past a strong mental barrier to hear them.

Which I wouldn't because he was one of Amiah's mates and that was rude.

When we got the Heart — and we *would* get it — I knew Amiah wasn't going to use it to free Rin. It was clear they both realized their soul bond wasn't the nightmare she'd thought it was, and while Rin was still permanently connected with her, I knew from the way he glanced at her when he thought we weren't looking — or maybe when he stopped worrying that we were looking — that he was hers and she his.

"I'm sorry he hurt you for not killing them," Amiah said, as if she'd known what he was thinking, and with their soul bond, perhaps she did.

"It is what it is." He met her gaze and the hint of a smile lightened his eyes. "And it's over now."

"Not quite yet," Cassius said, stretching out his wings and jumping out the window. "First, how long is it going to take to get to the temple? Bane, do you need protection from the Wilds? Does Amiah since she's still glowing like a high fae?"

Probably not a bad idea, I replied in everyone's head, following Cassius out the window and spreading my wings wide to catch an updraft and soar away from the aerie. *I don't know if Faerie wants us to get there quickly or not.*

"One protection coming up," Seireadan said.

"You sure you're up for this?" Hawk asked. "Your magic is still low and you've already committed to casting a containment spell and a spell to prevent shadow hopping. The last time you tried to take Deaglan's keys he almost killed you. Stop wasting your magic. You have to survive this mess, too."

"The spell preventing Faerie from ripping out mine and what's left of Amiah's fae magic is temporary, and I'll use one of my glyphs to focus it so it doesn't take up as much magic," Seireadan said with a huff. "And look a little deeper, Mr. Sensitive. Remember, I'm keeping as much as possible back so Deaglan doesn't know how powerful I actually am and I can catch him off guard. I'm a lot more powerful than I look right now."

"Good," Cassius said. "I think you have to be the one who has to fight him. He can redirect my fire and bind Titus and Rin with shadows. We'll back you up as best as we can, but we're better off dealing with the couple hundred men he brings with him."

I turned east toward the hint of pink that was starting to edge the horizon and Amiah and Cassius turned with me.

Below us, steamy heat already rose from the Wilds' jungle even though the day had barely started, and the vegetation was thicker than I'd ever seen it before with no patches of wasteland scattered amongst the trees.

"Final thing," Cassius said, his angel glow flaring as he glanced at Amiah. "I think our first strike should be Amiah trying to take the life forces of Deaglan's army."

"No way in hell," Hawk snapped back. "It's too dangerous. It's bad enough you want her in the center of this mess."

"That first strike will be the only time it's safest. We'll all be close and able to touch her. Even if she doesn't connect and kill any of them, that quick first strike should help to thin Deaglan's army or drain him, and either one would be extremely helpful."

"It's okay," she said to Hawk even as her worried thoughts grew stronger. "There are only six of us. We need every advantage we can get."

"Now that you actually have a mental door to control your power, I'll be able to help you a bit," Seireadan said. "You'll only need to open it a crack and you don't have to connect to everyone. Connecting with a few of Deaglan's men will do, especially if we can target the other sorcerers. Deaglan will probably work harder to protect them more than his foot soldiers."

Hey, I said in her head, drawing her brilliant gaze to mine and making my heart skip a beat. I didn't think I'd ever stop being awed that this incredible woman was my mate. I didn't think any of us would. *I won't let anything happen to you.*

I know you won't, she replied, but her fear stayed strong, a heavy darkness that encroached on her thoughts despite her determination to be brave.

After that, we flew in grim silence. We all knew what we had to do and we all knew what was at stake. And while Seireadan and I were the only ones from Faerie, I had no doubt that the others knew Deaglan wouldn't be satisfied with just reigning over this realm.

We reached what should have been the edge of the temple as the sun crested the horizon. I could sort of see the temple's massive crater, sloping toward the wide, flat stone altar at the center, and caught a glimpse of one of the four dragon statues that marked the edge of the temple. But the jungle had overtaken most of it with the trees and vines crowded down the slope where the elders used to sit to observe our most sacred rituals.

Of course, the last time the temple had been used had been years before the Heart had awoken the previous time, and now with only one dragon remaining, there was no one left to perform our rituals.

My throat tightened at the thought, making my fire curl into my chest. I'd been a long way off from becoming an elder, so I'd never been taught the rituals and had only ever attended one ritual with my grandmother when I'd been a child.

But even if I knew the rituals, would there even be a point?

Faerie was already letting the Wilds reclaim the land. It had decided that I alone wasn't enough to keep my species alive. The only reason the aerie probably hadn't been overgrown was because of the magic protecting it from the Wilds, and in time those protections would fade and even the aerie would be gone, too.

I flew to the center of the temple, my beast furious that this was the fate of my people, fading away and soon forgotten. It had been foolish of dragons to think they could protect the residents of Faerie from their own greed, that it was even their duty to try. The cost had been too great. It had been everyone I loved and five hundred years in captivity by someone who I'd thought had been a friend.

Below me, the altar, a large flat stone that was as wide as a dragon's wingspan hadn't been taken over yet, but vines and shrubs crowded close and there was barely enough room for me to land without actually landing on the altar itself. The stone was engraved with the symbols of our primal natures: fire, water, earth, and air, the water and air symbols soft and flowing, reminding me of the delicate golden lines of Amiah's mating brand embedded in my skin.

My fire curled tighter and a growl bubbled in my throat. I couldn't lose my soul's mate in this fight and I couldn't lose my pack. I had to protect them with everything I had, even if that meant foregoing my revenge on the monster who'd betrayed me and kept me a prisoner unable to shift for five hundred years.

"Can I clear some of this growth away?" Cassius asked, giving me the respect of asking first before releasing his fire into one of my people's most sacred places. "It'll be easier to fight if those who don't have projectile weapons have to cross an open space before they get to us."

I answered by spitting a ring of fire into the overgrowth around the altar. Cassius followed, adding to my ring, creating a massive wave of hot air that rushed over us, and sent the fire sweeping out in a great circle, burning the vegetation with flames so hot even the thickest tree trunks started to crumble and turn to ash.

I landed, sending a cloud of ash billowing around my feet, and knocked over the remains of a nearby trunk with my tail. Seireadan, Hawk, and Rin, hopped off my back and Amiah and Cassius landed beside them and pulled their wings back into their bodies with a flash of angelic magic. I didn't bother shifting. I was more powerful in my dragon form and returning to my human form before the fight was just a waste of time. We hadn't even brought clothes for me, since I'd probably end up shifting and that would just ruin a perfectly good set of clothes. But even if I had to shift into my human form, I didn't care about clothes. It didn't matter if I ended up fighting naked. I'd done it before and I could do it again.

Cassius swept his gaze over the area around us. "Eyes open, everyone. We may have gotten here first, but I doubt Deaglan will be far behind."

A low dark laugh echoed in the temple's natural amphitheater, making my fire burn hotter in my throat and the ridges on my neck rise. That laugh used to mean Deaglan was paying me a visit to remind me I was only useful as a compass to find the keys and unlock the Heart, that I'd been a fool to trust him, that no one was looking for me, and everyone in my pack was dead.

Well now I had a new pack, and I would be damned if I let him kill any of them.

AMIAH

Deaglan's laugh echoed around us, amplified by the temple's natural acoustics and without a doubt a little magic, making it impossible to tell which direction it was coming from.

I raked my gaze over the jungle, now a hundred feet beyond a circle of ash, as my new magic seeped past the door inside me and connected with over a hundred dark, thick, shadow fae life forces that were positioned all around us in the jungle, any of which could have been Deaglan.

There were also another eighty or so life forces that were a mix of shifters and demons, and while I knew my guys were strong, I couldn't quiet that little voice of fear that cried that I was going to lose them, that I was going to be trapped in darkness, forgotten, and helpless, and no one would come to save me.

"You really think you got here first?" Deaglan asked. "I knew you were a fool, Seireadan, but do you honestly think you can beat me at anything? You're slow and weak. You haven't grown in strength since I fucked your fiancé, and you won't be strong enough to stop me from fucking your wife."

Titus snarled and bared his teeth, making Deaglan howl with laughter.

"Of course, you probably won't mind," Deaglan sneered. "It's obvious you're already letting that animal fuck her and probably the incubus, too. Are you also sharing her with the angel and my assassin?"

"There are over a hundred shadow fae," I whispered, keeping my voice low and hoping Deaglan wasn't also magically eavesdropping on us. "And at least eighty others, a mix of shifters and demons."

"Swell," Sebastian said, as he turned to cast the spell on the altar to prevent Deaglan's shadow fae from using its shadow to surround us.

"Shit," Hawk hissed. "Incoming." He grabbed Sebastian's shoulder, not bothering to say what the spell was and choosing to just show Sebastian by making contact with him.

Sebastian also swore and a small glyph along his right side burst to life as a cloud of shadows crashed around us. The shadows forced all of us except Titus to our knees before Sebastian shot a stream of light through the cloud, tearing it apart.

"Amiah, now," Cassius hissed, as he grabbed my wrist, yanked me to my feet, and shoved me against Titus's side.

The others jerked up as well, grabbing my hands and wrists, their life forces surging against my senses. My soul snapped closer into alignment, close but not quite perfect, and my pulse roared in my ears with fear, as Sebastian slipped a tendril of icy magic into my chest and around the core of my new power.

It didn't matter that we still couldn't see any of Deaglan's men or that I had no idea which of the life forces belonged to the other sorcerers or even Deaglan. It didn't even matter if I could break through Deaglan's shields protecting his men's souls like I had when I'd tried to save Cassius, or that my goal was to kill as many of them as I could to help even the odds. I'd deal with the emotional and psychological fallout of killing them later. This was going to be my only chance to safely use my power, and the only opportunity to catch Deaglan unaware, and I had to do whatever it took to stop him.

I quickly brought to mind the plain heavy door that I'd imagined when Sebastian had begged me to create it while my magic had been consuming me.

Golden light radiated around the edges, seeping from the cracks between the door and the nothingness surrounding it as if even my imagination was staying true to the fact that I hadn't fully contained my power. I could feel the magic on the other side, an enormous fiery pressure waiting to break free and sweep me away, but I could also feel the life forces of my guys keeping me steady and the strength of Sebastian's magic ready to help me.

And the second I thought about opening the door, it burst open.

Oh, my God.

Power roared out of me and my senses snapped, suddenly hyper focused. I could feel the power in the life forces of Deaglan's men and I could feel the shields protecting them. I could also feel the life in the lush vegetation and all the creatures and bugs hidden within, and even a low-level hum of life in the Wilds itself. There was life everywhere, completely surrounding me for as far as I could sense.

My senses swept farther and farther away on a massive wave of power that burned around my heart and for a second there was only a brilliant golden radiance and life, so much life, flooding over me, in me, through me, whipping me around and around and around.

Then Sebastian's icy magic shoved my door mostly closed and wrenched my soul back into my body, and I heaved my attention to Deaglan's men, ramming my power against Deaglan's shields not bothering to search for a weak point. I didn't have to get in. I just had to make Deaglan use more power to keep reinforcing his shields before he retaliated and forced my guys to start fighting.

"So that's your big plan?" Deaglan called in a singsong. "Make your bitch fight your battles, Seireadan?"

Power swelled into the shields, thickening them and muting the life forces and a whirlwind of shadows crashed around us. Sebastian's icy power inside me flickered as he swept up a shield, and my door crashed open again.

Golden magic roared out of me, burning through my magical channels and heating my skin, and punched through the shields of a quarter of Deaglan's men. It seized their life forces, filling the amphitheater with screams of agony, and flooded me with more power, writhing, churning life. It stole my breath and seared through me, adding to the pressure and fire inside me with no place to go.

I fought to release it and close the door, but the power I was ripping out of Deaglan's men needed to be used and I had nothing to heal.

For a second, darkness and cold enveloped me, freezing me, trapping me, stealing all breath, my soul crying for help, to be free, to be remembered.

Then Sebastian's magic swept back in, bringing me back, but

Deaglan roared with rage. His whirlwind tore through Sebastian's shield, crushing me against Titus's side and tearing the others away from me.

My soul shuddered farther out of alignment, but Sebastian twisted some of the extra magic pouring into me and used it to slam the door shut before my magic could consume me. I sagged to my knees, mentally fighting to keep the door shut, as Deaglan's men rushed out of the jungle all around us, the demons and shifters first and the shadow fae popping up in the moving shadows created by their comrades.

Hawk scrambled to my side and helped me stand as Titus leaped up, flapped his wings, sending air and ash whirling around us, and flew toward a group with a dozen weretigers who were quickly closing the distance. Cassius also released his wings and took to the sky, while Rin, who'd been thrown thirty feet from me, stood, drew his katana, and waited for the enemy to come to him.

Sebastian, who'd also been tossed away, rose, and the large glyph that curled around his shoulder blade flared to life, glowing through his thin cotton shirt. But he didn't release the spell. Deaglan had yet to step out of the jungle and he had no idea where to aim, and the whole point was to lure Deaglan out so Sebastian could take the keys.

Another whirlwind of shadows swept toward me, and Sebastian grabbed his left forearm activating another glyph while still keeping the spell tattooed on his back ready. He sent a force-wave through the whirlwind, tearing it apart before it reached me and Hawk. But the whirlwind quickly reformed and slammed me against the side of the altar while tossing Hawk over top of it.

A shadow fae popped out of the shadow created by the altar, grabbed Hawk's arm, and rammed his knife into Hawk's side.

He screamed and my magic flickered to him, but his own rapid healing healed the injury before I could. Which was good, because even though I now had access to an enormous amount of power, I was still sure the rules from before still applied. Healing the others would take the least amount of magic, and healing Hawk and Rin would take the most. And now I wouldn't just run out of power when I was exhausted, I'd burn up.

Titus released a blast of fire into the midst of the pack of rampaging weretigers, and my healing magic surged to four of them who were on fire and badly burned.

I clenched my jaw, fighting to keep my power contained. I'd known going into this mess that staying in control was going to be the hardest part of this fight and yet I knew in my soul that this was where I had to be. Which was why I hadn't pointed out my situation when we'd been planning and most likely why Cassius, who was fully aware of how my magic worked, hadn't pointed it out, either. I couldn't stay behind in the aerie and wait to find out if one of my guys was dead, and I was damned well going to choose who I healed and not let my power turn in on me with any degree of backlash.

A hint of my magic leaked past my control and shot into one of the seriously injured weretigers, but I managed to wrench it back before fully making contact and healing him.

Titus released another blast, making my magic jerk again to two more seriously burned shadow fae, and a flurry of shadows shot out from the dense trees, seized him, and yanked him to the ground.

He landed on his feet and swiped his tail through a shadow rope, freeing one of his front feet then used his claws to tear into the other ropes. But more ropes formed, whipping around and around him, pinning him to the ground.

A dozen more weretigers in their beast forms bounded toward him while ten more shadow fae popped up in the shadow created by his large body.

He spat fire at the tigers, catching three of them in the direct blast — thankfully killing them quickly —while injuring half a dozen more who weren't fast enough getting out of the way, making my healing magic heave against my control toward them.

The shadow fae sliced in with their knives and somehow Titus managed to tear his tail free from the reformed shadow ropes and bat most of them away before they struck him. The blades of those who'd gotten out of the way slipped between his scales and sliced into his flesh, but not deep enough to really hurt him, only enough to make him roar with rage and blast flames at them, catching four of them who weren't fast enough to disappear back into his shadow.

I wrenched my gaze around the battlefield, looking for someone to help Titus break free of the shadow ropes, but Rin was completely surrounded, his black katana a deadly whirl of steel, efficiently killing fae and demons, while Cassius was fighting a flurry of shadow ropes from another sorcerer.

He swept his fire whip through them then sent a blast of fire at a pack of nagas — demons that were half man and half snake with red scales covering their bodies and their prehensile tails. The nagas, who were barreling across the charred ground toward the altar, jumped out of the way of the blast, but the split second he'd taken to fire at the nagas was enough for a shadow rope to seize his ankle and yank him out of the sky.

He sliced through the rope, just before he hit the ground, and a shadow fae popped out of his shadow and jabbed at him. With a grunt, he wrenched back and shot a blast of fire into the fae's face. The fae screamed and staggered back as more shadow ropes rushed out of the jungle and snared Cassius.

Cassius twisted his arm around the ropes and yanked, heaving the sorcerer out of the jungle and into the open. It was a shadow fae woman with shadows undulating under her pale skin and curling around her, and her eyes were hard with determination.

She sneered as two more shadow fae popped out of Cassius's shadow and attacked him, and a werebear barreled into him.

My heart leaped into my throat as they tumbled to the ground, but movement out of the corner of my eye caught my attention. It was close. Right beside me.

I jerked to the side as a shadow fae grabbed for me. The back of my thighs hit the altar as my healing magic snapped to someone behind me, and I lost my balance and fell onto the flat, intricately carved stone.

Hawk jerked the knife he'd thankfully stolen out of the stomach of a shadow fae — the injury that had just yanked at my magic — and ducked out of the way of a green-skinned demon who was swiping at him with her razor-sharp claws.

My power heaved and snapped, screaming to be released, to heal all of them, now now now. More divine magic leaked past my door, the pressure inside me making it bulge.

I wasn't going to last much longer, not without concentrating on my guys' life forces or touching one of them, and right now it was all I could do to hold on and avoid the shadow fae attacking me.

He reached to grab me again, and I kicked at him, managing to hit him in the chest, making him stumble. I tried to scramble away, but another shadow fae leaped at me, seized my ankle, and yanked me off the altar.

My head cracked against the altar's side and darkness swept through my consciousness, squeezing around me, immobilizing me. My soul screamed for help, but I knew no one could hear me, no one was looking for me, no one even knew I existed.

Then my divine power flashed, a brilliant golden light against the back of my lids, and a spark burst past my door and swept healing magic into the injuries of everyone within the temple's radius.

Men and women screamed and shifters howled and roared with the sudden, painful, blast of magic that wrenched their cells back to the way they used to be.

"Fuck," Hawk hissed on the other side of the altar. "Just stay down."

The shadow fae who'd yanked me off the altar, grabbed for my throat as my healing magic lurched to the green-skinned demon attacking Hawk and the fresh laceration across her arm.

No. I won't heal them. I can't. We can't lose this. I tried to get out of the way while heaving my power back again. But the fae grabbed my hair, yanked me back, and wrapped a hand around my throat.

I clawed at his wrist and kicked him in the groin. His grip loosened for a split second, then a knife flew through the air and landed in his temple with a heavy, wet *thunk*.

The fae's eyes rolled back and he collapsed. I shoved him away and scrambled to my feet, my gaze jumping in the direction from which the knife had come. Rin. He decapitated another man, with one swift swing, dropped to one knee, grabbed another knife from the pile of bodies around him, and tossed it. It flew past me and killed a shadow fae rushing up behind Hawk, while Hawk was busy fighting two others.

"Fuck. I wish Bane had gotten that spell on the altar," Hawk hissed, breaking the knee of one of his assailants with a swift kick then scrambling back over the altar to my side.

I jerked my attention away from him to look for Sebastian. He was still fifty feet away and surrounded by a ferocious shadow storm. More glyphs on his body blazed with power, making it possible to see him through the storm of shadow, ash, and debris flying around him.

"I can't believe you're a coward," Sebastian screamed into the vortex as he sent a blast of light tearing through the storm.

But the storm quickly reformed and shoved him to his knees.

"Staying behind cover isn't cowardice," Deaglan yelled back, his voice booming around the temple and making my ears ring. "It's what you should have done. Do you honestly think you can keep me from reaching the altar?"

And right now, there wasn't anything stopping him. In fact, we'd been hoping he'd make a run for it so Sebastian could grab his keys before he could release the Heart.

So why wasn't he jumping through the shadows like his assassins? Did he know Sebastian was hiding his true strength?

Hawk grabbed my arm and jerked me out of the way as a shadow fae lunged for me.

"Eyes on *our* fight, gorgeous," he said. "They can handle themselves."

He jabbed his knife at the fae's stomach, but the fae, a man with a thick scar running down his cheek, sidestepped, and slashed Hawk's forearm.

My magic snapped to him, wrenching against my control, then wrenched to the shadow fae Titus was still fighting, then to Cassius. Cassius had been hit with a shadow spear and was bleeding profusely. And while I could feel him still fighting, the strength was draining out of him.

I released a blast of healing magic, fighting to soften it while still being quick. But another shadow fae popped out of the shadows beside me, grabbed my arm, and Hawk cut his throat, making my healing magic split and slam into Cassius while also crashing into the shadow fae.

He screamed as I healed him and the ghostly whirl of my ferocious life force magic surged, connecting with his shadowy life then spinning my senses, reaching out to everyone in the temple again, reminding me of the golden light inside that would consume me if I couldn't control it.

I heaved my soul and power back into my body and yanked on the soul of the shadow fae I'd just healed.

The fae screamed, his eyes wide, as my magic tore out his life force, but the sudden addition of power shot cracks through the door inside me, and more divine power leaked out of me as the man dropped dead at my feet.

I stumbled back and hit the edge of the altar. Two more shadow fae popped out of the altar's shadow, not giving Hawk a chance to catch his breath.

God, there were so many, and my door just kept getting weaker.

Help me. Remember me. Save me.

I scrambled to find my connection with my guys and keep my soul in my body, but there was too much I had to focus on, and with the roar of my healing magic wrenching me this way and that, threatening to turn inward and consume me with a crushing backlash, I couldn't sense them. I wasn't sure I could sense anything.

The only way I was going to ground myself was with physical contact.

I jerked forward to touch Hawk, but a shadow fae scrambled over the altar, grabbed my hair, and yanked me back.

Hawk screamed, and far off behind him, Rin saw the fae attack me and his eyes widened. He seized a knife out of another fae's hand and threw it. The dagger hit the fae holding me between the eyes, killing him, but another fae jumped onto the altar beside me and clamped a metal collar around my neck.

AMIAH

THICK DARK POWER EXPLODED AROUND MY NECK, SANK INTO MY SKIN, AND surged around my heart. It blotted out the golden magic within me with a crushing pressure that stole my breath then rushed through my veins and flooded every inch of my body.

Hawk grabbed the back of the shirt of the fae who'd collared me and pulled him off me, and I grabbed the collar, desperate to get it off. But it was perfectly smooth, sealed by magic. There wasn't even a catch for me to try to pry open.

I was trapped, the weight of Deaglan's shadows getting heavier and heavier.

I fought to breathe against the pressure, fought to focus my thoughts. I might not be able to get the collar off, but I wasn't going to helplessly lie there. Except I couldn't make myself move, couldn't get off the altar, could barely hold on to the collar with muscles that were getting weaker by the second.

Hawk killed the fae who'd collared me. My healing magic stuttered, connecting with the dying man for a second before Deaglan's sticky darkness overwhelmed that power too.

His eyes wide with fear and his hellfire blazing, Hawk scrambled onto the altar beside me, but two more shadow fae yanked him off.

Behind him, Rin bolted toward us, while Sebastian was being crushed by the shadow storm, his brilliant white magic sudden flashes that were consumed by the storm as quickly as my healing magic had been consumed by the collar.

A demon lunged into Rin's way and he decapitated her without losing his stride. Hellfire blazed in his eyes and terror leaked through our soul bond before it, too, was consumed by Deaglan's darkness.

Black specs swarmed my vision and my lungs screamed for air.

I gasped in a shallow breath. I had to get up, had to get to—

I had no idea who.

Everyone was fighting multiple assailants. Even Hawk, who was only a few feet away couldn't break free from the shadow fae attacking him. There was no one who could help me.

An onyx-skinned demon with long horns shot lightning at Rin. I tried to draw in another breath to warn him, but choked as Deaglan's shadows flooded up my throat and into my mouth.

The lightning hit Rin in the shoulder, making him stumble, but he kept running toward me.

"Bane!" Hawk screamed, his voice cracking with desperation as he fought to get to me.

The shadow storm surrounding Sebastian wrenched him up, slammed him back onto the ground, then went out. For a second I was relieved. The storm had vanished.

Then relief quickly turned into frozen fear.

Sebastian wasn't getting up and I couldn't tell with Deaglan's darkness threatening my vision and the distance between us if Sebastian was even breathing.

I strained to connect my healing magic with him, but I couldn't push through the shadows crushing my insides. It took everything I had just to keep breathing and stay conscious.

Then the shadows around the altar surged. They shoved Hawk and the shadow fae back, creating a man-sized cloud, and Deaglan stepped out. With a sneer, he hopped onto the altar, grabbed my hair, and yanked me to my knees like Balwyrdan had done when he'd been about to punch me in the face.

I weakly wrenched against Deaglan's grip and clawed at his hand, trying to get free with what little strength I had left. I wouldn't be afraid of this monster and I wouldn't let him imprison me. But my efforts made the darkness inside me swell and the burning in my lungs grew. Each breath was getting weaker and weaker, the trickle of air I was able to suck in not enough to sustain me, just enough to draw out my suffering.

The darkness in my vision grew and my soul started screaming.

Help me. Free me. Please. Please.

White light blazed across my vision and Deaglan jerked me up into the path of the light. He clamped a hand under my jaw and held me against his body as a shield. The light rushed around me and poured into Deaglan, but the shadows inside me swelled, increasing the pressure and sending agony tearing through me. On instinct, I gasped, about to scream, but couldn't draw in more than a shallow trickle of air, and my cry came out as a desperate, strangled whimper.

More shadows swept from the collar, flooding around my head, choking me and darkening my vision.

Free me. Please. Help.

Sebastian's magic leaped from Deaglan to me, clawing at the shadows, drawing more agony, but unable to break through.

Deaglan howled with laughter. "Go on," he sneered. "You can't free her. You can't even kill her. You'll just make her suffer."

Sebastian wrenched his magic back and I fought to clear the specks from my vision and stay conscious.

Before me, Hawk stood in a standoff with three shadow fae between him and me, all of them glaring at each other, and all of them breathing heavily from the exertion of the fight. Sebastian stood forty feet away, all of the light in his tattoos gone and blood trickling down the side of his face from a laceration in his hair above his temple, and I had no idea if he was still trying to act weak or if he actually was now.

Beside him, Rin fought, his katana never stopping, blood splattering his clothes, hands, arms, and face, as he protected both himself and Sebastian so Sebastian could battle Deaglan. Behind them, close to the edge of the jungle, Cassius dropped a massive pillar of fire on the sorcerer he'd been fighting, along with a dozen of Deaglan's men, and took back up into the sky.

I'm coming, Titus said in my head as he roared from somewhere behind me. *Just hold on.*

"Bend your knee, Seireadan. Recognize me as the King of Faerie and I'll let you live," Deaglan snarled. "I'll even let you watch me fuck your wife so you know she's still alive."

"Kill me and you kill her," Sebastian called back. "We're soul bonded."

"That won't save you. My collar will keep her alive." The shadows inside me weakened, allowing me a desperate, shallow gasp while still smothering all my magic before swelling back into an agonizing pressure. "She'll go insane, but I don't need her sane to use her power or her body."

Help me. Please.

Cassius flew toward me at top speed, sweeping a massive swath of fire through Deaglan's men as he went and drawing screams of agony that should have made my healing magic lurch inside me, desperate to save those being burned alive. But I felt nothing. Not even a glimmer of my power.

"Bend a knee or I'll make her suffer for as long as it takes you to fade."

Behind me, Titus roared again and Deaglan jerked us around. "Back off, beast."

Shadows surged from the collar and enveloped my head, completely cutting off my air.

Please. I can't be trapped anymore.

Hold on, Titus said in my head, his mental voice sharp with fear. *We'll free you.*

A trickle of icy power whispered along my ribs in Sebastian's brand. Hope fluttered in my chest. He couldn't break Deaglan's spell on me from a straightforward attack, so he was going to try to break it from the inside.

But at the same time, I could feel the crackle of power from the keys inside Deaglan, a brilliant white power so much like Sebastian's and yet more raw and primal. It was Faerie's core tinged with the ferocity of the entire dragon race, and the Shadow King was activating it and going to release the Heart.

The icy brightness in my brand grew, but I knew Sebastian wasn't going to be fast enough. He wasn't going to be able to save me *and* stop Deaglan. It was one or the other.

I tried to scream at them to stop Deaglan, but only a gurgling whimper escaped my lips, and the darkness inside me surged stronger. God, I didn't want to pass out. I didn't want to be helpless.

Titus, please. Sebastian has to stop Deaglan. Now, I mentally cried.

I turned my gaze to Rin. *Stop Deaglan. Please.*

I strained to put everything I had into those thoughts. Titus could hear me, but I didn't know if he'd relay my message to Sebastian, and while Rin and I couldn't communicate telepathically, I was able to get a strong sense of what he was feeling and why. I could only hope the connection went both ways. *Please, stop him!*

The shadows clamped down, stealing the last of my air. Darkness crushed around and in me, cold and encompassing, and squeezing me tight. I couldn't move and couldn't breathe.

Help me. Please, help me.

Then a brilliant light tore through the darkness. Joy flooded me. I was free. I hadn't been forgotten. I was—

The light clenched tight, binding me as securely as the darkness. I wrenched against it but couldn't move. I clawed and screamed and fought, but the light was as powerful as the darkness had been and my screams were devoured by the void I'd been imprisoned in for too long. I strained to reach past the light, to connect and found—

Me?

Which didn't make any sense. I was trapped... except I wasn't trapped. Deaglan's darkness was suffocating and immobilizing me, but I hadn't been crushed in a void, locked away for an eternity.

At the thought of it, the shadows inside me swelled, overwhelming my new blinding prison—

Except it hadn't been *my* prison. It had been someone else's.

My pulse stuttered with realization and a glimmer of golden magic swelled around my heart. I connected with life forces. *All* life forces. I'd sensed the life forces of every man and women and creature within the temple. I'd even sensed the life in the vegetation and a low-level tingle of life from the Wilds itself. I knew if I went there, or God, even just broke free of Deaglan's spell and stretched my new senses, I'd be able to feel the life of all the high fae in their courts and the life force of the courts themselves.

Faerie's Heart wasn't just a powerful magic for Deaglan or anyone else to control. It *was* Faerie. Somehow, a long long time ago, someone had ripped out the realm's actual heart not realizing what it really was, and the dragons, also not knowing, had just locked it away. It was actually a miracle that the high fae sorcerers from all the courts hadn't banded together to destroy the Heart because they would have inadvertently destroyed their entire realm.

A spear of icy magic shot through the shadows inside me, then another and another, tearing through Deaglan's spell.

I gasped, drawing a desperate breath, and the collar shattered in my hands. My magic roared to life and I instantly connected with Faerie. I had no idea how I hadn't realized how seriously it was injured. The shattered Autumn Court with its broken and twisted landscape where there was no up or down or even a horizon, was only a fraction of the festering rot slowly consuming the realm. All the courts had erected barriers, trying to hold themselves together. They tore through the high fae, ripping out the fae's magic until someone was strong enough to withstand them, because Faerie was trying to keep itself alive and needed more magic to sustain itself.

"Too little too late, Seireadan," Deaglan sneered, and the ferocious power of the Heart surged inside him. It was all the power of the realm, not just a direct connection to it like what he had with his sorcerer's ability, a highway that allowed the power to flood into him while protecting him from the dangers of burning up.

He could do anything without cost to himself with just a thought, and that was something I couldn't allow. No one should have that kind of power. Especially a monster like Deaglan.

I had to get the Heart away from him and I had to heal the realm. And I couldn't hesitate. I couldn't use the Heart to do anything else, no matter how tempting it would be to remove the pain imprinted in Rin's cells or heal Cassius's heartache over the murder of his brother. I couldn't succumb to the temptation of keeping it, of using it to save lives, to heal the Autumn Court, to heal everyone.

Just like how the Heart had gone from its cold dark prison to one of light inside Deaglan, taking the Heart and using it, even using it for good, would keep it imprisoned. And really, where would I stop? Would I allow people to make foolish decisions and hurt themselves when I knew I could stop them?

I'd been right when I'd first sensed that the Heart was too powerful and that it would warp even the best of intentions. No matter what else I wanted, I couldn't keep or use the heart. The realm had to be healed.

And to do that, I had to get the Heart.

AMIAH

The Heart's power crackled around Deaglan, surging toward his heart, and I grabbed at the golden magic spilling around my door and shoved it into him. His grip in my hair tightened and he jerked my neck back to a painful angle.

"Don't even think about it, bitch," he snarled and the Heart's ferocious power slammed into me.

It ignited every cell in my body, filling me with an agonizing fire that tore a scream from my throat. Strength flooded through my soul bonds, and Sebastian shoved his magic inside me, fighting the Heart's power.

Titus divebombed Deaglan, but the Shadow King, without even looking, blasted power at him, tearing through one of his enormous leathery wings and sending him tumbling through the sky to the far side of the temple and crashing into the jungle.

My soul lurched and my healing magic snapped to him, but I wrenched it back. He could survive, his wing would heal, and I needed to take the Heart away from Deaglan. Now. It was the only way to end this and save my guys.

Hawk leaped onto the altar and lunged to grab me, and Deaglan blasted him with power, ripping a hole through his side and tossing him into Sebastian. The force sent them crashing into a group of shadow fae. Everything within me stalled and the world stuttered into horrific slow motion. Hawk's injury was too great, his enhanced healing wasn't going to save him and the shadow fae were lunging in to finish the job.

God, this had to stop. Please, make it stop.

Sebastian blasted the assassins with a force-wave, shoving them away from him and Hawk. His icy power protecting me weakened and the Heart's magic ripped back through my body, tearing a scream of agony from my lips.

"Hold on, Amiah," Cassius yelled, as he and Rin barreled toward me.

But I could feel the Heart's power building, readying another blast not because that was the only defense Deaglan had, but because it caused the most suffering. He could kill them with a thought, but he wasn't. He wanted to draw out the torture for as long as possible.

And that was unacceptable.

I released my hold on the door inside me and my divine magic roared out, tearing the door off its hinges and burning it up. The power blazed into the Heart's magic, twisting around it and blending into it. It exploded out of me and rushed into Deaglan.

Desperate to save Hawk, I managed to break off a thread of power, and shove a blast of healing magic into him with what I knew was a sudden painful blast, but I couldn't hear him scream. I couldn't hear anything beyond the roar of power consuming everything inside me.

Then my power wrenched me away from Hawk, and I was whirling in a vortex of both divine and healing magic. It latched onto the Heart inside Deaglan. That was the greatest injury my power could sense. The tear in Faerie's soul was greater than my guys' injuries or the men and woman from Deaglan's army who were dying in the open-air temple. And I *had* to heal it. The compulsion was overwhelming. Even if I wanted to resist it, I couldn't.

"You can't have it," Deaglan cried, his shadows twisting around and into the Heart, anchoring his soul inside it.

He blasted more power into me, trying to overwhelm my own magic and burn me up. The fire and pressure inside me grew, the agony blinding, filling my vision with a searing white light. It was consuming my body, both the Heart's magic and my own, and I'd become nothing more than a vessel for the divine power. A disposable vessel.

Far off, at the very edge of my senses, I could feel my guys' terror and desperation. It poured through our soul bonds but was quickly devoured by the fiery maelstrom raging inside me.

I tried to cry out to them, tell them that I loved them, tell them that I was sorry. I wanted to be able to control my power, and I knew I needed to connect with their life forces to save myself, but there was just too much power tearing through me that I couldn't concentrate enough to feel them.

I needed help. I needed them touching me.

But all I could do was try to hang on, and I knew even that wasn't going to be enough. The divine magic wasn't going to stop until Faerie had its heart back, and it was going to burn me and Deaglan up in the process.

Except Deaglan didn't have to die. If he released the Heart, my magic would rush out of him.

"Let go," I gasped. "My magic only wants the Heart."

"No," he screamed. "It's mine. My destiny. I won't let Seireadan have it."

"He won't," I gasped. "No one will."

"You can't destroy it. No one can." He swept more shadows into the Heart, strengthening his grip on it while shoving more of the Heart's burning brilliant power into me.

But that only made the maelstrom of divine magic surge stronger. It merged with the brilliant power with searing agony and devoured Deaglan's shadows.

"I won't let you have it," he screamed and he fully opened his sorcerer's connection to Faerie, not caring if it burned him up.

More shadows flooded in, but my magic consumed them as quickly as they formed then tore into Deaglan's essence. His dark thick life force flared and heaved, fighting to stay lit, but it wasn't strong enough to resist the ferocious primal power of the universe. Not even Faerie's magic was as strong as the golden magic that bound all the realms together.

It burned his life force and soul, drawing a howl of agony, and consumed his body, turning him to ash.

I sagged to my knees as the firestorm then consumed Deaglan's ash, destroying every last one of his cells, then turned in on me.

The Heart's power morphed into an agonizing backlash, making me howl in pain, and my divine magic raged out of control, even as my healing magic strained to return the Heart to the realm.

The golden power wrenched me this way and that, shredding my soul and tearing away chunks. It dragged me farther and farther from myself, numbing my body, thoughts, and soul. I'd find peace if I just let go. I'd join the primal power of the universe. I'd no longer be in pain. I wouldn't have my guys, but they'd get by without me. They were strong.

Except I knew they couldn't. The angelic mating brand would kill them or drive them crazy. Even Hawk who I hadn't branded would lose his mind if I gave in to the power devouring my soul.

I tried to heave against it, but I was small and weak compared to its endless power. I was a speck. Nothing compared to it. I couldn't fight the universe no matter how desperately I wanted to.

Then Titus and Rin grabbed my arms and their life forces surged against my senses, wrenching my soul back into my body. Agony roared through me again, but I clung to it, using the physical sensation as another anchor to keep me with them.

"Close the door," Sebastian said, his voice barely audible over the roar of power.

He interlaced his fingers with mine, adding more strength to my soul and heaving it closer into proper alignment.

I mentally searched for the door I'd made the first time, but it had been destroyed, consumed by the divine magic and the Heart.

Cassius shoved his hands under the back of my shirt and pressed his palms against my skin. His flesh was frozen against the fire inflaming my body even as his powerful fiery life force joined Titus's, Rin's, and Sebastian's life forces.

"Come on, sweetheart," Sebastian begged. "I can't do it for you."

"Please," Hawk said, cupping my cheeks and pressing his forehead to mine, adding his life force and yanking me closer into alignment.

I strained to focus so I could put the door back together. I had all five of my anchors touching me. I could feel their life forces straining to hold my soul in my body against the enormous power trying to rip me away.

Except I couldn't shut my magic away. Not yet. I had to put the Heart back where it belonged. I had to heal Faerie.

I heaved my focus to my healing magic and the agony of the realm exploded inside me. So much pain, tearing and slicing and burning without an end for so long. I didn't understand how I hadn't noticed its suffering before. How had no one noticed?

My thoughts jumped to Karthick half consumed by Faerie, pleading for the suffering to end even though he hadn't been in pain. It hadn't been his suffering he was begging me to heal. It had been Faerie's.

And I was the only one who could.

The thought steadied me and my guys' life forces swelled. Their fear and love and determination surged through our soul bonds, and I concentrated on holding onto them while my power roared out of me and into the Heart and Faerie.

Except my power needed more. Even with my connection to the divine magic fully open, my healing magic knew it wasn't going to be enough. My senses reached out to all of Deaglan's men, those too injured to flee and those in the jungle trying to escape. I connected with their life forces, then connected with the animals and foliage and bugs.

But my power didn't stop. I reached farther, needing more. If I had more, I wouldn't have to kill anyone. I could just take a little. Faerie had given a part of itself to every living being and thing in its realm, a tiny glimmer of magic imbued into every cell, and every life needed to give a little back to save it.

I reached in all directions, stretching farther and farther, my soul getting thinner and thinner. I couldn't stop its stretch, and the thinner I got, the harder it was to stay in my body.

"Amiah, stop, please," Hawk begged.

But I couldn't. I needed to connect with everyone and everything to properly place the Heart where it belonged without killing anyone.

Except if I didn't strengthen my soul, I was going to be swept away, and the only way my connection with my guys could get stronger was if one of them was inside me.

I dragged my eyes open and met Hawk's desperate gaze. The vortex of my power ripped the hellfire from his eyes, revealing how clear and gray-blue they were. Beautiful and unusual and amazing. He was the first one to fully accept me. He didn't care if Cassius and I were supposed to be mates. He'd said he'd make love to me anytime and anywhere, and he, out of all of my guys could handle this. Even terrified, he could make himself erect, and with his magic, he could make me wet and ready in an instant.

"I need you," I gasped. "I need a stronger anchor."

His magic flooded my core in response, slicking between my thighs and making me ache with sudden need despite the agonizing power raging inside me.

"Get her pants off," Hawk said, ripping out the laces of his fly and freeing his full erection.

Rin and Titus didn't question Hawk or hesitate. They tore open the sides of my pants with their claws and yanked the pieces away as Hawk ran a hand down his shaft, adding a glistening layer of lube.

Cassius grabbed my waist, lifted me up, and helped me slide onto Hawk's erection. He sank all the way in with just enough friction to heighten my desire before his life force surged inside me, fiery and dark and sensual. It stole my breath and for a second there was only him and me in the eye of a wild storm. A calmness filled the air around us, and need and love swelled around my heart.

Then the golden threads of my mating brands flared, adding the others' life forces to the mix and my soul snapped into perfect alignment. Divine power still poured out of me, intertwined with my healing magic and worked on joining Faerie with its heart, but my guys held me stable. I could do what had to be done. All I had to do was give in to fate's will and my magic's desires.

I let my power go, not fighting it. It stretched me farther, reaching to every corner in the realm, invading and connecting with all the courts and all the courts' residents and took a glimmer of power from all of them.

Then it surged back into me, channeling all the extra power and all the divine power into Faerie with a fiery blaze that threatened to burn me up even though I knew this was how it was supposed to happen.

I screamed, clinging to my soul and praying my magic would hurry up and heal Faerie before it burned me away. Hawk clutched me tight to his chest, and I buried my face in his neck, my tears evaporating the second they leaked from my eyes.

It was too much, too hot. But I could feel the Heart sinking into the fabric of the realm and I could feel my magic knitting the realm's life force back together and making it whole.

I just needed to hold on. Just a little longer. *Please, God. Just a little longer.*

Then the Heart fully sank back into Faerie, my power released me, returning to the core of my being, and the remaining fae magic I'd gathered sank into my cells. The realm's life force surged, strong and sure, enveloping me in a brilliant white nimbus, and a powerful *thu-thud* resounded through my soul, then another and another. The realm's heartbeat. Something I hadn't even known was missing.

Thank God.

No. Thank you, a soft voice whispered inside me. *I'm whole again.*

The nimbus swelled, turning into a gentle breeze that caressed my skin, wrapped around me, and became a silky, soft gown, and the light faded away.

I sagged against Hawk, exhausted and weak and sore, but not screaming in agony from what should have been horrible burns. My soul was also still fully intact, and my divine magic was now locked behind a new door inside me that was woven out of the golden threads of my soul bonds.

All *five* soul bonds.

I dragged my eyes open and my gaze was instantly drawn to the delicate golden lines glowing through Hawk's shirt around his heart. I pressed my palm to his chest, savoring the warmth and love radiating through the matching brand that I knew was overtop of my heart.

This was the way it was supposed to be and who I was supposed to be with. The angelic mating brand *was* sacred and beautiful. And it most certainly wasn't something that could be controlled. I'd been a fool to think I could.

AMIAH

WE RETURNED TO THE AERIE TO FIND KARTHICK SITTING ON THE FLOOR OF the pantry, a huge chunk of cheese in one hand and a half-eaten apple-like fruit in the other. Faerie had released him when I'd healed its life force and while he was still certain the realm wouldn't let him leave, he was more than happy to create a portal and send us back to the mortal realm when we were ready.

Too exhausted to do anything even just leave the aerie, we'd collapsed in a pile on the bed, and I slept soundly with my guys' life forces softly caressing my senses and singing through my soul bonds while Faerie's magic glimmered inside me.

I woke the next day with Cassius behind me, his arms wrapped around me, and Sebastian in front of me with his forehead pressed against mine. I could sense Rin's life force in the sitting room and Hawk's in the bathroom, and I could feel Titus, far off, soaring over the Wilds.

Somehow, I managed to ease out of Cassius's embrace without waking him or Sebastian — although from the exhaustion radiating through their soul bonds, it shouldn't have surprised me. Both of them had been expending enormous amounts of power for days. It was actually a miracle they hadn't collapsed before or during the final battle with Deaglan.

I was still in the soft white gown Faerie had made for me. Somehow, even though we'd all collapsed in bed covered in filth and blood, too tired to clean up, it was still pristine.

The skirt's soft fabric fluttered against my ankles as I tiptoed out of the bedroom and stepped into the warm, radiant sunlight streaming through the massive window.

Rin sat cross-legged in the sun, his demonic half protecting his vampire half from the harmful rays, his face turned into the light. He stood when I approached, and turned his attention to me, sending a shiver of desire and love rushing through me. His hellfire was back to smoldering red pinpricks and his expression without emotion, but the sense of harsh control was gone, replaced with a calm, comfortable stillness.

Out of all of my guys, he was the one I knew the least, and he would probably be the hardest to get to know. But we had a lifetime to figure it out, because he was mine and I was his. And even if I'd been able to use the Heart to break our soul bond, he would have refused. I'd been a fool to have ever thought our soul bond had been a mistake.

"You're still glowing," Rin whispered with his barely-there voice.

I glanced at my hands and the soft, fae glow still emanating from my skin. I had no idea if the magic would eventually fade from my system or not, but I could live with it if it didn't, especially when the alternative outcome had been losing some or all of my guys.

"Are you still claimed by a court or Faerie itself?" Worry whispered through our soul bond before being overwhelmed with a determination to fight to ensure I was free.

I stepped into the light with him and took his hand, interlacing our fingers as I searched inside me for a connection to one of the courts or Faerie. But the power inside me didn't feel like it chained me to anything. It felt more like the result of taking all that power from every life force in Faerie had permanently etched some of that magic into my essence.

"I'm free," I assured him. "But I think I'm going to be glowing for the rest of my life."

The worry coming from the bond changed to relief. "We all have scars."

My gaze dipped to the silvery scar across his throat, the wound that had killed him so Deaglan could turn him into a vampire.

Out of all my guys, Rin's scars were the worst, and his neck was the least of them.

Deaglan might have betrayed and locked up Titus for five hundred years, but he hadn't tortured my dragon like he'd tortured Rin.

"If you're up for it… when you're ready," I said, "there's someone who I think can help you."

I didn't know if Essie with her empathic healing magic would be able to heal everything, but I was sure she could help. And while I was still softly healing the pain embedded in his cells and knew that someday I'll have eased all of that pain, he still had psychological wounds that I couldn't heal.

"Although I'm not sure when we'll return to the mortal realm," I added. "I don't know if Sebastian or Titus will want to stay in Faerie for a little bit."

I didn't know if they still had things to take care of now that we weren't running for our lives. And while a part of me was fascinated by the realm, a stronger part of me just wanted to go home.

Except there was a chance home wasn't home anymore and Cassius and I would be forced to move out of Operations because we no longer worked for the JP. But all things considered, it wasn't much of a price to pay. My guys were alive and whole, and so was Faerie.

I have nothing here, Titus said in my head as his life force drew closer.

A second later, he soared around the mountain, flew through toward the wide window, and shifted. He landed before me, completely naked and I couldn't help but take in his large, muscular body.

"You're my pack," he said. "I go where you go."

"This is still your ancestral home. We should still figure out how we're going to visit." I held out my free hand to him, but instead of taking it, he wrapped me in a firm embrace, while still allowing for Rin and me to continue holding hands.

"I don't know if I want to," he said, his voice gruff. "I'm the last and being here is a constant reminder of that. Faerie was already reclaiming our temple. It'll eventually reclaim the aerie, too, and I won't insist that we live here just to keep the magic active." His grip around me tightened. "I doubt Padraigin has given up on her desire to have you as her personal healer and I won't risk your life for anything."

"I can keep the magic active," Karthick said from the doorway to our suite. "I might, in time, even be able to set up a private, permanent portal so you wouldn't have to travel to Faerie through one of the courts or use one of the unpredictable portals in the Wilds."

"That isn't necessary," Titus said.

Karthick shrugged. "Not everything has to be necessary."

"And what will we owe you for that?" Sebastian asked coming out of the bedroom with Cassius.

Titus released me and Cassius brushed his lips against mine before Sebastian drew up behind me, wrapped his arms around my waist, and tugged me into his embrace.

"All of Faerie owes your wife a debt it can't ever repay," Karthick said, and his lips quirked in a smile. "That and she's now not just a child of celestial light, she's also a child of Faerie. She'll always have a home here."

"So the glow won't go away?" Cassius asked.

"No," Karthick replied, his smile turning apologetic. "I realize that might cause some problems with other angels and those in the mortal realm."

"We can deal with it," Hawk said as he strode out of the bathroom, water dripping from his jaw-length sandy-blond hair onto his bare chest, and curling over the delicate golden lines swirling over his left pec. "And I bet she'll still light up when she's satisfied. Now the rest of you will be able to tell if you've done your job right."

"I don't need her glowing to know I've satisfied my mate," Titus huffed.

"None of us do," Cassius added.

Hawk shrugged and flashed me a wicked smile that unfurled a delicious, seductive heat low within me. "I think we should thoroughly test that theory to make sure."

"I think that's my cue to get out of here," Karthick said with a chuckle. "I'll be in the orchard. Call me when you want to portal back to the mortal realm."

We cleaned up and tested the guys' assumption that they knew how to satisfy me... multiple times, starting in the enormous tub then moving to a clean bedroom. We made love and ate and slept, recovering from our ordeal for another day, before we asked Karthick to return us to the mortal realm.

As expected, Priam and Chris hadn't managed to hide the fact that Cassius and I had abandoned our duties. Much to my surprise, however, after the Director of the Joined Parliament Bureau of Supernatural Law Enforcement had interviewed all of us personally — including Sebastian, Hawk, Titus, and Rin — he'd determined that given the circumstances, distancing ourselves from the JP and all civilians in the mortal realm had been necessary to ensure the least number of casualties.

We'd still been written up for not properly communicating and given a six-week suspension without pay, but given that we could have been fired or even arrested, being suspended and having that on our permanent records was more than acceptable.

And really, those six weeks off had actually been helpful for the six of us to figure out our new lives together in the mortal realm and to strengthen our soul bonds with a whole lot of intimacy.

Sebastian bought the seven-story building across the street from Operations — because there was no way in hell he was going to live there — and turned the top two floors into a penthouse apartment with lots of space for all of us. The primary team returned from their advanced training in Rome, and I gave Essie the apology I should have given her from the beginning. I hadn't realized just how insane finding my soul mates could be or what lengths I'd go to in order to keep them safe.

When the six weeks were done, Cassius, Titus, and Rin had all had a healing session with Essie and their emotional pain had eased — although every now and then, Rin still had flareups in his cells — and Rin and Titus had joined the JP. They, along with Cassius and Chris, made up an elite team that offered additional tactical and investigative support to JP teams all over North America.

I returned to Operations as the chief physician, and somehow — Sebastian suspected it was because I'd established mental control of my divine magic which also helped my healing magic — I managed to mostly control my healing compulsion, thankfully saving me from constantly healing people and exhausting myself whether I wanted to or not.

Sebastian and Hawk went into a legal, legitimate business together and had a new office on the main floor of our building. With their magical sensitivity, abilities, and knowledge, I had no doubt they'd be a success... not that any of us needed to work or be successful. Sebastian had more than enough money and investments to support our new family, and, much to everyone's surprise, it had all been legally obtained, which was a huge relief to Cassius.

On top of that, Priam reported that Voth hadn't been upset that we'd trashed his private suite. He understood that finding one's soul mate was a messy business, although he did make a point to point out that we were indebted to him.

And not at all surprising, Karthick sent word that Padraigin had completely taken the Winter Court from her mother. Healing Faerie had brought down the barriers between the courts and the Wilds, and the courts now had a stronger voice and could actually be heard by their monarchs, which so far had tempered a bit of Padraigin's cutthroatness. I still wasn't going to be visiting my fae in-laws anytime soon, but I had hope that eventually Sebastian would be able to have some kind of relationship with his family.

Now I sat in a lounge chair on our large-enough-for-a-dragon-to-land-on rooftop patio, soaking in the summer heat.

It was once again July, and I found it hard to believe that it had been a year since my life had been turned upside down and I'd found my five soul mates. They still surprised me and frustrated me and filled me with incredible joy, and I had a feeling it was going to be like that for the rest of our lives. Which was just fine with me.

Cassius chuckled, drawing my attention to him, Gideon, and Hawk standing on the far side of the patio around the barbeque about to fire it up to start dinner.

Gideon rolled his eyes at something Cassius said, and Cassius gave him the smile that I loved that had been missing since the war then sent a spark into the grill, lighting it.

Hawk laughed at the both of them and cooed something to three-month-old Dominic — named after Cassius's and Gideon's fallen brother — who he held in his arms.

The baby turned his bright blue eyes, filled with an angelic glow up to Hawk, smiled, and drooled down the front of Hawk's T-shirt.

The smile was new, only a few weeks old, and it melted my heart every time I saw it, especially since Dominic smiled at all of his dads.

I also had a feeling Dominic was going to melt a whole lot of hearts when he got older, because I could already tell he, like his twin sister, Imogen, was going to be stunningly beautiful.

But then their biological father was beautiful and they both clearly took after him, with a full-body fae glow, wisps of white-silver hair — that while it was falling out right now would come back beautiful and thick — and ears that extended into delicate points as if they were full fae and not half. They also had my bright blue eyes with my angel glow and little nubs just beside their shoulder blades that would eventually sink beneath their skin and become wings.

Technically, I wasn't supposed to be able to have children with anyone but Cassius. Angels could only conceive with other angels, but I wasn't entirely an angel anymore.

My full-body fae glow had dimmed but hadn't completely gone away, and while it wasn't noticeable in the light, it was obvious in dim or dark rooms and blatantly obvious after making love with the guys, since I still lit up like the sun when I orgasmed.

And while I didn't really care that Faerie had gifted me with an orgasmic light show, I loved that it had blessed me with Dominic and Imogen.

I slid my gaze to Imogen who dozed in Rin's arms while he lounged in the chair beside me, looking still as a statue and yet perfectly at ease. Love, satisfaction, and contentment radiated through our soul bond as he met my gaze. The bond was still the best way to tell what he was feeling, and even after living with him for a year now, he still remained soft spoken.

I knew he loved me. He showed me every day how deeply he cared for me with little thoughtful gestures and gentle smiles. I wouldn't have needed to sense his emotions through our soul bond to know he cared. But unless it was something extremely important to him, he still didn't speak up.

He gently rubbed Imogen's back and his contentment swelled stronger. He'd fallen in love with the twins the day they'd been born, all of my guys had even though genetically Sebastian was their father, and the twins, especially Imogen, found Rin's stillness, peaceful and calming.

The screen door on the patio slid open and Essie, Marcus, and Kol stepped into the sunlight carrying a couple cases of local craft beer, since neither Cassius, Gideon, or Hawk would stand for just regular beer, and a couple bags with a mix of white and rose wines because Sebastian, Rin, and I, and shockingly Titus, didn't drink beer.

Essie snagged a beer and dropped onto a lounge chair beside me and the guys took the rest of the drinks to the fridge built into the barbecue's station. She twisted off the cap, her gaze lingering on her guys, leaned back, and sighed, looking happy and content.

It had taken her a long time to get comfortable in her own skin and there were times when I saw a ghost of the fear that she'd lived with most of her life that people were going to hate and fear her.

She was a nephilim, an archnephilim actually — half archangel and half greater demon. She'd been made in a laboratory with dark magic intended to help eradicate all humans and supernatural beings from earth. And while she'd proven herself time and again that she wasn't the monster Michael and Lilith had wanted her to be, some people still looked at her with fear.

The thought made my chest tighten. People were going to look at the twins that way, too. They were clearly nephilim, half angel and half high fae. But, as much as I feared how the world would see my children, I also knew they had their aunt Essie to help them when things became confusing or difficult. They weren't alone like Essie had been during her childhood, and they didn't have to hide who or what they were.

Essie took a swig of her beer and leaned back in the chair, the movement drawing my gaze to the delicate gold swirls trailing from her wrist to her shoulder and across her collarbone to disappear beneath her tank top where I knew it curled around her heart.

"Does Hawk ever put Dominic down?" she asked.

"Only for diaper duty," Cassius said, grabbing a beer from Marcus "And then he's nowhere to be found."

"Hey, I change my fair share of diapers," Hawk said, "You're just pissed the last time you changed Dominic he pissed on you."

"Because whoever changed him last didn't point him down when they finished up," Cassius huffed.

"Follow the protocol and no one will get peed on," Sebastian snickered, making me wonder if he'd been the one to leave Dominic booby-trapped for Cassius... because now that our lives weren't in danger, neither Sebastian nor Hawk could completely resist pushing Cassius's buttons.

And really, Cassius didn't mind. It was just how our family worked, and he managed to get in a few good jabs of his own, so it wasn't completely one-sided.

Essie chuckled and turned her attention to me. Both the angel glow and hellfire in her eyes flared and a small smile tugged at her lips. "So, are you going crazy yet?"

"It's actually going pretty good with the six of us. Each of us only has to deal with one-sixth of the diapers and we each get at least a few full nights' sleep before it's our turn for the middle of the night feedings."

"Bet she's got you on a schedule," Kol said. "If I go into the kitchen will there be a chart on the fridge?"

"You bet your ass there is," Sebastian replied. "And I, for one, won't argue with it."

Hawk chuckled. "You know she won't cut you off for being an asshole. Pretty sure that's why she fell in love with you."

"I thought she fell in love with me because I'm that good in bed."

Both of the incubi, Hawk and Kol, snorted at that, and the rest of the guys, even Rin, chuckled.

I laughed as well at the easy comradery between all the men. I wouldn't have been able to do this a year ago. I'd been heartbroken at Marcus becoming Essie's mate and terrified at what my angelic mating brand would mean. Now I had my own delicate golden swirls curling from the middle of my left thigh, up my side, and over my shoulder. Five unexpected, unwanted, amazing men who anchored my soul against the ferocious power of my divine magic that for the most part, I kept locked behind my door.

Sebastian had been giving me lessons on how to control it, but when I hit my second trimester, all of my power, both healing and divine, had become unpredictable, and we'd decided it was too dangerous to continue. My magic was still unpredictable, at times driving me crazy with the need to heal someone, anyone, and at other times completely nonexistent, suggesting that it was my hormones making it unpredictable. But the irony of that was that I couldn't quite tell and doubted I would until it was over and my magic returned to normal.

"I wasn't actually talking about the babies," Essie said. "You've been on maternity leave for almost six months now. I would have thought even with your magic acting up, not working would have driven you crazy by now."

"She sneaks out to Mercy Memorial when she thinks we aren't paying attention," Hawk cooed to Dominic, getting the baby to smile at him again.

"I don't like feeling useless and when I need to release my healing magic, I need to release it. There's nothing I can do to resist the compulsion when it comes on strong. Better than me releasing my magic from afar." That still took more power than physical contact and in my current state, it sometimes exhausted me to the point of passing out. And that was something I wasn't going to do again, not after the last time, when Titus found me and went all alpha, overprotective dragon on me. He wouldn't let me out of his sight for a week and he'd almost lost his job at the JP until Cassius had managed to explain the situation to the Director.

As if thinking about Titus made him appear, he and Jacob stepped onto the patio carrying trays of hamburger patties and chicken breasts. The guys cheered the arrival of the meat and set about loading up the BBQ.

Essie shifted closer to me. "And have you told them?" she asked, her voice low — although not quiet enough for either of the vampires' with their enhanced hearing to not hear.

She dipped her gaze to my belly and up again.

Jeez. How had she figured it out? The twins were only three months old and somehow — probably thanks to the magic of Faerie — I was pregnant again. Barely, but I was. I just didn't know how my guys would react to adding another member to our family so soon and hadn't figured out how to tell them.

"Told us what?" Titus asked, nudging me forward on my lounge chair, settling behind me with his legs on either side, and wrapping his arms around me. "That you're pregnant again?"

"How do you know?" I asked him.

"Your scent changed," he replied.

"So has the feel of your magic," Sebastian added.

Hawk gave me a wicked smile. "Your aura changed as well."

"And the flavor of your blood," Rin said in his soft voice.

Cassius set a patty on the grill. "Hey, even I know. You keep looking at the twins and then trying not to touch your belly."

Well, fine then. "Yes, I'm pregnant again."

"So we can officially congratulate the new dad," Sebastian said, raising his wine glass in a salute to Cassius.

I pursed my lips.

"Oh, I'm not the father," Cassius chuckled, not at all upset. "Look at her face."

"How's that possible?" Hawk asked, turning to Sebastian. "I thought you said the twins were because of the spell your mother made when you two were supposed to consummate your marriage."

"One last gift from Faerie," Sebastian said. "That's what I thought. I guess I was wrong."

Titus kissed the top of my head. "It's because she's life itself."

"So you already know whose it is?" Hawk asked.

"Her," I said, and even though I knew the fetus was still too new to have developed sexual organs, I knew my baby would be a girl. "Her energy is already different from the twins. There's very little angel in her so even only a handful of weeks along it's easy to tell who her biological father is." I looked up into Titus's stunning golden eyes. "You're no longer alone."

Those amazing eyes widened.

"You're not the last dragon."

Titus captured my lips in a breathtaking kiss and everyone congratulated him.

I swept my gaze over my guys, my heart overflowing with the joy and contentment and love I saw in their eyes.

When this had all begun, I'd wanted to fall in love just like everyone else, not be forced into a relationship because of my mating brand.

And I had.

I'd fallen in love with Hawk with his unconditional love, Sebastian with his quick wit, Titus with his fierce passion, Rin with his calming stillness, and Cassius with his stalwart determination.

They had been the keys to unlocking *my* heart and the mates I'd always been fated to have.

OTHER BOOKS BY TESSA COLE

NEPHILIM'S DESTINY
Destined Shadows, prequel story
Destined Darkness, book 1
Destined Blood, book 2
Destined Fire, book 3
Destined Storm, book 4
Destined Radiance, book 5

ANGEL'S FATE
Fated Bonds, book 1
Fated Winter, book 2
Fated Fear, book 3
Fated Despair, book 4
Fated Resolve, book 5
Fated Heart, book 6

THE GRECIAN GODDESS TRILOGY
Kiss of the Goddess, book 1
Power of the Goddess, book 2
Bonds of the Goddess, book 3

ENSNARED BY THE PACK
Wolf Deceived, book 1
Wolf Denied, book 2
Wolf Desired, book 3
Wolf Distressed, book 4
Wolf Decided, book 5

CPSIA information can be obtained
at www.ICGtesting.com
Printed in the USA
BVHW050807230123
656726BV00033B/367